Also by
Stephen Markley

OHIO

THE
DELUGE

Stephen Markley

Simon & Schuster

New York   London   Toronto
Sydney   New Delhi

Simon & Schuster
1230 Avenue of the Americas
New York, NY 10020

First Simon & Schuster hardcover edition September 2022

SIMON & SCHUSTER and colophon are registered trademarks of Simon & Schuster, Inc.

For information about special discounts for bulk purchases, please contact Simon & Schuster Special Sales at 1-866-506-1949 or business@simonandschuster.com.

The Simon & Schuster Speakers Bureau can bring authors to your live event. For more information or to book an event, contact the Simon & Schuster Speakers Bureau at 1-866-248-3049 or visit our website at www.simonspeakers.com.

Interior design by Lewelin Polanco

Manufactured in Malaysia

1 3 5 7 9 10 8 6 4 2

Library of Congress Cataloging-in-Publication Data has been applied for.

ISBN 978-1-9821-2309-3
ISBN 978-1-9821-2311-6 (ebook)

For their edits and insights on early drafts of this book, the author would like to thank Stuart Roberts, Susan Golomb, Emily Simonson, Jonathan Evans, Dominick Montalto, Fatima Mirza, Jed Coen, Ben Phillipe, Robbie Orvis, Sarah Spengeman, and Hannah Markley.

For my mom.
All this began when I was a child
and you sat me on your lap in front of an MS-DOS computer
and asked me what story I wanted to tell.

THE
DELUGE

Book I

ONE LAST CHANCE

THE PHASE TRANSITIONS
OF METHANE HYDRATES

2013

One of the grad assistants had left the mail in a pile by the lab's primary com-
puter. The first envelope Tony Pietrus opened was a confirmation letter
from the American Geophysical Union for an appearance at the annual
AGU conference to present initial research findings. The second envelope
would change the way Tony felt about the world. He never got around to the
rest of the day's mail.

He opened this letter with his eyes diverted, still on the screen, lunch
settling in his stomach and his dad's advice—"Grants can't read denser than
the actual science"—still irritating him. He'd often do his best thinking when
he let his mind go, perhaps while playing with his daughters or after making
love to Gail, so he tried to grasp the gist of this latest round of data without
diving too deeply into the morass. Reading over the cluttered integers cross-
stitched onto the screen, he found himself compelled by the data set the way
his kids might anticipate a lesser holiday, like Easter, and he couldn't resist
a peak at the chocolate eggs. The issue of his dwindling NSF funds and failure, thus far, to secure another grant also nagged at him. As if competing for
money, lab space, and computational resources at Scripps wasn't already
pain enough in the ass, he and Niko had no "charismatic megafauna" involved. Only the maddening mystery of methane hydrate phase transitions.

To him, the obviousness of studying deep-sea methane molecules felt
like a bright red elephant walking down La Jolla Shores Drive, but explaining it to the layperson required a convoluted story, especially as to why hydrates deserved to take money from vanishing schools of tuna or adorable
chirping dolphins. It began with the model his eyes crept over now: He and
his fellow researcher, Niko, had concocted a Monte Carlo simulation to predict the behavior of clathrates under changing conditions of temperature
and pressure. He and Niko spent so much time in the lab playing with the
input parameters that they sometimes forgot this could all sound unbearably tedious and impossible to grasp. Gail lent her more poetic mind to the
task of making the clathrates' story cogent.

"So you're trying to figure out when some ice will melt," Gail said at dinner the night before.

"I'm *bored*," groused their youngest daughter, Catherine, while smushing her face in her hands. "Stop talking about this."

"Ah. 'Ice.' Yes, very funny." He stabbed at Gail's chicken. "You're more of an a-hole than the porpoise folks dropping a few hundred grand on new sonar equipment to measure dolphin clicks."

"I know what that word means, Daddy," Holly scolded.

In between his daughters' complaints, Gail helped talk him through a more "user-friendly" description of molecular interactions, specifically the ones that governed phase transitions. Warmer temperatures were one variable that could trigger the abrupt transition from ordered to disordered states: solid to liquid, liquid to gas. The Monte Carlo method—so named for its resemblance to random dice rolls—allowed scientists, economists, and mathematicians to perform all kinds of experiments to model natural phenomena that have irregular and unpredictable inputs.

The clathrates littering the floors of the world's oceans were just such a phenomenon. He, Niko, and their team of grad assistants spent their days running these computational algorithms, constantly adjusting variables like temperature and pressure. The idea was to mimic the random real-world fluctuations of molecular behavior.

A scattershot career that began in theoretical physics had taken Tony to Yale, where he ended up in the Department of Geology and Geophysics before finally developing a more permanent interest in oceanography. In the crisp salt air of Scripps's beachside campus, he'd found a way to apply his theoretical imagination to hard earth sciences. He spent a fair amount of time sunburning on the beaches of La Jolla with his girls, pondering the pore width and cage structures of clathrates while showing his four-year-old how to build a better sand castle.

Now he picked up the tan nine-by-eleven envelope, but his eyes left the screen only momentarily to catch a glimpse of the handwritten address, his name in the center in neat block letters, SCRIPPS INSTITUTE OF OCEANOGRAPHY beneath. It felt light, maybe only a slice or two of paper inside.

Bacterial degradation of organic matter in the oceans produced methane, he'd once told his dad, a math professor without much interest in physical nature. Basically, plants and animals that rotted in a low-oxygen environment became trapped in crystals of frozen water. It took thousands of years for methanogenic bacteria and sediment to do their work and trap the methane molecules where the conditions of temperature and pressure were right, either in the Arctic permafrost, beneath the seafloor, or on its surface clutching the rock in frozen chunks. Every gas hydrate had a similar structure, but methane was the most prolific prisoner, and in some places it was a prominent feature of deep-sea ecosystems, which first drove the interest at Scripps.

When he applied as a postdoctoral researcher, several faculty members had pointed him to Nikolaos Stubos, the Greek wunderkind from Berkeley, who had similar areas of interest. They'd gone from colleagues to friends when that NSF grant had come through. Together, they began plotting how to best understand the strange combination of circumstances that permitted the formation and enduring stability of this particular hydrate. In 2010, the BP oil spill gave their research subject the equivalent of a Hollywood close-up. One of the first schemes BP scientists employed to stop the well spewing oil into the Gulf of Mexico from five thousand feet below the surface was a containment dome. The idea was to lower this massive dome to collect the oil and eventually cap the well, but as the dome descended through the depths it began to clog with hydrates, formed as methane gas spewed from the breach. He and Niko had to listen to endless media mischaracterizations of their research subject, from the obnoxious "methane ice" to the downright vacuous "ice crystals." The methane wasn't frozen; it was just trapped inside a lattice-like matrix of ice. Niko was mystified that journalists could toss off such inaccurate information, while Tony scoffed that given the general state of science education, it was surprising they'd showed up at the right ocean. Lately, methane hydrates had been resurfacing in the news because the oil and gas industry had grown bullish on the prospect of developing hydrates into a fuel source. Estimates always varied, but in the sediments considered part of US ocean territory, there was thought to be roughly a thousand-year supply of natural gas.

"Doesn't that mean you guys could get some of that sweet, sweet petroleum money?" Gail wondered when he was bitching about grants. "Isn't that how most geologists get funded?"

Most days they met for lunch at a Panera near campus. He'd show up late and find her curled up in a booth, eyes poring over whatever lit crit text she was abusing for her doctorate.

"Turns out our work puts us at odds with the predilections of the extraction interests."

Her eyes widened. "Tony, no! Get the girls out of ExxonMobil Little Tots Academy right now."

He snorted a bit of Diet Pepsi. Her jokes were so dorky.

The envelope's return address did not pierce his concentration other than the "Louisville, KY" because he recalled that Scripps sometimes bought lab equipment from a manufacturer in Kentucky.

Tony always found himself detouring into the work of his pen pals in Melbourne—a team of researchers attempting to create a more precise estimate of the ocean's total reserves. The largest reservoirs of hydrates could be found on continental shelves, mostly in coastal zones with high biological production and the right conditions of pressure and temperature. Given this, a map of deposits looked like his youngest, Catherine, had outlined the world's continents in crayon. Off the East Siberian continental shelf alone lay an estimated 1,400 billion tons. In other words, the stuff was everywhere.

There was also a great deal of historical evidence that hydrates were more prevalent now than at any other time in Earth's history. Because Earth had experienced a rather cool, temperate climate over the last few tens of millions of years, biological matter continued to form methane, freeze, and accumulate, uninterrupted by the planet's periodic bursts of heat. Niko, in that assertive, unflappable ("a smidge chauvinist," according to Gail) Greek way of his, never got tired of pointing out that the study of "how much" was the business of those petroleum geologists, not real scientists. Their only concern was "how warm." He and Niko spent years mining clues from the Paleocene–Eocene Thermal Maximum, which Tony now referred to as the "Pet'em" because of his older daughter, whom he usually called "Older One" as a solemn title of nobility.

In her heroic efforts to teach herself to read ahead of schedule, Holly had seen Tony perusing a book on the subject, which had used the common acronym PETM. She'd asked, "What's a Pet'em?" He explained the Pet'em was the far less famous extinction event, a redheaded stepchild to the die-off that inspired *Jurassic Park* and the entire dino-subsection of pop culture for little boys.

"To understand the Pet'em," he told her, "it's instructive to first look at the end-Permian extinction."

"What's a redhead stop-child?" she asked.

The idiom proved more difficult to explain to a six-year-old than the mystery of the end-Permian, the event that wiped nearly all life off the face of the planet. Scientists thought that a million years' worth of volcanic eruptions in Siberia was the likely culprit, but the math didn't add up. The volcanoes simply couldn't have produced enough carbon dioxide in a quick enough time span to raise the earth's temperature six degrees Celsius. One had to account for all the light carbon found in rocks from the end-Permian. It was like the entire goddamn planet's supply of coal had suddenly oxidized right into the atmosphere, but there weren't a lot of coal miners running around back then, mostly just fish and bugs. Yet that light carbon was the reason 96 percent of life in the water and 70 percent of the land-based variety were wiped out almost overnight in geologic terms, clearing the plate for the dinosaurs. There remained only one desperado that could plausibly hold enough light carbon to explain the end-Permian extinction: methane hydrates. This explanation allowed the math to add up.

Cut to approximately 55 million years ago and the PETM, a more minor extinction event than either the end-Permian or the meteor that wiped out the dinosaurs. Yet the Pet'em certainly mattered to quite a few marine species that didn't make it. The earth experienced a rapid heating of five to six degrees Celsius in only twenty thousand years. When you looked at sediments deposited during the Pet'em, you saw a massive spike in light carbon, which meant that something injected over three thousand gigatons in two quick bursts that each only took a few tens of thousands of years.

Again, the only explanation for this appeared to be a rapid melting of undersea methane hydrates.

Tony pinched open the metal clasp of the envelope and slid a finger beneath the fold to give it a quick, ineffectual tear that simply created a flap of paper. Nevertheless, there was a hole for his finger to work as he continued to study the data.

"Twice the hydrates melted," he'd told Holly. "And twice there were catastrophic extinction events."

So the question became: What caused the hydrates to melt in the first place? By looking at other PETM-like events in the Paleocene and Jurassic eras—and coupled with the end-Permian hypothesis—scientists had established that the hydrates did not melt due to some outside trigger, like a meteor strike, but rather an unambiguous feedback loop.

When the Earth warmed during climate oscillations caused by solar activity, widespread volcanic eruptions, or perturbations in Earth's orbit, at a certain point the methane release occurred, spiking CH4 and CO2 levels in the atmosphere and raising the temperature even more. The best theory for how that worked involved ocean circulation: During the Pet'em, warmer, saltier water began flowing to the deep oceans, which in all likelihood began melting the top surface of hydrates. This exposed deeper reservoirs of hydrates, which in turn melted, exposing more. Why ocean circulation changed during these periods was still a mystery, but you didn't need a doctorate from Yale to guess that the two-to-three-degree Celsius rise in global average temperature prior to the Pet'em probably had something to do with it. Luckily, it only took a little over one hundred thousand years for the carbon cycle to return that excess carbon to the earth, so the mammals of the day could get on with their humping and eventually produce humans.

Last summer he'd found himself on a Gulf Coast beach going mad trying to explain why this mattered to Gail's obnoxious talk-radio-obsessed younger brother, Corey, who frequently directed his snide country-club snark toward Tony's "mind-and-dick-numbing" job. On their first date when Gail explained she was adopted, Tony had pictured her younger brother as an enlightened liberal, proudly championing his biracial family. Corey, it turned out, was the type of adult who found it amusing to joke about Tony's bald spot and old acne scars. Though the sun was setting, he felt his face grow hotter as he explained that given humanity's little science experiment of pumping all the carbon it could find into the atmosphere ten times faster than during the PETM, it was probably worth figuring out how soon the goddamn hydrates might melt and turn Corey's Sarasota beachfront condo into a pretty shitty fucking investment.

Gail shot him a look over the top of her sunglasses that said *Play nice*, and he again wondered if it was too late for his wife to un-adopt herself from her dynastic, self-consumed Floridian family.

He was somewhere here—among the numbers from the latest simulation and memories of their last trip to Florida and his brother-in-law and Catherine, whom he always called "Khaleesi" because it suited her magnetism and temper, either of which might be on display at her birthday party this weekend—when two things happened at once.

First, he aggregated what he'd read on the screen in the simulated clathrate analysis. Second, he turned his full attention to the envelope, which he succeeded in opening by using his finger as an impromptu letter opener. There was only one sheet of paper inside, and he pulled it out. The big block letters were similar to those of the address.

AFTER THIS YOU AND YOUR PEERS COLLUSION WILL BE
EXPOSED AND YOULL BE CHARGED WITH THE GREATEST
FRAUD EVER PERPETRATED IN THIS CENTURY. YOU WILL
BE DISCOVERED BUT I FEAR EVEN THIS ISN'T ENOUGH
PUNISHMENT FOR WHAT YOU DESERVE.

He snorted a laugh at the missing apostrophe in "youll."

This was a first for him. He'd certainly heard of other scientists receiving crass and intimidating notes from the right-wing or conspiratorially minded agitators who seemed to take up all the oxygen on the internet. Tony stayed out of all that, though. He hated politics. As far as he was concerned, all this fury directed at people taking passionless, unbiased measurements of phenomena was nothing more than the sad hobby of frustrated losers ranting into the ether. He imagined Gail's response, some nerdy joke like "At least this balances out all the bras and panties you usually get!" Imagining her voice gave him comfort. Milling outside a Yale lecture hall years ago Tony found himself unexpectedly talking to a young woman, Black and wide-hipped with round breasts stretching a T-shirt with a picture of Lando Calrissian lying seductively on a bearskin rug. He thought she was gorgeous then and would continue to think that past a decade and two children whose faces grew into hers year by year.

This was the kind of woman you needed when the world was teeming with morons, and you got hate mail for studying the phase transitions of methane hydrates.

His eyes crept back to the beginning of the letter. "After this," it began. After what? Tony wondered if he should call campus security. This seemed silly, though. He wasn't worried about a guy being camped out in the bushes. Some idiot had scanned the Scripps faculty page on the website and picked his name out of a lineup.

He set the letter down on his desk, ready to forget about it for the rest of the day when he noticed something white with a pale yellowish tint on his right hand. He rubbed the tips of his fingers together and the substance sifted off. Still holding the envelope with his left, he now felt a remaining weight to it. There was something else inside.

Without thinking, he tilted the envelope over the desk to empty the rest of the contents. A powder of the same color, maybe a couple spoonfuls, spilled out onto the marred wooden surface.

It was impossible for Tony to remember how long he sat there staring at it, but it was a very long time. His mind, chaotic and symphonic only moments before, halted entirely.

This obviously wasn't real. It was likely chalk or some other anodyne substance. This was an easy laugh for a sick crank.

He tried to think of everything he knew about *Bacillus anthracis*, but it wasn't much. Cutaneous, pulmonary, or gastrointestinal methods of infection were all possible—but here he was just breathing, just sitting there, staring at his hands, some of it still on his fingers. But what were the odds that a clueless loser who couldn't spell "youll" somehow had access or the wherewithal to cultivate *Bacillus* spores? Then again, the historical mortality rate had to be incredibly high. He became aware of a piece of food stuck in his teeth, leftover from lunch, and realized he was still just staring at the powder on his fingers.

As if born back into his surroundings, he looked up and around. He shared the lab in Nierenberg Hall on the east side of the Scripps campus with Niko, but since they only dealt in computer models they treated it as an overflow office. The cabinets that had once held equipment now stored files. The countertops that might have held aquariums of marine specimens now provided a home to mountains of paper flotsam. But there was still a working sink.

Tony stood, wondering if he could inadvertently wash the spores into someone's drinking water. Because he had no answer to this question, he dismissed it and knocked the faucet on with his elbow. The powder disappeared under the scalding water. He emptied a handful of the pearled gel from the soap dispenser onto his palms and scrubbed until his skin was pink and painful.

When he finished, he dried his hands and dialed 911 from his cell phone. He'd barely explained the situation before the operator was putting him in touch with the FBI.

By the time he hung up, he was confused. The FBI was coming, but what about an ambulance? He remembered from the scares of 2001 that bacillus wasn't contagious from person to person, so could he just drive to the hospital himself? He didn't want to go anywhere near the substance, so he took Niko's desk chair and sat by the opposite wall, as far away from his desk as he could, and wondered if he should lay a piece of plastic over the powder. Then again, he didn't want to go near it. He perched forward with his arms crossed over his chest, hugging himself. Even though it was surely a hoax, almost definitely a hoax, maybe it wasn't a hoax. The less he tried to think about this, the more he could only think about it. He felt a tickle in his throat. He wondered if in a few minutes he'd start coughing. Wishing for the antianxiety meds he'd dabbled with as an undergrad, he tried to focus on something else, and he wanted that to be his family.

But that wasn't where his mind went. Instead, he was overcome by an image of tiny bubbles rising inexorably through dark water. It was what he'd seen just before he pulled the letter from the envelope. With this data set, the trend was becoming unmistakable. And powerful. He and Niko kept fiddling with the simulation, making the stresses milder, but in the end, the hypothetical hydrates kept coming apart. He tried to focus on other things: Gail working on her dissertation in the kitchen of their first rental home in La Jolla while he kept Holly—not Older One yet—distracted in the living room by handing her baby toys to suck on while he read research papers a paragraph at a time. Gail had Holly by day, so he took her by night. They both pursued their careers while they fed and burped this chubby babbling machine, and when she finally began going down at a reasonable hour, they'd watch DVRed episodes of *Lost*, which Gail claimed offended her as a reader of literature, even though she never let him watch without her.

When Catherine arrived they talked about how their girls would be the most dissimilar siblings, as fundamentally different as Gail and Corey. Older One got the hang of reading by age six, and she seemed in a competition with herself to comprehend the most challenging novel her young mind could follow. Only a first-grader, they had to take books away from her at bedtime. She objected to so little, she threw no tantrums, and yet she almost seemed to carry around a latent fear or stress that she would never manage to finish every great book in the world. He'd swing the door open to her bedroom, and her surprised face and big head of curls would go dark as she snapped off the flashlight she'd sneaked. The ways she put that unrelenting curiosity to work never failed to astonish Tony, like when Gail taught her what it meant to call something "gender essentialist," and she began identifying everything in the modern world as "gendered essentialist," including TV commercials, children's shows, movies, all sports, and everything her uncle Corey ever said.

And her younger sister—Jesus Christ. Even as an infant she had a knack for the bold entrance and destructive tantrum. She was lighter-skinned than Holly, had a splash of spunky red-brown freckles on her cheeks and nose, and a beautiful red tint to her hair. She could charm an entire room or, if she didn't like the vibe, as Gail put it, "She'd spit at us if she could get her lips to work." Then she learned to talk, and in complete contrast to Older One, the words never stopped. They just came in an indomitable stream of thoughts, ideas, stories, questions, and wonders. And her crazy streak: When Niko, his wife, and some other friends had come over for dinner once, he and Gail had returned from the kitchen to find their youngest daughter bare-ass naked demonstrating her toddler gymnastics for the assembled guests, causing the rarest of lost tempers from her parents. But then, that was why she was a conqueror, a wild one, fearless and fierce, the Mother of Dragons.

He shut his eyes and tried to grip these memories, but each one became subsumed by the image and weight of a dark ocean boiling. Eventually, there was a knock on the lab door.

———

He dealt with an FBI agent named Chen, who could not have been more out of central casting. Neat, combed hair, workaday suit over a muscular build, pen, pad, and latex gloves. He was so no-nonsense that after the biohazard unit had put police tape across the door and collected the powder, Tony felt a simmering panic at the man's calm.

"Should I go to the hospital?"

The agent's eyes flitted up and back down to a notepad where his hand moved furiously.

"Do you feel any of the symptoms we talked about?"

"No. I mean, my throat tickles a little but it kind of did this morning."

"Anthrax poisoning tends to produce a little more than a throat tickle. You said you have a change of clothes—put those on, give us yours. Go home, shower, and if you start to feel real symptoms, go to the hospital. I'll call you tomorrow as soon as the lab looks at this."

The farther away Tony got from the office and the envelope the less plausible the threat felt. By the time he got home and told Gail, he was behaving as though it was nothing more than the stupidest of pranks, with the entire floor of Nierenberg having to evacuate when the FBI unit descended.

Gail spent a minute staring at him in uncomprehending horror, a minute hurling profanities at him for not going to the hospital immediately, and then several more reading the anthrax Wikipedia page.

"So we're assuming you haven't been poisoned? That's the assumption we're all operating under?" Her eyes still as wide as when he first told the story.

"The FBI seemed to think it wasn't worth worrying about unless I felt ill."

Gail squirted air through the small gap in her top front teeth, a very Gail tell for a snarky comment forthcoming. "I really hope whoever this guy is, he understands the dramatic irony of being scientifically literate enough to use science to make an antiscience terrorist attack."

"They really didn't seem to think it was necessary, I swear. If they thought there was a reason to worry I'd be there right now."

"Fine," she said, embracing him and tucking her head underneath his chin so that her ear aligned with his heart. "But, Tone, if you die, where am I ever going to find another nerdy white grouch with no meaningful social skills?"

The next day Agent Chen called Tony to tell him he was in the clear. The powder had been cornmeal.

"Cornmeal," Tony repeated. "To what goddamn end?"

"No cheaper way to put a scare into someone. It's why we tend not to break out Seal Team Six every time someone gets the idea." Chen had a conversational presence like he was reading out of a phone book. "We're still going to try to trace this letter. A powder threat—even if it's a hoax—is still a felony."

But they never found the guy who mailed cornmeal and the letter with its big block font. Tony never received another such threat, though when he and Niko secured a grant to finish their work and published their findings a year later, the emails did start to trickle in. These were less death threats and more hateful accusations and childish name-calling. He learned to ignore them. Gail took to calling Tony "Anthrax" every now and again, but she mostly employed the nickname after the speaking offers began to roll in. The story of the letter became a party anecdote.

"I like the way it makes you sound," she once explained when he asked why she made him tell it. "Brave and fearless." She cupped his aging butt and winked.

"Why?" he said, smiling. "All I did was shit my pants and call the FBI."

The story disappeared into the archive of memories that lose all urgency. Except that wasn't quite right. What he never could have predicted was the part of that experience that did stick with him. That of the image that overwhelmed him as he sat in Niko's chair waiting for the cavalry. It washed him away for a moment. The walls of the lab had not closed in like a tomb but rather expanded and deepened to almost infinite space and depth. Down there in the vivid blue darkness, in the cold, crushing rapture of the pressure, there was imperceptible warmth. The mounds of dirty yellow ice—the color of urine on snow—were leaking. Other clumps of the whitest frozen latticework, opaque crystals, fizzed like Alka-Seltzer. Or belching up from cracks in the rock, little farts in the dark, that sent schools of pebble-sized bubbles ascending. Or gurgling from invisible pores in the sediment of the ocean floor, beading up, clinging momentarily, and then writhing free of a soft sand carpet. Zipping back and forth, they climbed through frigid water. A mad poetry scrawled in the unseen corners of the oceans' expanse.

In the years that would follow, this image would settle upon him in moments of his most pressing fear. When Gail came home and told him her doctor had found a metastatic lump in her breast at her improbably young age. When they'd found out that it had already spread to her bones, her spine, her brain, that this wasn't the kind of breast cancer where you got to traipse around with a pink ribbon for a few years. This was the kind that took you. And when it took her, so rapidly and without mercy or time to come to grips or even fucking think, sitting at her bedside as she slipped away, he felt it.

He felt it after the funeral when he told Older One that he'd probably need help cooking dinner for a while, and she'd whispered that this was kind of gender essentialist without understanding how violently this would crack open his heart. And he felt it then again, years later, when a teenage Khaleesi got into a car accident, and the idiot father of the idiot boy she'd been with couldn't remember the name of the hospital they'd been taken to. He felt it when he saw the Mother of Dragons in a hospital bed with her arm in a sling, dried blood in her kinky red-brown hair, and a couple of nasty black eyes that would set her accelerating beauty back for a few months. He felt it when he went to her, and she said his name the way she had as a child. Like he could protect her from anything.

He'd feel that same eclipsing terror, born on the day of the letter, in the same familiar way, and all he could see were the bubbles, and then beyond into the molecule itself. This invaluable atomic combination in a prison of ice, struggling its eternal life away in a tomb until it broke free and began its journey through the depths and on to the invisible wastes at the crown of the world.

Shane and Murdock
Get Breakfast
2014

*S*hane watched Murdock shred three sugar packets open and dump them in his coffee. Bob Evans made her think of a barn as conceived by a dying old woman doped out of her mind on laudanum. Woven baskets tacked to the wall over a three-dollar painting of a rustic countryside. The other patrons were geriatric with flesh the texture of the snow slurry outside. They ate tediously, automatically, knives struggling through country fried steak, forks impaling scrambled eggs or scooping home fries. She counted four oxygen tanks in the main dining room, one of them hooked to a man so obese that the sides of his butt drooped over the edge of the chair. She watched him eat a small potpie in methodical, dignified bites.

The waitress had come by twice, once for the coffee order and again to deliver the brew. Shane told her they'd wait to get breakfast. Now they were sipping the not-terrible roast and talking about movies.

"That was some garbage. Military hates that movie. Specially EODs," said Murdock.

"I don't know, man. I felt like I needed a defibrillator by the time I walked out of the theater." She blew at the steam rising from the mug.

"Total fairy tale. So ridiculous, I couldn't watch it again."

Shane had gained weight in the past seven years, but Murdock had put on more, maybe thirty, forty pounds, mostly in the gut. He wore a white Affliction Chuck Liddell tee with the roaring winged skull across the front and had the same cut as when they met, shaved on the sides and a cap of blond on top, now with a bit of gray frost. His ears, always big, looked bigger, the slack of his lips slacker, which made his drawl deeper. Tormented blue punching bags hung under his eyes. Maybe every soldier came home older, but that older was nothing compared to the older of seven years on.

"There's this one EOD guy running around by himself," he said. "Running off the FOB alone to question an Iraqi, getting into a sniper fight, grabbing a Humvee to drive out to nowhere to detonate ordnance in a one-man

**BECAUSE HE DIDN'T
WANT TO EXPLAIN**
Even twenty-five would be
rolling light. By his second
deployment they were
escorted by a whole platoon
with Humvees, Strykers,
MRAPs, and sometimes
tanks for the neighborhoods
where even the toddlers shot
at them. During the dark
days when no-shit-fuck-you
civil war broke out, they'd
have escorts of one-hundred-
plus soldiers with an Iraqi
army unit to match.

convoy. Fucking absurd. When we rolled out
the wire, we never went anywhere without at
least twenty-five guys."

She'd been organizing a rally with Iraq Veterans Against the War in D.C. This was '07, Bush
II still president. Prior to the march, at a lunch
of turkey wraps delivered by the garbage bag,
she'd been introduced to this bomb-tech peace
activist, part autodidact, part swinging-dick
male trope. Though she'd mostly been dating
women at the time, she told him, "I doubt you
could have activated my fourth-wave feminist
impulses more completely." They did the thing
where after they slept together they became
Facebook friends, and over the years he'd drop her a line now and then.
The messages were tinged with puppy dog yearning (*Heya gal, hope you're
well. Was thinking of you the other day. Wondering where the wind blew you. –
Murdock*). Years later, when she reached out to him via postcard with a new
number, he'd called the same day.

"The whole lot of movies about OIF are such a pile of dog shit. It's like
they're making a movie about waitressing, and waitresses go and watch
it and see all these sexy characters meeting dashing, dangerous men, and
every encounter is some bullshit verbal joust—*Fuck no*. You serve old fucking fat people shit food for ten hours, some tip you, some stiff you, you wake
up and do it again. Iraq was mundane. Boring as beans until you got a call
and all of a sudden it wasn't. No one's seeing a movie like that, though."

"You know why there will never be a great movie or great art about the
Iraq War?" she asked.

"Why's that?"

"Because it hewed too didactically to its own absurdity." She looked off
at the cold parking lot. "Like, most war is stupid in the existential sense,
but this one was bad-joke stupid. You can't get a piece of art to grapple with
what's already brain-dead, you know? I mean, the fucking child-boy president landed on an aircraft carrier with a sock stuffed in the crotch of his
flight suit and stood in front of a banner that said— Well, you know what it
said. How can you make subtle, contemplative art about that? The whole
thing was an unknowing satire of itself from word one."

"Well, Eastwood's got a sniper flick coming out. I'm sure that'll be the subtle contemplation you're looking for, Ebert."

She laughed and remembered standing with him outside a bar, shadows splayed on the pavement of a dead D.C. street. He'd pulled two cigarettes from the pack with his teeth, handed her one, and said, "Wanna ditch these losers and go throw rocks at the moon?" He was wounded in that perfect, unfixable way that compelled her as a young woman, at least for a night.

"Not sure I ever asked . . ." She ratcheted the conversation closer to her mark, as carefully as if she were handling one of Kellan Murdock's IEDs. "How did you end up doing bomb disposal?"

He flipped a hand in the air and farted with his lips.

FOR HIS PART Murdock felt embarrassment and small-hold bitterness for how he must look to her. She was still Good Curvy, as Troy Ta'amu used to say. Her hair was longer now, a shaggy black mess with a mullet shape to it. She'd taken the stud out of her nostril, and he could see the small hole it had left. Her hooded eyes should have made her look naturally bored, but they drilled into him. Like what he said mattered. He remembered gripping the white of her love handles, and the tributaries of purple stretch marks crawling beneath pale brown skin. She still radiated fearlessness and a self-aware acid Zen. He ate up the way she spoke, the way she thought. Every honed, spear-sharp sentence came tumbling out of her mouth like it had just occurred to her. She'd never treated him with faux reverence. She was the first woman who slept with him after he got back, and at first it made him so achingly distraught, thinking this was what he'd missed: When he went to play with the bang, all the kids like her went to college and just fucked and fucked until they were bored with it. While he jerked off in KBR porta-pots and played endless video games with Slade, Hermoza, and Beech, his peers stateside lived in another dimension. He'd thought this was what his life could be like now that he was back. He'd been so sure she was a kind of mystic signal or road sign that life still remained, glorious and unexpected, on the other side of the war.

"Us guys from the Alabama part of Pennsylvania either go military or go to jail. Once I got deployed and started really meeting people—I mean, meeting guys from every fucking corner of the world where the American experiment got its hooks in—Samoa, Guam, Northern Mariana Islands—places I'd never heard of, it was funny how many of the stories were the same. Guy got in trouble with the law or was on the verge of getting shot over some bullshit or just owing too much money to turn down the signing bonus. Regular army's mostly ex–drug dealers from what I could tell."

"But why did you join?"

"I was rah-rah America. Wanted to go hunt al-Qaeda, put my boot in the

> **EOD SCHOOL** Some recruits were already engineers. Murdock was more like a savant, who'd gotten a lot of mechanical training by accident working in his mom's boyfriend's auto shop since he was ten. Some guys can just tell how the lock balls and gears of a setback-armed, mechanically timed, graze-impact-fired mortar fuze are gonna work.

ass, all that. Thought I'd be infantry, but I was always kind of a cerebral hick. An enlisted guy suggested I try for EOD school, and shit—guess you could just say I had an aptitude. Politics didn't even occur to me."

Her eyebrows made a skeptical bounce. "But what you're describing, Kel—that's a political attitude."

"Yeah, but I didn't know that. Plus, it all went away quick for me. By the time I started my third tour I couldn't have given a fuck less what hajji wanted to do with their sand. So even after I stopped caring personally, I still didn't really question the mission." He sipped his coffee. "Why, after all, would so many brilliant, hardworking, talented motherfuckers be pouring this much passion and energy and courage into a thing if it wasn't absolutely the correct undertaking? Get me?"

The waitress came by again, and Shane sent her away with a polite scuttle of her hand and a "Not quite ready." The cute little Bambi waitress pursed her lips like this made her anxious but didn't argue. Shane's sleeve slid down her arm, and she instinctively tugged it back down over the tattoo.

When she left, Shane turned back to Murdock. "Do you keep up with anybody from IVAW?"

"Nah. Didn't see the point. War's over. Might as well be the Spanish-American imbroglio as

> **TA'AMU** He'd spent an entire deployment grilling his captain, Ta'amu, about American Samoa, because what the fuck was that, right? Like a place Frodo's gotta go in *Lord of the Rings*? Ta'amu was a hulking engineer turned EOD commander with a body like a fatty stone pillar and a smashed-pan face topped off by a dark and handsome unibrow. Ta'amu was the guy who put him in the Suit, who sent specialists, technical eggheads like Murdock, on the lonesome walk. He was a bizarre dude. Hysterically funny on occasion. Everyone in the army was funny to some degree—maybe not in a laugh-out-loud kinda way; sometimes in a strange, grim, you-know-this-constant-talk-of-sodomy-and-incest-has-a-home-base-in-his-gray-matter kinda way, but Ta'amu could be both. "Dog tags and blood type go in the laces of the boot," he told Murdock early on. When he inquired why this was, Ta'amu replied, "Get with the program, Murder! What's left when the bang goes off? Hands and feet! What do you think they'll find of you after you go from a complex consciousness to a rapidly unwinding miscellany of gore and Pentagon-issued gear?" Then he started laughing like a lunatic.

> **NICKNAMES** Cropped up faster than IEDs: He was all at once "Kel," "Kelter," "Skelter," "Docker," "Dick," "D," "Murder," and "Manfuck."

far as anybody remembers or gives a fuck." He pronounced the word with a hard *g*.

"Sometimes I think it was better when American kids were dying and getting maimed. It put invisible infrastructures in front of people. On their television screens. Now that you've got a liberal—whatever that dubious word means—a liberal building a surveillance state and assassinating extrajudicially via robot, no one seems all that bothered."

"Yeah, well, time marches on. Getting caught up in causes don't interest me. Not anymore. Especially when you see the scope of what *this* is." He took the Heinz ketchup bottle from the condiment holder. "That's the thing: Most people don't understand this. The ingredients, what it goes on, where the energy comes from to create it, the ways the world's gotta be directed and coaxed and violated and controlled to get this one little fucked bottle. And once you see how ketchup relates to imperial maintenance it's tough to not get an overwhelmed quality to your thinking. Like one of them Magic Eye thingamajobs—hard the first time, but once you get it, you'll never unsee it."

"Did you have to kill anyone for the ketchup?"

Once she let loose the question, she wondered if she'd blown it. It felt rehearsed coming out of her mouth, like she'd used the whole conversation to

---

TATTOOS Murdock clocked Shane's lone tattoo (**BUILD THE PATH**—some drippy lib meaning he could no longer recall), and it set his mind off like daisy-chained 130-millimeter artillery rounds. First to the EOD Crab with its blue-bomb heart, now looking a little droopy as its home on his pec sagged. Then to Captain Ta'amu, who had an enormous design coating an arm as meaty as a chuck eye roast. "This here, Manfuck, is the Marquesan Cross. That's Polynesian warrior shit—not suitable for southern-fried baby-men like yourself." This fit because Ta'amu had the energy of a guy who'd prefer to charge the enemy with a stone axe. Once when they came under fire on a bridge, their security started pounding a riverbank, and some kid's SAW jammed, so he was pinned down behind a railing, frustrated and terrified as he tried to fix his weapon. This infantry escort was new, and it might've been the kid's first firefight. He looked about fourteen years old. From EOD's position behind an armored Humvee, you could see the kid's resolve cracking. Panic swelling. Tears beginning to well in his blue farm-boy eyes. When Ta'amu finally saw this, he tightened his boot laces, leaped up, and went jogging over through the bullets to plop down beside the boy. He took the SAW from him, unjammed the jam in about thirty seconds, and handed the mighty weapon off, yelling, "Remember, son. The tears of strangers are only water." Then he jogged back through the bullets pinging off the Humvee, took one hit in the Kevlar, which barely threw him off his stride, and when he got back to safety remarked, "What suspense! Didn't need to pay for the whole seat 'cause all I needed was the edge."

WHITEHALL While at Penn State working on his degree, he took a class on military history. Turned out the professor was a real fucking communist named Whitehall, who went on in class about American imperialism and militarism, which so enraged him that Murdock went to Whitehall's office hours and basically said, "Fuck you, I put my life on the line for this fucking country, so keep your faggoty fucking liberal mouth shut about it" (or something to that effect). And Whitehall, without flinching, immediately asked, "How many people dja kill?" When he responded none, he'd killed none, Whitehall went on. "You're lucky. What you've got here is nothing. It's not good, I'll grant you that, but what you guys are losing every two months, we lost in a day. That made us jumpy. I shot a woman through the head because I thought she had a rifle, but it was just an axe. She'd been chopping some wood. But when all your best friends are getting killed, one young woman in a sea of gore doesn't really weigh on you at the time. Then I got back and couldn't figure out why I was so messed up in the head, so angry all the time, and—oh, wouldn't you know?" He threw up his hands and rolled his eyes at the ceiling. "I'd spent two years killing people. Do yourself a favor and get over the posturing, get over your masculine bullshit, and go find some psychotherapist and have a good cry." He'd asked what war Whitehall was talking about. "'Nam, my son! Jesus Christ, I know we haven't gotten there in class yet, but I'd have thought some of you kids'd heard of it."

⬂   ⬂   ⬂   ⬂   ⬂   ⬂

ON THAT TOPIC He'd fired his weapon a handful of times, but only when shit got real sticky and even EOD was expected to return fire. He'd never hit anyone as far as he knew. Yet to say he'd killed no one? Not exactly nail-meets-head. For instance, there'd been the Iraqi woman approaching their infantry escort, and he'd been asked to assess if she was wearing a suicide vest. Who the fuck could tell? The burkas made them all look strapped to boom. So when she ignored the terp's instructions and kept walking, American brass spilled. No bomb, though, it turned out. She'd just been pregnant.

get there. Which she more or less had.

"Zero. I was purely a technician. I saved lives. Best way to see the war. Blow shit up all the time, but you ain't gotta kill no one. Thought that'd be perfect."

"We don't have to talk about this." It wasn't so much an offer to change the subject as it was a request to go on.

"I'll tell you, Shane: I got a pretty good idea of when I'm being probed. After every tour we had to take a psych stop to make sure we wouldn't go murdering our families when we got home. Part of me wondered if you were getting in touch to *get in touch*, but this is all about whatever you're working on, I gather."

Her smile flared before she tucked her lips back over her teeth, just enough to leave the flirtation hanging, but with a reminder that she wasn't interested. Touching his hand would be too much, so she went ahead and could feel in his palm how much he ached for it.

"Right. This is about a project I've started. As long as you're okay with that." Murdock waited, and she took the hand away. She weighed her options and decided to stay with EOD. She'd done her research, but again, there was the thrill of hearing about it from a man who carried the wreckage. "So you saw a lot of bombs?"

He snorted. "You could say that. If you count two or three a day, then yeah. A lot. Now, mind you, some of them had already gone off. We'd get the call or we'd see smoke rising from the FOB, and twenty minutes later we're in the thick of it. Half the job was investigations. Trying to collect all the evidence so we could find these guys. Some intense shit."

"More intense than defusing an IED?"

"In a lotta ways. Say you're out there, and a bomb's gone off, right? You got ten minutes to collect all the evidence you can 'cause after that, the snipers and other insurgents

EXPLOSIVE THEORY Understand how a pinch of extremely unstable or reactive compound can produce an expansion of material, heat, light, and pressure through a supersonic chemical reaction. Understand how the wave speed flowing through a brick of C4 will get a velocity of frag they called Mach Fuck Me. Know your frag: nails, bolts, ball bearings, steel shavings, human shit, pieces of dead dog. Know the ordnance better than the people who built the ordnance. Understand how to shear a firing pin, melt a land mine pressure pad, shoot buckshot, water, or steel bits into the mechanisms of a device to safe it. The US came to fight one war but got another, and EOD had to learn on the fly in this brave new hyper-creative world. They saw spray-foam-encased EFPs, sandbags filled with radio-triggered mortar shells, pressure-plate-activated devices, dual-tone multifrequency decoder board setups, 122-millimeter projectiles lashed like Christmas lights to pressure-switch contacts, improvised Claymores with two scoops of nuts and bolts for frag, VBIEDs with a suicide switch coiled around the transmission lever, the wiring running to a car battery in the back seat, sitting on a pile of propane tanks and plastic explosive all strapped tight with evil black electrical tape. Fill a pressure cooker with some diesel fuel and fertilizer, bury it in the road, touch two wires to a dinky double-A battery. Boomtown.

AND THEY FOUGHT BACK With the Suit, bang sticks, det cord, blast caps, time fuzes, shock tubes, EXIT charges, the British BootBanger, Bottlers, Maxi candles, Semtex, PE4, C4, and TNT. They safed IEDs with robots, from the four-hundred-pound monster the F6A, to the light, maneuverable PackBots, to his buddy SPC Kieran Slade's preference, the TALON. They handed the robots Gatorade bottles filled with water and explosives and sent them to get blown to shit and end their miserable robot lives. And the key: the Warlocks—the electronic jammers that saved so many lives, they should've won the Medal of Fucking Honor. He still saw the random digits of the glowing green LED displays cycling through threat frequencies in his dreams.

descend. So you're telling the Iraqi police to stand down, you're telling a Marine or army captain about ten pay grades above you to back the fuck off, you're telling family members of the victims, 'Sorry, ma'am, you ain't getting your son's disemboweled corpse,' or 'No, sir, your daughter's hands and feet belong to the US Army.' Because you need that shit. That's evidence.

That's going to help you find these motherfuckers and ventilate them. Then you start getting shot at, mortars are falling on your head, you're trying to swab everyone at the scene for DNA samples." His left eye spasmed, and he blinked furiously to clear it. "All that'll get your butthole puckered every time."

"But you made it out without a scratch," she said, not without admiration. "Three tours and you're sitting here like, like . . ."

"Like Jesus walked through gunfire." Shane smiled.

"I got scars. Shrapnel still under the skin. And I'm TBIed as fuck. I never sleep more'n four or five hours at a time since I been back."

"TBI is Something-Brain-Something?"

"Traumatic brain injury. Standing next to bomb blasts for a few years turns out to not be so hot for your think box."

"So like football players with concussions."

"Sorta. Concussion is when you come to a sudden stop and your brain kinda"—he thumped a fist into his open palm—

KELLY WILEY Bitched to her manager that she kept getting stiffed on tips, and Marcia snapped, "'Cause you don't pay attention to your tables, you let everyone see the bottom of the mug, and the cooks redo your orders twice a day when you bunk 'em." Now Kelly watched Table #19 like the pot about to boil. Table #19 was not the normal Tuesday-morning pairing. She'd guessed a quick first date for coffee, but they'd been talking for nearly an hour like they had nowhere to be. Old friends maybe. But the chat looked too intense. The woman with the darkish skin and messy black hair studied the fat guy, really peering into him. She tried to beam her wish into the lady's brain: *Order the skillet so I can stop worrying about you! Quit sitting there stewing on one freaking cup of coffee!* Maybe she should give trade school another try. She was not cut out for waitressing.

THE ONLY OTHER PERSON TO NOTICE Was Richard Lee Haas, whom everyone called Ricky Lee. He'd finished his Bob's potpie and was waiting for his waitress to notice he was done. She was just standing there staring off into space, and he hated being one of those unpleasant people who stuck his hand in the air and made a little check-signing gesture. Something very rushed, rude, and modern about that. His eyes passed over the young couple. The pretty woman focused on this young buck like she was practically interviewing him. Poor choice of time and place for a date, but they looked like they could be happy enough. "Everyone deserves a little." That was what Ricky Lee's late wife had always said.

"smushes up against the inside of the skull. What happened to us was a little different. Had to do with the blasts that got your brain all tore the fuck up."

"I'm sorry, Kel. That sounds awful."

"It gives me the sleep problems like I said, but there's some damage memory-wise too."

"Yeah?" She was circling him, but Shane also did love hearing about war. Though she'd begun her adulthood organizing against the country's major military misadventures, a part of her ached for combat. She envied the sense of purpose, the action, the definitive stamp of reality, finality, and meaning war seemed to imprint on its participants.

"My memory—especially before Iraq—is so fucking shot, it's almost like I was never that person. Can barely remember my hometown, my mom. Can't remember anything about high school— almost at all. Like, at some point, I know I learned algebra, but I couldn't tell you

READ UP ON SCIENCE Explosive waves that come off the bang either speed up or slow down depending on the density of the medium they travel through. So the time they rolled up on a car bomb only to have another one go off a few dozen yards away, those compression waves traveled slowly through the air, but then sped up as soon as they reached their skulls. Density was key. Density creates shredding, ripping-type forces. The misconception was that explosions killed people with their fire and whatnot—no, no, no. It was always blast lung. The blast cut these little air pockets in the lungs, and motherfuckers drowned on their own blood. Those same compression waves worked a number on your brain. Occupational blast exposure was what the MDs called it. Before they'd stopped speaking, his buddies from EOD all talked about lost memories, lost sleep, and losing the ability to make a decision at random moments. Murdock hadn't thought much of any of the memories he'd tagged before leaving for basic. Now that his whole life more or less began when he got to EOD school, he had to tell himself that.

MEMORIES MOST AVAILABLE Aluminum bunk trailers and the plywood offices, the phone on the ops desk that rang with their missions, garbage piles on the streets, dead dogs left to rot, endless situation reports, popping open the dust cover on the optical sight of his M4, cigarettes smoked at a lung-cancering pace, bomb scene investigation that earned him a familiarity with the human anatomy, sorting through intestines, burned chunks of automobile, fingers, ball bearings, feces, brake fluid, bloody fragments of bone, black coffee that tasted of desert grit, camel spiders, and endless, routinized interactions with gear: body armor, M4 rifle with three-point sling (pistol grip high, right hand ready), pistol in cross-draw holster on the front left side, ammo, night-vision, GPS, flashlight, crimpers, helmet, gloves, earplugs, sunglasses, Leatherman, knife, heart.

who was in my class or what teacher I had or what girl I liked. Some guys I know can't remember anything about their kids being born. Some don't remember meeting their wives. But even that's not the whole thing."

"What's the whole thing?"

"Hard to describe. Ain't quite anxiety, ain't quite depression. Not quite wanting to punch people out. It's just this clawing feeling like something's about to happen. Gets worse in crowds. Like I hate being at a football game or the airport. Anywhere there's too many people. Also, whenever I don't got my M9 nearby."

"That sounds pretty fucked."

He offered her a tepid bob of his head side to side. "You learn to get by. Iraq taught me you can get used to just about anything. I mean, shit, don't ask me to take a memory quiz or nothing, but I can still work. Been a product development engineer for a few years. Braking and transmission systems. But compared to EOD the stakes are so low—you know, if you fuck up no one's getting killed. Basically feels like I can sleepwalk through it. Don't tell my boss."

"Ever go home? Do you have family around?"

"Mom got smoked by cancer of the thyroid a few years ago—I swear it's that shit they're putting in the ground to get at the gas. No Pops to speak of. Gone before I was even abortion material."

"Any love life?" she pushed on.

"Between exes right now. Was hooking up with a girl I met online for a while, but she didn't work out." His hard stare told her to get to the point.

"Who do you spend your time with?"

"A few buddies at work, a few from Iraq who I still see now and then."

"No best friend?"

"Nah, I keep to myself. So are you like writing a screenplay about me, Alvarez? Christ."

Alvarez. She hadn't gone by that surname in five years. She did not correct him as to what was on her driver's license now, though. She pushed forward, sensing his itching curiosity. Allen Ford Jr., her mentor and comrade, had once clued her in that people mostly just wanted to be listened to. They wanted to tell their story, and if you could get to their story, you could get to their conscience.

"That first time we met, back in D.C., you told me you missed it. The war. Do you still?"

Murdock considered the advertisement for the Wildfire Chicken Salad on the laminated card propped up out of the condiment basket.

"Not as much no more. Sometimes. There's the brotherhood, the camaraderie of it, combat love, that's one thing. And there's the adrenaline—best

UNTRUE He never saw the EOD guys anymore. Once he got involved with IVAW, Murdock's views left him with the loneliness of both the prophet and the traitor. They didn't get how he could shit on the cause that some of them had given it all for, and he didn't want to argue with the people he cared for most in the world. Loving your brother in arms was a more profound experience than loving God. Better if they speak of it all in another life. Kieran Slade had called him up when he found out the guy they'd nicknamed Murder was going to IVAW protests. "So you're with these fucking brain-damaged Marines telling everyone we're war criminals? All so a bunch of fat, happy, self-righteous pussies who've never been afraid of shit in their lives can sit back and judge us? Fuck that, man, and fuck you. T would fucking lay you out, man. He'd fucking cripple you if he saw this. You're a coward, Docker."

high you'll ever get. No such thing as blood pressure meds for a heart attack, right? But there's also a calm to it that you can't really get back here."

"How was the war *calm*?"

"When I got back, I was dating this girl at Penn State—she'd sort of latched on to me even though I kept telling her I wasn't much in the mood to get married, and that's clearly what she was after. I remember this one time we were driving through a McDonald's, okay? And we're picking up food to take to her family's house for dinner, and she's got this huge list of everyone's orders. But the speaker box or whatever that is don't work so well. It keeps cutting out, so the lady on the other end keeps missing stuff and she needs to keep repeating herself, and then they're confused about what she's already ordered and what she hasn't, and I'll tell you—right in that moment, I would have given anything to be back in Baghdad. *Any fucking thing in the world* if it meant I could go back and get shot at."

His water glass was nothing but ice at the bottom, so he tossed back a few cubes and crunched them loudly with his molars. He began nodding as his story morphed.

"There was this guy over there. This bomb maker we called Toy because his devices always used the radio frequency from kids' toys. Remote-control cars and Buzz Lightyear dolls and such. He came up with some real ingenious shit. Like he'd find a way around our Warlocks—our electronic jammers. He'd plant decoys. He'd wire a bomb with a different trigger three times out of five and then the other two would be callbacks. He was a meticulous cat. And we never caught him. Thought we did a few times. Once, near a bomb site, we took DNA swabs from everyone at the scene, and this shopkeeper matched. So a unit rolls up on the shopkeeper. Bingo-bango-bongo. No more shopkeeper. But a month later, there's a new bomb, and you could just tell it was his. The Warlock Red jammed it—we were in that protective bubble. But the style was his, the way the wire braided from the battery to the blasting cap. Had a little receiver from a remote-control helicopter for the detonator. He'd put his signature on the IED, you know? Cuz he wanted us to know he was still out there. Now, don't get me wrong, we all wanted to find that motherfucker and put a few through him, but at the same time I had this respect for him because I had to be better, smarter, quicker."

The waitress tried to come over again, thinking they might be ready, but Shane gave her

> **HE RETURNED** To Whitehall's office hours because he liked having someone who could talk honestly about the thing. Whitehall didn't give two fucks what you were supposed to say to fellow vets. "Don't dwell on what's been done," he said. "When I got back I threw every medal and patch and memento and symbol of the American empire into a lake." He handed Murdock books, a lot of Chomsky, Hobsbawm, Bacevich, and Chalmers Johnson. He read them at the dining room table of his one-bedroom apartment while loading and unloading his M9. It was dismaying how quickly his illusions eroded, a bad paint job that once attacked with mere sandpaper just flakes to the floor on its way to dust. He hadn't understood how ready he was, and the puzzle pieces of his reading and his experience began to snap together. He carried it around in the back of his throat. However fury, sorrow, and undefended humiliation tastes. It made him want to go back to Iraq, finally hunt down Toy, and say, "I've had some time to think about it, and I sorta see your point, dawg."

a too-impatient *Halt* gesture. "We're still going to need another minute." Bambi smiled impatiently and turned heel. "What about IVAW? Do you have a foot in activism anymore?"

"Nah. I did a year more after we met, but the surge started to settle things down, and troops were on their way out. Got tired of lefty activist types explaining the war to me." He ticked one cheek in a partial grin.

"Turns out you might've been premature given the whole situation over there now."

"Not too hard to predict, I guess." Murdock took the fork from the silverware and began twirling a tine against his thumb. "And I'll tell you something else—the beheadings, the torture, this shit ain't going nowhere. Barbarity is a powerful thing. Almost a faith in and of itself. We opened a can of worms there that's gonna writhe for twenty, thirty, fifty years."

Shane watched as his eye twitched, and he looked down at his cold coffee.

"So," Murdock grumbled. "Maybe it's about time you got around to telling me what this is all about. Why I drove halfway to Pittsburgh to not eat breakfast."

THE LOVE OF THE SUIT Like bundling up for a Pennsylvania winter. First, armor: leggings, collar, breastplate of Kevlar. Then pants with suspenders and spine guard, the diaper that encases the groin. Slip on the overcoat. All of it weighing "half a good woman," as Ta'amu liked to say. Your buddies helping you in, checking all the zippers, ties, and quick-release tabs in case you caught fire. Finally, pop on the helmet, check the microphone, the air snorkel, and above all, make sure that power fan works and the batteries are fresh because it's probably 120 fucked-up degrees out. Then it's just you peering through a visor two inches thick that gets dustier every minute you're out. Like wearing the chitinous molt of a prehistoric colossus. Ta'amu would babble reassuringly in his ear on the lonesome walk. Just the captain's way of creating the calm: "I've been meaning to give you your performance review: You're a funny little monkey, Manfuck. Think about the millennium of your progenitors who've lived and died, son, so that when the cum spilled out of your mommy's asshole at the wrong angle a mastermind hick like yourself could be born into the light of consciousness. You are *Blown Away*, kid. Bombs don't survive you. You make IEDs IEDon'ts. Just remember, my man, if you offer to carry the weight then you can't complain about the load." Then it was just the safe. When all the focus and training came zipping down to a zero-point, a moment of creation. Peeling apart foam chunks to get at the plastic-encased detonating cord of an EFP. The bomb makers versus the EOD. It was a battle of intellect and observation and obsessive skill. He crouched in his own airtight astronaut-suit world, a piercing attention for the detail that tells no story or tells the whole one. You matched wits. There was no syllabus, there were no rules. Only adaptation and improvisation or mutilation and incineration. Blast lungization.

"What do you think it's about, Kel?"

He threw up a hand. "Hell if I know. Maybe you *are* writing a movie. People love war stories."

"It's good to see you," she said. "When my partners and I started this thing, this venture, I thought of you. But I'd been thinking of you for a few years anyway."

Murdock watched through a window as a woman struggled to her car on a walker, helped along by a husband with thinning gray carefully moussed back.

"So this ain't about *Hurt Locker 2: Hurt Harder*?"

"Do you remember," she said carefully, "when we met that weekend in D.C., we had a conversation about what it would take—what would have to happen—to actually change this country?"

He lowered his voice.

"I'd consider myself still a kid at that point. Feeling angry and alone and saying stupid kid shit." He scanned the Bob Evans to see what the other diners were doing. "My point wasn't that I wanted to do shit like that. It's that *there ain't no point* in doing shit like that."

"I'm not trying to sell you on anything here." She said this with great care, each word handled, examined, and chosen. "I've been where you've been, Kel. You didn't have to go to Iraq to feel despair about what's happened and what's happening now. All I'm asking is for you to hear me out on this." She could feel the agitation wafting off him. "And if you don't like our idea, no problem. You walk away, we walk away. No hard feelings."

"Christ, you got a hell of a way of piquing a guy's interest." He relaxed back into the booth. "Not just a cerebral hick here. Also an open-minded hick."

Shane was not satisfied yet.

"Here's what I mean by that: This is going to be a conversation you can't ever

HOME Ta'amu saw that Murdock rarely made calls home, mostly because his mom didn't have a computer or phone and had to go to the neighbors' to take the call. He started inviting Murdock to join him on the video phone when he called his family back in LA. This consisted of his wife, the dogs, and like seven little brown kids running around screaming the whole time (though he understood only three of these were Ta'amu spawn and the others belonged to a sister in rehab). His wife was a phat collection of gorgeous curves and beautiful Samoan-next-door features. The first time he made Murdock sit in on the herky-jerky, screen-frozen call, Ta'amu told them this was Uncle Murder, and after the children bombarded him with questions about war and how cool was their dad and did he know how to play *Call of Duty* and was he coming to Los Angeles with their dad after it was all over, Ta'amu replied that he'd have no white Shit-Demon from the Sticks in his house and the kids screamed with laughter and the wife reprimanded him for cursing, and Murdock had to get up and leave, at which point he began to cry, violently, until Ta'amu found him at the entrance to the HAS and told him to stop being a pussy—of course Manfuck could come visit him in LA. They'd grill steaks.

repeat. To anyone. We don't know what this thing will be, but I need your word this is only between us."

"And you got it."

"I'm not being clear." She put her hand over his again and squeezed. "This is not about hurting anyone, but we could get into trouble just talking about it."

"I'm telling you, gal, you got my ear. Start her up."

"I think you understand, Kel, that you have an important set of skills. First, I tell you the bones of what we're doing. Then if you dig that, we move on to the next step, and you meet my partners."

"Who are your partners?"

"You don't need to know who they are until you need to."

"Inscrutable doesn't really do it for me, Alvarez. If you hadn't noticed, I'm a detail-oriented fella."

"It's actually Acosta now," she said. "You'd call me Shane Acosta."

THE RON KOVIC FANTASY Whitehall's self-flagellating term. That once you got home you could take up the righteous cause because you'd been there and you knew. He could only read so much about the fat margins of the contractors making fortunes not just off Iraq and Afghanistan but the empire of bases, exporting their equipment and training to a world hungry for a taste of American military supremacy; or about the symbiotic tether between the Pentagon and petroleum—the work of the oil companies guarded and protected by taxpayer dollars; or how rapid and unchecked free-market globalization incubated inequality, which incubated instability, which would eventually incubate more excuses for militarism. He'd seen the way the American empire operates. He understood its vascular system and the grainy detail of its red cells. He could wage peaceful war against its patriotic heart. "That's the only impulse to follow," Whitehall told him. "Find yourself purpose in dissent and dig in. Maybe it feels pointless, but it will give you direction, and really, who knows—it might even bring a couple kids home who would've got packed into boxes otherwise. Don't think about your life before, don't dwell on the people you lost, over there or at home, and whatever you do don't start drinking. Once you open the bottle, you'll never put the cap back on."

RAGE Shane could sense this restless anger in him, he was sure. His left eye still went through spasms of uncontrollable twitching, and he still thrashed in bed half of every night, and he still got that uncategorizable panic bubbling in his chest in crowds, and he would still hear the distinctive sound of bullets snapping by his head, that noise they made as they broke the sound barrier when they zipped by your ear, and he could still never remember his mom's face or where she'd first showed him how to tie a turle knot. Because all that rage reading—fuck. How inadequate those explanations ultimately felt for all that he'd seen and lived through. There was still no account, no explanation, and no going back. Just him and his ghosts gazing in shared awe over the edge of darkness.

His lip curled and relaxed. "Do I even know who you are? Seems like maybe we start there."

"You know me, Kel. Even if you don't know who I am." She held his gaze to make sure he understood. "There's four of us. This started back when I worked on the wetlands."

"What's up with the wetlands?"

"Just another harbinger on a long list. The point is, the four of us are kind of, I don't know what you'd call it—the hub of the spokes. The core of the thing."

"Yeah, Shane, well, what's the fucking thing?"

"We would want you to be our fifth."

"You know . . ." He chewed on his tongue and spent so long thinking, she wondered if he'd say anything. Finally, he went on. "I spent a lot of time in IVAW dealing with folks who wanted to tell me about my life and what I'd done. They tended to sound a lot like you, no offense. So while you're dancing around whatever you're dancing around, let me ask you something first: What did *you do* during the war?"

He said this with great hostility. Ferocity. She had never heard either of those things in him before.

"I went to college," she said calmly. "Bounced around a bit after that."

"You ever feel guilty?"

"About what?"

"That guys like me and more'n a few gals like you went and wasted the best years of our lives in that sorry misadventure while y'all blew each other in dorm rooms and your parents got a supply-side tax cut?"

"I don't know. How guilty do you feel that you came home, and there's some Iraqi kid who got incinerated by American-brand white phosphorous?"

She couldn't read his face, but something dark passed across it. He carried a great misery inside, and he couldn't do a remotely satisfactory job of hiding it.

Shane picked up the saltshaker, cupped it in her palm. "What?" she asked.

"Nothing." He rolled his tongue around the inside of his cheek. "Small world that you and I ever met."

"So small, it makes you understand the difference that can be made if you go about it the right way."

"Color me skeptical. Alls I ever think is how the guys who died in Baghdad or Kandahar had all the sweet-berry luck. Didn't have to come home and sit with a stinking pile of shit in themselves. They got the hero's parade."

She sighed. "Don't talk like that."

He waited for a second, like he was trying to decide. "Like what? That dying can be lucky?"

"No, man. You can wish you were dead all you want. But don't pretend there's anything heroic about it. All the bumper stickers and parades and 'thank a veteran for your freedom' bullshit—all the pedestalizing. All the movies. All that isn't for you guys who went. It's for the next time. How else do you get children in Oklahoma City or Fallujah to kill people they've never met? Convince them they'll be heroes."

Murdock ran his finger around the wet rim of the coffee mug and stared glumly at the snow. He looked far away, like he was no longer listening.

"Look, Kel." She slid the saltshaker from one hand to the other. It scraped across the table. She kept right on staring at Murdock. "We can go through this shit to the moon and back. In fact, at some point I'm sure we will. But for now, I just want to know"—she slid the saltshaker back to the

ANAMNESIS He liked to think it'd been Toy's triumph that finally got them good, but that was specious and relied on a certain Hollywood symmetry. Anbar had dozens of skilled bomb builders and trained more every day. Toy himself may have been a composite of every operator that ever outsmarted them, a concrete antagonist to hunt. Still, his gut would always tell him Toy left the suspicious package in the intersection where the choke points were obvious and the convoy had to set up fifty yards back. After they'd rolled the TALON down to the package and discovered that it was only some men's shirts—false alarm, not unusual—Ta'amu cracked, "Man, I just got a baller idea for a GAP ad," as the EFP hidden under a garbage pile went off and pretty much liquefied the captain in front of his eyes. SSG Jim Matthews was killed as well, and SPC Cort Kronlan lost an arm. Someone had triggered it through a wire hidden in the ground, so the Warlock couldn't save them, and it was some five hundred pounds of armor, tactical vest, ammo, rifle, and man vanishing except the feet still in the boots. Ears droning, concrete chunks raining, molten steel popping holes in the armored Humvee, Murdock didn't stop to think of all the bits of Ta'amu he had in his eyes and mouth. The gunfire began.

INSTINCT One thing you could say about the US military is that when they trained you to do something, you fucking well remembered it. Even with pieces of Ta'amu coating him and a hail of bullets thwapping from a nearby building and the Muslim call to prayer suddenly ringing out from a nearby Statue of Liberty–colored minaret and someone screaming, "Tell 'em we got a TIC! Put the fifty on those niggers!" and SSG Mason Saunders going cyclic with the SAW right by his ear, spitting through nine hundred rounds in about a minute—melting the barrel in the process—Murdock still did what his trauma training told him to. He leaped on top of Kronlan, this shrieking nineteen-year-old child of Texas, ripped the med pack from his vest, ground his knee into the bicep above Kronlan's severed arm to stop the blood flow (between the heart and the wound, America told you), got the tourniquet ready, spitting out pieces of his brother that tasted more like diesel than blood, *not* thinking *Captain's dead, Captain's juice*, letting the pressure go long enough to slip the tourniquet around the Limb Formerly Known as Cort Kronlan's Arm, spitting, spitting, spitting, but Kronlan wouldn't stop thrashing and screaming long enough to get his life saved (*Kronlan, for the sweet cunt of fuck*), so he cracked him in the face with his elbow, broke his nose, but stunned the Texan long enough to get the tourniquet tightened—until the limb stopped the spurts that timed eerily with the pulse Murdock could feel humming through Kronlan's whole body—and then packed the wound cavity with this handy little Kerlix super sponge stuff they gave you. With sticky fingers, packing it into a stump the color of grilled brook trout he and his mother once caught, long ago, in Wiconisco Creek.

AND LATER When Kronlan was saved and people were already telling Murdock about the Bronze Star Medal coming his way, Slade found him picking at a bit of bloody material still stuck in his teeth, and SPC Slade looked at him and, channeling Ta'amu himself, Murder said, "Tastes like chicken," and laughed. Slade thought this was inappropriate, but Murdock was drenched in so much of Ta'amu's and Kronlan's blood he didn't much give a fuck. You put that shit somewhere deep and beat a stray cat to death with a hammer five years on to try to work those feelings out.

NOW THAT WE'RE DOWN THIS ROAD Two springs ago he'd driven down to Fort Walton Beach, Florida, for the annual May ceremony to induct the recently juiced on the EOD Memorial Wall. He sat among the family and friends of that year's fallen EOD in the sweltering, swampy heat and marveled at how many people in the audience were missing limbs. All manner of hooks, tennis-shoed prosthetics, grippers, and angled titanium protruded in place of bone and flesh. One woman had half her face burned away and wore a large hat tilted to cast a shadow over the ruined portion. The wall, a pale gray slab of concrete resembling a highway divider, had four cenotaphs, one for each branch of the military, with EOD dead dating back to World War II. A bedsheet of an American flag riding above. The keynote speaker was the air force chief of staff. "This is EOD," he'd said, and Murdock felt his throat close, his eyes well. "The brains of an engineer, the hands of a surgeon, the heart of a martyr." They played "Amazing Grace," and he went to the wall and ran his fingers across the slim bronze tablet affixed to the army's cenotaph, the one that said CPT TROY J. TA'AMU 2/07. Then he tossed his Bronze Star Medal at the ground because that was the cliché most appropriate to the moment. In war, cliché was as inescapable as the dread of your own death. They'd gone over there having already learned all the clichés from the movies, and they took them up with ease: the brotherhood and adrenaline that made you cuss and laugh and feel as if this was the only place you belonged, and then you saw fucked-up shit and did fucked-up shit and it changed you, the way the movies told you it would. How frustrating to watch your life, your misery, your madness depicted absolutely accurately by cliché. Because it felt so real and original when it was you with these wives, husbands, parents, brothers, sisters, and children milling in the heat. And what was he left with? What could he do when his head was a mess of forgotten voices and errant whispers of memories with no value and no sustained narrative, just purposeless minutiae and fragments he'd take with him to the void?

AND YET There was a memory that never happened: of eating steak and drinking beer and watching all these children with his friend's eyes play in a sunny yard, and it made him so fucking furious, so fucking crazy and desperate and sorrowful that he pressed his face against the surface of that bronze tablet and through gritted teeth and layered time sobbed into the metal, hot with the warmth of the Florida sun. An older Black lady, probably the mother of some other poor dead motherfucker, knelt beside him and took him in her arms. She whispered, "I know, baby. I know. We'll all be with God soon," while she stroked his back with one hand and held his heart with the other.

original hand—"if you've got one more war in you?"

There was the tinkering clitter-clatter of silverware on plates, murmured conversations ebbing and flowing, hash browns and eggs being lapped up. Outside on the highway, the pickups and SUVs sluiced by, spraying mocha slush from their wheels. By now the pristine white had all but disappeared. The waitress returned, and Shane and Murdock ordered breakfast.

THE ACTOR

I saw him in the bookstore without recognizing him at first. I was stewing from the last meeting of the week. Darren would get the promotion, and my eyes were still threatening tears. This news had enveloped me so thoroughly since leaving the office that my gaze passed over this man I'd watched so many times in other contexts. He was poorly incognito. He wore a crisp blue Cubs baseball cap and thick sunglasses that were a rectangular mask across his eyes. Yet I could see those distinct lips, naturally pursed like a blooming flower. The straight nose with its squarish point. The five-o'clock shadow, pinpricks of black on a flawless tan.

I'd wound my way from the office to the downtown Barnes & Noble because I did not feel like getting on the train at rush hour, not with the pulse of indignation still beating in my head, and decided to calm myself by browsing books. That meeting evaporated as I took in the rest of him. Dark blue jeans with the requisite fade, a tan jacket over a light blue shirt, brown leather shoes. He was shorter than I would have imagined, but you always hear that about actors. What surprised me more was his build—clearly in shape, but so slender. Those muscles that graced the posters were more compact in real life.

I thought of that peculiar phrase then, my eyes darting away from him as I sensed his glance: *in real life.* A cliché so far removed from what it ever meant, if anything. I could even remember watching one of his thrillers a few years back on one of those early dates with Jefferey; he was not exactly an A-lister, but his films were unavoidable if one saw enough American movies. I picked a book off the shelf just to have something to do with my hands.

Then he spoke to me. I missed what he said because I was trying to see the eyes behind the sunglasses. His lips curled expectantly, and my words came out with a defensive tinge that sounded crass to my own ears.

"Excuse me?"

"McCarthy," he said, pointing to the book I held. "Do you like McCarthy?"

Blood Meridian lay in my hand, a limp accessory. I had never read anything by McCarthy. I'm one of those people constantly trying to read short stories by Flannery O'Connor yet reverting to Jodi Picoult and Gillian Flynn at the first pang of boredom.

"I haven't read much of him."

"He's one of my favorite authors. *The Road* is incredible and an easier read. *Blood Meridian* has the Judge, who's one of the best characters in modern literature, but it takes a lot of concentration. At least that's my expert recommendation."

He smiled and that institutional bookstore light almost created a glare on his whitened teeth. I set *Blood Meridian* down and picked up *The Road.*

"The problem is this is a movie, so I know I'll quit halfway through and finish it on Netflix."

It was a feeble joke, and I immediately hated the dynamic, as if he was the authority because he'd read this one book. At the office I had learned never to give the guys ammunition or I'd watch their entitlement bloat. This is exactly how Darren Grinspoon muscled in and took credit for my work on his way to leap-frogging me to executive creative director: I let men explain novels to me in bookstores.

He laughed. "Eh, movies are cheap facsimiles of what novels accomplish."

"Strange coming from someone in your line of work."

His sandy eyebrows perked upward. "Ah, so you saw around the disguise."

"Oh, I'm calling my mother about this as soon as I walk out of here."

He smiled and leaned into the shelf in the manner of a high school boy at your locker.

"In that case, can I tell you why you should read that book rather than see the movie?"

"They passed you over for the starring role?"

I put a foot forward, moving closer, challenging him. There in the pit of my belly was the kind of squirming excitement you feel so rarely as an adult, the joyous ache of a crush whose face you want to push into the mud. While my celebrity infatuations tended toward the older, more distinguished type (Harrison Ford from the eighties, please and thank you), I still had a pulse, and this attention from a man I'd learned about mostly through issues of *People* was undeniably thrilling.

"No, they wouldn't even take my agent's call," he said. "But McCarthy has this way with his prose, so you're always chasing sentences down these caverns of meaning. You just can't translate that to film. No actor, no screenwriter, no director, no team of studio wizards can do in a lifetime what Cormac McCarthy can do in an afternoon."

He said this with a wry smile that let me know he was as serious as he was aware of his own bullshit.

"That's good," I told him. "Do you have to wait for women to pick up a McCarthy novel to plagiarize a *New Yorker* review or . . . ?"

His head bobbed back when he laughed.

"C'mon, I'm serious. Let me be corny!" His finger brushed against mine as he took the book from my hand. He lobbed his head toward the front of the store. "This is on me."

"Don't," I said, reaching for it.

He brushed my arm back, a little too forcefully. "Seriously, it's my pleasure—just in case you don't like it."

In my head, my friend Linda's voice rose in pitch: *Let the famous actor flirt, dummy!*

"I wasn't planning on buying anything," I said when we reached the register. "I was just killing time before I met a friend."

"What kind of friend?"

"What kinds are there?"

"Boyfriend?"

"No, a girlfriend. We were going to get a drink, maybe see a movie. Do you have anything out? I need at least a sixty percent on Rotten Tomatoes before I commit."

I stood awkwardly beside him as he produced an AmEx. My face flushed as I felt other people in line watching us, and I still wanted to snatch the book before he could buy it for me. He thanked the clerk, her bored eyebrow ring never rising in recognition, and glanced back at me. I was supposed to follow him now, and I did, slipping *The Road* into my bag.

Outside, early-evening pale had settled in. He took off his sunglasses, a full reveal. The high cheekbones and irresolute brown eyes. I remembered them as blue in his films and now took that as the work of contacts. It made me wonder how much of that fresh, taut look was surgery or Botox.

"I'll tell my mom you said hi."

"What if . . ." He looked off into the headlights and taillights of traffic. "You canceled on your friend and we grab a drink instead?"

The truth was I wasn't meeting a friend. It had been a spur-of-the-moment lie, the kind you tell when you want someone to think you have plans. A single twenty-seven-year-old wandering the shelves of a bookstore on a

Friday evening with nothing better to do? Though I hated that it made me feel anxious, it did. The drink offer wasn't shocking—his flirting was hardly subtle—but now my mind jammed with thoughts of how I looked. What did he see? Chestnut hair, I'd recently had drastically shortened and highlighted for the coming summer. The small bulb of my father's nose mixing with my mother's darker Mediterranean eyes. I attempted to not let my insecurities wash over me and thought of all the yoga and treadmill miles I'd logged during the city's hibernating months.

"Aren't you dating Scarlett Johansson or someone?"

Again, the laugh was surprised and genuine. "I'm between destructive relationships with coworkers at the moment. Here's my perspective: I'll either go drink at the hotel bar by myself until someone recognizes me and I get annoyed . . . or I can buy you dinner."

"Now it's dinner?"

"If you're hungry."

Of course I was going to say yes. But I told myself I was saying yes only because the initial shock at his fame had worn away. He was just another guy trying his hand at a pickup line.

We took a cab, sitting a comfortable distance apart in the back. The butterflies that flapped and spun kamikaze in my stomach when he first spoke to me now lay dormant, reverse-aging back into their chrysalises. The cab rounded the corner of Wacker, passing the river on our left and the gleaming silver phallus of Trump Tower. The setting sun reflected off its miles of mirrored glass and cast light over the city, lighting from a painting or a dream. After a bit of awkward silence, he said:

"You got into this cab and still haven't told me your name."

"Jackie." I shook his palm, and the grip lingered. That smile, how he flashed it like a knife, knowing it was dangerous. No wonder his dumb movies made so much money.

*

In the restaurant, we were led up the stairs to the second floor and a series of private tables. He was ordering a bottle of wine before I'd sat all the way down.

"Did we just screw everyone on the waiting list?"

"They don't give us half-famous folk a choice."

As the wine arrived, he went with the standard barrage of first-date questions, not all that different from a Tinder date: What do you do? Where are you from? (Consumer advertising, creative director; Iowa originally.)

"Do you like advertising?"

"It's a job," I said, only because I did not feel like talking about it. I was obsessed with my work in the way one is obsessed with a cruel lover, but I was saving my rant and fury about Grinspoon and the general chauvinism of advertising for my therapist.

"That's too bad. People should have passion for what they do."

I gave him my meanest laugh. "That's a pretty asinine thing for someone like you to say."

He'd taken off the Cubs cap and hung it on the back of his chair. His oak-colored hair, matted from the hat, swept back from his forehead.

"I don't see how I'm asinine because I love what I do."

"I said what you said was asinine. Because it was. You know, most people take whatever job they're offered. That's how you pay a student loan or buy a burrito for lunch."

"All I meant is that I love what I do, and I love it aside from the money. Aside from all that bullshit of being known."

"How can you separate the two?" Suddenly this guy was Darren Grinspoon and every other mediocre man I'd ever dealt with professionally. Linda Holiday had once called this "the conundrum of contemporary straight women": We understand better than ever that men are selfish, arrogant, awful, and entitled, and yet we nevertheless spend most of our energy and intellect trying to find one who seems okay enough and will love us. Leftover emotional energy is then wasted on not wanting to want that.

"I think you know how you sound," I told him. "It's easy to love what you do in your circumstances."

He didn't quite look like I'd taken the air out of him, but his gaze was puzzled, maybe put off. Then he smiled. "Hope you don't dissect every chunk of blather that comes out of your dates' mouths like this."

"If you'd like, I could sit across from you all night googly-eyed, asking what it's like to work with De Niro."

He laughed uncomfortably, and his eyes wandered, unable to settle.

"Yeah, okay, but you realize that I didn't get to that point for almost a decade after I dropped out of college. Until then I was a broke stage actor living in a shitty apartment, doing odd jobs for spare cash. I'm just saying I never cared. I've loved this since I was seven years old and my second-grade teacher suggested I try out for *Oliver Twist*. I just meant I've always loved performing, and I'd still do it even if it was community theater back in my hometown, which by the way, is Omaha, not Orange County or something."

"Fair enough." I looked back at the menu, face turning hot, feeling as though this whole thing had been a bad idea. I opened my mouth to say as much, but he cut me off.

"I'm hearing how defensive that sounded. Sorry, I don't have a lot of conversations anymore with people who aren't in the business. It's a bad bubble. Please do feel free to call me out as an asshole."

I closed my mouth, felt the flush recede. "I think I just began by assuming you'd sound like an asshole."

"Want to start over?" he suggested. "Maybe about how great Omaha and Iowa are? Real salt of the fucking earth, right?"

The waitress interrupted us. He ordered the grilled corn tamales and the fettuccini with artichoke, and she took the menu and said, "Yeah dude, whatever—like you're not a figment of my imagination right now," which made all of us laugh.

I ordered the pearled barley risotto and handed over my menu. In that moment, the trailing tail of a memory came to me like a song lyric I could remember but not place with a musician: Jefferey on a similar early date. We'd gone to dinner, and when the bored, ill-tempered waiter took our menus and stalked off, Jefferey whispered to me, "So that's your ex, and this is some psychosexual mind game? 'Cause I'm in. I'll bring the ice pick and boil my own rabbit." Every last word was so weird I couldn't help but crack up.

The actor and I talked about our salt-of-the-earth childhoods, his as familiar and mundane as mine. In turn, I told him about Iowa. My dad the farmer, Friday night football games, country bonfires, the town square where we all gathered on weekend nights and cupped cigarettes in our palms when the police cruisers passed. Most of our fathers wore the same Carhartt jackets and bitched about bailers and planters, fertilizers and Monsanto seed prices. Most of us went to one of two state schools when we graduated. I left off the story just before my dad was forced to sell the farm following my parents' bankruptcy. A decade later, he still wasn't over it, and I worried he was depressed or about to divorce my mom. My siblings and I couldn't be in the same room without arguing about it.

"Ever think you'll go back?" he asked.

"The same time you go back to Omaha." We exchanged a smile. "Maybe that'll change someday when I have kids, but I doubt it. Plus, I've been thinking of moving to Venice."

"Really?"

I nodded. This was not exactly true, but it was true in that I'd spent some unremembered period of time in the fall of the previous year searching for potential jobs that could allow me to move to the city I'd dreamed of living in since I was a teenager. When my mom and dad were arguing at the height of their financial stress, I'd put on headphones and click through images of the strange and wonderful city on our old Dell desktop.

"I'm aching for a change of pace. I know there's always nostalgia for ten minutes ago, but the country seems ugly to me in a way it never did before. It's reached some kind of new temperature lately."

"Couldn't agree more," he said.

This was a clichéd sentiment on my part, completely unoriginal, and not something I was even sure I believed. Mostly I was tired of my job. I'd gone from art director to senior art director to creative director as fast as anyone ever had in my company, but that progress had stalled. The higher I climbed, the more enraging the office politics became, and I had this sense every time I sat down in a meeting that my coworkers still considered me an intern. I'd moved to Chicago during the recession, determined to make my way, and after a year of unpaid internships, I thought I'd have to return to my little town in Iowa and live with my parents and waitress at one of the chains by the freeway where so many of my high school peers found work. The entry-level advertising job came just in time with my rent due and my bank account overdrawn and my three credit cards maxed. I was determined to prove I could do it, and when I got passed over for the Grinspoons of the world it reminded me of that desperation all over again.

I had five people working under me now, and on more than one occasion I'd hear the younger guys repeating back to me ideas I'd pitched earlier, regurgitating them as their own and congratulating each other. The worst of these was Darren, an ultra-nice young backslapper and Dartmouth grad who came from money and had connections littered throughout the agency. Marketing still retained its boys' club formulation, and this gave the women sharp elbows. Even after I'd piloted two very successful campaigns (a new home water purifier and a mind-numbing financial product called closed-end funds) my boss, the senior VP, Beth McClann still spoke to me like a kid sister being allowed to go off on her own at the fair for the first time. When she gave Darren the promotion that by the whole office's estimation should have been mine, I'd almost burst into hot tears. This blithely sweet guy who never missed an opportunity to second-guess me in front of my team, who acted like my seniority was ephemeral and temporary, I would now effectively have to answer to. I'd waited until I got to the bathroom to cry and thought about quitting and moving to Venice.

*

We split vegan chocolate cake for dessert, dueling over it with two short-tined forks. He asked me about my family, and I told him about my brother and sister, the former a lawyer in Tampa with a wife and two sons, the latter a physician's assistant in Davenport, married to her second husband, recently pregnant. I even found myself telling him of our lifelong emotional combat: her easily wounded nature, my impatience with her. My dad's insistence that his daughters could succeed at anything, from youth basketball to a high-powered city job, engrained in me and utterly lost on her. My warnings about both of her quick marriages. He asked about her new husband.

"He's older," I said. "Midforties. They met because she worked for him."

"He was the physician she was assisting." He grinned, a flash of the teeth that I recalled were crooked in some of his earlier films and now as straight as wall tiles.

"Exactly." I twisted the stem of my wineglass, staring at the purple murk within. "My sister is one of those people who leaps without thinking. It's been her MO since we were little and she threw tantrums in the supermarket over Fruit Roll-Ups."

"And you're not the tantrum-throwing type?"

No, I thought, Jefferey in mind. *Unfortunately.*

The waitress returned and he handed her his AmEx. I thanked him for dinner.

"It's my pleasure. You up for a drink? I know a great place."

"I'm sure you do, but I think I'd better get home." It's so stupid, the little dances we do even when we know they're dances.

"Come on, come have a drink with me," he said as if reading from one of his scripts. "It's good to have a conversation with someone who's not pretending."

"See, but you're saying that so I think, 'Oh, he likes me because I'm treating him like a real person and not fawning over how famous and gorgeous he is.'"

His lovely eyes dashed away from mine, and I knew I'd at least called him on his method.

"You know what I think?" he said. "I think you're the one who knows she's pretty goddamn intelligent, interesting, and beautiful but has to put up all these guards against pricks. And hey, I understand why you'd assume the worst about me, but honestly, right now? I've had a good time with you, and I'd like to continue. I'd like to buy you another glass of wine that you can sip at a pace best measured on a geologic timescale."

The laugh escaped before I could clamp down on it. I rolled my eyes.

"You're not as awful as you could be, I guess."

We walked back down through the restaurant where all but a few sets of eyes turned to us. Admittedly, it was more than a thrill. My stomach felt light, and I wished I had a dress on or at least something sexier than the jeans and blouse I'd worn to work. Wishing I'd done something with my hair that day—at least a chance to blow-dry and run a straightener through it—for this little walk of beauty and celebrity and mystery.

This time in the cab there was nothing left of the sun but a rumor on a dark horizon, and the distant lights of the skyscrapers backlit our drive. I knew it might be the wine, but there it was nevertheless: I felt good. This was exciting and unexpected and fun, and I couldn't recall the last time I'd felt any of that.

The bar was just a dim blue bulb above an unmarked door. Small tables surrounded by plush chairs with tall backs, the bustle of your standard chic nightspot. The host led us to a table in a corner at the back. We had to stop twice for people requesting selfies.

"There are all kinds of downsides to this," he told me as we sat. "I know that sounds like a whiny millionaire problem—"

"Multimillionaire problem," I corrected.

He smiled. "But it doesn't take long to see why it becomes awful. The temptation to sit in your mansion or penthouse like Citizen Kane and never be in the world is real. You get strange letters and social media shit, and people say things that you have to report to the authorities. Outright death threats become routine. Every interview, everything you say is scrutinized to the point where you want to pass every sentence by a PR rep because you never know who you'll offend. There are land mines out there you don't even know about and internet warriors always trying to plant new ones under you. You can't eat a meal or have a drink or buy a book because people are filming you everywhere you go. You're basically a zoo animal when you're in public. Every room or space is a set, and the director's told everyone with names A through M to notice you when you walk in, and names N to Z to notice exactly thirty seconds later. And that's coming from someone whose career has been absolute shit the last few years. People underestimate the wonder of anonymity. Once you've lost it completely, that's all you ever really want back."

I gazed at him with my chin propped on a fist.

"Cry me a river," I giggled.

"I know. And those Syrian refugees think they've got problems."

The wine arrived—red again—and we toasted.

"Do you get back home much?" I asked.

"To Omaha? Sometimes." He took a long gulp from his glass. "Not really. My folks are much older. My dad used to be a pastor at a megachurch. One of those places where the minister walks around with the Britney Spears headset. But he ended up with dementia pretty young."

"I'm sorry. That sounds like it could be rewarding, though, to grow up like that."

"Oh, it was mostly a childhood of bigotry against gay people and anti-abortion rants washed down with some syrupy Jesusy swill." He took another long pull, his glass nearly drained. "My folks didn't really approve of what I went and did with my life. Hardly original, right?"

When he spoke of his family, I could see the haggard quality of his features. In the bathroom at the restaurant, I'd googled and learned that he was twelve years older than me, but only now did I see that age in him. He picked at his thumbnail, peeling back a sliver and discarding it on the floor. My eyes fell to the wine bottle. We'd once pitched for an Italian wine brand, and my idea had been "Open to Life" with the image visually connecting to the emotional sensation of an open wine bottle. Of course, what I actually drew was myself and Jefferey looking out over what had once been my family's farm. When you want to create an emotional response in a stranger, you first look to your own joy or melancholy or nostalgia. Beth McClann didn't like the pitch.

"Why did you ask me to dinner?" I said, breaking the long quiet that had settled. "Honestly."

His eyebrows arched in an expression that could have been worry.

"You were in that bookstore. You were beautiful. Then you were smart. It was really nothing more than that—spur of the moment."

"I just want to know why you're doing this." I hated how this comment made me sound, but it was honest. "If this is some kind of shtick you put on to sleep with civilians."

"Look, you can go anytime you'd like. I'm not holding you hostage here. I thought we were having a good time."

"We are."

"Then why can't you just enjoy it? Why do you have to question it every ten minutes?"

"You want to sleep with me," I said, as if accusing my younger sister of stealing my clothes.

He rolled his eyes. "Of course I want to sleep with you. I don't have a charity where I take out spinsters."

"That's what you're after."

"Is it that surprising?"

"I've just never heard it stated that bluntly. How often do you do this?"

"I'm not going through twenty questions with you."

"I just want to know where I stand. What happens afterward."

"Afterward, we fall asleep. In the morning, we get breakfast. Then I catch a flight in the afternoon back to LA. But I'll be back in about a month when we start filming."

I nodded and pretended to consider this. It was so stupid. All of it. I could think of a half dozen of my closest friends who would throw themselves at this opportunity—maybe even wreck a marriage over it. Yet here I was simply wishing I'd never gone to the bookstore that day.

In the cab, once again we were quiet, and I found myself pointlessly thinking of Jefferey. None of this would have happened if he could have just grown up, if he could have just been the person I wanted him to be, but that's silly. That's putting such a massive "if" into the formula it topples the entire equation.

When we met I was so unsure about him and yet grew to be so certain so quickly. Maybe I saw what I wanted to see. He'd been so confident texting on the app that I distrusted him. But he was also cute in that way we learned boys were cute where I grew up: tall and sturdy, an Opie-like face with big features. Big ears, big chin, big nose, big jaw, big lips. Blond hair parted on the side with a cowlick bursting out of the product he used to tame it. A face where you could still see the pudge that had covered it as a boy but had stretched out handsome. When we went out, he was not the brazen jock I'd expected from our brief interaction on the app. He was a goof, witty in a dumb, self-aware way. He also had the widest, most beautiful smile.

He worked in supply chain logistics but said he wanted to go back to school to become a high school history teacher; he loved graphic novels; he watched loud, idiotic superhero movies but in a way that I enjoyed, deconstructing the tropes in endlessly amusing fashion. He traced patterns on my back that made the hairs on my neck stand up. We waited a full month before we finally had sex, which when you're a young person in the city is practically abstinence. We deleted the app together.

After a year I was sure I would marry him. My family adored him. We went down to Florida to see my brother, and while I chatted with my sister-in-law and ogled the new baby, my brother and Jefferey laughed like donkeys in the kitchen, tossing Corona caps into plastic cups and loudly debating college football. The other men I'd seriously dated in my life came to feel like filler, ways to learn the lessons young people need to learn before they're ready for the real thing.

When we moved in together, the high lasted for months. I'd never lived with a boyfriend before, and there were so many weird things about it. The little razor clippings he left behind in the sink or how there were these sacrosanct times when the television absolutely had to be on a sport of some kind, and I came to find the white noise of a football broadcast oddly soothing. He had an old Nintendo 64 that he refused to throw away, and finally he forced me to learn how to play *Mario Kart* with him. We would stay in on Friday nights, drink wine, and play every level of *Mario Kart*, screaming whenever the lightning shrunk the other down to miniature go-cart size. In the mornings, when we were both grouchy with sleep, he'd sometimes start dancing in his boxers, swaying his hips wildly while eating cereal or cooking eggs. "You like my moves?" If I ignored him, he'd start jittering his thick legs with all that blond thigh hair. "How 'bout these moves? Bae likes these moves, don't she?" It was so stupid, and it made me laugh so hard. He knew he could just go on like that and keep me in hysterics for hours. We hosted parties, and once he came up behind me about ten minutes before people were supposed to arrive and started kissing my neck. Without turning around, I unbuckled his belt, and he hiked up my dress. The way two people can learn each other, what the other enjoys and how to do things in a certain way. The right angle, the right way to move, the right way to hold me. He knew me. I would cradle his face and practically black out, holding the cheeks where those razor clippings began.

*

As we waited for the elevator in the hotel, his hand came to the small of my back, and I realized it was the first time he'd touched me intimately. In the elevator we were quiet. I stared at the floor and played with the jewel of my earring, felt how the stone was loose in the metal.

"Are you okay?" he asked.

"Yes," I said. "Just nervous."

"Don't be."

"That's easier said."

His hand crept into my hair and his breath drew near. He smelled of neutral shampoo and the mint he'd popped. The kiss felt entirely natural.

He didn't give me another chance to think about it. As soon as the door to his room closed (and this room was enormous—a separate bedroom adjacent to the living room, a wide view of the vast, blinking cityscape through the windows), he was kissing my neck. He worked quickly, popping open each button of my blouse, finding the zipper on my jeans. I sat on the bed, and he slid them off.

"Work underwear," I tried to joke.

He looked up at me. "You're so gorgeous, Jackie."

He kissed my stomach, tickling but in that good way, pulling at my insides, arousing all the equipment I'd been neglecting in my long self-imposed chastity. It wasn't until he pulled off his jacket and shirt to reveal the clean muscles of his chest that I felt overcome. He did look slimmer than in his films, but the curves of his muscles were beautiful, maybe a bit of flab around the love handles, but still sculpted and lovely. I ran my hands over his chest and stomach. I kissed the hair on his abs.

I avoided looking at his groin, pushing away the thoughts of all the women he'd likely been with, whatever background afflictions he might carry. He didn't offer to use a condom, and though this seemed incredible (*Think of the potential for paternity suits, darling!*), I didn't ask him to. I hadn't been on birth control since Jefferey. All of this seemed far away.

The pleasure was climbing back onto an abdicated throne—not an orgasm but that kind of aching skin-tight throb that felt triumphant and divine. He kept asking me what he could do for me, but I only urged him on.

I knew I'd never be comfortable enough to orgasm, not with this being the first time.

And only time. Over his shoulder I could see the city's stars. *The only time.*

*

When people began to ask when Jefferey and I would get engaged, I'd shrug and say, "There's no rush." Yet their curiosity was dwarfed by mine. The longer it went on, the more it upset me—as I feel it would have upset anyone. We lived together. We spent holidays with each other's families. We were both comfortable in our jobs. Yet he never so much as put a toe in the water on the subject, leaving me to broach it in the most oblique ways, talking hypothetically about buying a condo or a house. I began entertaining the awful notion of getting forgetful about my birth control.

It was a slow-rolling panic, a premonition of getting hurt, that made me finally use the very distant possibility of a job opening at my company's New York office as a way to talk about the future. An insidious white lie, but I had to know.

The conversation lasted from Tuesday night into Wednesday morning. There were all the typical platitudes—"I'm just not ready," "We're still young," "I'm not sure I even want marriage or children." Argued around and around for hours. It made no sense to me and still doesn't. Why be together for three years then? Why move in for those last two if he didn't think that was where it was going? It made me hate him so intensely, how he could lead me on that long. Of course, he didn't see it that way, but it was hard for me to draw any other conclusion: I'd spent three years with a man who always had one foot out the door, who'd conned me into falling in love with him even as he kept it secret in the back of his mind that he did not think of our future the same way. I wanted to curl into myself until the world vanished.

He stayed another month until the lease was up. A month of so many protracted hours-long weeping sessions, so much goodbye sex, so many terrible things said and then immediately retracted. He could still make me laugh even in the midst of the most painful thing I'd ever known, and I'd think, *This person is ruining my life.* And when he left, he left. We had some contact at first, two Starbucks meetups, emails exchanged, a few phone calls. The last time we spoke only because I drank too much with Linda. I woke him up and cried into the phone about how much I missed him. "You already know I feel the same way," he said. But this didn't change the bottom line. In the morning I deleted his number. What followed, everyone knows: a grief like death, only the person who haunts you is still of the world. Before him, I had no idea how fury and longing are barely any different at all.

*

He pulled out of me, and I felt what he'd left, slick, running between my thighs, pooling around my anus. I'd go to the pharmacy the next day for the morning after pill. My heart thundered, and my left breast throbbed where he'd pinched it in the heat of the moment. He turned onto his side and took my face in his palm. I kept my eyes on the hard line of his jaw.

"You all right?" he asked.

I nodded.

We stayed like that for a while, talking sporadically, but mostly I lay with my head on his chest, plucking at the hairs on his stomach while he stroked my back. The patterns of his fingers reminded me of Jefferey. Maybe all men just learn how to do that.

Finally, I pulled away from him. "I'm going to go," I said.

He looked confused. "Why? Stay. We'll get breakfast in the morning."

I didn't know how to explain it to him. How I didn't think I could bear to wake up beside him and eat overpriced room service.

"I'm a light sleeper," I said. "And I have a million things to do tomorrow."

"I don't want you to feel—" he began. "I don't want you to think I'm—"

I shook my head, pulling on that plain pair of cotton underwear. "It's nothing like that. You've been really sweet. I had a great time."

I was dressing quickly, checking myself in the mirror. It occurred to me that when I walked out, the concierge would probably think I was a call girl.

"Did I say something?" he asked, looking genuinely dismayed.

"Not at all. Really." I paused, fumbling with the buttons of my blouse. I grabbed my bag, and there was *The Road* sitting right on top. "I just think we should leave it here. That's all."

I managed to get through the door with only a few more protests and one long kiss goodbye.

I hurtled out of the elevator, through the lobby, and out into the brisk night. I moved like a wind coming off the lake, slowing for nothing. Then I stood at a corner of State and Wacker, just north of the hotel and there wasn't a single car in sight. It felt like a premonition, these empty streets, how hollow the city would feel if it was abandoned. The air felt cool on my skin, which was still as hot and sticky as candy in the mouth, and I could feel the pent-up desire soaking into my underwear. Already I wanted nothing more than to go back into that hotel, knock on his door, and again grip the muscles of his chest. I finally spotted a cab, and as I slid into the seat I couldn't tell if I was joyful or sad, empty or fulfilled, coursing with a new energy, a renewed love of life's possibilities, or simply mourning all the people and places I hadn't even realized I'd left behind.

Donald J. Trump ✓
@realDonaldTrump

One year ago I started calling President Obama INCOMPETENT and people thought it was too tough.   Tonight everyone is using that word!

5 Nov 2014 · 02:57

"We build the path as we can, rock by rock."

BEWARE: DANGEROUS FEMINIST PANICS SEND MALE SEXUALITY INTO CRISIS

*"You clearly don't know who you're talking to, so let me clue you in. I am not in danger, Skyler. I am the danger. A guy opens his door and gets shot, and you think that of me? No. **I am the one who knocks.**"*

#BringBackOurGirls

"Hands Up, Don't Shoot! Hands Up, Don't Shoot! Hands Up, Don't Shoot!"

DROUGHT LEAVES CALIFORNIA REELING

ISIS Insurgents Capture Mosul

Whether or not this particular quarterback is guilty, the sheer volume of college athletes accused of sexual assault who then go unpunished highlights the obvious intersection of football culture and rape culture. Football culture demands these athletes are given the benefit of the doubt. Rape culture demands that we view the victim as a questionable and promiscuous attention-seeker. The wider impact of this dynamic permeates society and goes almost completely unchallenged.

Vladimir Putin, his proxies, and the ring of oligarchs who pass for governance in Russia have, in just one year, illegally annexed Crimea, shot down a passenger airliner, and most alarmingly interfered in Ukraine's election, sparking widespread violence and protests. Worryingly, the Obama administration has been dozing on this bellicosity like a freckle-faced boy on a fishing raft. Russia may be a brittle and aging petro-state, but Putin remains one of the most dangerous actors on the world stage . . .

MALAYSIAN FLIGHT MH370 VANISHES WITHOUT A TRACE

"I CAN'T BREATHE."

KIM AND KANYE TIE THE KNOT IN $2.8 MILLION ITALIAN WEDDING

POLAR VORTEX SWEEPS ACROSS U.S.
SUBZERO TEMPS BREAK RECORDS

The Ebola virus has now killed more than 11,000 people across Sierra Leone, Liberia, and Guinea, and ushered in a tsunami of media panic. A nurse is suing New Jersey governor Chris Christie, claiming she was illegally detained and raising the question if governments can unilaterally imprison people if they may carry a pandemic disease . . .

Donald J. Trump ✓
@realDonaldTrump

A really bad night for President Obama. Now the Republicans have to get together and get the job done!

5 Nov 2014 · 10:25

Donald J. Trump ✓
@realDonaldTrump

Obama has now had two record & historic midterm losses. There is Hope & Change for America.

5 Nov 2014 · 21:26

The Absolute Most Insane Thing to Ever Happen:
Did Kim Jong Un hack Sony because of a Seth Rogen movie?

"And it's even worse because Bill Cosby has the fucking smuggest old black man public persona that I hate. *Pull your pants up, black people. I was on TV in the '80s. I can talk down to you because I had a successful sitcom*. Yeah, but you raped women, Bill Cosby. So, brings you down a couple notches."

THE LION
AND THE FIELD

2015

You decide to leave home for good after you win the lottery, a Shell station scratch-off that abruptly puts three hundred dollars in your pocket. You're fresh off one last blowout fight with your mom. You'll have to go back eventually, if for no other reason than to get your stuff, the box of minor valuables beneath your bed.

You're sick of Trotwood, sick of Dayton. It's time for a change anyway. You collect your winnings, the cashier laying twenty after twenty in your palm, and go pick up Claire Ann from the Jiffy Lube where she works. It's a sauna-hot evening, and you drive with the windows down because your AC's wrecked. You don't bother to call in to your job, and you don't answer when your boss puts in call after call, the buzzing phone annoying your thigh.

You deliver for Domino's, $4.50 an hour plus tips, and spend most of your time with Claire Ann, driving to the park so you can fuck without your mom interrupting. You have dreams—not as in hopes and aspirations, which you figure at age twenty are not yet your concern, but bad dreams. One in particular that won't stop.

You text McHenry, a dealer your childhood buddy Casey Wheeler put you in touch with before he fled to Coshocton on account of a dispute with his girlfriend's father. McHenry meets you on West Third with a baggie of coke. He's a mean-looking fucker with the eyes of a hound dog and three teeth missing from his upper row, but his shit is solid.

"Also got some of them X," he says, eyes wandering over Claire Ann in the passenger seat.

You ask how much.

"Give y'all two for ten. Less you wanna buy in bulk."

"Not tonight," you say and hand over another ten bucks.

You drive to a part of town more suited for two people of the white race, stopping in a gas station bathroom where you and Claire Ann cut and snort two lines each using a compact mirror and a credit card. You pop the X. You ask what she wants to do.

"My friend Dee's at a party down at UC. She texted me earlier."

Cincinnati's an hour's drive, but with all the coke and X and the bottle of Maker's you're about to buy, it'll feel like ten minutes.

You drive, and the headlights on I-75 glide over the ornate black cross tattooed on your forearm. You haven't been to church since you were twelve, yet you know God has plans for you. You first started having this dream two or three years ago. It never comes on consecutive nights. Sometimes weeks will go by. It always comes back, though. Sooner or later, you will always return.

You thought the heat would dissipate as the night came on, but the air still sweats and you feel moisture run from your balls down your thigh. That's the X kicking in. Claire Ann tried sucking you off on the drive down, but you were too keyed up to come. Stepping into this house party, you're too hot and thirsty to talk, so you cling to the bottle of whiskey. You pull and pull. The names come so fast, you can't remember which face belongs to which "Eric" or "Megan." Claire Ann introduces you only as "Keeper." Her friend Dee she knows from high school. Dee knows someone who goes to UC and lives in this sterile, bright apartment. You want to fuck Dee the moment you shake her hand. Not because she's attractive. She isn't. She's overweight with a bad black dye job, black nail polish, and too many piercings. Yet she has a look to her, a sexiness that speaks of highly limited inhibitions. You keep thinking of the dream, always the same: Running through the woods behind your old house. Trying to get to the field. But no matter which way you go, the pink umbrella always finds you.

You are thinking of ways to fuck Dee when a joint travels into your hand, which gets everything swimming further. Someone flips a switch and the room is swathed in red light. Spilling like a puddle of hot blood. Claire Ann motions for you to follow her into the bathroom. You met her last fall at a Trotwood-Madison High football game. She was a junior and you went because you had nothing better to do that night. You had a flask in the inner pocket of your jean jacket and she kept looking at you from the student section of the stands, stealing glances across the aisle until you went up and started talking to her. You'd been meaning to leave Trotwood for a while, but then you met this cute little sun-soaked kid with haunting green eyes, filmy, gray-stained teeth that overlapped each other, and an ass the shape of a full moon. You want to take her with you wherever you go, but she has to graduate first.

In the bathroom you both snort another couple of lines, then you reach a hand up her skirt and pull her thong to the side. You lick her clit while she sits on the closed toilet. She stops you because she says she has to pee. Then she says she has to tell you something. The pink umbrella is never open when it comes floating through the trees looking for you. It only opens once its handle has hooked the back of your collar and hoisted you into the air. At that point, you're helpless.

Claire Ann passes out on the couch, and you overhear Dee talking to some of her friends about going to a bar. You leave Claire Ann and end up in a car with five people, speeding over highway through vapor moonlight. Taking drags on a cigarette, window down for the smoke, crushed against the thigh of some guy in the back seat, everyone chirping. Birds in a hurricane. The air barely feels refreshing, the heat's so intense. You're coated in a film of sweat and grime that keeps replenishing itself. The guy next to you remarks, "Hundred-and-two's the high tomorrow."

"Not all that hot," you hear yourself saying. "It's the humidity that gets you."

You feel the eyes and ears of the car attuned to you, uncomfortable, and you're reminded of high school, the way you could say things and people would shut down their conversation. No one has ever liked you; no one has ever trusted you. You want to be out of the car and away from these preppy college faggots. In the dream, the pink umbrella takes you to the dot in the woods and leaves you. The yellow dot is vibrating in the dark, then darting back and forth with gathering speed, tracing lines of yellow in its path, printing a three-dimensional shape right there in the murk. The dot speeds and blurs, and a form begins to emerge—first the enormous body, then the mane, then the claws. The lion blinks, and it is alive. There's nowhere to go. You scream as the lion devours you, flesh shredding from bone, the crunch and snap of cartilage, the gush and geyser of your life's blood, until all that remains are your eyes. The powerful jaws descend and all goes dark. That's when you wake up, never more relieved for the dampness of your sheets and the murmur of your mother's television a room away.

Your hometown is a shoddy collection of breaking or broken families and people with too much time on their hands living off unemployment or disability. You hit the bars, you watch Little League and high school games and drink forties in paper bags. You sell plasma nearly every week, usually before Friday night to put twenty-five bucks in your pocket. You drive by the old house sometimes, the one your mom lost to Ameritrade, and you think of the field behind it. Beyond the backyard, through a tunnel of black oaks, there was the field littered with discarded farm equipment. You used to go there as a kid and sit among the rusted-out tractors and listen to the croaking of the frogs in the nearby pond. Now the field is gone. Replaced with a Kmart, a Verizon, a Dairy Queen, and a Payless. Some of your old high school frenemies are married, some have kids, a couple are dead. You've felt the urge to leave before, but never like this. After what Claire Ann has told you.

In the bar, you take a shot, and it puts you over the top. You hustle outside, to the alley, and puke up whatever you've eaten that day. A suctioning tube in your stomach, sharp fingernails in your throat. In a moment you feel better and try to go back inside. The bouncer, a large Indian guy—the dot, not the feather (one of your favorite jokes)—won't let you back in. You argue with him, swear at him, call him a monkey.

The people huddled outside laugh in disbelief, and he steps to you and says, "You have two choices, man: Get the fuck out of my face right now or take a ride in a police cruiser with a broken nose."

You feel sobriety lapping at you, which makes you embarrassed, which gets shame flooding your neck, heat on heat.

"Suck me, fag," you mumble as you walk away. You have no way to call Dee or any of the others. You stumble down an unfamiliar street, cars hurtling by. Some jackass has put an enormous handmade TRUMP4PREZ!!! sign in the window of his duplex along with a picture of Hillary Clinton with a bull's-eye over her face. You did like his show, though. You and your mom used to watch it. You remember Claire Ann back at that apartment with strangers. You vaguely understand that you need to get her, that she's seventeen and passed out alone, but first you need to finish the coke. The dream never stops. You'd think after so many times, you'd be used to it, but it still terrifies you. You try different things in the dream. At the beginning you take different paths through the woods, you run from the pink umbrella, you try to hide from the dot that becomes the lion. But the lion blinks, and it always, always chases you down, ripping away pieces of you until nothing is left but your eyes.

In a bathroom at another bar, you snort the rest of the coke, which is probably too much. You're not just flying, you're hurtling, atmosphere-bound. You wander down a street and see a huge house with a party going on. There are people on the lawn taking turns at a keg, Solo cups in hand. You pluck one off the lawn, walk up like you belong, and pour yourself a foamy beer. Some faggots stare at you but don't say anything. Inside, there is music that makes the blood in the veins of your scalp pulse. It's maddeningly hot inside. Cheap plastic fans try to circulate air, but there are too many bodies. Many of the guys have their shirts off, many of the girls are in strapless dresses. Every set of tits swells, every color radiates with magic and glitter, the walls inhale and exhale, every drop of sweat sparkles in the frosty light. Maybe you're dizzy. You decide to take a seat on the melting cushions of a couch. You sip your beer. After a while a guy comes and sits beside you, black hair, tall, pores like elevator shafts.

"What's the word," he says.

You pretend like you don't hear. You drink.

"You look like my cousin's boyfriend," he says. He has a huge tattoo on his neck, cursive scrawl. *Threnody*, it says. Probably his band or something equally retarded.

He's asking for your name, so you mutter about taking a piss and stalk off. There's a staircase, and you find a bathroom at the top. Rather than fumble for a light switch, you do your business in the dark and hear urine splashing on the floor.

In the hallway, you see the bedrooms now. There's just enough light coming from the bottom of the stairs that you can see these rooms belong to people with stuff. Computers. Televisions. Maybe jewelry or expensive shoes. You poke your head into one. An even deeper heat envelops you. It looks like there's a pile of clothes on the bed, but as you move closer you realize it's a girl sleeping. She's got her knees turned to the side and her arms splayed like goalposts. You touch the sticky skin of her shoulder but she only breathes shallow, husky breaths. She's wearing a black dress with spaghetti straps, black hair flowing like a still wave across her face. A weak chin and thunder thighs. You can see the air swimming around her.

You go to the door and close it. There's no lock. You undo your belt and pull her knees apart. Lowering your cargo shorts, you get your cock out and scoot her dress up. Silky thong underwear. She doesn't even stir. Your mouth is dry, so you swig some beer and set the cup on the windowsill where a thin gruel of light splits each slit of the blinds. You crouch over her and push in. She makes a sound in the back of her throat and tries to lift her head but sets it back down. You begin. It's that awful feeling like in the car on the way down with Claire Ann. You're hard, you're horny, but there's no sensation there. And it's so very hot in the room. The sweat comes broiling off your face. You squeeze her breast and wonder if this will wake her. You keep going until you can feel the sensation creeping in. You're so hot, your back is soaked, you feel like you're in an oven, you feel like you might pass out. You lower your face to hers. Her breath is vodka and corn syrup. She whimpers but doesn't wake. Then abruptly, you come.

You pull out and stare at her dress bunched around her thick thighs glowing in the timid light. Her head lolls from side to side, and then she goes still again. You pull up your shorts and buckle your belt. You take your beer and go back downstairs.

On the couch again, you drink. Then he's standing over you, Threnody. He thrusts a finger at you.

"Man, you don't know anyone here," he says. You sip. Your hair drips like mop water. "You don't know anyone," he says again.

That night, you sleep sitting up in a bank vestibule, and of course you dream of the lion. You sit on the forest floor and wait for the pink umbrella to find you. You watch as the dot zips the lion into existence. It blinks, and stands for a second, eyeing you with those cool predator eyes. It opens its cavern full of slick, wet teeth, and you plunge into those jaws headfirst, aiming to immediately gouge your eyes on the two longest, sharpest canines you can find. Your scream thunders in your throat and echoes in the forest, with tone and pitch. In fact, it's nearly a song. You feel the lion's jaws close and that bizarre dream-pain, which doesn't hurt so much as imply what hurting could feel like.

The next day you have a hangover for the ages, and Claire Ann is furious. She picks you up in your truck, and she's immediately bawling that she thought you were dead or arrested, and you try to explain, but you can't entirely remember what happened that got you separated. Eventually she falls asleep in the passenger seat. You stop for gas and a Red Bull. It's a day where the sun has the tar on the roads melting. Between the lingering booze, coke, X, weed, and heat, your consciousness feels like the wreckage of a storm.

Back on the road, you stare at the macadam traveling under the bumper and almost believe it doesn't really exist, that right now you're living a dream and if you steered the car onto the other side of the highway, you would pass through the other vehicles as if they were made of fog. You're already forming a plan. After you drop Claire Ann off, you'll nap and then you'll pack. After all, you have a car and a little money for gas. You can go practically anywhere you want.

Your head rocks with the rhythm of the truck, and you think of the field behind your old house, well after Ameritrade took it but before they bulldozed. You went there the day it happened, when you didn't know where else to go. Through the tunnel of oaks to the field. You slunk past old tractor tires, a combine, a few plows, a piss-yellow rotary tiller—all coated in rust. On the horizon there was a barbed-wire fence staked too far apart so the lines sagged. Penning in some farmer's marbled cows, still as sculptures. You sat in the grass between the decaying blades of the combine, pulling up fistfuls of tall cool grass and smushing ants with your thumb until the sun dipped too low, and the darkness frightened you back over the field to your home.

alHasan_May2016.docx

2016

Abstract: Today my mother and I had a conversation that excavated certain emotional reactions I've lately experienced due to my family, my work, my father's funeral, and, for reasons I have difficulty articulating, the National Basketball Association. Consider this an effort to understand the ways in which they refract and reflect one another. I'll begin with the context: a recent trip to Las Vegas with my financier, Peter, and the success of our proprietary black box, the Sports Almanac.

//

My final semester at MIT, I went in search of a professional gambler to finance the development of my modeling system for predicting the outcomes of NBA games. As was typical, major financial institutions had been circling us young quants, and I had lavish offers from firms in Boston, New York, London, and Tokyo—institutions eager to exploit the hard-won mastery of those with superior neurochemical wiring in the interest of market share. My peers failed to appreciate the dark humor I found obvious: that if they could, these elaborate boxes of capital would lobotomize us for this wiring without hesitation. If I was going to gamble for a living, I knew I'd prefer to do it on basketball, which had been a childhood obsession and which I still followed with more scrutiny than my studies. I should make clear I bore no resentment toward my peers who chose Wall Street. Mostly I found the thought of hopping from one bubble to the next tedious. It does not take an intellect capable of navigating higher order differential equations to understand that these firms are not in the business of creating economic value. I had no interest in joining a hedge fund. It seemed too easy.

I met Peter O'Connell in his Back Bay condo, a yawning cavern filled with only a square of living room furniture, a TV like an obsidian window, and a titanium couch-side refrigerator, stocked entirely with energy drinks and Michelob ULTRA. Peter was young, only a few years older than me, with the fair skin and crisp, red-brown hair of unspoiled Irish ancestry. The

blue of his eyes gave me a vivid recollection of the Fuller Park Pool in Ann
Arbor where my father tried to force swimming lessons on me, only to learn
I could scream effectively for the duration of the lesson. Behind Peter, a
pool table attempted to add presence, but it looked stranded, an abandoned
felt island. Peter seemed to know very little about the project for which he
would potentially serve as the source of financing. He had many frivolous
questions.

"You're a hoops superfan, right? So who was your favorite player as a
rugrat?"

"I wouldn't say I had one. It's the analytics that have always interested
me. As a child, I kept notebooks of statistics. One of the first variables I
studied was Scottie Pippen's perimeter defense on the opposing team's best
wing player, which was likely as responsible for the Bulls' success as Michael
Jordan's scoring prowess. That made the game fun, though it likely began as
a way of attempting to be close to my father, with whom I had some difficulty relating."

After a pause, Peter raised his hand: "Damn. Didn't know we were going
that deep, bro, but literal same!"

Peter O'Connell came from relative means. His family owned a concrete
business in western Massachusetts, and during an unimpressive stint at the
University of Massachusetts he'd used some of his allowance to gamble on
his favorite pastime. Peter explained that he made a veritable fortune by
exploiting an edge dealing with how bookmakers calculated their halftime
totals. For two NBA seasons his winning percentage was:

"Unholy as fuck. Like Vegas must have thought someone finally managed to sell their soul to the devil."

His method was far more clever than I would have expected given his
personality. However, he'd merely stumbled into the tail end of a fad as
bookmakers caught on and adjusted their method for allocating points each
half. Peter's edge became useless. He experienced the simplest rule in statistical probability: Whenever a variable is affected by stable factors a few
random samples prove nothing; the variable will soon regress to the mean.
In the following two years, he lost $4 million. He'd been living in Las Vegas
in the fashion you'd expect from a twenty-two-year-old male who suddenly
comes into such wealth. Yet one does not get into MIT without understanding that if you find gambling exciting, you are doing it wrong. As was the
case with Peter, who began betting more subjectively. He explained that this
was called:

"Being on tilt. Finally, I started to read a lot about APBRmetrics and modeling and all that shit. I mean, I didn't even know about the Kelly growth criterion, but c'mon, bro, they're not teaching that in high school algebra."

I'd reached out to several other high-profile sports gamblers but found that Peter was already searching for what I was proposing: a modeling system, a proprietary black box, to create a new edge. It was at this point that I realized Peter thought he was interviewing me. I allowed him to continue to believe this.

"I can't pay you hedge fund money," said Peter, extending his hand. "But this shit'll be way more fun. We're gonna build Biff's fucking *Sports Almanac* from *bee-too-tee-eff-too.*"

It took many more months of conversation before I understood that Peter was referring to the film *Back to the Future II*, and it did not help that he'd invent nicknames for our modeling system spontaneously and with decreasing sense. The black box was all at once: "the Sports Almanac," "Biff," "Biff Tannen," "BT," and then he began referring to it after his favorite basketball player, Larry Bird, as in: "Larry Legend," "Larry," "LB," "Birdman," and finally and most inexplicably, "Birdman Tannen."

My primary concern was not the humble working salary of $68,800, which was more than adequate for my post-collegiate needs, and it was not the challenge. At MIT, I'd worked under Dr. Sri Thankankur and Dr. Jane Tufariello on Earth System Models, weighing various scenarios for greenhouse gas accumulation in the twenty-first and twenty-second centuries, which required far more complicated interactions of variables than basketball. My primary concern was in fact my parents, who of course viewed gambling as haram. My earliest memories are of my preschool in Ann Arbor where I'd walk in circles around the perimeter of the jungle gym because I had no idea what these other children wanted from me. I learned how to be by myself in some safe corner, arranging wood chips in ascending order of quality. My sole interest might still be those wood chips were it not for the Chicago Bulls. The lonesomeness of my own mind made school difficult and mosque impossible. Though my mother would often repeat that I suffered from no disability, that I simply thought differently, this was not the way she treated me in practice. When the Bulls began the second run of their dynasty, however, my father enjoyed tuning in to the games. Soon, the dynamic interactions playing out on our television captured my attention as well, and I began keeping track of basic statistics in my notebooks. My father was clearly overjoyed that I watched with him, and his cues of approval meant a great deal to me.

Still, a career in gambling was in no way acceptable, and at first I kept this from my family. They knew Peter had hired me to work on sports analytics but did not know it was about wagering money. When I began working with Peter, I thought he was familiar: a protozoan high school jock turned college fraternity brother turned entrepreneur wishing to live out a twentysomething playboy fantasy any way he could, the type of individual who had long filled me with gruesome purple dread. Yet Peter was not what I expected. He treated our partnership seriously, taking notes and asking questions. I wondered if he was lonely, but that explanation felt inadequate. He had plenty of friends, a family so sprawling that I could never keep it ordered despite my exceptional recall, and a very pretty girlfriend, Rachel Franklin, who with her pert looks and urbane manner reminded me of the portrayal of young women on television sitcoms. Yet during the 2013–2014 season, he kept inviting me to watch the games as if they were social occasions rather than the raw data I was using to develop the model. He enjoyed conversation immensely and took no issue that I frequently recorded our interactions in a pocket pad notebook.

Peter employs a self-effacing jocularity. He is an individual who should be entrenched in his entitlement, and yet my experience of these three years has been quite the opposite. Peter is without artifice. Even when he uses the word *bro*, which he does with hyper-frequency, each *bro* has built within it a statement about the preposterousness of his own subculture. It took me perhaps too long to understand that Peter's insistence that I make the short T ride from my apartment in Cambridge to his Back Bay condo went beyond my work on the black box. It dawned on me that his perpetual motion machine of conversation was not transactional. He simply enjoyed my company. Outside of the members of my family—who I often thought were pretending anyway—I'd never met anyone who did.

//

As children, my younger sister, Haniya, once asked what it felt like to be me. I'd recently caused some conflict between us, spoiling her tenth birthday party because I could not bear the sound of her and her friends talking over each other, so I began screaming for it to stop. I was thirteen at the time and mortified by my own outburst. Unlike most adults, Haniya had no interest in the arbitrary mores that made it inappropriate to explore issues of neuro-diversity. When I attempted an apology the next day she said:

"Dad says it's like you got dropped off in a foreign country and only know bits of the language."

"I wouldn't know. I only know how I feel. I've never felt any other way."

She assessed me like I was an experiment: "I'd say that's not exactly true. I'd say you know the language. You just have to speak it your own way."

"That's an intriguing interpretation. Maybe."

She sighed. "I'd do anything for a normal brother." And then she bounced off her bed and went to watch TV at too loud a volume.

We've never understood each other. Haniya is charming, articulate, funny, and socially adept, and at school she made it clear that I should not acknowledge her in the hallways. In February of my freshman year at MIT when I was pulled from the Charles River and my mother and father came to stay with me, I was surprised that Haniya came as well. When our father was diagnosed she decided to transfer closer to home to help take care of him, but I made no offer to return to Michigan myself, for which I knew she resented me. Whatever difficulties my sister and mother experienced during Haniya's rebellious youth, they were memories by then. The two of them grew close during his illness, while I'd never felt more remote. It was a difficult time.

For over a year, I could sense my mother's terror at Papa's impending death. They'd wedded in India as teenagers, and she'd followed him to Michigan, USA, through med school, two children (one of whom was nonverbal for four years), and a cancer diagnosis. Haniya could weep with her and console her, whereas I was no comfort. I simply did not have the capacity to help her grieve. By my father's deathbed, I'd stood aside while Haniya held our mother's hand, and I felt as if I shouldn't be in the room. As cancerous cells destroyed his body's capacity to maintain brain function, she asked me:

"Ashir, you'll pray with us?"

"I don't see the purpose."

She begged me: "Just try. And Allah will come to you."

This bored me, and I left. My father's sickness has been the nadir of our relationship. Many-sided chance makes it outrageous for us to accept the possibility of just one cold life. How to explain to her that those relentless cells in my father's pancreas were just a matter of math? No intervention, no respite, no miracle would be forthcoming. The universe was written in equations, and so was my father's adenocarcinoma, a statistical probability infused into the cells of a macroscopic lesion. That was the only Truth. Just as the number 12 exists not because we call it "twelve" but because 12 is actually True and a mystical fairy wizard coming down from the sky to save a sixty-two-year-old doctor because his family is unprepared for his entropy is Bullshit. Haniya later called to berate me: "I don't care what you believe or don't believe, Ash, but stop sharing your fucking diagnosis of the human condition with Mumma."

When I returned to Boston after that trip, Peter invited me over to watch basketball. Rachel was there, curled into him on the couch like the logarithmic spiral of a nautilus shell. As soon as I came through the door her head popped off his chest. She found an excuse to leave, as she often did. I knew I made her uncomfortable, but I was very grateful to be alone with Peter. I realized he was the only person whose presence actually comforted me.

We did not talk about my father's illness at all. We simply watched the Cleveland Cavaliers play the Boston Celtics while Peter prattled away soothingly. At one point, LeBron James caught a pass on the wing with two seconds left on the shot clock. He spun away from a double team and launched a difficult fadeaway jumper. Yet his arm was a perfect sixty-degree angle with his ear (the real secret to shooting technique), and the ball fell softly through the basket with that sensuous whipping sound. He ambled back on defense. Peter howled:

"Bron-bron! What a freak show. What a fucking cyborg. We should put him in one of those prison cells where they keep Magneto."

My father died two months later.

//

Peter and I had been disappointed that the Sports Almanac barely broke even for the 2014–2015 season. It predicted the lines with 51 percent accuracy, which is not worth betting on.

As my father's illness worsened, I'd spent much of the following year avoiding communication with my family while trying to assess where I'd gone wrong with the model. It was in thinking of LeBron James and the few defenders in the league who could hope to disrupt his offensive potential that provided me with a succession of insights, beginning with the mathematical value of each player based on individual matchups. Though this sounds simple now, I was spending fourteen-hour days at my computers tinkering with the feeder models. By the end of this 2015–2016 season, the almanac had expelled a rather eerie data set. It forecasted nearly 62 percent of that season's games correctly. That isn't predicting the future, but it's quite close, and both Peter and I were eager to make a test run of the Sports Almanac on several playoff series. He also very much wanted to return to the city where he'd experienced so much initial success. Unhappily, I had just landed in Las Vegas when I heard the news. As per custom, my father's *Janazah* was supposed to be held within twenty-four hours. When I asked my mother to delay it a day so I could join Peter to go over the Almanac's initial results, she grew very upset.

"You wish me to break this tradition so that you can watch silly games in Las Vegas?"

"I'll still be attending. Papa is deceased, yes, but it need not interfere with my work."

She replied with fury: "Work is a ridiculous word for what you do."

Ultimately, she agreed to delay the services a day.

Immediately after checking in to the Mirage Hotel and Casino with its shrill, discomfiting window glass, Peter joined me in the lobby, Boston Bruins hat cocked to the side, clopping along in unlaced Nike high-tops. He'd been in Las Vegas for a week, placing bets based on the Sports Almanac, and we went to the sportsbook where he put an additional $10,000 on the Oklahoma City Thunder to break the 2–2 tie with San Antonio and win the series in six games. When Peter received his ticket, I felt a cheap thrill, not because of the bet but because of the work it reminded me of. It was the reason I had not wanted to fly to Michigan that night. The years spent building this model and taking Peter through it step-by-step have been profoundly psychologically satisfying. There are certain activities we pursue to attain a state of concentration, and those states of concentration are often more deeply enjoyable than the activities we're indoctrinated to view as enjoyable. I cherish this sensation by thinking of my lowest moment: crossing the Harvard Bridge, and the twilight sky had given the water a blue-purple shade. I wonder about this in relation to the Zoloft my father forced me to take after he came to Boston. That chemical crutch took care of some of the worst entropic musings, but I felt fuzzy, brain-dead, and could achieve neither a sense of sadness nor enjoyment. I was forced to see one of the mental health professionals the university makes available, and I admit the young woman gave me many useful ideas: I took up running, traversing Boston's gray-water bay in warm weather and a treadmill's running belt during the winter. She also suggested I try writing as a way to work out anxiety, and while at first I found this activity onanistic, I managed to find a format that suited me, and experiments in the alien landscapes of simile and metaphor ensued, difficult yet strangely engaging and diverting. Still, all of this felt ephemeral, and those haunted feelings I always associate with the color mauve remained nearby and perpetually accessible. It was only in the past three years, working with Peter, in the grip of a project I found so fascinating, that the dawn-colored sensation receded nearly beyond my horizon.

//

After placing the bet, Peter spent the rest of the day gambling. He kept insisting I join, and I kept repeating I had no interest. I was content to listen to his chatter and watch people try to shake and rattle the bias from their die. Casinos being foolproof moneymaking ventures, the best way to approach Las Vegas, I explained, would be to take all the money one is comfortable losing and place it on red or black at the roulette wheel where the odds are at least 46.7 percent. Then, win or lose, walk away. Peter did not see the fun in that, but it did lead to him switching from craps to roulette. Three of his friends from Las Vegas joined us, and they all became increasingly intoxicated as the afternoon wore on. They were extremely boorish, particularly "Jame-O," a squashed, preppy Caucasian with a ring of fat embracing his torso and cheeks that recalled two pockets of berries. I have little to say about these men except to relate this incident.

Jame-O called me "Taj Mahal Badalandabad" after a character in a comedic film (I was familiar with this slur, as I'd heard it before), and Peter, hostile and inebriated, exploded at his friend:

"Bro. Learn some *fucking* manners. This guy here's got more to offer in his fingernail than your entire sorry fucking existence."

I'd long been accustomed to how people become subject to narratives outside their control. Throughout prep school, my peers had christened me all manner of nicknames with and without intended animosity, one of which ("Osama bin Spock") gained particular currency. Since graduation in 2009, I've noticed their furious efforts to remove these "jokes" from social media, deleting comments from the deep recesses of various online forums making reference to me as the South Asian American math geek.

I accepted Jame-O's effort at an apology, but Peter's outburst left me disquieted. As they carried on gambling, I couldn't help but wonder, had I been blind to how Peter actually viewed me? After all, here we were in a gambler's mecca, so to speak, and was I not just his nifty multitool, an unwitting Dustin Hoffman card counter to his Tom Cruise? And were these transactional relationships not just the way of the hyper-capitalist-extractivist system? I thought of how I'd dismissed my MIT peers now performing various high-speed grifts for the boardrooms of financial empires in Manhattan. Embarrassment swelled that I'd come to think of Peter as my friend.

I left and went down to the street in search of sensations beyond the claustrophobic casino. Sweat ran a torrent down my back in the searing heat of the Vegas Strip. I saw a city of abstract fractal shapes, an artificial construct built only through a massive project of water diversion to create a mirage in inhospitable desert. A proper analogy for the discharging of consequences that people sought here. For all the hype constructed around the city, it is a plastic and uninspired place. Turn the temperature up a few more degrees, and I could picture the whole façade melting like a LEGO city in a microwave. I felt a great anti-magnetism, a desire to flee. Despite my best efforts, agitation turned to panic. Soon back in the hotel room, I sat in a corner running the cool back of the TV remote over my arm to still the particle accelerator speed of my mind.

//

Hours later, when I'd calmed down, I checked my phone. My mother had left yet another dissatisfied voice mail. Haniya promised me the delay had been helpful. Family we rarely saw had time to fly from Gujarat, and the imam had been away as well. The thought of going inside mosque for the first time in fifteen years, since my last outburst, weighed on me. My sister texted me: *Hey I know Mummas at maximum anxiety right now. Stay chill and just get here when you can.*

I did not reply to her. In high school, my sister had changed her speech, dress, opinions, gait, wore pro-choice buttons pinned to the end of her hijab, used strange slang, and performed complicated handshakes of greeting with her male Caucasian and African American friends. I learned not to take offense that she ignored me. She and my mother fought over her rebellious streak—she made trouble in the community over women's equity issues and dated Caucasian men, but Haniya was still faithful. She bore the envious gifts of intelligence and agile charm, which is why she and she alone would eulogize our father. I had not been asked to speak.

The next morning, with five hours until my flight, Peter asked if I would accompany him to a pawn shop. He alluded that he'd had his fill of Jame-O and the others and asked if I wanted to accompany him on a quick but important errand. In the cab, he began probing me about the player efficiency rating, and I explained, for perhaps the third time, the dubiousness of the PER metric. Peter often reengages me in conversations we've already had because he needs to use safe angles to approach subjects that make him uncomfortable, as I believe he did here:

"Efficiency's the game, right, Ash? That's why the Warriors are a lock."

"They're a special case. There's no comparable precedent for their achievements this season."

"Lock." Then Peter abruptly said to the driver: "A pawn shop on the Strip? Do we look like we're in the church group from Tulsa? Take us off-Strip, my man." He turned back to me.

I said: "I don't believe in locks. However, the Warriors are the dominant team in offensive and defensive metrics. That's how they won seventy-three contests. Over the course of seven games against an opponent like the Thunder or Cavaliers, the inferior team will tend to regress toward the mean."

"Ah, like you said about roulette. Speaking of, that's why I'm cashing this in."

He removed from his pocket a small lavender box, which he opened to reveal an engagement ring with a cluster of diamonds mounted on a band of white gold.

"Bought this for Rachel, but . . . Guess I threw up a fat fucking brick."

"You proposed? I wasn't aware."

"She said she had to think about it. Then thinking became driving back to Providence to stay with her parents. She called the other night to say it's over."

On the outskirts of the city now we passed a strip mall with only a dollar bargain store and cash-advance outlet still open. Beyond the mall were empty crabgrass lots and half-built domiciles flapping flags of forgotten plastic. I'd of course noticed Rachel's absence in the past few weeks. I tried:

"You could save it for the woman you will eventually marry."

Peter grinned, and in doing so looked quite handsome. "Whoa—what, am I trying to hex myself? I just want to get rid of it. Figured pawning it in Vegas would be a bad man's move. As per your wisdom nugget, I'll put all the money on black and walk away."

The cabbie pulled over at a random intersection of a six-lane road called Eastern Avenue. Palm trees bisected the lanes of traffic while telephone poles and wire offered the only skyline along the flat expanse of desert sky.

The pawn shop was set in the same building as a store called Sinaloa Video, still clinging to its business model in the age of streaming movies. Beyond it was a series of shoddy one-story houses with bars on many of the windows.

Peter's bartering took place with an overweight man in a black Pantera T-shirt who wore socks under his sandals and heaved a breath with each movement. It was a quick transaction. Peter accepted just over $1,700 from him, mostly in rust-green twenties, and dropped the ring into his fist like he was tossing a coin to a vagrant. On the drive back through the authentic Las Vegas of shuttered stores, battered used cars, and a heat that had weight, I commented:

"That ring was likely worth more."

"Less than half what I paid and much more than it was worth to me. I didn't want to have it in my drawer another day. Who would've thought getting your heart broken—that actually sounds like how it feels. I dunno. She might not have been the person I thought."

"What does that mean?"

After a long silence: "She came to me with this story from the *Globe* about how you took a swim in the Charles a few years back and some dude had to fish you out. I told her, So fucking what? But she didn't want you around."

My anxiety swelled, and I chose my next words carefully: "Peter, I'm sorry if I caused this. I would have gladly resigned if you'd just explained the situation to me."

"What, are you fucking kidding me? She doesn't get to decide who you are. So what if you had a death wish once? We all do—it's in the *Mad Men* pilot! You're a fucking brilliant, funny, stand-up fucking guy, and if she didn't want to get to know you like I know you that's her fucking problem."

I was at a deep, cavernous loss for something to say. Luckily, Peter spared me:

"And like I said, maybe it showed another side of her I couldn't see before. When I lived here I was a fucking psychopath, sleeping with a different girl every weekend. Then I met Rachel right when I got back to Boston and I was fucking humbled and ready to take a breath and be in fucking love, you know? It's like they say: 'Ruined love, when it is built anew, grows fairer than at first, more strong.'"

"Who says that?"

"Shakespeare, bro."

"I wasn't aware you read Shakespeare."

"Oh, I don't. BFQ, dude. That shit knows all."

"BFQ?"

"*Bartlett's Familiar*, bro. BartFam. 'Bartleby, the Scrivener.' That thing basically wrote the intro to every paper I ever had in college."

"You're a perspicacious man, Peter."

He patted me absently on the knee: "Stick with me, kid. I'll take you to the stars."

//

On the flight home, I tried to avoid thinking of the two days of dressing, praying, smiling, and emoting that lay ahead. The scent of my childhood home, of meticulously groomed plants and flowers in every corner of every room, greeted me as powerfully as my mother's worried kiss or my sister's careful embrace or the eerie sensation of walking into a tomb of memories echoing with an absence. We ate dinner, Haniya and Mumma bickering over her biryani recipe. I stared over Haniya's shoulder at the rows of old embossed books with gold-leaf lettering, all my parents' confused texts on the Qur'an. As a child, I'd viewed them with fear because the teachings were as difficult for me to believe as the khutbahs of the imam. I refused to walk by the shelf or sit on the side of the table where I couldn't keep an eye on them.

Haniya went on about college while my mother stole glances at the muted TV tuned to CNN, something she never would have allowed in our childhood. She watched with worry as the subject never wavered from failed casino owner Donald J. Trump, who it seemed would soon secure enough delegates to clinch the Republican nomination. Hani attempted to explicate silver linings:

"He's going to drag down every Republican on the ticket, Mumma. This is a blessing in disguise, trust me."

"This is a cursed year. The hateful people are winning everywhere. What about Brexit?"

"That's not going to happen either, Mumma."

"When you see your aunties, they will tell you what's happening in Gujarat. The violence against Muslims is so normal now, and this—this is the beginning of it here." Mumma shook her head while stock footage of Trump ad-libbing at a political rally played on-screen. Talking heads debated the odds of his unconventional candidacy. Our mother continued: "This is real, Haniya, and when he wins—"

Haniya laughed loudly at our mother's foolishness. "He's not going to win! This idiot can't tie his shoes! He's probably incontinent. He probably has to wear a diaper onstage!"

My mother slapped Haniya's hand, though she had lost control of Hani's foul mouth in her teenage years. Haniya swung her head to me, the crass yellow of her hijab sliding back and a lock of blond-dyed hair spilling out over her forehead.

"Ashir, tell her about the statistical likelihood of this doofus winning."

My mother continued to stare at the TV and the amateur politician that had so captured the public imagination.

"It's of negligible probability, according to most polling. But I'm far from an expert."

Later, when our mother went to bed, I sat in the living room watching game six of Oklahoma City–San Antonio. When Oklahoma City completed its upset, Peter texted me:

Birdman Tannen nails it. When we're millionaires don't change on me bro.

I texted back, in an effort to be teasing: *Are you concerned that when you achieve what you've worked for so vigorously, you'll find yourself feeling empty? What will you do if you conquer NBA gambling, Peter?*

Peter replied: *Easy-peasy, bro. We buy a basketball team.*

That was when Haniya poked her head in.

"Hey, look what I found."

She held aloft a bottle of Macallan twenty-year single malt scotch. I'd always known my father hid alcohol in the garage and that his surly moods grew worse if he spent too much time there, but I did not know that Haniya knew.

"Oh, I knew for years," she said, pouring us each a glass, the incongruity of her bright yellow hijab and the swishing amber liquid notwithstanding. "A son who's a professional gambler and a daughter who loves a stiff drink." She clinked her glass against mine, winking at her revelation of what I thought was my secret. "We are bad *haraming* kids, Ash. *Haram*-alam-a-dingdong. I'd say Papa would roll over in his grave if he knew, but this probably isn't the right night for that comment."

I laughed, and Haniya couldn't believe it: "Now I have to make it a double to celebrate."

Before that night, I'd always felt like my sister was alien to me: religious but progressive, bold but closed off. The night before our father's *Janazah* was the first time I felt close to her and finally understood what that phrase meant. I could admit to myself that it was good to be with her, that perhaps with the long ordeal of our father's illness now behind us, a new phase of our relationship might emerge.

The next morning, my head aching from the dehydration of the scotch, my mother asked me to drive her to mosque to help with some final arrangements. I agreed, knowing this was her transparent method to have whatever conversation she wanted to have.

"So your work in Las Vegas. You find this a good use of your talents?"

"It's lucrative, and it makes me happy."

"You know what your schoolteacher once told me and your father? Do you remember Miss Addie? Fourth-grade Miss Addie."

Miss Addie had been my third-grade teacher, but my mother quickly shooed away this point in the manner she had when she was very frustrated with me. My mother's accent deepened with her intolerance:

"She tells us that she's never seen someone so young so good with maths. She tells us that we are raising a genius." Then she arrived at what she actually wanted to say: "You realize I worry. I don't want you to do it again. It is never far from my thoughts. Or far from my fears."

"You've only seen me for a day. What could you know about my relative state of mind? I'm doing well."

"You make that impossible to know."

The picturesque homes of Ann Arbor looked cheerful in the spring sun. I chose to focus on the cool green lawns rather than engage in what I viewed as a tired and unwinnable debate. She persisted:

"Your father was a good man who helped many, many people, Ashir. And some of those sick people that he helped years ago, they are coming for the *Janazah*. He was so generous. Give, give, give."

Of course, the service would include hagiographic words from his friends, fellow doctors, and members of the community. But these were the memories of the bereaved—rose-colored and necessary to the circumstances. They couldn't know of my father's curt, dismissive treatment of my mother, how he'd freeze her out for days at a time, barely grunting replies, or that despite the dogma he adhered to, he hid liquor and Budweisers in the garage, from which we were all forbidden, and drank many nights after work and spent the mornings hungover, or that despite his assurances, he found me an impossible child, and it made him an exhausted and bitter parent. The dead don't receive honest criticism. Everyone is too stunned for impartial assessments, though they shouldn't be. Death is only the second law of thermodynamics—everything evolves to a state of maximum entropy.

Everything decays. The ultimate regression to the mean. I find this principle almost too useful. The human mind is dead set on resisting regression to the mean. Even those who are secular reject it at all costs. From religion to basketball, the mind yearns to believe in the extraordinary, the mighty, and this explicates so much about our fears, insecurities, and delusions. Perhaps this knowledge made me speak too curtly:

"Papa's death, my work—these subjects have nothing to do with each other. I had no interest in finance, and I wish you would learn to keep your feeble opinions to yourself."

My mother's jaw snapped open: "Do *not* speak at me like that. I know you think I'm a silly old woman, but when you have all these amazing offers from these financial peoples, what did I ask? That you take those jobs and make yourself wealthy?"

I agreed she had not. I apologized. I hoped that would be the end of the discussion. Sitting at a long red light, a tree lush with spring's nutrients hovered over the car, and a wild light seeped through slits in the leaves, running over my mother's face like the shadows cast by sun-dappled water. She said:

"You have come so far, Ashir. God gave you an amazing talent. He put something inside you that very few people have. I only want you to learn that happiness is about using such gifts for that which is beyond yourself. I am not even talking about something holy. Just something higher."

Conclusion: Sitting at the desk in my childhood room, I'll finish this rambling excursion by saying only that my problem, I suppose, is that the model worked. Perhaps Peter and I will begin to win a great deal of money, but that is of no interest to me. What is of interest is recapturing that moment of profound focus and pleasure spawned during the three years of working on the model. Because here I am despite it all, stranded in a universe of colossal scope and maximum entropy where human concerns are infinitesimally purposeless dust motes. And yet when one views those motes under a microscope it becomes clear that they too are each a colossus. They are formations worthy of our dedication, what I've heard people call "love" or our "heart." But they are really more like a fever. Or a fugue.

Warmed-Over Bunk

One of global warming's most spectacular and dangerous ideologues emerges. Why claims of "environmental crisis" will never go away.

By *John Taylor Jr.*

July 19, 2017

For those who view "Green New Deal" environmentalism as virtuous at best or benign at worst, I beseech you to pick up a copy of *One Last Chance: How to Save Civilization by Moving to Total War on Climate Change* by Dr. Anthony Pietrus.

Pietrus, an oceanographer, climatologist, and contributor to the Intergovernmental Panel on Climate Change, exemplifies the kind of near-psychotic delusions that have come to characterize the environmental Left. His new book, which is being touted as the New Testament of global-warming action plans, is a frightening reminder of what lies in store should such extremists ever gain electoral power.

"We are not at a crossroads," Pietrus writes in his introduction. "We long ago took the wrong fork. Now we must do everything in our power, including sacrificing our comfort, our livelihoods, our economy, and partial, carefully excised pieces of our democracy, to save our species and all species."

Much of Pietrus's radical wish list is unremarkable, well-trod territory of the climate vanguard. What differentiates *One Last Chance* is that last part, the "carefully excised pieces." It's also what should send a chill down the spine of every American.

First, however, his stunning grab bag of policies deserves comment, if only to deracinate it: the purchase and stranding of all US coal supplies and shuttering of all coal plants within five years; the nationalization of the thirty largest fossil-fuel-producing companies in order to "unwind" their operations; limits to production on virgin aluminum, cement, iron, plastics, and forest products; a buyback program to replace the entire US vehicle fleet with electric vehicles within ten years; achieving a 50 percent reduction in air travel by levying heavy taxes on each ticket; a rapid buildout of nuclear power plants; and massive public works projects ranging from the construction of a smart grid to carbon capture systems that would draw CO_2 from the air and sequester it in the ground and offshore.

The nation's farmers will not escape either. Pietrus also insists on draconian taxes to lower dairy and beef consumption and advocates a price collar system on agricultural emissions with auctioned credits, which would "quickly and effectively shift the economy toward zero-carbon energy and food production."

To pay for all this, a "project on par with the rapid militarization of the US economy following Pearl Harbor," he proposes levying taxes not only on carbon but increasing the marginal income tax rate, instituting a consumption tax on "luxury" goods (i.e., nearly everything the average American household might want to purchase other than basic foodstuffs), and the issuing of "climate bonds."

Lest other countries push back against this lunacy, he proposes economic war to force compliance. "The US, China, and the EU could easily draw the rest of the world into joining the new carbon compact by instituting a tariff on goods from any nation without similar carbon pricing." However, the US must be ready to go it alone: "The current economic order did not emerge without the political and military will of the largest empire the planet has ever seen, and similarly, a new carbon-free regime can be forced upon the world with greater ease than trying to get 190 nations to sign on to a new protocol."

If this all doesn't sound like madness yet, just wait. Pietrus claims he's spent "many years studying how such aims may be achieved. I've concluded that the only way forward is a new governing paradigm similar to war mobilization."

He would create two new government bureaucracies. The first would be modeled on the War Production Board, Franklin Roosevelt's agency that took control of the US economy during World War II and dictated what would be built and how much of it. Rather than being housed in the executive branch, however, the agency would be independent, an "environmental Federal Reserve," tasked with building wind farms and solar panels in order to "insulate it from near-term politicization and weathervane cold feet." To put it bluntly, he'd put the entire American economy under the aegis of an unelected scientific bureaucracy. To play the role of watchdog, he suggests a separate agency, an overseer, that reports to Congress and ensures the "climate Fed" doesn't run amuck or become invested in "crony capitalism."

Is your jaw on the floor yet? If not, take this brazen admission: "As in the Second World War, mobilization strategies will, by necessity, not involve much participatory democracy. Therefore, maintaining public support through information campaigns designed to shape the public psyche by highlighting the consequences of failure in the '1.5-degree war' will be paramount."

He wants not only to create an authoritarian environmental regime— he wants to build a propaganda department right alongside. Even George Orwell couldn't envision so audacious a plan.

Even if one does believe in anthropogenic climate change, *One Last Chance* at no point engages in a measured debate on the matter. Rather, it pulls the curtain back on what global warming and other attenuated environmental concerns are typically deployed for: Trojan horses for socialist policies. The Trump administration recognizes the threat posed by environmental socialism by fiat, and over the course of his tenure Trump and EPA administrator Scott Pruitt have bravely moved to return the agency to its traditional role. Pruitt has stalled or slowed agency actions, legacies of the Obama administration, despite widespread condemnation from the radical Left and intransigence in the courts. According to insiders, he will soon put forward a proposal to end the toxic Clean Power Plan, crippling to American industry. The administration has shown courageous leadership in defending American families and American business as the Left reveals its true radical aspirations.

Pietrus, meanwhile, spends much of his manifesto shamelessly invoking World War II, the threat of Nazism, and the Holocaust to build urgency. The difference between the Nazis and global warming is that the Nazis were indisputably real. Global warming is a potential problem that may in the distant future have negative consequences, or perhaps benefits.

As most of us long ago figured out, global warming and its sister "threat" ocean acidification are manufactured crises, and if those both fall through, you can count on environmentalists coming up with another. Their ideology, which includes a profound hatred of the free market, industry, and yes, as demonstrated by Pietrus's book, democratic rule, insists they devise a threat of apocalyptic terror to justify their notions of redistribution and central planning.

The Years of Rain
and Thunder: Part I
2017

The first time I saw Kate, she was walking down the dock on Jackson Lake, a backpack slung over her shoulder, sturdy hiking boots clomping on wood. Her legs and shoulders held the bronze of the summer sun, and she had a mass of dark blond curls piled in a makeshift bun. She was smiling like someone was telling her a joke in one of her earbuds.

I'd come to work in Wyoming after graduation, driven by directionless aspirations to become a writer. My cap and gown barely hit the floor of my room before I was striking off from Chapel Hill to the wild blue yonder of the American West. My senior year I happened to read a book of short stories about Wyoming by Annie Proulx, and it lingered as inspiration. Why not light out for the territories? I found ads for seasonal positions at Grand Teton National Park and landed on the docks of Colter Bay about fifty minutes north of Jackson. Most of my belongings went back to my parents' house in Raleigh where my dad made nervous rumblings about this half-baked plan. Law school would always be there, I told him.

I'd been working for about a month the day I met Kate. We marina employees wore white polo shirts with a green GRAND TETON NATIONAL PARK logo on the breast and spent most of our time renting canoes and motorboats to tourists who'd putter around the lake for a few hours. Captain Ray was our manager, a white mustachioed, beer-bellied man of few, though creative, words. He had a nose of burst capillaries like a misshapen beet and chuckled a lot—a raspy cigarette-smoker's laugh that came chuffing out whenever one of us did something stupid. On my second day, this foreign kid, Ghezi, was trying to take a broken Yamaha 9.9 off one of the motorboats, which was at least a two-person job. Captain Ray saw him struggling to lift the engine and came ambling over with a cigarette dangling from under his mustache, green Teton ballcap perched in defense of his sunspotted dome.

"If that winds up in the lake, you're going down there with a snorkel mask to dredge it up."

Sheepishly, Ghezi stopped his struggle.

"Hey, you. Tar Heel," Ray called across the dock. "Give us a hand." I set my book down and made my way to them. "Snorkel, you lift, we pull."

Together, the three of us lifted the engine, and I carted it back to the boathouse where Captain Ray tinkered all afternoon while I handed him tools as he chain-smoked. Ghezi forever became "Snorkel." I became "Tar Heel." Ray was one of those unintentional linguistic wizards I thought I'd someday figure into a novel.

We were a small crew. Ghezi, from Macedonia, spoke in halting English, had big bug eyes, a face like a crustacean, and was extremely good-natured about all the xenophobic shit Ray gave him. "We got plumbing and TP in America, Snorkel. No more shitting in a hole and wiping with your hand." Maybe Ghezi didn't find this hilarious, but he laughed like he did. Damien became my best friend, a pothead who'd just graduated from the University of Arizona. He had buried a jar of weed in the woods because the company had a one-strike rule on drugs. Sometimes after work, we'd trek out to this quiet spot, dig for a minute, and split a bowl in the still summer evening.

A month in, I'd begun to worry about the mundane flow of my days, fearing this job might not give me as much writerly inspiration as I'd imagined, when Kate came down the dock with a pink canoe slip in her hand.

Ghezi elbowed me in the side and said in that goofball Macedonian way of his, "Ah. Babe o'clock."

I'd quickly realized Colter Bay wasn't exactly awash in attractive women, and our clientele was mostly Asian tourists and the minivan set. Even if we'd been renting canoes strictly to beauties, Kate would have caught anyone's attention. Tall and athletic, her stride registered in the world. First, I took in her dark skin and huge head of curls. Then, as she got closer, her pretty snub nose, full lips, and a wide, hungry smile.

She held out the slip and looked at the three of us like she'd caught us comparing scrotums.

"Tourists need this much help getting into canoes?"

Ghezi took the paper and pinned it to the clipboard. "We aim to please," he said, tipping an imaginary hat. Damien snorted in disbelief. He brought a canoe around by its rope, and I took it from him before Ghezi could.

"Got it." I sat on the dock with my feet inside to steady it. "Just you?" I asked her.

She unslung the backpack and tossed it in the center of the canoe. Damien handed her a life vest and a seat cushion.

"No, my friend's in the bathroom."

"So we have a spiel we have to give you, and you can give your friend the CliffsNotes."

"Lay it on me."

"You're going to go out with two seat cushions, two paddles, two life vests, and we expect you to bring them all back. If you don't, we prosecute you, and in Wyoming that means you have to fight a bear in a pit."

"Yeah, that's just called justice."

"You may canoe anywhere you wish but be careful about going out too far on the lake, and whatever you do, do not try to cross to the other side. It's really far, and I don't want to have to come out at dusk to rescue you."

"But you'd be my hero." She finally popped out the earbuds and buckled the vest over a sky-blue tank top. She sat down beside me on the dock, resting her boots beside mine. I saw her eyes now, brown and icy, but with chips of green, a color impossible to pin down.

"Also, we have a gift shop where you can buy overpriced, Chinese-manufactured Grand Teton swag. Do you enjoy key chains?"

"Get out of my head, kid. They're only my favorite ever."

I could have sat there all day doing this. It was something I'd come to see about her: that she could play to the personality of whoever she was talking to, match wits. Only later would I learn she always had you at match point. I stole a glance at her legs, brown and smooth but peppered with scratches and mosquito bites.

As I prepared to ask her name, she looked behind me and said, "Get your tinkle out, Luce?"

The friend was short, wide-hipped, her face hidden behind a big pair of sunglasses. She had her black hair buzzed. She wore a cutoff shirt over a sports bra and didn't bother to buckle the life vest after shrugging into it. She looked strong, sturdy, and like she wanted to shove me into the lake as she slid beside Kate on the dock. Without saying anything, she leaned over and kissed her on the mouth. I heard Ghezi behind me let out a quick, sharp breath while I saw one of Damien's bored eyebrows ratchet up in intrigue. He nodded his head once approvingly. Of course, I felt caught. This butch woman had seen me bantering with her girlfriend and wanted to demonstrate what the situation was to everyone. When their mouths parted, Kate looked amused, dazzled, invigorated. "Let's do this, lady," she said. They each slipped into the canoe quickly and expertly, thanked us, and with a thrust of their arms, shoved the canoe away from the dock.

"That was, uh, amazing," said Ghezi mournfully.

"She was a cutie," Damien admitted. "Matt, you about knocked Ghezi into the lake to get to her."

We laughed and ragged on each other the way we would all summer, while I stole glances until she disappeared onto the sun-rippled folds of the lake.

~ ~ ~

I was up in the office running an errand when they returned. The butch girlfriend hopped out without a totter and offered Kate a hand, both of them laughing. As they came up the dock, she kept a hand on the small of Kate's back, and then headed into the office to pay while Kate veered toward the marina's bathrooms.

Ray called me over. He spent most of his day sitting on the tailgate of the shit-colored marina truck, surveying the docks and waiting for his moment to troubleshoot, as in the case of Snorkel and the Yamaha motor.

"What's up, Captain?"

He tilted his cap back to scratch at the vanishing gray stubble beneath.

"Tar Heel, you might as well've shit your eyes outta your head. That how lovestruck you get every time you spot a pretty girl? You ain't gonna see twenty-five years, son."

I laughed him off. "We don't get a lot of them out here. I gotta stare at your ugly face all day."

Ray bobbed his head to grant me the point. "Snorkel's about the prettiest thing out here, ain't he?"

I laughed again. "Jesus, Ray."

"Just don't say I never did nothing for you, Tar Heel." Before I understood what he meant, he called out behind me. "Hey, darling. These guys are all too stupid and chickenshit to approach you like a gentleman. But this one's the least stupid of 'em."

Of course, there she was, walking back from the bathroom, drying her hands on her shorts. She looked neither surprised nor offended, though I felt a flush brighten my neck and creep into my cheeks.

"Least stupid, huh?" she said. Her voice was deep and had a smoky quality that ended all her comments in a trail of vocal fry.

"They're all some kinda stupid nowadays," Ray muttered. He scooched off the tailgate and stalked into the garage, flicking his cigarette onto the pavement. I was left alone with her.

"This all looks very glamorous, I know, but we spend most of the day cleaning up Ray's cigarette butts."

"Does he help you pick up every woman who rents a canoe?"

"Yeah, Ray's a model wingman. Have a good time?"

"Very. The view of the Tetons is better up here. I'm used to Jackson, but here you get a better look at the Skillet on Mount Moran."

I was embarrassed to have already forgotten which peak Moran was.

"Do you live up here?" she asked.

I explained I had a one-bedroom in Jackson.

"Wow. You're not Harrison Ford's kid, are you?"

I felt a flare of embarrassment at the reference to Jackson's most famous ranch owner. Graduation gifts from grandparents, parents, and family friends had accumulated into a healthy nest egg. Funding a one-bedroom hadn't been a problem or something I'd even thought twice about.

Before I could retort, her eyes moved behind me, and she nodded. I glanced back and saw Buzzcut exiting the marina office, surely glaring at me behind the sunglasses.

"Nice meeting you." She offered her hand and when I shook it, I could feel all the calluses. I felt a disappointment not commensurate with the moment.

"You too."

"This is the part where you say your name."

"Right. I'm Matt."

"Kate," she said. "Nice to meet you, Matt." Our hands parted and she walked away, turning one last time. "You should come by the Cowboy sometime on a Saturday. I bartend."

~ ~ ~

"You can't go this Saturday," Damien told me. "She'll think you're a fucking psycho."

We sat on the life jacket bin watching the sun set behind the Teton Range. It spilled through the gaps in the mountains and appeared through my sunglasses in stark spikes of yellow. We'd gone to the woods after our dinner break for a bowl. Even after a month on the job, this was still breathtaking.

"I know, but I feel like I'm going to do it anyway. Which one's Mount Moran again?"

"This one with the glacier shaped like an electric guitar." He chucked his hand to the west. Damien never pointed at anything, just whipped fingertips in a direction like he was releasing a Frisbee. "As your friend for the summer, I can't condone a Ted Bundy–style move like that. She has a girlfriend. She sees you as tip fodder. You'll get a buzz on, she'll flirt, pretty soon you'll be tipping like it's a strip club."

"Shit, why'd you just tell me that? That could be exactly what she's up to."

Damien shrugged but his face remained stoner placid.

"Bad weed makes you paranoid, good weed makes you understand why you should be paranoid."

The sun finally receded behind the mountains, leaving only a red glow that trailed purple to the heights of the sky where the first stars broke through. You could see every stage of twilight, like sediment layers in an exposed cliff face.

Damien finally said, "Wow, man. That's something else."

~ ~ ~

Of course I went to the Cowboy that Saturday.

The full name was actually the Million Dollar Cowboy Bar, and inside it was everything that name implies. I passed under the sign, lit with hundreds of red, white, and yellow bulbs and a bucking rodeo cowboy above. Inside, paintings of the Tetons covered the walls, a stuffed grizzly roared from behind a glass case, and dozens of patrons competed for angles at the pool tables alongside murals of cowboys having firefights with bears and Indians. The bar itself was even busier, and there was Kate holding court while she abused a tumbler.

I found a saddle—in place of barstools, naturally—stuffed my thighs on either side in a dumb-looking straddle, and waited for her to notice me. Her bartending look was scrubbed, polished, and pinched, her bun now glossy and scalp-tight, her skirt and top serious tip fodder.

"Good. You can pretend like you're my date." She slammed a tumbler into the ice bin in front of me, scooping up a chunk. "This dude's been nagging me all night like I'm carrying his baby." Her head ticked to the other end of the bar where a muscle-bound guy in a tight white T-shirt and cowboy hat held a whiskey and stared blankly at the murals.

Before I could say anything, she thunked a Budweiser in front of me and was off, snatching the caps off bottles, collecting cash, doling out coasters with flips of her wrists.

Back a moment later, she asked, "How's that treating you?"

"Really, a Bud?"

"Are you crying about a free beer, Tar Heel? It's expired. We gotta get rid of it."

The night went like that, with her dipping in and out of conversation.

"Just a warning: This guy does not like you." She bobbed her head quickly at Cowboy Hat.

"Are you getting me in a bar fight?"

"Only cowards throw punches." Then she spun away to douse four shot glasses in Jameson.

Over the next three hours while I nursed free beers, I learned about her in this piecemeal way. She breezed by to ask, "So where in North Carolina?" "Why Jackson?" "What have you hiked so far?" In turn, I got all those crucial biographical details. From Phoenix originally but moved with her mom to Portland at age thirteen when her parents divorced. She'd studied philosophy at Oregon and graduated two years ago. Her dad used to bring her to Jackson in the summers. She came to the mountains right out of college to ski, hike, climb, raft, and "do activist shit" and now worked for a group called the Bison Project.

"What's that?"

She gave me an astonished look. "It's a buffalo, dude."

"No," I laughed. "What's the Bison Project?"

"The cattle ranchers have a lot of political pull in these parts, and they claim the bison have brucellosis and that if they don't slaughter them by the thousands, it'll spread to the cattle. But that's bullshit—the truth is it's about grazing rights. The bison graze on land the ranchers want. So a bunch of dumb, beautiful, amazing creatures get their throats cut. It's a real playback of what the US Army did when they were getting their asses handed to them by the tribes back in the day and they had to eradicate the enemy's food supply to make way for settler capitalism. Violence against nature always goes hand in hand with violence against people."

She blew by like she now had to deliver that same monologue to the other end of the bar.

An hour later, the lights brightened for last call. Cowboy Hat waved goodbye to her and departed.

"If you wanna stick around while I close, I'll walk you home after," she said.

Later, we stepped into a pleasantly cool Jackson Hole night, lit by the garish glow of the Cowboy Bar. Walking beside her, I could almost feel her internal heat radiating to the back of my hand.

"So the cowboy hat guy?"

"That's Trent. I keep telling him I don't date cowboys, especially Trump-voting ones, but he hasn't gotten the picture."

She led me south down Cache Street. We passed a neon-lit motel where a group of drunk cowboys and cowgirls stood outside smoking cigarettes and guffawing. One of them whooped as we went by.

"But he knows you're taken?"

"Huh?" She curled a lip in semi-mock horror. "Taken?"

"You have a girlfriend."

"What?"

"The woman at the lake."

"Lucy?" She pshawed. "Please. Queer New Agey ski bums make for the worst dating material. We're just friends. I mean, yeah, we fuck, but dating would mean I'd have to listen to her theories on my astrological chart or get my tarot cards read or whatever. Honestly, I'd rather go back to fucking Trent."

I navigated some steep and rough emotional switchbacks during this explanation.

"You're an interesting chick," I said.

"Am I? An interesting *chick*? Okay. Well, on paper, you sound really dull, but I'm optimistic."

I laughed and got self-conscious. "Does that mean we can hang out again? Maybe when you're not running around on your job?"

"Depends on what 'hang out' means."

She pulled the hair tie from her bun and slipped out a couple of bobby pins. The blond mess spilled across her shoulders, and she corralled it back.

"How about dinner? I've been meaning to try that Thai place everyone raves about."

"Ugh, dinner?" she moaned. "You are going to be a total cornball, aren't you?"

Before I could fire back, she stopped, grabbed my face, and brought her lips to mine. I wasn't prepared, and her open mouth locked over my closed one. Then I got with the program, and her tongue corkscrewed through the tunnel of our lips.

She pulled away and said, "Phone." Numbly, I handed it over.

She punched her number in and slapped it back in my palm. "This is me," she said, nodding her head toward a house of separate units behind a white picket fence.

She was up the stairs before I could think of anything to say.

~ ~ ~

Though I arrived at Teton Thai fifteen minutes early, Kate was already sitting outside under an umbrella reading a book. Wearing an airy white dress and her hair down for the first time, she looked altered, like the bartender and day at the marina had been different women, which is to say each incarnation felt like a fresh season—beautiful in its own way. She spent dinner kicking off a sandal and picking it up again with her foot.

We ordered drinks, and I asked her what she was reading.

"Rereading. Some Hannah Arendt."

"What's that?"

"Philosophy, I guess you could say. Suddenly she seems pretty motherfucking apropos."

The title was *Men in Dark Times.* It would not be the last instance of feeling out of my depth around her. On the walk over I'd cycled through every interesting thing I'd ever thought or done. I had "studied in Paris for a summer," "volunteered five weekends for Habitat for Humanity in high school," and "the collected works of Jack Kerouac" in my back pocket.

"So philosophy? That's your bag."

"I don't know about my bag. I was kind of one of those people just taking classes that sounded interesting, and a few of them happened to be in philosophy. It's like I majored in a hobby. Toward the end, when you've had four years of 'What is reality?' 'There is no reality!' 'Everyone just creates their own reality and nothing means anything!'—that bullshit—it got old and I kind of wished I'd done something else."

"Like what?"

"Environmental science, probably. If I'd just gone full granola from the start." The waiter approached. "Speaking of which, I'm also one of these militant vegans that basically can't stand to sit across from people eating meat. I'm not saying you can't get meat, but it's going to make me want to stab you."

I handed the menu to the waiter. "Vegetarian pad thai for me."

She laughed and ordered the pad gar pow with tofu.

We went on to talk about her Left Coast upbringing: the daughter of teachers and activists trying to gut it out during the Clinton years. After her parents' divorce, her father moved back to teach on the Navajo reservation where he'd grown up with his new wife. Kate rarely saw him more than once a year. Her mother was originally from Sweden and now worked for an Oregon nonprofit protecting the Columbia River and other waterways. Her folks had met doing antinuclear activism, and she'd grown up surrounded by heated discussions about intersectionality and the rights of nature. She also had a Jamaican grandfather, who'd been a prominent civil rights attorney. She joked that she would have rebelled by going to work for the Republican National Committee, but she doubted they served a whole lot of vegan fare.

"I'm sorry—I'm not a full-fledged PETA psycho, I swear." She laughed with her mouth wide open so I could see the back of her throat. "Let me say, I kill flies all the time. I'm a genocidal maniac when it comes to killing flies. We can pull their wings off if you want. Wow, what a weirdo. Okay, what's your deal, Matthew?"

I elided my family's story, which was that my father designed and built golf courses all over the South and Mid-Atlantic. Instead, I talked about majoring in English. To my dad, who was a booster of UNC's business school, this had been borderline mad. "I explained it to him as a stepping-stone to law school or an MBA, but I ended up falling in love with writing. That's kind of why I came out here." This sounded notably lame even as I said it. "To find something to write about."

"Found anything yet?" A breeze pushed over the patio. After spending a hot day on the docks, the temperature had melted to that perfect point of equilibrium it can hit in the summer dusk.

"Tourists can be really fucking stupid and shouldn't be allowed to drive motorboats."

Her eyes widened, mock impressed. "National Book Award, here you come."

A sheepish sound burped out of me. "No, I don't know. I just started realizing that I've never lived outside North Carolina. I've never really been anywhere other than on study abroad, and this seems like the time to do it. Broke it off with my college girlfriend, packed my bags . . . Maybe I'll stay out here for a few years."

She wrinkled her nose. "It gets old faster than you think. It attracts a lot of people with simplistic narratives and epistemologies who are nevertheless very impressed with themselves. Remember Lucy?"

How could I forget.

"She's the textbook example. These folks work seasonal jobs and then spend all their time skiing and climbing—which is cool, don't get me wrong. Part of why I came out here was to bag peaks and break my arm on a slope. But they're the surf bums of the mountains. Not engaged with the world, just passengers who figure as long as the train's running, what's the point of paying attention to how it operates? Enjoy the scenery. It's an attitude . . ." She paused and put her fingers to her temples. "It makes me insane. Lucy and I had it out about that while she was yapping bullshit about chakras. They ski down these beautiful slopes and don't care about why the snowpack is vanishing beneath them."

I didn't know what to say to this, so I said, "Interesting." And picked at a cuticle.

She bugged out her eyes again—what I'd come to know as a very Kate expression. "And the men—ugh!—they have a real fucking holier than thou attitude about it." She lowered her voice. "'Bro, I could never be one of those robots working in a cubicle all day. I gotta live for my maker!'" She smirked. "Jesus. Okay, I'm done with self-righteous monologues. Don't let me sit here and yak at you, Tar Heel. Give me more of your deal. How 'bout that ex?"

The waiter came with our meals, sliding gleaming white plates piled high with photogenic Thai food beneath our conversation. I sped through my ex, Candace, and our amicable breakup that took her to Atlanta to work in finance. She pressed me for more: My older sister now working in Charlotte, my mother's role in running charity golf tournaments, and then out came the family business. I could feel myself sounding so dull. I searched to change this narrative I could feel developing.

"I saw all my friends getting ready to keep doing the same things we'd been doing in Chapel Hill, and with Candace going to Atlanta, I saw what that path looked like and just wanted to try anything else. See where it goes with no expectations. And hey, I'm friends with a Macedonian guy, so I'm already feeling more worldly."

I stared at the peaks of the Tetons, afraid to meet her bored gaze.

"Does all that sound so stupid?"

"No." And when I looked, she was not bored. Her smile reached to her eyes. "You're cute, kid."

~ ~ ~

After that night, she really got into my head in that way a new person does, making you feel buoyant. After dinner we'd spent hours in a bar drinking cheap beer and pumping quarters into the jukebox until Kate said she had to go home, citing an early drive to Yellowstone the next morning for work.

"Was this like a onetime polite dinner thing or can I ask you out again?"

"I don't go on dates," she said, picking up her pint glass with a heart-achingly small amount of beer left at the bottom. "And I don't do boyfriends. The last time I had a boyfriend was in middle school."

"What I'm asking is can we hang out again?"

"Sure. But we're doing something fun next time." She threw back the last of her beer, slammed the glass down, and straight up shouted in my face, "None of this bitch stuff!" before erupting into her husky giggles.

She suggested the Paintbrush Canyon-Cascade Canyon Loop, her favorite hike in the Tetons. It was just under twenty miles. She'd reserved a campsite on the Paintbrush and we'd finish on the back side of the Teton Range in Cascade Canyon. I wanted to leap right out of my skin and wave it around my head like a victory towel.

What I did not anticipate when we began the Paintbrush Trail, hiking up steep switchbacks, the path like a tunnel through the towering pines, was how goddamn exhausting this "date" would be. We set out at 9:30 a.m., Kate in the lead. Twenty minutes after that I'd broken my first sweat. An hour later, I'd stripped out of my flannel shirt and soaked through my T-shirt. I'd volunteered to take the first shift carrying the tent. Kate had warned me that it was heavy and that we should probably switch off every couple hours, but I'd planned to forge ahead the whole day with the yellow bundle strapped to the bottom of my pack. Two hours in, my shoulders and back were throbbing, and I was checking my phone to determine an appropriate time to let her take it. I'd caddied every summer for ten years. I'd thought I was in fine shape.

She finally suggested we break. I unstrapped my backpack and let it clatter to the dirt with relief.

"How you doing?" she asked, pulling an apple and a Clif Bar from her pack.

"You can leave me here for the wolves," I gasped, then took a long pull from my water bottle.

"We're doing about a four-thousand-foot gain. If this is your first hike since you got here, it's probably not the best place to start. Just don't collapse. I can't carry you and the tent."

As far as dates go, it didn't have much to recommend it: one foot in front of the other, eyes set on Kate's heels and muscular backside (okay, it had that going), trying to keep pace with her and feeling like an epic wuss, my legs, back, and shoulders burning. She took the tent and that helped a little on the next two-hour leg, but the dread settled in and stayed. What if I actually couldn't finish this? We stopped around one thirty to eat again. Kate propped her bag on a rock and dug past a can of bear spray. She checked the trail map on her phone. I uncapped my camera, an expensive Canon EOS that had been another graduation gift from my mom. I snapped away at the woods, too tired to put much effort into it.

"Okay, we have a choice," said Kate. "Our campsite, the one we reserved, it's only about an hour short of the Paintbrush Divide."

"Which is what again?"

"That's like the peak of the hike. I'm kind of thinking we push on and camp on the divide. It'll be windy as hell—not to mention illegal—but the chances a park ranger will come by are virtually zero."

"And the upside?"

She squinted like, *Um, should we start back at the ABCs?* "We'll see the sunset from the most beautiful place in Wyoming, which means it's close to the most beautiful place in the world."

Without a doubt, I did not want to do this. I was seriously wondering if I'd get altitude sickness and have to be rescued by chopper. Yet I sensed the test inherent in her suggestion. This wasn't a test of my masculinity, but a test of how I dealt with being out of my element. Our every interaction felt like an exam, and now I wondered if maybe this woman was just too much for me. If she'd test me to collapse.

I forced a smile. "As long as you can carry me all day tomorrow."

As we climbed higher, the trees disappeared, and soon the trail was nothing more than a dirt path cut into an enormous slab of sloping mountain, loose stones skittering down an abyss with every footstep. Huge patches of snow still covered the ground, and we could see the beaten, muddy trail of those who'd marched before us. We were ascending again, and my legs almost couldn't comply. The burn shot from my hips down to my calves. My back and shoulders were on fire; the tent felt like an anchor. Perspiration again soaked my T-shirt and yet at this altitude the air was frigid, the wind icy, so I had my flannel and a windbreaker on, which only made me sweat harder. Even Kate finally looked like she felt it. Her tireless pace slowed. The back of her gray tank top was soaked through, and she stopped to pull her jacket on. If breathing was a chore before, now I felt a bit of terror at the conscious effort of each inhalation. I felt not just tired but ill. Sick to my stomach, sick in my head, dizzy, and diarrheal. I could only stare into the violet of the fading daylight and wait for it to pass.

Then we reached the peak of Paintbrush Divide, this massive ridge of rock, and I could see so far to the west it was like peering around the corner of the earth. The Tetons rose to the left and right, and looking out across the border to the vast, jagged carapace of Idaho, the evening sun lighting the mountains behind us, joy flooded into me. I'll always wonder if everything I ever came to feel for her was bound to the endorphins that soaked into me then, the miracle of oxygen finally steeping the red cells. I saw this sacred piece of the world through that prism and had a premonition of feeling deeply and mournfully for another person. Before she broke the silence by tapping the sign that read PAINTBRUSH DIVIDE EL. 10,700 and said, "You can't wear your church panties for this one," before we sat together eating a dinner of trail mix and hummus and cucumber sandwiches, watching the sun set over the Idaho mountains, peeling back the night and revealing so many stars it was like we sat on a plank stranded in the middle of space, while we stood on the divide with our hands on our hips sucking wind to slow our pounding hearts, I felt the gravity of what would come. That I loved this girl totally and ferociously and elementally.

~ ~ ~

When night fell and the temperature dropped, the wind had fangs. We'd set up the tent a few hundred feet on the other side of the divide where the gusts weren't as nasty. We'd hung our food in a tree, a standard precaution for bears. Now I had on every piece of clothing I'd brought. We huddled side by side in the dirt taking pulls of whiskey from my flask.

"I can't believe you were ten years old when you first did this," I said.

"Yeah, well, my dad kinda believes in throwing children into the deep end. It'll be a miracle if my brothers don't turn out as crazy as me."

"Brothers? Older or younger?"

"Ha. Younger. As in one of them is in the terrible twos and the other just popped out of my dad's wife last Christmas. Good luck to my fifty-one-year-old father with that."

The wind turned up and a frigid gust pierced all my layers. Kate held the flask with her sleeve tucked over her hand in lieu of a glove.

"I'm sorry. That sounds messy."

She threw me a skeptical look over the flask. "I've never drank anything but potable water. I've never gone a day without a meal. And I choose when I sleep outside. I think I'll step over that hurdle and continue on my way." She passed the flask to me.

"Hey, I just mean maybe that's why you don't want a boyfriend. You're afraid of emulating your parents' marriage."

"Oh my God." She put her face in her hands. "You're going with Psychoanalysis 101, Tar Heel? If you're going to be a writer, you'll have to tell more original stories than that." She took the flask back from me, maybe not realizing I hadn't yet drank. I was quiet after that, uncertain if what she'd said had hurt me.

"When we first moved to Portland, we were supposed to stay with my mom's friend, but the friend had moved, so she didn't know anybody. And she was so hurt by everything that had happened with my dad that she refused to call him and ask for money. The whole first month we slept in the car." She laughed. "I just remember thinking, Lady, I should be taking care of you, not the other way around. At some point you have to learn to take your parents for who they are and not let it rule your life one way or the other."

All along the rim of the Idaho mountains, flashes of golden light began to ripple. They flickered like incandescent bulbs eating away the last of the tungsten. She explained it was heat lightning. "Better than the sunset."

The gold bursts illuminated the clouds and made dark castles of shadows in the atmosphere. We watched the lightning for a long time, until she said, "Let's go to bed." Crawling inside the tent and zipping the flap closed behind us, I began to unroll my sleeping bag but never finished. She took my crotch in one hand and the back of my neck with the other. Kate moved unlike any woman I'd ever been with. With Candace, it had been implied that I was directing, that it was more or less my show to pull off. But Kate yanked her tank top over her head and directed my hands to her tough nipples. She got my pants down and her mouth was like a storm, slick and powerful and cleansing. Finally, she urged me into her sleeping bag and handed me a condom. Tugging it on, I felt squeamish and young. Then we broke sweats despite the cold. Afterward, we unzipped the inner flap and lay there while I ran my hands over the mosquito bites on her thighs. We watched the heat lightning through the mesh screen. The thunder was distant, but when my heart finally slowed down, I could hear it.

~ ~ ~

The next day we packed our gear and started down Cascade Canyon to Lake Solitude, a glittering blue pool of glacial runoff at the bottom of the valley. The mountains towered in all directions, and it felt a bit like photographing the sides of an enormous bowl. We stripped down to our underwear, dove from a rock into the frigid water, and I cried out when the surface first slapped my skin. We swam for as long as we could stand, then pulled ourselves out to dry on a rock in the sun. She sat up, leaning forward to hug her knees and look into the distance. Then I said something silly, and she smiled. I forget what it was I said—something errant and forgettable, but at the moment it worked. That was when I chose to pick up my camera and take a picture. Head turned, hair still wet and pulled back into her signature messy bun with strands pulling free in the wind, the peaks of Idaho behind her. It turned out to be a damn good picture. She seemed at once larger than life and the most remote grain of sand in the gutter of the cosmos. Later, I'd make a print of it in black and white. Much later, it would appear in a magazine profile. After that, it would show up on dorm room posters and T-shirts. Then billboards. It didn't feel iconic when I took it, but it would come to serve as shorthand for ideas and endeavors epic in scale. I'd dwell on the story it told about Kate: the way her eyes seemed to look off to places the viewer could only hope to comprehend, her playful smile hinting at an understanding of a secret beyond even that.

~ ~ ~

Captain Ray gave me shit about being over the moon, and I could hardly deny it. One time, when Kate picked me up after work, she sat with Ray on the tailgate of the marina truck. Ray said something in his Ray way (arms hugging his chest, looking off in the distance like he could care less), and she doubled over with laughter. Then to my astonishment Ray was laughing too, his nicotine teeth on display. The next day he told me, "That girl of yours has got some serious goddamn charm, Tar Heel."

But it wasn't just charm. I was fascinated by her. She'd read everything, she was opinionated, she cared about more topics than I even knew about.

When I mentioned that my favorite novel was *Hocus Pocus* by Kurt Vonnegut and had it with me, she borrowed my copy and finished it in two days ("The head of a human being pillowed in the spilled guts of a water buffalo is about the perfect image to describe the Vietnam War," she said, and I worried that I should have named a book that would take her longer than two days to read). And, of course, we had the sex of people who've just discovered a new toy.

So much of that summer was learning how to be with her and her blunt, unapologetic approach. She'd lost her virginity at thirteen to a college freshman she picked up in Powell's Books; when she was nineteen she booked a flight to Honduras, spent a week in a place called the Mosquito Coast by herself hiking and meeting people, and found out only after she got back that the US government had issued a travel warning for drug cartel and kidnapping activity; she had an abortion in college and the nurse invited her to her birthday party. I'd file away all of this in my ever-expanding Kate Chaos file.

We hiked, we climbed, we rafted, we went to the rodeo and watched the bulls toss the cowboys free. "Told ya, I'm not that PETA," she said. I brought Damien down from Colter Bay each Saturday, and we drank for free at the Cowboy Bar until she closed.

"You don't care that he won?" she demanded.

"No."

"You don't care this racist monstrosity is president at all?"

We sat in the Cowboy with all the lights on and the booths and stools cleared, Kate Windexing and wiping down the bar while she looked at Damien like he was insane. This was literally days after the riots in Charlottesville and the death of Heather Heyer, when a white supremacist drove his car into a crowd.

"It's not that I want him to be president," said Damien. "I just think it's another thing that happened in a system that's designed for things like this to happen. Bet you anything in fifteen years, this whole era will be pure bar trivia and people will be on to complaining about what a dictator the next guy is."

Kate set her spray bottle down and rubbed her temples. "This is hard to listen to for someone who spent last year getting hosed down with freezing water by corporate security firms."

"Oh, at Dakota Access?" asked Damien.

"It was called Sacred Stone," she snapped back.

I'd been silent, listening to them, hoping my best friend in Wyoming wouldn't piss Kate off and leave me trying to mend fences over topics I didn't dare comment on. I asked, "What's Dakota Access?"

Still looking at Damien with irritation, Kate said, "It's an oil pipeline. We were blockading into last fall, and they fucking cleared us with dogs and hoses."

"But even that," said Damien, sipping his glass of free whiskey through a straw, ice cubes tinkling, "it's like you're really upset that our species is destroying the atmosphere with smokestacks and cow farts, but back in the Proterozoic, when it was just mats of dumb algae calling the shots, the algae was like, 'Fuck yeah, this planet is rad, and it's all ours!' And then they went and farted out a bunch of oxygen and exterminated themselves." He folded his arms and nodded his head once.

Kate said, "You're sitting there very satisfied like you've made any kind of point."

"Just that everyone's running 'round trying to fix humanity but the only fixed thing is change. You gotta let go, dude. Embrace the chaos."

"How 'bout I fucking punch you instead?"

And until she threw the bar towel down and walked away, she really looked like she was going to.

Kate showed me her office, if you could call it that, and suddenly her pipeline story made all the sense. The Bison Project worked out of a small apartment above a Laundromat. When she'd described the operation to me, I'd envisioned a bustling war room. After all, it was an advocacy group attempting to influence state governments and battle a powerful business interest that spanned Wyoming, Montana, and Idaho. But it turned out to be four people working at card tables. I came to understand that Kate more or less had *become* the Bison Project. She'd organized protests on six college campuses and successfully lobbied members in all three state legislatures to put forward bills that would halt the indiscriminate slaughter of bison. Though none of them seemed likely to pass, Kate's coworkers told me she'd orchestrated all this mostly by sheer force of personality. She explained how she'd landed on this particular fight.

"After the election, I just wasn't in the right headspace for much of any-thing—I was too shocked. It seemed like I could come here and do some-thing righteous without also investing in the frenzy. You just can't keep up the fury of the Women's March twenty-four-seven-three-sixty-five, but now . . . Obviously it's beginning to frustrate me how little this one issue might matter in the scheme of what's going on."

Her apartment was awash in file folders and binders. A bulletin board dominated one wall, loaded to the point of collapse with pictures, papers, note cards, receipts, bills, reminders, and anything else that could be hung by thumbtack.

"It's a system," she assured me. We rarely stayed there, as she had three roommates and her bed was always covered in books and papers anyway. Frankly that was fine with me because she also had dozens of photos of dead bison on the walls, their throats cut, disemboweled, maimed, or tortured in ways that didn't seem like a systematic culling so much as a war zone. Hundreds of dead-eyed heads trailing blood and knots of spine still held together by cartilage piled in the grass. I never understood how she could sleep in that room. And I'd never realized how intoxicating passion could be in a person because I'd never really encountered it before.

~ ~ ~

As the dewiest part of me took over, and I began scouting out winter ski jobs in Jackson, as I began describing her to my folks and my sister in phone calls, I could hear my own gushing. Eager to impress her, I pushed her to read some of the short stories I'd been working on that summer. Again and again, she demurred.

One night while we were making pasta for dinner at my place, I found myself pressing her on it.

"It's a no-win situation." She tested the sauce, blowing at the steam before slurping off the wooden spoon. "Either I'll lie to you and feel like shit or tell you the truth and feel like shit."

I made a sound resembling a laugh. "So you're assuming I'll suck?" I'd been nervous enough about asking her to read something in the first place. To have her blow it off like this felt like a stamp of what she thought of me intellectually.

"No, not *suck*. I just have such a low threshold for fiction written by men. I can't even open a novel written by a man anymore—"

"What about the Vonnegut?"

She dipped the spoon back in the sauce for another round. "First novel I've read by a man in two years."

"Is that a joke? That's reductive."

"Maybe it is. I'm just trying to explain why I might not be the best reader for you."

"So explain."

She steeled her mouth in that way she had when she was preparing to lay down some Kate Truth. "Contemporary fiction is all status quo white male entitlement regurgitated over and over with almost no perception of what's unspooling outside of its closed circuit. All this literature of late capitalist exhaustion and alienation ad nauseam—no thanks."

"And you just assume that's me too?" I kept my voice light, but for the first time since we'd met, she'd pissed me off. I felt the frustration of all her small condescensions trapped in a vein near my skull.

Licking the spoon, she assessed me. "Don't use that bitchy tone, dude. This is not personal. I thought all this long before I met you."

"I'm just asking why you assume that about me?"

She cocked her head. "It's not hard to look at you out here, Matt, trying to have your little adventure in Jackson, Wyoming—the ultimate Jeffersonian yeoman's fantasyland serving as stage dressing for investment properties for the global elite and the celebrities living on ranches that they pay Mexican immigrants to maintain—and see what your quote-unquote *fiction* will look like. For Christ's sake, the Fed has its annual conference out here. You've never given a thought to what fuels these fantasies. Open-pit mining and mountain-top removal and systems of white supremacy and sexual violence—"

"Okay, Kate, I've been on a fucking college campus lately, I know the spiel." She gave me a cold, fixed stare. I didn't understand what I felt then. I'd passed for depth around my fraternity because I read books for my major, and it was suddenly frightening to realize how unmoored I was—without even a set of tools to calculate an opinion. "Because none of that is original," I went on. "You don't need to remind me I'm a privileged white man. I get it. That has nothing to do with why I want to write."

She watched me with infuriating calm. "Matt, it has everything to do with why you want to write . . ." She ticked off her fingers. "Because you view it as your inheritance, your birthright, your entitlement. It is your prerogative to look across the human condition and describe it through your ears and eyes, all while you cluelessly disregard what those ears and eyes are attached to. And more than that, you ignore the long chain of affluence that allows you the time to read and write and dream. You're ignorant of how your dad came to build those golf courses he builds, of the water it takes to

maintain them, of the carbon they're responsible for that's rapidly destroying the biosphere. None of it's even remotely a part of your worldview." As
she was saying this, my smile was growing larger and smarmier. "And I guess
that's why I'm not all that interested in reading some *Paris Review* rip-off
about you wagging your dick around a North Carolina prep school."

I laughed abrasively to show her that this was not the case, even though,
eerily, it was.

"You got me, Kate." I didn't want her to see the fear of my own empty
center. Because of that fear, I felt like I had to score a point, and I reached
for the only arrow I knew, the one all men learn at an impossibly young age.
"Maybe we should do dinner some other time when you're not being a cunt."

As soon as it left my mouth, I felt how childish it sounded, and I loathed
every male example who'd taught me that this was how you wound a woman.
I could tell Kate was only embarrassed for me.

She walked over and kissed me on the cheek. "This is a stupid argument. I'll call you later this week when work calms down."

After she left, I ate by myself in front of my computer.

~ ~ ~

It wasn't until Lucy introduced herself to me in the library a week later that
I understood the summer in the proper context. Our fight behind us, I was
determined to expand my reading list with Kate's recommendations. I had
just pulled Margaret Murie's memoir *Two in the Far North* from the shelf
when someone tapped me on the shoulder, and I turned to see Lucy. She
didn't mince words.

"You're hanging out with Kate Morris now, right?" I said that I was. She
nodded like this was exactly what she expected and it mattered nothing to
her. "Yeah, small town here. Word gets around. She do the thing where she
brings some brick of a book on the first date?"

She didn't sound jealous. Only curious. I said, "Arendt. *Men in Dark
Times.*"

She laughed and rummaged in her backpack. "Man, what a total crazy.
You, me, probably another guy or gal somewhere in between this summer. I
honestly wonder how she keeps all the plates spinning, you know?"

A coldness crept over my skin, but I smiled like I was in on the joke.

"Hey." She finally found what she was looking for in her backpack. "I
actually have this of hers. Give it back to her for me, will ya?"

She handed me my copy of *Hocus Pocus*.

"Yeah," I said. "No problem."

~ ~ ~

The next time I saw Kate, she told me she was leaving. She'd been offered a job with a new organization that would focus on political races vis-à-vis global warming. "Climate justice, but with sharp elbows. Really fucking people up," she explained. I could hear her trying to keep the undercurrent of excitement out of her voice and failing. "I'll be coming on as organizing director. It's a pretty amazing gig."

I told her that was great while my gut bottomed out. The job was in D.C.

"So I put in my two weeks both at the Cowboy and the Bison Project."

All of it came crashing down then. Maybe I should have understood this moment as inevitable—she'd never led me to believe otherwise—but I hadn't. This is how I ended up bringing up Lucy. The artillery I had wasn't working so I reached for the napalm. She took in that I knew she'd been seeing other people unfazed.

"I didn't think I could have been more clear with you." Her voice clinical. "On how I feel about being possessed. I'm not yours to tell who I can and can't see."

I fumed into my own crossed arms, unable to even look at her now. "You honestly spent all this time with me, and it didn't occur to you that I'd care that you were fucking someone else?"

She smiled. "Kid, I don't go in for slut-shaming. Not any more than I go in for the bullshit notion of possessive monogamy. I doubt there's any way I could've made that more apparent to you short of texting you every time I got off with someone else."

Trent, the big beefy cowboy made more sense. When I saw him twisting his whiskey at the bar, he was probably just going through what I was going through now. "Were you seeing Trent while we were together too?"

"So what if I fucking was?" Kate exploded. "Who are you to judge me for him or anyone else? What century did you grow up in, dude? What did you think, I want to be your housewife back in North Carolina? I'm not ashamed that I fuck who I want when I want. If you can't handle that, it's your problem, not mine."

"I never wanted to make you a housewife—I just . . ." She left me stuttering. Embarrassed that this was more or less exactly the fantasy I'd harbored.

She could be so raw, so unapologetic. "What do you think I was feeling for you this whole time?"

"What were you feeling?" she asked. Humoring me.

"Oh fuck you, come on." I felt the burn in the back of my throat that comes with the push of first tears. "That I was falling in love with you, that . . ." I'd felt like I had a speech, but as soon as the word was out there it only sounded stupid. "So."

She was quiet for a while.

"Maybe I was clumsy in what I just said," she decided. "I don't mean that I haven't developed many strong—very strong feelings for you. But I'm not yours to get jealous of. And I never will be. I've noticed most men absolutely cannot handle that. I thought I was sparing you by keeping it all from you."

And of course, she was right about that.

~ ~ ~

I texted to ask if we could get together before she left, but she never replied, and I expected she never would. I began to feel what it would be like to never see her again, what kind of void she would leave. Yet, she'd shown me I was a person who could stitch up his wounds before he could even feel them. I read what I'd written that summer, and I could hear her voice in my head pointing out the inanity. Suddenly, my whole life looked silly to me, a spoiled rich kid phony who's read too much Kerouac playing at profundity. On the docks, I mostly shut down. While I was gassing up one of the private boats, Captain Ray called me from the marina. He sat on the truck tailgate smoking.

"I asked the guys, 'What's going on with Tar Heel?' Damien tells me you got your heart shit on."

"Something like that." I didn't want to have this conversation with Ray. What I wanted to do was quit my job early. Get the hell out of Wyoming. I wanted to go back to Raleigh, start applying to law schools, and forget I'd ever come out here. "Is this where you give me the 'plenty of fish in the sea' talk?"

"Sure," he said. "Pussy comes and pussy goes. Everyone knows that." He took a drag of the cigarette. "Doesn't mean it can't be goddamn awful when it goes."

We sat looking out over the mountains, granite-colored, pocked with white snow and dark green forest. Mountains are chaos disguised as still-ness, Kate had explained once. "We carve out these places in the world, spare them from our cruelties, but only because it's one of the last ways we can still feel mystery. And then even our sense of mystery becomes another consumer edifice."

~ ~ ~

I woke to my phone buzzing, and when I saw it was Kate, I thought I might still be moving through the ends of a dream. She told me to come downstairs. I dressed quickly, my hair sticking up all over the place, and found that downstairs meant she was in her truck. Its red bulk sat at the curb, engine off. She had her arm draped out the window, sunglasses blocking her eyes. The bed was packed with her bike, several duffel bags, and a slew of boxes restrained with a web of bungie cords. I smoothed my bedhead and hastily wiped the sleep gunk from my eyes as I approached. I wasn't sure if I was furious at her for coming to say goodbye like this—basically slowing down on her way out of town—or forever grateful that she hadn't left without doing so. Either way, I could already feel the despair deep in my chest, waiting to be set free.

"You at least going to get out of the car?" My tone as unkind as I could manage.

She looked at me as if deciding what to say, then picked at a scratch in the door's upholstery.

"I'm not really a goodbye kinda person," she said.

"There are a lot of things you're not, Kate."

She looked at the steering wheel, and I waited.

"Look, Matt." Her grip on the wheel tightened. "I'm going to try to say this as clearly as I can, and I want you to think about it without your preconceived notions and social constructs—"

"Talk to me like a fucking person," I begged. "Quit with the PC-robot jargonese."

She smiled at me, and I wanted to scream.

"Okay, fine." The smile faded. "Despite my best intentions, yes, I have grown quite fond of you as well. By which I mean, I went out of my way to make you feel like shit, like what you told me was one-sided. I promise you it is not. I've spent a lot of time telling myself it's better that we just part ways. That would be the easiest path to sorting all this out." Her blinding smile cracked open again and reached all the way back to her molars. I wanted to hold on to my anger, but the smile was so mischievous, so in love with life and all its bizarre possibilities. "Goddamnit, what I adore about you is you're exactly what you say you are. I guess I didn't realize how much I appreciate that or how good it did me in my own fucked headspace. So what I'm offering is this: If you can take me for who I am—and I mean, not try to change me, not try to make me into the person you wish I was, but just take me for the person I've told you I am . . . Then instead of goodbye, just get in my truck, dude. I'm thinking Cheyenne tonight, Lincoln tomorrow, Chicago the day after that. D.C. eventually. Go on this journey with me, and maybe it'll be a huge mistake but that's what life's for, right? And it's better to go with the wild, outrageous mistakes."

Before she'd even finished her proposal, I knew I'd go back up to the apartment, pack the few things I cared about, and leave the rest behind. I was already gaming out how I'd abandon my lease and ask Damien to give away my furniture. I was already dreaming of the motel rooms Kate and I would stay in on the plains of Nebraska or in the palm of the Appalachian Mountains. How could I know then what would be born of that decision? The places I'd follow Kate, the people she'd draw into this cause, the passion she would spark within me, the years of rain and thunder—she once called them—that lay ahead. At that moment I was a twenty-two-year-old kid offered an adventure by a woman he'd never learn to refuse.

Kate grinned, and the dawn reflected off her sunglasses, the light flaring into my face, as bright and powerful as I'd ever known.

Book II

FEEDBACKS

RollingStone

What is 6Degrees? Feds Respond to Shadowy Heartland Saboteurs

How an Elusive Group of Monkeywrenchers Has Cost Energy Giants Millions while Evading the FBI

By JENJI FISCHER

MARCH 30, 2025

The charred stalk of the pipeline twists up from the ground like an exposed root. George Wisniewski squats near the crater, a divot of metal and blackened earth. Here on the golden plains near the Colorado-Nebraska border, the damage looks almost artistic.

"They hit it in three different places. They knew to space out the charges, which makes repairs more costly," he says. "It'll probably take six months, but see this here"—he points to the carnage of the pipeline—"this is scrap now. We'll have to tear all this out and rebuild. We got detection systems—the PIGs—that can locate a leak of around eight percent of max flow in under fifteen minutes, but it didn't matter because they called the operator and told them to shut the pipeline off."

Wisniewski is an engineer for Envige Energy. It's his job to reconstruct this oil trunk pipeline—just a sliver of the 2.5 million miles of oil and natural gas pipelines that crisscross the country. At forty-two inches in diameter, this particular trunk line was carrying a load of around 800,000 barrels a day. It won't take long, nor will it even be that expensive in the grand scheme of the oil economy. The problem is that the invisible infrastructure of gathering lines, trunk lines, refined product lines, and natural gas lines that supply American energy is highly vulnerable to these small-scale attacks. Groups like the Movement for the Emancipation of the Niger Delta in Nigeria or al-Qaeda in Yemen utilized pipeline attacks to further their political goals. Now they have an American equivalent.

Following the ransomware attacks of 2021 against Colonial Pipeline and a meat processing plant, the Department of Justice began working with the private sector to beef up cybersecurity protocols in vital infrastructure. Those ransom schemes were thought to be the work of cyber criminals with links to the Russian government, which is largely why the series of bombings beginning in early 2023 have been so misunderstood.

"If you worked in pipelines, you knew these attacks were more than just some computer geeks trying to make a buck," said Wisniewski, adjusting his glasses and looking off at a field of picturesque golden wheat. "Not sure what took everyone so long to wake up to that."

BENEATH THE RADAR, MONKEYWRENCHING IS NOT UNHEARD OF: wellheads cemented shut, gas pads vandalized, equipment destroyed, trees felled on access roads. These are common reactions of angry folks who don't want to see their water sources compromised or the value of their homes go down. Resentment at fracking operations has been growing for some years in the heartland. Despite the promise of jobs, communities that have to live in the dense webs of oil and gas networks find themselves racked by everything from mysterious skin rashes to aborting farm animals. At first, local police thought the bombings were the work of antagonized locals. Until this group started leaving a tag:

6DEGREES IS COMING, read the graffiti at several of the attacks.

"Law enforcement, the energy and pipeline companies—they didn't think this was the work of the same group," said former FBI agent Sheryl Carney, who now consults for the ACLU. "They were dispersed geographically, and it looked like the work of amateurs, not Russian commandos suddenly invading Nebraska. It's in the interest of the private sector to slow walk cybersecurity because it's expensive. By the third or fourth pipeline bombing, though, they were screaming for the FBI and their allies in the media to do something."

Oil and gas, already under pressure from the economic whiplash of Covid-19, lawsuits, environmental activists, and shareholder revolt, have indeed raised the profile of the attackers. In the winter of 2024–25, following the arrest of Miles Kroll, a twenty-one-year-old student from Brigham Young, Fox News and other conservative outlets turned their attention from a bad election defeat to this new "radical eco-terrorist." Kroll admitted to having planted an IED after the Explosives Unit of the FBI Laboratory found scraps of a backpack used as a container at a bombing site in Colorado. He pled guilty and is serving a twenty-three-year sentence due to a "terrorism enhancement" at the Terre Haute, Indiana, communications management unit, one of three secretive sites intended for prisoners with "inspirational significance." No further arrests have been made, and the attacks have continued.

The right wing has been using the specter of eco-terrorism, among many other cudgels, to hamstring President Joanna Hogan before her historic first term is even off the ground. Though she already backtracked ferociously on Green New Deal promises made during the Democratic primary, the Republicans have been merciless at tying Hogan and the GND to the bombings of pipelines and wellheads.

Nebraska republican Bob Syracuse described the instances of sabotage as "the most dangerous terrorist activity since 9/11." Along with fifteen cosponsors, Syracuse has introduced eco-terror legislation. The bombings have caused no fatalities or injuries.

Federal law enforcement now presumes these are not copycat attacks being carried out under the same loose umbrella. It believes the actions are centrally coordinated.

"6Degrees is not a fringe conspiracy theory," Loren Victor Love, CEO of Xuritas Corporate Services, told CNN. "This is happening, and us Democrats must face up to the danger to the nation's energy infrastructure." Love's company has received numerous contracts to protect pipelines, and he is widely viewed as the party's best chance to pick up a Senate seat in Montana in 2026.

President Hogan, feeling the pressure and playing into her "tough-as-old-boots, monster-truck-loving grandma" persona she cultivated as a candidate, has trumpeted the creation of a Joint Terrorism Task Force. Working out of a fusion center in Denver, the FBI, ATF, and local officials from seven states have dubbed their investigation Operation Weathermen, a reference to both the legendary antiwar activists and the new group's focus on attacking the fossil-fuel infrastructure that is radically altering weather patterns. Crafty nicknames aside, the bureau has turned up no further prints or DNA, and Kroll's cooperation has yielded little insight into the group's operational core.

Kroll is described by friends and family as a quiet, conservative Mormon student and husband, who took to social media to denounce the oil and gas giant he blamed for his wife's miscarriage. In his plea agreement, Kroll claimed he was recruited online and never met his handlers in person, according to a source close to the investigation. The FBI says it is looking into a number of leads.

Where previous environmental sabotage has been undisciplined and unfocused, 6Degrees has been tactical and precise, striking surgically and vanishing. Their targets are uniformly pipeline infrastructure, and as Wisniewski pointed out, they call ahead of time to warn operators to shut off the pipelines they're about to destroy.

"We condemn these attacks, absolutely and without qualification," said Rekia Reynolds, a spokesperson for A Fierce Blue Fire, the climate justice organization du jour. "However, since 9/11, the word 'terrorist' has been redefined again and again. It's been used against Black and brown people with increasing frequency, even as right-wing white supremacist violence has never been worse. The aim of all this oil and gas legislation is to extend surveillance and harassment to nonviolent activists. We can't allow law enforcement to become a tool of oil and gas companies, who are the real criminals of our planet."

During the past decade as protests over the Keystone XL and Dakota Access pipelines heated up, states have put together a host of antiterrorism laws of dubious constitutional legitimacy. Several states have made it a felony to protest within two thousand yards of an energy producer. "Eco-terror" legislation written by the American Legislative Exchange Council in Texas has attempted to recategorize civil disobedience as terrorism. The language singles out "all activities intended to influence government policy or damage economic interests by coercion." It also widens the net by outlawing action "that publicizes or promotes terrorism against energy producers."

Senator Syracuse's proposal—the Protecting American Energy Independence Act—copies this language while also aiming to create a registry for eco-terrorists and environmental monkeywrenchers similar to that used for sex offenders. If you sat in a tree in Eugene, Oregon, when you were eighteen you could be on this list along with a photo and a public address. If you carried a sign tying racial justice to climate justice in a Black Lives Matter protest, you could potentially expect to be a surveillance target. Nonviolent organizers have come under FBI scrutiny. As the threat of disruptive civil disobedience has emerged, agents have begun to keep tabs on individuals in these movements, intimidating people at their workplaces and gathering intelligence from public records.

"Energy is key to America's security and prosperity, and therefore these businesses need enhanced protection. They should be viewed as part of the critical infrastructure we need to keep America safe," Syracuse said while introducing the bill on the Senate floor.

Diving into the online forums, it's not hard to see why a company like Envige is worried. For the environmental left, action on the climate crisis has advanced at a terrifyingly slow pace. When they're not speculating that anarchist rapper Haydukai is the group's ringleader (his songs apparently contain coded instructions) or spinning conspiracies involving Mark Ruffalo (he's supposedly bankrolling the operations, hence all the new *Hulk* sequels), they clearly see these new monkey-wrenchers as folk heroes.

"It had to come to ecotage," writes one user, Isai89. "People were kidding themselves if they thought the powers that be and their political minions would ever back down. They will sooner support true fascists rising through the ranks of their political parties. Now at least we know the only path is war."

One imagines Isai89 will soon be getting a call from the FBI.*

ON THE PLAINS BETWEEN TWO STATES, WE LEAVE THE BLACK-ened crater behind. Wisniewski and I return to his truck and start back to town on roads that are sheets of ice glittering in the sunset. Envige is offering a million-dollar reward for information leading to the arrests of the perpetrators. It has contracted with Xuritas to conduct expensive nighttime patrols of all its operations.

"The problem is how do you guard it all?" wonders Wisniewski. "These security costs are a huge expense in a tight energy market." His voice is low and mournful. "This is people's livelihoods they're attacking, and no one cares, and no one's stopping it, and they keep pulling it off like they're apparitions. Obviously, it makes me afraid of what might be next."

---

* An FBI spokesperson had the following response to multiple queries about its targeting of activists: "The FBI has a very restrictive media policy, so I apologize that my answers will not provide the details you're hoping to receive. The FBI takes care to distinguish between constitutionally protected activities and illegal activities undertaken to further an ideological agenda. The FBI has the authority to conduct an investigation when it has reasonable grounds to believe that an individual has engaged in criminal activity or is planning to do so. This authority is based on the illegal activity, not on the individual's political views, position, or any other beliefs."

THE WATCH AND THE BLOOD BANK

2025

*Y*ou *find the note in the handle of the screen door of your trailer. It's all caps* and exclamation points, telling you you're now two months overdue on rent and the next letter will be an eviction notice. A hangover soaks your brain from the night before at the bowling alley. You regret the blow Casey found; it was expensive and cut like shit. Matters worsen when you find the mail, fed through the slot and scattered over the carpet. There's a letter from Claire Ann. You bite the inside of your cheek until you taste blood.

Bottom line is you need money. Three hundred fifty at least to get Claire Ann off your back, another $300 to hold off your landlord. How they got away with charging $300 a week for a heap of shit in the dubiously named Fairview Manor Trailer Courts is beyond you, but the whole town has been a landlords' market for years. Add to that the fierce cramps in your legs, warning of the comedown on the way, and you're settling in for a pretty bad week.

When you got fired from Tuscarawas, there was the typical spiral. It had taken all you had to land that job. Your old pal Casey Wheeler had an uncle who worked at the Tuscarawas Power Station, and you had been looking for any kind of steady work since moving out on your own. Casey hooked you up, and you put in your most earnest effort. Uncle Wheeler liked you well enough, and got you in for the test that Casey, his own nephew, had failed badly. You had to memorize the answers to questions like: If you're a drop of water how will you flow from the feedwater pump, become steam, blow through the turbine, and end up back as water again? Five months it took you to get in as a utility operator, a hot, dirty job reaching into the furnace with the spud bar to tamp down the ash bed all day. Less than seven months later you were done. The first time you showed up drunk, Uncle Wheeler reamed you. The second time he warned you, cold as shit. The third, you were only a little hungover, but he fired your ass. Not that you don't see your own culpability. No matter. Everyone in the plant was always talking about how it would be shut down any day now with the war on coal and all, so maybe you just fast-tracked the process for yourself. In some ways, it's better when you don't have money. Having money in your pocket has always gotten you into trouble.

Now the question becomes how to put together a few hundred dollars in a hurry. Your first thought is the blood bank, which of course deals in plasma but "banking" is a more apt description for what goes on there. Coshocton's has an okay price. Thirty-five for an hour with a needle in your arm. It won't solve your troubles, but it'll let you score a couple pills to get the immediate physical demon off your back. You're no addict—all you fuck with is the new Oxy—no heroin, no fent. But in a day, the withdrawal kicks are going to be psychotic, and you don't want to deal with the valley of bones on top of the current predicament. You walk to save the gas.

Needle in your arm, you have a couple thoughts.

Staring around a clinical-white donation room filled with the steady hum of PCS machines, you lay on the black leather bed with the footrest and flex your hand to keep the flow light green and the blood hustling. The tech must be new because he started in on a long explanation of how the anticoagulant separates the blood from the plasma, and you had to tell him, "Bitch, just get on with it." You said it in a jokey, friendly way, but he seized up and went quiet. Then the pressure, the needle tight in the vein.

You all lay there, middle-aged women, old-timers, a Black guy listening to his phone with earbuds and rapping away silently. Another dude has a pair of VR goggles on and cranes his neck back, as if peering up the sheer face of a cliff. All of your hands flapping open and closed like fish spluttering on the dock.

You watch superheroes throw each other into buildings on the one flat-screen framed in Christmas lights and think about what you can pawn. Your TV is worthless, your furniture hand-me-downs and garbage pieced together from Goodwill. You already pawned your PlayStation VR. You have a title loan for your truck, and it's a month away from getting repossessed. You begin to wonder what your mom might have lying around that she doesn't need. Probably nothing, but then you remember that watch, which has flitted through your mind when you've been in tight spots before. Back in your hometown on the other side of the state is a watch you got when you were a kid. You know exactly where it is in your mom's place. Still in the shoebox with some other childhood bullshit. What had Joe Biggs told you at the time? That men size each other up by looking at the wrist when they shake. You needed a decent watch, he'd said. Then he'd handed it over and, if memory serves, said, "That's five hundred bucks on your wrist." If you could get back home and get that watch that might hold off either the landlord or Claire Ann.

As you entertain this notion, a young Black girl comes down the stairs and gets pointed to a nearby bed to get her needle. While she waits, she taps away at her phone with the slack expression of a donation veteran. You stare at her the way you stare at the Glocks in a gun store case—something you want that seems like a bad idea. She's got tits, one of your prereqs, but also a delicate face. You imagine the bones beneath as translucent. She's very pretty. Very dark skin. She's still wearing her winter coat, but you can spot some of what's working with her seat. Worth-the-rape-charges pretty, as you and Casey sometimes joke. Except you don't like that joke about her. You more want to make her an omelet in the morning. You stare at her awhile, trying to catch her glazed gaze. She looks up once, and maybe her eyes catch yours, but they're immediately back down. You saw the deep brown of the iris, though. The color of good soil.

You feel the icy tingle of the saline, meaning you're almost done. It crawls up your bicep and down your forearm, a cool wonderful glow.

The tech comes by to finish you up.

"You got the veins for this," he says by way of saying nothing. All the techs here are exhausted stoner types, but this guy's pep makes your head ache. Reminds you of your hangover. If there was a way to donate at another place you'd head there now, but there's the invisible ink they mark your finger with. You learned it takes two days and too much scrubbing to get it off.

You owe plenty of payday lenders in Kentucky, West Virginia, and Pennsylvania. You're in hock everywhere. Your truck's looking like a lost cause, repossession imminent. You owe Casey like $1,200 and assume you'll both forgive and forget all debts when you're old men on the porch. So while you may owe more than the six-fifty, it's an attainable goal, something to work for in the immediate here and now. After hitting up the food pantry in Millersburg, you drive down to Cassingham Hollow Drive, texting Tawrny to let him know you're coming by.

Tawrny is the guy you go to for a fix. He fancies himself a regular kingpin, but mostly he deals from a connection in a pharma distribution center.

No black tar for him. The Covid-era spike in ODs led to crackdowns on fentanyl, which sent the docs back to prescribing Oxy because at least it was less deadly, and as such, the region is once again happily flush with it. Police whack the head of one mole and an old tired one just comes shooting up. Local dealers like Tawrny know how to read these peaks and valleys like the stock market and sell their wares accordingly. You got to know him pretty quick after you landed in Coshocton almost ten years ago now. Right after Claire Ann cornered you.

He's sitting out on the porch smoking a cigarette when you roll up to his house, a massive, falling-to-shit Queen Anne with pink trim that probably dates back to the Civil War. Half blue paint, half the faded wood beneath. You park, and he watches you approach, hunched forward on his elbows, smoking the cig in slow, laconic drags.

"What up, T?"

He nods. "Keeper."

A big, powerful man, all shoulders and haunches. He has long salty hair and a snow-white goatee. Restless gray eyes that assess everything, miss nothing. He wears carpenter jeans and a light brown Carhartt, but you know beneath that he has a quilted coat he claims will block radio waves and tracking devices and whatever other tools cops used to put the pinch on folks. He looks perfectly comfortable sitting in the cold.

"Ain't you freezing? Fuck."

"Bets won't let me smoke in the house." Betsy is the wife you've seen only once. "Plus, we got this storm coming through. They're telling us to batten down the hatches. Get me some fresh air while I still can."

You ask if you can get a handful of Oxy floated on credit, already knowing the answer.

"This ain't the country grocery, kid."

"Well, what can I get?"

"How much you got?"

"Thirty bucks."

"Got some of them thirty milligram ones. Hard to crush, though. Give you two for thirty."

"C'mon, T."

Tawrny never negotiates. He looks off into the bitter sky and blows a breath of smoke the same color.

"Look like you're gonna need it soon."

You're sniffling. Your nose is a busted faucet, and you keep tasting the salty flavor on your lip. Your muscles buzz and it has you bouncing around on your feet like a fucking tweaker. You have your hands stuffed in your pockets because of the cold, but if they were out they'd be flying around your body like rabid bats.

"Aight, I'll take 'em. Hey, T, you don't got any work, do you? Maybe sales department's hiring?"

"I don't trust junkies with product."

"I ain't exactly a junkie." You give him a goofy and—you hope—winning grin. "More a dabbler who's fighting through a rough patch."

"Well, I'm sorry to hear that, Keeper, I truly am. But maybe you shouldn't've got yourself fired from Tuscarawas. Then there's no rough patch."

"Man, they're about to evict me from Fairview. I'm trying here. You know a job where they hire ex-cons? By all means, I'll put in an application. Wanna write me a recommendation? 'He's a self-starter, good eye contact,' that sorta thing?"

Tawrny smirks. A tic in the corner of his mouth is about the most amused expression he ever lets rip.

"You got a good white-trash sense a humor, Keeper. That'll see you through, boy."

You grind one of the pills with a Dremel tool to get around the time-release agent. It's a hassle, but you've just known too many dumbasses who've lost their lives to black tar and the rest. You heat the powder in the microwave to destroy the binders, until the powder's a pale yellow, scrape it up with a defunct debit card, and snort away.

Immediately the world is a silkier place.

You sit on your couch and eat a few Oreos. Now that you've conquered this level, you can move on to the next, which is figuring a way to get that watch with only five bucks in your pocket. If you can get a few hundred dollars for that watch at a pawn shop, you'll be able to split it between Claire Ann and the landlord. Buy yourself another day or two to figure something out. The problem is gas. If you have to spend forty or fifty bucks getting over to Dayton and back, it kind of eats into your profit margins. You sleep on it.

The next day, you hold off snorting the other pill, and instead go out to a gas station in Newcomerstown, just off 77. You park down the highway and wait in the shadows, black-and-white camo cap on your head. Someone finally leaves their vehicle with the pump going. A Tundra owner goes inside to buy Skittles or take a piss, and you walk over casually with your plastic gas tank. You slip the nozzle from the Tundra and fill up. Guy who owns a newish-looking Tundra probably just swipes the plastic and doesn't even notice the final price. The clerk, a dark Muslim type, spots you and goes for the phone like it's a bank robbery. You don't panic. By the time any cop could possibly get worked up over this, you're bound for Dayton.

––––––––––

The drive takes over three hours. Sitting in the stop-and-go traffic of Columbus, you think about this watch, which you hid under your bed at age twelve. It was way too big for your wrist, and even though Joe Biggs said he could take you to the jeweler, there were other reasons to keep it safe. You didn't dare wear it to school. There were plenty of big tank hicks who'd beat the blood out of your nose and make it disappear.

Joe Biggs had been your mom's boyfriend for a year bridging your little fourth- to fifth-grade life. He didn't just give you the watch: He gave you the name Keeper.

Big and bald with fiery red hair still holding on around the crown, Joe was a good ole boy from Toledo who'd taught himself how to install heating and air-conditioning systems, which eventually earned him his fortune. When Mom started dating him, he took you to the Ohio State Fair, to Cedar Point, to Kings Island. He bought you gifts. You wanted to impress Joe Biggs, and you were all right at baseball. So when Little League started up that summer, you begged him to make it to the games. But the first game he did, you struck out all three times. The last one, you couldn't help but go nuclear on the umpire, screaming, tears running down your cheeks, crying all the harder because everyone in the stands was looking at you, the other kids snickering into their gloves. Then you felt the hand on your back, and when you turned, Joe Biggs was there. "C'mon, kid."

Joe led you off the field and down to the parking lot while you tried to vacuum back your tears. Finally, he stopped and pulled out the grossest, stiffest handkerchief and put it in your hand.

"Dry your eyes, my little friend." You took it and wiped at the tears, added your snot to his. You could sense your mom hanging back, watching from afar. "Freddie getting ready," Joe suddenly said. "Rock steady. When Johnny strikes up the band."

Then Joe laughed, a big booming noise. You couldn't help but smile at the sound.

"Huh?" you asked.

"Naw, nothing. You're the keeper of the keys, kid."

After that, Joe started calling you the Keeper of the Keys and soon just Keeper. When you switched schools that fall, you told the teacher that was your name.

Years later, you were listening to the radio and a song came on by an old, dead rock star, and you recognized your namesake. At that point you'd put Joe Biggs out of mind because after nearly a year with your mom, he was suddenly gone. Either he left or she told him off—she never said. At the time you were furious. Assumed she'd fucked it up somehow. You never heard from Joe Biggs again, but sometimes you'd take the watch out and admire it.

———————

Dayton looks terrible. You haven't been back in a while, but driving through, the whole city looks like a fucking bomb went off. Shuttered factories clutter the waterfront of the Great Miami River. They squat on the riverbanks like ass-ugly ghosts. You pass some half torn down, others mostly intact, and one is well illuminated by the lights of the city, and inside you can make out enormous piles of junk crowding up against the window: scrapped flat-screen TVs and detached mannequin arms trying to claw their way out. There's a new Walmart Supercenter, lit like a space station, with armed guards patrolling the entrance. Cruising past the city proper, the first-ring suburbs don't look much better. Maybe every other home is dark and empty, sidewalks and yards littered with trash, some with boarded windows, others with fresh foreclosure signs in the yards. When your mom told you she wasn't going to let you borrow one more red cent, you stopped coming back here altogether.

You work your way over to your mom's place in Trotwood. It's a one-story split-unit with two bedrooms and shitty memories. Pulling up, you see the windows dark. When you first moved here in high school, there'd still been some white people left in the neighborhood, but from the looks of things there wasn't much of anyone left. Dark house after dark house, and the lit ones all had some kind of porch-monkey vibe to them.

It isn't until you see one with blue lights dangling from the gutters, mimicking icicles, that you remember it will be Christmas in a few days.

You leave your truck on the street and dash across the lawn. It takes you about ten seconds to locate that stupid fake rock where your mom has always kept the spare key. You let yourself in without turning on the light, eyes adjusting, gathering the gloom.

Through the dark living room and down the hall, you feel your way to the bedroom where you moved your stuff after she lost the job at the Moraine plant, lost the house, and set the two of you up in this place.

You see pale blue light flickering through a crack in the door at the end of the hall. You duck into the room just before it and close the door quietly behind you. You don't turn on the light. Instead, you use your phone to make your way to the bed. On your hands and knees, you dig past Rubbermaid tubs full of your old clothes until you finally find the Nike box in the exact place you left it. The gray metal tin has a pebbled texture and the red placard of Swiss Army by Victorinox. Pop off the top, and the watch is looped around a pillow. The hands don't tick, the battery long dead, but there's the gleaming blue face and silver numbers beneath the sapphire crystal. Stainless steel casing with a steel band.

While you're busy admiring it by the blurry light of your phone, the door scrapes open behind you and the harsh bulb momentarily blinds. Your mom in flannel pajama pants and a Flyers tee.

"What the hell," she says.

You palm the watch behind your back and, standing, slip it into your pocket.

"Nothing. Was in the neighborhood and wanted to get some of my stuff."

"You just waltz in unannounced? You're lucky I don't got a gun."

You're angry with her that she doesn't, angry that she heard an intruder and doesn't even have a baseball bat near her bed. Especially in a neighborhood like this one.

"Nothing to worry about, I was just on my way."

You breeze past her into the hallway. She follows.

"You know I get collection agencies calling nonstop for you."

"I'm taking care of it."

"Doesn't seem like it. I got most of the numbers down now so I don't gotta answer, but I'll tell you what, they fill up my voice mail in about two days."

"I said I'm taking care of it."

"Claire Ann's called too."

"I know. I'm on it, Mom. For fuck's sake."

You reach the front door, your hand on the knob.

"Well, have you at least eaten something?"

You pause. Now that the Oxy has worn off, and all you've eaten is Oreos and Ritz crackers, you're starving.

"Wouldn't that be like borrowing money?" you ask.

"It's food, Johnny. C'mon, I'll fix you a plate."

She goes to the kitchen without waiting to see if you'll follow.

"Can I borrow some money?"

"Don't you even breathe a word to me on that subject." She pulls bread, butter, and American cheese from the refrigerator.

"Just joking."

She butters the bread and throws it in the pan on the stove.

"Where you working these days?" you ask.

"Over by the mall near Indian Ripple. It's a Tim Hortons. How 'bout you? You got a job with all these collections people after you?"

"Yeah, I got a job at a blood bank."

"Blood bank? What do you know about that?"

You pretend you can't be bothered to explain. There's a picture on the refrigerator. You at about nine or ten, splash of freckles, smile missing a front tooth. You're at the wave pool in the Soak City Water Park, pale chest on display. You know Joe Biggs took this picture.

You eat the grilled cheese and leave, drive down the block and park. You sleep in the car that night, and in the morning when your mom leaves, you let yourself back in with the key you pocketed. You grind up the second Oxy, microwave the powder, and snort it. She doesn't own a VR system, so you take the TV in the living room, a nice HD flat-screen, relatively new, but leave her the old one in the bedroom.

―――――

You figure it would be a bad idea to pawn the TV anywhere near Dayton in case your mom thinks it was actually stolen and calls the police. So you go to a shop in Columbus. The clerk says he'll give you $50 for the TV but won't take the watch.

"We ain't supposed to take watches unless they run."

Back in Coshocton, you drop the watch off at a jeweler who says she'll replace the battery for ten bucks. There's another note from the landlord waiting for you in the trailer door. Rent by tomorrow or you're out. The next day, after a night of aches and chilling sweats, you pick up the watch and drive to another pawnshop called Money and More. The one where you sometimes stare at the guns in the case. The clerk offers you $30.

"Man, this is a five-hundred-fucking-dollar watch!" You demand he look up at you. He's a big guy with hoop earrings stretching the lobes. Hairy arms and a beard that reaches his chest.

"You know the expression." He's fiddling with a small black safe on the counter that he can't get to lock. "Take it or leave it."

You want to walk out. You want to tell this guy to fuck himself, but after the new battery you only have $40.

"Fine." You slap the watch on the glass of the counter, hard enough to make it ring out with a crack. The clerk's head doesn't move but his eyes roll up at you. Undoubtedly, he's thinking of some weapon behind the counter.

He takes his time getting your money and the little slip of paper you have to sign. Amount financed: 36.00. Finance charge: 6.00. Total of payments: 30.00. Annual percentage rate: 243.33%.

———————

Just as the snow starts, your skin begins to crawl. You drive back over to Cassingham Hollow, almost out of the stolen gas. The flakes come down in thick bundles and the wind tries to nudge your truck from the road. When you get to Tawrny's place he meets you on the porch.

"You listened to the news at all, boy? This is 'bout to be the mother of all storms, and you're out driving around like a damn fool." Tawrny slaps at a pack of cigarettes. He offers you one, and you take it gratefully.

"I got seventy, man. Can you give me a deal?"

"Give you four for sixty. Price hasn't changed in the last three days, Keeper."

"C'mon, man, gimme five, all right? It's only a five-fucking-dollar discount. C'mon, please."

Tawrny eyes you. Without saying anything, he goes back inside. You stand on the porch in the blazing snow, the wind sliding up the cracks of your jacket and shirt. Your hand is frigid, but the cigarette tastes great, and the warmth glows in your lungs. Tawrny returns with a plastic baggie and five pills.

"Don't do all that shit at once. You'll OD."

"Man, you gotta need some help, right? Gimme anything to do, man. I'm not some unreliable asshole. Even if it ain't selling I can carry, you know? I got a truck. I can go wherever you want."

Tawrny watches the snow. It's already blanketing the streets. The sky is so dark it feels like night's descended five hours early.

"They're saying this is the real deal, Keeper. Record-setting snow, record-setting winds. You need to go home and stay inside. You got a generator?"

He's frustrating you.

"Man, I've lived through fucking winter before. I'm just asking for a little work. I got all this back rent, and my . . ." You stop. You don't even want to say it.

Tawrny finally looks at you.

"Go home, kid. Be safe." Then he walks inside.

———————

On the drive home, the roads are already treacherous. The wind wails and gusts shove your truck from its true direction. Only a few other cars are on the road, and you pass house after house that glows with the warmth of home and safety and shelter.

In your trailer, you grind, microwave, and snort two of the Oxy. You know you should just take one, but you need two. You do.

You sit on the couch and feel the warmth spread through you, the calm. You close your eyes and listen to the wind and think about how you're still alive.

You only come around when you hear the buzzing of your phone. You find it in your jacket. There's a fresh text with an image attached. You press the pad of your thumb to the sensor, and before you see that it's from Claire Ann, the picture loads.

A young girl in pink shorts and a white tank top bares her teeth at you. She has blond hair going brown and a smatter of freckles on her nose and cheeks. She's clutching her hands together and smiling with eyes squeezed shut, like someone just tickled her or asked her to goof for the camera. She wears a pointy party hat, poised over a cake with a candle in the shape of a *10*. There are no actual words in this message.

You stand there for a moment staring at the small image. Then you click the phone to black. Outside the wind has died down momentarily, blanketing the trailer in silence. The best of the Oxy has worn off.

You punch the phone back on. You scroll through the Cs until you reach Claire Ann. You dial.

The line rings and rings. She sent the picture two hours ago, according to the time stamp. She doesn't answer. Finally, her phone goes to voice mail.

"Listen to me, you bitch, don't you ever fucking pull that bullshit again. You fucking whore. I'm fucking out here working. I'll get you your money, so shut the fuck up and stop *fucking harassing me*!" Your voice hits a note of musical rage, and your hands shake when you scream, and fuck does it feel good to scream.

"*Don't you fucking send me that shit, you cunt!* If you pull that fucking bullshit again, I'll drive back there and fucking beat your face in, whore. I'll fucking kill you. I'll kill you and every little dick you're sucking, slut. *So don't fucking call me!* Or write me or text me or any-fucking-thing. You do it again, I'll fucking cut your head off. I'll stab you in the gut and fuck the holes."

That note feels triumphant enough and you jam your thumb at the screen to end the call, but as soon as this is done you picture Claire Ann letting her mother listen or even the police, which reminds you of your six awful months in Muskingum County, and you know you've made a mistake, a bad one, and you scream and hurl the phone at the wall where it cracks and the casing snaps apart.

"*Fuck!*" you scream at the wall. You walk to the kitchenette. You walk back. "*Fuckfuckfuckfuckfuck!*"

Your heart hammers. You're sweating. Everything is too stark, too bright, as if you see in this moment the dismal hole of your home for the first time. The sad walls and empty cupboards and scattered fast-food bags and the smell of old pot and cigarettes. You understand where you are for the first time in your life. You're the drop of water in the feedwater pump. You're the one getting pawned, and whoever's doing the bartering, they're laughing because the joke is on you. You alone in your valley of bones.

You grab the baggie with the three pills from the drawer and begin grinding them onto a paper towel with the Dremel. You lose some of the powder over the side and curse loudly. You try to scoop it up with a wet finger, but it's lost. You microwave the remainder, cut it into three lines on the kitchen counter with the debit card, and snort the first.

You pace around the trailer for fifteen minutes, but you don't feel better. Then you snort the other two.

That works. You lie on the couch and feel okay for a while. You listen to the wind rattle your trailer.

When you open your eyes, the high has already begun to wear away. Tawrny's warning about ODing rattles, makes its presence known, but you'd do anything for another pill. Those were supposed to last you at least through the week. You go to the cabinet above the sink. There's a thin amber gruel left at the bottom of a handle of Wild Turkey. You chug this down, but it only serves to whet your thirst. Fuck the wind, fuck the snow, fuck the cold, you need to get drunk. That has promise.

But you're out of money. Not even a buck or two for a bottle of King Cobra.

You pull your jacket on, thinking. You can't call Casey because you just destroyed your phone. Steal whatever you can carry from a gas station and run? But you could get busted, which would be a disaster in terms of criminal record issues—not to mention your options would be limited to beer.

According to the clock on the microwave, it's only 5:43, which means the blood bank is still open for another hour and seventeen minutes. You're allowed to donate today.

Zipping up, you step into your boots and set off into the storm. Of course, your truck won't start, as the fumes of the stolen gas fail to get it going.

The blood bank is usually about a ten-minute walk but it takes you thirty. The storm is something else. As soon as you're outside, the wind hits you with a chill that's goddamn near unbelievable. You pull on a toboggan cap but the wind cuts right through it.

You trudge through the dark, one foot in front of the other, sticking to the side of the road where you can see the headlights coming. The snow is already thick under foot. Each step sends you sliding backward, and it takes energy to make up the ground. You try to tuck your hands into your pockets and clutch your body. Past the Dairy Queen and the lumber supply. The stoplights sway wildly in the wind, bouncing frantically on their wires, the green glow falling across empty bone-white roads.

When you finally reach the strip mall lot where the blood bank does business, your entire body trembles uncontrollably. Your toes are chips of ice. Your ears have gone hot with pain even beneath the cap, and you lick the ice forming on the tips of the hairs that ring your mouth. The wind screams across the frozen desert. The parking lot lights barely cut through the white-out. Jesus. It's like a hurricane. A freezing fucking hurricane. Nearing the blood bank, you begin to understand that the lights aren't on behind the glass. The offices are dark. You know you checked the time, you know it should still be open, and for a moment none of this makes any sense.

Then you see the handwritten sign taped to the inside of the glass: *Closed for Christmas Eve and Day.* Of course. Tonight is Christmas Eve.

The cold encompasses you, but not just physically. The blade of the night wind shears all thought, all memory. The wind senses your despair and almost takes you off your feet.

You try to turn your back, and it seems you could fall into the gust and it would keep you standing upright. Then you're just turning pointlessly in circles. Looking off into the dark. Again, you have that sensation of seeing everything for the first time. The stores are all closed. The cars are empty and abandoned. It feels like you're not wearing a jacket anymore. Just the freezing hand of the wind clutching you now, fingers puncturing your body, digging inside of you.

You have no energy to walk back. The cold has knocked the high out of you. You might as well sit down. Pretty soon you'll get warm again. You're about to do just this when a dim honk issues from across the lot. One of the cars you thought empty flashes its brights at you. Loping over, you almost stumble and fall. You manage to make it over to the driver's side. The window hums down an inch.

"It's closed." A woman's voice. "Thought it would be open but it ain't."

"Can I come in and get warm?" you shout over the wind. "Just for a minute? I walked here, and this is fucking crazy. I'm freezing."

There's a long hesitation. Dimly, you understand this is a big ask for a woman alone in a deserted parking lot with a stranger.

"Please."

You hustle to the passenger side and, climbing in, you can feel the heater on full blast, pouring forth wonderful hot air. In the cocoon of the car, you rub your hands furiously, rip your boots off, and try to massage warmth back into your toes.

"Sorry," you say. "My feet stink, but I think I'm close to frostbite."

"This is unbelievable," she says, watching you. "It's all the way from Canada to Mississippi. It was on the news."

"Why're you sitting out here?" you ask. And now that you're finally looking at her, you realize you know her. The black girl from the other day. "I seen you here before," you add.

"Just need the cash."

"I mean, it's closed. Why don't you leave?"

She looked out the window. "Can't go back to where I'm living. Got problems there. Was trying to get me money for a hotel room."

"I'm trying to get some booze. Or Oxy. You don't got any of either, do you?"

She looks uncertain of both you and herself. You're glad you didn't tip-toe around the issue. You want it so bad, and you can just feel it humming in the veins of the universe that she's got some. You just know it.

"Not Oxy," she says, and a bag crinkles as she pulls it from her jacket. "This."

You stare longingly at the powder secured in the corner of the baggie with a rubber band.

"You got stuff to shoot it with?"

She nods.

"Tell you what, you can stay with me if you let me have a taste."

She looks miserable at this prospect. A misery that makes her so beautiful. "Where do you live?"

"Fairview. A trailer home."

She considers this. Snow accumulates on the windshield, darkening the interior.

"This ain't about me doing you, right? I don't do that."

All you're thinking about is that bag of white powder in her hand, a rib eye steak to your salivating dog.

"Nothing like that, girl. Just wanna get high. You can have the couch."

She has a spoon, a bottle of water, a syringe, a lighter. She has a piece of rubber tubing. She lets you go first. You've got the veins for this, as they say, and when the blood blossoms into the potion and then pushes back into your bloodstream, you don't even have to wait for her to take the needle from you. You are bliss. You are warmth. You are light.

The world is radiant and sublime. There is no joke being played on you. There is no valley of bones. There is only this wonderful womb, this place of peace and awe. She's fixed the next needle and gone about her own journey. Her hand slips over and takes yours. The idle of the car mingles with the sound of the wind, and it's beautiful. Everything is so fucking beautiful it hurts.

As the snow piles on the windshield and the car goes dark, a memory comes to you: of Christmas, a tree you and your mother decorated, wrapped in multicolored lights and sparkly green ribbon and snowflake ornaments. The gleam of wrapping paper as it catches all the sources of illumination.

Chips of light filter through the storm. Christmas Day nears, and the snow continues to fall, until it feels like a thick curtain closing over the earth.

KATE CHAOS AND THE PLANET'S LAST STAND

Once an anonymous foot soldier in an underfunded climate justice group, Kate Morris and A Fierce Blue Fire defied party politics, upended the midterm elections, and have reignited momentum on the climate crisis. Moniza Farooki profiles the frank, funny, fearless woman who has stormed to the front of the movement—even though she may not be welcome there.

BY MONIZA FAROOKI
DECEMBER 13, 2026

For those who've attempted to look away from the global cataclysm unfolding before their eyes, reality is finally descending. The news of the past year has been so grim, so terrifying, that it saturates the headlines and deadens the will. From apocalyptic western wildfires that incinerate entire sleeping towns before an alarm so much as sounds to Hurricane Alberto wiping Virginia Beach off the map to the Come to Jesus Storm killing dozens and plunging millions into cold and darkness across the Midwest, it is difficult not to despair. In that context Kate Morris's demeanor can feel offensively incongruous to the moment.

"I get that we're supposed to be funereal at all times, that joking about civilization-ending doom will get you excommunicated by the Twitterati, but if you think about it, this is all *kind of* funny. Don't write that down, bitch!" she quickly adds, and then begins laughing loudly at herself.

We're on the South Phoenix campus of Morris's organization, A Fierce Blue Fire—what the group calls one of its "Outposts." It includes a community center, urban garden, water recycling system, solar arrays, and vertical wind turbines. Heroin addicts wander the grounds, taking advantage of the addiction services and counseling.

"Our idea is that it's fucking gut-check time," Morris continues. "Nothing has worked so far. So it's time to throw everything at the wall, leave everything on the field, knock down doors, get into the streets, get into the towns, and here's a wild idea, even talk to people you disagree with. Personally, I think that requires some motherfucking gallows humor to keep your shit level, but to each her own, right?"

Until six months ago, no one but a handful of infighting climate activists even knew who Kate Morris was. Now she takes fire from all sides. She's been called, among other things, "a feminist traitor making nice with Trump country," and "the manic pixie dream girl of global warming." The vitriol is obviously more extreme on the right after A Fierce Blue Fire made a raucous intrusion in the 2026 midterms. Now Morris is escaping D.C. to barnstorm the country in her dust-encased Nissan Leaf, energizing the troops. She claims she's long harbored a dread of the spotlight.

"I get it. I get why people look at me like, 'I'm fucking sick of these whacky socialist bitches trying to take away my hamburger.' Hell, even I'm sick of Greta! I'm sick of AOC! I'm sick of the perverse media logic that takes this elemental emergency and juices it through the filter of celebrity at every opportunity. But we can't stop. None of us can stop. We have to circumvent the culture wars, get past personalities, and build a multiyear, even multi-decadal, movement."

An unbuttoned flannel flaps in the wind. Her skin has the weathered quality of a woman who's spent a great deal of time in sun and dry air. She never wears makeup. Her curls must require maintenance, though, and her hands never leave them alone, always sweeping, tugging, or corralling. She tends to be fidgety and wired, careening from topic to topic. Her stories never cohere or conclude. She frequently gives me instructions to meet her in cities that she's already left. She smiles.

"It's pretty simple: We fight to the fucked and bitter end or we die."

The founding of A Fierce Blue Fire dates to the tumultuous final year of the Trump administration when Morris and Harvard computer scientist Liza Yudong departed the climate advocacy organization that had brought them both to D.C. They wanted to build their own platform.

"The trauma of that time, especially the storming of the Capitol, lit a new fire under me," says Morris. At that point, her only experience was at a small bison advocacy group in Wyoming and a few years of fundraising for climate action. She and Yudong utilized connections to environmentalism's financial elite, billionaire families with familiar names, while also building a formidable small-dollar donation machine on the new social VR platforms. They were determined to expand beyond the strategy of running primary challenges against Democrats with fossil-fuel ties.

Yudong explains: "Kate mostly has weird or bad ideas. That's your starting point with her." Yudong is possibly the most meta-sardonic person I've ever interviewed, dressing up her intellect in an ironic veneer so thick it's almost impossible to pinpoint where her actual personality lies. "But then Kate'll be like, 'Hey, Liz, let's build the new world from the ashes of the old. Find me some places where we can build solar panel basketball courts and hold roots-rock concerts.' There's an uncomfortable amount of roots-rock."

This is how the idea of the Outposts began: taking the values of climate justice into communities abandoned as ecological or economic sacrifice zones. Staff, money, and volunteers began to flood into places like Flint, Michigan; Kemmerer, Wyoming; and Zanesville, Ohio. Amid decay they've built jewels of renewable energy, open green space, concert venues, addiction services, and small farms. Out of thin air, they create a vocal stakeholder, with roots in the community, waging a perpetual influence campaign on the district's congressperson and the state's public utility commission—a board of influential decision-makers in each state who have their hands on the levers of enormous amounts of carbon energy. They've also fostered a growing mutual aid network that springs to work after disasters. During the Come to Jesus polar storm that killed ninety-three people in seven states last Christmas, FBF used its vast peer-to-peer organizing app to crowdsource food, water, and shelter for those stranded in subzero homes or on highways.

"My thinking is," said Morris, "even if we don't win a political race, at least we're giving people a vision of what's possible. We teach kids how to grow a tomato. But to grow a tomato, you have to know about the weather, and to know about the weather you have to intimately understand what is happening to our climate. Fossil-fuel capitalism makes us feel atomized and isolated. Growing tomatoes and roots-rock makes us feel together."

IF THIS WAS ALL MORRIS AND FBF WERE DOING IT WOULD BE REmarkable, but it is not what has propelled her into the public eye and earned her the nickname "the Rottweiler of the climate crisis." She garnered this notoriety by putting an unthinkable head on a pike for all Democrats to see.

Senator Elmer Nolan was a five-term West Virginia legend, who'd long championed coal and gas interests in the hydrocarbon state and survived the state's lurch toward right-wing politics. Then FBF began its primary challenge.

One source intimate with that contentious campaign said that Morris sat across from Nolan at an early meeting and "told him point-blank that if he didn't agree to back the GND, her candidate might not win, but Nolan would never make it back to the Senate again. Morris told Elmer to get with her program or she'd take his scalp. And she did."

The result, some might argue, was catastrophe. In the general election, the precious Democratic Senate seat swung to Republican challenger Russ Mackowski, a neo-Confederate, hard-core climate denialist of the first order. Mackowski is now considered a leader of the hard right wing of the party.

Embattled president Joanna Hogan is apparently furious at the loss of Nolan, her Senate majority, and several key allies in the House. One source, close to the White House and speaking anonymously for reasons that will become obvious, had the following to say:

"You want my opinion of [Morris]? She's a toxic cunt."

The source went on. "She ousted Nolan, and now we're going to have Mackowski, who's not just a climate denier but practically a Holocaust denier. Not to mention her eco-socialist recruits in our party are all zealots you can't work with. She's torching [the Democrats] at a time when demographically we should be ascendant and when the other party has an openly fascist wing."

Since Morris arrived on the scene, the apostasies of A Fierce Blue Fire have stoked controversy: She allies with pro-life groups; she decries antinuclear activists as "climate denialists in their own right"; and she once called President Hogan's version of the Green New Deal "a five-trillion-dollar healthcare bill with a green coat of paint." Yet nothing has stirred more outrage than FBF's strategy of aggressively recruiting, cultivating, and supporting Republican candidates to run primary challenges. Forget about stances on abortion rights, gun control, LGBTQIAA+ issues. All these Republican challengers have to do to access FBF's money is run campaigns based on "the scientific consensus of anthropogenic climate change" and pledge to vote affirmatively on FBF's model legislation.

"People are going ape, sure, and maybe they're not wrong," says Morris. "But I've come to believe there are limits to activating the hard core, that what we were building was a clubhouse rather than a movement. Self-sorting political behavior is toxic, not just for QAnon dweebs but for the Left as well, because we have to create a durable, sustainable governing consensus. It's shortsighted to ignore people who vote Republican by habit. We have a moral duty to talk to people we disagree with. We have to build on-ramps to the movement."

Many viewed entering the Republican civil war in the post-Trump era as a fool's errand, but Morris has proved them wrong. The House now includes a "Green Tea" caucus, and Republican senator Ryan Doup, widely expected to become Senate majority leader, has promised action on climate. The unambiguous victor of this strategy is, of course, Mary Randall. The thirty-nine-year-old Republican came from the dredges of the statehouse in Albany and will become the first woman of color to occupy the governor's mansion in New York history. Poised, confident, and a full-throated advocate of action on climate change, Randall is already being championed by Republican moderates as a candidate for 2028 when the field will be anybody's game. It's no secret that Randall got a huge bump from FBF's Super PAC, which enraged some on the left: Randall, a Black woman, is also devoutly Catholic and a pro-life conservative.

"I don't necessarily endorse every last policy prescription from those folks," Randall told CBS's *Face the Nation*. "But we have a wide array of tools available within our free-market system to cut emissions and arrest the climate crisis. True conservatives have already left denialism in the dustbin of history because they see the enormous economic opportunities presented by the zero-emissions revolution. It's already begun. Now it's just a matter of how quickly we move and who is going to capitalize on it."

Meanwhile, the Left continues its vexed relationship with the current commander-in-chief. While pursuing only meager efforts on climate, Joanna Hogan has had her time in office consumed by global chaos. She's vastly increased troop levels across the Middle East, Southeast Asia, and North Africa, approved hundreds more drone strikes than Presidents Obama, Trump, and Biden combined, ramped up deportations, increased the military presence at the US-Mexico border, and opened people's data to new heights of exploitation by signing the Freedom of Data and Corporate Accountability Act. She's also embraced the "eco-terrorist" label for the pipeline saboteurs and applauded the heavy sentence of a college student who planted an explosive in Colorado. Perhaps most importantly, she's spoken with exasperation and occasional scorn for youth-led movements like A Fierce Blue Fire for their "pie-in-the-sky, gimme-gimme, baby-wanna-bottle attitude" as she infamously told a reporter following the abandonment of climate legislation early in her term.

This is in stark contrast to Governor-elect Randall.

When I ask Morris if she would support Mary Randall as a presidential candidate, Morris responds, "Depends. She's talked a good game, but if it comes down to it, will she bite the chain saw? Hard to say."

But can it be a coincidence that FBF's model legislation bears a striking resemblance to a policy touted by Randall, which she calls "the Green Trident"?

"Oh my god, that name is brutal," says Morris. "I just don't want to hear the word 'green' attached to anything ever a-fucking-gain. Besides, it's a total misnomer. During extinction events, the oceans acidify, carbonate-forming species get wiped out, and it's all replaced by green plankton. 'Disaster plankton' scientists call it. The oceans bloom with that shit. After the end-Triassic, the whole planet turned green. And that's what it'll look like again—a muddy tennis ball—unless we stop it. That's why we monkeyed with the Phil Shabecoff phrase for our name, because green, at this point, is a dead fucking brand."

FROM WHAT PRIMORDIAL AMERICAN STEW DID MORRIS ARISE?

She is tight-lipped about her father, Earl Morris, an antinuclear activist, who spent a year in prison on trespassing and vandalism charges. Social and political engagement courses through her blood: Earl was the son of a Navajo schoolteacher and a Jamaican civil rights lawyer. Earl's uncle, Mervyn Morris, was Jamaica's poet laureate. Kate's mother, Sonja Sundstrom, came to the US from Sweden on a student visa and never left. Sonja and Earl separated in 2006, and Kate moved with her mother to Portland. Her father and two younger brothers still live in Arizona, but she won't allow me an interview, and the situation smells of tension.

In Portland, however, I convince her to let me sit down with her mother.

Sundstrom looks like a mythical Nordic matriarch: tall with bleach-white hair that hangs down to the small of her back. She lives in a two-bedroom bungalow in Beaverton and works for the Columbia River Cooperative. She has a great deal to vent about her daughter.

"Kate has always been the most stubborn, most hard-headed girl," she says, her English carrying a crisp accent. "When she was young we fought all the time about everything. Not like mean, nasty 'I hate you, I hate you' fighting. We just argued. I only argue because I don't want her to do stupid things."

For instance, she points to her daughter's 2016 arrest during the Dakota Access Pipeline protest.

"Go to jail if you want, just like your father. I tell Matthew he can't get arrested." She refers to Morris's longtime partner, Matthew Stanton, who works under Morris at FBF. "'You get ready to rescue her as soon as she screws up too bad.'"

I ask Sundstrom what she thinks of her daughter's rise to prominence.

"Oh, she needs to stop wearing so many tight outfits."

I ask how that is relevant.

"Kate gets what she wants. So maybe she'll get what she wants this time, like always, and she'll save the world. But I keep telling her she's making many people angry and horny. It's a bad combination. Are you a mother? I'll tell you being a mother is just worry—especially if you have a crazy person for a daughter. When she was a teenager Kate would run away from home for weeks at a time, never tell me where she was going, who she was with, always scaring me. But Matthew is the finest thing to ever happen to her. I told him, if she's ever stupid and decides to leave him, he can come be my son."

The rest of the interview is spent allowing Sundstrom's inexhaustible repository of opinions about her daughter to spool out. Her nickname for Kate catches my attention.

"I call her Kate Chaos because that's what she's like to be with. All the time, her and chaos holding hands. She loves it, she causes it, she *is* it."

BEFORE JOINING HER ON THE ROAD, I FIRST MET MORRIS IN WASHington, D.C., where she indulged me with a tour of A Fierce Blue Fire's offices in Adams Morgan. Organizers drank from a keg midday, propped feet on carboard boxes, and flitted digits across five screens at once. All their work takes place beneath an enormous mural, a quote emerging from a conflagration of blue flames: PATHWALKER, THERE IS NO PATH. YOU MAKE THE PATH AS YOU WALK.

Morris has proven adept at siphoning talent from other organizations. Rekia Reynolds, twenty-five, grew up in Englewood, on Chicago's South Side, and went on to graduate at the top of her high school class and receive a scholarship to Northwestern.

Reynolds said it was an environmental science class that first alerted her to inequities she had not considered before. "I got my head spun by this professor who was talking about air quality on the South Side, and I was like, 'Yes, that was me!' Everyone I knew had some respiratory issue growing up."

Reynolds never considered environmentalism or the climate crisis as having any impact on her life.

"I thought it was about white people telling you to take the bus and never drive a car. I was like, 'Fuck you, you take the bus—I'm buying a ride.' But a lot of that comes from never having seen anyone in this movement who looked like me. It was all rich people hectoring. But the fact is, when you talk about structural racism, there is no greater purveyor or promoter than the fossil-fuel lobby and other polluting industries—not just the right-wing politicians they sponsor—because their products poison Black and brown people. They use our communities as dumping grounds."

Reynolds now does environmental justice outreach, a huge portfolio that includes everything from organizing and registering Black voters to coordinating with lawyers to file lawsuits against corporate polluters.

"Yeah, I'm here 'cause of the white girl," she jokes with a sly shift of her eyes to Kate. "Kate and I work well because we're both alphas, both big personalities, both Aries, so we can knock heads and then be chill almost twenty minutes later. But she is the one who convinced me that we need to connect these movements, BLM and the climate crisis, because they are absolutely the same fight."

Tom Levine, a Hill veteran, began his career in Nancy Pelosi's office before moving on to hold a number of jobs in the progressive wing of the Democratic Party. A muscular southern Jewish boy, he wears thick-rimmed hipster glasses and speaks with the slight drawl of his native Alabama.

"I've been around long enough, I remember the death of cap-and-trade, let alone the big talk and meager action of Biden-Harris. I thought Jo Hogan was going to take a swing at climate legislation first thing. When that didn't happen, I jumped ship and went to work for the barbarians. So, I lost my good apartment and my girlfriend left me for a lobbyist." He spits into an empty Red Bull can, and I realize he has chewing tobacco in his mouth. "That's all part and parcel for this town, so maybe I'm a double agent—maybe I'm just trying to drown this miserable fucking city."

Coral Sloane was recruited from a think tank to serve as FBF policy director.

"The Chewbacca to Kate's Han Solo," jokes Sloane. Sleeved in tattoos with a bowl of messy orange hair and a lip ring that gets in the way of their every word, Sloane is a graduate of Yale and the Harvard Kennedy School, where they did their master's in public policy. Sloane is a super-wonk who has helped draft their three-pronged model legislation. They believe any policy should lead with a pledge to the workers who've proven most resistant to the end of fossil fuels.

"Job security, a union, health insurance, a pension—people fight to keep all that for good reason. For communities battered by scarcity, they don't want to see one more plant or business close ever again. We want to guarantee that on the other side of the carbon economy is something better for working people."

A clean electricity standard, a zero-emissions vehicle mandate, and the shuttering of all coal plants by 2030 are the low-hanging fruit. A ten-trillion-dollar investment over ten years will pay for the "big-ticket items of deep decarbonization," like reducing transportation and industrial emissions. This also includes what they call the "1,000 Counties Project," which will direct half the money to the poorest and most environmentally degraded counties in the country. Much of this is old hat to GND-heads, but the final component of the legislation is something new, a hybrid proposal that has the climate policy world buzzing. "The central problem of climate action of the 2020s is that emissions have not fallen," says Sloane. "Even as renewables have become cheap, accessible, and ubiquitous, the Carbon Majors are still reaping huge profits. Carbon pricing got a bad rap as a half measure, but it's only a half measure if it's weak."

Morris, Sloane, and their cheerleaders envision an economy-wide tax on carbon pollution, no exemptions, with 100 percent of the revenues returned to citizens in quarterly rebate checks that will dwarf any rise in energy prices, similar to Canadian policy. The tax will begin at $50 a ton but be tied to emissions reductions, so it increases if emissions goals are not met. It will also include a border adjustment tariff to link carbon policy globally.

"We're making sure the fossil fuels have nowhere to go. No market left," Morris explains. "The carbon lobby is a big bad dog, so first we're going to tame it, then we're going to put it down." Morris's smile is vicious. "That's why we call it the 'shock collar.'"

Morris's partner, Matthew Stanton, was not what I expected. He is tall, slender, boyishly handsome with high, delicate cheekbones and mournful eyes. He spends a lot of time during our interview sweeping thick brown locks from his brow. He comes across as shy, amused, unassuming, and melancholy. Morris calls him "Tar Heel," a nod to his North Carolina roots.

Though he is a writer and photographer, he says, "Mostly my real gig is being Kate's amanuensis."

Stanton joined FBF in 2022 and now serves as assistant to the executive director and helps coordinate her speaking engagements and public outreach. He explains his own internalization of the climate threat.

"When we first came to D.C. I was pretty much like, 'Global warming, sure, whatever. Maybe someday you can get back to the bison, Crazy Lady I Love.' But suddenly I was living with a woman who gave me homework, and it really was like a religious conversion. I get why sometimes even smart people can't look directly at it. The implications are just so profound and frightening."

I ask if he worries about the constant barrage of criticism, outrage, death threats, rape threats, and defamation that Morris collects, especially now that she has become a topic of obsession in right-wing media.

"Nothing we can do about it," he says. "It fazes me more than it does her. If she reads them, she's like, 'Look at this masturbating idiot.' She puts the funny ones on a corkboard."

Though it's a touchy subject, I bring up the rumors, mostly circulating in said right-wing media, that Morris was detained in a New York City restaurant for having sex in the bathroom with Lucas Frisk, the lead singer of Dead Patriots. Frisk, the rumor goes, paid off the management to avoid indecency charges.

"I won't comment on that," says Stanton. "Except to say that Kate and I trust each other, and that's our bottom line."

Morris slinks back into the conversation, wrapping an arm around his neck. "Want to also tell *Vanity Fair* about our last ménage à trois?"

Levine, Sloane, and Yudong snicker at this. Stanton's face turns the color of sunburn, and he adds an embarrassed smile that his childhood orthodontist should advertise. "Jesus, Kate. That's off the record. See, she's just an unrepentant show-off."

Morris falls into his lap, tugging him by his thick head of hair and graphically sticking her tongue in his mouth. In our time together, I've often wondered how much of Kate Morris is calculation—even her crude jokes—and how much is simply an unfiltered expression of the drive within her. Here with her mates, as my recorder goes off and the inside jokes and old stories proliferate, I watch her happy-warrior armor fall away, plate by plate, and there is only her joy at being in the world, among people she clearly loves quite profoundly.

In Phoenix, the day is bright and beautiful, a pleasant sixty-seven degrees, making Armageddon feel very distant. On July 12 this past summer, Sky Harbor International Airport—where planes are now regularly grounded during the summer because the heat won't allow the aerodynamics of the wings to achieve lift—hit a record temperature of 125 degrees Fahrenheit. The Salt River Project, Arizona's largest utility, buckled under the energy demand and rolling brownouts ensued. Maricopa County reported at least twenty-five deaths, mostly infants and the elderly who roasted without power. Heat is not the only agent of chaos. The dust storms that have befallen the region in recent years are specters of biblical proportions. These ratcheting circumambient storms—known as haboobs—swamp Phoenix for days at a time. Six weeks after the brownouts, ninety-mile-per-hour winds blew a light orange fog of loose desert soil across Maricopa. Highways shut down and sand scoured windows until holes melted in the panes. The dust hung in a purple-mustard haze for several days.

Despite this, the state legislature remains a hotbed of climate denial intent on keeping the unchecked growth in the Phoenix Basin going any way it can. The state's troubles also manifest as xenophobic zeal, as migrants fleeing heat, drought, storms, collapsing crop production, and violent cartels in Central and South America arrive to find a police state on the Arizona border. This provides ample oxygen for the likes of far-right VR star Jennifer Braden, who's based out of Prescott. Braden continues to propose that men caught sneaking across the border should be chemically castrated and women forced into hysterectomies before deportation. She has the third-most-visited "worlde" on the popular new social VR platform Slapdish. Attendees log in so they can sit for three hours in an airplane hangar from the 1940s while Braden spews invective through a vintage retro microphone. A silver dual-propellered plane gleams in the background. CGI bodyguards wear sharp black suits with red accents in their lapels. Sepia-tinted American flags hang behind her, but one questions what aesthetic she's invoking.

Pushing back against the weather and the rage is A Fierce Blue Fire's South Phoenix campus. Across the street from its auditorium on the day of Morris's speech, men wear flak jackets and carry AR-15s with the muzzles pointed at the ground. They hold signs decrying global warming as a hoax, and there is Braden's face and a quote often attributed to her about undocumented migrants and those who want to protect them ("Hunt All Traitors to Extinction"). There is also a surprisingly strong anarchist-type contingent with signage proclaiming KATE MORRIS = CORPORATE STOOGE and images of the three-eyed nuclear fish from *The Simpsons.* Many wear FREE MILES KROLL T-shirts with the pristine face of that Mormon eco-revolutionary.

Inside, all two thousand seats of the auditorium are vouched for, and screens have been erected in every classroom and office to accommodate spillover. When the local director introduces Morris, the crowd—young, multicultural, eager—breaks into a rowdy welcome. Morris beams as she takes to the podium, flipping open a tattered spiral-bound notebook, and waits through several waves of applause.

"Okay, okay, sit the hell down," she says when she can finally get a word in. "Man, this is the best-looking audience I've seen in my life. Not kidding, I'd sleep with everyone in this room, gender agnostic."

Her choice of outfit is beyond casual. She wears sand-coated hiking boots, khaki cargo pants, and a sky-blue tank top that exposes the smoky brown of her shoulders. There's an immense screen behind her with the organization's blazing blue logo.

The laughter is genuine but also imbued with a bit of, *Really? Would you, please?*

"Now I'm sorry to say that's probably our last laugh for the evening." The crowd whispers itself to silence. She turns to the screen. "So. Here is my whole presentation. Soak it up."

The logo switches to 430 PPM.

"I'm not telling you anything new. That is the carbon dioxide level of the atmosphere today. We started at around two hundred eighty before the Industrial Revolution. We know the absolute safe upper threshold is three hundred fifty, which the world blew by in the nineties, and it's still rising at the rate of two to three parts per million every year. It's as simple as this: The fate of every man, woman, child, and species on this planet is bound to this number. Nothing matters unless we can *stop and eventually reverse that number.*"

She steps back from the podium and decides to pull her hair into a bun, swiftly snatching a hair tie from her wrist and running her hand over her face to collect loose strands as she speaks. She gives a quick lesson in the basic physics and chemistry of greenhouse gas emissions, "simple enough that when Svante Arrhenius made a few back-of-the-envelope calculations in 1896, he predicted that if smokestacks continued to belch CO2, the planet would eventually warm by three to six degrees centigrade. This remains exactly in line with what the most sophisticated computer models still say today.

"What most scientists have been wrong about," Morris continues, "is how quickly our planet's systems could unravel given this additional heat. The chaos we're seeing is from just a 1.2-degree temperature rise. Now we have feedback loops to fear."

Her hands make swift, enormous gesticulations, a conductor building urgency for her symphony, as she describes the Amazon's epic droughts releasing six billion tons of CO2, equivalent to annual US emissions. She moves on to the permafrost in the tundra of Alaska, northern Canada, and Siberia.

"Scientists believe by the end of this century"—she skips one palm across the other to send it riding to the sky—"the permafrost could release one hundred billion tons of methane, which is equivalent to two hundred seventy years of emissions at our current levels."

Finally, she describes the deposits of methane throughout the world's oceans. Scientists hoped it would take centuries for methane clathrates to melt, but they're already discovering plumes venting from the Arctic Ocean during sea ice retreats. The first ice-free Arctic summer will probably arrive in the next five to ten years—and rather than white ice reflecting sunlight, the dark ocean absorbs it. Yet another feedback loop imperiling the highly dangerous clathrates.

"For anyone who hasn't read Anthony Pietrus's terrifying book, at that point, there is no adaptation, no survival, no Earth. The entire surface of the planet will be too hot to sustain life. So we're not just talking about fucking polar bears here. We're talking about the violent disintegration of civilization followed by a slow-rolling global genocide, and it's underway right now. In other words, it might already be too late. Here is the absolute best-case scenario of where we are."

She leaves the podium and approaches the edge of the stage. She stops with her toes on the precipice and leans forward, outstretched arms quivering in tight, tiny circles for balance. She teeters forward impossibly far, and one can easily picture her sprawling face-first into the front row, cracking her chin open, or worse. There's a palpable anxiety to watching her perform this feat, the crowd tensing at this gut-clenching display, the spotlights spilling her long shadow across the stage. Two thousand mouths exhale with relief when she finally catches hold of her momentum and tilts back from the edge. She smiles at herself and returns to the podium.

"Again, that is our best-case scenario. We have a precious handful of years left to act, and I promise you this: If you do not join this movement now, you will wake up ten, fifteen, twenty years from now and feel sick that you didn't do everything you could during the sliver of time when we still had a chance. When we hadn't yet fallen over the brink."

I've heard this speech multiple times by now, but there is something acute about the blanket silence that engulfs this crowd. Morris checks her notebook on the lectern.

"So what does that mean? First of all, forget about your carbon footprint. 'Carbon footprint' is a PR term invented by an oil company. I want you to remember two words . . ."

These words replace 430 behind her: **THEY KNEW.**

"*'They'* are the Carbon Majors, the one hundred companies responsible for over seventy percent of emissions since the eighties. Their own scientists knew what would happen. They knew if they kept burning their reserves they would threaten the future of the human race. They knew, and they built their oil rigs to account for higher sea levels and more intense storms. They knew, and they told us to focus on our consumer behavior while they locked us all into structures of hyperconsumption. They knew, and they waged a propaganda war of denial and delay. They knew, and they're still doing it! There is no other way to put it, they are committing the greatest atrocity in human history and *they knew*. They knew, and they told us to worry about our fucking carbon footprints."

She thrusts her right hand toward the sky. Three fingers stretch upward, and her voice thunders.

"So what do we do? Climate. Inequality. Democracy. They are inextricably linked, so our only choice is to seize power beginning right here in the US, right here in Arizona, right here in Phoenix."

A smattering of applause breaks out, but Morris quickly speaks over it.

"That's the philosophy of Climate X. There is no one deal—there is only this crisis as far as the eye can see. We won't stop until the global economy is circular, zero-carbon, near-zero waste with contraception and education for all, with population stabilized, healthy, and thriving and with our ecosystems restored and managed. We won't stop until half the earth is wild again. But right now, we have a dangerous waste disposal problem, and nothing else matters because this number has not stopped."

430 again appears on the screen.

"When you climb a mountain, you don't just materialize at the peak. You cannot ignore the first step. Which is why we have a plan that will deliver investment and opportunity to regions that have known only poverty, neglect, and exploitation. That means a rebirth right here in South Phoenix, in the decimated mountains of West Virginia, in the redlined neighborhoods of Chicago, in the Navajo Nation where my grandmother grew up. We will create a mass political movement that crosses race, region, religion, and any other category you can come up with. That binds us all in restoration and reparation.

"Yes, climate is a reckoning, a deadline, but this is also the keyhole through which we build a more just and equitable world. A Fierce Blue Fire has been told a lot of things: that we're spoiling things for the Democrats, that we're compromising with problematic people or we're too uncompromising in our demands—but look, when you understand what's happening, how can you not spill the whole toolkit on the floor? When I sit across from politicians that I'm trying to either get in or out of office, what can I say except 'I don't care about your stance on abortion or gun control or prayer in school, I don't care about your sex scandal, I don't care if you're a Republican, Democrat, Whig, Tory, or Ostrogoth. I don't care about anything except whether you're ready to fight back.'"

She's still talking, but the clapping slowly overwhelms her voice. Then people rise from their seats, thousands of hands beating themselves pink.

"We have an election coming in two years," Morris cries over the applause. "And we need to blow the fucking roof off this thing." A scream rises from the crowd, a war whoop. "We follow every candidate everywhere they go and ask, 'What are you doing about this crisis?' We protest, invest, divest, blockade, persuade, disobey, make nonviolent trouble, and most importantly, we vote, every race, no matter what. And if there's no one worth voting for, bitch, get yourself a clipboard, get your signatures, and get yourself on that motherfucking ballot."

The ovation overwhelms. It is a surge of passion, exploding from a crowd that has just been informed that the world as they know it will be gone within their lifetimes.

BACK IN WASHINGTON, MORRIS AND I MEET AT THE REFLECTING pond near the Lincoln Memorial and wander down its length. It's a brisk winter day, and Morris's cheeks are a healthy fuchsia from the cold. I ask if she's trepidatious about this profile.

"Obviously. But there's a reason I decided to quit fighting celebrity. Not embrace it, but at least use it. And if I somehow came to believe that posing nekked for *Penthouse* would help, I'd drop trou right here."

She stops to laugh. A burnt-orange leaf parachutes down from a tree and lands on her shoulder. She plucks it off and shares her laughter with it. "During Covid, Matt got me to watch that old show *Friday Night Lights*. I was like, 'Football melodrama? Fuck off.' But of course, I got hooked, and I think it sort of made me fall in love with him even harder. I still watch certain episodes when I want a good cry." She twirls the leaf by the stem. "There's this scene where Coach Taylor goes to Saracen, the QB, in the fourth quarter of the state championship and Coach says to him, 'Son, have you got one more in you?' And Saracen just gives him this earnest-as-hell look and goes, 'I always got one more in me, Coach.' And goddamn, for whatever reason, that scene moves me." She slips the leaf into the pocket of her peacoat, and we continue walking. I tell her I don't quite get it.

"What I mean is, I've got my eyes wide fucking open. Maybe our notions of liberty and democracy are fictions built on exploitation, and we just happen to have lucked into the moment of the greatest plunder and consumption and called it freedom. But I really do believe what we have here . . ." She searches for the words. "We have the two most consequential experiments in the history of humankind. The first is the uncontrolled dumping of greenhouse gases into the atmosphere. We know how that ends. But the second is an experiment in human community. In democracy and organization and compassion and our willingness and ability to confront this emergency, arm in arm, together."

She stops at the edge of the reflecting pool. Her gaze fixes on the Washington Monument, pointing drab and gray to the overcast sky.

"That's why we need to keep adapting, keep switching tactics, and if those tactics don't work, switch them again. We can't be in denial about what's going on—this is a last stand for our world. But who would have thought a last stand could be so much fun? Or just so beautiful."

MAGIC MOUNTAIN

2027

On his way to the World Economic Forum, Tony got lost in the muck.

A meter of snow had fallen on Davos the week before, followed by a warm snap. The temperature rose to nearly thirteen degrees Celsius while the city's street cleaners worked round the clock to truck snow from the streets and dump it in Lake Davos, but the whole alpine city was still soaked with slush and meltwater. His panel wasn't until the next day, but he wanted to sit in on some of the others, particularly his friend Marty Rathbone's. Marty was discussing macroeconomic trends with the CEO of Google and the EU's chief economist. Limo tires sluiced and pedestrians flattened themselves against quaint Swiss brick to avoid the spray. Nestled among four snow-coated mountains in postcard perfection, the picturesque town looked rotten. Like it was moldering.

He found his way when he spotted the protestors: five hundred people held behind a fence, signs declaring every manner of grievance, justified or conspiratorial. One young woman held a sign that read **GANGSTERS PARTY IN DAVOS**. Another, **OFF WITH THEIR FUCKING HEADS**. Following near-riots after the last NATO summit and the G-20, most of Europe had imposed severe restrictions on protestors, herding them into little pop-up concentration camps for the afternoon where they could be tear-gassed if someone shook their fist too hard at a cop. As he shuffled through redundant checkpoints, barbed-wired barricades, FaceRec scanners, and a quick Covid swab lest anyone smuggle in a new variant of the troublesome virus, he eyed the Polizei. Riot gear masked every feature except cold eyes. The Davos church spire shared the skyline with all the SWAT-looking characters perched on rooftops, idling their tripod-mounted sniper rifles.

When Marty Rathbone told Tony he'd nominated him for a much-coveted invite to Davos, Tony had given him grief over "capitalism's biggest cocktail party." But Marty, Harvard's star, had become a fixture, and he wanted Tony to take his show on the road. Ever since the publication of his book, Tony hadn't had a problem hopping back on the lecture circuit. He had that odd type of celebrity: unrecognizable to the vast majority of the hoi polloi, but instantly controversial in certain circles, iconoclast or heretic depending on one's prism.

Holly called him "our idolater father," but he scoffed at this. He'd simply laid out some ideas based on the science, and the world could take it or leave it. His old partner in crime from Scripps, Niko, had introduced him to Marty. "You two will annoy and argue and despise each other," he'd written. Later, Tony and Marty decided to partner on a paper. Marty was a slick academic, well aware of his brilliance, which he leveraged into book contracts, Treasury Department roles in Dem administrations, well-paying consulting gigs, and grad students' panties. He was a financial economist and devout free marketeer, who'd read Tony's book and come around to his own climate Cassandra conclusion. Their paper, examining the potential economic impacts of a real estate collapse on the Gulf Coast and Eastern Seaboard, had created a stir—though mostly of denial, data nitpickery, and debunkification.

As he passed through the final security barrier of the Congress Centre, flashing his low-level white badge branding him as a member of civil society who didn't pay upward of $100,000 to attend, Tony saw Marty's text.

Just heard Clinton speak. That guy is looking like the Crypt Keeper!

They met in the main hall and picked at finger food from one of the many catered spreads. Tony overheard all kinds of nonsense from nearby conversations:

"India? What's left to export? Mud and suicidal farmers?"

"I underestimated Argentina."

"That's Adjaye. He's a starchitect and a real cocksucker."

"Asteroid mining is hot, and Luxembourg is making a big play."

Bono, looking Botoxed and pallid, went striding through the center of the room, collecting gazes, smartphone videos, and whispers.

"Shit, where's the Edge?" said Marty, watching the short Irishman flanked by what looked like two ex-football players. Bono wasn't the half of it. Tony had read a bit about the attendees on the flight to Zurich: Facebook's new CEO, the director of the IMF, a performance by Coldplay, a South African novelist, a Turkish artist, and the usual interchangeable billionaire axis of Bezos, Branson, Musk. Natalie Portman was on a panel that overlapped with a speech from the Iranian president—so who knew which would be the bigger draw. The CEO of Goldman Sachs. Top executives of Lufthansa and Deutsche Bank. Rao Ling-Mosgrave, one of Slapdish's founding wunderkinds, and the first person with a $500 billion net worth. According to the folks who kept score, the three richest people in the world now had the same wealth as the bottom half of the global population.

"You're a real starfucker, aren't you, Rathbone?" said Tony. "Also, is it just me or do they still barely invite any women?"

"Tell me about it," said Marty, scanning the ass of one of the caterers. "Later, though. The after-parties are called nightcaps. The Steigenberger Grandhotel Belvédère is the big one, but last year Apple had an augmented reality party that was pretty neat. You looked around and there were all these celebs hanging out as holograms. You could walk right up to Leo and talk to him in LA." Marty brushed a hand through his carefully parted gray and tugged at his suit. His panel was that afternoon, and he was wearing makeup. Tony had brought only the blue Brooks Brothers he wore for all weddings and funerals. "At the Tonic Piano Bar in the Hotel Europe, Norman Nate flew in this Michelin-starred chef from London and was just giving away Château Cheval Blanc and Château d'Yquem."

Tony stared at him blankly.

"Those are wines, Tone."

"Whatever. Who the hell is Norman Nate?"

"Tech guy. Had a big stake in Slapdish, and now he's onto human intelligence enhancement, radical life extension, nanotech, and the like. They call him 'the homeless billionaire' because he doesn't own a house, he just stays in luxury hotels around the world and lives out of his jet."

"Jesus Christ. Don't expect me to join you for any of that horseshit."

"Tony, I'd never try to tear you away from your single-minded devotion to your own misery."

They argued about which panels to attend. The jet lag was making Tony crankier than normal. They settled on "Capitalism: To Infinity and Beyond," about the ongoing privatization of space, during which Tony fell asleep and later "The End Game for the Middle East," in which the Saudi head of security painted a grim picture of the now two-and-a-half-decades-long state of war that stretched from Syria to Pakistan and had recently spilled into the kingdom. Though this year's conference was supposed to have a focus on climate and water security, the capture of several Saudi oil fields in the northeast by radical Islamist groups was the only thing in the news. Bomb them, don't bomb them—the usual debate, but oil was at stake again, so those nutty Muslims were going to get bombed. Marty's panel featured him jawing with five other economists about development issues, and the usual conclusions were bandied about. Grow that pie bigger, get that rising tide to lift all those boats in the Global South. Tony fell asleep again.

———

That night he dialed Catherine in LA.

"What is this thing you're at?" she asked. She sat on her bed, a mess of dirty-looking sheets and pillows. He could see a pink bra stuffed into the crease between bed and wall.

"From what I can tell it's an excuse to go to tech billionaires' blowout bacchanals."

"Guessing that's why you're hiding in your hotel room?"

"My colleague wanted me to go to one of these parties with oxygen bars or hula-hoop go-go dancers or some such dogshit, but I thought I'd talk to my brats then read a book."

His youngest looked thoughtful. "I didn't think a human being could survive on so little fun, but you're like an experiment, Dad. You should get your scientist friends to study you."

She checked something to the right of the screen, no doubt her phone. She wore a pair of red shorts and a gray USC T-shirt, flaunting her school colors like all the undergrads did. She'd gained a little weight, and it hung under her chin, much the way it had with Gail, especially when she was pregnant with this very girl to whom he spoke. Tony let that painful thought come and gladly go.

"What do you want from Switzerland?" he asked.

"Duty-free booze?"

"How 'bout a Swiss Army knife."

"I was just thinking I had to cut . . . something . . ." She looked around, faux-puzzled. "But it's really small so it doesn't require a real knife. Just a really small knife."

"Har-har." Tony smiled.

She didn't look exactly like Gail. The round cheeks, yes, and the nose were similar, but of course she had lighter skin, an invasion of Tony's freck-les, a red hue to her hair, and bright champagne eyes. They had small bags under them now, but he wouldn't ask if she was getting enough sleep. As she edged hesitatingly toward adulthood, he'd gotten hip to what annoyed her.

"Dad," she said, picking at some half-scraped nail polish on her thumb. "I'm going to tell you something, but don't freak out." Of course, if one's child opens a conversation with such a phrase, the gut tightens. "I'm taking this semester off. I already did all the registration stuff—or un-registration stuff, I guess. But look, I'm just so totally burned out. I've been working a lot at the restaurant—"

There was first relief that she wasn't pregnant with some idiot's baby, then annoyance, then regret at the annoyance.

"I told you I'll send you more money if you need it."

"No, it's not the money." She picked at the nail. "It was just like a hell semester last fall. I didn't get into the business program. I've got a shit GPA. It's a lot of stress at once, and I think it would be good if I just worked for a while and sort of recharged my batteries."

Tony stared at the screen on his lap.

"I think that's a goddamned awful idea," he said.

"Daddy." She said it in that way she had. That made her sound like a child again. He figured he would never stop getting surprising phone calls from her or about her. The accident in high school. To tell him she was staying in California after he got the job at Yale and was overseeing the move to New Haven. That she'd go to USC instead of Connecticut despite his lobbying. He'd taken the Yale job partially because he wanted to move them closer to Holly, to reunite the family at least in the same region. The harder he tried to get the three of them in similar zip codes, the more she resisted.

"I was so well aware," she said, "that you would not like this. Trust me. That's why I didn't tell you. But you have to understand, I'm not Holly. I'm not naturally smart."

He rolled his eyes. "That's preposterous. You're not motivated, Khaleesi. You just haven't found something yet that makes you want to focus."

"So that's what I'm trying to do here! I was in my business communications class and I was like, 'Wait, I could not give a shit less about this'—and please, please, please don't do the name, Dad."

Tony was about to get irritated with her, but he stayed himself. First, he knew if he had an argument with his younger daughter via laptop it would ruin his entire week. He'd probably go blank onstage the next day because he'd be feeling guilt over whatever he'd said to her that might not have been fair. Second, he saw hope in her "taking this semester off." Maybe this was the first step in her moving to the East Coast.

"Tell you what," he said. "Why don't I buy you a plane ticket for next weekend? Holly was going to come up from the city anyway. If you're not in school, you might as well come see us."

She stared at her bedspread like an ashamed duckling but now her eyes traveled up to him.

"You promise this isn't a rouse to get me there so you can yell at me?"

"I promise. You can tell me what you're thinking of doing next. Maybe we can give you some ideas."

"And you'll tell Holly not to bitch me out? She lives to bitch me out, Dad."

"Holly's her own woman, Catherine," he said. "But I'll tell her to go easy."

————

"What did you expect?" said Holly when he called her next. "Have you seen her Instagram? It looks like she's drinking every night of the week. She has zero sense of responsibility."

"Okay, okay," said Tony. "I get it, kiddo. But look, you've got to play nice, okay? If you just start badgering her, she'll get defensive. She'll feel ganged up on."

"So what am I supposed to do, Dad? Encourage her to drop out and become a full-time waitress?"

Holly sat at her kitchen table sipping from a mug, the string of a tea bag hanging like a graduation tassel. A spice rack affixed to the wall behind her and below it a shelf with a row of cookbooks. Her cat, an orange tabby, tried to hop up on her lap, and she told it, "Not now."

"She's coming to New Haven next weekend when you'll be here."

Her eyes exploded in incredulity, twin flashes of eyebrow and flared nostrils that made him think the lenses of her glasses might crack. "How?"

"I bought her a ticket."

She blasted air through her lips. "Great incentive system, Dad. She drops out, you buy her a cross-country flight."

"You've made your point," he said, hitting the note of gentle sternness that Holly sometimes needed to end the conversation. "The three of us haven't all been together since the summer. It'll be good."

Holly was only two and a half hours by train to New York, so they saw each other frequently. They'd pick a museum or a sightseeing activity, get lunch, and spend the afternoon together. He flew to California once every three months to see Catherine. During the summer the three of them often visited Corey's place in Florida, and though the guy's entire engagement with reality consisted of memorizing Fox talking points, Corey had made considerable effort to stay in the girls' lives after Gail passed. Begrudgingly, Tony did want to honor that.

Holly looked off-screen and said, "Hey. Yeah. Talking to my dad. He's at the Burning Man for billionaires. Say hi."

Dean's grinning, mop-topped head edged in from the right side of the frame. "Tony! How's it going? Here, make room, babe—" He brought a stool swiveling around and perched beside Holly, who scooted left. "I was telling my friends you were at Davos, and they were asking me if you were an international playboy or something. How is it? Is it so cool? Who've you glad-handed with?"

"Glad-handing's not so much my thing. Not sure if you could tell."

Dean laughed far too hard. When Holly first introduced Dean, Tony thought the guy was mocking him, but it turned out, no, that was just Dean, an eager beaver. He was a slender Korean kid with a wispy hipster mustache that made him look like he'd just figured out puberty. Tony was certain he'd never like any of the idiots his daughters dated, but Dean wasn't so bad. The first time Holly brought him to dinner, he excitedly debriefed Tony, with genuine interest, about ice sheet flow rates. For whatever reason, the kid could not get enough of Tony, and this seemed to make Holly happy. Dean injected new flavor.

"We're going to watch your panel tomorrow, Dad. You can livestream all of them on Slapdish."

"People sit in virtual reality to watch Davos panels?"

"Tony, man, people sit in VR to watch flies land on countertops," Dean said. "Now you gotta give these people all the shit, man. Who else is on your panel?"

"Randall," said Holly.

"Randall? Like Mary Randall!" His eyebrows shot up as he looked between Holly and the laptop camera. "Tony, she could be president."

"She's not going to be president," said Holly. "She won't even get the nomination."

"No," Dean clapped his hands, "I read this thing about how the RNC is changing all the nominating rules in Iowa and New Hampshire to avoid getting themselves another lunatic Twitter-troll game-show host! They're clearing the way for her. Tony—holy hell—get her autograph, man."

"I thought you wanted me to give her shit?"

"Yeah! Get her autograph then give her shit! That'll be badass."

He stayed on the line for another hour talking to Holly and Dean. When he closed his laptop, he had that feeling he got when he'd had a particularly good conversation with one of his daughters. Satisfaction colliding with melancholy. Missing them.

He put his shoes and jacket back on and went down to the lobby, where he bought a pack of cigarettes with a gruesome picture of gum cancer. He'd picked up the habit in undergrad and had been a pack a day chain-smoker through grad school and his PhD when the nicotine let him burn through work, feverish. At Gail's insistence, he'd given it up when Holly was born, and other than the errant loosy here and there, remained quit of it until he moved back to Connecticut. When Catherine didn't follow him to New Haven, he'd bought his first pack in over twenty years.

Davos Klosters was the perfect place for a smoke. He stood outside the hotel and took a drag. The temperature had dropped to a properly frigid position on the thermostat, and the day's slush had frozen solid. Trucks went by spewing sand and salt on the steel-hard ice. The smoke warmed his lungs. The lights of the city glowed gold, and the air had streaks of pale blue and purple lingering from the fallen sun. Beyond the city, he could see the outlines of the mountains. Dark and slumbering behemoths.

———

As one of the emissaries of Davos guided him to his seat on the stage, his dream from the previous night was still fresh. He'd been swimming or on a boat—somehow in the ocean—trying to navigate a storm overhead that looked like a dark gray city turned upside down in the sky, monolithic, with jets of black billowing from the edges. Multiple tornadoes descended and whipsawed in the surf. Red lightning flickered across the horizon, and descending from this cloud, like alien spacecraft, were deep-sea drilling rigs. They crashed into the water in a perfect row, impossibly immense, city-sized themselves, and as they fixed into place, they got to work. The tubes siphoned a briny liquid from the depths, and in that liquid were naked bodies, one after another. The machinery hummed until he had to cover his ears.

Not too difficult to interpret that one, at least.

He would share the stage with the former head of the World Bank, a Japanese American banking mogul with a bad comb-over; the Nigerian finance minister, a large woman in brightly colored African dress who would supposedly represent the developing world in the conversation;

the spokeswoman for a laughable organization of fossil-fuel players called the Sustainable Future Coalition, which claimed it wanted to see action on climate; and finally, the New York governor herself. Randall had hooded, sleepy eyes that nevertheless crackled with confidence and cunning. She was attractive, like a gracefully aging movie star, and her hair was styled smooth with bangs nearly falling into her eyes. The political-gossip rags all loved talking about her hair, and maybe it was his imagination, but the room did feel whispery and electric with her presence. Here she was, the Republican Party's resurrection, its woke rebirth after a decade of Trumpism.

The stage was what he imagined one of those old single-camera sitcom sets would be like. They sat in a semicircle in front of a wall with repeating logos for the World Economic Forum. He clutched six note cards he'd never look at. This had been Gail's suggestion about his public-speaking skills. "You need something to do with your hands. You're fidgety," she'd chided. Had she lived to see the publication of his book, he doubted she would have seen much improvement.

The lights bore down so the audience was nothing but indistinct shadows, but he could feel perspiration struggling free on his brow. He sipped the glass of water on the table beside him, from which the wire microphone sprouted. The moderator, an unsettlingly young, pretty British journalist whose name he immediately spaced on, began by introducing their panel on the climate crisis and the transition to a zero-emissions economy. Of course, she had to tally the carnage first.

"The typhoon that devastated the southern coast of South Korea this past year," the reporter began. "The persistent droughts in Australia, the Middle East, Pakistan, South Africa, and the American Southwest—some of which have required major investment in emissions-heavy desalinization efforts, the flooding last spring that inundated parts of the United Kingdom, the Netherlands, and Germany. We have the paradoxical effect of a warming Arctic creating more intense blizzards in northern latitudes. The so-called Come to Jesus Storm a little over a year ago was only the latest example, breaking every regional snowfall record in Canada and the United States while killing nearly a hundred people. These increasingly destructive events are becoming more frequent, more expensive, and more deadly. We are deep into the new normal and our panel will discuss how we navigate a changing global climate."

He found himself tuning in and out as the reporter began with softballs.

He kept thinking of the rigs descending from the storm. The inky steel back-lit by the wicked scarlet cast of the lightning.

The former head of the World Bank spoke of the ongoing fight to decouple greenhouse gas emissions from growth while cautioning that the world was still recovering from the residual effects of the Covid-19 pandemic and would need to continue to grow the economy to bring people out of poverty. The finance minister described the flooding hammering the Nigerian coast, the saltwater intrusion destroying the livelihoods of farmers, who then went to Lagos to find work as the megacity exploded. Amazingly, the reporter did not ask the minister if her country planned to stop selling its petroleum anytime soon.

The woman from the Sustainable Future Coalition, Emii Li Song, projected an air of practiced reasonableness. Though her organization's members were among the worst polluters in the history of humanity, she had a solution. "We need a carbon pricing mechanism, it's that simple. And frankly, we also have to be concerned about the spate of attacks by eco-terrorists. We believe that Congress has to act on both fronts—on climate but also on the security of our energy systems."

Finally, the belle of the ball got her close-up.

"In my state of New York, we're planning to install nearly thirteen hundred megawatts of new solar capacity before the end of my first year in office," said Mary Randall, and he could almost feel the audience perch forward. "We've only intensified our efforts, bringing down emissions and saving consumers money. It's true that some carbon interests and utility companies have worked to pass laws to slow the progress of renewables—this just happened in Ohio where the state government extended the life of three of its dinosaur coal plants again—but the market will win this in the end."

The reporter changed the subject. "There are rumors that you're considering a run for president. Given the track record of the Republican Party on the climate issue, particularly under Donald Trump, do you feel as though people can trust your seriousness on the matter of climate change?"

"I'm committed to turning the page," Randall said with the confidence of Cleopatra. Her voice was low, breathy, and seemed to curl in the air like smoke. "What's done is done, but I believe in the threat of climate change. If I were to run, it would be because I understand market mechanisms are the best solution, my campaign has no ties to Russian intelligence, and I don't even have a Twitter account."

The crowd burst into knee-slapping laughter at this deflecting, canned response.

Tony tried not to make his opening remarks too prickly, but he could already feel the edge in his voice as he ran through his spiel: He'd published a book on what it would take to save the world from calamity almost ten years ago, and he'd called it *One Last Chance* for a reason—because if the world waited much longer, there would be no chance. Since then, global emissions had continued to rise, on their way to 600 to 700 ppm by the end of the century. If the world didn't move to a war footing, there would be no way to draw down emissions or remediate carbon quickly enough to avoid cataclysm. "I may admire certain things that the esteemed members of the panel are saying here," he said, feeling himself slipping into his preferred mumble. Then Gail's voice popped into his head and he cleared his throat and spoke up. "But they're still trapped in a paradigm of thinking that, frankly, we should have abandoned by 2008. We don't have time for anything but the equivalent of a planetary wartime mobilization. Otherwise, it's Welcome to Hobbes."

"Hobbes?" asked the reporter.

"As in Thomas. As I wrote in my book, these feedbacks are tombstone dominoes. We've documented the first of the methane hydrates beginning to melt as the ocean warms, but we have no idea how sensitive this feedback loop might be. Along with the permafrost, it's the other slow-rolling time bomb, and it's starting to go off." He thought he had more to say, but he petered out.

The reporter asked the former head of the World Bank to respond.

"At the same time, as we recognize that this is a very serious issue, we can't allow a singular focus on emissions to throw the world into economic uncertainty or deny opportunity to those trying to climb out of poverty. I'd also add that some of the more extreme scenarios proposed by the IPCC and others may be overwrought."

Tony became more annoyed from there.

You understand chemistry, math, physics, Gail said when he told her he wanted to write a book and truly engage this issue politically, *but you have near-zero intelligence about people. You want the world to be this place of rational actors, but no one's rational, Tony. We're all guided by our crazy.*

He'd never managed to take this to heart. People devised all sorts of ways of putting their heads in the sand even when they should've known better. When the evidence of their own illogic stared them right in the face.

His irritation finally bubbled over at the person who added the final piece of straw to the camel.

"I do not buy this idea that we need to impose state controls," said Governor Randall. "I think that's been the fear from conservatives for a while, but it's not a necessary fear. We can solve this problem utilizing the brilliance of the market." She gestured to Li Song. "If the next administration passes even a basic price, it will set off a whole series of tipping points, and in a decade we'll be running most of America on renewable energy. So this idea that we need a quote-unquote war mobilization is totally hysterical when you take into account the progress we can make with a very unintrusive, inexpensive policy."

Tony's hand shot up like he was an undergrad, and the reporter said, "Yes, you'd like to respond."

"I would." Tony had to adjust the wire microphone so he could lean across the others to address Randall. Her face never changed. She held her knee and watched him with those intense, sleepy eyes.

"Here's the bad news for all of you: We've reached the end of growth. Raising people out of poverty and maintaining Western standards of consumption are simply no longer possible. That's why I didn't want to come to this bullshit charade. Frankly, you people are exactly the reason real action on our ecological situation cannot move forward, because the only real way to do it is to not have lone wealthy individuals consuming the resources of small nations, which as far as I can tell is the premise of this entire gathering. Look at the list of attendees you have here, how many of them come from companies that suck hydrocarbons out of the ground? No offense, but those are the dues-paying members of Davos and the Sustainable Future Coalition, and that's a joke, and you all are a joke. Tomorrow there's a panel called the Future of Extractives, which I guess is yet another joke since there can be no future for extractives, at least not if we want to survive this. Davos brings in a pop star or teenager every year to yell at them, but the market is still more real to the people here than nature. Furthermore, to gird our infrastructure and pay for an aging population in China and the West, we'll need a drastic reallocation of financial resources. There's simply no other way, and yes, it will come at the cost of growth. You people are living in a bell jar if you think differently. So, you can keep convening your panels and trotting out your woke women POC candidates and all the diversity hires of the corporate carbon establishment, and you can tell yourselves that everything's going to be A-OK, but I can assure you, it is not. And I pray there's somebody watching this video in about twenty years because all four of you are going to look very, very fucking stupid."

———

On the flight back from Zurich to Kennedy, Tony woke to turbulence.

He'd picked up a copy of *Vanity Fair* in the airport after he spotted the cover, *Kate Morris: The Rottweiler of the Climate Crisis*. When Holly had taken the position at the Brooklyn office of the climate organization that summer they'd joked about her getting into the family business. Still, Tony had never really believed this incarnation of young people chanting tired slogans and setting papier-mâché Earths on fire would be any different. Activists, for all their passion, usually knew less about earth systems than the oil men. Holly had pestered him to check out this Morris woman, but it sounded more like Holly had a bit of a hero crush than anything else. Reading this piece of hagiography, he could grant that the Morris kid didn't sound like a total idiot, but if she thought scaring a few Democrats was going to change people's calculations, she was Pollyanna. Green New Deal politics, the Sunrise Movement, the half-measures of the Biden and Hogan years—it had all been so much hand-waving while the guts of the carbon economy chugged along. When he read Governor Randall's name he smirked, thinking of the withering look she'd assessed him with as they left the stage. *Wow. Even for you, that was something else*, Rathbone had texted him.

When he fell asleep on the plane, there was another dream. A dark space, like a Gothic church built into the side of a hill, and he could just see outside, the blue sky and sunlight beyond the buried shadows. Then he woke with a jolt.

The woman beside him was gripping the armrests, white-knuckled. The plane took another abrupt dip before righting itself. There were gasps from the rows ahead. He pulled his seat belt taut. The plane bounced violently again. The pilot came on to say they should all be buckled in at this point, as if he needed to tell them that. Tony knew the odds of a plane going down were insignificant, but that was cold comfort as it lurched side to side and a bag rattled in the overhead compartment, trying to make a prison break.

"I don't know how you slept that long," said the woman beside him. Well-heeled, clutching an expensive silk scarf, she looked green. "It's been like this for twenty minutes."

"Clear-air turbulence," said Tony. "The jet stream is getting stronger."

"What?" she said.

"At high altitudes the temperature difference between the poles and the tropics is growing. I mean, on the ground it's been shrinking, but at these high altitudes, it's getting bigger. Eventually, a plane will fall out of the sky when it gets bad enough."

The woman turned her head to the window and didn't speak to him for the rest of the flight. When the skies calmed down, Tony fell back asleep.

————

That week, on their way to pick up Catherine from the airport, Holly gave him an earful about his panel at Davos.

"You realize that just being the biggest ornery asshole you can manage is not going to win people over to your way of thinking?"

"I didn't say anything I don't always say."

"Diversity hire? Dad, you don't hear how offensive that sounds? Have you even read what they're saying about you on the internet?"

He gave her a puzzled look. "Oh no, is someone angry about something on the internet? *The internet?*"

"*Daaad,*" she growled. "The idea is you change people's minds, not call them stupid to their faces while your whiteness explodes out of you."

"You're the one who pointed out their game to me, Holly! I'm just quoting you! Hire a bunch of brown women to front for you while you burn the planet to ashes and call it progress."

"I don't think I put it quite like that," she said, gritting her teeth. "I'm talking about tact, Father. Tact."

"It wasn't that bad."

"That woman could be the president in two years! Don't you think it might have been useful to get on her good side? Then, I don't know, she's making some policy, and she thinks, 'What about that really smart scientist guy I met at Davos?' Instead of, 'Oh, that old racist asshole who publicly berated me.'"

"You know, Older One, you get more dramatic with every passing year. You're more of a cranky old white man than me."

She guffawed a fake laugh, craning her head back so that her long neck stretched to gazelle lengths. "That's, like, totally hysterical given every acid reflux grumbling I've heard come out of your mouth since I was aware of language."

They were silent for a second and then he laughed. "Acid reflux grumbling?"

"I don't know. It just came out."

Catherine was especially ebullient when they picked her up, bouncing around in the back seat even after Holly scolded her to put her seat belt on. They didn't bring up school, and she seemed happier than she had the last few times they'd been together. After he got both girls situated in the guest room, they went to dinner at his favorite Italian place in downtown New Haven.

"I watched your thing, Dad," Catherine told him. "On Slapdish. It's got like two hundred thousand views. Loved it when you gave it cold to those bitches."

"Don't encourage him," said Holly.

"Do you see what everyone's saying about you?" she asked. "You have your own hashtag. And there's a deepfake vid of you making out with that lady governor."

Holly sighed loudly. "Not 'lady' governor, Cat. Just 'governor.' Jesus."

Catherine tossed back her wine. She'd already lapped her sister by a glass. "Whatever. I'm not voting for any of them."

"Cat," said Holly, who should have known her younger sister was baiting her but, like a fish, could never seem to resist the gleaming bit of tinfoil. "You really want to have this argument?"

"What? They're all a bunch of jabronis. I'm not taking part in their little stage play."

Before Holly could go into a full-bore lecture, Tony kept the peace. "You're voting, Khaleesi," he told her. "And you're voting for whoever your sister tells you to vote for."

The next day it was too cold to do anything other than go to a movie— some claptrap piece of shit with a crumbling Brad Pitt. Then they walked around the mall, and he let them pry whatever they wanted from him. He bought Holly a new dress and Catherine got him for two pairs of jeans, a revealing top he'd prefer not to imagine her wearing, and an extremely expensive Coach handbag.

While they waited for her to come out of another dressing room, Tony asked Holly about work.

"So have you met the Anointed One yet? Has Morris even come to the New York offices?"

"Not yet. I'm still bottom of the pile," she said, shrugging. "It's what I expected."

"Don't they know your father wrote the book on this subject?"

"I think that's why I'm not getting any special favors. Why I'm stuck in a VR set asking people in Slapdish worldes for spare change."

He rubbed her back. "You're probably already the smartest person in that whole organization."

She smiled. Holly was still only a glorified canvasser at A Fierce Blue Fire. He knew she felt like her talents, energy, and ambition were spoiling. "Dad, you're not a reliable source of comfort. Too many biases."

"Bullshit. I read the *Vanity Fair* article. You'll be running that place like it's your pet goat in no time."

Holly cracked up. "What?"

"I don't know. Just came out." Tony smiled at her. He'd lost his mom as a teenager, his wife in his thirties, and his dad had passed away in '21. At that point, it felt like his life's skin was sloughing off, and he'd grown coldly accustomed to the people he loved leaving him. Then at his dad's funeral, Holly had given the funniest, most moving eulogy about her grandfather, and Tony had gritted through this moment, his few remaining hairs blown back in shock. His daughter was an adult, and she would do things he would never be able to predict.

She twisted a simple metal ring around her index finger, taking it from knuckle to nail and back again.

"Dean and I are probably going to get married this summer."

A lump crawled into his throat, and he gulped it back down. "Really?"

"Yeah. Probably nothing big. Don't worry. We were going to go down to city hall and then maybe have a small party for you and his parents and a few friends. What do you think?"

"I like Dean."

"So do I."

"You guys are young."

"You and Mom were about the same age."

"We were."

"You two seemed to do all right."

Tony exhaled his agreement. "Marriage is hard. It's a lot of compromise, especially if you want to have a real career." He reached out and touched the cotton material of some flimsy top. "But there's really no equation for it. And you know what, if it doesn't work out, you can always get divorced."

She laughed. "You give the best fatherly advice. That should be the next book."

He put his arm around her and hugged her to his chest. "You just tell me where to show up. I'll have your back come marriage, divorce, or murder trial."

That night at dinner, they celebrated. Catherine and Holly went at another bottle of wine. Holly told her sister that she'd have to make time that summer to be her maid of honor.

"I'm not sure if the summer will work," said Catherine.

"What does that mean?"

"I don't know. I might travel."

"Travel?" said Tony.

"I have some friends going to Europe in May, and I was thinking of going."

"On whose dime?" said Holly.

"I'm working more now. I have money."

"From the bar?" Holly's tone was not without acid.

"Yes, from the bar."

"So you weren't planning on going back to school then."

He could see Catherine retreating into her armor, gearing up to take on her sister. "The point of taking time off is to take time off."

"Going to Europe to find yourself," said Holly. "Real original, Cat."

"Jesus Christ, could you be more condescending?"

"All right, guys," said Tony.

"You have pretty much zero idea of anything going on outside the walls of Catherine, don't you?"

"It's just that beyond these walls all I see is a humorless bitch."

"Hey," said Tony in full Dad Voice. Then he brought out a word he'd used when they fought as little girls. "Détente, guys. All right? We're moving into détente."

They both sat back in their seats, glowering, until they'd had enough wine that they'd forgotten the argument.

———

On the last night of their visit, Tony made a fire, and they stayed up until midnight talking. He wanted it to last longer, but his normal bedtime was around ten, and he couldn't stay awake. He kissed them each good night, and when he slipped under the covers, exhausted, he realized he could still hear their voices drifting through a grate in his bedroom wall. When he moved back to New Haven, he'd found a cozy one-story on the west side, three bedrooms, one of which he used as an office and the other as a guest room for when the girls visited. But he'd never left them like this, alone in the living room after he went to bed. He could hear everything they were saying.

"Will you take his last name?" Catherine asked. "Yu? Holly Yu? I dunno."

"No way. I told him I'm not doing that patriarchal bullshit. His parents were not thrilled with me. Now I'm in the phase of winning them over."

"He's cute. He's got kind of an Asian James Dean thing. I only met him that one time."

"His dad likes me, but his mom—not only does she have the whole complex of 'This is my baby, and you are not good enough for him,' but I think I might be the first Black girl she's ever had in her house."

"Will you stay in New York?"

"Oh, I think we're lifers. I actually don't know how people survive in places where you can't buy pantyhose or antacid at any time of night."

Tony's exhaustion stalled. He lay with his eyes closed and hands folded on his stomach, listening.

"What about you, Miss Traveler? Will you go back to LA after Europe?"

"I don't know if I'm serious about that. That guy I told you about? Xander—"

"Awful name." Holly retched. "Awful, awful name."

"He's got this plan to live in Europe working on these farms where people give you room and board. Just not sure how much I want to pull up rutabagas."

"You're together?"

"We're hooking up, but I don't think it's serious."

"Sounds like a d-bag, Cat."

"You don't know him."

"I know the Xanders. Remember Antwan? He was a Xander. Caught him when he left his cell phone unlocked, and I was like, 'Oh, you're talking to ten different bitches right now? Cool. See ya.'"

"This is what I'm talking about. You don't know my friends, and you don't know him. Can you just reserve judgment for ten seconds at any point in your life?"

Holly was quiet for a moment.

"Sorry," she finally said. "But you stress Dad out, and then it like shoots down the invisible umbilical cord that tethers all children to their parents forever, and it stresses me out."

"It's like with Uncle Corey. You can't just let him have his opinion, you have to come crashing in with all your Hollyosity and then pretty soon we're all just losing our shit and Thanksgiving's a pain in the ass."

"Uncle Corey is a savage."

"Yeah, but I'm saying you—and Dad too—you guys need to learn to exercise some fucking patience. I'm not dropping out; I'm taking a semester off to catch my breath."

"Dad said your grades are weak."

"Yeah, he doesn't know the half of it. I failed a class last semester and had two Ds on top."

"Catherine P., for Elsa's sake."

Then without warning they both started laughing loudly.

"What was that?" Catherine asked through hitching breaths.

"I don't know! Just came out. I want another *Frozen* sequel! An F and two Ds? You're the daughter of two PhDs!"

"I know, I'm a total degenerate. School's just not my thing. Maybe I'll be an actress."

"Oh, good. That'll make Dad's head explode."

"I'm serious. I think it's something I could do. I took theater, and it's the only thing I've really been interested in."

"Here, finish this." And they were both quiet for a moment as Holly poured out the rest of the wine. "You obviously get that he wants you to move out here," she said.

"I don't know how you deal with him being this close."

"It's good. We get to spend time together."

"He's a hoverer."

"He's a dad."

"When he moved, and I decided to stay with Miriam's family and finish high school in La Jolla, I thought he was going to lose his shit."

"Oh, he briefly lost his shit."

"If I moved out here, I'd probably go insane."

"It's an option."

"Do you remember when I got in the accident in high school?"

"Hard to forget."

"Even when the car rolled it wasn't like I was afraid. You know? I knew everything would be fine. But I could already picture the look on Dad's face. All the disappointment and that snarl he has. You'd already left for school, but I just couldn't deal with his hovering. I wanted to be on my own."

"You should give him credit. People have way worse dads than Dad."

"Oh, believe me, I know. Xander's dad's in jail for selling methamphetamines."

"Wow, you should definitely marry this guy."

They both cracked up, and when it died down, there was a pause.

Then Catherine: "So are you looking forward to getting deflowered on your wedding night?"

Holly burst into even harder laughter, and he could almost picture the two of them falling into each other, grabbing the other's arms to steady themselves as they howled. Not long after this, he drifted to sleep, sediment-slow, and he dreamed of Holly's wedding, outdoors in the midst of a blizzard. The snow fell like clumps of wet cotton, and Gail was there. The four of them walked up a slope to where the preacher waited, their feet carving a path into the white blanket coating the hillside.

THE YEARS OF RAIN AND THUNDER: PART II

2028

Eleven years earlier, I got into her truck.

After four days on the road and a night camping in the Smoky Mountains, we crossed the Teddy Roosevelt Bridge in the morning dawn. A tired wind pushed river mist over the Potomac, and this city that would become my home for over a decade had a stillness to it, a gray-born mystery. At first, we lived two blocks from the Capitol in a dingy brick-block apartment building called Hill House. It was home mostly to congressional staffers, bouncing out of their overpriced shoebox hovels by 6 a.m. with a thermos of coffee and a bagel. The Republican National Committee was close by, and during the grim days of the Trump presidency, this felt like enemy territory, a dangerous movement's dark core. Kate rode her bike to her offices over on the H Street Corridor, making $37,000 a year, which in D.C. is close to a poverty wage. I struggled to find any kind of work, and for the first seven months did a lot of paid line-standing for lobbyists outside congressional hearings. Eventually I found an internship with a social services organization that worked with sexual assault survivors, though I'd be let go when Covid came. I plowed through the last of my savings to help make rent while Kate tended bar on the weekends. Even though we were broke, everything was new and came with the thrill of early, hungry adulthood. That era now has the blur one's twenties take on over time, especially after the chaos descended in 2020. My parents visited that March, and we were all sitting in Hawk 'n' Dove, Kate bickering good-naturedly with my dad about Trump's first impeachment, when we heard news of the lockdowns.

Twenty-twenty was our first blush with that sensation of true global emergency, and because we spent that year initially secluded, then in the streets as Kate and her coworkers took part in the Black Lives Matter protests, then working furiously on the 2020 election, and then back to a curfew after the attack on the Capitol and another Covid surge, and then . . . well, you know.

To say there was ever any return to normality isn't quite right, but there was an acquiescence, a decision that a certain amount of chaos would be tolerated in order to let the world grind on, and within the context of the climate crisis, this was very bad news indeed.

By then, Kate was deeply unhappy with the job she'd come to D.C. for, and she and Liza set off on their own. They started a 501(c)(4) and 501(c)(3), opened offices in thirty states with field directors, and a slew of hubs with neighborhood organizers, but, as she pointed out every night at dinner, this was not much different from anything else folks had been trying for thirty years. As Kate put it to me over wine and a very potent weed gummy, "We need to shock the system."

"How do you expect to do that?" I asked.

"First and foremost," said Kate, "fuck off with the messaging apparatus that can only preach to the converted. It's dour, man. We live on this incredible, joyful, one-in-a-trillion blue marble in the depths of cold black infinite space! We can either be another feeble assemblage of do-gooders patting themselves on the back or we can get rowdy. We set off a riot in the American political system and give all sides of the spectrum unshirted hell."

In less than three years, they raised astonishing money and built an incredible, daring organization. Even before they began gaining attention, fame, notoriety, I knew Kate and A Fierce Blue Fire were heading for something big. Even when it was just her and Liza working on laptops in our apartment, and the idea that she would be splashed across the front page of a glossy magazine seemed ludicrous, I already knew. It was my first encounter with the sensation of destiny. How that word feels like living inside a bright, wet fog. If you close your eyes you know it's still there, a premonition made tactile.

I was thinking about this long journey, from hopping into Kate's truck in Wyoming to her explosion into the public realm, as we sat in the hideaway of one of the most powerful Democrats in the Senate. I thought of how my life's path had careened, and remembered that ride with her out of the Wind River Range and across the blunt plains east of the Rockies.

"I was an actual working-class hero," Senator Cy Fitzpatrick whittered on to Kate, his cotton-ball eyebrows bouncing. "I worked in a meatpacking plant with a bunch of Mexicans to put myself through college." Hideaways are small, secluded offices, and the most senior senators got the ones even the staffers didn't know about. Supposedly only two keys exist, one for the senator and one for his or her chief of staff. Like most things about Washington, it was not as impressive as it sounds, but now here we were in Cy's. He made no secret how happy he was to have a pretty audience, and Kate flirted enough to delight the wheelchair-bound Pennsylvania senator. Whatever this cloak-and-dagger meeting was about, it had been brokered by Fitzpatrick, one of the first senators to take FBF's radical approach seriously.

The door popped and scraped open loudly, and finally Russ Mackowski, West Virginia's Far Right firebrand, arrived, trailed by his chief of staff, Dave Montreff. Mackowski made the rounds, shaking hands with curt hellos. He was big and barrel-chested with steel-gray hair and a red, weathered face. When he shook my hand, his palm felt like tree bark. He pumped my hand once and said "Goodtoseeya" before moving on.

Tom Levine, our Capitol Hill vet, now whispered in the ear of Coral Sloane, our policy director, while Kate herself took Mackowski's hand, smiled huge, and gave him a joyful "Senator!" The old Republican did not return the enthusiasm despite the fact that Kate practically got him elected over Elmer Nolan.

In addition to the four of us from FBF, Fitzpatrick had invited only one advisor, a man of South Asian descent, thin, intense, and severe looking. He stood with his arms crossed and shoulders hunched, staring through rectangular glasses directly at the floor. He had not bothered to introduce himself but appeared to be listening so intently, the effect was somewhat creepy.

The eight of us—four civilians, two politicians, and their aides—crammed together in that little office with a window overlooking the darkling Capitol—felt uncomfortably intimate. As the introductory chatter wound down, Tom Levine leaned into my ear to mutter, "You're in the big leagues now, Stanton. But don't worry. Once you watch these esteemed members finger every turkey wrap on the tray before picking one, you quit going gooey. Generally, all these fuckers live solely to get on TV."

"Enough with the throat clearing, Cy." Mackowski's voice boomed inside the small room as he cut off Fitzpatrick's efforts at glad-handing. Mackowski popped his index finger at Kate. "This meeting *that doesn't exist* has one objective: me and this gal."

"We're just as curious why we're here," said Coral. Their words stuck on their lip ring. They wore a black short-sleeve button-up and tan slacks, dressed like they were going bowling rather than meeting with senators. "We've got an election in less than two weeks, and it's hard to see how our interests might align."

"Cy didn't mention that we may have found a piece of common ground?" Mackowski's disdain with them was plain to see. He projected a military bearing (though he'd never served) and stood stock-straight with his ample arms crossed over his chest like a drill sergeant.

"'Common ground' is a phrase usually reserved for people who don't quote white supremacists in speeches," said Tom.

"Oh, fuck off, Tom," groused his chief of staff. Dave Montreff was a slick cardboard College Republican, who made sure to lounge with his hands in the pockets of his Dockers. "That story was bullshit—"

"Okay, children!" said Fitzpatrick, calmly pushing the air down. "How 'bout we get some facts on the table? First, Mary Randall is going to win. If the numbers hold, she'll be governing with a Republican Senate and a Democratic House. Maybe a recipe for four more years of fuckery, but maybe an opportunity to actually pass something big. Second, this Climate X nonsense you"—he nodded at Kate—"have been plugging on the talk-show circuit, that's not going to happen without a hell of a lot of ball-busting and backdoor dealing."

Kate twisted a pen in her large, rough hands; she never wrote notes but liked to fiddle with the tool while she listened, the notepad on her lap so pristine it could be resold.

"All Climate X means is we treat the most important issue in the world like it's actually the most fucking important issue in the world. And we're not settling for anything less than the whole package. Shock collar, tough new regs, Just Transition, and a big helping of investment and redistribution. You're going to love it, Senator," she said, teeth shining in Mackowski's direction.

"Sure, and the rainbows will break through the clouds and the nymphets will start feeding me grapes. Ha!" Fitzpatrick barked at his own joke. Behind him, his aide took a pen and pad from his breast pocket and began furiously scribbling notes. His concentration was so intense, I couldn't help but be distracted by it. "Point is, legislation is coming down the pike. These kids made sure of that."

"And there'll be resistance," said Montreff.

"And we're ready," I added, and felt sweat on my brow as all eyes briefly found me. Kate threw me a smile, and I could tell she was happy with that line. Nevertheless, I settled into holding my tongue.

Mackowski expelled a condescending snort. "What did you call me?" He smiled big at Kate. "The oil industry's meat puppet?"

"Sounds like me," said Kate.

He scratched his eyebrows and bits of dandruff flaked off. I could smell his aftershave from five feet. "That a good idea? Making enemies of those who might be holding an awful lot of power someday?"

"You got, what? Thirty-seven delegates in your lame bid for the Republican nomination?" said Tom.

"He entered the race late," said Montreff.

"Yeah, as an alternative nobody wanted. The Trump years are history, Senator." Tom adjusted thick black glasses. From where I was sitting, I could see little spouts of AR information—his meeting notes most likely—glowing dimly within the lens. I didn't understand how people focused with those things on their faces. "Look at Tracy Aamanzaihou in Houston. Oil and gas districts are flipping to renewable-energy labor leaders. My professional political opinion is that you and your whole coalition are about to be deeply fucked."

Tom crossed muscular arms over his chest and sat back, very satisfied. He was a good enough guy, but also enthralled with himself. Montreff looked like he wanted to kill Tom, which meant they'd likely been in some kind of political knife fight previously. He looked at us the way many staffers did these days, with disdain, fear, and often envy. We were the upstarts. Every room we entered, eyes darted, and I felt like I had some bold new haircut. All through the mid-2020s one could feel the momentum shifting. Randall's win in the Republican primary cemented it. Still, what happened next took us all by surprise.

"Aren't you even curious about what I want?" said Mackowski.

Coral, Kate, and Fitzpatrick simultaneously replied: "We are, Senator," "So let's hear it," "Batten down the hatches!"

Mackowski cracked his knuckles. He motioned to Fitzpatrick. "We want A Fierce Blue Fire to endorse Randall for president. Right now. In the eleventh hour."

We all sat there for a minute, stunned. Coral said it first: "What?"

Mackowski shrugged, big boulder shoulders lifting his suit. "We all have our reasons."

I looked to Fitzpatrick. "You want us to endorse the Republican running to unseat your party's president?"

Fitzpatrick tilted his big head back and forth in a gesture of indifference, his wheelchair creaking as he did so. "Let's just say, I'm a team player, but sometimes you get a quarterback who keeps tossing passes into the bleachers. Jo is not a bad person, but she is a bad president. For reasons I'm sure you're familiar with and a few you probably aren't."

"Oooh! Palace intrigue! I've got the shivers," cried Kate.

"Look, my sweet darlings," said Fitzpatrick, swiveling in his wheelchair and then rolling to his desk. "You turned this into a one-issue election. Climate, climate, climate. Biospheric crisis *this*, ocean acid bath *that*. Set your hair on fire, start screaming, grab the first gal you see, and ask her to dance—and I'll tell you something: I'm not far from the finish line here. And I don't work for the Democratic Party, I work for the American goddamn people, fucking lunatics though they may be. A Republican president, a Black woman no less, can get the glory for finally turning the dime on the climate issue. She's captured the folks' imagination, and we need to ride that wave to a better world. Meanwhile, Jo Hogan . . ." He let out a slow whistle. "All she really cares about is slaughtering uppity A-rabs half a world away because she knows it gets the Blob, the press, everyone in this town, hard as a rock."

I looked to the quiet man behind Fitzpatrick who'd not lifted his eyes from his notepad even once. He was making a strange shadow puppet gesture with his pen. At the mention of "A-rabs" he quickly scribbled another line or two, and like me, Mackowski watched him.

"This meeting is off the record," Mackowski told him. I thought of how he'd won his Senate seat promising the mass surveillance of mosques and an end to all Muslim immigration.

"Don't mind him," said Fitzpatrick. "He's just a thinker."

When I later came to know Ashir al-Hasan, I'd learn this was quite the understatement.

"What's your angle, Senator Mackowski?" Coral asked, always about the bottom line.

Mackowski blew a long breath and seemed to contemplate how much he should share. "I like to gamble. Mostly craps, some slots, and I can't get enough Texas hold 'em. I'll sit in a casino for a day without blinking, swear to Christ. My thinking is gambler's thinking. You endorse Randall, she probably still wins, but the base hates her even more than they already do. Then in four years, eight years, whatever it might be, a lane opens up for me again. Simple as that."

"You want us to torpedo Randall with the right wing for you?" asked Tom. "Even by D.C.'s rat-fuck standards, that seems weird."

"Look, I can't promise you I'll vote for your socialist superbill when it comes down the pike, because I won't. Ryan Doup and the rest of the RINOs will do what their president says, and I'll resist. But I can promise that I'll make strategic choices about who I'm pressuring. I can offer you breathing room. Hell, if a Green New Deal passes, it'll give me something to run against in '32 or '36."

We all sat there for a minute, stunned. In all the years I'd been in D.C. I'd never been surprised by the cold calculations people made, but they rarely phrased them so overtly.

Finally, Kate oozed forward in her chair and looked Mackowski dead in the eye, almost seductively.

"Senator, you're never going to be president."

"Oh no?"

"I'd never let it happen," she said, nonchalant, like she was the actual puppeteer of the universe and really did hold that power. "If it came to it, I'd drive every swing-state voter to the polls myself. And please. You're a total phony anyway. Little prep school kid with a fake drawl playing at right-wing populist." She was smiling so happily, her eyes locked on his.

"That a fact, huh?" said Mackowski.

"Oh, I'd rock that ass, boy," said Kate. "I promise you that."

Fitzpatrick's aide abruptly snorted a laugh and then quickly touched a hand to his mouth to stifle it. Other than that, the hideaway was silent, all eyes on Kate and the senator.

~ ~ ~

Driving out of Wyoming and across the empty expanse of Nebraska, Missouri, and Illinois, wind roaring through the windows because her truck's AC was broken, how was I to know that I'd one day work for Kate? In 2022, as A Fierce Blue Fire gained steam, she offered me a job doing media outreach. The boss hiring her boyfriend made "logistical, financial, emotional, and unethical sense," she joked.

This was right as they were able to afford office space and Kate began to grow her trusted inner circle. My desk was beside that of Coral Sloane and their encyclopedic brain. At first, I couldn't help but study their tattoos: a red shooting star on a forearm, David Bowie in full alien garb on their bicep, Winnie the Pooh, sitting contentedly in the crotch of a tree with his pot of honey, on their shoulder. It was such a strange collection of ink for someone so sober and unrelentingly level-headed. Coral could listen to an argument or idea and instantly deliver a complex analysis of its merits and drawbacks. It was Coral who began laying the seeds of doubt around the version of the Green New Deal that emerged early in Hogan's term. "It's become a catchall for any and all progressive ideation while also letting industry off the hook," they said.

Coral led the charge in developing a fifty-state strategy, particularly in congressional districts with a coastline vulnerable to sea level rise and climate disruption. They led the push to begin funding climate Republicans and third-party challengers in select districts and supported Kate in building the Outposts.

But Coral was also not the ultra-serious, Harvard Kennedy taskmaster I'd expected. The first day, as I set up my desk, I noticed the *Alien* action figure from my favorite movie franchise. Its eyeless banana head glowered from Coral's desk.

"Which one is your favorite?" I asked. Coral looked at me with pure befuddlement.

"That's an absurd question to even ask, Stanton."

"Obviously, it's the Cameron?"

"Game over, man! Game over!"

We quickly became friends, and when Kate was out of town, traveling to new Outposts and offices, Coral and I would get together for movie marathons or to play VR games. Kate called me from the road once, and I said I'd have to call her back because Coral and I were watching *Starship Troopers*. She laughed.

"What?" I asked.

"Nothing," said Kate. "You guys are cute is all."

The quagmire produced by the climate politics of the Biden years influenced Kate's next two hires. The first was Tom Levine, who came to Kate's attention through the D.C. grapevine. The organization needed an outside game, an infestation of climate in every facet of public life, but it also needed a better inside game, a creature of the swamp with sharp elbows. Foul-mouthed, funny, and occasionally a vitriolic asshole, Tom Levine chomped through a tin of tobacco a day, kept whiskey in his desk, and always seemed to have cocaine on him. He was also a damn smart guy who hated every faction in American politics. This included the entire wingnut Republican establishment and spineless Third Way Democrats, but he reserved his most vicious rancor for the self-righteous progressives he'd spent his career working for.

"The first thing you've got to remember about this town," he told me soon after I came aboard, "is that every lawyer is angling for the Supreme Court, every doctor for surgeon general, every cashier for a lobbying gig. No one actually does their job. They all have a mental chessboard and are calculating five moves ahead." He lit a cigarette at his desk and walked away, spraying a bottle of Febreze behind him.

Rekia Reynolds came aboard in '24. Rekia, a veteran of Black Lives Matter, had first come to our attention when she wrote a piece decrying Kate as a "white apologist's fantasy girl for deracialized discourse," and that her vision "glossed over the country's foundational organizing principle of white supremacy in favor of a kumbaya story about post-racial eco-camaraderie." This was the first true blowback we'd gotten from the Left, and it felt deeply unfair. I spent two nights up until 3 a.m. drafting a detailed rebuttal to Rekia's argument: all of our outreach to BLM groups, the Outposts we were building in urban centers, and oh yeah, the fact that Kate was actually biracial, which this stupid woman had not even bothered to learn.

Kate took one quick skim of the letter and said, "Dude, don't publish this."

"Why the hell not?"

"Because she's got a point. We very intentionally gloss over all kinds of histories of power in America. Purposefully, though! Purposefully."

"Oh, great, Kate. Agree with this identity politics witch who just trashed you."

"I think we should offer her a job."

During Rekia's interview, she stuck to her guns, lecturing Kate about the legacy of environmental racism and the movement's inhospitable stance toward communities of color. She was short, curvy, and dark-skinned, with an urgency to her every word and gesture. I'd come to learn that Rekia ordered takeout like she was telling people there was a fire in the kitchen, and I got my first glimpse of this energy during her interview.

"Rekia, let's take a breath," said Kate when she finally got a turn to talk. "The fact of the matter is that we are having this fight in the context of a demographically changing country with a toxic history of racism. It's also a fact that our political system gives rural, mostly white regions disproportionate influence in the electorate. That's an iron-clad reality we must deal with as we navigate this emergency. So we need to go out and start winning those regions and not cede them to the Trumpists and Mackowskiites. Not just because it's the tactically correct path but because it's the morally correct one. We offer our hand even when it's slapped away. We have to meet people where they are, and that means not cramming various guilts down their throats—"

"How the hell?" Rekia demanded. "You're spinning this fantasy and forgiving behavior—"

"We're trying to forge an effective counterforce against powerful institutions, and we need an aspirational vision of our common humanity.

Solidarity! Now do you want to continue lobbing tweets from the sidelines or do you want to actually join a movement that's trying to remake the world? In other words, do you want this fucking job, bitch, or not?"

Through all of this, Liza Yudong remained the innovator, the unsung brains behind our social platform, small-donation operation, voter data project, and finally, as Slapdish exploded in the public consciousness, our "worlde." Liza tutored me on the new terrain: a "worlde" was an interactive virtual stage where people could gather to hang out, debate, listen to a speaker, or, for our purposes, fundraise. Our worldes were all pristine nature, from golden meadows surrounded by snowy mountaintops to glistening wild rivers. "Xperes," on the other hand, were experiences. The user didn't interact, they watched. Liza's xperes were much darker. Fires raging, floodwaters crashing, refugees trudging by your eyeballs, gazing at you miserably, and though these people were looking at a camera operator perhaps years earlier, one could not help but cast their eyes down. These tools proved astonishingly effective and our fundraising soared. Liza was a "one-woman Cambridge Analytica," according to Tom. Though each and every candidate and cause had its own chop shop of psychological profiling and voter suasion, it always felt like Liza was a step ahead. She was also, I thought, quite funny, though her sense of humor was an acquired taste. Pretty and petite, she dressed like she'd pieced together a brand-new outfit from a vintage store every day. Once, I heard her tell Rekia and Coral, "I feel like I would be a more full-throated eco-socialist revolutionary if anyone could convince me that there will still be cute outfits after capitalism crumbles. I refuse to wear Birks."

"Sure, there could be cute outfits," Rekia assured her. "Why not?"

"From my understanding, socialist countries tend not to have cute outfits. Also, every day I get to see how Kate dresses." And she went back to typing.

Liza designed our logo, blue flames conflagrating against a black background. It was a trip when I began seeing that image on social media profiles or graffitied onto a wall or tattooed on someone's arm.

We were just kids trying to find something that worked. The trajectories of the two major political parties shaped much of our lobbying experience, the Republicans in wounded disarray, trying to rebuild their party while frequently staving off primary challenges from suburban neo-Nazis, the Democrats playing a perpetual game of three-card monte, releasing aspirational platforms and progressive wish lists while mostly doing the bidding of Wall Street, Big Tech, and the military–national security–industrial complex.

There was a great deal of excitement when Joanna Hogan took office, but that dissipated as her schizophrenic presidency advanced and Green New Deal aspirations died quickly. The memes of Hogan's face and blond bob photoshopped onto a former WWF star's body as she appeared to tear apart yellow spandex swarmed, and Democrats spent a full week rejoicing at that eye-rolling moment in the last debate of '24 when she told her Republican opponent, "Eat your vitamins and say your prayers because next thing you know I'll be hanging curtains in the White House." But Kate knew who Hogan was as a president before Hogan probably did, and the former governor had no appetite for confronting the coal and gas interests she'd gotten comfortable with in the Missouri statehouse. In public, Kate struck as respectful a tone as she could manage, but in private, she despised Hogan.

At first we were ignored, mostly meeting with low-level aides and science advisors. But then a few key House Democrats began to coalesce around FBF's policy ideas. Joy LaFray of Oregon began backing the "shock collar" while Tracy Aamanzaihou of the Clean Energy Labor Coalition publicly pronounced FBF "the insurgents the movement needs." Then *Vanity Fair* called.

Following Moniza's article, there was nary a podcast, talk show, or Slapdish worlde that didn't want Kate. She was a natural in any format, attractive but accessible, playful but passionate. She delivered her galvanic message with a smile and her armpit hair showing. Even when things got testy, as they did on Colbert when she challenged the show's sponsorship arrangements, she was too agile to lose either host or audience.

"Okay, but how do I change anything, Kate!" Colbert cried, after she'd rattled off a dire assessment of the world's overheating oceans and their falling pH levels. "I'm just a guy with a television show, and if I tell people to turn off their air-conditioning, Fox News will be mad at me."

"I'll tell you what you can do, first and foremost, is drop your sponsorships from oil and gas companies. Tell them you won't accept their advertising, no matter how much money they throw at you."

Colbert threw the camera a comedic *Uh-oh*. The happy-go-lucky *We're working on algae fuels, we swear!* advertising had just preceded Kate's segment. Kate shot the audience a quick, wry glance, and there were uneasy titters as she launched in.

"These fossil-fuel companies are creating the conditions for mass planetary extinction and then funding a political force to stall action on it. Our grandchildren will look at Chevron and Exxon ads the way you and I look at swastikas." Colbert began objecting to that, but Kate talked over him, practically snatching the entire show for herself. "No, no—see, this is why you should go back to the Comedy Central days and forget this 'reasonable shill for the center-left' persona."

And with that small joke, Colbert couldn't help but laugh, and Kate took her moment. "I know that sounds hyperbolic, but those are the facts. That is what is happening. People ask what they can do, but usually they *are* in a position to do something, they just don't want to see it. Now this industry, oil and gas, has been going state by state for a decade, passing laws essentially making resistance to their operations illegal. They're codifying the illegality of our speech, assembly, and dissent. So, what shows like yours and sports leagues that claim to care about Black lives and any other powerful person can do is stop accepting money for their propaganda. And if they want to keep passing laws to make our speech and assembly and resistance illegal—then fuck it, man. Make me an outlaw."

Without even trying, she forged these clips that surged across the internet. Fox News raged that she would compare patriotic American companies to Nazis. Our allies despaired that Kate had tripped so easily over Godwin's law and invoked the laziest analogy. Even Coral was unhappy with her: "What happened to creating on-ramps to the movement?" they wondered sharply. But that clip lived on, and within a month it wasn't just Colbert dropping those sponsorships. Even the *New York Times* was forced to confront its advertising arrangements with Big Oil.

She could describe the situation with such magnetism, simplicity, conviction, doom, and hope. Before I met her, I'm sure I never thought about the issue for longer than thirty seconds, and if I did, figured it was still an open debate. Then I started to do my due diligence. It's difficult to describe what happened to me during that time. I came home to the person I loved, we adopted a timid little Australian cattle dog we both adored and named it Dizzy, I congratulated my sister on her wedding plans, I chipped balls at the Langston Golf Course and felt that little glow of accomplishment when they dropped right—yet looming over all of it now was this monolith of dread. This dark pillar was overwhelming, painful to confront; it began to nag at me absently all the time. Because even the people who do understand the science, who are maximally frightened, they're in denial as well. When I first heard of the "climate Robin Hoods" blowing up pipelines on the plains, I wondered what kind of lunacy it took to do that, but really, I was the mad one. I'd lived my whole life thinking nothing about this. I hadn't realized that the natural cycles of the earth warming and cooling were laughably insufficient explanations, like saying your house fire began because of the arrival of spring. I didn't know that scientists could easily trace the carbon produced by human fossil-fuel burning in the atmosphere or the truly horrifying changes that befell the planet when carbon concentrations had been this high in the past. I hadn't understood the speed at which it was all occurring, that in just a single human lifetime we were precipitating changes that had before taken hundreds of thousands of years. Because once you've taken that journey and understand the alarmingly simple science, you can't unknow it. For a while, I stopped sleeping. I'd lie awake staring at the ceiling and a despair would come over me. I'd reach for Kate, who fell asleep instantaneously whenever she felt like, and I would grip her, stuff my face in her thick, fragrant hair, and imagine our children, what kind of frightening, disintegrating civilization they would be born into.

~ ~ ~

Kate and I were supposed to leave for North Carolina that Monday, but first she called a meeting to discuss the offer from Senators Mackowski and Fitzpatrick. We were spending Halloween at my parents' house on the coast even though it was a week out from a landmark election we'd been working toward for upwards of a decade. My mom, who treated Halloween with more reverence than Christmas, badly wanted the whole family there and twisted both our arms until we agreed.

The Mackowski-Fitzpatrick offer required urgency. Not that any of us really knew what to make of it, but it was tantalizing: the potential for a Republican president to shatter the stalemate and pass a comprehensive climate agenda.

"Now that Randall's pummeling Hogan on the issue," said Tom, "man, I think it's fucking time. Mary's practically reading our press releases at this point. Let's do it. Let's endorse."

I could tell Tom had felt gung ho since leaving the meeting, and now with a dip puffing out his lower lip, buzzed from the nicotine, he was humming like a tuning fork.

"This is a huge last-second shift," warned Rekia. "We've always intended to stay neutral."

"Look, the polls are what they are. Jo is a lame duck already. Tell 'em, Sand."

Sandeep Goswami was a Georgetown poli sci major who'd interned with us for three years. He'd taken the semester off to work grueling hours for Liza. Tall and handsome with a thick unibrow, he had a kind of dazzled face, like he was always half-amused to be in the middle of all this. Sandeep had taken on the thankless task of monitoring every poll, model, and betting market for every race all the way down to public utility commissioner in Arizona. Other than the core brain trust of me, Coral, Liza, Rekia, and Tom, he was the only "minion" Kate invited to this highly classified meeting. He laughed now as the spotlight fell on him.

"Ha, sure, stick me with this—umm . . ." He rubbed a healthy five-o'clock shadow. "It's like you say, Tom, the polls are what they are. Eight years of Democrats in the White House, and Jo is the least popular incumbent since Carter. She'd have to run the table. But that's all I'm really willing to say."

Kate leaned against my desk with her arms crossed, looking pensive and overcaffeinated. "What's the advantage of an endorsement then?"

"The advantage," said Tom, "is riding the wave of momentum, only looking like we caused the momentum with this bombshell October Surprise."

"Excuse me," said Liza, pointing to the wall where the Machado quote was engulfed by her blue flames. "We did cause this. I drew that, and the politics people were like, 'Oh hey, climate-climate, carbon-carbon.'"

"But if the polls are wrong, and Jo pulls it out, we still have to work with her." Coral was A. C. Slatering their chair, arms resting on the back. "It would poison the well with her forever."

Liza said, "I feel like the well may have been poisoned when Kate called her the 'drone-assassin-in-chief with a vagina.' Call me crazy."

Tom was not without reason for his passion. He'd long been adamant that it had been Hogan herself who'd given *Vanity Fair* the "toxic cunt" line about Kate. Tom now threw his arms overhead.

"Fuck this woman! Hogan won't even fucking meet with us! She pours our ass from vial to vial, and I'm sick of being in a fucking test tube listening to her excuses. She made her career by busting challenges on her left flank— remind me why we aren't trying to defeat her outright?"

"Tom, my dude, take a breath," said Kate. She pushed herself up to sit on my desk.

"We don't know that we can trust Randall any more than Hogan—or at all," said Rekia. "Green Trident or not, her caucus does not want a climate bill—"

"She's a Black woman tackling the issue, Rek, what is your prob—"

"Who will be in charge of a caucus with legit white supremacists."

Then Tom and Rekia were at it. Tom often groused about Rekia in an uneasy-making way, saying she suffered from "social justice warrior apophenia," and Rekia obviously had her issues with Tom. They clashed frequently about the Outposts, mostly because Rek viewed lobbying public utility commissions as a waste of time compared to energizing voters of color, who she thought we often ignored with our strategies. This once came to a head when a photo went up on the website of our Ohio outpost featuring no people of color (there was one Latino guy, but Rek called him "white-passing," and Tom's head nearly exploded). This infamous meltdown between the two of them became office lore. As the argument escalated now, I tried to calm everyone's nerves.

"You gotta admit, Randall is astonishing," I said. Tom and Rekia stopped to look at me. "Imagine five years ago, a climate justice movement endorsing a Republican? This is an absolute historic opportunity."

"But why does Mackowski want it?" said Coral.

"Because he's a poser!" said Tom. "He burnishes this image of Nathan Bedford Mackowski, but Republicans want to put this faction of the party to sleep. Look at the way the RNC rejiggered the rules of the nominating process—to get Randall through and purge those hooting rebel-redneck Nazi fucks once and for all. We back Mary now, hard, and the movement will go with us. Then it's an all-out sprint to pass our bill in the first hundred days. The Republican Party takes credit for saving the planet, Randall's face goes up on Mount Rushmore, and everyone fucking wins."

"Bipartisan Black women save the planet," I said, nodding to Kate.

"Our neutrality to political personalities is a strength," Rekia pleaded. "They will always come and go, and they can always betray the cause in the blink of an eye." Rekia thrust her hand at Kate so hard that her earrings rattled. "Randall feels nice because she comes with that deceptive post-racial afterglow, and y'all feel like Kate here grew her in a vat for the movement and this moment. She's proof of concept to you. That does not mean she'll do what needs to be done, though."

"Okay," said Kate, hopping off the desk. "I'm wondering if we can make it through one meeting without referencing how Black or not Black I may be—"

I held up my hands. "I'm sorry, I meant that in an entirely jokey way . . ."

Liza had begun to paint her nails an amber color and shot me a look, *No backpedaling now!* Sandeep started to say something about the polling, but Rekia spoke over him.

"If we endorse her, do we put money behind her?" Rekia was now talking only to Kate, her voice rising. "I feel like I'm the only one pressing the brake pedal on this. Do we tell our supporters to not worry about reproductive rights or police brutality or Medicare for All or immigration detention or any of the other issues where Randall walks on the other side of the street? I just loved her speech telling Black mothers to take responsibility for their lives so they wouldn't have to visit the abortion clinic."

This was actually what I'd come to like about Rekia. That she could stir the pot over minutiae, there was no question, but she was so genuinely smart, tough, hardworking, and passionate; Kate had been right to hire her. Yet, in a reversal, as Rekia Reynolds grew on me, she began to grate on Kate. Their relationship was something of a black box. One day they'd be feeding off each other's jokes, and in those moments, they'd seem as close as sisters. Then there were moments like this.

"Okay, Rek, take it down a few degrees." Kate glared at her. "We're just talking this through."

"Like we talked through funding the next round of your Scientology-NXIVM centers? Or any of the other thirty thousand decisions that get made around here basically by you and you alone while you pretend there's any kind of consensus-building or democratic input? We're supposed to be building to action after the election, and you want all our financial operations working toward more vegetable gardens in Arkansas."

"How is that relevant to Randall?" Kate demanded.

"Because, Kate, Mary Randall fits into *your* model. She benefits *your* vision. You want to have it every which way for every kind of audience. Traipse through the world like you're a pretty little white gal, gather the eyeballs and accolades, the ease of movement, and then when it suits you, remind everyone that you're a quarter Black and a dime Indigenous and collect yet more fawning."

Kate slammed her heel back into my desk, a clap of metal thunder. "*What the fuck* does that have to do with anything?" Coral flinched. My eyes found the carpet. "Do you even have a fucking personality, Reynolds? Or is it all just pointless virtue signaling and identity politics down to your empty fucking core?"

And Kate stormed out of the office. We heard the door to the stairs crash open and slowly settle shut.

Liza blew on her nails to dry them. "So meeting adjourned, I guess?"

~ ~ ~

When we reached Nashville in late summer 2017, Kate left me at a honky-tonk bar. She didn't answer her phone, and it took me an hour to track her down at a greasy spoon where she'd joined a group of drunk partygoers. I remember thinking, *This is Day 3, and you're planning on a life with this woman?* I got to thinking about this selfish side of Kate. Eleven years later, I could still feel the desperation of that night, searching the karaoke bars of Nashville.

I found Rekia in her office. The lights were off. There were tears on her cheeks and embarrassment as well. She was so self-assured that it was unnerving to see her cry.

"I wanted to apologize, Rekia," I began. "That was my fault. I thought I was making an innocuous comment, and it exploded into this—"

"It's not your fault, Matt." Those words were followed by half a sob. She collected herself. "I swear. I feel like I'm going to have a nervous breakdown."

"When Kate gets these threats," I tried to explain, "those people don't think she's white."

They were worse and more frequent than ever. Recently, we'd gotten a deepfake video of Kate being assaulted by multiple men.

"Then why doesn't she feel this?" Rekia shot back. "You say that, Matt, but she doesn't feel what this decade has been. She thinks I'm the one who doesn't get it, but her only plan ever is to make nice with people who think I'm less than human."

"I don't think that's fair, Rek. But we're all stressed and exhausted. So is Kate."

"And if Kate doesn't get her way," Rekia went on, "she can be so fucking mean."

I left her alone and went to meet Tom and Coral. The closest bar was a sliver of stools and booths carved between D.C. row houses, with wood paneling and a handful of alcoholic regulars in suits. In those years, we did a lot of our drinking there.

"I was carrying Pelosi's purse when the Republicans were trying to default on the debt ceiling," said Tom. "I was around when Trump wanted to call the tax bill the 'Cuts! Cuts! Cuts! Act' but Paul Ryan wouldn't let him. I don't know what I'm still doing in this evil fucking city, but I know enough to know Rekia's wrong."

He downed an old fashioned and ordered another before I was a quarter of the way into my beer.

"She's wrong about the endorsement?" I asked.

"If Randall loses and we've still got Hogan's vindictive fat ass in the Oval Office?" said Tom. "Fuck that, Stanton. We've worked too long and hard to maneuver the GOP into confronting the carbon problem. Randall has the chance to be transformative. We can't sit on the fucking fence now."

I looked to Coral, who shrugged with their typical unexcitable neutrality.

"I see the merits to both arguments, honestly." Tufts of their red hair stuck up in the back and several juicy zits crowded their temples and forehead, making Coral look even more like an awkward teenager than usual. Yet when they spoke, it was always with confidence and nuance. "The meeting got personal before we even took up other important issues."

"More important than the fucking presidential election ten days away?" asked Tom.

I felt my pocket buzz. I thought it was going to be from Moniza Farooki, and if so, I wondered if I should float the Mackowski offer by a journalist who worked the climate politics angle professionally.

"Yeah," said Coral. "Such as the New York office. We need a new director. The last three haven't made it longer than five months apiece. The current one faked a case of Covid so she could walk away from the job for three weeks. I wanted to talk about Holly Pietrus."

"What about her?" asked Tom.

But the text was from Kate: *I calmed down a bit. Anyone at the bar with you? Katepologies forthcoming.*

"She's been angling for it," said Coral. "Holly turned out crowds for those city council meetings, she's hassling the mayor, she's even got the Staten Island rep running scared that the Dem will pull an upset."

"She's ready for the big-girl job?" asked Tom. "The New York office eats people alive."

"Not now," said Kate, materializing behind us, dragging a stool to prop herself between me and Coral. I looked down at her text. She must have sent it from outside the door to the bar. "Holly's father is still radioactive. Guy can't stop himself from blaming affirmative action for climate change." She pecked me on the cheek, her thick lips warm and wet and smelling of booze.

"Just want to say sorry for the outburst. I'm what you might call 'a white-hot ball of fucking nerves' right now."

"Holly's not responsible for her father," said Coral.

"Yeah, but we put her in the spotlight, and suddenly he's the story," said Tom. "We need to keep Tony Pietrus as far the fuck away from the movement as we can. He doesn't put his foot in his mouth, he shoves in the whole leg up to the fucking hip socket."

I wondered if Tom sat around thinking up these crude bon mots.

Kate said to Coral, "Let Holly keep doing good work." She nabbed the bartender, ordered a whiskey ginger, then slipped her hand into mine, and this cue told me her heart had stopped racing from the fight with Rekia. "We'll come back to it after the election."

Kate used *that* voice she deployed to end all debates. Her final word could feel like a boulder being rolled up against a tomb, and I could see the small muscles of Coral's face fall in disappointment. Rekia was right about one thing: Though FBF purported to be a democratic organization, there was one woman running the show. A pharaoh hiding in plain sight.

We had an early-morning drive to North Carolina, so we finished our drinks and left Coral and Tom at the bar. We walked through the lights of nighttime D.C., Kate pushing her bike along. Drunken twentysomethings in Halloween costumes were already streaking down the streets.

"Do you think I embarrassed myself today?" Kate asked.

"No more than you usually do." I smiled at her.

"I'm sorry," she said. "Is Reynolds furious?"

"Maybe you both said stuff that you both needed to hear." I could feel her looking at me as she rolled her bike along the sidewalk, like she was trying to decide something. I laughed and finally asked, "What?"

"Nothing, Tar Heel. Just trying to figure out what I did in another life to deserve you."

"Probably charged a Confederate line, just you and your bayonet."

"Ugh, such a masculine interpretation of heroism."

"You're a masculine interpretation of heroism!"

As we giggled, a group of loud, drunken women spilling out of a bar stopped me cold. "Holy shit," I said, pointing to the five of them. They all wore hiking boots and cargo pants, along with sky-blue tank tops, their bare shoulders goose-pimpled in the cool October air. A few wore huge wigs, but others had permed and dyed their hair to get the proper color and volume. Kate burst out laughing.

"Are you fucking kidding? Look at these fire-hot bitches!"

They all turned to her. The first woman shrieked, screaming like in those VR worldes where Zeden showed up to surprise random fans at their sweet sixteens. Then the rest of them realized what was happening, and they too launched into a fit of screaming, gushing, and hugging. We were there for nearly twenty minutes while I held Kate's bike and each of them got a selfie, followed by a group photo. I took a couple on my phone. They were drunk, emotions heightened, but a heavier white woman, who looked maybe all of a year out of college, started tearing up. She apologized to Kate, and the more she apologized, the harder she cried. She said, inexplicably, "This is better than meeting Cate Blanchett."

For whatever reason, this made everyone laugh very, very hard.

~ ~ ~

We arrived at my parents' house in Wildwood a few hours before the party. The wind swept cool air off the ocean as we walked into the decorative maelstrom my mother had organized with the acuity and determination of Spielberg re-creating D-Day. Several full-size skeletons crawled up the sides of the house, peering in windows while an enormous black plastic spider the size of a car crept over the roof. When we got closer, I saw these decorations were actually moving, the skeletons craning to watch us approach, the spider snapping its mandibles: robotics.

"It's kinda cute?" I suggested. Kate bulged her eyes.

My dad shoved Oktoberfest beers in our hands, my mom threw my niece, Gwen, into my arms. Gwen, riled to the nines by her grandma's Halloween spirit, breathlessly explained to her uncle that she was dressed as a ballerina. My mom was a "basic witch," including heavy pentagram earrings along with yoga pants and a Jamba Juice smoothie. My sister, Cara, and her husband, who we all called Habswam because his first name was also Matt, wore the gauzy outfits of Beyoncé and Jay-Z from their latest album cover.

"Hey, Matty," said Cara, hugging me. She had her phone out and was making a twisted, pained face.

"What?"

She shook her head. "Sorry. Putting it away. A school shooting in Minneapolis."

Morbid curiosity led me to check my news app and find that fourteen children, Somali refugees, had been murdered by a gunman who'd stormed into their school. I put my phone away because my sister was right. These horrors occurred with such frequency now, it left one numb to fourteen-child body counts.

"What are you waiting for?" my dad demanded. He was dressed as Indiana Jones, with a fedora and a bullwhip hanging from his belt, white hair popping out of his shirt. "Get your costumes on!"

As we changed in the room that had been mine during summers on the coast, Kate asked, "What do you think we should do?"

I held my elfin ears and had my green tights halfway up my legs, afraid I'd shred them because I'd bought a pair a size too small. "About what?"

She shook her head and the turquoise beads on her cowboy hat rattled. Farm Girl was the idea, but it was hard not to inject the word *sexy* in front of it. "About Randall. The endorsement."

I just shook my head. "Above my pay grade, sister."

"In your heart of hearts?"

"There is no path, remember? We make the path as we walk."

"Kid, that's not an answer."

I held my hands out in utter unknowing. "It means whatever we choose, that's the path we'll walk."

Kate's eyes fell to my bare thighs, and she started laughing. "God help me, you're cute."

She flicked the button lock on the door, the same one I used to engage when I got out the lotion as a teenager. "I'm going to call Rekia to apologize. But I'm telling her we're going for it with the endorsement. Time for bold moves."

"Then that's the path."

She slipped the overall straps off her shoulders and dropped them to the floor, kicking them away with her boots; the plaid shirt was next, but she kept the cowboy hat on.

Twenty minutes later, we were back downstairs, and the party was roaring. Kate split off to play with Gwen and talk to Cara, while my parents' friends were eager to hear what little Matty Stanton was up to. None of them gave much of a rip about the climate, and it was almost eerie to hear them ask, "A fierce blue what?"

One must constantly remind oneself that American life is divided into pockets that, at this point, were nearly hermetically sealed. If Gombo Bolorchuluun, the Mongolian Master, who'd put together incredible back-to-back wins at the PGA Championship and the British Open, had walked in this would have blown their minds, yet most didn't seem to know who Kate was. In a way, it was nice. No one wanted to talk about the election, and all our rancorous meetings were scenes from another person's life. Then my sister found me.

"Hey, I think you better come break this up."

I followed Cara to the dining room where a crowd had gathered around Kate and my father.

My dad was in the middle of ". . . he barely even plays anymore since he moved there."

"What the hell does that have to do with anything?" Kate demanded. "What does that have to do with children getting murdered at their school, Dan?"

"He doesn't play." My dad shook his head; he was drunk and slurring. Kate was drunk and furious, a pink heat scalding her cheeks. "He doesn't play, and it's 'cause you got him running around chasing socialism fantasies." He poofed his hands in the air like he was flicking water in her face.

"So what? Children. Murdered. I didn't think it would be controversial to be Con on that."

"Young people don't even play anymore!" he cried. "The game's dying because young people don't even play!"

Some tubby guy dressed as Pennywise the Clown roared at Kate, "He's saying Hogan's a Democrat! And she doesn't even want the Somalians here, so why should anyone else?"

Kate ignored him. Now the entire party was more or less silent except for a faction still chatting in the kitchen. "No one's playing golf, Dan, because it's a hundred fucking degrees out, and you're using fans to cool the greens and slurping up an aquifer to keep the fucking courses from going brown."

"Whatever, Kate." My dad reached to the table to grab a handful of potato chips, which he stuffed in his mouth. "You're a little girl. Doesn't know a thing about anything."

When my dad said this, Kate's eyes bulged and the muscles in her neck tightened. I hadn't stepped in yet because I didn't want to make it worse, and Kate was usually so expert at defusing these situations. I quickly took her by the waist.

"C'mon, let's go outside."

She kept glaring at my dad. Then she slipped free of me, stepped to him, and shoved her index finger in his face. "Fuck you, you privileged prick. You're a fucking cancer."

My dad rolled his eyes drunkenly and pushed another handful of chips into his mouth. I saw my mom across the room holding her cheek in her hand. The only sound in the room was him munching until someone snickered softly. Kate let me lead her outside then, and we walked silently through my mother's Halloween fantasyland and then through the salt wind to the darkened beach where we stayed for the rest of the party.

~ ~ ~

In the morning Kate insisted we leave first thing. She didn't say goodbye to anyone. I couldn't tell if this was out of embarrassment or fury.

After leaving Wyoming eleven years earlier, between our spat in Tennessee and arriving in D.C., we took a detour to Asheville where Kate had friends. At that point, I hadn't even realized she'd been to North Carolina before, and I met this whole crew of crunchy types living together in a five-bedroom house. The friends were nice enough, but as the stories and inside jokes whizzed over my head, I couldn't help but feel like Kate had already lived two lifetimes before she'd even met me.

On our last day we hiked out to a waterfall. Dozens of people swam in the shallow pools formed by the river tumbling down the mountainside. Others lay on boulders, sunbathing. Women went topless and men had beards down to their nipples. We hopped from slick rock to slick rock, and while Kate's bare feet gripped the stones with ease, with each precarious step I worried I'd slip and crack an ankle. Along the way, she pointed out flora: a leatherback milkcap mushroom, which squeezed out a milky white juice and made your fingers smell like fish, a turkey tail she claimed could help boost the immune system of cancer patients, a little red partridge berry she fed me that tasted like wet cotton.

"I swear I'm not trying to poison you to get at the golf empire," she said when I grimaced and spit it out.

"How do you know all this stuff?"

She made a face like she was sniffing the juice of a leatherback milkcap. "Dude, I read a book."

We stripped down and crawled into a churning pool of freezing river water. This high in the mountains, the day could be hot and the water positively frigid. The trees towered overhead, catching the sun and sending light and shadows glittering across the forest. We swam over to the rocks by the waterfall because Kate wanted to look for salamanders in the crevices.

"Salamanders have the most biomass of any wild creature living in western North Carolina," she said definitively, and when I only nodded, she looked at me. "Don't you think that's incredible?"

"Sure."

"Matt, just think about how many salamanders you'd need to make up one bear!"

This made me laugh very hard.

We disappeared beneath the waterfall, scooting together, the skin of her hip chill but the thick muscle beneath it warm. Frigid water pounded my lap. Our backs rested against slimy green moss, which, Kate told me, was called rock snot.

"Really?"

"No, I have no idea what it's called."

"You're impossible."

"Tell me about it. Believe it or not, when I was a kid, it was not cool to know all the names of fungi and edible berries."

"Yeah, I'm sure you really struggled socially."

"Dude, I was a dork and a tomboy! You were the one who grew up popular and good-looking." When I gave her a skeptical look, she said, "Really! Boys thought I was weird, and I hated everything girls talked about. Also, I was this tall when I was in sixth grade. I looked like a fucking circus act."

Shivering under the cold thunder of the water, with sunlight cutting through the roaring shroud, there was no way I was buying that. She looked so beautiful, it scared me.

"Want to make out under this waterfall?" I asked.

"Why do you think I brought you here? Pretend like this is the first time."

And so the kiss began delicately, tentatively, as pretend-Matt and pretend-Kate grew more confident. Later, we emerged to dry ourselves on a rock in the sun while she cut slices from an apple with a knife and fed every other one to me. Then we put our clothes back on as the sun set and the stars came out and the green forested mountains were limned with the silver light of a quarter moon. Of course, she knew most of the constellations. She put her head against mine so I could follow her index finger as she traced the line of Cassiopeia and told me stories I've long forgotten about this queen of the northern sky.

SHANE RIDES
THE PANOPTICON
2028

She left for Kansas in a driving rain. The downpour had lasted two days, and even the dash from the back door of the safe house to her car left her half-soaked. Driving out of Berlin, New Hampshire, she cruised along the raging Androscoggin River. The muddy water crawled up the trees along the banks, threatening a blue-yellow NAPA Auto Parts store built too close to the floodplain. In the White Mountain Forest, a gray-black mist shrouded Mount Washington. She imagined illogical, long-lost beasts huddled from the storm: eastern elk lowering wet snouts and six-foot antlers or mountain gorillas sheltered beneath the sweet green depths of the red pine and balsam fir canopy.

She passed between the lakes dashed across the midsection of the state like spilled paint and stopped for lunch at a Subway outside Concord. She used the mirror to pin her hair back and affix the wig of dirty blond over her scalp, followed by a logo-less gray ballcap. When she held the switch hidden beneath the cloth, a low buzz briefly enveloped her skull. She paid cash for the sandwich. On returning to the car, tuna melt in hand, a bird fell out of the sky.

She jumped as it cracked wetly off the pavement. Like a bolt from the storm had hit both her and the bird. It was still alive, twitching on the wet macadam, hammered by the downpour. Kneeling, she saw one of its wings mangled. Gray and white feathers torn. She couldn't recognize the species, but Allen would know. She found a shoebox in the trunk and lifted the bird's shivering

JANSI Had watched her drive away. When Jansi asked who she would be working with Shane With No Last Name gave her an impatient look but answered anyway: Jansi would be connected via a post office box to an engineering dropout in Georgia, an organic farmer in Maine, and a lawyer in Boston. Five years of proving herself useful, careful, and smart, three years of fortifying her cover, and now she was all the way in. It was going to be hard as hell to return to teaching seventh-graders geography after Thanksgiving break ended. "Will we see each other again?" Jansi asked. "No," said Shane. "Definitely not." Then, as an afterthought: "We're calling you the Second Cell."

body inside. It lay by her on the passenger seat for seventy miles. By the time she stopped again, it was dead.

———

The wipers raced back and forth in a frenzy. The rain was a white-noise thunder against the windshield. She drove the speed limit, and when impatient semis blew past, they sent up a blinding spray. She kept thinking of her mother, and the way rain had put her to sleep when she was a child and young to sorrow.

Because the highways were so heavily monitored now, she traveled outside the system of interstate rest stops. Rural highway bathrooms could be a dice roll. After a cup of coffee and sufficient pressure on her bowels, she pulled into a tidy-looking gas station in a one-stoplight town and got the key for the toilet. She regretted the meat and mayo at lunch. She could no longer reliably lose weight, so she went through phases of diet, and her pants size seemed to change with each meal or shit. Sitting on the toilet, listening to the raindrops chime on the aluminum roof, she noticed a marker left on the floor, some graffitist's forgotten tool. She picked up the marker, tested it on the white surface. Between the nastiness, swastikas, and tired limericks, she childishly tagged their line. She bolded each letter, outlined the 6 and the D, washed her hands, and tossed the marker in the trash on her way out. 6DEGREES IS COMING.

———

The drive took another five hours. By the time she arrived at the next safe house a few miles outside Altoona, Pennsylvania, it was well past dark. Down a gravel lane, isolated from the road, sat a nondescript, one-story home, vinyl-sided and squat. She grabbed her pack and found the key taped to the underside of one of the green plastic lawn chairs sitting on the concrete slab that served as a porch. She let herself in. Without bothering to explore, she went to the freezer, which was empty except for three frozen dinners. She microwaved two and wolfed them down. Then she took a shower in the too-bright bathroom, unrolled her pad and sleeping bag on the living room's empty carpet, and slept beneath the hum of the rain.

She woke to a knock on the back door. Though she knew it would be Allen, she looked out the side window and saw him waiting in a black rain slicker with the hood tucked over his smooth pink skull, still, when she put her hand on the doorknob, she almost couldn't bring herself to turn it.

She ushered him into the kitchen, scanning the woods behind the house.

"Where'd you park?" she asked.

"Church lot 'bout a mile away. Too far in this muck."

His boots and the cuffs of his pant legs were soaked, and he squeaked with each step. He kicked some of the mud onto the white linoleum. When she'd seen him last summer, he'd worn one of his disguises: false beard, eyebrows, salt-and-pepper wig. Without it he looked like a newborn mouse. After he got the slicker off, they embraced. They sat at the kitchen table. He'd brought her McDonald's coffee.

"Any trouble?" she asked him.

"Had my face scanned at a tollbooth but nothing I wasn't ready for." He held aloft a medical mask, still in vogue enough after all these years. He slid her a slip of paper with a Tennessee address. "Van's here. I talked to our operator today. It's stripped clean. No VIN, and our mechanic swapped out every part with a CVIN number. Plates go to a false identity. Should be a nightmare to ID. Pickup spot's close to where you're going but not too close. Drive the limit the whole way."

"Trust me, I've done scarier."

The kitchen hummed with the cheap white fluorescence and dead drift silence of a hollow house. She worried about drones watching from overhead, but if she worried about that, she'd also have to worry about long-distance microphones or the cameras that could scan for biometric data or aerial spycraft that looked and moved just like birds or even houseflies. There was only so much paranoia one could accommodate.

He blinked several times, all that old pink skin pinching around

ALLEN Hoped Shane was taking care of herself. She looked tired and raw. Eating poorly and not sleeping enough. They discussed the Second Cell. They discussed Allen's recruiters, his network of mostly college professors and low-level activists working aboveground, people he could trust but who kept themselves absolutely separate from the operations, who knew nothing except how to spot those either dedicated to the cause or those they could use for their ends. The recruiters felt out potential subjects and alerted Allen (**THE HANDLER**, as he liked to think of himself in *Ocean's Eleven* font). Shane made no secret she disliked how long this all took. Building this infrastructure took precious years the planet didn't have, but they needed impenetrable protections against infiltrators and informants. Paranoia was survival. They couldn't skimp on these measures. Allen was the oldest of the Principals, their core five, and often felt a paternal responsibility, especially to Shane. Sometimes he used their code just to check in on her. Once, he'd driven all the way to Missouri to meet her for a day and let her vent for a bit.

his eyes. He pointed to the shoe box she'd left on the counter. "You do some shopping?"

"No. I found a bird. Fell right out of the sky. Not ominous at all, right?"

Allen heaved his considerable girth from the chair and went for a look. "Guess you didn't find her soon enough."

"Stopping at a vet seemed ill-advised. I was going to see if you'd adopt her."

Allen's hand remained in the box, carefully turning the bird back and forth. "Yeah, except I'm not sure the farm can accommodate one more rescue animal. Emmy and the kids have basically adopted every Hard Times critter in western South Carolina— Smokes! You know what this sucker is?"

"Smokes," Shane repeated, snorting a laugh.

"They're tough to ID, but I'm pretty sure this is a blackpoll warbler."

"Yeah?"

"Shame. They're a songbird with a miracle migration. All the way from New England to Venezuela, sometimes Colombia." He looked at her knowingly, as if she and this bird were therefore related. He continued to stare into the box, puzzled. "She should be well south of here by now, though." He'd always be more amicable yeoman professor than Radical, and that was why she trusted him. Sometimes, she thought it was only these small doses of his presence that made her secret life bearable. He scraped the van key across the table to her and sighed. "I should get going. The op drops the van, drops the key to me, I give the key to you, you pick up the van—I mean, at some point we gotta ask if all this is necessary."

"Firewalls, Allen. The point is to keep our movements and connections convoluted. You think I like hauling thousands of miles from Kansas to New England to Tennessee?"

But the truth was, her urgency to get home often did battle with an itch to never go back.

"Speaking of Kansas . . ." He raised the flesh where his eyebrows once lived. "You seen pictures of this dust storm yet?"

She held up her palms. "Is that a bluff check? I haven't touched anything networked since I left."

"Started in northern Texas and the Oklahoma Panhandle and been moving east. My guess is you might get a good look-see on your way home."

Allen donned his slicker and set off, back through the dreary woods to the church lot. Shane watched the low fog close around him until it swallowed his figure, and there was only the dwindling sound of his boots slogging across the mud.

———

The rain finally let up. The flint banks of clouds looked like dunes turned upside down, casting shadows on the Appalachians and its footnote towns.

THE FIRST WOMAN OF COLOR ELECTED PRESIDENT *"Mary Randall won in a veritable landslide, collecting the largest percentage of Black and brown votes for a Republican candidate in the modern era. Liberals failed to turn out for Jo Hogan, and many even crossed over after a climate organization's unprecedented endorsement of Randall, who has promised a grand bargain on climate, energy, and taxes. Clea, what do you make of all this?" "Well, Senate majority leader Doup has signaled his willingness to move forward on climate. But there's no doubt the House, goaded by the likes of LaFray, AOC, and Aamanzaihou, will want much stronger legislation than Republicans are willing to offer." "But could this actually happen?" "You know, there are climate activists right now who are as breathless as a teenager at a Zeden concert—"* [Laughter] *"But President-elect Randall will ultimately be the brake or the gas pedal."*

She ate a drive-thru breakfast, snatching fries with one hand while listening to NPR. The dust storm led, followed by the Sahel civil war where people were murdering each other over the last boreholes; if water was found, the armies swarmed and drank it down to the mud. This cheery story was displaced by recycled recitations of post-election news.

Shane shut it off. Over the years, she'd found she didn't mind letting these trips pass in silence, watching the cows of the countryside, the miles of weathered fence and red-roof barns, or the species of tree change as new forests rolled over the hills. Her pique at another insipid sham election in which one corporate-backed ticket defeated another while a fascist movement thrashed in its chains dissolved back to dread. It wasn't hard to see how all those fantasies of the chattering class would play out in the end.

Before she'd left for her "Thanksgiving vacation," a busboy at the restaurant where she worked had caught her using his phone. Ramón stuck the old, cracked iPhone in her face in front of their coworkers and demanded, "*¿Por qué estás usando todos mis datos, perra blanca?*"

White bitch. A very particular slur for her, the only Spanish-speaking server. She felt a sweat break out on her brow as the other servers, bartenders, and a couple early-drinking patrons popped their heads up, curious about what could have so upset this small Mexican dishwasher.

She tried to play it off.

"Calm down, Ramón. *Lo siento. Tuve que comprobar algo. ¿Vivir y dejar vivir?*"

"*¡Tomas mi teléfono y usas todo el internet!*" he barked, and his anger chilled her. Teddy made his way over from the front of the house to stare at the two of them worriedly. She thought she had a good relationship with Ramón and the other immigrant workers. She often took his phone not just because he didn't use a password but because, if she was being honest with herself, he was powerless, at the bottom of the pecking order, so he would not be able to complain to anyone if he caught her. She used it to search for terms she could not on her own devices: "eco-terrorists," "6Degrees," "Colorado pipeline attack," "FBI eco-terrorist investigation." On her breaks, she watched videos about law enforcement's hunt for a group of "student terrorists," as one article put it. Maybe she'd underestimated just how many videos she'd actually watched, though. She hadn't realized she'd used so much of his data, and of course, that had cost Ramón money he didn't have.

Shane made her voice small and contrite.

"*Lo siento*, Ramón. My phone ran out of battery. *No batería. Lo siento.*"

"Is been you this whole time!" he cried. "*¿Usas mis datos para gorilas?*"

Browsing a bit on his phone, she'd come across a news segment about the search for the last mountain gorillas. No researcher had seen one in over a year, and biologists were prepared to declare the subspecies extinct.

"*Lo siento,*" she repeated. Her eyes shifted to their coworkers. "But *respetame por favor. Todos estan mirando.*"

"Why?" he said. "You no respect me."

He shoved aside the swinging kitchen doors and stormed to the back of the house before she could say anything more.

She fell into the trap of pointlessly spinning her mind in worry about seeing Ramón when she next went to work, which metastasized into worrying about every aspect of life in the hilly college town she called home. Chosen only for its geographic utility to their operations, how lonesome she was there. She tried to drag her mind away from all this, but paranoia and loneliness—one always felt like the answer to the other. She was so caught up that when she stopped at a gas station somewhere outside Parkersburg, West Virginia, for a snack and a coffee, she made a mistake. While standing in line, her eyes landed on an electronic advertisement for chewing tobacco. Abruptly, the screen changed to an ad for Subway, and she almost sprinted out the door. She had on the wig but no mask and no hat with its disruptive infrared lights hidden in the bill. The strands of fake blond didn't fool the ad's facial recognition software. She forced herself to stand and wait, even as she broke into a sweat and her stomach revolted in queasy cramps. After making her purchase, she went to the side of the building and vomited.

Then she drove on, crossing the Ohio River as night fell.

By the time she followed the handwritten directions to the address (all GPS, including the theft recovery system, neutered), she was exhausted. Their op had parked the van behind an abandoned shotgun house, and Shane hauled her gear from the trunk of the old Camry Kai had set her up with to the van's passenger seat. She'd get a ride back to the car in the morning. She drove the speed limit, used her turn signals. When a police cruiser pulled behind her, she tightened her grip on the wheel and nearly stomped the gas pedal. Feedback loops of panic washed over her as she sat waiting for the light to change. Most police departments now had at least one X-ray device that allowed them to peer through walls or into vehicles. It was unlikely this car was equipped with one, but it surely had cameras.

She turned into a gas station rather than drive another second in front of the cruiser. Shane took a breath, closed her eyes. Years ago, in a secluded cabin in Wisconsin, they'd asked each other: How could they disappear?

Caught between the vicious crosswinds of surveillance capitalism and the surveillance state, between a beast demanding profit and a beast demanding law, order, and lethality, most people had given up, accepted this as the natural state and buried their heads in as much sand as they could find. No need to stand over all 346 million US residents with weapons twenty-four hours a day. The algorithms could classify you as part of a "community of interest" for law enforcement if you sat by the wrong stranger in a restaurant as easily as they could determine your favorite soda brand. For the average Jane pecking at her phone, the world became more confusing

THAT CRUISER The dash cam recorded her. The body cam as well. That data then downloaded to a server for a corporate surveillance company that would use AI to filter and analyze every face it came across. Along with the Subway sandwich ad, there were now at least these two data points of her journey. No matter how careful she'd been in her weeklong trip up the plains, along the Great Lakes, across eleven states and dozens of law enforcement jurisdictions, she left a trail. Quinn Worthington, her feet up on a desk out in the new Master's house of Silicon Valley, would go after this trail later, scrubbing and polluting until Shane vanished from digital sight. At this point, complex data still awaited a tool capable of narrative organization.

and assaulting, while the dark data cycle mined her psychology and watchers of all stripes bartered for its value.

She waited half an hour before pulling back onto the street.

On the northeast side of Memphis, ten miles from the city, there was a road called Cowtown Way that dead-ended in a grove of battered blue ash trees. An unmarked dirt driveway led to a padlocked gate with a NO TRES-PASSING sign. Shane had the lock's combination memorized and glanced into the trees where hidden cameras surely tracked her arrival. She drove the van a mile more into the woods until she came to a long, low aluminum shed. An anonymous gray sedan with Mississippi plates sat outside. Shouldering her pack, she knocked on the heavy door. Kellan Murdock, half a smile on his face and purple bags beneath his eyes, swung the door wide.

"You make a pretty blonde," he said. "Or do gals not like being called pretty anymore on account of the MeToo?"

She embraced him. "How long have you been waiting to use that one?" And for a moment she forgot about the sky's drone and satellite denizens.

Murdock had built the shed into a survivalist fantasy redoubt, cruddy but cozy, with a bed, kitchenette, and bathroom separated by a curtain that ran on metal rings suspended from the ceiling. Solar panels and a battery storage unit supplied the energy off-grid. The wood-burning stove was unlit but had a pile of dry wood waiting nearby. On a tablet, two UFC fighters swung fists at each other's bleeding, busted faces, and a VR set hung in its dock, charging. On the walls: a poster of President Hogan, stout, enormous, crazed, and snarling, doing a leg drop off a pylon as the warriors from *300* awaited her undercarriage with shields and spears; a bumper sticker, RUSSELL MACK 2028; a black American flag with a red assault rifle and the words COME AND TAKE IT; and a photo of Mary Randall, eyes popping wide in a rare moment of looking frightened and insecure, NO MORE PUSSIES IN THE WHITE HOUSE.

"When did you get in?" she asked.

"Yesterday. Drove through a goddamn monster of a storm for most of it."

Her eyes ran over the rifle propped in the corner, the shelves stocked with cans of food, dry pasta, cereal, and an inordinate number of hot sauces. Murdock reached behind a box of Cap'n Crunch for some unseen switch. The mantel on which the stove sat abruptly popped upward. He dragged it aside, the chimney flute detaching with a metallic twang, revealing a cramped flight of stairs leading down to the hidden room.

MURDOCK'S STRAW BUYERS Mostly underemployed men across the South and Midwest, guys recently laid off or perpetually out of work, family men with much to lose. Quite a few churchgoers. Blighted by decades of deindustrialization, deunionization, offshoring, and finally a pandemic, the heartland was now being hammered by drought and flood, polar storms, and heat waves that crippled the economy in fun new ways each time. Murdock sent Allen to approach these men with a script, and the bald prof would strike up a conversation at a bar or a Mickey D's at lunch hour. Allen would claim he worked for a landscaping company, and man, they were just getting killed by taxes and healthcare costs. They were a small business, you know? They happened to be looking for a few off-the-books employees to run a few bullshit errands. But: "Nah, it wouldn't work out for you, man, sorry. Company's based in Indiana/Illinois/Florida/ Kentucky/Mississippi. They were just down/ up/over in these parts for a job that was about done. Shame, though. Company could use a guy like you. Here, let me get your number just in case."

THEN A FEW WEEKS LATER After the mark had given up hope that such a dream gig would come through, Allen would put in the call. "Could you deliver some shit to the company's storage locker over in [Insert Small Town Here]? We'll reimburse you for the materials, plus gas, plus $500 for the day's work? Here, write this down: rotary cutter blades, a timing belt for a box scraper, a rake, four fifty-pound bags of fertilizer, and blasting caps for removing stubborn tree stumps. Yeah, drop it all off at this locker—write the lock combo down—and I'll come pick it up in a couple days. Thanks, man, you're really saving our asses. Just can't afford to have the IRS penalizing us for a fiftieth employee." For the guy trying to feed a wife and three kids, it was too good to be true, which meant they never questioned it. All the materials remained two steps removed from Murdock.

He gave her work gloves, and they went about unloading the van. Shane had to swallow her sandpaper throat just to touch the two fifty-pound bags of ammonium nitrate fertilizer or the fifty-five-gallon plastic barrels the color of a cloudless sky. Even disassembled, the materials felt terrifying, holy. When she reached for a bundle secured with brown paper and duct tape, Kel took the package from her.

"Tovex sausage," he said. "But probably we don't wanna grill it."

She tried to sound casual as she retracted her hand and let him take it. "How fucked would I have been if I got stopped with all this?"

"Pretty good and fucked. Just think about my ass. I gotta drive three vans of this shit to the drop site in Kentucky."

She hauled a bag of fertilizer down the stairs into Kel's office. Lit by a single overhead fluorescent, the workspace was dense with blue drums, fertilizer, Tovex bundles, and plastic jugs of nitromethane. Tools lay scattered on a workbench: wire, pliers, grinders, gloves, safety goggles, pink prills, detonating cord, boxes of little sticks she knew to be blasting caps. She'd never seen the ingredients like this—just the results, which always seemed weak and ineffectual through the scrim of the news networks. It was why the media still referred to them as "student terrorists."

Her hip grazed one of the empty plastic barrels, and she jerked away as if her touch might set off the room. "So don't light a match down here," she said.

"Light all the matches you want. Motherfuckers'll see it from space."

"How are you on this stuff?"

"Slow-going. Straw buyers are mostly working out. One guy got sent up six months for forging a check, so he's out. But Kai is right about one thing: You send someone to buy two hundred pounds of fertilizer, and he ain't from the fucking Mid-Tennessee Farming Co-op, you're raising red flags. Same for all this shit."

"But now we have all the vans."

"Sure." He snatched up the pliers. "I'll probably get all the materials by February. Maybe March. That ain't the issue so much. We still got what you might call reconnaissance problems. How to approach the targets."

"We're working on it."

"Well," he picked at the skin of his thumb with the pliers, as if digging for a splinter, "work harder."

Shane's eyes wandered to the shelves behind the workbench: a water purifier, a machete, boxes of ammo, a med pack, a flashlight radio, and two handguns with full clips lying beside them. A Tyvek suit with masks, gloves, booties, and dozens of jugs of bleach to wipe down materials and vehicles. Their own DNA was perpetually trying to snitch. There was only so

MURDOCK Trusted Shane and Kai but did not always appreciate the contortions they built into every operation. You left keys under passenger-side doors, and some unknown kid from Atlanta picked up the vehicle two days later. It was a lot for his brain to keep straight. Still, he'd told Shane and himself: "I'm along for this ride as far as it takes me." Whenever he briefly forgot what the others looked like, he'd review a note he'd written to himself that he kept in a junk drawer at home. Probably not great to have around if the ATF ever descended but it kept him straight when he got their coded messages and couldn't remember who they were from or what he was doing.

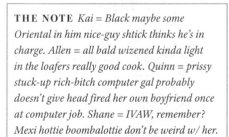

THE NOTE *Kai = Black maybe some Oriental in him nice-guy shtick thinks he's in charge. Allen = all bald wizened kinda light in the loafers really good cook. Quinn = prissy stuck-up rich-bitch computer gal probably doesn't give head fired her own boyfriend once at computer job. Shane = IVAW, remember? Mexi hottie boombalottie don't be weird w/ her.*

much their data scientist, Quinn, could do with her backdoors into the FBI's Terrorist Explosive Device Analytical Center.

"You're going full survivalist on me, Kel."

"Y'all keep telling me the world's coming to an end." He rubbed a hand over his paunch. "You and me could be real cozy in this place is all I'm saying."

She tried to return his smile but couldn't take her attention from the full clips lying beside each weapon. "C'mon. Cook me dinner with your nuclear bunker food."

Disappearing meant something different for each of them. Murdock had been to antiwar rallies, but he could retrench into his stereotype: posting to Facebook the hyper-conservative screeds of a revanchist rural white male. His digital trail consisted of ranting about Joanna Hogan and the Democrats, extolling the virtues of the Trump era, and sharing obnoxious Russ Mackowski bromides. If you were, say, the NSA and scrutinizing these bread crumbs, you'd find a lonely bachelor, an engineer, and the veteran of a war no one wanted to remember, who thought Randall was a socialist, who celebrated the anniversary of the Henderson-Rua fight as the greatest of all time. You'd see a man with a mortgage on a humble one-story in suburban Nashville, who drank too much beer, had put on a considerable amount of weight since his army days, and had a spartan Match.com profile. If you were taking a serious look, you'd find that back in 2014, he'd broken digital ties with one Luciana Alvarez of New Orleans on multiple platforms.

They'd underestimated what they were taking on. Shane's activism had taken her from post-Katrina New Orleans to Bolivia, Venezuela, Colombia, and back to the post–Deepwater Horizon Gulf. This surely made her a target for the security state's algorithms.

"We have to assume we've all been red-flagged for our personalities and politics," Quinn explained to them in their first meeting together at the cabin in Wisconsin. "We have to assume EOD techs are all under soft surveillance due to their skill sets." This was Shane's first time meeting the woman and her first wake-up call about what they were actually embarking upon, launching her down this endless road of passion, loneliness, paranoia, and fear. You could read about corporate and government tracking capabilities, you could study the unchecked organism with roots in the CIA, FBI, NSA, DHS, and the Pentagon, but the average citizen could not wrap their head around its true scope. "And so much of it is our own fault," Quinn had said coldly, her chin propped on her knuckles, firelight on her pretty but severe face. "We all gladly and willingly herded ourselves into this state of technofascism."

"All I'm hearing from you," Shane said, "is why this won't work. Why are you here if you're this scared?"

An argument erupted. For days, they'd been close to concluding that they should all just melt away and pretend none of this had ever been on the table. Not for the last time, Shane took control of the conversation.

"We shouldn't be afraid," she said. "It's a panopticon."

"I know," said Allen. "That's what Quinn is saying."

Shane took the problem into her hands, cupping it in front of these new comrades. "You misunderstand the panopticon. The point isn't to watch everyone; it's to give the illusion of total surveillance. For the actual watchers, they can only point their eyes in so many directions at once. The amount of data overwhelms and confounds. It helps us."

QUINN Frequently wondered how Shane managed this. Quinn, who'd dealt with supposedly nonhierarchical consensus decision making in her hacktivist days, figured the dynamic out quickly. It was clear, Shane was their quiet internal compass, and she appeared not to have hesitation or indecision inside of her. Meanwhile, Quinn crawled into a new life of suffocating emotional isolation. She would be on dates in San Francisco sometimes and feel the urge to simply confess the entire operation to a boring programmer talking himself up. She often woke from nightmares of being caught while simultaneously wishing, sometimes, that it would just happen.

While Kai and Quinn wanted to recruit computer programmers and hi-tech savants to build them anonymizing software that would bounce their IP addresses all over the world, Shane told them: "No. We take it the other way. Like every good insurgency, we defeat hi-tech with low-tech."

So they dispersed. They adopted normal lives. They stayed patient. They deactivated their activism. They encrypted nothing. They'd all be red-flagged for the rest of their lives with user scores utilizing logistic regression to estimate the likelihood they were involved in illegal activities, but so would an Everest-sized haystack of ordinary people. So they Googled. They Facebooked. And now they Slapdished. They bought face creams and eyeliners and power saws on Amazon. They polluted their data with tedium. They built profiles of themselves as average, boring, troubled, lonesome

Americans who looked like anyone else enjoying the privileges and rewards of conformity.

Meanwhile, they sent messages via PO boxes and safe houses, which, like the old Camry, were owned by one of a few different limited liability companies in New Mexico. They coordinated mostly through junk-mail flyers: YOU COULD ALREADY BE A MILLIONAIRE! A delighted woman held a lotto ticket crammed with numbers, small enough that you needed a magnifying glass to read, which corresponded to pages, lines, words, and characters in the Signet mass-market paperback edition of Stephen King's *The Stand*. If the FBI kicked down their doors, the flyers would be ashes and *The Stand* would sit unassuming on a bookshelf.

This was how she'd received Kai's message in early November: *We need you on the road*.

Due to the firewalls, it had to be Shane to activate the Second Cell by delivering the contact info to Jansi, and if she was going to New Hampshire, she could also make a delivery to Tennessee. And if she was doing all that, she could run an errand of her own and check a mailbox in Tonganoxie on her way home.

"Randall says she's gonna pass a New Green Dealy, first order of bidness," Murdock said over a wagging cigarette. He stirred a powdered pesto sauce into water and olive oil. "What say you, Shane? Victory is ours?"

"Yeah, and more tax cuts for the oligarchs and more detention centers." She sat on his bed, paging through a book he was reading. *The Last of the Wild*. Free of the wig, her scalp still itched. "And a fully militarized border."

"She's got Saudi Arabia and Nigeria on her plate, gas prices spiking, price of solar is cheap as ever, her party only controls one thingy in the Congress, so she needs Dems if she wants to do anything. Might could happen, as they say."

"Wake me up when it does."

She opened to his bookmark and read from an underlined paragraph: *How did the creatures of the Pleistocene deal with these catastrophic temperature swings? They ran—migrating on immense, continental scales.*

"To fight the empire, you fight the source of its power." He dropped a handful of angel hair into the pot of boiling water, mashed it down with a wooden spoon. "You told me that in the Bob Evans, remember? Way before the ecology shit."

"That's what we're doing."

"Fighting? Are we? Or are we just horseflies? Biting at the murderer's ankles while the shit goes down."

"That's why Kai pushed for this escalation. No more pipelines."

He clucked his tongue. "Kai. The man with his hand in every pot, plot, and plan."

Murdock was given to talking like this, good-naturedly testing his compatriots' assumptions. When they first got together, he was eager to build bombs, even though he was skeptical of the "global heating hoopla."

They ate in collapsible lawn chairs near the warmth of the stove, plates balanced on knees. Kel drank from a cup of whiskey while Shane stuck with water. The lamp cast a long shadow over a gruesome poster she hadn't noticed before: HATE above a picture of militiamen bravely charging across the desert borderlands.

He pulled out his phone to show her what she'd be driving into: video of Oklahoma in a dust storm so thick the shapes of roads and buildings looked like the infrastructure from a city of ghosts.

"Lawrence is far enough east you won't be going right through it, but you'll get a taste."

She watched as a woman wearing swimming goggles and holding a scarf to her face guided a group of teenage students into one of those quickly erectable annex classrooms, the kind they threw up when schools got too crowded and didn't have money for new construction.

HATE Murdock loved his posters. This one popularized by the Jen Braden crowd. "It's not offensive," they insisted, and Kel Murdock found this deeply funny in that gallows way he most appreciated. It gave him a laugh, all these hard-core War on Terror vets following the panpipe of this rich, racist princess: Nothing to be offended about, these patriots swore. All it meant was HUNT ALL TRAITORS TO EXTINCTION.

"This is it," she said, keeping all the dread she felt out of her voice. "The new Dust Bowl." Shane set down her plate, her taste buds sore from all the salt of Kel's recipe. "Is your apprentice ready?"

Murdock nodded as if satisfied by a child's success on a soccer field. "He's sharp. Even had some halfway good ideas for our next operation." The new bomb maker had been the culmination of a two-year search, the screening process heightened and sensitive beyond their norms. They'd dropped contact with three other candidates before finding a student from the Georgia Institute of Technology. "Now that we're cutting ties, and he's going with your girl, Jansi, I realize I'm gonna miss the kid. He loved learning. Makes me think I should go into teaching."

"They don't have your kind of classroom at your average technical college." Her eyes fell on the rifle in the corner, the smooth grain of the wood finish. "I'm thinking we should meet up. The Principals," she said. "After this op."

He scraped at pesto sauce and licked the tines of his fork. "If you insist."

He finished his whiskey in one pull and set it on the floor. He put his hand on her knee and leaned over from his chair. She let herself be kissed but did not open her mouth to return it. He eased away from her. The pesto smell of his breath lingered.

"Probably a bad idea," he admitted.

"Probably."

Embarrassed, he snatched the plates up, took them to the small sink with the piping exposed and tangled like a toy model of a refinery. She wondered how he could possibly still feel this for her. The gray in her hair, the weight she kept adding. Before she'd left Kansas, she'd taken a picture of her face, and the image rocked her. She looked like she was melting.

"Can I—" he stopped. "Will you sleep next to me tonight? Promise I'll keep my hands to myself."

He sounded like a child asking his mother if he could crawl into her bed during a thunderstorm. She hated that it made her wish for her own mother—on the street, dead, wherever she might be.

Beneath the comforter, in her sweats and tank top, Shane let him put his arms around her and dip his face into her neck where his breath whistled.

Before she fell asleep, he asked her what she was afraid of. "If you get afraid of anything, that is."

So she told him.

―――――――

On the highway west over the plains of Missouri, the sky was a color she'd never seen before, a hellfire arterial crimson. According to the radio, this was the soil of the plains, ripped from the roots by a hard wind and borne skyward. She knew the color was the result of the grains in these galaxies of dust performing with the dissipating sunlight. It gave the air texture. The fibrous atmosphere on the approach to Hades. Now her mask was for more than just disrupting FaceRec cameras. When she stopped, she could rub her fingertips and come away with a thin black resin and imagined what this must look like inside people's lungs. The dust coalesced in pockets that hung in the air like jellyfish. The farther west she drove, the larger the dust piles grew, brown snowdrifts against the sides of homes and strip malls, piled in parking lot dunes, stirred into a miasmic cloak by traffic. She took the highway through Kansas City. Even with the lights of the cars—bright white dyads in the oncoming lane, cheap red in hers—the city had a feeling of abandonment, a shrouded necropolis. The few haunted figures she saw slogging through the streets wore masks and goggles and carried flashlights, the beams of which looked solid when interacting with the dust. Overpass signs warned caution. Reduce speed. Wear a mask or particulate filter even indoors. The lights of police cars and ambulances strobed through the dusk. And this was just the tail end of the storm, the dissipation of the cloud that had torn across the plains. A state of emergency in five states.

At the Merriam Town Center mall, Shane parked in an underground garage and left the key in a magnetic box beneath the passenger door. She grabbed her battered Osprey and made her way to another garage. Her old gray Chevy Cruze waited, the key in another magnetic box beneath the door. She'd had this sad beater for six years, had sunk too much money into repairs, and the very sight of it filled her with melancholy. She threw her gear in the trunk and took off, shedding her clandestine life yet again. Putting the old disguise back on. Her white server's apron, hopelessly stained, lay on the passenger seat, and she remembered Teddy begging her to either use bleach on it or buy a new one.

She had one last stop outside Tonganoxie. Just south of a state fishing lake there was an unassuming two-bedroom cabin typically rented to area fishermen. Guests were asked to politely leave the mailbox for the owner to clean out. Here, Shane sifted through the junk mail until she found the flyer for cable and internet (*Your New Smart HD VR Includes These Fully Integrated Apps*). She couldn't wait. Back in her car, she grabbed the order pad from her apron and found the paperback copy of Octavia Butler's *Parable of the Sower* stuffed beneath the seat. It took her ten minutes to decode the message, and after that, she had to sit for a while, flooded with a new dread unrelated to the burning orange sky over the lake and trees.

The porchlight of her rented bungalow on the edge of Lawrence cast an eerie glow into the dust. Before she could put her key in, the deadbolt turned and the door opened. Shane felt a pang of fear even though she knew who would be there.

"I've been dusting," said Kai, and he hugged her as she stepped inside.

"Is she asleep?" she asked him. He wore a dark denim shirt with a pocket on each breast and shiny faux-ivory buttons, the sleeves rolled up on handsome forearms. The shirt matched the shadow of his stubble and hair poofing up like a crown on his scalp and showing a bit of recession.

"I just put her down."

She made her way back through the clutter of her house: shelves of books, stacks of paper, a piano where she pretended to still be learning Norah Jones from the songbook.

"And we're not even getting the worst of this. Oklahoma City is shut down," he said.

She motioned for him to be quiet. She opened the bedroom door softly and crept in. It would be a nightmare to wake her right now, but Shane had to put eyes on her.

Lali slept in the small bed, positioned in that goofy way: Her arms shot straight up over her head like she was about to inbound a soccer ball. She'd kicked off her blanket, which was now spiraled around her footie pajamas, the ones with robots that she currently favored. Her mouth was wide open and her tongue poked out. Her drool collected on her cheek in a thick paste. Shane resisted the urge to pick her up and hold her. It was never worth waking her up once sleeping, not for anything. Yet there was that mix of grief and guilt and a love so terrible it made her stomach roil. When she'd departed on this trip there'd been the pain of leaving her daughter for a week, but also the sheer, unbridled relief of being free of her for a moment. The diametrically opposed impulses to race back home as soon as possible and to keep going, to forget about drop boxes, safe houses, nitromethane, and coded letters, to take whatever ghost vehicle Kai had set up for her and keep driving forever.

> **KAI** Saw Shane begin to reach for Lali and sucked in his breath, ready to beg her *Please don't*. Lali had spent the entire week throwing tantrums before bedtime. At some point, he had to just let her go until she exhausted herself. He had a student who, like Shane, was a single mom, and it was disconcerting how quickly sympathy for this tough circumstance could rot away into *Please do a better job raising this kid, lady.*

As she watched Lali sleep in the toddler bed Teddy had given her, Shane despised herself for daydreaming about such a thing.

She eased the door closed on her four-year-old and picked up the baby monitor.

"We should talk outside," she told Kai.

"You think that's okay?"

She held up the monitor. "Only one potential surveillance device that way."

They walked through the dusty night, an N95 mask cupping her mouth and nose. Shane wanted to walk away from her house but no farther than the monitor's reach. Every now and then she took a glance at Lali dozing peacefully on the screen. She wondered how much the dust would obscure them in all the cameras they passed.

"Some spooky shit, huh," said Kai, his voice muffled by his own mask. "I've seen the skies from a wildfire before, but I've never seen anything like this."

Shane hesitated, uncertain what to bring up first. She decided to start with practicalities.

"I need more money."

Kai looked at her, surprised. His eyes still had that quiet cunning that had first drawn her to him in New Orleans, irises dark and searching. "I'm slipping you what I can. The funds are for our operations, not our personal pleasure."

"Pleasure? Kai, I'm working a serving gig. I'm driving thousands of miles on county highways and switching vehicles while you do what? Kick back in your condo in Saint Louis and occasionally babysit?"

"It's your cell, Shane. We have to keep the firewalls in place. That's protocol."

"I'm not asking for much. A couple hundred dollars a month maybe."

"All it takes is one IRS audit. Just one accountant poking into your financial life to see that you're collecting money from somewhere. Get in touch with Tracy Aamanzaihou if you like, but last time I checked there's no collective bargaining in an insurgency." He looked around then lowered his voice. "I mean, no one told you to go and get pregnant, Shane."

Shane stopped.

From the look on his face, he knew he'd gone too far. He stuck his hands in his pockets and shook his head. "I'm sorry. I'm just tired. But you've made this bed, and you have to work around Lali just like the rest of us have to work around our covers."

Rage rose and receded, the way it did so often. One becomes accustomed to the contempt the world feels for unwed mothers and swallowing a blooming rage to get done what needs to get done—that was just her life. Whether it was a preschool teacher side-eyeing her for showing up late or Teddy getting pissy when she called out for a shift at the last second because Lali was throwing up, she could hear them all thinking, *God, these sneaky sluts sure know how to game the system for themselves, don't they?* It didn't matter if she'd gone to college and read Barbara Ehrenreich, after a few years as a single mom, this sensation tunneled into her. She marveled at how much contempt she could sometimes feel for herself.

They walked in silence to the end of the block. At the intersection they reached a shrouded brick YMCA that had become a full-time shelter. All the towns west of here were blowing away. Pretty much every burg except Wichita and Topeka had emptied out. Ghost towns. The cities were the only places that could afford the water. The Ogallala was running dry, so now they had companies trying to drill to the center of the earth to find water. The University of Kansas was putting millions into it, but it was hard to see how enrollment would fare after this. Kai made an effort to move on.

"This won't be like Kroll. They think they're closing in. Once this goes down, the tactics will get tougher. They're going to come after us in more ways than we can imagine."

The operative, Miles Kroll, who'd driven the van and planted the bomb in northern Colorado, had gotten picked up because he'd put the device in his own backpack, which he'd purchased at a campus bookstore with a credit card. They were sure he'd ratted everything he knew, which, thanks to their system, was nothing more than a guy in a wig telling him where to find a van and what to do with its contents.

She licked at the dust that got by the mask, a fine sandy refuse on her tongue and lips. "Thirteen missions later, only one low-level operative caught. Give a gal some credit, it's all working."

"I'm just saying, after this they'll break down doors looking for us."

"We keep to what we've been doing. Keep the protocol and precautions in place."

He lifted his mask to spit dust from his tongue. "Yeah, and that's why you had to activate the new cell, and that's why Allen and Quinn and Clay and everyone else sticks to those protocols—"

"You don't have to tell me, Kai, I'm the one who came up with it."

"So you've done your job. And I'm doing mine."

A woman on a hoverboard came zipping toward them on the sidewalk. She had a scarf wrapped around her face and on the side of her skull was a tattoo like a saprophytic mushroom. Shane waited for her and her humming gadget to pass. "There's something I need to tell you."

As though he hadn't heard her, he said, "We're still gathering information on our targets, but I'm looking at summer right now. Less than eight months."

"There's something you need to know," she tried again. "There's something new. A threat."

He stopped and the dust circled his head like a spiral galaxy.

"How many pieces of our bombs have they picked up? Not a mote of DNA on any of it," he said. "What more can we plan for?"

Just by opening her mouth to describe it, Shane felt the urge to get off the street, to get away from Kai, to flee, but then again, she wouldn't have felt safe in a lead box at the bottom of the ocean. She didn't feel safe in her own skin. Her very cells were a telltale heart beneath the floorboards. And now this thing Tinkerbell had described to her via a coded message in a Tonganoxie mailbox.

"It's a new AI project working with megadata. Apparently, it can identify and conceptualize data points in ways even the people who built it can't understand. The way it was explained to me, you give these algorithms a suspect, and they can backfill their entire inner lives. Basically read a person's mind."

"How?" Kai asked. She assumed he meant how was it legal.

"I don't know, you're an adult. The same way drones and torture and data mining and the rest of it is."

"No. I mean, how the hell do you know about this?"

She shifted her eyes away from him. Five years of keeping this a secret, longer than Lali had even been alive, but it was time to bring him in. "I have someone," she said, "in a national security consulting firm, GBI. It's a corporate partner of the FBI's NatSec Branch. I recruited her in 2020 when I was in New York. She worked her way into domestic terrorism, and now she's working with the JTTF."

Beneath the mask, she was sure his mouth was agape. "There's someone on the fucking JTTF who knows about us?"

#MOVEMENTS An off-campus apartment flying a Jayhawk flag with each of its three windows draped with enormous banners: **BLACK LIVES MATTER | GREEN NEW DEAL | A FIERCE BLUE FIRE**. Here in a campus bubble it was easy to look around and believe the country was swept up in a wave of change and possibility, a narrative propagated and commodified by the social media companies inflicting a new colonialism on people's minds. But it was a false revolution that Kai had spent his entire twenties gazing at in disbelief. "Activists" thinking themselves impossibly brave for leading the charge to cancel a celebrity or barrage some hapless prole for her racial, gender, or religious insensitivity. All just to build new mansions for the Silicon Valley plutocracy. The righteous energy of the past decade-plus of hashtag "movements" could occasionally summon the angry poor to the streets or sympathetic liberals to their Twitter accounts, but it stood no chance of fomenting the necessary revolution. As a young Black activist, he'd been in disbelief that his peers could be so easily snookered, that they couldn't see these hashtags for the marketing campaigns they were, the Masters' best tool yet to misinform, disinform, and sow discord as they tightened their grip on power. Now that the Morris woman had forced the biosphere into the role of cause celeb, her movement was following the same familiar route: immense self-congratulation, vast internet hot takes, enormous promises of change, light, sound, and fury, all empty, all signifying absolutely nothing. He'd known that no movement would succeed in this fight without a major disruption. He'd just never had any idea how to create such a resistance until he met Allen and this woman walking beside him.

"I had to keep it compartmentalized. It's a firewall. Same as the new bomb maker and the others in the Second Cell. This woman, though, she's in a much more sensitive situation. She's had to beat polygraphs, Kai. I didn't want to tell anyone about her unless I needed to. But now I need to."

Kai made an exasperated sound in his throat, but he was still processing.

"The good news is, she's feeding me everything. And right now, they're not even close to us. You're right. They think Kroll was the mastermind. They've been sweating him in a hole for four years and he's down to making stuff up to try to get out of it. Painting a crazy portrait of us."

The sky was a draining vein. Above the door of a one-story home, flies did jet-fighter moves around a muted lamp. She could see the dead ones curled up inside the fixture.

"This spy versus spy shit," he warned. "It's dangerous."

"I trust her. And she doesn't know who any of you are—or the new cell. The firewalls will hold."

He seemed to wilt into his acceptance of this new information. "This AI thing—that's fucking dystopic."

"It's what we should've seen coming."

He started walking again, and she nodded to the blue flame in the window of an apartment. "Then there's this bullshit."

"What about it?"

"Of all the do-gooders, Kate Morris is the apotheosis of liberalism's pitiful fucking response to environmental collapse."

"Right. So who fucking cares? She's out to write the screenplay for her own biopic."

"That's why we need to move faster, Kai. Idiots like her are out there trying to lifestyle brand our way to better consumption in an extinction event, but what have we done, Kai? I mean, really, *what have we done*? Maybe we're just as pitiful."

"Yeah, well," he scoffed. Then he started laughing, a slightly manic and infuriating sound. "At least she's foxy, right?"

A weight came bearing down on her then. "Glad this is funny to you." They'd been ambling, but now she bolted ahead of him, into the dust and dark. He was maddening. Over a decade of learning to be idle, to slink into these quiet lives of mud. Fifteen years of the plans and protocols, and what did they have to show for it? A few busted oil and gas pipelines? She was a lonely waitress and broke single mother shuttling coded messages over the mountains while the world cooked.

Kai caught up to her on the road. He snatched her elbow, and she wrested free of his grip.

"The fuck," he said.

"I didn't drive two thousand miles so you can treat this like a joke."

On the street, crows descended giddily on a possum ground into the pavement. Kai released an exaggerated, exasperated breath. Finally, he said, "Obviously, I don't think it's a joke, Alvarez." Her old name left his mouth gently.

"We're moving too slowly," she said. "We're wasting our time on cheap bullshit."

"I wouldn't call what we're planning cheap bullshit by any measure."

"We need to escalate. And we need to start executing more quickly."

"Quick gets us caught."

"And slow gets us killed. Slow ends our world."

They'd walked too far. She was suddenly filled with the sensation that she'd check the baby monitor, slick in her sweating palm, and there'd be a man standing over her daughter, glowing black-and-white in the night-vision camera.

"We meet at the cabin," said Shane. "After this operation. All the Principals. To plan what comes next."

When they got back to her place, she asked him to stay one more night before heading back to St. Louis. It wasn't about sex or intimacy—he would sleep on the couch—it was about having someone there, in her home. They stayed up another hour, and he showed her maps of the facility. They studied the routes until the conversation winnowed and they had nothing to turn over but errant memories of the muggy days in New Orleans when they'd been young. He made up the couch and then went to shower the dust from his hair.

While he was using the bathroom, she picked with compulsion at the lattice structures the windblown soil had created in each nostril. He'd been sleeping in her bedroom, and now he'd moved his pack next to the couch. She couldn't help herself. Smushed inside along with some basic T-shirt and jeans outfits, he had his copy of *The Stand*, and stuck inside, one of their flyers. She hadn't seen this one before, though. It was addressed to Styx Capital Management in New York City. She replaced it and zipped the pocket shut.

That night, she couldn't sleep and found herself thinking of the last of the gorillas, the tigers, the blackpoll warblers. The last of the wild. All those eyes in the sky incidentally bearing witness to a holocaust the scale of which had only occurred five other times in Earth's four billion years. She often lay awake with this dark clarity of the world her daughter would know.

In the morning, Kai bid her farewell, dropping Lali off at daycare on his way out of town. Shane put on a new mask and went outside to brush the dust from her windows with a snow scraper. Her shift began at two. She drove under the bonfire heavens, but the dust was moving on. By the time she reached the highway, the billboards again beamed brightly. All around her, omnicidal frequencies cruised the airwaves, and she could feel each and every one of them adrift, sagging into the long night of extinction that lay in wait.

.

OPINION | GUEST ESSAY

A New Hope for the Planet

Al Gore, Bill McKibben, and James Hansen

December 10, 2028

Following the haunting dust storm that descended on the East Coast this Thanksgiving, we would warn citizens and policymakers not to bury their heads in the accumulating drifts of soil from the plains, but to consider the patient crisis that can no longer be ignored.

Forty years ago, one of the authors, Dr. James Hansen, testified before Congress about the threat posed by the accumulation of greenhouse gases in the atmosphere. Global warming, as an idea, a threat, and a policy priority, entered the mainstream conversation. In the intervening decades we have seen from politicians, business leaders, and the media equivocation, delay, and denial in confronting the most urgent matter not only of our time but of all human history. All three of the authors have dedicated their lives to warning that a reckoning is near.

Delay has cost the world dearly. The global average temperature is now 1.2 degrees centigrade above preindustrial levels and rising faster than predicted. At just a 0.8–1.2-degree rise we have seen unprecedented weather events strike our planet with increasing regularity: record-setting floods, heat waves, and hurricanes. A decade of extreme heat, drought, and voracious wildfires have tormented California and the Southwest, destroying homes, farms, and lives while rattling the insurance industry and real estate market. In the African Sahel, the Middle East, the Mediterranean, and Central Asia, water scarcity is killing people by the thousands each month and sparking further refugee flows to Europe. Climate refugees will continue to surge into Western countries in numbers that will make accommodation increasingly difficult. The effects on food security and disease vectors are also frightening. Tropical diseases now thrive in regions where no doctor had ever before seen a case in her lifetime. Having fought back the scourge of Covid-19, the world waits with anxiety as each year new pathogens emerge while the epidemiology of known diseases mutates. Scientists have no clear playbook for when one of these new mass killers may break loose, but Covid-19 may simply be a harbinger of things to come.

As dire as these consequences may be, none of it holds a candle to the threat of sea level rise. This past summer, in the middle of a heated presidential campaign, the Thwaites Glacier in Antarctica experienced a partial collapse. Half a Pennsylvania's worth of ice broke away over a long weekend. Scientists estimate the other half may be lost in the next two years. This is a frightening development not because the Thwaites itself will raise sea levels, but because it buttresses a mountain of ice in West Antarctica. If and when the Thwaites collapses for good, the West Antarctic ice sheet will begin sliding into the ocean. This could raise sea levels by nine to thirteen feet, which is doomsday for every coastal city in the world.

Given the severity of events we've witnessed at one degree, one might think the world would mobilize, but delay continues to be the operating principle of our economic and political leaders. We've squandered precious years and staying below the 1.5-degree threshold is in all likelihood now impossible. Two degrees looms, and any temperature increase beyond that would likely be the end of global civilization as we understand it today.

Mary Randall's historic win should rightfully be celebrated as a joyful sign of our country's progress. However, given the enormity of the challenge, there is no time for a honeymoon. President-elect Randall was elected to office promising action, and she cannot waste even a single day. She and Congress must pass legislation to deal, once and for all, with the coming storm. We urge her to seize the moment.

What would that action look like? At the very least, it should include a zero-carbon electricity standard to finish electrifying the power sector as quickly as possible; the shuttering of all coal plants within three years and a ban on mining to follow; a zero-emissions vehicle mandate for 2035, including trucking, and a cash-for-combustion-engine policy to electrify the transportation sector; standards for heavy industry to begin switching to clean fuels, banning certain refrigerants, eradicating methane leaks, and lowering process emissions; investment in building retrofit and new codes to electrify building stock; targets for increasing aviation efficiency and mandating sustainably produced "drop-in" biofuels, which can work in existing aircraft. Just Transition funds should be targeted at workers in the carbon economy and those people and regions most hurt by polluting practices, which will require major investments in clean electricity deployment, adaptation measures, and afforestation and land management projects. Money must flow to those most affected by the clean energy transition and climate damage. R&D should focus on hard-to-decarbonize sectors with a special emphasis on bringing green hydrogen to scale and carbon sequestration and utilization. Lowering emissions is no longer adequate. We must remediate carbon from the atmosphere or utilize it in cement, polymers, fuels, or create hydrogen via electrolysis to begin tightening the earth's carbon cycle. Of course, the United States cannot go it alone, which is why the proposal from the organization A Fierce Blue Fire has received so much attention.

The "shock collar" is, at its core, a carbon price with 100 percent of the money rebated to taxpayers in the form of a climate dividend. Starting at $50 a ton, it will have the effect of not only making emissions more expensive but will give every American a quarterly check that will invest them in the process of decarbonization. The "justice" element of this plan should not be overlooked. As research has shown, putting money in people's pockets will allow a strapped populace financial breathing room while also stimulating the economy. The innovative element of the shock collar is that the price is tied directly to emissions. The price to burn a ton of carbon will rise steadily at 3 percent per year plus inflation unless emissions do not decrease, in which case the price jumps by 7 percent the next year. If emissions decrease but miss the target, the tax will increase 5 percent. This addresses the concern that a tax might not necessarily lower emissions. With this policy we can quickly ramp up emissions reductions to meet the 10–15 percent per year target we must hit in order to avert catastrophe.

Crucially, the policy will levy a border adjustment tariff on goods coming from countries that fail to apply a similarly ambitious carbon price. This will keep heavy industry from fleeing the US and allow us to decarbonize without outsourcing our polluting practices (known as "leakage"). It offers an enormous incentive for recalcitrant countries to pursue deep decarbonization. If we can link carbon price policy with just China and the EU, it will effectively create a World Carbon Price, and the rest of the global economy will have little choice but to embark on its own accelerated timeline.

This, of course, does not in any way abrogate the US and other developed countries from fully financing sustainable development and adaptation measures for the developing countries through the Green Climate Fund. A proposal to levy a global tax on corporations to create a strict and sustainable funding source should be considered. To pay for mitigation and adaptation investments, high-income earners and concentrated wealth must finally pay its fair share. Tax justice is climate justice.

What we have lacked over these past forty years is political will. Nothing in our experience of fighting for the planet has heartened us more than witnessing this generation of young activists take the lead, from Greta Thunberg and Alexandria Ocasio-Cortez to Kate Morris and newly elected congresswoman Tracy Aamanzaihou. All have been ruthless, resilient, and indomitable in their advocacy. The result has been a new coalition of "climate hawks" in Congress, and now Mary Randall, a candidate who has courageously led her negligent party on the issue.

This is no longer a country for old men, and soon we will fully give way to this new generation—progressive, multiracial, multigendered, talented, and passionate. They have been handed the unenviable task of saving humanity as we know it. We urge these young people to keep the pressure on. We urge Congress to seize this historic opportunity. We urge action.

EXECUTIVE SUMMARY ON LEGISLATIVE NEGOTIATIONS FOR THE POLLUTION REDUCTION, INFRASTRUCTURE, AND REFUND ACT OF 2029

EYES ONLY:

Sen. Cyrus Fitzpatrick, Chair of the Senate
Select Committee on the Climate Crisis

Rep. Joy Barry LaFray, Chair of the House
Committee on Science, Space, and Technology

Ashir al-Hasan

January 29, 2029

Abstract: As chief of staff for the Senate Select Committee on the Climate Crisis and leader of the informal White Paper Group assembled by the new administration to draft legislation aimed at the rapid reduction of greenhouse gas emissions, I initially feared my expertise would fall outside the parameters of this tortured task, yet I now realize my years spent modeling the googolplex's worth of interactions within various Earth System Models for NOAA was small bore. A joke, apologies. I'll try to keep my comments focused on the model's analysis of differing iterations of the Pollution Reduction, Infrastructure, and Refund Act (PRIRA), but will have to occasionally comment on the inanity and profiteering that surrounds the legislative process. I will conclude with the summary of my clandestine meeting with Dr. Anthony Pietrus, formerly of the Yale Program on Climate Change Communication.

The new administration has deemed the chances of success for climate legislation as high due to a Republican president and Senate majority vowing to work with a Democratic House of Representatives. In order to provide an understanding of the institutional obstacles, allow me to use my notes from the third assembly of the White Paper Group, as we attempt to create an outline for so-called grand bargain legislation that advances deep decarbonization schemes, to explain the dynamic. These meetings have primarily consisted of legislative staffers, experts, and low-level aides. I was surprised to learn that representatives and senators rarely draft legislation or even attend the meetings during which provisions are debated. In this early backdoor meeting, the argument centered on whether the bill would include a carbon-pricing scheme. Kaye Martine, the Democratic staff director for the House Committee on Energy and Commerce, was concerned with the public relations optics of the final legislation. At under five feet, she is always the smallest person in the room and yet the high pitch of her voice allows her to override the conversation whenever she pleases:

"Your party's leader—the fucking president—wants a carbon price. That's her idea."

"The president has her priorities, and so do Senate Republicans." This was from Joe Otero. President-elect Randall has deputized Senate leader Ryan Doup with the burden of persuading obstinate conservatives to vote for climate legislation. However, it would be Doup's top energy and climate advisor, Otero, who would be doing the bargaining. Otero and Martine are garrulous, profane characters, often at odds in a near-flirtatious way. Martine tends to wear more mascara and blush at these meetings, while Otero will roll up his sleeves to expose tattoos that begin at the wrist, a legacy of his aborted punk-rock career. He has the physique of a former bodybuilder gone soft and an oily black ponytail that gives him a certain air of rebellion in the staid circles of the GOP.

Though this meeting included seven of us, this exchange was approaching ten minutes. As Martine drew a breath to respond, Dr. Jane Tufariello gratefully interrupted: "Would you mind if we returned to the pricing mechanism? That's all we're debating right now."

As you know, when she is reconfirmed, Tufariello will be the longest-serving undersecretary of Commerce for Oceans and Atmosphere and administrator of NOAA. In addition to being a key mentor during my time at MIT and encouraging me to join the committee staff so that I might work on this legislation, we sometimes watch WNBA basketball together. Dr. Tufariello is one of the most competent and dedicated scientists working in the government, and I wish she'd interrupt more.

"Christ, Jane, how do you not get that the pricing mechanism is a bait and switch?" Martine pointed to Martin Rathbone, the Harvard economist, expected to head the president's National Economic Council. "The scientists and economists keep telling us we don't understand the science or the economics. But eat shit, because you don't understand the politics. None of this matters if the bill can't pass."

"And the way we do that is we broaden the appeal body," said Otero.

"I love that term," Dr. Rathbone mused, slouching so far back he appeared to be close to napping. "An 'appealing body' has nothing to do with this. *This bill* is a paper hangover. But I do love an appealing body."

Rathbone scanned Kaye Martine when he said this, and Martine gave a perfunctory roll of her eyes, though this appeared to be a routine long worked out between them. That the highest levels of government seem to spend so much time behaving like it's seventh grade never fails to astonish me. I wrote all this down because I found it as fascinating as I did obnoxious.

Dr. Tufariello, who loathes Rathbone, once remarked to me that it never pays to lose your temper at a white man in Washington, as they would find a way to weaponize it against you. Instead of acknowledging his comment, she focused on Otero: "Yes, but the legislation has to actually *work*." The last word snapped out of her mouth, and I pictured it crackling above her head like a dissipating spark.

No offense, Senator Fitzpatrick and Congresswoman LaFray, but of the 535 members of the US Congress, those who have a sophisticated understanding of climate and energy policy would not fill an NBA roster. People luxuriate in the comforts bestowed by science without any interest in the empirical mechanisms that make those comforts possible. This leaves much of the lobbying to the likes of Tom Levine, representing the gadfly climate organization A Fierce Blue Fire, who felt entitled to interrupt next:

"Question is, who are you negotiating for here, Joe? If this is just about pleasing the literal pig-fuckers from rural Missouri who think the earth is six thousand years old, then why waste the time?"

Laughter ensued, and Alice McCowen slapped the table to cut it off:

"Enough. The Republican Study Committee can wag its limp QAnon dick all it wants; it doesn't mean they have the votes to block anything."

A new entrant to these meetings from the White House Office of Legislative Affairs, McCowen became a household name during the 2028 campaign as Mary Randall's Svengali in the mode of other political pseudo-celebrities (with each administration comes a new one: Carville, Rove, Axelrod, Bannon). She seems to me a master of self-styling. On the campaign trail, she received criticism for referring to herself as a "hard-charging Texas bull dyke" and seems to be performing that character at all times. The media called it a gaffe, but it seemed much more a calculated move to demonstrate her candidate's moderate social views. McCowen is taller and larger than most of the men in the room and swings the White House bat with ferocity.

"Now, my boss sent me here because, frankly, she heard the first meetings were coming up with fuck-all. From now on, the administration will have its hands deep in this cow, delivering this thing, so hear me: Speed is of the essence. We want a bill ready for Leg Counsel by the time Congress convenes."

An argument erupted, with enough cross-talk that I lost the ability to record it all. Levine demanded the FBF's "shock collar" while Martine argued the Democrats wanted Republican buy-in for any kind of pricing mechanism, and Otero interrupted to push the Republicans' preferred policy of an extremely weak cap-and-trade scheme. This led to Dr. Tufariello saying what was obvious but politically intolerable:

"The primary thing the bill has to do immediately is shut down coal forever."

Leading Ms. McCowen to bark at her: "Jesus Christ, Jane, don't say that outside of this room *ever*. The Sinclair Broadcast–Jennifer Braden–Renaissance Media kook machine will come for Madam President before she even puts her hand on the Bible."

Perhaps it was the volatile cul-de-sac in which the discussion had bottomed out or just the brittle sound of all those voices fighting to be heard that created a sensation on my skin like someone pelting me with rocks. My frustration neared a tipping point, so I chose this moment to speak up:

"It seems rather idiotic to begin this discussion by trying to form a consensus about what has the most political viability." This quieted everyone, so I continued. "Any policy designed to achieve the goal of lowering emissions will necessarily inflict some economic pain, and therefore the policy must also alleviate that pain. We can simply run those numbers and decide what's best, empirically speaking. To spend our time dawdling about political constituencies seems to me rather fruitless."

I left my pen poised over my notepad in case anyone had an interesting response.

Ms. McCowen stared at me as silence took hold: "Who in the sweet brandy fuck is this guy?"

Dr. Tufariello volunteered that information: "This is Dr. Ashir al-Hasan."

I added: "Chief of Staff for the Senate Select Committee on the Climate Crisis and advisor to Senator Cyrus Fitzpatrick of Pennsylvania," while also favoring Ms. McCowen with what my brother-in-law, Peter, calls a *fuck you gaze*. Mostly I was just happy they all stopped speaking over one another.

Dr. Tufariello said: "Ash was also one of NOAA's top Earth System modelers. We listen when he talks."

Ms. McCowen glared at me. "Yeah? Well, let me tell you something, Doctor Dicksucker: On my daddy's farm we used to do rectal palpitations on cows, and if you call me an idiot again, I'll come for you with two fists."

Hopefully this example gives you some idea of the tenor of these meetings. They are also too often catered with the same bland turkey and portobello wraps.

//

In college, I discovered that running was an excellent way of alleviating anxiety. When I moved to Georgetown, I found a running club online, the project of a man named Seth Young, who was "a recovering political operative."

Young had worked in the Obama administration and quit politics after burnout from Hillary Clinton's 2016 race. Instead, he formed a fitness and wellness business, one aspect of which was taking moribund, desk-shackled Washingtonians on runs around the capital. I found the experience enjoyable, and it eased my transition from Tennessee, where my home was proximate to many excellent paths. As you may recall, I took the Senate Select Committee's offer with a bit of trepidation. After my years consulting with the New England Complex Systems Institute, I moved on to NOAA's Oak Ridge facility. This was powerful, cutting-edge modeling. Working under Dr. Tufariello, I helped pioneer an integrated assessment model (IAM) that broke new ground with its accounting of biospheric inputs, population, economic activity, national and international policies, and technological options available on decadal and century timescales. That's largely why I'm here: because Dr. Tufariello wants to put each draft of the PRIRA legislation through our IAM to show how it might affect the climate under ideal circumstances of implementation.

It was after that most recent meeting in which Ms. McCowen threatened me with a bovine medical procedure that I decided to join the evening run. The weather was bitter cold, fifteen degrees Fahrenheit, and we well-bundled runners crunched across the thin veneer of leftover snow. Mostly this group consisted of staffers and lobbyists plugged into the D.C. ecosystem, who seem to use the club as much for networking as physical fitness. We jogged up Constitution Avenue, past the Washington Monument, and then cut over onto the Mall at the Smithsonian. I fell beside Seth, our legs falling into synchronized rhythm as we beat across the gravel. Seth not only leads these runs but is a rather impressive repository of D.C. history. When we ran past the Washington National Cathedral, he stopped and led us inside to show us the Space Window. The blue and black stained-glass window depicts constellations in motion, green planets and red stars, and even though the cuts of glass were obviously still, one's eye seemed determined to watch them swell and swirl.

"Neil Armstrong and Buzz Aldrin brought back a piece of the moon, and it's actually embedded in the glass," said Seth. "Not to get corny, but it's remarkable, right? That a sliver of the moon would meet the sands of our planet and be joined together to create something beautiful."

I'm not sure why, but when he said that I felt deeply emotional for a moment. That evening, as we rounded the path just shy of the Reflecting Pool outside the Capitol Building, most of the group dropped away. Seth finally stopped and laced his fingers behind his head. The five of us who'd stuck with him trotted alongside. Until:

"I usually only see you in the morning."

I explained: "I had a maddening day at work."

Seth grinned and briefly touched my arm. "You work on the Hill. They're all maddening."

Until that moment I was unaware that Seth knew of my position. When I inquired how, he shrugged, an almost bashful expression: "You're sort of dork-famous to a certain set. All the wonks whisper. You're the NOAA modeler working on the top secret bill. Trust me, Ashir, that makes you famous in this town. I was around that game once upon a time, remember?"

As the rest of the group said their goodbyes, Seth and I continued down the Mall until we reached the Potomac. The water glittered in the city's lights. Though I've become adept at meeting people's gazes to signal that they have my attention, Seth was difficult to look in the eye. He was Germanic, with bright blond hair and startlingly blue eyes that gave me anxiety. He said:

"I have such an urge to interrogate you about what Randall is up to."

"I can't share specifics of the negotiations for reasons I'm sure you understand."

"No, no, I get it. Hard not to wonder, though. You leave the game, but the game never leaves you."

"On the other hand, perhaps it would be helpful for me to ask about your experience."

"What if we got dinner this weekend? You can pick my brain on all of the government's doomed efforts to curb emissions, and I can tell bad jokes until maybe I see what your smile looks like."

I felt an old terror claw. Whenever I have a moment like this, I think of my brother-in-law, Peter, who was the person who taught me to be myself unashamedly. I told Seth that was quite the hokey line—and that I'd gladly have dinner with him.

/ /

I bring up Seth Young only because our dinner included insight into his experience with the failed Obama-era effort. Many of us are optimistic that this time will be different. In the last year, with two Category 3 hurricanes making landfall, record-setting wildfire activity in California, and finally, the Great Plains dust storm blowing in from the west and coating D.C. in a pink-orange haze, the political establishment finally seems sufficiently terrified. Yet the politics of action remains a vipers' nest of complications. Yes, clearly, the conservative movement and its proxies practice bad science, but the so-called climate hawk community is often guilty of the same.

It has become internalized in the climate activist culture that in order to alleviate destructive hurricanes and wildfires, certain social policies must be enacted, many of which have virtually nothing to do with greenhouse gas reduction. In other words, universal healthcare schemes are a dangerous distraction, though activists keep demanding they be attached to any bill. To point this out, however, has become heretical. As you may understand from some of the correspondence your office received upon hiring me, there is a contingent of political activists in online forums who believe me to be a "stalking horse for neoliberalism." Online harassment has followed. As I've tried to make clear to politicians and activists alike, science and advocacy make poor bedfellows, no matter the circumstances. Dispassionate empiricism is the only methodological approach that should be pursued.

At our dinner at Charlie Palmer Steak, Seth Young was eager to share his experience in D.C.

"I still can't stop reading *Roll Call*. It's pathetic. But when I was in politics, I was twenty-three and had an ulcer that wouldn't go away. I was snorting Adderall every day, working seventy hours a week. Starting my business probably saved me from dying of a heart attack at forty. Also, I'm like the only guy from the Obama era who didn't get a lobbying job or become a bro media guru. But I still can't help but live and die on the gossip."

The waitress came, and Seth ordered for us. He'd declared that he would be paying for the meal, but I did not see how that entitled him to choose for me an animal-free steak grown from cell culture with plant-based imitation butter-bacon sauce. When she left, I asked:

"Any gossip you could potentially share that might be of help in passing the legislation?"

Seth let out a low whistle and sipped his wine. He was on his second glass to my first.

"You guys have a tougher climb than you think. When I was meeting with USCAP, everyone thought we'd get something passed, at least the framework of a cap-and-trade system."

"I'm aware. I've read the Skocpol report."

Our meals arrived. Seth dug into his while I allowed mine to sit for the moment. Through a mouthful of plant protein, Seth went on:

"I train this congressman, a Dem from a gas state who wants this bill gone. Whichever version the Senate passes, whether it's cap and trade or a tax-and-dividend scheme or a set of regulations, he's going to back something else. It's clever. You have these mechanisms which enviros have disagreed on going back to the nineties, and it's a surefire way to divide and conquer."

"That's already what's happening in our meetings. In my estimation, simply phasing out fossil fuels is no longer adequate. We need to embark on major R&D to jump-start next-generation nuclear power and carbon sequestration and utilization. There is still a great deal of momentum for the tax-and-dividend approach."

Seth favored me with a skeptical glare. "This is the 'shock collar' fantasy?"

"Yes. Tom Levine has been invited to participate on behalf of A Fierce Blue Fire."

"Oh Jesus. That degenerate Bernie bro. I'll grant you they've created the political opportunity in a surprising way, but no one has proven yet that the GOP will actually play poker. Randall thinks she's going to get a pass because she has an R beside her name, which is lunacy if you ask me. Once all those industries are threatened, money will start flowing to other options. The base is primed to turn on her the second it gets a signal from Fox News and the right-wing armada." He pointed behind me to the TV playing on mute over the bar where a striking woman with bright red lipstick and lustrous black hair chopped a hand in the air to make her point. "This Jen Braden floozy is taking it to Randall. People think outlets like Renaissance Media are the white supremacist, conspiratorial fringe, but they're the vanguard now. Aren't you going to eat your steak?"

"Actually, I prefer real cow flesh."

I betray Seth's confidence here only because I think it's vital for you to understand that the granular details of the bill matter almost nothing until we have a better understanding of what's going on within the unreported, unchecked halls of the influence peddlers behind the façade of the state. At heart, though, I remain a mathematician, and when I look at passage of this bill I see simple math: In the Democratic-controlled House, 35 percent of the prospective yes votes will come from New York, California, Oregon, and Washington, low-carbon states that stand to lose little economically from the legislation. However, these states represent merely one-twenty-fifth of the Senate, or 4 percent. Your body, Senator Fitzpatrick, an anachronistic and vigorously antidemocratic institution, will, as it has throughout history, prove the most intractable obstacle to major reform.

//

Three weeks later, Dr. Tufariello felt the need to recruit me for a subaltern mission involving a scientist no longer welcome in the public sphere. In the privacy of her office, she confided to me: "The Randall transition team has a white paper ready, and they want us to take it to outside sources. You've worked with Tony Pietrus?"

If I have not made it clear, Dr. Tufariello has earned my utmost respect. After growing up in rather discomfiting circumstances in West Baltimore, she has become one of the most energetic scientists in her field. I would honor any request within reason, yet this one seemed strange.

"I did. We met at the Global Change Research Program modeling forum. We did not exchange life stories, as they say, but we're well aware of each other."

She said, very carefully: "The president-elect wants Tony's opinion. Without anyone knowing about it."

This made halting sense. Dr. Pietrus became something of a celebrity based on his popular book *One Last Chance*, and then a pariah. Scientifically, his work on the parameterization of clathrates has been key to some models. He's contributed to process and observational understandings of methane clathrates, one of the key unresolved climate-relevant processes. However, when the Seventh Assessment Report came out in early 2028, he called the IPCC "a joke that still bends to the whims of petrostates like Saudi Arabia, Russia, Brazil, and the US." Pietrus gave interviews denouncing the report as a "genocidal document" and promoted his histrionic "Tombstone Domino Theory." He alienated himself completely with an outburst at a World Economic Forum panel, when "he called the future president of the United States an 'affirmative action hire,'" as Dr. Tufariello put it. He's been labeled a racist by detractors, a truth-teller by admirers. He remains a controversial figure, and his early retirement from Yale has not calmed his critics.

"I'd be glad to meet with him," I said. "But why not use Marty Rathbone? I believe the two are colleagues and friends."

"Rathbone is an ape. He knows how to get himself on TV and duck a sexual harassment complaint. But also, no way can the head of the NEC talk to Pietrus. The wingnuts are already dreaming up conspiracy theories about Randall's win in the primaries, and Tony would be even more toxic on the right than the left. You've gotten a taste of what it's like to be at the center of a politicized issue, but nothing like this guy."

"But Mary Randall wants his blessing on the bill?"

"She *wanted* to nominate him for the EPA actually. I guess she liked him for whatever insane reason. But McCowen shut that down because obviously getting him confirmed would be a nightmare no one wants. He's seen as the most hardline scientist alive, so if he's on board, it can protect our scientific flank. But we also have to protect our social justice flank. We keep those intact, and the Left as a whole will follow, even if the bill isn't perfect. Which it won't be."

"If you don't mind me saying, Jane, it feels as though we're consistently attempting to craft a coalition before we even have the policy in place."

"Yeah, well, welcome to politics. And listen, Ash, you need to exercise extreme discretion about meeting with Pietrus. Don't use anything that goes out on a broadband connection. No phone, email, HoloChat, or Slapdish. In person. Make it a hotel and pick the conference room the day of."

Perhaps this was paranoid of her, but everyone in Washington frets about being monitored or hacked, and working on sensitive legislation means that assumption is not without merit. Private spy networks, corporate data collection, and foreign espionage are all possibilities. Xuritas Corporate Services has rapidly increased its market share by promoting and gaming fears of terrorism, and it's hardly a coincidence that its founder, Loren Victor Love, managed to secure himself a Democratic Senate seat in Montana. Meanwhile, Russia's FSB, China's MSS, and Mossad have now penetrated multiple presidential administrations and countless senatorial and congressional offices.

For instance, when I walked from my office to the Metro stop that would take me to Seth Young's apartment, I passed through the sights of dozens of video analytics programs scanning multiple security cameras and processing huge amounts of data, including facial muscle observation, walking speed, heart rate, and other biometric data that might indicate if an individual was nervous or ill. People move through D.C. as if it were still a free city, but there is not a word, motion, website, photo, or sneeze that is not monitored, catalogued, and shuffled through the scrutiny of governmental and corporate AIs. That night, I told Seth we could not see each other for the week following, as my sister and her husband would be staying with me.

// /

When I returned to MIT to pursue my doctorate in applied mathematics, I left behind a lucrative career as a professional gambler. My partner, Peter O'Connell, remained a good friend, and in my final year of doctoral work, my sister, Haniya, moved to Cambridge to pursue her doctorate in economics at MIT. This is how she met Peter. I moved on to work at the New England Complex Systems Institute, and then my mentors Dr. Sri Thankankur and Dr. Tufariello steered me toward work at NOAA. It was during my first months there that I received a call from Peter. We talked about basketball for a great deal of time, which usually indicates that he has something else troubling him:

"It's the kind of thing where you could hate me, and it'll rip the guts out of our friendship, get me?"

"Please continue."

"Argh. Shit. All right. Ash, I love you dude. Okay: Haniya and I have been hooking up."

This was indeed quite surprising: "Really."

"Yeah, like a lot. For a long time."

"Okay." I paused for perhaps too long, lost in thought and forgetting how this cue might be interpreted.

"That's like the bad news, dude. The really bad news is I'm pretty sure I'm head over heels fucking in love with her."

"I see."

"Yeah, man. At first, I just thought she was a fucking sexy whack job in bed, but . . . Nah. She's Haniya. The Han dynasty. Han Solo. Harrison Ford. Ford Fusion EV, range of three hundred forty miles. When I told her how I felt, all she said to me was 'I know.' I fucking love her, Ash."

At first, I harbored not just trepidation about this relationship but jealousy. They'd been having sex for nearly two years without telling me, and I resented this. After our father died, I became closer to my sister, our youthful misunderstandings dissipating. Peter, meanwhile—I'll only say that I met him at a point in my life when I still harbored a great deal of anxiety and loneliness. Only years later did I understand what his friendship meant to me, the ways he taught me to be unafraid, to approach life with humor and bravery. Beyond that, I came to realize I was attracted to him, a problematic episode that I've never broached and never will. For a time, I kept my distance from both of them, hoping the relationship would run its course, until they visited me in Tennessee. I remember giving them a tour of my lab in Oak Ridge. I had a whiteboard hanging on the door and while I explained to Haniya how we were attempting to tackle the extreme-scale computing challenges of increasing spatial resolutions and representations of parameterizations, Peter, behind our backs, doodled an intricate portrait of the Millennium Falcon doing battle with a TIE fighter. The caption read, *The Al-Hasan Brainbox Showdown.* It made Haniya laugh very hard, and she took multiple pictures of it with her iPhone. After they left, I sat to write about the episode, as I sometimes do when attempting to work through moments of psychological complexity and decided that it was low of me to resent these two. They have become my closest confidants ever since. It so happened that while working on the white paper, Haniya and Peter visited me in D.C. It was their first vacation since the birth of my niece, Noor, and though I was eager to see her again, Haniya and Peter were more eager for respite and a few alcoholic beverages. My mother flew to Boston to spend the weekend with Noor. Peter, always a playful, slippery, logic-defying linguist, had dubbed my mother, Amala, "Grandmamala," and it was one of Noor's favorite words to hear. Perhaps the most surprising element of

Peter's romance with my sister was that my mother seemed to genuinely like him. It also helped that Peter had undergone "a half-conversion to Islam."

Haniya, by this point, had stopped wearing hijab, but this was not an easy journey. She'd been independent-minded and rebellious the moment she could stand on two feet, and as a teenager had started a website with photographs displaying the difference between worship facilities for men and women in various mosques around the US: women's prayer spaces baking with no windows or air-conditioning or only one dirty sink to perform wudu. My parents and the imam were far from pleased. This defiance continued into college, when Haniya started a Muslim women's group at Michigan. Most of her activism involved combating misogyny, sexual violence, and domestic abuse, and I know Haniya received a great deal of online vitriol, both from Muslims and their just-as-strident Islamophobic counterparts. She was caught between the imperative to defend her faith, which was precious to her, and to try to change the things within that faith community that she saw as unjust. She claimed that Peter, raised Irish Catholic, had been instrumental in helping her through this crisis.

"He would always say I should approach my faith and my relationship with Allah on my own terms and doing it any other way would not be keeping true to myself. Then we started praying together. He even read the Qur'an."

"Peter? Read the Qur'an? And prays with you?"

"Don't say it like that. He's different than you think, Ash."

"I'm only attempting to assimilate new information."

While staying the weekend in the guest room of my condominium, Haniya met up with a few college friends while Peter and I attended a Wizards game, where he filled my ear with his plans to use proprietary models I'd created for him to start a hedge fund. This was indeed news, as that line of financial speculation was not for the amateur, but he claimed he had multiple investors and a "major, boffo, super-god of the PR world" on board. On their last night, we ate a barbecue dinner in Adams Morgan. While Peter kept halal and ate chicken, Haniya had a taste for the food our parents would never let us eat growing up and greedily sucked the meat off a rack of ribs. Our talk eventually turned to the legislation. She asked: "Can I take a look at what you're proposing?"

After becoming curious about my work, Haniya wrote her dissertation on the intersection of economics and democratic systems in a changing climatic regime. She now works at the Eunice N. Foote Institute, a think tank dedicated to climate policy. Similar to Dr. Pietrus, she harbors great skepticism that any policy would sufficiently address greenhouse gas emissions other than governments putting a heavy thumb on market forces. I called up the white paper on my phone, and while she skimmed with her thumb and snacked on ribs with the other hand, Peter made his feelings known:

"Problem is we gotta think of this as an engineering problem, not a social one. Why can't we fix poverty? Why can't we fix our schools? Because those shits are tough-as-balls social problems with complex moving parts. But shoot a guy to fucking Mars? Hell, that's just getting the math right. So why don't we just pump some volcano dust into the air like all these scientists say and chill the planet out? *Snowpiercer* that shit, bro."

"It's certainly a proposal that gets more serious attention with each passing year."

"Oh Christ, look at your fucking face, dude. What's the problem?"

"Almost too many to name. Also, if I recall, *Snowpiercer* was a disaster narrative."

"What disaster? Four-fifths of that train was dope! You heard Ed Harris."

In due time, Haniya finished scanning the white paper. She gave me two pumps of her dark eyebrows.

I noted: "You disapprove."

"No, look, I support *anything* at this point. But in the past five years alone IT infrastructure, like data centers storing VR worldes, has eaten up all the gains of renewables and then some. Global energy growth is outpacing decarbonization. That's why we liked the shock collar or even Randall's Green Trident. Price signals got a bad name because they were often badly designed, but without one, these companies can keep finding ways to bring their carbon to market. They win by stalling. Carbon will always be useful, so unless you make it expensive or illegal to burn, those interests will find a way to do so." Peter was staring at her with his mouth slightly agape. Haniya looked at him: "What? Stop being weird."

"Mama, you're so fucking sexy and beautiful, I want to put my fist through a wall."

I slipped my phone back into my pocket. Once back at my condominium, Haniya and Peter drank heavily, and when I left them in my living room to go to bed, they were kissing quietly on the couch. In my bedroom, I put in earbuds and listened to the sound of rain. I thought about how there will always be something about me that finds happiness too painful.

/ /

Which brings me to my final conversation regarding the white paper. On Saturday, January 20, while the rest of Washington streamed to the Capitol to witness the swearing in of Mary Randall as president, I took the train north. Dr. Pietrus had agreed to meet me halfway between New Haven and D.C., and I arranged for a small conference room at a Hilton hotel. A concierge showed me to the secure space where a pitcher of ice water, two glasses, two legal pads, and two Hilton pens were arranged in flawless symmetry. I passed the time by exchanging text messages with Seth. We were in the middle of a minor disagreement because I hadn't invited him to meet my sister and Peter when they were in town.

I texted: *I'm not comfortable with you meeting them yet. You'll simply have to accept that.*

Seth replied: *I feel like you're not comfortable with anything until someone forces you to be comfortable with it.*

Haniya had expressed a similar sentiment before she left when she attempted to broach the topic of our mother: "I don't think you get how much she's changed. Since Papa died, it's been one step after another. She didn't blink when she met Pete. She has a new best friend at the country club who's Black. Black, Ash. I remember back when she used to tell us that the races don't belong mixing."

"The issue is not that this person in my life is white, Hani."

That single, terrifying sentence was as close as I'd ever come to admitting to my sister what I'm sure she'd already long known.

"I'm just saying, Ash, you have to give people the chance to not disappoint you."

By the time Dr. Pietrus arrived, forty minutes late, I was so lost in thought on these personal issues that his entrance was akin to a plate shattering on the floor.

"I apologize," he said without a hint of apology. "I met my daughter in New York for brunch and it was— You know, it was a whole thing."

He slid into his chair and dispensed water into his glass. He wore a rumpled suit, and I was reminded that he was constantly in a state of dishevelment. His skin was dry and pallid, his lips chapped and peeling. He looked ten years older than he should and reeked of cigarettes. While searching the pockets of his jacket and pants, he muttered the question:

"You don't have kids, do you?"

"No."

"They get old enough so you can't just give them a time-out or take away their doll. And they don't listen to you anymore. You try to give them advice, but it's useless." He removed a tablet from his breast pocket and slid his finger across the screen to bring up his notes. He took the stylus and scrawled something, crossing his legs tight and pinching his lips. "I gotta say, it's some pretty weak tea bullshit of Jane to send you. I'm insulted she didn't at least come begging on her own."

"What do you mean?"

"Oh, you've both drank the Kool-Aid. You're political totems now."

"That's not how we see it."

"Then get your eyesight checked."

Dr. Pietrus has never been accused of tact. One learns not to take too much offense at his brusque demeanor, but in my opinion, he's been politicized into a rather rabid paranoia. I told him:

"I would think you'd be happy that the Randall administration views climate policy as its top priority and has brought in respected scientists to shape legislation."

"Hasan, don't be a dimwit. You won't have a fingerprint on this thing by the time it gets through. If it gets through."

"We're modeling the legislation in NOAA's IAM. We'll be able to present the politicians with firm evidence of how the legislation will affect processes."

"Right. Because politicians are always interested in sober evidence. Congress is just another neon-lit whorehouse." He set his tablet down, leaned back, and laced his fingers over his small belly. His shirt had a stain near the third button and another on his jacket. "I was thinking on the ride down here, part of the problem is that you guys come from the world of modeling. That's fine. I've done some myself. But it's all hypothetical to you. The models haven't kept pace with the chaos we're observing. The modeling community is always lagging behind the observed trends. And that's not to say you haven't done impressive stuff. You get a computer with ten petaflops and grid spacing at six to ten kilometers, and you'll turn some heads. But it doesn't matter outside of what's actually *happening*. You're playing video games, boss. Complex systems with multiple processes and feedbacks will always exhibit emergent behavior that will surprise you. Too many dynamical pathways linking cause and effect, which is why our hypotheses that get encouraged by the models tend to break down in the real world."

"Perhaps. But in your public advocacy, you display certainty. I don't believe in certainty. It makes for bad science."

"You've been giving denialists and slow-walkers ammunition for years, Hasan. And speaking of sloppy science, your models have been a disaster when it comes to soil respiration. Shifts in ecosystems are tilting to a net carbon loss."

"The models still don't agree on that."

"Fuck the models. You saw the numbers coming in from Greenland this summer. Surface melting and ocean warming at the intermediate depths is now in overdrive. Greenland and the Antarctic ice sheets are frying. Hell, the West Antarctic sheet alone, once that melts—global civilization is a complex entity extremely vulnerable to disruption. This isn't a pissant cold virus with a mortality rate a tick higher, this is nearly a million cubic miles of sea and glacier ice that'll spill. Even mild regional effects could have dire consequences for humanity's survival, and you're sitting there with all the concern of a happy baby in a fresh diaper."

"That's not the matter at hand, Tony. If industrial chemists had used bromine instead of chlorine in the development of CFCs, it would have eradicated the ozone layer within a few decades, probably leading to the collapse of most societies. It's only an accident of economies of scale that we avoided this. We do what we can with the information we have available. I'll remind you that the job of a scientist is to view the world empirically, even if the results are in occasional disagreement with our ideological preferences."

He smirked, nodding his head as if he'd anticipated this line of argument.

"Why am I here? Why did you and Jane make me truck three hours on a train to listen to this beshitted lecture?"

"Jane says the president wants your endorsement of the legislation. Or if you can't give us that, then at least neutrality."

"Are you kidding? I'm canceled! I have no say in anything! I lost my book contract, I got shuttled to an emeritus role at Yale. No one's listening to me."

"Jane seems to think you are one of the few people with the ability to detonate the policy if you speak out against it. Which, knowing you, I somewhat assume."

"You see this graffiti the so-called terrorists are putting up? Weathermen or 6Degrees—whatever they're called? 'You are not a neutral witness.' If it's a bad bill, I'm gonna say so—I promise you that."

"What would you have us do? If you were in our position?"

Dr. Pietrus laughed darkly at this question. "Are you kidding? I literally wrote the book on this."

I was growing impatient with him, and the feeling seemed mutual. "Those involved seem to think it's politically impossible to enact virtually any of your recommendations."

"And guess what, the biosphere doesn't give a shit about the craven vicissitudes of the American political system. You're pushing modest standards, which can all be eviscerated if the administration changes, when we need a two hundred dollar per metric ton tax rising twenty dollars a year, every year, *at minimum*. We need to phase out coal in the next two years. That means beginning to shut down plants by fiat and have the government nationalize all coal stocks. Preferably we'd buy fifty-one percent stakes in every major carbon producer and unwind them as rapidly as possible. We need to be commissioning five new nuclear reactors a year for the next twenty. Then we need to hammer the shit out of India and China until they're on board. The bottom line is no one really has any idea how rapidly we can decarbonize the global economy at this point, but we're going to have to find out."

It took many years for me to learn how to look people in the eye. Dr. Pietrus now drilled his into mine, and I reverted to a past self and cast my gaze down.

I said: "You have read the white paper then."

"Oh, I've read it."

"And your assessment."

"My assessment? You've got no carbon price, a toothless set of standards for buildings, vehicles, and the utility sector that, best case, will let business-as-usual roll on another ten years, money to ill-advisedly arm coastal real estate, and on top of it all, a tax cut? No one involved in this legislation appears to understand the gravity of the situation. If we'd enacted this forty years ago, yeah, sure, maybe the economy would have moved toward a less carbon-intensive path. But it's too late for that. We're going to be at two degrees by the end of the next decade, on our way to at least four and maybe even six. We need all hands on deck. We need to go to war. And this? This is a joke. So my assessment is that this plan falls under the category of Don't Even Fucking Bother."

With that, he stood, buttoned his jacket, and walked out the door.

Conclusion: At the end of all this, I remain optimistic about the chances of passing the legislation outlined in the white paper. The objections registered by Dr. Pietrus, my sister, Seth, and members of the political team—these all serve to underscore the complex nature of the endeavor. There is no legislation that will look ideal to every constituency. However, I agree with Ms. McCowen, who pointed out that a reduction in the income tax will make the bill just palatable enough to sell to the key moderate members of the Republican caucus. Whether Dr. Pietrus supports the bill or not, A Fierce Blue Fire and other environmental groups will be under too much pressure to let this effort fail. The same goes for the administration. I will conclude by sharing the preliminary results from NOAA's IAM about the modeled effects of the legislation: Currently the US is on course for a 33 percent reduction of carbon-equivalent emissions over 2005 levels by 2040. The bill would accelerate that to 41 percent, according to models. Without a carbon tariff, it will have little effect on global emissions and many carbon-intensive industries will relocate to other countries. A range of economic impacts could emerge. The models foresee carbon concentration rising to 550 ppm by midcentury with a range of adverse climatic effects possible, including but not limited to a sea level rise of seven to fifteen feet by 2100.

#HoldSlapdishAccountable

CONGRESSWOMAN TRACY AAMANZAIHOU DEFENDS CELC'S WILDCAT STRIKES

"Kobe is alive. This is not QAnon. This is real. He was made a Prime Marshal and is controlling events with his sentient supercomputer."

Years later, survivors of Hurricane Alberto continue to live out of their cars or in temporary shelters that no one is calling IDP camps.

New World Solidarity

3D printing has not changed weaponry as much as critics have feared. Basic assault rifles remain so cheap and accessible that black market, self-assembled weapons are scarcely worth the trouble. It is guided bullets that are a grave concern, because amateurs need never have practiced firing a shot.

China Executes Over 300 Dissidents:
State Department issues condemnation

SLAPDISH AND VIRTUAL REALITY WILL ALMOST CERTAINLY RESHAPE THE WORLD. CAN UNLIMITED CONNECTIVITY BRING HUMANITY TOGETHER?

"As they lick their wounds in a post-Hogan world, Loren Victor Love may well be the Democrats' savior: a gay military veteran and businessman who takes no guff, suffers no fools, and is easy on the eyes."

"The young, especially the men, have been neutered, spayed, defanged because as a society we lack belief. We have empty vessels like fame, feminism, money, and multiculturalism, but we have no belief. Belief delivers power and purpose. Lack of belief is at the root of your woes. It is why you are poor, unhappy, anxious, depressed, alcoholic, drug-addicted, and full of misery."

RANDALL VOWS CLIMATE LEGISLATION IN FIRST 100 DAYS

ⓍURITAS

RENAISSANCE MEDIA SURGES TO FOREFRONT

A white supremacist billionaire and his frightening new star, Jennifer Braden, have redefined the Far Right.

A GROUP OF PARENTS HAVE A MISSION TO END THE OFFENSIVE VR COMEDY DUO HENNY & DILLPICKLE

"I was raped by my commanding officer while serving our country in Saudi Arabia. I am not the only one. Over and over, our leaders have ignored the culture that makes this possible. Women need to know they are not safe if they join the military."

SLAPDISH MIRACLE ALLOWS VR USERS TO ATTEND '28 OLYMPICS

"Has a president's hair ever received more scrutiny? You would've thought she invaded Texas after she let her natural curls show."

"Why am I wearing it? Because they're the climate Robin Hood. They're the only people actually doing something about this. Why are you wearing that stupid fucking tie?"

"Run, do not walk. Sprint from all fossil-fuel energy stocks. This stuff, guys, this stuff, mark my words, is about to tank worse than the Harry Potter reboots."

ENVIGE ENERGY FILES FOR BANKRUPTCY, CITING LOSSES FROM ECO-TERRORISM ATTACKS

KATE MORRIS INVOLVED IN "THROUPLE," INDECENT SEX WITH LUCAS FRISK AS ENVIRO-SOCIALISTS DISMANTLE THEMSELVES

FORMER PRESIDENT HOGAN LASHES OUT AT REPORTS OF BLACK-SITE TORTURE

SCOTUS UPHOLDS LAW STRIPPING RIGHT TO VOTE FROM THOSE CONVICTED OF AIDING ILLEGALS

Israel's "semi-sentient" border wall with Gaza has in recent years undergone such rapid evolution that it may have developed its own prerogatives. The "auto-kill zone" surrounding the territory means that a computer algorithm has been responsible for the instantaneous trial and execution of over five hundred Palestinians. This technology is being deployed with even fewer safeguards in Kashmir and on India's border with Bangladesh.

TRANSCRIPT EXCERPT FROM *THE CONVERSATION* WITH ALANA AFZEL ON *NEW YORK TIMES* PODCASTS

Kate Morris Discusses Recent Controversies and Where Climate Legislation Now Stands

March 28, 2029

Alana Afzel   Today on *The Conversation*, we have a special guest, who needs, I'm guessing, very little introduction. From the trenches of the climate crisis, executive director of A Fierce Blue Fire, Kate Morris. Kate, how are you?

Kate Morris   Oh, ya know: the Dude abides.

Alana Afzel   [Laughter] Okay, I know you're short on time, so let's get straight to it. You're finding yourself in the middle of multiple controversies, but let's start with the big one. Explain to our listeners what has happened with the House bill, the so-called PRIRA legislation, why FBF nearly revolted, and what just passed the House of Representatives over the weekend.

Kate Morris   We threw a f—— fit.

Alana Afzel   Yes, explain the fit.

Kate Morris   We found ourselves in this bizarre position where our supposed allies were actually proposing something weaker than the Republican president. Democrats have basically convinced themselves that they will lose seats if they vote for any kind of price on carbon.

Alana Afzel   You're specifically talking about the shock collar?

Kate Morris   Yeah, that's right. The Dems want to spend money but they're nervous about trying to actually keep carbon in the ground. They don't want to use the best tools because they view those tools as making them politically vulnerable. So, what was being proposed in Congress was middling investments in renewables and frontline communities, but as we've seen, that doesn't get the job done with decarbonization, so we had to make it clear that this was not acceptable.

Alana Afzel   You don't think using regulations and standards can achieve the needed greenhouse gas reductions?

Kate Morris   Well, they could if given the chance, and any plan should include strong standards. The problem is Republicans and oilmen drag them into the courts, which can affect implementation. On top of that, the average American worker sees no benefit and has no skin in the game. The shock collar's rebate checks create a political constituency for decarbonization that will be extremely difficult, if not impossible, to dislodge. Then there's the global element. We've f—ed around with these nonbinding international accords like Paris for too long. This plan starts a race to the top, so if China is making high-carbon steel and Sweden is making incredibly efficient low-carbon steel, suddenly the Swedish steel is the cheap stuff. We build the largest economic bloc in the world and lock these countries, including ourselves, into this program of accelerated action. So in one policy, one bill, we can address global emissions, workers, and justice all at once. None of this is a panacea, but it's the best way of moving faster than f— in an emergency."

Alana Afzel   And that's the bill that your allies have muscled through in the House.

Kate Morris   Yeah, I mean, it's missing some stuff we'd like to see put back in. The tax starts at $30 a ton, and $3 trillion is not nearly enough in investment. Then there's a miserable chunk of money that goes to arming rich communities on the coasts, some insurance bailouts—look, it's not perfect, but the framework is there. Joy [LaFray] and Tracy [Aamanzaihou] have been key in getting Democrats in line, and now we're counting on Cy

Fitzpatrick to help push this over the finish line in the Senate. But we are as close to major action as we've ever been.

Alana Afzel   The bill has come under criticism from some environmental justice groups that say it fails to properly address racial and gender hierarchies.

Kate Morris   That's horse———. This is a frontal assault on chronic inequality. Folks are trying to hold climate policy hostage to single-payer health care and jobs guarantees and slavery reparations and police reform and other forms of social policy while our planet collapses. It's all backward. They're trying to put Band-Aids on a gunshot wound before we go in and get the bullet out. That's the climate crisis. Folks keep touting these reparations proposals that are deficit-financed conscience-laundering for affluent white liberals, and it pisses me off when those same people scoff at the tax-and-dividend plan. We are literally taking money from rich polluters and putting it in the pockets of working people as a foundational piece of a reparative project. It doesn't just offer the fiction of "Hey, here's a few bucks so you can build generational wealth, even though yours is the last generation to enjoy a functioning atmosphere." That would be a funny joke by white people, I guess.

Alana Afzel   Yes, but I think their point is you rarely comment on patriarchy or white power structures. That you're focused on technocratic solutions.

Kate Morris   Alana, girl, for real. If that's what people think, then they're not listening to me. That's all I comment on. Who I will work with—that's a different story. You think I don't get pissed when some conservative pol tells me all I care about is identity politics? I'm like, dude, if you were constantly reminded of your identity in every f——— interaction of your life, you'd probably form some opinions of it yourself. But none of this stuff is metaphysical. We are not interested in bettering this world into a woke ash heap. We are committed to taking capital, and therefore political power, out of the hands of a fossil-fuel oligarchy. That is the global recipe to attack a primary source of misogyny, racism, and endemic inequality. Distributed systems of energy will redistribute political and economic power faster and more decisively than any other action, period.

Alana Afzel   And your embrace of nuclear energy? Which is also in this bill? How's that for "distributed systems of power"?

Kate Morris   I embrace nuclear energy because I can do math. The coal-fired power plants set to come online in India and China alone—it's apocalypse. But those countries also need energy, particularly air-conditioning, because they're facing land temperatures that are killing people by the tens of thousands every year. Renewables won't provide that quickly enough, and the only way to square the circle is nuclear. Do we need to pay attention to the trade-offs involved? Absolutely. We can't put our heads in the sand even about the impacts of solar power and wind on ecosystems or mining waste. Trade-offs are inevitable because we are in deeply uncharted territory now.

Alana Afzel   Not to switch gears from, you know, the fate of the planet to gossip—but you've also been in the news lately for a different reason that has gotten you a lot of heat. Allegedly you were arrested in 2026 for an indecent act in a restaurant bathroom with the musician Lucas Frisk, who then bribed the arresting officers.

Kate Morris   That's an oldie but a goodie. Right-wing media dragged it back out, now joined by lefty internet trolls. It's the convergence of the hard right with left-wing cancel-mania, and yes, am I having a blast with all the slut-shaming. Great fun.

Alana Afzel   Did the incident happen?

Kate Morris   Well, I can neither confirm nor deny. I'll say three things: I'm still madly in love with my partner. We don't believe in monogamy. And this is clearly an awkward political hit job, so ultimately, I have no comment.

Alana Afzel   But do you understand why feminist writers have taken issue with this? You proudly speak about nonmonogamy and flaunt the freedom of your own sexuality while allying yourself with politicians who want to restrict abortion access and contraception. How has Mary Randall been on women's issues, for instance? She reinstated the global gag rule, and she's assured conservatives and the Christian Right that she will appoint yet another pro-life justice to the Supreme Court.

Kate Morris   These are acceptable trade-offs in a tactical war. We've been clear that we will make political accommodation with anyone who's committed to treating the biospheric crisis as the priority, and my personal life shouldn't play any role in that.

Alana Afzel   But there are groups you won't make accommodation with— for example, the one that's been blowing up oil pipelines.

Kate Morris   No. We categorically reject violence, even against property. These people think they're heroes, but they don't understand what they're opening the door to. The entire movement is now dealing with law enforcement scrutiny and harassment. Right-wing violence has never been worse, and these pipeline bombers—they will exacerbate that. They're endangering everything we're working for. On a more philosophically macro level, as soon as you pick up a brick, bat, or gun and tell yourself that this is the only way, then there is no end to what you will do.

Alana Afzel   It's interesting how malleable your philosophy seems. I read your honors thesis on ecofeminism, and that young woman sounded much more—I don't know—ecofeminist?

Kate Morris   Jesus, you are going to the bone, aren't you? There are undoubtedly components of ecofeminism I find compelling, just like there are components of Marx or Adam Smith or Heidegger I find compelling. But any earth-goddess-mother-hen squawking, no f—— thank you. I enjoy a grand vista as much as the next gal, but ultimately the solutions to our crisis are going to come from stuff like industrial carbon capture to produce building materials and hydrogen by electrolysis. We need the technocrats, scientists, wonks, and we need hard-headed women thinking about the built environment of our societies. As for what ecofeminism means to me, it's like— Ha, okay. You want a rant that will make Sean Hannity shit his tampon? The history of capital accumulation has also been a history of women's subordination and environmental degradation. Those three things are so intimately connected that you can't unwind them. Our current order was built on the enslavement of women who were treated as free, on-call labor in the home. Until recently, any woman who bucked this domesticated chattel system and displayed any economic or sexual autonomy was imprisoned, tortured, burned at the stake, drowned—before the term "witch hunt" was used exclusively by insecure, baby-dicked men.

Alana Afzel   You don't think that's still ongoing?

Kate Morris   Of course it's still ongoing! The institution of marriage still exists, doesn't it? Shit, man, we're a colonized gender, some of us just know how to get off with our preferred colonizing man better. What's happened to women, it seems to me—and I think Mies and Bennholdt-Thomsen got this exactly right—is that we are in the process of achieving the dream of all oppressed peoples: we're moving into the Master's house, when really what we should be doing is burning the house down. Instead, we're clamoring to be a part of the patriarchal, phallocentric political, economic, and social ecology. Look at the *Wonder Woman*–themed presidency of Joanna Hogan. This is what we define as a powerful, accomplished woman because she's cracked the capitalist patriarchy. But there has to be an "other" for that system to maintain because it sees a world of scarcity and the only solution is an inequitable hoarding of resources. Part of that "other" will always be women, and bitches are kidding ourselves if we think otherwise. If a system views everything in the biosphere as a resource, whether it's buffalo, maize, fresh water, a gas deposit, or our internet data, it's going to view women as extractive resources as well. [*Laughter*] Alana, c'mon, who the f—— is going to want to listen to this interview?

How to Stop
a Revolution
2029

I was visiting my mother when I got the call that we lost Procter & Gamble. It wasn't that this was worse than my father's passing, but when I got the news from Linda Holiday in Chicago, I felt a resurgence of that grief. P&G had been unhappy for some time. They were a generations-old institution suddenly caught up in an inexplicable fad that sneered at home bathroom products. You know those cosmetics we've been smearing on ourselves for more than a century? Turns out they're vile markers of hyper-consumption, poisoning our water, and one can get by just fine with a simple bar of soap. Profits go down for a few consecutive quarters, and the easiest, oddly ritualistic, sacrifice is the ad agency.

"Mom?" I came out of the bathroom. "Hey, I need to make a call for work. It'll just be a minute."

Mom sat at the kitchen table folding my dad's clothes before delicately packing each item in a garbage bag. It was all going to a secondhand shop in Anamosa. Though I'd forced her to get to his clothes during this trip, she'd failed to put a dent in the stacks of agricultural almanacs, magazines, and bulletins he'd compulsively hoarded in the den. *Today's Farmer, The Corn Producer*, and the Iowa Farm Bureau's *Spokesman*. Why he'd kept issues from the nineties was anyone's guess.

"Jack, do you think Erik will want Daddy's sweaters?" she asked. I couldn't see my brother wearing any sweater Dad had ever worn. He also lived in Florida, but pointing this out would only lead my mother to accuse me of being flip.

"You'll have to ask him."

On my way outside I passed through the modern quadrant of kitchen that Dad had built onto the side of the house, which had been in the family since 1902. Survivor of two tornadoes, according to family lore. Hanging on the peg by the door was his hunting vest, Mossy Oak camo, the pockets still bulging with shotgun shells. On another peg hung a wooden turkey call and duck-cloth bibs. His work boots neatly twinned on the shoe rack, covered in creamy streaks of last fall's dried mud.

On the porch, I dialed Gruber and walked farther into the backyard twilight so my voice wouldn't carry. I stared out over the eight hundred acres of corn and soy my father had been forced to sell as the profits in small plots dwindled. He would have had to grow the farm to an enormous size to compete with Cargill. "You farm small, you might as well take a vow of poverty," he'd muttered to Mom just before the sale that changed his life.

A foreign haze hung in the winter air. I thought of "walking the beans" with Erik and Allie. Dad would hand us machetes to hack away at weeds in the soybean rows, one of the only chores he ever made us do. Erik hated it. He hated everything about the farm.

"How you doing, Jackie?" asked Gruber, my art director. It was eerie. The voice tech on the new generation of phones made it sound like the person was standing next to you.

"We saw this coming. P&G thinks it can rebrand something that's more structural than they realize. Fine. Let them try."

"McClann is pretty pissed off," he said. "She thought we could hold on to them."

No matter how successful you got in this business, you were only measured by your most recent victory or defeat, and this implosion lay heaped at my feet. Maybe the "Live Simply" campaign had been defeatist and uninspired, as Beth had warned, but my specialty was steering into the skid, and that's what I'd done.

"All Beth needs to worry about is Thursday's pitch."

"Are you two even on speaking terms?"

The people with whom I wasn't on speaking terms were my brother and the man whose miscarriage I'd had the year before. Beth McClann and I were just competitive.

"We're fine. How's the art coming along?"

"We're ready. Beth doesn't like that you took two days off before this pitch."

"My mother's bereaved and my selfish siblings won't handle anything. Tell her I'll be good to go. I'm driving back first thing tomorrow."

"He'll be there, by the way."

"Who?"

"Who else? Wimpel. Dark Arts himself."

I hung up but stayed outside a moment, hugging myself in the chill. To the south, the three large grain bins that once stored the corn and soy no longer looked like skyscrapers as they had in my childhood. To the north were the two Morton sheds that held my dad's tools, equipment, his tractor and wagon. There'd been a barn that my great-grandfather built, but when I was in junior high it blew apart in a storm. An acrid smell hung in the air now. The remnants of a dust storm coming up from the plains, carrying a fog across Amber, Iowa. I thought of what Allie had told me: that Dad had been seeing the woman from church even at the end. She'd come to the hospital when my mother wasn't there.

When I returned to the house, my mom had CNN on, and I couldn't help but stop and watch, as the anchor reported on a once-famous actor who'd just legally changed his name.

The next day, on the plane from O'Hare to LaGuardia, I overheard two middle-aged women talking about the actor. I ordered a screwdriver and instead of scanning through content on the VR set, I listened to the two women. He's gone full cuckoo clock, they said.

I tried to think if I'd ever told anyone the story. Maybe Trish, before she moved to Naperville and our friendship dried up. I could picture us drinking wine in her last apartment in the city, her jaw on the floor when I divulged, but then it also had the tinge of an invented memory. Maybe I'd never told anyone.

Eventually, I put on headphones and opened the file on my AR glasses. I looked over the artwork and my notes. Stirring in my gut, the anticipation of the pitch at least distracted me from all the raucous hurt banging the walls for my attention. I messaged Gruber: *There's still too much green in here. Green's a dead brand.*

He wrote back, *The earth is not without shades of green to it.*

Darken it. A forest green. Not a limp "recycle more" green. Make that blue of the water pop.

When measuring grief, I'm always surprised by what lingers and what dissipates. That night I thought often of the actor—how his eyes had grown sad and wet in that violet bar—and occasionally about Procter & Gamble, and almost not at all about my father.

*

Everyone from our agency met an hour in advance in the creamy Manhattan lobby of Palacio-Wimpel to go over the game plan, and how to pivot if my "unorthodox approach," as McClann called it, bombed.

The way I saw it, our team felt fifty-fifty on this bid. Linda Holiday, our global chief creative officer, and Darnell Greene, our chief strategy officer, had backed my approach. McClann had fought it every step of the way, and seeing as how it was her account, this had produced a month of turbulence and backbiting in the office. Our CEO, Patrick Yeats, only a year into the job, had a consummate poker face. It was my first pitch with him in the room, and I couldn't read where his head was at. I'd come up in the company under Linda, a chain-smoking, twice-divorced munchkin spitfire who claimed she'd never actually had a good idea in all her years in advertising but knew how to spot secret artists when she saw them. We became close, and she mentored me to never think of the audience. Let the work speak.

"My question," said McClann, pointing to Gruber, "is do we keep him in the room?"

As expected, Gruber showed up to a meeting of professionals wearing a short-sleeve denim shirt buttoned to his neck. The tattoos coating his arms glowed darkly, and the word written across the right ridge of his jaw that looked almost like an odd birthmark: COLLIDE. Gruber had been my right hand for two years.

"He's my art director," I said. "This pitch wouldn't exist without him."

"These aren't the kind of clients who want to see Post Malone," said Darnell.

"It's meeting theater," I explained. "Part of the client problem is generational. Gruber represents the demographic that grew up not trusting them."

"*You're* the meeting theater," said Yeats. "A young, attractive woman who calls to mind a kind of . . ." he spun his hands around in the air, not in a hurry to get to his point, "Kate Morris for the rational set."

"She Who Must Not Be Named," said Darnell, and he laughed at his own joke.

The debate went around for a bit. Finally, I interrupted Beth McClann to say, "Gruber stays. I need him in case there are questions about the art."

McClann glared at me. Over the years, you learn to say things in such a way that people stop arguing with you.

*

These corporate boardrooms always gave off a sense of desperation. They are spaces meant to demonstrate wealth and control, but no matter how historic the client, the room and the people in it are ephemeral, trying to hold on to the market share that allows them the skylight and high-end seating. This particular boardroom required a long, supervised walk through the tight security of Palacio-Wimpel, the PR firm specializing in crisis management. Then it was our choice of bottled water or coffee and a tray of fruit and pastries that no one touched. The Sustainable Future Coalition was an unprecedented black box of money that counted among its members the National Association of Manufacturers, the Aluminum Association, GM, Ford, four agribusiness firms, several railroad companies, a dozen electric utilities, fifteen major real estate developers, three private security and logistics firms, including the behemoths of the field, Sentry and Xuritas, and every major player in the oil, coal, and gas sectors, from primary energy developers to the associated industries that serviced exploration and transportation of fuels. We shook hands with several junior-level railbirds, two middle-aged men, a tight-lipped Asian woman, and the president of the SFC, former Exxon chief Tom Duncan-Michaels. They were led into the room and shown around the table by Dark Arts himself. Though I'd seen him before in some of our HoloChat meetings, in person Fred Wimpel reminded me of the actor. They had the same kind of faux-rugged handsomeness that was likely more the product of fighting off middle age through Botox and light plastic surgery than it was honest weathering. He wore a short brown beard streaked with gray. Despite his and his firm's reputation, he didn't demand attention in the pre-meeting scrum of handshakes. When he reached me, he put his hand on my elbow. "I'm a big fan of your work." His voice was unexpectedly high and melodic for a man I was certain had Sun Tzu on his office bookshelf. "I've been showing Tom and Emii what *Sine qua non* did for Adidas. Not to mention your work for the Pentagon. Beyond impressive."

I smiled. Like any artist, I viewed past hits with some amount of embarrassment.

"Keep an open mind about this one," I said, and I liked the expression he gave me: reassurance, confidence, with a skewed smile that seemed to acknowledge what a grand, fine joke this all was. As if he knew the only people who actually believed in the power of public relations and advertising were the troubled boardrooms that thought it could save their skin. One had to play into the myth of the fixer. The puppeteer. Merlin.

Yeats began the meeting by introducing our team, his fingers twiddling;
Beth McClann then took center stage, sucking the presentation into the vortex of her rigid bearing. She sat in every chair with her legs crossed, hands
clasped, hair wound into a bun so tight it straightened her posture.

"Though what we will outline for you is an all-of-the-above strategy,"
said Beth, "we want to highlight the 'persuadable special public' or the 'persuadable middle.' Now that the House has passed legislation, the persuadable middle has crossed the Rubicon, and you and your clients cannot waste
another day. This is happening. And while your lobbyists will attempt to
introduce every rider and poison pill on the menu, what you need more
than anything is an open revolt of public opinion. Without further ado . . ."

Gruber activated the 3D projector, and it cast the image of a hipster
hoverboarding into a glass door, coffee splattering across his shirt as he
sprawled onto his butt. Genuine laughter. This corporate meme of starting
high-pressure meetings with a gag projection had gotten a little rote for my
taste, but the room liked it.

I smiled at the clients, looking each of them in the eye. Through the windows, the evening light was burning away. New York's cityscape lay beyond,
winking to life.

"There's bad news," I said. "There's more bad news. And finally, there's
desperate news—where should I begin?"

Mild laughter. The Asian woman, Emii, didn't so much as smirk, and I
suspected she might be a secret fulcrum of power within the client.

"Your organization sees what's coming. Perhaps at some point you harbored fantasies that a Randall administration wouldn't pursue legislation
to restrict greenhouse emissions. When A Fierce Blue Fire and the Clean
Energy Labor Coalition remained neutral during the early stages of the
election that should have raised a red flag. When FBF endorsed Randall at
the last second, well, they bet on her, and they bet on transformative policy. Let's just say there are now quite a few members of Congress who are
risking their careers if they vote against this legislation. Furthering the bad
news, what you'll be facing will not be a reasonable cap-and-trade scheme,
but a law that could be further-reaching and more invasive than anything
American business has seen since the New Deal. In other words, you're right
to be worried."

Wimpel rested his chin in the ninety-degree angle of his thumb and
index finger. The glowing projector cycled through images of pipeline

protestors and oil-soaked birds. A man with dreadlocks and a septum piercing marched across the table pumping his fist.

"Your coal, oil, and gas members have long been suffering from deep reputational crises. They're the supervillains of public opinion, and others, such as the utilities and agricultural producers, are feeling the heat as well. Make no mistake, we cannot misdiagnose this as a 'communications problem.' This threat is structural, and we cannot do much to change that structure. Oil companies profit from selling oil. And now their conventionally weaker adversaries suddenly have enhanced influence. Ben."

Gruber tapped for the next hologram. The room faced the miniaturized image of an earthy woman standing on the boardroom table, arms crossed, blue flames burning behind her.

"Morris and FBF are the culmination of a long trend in which credible, law-abiding institutions have become vulnerable to an agenda-driven, organic disruption. Morris has become such a force so quickly, she almost counts as a conventional power herself now. Her ruthless attacks on your members, her tactical acumen politically, her attractiveness as a spokesperson and cultural figure—all this has shifted the political economy. Coupled with the surprisingly effective advocacy of the CELC"—the image switched to Tracy Aamanzaihou in all her frumpy, jowly glory, forming a picket line with other workers—"not to mention a series of weather-related disasters that can be easily scapegoated . . ." Images of people scrambling out of the ruins of Hurricane Alberto, of homes burned to the ground in California, of a flood ripping buildings from their foundations and carrying them downriver. The 3D projector fritzed on the image of a weeping Black woman standing waist-deep in water, trying to lift her child to a man in a helicopter. Finally, scenes from the massive Thanksgiving dust storm of 2028 rolling east, blanketing cities, in this case Pittsburgh and fans looking up in Heinz Field as the football team exited the stadium under a red-brown blizzard. "Suddenly what seemed impossible just a few years ago now seems likely."

Duncan-Michaels, the oil tycoon with a stye on the ridge of his eyelid, took a sip of bottled water, and some of it dribbled onto his chin and then his tie. Gruber's eyes were sleepy slits that never blinked. He looked bored and Gen Z, which was what I'd wanted.

"The response from industry has been familiar, straight from the playbook: Use backdoor groups to continue casting doubt on the science, question the cost of taking action, debate the motives of those demanding action while facing outward with a pro-environmental agenda. The disutility of denialism was revealed by Russ Mackowski's presidential bid. The conversation has changed, and you must change with it."

Yeats coughed.

"Never once has climate been a first-tier campaign issue. Yet in the past election it sometimes felt as if it was the only thing anyone was talking about. Impassioning hard-core resistance will be a given, but it's that persuadable middle this campaign must rally. We've spent two months analyzing strategies in four test markets: Chattanooga, Champaign-Urbana, Flagstaff, and Columbus. I'll tell you what we found: People like Kate Morris. They like her message, her optimism, her spirit, her bluntness. Most of all, they like that this attractive young wildwoman worked to help elect a moderate Republican administration that seems to want to do something about this issue. Where does that leave us? I'm sure some of our competitors have told you that you need to reposition this choice as being about freedom. Keep the heavy hand of government away from my SUV, et cetera. Well, my father had this expression: 'Kid, that dog won't hunt.'"

McClann had her lips pursed in an excruciating pucker. She looked like she was watching her cat burn to death but had been told if she intervened, her other cat would get it as well.

"What is the alternative? The key is for you and your members to charge the problem head on."

At this cue, Gruber flipped to an image of young, diverse workers erecting carbon capture devices.

"For a public that has stopped trusting these companies, you must now say . . ."

I read the caption aloud as it floated in misty block letters on the table.

"*We are faced with a challenge unlike anything in the history of the human race.*"

An image of Obama at his inauguration. The next, of children planting trees in a barren landscape.

"*We are told calamity will be impossible to prevent.*"

An image of doctors and nurses administering to patients during the Covid-19 pandemic, followed by another of wind farms and solar panels.

"*We are told there is no hope.*"

An image of a coastal town laid waste by a hurricane and a family in silver foil blankets, a woman weeping upon finding her home burned down to the foundation.

"*We say: Not on our watch.*"

Gruber ripped through the rest of the 3D slides: forests, oceans, mountains, Black Lives Matter protests, hard-hat workers erecting wind turbines and lowering solar panels onto roofs, a majestic humpback whale, a multicultural cast of students working diligently in labs, a woman carrying a sign that says WE DEMAND A FUTURE and a face mask that reads HOPE, followed by a coal plant with the words CARBON CAPTURE FACILITY.

"From scientists to teachers, engineers to urban planners, students to community organizers, we are coming together to face the incredible challenge of climate change. Joined by millions of activists across the country, the Sustainable Future Coalition is an unprecedented collaboration of over one hundred major American companies pursuing one goal: the transformation of the American economy to a zero-carbon future. Together, we can win the battle against climate change and ensure generations of Americans a brighter, healthier, happier future. We are stronger together. And together we are the Green New Deal."

Beneath WE ARE THE GREEN NEW DEAL, spaceship Earth spun against the black tapestry of space.

I waited in case anyone felt like applauding. They did not.

"The message," I went on, as if I'd always planned to explain, "is one of inclusiveness, of working together against impossible odds. The heuristic is that industry is not just embracing the Green New Deal—you *are* the Green New Deal."

I felt myself wanting to ramble, to add one weak, pleading explanation, but Linda's gaze kept me straight: *Stop punching, the bell has rung.* I closed my jaw with a smile. A phone buzzed in someone's pocket.

"The approach is strategic accommodation," said Darnell, cracking the silence. "But it's also bold—"

"Oh, it's bold all right," said Duncan-Michaels. He looked to his team. "I'm not going to lie, I have a lot of skepticism about this approach." The minions nodded. My stomach fell.

"My first thought," said a man with hair so white, it glowed a powdery blue, "is that this is very similar to what BP tried decades ago with 'Beyond Petroleum.' At the end of the day, no one bought the rebrand for a second. Then they dumped two hundred million gallons of oil into the Gulf of Mexico."

"I have to push back against that," said Linda. "This is more than greenwashing. Polling tells us this message resonates and that people are less likely to support Randall's legislation if they believe industry—"

"Green New Deal? Why in the hell," Duncan-Michaels slapped the table, "are we reanimating that goddamn term? We killed 'Green New Deal' deader than a doornail. We hung so much baggage around that watermelon bullshit it immolated on its own, so why are we trying to claim it now?"

"Because," said McClann, her voice eking between her teeth, "that term was once the vanguard of the climate movement. It's now been supplanted by a more complicated notion, this Climate X thing that Morris can never actually explain, which makes it difficult to get lead on the target. Resurrecting the Green New Deal on *our terms* means we can co-opt the political center while inflaming the passions of the Right and hard Left."

I found myself speaking. "Our aim is not to rebrand any particular company but to create a compelling case for your members to maintain the social license to operate."

"We shouldn't have to *beg* for the social license," said Emii, her voice and face passionless. "There is no economy without our members. What about expanded Arctic drilling? The new energy horizons? You haven't addressed that."

"You're on defense right now," said McClann. "Once we get the ball back, we can go on offense again."

"Why not stick with what works? That this stuff is all watermelon bullshit?" Duncan-Michaels repeated. "Green on the outside, red on the inside. It's the Left cramming a socialist agenda down our throats."

"Because that argument has no weight," I said patiently. "A plurality of young voters under thirty-five are happy to identify themselves as socialists now."

Emii absently tugged at a tight black braid, pulling it over her shoulder and fiddling with the tip. She exchanged a glance with Duncan-Michaels. He said, "And what do we do when SFC members don't want to endorse the goddamned Green New Deal?"

I couldn't keep the annoyance from my voice. "The Green New Deal will be whatever we say it is. This includes solar radiation management and other geoengineering techniques that, according to studies, could allow your members to continue exploiting their reserves well into the twenty-second century. There are sub-strategies as well. You get on board with renewable deployment as panacea and shift the attention and passion to environmental justice by highlighting diverse hiring practices in minority communities. The polling on this is impressive."

"We want a candidate, a spokesperson," said Emii, ignoring everything I'd said. "Someone beyond the political arena to advocate for a carbon-fueled future."

"But that's not what you need," I protested, hearing the wheedling in my own voice. "You have the Mackowskis and conservative media making that argument already. You need *this* new angle."

I could feel the meeting growing combative. The client hated the pitch, and they weren't even being polite about it.

"Yes, but this means we're admitting *that it's real*." Duncan-Michaels brought his hand down on the table in a karate chop, and with each phrase chopped again. "That has always been our last line of defense, and then it's only a matter of time before we have nowhere left to retreat."

"I'm sorry," I said, feeling the room's gaze as my tone gained a blade. "Why are we even here then? Did you want us to tell you that all will be well if you just keep running ads extolling the virtues of algae fuels? You're look-ing at the birth of a revolution."

"But we don't want to simply delay the birth," said Emii, each word car-rying the bite of a snapping turtle. "We want to strangle it in the womb. By the time we're through, we want this issue to be a political albatross so heavy, no one ever tries it again. And if that means cratering the Randall administration, so be it."

"I'm sick of these fucking rope-a-dope strategies." Duncan-Michaels blinked hard, and I could almost imagine the wet sound the stye made as it slid across his eyeball. "We built this fucking world, and now these ungrate-ful idiots want to dismantle it, and you want to hand them that ammunition."

Fred Wimpel, who sat to Duncan-Michaels's left, placed his hands flat on the table. "If I may." Everyone in the room turned to him. He looked me in the eye. "This is excellent work, Ms. Shipman. I want to make that clear. And I know it's good"—he looked at his clients, specifically Emii—"because it makes you all uncomfortable. Ms. Shipman's correct, I'm sorry to say. Your members had no idea how dangerous this new iteration of the climate movement really was until last year, and you've been caught flat-footed. Those other multinational advertising conglomerates want to sell you what you want to hear. Safe ideas that won't get anyone fired."

As he spoke, I felt the thrill of the embattled boxer striking back.

Yeats was nodding along. He pointed two thumbs at his chest. "And hey, not all multinational advertising conglomerates are so bad."

There was tepid laughter. Duncan-Michaels, Emii, and the minions looked like they knew they were about to eat their own intestines.

*

At the hotel bar, Gruber ordered our drinks. Yeats had gone home to his penthouse and Darnell left to catch his flight back to Chicago. The rest of us were out the next morning.

"We're either fucked or we got it with that meeting alone," Linda decided.

McClann looked at me. "You were good, Jackie." I felt a bit of the tension between us that had built over the last six months deflate.

"We'll see," I said. "If even a few of their members have doubts we'll be dead in the water."

"Yeah, but the more I think about it," said Linda, "the more I take Wimpel's point. They've probably met with four or five other agencies, and I'm sure they're all saying play it safe."

Gruber returned to the table with overpriced cocktails. We cheersed and practically chugged our first drinks. By the second, Linda was saying, "C'mon, doesn't good ole Duncan-Michaels just look like a guy who jets off to Thailand to buy child prostitutes?"

We laughed, ridiculed the minions, drank more, and ate a dinner of appetizers. I watched to see if Gruber would get on his phone, possibly to scan the hookup apps for local tail, but he remained with the old ladies. Around nine o'clock, Linda announced she had to call her husband and get some sleep. McClann seconded the motion and came around the table to hug me. "Great freaking job, Jackie." And she lowered her voice to say, "And I'm so sorry about everything you're going through with losing your dad."

"Thank you, Mac," I told her, feeling a genuine affection that wasn't entirely the alcohol. They both tottered toward the elevators.

Gruber ordered us each another drink, then the bill. When he tried to pay for it, I snatched his card away and inserted my own. "You don't make half my salary." He smiled, held his drink lazily in two fingers, one of which had a tattoo of the Star of David on the knuckle.

"Would you want to come up for one more drink?" he asked.

I was tipsy and still buzzed on the energy I'd summoned for the pitch.

"That's probably not the best idea," I said.

He nodded. "Will it be a good idea ever again, you think?"

"You're fifteen years younger than me. And my employee. So I'm going to say probably not."

"Yeah, but fifteen years is . . ." he flipped a hand. "I'm roughed up from alcohol and occasional intravenous drug use. You still look younger than me." He waved this away. "I'm just saying if all you want is the night, all it has to be is the night."

Vines crawled up his forearm onto his shoulder. I thought about the red-and-black knife sheathed into the muscle below his groin and the exploding galaxy on his chest. His sleepy eyes watched me.

"I'm going to bed," I said.

We went to the elevator, and he got off on his floor, and I got off on mine. I cracked open the minibar, mixed whiskey with ginger ale, and fumed that the room didn't have a VR set. I had to settle for old-fashioned television.

When my phone buzzed on the nightstand, I expected to see Gruber's name. But it was a new number.

Hi, it's Fred. Wondering if you had time to grab a drink or a bite? Talk about the pitch?

I was drunk. My fingers dashed across the glass, and I hit Send before I had a chance to question myself.

In for the night. Want to come by my room?

It wasn't that I invited Fred Wimpel with any intention, but his text told me something. I'd felt it in how he shook my hand when we parted ways after the pitch. A subterranean attraction that tugs at both people simultaneously. Each of them searching for an excuse to act on it.

I mixed him a vodka tonic, and he sat at the desk chair while I perched on the bed. We at least had the pretense of talking business.

"He didn't like you," he said, referring to Duncan-Michaels.

"I gathered."

"These guys, they're real retrograde. They still think they can sell doubt. They don't understand they're about to lose that game the way tobacco did in the nineties. All at once." He sipped, bringing the drink to thin, pale lips framed by his beard. "But Emii Li Song, she's a secret advocate of the plan."

"It didn't seem like it."

"It's her strategy for handling the Coalition's more intractable members. To be blunt, I can talk them into your firm, but you've gotta come up with, I dunno, a Kate Morris vaccine. They want a strategy for her."

This issue had not come up in the meeting, but I'd been preparing for it for months. There was a recent interview with her addressing the House bill and the Lucas Frisk story, and I'd listened to it over and over. Morris was compelling, confident, and brash, and in that combination, I saw weaknesses she likely didn't think she had. I crossed my leg over my knee and tugged at the hem of my skirt.

"Everyone's trying to get at her from the right. She's too savvy. The way at her is to steer into the skid."

"What does that mean?"

I felt him hanging on my words, and I liked it. "When I won the Cannes Lion for *Sine qua non* . . ." I laughed. "Sorry. What a braggy way to start. But when I won that, it was just a nice idea that got lucky. Adidas was never going to beat Nike at anything because Nike was the indispensable athletic brand. But you marry a charitable campaign to an advertising strategy, and you create a movement. Get shoes to every child in the world. Troubling images of African kids trekking miles for water in bare feet. Adidas could raise prices, sell more shoes, and make sure that growing markets in the developing world would be wearing Adidas, not Nike."

"I guess I don't see your point."

"Adidas wasn't in a crisis. We just summoned an emotional narrative in people. And that's crucial. It doesn't matter how many think pieces are written about the conditions in Adidas factories in some of those same countries. Nobody cares about Bangladeshi sweatshops when they feel like they can be doing some good with their shoe purchase. Intellectually, they might know it's bullshit, but emotionally they connect."

"Same thing with the army campaign?"

When a pretty young Texan named Brandy Squires published a piece about her repeated rape by her commander while she served in Saudi Arabia, suddenly military women began pouring into the public sphere, and each story was more horrific than the last. Women's enlistment fell off a cliff. It wasn't like it was any secret the military had a huge sexual assault problem, but then it emerged just how hard the Pentagon worked to keep those stories out of the media and cover the tracks of abusers. Reputational fires began with representative stories or images—a spark like Brandy Squires.

"The armed services people we dealt with were the same kind of skeptical," I said, pointing to the door as if Emii and Duncan-Michaels were standing in the hall. "But you steer into the skid. You put images of suffragettes, Rosa Parks, Jo Hogan, and yeah, you put the image of Brandy Squires testifying before Congress."

The ad's music and voice-over swelled pleasantly in memory. *Progress has never been easy. That's why the story of history is the story of women who fought. For their rights, for their families, for their humanity, for their country.*

"If you're the army, you're not admitting guilt, you're not admitting to the cover-up. You're saying, Yeah, ladies, we're with you. And by the way, we're looking for tough-as-nails bitches to go fight for our freedom around the world."

Wimpel swirled his drink. Moisture beaded on the glass, and a drop broke free and fell to the carpet.

"So what's the equivalent with A Fierce Blue Fire?"

"First, attack Morris from the left. I assume you'll be bringing much of this fight to the shadows? Stir up dust with her allies first. Any hard-left movement is susceptible to purity attacks. If you spend a handful of dollars creating the sense that she is not pure, that she's ignoring queer Latinx voices or silencing frontline communities or marginalizing this group or that group, they'll turn on her. Stoke proxies that call her a sellout doing the bidding of the nuclear industry. That's a huge wedge in their movement. Find a way to discredit her in the eyes of her fans and turn her greatest asset into a liability."

"Nobody can destroy a lefty movement like lefties themselves."

"They can't help it. They love eating their own. Next, get into her personal life, but be careful. It has to reach the public eye by accident. You can't slime her outright, but she proudly talks about her open relationship. There are opportunities in that."

He nodded. "No, I know, but that's been tough. She's been bulletproof. You and I should stay away from talking about this, but whatever can be dredged up about her allies in Congress will be dredged. Although," he smirked, "from what I hear, Joy LaFray has some serious kompromat lying around, and her ego won't let her not put the name LaFray on this bill . . ."

"Well, all of that takes a back seat to the most vital element anyway."

"Which is?"

"The word 'terrorism' is the most powerful marketing tool of the twenty-first century. It doesn't matter that Morris keeps disavowing these people blowing up oil pipelines and gas pads, you have to make her do it again and again and again every time she's near a microphone. See if she can swim with that shackle on her ankle."

"You have a lot of swagger."

I gave one shoulder a twitch of an uncaring shrug. "Maybe. Female recruitment reached record levels by the time I was done with the Pentagon's ad campaign. But who knows?"

I liked drunk bragging. I didn't do it enough when I was sober. The sounds of New York traffic penetrated the hotel walls and called to mind a river of whispers. "Dim lights." The room responded by lowering the lights. I reclined, arching my back to stretch. "Was that too cheesy, too forward, or both?"

He twisted his wedding ring. "You should know my wife and I are separated right now."

"I don't really care about that." And I didn't. "We're all adults."

He let out a troubled, excited breath and set the drink on the desk. As he walked over, I slid my hands up my skirt and pulled my underwear off. I put one foot on his chest and the other on his belt and guided him down to his knees. We didn't fall asleep until dawn, and I had to reschedule my flight.

*

My father never went to the doctor; he distrusted the entire profession. It was an untreated kidney infection, a pain in his lower back he refused to believe was anything, which in turn led to sepsis. By the time I got to the hospital in Anamosa, he was in a coma, unresponsive to antibiotics. And then gone. Allie and her husband, Burt, were already there, Burt doing his doctor routine, nodding gravely and knowingly at the diagnoses of the brothers of his medical fraternity.

My dad had been allergic to cats. Even though we had dogs my entire childhood, only once, when I was ten, did he allow me to adopt a stray mama cat. "As long as she's an outdoor cat," he'd said. I found her later under the chicken coop where she'd given birth to about ten kittens. For the two weeks we had all of them, I thought life couldn't get any better. Then he made me give away all but one, and I told him I'd never forgive him. Each night I sat sullen and refused to speak to him. He just ate his dinner. A few days into this act, he called me into the kitchen.

"Jackie-O!" I thought about ignoring him but there was too much excitement in his voice. He hoisted me up to the kitchen window above the sink. "Look at this." Outside in the mist, there was a doe no bigger than a Labrador sniffing around my new kitten, who I'd named Britney. Britney batted her paws around the young doe's face, and the doe seemed to love it. We watched them circle each other in a bed of ocher leaves. Finally, Britney's mama cat came darting out from under the house, and the doe took off, back to her own mother, galloping through our ghostly autumn field.

"That was something, huh?" said my dad. "I couldn't tell if Britney wanted to be a deer or the deer was hoping to become a kitten." He had a mole where the bridge of his nose met the bone of his eye socket. He called it "Little Mike" and it looked like a head of broccoli in Mom's garden.

"Maybe a little of both," I said, and I knew our fight was over when he laughed at this. I loved when he laughed. He didn't do it very often, and, I liked to think, only at my quips. The sound made me love him.

When I returned to Amber that Friday evening, I found my mom sitting in the living room with the family photo albums spread on the coffee table in front of her. They ran from my parents' wedding all the way to Allie's graduation and then abruptly stopped, demarcating the cultural moment when most photography moved online. There were fast-food bags crumpled around the room. I'd never before known my mother to eat fast food.

"She's depressed," Allie said when I'd called her on the drive. "She needs people around."

"Aren't you and Burt the ones who live in the state?" I shot back. "It's a four-hour drive for me, and you know, I sort of have a career I'd like to not toilet."

"Jackie. I'm so sick of that argument. You know how much time I spend going up there? I'm doing it all. Who arranged everything for the funeral and the will?"

She was right, and she also wasn't. Erik was as absent as he could manage. He'd flown back for the funeral and once more to stay with Mom for a weekend, but it was the most he'd been home in three years. Since Dad's death, Mom wouldn't shop for herself. She wouldn't see a doctor. She wouldn't leave the house except for church, which she was attending four or five days a week.

I regarded Mom now. She'd been gaining weight for a few years, becoming more sedentary with each passing trauma. She had a swollen look to her eyes and the skin of her face was pale and loose. She moved like every step shot daggers into her hip. I asked if maybe she'd like to get back to gardening this summer.

She hummed and watched a fly trapped between the windowpane and the screen. "I suppose I will. I'll have to go get some supplies. Haven't given much thought to it since Daddy got sick."

She was in the habit of repeating stories I obviously knew. The fly buzzed its panic.

"Why don't we go now?" I suggested. "The Walmart will still be open."

She did not appear to want to do this, but I coaxed her along. In the car, I asked if she thought she might come visit me in Chicago soon. "We can do a girls-night-out type thing." Whenever my parents visited me over the years, it did not escape my attention the way my mom seemed to shrink from every sound of the city. She hated the motion of the train, and even escalators gave her pause. My ex, Jefferey, used to chatter with her on the L because he could see how unnerved she was by every young Black or brown male passenger.

"Will I meet anyone?" she asked.

"Anyone like who?"

That Midwestern look of disapproval. It was all in the absence of any outward sign of disapproval. "Anyone you might marry."

"Unlikely, Mom." The encounter with Fred was already draining away, as though it had never happened. The way I had come to like it.

"Hmmm." She was quiet for a moment. "You've really disappointed me," she said.

My skin went numb with the brutality of those words. "Excuse me?" She stared out the window and said nothing. "What does that mean?"

"Never mind," she muttered.

I took a breath.

"So how long did you know Dad was seeing that woman? Do I use that to accuse you? No. I don't. Because it's not my friggin' business, Mom. I don't judge you about that." This barely felt cruel. Because what I really wanted to say was, *Fuck you, you numb, grieving cow*. How insular and pathetic my parents seemed to me now. My father stepping out on his wife and ignoring a kidney infection until it was too late and my mother still going to the church where he met his mistress. How utterly false my entire childhood felt.

Mom didn't speak to me again until we were in the gardening section of the Walmart superstore. Pointing to the soil choices, she finally said, "Get the Miracle-Gro, but just the gardening soil, not the Organic Choice. Organic's just a marketing scam they made up to tack a couple dollars to the price."

*

Driving east on 80, one of the most familiar stretches of highway in my life, fuming about my mother, I was struck by the landscape. What I'd loved as a girl now filled me with a sense of desolation: the yawning expanses of corn and soy in every direction, interrupted occasionally by an evergreen shelter-belt or a cropping of maples and oaks, the repeating farmhouses and grain elevators battered by prairie winds, the scent of cut grass, pavement, and pig shit, that particular manure stench that was never far from the back of one's nostrils. It began well before Dad's death, this quiet revulsion at the bucolic, at the chopped and spliced lands for which he'd had bottomless loyalty.

While I was listening to that one Kate Morris interview for possibly the tenth time, my Tesla interrupted to read me a text from Linda Holiday: "We got the account."

Back in the office that Monday, Darnell, Linda, Beth, and I sat around a linkup of Yeats beaming in from New York.

"I wanted to congratulate all of you on this. Beth and Jackie, especially. You two brought this home, and let me tell you: I think it's going to have a cascading effect. Fred Wimpel is already advising several of the member companies and trade groups to move their accounts to us. We're talking top oil and gas, Xuritas, aluminum, and even huge, huge fish like GM and Ford are going to take meetings. They want to coordinate this message across social media, TV, whatever's left of print—everything."

"It's wild," said Linda. "We're talking potentially hundreds of millions of dollars of new business."

McClann looked happy but humbled. All the weeks she'd fought me on this, all the passive-aggressive emails and worried, constipated looks when she didn't like my direction. All obliterated by this news.

"You ready, Don Draper?" Yeats asked me. "You just wrangled us an asteroid made of money."

Like that, my mom's cruelty was forgotten. My head swam with what I'd do with this artist's heyday. For me, creativity has always come from a place of opportunity. It's what electrified me about advertising—there was simply no purer rush in all of business. Every client has a problem, and you must solve that problem in color, light, sound, and suggestion. Everyone now spoke of the algorithms of persuasion, and yes, we had those tools. But at the end of the day, the job came down to crafting a narrative that would win out over Kate Morris and her ilk. I'd just been handed the keys to one of the largest, most expensive campaigns of the century. It was the chance to charge into the fray, shape the American consciousness, and make my name in this business for a generation.

"Forget the nudge tactics for now. We want images of abundance, symbols of health and well-being," I told my team in a conference room. Gruber twiddled a pen on a pad and favored me with his punk smile. Two of my favorite copywriters, Michelle and Sophie, who looked like little blond twins and wore their hair in the bouffant sixties style that was suddenly in, gazed at me with wide eyes. Sophie had once confessed, "I've been looking for a mentor my whole life, and I just really want it to be you. You're the reason I came to work here."

"Abundance is not just economic, though," I told them. "It's the natural world, and we want that imagery suffusing the campaign. Yes, this is industry declaring itself reformed, that it's all in for the future—"

"Oh!" said Sophie, perking up. "That's not a bad tag!"

Everyone laughed. "And they say we're all failed novelists and art school rejects!" My mom might as well have lived on another planet. Procter & Gamble might as well have been an ex-boyfriend from another lifetime. "But we also want images of aliveness," I went on. "Of people expressing almost a subversive joy."

"Sort of that carnivalesque attitude," said Gruber. "We can save the world in a sex, drugs, and rock 'n' roll way."

"Exactly," I said. "People living vital, rebellious lives and becoming a part of this transformation."

We stayed until midnight, ordering pizza and filling up dozens of e-board screens with our brainstorming. My team could sense the energy that had dimmed in recent months and left me cold and snapping at their efforts abruptly renewed. Now they were all too happy to shovel fuel on the blaze.

*

Fred's text landed two days later. *Congratulations.* I teased him about getting the job after sleeping with him (*Coincidence?*). Still, when he asked me if I was free on the weekend, that he would be in Chicago to meet with a client, I hesitated. Sleeping with a married man was one thing—all the premium shows were teaching us that open relationships and polyamory were no longer taboo, after all. But twice would mean we were having an affair. Twice would mean I'd probably spend the night in his hotel. Maybe even the one downtown, where long ago I'd followed an actor to his room.

Ultimately, I decided against it. Told him I had plans.

In my condo, I'd turned the master bedroom into my workspace while I did my sleeping in the guest room. I wanted to spend the weekend with storyboards, tags, and ad proposals. I only left for runs and yoga. The older I got, the more addicted I became to my exercise routine. Part of that might have been the vanity that accelerated with age, especially if one was still single.

That Saturday, I got back from a run. I drank a glass of water and ate a yogurt with my tablet on my thigh. The blue Earth spun, half in and half out of darkness. Lights winked on as the hemispheres changed from day to night. Translucent type floated across the screen. WE ARE THE GREEN NEW DEAL.

Not there yet. I drew arrows to elements I wanted to highlight, typed a few notes, and sent them back to the crew. I needed a break, so I got a glass of wine, slipped on my VR set, and found myself scanning through news of the actor's full-blown career change.

Of course, I'd followed him over the years from afar ever since I left his hotel without giving him my number or even telling him my last name. I'd even gone to a few of his movies before he kept putting his foot in his mouth. His films were increasingly downgraded to the far reaches of cut-rate streaming services. His roles dried up, and he couldn't appear in an interview without blaming diversity politics. Now I studied his clean, taut face almost unchanged in the intervening fifteen years. He meant something to me, yes, but not what one might suspect. I didn't pine or ache for him in the slightest. He was more a totem of what I'd consciously changed about my life. After Jefferey, I made up my mind to never again allow a man to determine the course of my happiness. Maybe one forms scar tissue too thick for any more hurt to pierce them, but I likened it more to living on my own terms. There'd been a couple partners and several fleeting encounters since then, but mostly I slipped away, leaving behind a few wounded people myself. *Don't let yourself be sold and sold* to *like that*, I wanted to tell these men. Love can often be a conjurer's trick. J. Walter Thompson once said, "This is an age of faith. All ages have been ages of faith. Disbelief requires an effort of the will while belief requires only acquiescence."

But this didn't mean I couldn't wonder if the actor ever thought of me.

"I had a vision of a plague, and when both my parents passed during Covid—a crisis I foresaw—that's when I knew. I had to quit acting. I had to escape the secular media, go back home and begin rededicating myself to Jesus Christ."

He sat on the edge of his garish CGI stage in his Slapdish worlde. It was a vulgar mix of a Gothic cathedral and a sports arena, titanic crossbeams soaring overhead (and there I was craning my neck to take it all in). He wore flowing white linen pants and a rugged tan shirt, his voice mournful. Despite years of owning the VR set, I found myself instinctively reaching up to touch his stubbled cheek. I was filled with sadness for this version of him. He wore the born-again shtick clownishly, his easy confidence replaced by the kind of evangelical desperation I'd seen in my childhood. It was hard not to be cynical about his motives—I vividly recalled his quick dismissiveness of religion—but maybe he thought it was a sincere transformation. One came to understand that we all purchased, voted, worshiped, and loved in unconscious obedience to narratives we thought were original, but which were largely dreamed up in sterile boardrooms like the one in New York. Then we went and called these stories our passions and dreams.

"We carry the sadness. The sadnesses of my life were drinking, loneliness, and walking away from my parents' mission of carrying the news of Christ. I was on a journey to my judgment."

His voice lowered. He looked as young as when I'd met him, but now he wore his hair slicked back. His eyes were still a deep and arresting blue from his contacts. His mic hand had a gold ring on the pinkie, glinting in the imaginary light of his virtual realm. I reached for the messaging function.

"We are living through yet another scourge, a plague, this one borne not on the back of a virus but a plague of consumption, addiction, and poverty of the soul, and man oh man, the times they just grow darker and darker, don't they? And it means something, my friends. It does."

"Text Linda Holiday," I told my VR set. "What about this guy who just changed his name to The Pastor? Might be a good candidate for Emii and the gang. His Slapdish ratings are big. Send."

"The times we live in—what we are seeing—call to mind Matthew twenty-four, six through eight: 'And ye shall hear of wars and rumors of wars: see that ye be not troubled: for all these things must come to pass, but the end is not yet. For nation shall rise against nation, and kingdom against kingdom: and there shall be famines and pestilences and droughts and great storms. All these are the beginning of sorrows.'"

A text bubble popped up in my peripheral vision, but it wasn't Linda replying. It was Fred: *Flight got canceled. Tornado watch. What if we got a drink?*

Pulling the bright scene from my eyes, The Pastor's voice fading, I suddenly wanted company. Ached for it. While I slid toward J. Walter's acquiescence, the sound of the rain came on like a switch. My living room had a view of the Chicago River and the former Trump Tower. Rain streaked down on the city. I texted Fred back to say there was no way I was going out in this.

Then I'll come to you.

When he arrived, neither of us had the patience for the pretense of wine. He was soaked, his hair matted. He dripped water onto my hardwood floor. "This is just from the car to your lobby," he said, and the part of me that felt how transactional this encounter could be was excited by it rather than guilty. Fred took his jacket off and kissed me with his hand fastened to my jaw, holding my face like a prize.

The wind and rain beat against the window. I led him to my bed and flipped the lights off. I hated having sex with the lights on—something to do with the way I could see the little blue veins in my breasts; a sign of age they hadn't invented a cosmetic solution for yet. With the room dark, the city glittered, and gusts of wind sent hard sheets of rain through the light in eerie pulses.

"Was your flight really canceled?" I asked when we finished. He tried to put an arm around me, but I gently took it away. "Give me a minute. I'm sweaty."

"I didn't even leave my hotel. It was canceled when they saw the storm coming in."

"You don't have your ring on this time."

He was quiet a moment. "I was thinking I should stop wearing it."

"Pick up more women you work with that way?"

"It's not like that."

"Whatever." I crawled out of bed onto the floor and pushed myself into an up-dog pose, feeling the stretch in my lower back and glutes. "You did a number on me."

"Sorry—question mark."

"No." I grunted, feeling my hip pop. He'd had my knees at my ears. "It's a good thing, trust me. My last relationship. I'll just say I was never good and sated. You're a sater. A satist."

He chuckled.

"What client were you meeting with?" I asked, coming out of up-dog.

"It's an ag company."

"In trouble?" I slipped back into bed and let him curl beside me. He was still wearing the condom he'd produced from his sports coat, and I could feel the latex on my leg.

"I've never seen a cultural environment worse for business than right now. Everyone should be watching their backs."

"It's probably the same guys my dad sold the farm to," I said.

Ice-blue lightning cracked the sky, sweeping the bedroom in staccato flashbulbs. The cannon fire of the thunder soon followed. When it was over, he said, "You know after this campaign, I'm looking to cash out and start this new thing. How do you like New York?"

"I'm more of a Midwest girl."

"So maybe it's time for a change of pace. This is me trying to say I really like the work you do. You think outside the box, and that's becoming increasingly hard to find. I'm moving into finance. I've hooked up with some sharp people, and it really could be worth a fortune—"

"Hey," I touched his shoulder. "Can we not talk shop? If you want to stay, that's fine," I said, hoping he heard the opposite in my voice. "I can't leave Chicago anyway. My father passed away, and my mom's not doing well with it."

"I'm sorry to hear that."

More lightning, now with the thunder right behind. We were quiet for a while. I thought he might be asleep, but then suddenly out of the dark, he said, "You should know that this is not about me being bored in my marriage. I told you my wife and I are living apart now."

"Okay."

"It's complicated."

"It usually is."

"Our son has had problems."

A sickness slid through me. I felt it first at the top of my head and then bubbling through the veins of my scalp down through my neck, lungs, and heart, only to settle somewhere in the bowels.

"That's too bad."

"We've been apart almost since it happened. This was two years ago now. My son's always been a kind of . . . I don't know, a handful, I guess you'd say. He has moments where he can be really sweet, but then he'll do things—just behavioral problems. We thought he was maturing for a while, and then— You know, I thought he was just being a kid. And then he did something truly . . ."

It slipped out of my mouth before I could catch it, this bit of the sickness coming up like bile. "What?"

"There was a kid a year younger than him, a sixth-grader, who he picked on. He hurt him pretty bad. After school. So they took my son away."

Maybe he'd shared this with me so I would tell him something. About my father's death or his mistress or my mother or siblings or the actor. But it wasn't a game I wanted to play. Instead I said, "Sometimes I have this . . . I guess you'd call it a nostalgia. A nostalgia for the worst moments of my life."

"That sounds terrible," he whispered.

"No, it's not. I like remembering them. Because those moments—that's what's vivid. Unforgettable."

He pulled me closer, and I let him. Outside, the thunder shook the whole building, and the lightning spiked again, and this time the entire sky raged with electric-blue fire.

Book III

WITH SPEED
AND VIOLENCE

The Derecho
and the Light

2030

It was the third such storm of the summer, and the pattern was becoming familiar. The thermometer soared toward triple digits, the sky darkened, the air turned that jaundiced green, and then, as though a vacuum cleaner sucked up the heat, the temperature plummeted. The wind and rain started up, and as Casey Wheeler explained, "Brother, you better be off the road and taking cover, 'cause who goddamn knows what's coming out the sky."

The first time you were coming home from work, and it was like a whiteout with rain. A five-minute drive turned into a twenty-minute white-knuckle-grip ordeal. You inched along in the battering-ram wind, tires sluicing through deepening water, until reaching the safety of your driveway. You've heard them called derechos, but a "land hurricane" is more apt. And tonight, when you get home to find Toby mashing a fistful of peas into pulp and Raquel anxiously watching the Weather Channel, you know another superstorm is on its way.

"They ain't even cleaned nothing up from the last one," Raquel bitches.

After putting Toby down, you climb into bed, exhausted, and drift off for what feels like a blink.

Then you wake to the wind. It's the sound of driving through a tunnel under a mountain. It surrounds your two-bedroom rental, the one you and Raquel worked so hard for so you could get out of the trailer court. As during the last two storms, you worry if the heap will hold together. The house has no basement, let alone a storm shelter. The rain begins, pummeling the siding. Raquel stirs. You lie in the dark and wait. The storm grows louder.

Finally, light flashes outside and the rattle of distant thunder wakes Toby, whose wails match the intensity of the storm.

"Baby," says Raquel, as a way of asking you to get him. And that's fine. You can't sleep through this shit anyway.

Pulling the howling Toby from his crib, his frightened hands grope for you. As you hoist him into your arms, the power goes out, and he screams louder.

You take him to the living room where the window looks out over the road, train tracks, and a small field. The streetlamp is out, along with electricity for the rest of the block, and you and Toby can only stare into a wall of darkness. Toby hates the thunder, and you can't really blame him. With each crack, you can hear the plates in the cupboards, the silverware in the drawers, jittering.

Lightning strikes and it blesses the whole neighborhood with a moment of purple daylight. In that instant you catch a glimpse of a figure across the tracks, struggling down the side of the road. You hope the guy is smart enough to get indoors fast. The last two storms, they were talking eighty-, ninety-mile-per-hour winds. When the lightning comes again, he's gone.

Toby moans at each boom, but he also appears fascinated by the lightning. He sucks on his fingers and watches wide-eyed for each round of illumination. His black hair has turned kinkier, but he has a smattering of your freckles. He reminds you of the picture on your mom's refrigerator, the one from Soak City Water Park.

"That's lightning, Toby. See, nothing to be scared of. Just lightning. Just rain."

But you know this isn't true because you can feel your blood racing with the fear of the storm. And when a bolt of lightning splits the sky and strikes a tree across the road, Toby screams, and you can't help but grip him against your chest in a full-body recoil. The tree explodes in sparks and splinters, half of it crashing onto the telephone wires. Your heart is as loud in your ears as the thunder.

You've never seen lightning that close before. It was more weapon than weather.

After an hour the storm passes, and Toby drifts off on your shoulder. You put him back in his crib. You think of going to bed, but you're too awake. Your skin too itchy.

Instead, you get a paper bag from the kitchen. Then you get a can of Raquel's hairspray. In the bathroom, you sit on the toilet and spray, gathering fumes. You hold it to your face and breathe. You do it again. It's a cheap high, but it helps. You sit back against the toilet, and in the blackness, you see that blue-purple bolt of lightning shredding that tree over and over.

In the morning, you have a headache from the hairspray. There's still no electricity, and the heat of the day is already descending. Raquel snaps at you when you open the freezer because the food might spoil. There are only a couple of soggy microwave dinners, though. The window AC units are useless, so Raquel will have to take Toby somewhere with air-conditioning, probably the Walmart with its generators. You're late for work because there are downed trees everywhere, and only so many road crews to clear them. You think with all these storms, maybe there's better work doing tree cleanup or repair, but this is your typical dead-end thinking. Ideas you'll never do anything about. You pass a house where the kids' trampoline has blown onto the roof and snagged on the chimney. Another house has a tree shot through its upper floor; an upstairs bedroom now exposed. Through downtown, past empty storefronts where the windows have soap cataracts, multiple cars have been crushed by fallen trees. One SUV has been cut nearly in half; the sturdy oak now embedded in its middle seat. You edge past a busted recliner mid-street. There are more stray dogs than ever, nosing through trash.

The Kroger is packed. People buying food and water while the power is out. Still, you'd almost rather be here with the store's generator-powered AC than stuck in your house, which you know is cooking. Julian, your manager, finds you.

"Could've used you on time today, Keeper."

You gesture back to the road. "You got any way to clear about a thousand trees, lemme know." You lost a tooth five months ago. There's another molar throbbing in your jaw, but you haven't had the money to go to the dentist to see about getting it pulled. It gives you this faggy, wisping lisp that you hate, especially in conversations with the doughy Julian, a guy you would beat up on a playground if adults could do such things.

"We're telling people, maximum of two bags," he says. "But I want you stocking for now."

The shelves are already picked over. You roll up your sleeves, exposing the crucifix on your arm, and get to work, thinking about how things could be worse.

When you met Raquel in the parking lot of the blood bank on Christmas Eve, both of you were sagging toward rock bottom. You were snowed in for five days, and you spent the Come to Jesus Storm fucking and shooting up, then the next six months becoming a full-blown heroin addict. Until you found a fentanyl connection. Far more economical and a lightning high. Raquel made for nice company. She didn't talk much, but she liked cooking and could whip up a decent meal. You hadn't been with anyone in a while, and it was nice. Then you got the bright idea to break into a shoe store downtown. Coming out, the Coshocton PD had been waiting for you. You'd heard tell of a way to avoid withdrawal in jail, and you tried cutting a gash in your thigh and rubbing in the last of your score. All it did was leave you bloody and in withdrawal—aching, cramping, shitting, barfing in a cell—anyway.

You served your sentence where the loneliness got bad. Why bother with anything. Do your time, get free, get the purest product you could on the street, and go OD somewhere. Out in eleven months for good behavior, and you figured you'd never see Raquel again. To your surprise, she was waiting when you got out. She'd somehow come by a car but didn't say how. The two of you drove straight home to score, and you OD'd. Not such a big deal, though, first responders carried Narcan everywhere now. It only felt like a strange blackout. Then you and Raquel were back in a motel, eating off a hot plate, getting fucked up every day on the dope you'd buy from Tawrny.

Love was a funny thing. You never thought you believed in it or that you'd find it or rather that it would find you. But Raquel treated you like you had some kind of value. When she came back from the clinic and told you she was pregnant, you thought of fleeing. At least it crossed your mind. The problem being there was nowhere to go. Your only people were in Dayton, and mostly they wanted nothing to do with you. You had no money. No way to get any. You'd be living under bridges if you tried to run.

"I'll get rid of it if you want. I done it before," Raquel said. You put your eyes in your hands. Of course, you thought of Claire Ann. She'd given up trying to get money out of you. You also knew who Raquel's other gotten-rid-of-babies probably belonged to. Raquel had been living with an older man since she was a girl. She'd finally run away. "But maybe we should keep it," she went on. "I mean, maybe this is a chance for us to get clean, get turned around, you know?"

"Turned around to what?" you asked bitterly.

She shrugged one shoulder, a limp, defeated movement. "I dunno. We get off junk. We get a place. Get a name for our baby. Maybe get married someday."

"Sounds so simple." You immediately regretted your tone. You could see the choke of tears in her eyes. Why did you have to be like this? Why did everything have to be like this? You took her in your arms but suddenly you were crying too.

You got through rehab somehow. You called your mom for the first time in years and told her what was happening. You told her you were going to be a father this time, and you were going to get clean. She wished you luck but clearly didn't believe it. Raquel found a place in Zanesville that wasn't like other rehab centers you'd drifted in and out of. Right in the middle of the city's busted downtown was this brand-new complex with a garden the size of a farm and a park beside it. There were weird kites tethered to the building and way up in the sky, you could see little propellers whirring, some kind of portable wind turbines you're told, along with solar panels that look like sunflowers sprouting from the ground. A mural of blue fire as you walked inside and a separate in-take office for the addicts. (It said above the door, bizarrely: WE'RE HERE TO HELP. DON'T WORRY, YOU DON'T HAVE TO BE-LIEVE IN CLIMATE CHANGE.) They started you and Raquel on a prescription and meetings. Later, they helped her out with job placement. Tougher for you because you're a felon. It hurt to get sober, but you do it. Or at least you mostly do it. You haven't touched an opiate for over two years.

Casey appears around the corner of Kroger's breakfast aisle.

"Thought you was off today," you tell him. Casey keeps getting fatter while also buying pants even bigger, and he never remembers a belt. He walks toward you hoisting them up every other step.

"I was. Julian called me in. Yo, you hear about Levi's girl, Missy?" Levi Basset was a guy you two were friendly with. You, Casey, Levi, and Dick Underwood sometimes bowled or got beers when you had a night to spare. Now that you'd had all this time off junk, you were starting to remember what it's like to have friends.

"Yeah man, she's in the hospital. Her trailer got tipped last night in the storm."

"No shit?"

"Broke both legs and her collarbone. Trailer's totally trashed too, I guess."

"That sucks a fat one."

"You guys come through okay?"

"Yeah, didn't touch us. Course Toby went fucking ballistic. He can't sleep through that shit, so I can't sleep through that shit. Saw this lightning come down—holy fuck. Now power's out, of course."

"Whole town's out. They're saying it'll be back tonight." He lifts his Kroger ballcap and scratches what gruel remains of his hair. "We didn't even get the worst, all the tornadoes missed us. Near two hundred people dead or missing to the south, not to mention Indiana and West Virginia."

"We still bowling tomorrow?"

"If it's open."

"Guys." Julian appeared in the aisle. You hate this face of his, this exaggerated exasperation. He points to his watch. "My time. Not your time. We're swamped here." He says this so a dozen shoppers piling the last of the Lucky Charms into their carts can hear. Trying to embarrass you. To prove he's the alpha in his stupid fucking grocery kingdom.

"Yep," said Casey. "Just had a question for Keep." Then to you, "I'll see ya."

You go back to unloading cereal boxes for $9.74 an hour.

When the rehab folks got Raquel her job at the McDonald's, you still had only the one connection and asked Casey to set you up at Kroger. He was wary of getting burned after you worked your ass off to get that power plant job only to fuck it up. Raquel got enrolled in Medicaid and food stamps. You couldn't get either because of your record and had to pretend you didn't live with your family when the government came around. This also proved a problem in finding work. Your eyes went numb filling out applications, and no one ever called. You just marched to the blood bank twice a week to get your $35. You went back to Tawrny, explaining that you'd gotten clean, but all he said was, "Still can't have you around product, kid. Glad to hear you're doing well, though."

You kept on Casey, and finally it paid off. Kroger fired a whole slew of people because they'd been talking with an organizer from the UFCW. The unions were suddenly flexing everywhere, encouraging wildcat strikes and other disruptions. The bosses were fighting back with companies that rooted around in your social media or whatever. Even talking union could get you blacklisted from every job in town. Good news was, suddenly, Kroger needed a lot of new workers. Casey got you an interview, and Julian barely glanced at the explanation of your incarceration. "I'll start you part-time, fifteen hours a week, and if you're on time and a hard worker, I'll up your hours. Sound fair?"

You couldn't believe how happy you were about this. You shook Julian's hand and thanked him profusely. Raquel helped you celebrate that night by baking a lemon meringue pie.

You work from 8 a.m. to 4 p.m. The store's a madhouse. The ongoing argument between Coshocton and the summer storms has given the whole town the feeling of a battered wife. It feels like every last resident is there, elbowing each other for bologna and beans. You have to settle a dispute between two women who think they were first to the last container of hummus.

You go home and find Raquel feeding Toby. Thankfully, the power is back. The previous outage lasted two days.

"Landlord called," she says. "She say we need the rent."

You think of your car, a junker Prius making a troublesome noise. You're up to twenty-eight hours a week, just enough so that Julian doesn't have to make you full-time. You think of how you and Raquel can't get married because with your shit car, the two of you will have too many assets for the Medicaid. You think of how Medicaid doesn't cover eyeglasses more than once every three years, so Raquel has to squint when she drives and can never read road signs.

"Can't make miracles," you tell her. "Get my check when I get my check."

———

Church the next day. Toby always fusses through it, but Raquel insists. Even when you and her were in the depths of your junkie lives, she always found a day of the week to go. It's not exactly a Black church, and it's not exactly a wetback church. There are at least enough white people there that you don't feel too fish out of water. It's just you'd rather be doing anything else. She doesn't ask much of you, though, and this keeps the peace at home. The minister natters on about resilience and forgiveness.

"These storms are not God's reckoning. Don't go down that old road. Some folks like to blame every hard rain and earthquake and fire on God, but the Lord isn't that kind of thinker. These are common tests like everything else. Tests of our humanity and our faith."

The church has a charity drive going for the families of the people who'd been killed by the summer storms. Raquel slips a five-dollar bill into the greasy collection plate, and you feel that money leave you and your family like the skin you lose after scraping a leg.

On your way out, the minister, a hardy old spic who doesn't sound like a spic, stops you. "We still got a date, don't we, Keeper? You let me know."

"Will do," you mutter. He wants to save you. You figure he needs your family because now half of every church congregation in the county stays home on Sundays to watch The Pastor yip and cavort around in VR. The rev needs the families who can't afford sets. Eventually, you'll let him do it just to shut him up but putting him off is fine too.

On the drive home, you pass a crew sawing a felled tree into more manageable pieces, sawdust misting around an orange-jacketed worker. While you wait to get the SLOW instead of the STOP, your phone vibrates. To your surprise it's Tawrny. He wants to know if you've got a second to talk that afternoon.

One-handed, you text him back and ask him about what.

Might have an opportunity for you, he writes.

You can't tell Raquel that you're going to see Tawrny because there's only one kind of work the man has, so you make up an excuse about Casey potentially having a line on a handyman gig.

"You didn't say nothing about that," says Raquel, but not with suspicion. Hope.

"Didn't want to make a deal of it, 'less it turned into something. Shouldn't take long. I'll be back by dinner."

On the way out to Cassingham Hollow, you pass the house with vinyl siding the sunny color of Raquel's lemon meringue, only to see that the roof collapsed in the storm. Now the family has all its belongings on the lawn. They squat in their possessions like exhausted hobos, confused. Like they can't find a missing couch.

Pulling up to Tawrny's Queen Anne, you expect to find him on the porch smoking, but instead, he opens the screen door and gestures you inside. He's never let you through the door before. He's grown his goatee into a full white beard, which makes him look like Truck Stop Santa. He shakes your hand.

"How you hanging in, Keeper?"

"Good, T. Good as can be expected."

He leads you to an old oak table in the kitchen.

"You getting through these storms all right?" His voice is still gruff, flinty.

"We been lucky. We don't got any trees too near the house, but I'm sure as hell losing sleep over 'em."

"Yeah, we had a tree come down." He motions with his cigarette hand, sort of waving the yellowed digits to the back of the house. "Just sorta glanced off the roof, but goddamn if it didn't sound like the whole fucking thing was caving in. Bets ain't doing too well, so she about lost her mind. Made me make up a bed for her in the basement."

"Sorry to hear that."

"You know what this reminds me of? I'm watching this old show about the blitzkrieg in World War Two when Hitler was trying to bomb Britain into submission. And they got some of the survivors talking on it. What it was like to worry every night about a bomb coming down on your house. The way they talked reminded me of these storms."

"Huh." You nod. You don't want to look too impatient for him to get to the point.

"Maybe that sounds like an exaggeration but this last one killed damn near three hundred people when you count all the tornadoes and flooding and wind." He takes from his jeans an old pocket watch, the glass murky, the hands still, and begins twisting the top to set it. "So the grapevine comes down saying you got clean."

You nod again. "Over two years now," you exaggerate. Without mentioning that this clean still lets you get down on a Budweiser or the occasional can of hairspray.

"Hell, boy, that's impressive. Seen many a man that looked tougher'n you fail abjectly at such a project."

"I swear, I'm good, T. I'll carry product. I'll sell. It might be tough for me to straw buy 'cause of my record, but whatever you need."

Tawrny twists and twists the crown of the pocket watch. He relaxes back into his chair to the tortured squeaking of the wood.

"Not that kind of job. One-off gig."

Disappointed, you try to keep your eagerness, your sobriety, on display.

"You used to work at Tuscarawas power plant, correct?"

"That's right."

He sucks on his teeth. He releases the crown, and the watch ticks satisfactorily.

"I got a guy—he's willing to pay a nice chunk of change for some information regarding the security concerns there. Told him I could get him that information."

You're confused. "Okay . . ."

"You understand the conversation we're having, Keeper." His eyebrows arch. "This don't go beyond us. This is the kinda thing you keep under your hat."

"Course. What do you need?"

"Say you wanted to break into that facility. How would you go about that? From what I understand there's a fence surrounding the property. And then a thumbprint scanner to the front door."

"Yeah, that's right."

"You don't have access anymore, do you?"

"Nah, they woulda dumped me from the system first thing."

"And there's only that one way to get to the plant?"

"Well, sure, to get inside the building, but to get in the perimeter, inside the fence, there's actually an access road that comes in from the back. I s'pose if you wanted to just sneak onto the property, all that's on that gate is a dinky padlock with a punch code."

You have no idea why anyone would want to break into the Tuscarawas power plant, but you're unbothered by the mystery.

"And what's that code?"

You cross your arms. "C'mon, man, I ain't just giving away all this. You told me you had a job for me. I got a kid now, brother. Tell me what you're paying."

"Think they've made any security upgrades since your termination?"

You fart with your lips and repeat what you've heard Casey say. "Ohio Valley Power ain't sinking a dime more into that place. As soon as the fucking Democrats get their way, that place is getting shut down."

Tawrny nods. He looks pleased. He has an ageless quality, a survivor's ferocity. Whatever he needed this information for, it's no oddball favor.

"Tell you what. You give me that code and you give me the time when that fence ain't being watched, I'll give you half of what this guy's paying me."

"How much is that?"

He hesitates. "Two grand."

Your head buzzes from the number and the notions of what you could do with that money: a couple months of rent, baby food, clothes, eyeglasses, repairs to the house, to the car, a new microwave. The possibilities bloom and recede, bloom and recede.

"Tawrny, man, if you're paying two grand, I'll get the shift changes, I'll draw you a map, I'll get the code—whatever you need."

Tawrny nods. "Got yourself a deal then, Keeper. Just a little information and that money'll be as good as in your pocket."

———

You take the next two days to make sure you get everything right. You tell Raquel that Casey hooked you up with the gig. Just some basic masonry work for a couple of rich farmers, you lie. You park out on Route 273 and hoof it down the access road past the tailing pond of the Tuscarawas plant. Squatting in the dark underbrush, you snack on Fritos. The smokestacks glitter in the night. Twin stars blinking from the top of each stack, that orange rocket-fuel color of the lights washing over the water. The shift changes over exactly as you remember. One group of hard-hatted workers slinks in, and soon after, another slinks out. Then quiet. You sidle up to the fence and see a camera perched over the road, and it's more than you could've hoped for: nothing's changed. Because the camera's angle is fixed, you approach it from the left, climb a bit of fence, and drape an opaque plastic bag over the lens. No one would think twice about the wind landing it there. You try the lock, and it's still the same code: 1-9-8-5, the year of the plant's commission.

You hand over all the information to Tawrny, and as promised he puts a stack of bills in front of you.

"Don't go telling your woman where it came from."

"Course. I may be an ex-addict, but I ain't retarded."

You already have your plan: Pay this month's rent and the next. Give Raquel $400 for baby supplies and whatever else she wants. Put $200 in the bank. Save $100 for miscellaneous spending. Blow $100 on a night out with Casey, Levi, and Dick Underwood.

"What's this business?" A waif of an old woman appears in Tawrny's kitchen. She is frail, emaciated, and a crumpled nightgown hangs from her skeletal frame. Tawrny moves quickly.

"Betsy, goddamnit. Back to bed." She looks confused. Strands of white hair float away from a scalp the color of a burlap sack, and she has patches of dry skin all over her face and neck, little white lesions that look like scales. She doesn't want to be led away, but Tawrny turns her around and moves her quickly back down the hall. The sight of her has made you ill, and when you leave, you wish greatly that you had never seen her.

You tell Raquel the extra work paid off, but you only pay one month's rent and give her $300. A week later, you and the guys get your Saturday at the bowling alley. They got a deal on Jell-O shots—$1 each—and Levi insists you all put down three before you start bowling. From there it's pitcher after pitcher. You bowl like shit, partly because you haven't played in five months, mostly because you're getting drunk really fast.

"Keeper, you roll like Obama," Dick Underwood says. He's in third place, then Casey, then you. Levi's like a pro. Bowls three or four times a week by himself. Casey's about at your level but he can hold his liquor better. You buy two rounds of tequila shots to even the field but somehow Levi bowls a 280.

You toss two gutters in a row.

"Jesus, you do roll like a bitch," says Levi.

You flip him the bird and wander off to buy another pitcher.

Returning to your lane with the beer, you hear Dick Underwood going on about the Ohio Light Foot, his little soldier-playing militia. Every few months a bunch of grown men got dressed up like Navy SEALs and pretended they were fighting off the jackbooted Feds or the Islamic Empire. "We got money coming in now through this partnership," he explains. "So we go to the Oath Keepers and Three Percenters and explain why we should absorb them under our command structure." He takes the pitcher from you and pours both of you a glass.

"Didn't y'all get broken up when those guys shot up the mosque school," says Casey.

"First off, that wasn't us. Second of all, that ain't the whole story and you know it. There's a lot of people think that was a false flag by the FBI to make some arrests."

"Killing a bunch of little kids is a false flag?" Casey wonders. "Interesting."

"You gotta watch where you're getting information. They were Somalis, and they weren't kids, they were prime recruiting age. Besides, that guy used smart bullets. Ain't no hunt to that!"

"Enough," you tell them. You know Underwood's looked at you sideways before because you've got a Black girlfriend and a mulatto son. When someone put a threatening letter under the door of Raquel's church, you're pretty sure Underwood would know the guy from the Ohio Light Foot. "Let's shut up and play."

You drink more tequila. You take your turn (three pins on the first roll, gutter on the second), and then stumble back to the bar. Before you can order, you get a call from Raquel.

"Y'all checked the weather?"

"Ain't no weather in a bowling alley," you explain.

"Weather says there's another one of them storms coming in tonight. Get coming back now."

"Aye, aye."

You go back to drinking.

You roll a 76. Then a 107. Then a 140. "You're better when you're skunk-drunk," says Levi.

"Suck cock," you tell him. Then the next few minutes blur. You're trying to order more from the bar, but the bartender's saying no. Then you're angry. Then you're in the parking lot by Underwood's truck, and he and Casey are trying to tell you the night's over. You're done. Levi's smoking a cigarette, looking off into the parking lot. Wind ripping around his greasy hair. Levi looking smug. You turn around and open the toolbox in the bed of Underwood's ride. You root around among the tools, looking for something interesting.

"Keeper, what the fuck, man?" says Casey, sounding exhausted with you. "Let's just go to another bar."

You find a pair of pliers. These are interesting. You shove past Casey and Underwood. You throw one forearm into Levi's chest and take him to the ground. The cigarette flies from his lips. You fall on top of him. Before he knows what's happened, you've pinched the top of his eyelid between your finger and thumb. You're drunk, sure, but you're like a surgeon when you're drunk. "Hold still." And you slip the needle-nose part of the pliers under his eyelid and clamp down.

He's screaming. You hear Underwood and Casey come running at the sound.

"Don't move, Basset. Don't move," you hiss at him. "You ain't been no-where, Bassy. You ain't been anywhere. I been places. I know things you ain't figured out yet."

The wind blasts over the four of you, struggling there on hard pavement. And you want to rip his eyelid off, jerk it from his socket to see how much of his face will come with it.

Then Underwood's foot crashes against your ear, and you fall into the side of a car. Levi's on his feet, holding his eye and shrieking. You hop up and walk off. Casey and Underwood are yelling after you. Fuck them. You find your keys, and then you're driving.

Gusts of wind thrash your car. The rain is steady but not violent. This is nowhere near as bad as the other storms. And yet on your road, you can see the red and blue emergency lights strobing over the night. You can see smoke billowing from a roof and for a horrified moment you're sure it is your own. All reason leaves you and you just know God is out for you. Everyone is out for you. Your cheap shitty fucking rental that you never wanted with the son you never wanted with the girlfriend you never wanted, and you want to drive over to Tawrny's and bash him on the head and dig up every last speck of dope in his place and hole up in a motel and shoot your veins back to their original size when you were a screaming infant.

But it's not your house. The smoke is billowing from too high a point.

This is a second-story sucker. About three houses down from you. For once, someone with more money has to eat the world's curb.

"Lightning strike," says the police officer directing traffic. "You'll have to go around." More lightning licks the sky. The rain picks up. At the base of the smoke you can see the yellow flicker of flames in the upper rooms. "Have you been drinking?" he asks. Of course, you didn't even consider all the booze on your breath. Without saying another word, you pull away, breaking for a street that'll help take you around.

In your driveway, you can see the other side of the fire trucks and ambulances and patrol cars. All that blue and red comes screaming past the curtains, lighting your whole living room. Raquel is asking if you're drunk, but you're already stumbling for the bottle of whiskey you've hidden in the closet. Toby is wailing. Your little nigger baby is wailing. How could you have done this? Your whole life spent trying to stay away from these ugly, disgusting animals and you go and have a baby with one. You got a white baby somewhere and you choose to stay with this half-breed and his dope-addict whore mother. Raquel is in your grille about something, and you bounce her face off the wall to back her up. The last thing you really recall is the door to the bedroom slamming closed, and you're too weak to kick it open, though you damn well try. You kick and you scream slurs at Raquel, and you threaten to put Toby out in the field for the stray dogs to get. But she's stuffed a chair under the knob or something. Eventually you lay down and watch the light slither under the door.

————————

For two days, Raquel does not speak a word to you. At work, Casey simply says, "No more bowling, I guess. You should think of finding another job." Once you are past the crush of the headache and reclaim the retrievable memories, you don't feel like apologizing so much as asking for apologies. From Levi for being a prick, from Casey for not taking your side, from Raquel for letting you pass out on the floor. And then after that, the shame. The shame of your whole of life. The shame of being.

The fourth derecho of the summer was not the worst. The power even stayed on. Yet it feels like it's drained the town completely. The second story of that house burned, and it's derelict now, its occupants hospitalized or homeless. The Kroger had a window blown out by a piece of flying debris. Your church lost its roof, and when you drive by you see an incredible hole sagging through the apex, like someone dropped a piano through it. Two trees in the field, dirt-clotted roots shredded from the ground.

"You ever gonna talk to me again?" you finally ask Raquel over dinner. Toby, unaware of anything else now that the awful night of the storm is over, happily puts a toy truck in his mouth while he paints the high chair with his food.

"I had anywhere else to go, I wouldn't be here right now," she says, not looking at you.

"Who brought you home this meat loaf?" you ask as you fork the meat into ketchup. Raquel just shakes her head to indicate this is as nonsensical as you know it is.

"You got a bad side," she tells you. "A serious bad side."

"What do you want me to do?" you ask. "Lemme make this better. I can't live with a woman who spends all her time hating me."

Toby hands you his slimy truck. You take it.

"Seems like you already hate me. And Toby. From what you said."

The wave of guilt is too much. You want to both beg her for forgiveness and punch her in the eye. The feeling makes you wish you'd ripped off Levi's eyelid. At least there would have been satisfaction.

"I won't drink again," you promise. "Never again."

Toby now wants his truck back, reaching his pudgy hands for it. You hand it over.

"You need more than being sober, Keeper. You need God in your life. Don't think I ever met no one who needs God in his life more than you do."

"I'll get saved."

She looks up from her meat loaf, which she's pushed around in her ketchup until it's a soup.

"I'll go get saved from what's-his-name."

"Reverend Andrade. Lord, Keeper, you don't even know his name?"

"I know his name. And yeah, I'll get saved."

She stares at you, her eyes bright twin questions. You understand you'll never be able to live without her and Toby. That if the two of them leave you, you'll take everything you have to the pawn shop, buy a gun, a bullet, and put it in your brain.

"The service this Sunday."

"How? The place's got a hole in its roof the size of a car."

"There's gonna be a service on the lawn."

Toby hands you the truck again. He smiles, giggles, thinking this an awesome game.

Sunday comes, and the temperature is 101. The weather calls it a heat dome. Temperatures ranging from 120 across the Southwest, to 110 in the South, to as high as 105 in the Northeast.

"He's still having this? Ain't old ladies gonna keel over dead?"

"Heat don't stop Jesus, Keeper."

You don't have any kind of suit, but you put on one of your two church shirts and gray pants. You fidget more than Toby on the drive over.

There are about thirty people out on the lawn beside the church, which now has a blue tarp over the hole in the roof. You shake hands with a few you barely know. Some of them appear leery, and you wonder if news of your antics last Saturday reached them.

Reverend Andrade calls the service to order. A semicircle gathers around him. People are fanning themselves with whatever's handy.

"All right folks, we're not going to be here too long on account of the heat," he begins. "But the plate will go around as always, and please maybe give a little extra on account of some repair work we have to do now." He smiles saying it, hesitates. He is old but smooth-faced. Pale brown skin. Graying black hair. Real smiley. Very straight teeth. You hate him. "You know, we've had a really tough summer in this community. Between all the storms and the lives lost and a couple of store closings with the layoffs, and of course our beautiful church"—he gestured—"taking the insult from nature that it did, it's been a rough go. Among our own members, Mrs. Slovic, who's in the hospital right now and may not be with us much longer, and Jaquan Daniels, who took his own life last year—you know it feels like the bad news just keeps coming and coming. But here's the thing: all bad news— it's nothing when stacked up against Jesus Christ's love."

A few amens float from the crowd. The reverend motions you to come forward. You do not want to. You do not want any part of this cheesy bull-shit. Your feet, you find, will not let you move.

"That's why for today's sermon, we've got something long overdue. This is our brother, Keeper. C'mon, Keeper, come forward. That's the devil that's got you rooted there."

Raquel nudges you, and you finally venture into the crisp brown grass. Reverend Andrade puts a hand on your shoulder.

"Keeper's what we call a long time coming. He's had his struggles. Him and his family have had a tough time. But recently they became a part of this church."

"*Amen*," "*Amen*," "*A-MEN!*"

"And today Keeper—Keeper, why don't you kneel down with me, let's kneel before God." The reverend takes a knee, and you follow his order and come to one knee on the ground. You're sweating. "Keeper has chosen today to let Jesus Christ into his heart. He's getting saved today. All this pain, all this misery we've all been enduring these last months, these years, these decades—none of it matters before the glory of Heaven, right? Before Kingdom Come."

He squeezes your shoulder.

"Bow your head and close your eyes, brother."

You do so. You should have drunk more water this morning. Your mouth is desert-dry, and the sun feels like a flamethrower. You're dizzy.

"God gave us a way past pain. He gave it to us, two thousand years ago, and that way is Jesus Christ."

"*Amen*," "*Amen*," "*Amen*."

"Ain't that right, Keeper? Now you know, son. God wants a relationship with us. If we come closer to Him, He comes closer to us. Trust in Him, Keeper. Repent. Turn away from your sins. You feel that?"

You nod, even though you feel nothing but hot and tired.

"Feel it in every muscle and nerve in your body. Let God touch you now. Repeat after me: Let the Holy Spirit come upon me now."

"Let the Holy Spirit come upon me now," you say.

"God, let the Holy Spirit take these evil things out of my life."

"God, let the Holy Spirit take these evil things out of my life," you say.

"Let me be saved, Lord."

"Let me be saved, Lord," you say.

"And having been saved, Lord, let me be born again."

"And having been saved, Lord, let me be born again," you whisper.

And then you feel something. From your head to your toes, you feel it, a light you cannot name, dusky but forever warm. The reverend continues.

"Let the Holy Spirit touch him right now. You spirits of rejection and loss and addiction, be gone. Fill him with your power, Lord. Fill him with the power to accomplish, to love. Take one breath, son."

At the command, your lungs fill of their own accord.

"Feel that. That's the glory of God. Evil spirits, get out of this man's life.

You're here with him now, Lord. You know his struggles. All the depression, all the loneliness, all the sorrow—let God take that away."

You can feel what has always been there but you've long ignored: an infinite sadness. With you all day, every day of your life. And when you open your eyes, you're weeping, but you don't know how long you've been doing so. A sob comes groaning out of your throat. Your life has always scared you.

"I'm sorry," you say.

"Don't be sorry. You feel that? That's Jesus Christ. He's here with you right now. He's beside you."

"I'm sorry. I'm so sorry," you repeat as the tears run down your face and drip from your chin into the grass. You feel why you got that cross tattooed on your arm in the first place.

"This grass will get its rain now. Those tears are the love of Christ, Keeper. That's the love of Christ."

The amens echo all around. When the sobs die down in your chest, when you can finally bring yourself to look up and around, when you can finally bring your arm to your face and clear your eyes of the tears, you see Raquel, holding Toby, wiping her own tears from her sweet brown cheeks.

The reverend pulls you to your feet. People are clapping and cheering.

"How was that?" he asks with a laugh. You laugh too.

"Good," you say.

As people cheer louder, the reverend pulls you into his arms. He says into your ear, "You let God do that to you all the time. As much as you need it. It'll keep you away from everything: the booze, the drugs, the hate. You let Jesus Christ into your life, and you don't need nothing else. Now go see your family."

You turn from the reverend and the spot of dry grass where you're sure your life just changed and go to Raquel and your son. You pull them into an embrace, Raquel laying her forehead against your cheek, both of you still weeping. Toby reaches up and touches your tears, curious about what could make his father do what he does when he's hungry or peed himself. When you open your eyes the light is different, as if it's refracting through a dragonfly's parchment wings.

That night you wake to a fearsome noise in the distance. As percussive as thunder, but lower and deeper. You sit up and look around. "Did you hear that?" you ask Raquel. She mumbles that she didn't hear anything. You remember what happened to you in the grass the day before. For the first time in as long as you can remember, you are awake and you don't think about getting high. You lower your head back to your pillow and put your arm around the woman you will someday find a way to make your wife.

When you're out of bed in the morning, Raquel is flipping a light switch back and forth. "Power's out again. Wasn't a storm yesterday, though."

You dress, get Toby fed, eat your cereal, and walk to the front door. You marvel that you have a home now. There was a time when you didn't, but now you do. And you managed that without this new power. You open the screen door. The wood of this door is warped, so it always squeaks and rattles when it pops out of the frame. This seems like a miracle now.

"Oh my Lord," Raquel says from the kitchen. You wander back in. She's looking at her phone. "Know that noise you heard?"

"Yeah?"

"Must've been the power plant up in Tuscarawas. There was an explosion last night." She holds up her phone. You can see a small picture of the Tuscarawas station, black smoke billowing from a hole in the guts of the structure, a redbrick wall fallen to rubble. Fire trucks streaming jets of water into the dark, smoldering wound. Without the AC units working, the day's heat begins to creep in. Raquel looks at her phone again. "This here says it was a bomb."

The Washington Post

SUNDAY REVIEW | NEWS ANALYSIS

A Political Storm Blows Washington Hard Right

By *HazelHorizon Political Analytics*

September 1, 2030

TERRORISM, White House resignations, and civil war within the GOP—all part and parcel of this strange and volatile summer—have sent Washington's weathervane into a tailspin.

With two months to go before midterm elections, President Mary Randall's party appears to be in open revolt, which has led the White House to shift priorities from energy and climate legislation to border control and national security.

The recalibration began in July with the "Ohio River Massacre," when truck bombs exploded outside three coal-fired power stations in Ohio and Kentucky, destroying generating capacity. Though the bombings produced no fatalities, they left two million people without power at the height of a record-breaking heat wave. A domestic terrorist network claimed responsibility. Public health officials estimate that at least thirty-four people died of heat-related effects across six Midwestern states during the periods of blackout, although whether these deaths could have been avoided is impossible to say.

Then this past week, President Randall canceled an event in Iowa after the Department of Homeland Security received credible intelligence of another domestic terror plot. Arrests were made of nine individuals with ties to the antigovernment extremist group the Hawkeye Brigade. The FBI and the Iowa attorney general have outlined felony domestic terrorism charges against the seven men and two women involved.

These plots, motivated by different ideological programs, are not being treated with equal severity. The eco-saboteurs known as "the Weathermen," in reference to the radical leftist group of the 1970s, has set both political parties on their heels, crippled what remains of the coal industry, and ignited a mutiny within the Randall administration, leading to the resignation of Secretary of Defense R. Holden Jons. In a statement explaining his departure, Jons took the unusual step of fiercely criticizing the president for her failure to confront "Islamic radicalism, narco-terrorists, and eco-fascists." Similar defections have followed among congressional Republicans, and Randall's most vociferous rival, West Virginia senator Russ Mackowski, continues to call on the president to resign.

Caught in the center of this storm is the hotly contested climate bill. The president and Senate Republicans face enormous pressure to scrap the year-and-a-half effort to pass LaFray-Kastor, also known as the Pollution Reduction, Infrastructure, and Refund Act.

Primary season treated Randall's allies particularly poorly. Several key Republican lawmakers who'd worked with Democrats to shepherd the bill through the House lost to Far Right challengers, including the legislation's Republican cosponsor, Judith Kastor. Republicans find themselves facing revolt from a rabid base crying out for answers to this summer's ongoing violence at the US-Mexico border.

Multiple incidents along Arizona border towns have created a siege mentality in a state rocked by water shortages and a struggling housing market. In April, a firefight in the desert between suspected drug cartel operatives and the paramilitary group the American Patriot League left five Americans and thirteen Mexican nationals dead. Meanwhile, refugees from Central America and Mexico continue to pour northward at an unprecedented rate, and Border Patrol estimates that attempted crossings have increased to nearly two thousand per day, with most of that increase being children. A spokesperson said the agency expects to process nearly 710,000 asylum seekers this year.

Jennifer Braden, star of the insurgent right-wing news network Renaissance Media, continues to draw criticism for emboldening groups like the APL and the Hawkeye Brigade. She has called for militarizing the border in a fashion similar to the partition between North and South Korea. Braden's views continue to find purchase on the right and have the backing of several billionaire financiers who are spending vast sums to fuel the Republicans' internal insurgency. The drumbeat to challenge Randall for the nomination in 2032 has grown louder, with names like R. Holden Jons and Russ Mackowski leading the conversation. Yet the Draft Braden movement has the fury of social VR and a newly formed Super PAC already behind it.

As President Randall moves to guard her right flank, her climate bill could be the first victim of that maneuver. In a Sunday interview, she told CBS's John Dickerson, "I've said over and over, we will not pass a bill that will harm American business. I cannot repeat that enough. The bill—if any bill passes at all, that is—the bill will not be punitive. These are the same companies, after all, working with their ingenuity and the power of the market to come up with the next technologies that will fix this issue."

Meanwhile, with four arrests made for the Ohio and Kentucky attacks, law enforcement seems to have begun unraveling the Weathermen's network. Yet for Washington, this is not enough. The Senate's bipartisan Gang of Nine has proposed combining elements of PRIRA with a security and immigration bill, the Protecting America's Borders and Energy Independence Act, introduced by Nebraska republican Bob Syracuse.

"We're looking at where our interests overlap," said Victor Love, the junior Democratic senator from Montana, during an interview with CNN. "I think my party and the Randall administration are taking our lead from the American people, who are clearly saying, 'Yes, we want to deal with climate change, but no, we don't want onerous new taxes and regulations, and we want to be secure."

Love's elevated voice in the Democratic Party has been greeted with hostility from the Left.

"Any politician who backs down now, we will campaign to remove from office come November," said Rekia Reynolds, spokesperson for the climate activist organization A Fierce Blue Fire.

However, Reynolds's threat may not be as potent as it was two years ago. Key allies like Pennsylvania senator Cy Fitzpatrick are behind in the polls while the House bill's primary Democratic sponsor, Joy LaFray, has become enmeshed in a scandal after a leaked Slapdish xpere revealed her interacting inappropriately with her seventeen-year-old stepson.

That a sex scandal involving a fifty-nine-year-old congresswoman and a minor has made only a glancing blow at the headlines of the day says something about the "derecho summer" of America in 2030.

HazelHorizon is a machine-learning language model. Azi Paybarah and Heather Abramowitz contributed reporting.

THE WEATHERMEN

2030

*T*he drive was eight hours of bitter winter scenery, up through Iowa and Minnesota, under low clouds hovering above glass office boxes and half-
abandoned strip malls with empty acres of parking lot, past endless
billboards advertising everything from Jesus Christ to laser sculpting to assault rifles with smart bullets. The day had begun at 5:30 a.m. when they
caught the Greyhound from Lawrence to Des Moines. Halfway into the five-
hour ride, Lali pulled the children's VR set from her face and demanded her
fiddle, which Shane had of course forgot. Lali started to cry, proclaiming
loudly and tearily that she didn't want to take a "robe trip" without her fiddle. Though she could play only basic notes, she carried the thing around
like other kids carried dolls.

Once upon a time Shane had packed carefree. Now journeying more
than a mile from home was like prepping for a military deployment, and the
worry that she might forget some crucial childcare item made it a certainty
that she would. She just never counted on the fiddle.

By the time they got to Des Moines, as she led her daughter by the hand
away from the bus station to the big-box parking lot a quarter mile down the
road, Lali started complaining she had to go to the bathroom. Shane quickly
found the car the op had left her, a forest-green Subaru Outback with the
GPS and LoJack disabled. But she couldn't find the magnetic box with the
key fob beneath the passenger door.

"Mama, I gotta go," Lali wheedled.

"No, no, no, c'mon." She scraped her hand in the muck beneath the door.
She tried under the driver's side, but it wasn't there either. Could the op have
forgotten to leave the fucking key? Just walked away with it still in his pocket?

"Mama, where are we?"

"Lali, just give me a second, okay?" She tried to keep her voice calm.
Don't make demands of children, the mothering hive mind said. Be firm, but
not harsh. Lali whined away, and she had to ignore her while she searched
beneath the other doors. People walked from their cars to stores in this clot

of cheap Midwestern retail, and she kept waiting, checking, scanning to make sure no one had narrowed their eyes at this woman looking like she was trying to boost a car. It was freezing out too. Her fingers were numb, and her nose wouldn't stop running.

"Mama," Lali's tone flipped to stern.

How had the fucking op forgotten to leave the key? She had no phone. No way of contacting Kai or the others. No emergency number to call. As she scraped her hand along the entire frame of the Subaru, she felt tears choking her throat. She hated crying in front of her daughter because she'd spent so much time doing it lately. Lali wouldn't be able to help herself, and her color would go from pale beige to bright pink as she flooded with shame. Her own weeping would soon follow.

"Mama," Lali moaned.

"Just one second, honey," Shane pleaded, and she had to bite down on the sob that trailed it. She jammed her finger on something and hissed. But the pain was momentary, and the magnetic box was there. The op had inexplicably left it under the back left wheel well. "Thank fuck," she whispered, pulling the key fob from inside. "C'mon, Lals, let's blow this popsicle stand. Outlaws forever, right?"

But when she turned, she saw the stain running down her daughter's little pink sweatpants and her mortified sourpuss face. "Okay, doll. First we change."

She had at least remembered another pair of pants.

Lali kept her head stuffed in VR for almost the entire drive. Shane once told herself she'd never stick screens in front of her daughter, but her boss, Teddy, had given her the set, and Shane had to admit it was a godsend in a situation like this. Shane, meanwhile, listened to the scattered FM stations, and by the time they were in Wisconsin, thin flurries had begun blowing over the windshield without sticking.

FRESH AIR Had Terry Gross interviewing Zeden, and Shane stopped the dial there. Gross asked the pop star about the controversy she'd stirred when she wore a tank top to the Grammys that said I'M WITH THE WEATHERMEN. Zeden's response wasn't the least defensive. *"Because they're doing what no one else has the guts to do."* Gross: *"So you endorse their use of violence?"* Zeden: *"What they're doing is not violence. What the people who owned those coal plants were doing—that's violence."* A pop star who'd gotten her start with a #1 single about her boyfriend's hair certainly had a better grasp on the situation than most journalists.

Far off the highway, down an obscure road between pine trees hardened by December cold, she squeezed into a yard beside two vehicles and a box truck that said FORD CUSTOM FURNISHING.

The two-story cabin, chocolate wood and dirty glass, looked like a piece of petrified mahogany grown right out of the forest floor. A plume of smoke curled from the chimney and drifted over the trees. A firelight glow beamed from the bay window into the dusk. She roused Lali, who'd long ago fallen asleep, her booster seat a mess of applesauce pouches and graham cracker crumbs. Shane grabbed their bags, and they climbed the steps to the porch, Lali rubbing sleepy eyes. She eased the front door open with a reedy "Hiii" as Lali shuffled in behind her, one hand tightly gripping the butt pocket of Shane's jeans.

Inside, warm light bathed the wood of the walls, floors, and ceiling. Across from the cushy furniture in the living room was the kitchen where Allen, Murdock, Kai, and Quinn colluded over pasta. Their chatter ceased abruptly. As Shane set her pack on the floor, a swarm of emotions passed over their faces. They'd surely watched Shane's car approach via a surveillance camera perched in a tree, but now they all stared at Lali. Allen was the first to speak.

"Hey there," he said, unloading his big, kind smile on her daughter. "Who's this?"

"This is Islali, but she likes Lali. Do you want to say hi? These are Mama's friends."

Lali clung to the back of her leg, wrecked from the long day of travel. She peeked one eye out and stuffed a fist against her lips.

Kai took a step forward from behind the island. Because they were all so quiet, his voice boomed: "Lali, you remember me, right? We've hung out before! Badman Kai, remember?"

Lali nodded twice. Murdock looked irritated but not enraged. That specific what-the-fuck simmer belonged to Quinn, who gazed at Shane like she might bolt across the living room and plunge the knife she was using to slice cucumbers into Shane's chest.

"Can I have a hug or at least a high five or something?" Kai begged. Lali repeated the nod and then left her grip on Shane to dash across the room to Kai and give him a bear hug. "Aw yeah, that's better!"

After a few minutes of stilted how-was-the-drive chat, Kai suggested, "Hey, Lali, why don't you let me show you the bed you and your mom are going to sleep in? How 'bout that?"

Lali was already following him. "What about a fort? Can there be a fort? Like, um, pillows and stuff?"

"Genius," said Kai.

When the two of them reached the second floor, staring only at Quinn, Shane said, "I know."

Quinn snorted and shook her head in disgust. "Are you out of your motherfucking mind, Shane?"

"I didn't have a choice."

"You brought your fucking daughter."

"She's here. It's done. Get over it."

Quinn started laughing. "You are a piece of work, lady. Honestly, I'm kind of speechless."

"She's what—six years old, Quinn?" Allen stood with one hand in his pocket and the other holding a beer. "What's she going to remember? Where's the harm?"

Quinn looked to Murdock, who sat on the kitchen counter. He'd gained more weight in the two years since she'd seen him in Tennessee. He wore a Nittany Lions sweatshirt and a bright red MAGA hat.

"Not ideal," he said, and swigged from a bottle of Coors.

"That's an understatement," said Quinn.

"Look, I didn't have a choice. The woman at her daycare was going to take her, but she's having surgery, and there's no one else I trust or even know well enough." She felt herself preparing to launch into a disquisition of how she spent more on childcare than rent and food, how the supplemental allowance they each got wasn't enough, and how she'd even thought of asking her boss if he could look after Lali, but what if something happened? What if Lali got sick or broke an arm and suddenly he had to get in touch? The lies would pile up and become dangerously convoluted. The two times she'd run operations since having Lali, she'd relied on Kai to come stay at her place, but in these circumstances—a meeting of the Princi-pals—that obviously wasn't possible. All of this died in her throat, however. Instead, she just said, "I brought her VR. She'll be in that the whole time we're working."

"Uhhh," said Quinn. She splayed out her hands like she could zap enti-tlement from her fingertips.

"It's the kind for kids, so it's not networked," Shane quickly explained. "She'll sit around and watch cartoon bugs splat into windshields. Relax."

Quinn shook her head and aimed her knife back at the cucumbers. Shane felt like the dumbest woman and worst mother humanity had ever coughed up.

"It's been a long day. We were up at five to catch a Greyhound. I need to pass out."

Allen rubbed his smooth, pink head. "Want some portabella pasta first?"

———————

Lali wouldn't eat anything with mushrooms and instead had cheddar Gold-fish and a juice box before Shane put her down. At least she was out as soon as her head hit the pillow. They ate at the oak dining table, Shane wolfing down three helpings and chasing it with Diet Pepsi.

"The next target. We should get a jump on that, but it's also valuable to talk about the people who got picked up." Kai was finished and had set his fork in the center of a plate scraped clean by a slice of buttered bread. He wore a dark blue sweater, lovely against his skin. He looked healthy and well rested. "They'll all be doing significant prison time."

"The lawyers have the prosecutors jammed up," said Quinn, unworried. "The sentences will get sliced away bit by bit. None of them will get time like Kroll."

"Maybe we should feel empathy, if not guilt, for the people we've led to prison," suggested Allen.

"Tabitha and Newman were the fault of Second Cell," said Shane. "That's ultimately with me. I'll debrief Jansi before the next op. They made avoidable mistakes."

"*Mmmph,*" said Murdock. He drooped in the dining room chair. "I dis-agree, Professor. Feeling guilt for patsies doing what patsies are supposed to do ain't exactly a productive use of our limited time here. Crying over spilled milk and all."

"Yes, well, they're still human beings who had free lives and now they won't. They didn't accept the risk we assigned them." Allen had opened champagne to celebrate the successful coal plant operations, only to take one sip and abandon the flute on the nicked surface of the table. Murdock huffed and rolled his eyes. Shane thought of the DNA they would leave everywhere.

"I agree with Kel," said Shane. "Spilled milk. Clean it up as best we can, and let's move on."

"Agreed," said Quinn.

"I more meant what message do we get to the lawyers?" said Kai. "Carrots and sticks to keep them quiet and doing their time."

CAUGHT Allen had followed the news at home while pretending to not care in front of Emmy. The FBI had picked up Mitchell C. Tabitha of Oregon, Daniel P. McCulloch of South Dakota, and Marie K. Newman of New Mexico. All of them had pieces of the IEDs, scraps of material (wiring, nitromethane, cell phones, detonators, and the vans), traced back to them by TEDAC. None of them had planted a bomb, though. None were good for so much as a speck of insight into even the lower ranks of their operations. John G. Gerald of Coshocton, Ohio, on the other hand, was a link closer than Allen would have liked. "You believe this, Allen?" his wife demanded. "They're railroading these poor people!" Allen shrugged it off like there was just too much to be outraged about these days.

"Seems to me they don't know enough to get to us. The guy with the closest link, according to you," Murdock looked to Allen, "is Gerald in Ohio, and all he knows is some drug dealer sent him out to look at a fence? Lasso his ass with a decent threat and carrot him with the promise that his family will get taken care of while he's away." Murdock downed his beer and shrugged his shoulders. "Simple pie."

"They have nothing on Gerald anyway," said Quinn. "Not enough proof for material support of terrorism, so the FBI's trying to make a case for felony trespassing, vandalism, attempted burglary—it's a joke. He has no idea who Allen is, and he has no connection whatsoever to Clay."

"That's right," added Shane. "According to my source, Gerald wouldn't roll, and they know their charges are over the top. They're puffing out their chest in the media, trying to shake people out of the trees by saying it's all unraveling, but that's bullshit. They're nowhere near any midlevel operative, just running in circles chasing ghosts."

"We need new recruits," said Kai. "We've asked so much of Clay these last few years. He has kids."

Shane thought about pointing out the obvious, but instead decided to

CLAY RO Was their man in Ohio, a plumber who ran his own business and had an econ degree from Ohio University. Kai had recruited him as an undergraduate, steering him into a humdrum cover. The driver and detonator of the bomb that took down Tuscarawas, Clay also had two pipelines and one gas pad under his belt. Kai feared for him, though, as they all feared for the people they'd brought in. Maybe Clay Ro's brother had once sent his DNA into an ancestry company because he was curious about how much Scottish or Korean he had in him. All it would take, in the end, was spit from a soda can or a random hair found at the scene of a bombing, and Clay would be sweating it out in a hole. He was a heroic kid.

JOHN GERALD Instead of Clay's, the FBI lifted the DNA of some hapless grocery store clerk from a Fritos bag, so they tried to threaten him with a terrorism enhancement. Kai scrambled to arrange a lawyer, who appeared out of the blue to work pro bono. Gerald weighed on Kai's conscience more than the others. Gerald hadn't sold them vans like Tabitha (who thought they'd be used to run heroin) or nitromethane from a construction site like Newman. Gerald was just a dupe who'd gotten roped in by circumstance more than anything.

familiarize herself with each knot in the wood of the rustic dining room table. She already knew the contours of the entire argument that would follow.

"We've already expanded," said Allen. "If you own a business, you know the death knell can be growing too fast."

"Insurgencies have to keep growing," Murdock replied. "They live and die on new recruits. For those of us who've fought real insurgents."

Ever since the first meeting in this cabin, they'd disagreed on how many operatives they should be adding. Allen always argued against new recruits, especially after their profile began to rise. He worried about potential defectors or, even worse, infiltrators. He'd demanded a moratorium after they activated the Second Cell. Allen had done so much of the initial scut work of recruiting with the cover of his handcrafted furniture business, which he used as a front to travel the country. He delivered his rustic tables, built out of reclaimed wood, anywhere east of the Mississippi. Over the years the Benefactor had purchased a good deal of these tables, which ended up being dropped off at Goodwill stores wherever Allen went to recruit. Beneath their own cell, they had thirty-seven active, in-the-know operatives muling supplies, moving cars, buying and selling safe houses, and of course planting bombs, and that, in Shane's opinion, was not nearly enough. Everything took too much time.

"Jansi had a few minor slipups, sure," said Quinn, "but they took out the Kentucky plant. And now Second is building a third cell?" She looked to Shane, and Shane nodded. "We should do the same."

Allen stretched his arms to place his chapped hands in the center of the table like he was setting down a Christmas ham. "The more people we bring in, the more complexity we add. Every new recruit—"

Murdock dropped his head back and snored loudly. "Boring! We've heard this before."

It was so juvenile that Allen began to scold him, and Quinn tried to interrupt with her ideas about new propaganda, and the argument spilled in three different directions at once.

Finally, Kai muttered through his hand, "Vote?" They all looked to him.

They voted four to one to add five new recruits in 2031 and elevate five operatives into a new cell.

The next morning, Shane rose early to get Lali fed and situate her upstairs with her VR, leaving her with only the educational cartridge. Allen made a breakfast of scrambled eggs, pancakes, fresh fruit, and bacon. Murdock doused his whole dish with hot sauce, stewed it together, and practically licked a hole in the china. They talked for five hours about copycats. The energy from the night before repeated itself, as they quagmired into the same frustrating, circular murk.

"Question is," said Murdock, "we took a few of the dirtiest power plants in the country off-line, maybe two thousand pounds of carbon dioxide per megawatt hour—something like that—but what of it?"

"What do you mean, 'What of it?'" asked Kai. "We blew a hole in OVP's share price."

"Yeah, but they're moving a lot of that generation to natural gas," said Quinn. "Not much better."

When they'd bankrupted Envige two years ago, they'd met at this same cabin, popping champagne, Mission Accomplished and all that. But what happened, one finds out, is that after a meticulous campaign to destroy crucial infrastructure and topple a carbon producer, the big fish turns out to be a little fish, and some oil and gas multinational just comes along and buys up their reserves and keeps digging, drilling, and fracking that carbon straight into the overloaded atmosphere. They didn't just need more operatives, they needed more followers. As Quinn was saying, "We need to get people off the message boards and into the game."

Shane, for her part, was bored by this line of debate. They had only two days. With the amount of deception it took to bring the five of them together from distant corners of the country, the bevy of lies they'd deployed to their friends, families, bosses—all of it riding on the specious premise that they'd forgotten, lost, or had their cellular devices, laptops, tablets, watches, smart clothes, pens, rings, and other techno-fashion and trackable gear stolen—they couldn't waste a moment. She only wanted to hear one word: *escalation.*

"It's a careful calibration," said Allen, "when we ask people to take things into their own hands. It's not like Murdock can set up a 'My First Claymore' workshop. We don't want people blowing themselves up with homemade pipe bombs."

Quinn's head ticked toward him, a spindly blond predator hearing a twig snap in the brush. "I thought the point of all this was to inspire people to resistance. Why else am I spending time encrypting and distributing these communiqués?"

Shane resisted rolling her eyes. Quinn's absurd communiqués calling people "to war" were, in her opinion, cringe-inducing. It made them sound like every dorm room revolutionary, and Quinn betrayed her hacktivist background with dopey leftist juvenile rhetoric that made Anonymous sound mature. Shane didn't want to acquiesce to her distaste for the only other woman among the Principals but every time they met in person, she could not help but bristle at Quinn's every little habit, motion, or notion.

"I'm reading about this group in the Niger Delta, and they've got all our identical rhetoric with an anti-colonial twist." Allen burped uncomfortably, his face pinching as the gas rose through his throat and he tried to muffle it. "Excuse me. But it's all the same: child soldiers drilling holes in people, torturing, executing. Same thing with the Maoist Naxalites in India's Red Corridor assassinating coal workers. This is not something we want to emulate, obviously, or trigger. When we ask people to join a resistance, we have to give them the tools

> **BUMPER STICKERS, T-SHIRTS, SLOGANS, TATTOOS** Quinn had flown from SFO to O'Hare before picking up the burner car to drive north. On the plane, she'd spent her time engaged in a dangerous hobby: looking at the world's reaction. A sign outside a barrister's office in Brisbane: **WE DIDN'T DO IT BUT WE DUG IT: THE OHIO RIVER MASSACRE 2030.** A banner draped across Times Square for nearly an hour before authorities cut it down: **6DEGREES IS COMING.** A quote from one of her first communiqués now on social media posts, T-shirts, bumper stickers: **DON'T TELL ME ABOUT YOUR CARBON FOOTPRINT UNLESS YOU'VE BLOWN UP A PIPELINE.** Her words now sizzling in the ether. Inspiring others. It did give her a tingle in the belly, there was no denying it.

to do so in a way that threatens no human or animal life."

Kai tapped his foot. Murdock looked irritated. Everyone stared at their plate for a moment, scrambled egg crumbs and syrup-soaked pancake bits going cold.

"It's hard," Kai finally said. "We had eleven years to prepare and put safeguards in place. There's no way to disseminate that information or that know-how without giving the FBI a manual to finding us."

"Which is why we need to build more cells," Quinn said for the fifth time that morning.

"We also don't know the effects of PRIRA," Allen added. "When we ask people to take matters into their own hands, they're facing down this amorphous, unconstitutional bill that no one really understands—"

DOMESTIC COPYCATS Crank calls and bomb threats to the New York Stock Exchange, Goldman Sachs, and Chevron corporate headquarters was about the best they'd inspired. A group of college kids in Texas bought materials to build an IED to target a refinery and had been caught before they even downloaded the instructions. When Kai first began seriously discussing this with Shane, he had known it would be vital that they appear as a hydra of cunning, the Great and Terrible Oz. The problem was, one could claim the mantle of 6Degrees, but without any of the discipline, one could measure the time it took to get caught in hours. He too was frustrated with the lack of movement from copycats. He'd imagined hordes rising up and sabotaging operations with everything from computer viruses to wrenches. He'd expected sledgehammers, axes, and screwdrivers as rebels dismantled infrastructure. Instead, there was the San Antonio 9, who didn't even bother to clear their search histories.

"PRIRA's a paper-fucking-tiger," grumbled Murdock. "We've got nothing to fear from it."

"Except drastically enhanced prison sentences," said Kai.

Murdock *pffft*ed at this. "If we're at that stage, it's all for shit anyway. Point is, they're already using every maximally extraconstitutional method on deck. What's gonna happen is they're gonna wrangle up a bunch of idiot trust fund kids like the San Antone 9, Mommy and Daddy will get lawyers, and these measures will get struck down. Meanwhile, they ain't got no fucking way of finding us. Doesn't help 'em there."

Kai and Allen were both shaking their heads. Kai said, "No one understands this bill yet."

"Tinkerbell understands it," Shane interrupted.

"Right," said Quinn. "Our fairy-fucking-godmother."

"Tinkerbell is actually just your standard-fare fairy, I think," said Murdock. Shane felt her blood beating fast because of Quinn.

"Why are you so pissed about her?" Shane demanded.

WHO WAS HUNTING THEM Quinn knew the list included the government's heavy hitters and multiple private intelligence contractors. All assembled into the Joint Terrorism Task Force, where Shane supposedly had her mole. Shane claimed that according to her woman, the JTTF was targeting mainstream environmental groups. The problem with shadowy national security apparatuses was that there was no accountability for lazy thinking. It was a multibillion-dollar Maginot Line. Nevertheless, Quinn was convinced that the gravest danger within their group was Shane's sole access to this mole. Meanwhile, Quinn, doing all the most dangerous hacking, was treated like a combination of the kid sister and the naggy aunt. She watched the girl, Lali, fret about her pissed pants, and the rest of them melt for Shane's single-mom act.

"I'm not."

"Tinkerbell is keeping us safe at great risk."

Quinn snorted. "So you say."

And then they were all talking over one another again, so that no one noticed Lali, who came down the stairs and stood at the edge of the room, wringing her hands at all the furious adults. She finally said, "Mama."

They all stopped. Lali stood looking guilty, the stain, mortifying and obvious, on the legs and inseam of her gray cotton pajama pants.

"I couldn't—I couldn't—I couldn't—I had to take a nap," she began to explain, her words coming out punctuated by the short breaths she excitedly took to avoid crying, "because I don't have my fiddle, and if I don't have my fiddle, it makes—it makes—it makes—"

"Okay, okay, dígame, mi amor. Let's get you changed." She took her daughter by the hand and led her back up the stairs.

"Me and Professor Ford are gonna walk on down to the lake. Get some fresh air." Murdock rattled a pack of Camels at Shane. "Care to join?"

Lali was playing a board game with Kai; they'd started with Clue but when that proved a bit complicated had moved a step backward to checkers. Quinn was in her room taking a nap. Kai nodded to Shane: "Go ahead. I got Lals."

"He's got Laaaals!" Lali brayed in her robot voice. She moved a black checker back and forth indecisively between two squares.

Shane bundled into her hat, boots, and gloves, yet when they stepped outside, the chill snaked into every slit. She, Allen, and Murdock stomped down the porch and into the woods, toward the bloodied lip of the sunset.

Allen led them onto a narrow trail that cut between the trees. They walked single file, with Shane bringing up the rear, as Allen pointed out the

Upper Cambrian sandstone and the forests of jack pine, oak, and aspen. The air smelled of snow.

"Invigorating," said Murdock, blowing smoke skyward. "Our benefactor's got good taste."

"She's about seven steps removed from actually making our real estate choices, Murdock," said Shane.

"Too bad—" Murdock stumbled over a hidden root, breathed a quick cuss, and sprang back up. "Speaking of! I'd be just delighted to know who she is."

"Get in line," said Allen.

They came to a fallen limb, and Murdock lifted one fat leg over it and then the other, gingerly, as if his kneecap might explode from the torque. He was huffing severely from just the short trip, his ruined body no secret to them.

PRIRA The Zombie Climate Bill, Allen's wife called it. Signed under duress during record-setting D.C. floods, a veneer of investment for renewable energy, worker retraining, and environmental justice initiatives coupled with a veritable deluge of money for national security to chase terrorist threats, including themselves. When Vic Love wasn't charming housewives by sitting for interviews on *Good Morning America* with his alarmingly handsome husband, he'd been cutting backdoor deals to include gobs of cash for military contractors, including his former company, Xuritas. Now he was the hero for pushing through what everyone was calling "the Green New Deal," even though it didn't even glance at fulfilling that daffy Keynesian castle in the sky. The bill was stuffed with money for beach sand replenishment on the coasts and loopholes that deputized private military contractors. It included money to replace lead pipes in cities but also allowed private security forces to patrol the streets of those cities. It was so expansive, so stuffed with provisions, even legal experts couldn't agree what to make of it yet. Allen had a few bets on that subject, though.

"Whoever she is, she's gotta be crazy," he said.

"Why's that?" asked Shane.

Murdock jerked a thumb back toward the cabin.

"You seen Kai, that handsome devil? How could anyone trust a bright, shiny smile like that?"

The path angled downward and the trees opened up further. The bed of red pine needles spread before them like a shag carpet. Greater volumes of white exhaust collected before Shane's face as her breathing picked up. Used to be she had to hike a mountain to get this kind of winded. Age took all kinds of things from you. She couldn't remember the last time she'd taken a walk for pleasure. Once she was off her feet after work, it was all she could do not to lock her brain into garbage television and finish an entire bag of chips.

ALLEN'S SECRET The Benefactor made
all this possible with what seemed like
bottomless funds. Part hawala, part two-bit
money laundering, her system utilized fake
online businesses to create a slush fund for
their operations. Yet it was Shane who'd really
created this. Allen met her when he quit
academia after failing to get tenure for the last
time. They were living off his wife's family's
money when he decided to find some use for
himself by joining a social justice campaign
during the BP crisis in the Gulf. As he and
Shane got to know each other (usually while
sharing some bad reefer), he'd been impressed,
engaged, activated. She spun radical fantasies
of resistance, but it wasn't like he hadn't had his
own dreams along these lines back in his youth.
Hell, it was why he'd made a career of studying
those radical movements in the first place.
Over the long years of crafting and executing
their plans, she'd taken up space in his head like
she was actually his oldest daughter. It pained
him that they had to stay so far away, that their
communication had to be so circumspect and
infrequent. When he saw her face wrench in
worry, over Lali or their cause, he wanted
nothing more than to take her hand and tell her
everything would be all right.

As the night crept closer, the lake came into view. A liquid keepsake of the Last Glacial Maximum. The pines surrounded this rippling black jewel, and the distant shores looked like a towering fortress wall. Crisp winds swayed the branches. Murdock lit one of his smokes and then handed one to Allen. The two men's faces drew together as Allen lit his off the ember of Murdock's.

"I don't know why Lali's still wetting herself." Shane hated that she felt compelled to apologize again, but she couldn't help it. "I thought I was done with that."

"My youngest, Perry, was peeing himself until he was seven," said Allen. He waved his cigarette hand around his be-hatted dome. "We thought it was because of the alopecia. It started in patches on my head and chest. He'd cry when he saw me until I finally just gave up and shaved everything, even my eyebrows. He got over it." He sighed his smoke out through his nose, and it drifted into the clear sheen of his hairless brow. "Then again, the boy is nearly twenty and still lives with us, so what do I know."

They were quiet for a moment, just enjoying the lake and the glow of the purple-gray sky while they trusted the ignorance of those who might watch from the heavens.

Shane finally said, "We need to talk about targets."

"Patience, Shane," Allen cautioned. "We'll get there."

She exhaled in frustration. "Now PRIRA is law, and it's proof the political process vomits up nothing—or worse than nothing. We have the chance to be who people turn to."

"I agree," said Murdock.

"You two," said Allen, "are running way ahead of yourselves."

She couldn't help but laugh. "We're running out of road to get ahead of ourselves on, Allen!"

Murdock meandered toward the crest of the lake where water lapped against stones, and she and Allen followed, polar darkness creeping east. Murdock stared out over the water. She watched the blue smoke whispering out of his lips.

"In Iraq, when we were near Fallujah, one of the things the insurgents liked to do was get you to go through a door, and then they'd have it wired to blow. For a while, it seemed like they were wiring bombs to every god-damn door in the city. But then there were civilians, women and little kids, running around everywhere. And none of 'em ever got blown up. Or hardly any. We couldn't figure out what the hell was going on. Even if these civilians were in on it, how was the information getting disseminated about every single door in an area with hundreds of thousands of people and nearly as many doors?" He picked up a rock and tried to skip it across the lake. It hit the water twice and then sank with a sound between a splat and a plop. "Then this guy I was EOD with, name of Kieran Slade, goes to our captain, this crazy weird fucker Ta'amu. He says, 'Captain, it's the house numbers.' See, the house numbers were always messed up, like falling off or upside down. What they were doing was, if the house was wired to blow, an odd number would be missing or turned upside down or painted over or scratched up. If it was an even—like Forty-Two Al-lahu Akbar Road—it would have a new odd number added to it. Like

MURDOCK Figured himself unlucky enough to be born in an era of murderous bipartisan military overreach. During Jo Hogan's term, it tickled him the way she conjoined feminism and militarism so seamlessly, her embrace of Brandy Squires's revelations and the Pentagon cover-up simultaneous. It was an open secret the military could be a real rape factory. Now the Dumbocrats ran vets at every level, and you could almost see in real time the wars coming home. He and his peers had cut their teeth on corralling, hunting, and monitoring brown people overseas. Now these veterans suddenly staffed every level of government. They brought skills and attitudes honed on the streets of Kabul and Fallujah and became cops and prison guards and senators and consultants to the defense industry. They chose their routes of right-wing extremism or intersectional patriotism. So when a Jo Hogan or Mary Randall or Vic Love inveighed against the threat of terrorism, almost no one blinked. In his time overseas, Murdock had gotten a sneak peek at what was gestating in the body politic, and the civvies would soon learn just how casual violence could be.

an upside-down five. Pretty simple. Sorta like our code with the books. You don't need nothing fancy because the other guy doesn't know what to look for."

A startled heron burst from the nearby shore and soared across the lake, its tucked feet skimming a line in the placid water.

"So you stopped them?" asked Allen.

"For a while. We pretended we were getting lucky. Like every once in a while, Ta'amu'd even send a robot through a door just so it could get blown up, but pretty soon the insurgents figured out we'd figured it out. They moved on."

He wetted dry lips so that they shone in the last of the light. "Those motherfuckers, AQI and the Mahdi Army, they were clever and barbaric and romantic. The civilians they'd killed—their families would be rooting for them anyway. That code? It became insurgent lore. Folk tales are inspiration. Reminds your people why you fight. Sometimes I think of us in that sense. If we're not giving people a story, there ain't no point. Might as well chuck our tears at the sky."

He met Shane's gaze when he said this, and she stepped away, to the shoreline's nearest pine.

"Some narratives are better than others, though, Murdock," Allen said.

"Oh sure, Professor."

"What about Slade?" Shane asked, running her fingers over cold bark. "He's dead, I take it. Got blown up going through a door after they switched the system."

"Nah. He's fine. Hates my guts for going antiwar, never spoke to me again, but he made it just fine."

To Shane it sounded like there was way more to that story, but it was almost dark. She said as much to her friends. The three of them turned and headed back up the hill where a bitter dark swallowed the cabin.

That night, unable to sleep, Shane left Lali in bed and crept down to the living room where she found Quinn awake, indulging in a twenty-four-hour news network and the copy of a print newspaper left on the end table. Volume hushed, her attention flitted between the newsprint and screen where a young Dan Rather, CBS's granite-faced star of the late twentieth century, held forth.

"Should you be watching that?" she said.

"Jesus!" Quinn clapped a hand to her chest.

"You scared the shit out of me, Shane."

"Sorry, I couldn't sleep."

Digital resurrection was a nifty trick, and on the TV, CGI Dan Rather sent it off to a correspondent reporting from CPAC where that woman Braden was the headliner. At every sight of her, Shane felt a darkness creep into her periphery, something she was sure every person of color felt from time to time, this unsettling understanding that you are a part of a place where you don't belong and have never belonged, where at any moment, the violence that made this world possible might erupt anew.

THE MIDTERMS The Republican Party had shattered its chains. Gone were the Obama-era Tea Partiers, careful to disguise their racism behind a veneer of concern for the deficit. Vanquished were the squishy Trumpist apparatchiks trying to remain obsequious under shifting sands of presidential whims. This new crop were honest-to-God Klansman, theocrats, and outspoken fascists. Top priorities included bringing the death penalty for abortion doctors and any woman who sought the procedure, an end to birthright citizenship, and a Muslim registry, once and for all.

THE WEATHERMEN, WANTED: DEAD OR ALIVE Read a sign above Jennifer Braden's worlde set.

CHINA Had its hands full. The Communist Party was arresting people by the thousands in an attempt to contain the Minyun democracy movement, which had cracked open the Great Firewall with multiple cyberattacks. The weather was also savaging the country: images of floods shredding whole towns to splinters and inundating cities to the second floors of office towers in Guangxi Province, while wildfires in Sichuan had killed 134 people in the past month.

AUSTRALIA Terrifying images of Perth. Dan Rather narrated over images of glowing orange hills, the city choking in smoke from wildfires. Protestors were lying down in front of the Carmichael Mine, but policy refused to acknowledge the obvious links, and the coal kept flowing.

MACKOWSKI AND BRADEN Mackowski had declared his intent to challenge President Randall for the nomination but was being taunted by the Right's vicious Barbie pit bull. Braden advocated that land mines be planted in the desert along the US-Mexico border. Mackowski, backed into a corner, promised to introduce a land mine bill in the next Congress. Rumor had it she had her own presidential aspirations. Announcement forthcoming.

MISCELLANEOUS
TERRORS Hindus massacring Muslims in India. A mutated strain of multidrug-resistant tuberculosis blazing through the Russian prison system, killing an average of nearly eight hundred prisoners a day. The island nation of Tuvalu preparing to abandon its land as seawater crippled the last of its infrastructure. Quinn ran her fingers along a faint scar on her left wrist: a teenage suicide effort. She'd undergone treatments of electroconvulsive therapy, and the induced seizures brought her peace like nothing else had. Now, she preferred ketamine treatments.

HORROR DRONES The combat footprint of the US now stretched from Kyrgyzstan to Angola. The latest imperial weapon was a hovering machine gun the size of a large dog that could buzz through doorways, caves, or sewers, fire its M4, launch grenades, or perform crowd control with high-decibel speakers and rubber bullets. The Northrup XR-32 earned its name from the pilots who tended to adorn the faceless sensor panel with the war paint of such iconic pop culture images as the hockey mask of serial killer Jason Voorhees or the metalloid-skeletal grin of the Terminator. In CBS's slavish story on the new sci-fi nightmare, one pilot petted his drone and said, "We chase terrorists through their holes flashing the strobe [lights] and blaring death metal. I can't imagine how terrifying that would be."

THE PASTOR This B-list actor turned jolly preacher-guru had erupted into mainstream stardom and now his fellow Evangelicals were having buyer's remorse. He misquoted the Bible or made up new passages, they moaned, yet his book *God Has a Plan for You* had sold 1.3 million copies in 2030. He claimed he'd prophesied Covid-19 as well as the "great storm coming to wash away the sinful" just before Hurricane Alberto hit Virginia Beach. Now he was declaring that the "vipers' nest of sin known as Hollywood" would "suffer in hellfire for shutting out Christianity." While Los Angeles County would certainly experience its standard round of wildfires every summer, one poll found an astonishing 39 percent of the country believed this idiot to be a prophet of God, according to Gallup. He was coming out with his own branded Bible.

"Join the club," said Quinn, and she muted the television. Shane moved to sit beside her.

"I thought we agreed to keep this unplugged," she said.

"Fine." Quinn got up and janked the plug from the wall, short-circuiting Braden's wet, red-lipsticked mouth as she joyfully inflamed the crowd. "I just couldn't think of anything else to do." Quinn tapped the newspaper on the end table. "They have a story about Kroll. Civil rights and enviro folks are trying to get him out of solitary confinement."

"And I hope they succeed."

"You think you could handle that? Twenty-three-hour lockdown?"

"I will if I have to."

Quinn nodded but this clearly did not satisfy her. She'd been Kai's recruit, their activist pasts overlapping somewhere that neither of them spoke of. She did her job well, but she also flaunted simple rules, like turning on the TV when she thought she was alone. Shane knew Quinn had grown up rich, attended an Ivy, and only toyed with hacktivism before moving on to one of the top cybersecurity firms in the Valley. All that blond arrogance made Shane deeply distrustful.

"So why do we let them dictate to us?" Quinn wondered. Her head bobbed at the stairs. "Those three. Especially Kai."

"I don't see it that way."

"Then what exactly do you see? He's got the Benefactor, so he's got the money. Wouldn't your life be easier with a couple grand a month more?"

"It's a firewall."

"Like you and Tinkerbell, huh? And what if you or Kai get caught. Where does that leave us?"

> **FREE MILES KROLL** Obnoxious that he'd become their public face. Stuck in prison, he had do-gooders raising money for his defense. But Miles was a gutless coward, who'd tried to sell their operation out for a few years off his sentence. After his capture, they'd put more safeguards in place and Quinn had doxxed, manipulated, and harassed his family into deep space, adding child pornography to his father's computer, ruining his mother's credit, and serving Kroll's whole sad life on a platter to the Feds to keep him in there permanently. She showed this example to operatives now, like a head on a pike.

> **QUINN** More or less feared Shane, and then resented herself for being afraid. Shane's eyes were sleepy, dark brown pools, and they simply betrayed nothing. No matter how much she dug into the woman's past, utilizing every tool at her disposal, there was nothing there before roughly 2013. Obviously, "Shane Acosta" was not her real name and yet that identity tracked. She looked like a real person, and Quinn could not figure out how she'd done it. It scared her that this frazzled single mother, who couldn't find a babysitter for her kid, might be smarter than her. Which was why, when she'd heard Shane awake and moving in her room, she'd gone downstairs and turned on the TV. To see if she could get her alone for a moment, away from the men. To put out the first simple feelers.

"There are contingencies in place. This woman—Tinkerbell—had to beat multiple brain scan polygraphs. She's the real deal, and she's putting herself at just as much risk as we are."

Quinn picked up an empty beer bottle that wasn't hers and began to glumly scrape the label free from the coffee-dark glass.

"Shane, if you want to broach subjects that no one else will . . ." Outside the window, dawn had begun to crack the night, and there was that eerie blue-gray glow overcoming the woods.

Quinn had a cruel and excited look, like a sorceress about to conjure black magic into the room. "I'm with you. One thing you should know, though. If we get caught"—a burst of winter wind rattled the windowpanes—"I have a bottle of prescription painkillers that I'm going to eat like cereal."

———————

On their last day, over dinner, talk turned to Kate Morris and A Fierce Blue Fire.

"We should thank our lucky stars," said Kai. "They're so obsessed with Morris, they have no idea what they're looking for. That's why I was saying PRIRA is our friend. Eviscerating civil liberties is every Fed, cop, and politician's first approach. It keeps them looking at all the wrong people in all the wrong places."

"And that dumb floozy helped to pass it," said Murdock.

"I think," said Allen, "that you folks should accept the idea that her movement has been complementary to ours. We're not antagonists."

"Yeah, screw that," said Kai. "She spent ten years pretending at revolution while she eff-you-see-kayed celebrities and spread memes. That's the Left, Allen. It's a Facebook page that occasionally sends its troops into the streets with cute signs before they hit the yoga studio."

"Mama," said Lali from the seat beside her. "I need a spoon. The fork doesn't work."

"She was the climate reality show du jour," said Quinn. "But now she's learning what all women learn: Don't get crow's-feet or they'll recast your ass."

"I still wouldn't kick her out of bed for eating crackers," said Murdock.

Shane slammed her fork down on the table. "Could we *please* give it a fucking rest?"

Lali popped her head up, alarmed more by the tone than the F-word. They were all looking at her now.

"I'm just so sick of everything about that woman."

There was a moment of quiet, and then Allen said, "Okay. New subject." And they all moved on.

After dinner, Lali was riled up, jumping on the bed in her pajamas and giggling while Badman Kai swooped around the room using a blanket as a cape. It was only in this moment that Shane realized Lali was saying "Badman" when she meant "Batman." This was another one of her malapropisms that actually made more sense, like how she called the shuttle bus that zipped around KU's campus the "shuffle bus." It did sort of shuffle, and Batman was a bad man, the spoiled son of a billionaire waging his own one-man paramilitary war. When she played Tracy Chapman, Lali would sing her favorite song loudly and enthusiastically, *"Don't you eat all the shiny apples / Don't you taste all of my fruit."*

"Lali, time to settle down," she said.

"I'm settling down!" Lali shrieked happily, then starfished backward onto the bed with a *whoomph* of the mattress and a giggle like the Joker. It took her and Kai another ten minutes and a mix of stern and sweet to cajole her under the covers. She worked herself into the crook of Kai's arm as he began to read to her.

> **KAI** It wasn't like he didn't share her disdain for the quasi-celebrities the climate non-movement kept spitting up. Hell, that was one of the first things he and Shane bonded over when they met in NOLA. This wasn't about Morris, though. For her to snap at them like that, something else must be going on. He'd been worried about Shane all weekend. She had a nervous edge to her, and he'd catch her face twitching like she was gritting through some kind of chronic pain. The way she looked at Lali worried him especially.

Ever since she made the decision to not drive two states over to find a clinic, it felt like seven years of failure. From forgetting to take folic acid to prevent spina bifida, to all the meconium they had to suction from Lali's lungs so that Shane couldn't hold her, and for an hour she thought her baby was dead. Lali didn't have a "social smile" until well past eight weeks. She didn't walk until twenty-one months, and she'd been nonverbal for nearly two years. At seven months, Shane had taught her to blink her little eyes hard whenever she heard *"¡Ojitos!"* But the ordeal of getting her fluent in one language destroyed any determination she had of raising her with two.

Kai turned a page, and Lali's *ojitos* grew heavy. Then, of course, there were the things no one told you in any parenting class: like how despite having another human being with you all the time, you'd be unbearably lonely. You'd ache for touch in a way you'd never ached in your life. Shane had gone the clichéd route and started sleeping with her boss. Because Teddy, overweight and friendly with the staff, had so looked and sounded like a manager who would sexually harass her, she gave him too much credit when he didn't. Still, he offered touch, and sometimes she needed that so badly.

"You okay with her?" she asked Kai.

He nodded. "We got this."

"We got this," Lali repeated sleepily.

"'Cause we're what?" Shane asked her.

"'Cause we're outlaws," Lali replied on cue.

"Okay, *mi amor. Duerme bien.*" She kissed her on the forehead.

Downstairs, she found the living room empty and saw Allen alone outside by the firepit. He'd whipped up a real blaze.

"The little one's asleep?" he asked.

She took a seat in the Adirondack chair and felt the heat from the flames on her legs. "Almost. Finally calmed down. She's driving me a little crazy."

"They'll do that to you."

Shane resisted pointing out that Allen's wife, Emmy, had done most of the work raising their kids while he pursued a career in academia.

"Earlier, Lali kept throwing acorns in the air?" said Allen. "It was all she wanted to do."

"Oh. She . . ." Shane laughed and shook her head. "She figured out this thing about bats."

"What about them?"

"Their sonar. How they'll dive at an acorn because they think it's a bug. She goes into our backyard and throws stuff at the sky to get the bats to dive at it. She thinks it's so funny."

Allen laughed loudly at this. It was a kind and beautiful sound. She'd first met him in the Gulf during the BP crisis as he was trying to transition from "the piss-pot of academia to doing something right for the world." She learned he'd spent his career writing about the School of the Americas, where the US military had spent decades training death squads. He'd traveled South America extensively, without speaking nearly enough Spanish. It wasn't that he reminded her of her dad, but he spoke like a father. His voice was calming. When she and Kai decided to take the first step in this plan, she'd gone to see Professor Allen Ford. They'd met in a Cracker Barrel near Clemson, and she pulled from her battered pack a dossier: law enforcement protocols, data collection practices, surveillance techniques, over a hundred pages on the civilian explosive tracking system and the "date/plant/shift code," and then targets—all that gas and drilling infrastructure lying out there, exposed. He hadn't laughed in her face. Instead, he had questions.

Twenty years later, she adored him because he looked at her with love and she felt so little of that in her life these days. She almost didn't mind what he asked next.

"Kai's not her father, is he?"

She leaned forward, into the intensity of the heat.

"That's not your business, Allen."

"No," he admitted. "It's not. But since you've had her—this can't be easy on you. I guess what I'm saying is if you ever want out, Shane, I'll be there for you. I'll talk to the others. I'll be on your side. We can make it so you can just fade away. I'll get you money. You can raise her somewhere safe."

She let out a humorless snort. "As if there is such a place." They were quiet for a while. "You know what I think about sometimes? I wonder about her future, but not like, what will happen as the planet buckles. What I think about is, 'Can we afford college?'"

"That seems reasonable, hon."

"No it's not," she said matter-of-factly. "It's really not. But I can't stand the thought of her life being like mine. Where she's constantly worried about her bank account. Where she's terrified of losing a tip and will put up with anything some pig customer says because if she doesn't get his five bucks, it's a minor catastrophe. I don't want her to ever live a life like the one I've had."

As Allen opened his mouth to reply, Quinn's boots creaked across the warped-wood porch.

"Should we finish this?" she said.

Shane and Allen rose to go inside, leaving the fire to smolder down to its coals.

It was closing in on midnight. They all had to be back on the road the next day. Shane sat on the living room's large plush couch, while Quinn sat pretzel-style at the other end, her wool-socked feet tucked under her. Allen hunched forward in the armchair breathing noisily through a deviated septum. Murdock stood at the kitchen counter, playing with a plastic clip for a potato chip bag. Kai sat sideways at the head of the dining table, his back straight, hands clenched as if at the helm of a ship fighting rough waves.

"A corporate headquarters is easier in some ways, harder in others," Murdock explained. "I could probably get it done with a hillbilly mix of some kind. Off the top of my head, a brew of gas, diesel, and glycerin tar soap—splash some of that around—but it's more time intensive."

"I don't like the idea of office buildings," said Kai. "So much harder to control."

"We still make a call to evacuate," Quinn argued. "Principally, it's the same procedure."

They agreed they needed escalation, but they'd been going around for hours about what that escalation should look like. All kinds of ideas had been floated.

"Industry is beefing up security—satellites tracking pipelines, drones watching power plants, engineers monitoring grids." Quinn shook her head. She'd been chewing her nails to splinters all night. Greasy strands of hair hung in her face, the same candlelit color as the homey lamps of the cabin. "An office building might actually be a softer target now."

"But much harder to control the variables of the attack," Kai repeated.

"It's also not *infrastructure*. An office building . . ." Allen made a troubled sound in the back of his throat. "It's personal. It's leaning toward humans instead of machinery."

Kai stood. They'd shut off the lights in the rest of the cabin. It created the illusion of isolation, an island of light. The wood crackled and hissed in the fireplace. Kai fed it another log but didn't sit back down.

"Okay," said Kai. "We have a few ideas on the table: Why not all of them?"

Quinn's eyes drifted up from her ragged nails. "All of them?"

"Yes. All of them. The refinery, the tar sands facility, the dragline manufacturer. We have two cells, dozens of operatives ready and willing, and we have this new delivery method"—he nodded at Murdock, clacking away with the potato chip clip—"that Kel is itching to try out. Our original goal was to create disastrous uncertainty in the market for dirty energy, make it too risky and expensive for investors, but it's all been surprisingly resilient. So let's hit the full fucking menu."

Shane felt an agitation bubbling in her core. The urge to interrupt a friend can itch worse than a hive.

"We keep it geographically dispersed. All in a twenty-four-hour period. We show them we're everywhere."

"What about the office building?" asked Quinn.

"We shouldn't hit office buildings," said Allen.

"Why is that so important to you?" she demanded.

"Our only goal is to inflict damage on the infrastructure," he reminded her.

"A corporate headquarters is infrastructure, Allen. It's where they make the decisions on how to best turn the world to ash for shareholder value."

"We don't want to inspire the wrong thing. It's not a far step from office buildings to playgrounds."

"They have significant equipment in their Calgary offices," said Kai. "I'm not saying it's a must."

They all jumped as a hard gust slammed the living room windows. It sounded like someone smacking the glass with a palm, and only the moan of the wind that followed reassured them they were still alone. Nevertheless, they sat in silence for a moment, and Shane knew their four hearts were pounding as hard as hers.

"Maybe." Quinn hugged her knees to her chest. "What I think—and what I've always thought—is we need to escalate toward some version of total war. Whatever that means for us. Destroy the *economic infrastructure*, and if that means bridges, railroads, the electric grid, server storage facilities, so be it."

Shane watched Allen squirm at this. "We'll garner no support for taking away people's comforts."

"I'm sorry, Quinn," Kai added. "But you have a bad habit of entertaining high-cost fantasies. We're not toppling capitalism in one fell swoop. We're propogandists eking out greenhouse gas reductions where we can and raising insurance, security, and operational costs. That's always been the plan."

"Have you seen how little this is working?" Quinn stabbed two fingers at the coffee table. The beer bottles and chip crumbs rattled. "We first came here in 2014, and we didn't execute our first operation until nearly a decade later. Now almost *another* decade has gone by. Seventeen years, and the situation has gone from catastrophic to apocalyptic. We are out of time, and you two show no fucking urgency."

And then the two of them were arguing, as juvenile and simple-minded as a debate in a Slapdish worlde. Quinn told Kai to go write press releases for Aamanzaihou. Kai told Quinn to go tack up a Che Guevara poster in her dorm room. And on they went. Murdock clacked his potato chip clip and pouted his lower lip like he was watching a good show. Allen rubbed his bald head. Finally, Shane stood and walked to the fire, interrupting their argument with her tired body.

"Enough," she said. They quieted. "Quinn's right."

"Right about what?" Allen asked.

"Our approach."

"That's cryptic," said Kai.

"We're not effective because we're not that frightening. Not really. We're cute. An amusing sideshow in the news cycle. A nuisance at best." She looked into the fire. "That's why they don't use our real name. They're calling us the same thing as the last cute little group of revolutionaries who changed nothing."

"Besides, what makes them think only men can pull this off?" Quinn joked. No one was in the mood.

"It's been seventeen years," she said, and those words lingered for a moment.

"Shane." Murdock tossed the clip on the counter. "It's late, and we're all gone tomorrow. Maybe just say what it is you want to say, huh?"

Shane looked directly at Kai when she said, brusquely, determinedly, "Targets. In politics and business. So-called civilians, if you believe in such a thing."

There was a moment of quiet as all their minds worked around the wording. Kai glared at her.

"Absolutely not." He crossed his arms and shook his head. "We're not even discussing that. Move on."

"That's not how this works. We hear each other out—"

"Move on."

"You don't have a veto, Kai."

"Move. The fuck. On."

"I want to hear what she has to say," said Quinn.

"*No,*" cried Kai. He gripped a living room chair and slammed its legs against the hardwood. "That is not what we're about. We're not even talking through it. That's not why we— That's not— We're not killers—"

KAI While driving across Illinois once as a teenager, on his way to visit his then girlfriend on winter break from college, his car hit a patch of ice and spun out at nearly seventy mph. There was that skidding, slippery sense of an absolute loss of control, of having one's fate served up to chance in a way that felt so unfair, so terrifying. Now he searched for any way to wrestle the wheel back.

"I'm a killer." Murdock took a seat on a living room chair, bringing a fat leg up under its partner so that he looked like an oversized version of the pudgy children in Lali's daycare. "I was part of a savage military campaign that killed hundreds of thousands and turned the Middle East to rubble. I don't shirk my complicity in that. Not anymore." He gestured to the chair

Kai had just rattled. "Now, before we go start calling each other 'murderer' I suggest we hear Shane out, as per the rules we established long ago and far away. Then we vote. Like always."

After a moment Kai did as Murdock demanded, pulled the chair out and sat back down, furious but silent. Murdock's eyes slid to Shane, offering her the floor again. She took it.

"What makes us think these elites are any different from all the other tyrants and kings who've come before? Because they wear suits? If anything, they're worse. We are talking about people who are happily incinerating the conditions for life on Earth for nothing more than a few quarters of profit. We can hem and haw about violence, but—fuck, man—they are the most violent people history's ever seen. And there's just *no time left.*"

She huffed a disbelieving breath and put her hands on her hips like she couldn't believe her daughter had wet herself again.

"There won't be any chance to look back and second-guess because we can't wait a few decades to build a worthwhile mass resistance. By then it'll be too late. So how will they be stopped? This is the only tactical move left. The corporate state is faceless. The fossil-fuel elite is anonymous, but behind this holocaust there are human beings, and they have addresses. We can rip those masks right off. I see three benefits to this. First, it's easy. Small bombs or a handgun. All you need are one or two operatives per target. We've built a clandestine network in an age when that's supposedly impossible. The second advantage is that it demonstrates what's *actually* at stake. This is life and death for all of us, and it's time to choose sides.

> QUINN Felt a thrill crawl up her legs and arms into the core of her chest. Finally, someone was going to say what she'd been thinking since roughly 2016 when the country went truly dark and all the evil men stepped right out into the spotlight. They needed to be stronger, fiercer, and crueler than the people they were up against, or they stood no chance. Kai tried to catch her eye because he surely thought he could persuade her back to his side, but she ignored him. Shane looked positively frightening standing there, this fattening, bedraggled mother suddenly picking up the sword.

> PROPAGANDA OF THE DEED Part of Allen's curriculum for his class about radical movements always included the anarchists of the 1880s and '90s who attempted to instigate insurrection by assassinating various "class enemies." How frustrating that history was so chockful of lessons that people so heedlessly ignored again and again. To lecture Shane on how those killings did far more to alienate the working classes than inspire them seemed, in this context, rather pointless: Where's the thrill in learning about history when you can make history? He'd feared this moment for some time now, that one of them might suggest such a thing. He just never thought it would be Shane.

We offer amnesty to anyone who turns against the fossil system, who joins us in sabotage or resistance. Otherwise, every defender and apparatchik of the regime is fair game." She paused. "Their families are fair game."

"Jesus Christ," whispered Kai, rubbing his face.

"You know what scares me?" She pointed upstairs, her voice straining. "That something awful is coming for my daughter. These people, the carbon profiteers and the politicians who do their bidding—they own every aspect of the system. They own the courts, the media, the political process at every level. That's why this has all been futile so far." She thumped her chest with a fist. "So they need to feel the fear *that I feel for her*. They need to feel that something is coming for them and theirs."

Kai massaged his eye sockets. The dishwasher hummed. Outside, the gentle tinkling of wind chimes.

"You said three," said Quinn. "Benefits, you said."

"The third is simple." Shane paused. "People enjoy killing. We'll recruit easily."

Kai shook his head, staring straight at the dark green carpet.

"Well," said Murdock. "This just got real. Someone tell me why Shane ain't right on this."

"If it's not self-evident, Murdock—" Kai began, and Allen cut him off with a palm.

"I've got three reasons for Shane's three reasons." He looked at her with a father's practiced disappointment and held his hand in the OK sign. "First, we've got to understand that the five of us—no matter how many new cells we start—we're never winning this in any military sense. It's, how they say, about hearts and minds. Right now, we're folk heroes to a certain set. We will lose popular support the minute we start killing people." Shane saw that he was sweating, and because he had no eyebrows to catch the beads, he had to swipe at his brow as he searched for the words. "The media might be calling us terrorists, but people do not think of us like ISIS or neo-Nazis. We take a

> **MURDOCK** Hadn't thought Shane had it in her. He'd pegged her as more the mother hen of the group or the glue guy, in sports terms. Not that he wasn't still in love with the lady. Speaking of inconvenient truths. When he looked between the professor, Kai, and Quinn Worthington, though, he could see far down the road. His brain fireworked, the way it sometimes did, and he wondered if he was back in Iraq or in this cabin or off in some restaurant in the future, discussing their endgame and watching darkening clouds roll in across stewing whitecapped water.

human life and that changes. Second"—he flashed a peace sign—"the way I see it, alls we'd be doing is killing cogs in a machine. Nothing more. It's time and work and risk to take out an interchangeable functionary. They mint thousands of new ones in the Ivy League every year. Finally"—he held his index finger high—"we differ with Morris and her ilk about what 'nonviolence' means, yes, but nonviolent movements ultimately succeed by flipping those within the power structure. Our goal shouldn't be to kill them but recruit them. Wake up their souls."

He appeared to want to say more but closed his mouth. Shane regarded each of them.

"Shall we vote?"

As she packed her and Lali's bags into the trunk of the Subaru and buckled her daughter into the booster seat, Shane marveled that Murdock's car was already gone. Still military in his ability to rise at the crack of dawn. Quinn was still showering, and Kai would be the last to leave, going over the house with bleach in addition to the deep-cleaning crew that would arrive the next day. She and Lali had eight hours to Des Moines and another five by bus back to Lawrence. She was brooding on the dread of that interminable trip when she spotted a figure in the woods. At first, her stomach dropped. Her vision grayed. Specters of blue-jacketed FBI agents and SWAT killers, guns drawn, surrounding the cabin, ready to put a bullet through her and take her daughter. Shane even began to put her hands in the air. Then she realized the figure was just Allen. Wearing his dark toboggan cap and smoking. He waved. The hazy winter sun had been in her eyes.

The lump shot up her throat without warning, and she turned away from Lali. *Do not let her see you cry again.*

But to do this, she had to leave her daughter. She had to stalk off toward the woods, down the path that led to the lake. The early morning was awash in blue-gray mist, and Shane wanted nothing more than to simply vanish into it.

"Mama?" Lali wondered behind her. "Mama!"

"Just a minute," Shane yelled back over her shoulder. But she kept walking, practically running. The tears broke, and her feet carried her farther until she was in the woods, alone, huffing and weeping, the crystal sheen of the lake visible just beyond the mist.

A moment later Allen emerged from the fog.

"Shane?" He approached her carefully, his old-man pants flapping around stocky legs. "You okay?"

She was trembling all over. He put a hand on her shoulder, and she whipped away from it. "Get off."

Tears coated her face, snot crusted her upper lip like Lali, who never felt embarrassed by letting a tantrum collect mucus there. Allen stayed a step back.

"You're upset we're not going to murder people."

"Fuck you, Allen," she spat. She started toward the shore to get away from him. He followed.

"Shane." She kept walking. "Shane, stop." He grabbed her elbow, and when she tried to yank it away, he held on. "Stop." He pulled her to him. "The vote went against you. It's over. Trust me, I know." He took her shoulders and looked her in the eyes. She thought of her parents and what had happened to them. "Shane, you made the argument that had to be made," he said.

Her cheeks were freezing, and her ears sang with pain. The CO2 plumed around each of their mouths and mingled between them. She was so lonely all the time.

"That's not why—" she sobbed. "What are we doing? It's too late. *We are too late.*"

"It's not too late." He pulled her against him. She let herself be held because what else could she do? She lay one pained ear against his shoulder, and he covered the other with his gloved hand, like he knew how much it hurt.

"Of course it's too late," she sobbed. "Of course it is."

Shane wept. Everyone stood by watching in disbelief as their home slipped away, looking at each other, wondering if anyone would do anything about it. The five of them were supposed to be the affirming flame. The last hope. Gazing through tears at the arachnid limbs of the trees, the wind blew frigid air into her eyes, and she knew they stood there, in this moment, at a fiery crossroads.

The Years of Rain and Thunder: Part III

2031

We were still in the office at midnight when Kate got a text and everything changed. We couldn't have known it then, but it was the moment when the bill began to fall apart, when the internal schisms of A Fierce Blue Fire widened into chasms, and nearly ten years of work began to evaporate in the span of a few weeks.

It was July 29, 2030, a grueling Monday because we'd already been in the office all weekend. Everyone had left for the night except myself, Kate, Liza, Tom, Coral, and Rekia. After being stalled for the past five months, our legislation had found life in the Senate. The addition of massive pork projects had a waffling Ohio senator coming aboard and another from Iowa said she was close. This would be enough to carry it at least into reconciliation with the House version. We were deep in an argument, Tom and Rekia butting heads, Coral trying to referee, when Kate interrupted.

"Liza," she said, staring at her phone. "Turn on CNN."

At first, there was still confusion as to what had happened, but by 3 a.m. of July 30 we had the basics: three bombs, three power plants, and a communiqué from 6Degrees, also known as the Weathermen, claiming responsibility. We all sat there, reading and watching until dawn. I remember Kate's face tight, her eyes haggard, and the one thing she uttered before she went home to collapse from exhaustion: "Motherfuckers just cost us our Ohio senator."

But it would be worse than that. A Fierce Blue Fire had made a huge bet: that we and our followers could fundamentally realign the American political system, and when Mary Randall won with a bipartisan coalition of voters, vowing to take aggressive action on climate change, it all felt within reach. Kate and the rest of us had done the slow, careful work of movement building. We'd constructed Outposts in communities long abandoned by the Left, and as renewable industries spread, it began to create politically contestable areas that had been rock-solid red for generations, all of it paving the way for Randall and a coalition of climate hawks to take control, a once-unthinkable development.

That night I recalled the euphoria following the '28 election, when our gamble on Randall held the promise of a religious awakening, and the dust storm that followed just weeks later. A decade of drought followed by insatiable winds that picked up what looked like most of the soil of Arizona, North Texas, and Oklahoma, and blew it eastward. We all watched it advance in real time on the internet, first as it rocked vehicles on their struts and choked livestock across the cattle states, packing their stomachs full of dirt. A handful of people who couldn't get out of the storm's path actually suffocated in the open air. Crossing over the Appalachians, the vast nebula finally reached the East Coast. Kate and I woke the morning of its arrival because Dizzy was going ballistic, pacing back and forth, running to the window and then running away. For two days most of the Mid-Atlantic watched through the dustlight of shifting red, orange, yellow, and blue as those fine grains of silt reflected sunlight fifty miles above in mesospheric clouds. It looked like the dawn of hell itself.

THE DUST BOWL RETURNS, trumpeted the *Post*. Masks and goggles sold out, people duct-taped their windows and still the grit penetrated everything. In our apartment, it came in through crevices we could never entirely seal. We opened the cupboards and the plates were all coated. You couldn't leave a glass of water out for a minute without it tasting like sand. Kate's hair turned stiff and gray, and I'd close my mouth and feel my molars crunch on the grit. We could look out the office windows, over the Potomac, and see nothing but the headlights and taillights of traffic, fuzzy in the beige gloom beneath an iridescent alien sky. As Randall took office and hearings began, one could tell there were a lot of Republican lawmakers who wanted to get climate legislation done, survive their future primaries, and never look out the window at anything like that ever again.

After the legislative process got off to a rocky start, our most important congressional ally, Joy LaFray, moved the shock collar through the House Energy Committee while Judith Kastor led a small but brave contingent of Green Tea Republicans to yea votes. While much of the political-entertainment complex focused for a month on what it meant that President Randall had begun to wear her hair in natural curls, LaFray-Kastor, a 2,500-page piece of legislation that would remake American life, was muscled through by seven votes in the second month of Randall's presidency. Of course, the Pollution Reduction, Infrastructure, and Refund Act was not perfect. Fresh enemies were made. Everyone accused everyone of various betrayals. The compromise was good enough, though: a rising tax on fossil fuels at the point of origin, with the money to be redistributed to every taxpayer and some set aside to buy off industry and invest in adaptation efforts; an additional host of regulations would be phased in, and the government would spend $2.8 trillion over ten years to accelerate decarbonization, help move displaced workers into the clean tech economy, and begin work on drawdown efforts and other environmental remediation projects with half the money to be targeted at a variety of impoverished and vulnerable communities. It wasn't everything we'd been angling for, but as one of the bill's principal authors, Ash al-Hasan, explained to me, "It puts in place the mechanisms. Future legislation can build from these efforts."

When I first met Ash through Joy LaFray, I recognized him as the pensive climate modeler who'd also advised Senator Cy Fitzpatrick. Strikingly handsome with a lean build, chiseled jaw, and menacing eyes, Ash was a strange and brilliant man. He wore the same suit and tie every day, wrote notes to himself mid-conversation, and made odd gestures without appearing to realize it. He was viewed as one of the most serious thinkers in climate policy circles, and many people loathed that he preferred math to ambitious vision. Senator Fitzpatrick said of him, "Guy's heart probably beats once an hour."

I was dispatched to a particularly tense meeting after a group of vacillating reps made clear the price of their support would be a subsidy for utilities that had coal plants still online. LaFray was apoplectic.

"Why should we buy any of them off?" she demanded. "We're going to end up with the European cap-and-trade system—just an ineffectual hodgepodge of goodies for the industries we're trying to snuff out."

"Trust no one but firemen," Ash said. Everyone in the meeting looked at him.

LaFray demanded, "What's that have to do with the price of tea in China, Hasan?"

"Just to say, the fireman has only one job, and that's to stop the fire any way he can. We are forcing a number of vested interests to walk the plank, so to speak, and these interests are demanding that instead of using a sword to walk them to the precipice, we use a shovel. Or a hammer. The only thing that matters is maintaining an incentive system that will degrade the political constituency currently invested in burning hydrocarbons."

He paused to look around the room. A bunch of blank faces gazed back at him. "Apologies. I've long been enamored with similes and metaphors. Mostly because I'm so bad at them."

"Man, I thought those were great," I chimed in. "I'll use the fireman thing on my dad."

After the meeting let out, he approached me to ask, "Would you like to eat a slushie with me?"

We began meeting outside the Russell Building to go for slushies near the Mall. Ash always ordered blue raspberry, his lips and tongue turning indigo as we spoke.

"We need the Senate to include a low-carbon tariff in its version," he explained, slurping syrupy ice. "So at least there's a chance we can force it through during reconciliation. I fear, though, industry is only beginning to organize. The alligator's jaw muscles are built to snap shut; they take a long while to wind open."

"Man, you're great at metaphors. I don't know who's telling you otherwise."

Ash was right, though. The carbon lobby was caught flat-footed by the speed with which Mary Randall captured the nomination, won election, and passed a bipartisan bill in the House. Even longtime Washington insiders were staggered by the lobbying campaign that followed. Over three thousand lobbyists were deployed, half of whom were former government officials. Aboveboard advertisements filled every niche of public life, from the NFL to the Oscars to Slapdish feeds. The chum slick of glossy greenwashing felt omnipresent, as oil and utilities declared themselves reformed and "working around the clock to bring a just version of the Green New Deal to our great country." Scuttling beneath the surface of this corporate sheen was a vicious subaudible smear campaign and conspiracy blitz. From Fox News to Renaissance, conservative media ran amok with rage. Russ Mackowski would get on the Sunday shows and fan all this nonsense, and the rest of the Right tended to follow his panpipe. Renaissance Media's star, Jen Braden, began calling our coalition the "new Gestapo," and that stuck while she dog-whistled at every scientist, politician, or activist who had any hint of a Jewish background. Tony Pietrus came in for particular vitriol when it was disseminated that he was a quarter on his mother's side, and his book became a virtual *Protocols of the Elders of Zion* of conspiracy baiting. White power groups began to harass every congressperson who'd voted for the House bill, filling up their social media, tailing them at public events, showing up with assault rifles outside town halls, and eventually circulating documents with addresses, as well as information on their aides, who then began quitting or demanding security or having nervous breakdowns as the intimidation ratcheted. One of our key congressional allies, Tracy Aamanzaihou, had to close her Houston offices after most of her staff quit following coordinated death threats against their families. As she told an interviewer, "You don't spill this much acid in public without consequences."

I didn't want to know about the threats we were getting. Liza's team handled that issue. But then she gave us a presentation on what was going on behind the scenes. It was easy enough to conjure a make-believe army to harass people online. There were stories about the troll farms set up in India, the Philippines, and Russia where wealthy interests could contract out an avalanche of hate and bile as easily as ordering food through an app. By simply dripping the nectar, one could draw real hornets. Then there was the sophisticated nudge tactics and AI targeting an individual's psychology, based on their perception of the issue using predictive analytics.

"Whether you're getting an ad telling you the bill is 'betraying Climate X philosophy' or a more standard Madison Avenue plug . . ." Behind Liza on the PowerPoint, a cartoon carbon capture plant hoovered black powder from a healthy blue sky with the SFC's tag, WE ARE THE GREEN NEW DEAL. It was the kind of crap you couldn't believe anyone fell for. "People are being fed news, opinion, and content tailored to specific fears and insecurities. On my feed, I might get a bit of body-shaming, warnings that my eggs might be dry, inter-Asian identity politics—it's a highly specific psychological package. It's not just the right wing getting goosed—*our* members and allies are being nudged like this. They're getting opinion filtered to them that the legislation is a betrayal."

"Some dystopian psyops shit," said Rekia.

Liza huffed. She wore a white kerchief around her neck, a black top, tan leather pants, and high-top Nikes, because she dressed hip even for the midnight meetings. "Think about how many times you two have exploded at each other," Liza said, bugging her eyes at Rekia and Tom. The two of them had just had a blowout the day before, during which Rekia accused him of having a problem with Black women and Tom snapped, "I don't have a problem with Black women, I have a problem with stupid Black women." Rekia demanded he be fired, and Tom said he couldn't be fired because he quit, and we all spent the rest of the day trying to calm them down.

Liza went on. "I wouldn't be surprised if analytical models understand you two have tension and exploit that."

Rekia and Tom exchanged a begrudgingly kind look and then went back to icing each other. I tentatively raised my hand to ask how many threats we were getting day to day.

"Unfathomable volumes," Liza warned. "Trust me, Matty, you don't want to look at any of it."

After she said that, I couldn't help myself. I stayed in the office all night, sifting through just one week's worth of the messages Liza's team had flagged and forwarded to the FBI. Certain phrases come back to me all the time:

Morris is going to die slow with dicks in her ass and mouth and eye sockets
Stuff a bottle in her pussy and smash it 2a thousand pieces cunt
You're going to regret your life, you evil slut. God is coming back
Lynch the nigger bitch
Cut her titttties off
Me n my crew will fuck her to death slow and painful

I closed my eyes at night, unable to sleep, and those images would linger for hours.

The town halls didn't even make the news anymore, all of them so full of cranks and crazies screaming into the microphone, occasionally unable to stop themselves from issuing death threats right then and there. Gun sales went through the roof. People burned President Randall in effigy. The major corporations of the day, of course, disavowed stirring the pot on this rhetoric, but the money flowed from these interests through intermediaries, all the way down to front organizations and unheard-of vitamin companies that advertised exclusively on Renaissance.

But in the end, the tipping point might not have been the right-wing fury or the astroturf group calling themselves the BIPOC-GND, which marshalled hundreds of thousands of social media posts claiming that the legislation ignored voices of color while appearing not to have one operational human being involved in the organization. It might not have been the venom and confusion. It might just have been a savvy Montana senator, a Democrat, who saw the perfect opening.

When Victor Love arrived on the political scene, he seemed an unremarkable politician even if the media had a bit of a love affair. A gay veteran who'd fought in Afghanistan and Iraq before starting his own military contracting business, which he built into a private security empire, he was a "reformed Republican," extremely handsome, and quick on his feet. He had, as Kate put it, "Hot dad energy. Like you're fourteen and meet your friend's father, and you're like, 'I totally would.'"

Love had a scar on his cheek from battle. He wore a turquoise bolo tie. He had a dashing husband with a blinding smile. Love exuded centrist reasonableness, which only meant that he was a foot-dragger, one of the senators who drove us crazy with their hemming and hawing. Still, he blindsided us after the Ohio River Massacre, when he held a press conference to say:

"If we do not address this country's security concerns, whether that's radical eco-terrorists, Islamists, or white supremacists, if we do not address the humanitarian crisis at the southern border, if we do not address the concerns raised by the coalitions of Black, Indigenous, and people of color, then I walk away from the bill, and I feel as though many of my fellow Democrats will follow."

It was a deft tap dance, attacking a Republican president from the right while hippie-punching his own party and walking the line on intersectional platitudes. His resistance would only stiffen from there.

As Cy Fitzpatrick told me in the days following his colleague's revolt, "Vic Love is exactly the reason I can't wait to die and get out of this place. Guy's been on the scene for all of a sneeze, and he's already throwing elbows." Cy beckoned me closer. His breath reeked of onion. "You tell that booty of yours, Kate, to watch this guy. He's a snake in the grass."

I relayed Cy's warning to Kate, but by then it was already too late. Defections in the Republican ranks had begun, and nervous Democrats from carbon-intensive states looked over their shoulder at Vic Love's early poll numbers against Randall and found their feet cold as well. When the Senate adjourned for the August recess without taking a vote, a sense of doom descended. Where Mary Randall had been steadfast in her 2030 State of the Union, jutting her finger at the sky and boldly challenging Congress, "This is our moment. This is how history changes. Those who step forward will be remembered for their courage and those who miss this opportunity will know the scorn of their descendants," now her tune was changing. In press conferences and interviews, she slowly began backing away from the bill. In a Fox News interview, she promised, "This bill will never raise energy prices, it will not threaten jobs, and it will not threaten small businesses."

"But what about a company in Ohio that manufactures equipment for natural gas producers?" asked Peter Doocy. "How can you say that to the workers in this company?"

"It will not threaten them," she said. Her eyes were cold stones. "Their livelihoods will be safe."

I never understood how she and her inner circle didn't see how craven she looked in these moments. Then in late September, the midterms little more than a month away, we got word from Ash al-Hasan that there would be a vote on PRIRA in the Senate.

"Wait, what?" Kate demanded. As we were increasingly shunned, abandoned, and finally vilified by those who'd championed our cause, Ash had remained our ally and our last conduit to what was happening behind closed doors. By the time Kate hung up with him, the whole office had gathered around her. "These fucking rumors are true. They're taking the Syracuse-Love version of the bill straight to a vote."

~ ~ ~

At her worst, Kate could make me feel like I was vanishing before my own eyes. She passed by me in the offices that night, eyes locked on her phone, and her arm caught me in the rib. I imagined my body briefly turning to dense smoke, which she simply passed through.

Later that night, I found Kate, Rekia, and Tom in our drab conference room. Everyone else had gone home. Tom's face was stitched tight with rage but not surprise. Rekia had a sob stuck halfway up her chest, and when I came in, she put a hand to her breast and sucked a little wind.

"Guess we did get them to vote on something in the end," said Tom. He held a Rubik's Cube, clicking the blocks around, the muscles of his forearms tense as he worked the colors. "We all might be in a gulag by the end of next month, is what they're voting on."

"Tom," I warned him. "Not now, man."

"We should have a response planned," said Rekia. "Get people in the streets."

Kate stood and, as if I emitted an anti-magnetism, seemed to just want to be in any room besides the one I was in. "They want me on MSNBC," she said. Then she went about turning me to smoke.

Knowing I shouldn't follow, I stood there dumbly.

"I'm the fucking sucker," Tom said as he tweaked the sides of the toy.

"Those cowards," Rekia moaned, and the tears burst from her eyes. Tom set the Rubik's Cube aside and went to his archnemesis. He removed his glasses, folded them into his pocket, and took her in his arms. Rekia wept loudly into his shoulder.

On my ride home, helicopters barbed-wired the skies, the thump of their blades ever-present, and the drones buzzed along their routes a level below, all that sky traffic as unremarkable now as the driverless delivery pods. The penitentiary feel of the city had spiked following the Weathermen attack.

Kate didn't come home that night. She'd been sleeping at the office a lot lately, sometimes elsewhere. I fed Dizzy, then smoked the only kind of weed that didn't make me completely distraught. With the dog on my lap, I watched Kate appear by hologram on MSNBC. Kate had taken to wearing makeup when she made these television appearances, surrendering more and more to vanity, and I couldn't blame her. Even with the makeup she still looked twitchy and sleepless. What I wasn't used to was the fear in her voice. She told Nicolle Wallace that all was not lost, but you could plainly see she didn't believe this.

"And the Senate?" Wallace asked with a newscaster's funereal mourning. *"We're hearing they're going to use the House bill to go to conference with new antiterrorism legislation?"*

"They're going to take her bill," I told Dizzy, high but lucid, stroking the spot between the Australian cattle dog's eyes. "They're going to take everything we worked for and use it to hang her."

"People will be in the streets," Kate promised. Her eye twitched, and she rubbed its lid with a finger.

The next day it rained, and it kept up for three straight days.

Advocating for climate legislation, you can't help but believe the weather to be a complicit force, an anthropomorphized boogeyman creeping closer and closer to the murder cabin even as all the partygoers assure you no one's out there with an axe. When we needed people to take to the streets, it was more or less impossible. Twelve inches of rain fell over the Beltway in three days. East Potomac Park was underwater, and the Southwest Waterfront had cars floating down the streets. As far north as the Ellipse, people were trudging to work wearing rubber boots in ankle-deep water. The Potomac crested at twenty-seven feet, washing out weaker bridges and roads farther upstream. The gray-blue color of a ripe storm hung over the city in what felt like permanent night. Three days is a long time. You almost forget what the sky looks like.

Protests were sparse, objections few, unless you count the brain-dead social media outrage machine. All the energy and passion we'd spent a decade building, it all drained away faster than the district's floodwaters. In the offices, the mood was total despair. I found Liza dabbing her eyes by the coffee machine. Tom was placing calls to building maintenance, trying to deal with a huge blister of water that had formed on the wall of the conference room. I heard Coral uncharacteristically raising their voice on the phone. In Rekia's office, I asked her if she had any understanding of what had happened, how we'd lost everything so fast. She chose the moment to root around for lipstick in her purse, retrieving a deep red color.

"What if this is what they wanted? Or planned?" she said.

"Who? Planned what?"

"Gut-and-go legislation." Rekia twisted the lipstick from the tube. "This is why I never trusted Randall. Our entire bill ransacked. Now it's a bunch of money for seawalls and levies and beach sand in wealthy coastal districts, but mostly it's the police state unbound. That's not an accident. This stuff was ready and waiting. Someone just pulled it off the shelf at the eleventh hour. You don't have to be the Weathermen to see that."

The Left was properly freaking out about what PRIRA had become, but at that point I still thought a lot of it was hysteria. No, it was not what we'd been pushing for, but the idea that the fossil-fuel industry had used the bill as a Trojan horse seemed to me like Covid truther stuff.

"Now that's paranoid. And please do not say that fucking terrorist group's name around this office."

Rekia finished her quick primp and picked up her phone to signal that she needed to get back to work. The rain hammered the windows. "Yeah, well, maybe they've been right this whole time."

On the street, an overflowing sewer grate had turned into a fountain and was spewing oily brown sludge five feet high as cars swerved to avoid it. I rode home, soaked immediately, my poncho of little use in the downpour. Often, I regretted giving up my car for a stupid e-bike. I showered, ate takeout leftovers, and fell asleep on the couch listening to the storm. Kate woke me when her keys rattled in the lock.

"Didn't mean to," she said. She dropped her bag and keys indifferently and oozed into the apartment. I could tell she'd been drinking.

"It's okay." I sat up. She went to the kitchen, ignoring Dizzy, who crept out from the bedroom to see her other human. I followed, feeling the first threads of anger but also because I missed her. She was never away for three entire days. She was wearing the same clothes as the day the bill died. "Where've you been?"

She pulled open the fridge and ducked her head inside. "Thought you knew better than to ask me that."

"Just wanted to make sure you didn't get kidnapped." Dizzy put her nose on Kate's leg, and she absently scratched beneath her jaw where she liked it. Yet that was all Dizzy got, as Kate shoved around cartons of spoiled coconut milk. Dizzy padded back to me. "You could have at least let me know you're okay."

"Did you eat that leftover Burmese?"

"It was going bad."

She shut the fridge and pulled out her phone for a take-out order. She still hadn't looked at me. I wanted to go to her, touch her dark gold curls, frizzy and wet from the rain, but I feared her hand whisking mine aside and an impatient *Not now.*

"I know how much you're hurting. Trust me, I am too. We all are."

She set down the phone and finally let her eyes find me.

"There's a thing coming out about me," she said. "It's a video."

"What do you mean, a video?" I asked, my skin tightening.

"With a guy. A guy I met up with in Philly last time I was there."

How many times I'd been in this position, my hurt so vivid and her disposition so matter of fact. *Here's how it's going to be, Matt. Don't let me see you cry now.*

"Anyone I know?"

She did not avert her gaze from mine. "He worked at our office. Yeah."

She peeled off toward the living room.

"That's impressive, Kate." I followed her. The rain drummed on monotonously. Dizzy, sensing unpleasantness, slinked away. "We're here on the eighteenth goddamn hole of our life's work, and you're making trips to Philly to fuck someone from the office?"

"I was in Philly speaking. It was an incidental fuck."

"Who is it?"

"Why does that matter?"

"Who is it?" I repeated. "Who is my family going to have to watch you screwing online?"

She had the hint of a smile. Because part of her was no doubt proud: Fuck the patriarchy, fuck my haters, fuck the world, and fuck my "colonizing male" for thinking he has any say over what I do.

"It was Sandeep."

I could feel my eyes strain out of their sockets. "The intern? The fucking kid intern?"

She turned away. "Enough, Matt."

"He couldn't even drink when we hired him! Do you ever stop and think for even a fucking—"

Before I could finish that thought, the sting of her palm spun my head sideways. My ear was ringing so hard that her next words were distant and half-lost in the fury of the raging cumulonimbus stalled over the city.

"Not the time, kid." And she stalked off to the bedroom, leaving me there with the pinking of my left cheek. I reached up and touched it like my whole face was suddenly new. She'd never done anything like that before. I sat down on the couch and the shock followed a moment later. I stared out the window at the rain until I fell asleep again.

She frightened me awake. I thought I was still dreaming because my nightmare evaporated into a thing I wanted so badly.

"Matt," she whispered. "Matt, come here." She pulled me into her arms. Of course, I let her. She was crying. "I'm so fucking sorry. I'm losing my mind. I can't even believe I did that. I'm so sorry."

Tears traveled the pretty bulb of her nose. She was so expressive in her joy, but when she cried, she did so with an inverse calm. Her hurt ran out of her like a trickle of water seeping from pressurized rock.

"Now I gotta go to the abused boyfriends shelter."

She laughed and said, "Don't joke. I'm so sorry. I'm so fucking sorry for everything. I adore you. I'm so lucky to have you."

It was dawn by then, and the rain had at long last quieted to gray-black clouds. They hung low over the district, slouching eastward. We took a walk, got ourselves coffee and a doughnut to share. In a month, there would be a video of her on Renaissance, on Slapdish, a think piece, a hate piece, a fuck piece on every sleaze and scandal and political site, but that morning we walked the city aimlessly, cataloguing the damage the flooding had wrought: the downed trees and shredded limbs, the cars carried into errant arrangements by floodwaters, all the city crews in white hard hats, the yellow and orange of officialdom organizing the cleanup. Receding waters had left the district with wind-blown scabs of trash and deltas of muck clinging to the streets and sidewalks. We eventually found ourselves at Arlington National Cemetery strolling past the tombstones, the grass verdant with rain. Finally, we came to Kennedy's gravesite, and looked out over the Potomac, the Lincoln Memorial, the Washington Monument, and the Capitol Dome all lined up.

"Why don't we get away?" I said. "Let Coral and Rekia take over for a few months. We can go see our families. We'll go camp and have sex in a tent. We can regroup."

Hands tucked in her jacket pockets, Kate toed a batch of roses near the gravesite. Who, after all this time, was still delivering fresh roses to Kennedy's grave?

"I love you, kid." She said it slowly, mournfully. "If only the world wasn't ending, I bet we could've made a real run."

"We're making a real run," I said. "This is only a speed bump."

She looked up at me. Thirteen years on. Thirteen years since I first saw her stomping down the dock in Colter Bay and couldn't take my eyes off her. Now she smiled.

"It would be fun to fuck in a tent again."

There, on the walkway surrounded by the faded white stones and beneath a sky nearly the same color, I kissed her as an unmarked helicopter thundered overhead.

After emerging from reconciliation, the bill went straight to Randall's desk with a signing ceremony in the White House. "We can have security, prosperity, and a healthy environment," she boiler-plated, her face grim, her words clipped. While most of the late-night quips were about the salad fleck in her teeth, Seth Meyers noted that she looked like a hostage. Her lips were tight and bleak, a flock of bipartisan politicians peering over her shoulder as she hastily scrawled her name, set the pen down, and seemed to drag her eyes up to meet the cameras. I wondered about the human being behind a moment like this. The quiet, whip-smart girl from Buffalo, who went from Catholic school to state government in a decade, from governor of that state to president of her country, who broke a political stalemate and seemed poised to usher in a revolution no one else could. Now she would live her life through the prism of this haunting compromise, having signed her name to doom. The bill added new surveillance techniques for law enforcement, broadened the scope of permissible FISA warrants, and earmarked nearly $30 billion for the deployment of AI technology in the monitoring of Americans suspected of terrorist activities. That the Supreme Court would uphold all this was barely a question. The Pollution Reduction, Infrastructure, and Research Act—the refund mechanism having been chopped out—was signed into law on October 4, 2030. A month later, most of the Far Right candidates denying the reality of climate change, promising new detention facilities for immigrants, and new curbs to the civil rights of Muslims, environmentalists, and other agitators against the state, won their elections.

~ ~ ~

We stayed in D.C. through the electoral bloodbath when so many of our allies lost, including Cy Fitzpatrick, deposed from the Senate seat he'd held for a generation. Though the polling had been telling us this was coming, that made it no less devastating. Joy LaFray resigned in scandal, and the details of her affair with her stepson were paraded across Fox News with triumphant glee. We planned to take at least four months off. Kate hadn't taken anything more than a three-day weekend in seven years. The morning we were supposed to leave, as I loaded our bags into our electric truck, she texted asking me to meet her, Rekia, and Tom at Lafayette Square across from the White House. *Why?* I asked, but she didn't respond.

A cold wind blew across the Potomac. Soon there would be snow, the bitterness of a D.C. winter. It wasn't an exaggeration to say I'd come to hate this place, what it represented and whatever the weather did. As I cut through Foggy Bottom, I marveled at the normality the city could produce in the face of cataclysm. The terrifying future becomes ever more certain, and yet after some television squawking, a few despairing tweets, op-eds, and news analysis AIs telling humans what to think, people go back to their lives.

Approaching Lafayette Square and the White House, following the pin Kate had dropped, I saw there was some kind of rally. There was chanting. A woman was straining to be heard over the noise, and it took me a moment to place her. Jennifer Braden wore a dark peacoat and punctuated her words with black-leathered fists. She was extremely beautiful, with coal-black hair, red lips glowing against porcelain skin, and a hat with netting over half her face, calling to mind a movie star of the 1930s. The PA system pushed her voice out over the park.

". . . And what we're asking for, what we demand: We want our country back! We want our borders impassible. We want security, and we want peace."

Her crowd beat its hands in approval. There was another contingent behind a police barrier, a raucous counterprotest. Several robocams dispatched from various news outlets hovered, broadcasting. These levitating bots still made me uneasy with their too-languid movements and the cold surveilling surface of their glassy eyes. A jowly woman in front of me held a red placard with a photo on it. This stopped me cold.

Braden continued, "What we have endured in this country for too long is an acceptance of multiculturalism, an erosion of our Christian character, of our European ancestry."

HUNT ALL TRAITORS TO EXTINCTION, read the sign. And above it a picture of a young girl in a headscarf with a bullet wound in her face. It took me a moment to understand the image as one of the Somali girls killed in Minneapolis in '28.

I felt ill. Because I was staring, the woman's eyes met mine. She looked like any overweight Middle American housewife. Pleased by my shock, she smugly returned her attention to the speaker.

"The white race, the Christian faith—my friends, we built the modern world. Every single achievement you see around you is because of us." Braden thumped a hand above her breast. "And that is why it's not enough to simply have pride. We must go out into the world, and we must *fight* for that truth."

A rousing cheer lifted from the crowd to the sky. *"Hell yeah!"* screamed a short man with a wispy mustache. Clipped to his belt, he had what looked like a combat knife. The woman with the sign locked her elbows to hold her grisly image higher: a bloody hole in the cheek of a girl not yet a teenager.

I found Kate, Rekia, and Tom on the fringe of the counterprotest, all with identical dour expressions. The counterprotestors chanted with rage, *"No Braden! No KKK! No fascist USA!"* while police in full combat gear lined the fence of the White House, weapons angled at the ground.

"What the hell is this?" I shouted to be heard.

Rekia chucked her head at Braden. "We heard the Hot Nazi was declaring. No permit or anything, she just showed up at Randall's front door." The whole scene was so jarring, I didn't quite register at first that Tom and Rekia were holding hands. Not until years later would I learn that the night PRIRA passed, Rekia and Tom had consummated their heated rivalry in our offices.

"And what has the so-called conservative Mary Randall done with her time in office?" Braden continued. "The country is terrorized by eco-fascists and Muslims while she coddles the socialist Left. She wants to raise the cost of energy, allow aliens to pour across the borders, tax you, restrict you, demean you, all so she can get a pat on the head from the *New York Times*."

"Jew York Times!" someone cried.

Tom, ever the instigator, laughed loudly and began heckling the guy, asking him his name and where he worked. "The Zionist conspiracy is coming to get you, motherfucker!"

Braden took a hand from her peacoat and jabbed it at the White House behind her.

"Mary Randall, let me tell you something, you stupid *bitch*." Braden salivated on the word, and the crowd went wild for it. "You are done! Your alliance with the greens, the dirt and scum leaking across our borders, the mongrels, the Black nationalists, the Muslim agenda—it is over! We are here! We are fighting back, and it *Starts. Right. Now.*"

The crowd roared in triumph. I watched a teenage girl beat her pink mittens together in applause.

"Can we please go?" I begged Kate.

"That is why, my friends, today I am declaring my candidacy for the presidency of the United States."

The crowd positively erupted. Signs and hats thrown skyward. Someone swept a large Confederate flag in a whirl. A muscular bald man, wearing a shirt with a picture of Anders Breivik, flexed every muscle of his arms and howled, *"Braaaaaden!"* Silently, the four of us agreed and slunk away down Connecticut Avenue. Braden's sultry voice, the applause of her rapturous fans, and the chant of the counterprotestors borne along by the PA, followed us for blocks. Kate slipped her arm around my waist.

"What a lovely way to start our vacation, huh?"

The video of Kate having sex with the intern broke that night, chasing the story of the Hot Nazi throwing her hat into the presidential ring.

~ ~ ~

We never understood why Renaissance sat on that video until after the election, the timing a twist of the knife instead of a bombshell, but we also didn't wait around to watch the news cycle enjoy it. That day we drove out of the district, breaking free of its clogged, gristled arteries, into the mountains of Virginia and down through the Shenandoah Valley, aiming to make the ridge of the Smoky Mountains by nightfall. We climbed in altitude, and snow appeared in the hills. Despite all that had happened in the past months, I felt immense gratitude that if the men and women of power let the continents vanish beneath the oceans, I would at least swallow seawater with Kate beside me.

We reached Pigeon River Campground on the Tennessee-North Carolina border after dark and unrolled our sleeping bags in the truck's camper.

Kate played music, something slow and plaintive, and took off my shirt by running her palms up my chest and flipping it over my head. We'd sleep without a single city sound for the first time in an eternity, but first we reached for each other, our troubles momentarily vaporizing in the hot contact of our flesh.

~ ~ ~

Our second stop was a hotel in Charlotte, to visit my sister and her family. Upon arriving Kate took out an infrared scanner, a radio frequency detector, and something called a nonlinear junction detector, and together we went over the entire room inch by inch.

"Lady, is this necessary?" I asked. She was perched on a chair, waving this buzzing box over a wall socket. "I know that video is fucking terrible, but . . ."

"Yeah, you think I filmed that, Matt?" She hopped off the chair. "Sandeep chose that hotel."

"Oh, so your boy toy is a sleeper agent now? Spy from the deep state? Paranoia is an excuse to ignore the reality of a situation, Kate."

She gave me an annoyed look. "And what reality is that?"

"That you're selfish and fucked an intern because you thought it would be fun."

"So I fucked an intern, so what?" She wagged the infrared scanner over a light fixture. "Jesus Christ, it was the best day of the kid's life. This is actually serious, Matt."

Kate was sure we were being monitored even before the Ohio River Massacre. We'd spoken to the FBI with our lawyers present about potential 6Degrees sympathizers within our organization. Kate was adamant that we cooperate, but the FBI was always pushing the line, asking for emails or employee data that we had to refuse to give up without a warrant. Kate never found a listening device in that room or any of the rooms we stayed in that year, but that never stopped her from searching.

We removed the batteries from our phones and stowed all the pieces in a Faraday bag. We'd left our laptops in a safety deposit box in D.C. We weren't going to even look, we promised each other. But when we did peek, the news was harrowing. The video of Kate with Sandeep had been adapted to VR, and after giving an interview calling his relationship with Kate "coercive," the backstabber had holed up behind lawyers. "Certainly, if you watch the video, she looks like a predator," said Tucker Carlson while also calling the encounter "consensual if energetic." Meanwhile, Kate's left-wing critics were also having a field day.

They could take a little clump of cells, a woman in an open relationship, and metastasize it into a cancer. What angered me was how few women spoke up in her defense. There was something bawdy about Kate that the feminist commentariat did not like. She was rough around the edges; she used "the language of toxic masculinity"; she worked with pro-life organizations and politicians; she rejected sloganeering and hashtags of various leftist movements in favor of more complex and nuanced examinations of power. She didn't perform the stations of the cross prescribed by the woke hive mind, and this made her enemies. Yet I do think Kate wore blinders when it came to being a public persona. She seethed that a woman couldn't get coked up and have sex with a musician in a high-end restaurant bathroom without inviting trouble or couldn't sleep with an intern a few times without it turning into a national spectacle. She wasn't a victim of slut-shaming so much as joy-shaming. People simply couldn't put up with all the ways she deviated, disappointed, and rejected conformity at every turn. I doubted Sandeep was any kind of spy for the national security state. I'm sure Kate slept with him a handful of times and then simply walked away and broke his heart.

"This is fucking unreal," Kate fumed to Coral over speakerphone. We were sitting on a log, petrified with shellac, outside a charge station near the South Carolina border. "Let's just spill my whole fucking sex life! Tell them I lost my virginity to a college student when I was thirteen, and I savored every last pump."

"*Do not* tell anyone that," I told Coral.

Coral was slow to respond. "You can continue to strike a pose as an apostate, but I'm warning you, Kate, this has cost us friends. Your activities have made us vulnerable."

Kate gripped the phone like she was going to hurl it into the woods.

"Another country heard from," she said brightly. "Don't worry, I'll stay out of sight for now. But, Coral, this new Congress is a true nightmare. This train's still moving even if I decided to get a piece of ass once."

We spent Christmas of 2030 camping in Tishomingo State Park in Mississippi then the Sam Houston National Forest in Texas until well into February. We hiked every trail we could find, swam in whatever freezing pool of water looked clear, and had sex at least once a day beneath a beautiful forest of spruce, aspen, and fir. We learned of the Mall of America shootings only after emerging from the wilderness. We were at a rest stop where a group of women in hijabs watched the news of an Islamist father-daughter team murdering thirty-three people in nine minutes. Mackowski and Braden hustled to outdo each other's venom.

We kept on west, driving beneath a sky with island-sized clouds.

~ ~ ~

For many years after Wyoming, a part of me still held on to this dream I had of my life with Kate. We would spend a few years in D.C., she would get all the crazy activist passion out of her system, and then we'd go to North Carolina where I could write while making good money at my dad's business. It's incredible to recall how long I held on to that fantasy. Our third month living in that first dumpy apartment in Hill House, Kate took a trip to Savannah with a "college friend." It wasn't just that Kate demanded an open relationship, it was the way she made me feel small for any discomfort I gave voice to. Whenever I let her see that her dalliances got under my skin, she would ridicule my conception of monogamy as purely a form of sexist, patriarchal control. She brought home fresh venereal diseases and told me I would've caught them one way or another. But we also brought women home, had more threesomes than I can count. Her attraction knew no specific type or gender. At a show at the 9:30 Club, Kate met an Asian woman with bangs and tattoo sleeves, and they hit it off. That night I sat in a chair in our living room and watched the two of them for a long time before joining. Even the memory of that night still makes me weak with a very base lust. "I love sex," Kate said during one of our early fights. "Our culture demands that a woman sleep with one man, loyal as a dog, for her entire life, and it's bullshit. You're beautiful and sexy and energized for only this fraction of a geologic nanosecond in all this darkness, so how can you not drink down to the last drop this thing that makes you feel vital and alive?"

"Because I don't have the energy to fuck every night," I said.

"Oh, I know," she shot back.

I never got over it. I probably still haven't. But after a while I stopped being surprised by it. I came to see these men she was with as passing fads, like she was reading a new book she couldn't put down. Yet she would always finish it, close it, and return to me. I stopped fearing she would leave me for someone else.

"It gets it out of my system," she explained after the embarrassment of the Frisk episode. "Half the reason people have quote-unquote affairs is they're just bored. They want new dick, ya know? You want new dick too, Tar Heel, I know it. And we can always come out the other side still loving each other."

Kate, in other words, encouraged me to sleep around. At first, I just couldn't. Even the thought of spending the night with another woman scared me. We would have sex, and I knew the second it was over I would hurt. I'd never meet another woman who spoke her own particular language, who'd accuse me of "wanting new dick," who I would hold at night and just feel such a deep, bone-pressure joy.

Moniza asked me if I would leave Kate.

Following her first feature as a cub writer for *Vanity Fair*, Moniza happened to be down in D.C. and asked if I wanted to grab a drink. We sat in a smoky bar without the smoke, drank cocktails, and talked transpolar shipping. Moniza was short and curvaceous, with deep brown skin, a round pixie face, and lustrous black hair she pulled over one shoulder and played with as we talked. She'd grown up in London and gone to Columbia, before working her way up at *Vanity Fair*. I made a joke about the expansion of shipping through the Northern Sea Route as the Arctic ice melted, and when she laughed, she put a hand on my thigh and leaned into my space, so that her long hair dropped briefly into my lap.

"Don't laugh at what a nerd I am," I scolded.

"It was a papa joke crossed with some nerdy book-reading," she declared in that immaculate British accent. We went back to her hotel, and it was the first time I'd been with a woman without Kate involved since my college girlfriend. When we woke up in the morning, I put her against the wall and one of her thighs on my shoulder, brushing her clit with my lips and pushing two fingers as far inside her as they would go, a technique Kate had trained me in, and one that sent Moniza into conniptions.

"Jesus Mary," she said after she came. "Jesus Mary, Tar Heel."

Later, I would ask her to not use that nickname.

I followed Kate's lead: We would tell the other that we had plans with a friend, and then one of us would take a leave of absence for twenty-four, thirty-six, forty-eight hours. At first, Moniza and I would simply get dinner and drinks and retire to her hotel room, but then we began taking trips. We actually had to evacuate from Ocean City as a hurricane bore down, and the ruined weekend became a small miracle as we stayed in a dumpy motel off the interstate and did nothing but have sex, order takeout, and listen to the rain. Then I began visiting her in New York.

We saw each other like that, intermittently, for a year and a half. As the 2028 election geared up and FBF sank more and more energy into the final push, I stopped having any time. I had to cancel on her twice, and when she finally did come down to D.C., everything felt off. After dinner, we took a walk past the Nationals stadium, a game in progress. She was awfully quiet.

"It's better if you just tell me what's on your mind," I said.

"I'm sorry." She stared at the ground. "It's just been so long since I've seen you. I've spent more than a bit of time telling myself this is all for fun and play, but it would be nice to know."

Then she didn't say anything for a while. I waited, but she only walked forward with her gorgeous brown eyes cast down.

"Need to know what?" I finally asked.

She stopped, looked at me. "Would you leave her?"

So stupid, I told myself. I'd basically fallen in love with every woman I'd ever dated. She gazed at me, confident in her question but as vulnerable as I'd ever seen her.

"It's not fair to ask me that. I've told you our situation. I've been totally honest about it."

Moniza looked away, her face crumpling ever so slightly.

"No, you have," she agreed quickly. She finally looked me in the eye. "She doesn't deserve you, Matt."

Embarrassed, I shook my head. "No one deserves anything or anyone. That's not how it works."

"I'm only saying—maybe you don't want to hear this, but—Kate is a manipulator. She's a user. I've known women like her my whole life. She takes endlessly from you. Charms you when she needs to, and then goes back to using you."

"Moniza," I said, as calmly as I could, "please, don't talk about what you don't understand."

She bit her lip, and the tears finally achieved their freedom.

"I love you," she said. "I hate how hurt you are all the time. I would never treat you like that."

"You don't know anything about how she treats me." Again, I said this with as much calm as I could summon, ignoring how she'd begun that statement.

She laughed, as if this explanation suddenly made total sense. "You're right, I don't . . ." Her voice choked with mourning. "I simply find myself missing you every day."

In her hotel, we made love for the last time. I slipped out in the middle of the night, after she'd fallen asleep, and back home, I got in bed next to Kate. Moniza and I stopped speaking after that, but of course, what she'd said stayed with me. I would smell her unique scent—whatever alchemy creates a person's odor—without warning, the way the pasture behind my childhood home would suddenly become fragrant after a heavy rain.

~ ~ ~

After months on the road, schlepping our gear from campsite to campsite, unshowered, unshaved, unmoored, we finally met Kate's family in Moab in early March. Her dad had rented a four-bedroom house for us, including Kate's two half brothers, Myra and Wakezi. The last time we saw Earl, he'd been married to Myra and Wakezi's mother, Macie, but she'd now become the third woman to walk out on him. Myra and Wakezi, both in the middle of tough teen years, were about as dissimilar to Kate as siblings could be. They grumbled about each hike we took into Arches or Canyonlands and spent every free second with their faces strapped in VR goggles, making indiscernible trigger pulls and karate chops, groping at other untethered fictions. Myra, the elder boy, was very heavy and had a spectacular case of acne, which simply coated his cheeks and forehead. Wakezi had a slightly better complexion but was even heavier and quieter. Both made no secret of their misery for the four days we spent in Utah. Kate did her best to engage them, but it was painful to watch how distant they were to her. She'd remained mostly locked out of their lives at the insistence of Macie until she left Earl. Her brothers hiked in flip-flops, heads down, trudging on until they were allowed to return to the car.

Now in his midsixties, Earl had aged in a bent, unhealthy way. He had the hooked nose and snarling mouth of a vulture, small eyes he always beaded further in suspicion. He wore his kinky hair in a long, stiff braid that jutted from the back of his head. He was also thinner than the last time I'd seen him, no longer simply lean, but spindly. Sonja once told me she didn't understand why Kate wanted her father in her life. "He's an unhappy man," she'd said. Kate's relationship with her father was a total black box to me. She put forth a mighty effort, but what Earl gave back was ephemeral, and then there were moments when Kate was nothing but a stranger to him. While packing sandwiches for our hike into Arches, Kate held hers up.

"I don't eat turkey, Pop."

Earl looked maximally confused. "You don't?"

"I've been a vegan since I was born, dude. Remember? You and Sonja raised me that way?"

He stood with the butter knife dripping mustard. "Didn't know," he muttered.

Earl behaved like a man who'd been robbed. He'd been a handsome, hot-blooded activist in the nineties, at a time when it was no longer in vogue to be a radical. He'd been arrested, beaten (according to him), had written a memoir he'd never published, floated from job to job, woman to woman, falling out to falling out. He now lived in a tract house in Tucson and taught at a prison. He still wore his radical politics on his sleeve, but in my opinion, as a shield against his own fall into conformity. He was bitter because his daughter was everything he'd never managed to be.

One too many glasses of wine, and Earl's issues came to a head at dinner on our last night. Myra begged to be released to his VR set within moments of sitting down, and he and Earl began to argue, loudly. Earl's parenting method was to mostly ignore the boys until he found a hill, at random, to die on. It was painful and embarrassing for everyone.

"Go play the goddamn thing," Early finally barked. "I don't want to hear your whining anymore."

And before he'd even finished the sentence, Myra was gone, his fork still rattling against the plate.

"Can I go too?" Wakezi asked.

"You're not going to spend the last night with us, Keys?" I asked. He twisted his glass of orange soda. I'm not sure that he'd actually responded to anything I'd said all weekend. Earl waved him away too.

"This generation deserves to wake up one day with the planet burned and drowned," he said.

"Eh, they're teenagers," said Kate. "They're invested in doing everything their parents hate. If you started playing VR shooters and talking shit about ecosystem restoration, they'd join Greenpeace tomorrow."

This at least got a smirk out of Earl.

"It's been good seeing you guys," I ventured. "Even if the boys didn't quite get the outdoors gene, we've had fun." One says things like this out loud to make them true.

"Where do you two go from here?"

"California," I said. "To hike Mount Whitney."

"And then you'll be back to Washington cutting deals with the corporate plutocracy? Get your picture on a few more magazine covers before the deluge?"

I coughed as a bit of water went down the wrong pipe. Kate glared at her father.

"That's hostile. Even for you."

Earl pumped his eyebrows. "Doesn't make it any less true, my child."

Kate chewed her tongue and twisted her fork against the plate. I felt like joining Myra and Wakezi.

"I hit a nerve?" asked Earl.

"Here's your chance, Dad." Kate set down her fork and splayed her hands in a *Bring it on* gesture. "You want to lay out everything I've done wrong, every opportunity I've taken to sell out—please, go ahead."

"No need to document your selling out. You were never anything but a product in the first place. A glossy, big-tittied mascot the normies could pin up while they watch the boxcars go by to Dachau."

"Earl, man. C'mon," I warned him.

"Shut the fuck up, you pale, spineless bitch. No one's talking to you."

"Dad!" Kate barked at him. "Cut it out. You're not impressing anyone."

Earl sniffed and took a dainty sip of his wine, his teeth now a deep purple. It dawned on me then that he'd already had several glasses that night. "You believed your own hype, girl. You figured you could bat your eyes and change the system. But you weren't using the system, gal, the system was using you. A flashy little piece of greenwashed pussy—"

"That's enough!" I snapped, but he kept going.

"And what've you got to show for it? No compromise from corporate power, not even an inch. Just another crackdown. Just another step along the way to nuclear-armed global fascism." Then he laughed, slapped his knee. "And you built them a little vehicle to get there. And all anyone'll remember about you, my child, is a fuck film in a hotel room. A fitting end for Supergirl herself. What a culture we live in."

Kate threw her napkin down, stood, and walked out, Earl chuckling as she went. The only reason I didn't follow was because I had to say something, and I searched for the most hurtful thing possible.

"You're a shit father, and a shit man," I said, struggling to get the words out. "Kate's done more in ten years than you've done in your entire sad lifetime. You're an embarrassment, Earl."

Earl sighed. "Oh Matty, Matty, Matty. I'm gonna laugh when she finally leaves your rich, boring ass."

We left Moab that night.

~ ~ ~

We drove through the canyons of the desert between crashing mountains. I closed my eyes and opened them to the berserk sky and a cruel and glorious land. When I asked Kate if she was okay, she waved it away. "That's Dad. He wants to make everyone around him as miserable as he is. But still, he might've had a point."

"He didn't even remotely have a point, Kate. Don't ever let him get to you."

She looked at me, nothing but two fingers on the wheel at six. "I've only ever let one man get to me." She snatched up my hand, kissed the back of it, then stuck my whole index finger in her mouth and practically swallowed it. We were both cracking up at how weird she was for miles to come.

What I wished I'd said to Earl was that Kate's talent for connection was singular. In those years, it was impossible not to see the gravity of a room bend around her. She offered people an invitation. She didn't judge and she didn't badger, she simply found a seed within a person that she might tend, garden, and grow. And that person would often have already accepted her invitation without even realizing it—just because they'd leaned in to hear what this wild woman had to say.

We rented a house in the shadow of the Sierras, and on a beautiful May night, we set out for Whitney, departing at 3 a.m., under a full moon as bright and white as an exposed piece of bone.

Several hours earlier, before trying to grab whatever sleep we could, Kate had drank too many beers and then found a half-empty handle of Ever-clear left in our rental by some past hikers. She demanded we do a shot. I told her absolutely not. But when we parked at the Whitney portal and shouldered our packs, adjusting our trekking poles and headlamps, she pulled the Everclear handle from the car.

"No way. Fuck yourself, Kate."

"One shot, Tar Heel. You'll do it if you love me."

We did the shot. When the antiseptic brine hit my throat, I thought I'd gag, but I muscled it down, choking. Kate, on the other hand, turned and projectile vomited into the road. I almost fell down, I was laughing so hard. She belched.

"What a way to start."

We picked our way over the initial boulder field, and then climbed through the corridor between mountains, bathed in a blue glow, catching sips of cool air rushing down through the mighty cavern of the John Muir Wilderness. The pines of the Inyo loomed on all sides, while the crags of the surrounding mountains lay hidden in shadow. We saw other hikers using AR glasses to make their way instead of headlamps, and it was eerie seeing them move like phantoms through the dark. Kate was heaving breaths, struggling from the booze. Two hours in, we'd climbed fifteen hundred feet, nearing Lone Pine Lake, this high-altitude body of water fed by all the mountain streams. We looked back into the first pink, yellow, and blue filaments of sunrise on the eastern horizon. Kate slipped her fingers into mine, and we stood there for a while, watching.

The day after summiting, after my anger at Kate's behavior on the upper reaches of a dangerous mountain had worn off and I had a chance to sleep for ten hours, ice my feet, and treat the plantar fasciitis that had lit in at the worst possible time, the flood of endorphins hit, "secondary fun" my mom calls it. Kate decided we had to make Everclear margaritas to celebrate, and this time I was more than game.

Though we'd seen the fire advisories all over California (Very High), the town of Lone Pine was nothing but vast, unyielding desert, so we built a fire in the pit out back and put on the wire mesh top so that the flames just barely licked out. We sipped the margs and put our bare toes by the fire.

After a while, Kate asked, "Have you given any thought to what we do now?"

"In regards to what?"

"In regards to Ivanka Trump's *Apprentice* reboot—dude, what do you think? You know, like our fucking planetary emergency? Where does FBF go from here?"

"You're asking me?"

"I am. I always do."

It was the first time I ever opened my mouth to give voice to the idea that maybe we should just run away. That we should walk into the future, however frightening that might be.

But instead, Kate's phone, for a month secured in a bag that blocked all transmissions, rang.

"It's Coral," she said, and we went inside to project the video on the wall.

The sight of Coral and their pageboy haircut, heavy glasses, lip ring, and that odd Winnie the Pooh tattoo coating their shoulder, flanked by Rekia and Tom, filled me with a buoyancy. These were not coworkers or even friends, they were my siblings in arms. They sat in the main conference room in the D.C. office. Above Rekia's new bouffant doo, the Antonio Machado quote hovered, and though I'd stared at it in meetings for years, its meaning, in that moment, filled me with purpose again. I saw I had a text from Tom. All it said was *I'm sorry man.* Kate was giddy, telling them how great it was to see their faces, when Coral cut her off.

"Kate, we need to tell you something. There's been a vote."

I thought they meant in Congress, and so did Kate because she said, puzzled, "There are no bills up right now."

"No," said Rekia. Kate stared up at the white plaster wall. Dust glittered in the path of the light spilling from the phone's projector. "There's been a vote internally. We've decided to remove you from the position of executive director, effective immediately."

I couldn't have been more stunned if they said they were endorsing Jennifer Braden for president. My mouth dropped open. Kate's face, on the other hand, betrayed nothing.

After a moment, Tom said, "I thought we should all call you to explain."

"We lost so many allies in the midterms, Kate." Coral removed their glasses and rubbed their left eye with the heel of their hand. "Now Senator Love is promising to investigate us. Our financial situation has grown dire."

"Wait, wait," I said, interrupting. "Kate didn't rewrite PRIRA. This isn't her fault."

"Oh, isn't it?" Rekia snapped. "Not sure if you heard, but news from the front is, we lost. Motherfuckers cut us to ribbons in about sixteen months. Kate wanted to live her tabloid life, treat all this like a vehicle for her brand, and when it blew up in our faces—who's expected to handle the mess?"

"An intern?" Tom implored. "Really, Kate?"

"What you do in bed," Rekia went on, "is immaterial. Hell, how you treat Matt is immaterial. But you stopped being an effective advocate a long time ago."

"Rekia, you're out of line," I warned her, and I could feel the petulance rising in my voice. "You're making this personal."

"That's not true."

"Yeah, and who's taking Kate's place?"

Rekia didn't hesitate. "I am."

I stood and began pacing, walking from the couch to the bookshelf full of guidebooks for the Sierras. Coral explained what would come next.

"We're issuing a press release tomorrow. Kate, it would be better if you didn't make a statement yet. We're in a very delicate position with our biggest donors, and these are relationships that must be repaired if we're to continue financing our operations at full capacity."

"Kate, I'm saying this because you're my friend, and I fucking care about you, okay?" said Tom, and because his voice was so genuine, because I knew he'd long acted as Kate's champion and loyal servant on the Hill, it enraged me even more. "It's time to get out of the spotlight."

"*We get it!*" I roared. I stormed back to the phone, resting on its stand, to make sure they could see my face. "We get what cowards you all are. We get you can't take the heat. But you goddamn well know there is one person in this organization who dragged it to relevance and made it a *force*. And it's *none of you*!" I jabbed my finger at Kate, still silent on the couch. "None of you have the creativity, the passion, the focus, or the courage to do what she did. And the first trouble that comes along, you all knife her in the *fucking back*."

"Matt," Kate said softly, and she put her hand on my waist, looked up at me. Her color-shifting eyes implored me to calm down. I had to walk away. I heard her say, "Thank you for calling, guys. Good luck to you."

Kate came to me in the bedroom after that. She put her head against my chest, and we lay there together, the margaritas forgotten, nothing left of the day but a pink hue over the serrated blade of the mountains.

Two days later, I'd wake to find her in the kitchen. She'd gotten up early and gone into town for coffee. Without a word, she handed me the first proper physical newspaper I'd held in years. While we were hiking, a wildfire had broken out in Northern California: seven thousand acres near Calistoga had gone up in twenty-four hours, killing at least two hundred people with hundreds more missing. It was the worst death toll from a wildfire in California history, and the flames were still spreading. The lede was a simple quote from a Cal Fire spokesman: "This is up there with some of the worst fires I've ever seen, and it's only May."

"This would've happened anyway," I said. "Nothing would've changed this."

She touched the image on the front page—a screaming little girl being carried by a fireman. "I know that," she said. "But for the rest of my life, I'll see things like this and remember how we failed."

We left Lone Pine that day as the fire spread: twenty-thousand acres and still uncontained. Kate barely spoke as we hurtled north. I had no idea then what dreams she was hiding, what burdens she was safekeeping. She kept her eyes on a mountain range and above it, the vivid blue ether. I held her hand and wished we had met in another time, someplace far away from this endless fear and grieving.

While the violent clash between police and protestors on the USC campus made headlines, a more ominous signal has arrived from a small liberal arts college in Iowa where a local pipeline company has leveled a $50 million lawsuit against two dozen eighteen-year-olds. With PRIRA removing many restrictions on SLAPP suits, your average oil company can now make life hell for any student-dissident it sees fit to harass.

Is sea level on the rise? Not according to these scientists.

"This man has actually rewritten the Bible, and his version is outselling the original. His followers are that rabid and that convinced of his divine connection."

(**Slapdish**)

The Republican-led Florida legislature is trying to pass a bill making it illegal to "spread fear, panic, and misinformation about the myth of global warming."

MEET TARA, THE CLIMATE-SAVVY WUNDERKIND HEDGE FUND

CYCLONE MALWAN DEVASTATES MUMBAI, AT LEAST 70,000 DEAD

FIRST ICE-FREE ARCTIC SUMMER COMES AND GOES WITH A SHRUG?

Al-Bawadis, the Mall of America killers, Have Links to the Weathermen, Morris, A Fierce Blue Fire, says confidential source

VIC for VICTORY 2032

"We saw it coming from the canyon to the south of us and the Pocket Fire was coming down from the north, and there was nowhere to go. One little ember, and our valley went up in flames. The roads were blocked, and we were stuck. We couldn't sleep, we just watched the peaks over in Sonoma burning. And all of our neighbors—all of them are dead. And we're here."

A Border in Flames
Hundreds of thousands fleeing violence and ecological devastation in Central and South America arrive at the US border while the American Patriot League murders migrants regularly and the private prison industry waits to capitalize.

"If you add these less headline-generating diseases together, you have a toll of death and suffering not seen since Native peoples first came in contact with Europeans."

SCOTUS has struck down birthright citizenship at a time when macroeconomic growth is slowing due to the aging of the population. The labor force is shrinking, age-related spending is rising, and the young, dynamic, innovative portion of the population is declining. We've never needed immigration so badly.

CALI FIRES EXPLODE, GROW TO 2.5 MILLION TOTAL ACRES

BRADEN AND MACKOWSKI NECK AND NECK WITH RANDALL IN EARLY IOWA POLLS

"The unnerving truth is that you and I, we don't have identity anymore. We vote, value, verify, vaccinate, and venerate based on the machine learning behind our many screens."

EL DEMONIO

2031

If he believed in omens, Tony might have paid more attention to his dreams. In the most disturbing one, he was pinned to a desert floor while screaming winds of silt and sand scoured him away. Paralyzed, as the sand removed his flesh grain by grain, he could feel the bones of his knuckles and cheeks exposed to the blasting air. Then there was a form in the wind-borne sand, a banshee smothering his bleeding limbs, smuggling her shriek into his mouth. He awoke in his hotel overlooking the Atlantic soaked in sweat. Through the window, the moon reflected orange off the ocean's horizon.

The next day the protestors were a cloud of flies on a carcass. He'd come to Miami at the invitation of the mayor to discuss the city's battle with the ocean, but wherever he traveled now, protests followed. They carried the typical signs proclaiming him a liar, a traitor, a cancer, part of the Jewish-media climate conspiracy. "Where do you get your money!" they shouted. Counterprotesting climate activists held Fierce Blue Fire placards and cardboard painted like tombstones with the markings of a domino, in reference to his theory; a few young women held signs that read PIETRUS CHECK YOUR PRIVILEGE, and they began chanting, greatly confusing their neo-Nazi bedfellows as to whose side they were on. After calling out the future president on her shell game at Davos, his publisher dropped him and Yale guided him into retirement. Now he mostly collected "consultant" fees by bringing city governments news they abjectly did not want to hear (nor do anything about). As was the case with the mayor's team, some of whom even nodded off during his presentation on saltwater upwelling.

"How'd the meeting go?" his brother-in-law, Corey, asked him when they met for a late lunch before his flight home.

"Oh, dandy," said Tony. He insisted they sit inside the restaurant so he could avoid sweating like a hog in the Florida heat. Their table overlooked Biscayne Bay, boats puttering around the water, traffic flowing idly over the bridge to Miami Beach. Clear blue sky.

"This place is great," said Corey. "How are my nieces doing?"

"Holly's great. She's taking over the New York office of FBF. Dean's teaching at the New School."

"A rabble-rouser like her dad. And Cat? Still holding out hope for her big break?"

"Guess so." Although he really had no idea. Even after Tony acquiesced to her dream of acting, Catherine forbade him from inquiring about her progress, claiming it put too much pressure on her. The waiter brought Tony's iced tea and Corey's wine spritzer.

"That's terrific." He quaffed the spritzer. "How 'bout you? Seeing anyone?"

"Absolutely not."

"Tony, come on, man! You can't just wank it in the VR set the rest of your days."

"God. Corey."

"Just saying. Check out this one I'm dating now." He held his phone aloft. A picture of him in a glossy blue suit with his arm around an uninspiring bleach blonde with a spray tan and enormous fake breasts.

"Wonderful," said Tony. He gazed dispiritedly around the restaurant. Mostly wealthy retirees adorned in every manner of sparkling mineral washed of the toxic slurry its extraction had left behind in some far-flung sacrifice zone. All of them albatrossed by credit cards, boat upkeep, and the perturbations of the stock market.

"I know, right?" Missing the irony in Tony's comment, Corey flipped through several more pictures of his latest conquest. Corey had married his college girlfriend, a woman both Tony and Gail had quite liked, only to divorce her when he started really making money in their father's business. The Briggs Group of Florida, a boutique firm specializing in unremarkable Stepford Wife luxury condos, wasn't even a top twenty player in the real estate market, but for half a century it had been impossible to not do well. You built a tower near the ocean and every unit was sold before you even broke ground. When Tony first began dating Gail, Corey had been a twerp prep school kid already eyeing fraternity rows at Florida's most debauched campuses, and Tony had never stopped looking at him that way. Even in his midforties, dressed dapper in a jet-black blazer over a gray polo and what looked like a thousand-dollar Seiko watch on his wrist, Tony still saw him as Gail's stupid little white brother who'd farted on Tony's arm when he met her family for the first time. Nine years after Gail's adoption, Corey had been the surprise pregnancy, and though it always seemed like her parents were prouder of their ultra-bright adopted Black daughter, boy, did they let this little biological shit get away with anything. Corey still had the same buzzed head, eyes that shrank mischievously when he smiled, and devil-may-care, brash individualism signaled to exhaustion in every detail of his person.

Corey pocketed his phone. "Don't you get groupies from all the fame, man? Like enviro-sluts?"

When Gail was dying, Tony had morbidly assumed the only silver lining to the whole situation was that he'd never have to see this arrogant little prick ever again. Oddly, Corey had not allowed that to happen. He'd stayed in close touch, invited Tony and the girls out to Florida once a year, and bought Holly and Cat an extravagant, over-the-top gift every birthday and Christmas. Corey still annoyed the hell out of Tony, but he would combat this by thinking of how he'd seen Corey once, unarmored, in Scripps Memorial, when Gail was really near the end. It had just been the three of them in the room, Gail wasted and failing, Corey holding her hand. He didn't just look young in that moment, he looked preadolescent, back to the obnoxious but vulnerable little boy Gail had helped raise. "You were a perfect big sister," he told her, gasping back tears. "You always kept me straight."

"And you were a total pain in the ass," Gail had said, her voice gone, her eyes too hollow to land the humor. Corey had buried his head in her fragile shoulder and cried so hard Tony thought he might choke.

"So." Corey now picked up a butter knife and began twirling it baton-style, gazing out at the sun-dappled waves. "This guy introduced a bill in the state senate, right? It would require real estate brokers to disclose any risk of sea level rise for the properties they sell. Friendly legislators killed it but . . ." He trailed off. It dawned on Tony that Corey hadn't driven over from Sarasota so they could simply grab lunch and catch up. He pointed off into the bay. "For sure, they have to elevate those highways connecting Miami Beach, but they can't raise taxes to do it. That'll just spook the market. The big thing—now that we've killed that monstrosity Randall was trying to pass—there's a vote coming on the National Flood Insurance Program. They always want to raise the rates without understanding the effect it has on housing prices, you know? Then the banks want a bigger percentage of the property's value insured, but the insurance companies don't want to write those bigger policies, and so the banks don't want to lend a thirty-year mortgage. You know?"

"Nope. Are you trying to ask me something?"

Lounging maximally, his arm draped over the back of the chair, Corey laughed. "You should retire down here man. I could set you up with a fabulous place. Nothing like wasting the day away in paradise."

"You know what the deal with Florida is, Corey? Florida's been underwater for most of the billions of years the planet's been around. It's only recently, geologically speaking, that Florida stuck its neck out. That's because all these organisms swimming around the shallow water shat and died. And all their shit and dead bodies piled up and cemented into limestone. Florida is literally a pile of shit and death."

Corey laughed some more, and Tony indulged his fantasy of Corey's properties all washing away.

"And I bet that shit-and-corpse limestone isn't looking as sturdy as it used to." Corey's laughter tapered off. The knife stopped in his hand as well. "We get the news up north. The spring rains? And the last couple of king tides? Septic tanks bursting out of the ground and riding down flooded streets. Our Lady of Mercy Cemetery, all those remains boiling out of the boxes like a zombie movie. Bet it's getting just a little harder to sell people on paradise."

Corey made a small, unamused sound. He set the knife down and sat up. "Okay, Tony. Level with me then. We've got sunny day flooding at high tide that's swamping our projects. Obviously, the cemetery incident was a bit of a black eye. But is this sea level rise—is this thing going to be real?"

Tony just stared at him, blinking.

"Are you fucking mad? Corey, I've been telling you this for twenty-five goddamn years. I wrote an *entire fucking book about it.*"

"Yeah, but what are we talking here? Like a foot, maybe a couple feet—that's manageable. But then you've got doomsayers going around telling people it's going to be six feet. Six feet? How's that even possible?"

Tony slapped his forehead without even thinking of how theatrical it might look.

"Corey, you'll be lucky as hell if it's only six. Do you know what the Thwaites Glacier is? Or the Pine Island Glacier? That's the whole reason I'm down here. That was my whole presentation to the city."

Corey pouted his lower lip and shook his head. "What's their deal?"

"Those are marine-terminating glaciers in West Antarctica that are disintegrating. Fast. And once they're gone? They're holding back a mountain of ice, enough to raise sea levels by a significant amount in the next fifty years. This . . ." He tossed his left hand at the bay and his right at the interior of the restaurant. "All this is *fucked*. All this is gone. I've been saying this to you since the girls were babies, and all you did was quote Fox News at me."

Corey gulped his spritzer. "What do we do about it? I read this thing—they can put sulfur up in the sky and we can cool down the planet that way?"

"Corey, even if we prematurely liquidated all the investments sunk into fossil-fuel infrastructure, even if we took those trillions of dollars and applied it to a crash course to save the world, Florida is still going under. Florida was probably doomed by 1995. Randall's bill? That was this generation's last-ditch effort to save the planet from mass extinction. You know what extinction is? That means you starve to death. That means your family drowns. That means everyone you know and love watches the world waste away until they're dead too."

Corey finished off his wine spritzer and signaled to the waiter for another.

"Jesus, Tony. No wonder you can't get any snatch."

───────────

His flight was delayed two hours going home, so he sat in Miami International Airport too distracted to read. His attention was momentarily captured by CNN. Rory Baumgart, the white nationalist billionaire, had dumped millions into Jennifer Braden's challenge, even as the Republican Party was changing the rules for the primaries to protect President Randall. Russ Mackowski was meeting with the evangelical leader The Pastor, in hopes of winning his support because he trailed both women. The two of them appeared together on-screen, Mackowski wind-burned, flinty, and impatient, the Evangelical handsome and well-kempt, his hair shellacked to his skull. Then the news moved out west where the worst wildfire season in history was raging across California, Oregon, Washington, Idaho, Colorado, and Montana with three Canadian provinces ablaze as well. Across the North American continent, fire season had killed nearly four hundred civilians and twenty-three firefighters.

And yet, the anchor moved on to a segment called "Shame on Who?" The subject: Holly's former boss.

He'd been skeptical of Kate Morris, and he'd told Holly as much, but for a minute, he'd wondered if they were going to do it. After they got Randall elected and flipped enough House and Senate seats, it did feel like there was momentum for a real piece of legislation. And his daughter, the stalwart optimist and bullheaded, nose-to-the-grindstone worker bee, would be a part of it. It would make him unbearably proud to watch her succeed where he had so miserably failed. Then to see how it had all ended last fall. Utterly ignominious and with an implosion that left this police-state wreckage in its wake. And now this: Two more FBF staffers had accused Morris of unwanted sexual advances. One young woman claimed she'd led her into a closet during a fundraising soiree in New York City and performed oral sex on her. Sure, the media's appetite for the salacious was appalling, but how could this Morris kid not learn to keep it in her pants? It was almost pathological.

He'd had enough and put in his earbuds and turned on some Bach. To let the infotainment bath of the day stream over you was to slowly scrub away at the skin of your own humanity.

You have a typo, he wrote to Holly the next day when he was back at his abode in New Haven. *Page 6 you wrote "seal level rise." Although an extreme seal level rise would be problem too.* And he added a smiley animation that did backflips before slipping on a banana.

One had to be careful with criticism when it came to daughters. He would never forget how in the first year after Gail died he'd picked up Holly from track practice and during an otherwise unremarkable ride home said something about how her baby weight looked like it was melting away. He'd thought nothing of it until months later, when Holly's arms and legs had turned to matchsticks and her face shriveled, cheekbones becoming uncomfortably prominent. He asked if she was eating, and she spat back in his face, "I thought it best if I lose my baby weight."

Or at least she spat it as much as quiet Holly could ever spit anything, with reasonableness and detachment and curiosity. He never really managed to backtrack from that one, and Holly saw a therapist for two years as she reluctantly returned to eating a normal diet. The incident had terrified and shamed him. How easy it was as a father, especially a single father, especially a workaholic single father, to let some innocuous comment slip free and have it go off in a child's life like a mortar shell. Maybe he was an occasional failure as a parent, but he trudged on. That's what parenting was, never getting over all the grave mistakes you'd made while cherishing a special fear: that this part of yourself, external to you, was in constant danger.

He was thinking of that teenage incident when Holly called him.

"Kiddo! Older One! I read the thing you sent. Also, I saw Uncle Corey when I was down in Miami. You won't believe what he asked me about . . ."

"Dad, have you seen the news?"

He stopped. That sound in her voice. "Not since yesterday?"

"The fires. Right in LA."

A quick Google search, and he was rewarded with images of the Hollywood sign burning.

"Two of them started yesterday, and there's a new one today."

"Where are they?" He was already pulling up a map of the city.

"One of them, the Canyonback, is west of the 405, but two of them are closer to Catherine. The Wisdom Tree Fire is really close to her."

The cursor churned as the page struggled to load, but Tony could already picture the chunk of Los Angeles she was talking about. The city's landmark mountain range where the wildland-urban interface stretched from Glendale to the Pacific Ocean.

"Have you talked to her?" he asked.

"No. She hasn't answered her phone. Or my texts."

"What's her address?"

"I have it here somewhere. She's on the border of Los Feliz and Silver Lake."

"Hold on."

He found the address in his phone and plugged it into the map.

"She looks pretty far south of the fires right now. She's definitely nowhere near the Hollywood sign." He clicked back over to the tab where the white letters were in flames. The picture was everywhere. "I'll keep trying her."

"Tell her to call me if you talk to her."

"Will do. Love you, Holl."

"Love you, Dad."

He called Catherine, but it went to voice mail. He left a message and texted her as well. *Hey Khaleesi, everything good there?* He wanted to add *Pack a bag just in case of these fires* but stopped himself. He knew it annoyed her when he was overbearing or when he worried. He clicked to video of the fire. The 405 was shut down because both sides of the Sepulveda Pass were ablaze. Seven hundred acres had burned in the heart of Los Angeles and an additional two thousand in the Verdugo Mountains. A lot of rich people's homes were on fire in the Hollywood Hills, but there were no fatalities and firefighters had the Canyonback 80 percent contained. He picked up his phone and added: *The fires have your dad a little freaked out. Just gimme a call when you can.*

Every channel was covering it. One legendary film director had lost both his homes. A rapper was having his wardrobe shipped out on trucks as the flames wrapped around Bel-Air. The Getty Museum was moving its collection to the basement. The smoke rose like a mushroom cloud. By eight thirty Catherine still hadn't called or texted, and it occurred to him to call Ash Hasan.

"Tony. How are you? Seth and I were just about to sit down to dinner."

"Sorry to bother you, man. I'm wondering if you've got any inside track on the Los Angeles fires?"

"I'm certainly keeping abreast of the news. What do you mean?"

Tony chewed his tongue. What was he asking exactly? He'd known Hasan for a few years now, and at first the guy had rubbed him all kinds of the wrong way, just a grab bag of peculiarities and quacking hands. Not that it was PC to be weirded out by these full-spectrum cases, but Tony couldn't help it. Over time, though, he came to appreciate that his distaste might be part and parcel of a thing other people called "jealousy." An undeniably brilliant man like Hasan got under his skin because of Tony's own ego. After Tony told him off during their secret conference back in '29, Hasan had nevertheless continued to seek his advice on drafting LaFray-Kastor. Begrudgingly, Tony began to admire the man. As the bill neared the vote in the House, Tony found himself at lunch with Hasan, awkwardly apologizing for his prickly nature.

"That's amusing," said Hasan sans any amusement. "I never noticed. You appreciate empiricism. One of the five people left in the world, I believe. That was a joke," he said too quickly, his timing woefully inhuman.

"Congresswoman Aamanzaihou has been dealing with emergency packages for the wildfires all summer," Hasan now offered. After the mutation of PRIRA, Hasan was tapped to lead the US Global Change Research Program, and because Joy LaFray got run off in disgrace, he now powwowed exclusively with the last card-carrying member of the decimated climate hawks. "I've drafted an executive summary on the situation. I could send it to you?"

Tony chuffed a laugh. "Ash, last time I read one of your summaries there was seven pages on you and your boyfriend shopping at Target."

"I find adding autobiographical detail aids in the writing process."

"Yeah, okay, send it to me when you get the chance."

Eventually, Tony fell into a restless sleep while the news recycled images of smoke gathering into a violent thunderhead over the city.

He woke at 6 a.m. when his cat, Tyrion, jumped into his lap. The cat stared at him with expectant, eerie intelligence. *Wake up, old man. You're running out of time.* Tony realized his phone was thrumming on the coffee table. Holly.

"You heard from Catherine?" he asked.

"No."

They were both silent.

"Dad, the fires are worse. There's a new one in Griffith Park. That's just to the north of her."

Tony rubbed his eye with the heel of his hand. "Well, why isn't she answering?"

"I don't know. She's home. Or at least her phone is. We've got find-a-friend turned on with each other."

"Is there anyone else you can call there? Any of her friends?"

"I don't know. She was seeing this guy, but nothing serious . . ." She trailed off.

"Okay, let me call my colleague in D.C. He might know something . . ." It was his turn to let his helpless sentence wither.

"Call me back."

"Okay."

Ash didn't answer, so Tony left a message. The news was grim. The Wisdom Tree Fire had raced east and south, threatening homes around the Hollywood Reservoir. Fire crews had been unable to contain it overnight. With nothing to do but wait for Ash to call, Tony showered and changed. When he returned, CNN was still replaying the footage of Hollywood ablaze. From ten thousand feet, a plane captured the massive plume of smoke. It looked like an enormous horned beast. He had a missed called, but it was neither from Hasan nor Holly. It was Dean. He dialed his son-in-law back.

"Hey, Tony, man."

"Dean. Everything okay?"

There was the sound of traffic white-noising in the background.

"So, you can't let Holly know I called you, okay? I've been sworn to secrecy too many times to count, but look, you're like a dad to me. I love you and respect you, man. I feel obligated."

"Okay . . ." Almost every time they spoke, Dean repeated that Tony was like a father to him, and he loved and respected him. Utterly cloying. He liked Dean just fine, but at some point, give it a rest.

"Holly's been worried about Catherine for a while now."

"Worried how?"

"She's been out to LA twice in the last year to take Catherine to *meetings.*"

"Meetings?" Tony choked. "Dean, what the fuck are you talking about?"

"Cat's just . . . She's a partier, man. She works at that bar, drinks every night. She's into harder stuff too. She goes on benders where she blacks out . . . Did you know she was arrested?"

"What?" Tony barked the word so loud that Tyrion darted behind the couch.

"For possession. But that's not a big deal, man. That was years ago. We're just worried because she's not answering and—I don't know. Holly didn't want to tell you, but I think— Fuck! Watch where you're going!" Dean muttered something he couldn't make out. "Sorry, Tone, I'm on my bike. Anyway, I just thought you should know. And don't be mad at Holly. She's just trying to look out for her sister but not betray her trust."

"Thanks for calling, Dean."

Tony stewed on this information while he watched Los Angeles burn. He tried calling his colleague Niko, thinking maybe Niko could drive up from La Jolla to find Catherine, but his wife answered and told Tony that was an absurd idea. People were driving *away* from Los Angeles. He tried the LA Fire Department next but got an automated message. Every emergency service in the city was engaged at this point. Then the news started coming very quickly.

"We're getting reports that the fire has jumped the 101 near the Hollywood Bowl, and at least thirteen firefighters and rescue workers are dead. The fire apparently leaped over the Cahuenga Pass when wind speeds picked up. We're now seeing winds gusting at upward of eighty miles per hour and that is pushing the flames down into the city . . ."

Tony had his phone out, looking at flights to Los Angeles, and of course this was stupid, there were no flights to Los Angeles. All of them delayed or canceled, LAX suffocating. Ten minutes later, the harried CNN reporter was back on: the governor had ordered the evacuation of Los Angeles.

"This is unprecedented. As many as five million people ordered to leave their homes, as multiple fires converge, and the winds—I think it's difficult to explain just how hard the wind is—"

Tony snatched up the remote and turned off the TV. He sat staring at the blank screen. Tyrion perched on the armrest, green eyes locked on him. *You're wasting time, old man.*

His phone rang. Holly.

"I know," he said.

"Dad, they're evacuating the city. I didn't even know that was possible."

"Yeah."

"What about Catherine? She's still not answering." Holly sounded less frightened than furious at her irresponsible little sister. Tony could not recall being this scared in his life. Not when his mom passed away when he was a boy. Not following Gail's diagnosis. Not when he opened the envelope and rubbed his fingers together to test the consistency of that powder.

"Your track-a-friend thing still says she's in her apartment?"

"Yes. Dad, I've called every emergency line in LA. It's fucking pandemonium. All her friends I know of are already gone. No one knows where she is, and they're sure as hell not turning around to go look for her."

"Okay," said Tony. "Okay." His phone beeped with an incoming call. "Hold on, Holly, it's my colleague. Let me take this."

"What's strange about these fires," said Hasan, not bothering with any phatic drivel, "is how far the flames are reaching into urban areas. The factors involved are quite interesting."

Tony rubbed his head and considered hanging up.

"What makes these particular fires so pernicious is fountain grass."

"Grass."

"Yes. It's an invasive species, highly flammable, and it grows best in areas burned by fire. On top of that, the horticultural trade actually promotes it. People plant this in their yards! Which is helping the flames carry down into the city."

"Ash. Stop." The other end of the line went quiet. "My daughter is in Los Angeles. I can't get a hold of her."

"Oh." He paused. "I'm sorry to hear that. Where does she live?"

"Silver Lake. Right around Sunset and Hollywood."

"That's . . ." He could almost hear Ash pulling up a map. "That is not a good place to be right now."

"I know."

"Have you tried contacting local officials?"

"Local officials appear to be busy."

"Of course." He hesitated, probably trying to come up with anything that didn't make him sound like a mutant. "Would you like me to send over the executive summary I've drafted for the congresswoman?"

Tony snorted. "Sure. I gotta go."

He hung up without waiting for a reply. He stood in his living room watching the same cell phone and helicopter footage repeat on CNN, though they'd changed the chyron to GOVERNOR ORDERS EVACUATION; CHAOS AS HIGHWAYS CLOG. Just in case anyone didn't know to panic. He felt detached from his own skin, unable to pull himself back into the moment. Tyrion whispered past his ankle. Then he remembered he'd hung up on Holly, but he didn't call her back. He didn't know what he'd say.

His phone buzzed. Hasan again.

"What."

"Tony? It's Ash."

"I know, it says that."

"This may be dangerous and perhaps unethical, but I think I've found a way you could get to Los Angeles before nightfall."

Tony sat down. "How?"

"The airports in the area surrounding Los Angeles are all closed, but there are special dispensations for disaster response professionals flying into emergency zones. I can get you on a FEMA plane bound for Ontario, California. President Randall is sending every available resource, so I'll recommend you as a climate variability expert—"

"A what?"

"It's a made-up title. Ontario is roughly an hour away from the city. Once there, I can have a car waiting for you through FEMA channels. Officials are turning all incoming highway lanes to the city outbound, but there will be an emergency route in. I'll figure that out while you're in the air. Of course, you have to understand the danger, and I simply can't ask anyone to accompany you—"

"No, of course not." Tony caught his breath, and then he hurried into his bedroom to pack a bag. "Ash—my God—thank you. Thank you so much. I can't even . . ."

It was like a wire had tripped inside him, the fear blown back by this chance he'd been given.

"If you can get to the New Haven airport in the next hour, I'll route you through Chicago where you can catch the FEMA plane. You should read my executive summary despite your skepticism of my methods. It would be best if you had some background on the behavior of large-scale fire events in case of emergency."

"This is incredible of you, man. I swear to Christ, I'll never forget this."

"I was thinking of how my sister and her husband, Peter, would behave if it were their child, and that allowed me to think creatively about the situation." He said it like such a fucking robot, and Tony felt such warmth for him. "I just hope you find your daughter."

He packed a change of clothes and a toothbrush. He called Holly on his way to the airport.

"Are you out of your fucking mind? Dad, the city's being evacuated. People are dying in car accidents on the highways trying to get out."

"What choice do I have, Holly? Your tracker still says she's in her apartment, right?"

"Yeah, but—"

"So I'll get into the city and find her. The fires are still well north of her."

"Not that far north! Dad, this is a terrible idea. You don't know if she's even—"

"What the hell do you want me to do, Holly?" He immediately regretted shouting at her. He had to keep a lid on his fear. He lowered his voice. "I can't sit in my goddamn house and watch the city burn down knowing she might be there. And you, Older One, should have told me about her problems."

Holly was silent for a moment. Tony was almost at the airport.

"I guess I thought if I told you, you'd do something stupid like fly to Los Angeles in a firestorm."

Tony couldn't help but laugh. God, these girls were just too much, all the time, they were too much, and he loved them so intensely it made him insane.

"We don't need to argue. I'll be fine."

———

Total flight time six hours. In Chicago, he transferred to a FEMA plane packed with bureaucracy, men and women huddling over maps and spreadsheets, wizarding away on phones, and a few watching movies or slumped into VR sets. Tony didn't make friends, and no one appeared to recognize him. He tried reading Ash's report to pass the time.

Fountain Grass, Soil Moisture, Wind Speeds, and the El Demonio-Los Angeles Complex Megafire in Context: Plans and Protocols for Containment was forty-six pages long and began with a tedious description of the proliferation of fountain grass that Tony mostly skipped. More importantly, Southern California had been in a state of periodic drought since the early 2000s with spates of wet years that would interrupt these longer spasms of rainless winters and diminishing snowpack in the mountains. The years of rain, however, simply grew more fuel, and when the heat returned, months of sun and wind depleted fuel moistures, leading to climatic whiplash. Bark beetles took their toll and chaparral was moving higher into the mountains as the region warmed. The summer of 2031, the entire North American West had been a tinderbox. Firestorms raged, leveling whole towns, sending people fleeing down highways on foot. There were currently two hundred large fires burning across twenty-one states with nearly forty thousand people fighting them, including volunteers from Mexico, South Africa, Portugal, Chile, and Australia. Many of the ignitions were due to humans, as was typical, but there was also lightning. The storm that had begun the Flower Lake Fire in Montana produced twenty thousand bolts of lightning in a single day. There was simply no precedent for that kind of pyrocumulonimbus behavior.

The Los Angeles megafire, now nicknamed El Demonio after folks got a gander at the eerie image of a demonic face formed by the smoke cloud, began as four separate fires, but grew due to mismanagement by firefighters in the Hollywood Hills. Wealthy residents employed private firefighting companies to protect their homes. They coated the houses in Phos-Chek, a Monsanto-developed chemical retardant, and tapped the public hydrants to beat back embers and spot fires. A company called Transpen Fire Services had engaged in a pitched battle with another called Firestop for water and staging areas. The result was that the hydrants went dry, and the fire leaped from unprotected home to unprotected home until entire neighborhoods went up, and the firefighters were forced to retreat. The flames eventually joined up with the Wisdom Tree Fire and were carried eastward by abrupt shifts in the wind. There was a link to a video in the report, cell phone footage of Route 101 near the Hollywood Bowl, cars inching along in traffic, and within seconds fire came barreling down the side of the highway, trees candling, flames blowing sideways across six lanes. As the video went on, the smoke became a dark blanket and you could see people in their cars panicking, screaming, a few trying to get out and run, but soon they were all engulfed.

Another link took him to a video of the "firenado" in Beverly Hills. It was actually called a fire whirl but the effect was basically the same: a red-hot cyclone of smoke, dust, and flame eating its way across Coldwater Canyon, and he could hear drunk people gabbing from a rooftop deck. Then the firenado picked up a landscaping truck, whipped it in a spiral, and sent it crashing through the side of a building.

Ash wrote that he'd been in contact with the US Naval Research Lab, and its models were predicting that no amount of airpower would put this out, and only containment was possible. Abruptly, Ash's paper detoured to his sister's work as an economist of climate disaster, which then jumped to a description of their relationship. Apparently, they'd grown quite close over the last few years ever since she married his best friend. The whole report culminated in a scene at his sister's wedding, in which they had a traditional Islamic ceremony on a Friday night and a standard American on Saturday.

"You're one weird fuck, Hasan."

Descending into California, the pilot warned they'd be in for a bumpy ride as the Santa Anas blew hot. They could all hear loose chunks of soil pelting the hull. To the north, there was no sun, just an impregnable wall of smoke like a fortress erected to guard the horizon.

———

Climbing down from the plane, his particulate mask on, overnight bag slung across his shoulder, the first thing Tony registered was the heat: 103 degrees was different. He futilely unbuttoned the top two buttons on his shirt as sweat soaked his back and stomach. The air smelled of a region-wide campfire.

A man, dirty, sweating, hands dark with grime, stood holding a handwritten sign with Tony's name. Hasan must have put all this together while Tony was on the plane, and for a moment he was humbled and felt guilty for how much Hasan had done for him.

"Hank Magdolin with Cal Fire." He shook Tony's hand while he crumpled the piece of paper with the other. His mask clutched a thick gray beard, and he was humming with adrenaline. "You're the crazy son of a gun who wants to drive into LA in the middle of the book of Revelation, I take it? Look," he said without waiting for a reply, bounding across the asphalt toward the airport gate. "I don't condone this, but I got a call from some muckety-muck Fed asking if I can get this guy a car and a clear shot into the city. You know much about wildfire?"

Tony half shrugged a shoulder. "More than the average prole, I guess, but I'm not taking a test on it."

"Wow. Huh. Well, let me warn you, fella, this thing is a real kettle of fish. We've got lightning and Santa Ana winds, which is not supposed to be possible. Fire's burning so hot it's making its own weather. It came outta the Angeles Forest this afternoon, taking houses down to the frames in a minute, going through a thousand acres an hour. Fire-line construction's been impossible. Too much fuel, and it's moving too fast."

Inside the blessed air-conditioning of the terminal, Tony sucked in a welcome breath of cool oxygen. None of the businesses were open. The entire airport had been converted into an emergency command center. Hank Magdolin tore his mask off, revealing a ring of soot around his beard.

"No smokejumpers available at first—everyone was busy in other states. Wind too strong to deploy aircraft anyway. You can't fly in 'em. Updrafts are a nightmare and when they collapse, it's like the devil breathing on the city. Water, electricity, and cell signals are all failing. Hydrants are dry." They made their way back outside and into the parking structure. Magdolin took the stairs two at a time. "We've got you set up with a Suburban from DHS. Obviously, don't use the self-driving mode. You're going to take the 210, then cut down on the 710 once you get near Pasadena."

"Why?"

Magdolin looked back at him, cocking one twitchy gray eyebrow. "Pasadena's burning down, fella."

He took out a paper map and slapped it on the hood of the SUV. "This son of a gun's not going to sleep tonight. It'll be hunting for fuel. Where exactly are you headed?" Tony gave him the street address and neighborhood. "*Phewww*. Doc. Okay. You sure about this?"

"My daughter's there," he said.

Magdolin nodded knowingly. "Yeah. Okay." He folded the map and handed it to him. "I'd say we could try to get a fire crew in there, but the whole city's spilling out. No way of knowing how long it would take. You gotta hustle. The crews are going to drop back to Highway 10 and use that wide strip of concrete as a fuel break. Try to make a stand there and save the other half of the city." He handed Tony a walkie-talkie-looking device with a screen. "Sat-nav. Sorry, you'll have to learn it on the fly, your cell definitely won't work."

"Thank you," said Tony.

He dropped the car's fob in Tony's hand. "Once you get there, if your kid's gone, don't dawdle. Be safe. This thing is alive, angry, and a total F-E-A-R fire."

Tony smirked, sensing good jargon. "And what's that stand for?"

Magdolin spit on the concrete. "Fuck Everything and Run, of course."

Tony drove faster than felt safe as gales tore across the freeway. Choppers clattered low where they could still fly. Bucket drops and slurry tanker runs. It had the feel of a military campaign. He watched one of them dump red fire retardant on a ridge, only to have the load blown sideways, vaporizing, then vanishing.

He shared the road only with LA County Fire convoys and other emergency vehicles, lighting up the tangerine haze with their reds and blues. White ash fell like snow. To the north, the peaks of the San Gabriel Mountains thrust upward like the backs of wild beasts, and every few moments he'd catch flashes from the corner of his eye, lightning in those massive clouds, somehow battling the Santa Anas. As night fell, and he neared the city, the full scope of the refugee flow became clear. The 210 was bumper to bumper in all twelve lanes. There were cars in ditches or pulled to the side of the road, out of gas or charge. People vehicularly trampling each other. In a subdivision adjacent to the freeway, he saw them carrying cardboard boxes, TVs, and VR sets, piling suitcases into their cars or strapping them tight to rooftops. The wind had blown over most of the trash and recycling bins, so cans and glass jars and plastic milk jugs crunched and exploded under escaping tires. He saw a man in a bulldozer plowing into a house, destroying the vinyl-sided one-story, probably to clear fuel around his own home. Perhaps it was foreclosed, or maybe the neighbors had just fled.

Then he saw his first flames.

Orange embers danced in the air, and it appeared some of the vicious stowaways had found a community of mobile homes off the highway. Three of the trailers in the center of the park were ablaze, smoke pouring skyward, some chemical in the siding giving the flames a purple tint.

He raced down the cleared emergency route until he found the exit from the 710. The surface roads were mostly empty going into the city, and he used the satellite device to send Holly a quick text: *Landed safe. Heading to find Cat now. Will call soon.* What a preposterously calm message, as he looked up to see the ridge of Griffith Park glowing a pitch-dark amber. He crossed into Franklin Hills, and he began to understand.

Many of the homes in the hills were ablaze, as if the fire was picking and choosing, executing at random like a bored king. The sound was deafening, a freight train roar. Trees candling, grasses smoldering. He had the windows up and still the bonfire smell overpowered him. Embers suspended in the air like fireflies, smoke and flakes of ash forming a permanent silk haze. The power was out, but those burning homes at the top of the hills made it bright as day. Dogs and cats ran wild in the streets, and he honked the horn to avoid flattening a lost retriever.

He turned onto Hyperion Avenue, following the sat-nav. As he sped down the empty street he came to an intersection where sparks sizzled from a downed electrical line. The frying wires looked like a firework, sparks spraying into nearby shrubbery, and he was forced to make a right turn. He whipped the Suburban left down another street as his navigation redirected. It was a residential neighborhood; big, beautiful homes, most still without fire, except here was one, with just the wooden porch aflame. And here were either homeowners or looters, carrying a couch to the back of a truck, risking their lives for whatever salvageable prizes lay inside. They didn't even glance at him as he drove by.

He heard the horse's whinny before he saw the animal. It came streaking out of a yard, its fur smoking, hurtling into the street in a panic, and Tony slammed the brakes. The horse had a choice—either dart across the road or pull back to avoid him—and it lost itself in indecision, so Tony made the choice, yanking the wheel hard left, missing the animal, crashing into a blue recycling bin, and he thought he was safe, when something to the right of the car exploded.

The way his skull smacked the window felt like a bat to the side of the head. He lost control of the SUV and found himself spinning, spinning, spinning, and he felt the tree catch the hood with the simultaneous crunch of metal and pop of the airbag, and he thought he was blacking out but maybe not. Maybe he was smelling himself burning alive.

———

It was hard to tell how long he sat there. He was awake but also not. Aware enough to hear the fading cries of the horse, but unable to recall why that mattered. At some point he realized he'd thrown up. A pile of vomit lay in his lap. Then he remembered Catherine, and he looked up and around, his fog blowing away. Something was on fire. He touched the side of his head where it had thunked off the window, but he wasn't bleeding. As a kid, he'd taken a hit to the head during a game of backyard tag. *Got your bell rung*, his father had said, examining the knot on his head. Then he was lost in a memory of his dad passing away.

Tony stumbled out of the car into the inferno. He'd driven into the trunk of a palm tree, and this tree was in the process of going up. On the other side of the car, he saw pieces of what looked like a rocket or mortar buried in the side of the vehicle, and he stupidly looked around, wondering if some *Mad Max* crew of postapocalyptic thugs had taken a shot at him. Then across the street he saw one of the burning homes, saw the mangled remains of a grill, and understood. Someone's propane tank had exploded. Launched sideways like a missile into the car.

He went back to the Suburban, spitting to clear the acrid taste of fumes, and of course the vehicle was done. The bucketing noises of an engine grinding uselessly. He couldn't find breathable air, so he grabbed the sat-nav and hurried out, eating smoke and then hacking it back up in painful upchucks. He tried to follow the blue line of the map pointing the way to Catherine, but he saw a gas station on the horizon, and he really needed water. His eyes, itchy and swollen, kept filling with tears, and he couldn't stop coughing. All he could picture was clear cold water.

The gas station convenience store was locked, but he found a cinder block around the side, threw it through the glass, and crawled through the shattered spikes. The air inside was marginally cooler. Barely able to see, he made his way to the back row of beverages and grabbed the first plastic bottle he found. He cracked a Gatorade open and dumped its sticky contents on his face. After he washed his eyes out, he swigged from another bottle. His nose was bleeding. His head spun and throbbed. His skin itched like crazy from the smoke. Outside, the roar of burning structures was like standing under a jet engine. Gas station not the place to be. Keep moving.

He bagged the remaining four bottles of Gatorade (there was no actual water left in the place) and crawled back through the door. There was a dog waiting for him. It could have been the brown retriever he'd swerved to avoid or, given the dizziness, it could have been a hallucination. It looked at him hopefully.

"Can't help you, dog."

He was less than half a mile from Catherine's. He went south as fast as he could, and the dog followed, trotting along at his side while a small metal heart tinkled on its collar. A glance back to the north and he saw the way the fire had marched out of the hills and into the city, sending its deadly ember emissaries as shock troops, all those tightly packed homes offering the perfect kindling.

Near a dark Goodwill store, the dog ran ahead of him to sniff at a pile of clothes heaped on the sidewalk. It took him a moment to realize that the pile was a man lying dead under a heap of rags. He was about to walk around it when the dead man spoke.

"Nice pup." He was older, Black, bald, and missing teeth.

"It's not mine," said Tony. He didn't want to stop. Not for anything, but he did. "Hey man, you've got to get out of here. Look around."

As if for the first time, the old man did. "Yeah, but where to go?"

"South, buddy. Get to the 10. That's where they're trying to hold it."

He smushed his lips in skepticism. "Nah. Thought I'd stick around and see if I couldn't move in one of them houses when everyone's gone."

This was not a conversation worth having. "Get out, pal. Right now. While you can. The fire's already hitting a few blocks away."

"God won't let it touch me. Know how many times God's had my back?"

"Whatever."

Tony kept on. For a moment the dog looked indecisive about who to follow, but when Tony turned the corner, the dog yipped and bounded after him.

Catherine's apartment building was as dark as the rest of the city, but the gate was propped open, likely by residents trying to carry out belongings as they fled. He bounded up the stairs to the second floor, found her number, and began pounding. The dog stood alongside him, tense, then it started barking.

"Catherine!" Tony screamed. "Catherine! Are you in there?" He slammed his fist over and over. The side of his head throbbed from where it had connected with the window, and the circumstances—well, it all felt too much like one of his dreams. "Catherine, goddamnit!"

He rammed his shoulder into the door, then tried to kick it, but he was kidding himself. He rattled the knob. Kept screaming her name. The dog barked and barked. He left and ran back around the side of the street to where the homeless guy was sitting under the Goodwill's awning, smoking a cigar or blunt and watching the city burn.

"Hey man," said Tony. "I'll give you all the money in my wallet if you help me break a door down."

"What kind of door?" he asked, curious but noncommittal.

"I don't know—a fucking door. A door I can't break down."

"Hold on, I got you."

He picked up a few of his rags and wandered into the unlocked Goodwill. Tony waited for a minute and thought about leaving. Then the man emerged from the store, carrying a crowbar like a sword. They reached Catherine's apartment, and Tony emptied his wallet into the man's hands, maybe sixty-five bucks.

"Thank you much," he said. "This illegal?"

"Look around, man," Tony said frantically. "There's nothing fucking illegal anymore. Now help me open the door or give that to me." He pointed madly at the crowbar. "My daughter's in there."

The man shot him a horrified look, big folds of his brow bunching into tension. "Well, why didn't you say. Here." He handed the bills back. "I can't take your money. Not for God's work."

Tony jabbed two fingers into his chest. "Keep the money. Open the fucking door."

The man slammed the end of the crowbar into the frame and pried. A minute of wrenching, each of them taking turns, and the door ripped open in a crack and shriek of splintering wood.

At first he thought he had the wrong apartment, and then he thought maybe looters had torn through, and he feared for his daughter. But then he recognized the place was just a dump. Pizza boxes and liquor bottles and fast-food containers littered every surface because the garbage bin was overflowing. Every dish in the sink, dirty laundry strewn over the furniture. He swung the sat-nav's flashlight back and forth, trying to make sense of the person who lived here, and it revealed yet another table where empty vodka and tequila bottles stood like mini skyscrapers in a diorama.

He made his way to the bedroom and found Catherine in a beanbag chair, a dead VR set and headphones wrapped around her face. Her mouth hung open and drool ran down her lip. She wore sweatpants and a T-shirt with no bra. There was a glass with a small pink straw poking out and the entire room reeked of booze. She was breathing, though. The dog trotted up to her and licked the tips of her dangling fingers, but she did not respond. He pulled the VR set from her face.

"Catherine," he said gently. Her eyes didn't even flutter. There were garbage bags taped across the window, blacking out the room. He didn't see her phone anywhere.

He still had the bag of Gatorades and splashed some of the sticky beverage on her cheeks. "Cat." She looked terrible. Her hair was matted. She'd put on weight since he saw her in December, and her skin was riddled with acne. He splashed more Gatorade. "Khaleesi," he said.

Finally, she swiveled her head to get away from the moisture. Her eyes slid open. She looked drunk, high, and confused. "Daddy?"

"Honey, we've gotta go."

"What?"

"We've gotta go. There's a fire."

"Huh?" She looked around her room, as if trying to remember where she was. "Whose dog is that?"

Tony took a moment to scan the room, looking for evidence of what else she might be on. He had a father's impulse to open all her drawers, ransack the medicine cabinet, search under her bed, but there was no time. She drank a bit of the Gatorade, but she couldn't walk without Tony's help. She laid an arm around his shoulder and leaned into him, feet dragging, eyes slipping open and shut.

"I fell asleep with the VR on," she mumbled. "It was a space journey. I was going to space."

When he got her outside the apartment, the homeless man was still standing there with the crowbar.

"She okay?" he asked.

"I don't know," said Tony. From their perch on the second floor, he could see the glow of the fire just over the hill, hear its steady raging thunder, watch its embers drifting down onto roofs. They would never outrun it, not with Catherine the way she was. She didn't have a car. The sat-nav still worked, but who would he call? And what was the likelihood any kind of rescue would reach them before the fire engulfed the neighborhood? He thought of Ash's report. Buried amid an unexpectedly tender story of his younger sister convincing him to reveal his sexuality to their mother, there'd been a few useful suggestions for what to do in a wildfire. "What's around here? Something brick and big. With a basement maybe. Something that won't ignite right away."

The homeless guy looked at the dog, as if it might know, and the dog looked right back at him.

"The middle school," Catherine slurred. "S'pose," she added. And she gestured vaguely to the south.

"Help me," Tony begged, but the man was already sliding under Catherine's arm to keep her upright.

"He smells," complained Catherine.

"You ain't fresh out the bath yourself, sister," said the man.

They struck off down Catherine's street, a savage wind raking heat and embers across their faces. The heat was so intense, it created a sunburned feeling on his skin. From the map it looked like there was some kind of movie studio to the left, but the flames had reached it. A few of the structures within the gated compound were already burning. The only other sound besides the fire was the dog barking at them as it bounded ahead, urging them on, Lassie-like. Catherine wasn't dead weight, but she was close, her feet barely carrying her.

Tony could've cried with relief when he saw the campus. Thomas Starr King Middle School had trailers and classroom annexes that would catch, but the main building was solid brick. A few of the houses surrounding the school were already igniting. The tops of the palm trees surrounding the PE field were torches, raining embers on the campus. Tony hustled their ragtag crew across the basketball courts, the soccer fields, and to the main building. The doors were locked, but it only took his friend a moment with the crowbar to bust out a window and crawl inside to let them in. Tony checked the sat-nav. There was an SOS button, and he activated it. He texted Holly anyway, telling her what had happened, where they were, and that he was sorry. Then he ducked into the school. They found the stairs to a basement, and there, along with a boiler and janitorial supplies, they hunkered down, soot-covered, smoke-reeking, and thirsty, hoping the walls of the building would hold, and the fire wouldn't eat all their oxygen.

———

It was hot as hell in that basement, lit only by a haze of orange splashing down from the window near the ceiling. He found a flashlight in a supply closet, but there was nothing else of use. No food, no water. The temperature ticked up the longer they sat there. The smell of smoke leaked down to them but not the substance itself. The second it crept under the metal door at the top of the stairs, it would mean they were done. Catherine had fallen back asleep in the corner of the room, using her arm as a pillow. The dog settled near her, resting its head on her feet. Tony tried to give her some of the last bottle of Gatorade, but she just wanted to pass out. He drank a little and offered the rest to the homeless man. Tony thanked him for everything he'd done. "Probably just so we can die down here instead of out there but thank you anyway."

"Nothing to think on," he said, gulping down the purple sugar water.

"What's your name?"

"Diamond."

"I'm Tony."

"Used to be I worked in this place."

"This school?"

"Naw, but one like it. Down the way a bit. Used to be. They took me away."

He didn't share anything more.

An hour after that, he checked on Catherine. She was slick with sweat and shivering. She'd wet herself. He'd read enough to understand she was going through the first stages of withdrawal. He could hope it was heroin but there were no needle tracks on her arms, which probably meant it was this concentrated fentanyl shit or worse. He'd asked plenty of questions but not enough; he'd sent her money every month when she needed it; he'd let her plead her way out of any reckoning. He was at least partly responsible for this, and now it was going to kill them both. When Catherine had been little she'd refused baths with borderline violence, especially if Dad was the one enforcing her hygiene. Once, trying to get her in the tub, she even bit him. Of course, once she was in the bath she'd have the time of her life and never want to leave and another fight would ensue to get her out. He'd pull the drain and she'd try to put it back in, stand in the water and stomp her feet furiously. How feeble these memories felt in the face of an inferno. That was when he coughed, tasting smoke yet again. He clicked the flashlight on, and there it was: wisps creeping under the door, gathering in the beam.

"Goddamnit," he moaned.

Diamond tore his coat off and stuffed it into the crack, but it was still seeping in around the edges. He stepped back beside Tony and Catherine. The dog whined.

"I'm sorry, brother," said Diamond.

"No," said Tony, stroking his daughter's face, thinking about the time she was seven and he wouldn't let her stay up so she shouted *You're a tyrant!* and launched a bowl of SpaghettiOs at the wall. "I'm sorry."

Smoke sipped in around the frame of the door, exploring the ceiling and crawling, a step at a time, toward them. Catherine woke as the smell became too powerful. He smiled and put his arm around her.

"Hey. How you doing?"

Her face crumpled with misery. "I'm sorry, Daddy. I'm so fucking sorry."

"For what? There's nothing to be sorry for."

"Holly's going to be so mad at me," she whimpered, and despite the dread filling him, he couldn't help but laugh at that. Diamond looked at him like he was a madman. Then, abruptly, all three of them started coughing. Choking on smoke, he had the urge to claw his throat open, as if this would siphon clean air into his lungs. He was going to die scratching his throat apart. They all were.

At first, he thought the sound of the siren was his imagination and ignored it. But then his friend, huddled against the wall with his knees drawn to his chest, trying to keep his face buried in his rags, heard it too. He looked at Tony. "Where it coming from?"

The brays of some kind of emergency vehicle. Tony left Catherine, held his breath, and climbed the stairs to the door. He put his hand on the metal, and it was too hot to touch. He ran right back down where the smoke was thinner. He looked up at the window with its orange slice of light. The sirens and the horn grew louder. The dog lifted its head and perked up its chocolate ears. Tony dragged a broken student desk below the window, ordered Diamond to hold it, and climbed up. The window had metal wire covering it, but he could at least see out. The sirens grew louder, then the strobing red and white lights began to splash across the burning night, and finally—never having flirted with religion for even a moment—Tony understood what it was like to watch an angel appear. An honest-to-Christ fire truck pulled to the curb outside the middle school, lumbering to a halt on the lawn. It was covered in ash, a sooty scorch mark slashing through the LAFD logo. Tony began screaming through his hoarse, burning throat.

"In here! Heyyyyy!!! In here!!!!"

Three firefighters leaped from the cab, and then the bulky angels were running toward the school, oxygen tanks bouncing, masks like deep-sea divers, wielding axes. How did they know?

"We're in the basement!" He smacked the window with both fists, and this sent pain shooting through his busted head and scorched lungs. The dog got the idea and began barking at a steady clip. *"The basement!"* And then his lungs exploded into another coughing fit, and it felt like he was choking on barbed wire.

Three more figures leaped off the rig, while one turned a water cannon on the building. He just couldn't believe it. He crawled off the desk, trying to stay the coughing of his smoke-scarred lungs long enough to command the others: "Scream!"

And the three of them began shouting all at once. The dog barked furiously. Tony bounded up the stairs to the door, pounding on the metal even as it burned his fist.

From the other side of the door: *"Stand back!"*

"It's unlocked!"

Nevertheless, the door burst inward, slamming against the wall and rebounding. Clad in orange jumpsuits, three women came hurtling through like Navy SEALs, rushing them with silver foil. One stuffed an oxygen mask over his face before he could even get a word out. The smoke stung his eyes, but he could clearly see this savior had a tattoo on her face. She was also missing most of her bottom teeth.

"C'mon, man, we gotta beat feet!" she cried.

"My daughter," he wheezed.

"They'll get her. Let's go."

One of the women was wrapping Catherine in a foil blanket and then hoisting her over her shoulder without asking, picking her up like a bag of laundry. The dog barked.

"C'mon, pup!" cried the third woman, who'd gone to Diamond.

Tony followed on the firewoman's heels. Through a smoke-choked hallway, sucking cool air from the oxygen mask, and out into the savage night. Fire everywhere. Burning so bright, the night was forgotten. Every home he could see was in some state of nature's arson, whether it was cinders spotting on the roof or the whole structure wrapped in flame. It felt like it was a thousand degrees outside, and the wind blew hot and spiteful into his face, peppered with a cool mist evaporating from the barrel of the truck's water cannon. The hellscape ran on in every direction, as far as his vision allowed.

The woman hauled Catherine to the fire truck, another carried the dog in two arms like a bag of concrete, and Diamond brought up the rear. As they reached the rig, he saw a man in a shirt and tie holding the door open, looking like he'd wandered out of a boardroom into the hell he most likely deserved. At first Tony figured him for another person the women had rescued. Then he realized who he was looking at.

"Corey?"

"Is she okay?" his brother-in-law shouted, trying to be heard above the blaze.

"She ate some smoke," said the woman loading her into the truck. "But she'll be fine."

Despite the searing knives in his chest and the ringing in his head, Tony was caught staring at his brother-in-law, stunned dumb. The firewoman grabbed him by the collar and practically threw him into the truck. He collapsed in a seat opposite Corey, still just staring. Corey's sleeves were rolled up, his blue button-up pit-stained, his tie askew, gray ash resting in the tips of his buzzed hair.

"Let's fucking go, ladies!" screamed the woman with the face tattoo, who seemed to be in charge.

"Corey, what the hell?" Tony whispered through the glass of his throat.

The siren wailed and the truck lurched up a hill, hanging a left on Sunset, racing down through a cool tunnel of air between burning shops and restaurants. Corey wrapped Tony in his arms, crying and laughing and slapping his back.

"You crazy motherfucker, Tony! Your balls are almost as big as these gals'!" He let him go and then threw his arm around the firefighter sitting next to him, an exhausted Black woman with a gap in her front teeth. He planted a kiss on her cheek. She shook her head, neither amused nor repulsed, just tired.

"That was a hell of a mission," she said. "A real check-your-State-Farm-policy for real."

"Uncle Corey?" Catherine looked as confused as Tony felt, but she was too tired to inquire further. One of the women slipped an oxygen mask over Catherine's face and she closed her eyes. Diamond gazed out the window at the city on fire. The brown Lab panted happily in a firewoman's lap. They raced south out of the inferno, and when Tony looked out, he could see the woman riding near the water cannon like a soldier poking up from a gunner's hatch. She gazed across the city, backlit by the burning mountains to the north. By the time they reached the containment line established at the 10, dawn was approaching, and they found safety under a sky as gray as the dead.

———

Later, Tony would get the whole story.

Unable to reach Tony, Corey had called Holly and learned of Tony's crazed cross-country flight to find Catherine. While Tony was getting on the FEMA plane in Chicago, Corey chartered a jet to get him as close to LA as possible, which turned out to be the former John Wayne Airport in Orange County. From there, he hitched a ride with a rescue helicopter (which probably meant he paid someone an exorbitant bribe). He was in constant touch with Holly, who was losing her mind. All she knew was that Cat appeared to still be in her apartment and that's where their dad was heading. Corey stalked the ranks of the firefighters and rescue workers trying their best to evacuate five to eight million people. This army included not just the obvious first responders. Take all the National Guard, smokejumpers, pilots, police, paramedics, doctors, nurses, hospital staff, and even Mexican fishermen coming up in their boats to evacuate people along the coast. Take FEMA officials and air traffic controllers and Cal Fire and military and off-duty everyone, get them on the phone and tell them they're needed. The miracle was not just that the death toll stopped short of four figures. The miracle was not just school bus drivers showing up to move whole neighborhoods of the homeless south as the fire advanced. The miracle was how many people just flat-out answered the call. Or as the mayor would later put it, in a speech many said would vault him into vice presidential contention for the Democrats, "We have to rebuild, so Hollywood can go about immortalizing this story."

But when Corey arrived at the fire line, that's not what he saw. All he found was chaos, disorganization, and fear. The people in charge, FEMA reps, police captains, fire chiefs, all told him the area he wanted to get to was already lost, and he needed to back off, let them do their jobs, and get to safety.

Corey approached every firefighter, paramedic, and cop—anyone with a vehicle—and begged them to help him get to Catherine's address. No one even considered it. "You're going to get yourself killed," one crew chief told him. "That whole area's going to be ash."

Then he found the women in orange. They wore this color because they were prison inmates. Based out of the women's correctional facility in Chino, they fought wildfires for $7 a day. They'd been mobilized more or less nonstop the entire summer, and now they were part of the force trying to save Los Angeles.

"Please," Corey pleaded. "It's not just my niece. It's my brother-in-law too—her dad. He went to try to get her, and I can't reach him." He looked from woman to woman. They sat on milk crates and fold-out chairs, chugging water, snacking on boxes of animal crackers. They had less than five hours before they were supposed to be back on the line.

"You don't get it," said their chief, Yolanda Quebrada, the woman with the design on her cheek. "Our truck, it ain't our truck. We take off in it, they could give us more time."

Corey, a delirious negotiator, a lifetime spent talking people into deals that may or may not work out for them, saw that crack of daylight. None of them had said no.

"I swear to God," he said. "I'm not just talking money. I will spend the next decade of my life hiring you all lawyers, calling the governor, getting your sentences commuted. I will find you jobs when you get out. Anything you need, anything your families need. This is my fucking family," he continued, his voice cracking. "I swear to Christ if you help me get to them, I will make you whole after this. I promise. I will make you whole."

One of the women, the one he'd later kiss on the cheek, was staring at her box. "My daughter calls these 'amnimal crackers,'" she said.

So seven of the inmates from the California Institution for Women in Chino, serving time for everything from drunk driving to armed robbery, drove their truck into the flaming east side hills. They knew to look in the school because Tony's text had reached Holly.

Listening to this story, Tony felt as if he were absent from the moment. While they drove south to the medical tents where he and Catherine would be treated for smoke inhalation, he was having enough trouble believing he was alive. The man who called himself Diamond melted away as soon as they reached the safety of the 10. And the women of Chino? He hadn't even had a moment to thank them. They had immediately plunged back into the dark flames, into the war, following the scent of smoke. Forty-eight hours later, the fire finally brought under control, he, Corey, and Catherine flew from Orange County with the dog in tow. That night, as they flew over the rubble of Los Angeles, a massive scar that stretched for thousands of acres before vanishing into the coal-black ocean, Tony thought of those women stepping off the rig. Looking out from the plane's window, he imagined them now among the cinders. The city looked like a gutted hole in the earth, indistinguishable from the night, this yawning abyss left behind by the fire.

FEDERAL BUREAU OF INVESTIGATION

Preference: ROUTINE   Date: 02/10/32

To: Washington Field

From: Washington Field

      Contact: ███████████████

Approved By: ███████████████

Drafted By: ███████████████

Case ID #: 838A-WF-3333897-USWEAIID (Pending)

Title: WEATHERMEN 6DEGREES

      MAJOR CASE 194

Synopsis: Report details low-priority persons of interest regarding eco-terrorist activities and attacks spanning nearly a decade. Despite several high-profile arrests, the Joint Terrorism Task Force assumes the investigation has neither found nor prosecuted primary suspects within the operational core of the organization. Several previous persons of interest may be ruled out as ongoing threats.

Details: As part of the investigation into ███████████████ ███████████████, sources and methods will be partially redacted. Disconnect remains between arrests and operations. While Mitchell Corbin Tabitha and John George Gerald Jr. did have minor infractions, arrests, and lawsuits against them, there is no evidence to indicate they were ongoing members of a cell. Daniel Porter McCulloch and Marie Karina Newman had no police records. None of those arrested appear to have been radicalized to an environmental cause, with the possible exception of Miles Russell Kroll. ███████████████ believed these operatives were largely recruited because of their nonideological posture and lack of knowledge of 6Degrees' operational capacities. It is recommended that limited resources be redirected from monitoring the suspects in custody and their networks. Predictive analytics conclude the same. ███████████

███████████████████████████████

███████████████████████████████

█████████████████████████████.

██████████ also stated that Gerald, McCulloch, Newman, and Tabitha should be viewed as low priorities. Bureau resources should be redirected, especially given that the budget for this operation has reached ████████ USD while overall budgetary considerations are now ██████████ USD.

6Degrees is adept at utilizing unsuspecting middlemen to perform the bulk of their procurement operations. ████████████████████████████████, a law firm with offices in ██ ██ ██ ████████████ also stated the firm has taken an interest in the suspects due to the high profile of the case, likely as a strategy that similar "saboteurs" utilize their services. ██ are not unsuspecting citizens, and it is here investigative efforts should continue to focus. TEDAC has helped investigators trace numerous components from the IEDs to various retail outlets and manufacturers. Ammonium nitrate and fuel oil provided the incendiary means for the attacks on three coal-fired power plants, while many pipeline and gas bombings were carried out with less sophisticated IEDs. Certain electrical components have been traced to various manufacturers. ██████████████████ revealed that ████████ ██ ██ ████████████.

The geographic diversity of the purchases of these electrical components has complicated the investigation. Electric detonator lead wires utilized in the Colorado Envige pipeline bombing were traced to a supplier in Saskatchewan, while fragments of 12V batteries used in the devices were purchased at a retail gas station in Laredo, Texas. The distinctive crimp of the detonator used in the Kentucky coal plant bombing eventually helped the lab identify McCulloch as the purchaser of the blasting caps. Newman worked in inventory for the construction company Otwellen Inc., ████████████ ██. ████████ ████████████████ revealed ████████████████████████████████ ██. The procurement of some items aligns with straw buyers like Mitchell Tabitha. The vans used in the coal plant bombings were procured illegally from Tabitha's business fleet. Use of a 3D printer allowed the bombers to replace certain components with CVIN numbers, which is why it took investigators so long to locate the vans' origins.

Investigative efforts of the 501(c)(4) A Fierce Blue Fire and 501(c)(3) A Fierce Blue Fire Mutual Aid continue to provide little investigative value. ███████ ████████████ stated that after Kate Morris's resignation, several top-level staff also resigned in protest, including Liza Yudong, a computer scientist who's received previous scrutiny. ████████████████████████████ ██████████████████████████. Rekia Reynolds, now in the leadership role, will receive similar protocols as Morris, but analytics demand attention elsewhere. ██ ██ ██ ██████████████████████████. Reynolds continues her affair with Tom Levine, though the two are antagonists internally and engage in disputes in front of staff. ██ ██ ██.

The heated political environment ████████████████████████ ██ ██ ████████████████████ militia members appearing outside polling stations en masse appears likely. An attack on the power grid at such a time could provoke ███ ██████████████████████████.

Kate Morris and Matthew Stanton, previously targets in POI investigations, have moved to Bend, Oregon, following Morris's dismissal. ████████████████ the conservative intelligence and disinformation network, recruited or co-erced individuals ██ ██ ██ ███ remains ██████ ████████████████████████████████████ deep political connections that have kept the Bureau investigation ████████████████████████████ stated ████████ ██ ██████ Congresswoman Joy LaFray, FBF's Sandeep Goswami, ████████████ ██.

Stanton made a single trip back to Washington, D.C., to collect belongings and their dog. They frequently travel to Portland to visit Morris's mother, Swedish national Sonja Sundstrom, ████████████████████████████
████████████████████████████████████. Contact between Morris, Stanton, and other members of A Fierce Blue Fire has remained limited. ███████████
███
███

███. Stanton used the opportunity to express his displeasure with Morris's dismissal while Levine justified it. ████████████████████████████████████
███. Morris continues to collaborate with Yudong regarding a project, a musical concert to raise awareness of the climate issue. They've associated with Seth Andrew Young, a former White House political aide, and applied for a permit from the National Park system. Morris has ceased contact with the three men with whom she was engaged in sexual relationships in the D.C. Metro area, including David L. Montreff, Senator Russ Mackowski's chief of staff. When Stanton is away, she currently engages in sexual activity with Arnith Jyle Cole, of Bend, Oregon, a clerk at the Central Oregon Locavore, a grocery.

In closing, it is the recommendation of investigators that limited resources be expended upon Morris, Stanton, and Yudong going forward. Several of these POIs have received over four thousand days of surveillance and ████████████
███
███
███
███

while that does not mean that they have no operational contact with the Weathermen/6Degrees, ██
███
███
██████████████████████████████████.

New Energy Horizons

2032

Fred was in a bad mood because security at the Tribeca Rush took nearly twenty minutes. Huddled under awnings while the rain blew sideways, we had to produce picture IDs and submit to a full body scan. Once upstairs, the event space was too crowded. Few people were willing to go out on the rooftop because an early tropical depression was still in the middle of dumping two days of rain on New York City. Event staff had erected a tent outside, but the force of the water kicked up a spray that made walking in heels a slick disaster. I watched Jennifer Lawrence and Ben Affleck come back inside, arm in arm, Affleck's pant legs soaked, Lawrence clutching her emerald gown so it wouldn't get the same treatment, the two of them tipsy and laughing.

I still loved these fleeting encounters with celebrity, even though we'd paid the same $300,000 for dinner, a few stand-up routines, musical performances, and cocktails on a flooding rooftop.

"Like have your act together," Fred went on. "You're throwing one of the most important charity events of the season, and you've got the Pink fucking Panther doing security."

He was still peeved about our table at dinner, which included a couple of bobbleheads from Fox News, their spouses, and a California marijuana magnate. Fred claimed he was fine sitting at a Nobody Table, as long as the people were good conversation, but well before the tenderloin arrived we understood the chatter was to be a root canal without anesthesia. My sister called twice, and I was almost bored enough to answer. Thankfully, the food came and the conversation dwindled. Now that I attended dinners like this, I always tried to think of the farms this food came from before I put it in my mouth, certain no one else in the room ever did.

Images of the Sunshine State were projected on walls and in holograms above our heads. Bouquets of California poppies adorned every surface. The charity event was expected to raise close to $100 million for the re-building of Los Angeles, with some of that money going to goad develop-ers to build low-income housing and the rest earmarked for the restoration of famed institutions and landmarks: the Hollywood sign, Griffith Observatory, and the vanquished Getty Museum, now a pile of ash and rubble with more than half its collection incinerated. For all its precautions, including a million-dollar sprinkler system, the heat, flames, and smoke of the El Demonio-Los Angeles Complex Fire had overwhelmed the Getty's defenses.

On entering the event space, each attendee was met by a series of enormous photographs: twin fire tornadoes drilling through the Hollywood Hills, a truck vacuumed up into the vortex. A bobcat and other wildlife fleeing down a mountainside. A Tesla melted into a freeway, the shape of the vehicle barely recognizable except the badge. All the images had been taken by a heat-resistant drone piloted by an artist in Berlin.

Tragedy transmogrified into an A-list gala. Hollywood royalty, from washed legends to impish teen stars, decorated the party, while senators and CEOs clinked martini glasses and traded encrypted messages on their phones, watches, and glasses. Fred needed to be there for the sheer volume of business being done by the slightly boozed wealth circulating. Talk of who'd lost homes in the blaze (Lachlan Murdoch, LeBron James, and Shonda Rhimes, but with Bel-Air incinerated, who hadn't?). Waiters delivered tray after tray of cocktails, and I caught a tall Black woman in a matte-black tuxedo, her hair done in a swooping bouffant with her skull shaved on the sides. Her smooth brown eyes were embedded in deep blue eyeshadow, and for a moment I was so struck by her beauty I thought I'd made a mortifying mistake, and she was a guest instead of a waiter.

"Hi," I said neutrally.

"Can I get you something?" she asked, and I breathed heavy relief.

"Just a plain old Negroni."

She smiled and walked off.

"I'm too tense," I told Fred.

"*Pshaw*," he said, somehow already with a drink, sliding a maraschino cherry off the plastic toothpick with his teeth. His eyes cased the room. "You're stunning. What's to worry about?"

"Who are you looking for?" I asked, slipping my arm around his waist and rubbing the tip of my nose into his soft beard, tasting those thin whiskers briefly. Since leaving Palacio-Wimpel, the PR firm he'd founded that made him his first "mid-minor" fortune, most of his time was spent on the lookout for investors. He turned to kiss my lips carefully because he knew of the lipstick's pairing with my earrings. Pink lipstick and rose gold achieved a delicate, detailed look that I didn't want smeared by his inability to keep his mouth off mine.

"Not sure yet. Norm Nate is here model hunting, but he'll be in Venice. Are you actually anxious?"

"No, I'm fine. I'd just like to get you home."

He smiled and kissed me again, softly on the side of my mouth.

"Nothing would make me happier. Let's give it one hour, huh?"

The waitress found me to deliver my drink, and we circulated.

California congressman and supreme dud Warren Hamby asked Fred what he thought about the plight of the Washington Nationals, while his blinking wife complimented my gown and earrings. Goldman's top trader, Noah Hosch, caught Fred's elbow, hastily filling his ear with news of the crisis in China (apparently the government was in dire straits as strikes crippled the mines where his firm had made sizable investments in rare earth minerals). Gombo Bolorchuluun, the golfing sensation, held forth for a gaggle of mostly blond women, including our Fox News tablemates from earlier. I recognized top talent from the law firm DLA Piper speaking with Renaissance CEO Rory Baumgart (the "alt-right Ted Turner" as he was known). I could see the rest of the room bending to avoid him, but you couldn't kick a billionaire out of a charity event. A Fierce Blue Fire's director, Rekia Reynolds, looked like a starlet in traditional African dress, while her partner, Tom Levine, wore a simple white tuxedo. In a sign of the times, they were speaking to none other than the president of the Sustainable Future Coalition, Emii Li Song, and I felt a small swell of pride. Three years earlier, the SFC had been sure FBF was going to replay the French Revolution in the role of the sans-culottes, and now they were rubbing elbows at the same party. With this less antagonistic posture toward industry, I was sure they'd start seeing better results. Emii's eyes met mine from across the room, and we exchanged smiles. I'd been an ally in goading the SFC to replace Tom Duncan-Michaels with a woman of color, and as the legislation inched closer, they finally submitted. "Sister Power," I'd told her at the time, and I mouthed these words to her now. Her mouth spread in an uncharacteristic grin, and she winked at me before returning to her conversation. I thought of Kate Morris then, which I didn't do much anymore now that she was gone from the limelight. It turned out she didn't need as much help as we'd thought, mostly kneecapping herself. However, I held a complicated portfolio of emotions from that effort. I almost missed her. Though she didn't know it, we'd been playing a chess game, and it almost made me wistful that I'd won so easily.

I heard his voice before I saw him, and I was stunned by a surge of déjà vu. I saw the past and future at once. It was only then I remembered that his voice sounded different in person. Lighter, cleaner. The Pastor wore a tuxedo so perfectly tailored it had the lines of a sports car. Slicked-back hair, skin flawless, surely from an expensive chemical peel, hand tucked casually in a pocket while the other moved fluidly for a crowd of spectators listening to him talk. I moved closer to do the same.

"President Randall is failing to beat back this challenge, but if you look at what the RNC did—they're shielding her. She's going to come away with more delegates even though she lost Iowa, and New Hampshire was basically a coin flip." Half the crowd appeared as rapt as the people who bought his "Bibles" while the other half stood on their toes as if ready to interject. He wouldn't allow it. "Now you can say that Braden's an inappropriate candidate, that you can't let her get the nomination, but there are consequences to bottling up the popular will like this. Especially with the illegal refugee situation."

It was almost more eerie to hear him sounding off about politics, to hear what a calm, reasonable presence he was in person. Since the LA fire he'd been all over his new TV network and Slapdish worlde, replaying his prediction that Hollywood would burn. I knew because my mom was one of those people who believed he was a prophet.

"You endorse the religious registry," a man accused him. "You said everyone in the country should have to enter their religion in a government database. You know what that reminds me of—"

The Pastor cut him off. "So what? The BIPOC-GND endorses a racial registry to allocate reparations payments. This is not an idea outside the mainstream, and we will have it soon in one form or another."

The man got fed up and walked away, leaving The Pastor to quip, "Can't get away from politics anywhere, can you?" His crowd laughed politely. The practiced self-deprecation was gone. He oozed wealth and confidence, fully grown into his role as the de facto leader of the Christian Right, surrounded by every Republican politician trying to chisel him for an endorsement in a primary race. He'd come a long way since finding his name trending beside a #Cancel for decrying "the ideology of wokeness infecting film like a plague." No longer chasing Hollywood tinsel, no longer a happy warrior for his version of Jesus, now he generated prophecies. From what I understood, his "Bible" was a strange alchemy of the book of Revelation and climatic apocalypse. Watching him from afar all these years, I'd thought it impossible that he actually believed his own bullshit, that he was anything but a grifter, but now, watching him, I had to wonder. I never told Fred about my night with him.

I was standing behind two people, clutching my drink with an arm crossed over my breast, and as if he heard that thought, his head turned, and his eyes found mine. His gaze was an unnerving horizon. He stared at me for so long with those crystal-blue contacts, I felt I had to say something. Uncertain words formed in the back of my throat, and now I was the one who felt infected.

"Jackie, come meet my friend." I flinched as Fred touched my elbow. He didn't notice, and when I looked back, The Pastor had resumed inveighing about the election. Maybe I would have dwelled longer on this surreal encounter were it not for whom Fred was dragging me to on the other side of the room.

"How you doing?" said Barack Obama, as Fred guided me into the former president's circle. "Good to see you."

I made a dumb sound with my lips, laughed at myself, held up a finger, and said, "Hold on. Let me swallow my spit."

The people gathered around us laughed, though their faces might as well have been blurred out. In a room of people who prided themselves on influencing the workings of the world, it was transparent how much each individual felt the need to effect a gravitational pull. Yet Obama displayed none of this need, and the way he simply tucked himself into a conversation with myself, Fred, and the small crowd around us, it was almost a more powerful display. As he shook my hand and I introduced myself, I studied the deepening wrinkles of his face. He looked old, his hair entirely white, and yet he still bounced within himself, as much energy and vigor as when I watched him, at seventeen, take to the podium of the Democratic National Convention to become a historic fixture in American life.

"You were the first vote I ever cast," I told him. "When I was living in Chicago, my boyfriend at the time, we had tickets to election night and waited nearly two hours to get in."

"To Grant Park?"

"No, it was 2012, so that convention center—um."

"McCormick Place."

"Yes!"

There was a small gap in the conversation as everyone stood around smiling, and I realized I'd begun a story without a conclusion.

"So how was it?" Obama teased.

"Not bad," I said, my face as bright as the red of his tie. I pretended to look over his shoulder. "So is Michelle coming? I only voted for you to get more Michelle."

Our little crowd roared at this, and Obama's laugh seemed genuine. "We all know she's the entire reason I became president twice. Actually, Michelle is in Texas working with a new voter turnout project, and I'm stuck wining and dining all the barnacles on the side of our democracy."

Obama gave a playful slap to Fred's shoulder, and even though I wasn't sure the quip was entirely playful, Fred was beaming almost as hard as I was.

"No, no," said Obama. "You've got a good one here. Fred's an amazing businessman, and one of the few people left who can talk to both sides of the aisle. Although, having only just met you, Jackie, I can already tell you're the brains behind the whole operation."

Hearing my name come out of his mouth was undeniably sexual, and I knew I'd be shamelessly thinking about this moment for days. The way Obama's tongue struck the consonants, that timbre in his voice, the unfathomably deep eye contact he made. If he asked me to go home with him, I would have entirely forgotten about how much I still loved Michelle.

I felt my phone buzzing relentlessly in my clutch, and one of the two people flanking Obama—his body man, perhaps—touched his shoulder and pointed him to another man standing in the group. As Obama reached for a new handshake, I saw the text. *WHERE ARE YOU?! CALL ME BACK! EMERGENCY*

Only my sister could summon so much dread and annoyance simultaneously. To my dismay, by the time I looked up, Obama had already been cocooned by the group. That I'd so quickly gained and lost this proximity pushed a flush into my face. I told Fred I needed to make a call. Furious, I slipped outside to escape the din, not that the rain was much quieter. Hugging myself in the cold air beneath the center of the tent and away from the splash of the rain, I dialed Allie.

"Where the hell are you?" My sister's voice in middle age had the sonic quality of an aggrieved stork.

"I'm at an event. What happened?"

"You're supposed to visit Mom."

"What?"

"When are you visiting Mom? You were supposed to go see her?"

"Huh? I am. In three weeks. After I'm back from Venice."

"Three weeks? Are you kidding me, Jackie? I've been driving up from Saint Louis every other weekend for a year. I'm exhausted. The kids have so much going on, and I don't have time to be Mom's only support—"

"What's the emergency?"

"When we moved down here, I told you I was going to need you to help! Hell, even Erik's been up to see her more than you, Jackie. And he's a deadbeat!"

"Allie, what's the emergency?" I repeated.

"That you haven't seen Mom in nearly six months. That she's a mess and you can't be bothered—"

"So there's no emergency? Mom's still Mom, and this is not, in fact, an emergency?"

"After Venice?" she screeched, circling back to the point I knew had upset her the most.

"It's for work. Stop stressing out."

"I'm stressed out? I have three kids! What do you have to look after? Who do you have to take care of? Our mother, Jackie. Our goddamn mother!"

"*Okay, Allie! Christ!*" I said it too loudly, so that a man smoking a cigarette paused from contemplating the rain and glanced at me. "Jesus. Okay. I'll get a plane and go see her next weekend." I immediately regretted the phrase even as it was leaving my mouth.

"You'll *get* a plane." Allie snorted.

We hung up. Of course, what really bothered my sister was the fact that she'd married a doctor, and they still found themselves struggling to pay for all their kids' cars as they came of driving age. That I lived in a penthouse overlooking Central Park, and they lived in a chintzy McMansion in a St. Louis suburb. Through the glass I saw that Obama and Fred had been swallowed by the crowd. Rubbing my arms in the cold, I turned back to the falling rain, the sound it made against the city like the breath of a massive beast at slumber.

*

The following weekend I flew on one of Tara Fund's company jets to Chicago then had my assistant arrange a driverless to Amber. Though I lived in the penthouse with Fred, I'd kept my condo in Chicago. I could have flown to the Quad Cities Airport, but I preferred the flat, bare scenery of the drive, a route I'd been taking since I was in college and my friends and I would journey to Chicago for music festivals. With the driverless, I could nap and then have my phone wake me just before my favorite part of the trip: crossing the Mississippi River near Moline. The windshield wipers pushed the drizzle aside, but the sun was breaking through in the west, and its light beamed across the river valley. A low cloud cast a shadow across the water and streaks of sunlight shot through as the car rumbled over the bridge that spanned Iowa and Illinois. The river was high, pushing right up to the yards of the dollhouse homes that dotted the banks. Allie was right that I didn't make this trip too often, but each time I did, I'd feel melancholy nick at my heart.

I continued over crumbling highways, past once-immutable towns in the last stages of drying up and blowing away. Gas stations abandoned, factories gone, warehouses now run by robots. Farming operations that once took hundreds of people could now produce corn, soy, or pork with a handful of technicians overseeing the machines. Gazing out over the flawless green of a soy field, I imagined how my father would have hated this new farming world. I missed my dad intensely in that moment and thought of sitting on his lap as he drove the tractor, that beast jostling beneath us, one of his heavy, chapped hands acting as my seat belt. It wasn't sepsis that killed him. It was giving up his work, his creativity, his communion with what was once our land. When the crisis of the eighties came and family farms were foreclosed across the country en masse, he and my grandpa beat the odds. As a young man, he'd stayed when the children of other farmers had run, only to lose it all in the end.

When the car pulled into the driveway, I barely recognized my childhood home. It looked feral. The yard was soggy, the grass yellow and pitted with mud puddles. The shingles were rotting, flaking off, and leaving the roof's tar paper exposed. The vinyl siding my father had put on before his illness was moldy and cracking, battered by the ferocious summer storms of the past few years.

I went to knock but could tell the door wasn't latched and let myself in, calling out to my mom.

Immediately, I wanted to scream at her.

My childhood home was a catastrophe. The TV was blaring, the living room coated in garbage. Old fast-food bags and take-out containers and pizza boxes. As kids, we'd never been allowed so much as a Happy Meal, and now I could see the crumpled Golden Arches in every crevice of the room. Flies buzzed around a stack of dishes in the sink. Everything I touched was sticky. There were wine bottles, half-finished, littered throughout each room. I couldn't remember my mother drinking alcohol at all before about 2026. Apparently, her preference was JP. Chenet Rosé Dry sparkling wine. A gas station brand.

The TV's volume was so high, I went sifting through a pile of unopened mail on the coffee table to try to find the remote. Finally, I remembered what decade I was living in and simply told the TV to turn itself down.

My mother emerged from the downstairs bathroom, though I'd not heard a flush.

"What are you doing here?" she asked, less surprised than suspicious.

"I told you I was coming." She still looked uncertain. "I called Monday?" She batted a hand. "Thought you was talking about another week."

Still wearing her nightgown, she shuffled to the couch. She'd never looked so old to me, and watching her move, in pain from both hips, it was almost difficult to imagine how she'd looked when she was young. She'd been beautiful, at least in the way most daughters find their mothers beautiful. I'd envied her blond hair because Allie's was also blond, but mine had been a mousy brown. Mom never wore makeup except for church, but I'd always been proud of this. My mom needed no makeup, I'd bragged to girlfriends.

The way the years took you—it was astonishing. In my circle, the game was defying age with simple cosmetic procedures. I looked at pictures of myself from ten years earlier and was pleased to see that the changes were imperceptible. A light facelift, a small surgery to smooth the cellulose from one's thighs—no one need ever feel vain about it. Mom was proof of what happened without these inexpensive adaptations. She had deep, drooping bags under each eye and flesh that simply hung, rippled, and swayed around every portion of her face: cheeks, jowls, and turkey throat all part of the same mass. The meat of her triceps wobbled, skin patched with psoriasis, moles spiraling ever higher. Her hair sat atop her head in an unkempt mat of gray and white. She eased into the seat nearest an end table where a mug of JP. Chenet awaited her return.

"You finally got yourself some time, huh?"

"It's been a busy start to the year," I said.

"Doing what?" Her eyes trained on the TV.

"Fred's fund has been growing. We're starting to get serious returns. I really would like to spend some money on this place. Fix up a few things."

My eyes landed on a missing spindle in the balustrade. Beyond that, the pictures of our family. Me and my siblings lined up like grinning hostages before the feet of our parents in a picture snapped at Walmart when I was six.

"Don't want your money, don't need your money," she sang.

I had developed a rule with my mother: only self-defense. Never take her bait. I walked to the sliding glass door at the back of the house. A gorgeous rainbow vaulted over the fields that once belonged to my family. I still loved this view from the back, where I could feel the ancient time of the prairie.

"What if you sold the house? Moved into my place in Chicago."

"Don't wanna go anywhere, especially not the city," she sighed. "Besides, you know what I'm likely to get for this place? Property values round here are a Big Zip. Maybe the meth guys would take it off my hands as a place to cook, that's about it."

There was nothing to eat, so we went to the Hy-Vee, which had an armed guard at the entrance, something I'd never seen before. It was a hassle because so many of the products were now behind locked glass, and it took forever to hunt down an associate to open them. I bought fixings for lasagna and back at the house, the two of us slapped it together, adding some cayenne pepper for kick. After that, I took a trash bag and moved through the downstairs, cleaning up.

"Don't have to do that," my mother said.

"Oh yes I do, Mom. Tomorrow I'm getting you some flowers too."

By the time the lasagna was ready, the living room, dining room, and kitchen looked habitable. We ate with the TV on, and when I sat down with my plate, I realized she had turned it to The Pastor's new channel. Not him, but a show that looked like the news with coiffed anchors blasting President Randall's response to the crisis on the US-Mexico border and "reporting" on what The Pastor had said about various issues of the day. They spoke of him, with newscaster intonation, as if he really was a prophet. They speculated on how God might guide his hand toward other revelations, and if the End of Days predictions would be coming soon or if they were still a few years away.

"This is the only place left you actually get at the truth," my mom noted. I'd noticed the family Bible on the mantel, but now next to it, The Pastor's "New Faith Translation" with a gold-leaf cross. It occurred to me that her eyes might light up if I told her I'd just seen the man in person, but I decided that might be more unsettling. Forget about what else I could tell her.

"Are you still going to church, Mom?"

"Of course. Not many people left in it, though. Don't suppose you ever go?"

"Not really," I admitted. "I'd go with you tomorrow, though."

"That'd be nice."

She didn't smile, but I did.

After a few minutes of silent eating, I said, "You know, it doesn't have to be Chicago. We could get you a place anywhere. Down in Saint Louis with Allie. Or Florida with Erik. I'd say New York near me but—"

"*I don't like the city!*" she cried. "What the heck don't you get about that, Jack? I don't like the city, and now stop frickin' bothering me about it."

I couldn't remember my mother ever raising her voice like that. My fork hung suspended over a noodle while she glared at me, eyes furious moons behind ornate glasses. Then she turned back to the TV.

"I'm just worried about you," I said.

"Why?"

"That's a silly thing to say, Mom. You're my mom. I love you."

"If you love me, you'd leave me be. I was born ten miles from here, I lived in Amber near all my life, I'm not moving nowhere else now. So just quit that idea, got it?"

"I got it. I'm just saying I'm doing well. I can afford to help you. Maybe move you to a posh retirement community where there are people around, and you can make friends."

She snorted and her voice dripped with contempt.

"What you have yet to learn, Jackie-O, is that all that money you got, it's an optical illusion. It ain't nothing."

For some reason, this was the thing that finally got to me. I could let so much go with her. Water off a duck's back and all that. My therapist had given me this technique once: When a person you love hurts or angers you, think of a thing they've done that made you love them. With my mom, I would remember her "lice checks." One time I'd come home from school quite excited because they'd checked our scalps for lice, and I thought it felt wonderful. Thereafter, my mom performed lice checks on my small head whenever I requested, and the feel of her careful fingers moving through my hair, nails gently scratching at the skin of my scalp always sent shivers of pleasure through me. She'd do this while the whole family sat around the TV, her fingernails performing with love.

"Mom, do you have any clue how much I made last year?"

"Think I heard your father say the same thing. Couple years before he had to sell the whole dang farm."

I set my fork down, pulled my hair back, and arranged it into a quick, angry bun so I'd have something for my hands to work.

"In a few years, our fund is going to be one of the most important on Wall Street. We're working with proprietary computer models and AI that will make other investors look like Stone Age bean counters."

"Oh, how impressive. I take it all back."

"And *I* worked for that!" I jammed myself in the breastbone with two fingers. "I didn't get knocked up by a doctor twenty years older than me like Allie, I didn't run away like Erik, I went out and worked my ass off and made myself invaluable. I've turned down more job offers from— I've done more than you or Dad ever could've dreamed for me. And as a woman! As a woman wading through sexist bullshit in every job my whole life. Because I had to watch you and Dad get your hearts broken by this goddamn place, and I wanted to be able to help you and take care of you guys. And are you grateful or even remotely happy for me? No. *You resent me for it.* And what have you done with your life, Mom? You go to the same church as Dad's fucking mistress."

I picked my fork back up and jammed a big piece of noodle into my mouth. My mother never looked away from the TV. She was quiet for a moment while the anchors squawked.

"You work for your boyfriend," she said.

"I left a six-figure salary to help him do something special. And we're doing it."

"And he won't marry you."

I shook my head. Though I should've known this was what she was driving at, it amazed me how deft she was at the sneak attack. "Fred and I live together. We're in love. It's by far the best relationship of my life."

"He's still married."

"He has a complicated situation, Mom."

She nodded. "You know the old phrase about the milk and the cow."

"Jesus Christ. Mom, they're separated. She lives in San Francisco. Fred and I live together. Just because that doesn't conform to your antiquated, white-wedding-dress idea of love . . ."

"You won't bring him here, you won't introduce him—"

"Is it any goddamn wonder?! I walk into this place and it looks like you haven't cleaned it—or yourself—in months."

"I read about his son."

Just the fact that she cared enough to use the internet. To find out about Fred Jr.

"What about his son."

"He killed a boy."

"No, he didn't."

"He might as well have." She sucked on her teeth to remove a piece of food, a disgusting sound she would have scolded me for thirty years ago. Staring down at my crossed arms, I thought about my skin: how the flesh would turn old and liver-spotted and psoriasized like hers.

Finally, I asked, "Are you trying to get me to leave?"

"Honey, I long ago stopped trying to get you to do anything."

The TV blared, on and on, a babbling brook of voices and light streaming quietly over our dark faces.

*

Two weeks later, Fred and I arrived in Venice for our working vacation. We stayed in the Aman Venice on the Grand Canal amid its gorgeous period furniture, frescoes, and gilded walls, waking to the crisp, cool morning air flowing through open patio doors. The saltwater and waste scent aside, I'm not sure I'd ever seen such a beautiful place in my life. Fred arranged for private tours of Saint Mark's Basilica and the Doge's Palace. Over the course of a day, our tour guide, a retired professor from the University of Padua, spun a fabulous portrait of fourteenth-century Venice, a mercantile superpower that drew together some of the most brilliant minds of the age, only to destroy itself when the city's oligarchy initiated La Serrata, or the Closure.

Later, Fred and I sipped champagne on a private water taxi up and down the Grand Canal and strolled hand in hand across the Piazza San Marco, nibbling at stracciatella. In the Murano Glass Museum, we watched one of the craftsmen fashion a vase and then had it shipped back to New York. That night at dinner, we drank a $1,000 bottle of champagne from the Trentino region in the Dolomites. According to our Bengali waiter, "the high peaks and the steep valleys make for the best champagne in the world."

During that week in Venice, work, my mother, my difficult, fractured family—it all melted away. And Fred, he did his typical Fred thing: So at ease, he put me at ease. When we'd first begun seeing each other I'd just assumed he'd come from money, and he laughed at this. He was born in Humboldt County, his mother had died young, and his father had gone through long stretches of unemployment, depression, and alcoholism after the timber companies were forced out following the battle over old-growth redwoods. "My dad and I were moving towns every year," he said. "We could never make rent, even when I started working. He became a really angry guy."

Hearing the echoes of my own father's life, it was the first time I felt something more than just attraction to him. It ran deeper than similar biographies. I recognized that specific pain of watching someone you love have their pride taken from them and the sad carapace it leaves behind. Fred escaped these bitter circumstances when he got into Stanford. From there, it was on to his first position at Leo Burnett, and then Galvani, the major D.C. PR firm. Finally, at thirty-three he cofounded Palacio-Wimpel and made a raucous name for himself in the industry. By the time I met him, he was plotting his move to become head of investor relations for a new hedge fund. Wall Street had chuckled at the cute little PR boy suddenly diving into the hedge fund game, and Fred had welcomed their scorn. It took him time to convince me to join him—not only because we were sleeping together but because I didn't see how my background as a creative could translate at all to the world of high finance. But he was persuasive. "I saw you in that room with those big-leaguers of the SFC, just this rough, pissy, old-boy network of backslappers, and you were fearless. Your creativity is what's going to make you so good at selling investors on us."

The night of the $1,000 champagne we made love and then wrapped ourselves in terry-cloth bathrobes and sat on the patio looking out over the lights of this priceless city.

"I love sharing this with you," he said quietly. "Promise me we'll do this every year for the rest of our lives."

I scoffed. "Don't need to ask me twice, buster."

Carrying on a romantic and professional relationship at the same time could have been disastrous, but Fred was too kind a man and the work too interesting. I buried myself in the literature of hedge funds and finance, an opaque, complex field. Fred had been recruited by a man named Peter O'Connell, who began his career in sports gambling and had gone on to make yet another small fortune betting on cryptocurrencies. Peter himself had no real computational talent, and in fact, was barely literate in programming, but he did have an impeccable instinct for talent in the field. He found brilliant programmers, and he owned a modeling system built by Ashir al-Hasan, widely thought to be one of the most important minds in the field of complex modeling. Fred brought a ferocious work ethic and a life-time's worth of connections to some of the richest players in the corporate world.

Their scrappy fund quickly gathered a lot of excitement due to the DNA of its proprietary model. They each put up $25 million of their own fortunes and were able to raise an additional $250 million. In the hedge fund world this was a modest beginning. But Peter's model and his team of analysts—these whiz kids plucked from the Ivy League, the acne still bright on their cheeks—had something special on their hands, making bets with forward-thinking algorithms accounting for environment, weather, and water in groundbreaking ways. Their model embraced risk assets at speed, dumping them at the exact moment before they could plummet in value.

As Fred once put it, "It's math but it's also narrative . . . What are the underlying stories beneath the trends? And more importantly, how do we manipulate those narratives to our advantage?"

Within the first year we'd grown the fund to $3 billion in assets, and I'd made my first small fortune. I could now become an accredited investor and put money into the fund. This was jarring. I hadn't been doing badly before, but I had the typical debts: student loans, a mortgage, credit cards, car payments. My retirement consisted only of my 401(k) and a bit of money in a Roth IRA I'd set up after college. Having learned the lessons of my father, I'd been prudent with money, and then suddenly, almost overnight, I was in a new class of investor. There was a grand casino, and very few people were even allowed to come through the doors and approach the tables. I understood why finance drew so many talented people. The competition, the adrenaline, the sense of permanent adventure was intoxicating the moment you had it at your fingertips.

In addition to my responsibilities with Tara Fund, Fred also turned over to me the keys to all his philanthropic work. His politics tended to skew much more libertarian than my own, but I created a series of regularized contributions to support the arts in the largest fifteen American cities, the American Cancer Society, the World Wildlife Fund, the Nature Conservancy, Planned Parenthood, Boys & Girls Clubs, three different LGBTQIAA+ organizations, a network of charter schools specializing in STEM education and no-excuses teaching philosophies, and of course, we gave a hefty contribution to A Fierce Blue Fire now that they'd embraced a less antagonistic philosophy.

After working at Tara only a year, I moved in with Fred. It was my first time living with a man since Jefferey, and though I had my hesitations, they proved baseless. Fred's marital problems notwithstanding, the troubles with his son, who I'd still never met, these all felt inconsequential when we were together. When Fred trimmed his beard, he never left a single razor clipping in the sink. I never even mentioned it, he just knew to wipe them away.

"Check this out." Fred handed me his phone as we descended in the elevator. At first I thought it was a puddle, but then understood it was a city, shot from an immense height.

"Oh my God. Is this real? Where is this?"

"Indianapolis. The whole city is underwater."

The headline said something about flooding in ten states.

"Jesus, now I feel awful for complaining about the rain in New York."

Peter waited for us at the table, a pair of aviator sunglasses masking his face, a white linen suit over a T-shirt with a picture of a rearing minotaur. I'd seen that same shirt for sale among the street vendors. He hugged Fred and kissed me on the cheek.

"Damn. This power couple. You put Bogie and Bacall to shame."

Fred put his hand on my thigh as we took a seat in the shade of the umbrella, pushing the edge of my dress up ever so slightly, and I quickly adjusted it back down.

"Did you guys ever think we'd be here?" Peter threw one leg over the other and bopped a brown-sandaled foot. "Taking meetings in Venice with three fucking rainmakers? Fuck. I had to take out insurance on myself just in case I woke up and it turned out to be a dream."

"Is that a product you're thinking of creating?" I asked. "Goldman would probably draw it up for you."

Peter looked from me to Fred. "See, this is why we're both in love with her. This-Is-All-A-Dream Default Swaps. TIADDSs. They pay out when you wake up and the whole thing was too good to be true."

Our three potential investors arrived at breakfast like a triptych of understated wealth. The first, Giuseppe Aleotti, was an Italian chemical magnate. Tan and weathered with thick black hair combed straight back and an enormous Blancpain watch on his wrist, he was the gaudiest person at the table. Norman Nate had earned (or self-coined) the nickname "the homeless billionaire." Nate had made his first billion by winning the race with Slapdish to become the all-purpose social VR platform. Now he had his hand in everything from the carbon nanotubes for the upcoming Mars mission to solar radiation management. He still looked like someone's little brother, tousle-haired, pug nose, and wearing a teenager's overlarge pink T-shirt and jean shorts.

Archana Bhattacharyya came in behind the two men, her net worth the least impressive at the table (other than my own). She was a short seller who'd left JPMorgan Chase to start her own shop, Styx Capital Management, and had struck a pot of gold when she shorted an ultra-hot energy company, Envige. Envige had been buying up competitors, expanding too quickly, burning through cash to make all its bids. While Wall Street was still in love, she was shorting their stock. Then the Weathermen blew up a couple of their pipelines, and investors sprinted away, but Bhattacharyya had seen their weakness first. Some people called short sellers leeches, but it seemed to me she'd just found the right neck on which to drop the guillotine.

Our pitch lasted fifteen minutes. I finished by setting reports in front of each potential investor with a detailed road map, but Bhattacharyya didn't touch the document.

"I'd like to dig in a bit more," she said in her highly provincial Long Island accent. She wore a lovely magenta jacket, and had her hair elegantly pinned up in a short side sweep. This made the accent all the more jarring. "What's the deal with CLK Metrics?"

"They're a small part of our portfolio," said Fred, lounging back in his chair, hands folded on his lap. "Minuscule is the word I would use."

"That's not what I hear. The word 'alliance' got tossed around by my source."

Fred smiled. Breakfast had come and gone. My plate sat with cold, congealing egg yolk.

"They're not a big deal. Just another psychometrics firm. Their sales pitch is strong, but like all these other guys, they're going to claim greater powers of persuasion than the tech can actually pull off. Everyone thinks they're Iago. But early indicators are promising."

I almost opened my mouth to ask Fred what this meant, but Norman Nate spoke first.

"That's not what I hear either."

"Okay, so what do you both hear?" asked Peter, who seemed as genuinely curious as I was.

"That CLK is working on revolutionary stuff. You knew their CEO from your PR days, right?"

Fred kept smiling. "Look, all I can say about CLK is they claim they've helped Vic Love vault out of a crowded Democratic primary to the front of the pack. Now, if you ask me, it's because he's the only sane candidate in a field packed with socialist yahoos who want to turn the States into 1960s Cuba. So CLK's value—we're investors, yes—but it's still less than proven. What we're trying to sell you on is *our* model." Fred leaned forward and put his hands on his chest like he was scooping out his heart. "We're cutting edge in highly unpredictable times."

The waiter came, and we all paused, sitting in silence as the thin Bengali man scraped crumbs off the table and inquired in halting Italian if we'd like more coffee. Our tour guide had explained to us that most of Venice's working class was from Bangladesh. They commuted in from mainland Italy where rents were affordable and made their living selling vegetables and knockoff sunglasses to tourists. They took up pizza-making and tossed the dough like they'd grown up in Napoli and played the violin for restaurant diners. He finally left. Nate's shirt lifted as he craned back, and he scratched his hairy belly. "I don't know, man, you've got a bunch of the SJW left swinging for a guy who was a radical right-winger a decade ago. How's Love pulling that off?"

Archie cocked an eyebrow. "His scandals are piling up. There's apparently a tape of him in 2022 saying to his buddies, 'The next time we storm the capitol, we plan to hold it.'"

Fred laughed. "And you think CLK's stemming the fallout from that somehow? Love came out of the closet. He has a husband. People love a redemption story. The States have a thousand billionaires who all stomp their feet because they want to play kingmaker. Folks have tried to guarantee themselves candidates since the advent of democracy. Trust me, it never quite works out."

Aleotti, who'd been concentrating on understanding the conversation, broke in.

"Yes, but you see, we have a saying in Italy: There are only three type of the people." Aleotti's fingers sprang up with each type. "The edible, the inedible, and the fed. Fred Wimpel I hear is the fed."

"Well, I hope so," said Fred, chuckling.

"Chopped liver over here, speaking up now," said Peter because it was, after all, his fund. "We've got a huge array of bets in a number of different sectors. If you look through those reports Jackie handed you, you won't be disappointed. We're in corners of the world where no one else is even looking yet."

"Depending on who wins the election," said Nate. "If Jen Braden wins . . ."

"We're hedged on beef jerky and water filtration devices," Peter quipped, and this got a good laugh out of the group.

Later that night, Fred and I met Peter for drinks near the Piazza San Marco. My sister had been calling me all afternoon, but I'd ignored her. Whatever "emergency" she wanted me to deal with could wait.

Peter said, "We'll get $260 million from the Italian stallion Aleotti, the Venetian creation—"

"Those words don't rhyme," I said, laughing.

"Maybe another hundo out of Nate, but I think Miss Archie's only in for a dozen mil."

"She plays tight," said Fred.

"She's also not that rich," I added.

"Still, not bad for a morning's work," said Fred. The three of us cheersed.

"Why was everyone so worked up about CLK?" I asked, and Fred rolled his eyes.

"Who knows where that came from. Everyone thinks one of these data firms is going to crack the code of the next level of psychometric manipulation for advertising, but it's all malarkey if you ask me. Our stake in them isn't even worth all that much. Are you staying on in Venice, Peter?"

"Got to. It'll probably be gone by the next time I have a chance to get here." We all laughed at this. "I've got a lady coming in from London. Black British chick—extinction-level hot. Just a total asteroid wiping out the dinosaurs. Fred told me about your romantic week and I got so jealous I chartered a fucking plane for a date. You guys sticking around?"

"We are." Fred nodded at me. "We need a bit more of this."

*

Our plan was to stay for the rest of the month, but two days later, my sister called. On FaceTime, she looked even more crazed than usual, her urgency full of inferences and histories of our childhood.

"Mom's not answering at all." She had her hair pulled back and her face, puffed, red, and fleshy, strained into her phone's camera.

"Okay, so she's not answering. Sometimes she doesn't answer."

"It's been two days, and we don't know if she got out."

"Got out of what?"

"Did you even look at my messages?"

I gained nothing from being pulled into an argument with her. I had to be the reasonable one and never let her encyclopedia of accusations faze me. Sometimes this meant not answering the question.

"What does Erik think?"

Her eyes bugged in disbelief. "Erik's here. We're at Erik's."

She thrust the phone, and there was my brother, staring at the table, a malingering beer held by the neck between thumb and forefinger. He looked heavy and old. It was the first time I'd seen him since his divorce. Allie thought he suffered from depression, but when I checked his social media he seemed to be having all the fun with friends in his new place in the Tampa burbs: grilling out, football games, beer after beer in his stupid koozie that read GO BIG OR GO HOME. My theory was that he was just a selfish alcoholic. Ask his kids, who only saw him once a month, and who could probably tell that their father was fine with the arrangement.

Erik gave me a bored little salute. "Hey, Jack."

"What are you doing down there?" I asked.

"The floods. We live by the Mississippi," said Allie. "Did you even read my messages?"

It was the guilt of not doing so coupled with the sensation one gets from having missed anything in our saturated-media age. There was a shooting where? This politician did what? This ignorance presaged a loss of moral and intellectual status: Do you not have CNN updates in your glasses?

"Just tell me what's happening, Allie. I've been busy with work."

She took the phone off my brother.

"The flooding! All over the goddamn Midwest and East Coast. We had to leave Saint Louis because the Mississippi was spilling into the suburbs! And now I've been looking at the FEMA site and Amber's right in the flood zone of the Wapsipinicon River, and Mom's not answering."

With each breathless word, I felt a tiny surge of discomfort in the center of my head, and now I tried to massage it away. "Okay, Al, what do you want me to do, I'm in Venice."

"Italy?"

"Yes, Italy."

There was a pause, and the phone angled so that her face was off-center. She was rubbing her head just like me, in the exact same way.

"We have the kids, and none of us can get back up there right now." She started crying. "I know, I know, I should've checked in with Mom before we left, but it all happened so fast, you know? Like we got the evacuation notification but it didn't occur to me that Mom and the house would be in any trouble . . ."

"Okay, okay," I said to stop her from cry-rambling. "I was just there. Mom's fine. She's going to be fine. I'll call her. You take a break, okay? If she hasn't gotten back to either of us in a day or so, I'll fly back? Honestly, Allie, even if the house got flooded, she probably left and just forgot her phone. Simplest answer's always the right answer, you know?"

Through her tears, my sister nodded.

That night, I couldn't sleep. Just when I'd gotten adjusted to Central European time, I found myself up and on my laptop, reading and watching videos of the flooding back in the States. The East Coast and much of the Midwest had been pummeled by heavy winter snowfall. The lethal super-cell storm that soaked Indianapolis had been accompanied by forty-three tornadoes in the past week, one of the deadliest outbreaks of severe weather in the past century, but the larger issue was rain. With the ground saturated and a series of heavy spring storms dropping record-breaking precipitation, the water had nowhere to go. River systems along the entire eastern half of the country were swollen, roaring, and dangerous. No estimate yet on how many people had been killed and how much property had been de-stroyed, but the *Times* assured that it would break records when all was said and done. Nearly 200 million people across twenty-five states were affected. I watched video of choked floodwaters surging across roads and washing away vehicles, homes wrecked and collapsed. Whole towns turned into lakes; highways swallowed so that only the tops of the trees along the road-ways poked above the water. Broken dams losing chunks of concrete as their imprisoned waters fought over the top. Correspondents splashed through in rain boots, clutching microphones and making authoritative pronounce-ments about the dangers to residents. Boats of all varieties chugged up and down city streets turned to rivers. From Charleston to Minneapolis, Phila-delphia to Lake Charles, levees were breached, and floodwaters surged into homes, businesses, farms, towns, cities, and highways, drowning vehicles, bridges, buildings, sandbags, and people.

I tried my mom again and got no answer. I went to bed still uncertain about what I should do.

*

"This mess is someone's fault, I'll tell you that."

I woke to Fred's voice integrating into my dream, and in the haze of sleep I thought he was talking about the floods, and he was. Just not the ones in America.

"So who do we call about getting out of here then?" A pause. "Well, I'm not going back downstairs with a literal tide of shit on the floor of the hotel, excuse my French." Another pause. "No, what I'd like is that you people prepare for events like this, and if you can't do that, at least comp us a night someplace that has its sewage issues under control. Christ, I thought this was the best hotel in the city." He hung up.

"What happened?" I asked, rubbing my eyes.

"The whole first floor is flooded and smells like a toilet exploded." He put his hands on his hips and stared at the corner of the room as if an answer would emanate from that intersection of molding. He looked on the verge of tears. "We'll have to either stay in the room all day or actually walk through it."

I wasn't much for signs from the universe, but this sent a stitch of crimson dread through me. As if the waters from home had come and found me. "We need to leave anyway. I think I need to go see my mom, Fred."

"Why?"

"These storms back home. Allie can't get a hold of her. I was up all night."

"So send someone to check on her! I'll pay for it."

"No, I can't. I can't explain. I just need to go home and be with her."

He looked at me, his handsome face despondent. I loved him for how much he wanted us to stay.

"You know I have to go to Hong Kong."

"You take the jet. I'll book something."

He took my hand and kissed it. "Why is it every time you leave me, I feel this pain. Like I'm never going to see you again. It scares me every time."

I'd brought no sensible shoes. We were given complimentary galoshes by the hotel, and they put our bags on an elevated luggage rack. Still, we had to wade through the hotel's muck-drenched interior and into the street. I held my breath the whole way, gagging when the stench slipped into my nostrils. I asked if there'd been a storm, but the bag man said it was simply *acqua alta*: a king tide. The moon brought an exceptionally high spring tide, and the lagoon came rushing in to claim the city. In the streets, water bubbled out of cracks in the stones and storm drains. We slogged away, the murky water waist-deep, and yet no one else in the streets seemed particularly concerned. They all wore waders and struggled against the water like it was second nature. A group of small girls paddled by in a tiny boat, slapping the water with red plastic oars and shouting at each other in Italian.

Only now could I see the way the water marked a line on all the buildings, the plaster and Istrian stone eroding below a certain height. It was not like I'd been unaware that Venice was dealing with flooding issues, but I hadn't realized the water was spilling into hotel lobbies.

I managed a first-class ticket to Chicago, but there was only a coach seat to Frankfurt. It had been two years since I'd flown on a commercial airliner, and I'd forgotten all the minor indignities. The scramble to claim overhead baggage space, the way you warred for the armrest with your seatmate, the disappointing entertainment options, the constant chirp and squawk of some child. I dozed on and off, and when I woke, I called Allie to say I was on my way to get Mom and take her to my condo.

*

In Chicago, I hired a car, but it came with a human driver. There was too much debris on the roads, he informed me, and traffic was logjammed. Bridges had fallen, roads were impassable, people had fled to high ground from anywhere with a floodplain. Driving southwest from O'Hare, trash coated the highway, washed down from overflowing sewer drains that had discharged the excess water after the Chicago Deep Tunnel had reached its limit. Sewage had spilled into Lake Michigan in volumes never before conceived by city planners, and now the whole population was scouring supermarkets for bottled water. Garbage collected at storm drains and was strewn across sidewalks: diapers, plastic bottles, traffic cones, children's toys, lawn chairs, aluminum siding, driftwood, water-logged paperbacks, and for some reason dozens of plastic baby doll heads bobbed along in the restless roadside rivers, staring dead-eyed wherever they pointed.

"I've been out of the country," I explained. "How long has this been going on?"

"Worst was last week." The driver was old and South Side, his accent dripping with loyalty to the White Sox. "It's better now. Last Friday the streets were all waist-deep."

"Jesus."

"Randall's just flying around the country declaring disaster areas here, disaster areas there. Whole states are underwater." He paused, then asked, "Who you voting for?"

Shocked by his forthrightness with a customer, I stammered, "Whoever gets the Democrat nomination. Formisano or Love."

"Good. As long as you're not for that nutjob Braden. I'm afraid she's

Trump all over again. But times a million. And we can't do another four years of that useless shithead Randall."

Put off by his vulgarity, I nodded and took out my phone, hoping a dome of etiquette would descend. We were quiet for the rest of the ride. I couldn't stop watching videos.

An entire McMansion, intact, carried down a river along with the basketball hoop attached to the garage. A sinkhole in a major highway with the rear ends of two cars jutting out. A man clutching a rope in a strong current, trying to pull himself to safety as rescuers urged him on, only to tire, give up, and let go.

The sun broke through the low clouds, and we drove by sight after sight, harrowing and spectacular: An SUV flipped on its head on the lawn of a half-collapsed home, outer walls ripped away, exposing soggy pink insulation. Trees bisecting roofs, crushing whole homes, pulverizing cars that had remained right-side up. Near the Illinois-Iowa border, traffic slowed to a crawl as the highway narrowed to one lane. I could see where the high-water mark had carried vehicles, chewed through foundations, cracked and cratered asphalt roads, and dragged entire buildings into rubble. A couch had beached itself on top of a gas station like it was just waiting for a family to jam into its moldy leather and start watching TV. Coming upon the Mississippi, which I'd seen from this vantage point only a few weeks earlier, I couldn't believe my eyes.

"Oh my God," I whispered.

"Yeah," said my driver as if he'd already seen this.

The Mississippi looked like an ocean. Muddy, viscous, and frothing. Normally the river was hundreds of feet below the bridge, but now it must have been only a few dozen. Weeks ago I'd seen it crawling up the banks, but the water had now swallowed the floodplain, and I could see the tops of those riverbank homes nearly submerged, the white steepled tips the only evidence of roofs. On the Illinois side, there'd been a gas station beneath the bridge, and it had vanished under the raging murk. Treetops emerging from the water had collected debris, driftwood, and plastic, including a blue and yellow inflatable raft. I tried not to let my dread grow—our house wasn't even that close to the floodplain—but I tried my mom again. Still no answer.

On Route 64, maybe five miles outside Amber, we finally arrived at a roadblock where a state trooper in a plastic-bagged hat stopped us. He approached the window, and my dread swelled.

"Can't go past here," he told the driver. "We got floodwaters from the Waps River still receding."

"Officer, my mother's at home, and I haven't been able to get a hold of her."

"She didn't evacuate?"

"I don't know. But if she's hurt or didn't get out . . . I don't know what to do."

He looked around. He was the only one out on this lonely stretch of road, waiting for the opportunity to warn people of danger. He looked like every kid I'd ever grown up with, white and ruddy and heavy in the face. "What's the address?"

I gave it to him. "It's really only about five miles from here."

"Okay. But promise me: Do not drive through any high water. Turn around. It's not worth your life."

I thanked him, and my driver, reluctantly, put the car in drive and eased around the roadblock. Crunching over leaves, branches, and smaller fallen limbs, we passed through this familiar route of my childhood, roadside trees chewed, battered, and torn from the ground with clotted dirt clutching the roots.

My house came into view, the yard flooded. But the beat-up Explorer my mom had been driving for the better part of the last decade was still in the driveway, and I couldn't tell if it had been caught in the flood.

"Will you wait here?" I asked the driver.

"Supposed to be back in the city tonight." He craned his neck to look back at me. "What's the plan?"

"I'll pay you to wait. If my mom's here, we'll just grab her things and take her back to the city with us."

"And if she ain't?"

I unbuckled my seat belt, done with his brusque shtick. "We'll figure that out."

I splashed into the driveway, water lapping at my boots, dark chestnut Ainsley Chelseas I'd bought in the Frankfurt airport, soon to be ruined. I texted Allie: *Hey, just got here. I think Mom stayed.* The water made soft gurgling sounds with each step. I almost stopped to fix the mailbox with our house number and SHIPMAN FAMILY FARM still on the side, but I left it. I was so exhausted, jet-lagged, and put off by my surly lib driver, I imagined going up to my old room and lying down on the guest bed.

Squishing through the muck, I reached the front steps. The water was right up against the house, deeper than it had looked, sloshing against the door. It was locked. I rang the bell, which I heard echoing inside. I called for my mom but got no reply. I unscrewed the outside light fixture and fished out the key my parents had always kept taped to the inside lip of the dome.

The first floor had almost a foot of water, some of it rushing out past my ankles as I stepped inside. Even as I thought about all the rot and damage this flooding would inflict on the structure of a home over a hundred years old, the smell hit me: a putrid, sewage stench. Exponentially more potent than Venice. I gripped my mouth and nose. I tried to breathe the scent of my palm as I called for my mom.

It had taken her almost no time to turn the place into a dump again. Though the flooding was what mattered, the dishes in the sink and the general chaos of fast-food wrappers had reasserted itself since my visit. There were pebbled splashes as water dripped from the ceiling.

"Mom!" I shouted. Then I saw her phone on the dining room table and slogged over to it, trying not to think of why this water stank so badly. The phone was dead. It made more sense now. A neighbor or someone from her church had come to get her when the flooding began and she'd simply forgotten her phone. Of course, she wouldn't just know my number or Allie's off the top of her head. Now it was only a matter of tracking her down. First, I had to get to town, though. Find out where people had evacuated to. I decided that as long as Mom's car was still running, I'd tell the driver to head back, and I'd stay in a hotel until I found her.

This meant finding the keys to the Explorer and hoping the water hadn't gotten to the engine. My parents always tossed them atop the bureau in the living room, and this is where I found them now—sitting on a white legal pad with what looked like a note. Overcome by relief, I splashed over to it.

It certainly was a note, written in her stunted, boxy handwriting. But it made no sense.

THE FLOORS WET

Was all it said.

I flipped to the next page looking for more. All she'd written was "the floors wet"? I tried to concoct a scenario that made sense, but my imagination struggled to piece it together. Who was this stupid complaint even for?

That drip again. Close by. The stairs of our house ascended to a loft-like hallway that led to all the second-floor bedrooms. As kids, Allie and I had spied on our parents whenever they had company, sneaking from our rooms to the banister, staying low, giggling at each other to be quiet. This was what I was thinking of as my eyes traveled up, first lighting on that one missing spindle, and then on my mother, hanging by her neck from an electrical cord secured around the banister where her daughters had once whispered.

At first, I just stared as my brain tried to make sense of it, and stupidly, I wondered if my mom had decided to play an extremely elaborate prank. The contortions our minds will attempt in order to tell us that what we are seeing is not real.

But no. It was my mom, wearing a soiled nightgown, her face a bloated blue-purple, her dry tongue lolling out of her mouth, red-veined eyes bulging, flies on her face. Her fingers pointed straight at the floor like she was trying to shoot lightning from the tips. The dripping was coming from beneath her nightgown, her fluids slowly draining into the water.

And still my shock was so total that I couldn't process what I was looking at or what had happened. My brain continued to swipe through explanatory scenarios, anything to render this moment inert and commonplace. I almost even said something to her, something along the lines of "That's not funny."

Then I gagged and fell down, backward onto my butt, so that the cold, reeking water swallowed me to my stomach. I turned my head and vomited, the reflex taking over, and I gagged again and again until my stomach ached, and after it was over, for a long time, I wanted to scream, but I could only sit there, my breath gone, bile coating my jaw, staring up at my mother's body, quietly dripping, distended eyes staring at nothing and everything. The house was quiet except for the sound of water. How very many mystifying noises still water can make.

EXECUTIVE SUMMARY
ON ELECTION 2032

Ashir al-Hasan

October 15, 2032

Destroy Document After Reading

Abstract: With two and a half months and an election still to go, 2032 has been a challenging year, personally and for our country. In many respects, it reminds me of 2020 when a rancorous presidential contest collided with exogenous emergencies that had the trappings of a waking nightmare. When I agreed to establish a back channel with you from my position at the Global Change Research Program, it was because I believed you to be one of the only elected officials still speaking with urgency on the climate issue and who understood that the Pollution Reduction, Infrastructure, and Research Act was a deeply flawed and counterproductive piece of legislation, even as I harbor concern for how often you request input on topics far outside my purview. However, I've become radicalized in the sense that politics have now infested the government's scientific agencies so thoroughly that we must essentially advocate for the continued existence of sound science and the policy it demands as this global emergency barrels forward. What follows here, I fear, will be less than helpful, and will cover the major domestic events of 2032 and their impact on an increasingly chaotic and unhinged political race that is fracturing as never before an already anomic American polity. In some sense, this will read as a treatise of my greatest fears about this moment, and concludes with a clandestine conference this September, which, I beg you, must remain ensconced in secrecy.

I spent the first part of this year back home in Michigan as my sister, Haniya, and I took turns staying with our mother, who'd recently been diagnosed with Alzheimer's. I was with her for Ramadan in January. It was Eid al-Fitr just before the Iowa caucuses, and at sundown my mother turned on the television during dinner. Her obsession with cable news was such that she could not be away from it for long, particularly when all the talk was of the verdict in Minneapolis. As you recall, a year earlier, in February 2031, Shariz al-Bawadi and his daughter Eman al-Bawadi killed thirty-three people at the Mall of America in Bloomington, Minnesota, the father flushing terrified shoppers down one hall with an AR-15 while his sixteen-year-old daughter perched in a rafter above a roller coaster firing guided EXACTO bullets from a high-powered rifle. Predictably, what followed was an outpouring of anti-Muslim vitriol. Muslims, Sikhs, and others of Middle Eastern or South Asian ancestry were attacked in cities around the country. The entire Somali population of Minneapolis has endured raids, arrests, and indefinite detention as the courts grow ever more comfortable with elasticizing the habeas writ. A year later, both al-Bawadis would receive life sentences.

I chose this moment to unburden myself. Haniya had admonished me that I tell our mother before she was too far gone. We'd finished our meal of stewed lamb, rice, and raisins when I told her I would be moving in with my partner, Seth. This was the first time she'd even heard of Seth, and it took me several attempts to explain who he was. She thrust her hand at me:

"Stop speaking. Stop speaking right now."

She left the room, and I gave her some time, clearing and washing the dishes before attempting to approach her again that night. When I did, I found her downstairs in my father's den, watching more TV in the dark.

From his opulent stage, translated to 2D from his Slapdish worlde, The Pastor excoriated: *"When a prophecy comes true, when fire destroys a city, and the liberal media, who've been lying to you for decades, they say, 'Don't pay attention to that prophesy. Don't listen to that man, he's a charlatan'— who would you believe? And now he foresees great floods coming. Yet they are hellbent on turning you away from him. 'The scientists tell us it's this reason or that reason.' They think you can't see with your own two eyes. My friends, do you really believe these events do not directly reveal the hand of God?"*

He stalked the stage, and his movements were leonine, his suit and hair impeccable, the enormous cross on his lapel gleaming in the stage lights. What drew my mother to this man's incoherent gospel, I assumed, had to do with fear. Gently, I asked her if I could turn the channel, and she flipped a hand in acquiescence.

"He is so dangerous. If he wins then what happens to Muslims in India will happen here. To you, me, Haniya, Noor, Gregory. All of us. You don't care about our people, and this man is what happens."

Of course, she has already lost a good deal of her ability to understand current events. I explained to her that The Pastor was not a presidential candidate, that soon the Democrats and Republicans would begin their primary season in Iowa, but she would not hear this and kept insisting The Pastor was going to hurt Muslims.

While her fears might have been confused, they were not exactly incorrect. In my position as executive director at the US Global Change Research Program, Asia has become a vector of grave concern. Home to the vast majority of the world's population, the continent is in the midst of a violent paroxysm of conflict and biophysical upheaval. It is greatly susceptible to extreme weather events, as Mumbai discovered during Cyclone Malwan, but also drought, flooding, food insecurity, sea level rise, and saltwater intrusion. There are few models left predicting benign climatological outcomes in India, Bangladesh, Vietnam, Nepal, Pakistan, or China. The catastrophic shortages of water are creating refugee flows, eruptions of conflict, and ethnoreligious carnage. Climatological calamity is driving widespread social and political unrest, which then manifests itself as conflict over ethnicity, caste, religion, race, gender, language, and other imagined communities. When my mother scolds me on my indifference toward "our people" she does so with the knowledge of the persecution Muslims in India are experiencing, all of it sanctioned by the right-wing Hindu government. Following the tens of thousands killed and displaced by Cyclone Malwan, spasms of extreme violence erupted, as disinformation spread that Muslims were hoarding food, water, and fuel.

As for The Pastor, I find him no more than a con man. After losing a string of roles to nonwhite actors, embroiled in scandal for decrying film and television's politically correct culture, his movies increasingly ridiculed, his profligate lifestyle constrained, this former actor simply recalibrated his ambitions to a different style of performance. He saw that the captive audience of American Evangelicals was ripe for a hostile takeover and that he could generate income by preying upon a group already eschewing critical thinking. Internet sleuths love to point to a villain's soliloquy in one of this man's underperforming films, the plot of which includes a Silicon Valley corporation attempting to introduce mind control technology to the internet. By the time of the film's streaming debut in 2024, this was hardly an original thought. More telling is the former actor's investment history. He spent years as the primary financier behind a venture capital firm, pouring money into virtual reality and technologies of targeted persuasion. His ambitions were thwarted when he bet on one of Slapdish's competitors, and his firm failed.

However, the villain's speech from the subpar action movie remains trenchant, if appallingly scripted: *"We live in a contemporary Tower Babel, and inside that tower is a sorcerer's stone. But only a lucky few understand how to wield it. Those who do can feel its power, and that power is seductive."*

Dreck, to be sure, and perhaps too simplistic an explanation for the media empire he has built. He is tapping into real emotions of frustration and disillusionment, but a con it remains. None of this would comfort my mother, however. She now gestured to the TV, where The Pastor had been replaced by a commercial for collectible coins. She began to weep:

"It will be like in India. The women endure the worst of it. My friend— she and I grow up together—her daughter was raped in front of her children. The men cut off her breasts, stole every possession the family had, and left her to die. She survived, but this is not just some scary story. This is what is happening to Muslims every single day in my home." She looked at me miserably. "Ashir, tell the people where you work, do not let this man hurt anyone."

She reached out and took my hand, this small woman who'd gestated me. I assured her I would pass this message along.

As you know, in the first contest in Iowa, Senator L. Victor Love and Governor Pat Formisano tied in the Democratic primary while on the Republican side, the white separatist talk-show host Jennifer Braden defeated the president of the United States by four points, setting off a political earthquake.

//

In April I returned to Michigan to move my mother out of her home as the country was upended by what became known as the Great Eastern Flood.

My colleagues and I had watched in awe from the offices on G Street as an astonishing confluence of hydrological events shattered our models, specifically a warm, wet winter saturating much of the Eastern Seaboard and Middle West, several tropical depressions moving from the Gulf to the Southeast, followed by three frontal cyclones, storms of phenomenal power, crossing eastward from the plains. As you well know, there was hardly a riverine municipality that did not experience some degree of flooding. Statistics are unwieldy, but I believe when viewing the flooding in aggregate, as one event, rather than a series of ill-timed, compounding disasters, FEMA will total approximately 3,800 fatalities across twenty-five states and $209 billion in damage, dwarfing Hurricane Alberto's record-setting tally. The cities of Memphis, Nashville, St. Louis, Kansas City, Chicago, Pittsburgh, Baton Rouge, and New Orleans account for much of that human toll, as levee failures, sewer system overloads, spillway collapses, and other infrastructure failures left residents with little time to escape. It's easy to forget that human lives exist behind the integer. I remind myself by thinking of the staff of a Missouri facility for the physically and mentally disabled who abandoned a bus full of patients in a roadway as a bridge began to wash out. The staff members escaped, and all forty patients drowned as the river flipped the bus and overtook it.

Back in Ann Arbor with my sister, her husband, Peter, and their two children, we had a glimpse of one of these extratropical cyclones, followed by four days of powerful microburst storms. The air turned green, and a tornado alarm began to blare. All the noise felt like broken glass being raked on the inside of my skin. I knew my panic was unnerving Noor and Gregory, and I had to retreat to a bathroom without windows and push the smooth side of a hairbrush over my arm to calm myself. The next day, on our way to the store, Peter and I saw homes with their walls ripped out, bikes, clothing, and lawn chairs in trees, cars blown onto their sides, and one structure where the roof had been cleanly removed. That particular storm system spawned three tornadoes across Michigan, none of which was as destructive as the flooding of the Huron River. Said Peter:

"Fuck me. Where's Bill Paxton and Helen Hunt when you need 'em?"

In addition to the storm, my mother was insisting I go to mosque with her, and this had led to a bitter argument. She insisted it would pry me from the grip of a "great sin."

Haniya tried to argue with her that my choices could be justified by

Qur'anic text while I sat there silently, recalling my childhood when mosque and the imam terrified me. I recalled how he would take me to task for refusing to go through the motions of raka'ah, or how he ridiculed my Arabic pronunciation. Now both my mother and sister were in tears, as Hani tried to build a bridge from the dogma of our ancestors to her brother's life. As they carried on, I marveled at how little power all of this wielded over me anymore. Finally, I left to go play trucks with Noor and Gregory.

That night, in my childhood bedroom where I'd once pinned up long reams of the basketball statistics I adored, Hani knocked on the door. We talked about the sale of the house until she finally asked a question I could not believe she didn't already know the answer to: "Have you ever believed, Ashir? Maybe as a child?"

I picked up a toy model of a pirate ship I had built as a seven-year-old with our father. It had remained on the bookshelf in my old room all these years. "Not to my recollection. The first time I remember hearing the idea of God, I was five. I went to the library with Papa to try to figure out where these realms or kingdoms could possibly exist within the physical structure of the atmosphere or deep mantle. For maybe two minutes, I wondered if the beings and locales of those stories were contained in the mesosphere because it lay between the stratosphere where the jets fly and the thermosphere where astronauts would clearly bump into such marvels as akhirah. Obviously, this all collapsed rather quickly."

My sister has a wide and beautiful face with cheekbones that stretch outward like they are trying to escape the skin. This gives her every utterance a calm that can often feel cold. Her social cues remain some of the most difficult I've ever had to read: "You were not actually that literal when you were five, Ash."

"It only shocked me that none of this had ever occurred to anyone before. I tried to tell Mumma, and she smacked me."

The sting of my mother's hand stayed with me, and not only because of the guilt and confusion that followed, but because her reaction seemed endemic. What I felt in the drill of her hand as a child, I hear in The Pastor's voice all these years later: The piffling anecdata of the faithful peddled as law and conscience. The world is in the throes of a desperate religious revival as believers plunk their heads into the sand to shield themselves from what is happening to the biophysical world. As she grows mentally frailer, I suppose there will be no reconciliation with my mother. Her moments of tenderness are fleeting, and her fury at my relationship with Seth seems the one thing she can easily recall. No doubt she will forget me before she forgives me.

//

It took us a week to make the arrangements for my mother to move to New York where Peter and Hani have been caring for her with their significant financial resources. I was left alone in Ann Arbor with the task of closing up our childhood home. Instead of ruminating pointlessly on uninteresting nostalgia, I took the opportunity to don my new VR set and enter The Pastor's Slapdish worlde. I'd first had the idea in January when a man I'll refer to as "Ned Stark" contacted me and asked that we meet clandestinely in VR. I thought of The Pastor's gaudy megachurch-theme-park worlde, which was dense, crowded, and allowed anonymous entrants. I'll spare you the description, only to say that Ned Stark and I met on a tower spire's precipice where I couldn't help but step my foot off the ledge repeatedly, musing at the strange disconnect between my brain telling me I would fall and my foot finding the carpet of my childhood bedroom.

"She wants to wait until after the primaries," he said. I call him Ned Stark because that is the avatar he'd chosen. I myself was dressed as early NBA analytics hero Shane Battier. "Love has got it in the bag, it looks like, but the RNC can't seem to manage to put Braden down. This all gets very different if Braden manages to pull this off."

I asked: "What is the eventual plan?"

"We're going to come together and reveal ourselves."

"I'm putting a great deal of trust in you with this."

The avatar made a cheap facsimile of a grimace. "Yeah, well, so am I."

Across the futuristic Christian theme park, Jumbotrons displayed the shellacked smile of The Pastor. He'd been busy celebrating the spring's flooding as his prophecy coming true rather than an excess of water vapor in the atmosphere powering the engines of devastating storm systems. He inveighed:

"And who is the one who foresaw this? Who, just a few months ago, warned you of this?" He flipped open his self-authored book of scripture and quoted: *"'For there will be fire and flood, and a man will appear giving warning of these tribulations. The vested powers will tell the people to ignore him for he may carry the blood of the Christ in his veins. This man will make rain, and he is the future.'"*

//

President Mary Randall had the misfortune to launch her reelection campaign touting her supposed victory over the climate crisis with the passage of PRIRA then presiding over the catastrophe of the Great Eastern Flood. To get into the missteps of FEMA here is a bit much, but suffice it to say she took much criticism in the press and from the Democratic nominee, Senator Love, while also suffering broadside attacks for her failures to curb terrorism and illegal immigration from Jennifer Braden. Braden had recently stated, without evidence, that Randall had ordered the CIA to supply the al-Bawadis with smart bullets, and her rabid followers launched this baseless theory into the mainstream. However, as soon as Senator Russ Mackowski dropped out of the race and endorsed Randall, the Republican Party locked arms, and Randall accrued an insurmountable delegate lead. Braden's rants grew more unhinged, and political prognosticators deemed her buried when she unleashed her taunt, "You dirty brown bitch," at the president during the last debate. The scene at the Republican National Convention was particularly troubling as Braden's followers, armed with assault rifles, attempted to surround the convention center in Charlotte.

On July 16, Seth and I happened to have a social occasion with Alice McCowen, former director of the White House Office of Legislative Affairs. Though our relationship began on rocky ground during the maneuvering around PRIRA, we became allies in its failed effort and a mutual respect emerged. McCowen also began a relationship with my friend and mentor Jane Tufariello. All three of us now viewed one another as survivors of the wreckage left behind by that devastating legislative fight. Alice and Jane had us over for dinner, and it was difficult not to slip into talk of the loud and unpleasant election dominating the news. Alice was particularly irate at what she saw as the efforts to destroy her former boss and friend, the president:

"Before I left, I told Mary, the campaign staff, everyone, this whacko-bird, the Hot Nazi, she's not to be taken lightly. And they all got caught flat-footed. I didn't drag the Republican Party kicking and screaming into the twenty-first century to be a part of this horseshit. Meanwhile, everyone knows the Dems' golden goddess first-female-feminist-idol Hogan basically watched a live feed of a guy getting tortured for thirty-six hours without blinking. The Beltway talks about how Mary doesn't have the stomach to fight terrorism but look at the psycho act she had to follow."

Jane put a hand on her arm: "Okay, Alice. Enough."

"What? Hogan was one bloodthirsty cunt."

Seth was laughing, finding this exchange very amusing, though I was irritated by the cross talk. It was at this moment when all of our phones, watches, and glasses issued simultaneous notifications of the events that would effectively end Mary Randall's chances at a second term.

//

That night Seth remarked: "Twenty thirty-two is one of those years you have to turn off the news alerts."

All we knew then was that a series of IEDs had destroyed a manufacturing facility in La Grange, Illinois. By the time Seth and I took a driverless home, several incendiary devices had set ablaze a processing plant for diluted bitumen in Fort McMurray, Alberta, while also nearly causing a forest fire. Multiple residents of Fort McMurray were injured, nearly a thousand evacuated, and forty-three structures destroyed. Finally, as we watched the news back at our condo, a third attack was reported at the Tucker Anacortes Refinery, seventy miles north of Seattle, when a missile struck the catalytic cracking unit. Seth gasped:

"A missile? What the hell is happening?"

The Anacortes attack had something new as well: fatalities. Two workers were killed in the strike.

Images played on a loop of the smoldering manufacturing plant in La Grange, the fire burning in the Canadian night, and the wrecked refinery in Washington, smoke and dark obscuring the damage. It was assumed on all the major networks that this was the work of the same faction responsible for the attacks on coal plants in the Midwest two years earlier, and both American and Canadian intelligence soon confirmed this. The media grappled for a nickname as catchy as the Ohio River Massacre but only managed the "July Surprise." Before I went to bed that night, I received a call from the FBI requesting my presence in Anacortes.

//

Following the coal plant attacks of 2030, at the behest of Ms. McCowen, I began consulting with the task force pursuing eco-terrorism suspects. I already had a relationship with the FBI ever since they opened a case into the various death threats I've received since PRIRA was thrust into the spotlight. This is how I met Special Agent John Chen, a task force leader, and he has sought my perspective on the motives and thinking of the so-called

Weathermen ever since. He feels they follow the science, economics, and politics of carbon pollution closely, and that I might provide insight into their thinking.

I arrived the next afternoon in Anacortes, a pristine town that abuts Puget Sound in the shadow of the Cascade Mountains, and checked into my hotel.

Special Agent Chen sent a car for me the next day. At the refinery, I filled out the access-control log and donned booties, though we were to remain on the demarcated entry and exit paths of the crime scene. SWAT officers with MP5 submachine guns surrounded the perimeter, scrutinizing my visitor's badge when we passed. Agent Chen greeted me with very little small talk:

"If there was any doubt after Ohio, this about wraps it up. These are not campus activists."

"The complexity of geolocating a missile strike should narrow down potential suspects."

"Not as much as we wish. Plenty of unscrupulous firms out there that will sell you discreet rush satellite tracking—every jihadi group in Africa and Arabia can buy them now. We think they 3D-printed most of the components and assembled the missile themselves, then launched it from a boat in the sound. Guided it via remote control the same way they did drones up in Fort McMurray. Satellite images haven't been helpful yet because of the weather, but we'll see."

Agent Chen's manner is lockstep professionalism. He is the consummate "by-the-book Boy Scout," as my colleague Dr. Anthony Pietrus, who's had previous dealings with Chen, once said. His silver hair was parted on a knife's edge at the side of his head. He wore glasses and a pen in a plastic pocket protector on his shirt, a prosaic style even I would hesitate to adopt, regardless of its clear utility. I asked him:

"And the men who were killed?"

"Two workers in the cracking unit. A call came in to the refinery roughly thirty minutes before the missile hit, and the facility operations manager initiated an evacuation. Those two either didn't hear the alarm or simply failed to heed it—we're not sure."

We approached the charred, burned hole in the side of the building. The missile had struck the base of the fluid catalytic cracking unit. Without this unit in operation, a refinery amounts to little more than a temporary storage facility for useless crude oil. Part of the wall had collapsed, and metal twisted into the sky. Orange hazard tape surrounded the site, and forensic chemists and other investigators in Tyvek coveralls combed the area while agents swarmed the scene with guns on their belts and clipboards in their hands. In the wreckage, I could see an intact coffee mug with the Seattle Seahawks logo, charred by fire, sitting atop a pile of blackened brick. Police drones swarmed overhead, surveilling the area. With their whirring rotor blades, they always appear to me as angry insects. I said:

"These fatalities were accidental then."

"Depends on how you look at it. When they blew up those coal plants in Ohio, and grandmas cooked in their homes at the height of summer, was that accidental?"

"They take a great deal of care to avoid casualties. Doesn't that tell you something about their motivation and psychology? Their objective seems persuasively aboveboard: trying to raise security and insurance costs for carbon industries to make them unprofitable."

Chen delivered what I might call a "who the hell knows?" expression: "I'm done speculating. The investigation's become so politicized—we're following wingnut hunches more than we're following actual leads. A QAnon senator picks up a conspiracy and suddenly the bureau is actually getting pressure to track down Kobe Bryant's widow in case she knows something. I mean, it's all just . . ."

He shook his head and trailed off. Aside from the activity of investigators tiptoeing over scattered detritus, the scene felt unnervingly still. The distillation tower reminded me of a forlorn lookout of an abandoned castle.

"The La Grange and McMurray devices were delivered by consumer drones?"

"TEDAC says it's ingenious work. Hell, my daughter could pilot a drone when she was five, but these things were carrying complex IEDs."

"Perhaps it's just a coincidence that this district is represented by the chairman of the Unmanned Systems Caucus in Congress."

"That's who we have to thank for the sky the way it is? Robots crashing into each other every damn day?" His hands tucked into his pants, a stain of sweat under each arm and more breaking out on his brow, Agent Chen scuffed a foot at the dirt unhappily. "Between you and me, this investigation is a catastrophe. Ten years, and we have almost nothing to show for chasing backpack scraps and fertilizer receipts. A handful of arrests, none of which have yielded any insight into the operational core. We've had two computer glitches that have lost reams of evidence. Mismanagement up and down the chain of command."

"I'm sympathetic to your predicament, Agent Chen. This group has catalyzed an ugly reaction to environmental remediation. No one would prefer that you arrest these conspirators more than myself. You flew me a long way. How I can be of service here?"

He removed a hand from his pocket and began picking at a cuticle. His black-pitted eyes searched the nail bed carefully. This made what he said next unnerving.

"The lists you've been compiling for me, of potential vulnerable infrastructure, it's helpful. But what I really need to get in your ear about, Dr. Hasan, is the political situation. I was coming up through Quantico after 9/11. I knew a lot of what was happening was counterproductive to the goal of finding and stopping the people who'd do the country harm. I was around during Trump when the bureau was effectively at war with a traitor. None of that scares me as much as the efforts to politicize us now. It would be helpful if you could alert certain allies in Congress and the White House."

"I assure you, Agent Chen, I will."

Chen propped a leg up on a piece of fallen concrete and then draped his arms across it. He reached out and touched a piece of twisted rebar, protruding from cement blocks. Then he glanced around to see who might be paying attention to our conversation. Satisfied, he looked back at me.

"I wanted you out here, Doctor, because holo-conferencing, VR, Face-Time—eyes and ears are everywhere now. What I need you to relay, it has to stay off-channel. Vic Love is going to win this election, and he has a track record with law enforcement. What he's done with policing in this country—and that was before he was even elected to public office. Word I'm hearing is he wants to turn the bureau upside down. Meanwhile, Republicans in Congress are goading us to shut down task forces on, if you ask me, much more dangerous groups. Militias and white nationalists. We're getting resources yanked from important operations left and right, and it's *all* political pressure."

"A troubling situation, I agree, but I'm not sure that 6Degrees doesn't constitute the more potent threat."

"You haven't seen the intelligence on the League then."

"Indiscriminate murder is hardly sophisticated. The materials involved cost a few hundred dollars and with the modern artillery available to civilians, hitting a number of targets can be accomplished with only a modicum of training. What 6Degrees has conducted is much more impressive—a sustained, multiyear campaign of clandestine bombings with absolutely zero penetration of its leadership. They've demonstrated not only expertise with explosives but law enforcement protocol, surveillance techniques, and most importantly, counterintelligence. The fact that neither the FBI Laboratory nor the ATF has been able to understand how they are procuring high-explosive material, particularly Tovex, Semtex H, and pentaerythritol tetranitrate, is troubling."

"Marie Newman gave us some clue. And 6Degrees is not more dangerous. Twenty-two years ago, this refinery had an industrial accident after a maintenance restart gone bad. The explosion killed seven. That toll exceeds 6Degrees' entire decade of operations."

"I've read your reports, Agent Chen. There were surely others like Marie Newman unwittingly supplying them. Still, other than the patsies, there has been no DNA evidence gathered, no latent fingerprints. Materials analysis, toolmark examinations, metallurgical analysis, device reconstruction have all yielded few leads other than the conclusion that you are now searching for more than one bomb maker. They are growing. And they understand how to cause greater chaos than their current efforts suggest. Should they ever decide to raise the stakes, that, Agent Chen, is what would put the fear of God into me, so to speak. L. Victor Love has called 6Degrees the number one threat to the security of the United States, and though I'm not typically given to agreeing with such promulgations, I have to say I see his point for one reason: effectiveness."

Agent Chen said nothing to this, he simply extended his hand to shake mine, and when he tucked the thumb drive into my palm, I finally understood why he'd flown me all the way out to the relative safety of a crime scene.

The government SUV took me around Fidalgo Bay under low iron clouds. Past the still beauty of the Pacific Northwest, skirting the belly of the temperate rain forests that make up Olympic National Park, I saw a field of horses grazing in the summer sun, and I thought about how little of the world I'd actually seen. How very much of my life has been spent in front of computer screens. How little opportunity I have had to explore in the brief shock of light and color between otherwise eternal respites.

Once back in the hotel, I packed away Agent Chen's thumb drive, slipped on my VR set, and entered The Pastor's worlde. While waiting, I looked out over the assembled avatars moving through a fluid lambency in the futuristic Christian megalopolis. The crenellated towers of this neo-Disney kingdom spiraled majestically into a mustard-colored sky, supposedly mimicking the sky under which Jesus walked with the cross. There would be a meeting soon, Ned Stark told me. And we would all take down our avatars.

//

When Seth and I moved into our apartment in Georgetown, he broached the subject of becoming fathers, either through adoption or a surrogate. I told him this was not something I wished to discuss so soon into our co-habitation and left it at that. There are many things about Seth I find distasteful. He's a poor cook, though he thinks he's a good one. Ideologically, he is heavily invested in identity claims to one's sexuality and pushes me to attend "Pride" events, though I find them tasteless, corporatized alcoholic displays. He doesn't rinse food from dishes before placing them in the dishwasher, which usually means some granule will cling on, and I'll have to wash them again by hand. When we hike, particularly our favorite trail, the Billy Goat at Great Falls, he prattles too much and too excitedly, which obviates the serenity of the forest. Nevertheless, I'm fond of him. Fond of his passion, optimism, and skewed Roman nose. His boyish blond cowlick and bright blue eyes tend to erase all petty grievances. And yet, how badly he wants to be a father. On the night of August 20 of this year, I returned from a run, and he put a picture of a lean, aesthetically pleasing African American woman in front of me.

"This is Janelle. She's twenty-seven. She wants to be our surrogate."

I did not take his phone. "I suppose she just approached you out of the blue and offered her services?"

"I wanted to get an idea of what our options would be. But she's perfect, babe. Just out of law school. Smart, kind, beautiful. Genes for days! And she'll accommodate us on everything."

He tried to touch my back, but I moved before he could do so. I removed my ARs. They were fogged from entering the air-conditioning. Seth took my hand.

"Ash, just meet her. That's all I'm asking. Meet her and tell me this isn't destiny."

"I'm sure you can guess my feelings about an insipid notion like destiny. The brain seeks patterns because that is what brains desperately do. This would be an irrevocable decision for us." The joy drained from his face. I'd punctured his enthusiasm, and as he deflated, I admit, I found it very gratifying.

"Okay, Ashir, that was uncalled for."

"I'm concerned about the irresponsibility of the decision. You act as though we bear no moral culpability for creating a consciousness at this particular social and environmental moment."

He brayed an obnoxious and exaggerated laugh: "Wow! Babe! How original! 'Oh, this world's so cruel, how can we bring life into it?' At least make an effort to not be cliché."

I took his outburst in stride, but there was an instance of mental forewarning, almost a premonition of mauve darkness billowing down.

"You keep track of your emissions footprint on your glasses, Seth. You scold my sister when she eats a hamburger, and we all had to suffer through the two of you arguing interminably about low-methane beef at Thanksgiving. You do understand that every metric ton of carbon you've saved as a moral crusader will immediately propel itself into the atmosphere after our second year of buying diapers?"

"That's so bogus, Ash. That's not what this is about." He walked behind our kitchen island and pretended to busy himself. Because our finances were so secure due to my investment strategies, he purchased an excess of upscale kitchen appliances. He now fiddled with the nutritional analyzer and a handful of chopped mushrooms. "You're afraid."

"I am. But not of what you think. You believe I'm afraid of late-night feedings and the responsibility of caregiving and perhaps the passing along of my insecurities and anxieties. My depression and suicidal ideation. These, Seth, are obviously banal concerns."

"Oh, are they? Could've fooled me."

Seth quit pretending at his concern over the mushrooms' quality, grabbed the kitchen island, and clutched it as if to steady himself. His blue eyes trained on me, his high blood pressure likely spiking. I said:

"Yes. And spare me the speech about the singular joy of becoming a parent. Haniya and Peter expressed sentiments just as boring after they had Noor, so I beg you not to be as uninteresting as them."

"Real nice."

I replaced my glasses and noticed an alert in the lens with your name, Congresswoman. I apologize for not responding. Instead, I went to our bookshelves, which lined the wall and surrounded the television. I pulled down my colleague Dr. Anthony Pietrus's book. I also took down those of James Hansen, Fred Pearce, and Elizabeth Kolbert. I pulled from the shelf every book of Seth's that dealt with the climatic impacts of greenhouse gas emissions and piled them under my arm, these cheap tomes of popular science meant to frighten and unsettle a particular class of college-educated, medium-to-high-income urban professionals of an energy and extraction-intensive economy, one who likely reads Moniza Farooki in the *New Yorker* and has a certain genre of documentary suggested to them by the algorithms of their streaming services. I carried the pile over to the kitchen island and dumped them on the food analyzer and the mushrooms. A few of the books spilled off the sides of the kitchen island.

"You're not ignorant, Seth. You read the material, or at least the material you can comprehend. So you understand there is a better than fifty-fifty chance that by the year 2100 civilization will be drastically altered in nearly every regard, and those deviations could include violence and turmoil on a scale never before experienced in the memory of humanity." I was glancing from the floor to Seth and back to the floor, as I did when I grew heated. "You also understand—at least if you paid attention to all these books you so proudly display—that there is a very real chance that runaway climate change could eradicate most human life, and that this could happen quickly, possibly within the lifetime of this hypothetical child you want to pay this impoverished, indebted law student to carry for you. And why do you seek this? Because of some fuzzy notion indoctrinated in you by the aspirational marketing of cloying lifestyle brands targeting the consumer habits and media diet of the yuppie homosexual? You chide the right wing for their intransigence, you chastise the working poor for their ignorance, but how are you any different? You want to maintain your beloved political signifiers out of a sense of self-righteousness while you enjoy the privileges you feel entitled to, but you are as selfish, blithe, and arrogant as the Middle American consumers you so decry."

We stood there for a moment, the mess of books scattered around us. Seth stared at me, and I stared at the edge of Tony's volume, with its picture of Hurricane Sandy clobbering the Eastern Seaboard. Seth said:

"It's amazing what an asshole you can be when you put your mind to it."

He left the room, and I slept on the futon in my office that night.

/ /

In the morning, I found Seth in front of the TV with an untouched bowl of cereal. Instead of preparing my morning tea, I was drawn to the CNN report he was watching. I'd forgotten to text you back, but I now knew why you'd tried contacting me: 542 people dead at Chicago's Wrigley Field in the worst mass shooting in American history.

The night before, the Chicago Cubs were competing in a baseball game against the Milwaukee Brewers when five men opened fire from nearby rooftops. Using high-powered military assault rifles and the same guided bullets popularized by the al-Bawadis, they shot into the stands for over an hour as panicked fans attempted to flee. With the exits covered, people simply ran into gunfire as they tried to escape. Nearly a thousand were wounded. What the so-called smart bullet has precluded is the utility of "running away." In an era of guided ammunition, to run is to ensure one's death. The five men had each purchased a ticket to various apartments and rooftop perches and then set themselves up behind heavily fortified shooter's nests so that the Chicago police were unable to effectively return fire. Instead, the bomb squad strapped explosive devices to separate crowd control drones, piloted those drones into the occupied apartments and, as a weeping Chicago police chief put it, "blew those monsters straight to hell." It is the first recorded use of drones to kill combatants on American soil.

Haniya had called me in a panic because she assumed these men had been Islamic extremists. They, of course, turned out to be white separatists from Indiana with ties to the wider militia movement, and I could not help but think of what Agent Chen had told me in Anacortes the month before. One of the shooters, Robert Lynn Carmichael, left behind his infamous appeal to:

"Wake the hell up, America! They're taking it all, and if you don't fight for your heritage and your skin, they will destroy you. This is a genocide, and you are already standing in the gas chamber!"

Remarkable how the people who cause the most chaos are also always the most boring and insecure. When I made this remark to Seth, the first words I'd spoken to him since our fight, he looked at me with contempt.

"I suppose you'll use this as evidence of your 'cruel, harsh world' theory."

"Not remotely. It's a mathematical certainty that in a country with such a proliferation of high-powered weaponry, citizens will find use for that weaponry. But still, the odds that our hypothetical child would die at the hands of murderous extremists remain vanishingly small."

"You know, Ash . . ." Seth pushed his hands through his thinning hair. "This isn't theoretical. You can't quantify why children are important on a fucking spreadsheet. This"—he jabbed a finger at the screen of our opulent television—"is why we need to do this. We can't control anything at all in this life, but if we can bring just a sliver of kindness and compassion into it, then *we are helping*. We are doing our part."

"Seth, you can reconfigure an ignorant bromide all you want but an ignorant bromide it will remain."

He looked like he wanted to say something more, but instead left for his kundalini yoga class. I poured his cereal down the garbage disposal.

//

Two days later, Senator L. Victor Love held a rally at Cellular Field baseball stadium in Chicago, assailing "all threats to our democracy, our diversity, and our way of life." The implications of his speech were clear. Though he led with the attack in Chicago, he spent a great deal of his speech reminding voters of 6Degrees, the al-Bawadis' slaughter, and the threat of terrorist infiltration along the US-Mexico border, concluding with:

"I have a message for all savages, murderers, and enemies of our country: We will hunt you, we will find you, we will end you."

The audience thundered its approval. If you recall, Congresswoman, one of the reasons we first came to an accord was over the backroom dealings Senator Love engaged in that transformed PRIRA into an expansion of surveillance and law enforcement while deploying only tepid antipodal climate adaptation measures. He showered his former company with billions in government contracts and walked away a hero of bipartisan deal-making. Ostensibly, this document began as a measured attempt to extrapolate if you and your supporters should throw your weight behind L. Victor Love in the presidential contest, and I apologize if I've traveled far afield. I'm told my memos can be convoluted. However, I believe everything I've included here is in service to the goal of thinking through the rise of Senator Love. The dynamics of the parties have changed a great deal since I've come to Washington. Mary Randall's near-certain political failure will resonate in perpetuity: The Republican establishment bent over backward to nominate a moderate woman of color, and its own voters and media apparatus rebelled. The conundrum facing the dedicated climate hawk such as Seth or yourself is that Mary Randall, who signed PRIRA, has been chastened and metaphorically gelded by her own party. She is now desperately behind in swing-state polling, and in only thirteen of one hundred simulations of Nate Silver's 538 models does she manage to win.

Meanwhile, true power in American politics has found other avenues. Wall Street, fossil-fuel interests, pharmaceuticals, and the military-, security-, and prison-industrial complexes all began backing Democratic challengers and pushing the socialist wing of the party into a spoiler role. It is a testament to the rightward march, not of the country but of the financiers of its politicians, that this has occurred in only a few election cycles. L. Victor Love's nomination is its crowning achievement; a handsome and masculine homosexual military veteran and businessman who, when posing with his husband shirtless in lifestyle magazines with their impressive abdominal muscles on display, seems to check every box. Yet even a dedicated Democrat like Seth can see that Love serves a specific constituency. His mantra this election has been "climate security," a refrain meant to assuage progressive voters, while signaling that we as a nation will continue to arm the lifeboats, as the expression goes.

You may recall this conversation we had in your office after Love essentially cleared away his competition following the April primaries. You said:

"Vic is not just a corporate, Third Way Democrat. He's what we used to call a right-wing Republican. He's a billionaire war profiteer who bought himself a Montana Senate seat. This is about the worst possible outcome I could've pictured. I don't understand how it turned this fast."

You were very agitated and looked like you hadn't slept much. I attempted to project optimism:

"He could become a reluctant mechanism for change. After all, Mary Randall came in with a promise to do something about climate and was thwarted. Perhaps if the donor class feels safe with Love, we can shock them."

Since that conversation, of course, troubling reporting has emerged about Loren Victor Love. Agent Chen's thumb drive, which I've now conveyed to you, suggests the bureau is also greatly worried about his candidacy. The thumb drive, which I've included, confirms rumors that during his combat tours he was twice investigated for the unlawful killing of civilians (including that he ate a cold hot dog while standing over a young boy, watching him die). But it also contains troubling information on the

unraveling of his primary political opponents. Both Governor Patrick Formisano and Congresswoman Sheila Wang dropped out of the Democratic
race not due to a lack of support or delegates but because of carefully designed scandals. The allegations of sexual misconduct by Formisano have
never been credibly verified, while the leaking of twenty-thousand pages
of Wang's personal texts and emails dating back to her career as an MMA
fighter contained, in my opinion, nothing disqualifying her from office (rib-
ald jokes about MDMA and cocaine use twenty years ago do not impede
one's ability to govern). Following my work for Congresswoman Joy LaFray
and her own collision with scandal and ignominy, I've become fascinated by
what historian Daniel Boorstin calls pseudo-events: orchestrated happen-
ings meant to spark, sway, or deter public opinion. Certain PR firms have
become adept at utilizing these bombshell moments for the political and
economic advantage of their clients. According to the FBI, Love's campaign
has worked closely with one of these unscrupulous firms.

Your misgivings about L. Victor Love, therefore, are perfectly valid, and
the *D* beside his name seems to lead liberal voters into a perilous cozenage.
One thing we've learned about dangerous men is that it's usually *how* they
are dangerous that surprises, and Love remains the down card in the poker
game. There is a fear and anger beneath the surface of every society, and
certainly every empire, waiting to be activated. The years of the Covid-19
pandemic, economic decline, increasing inequality, news of the plutocratic
class gorging itself on the commonweal, widespread addiction, extreme
weather events, and psychological despair have, I fear, primed the body
politic to accept radical interventions. L. Victor Love, I fear, may prove the
lesser evil as figures like Jennifer Braden become increasingly attractive candidates to a lost and desperate citizenry.

This brings me, finally, to a confidential meeting I had in a nondescript
virtual worlde. What I'm about to share with you I do so in confidence, and
I trust that you will in fact destroy this document upon reading it. For the
sake of plausible deniability, I will employ pseudonyms, though these will
likely prove transparent, as I find it difficult not to editorialize about these
personalities and the dangerous position they have put me in.

/ /

On September 29 of this dreadful year, Ned Stark contacted me with directions for how to access an encrypted Slapdish worlde, one in which it

would be safe for the assembled to lower our anonymizing avatars and sit face-to-face. Rarely have I encountered such a catastrophizing personality as Ned Stark. He'd called me once, panicked and begging for the use of a government plane to get him to Los Angeles in the midst of the El Demonio-Los Angeles Complex Fire. I obliged only because his child was apparently trapped in the city. I thought I'd never hear from him again. That he found and saved her—the odds were simply unrealistic. He thanked me awkwardly in a handwritten letter.

Rather than risk Seth coming home, I drove to a parking lot in Rock Creek Park, set the kinetic sensor on the dashboard to capture my movements, and lowered my headset over my eyes. After booting up, I entered my avatar through the anonymizing app, bouncing my IP address across the globe, and then input the code for the portal to the Slapdish worlde. I found myself sitting on a windswept cliff, supposedly seaside rural Ireland, a boiling red sun setting on the horizon. Sitting in a rough circle, from my left, were Ned Stark; Sigourney Weaver as Ellen Ripley from the *Alien* films, her flamethrower sizzling by her side; a cartoon version of Donald Trump as Donald Duck with no pants and ketchup stains all over his shirt and tie; Julia Roberts as Erin Brockovich; Michael Madsen as Mr. Blonde from the Quentin Tarantino film *Reservoir Dogs*; and, suspiciously, the wheelchair-bound Slapdish comedienne Henny. Of course, I was still Shane Battier. We all stared at one another for a moment. Donald Duck Trump let loose a burst of wild-horse laughter and said:

"I never use this shit—God, this is so stupid!"

"VR revolution, here we come," said Ned Stark. "It'll change everything, they said."

"Your avatar is deeply disturbing," said Mr. Blonde to Donald Duck Trump, whose avatar featured not just the cartoon beak under the infamous blond nest of hair but also splotchy and prolifically diseased genitals. A micro-penis and testicles flopping all too realistically.

"Are we safe to take these down?" Ellen Ripley scratched her face and the whole flamethrower appeared to wag at her nose.

"Oh my God, please," said Henny. One by one, we lowered our avatars, though I will continue using most of the pseudonyms here. It turned out I knew all these people.

Ned Stark I've already described as much as I dare. Ellen Ripley turned out to be a man I knew quite well from the legislative battles of 2028–2030, and with whom I used to trek to a slushie cart near Capitol Hill and muse in the summer's hottest days. We were collegial, if not friends. Donald Duck Trump was his partner, a woman with whom you're intimately familiar from her years in the limelight. Erin Brockovich and Mr. Blonde were part of the same organization, though I knew Erin Brockovich to have quit after Donald Duck Trump's dismissal. Finally, Henny's rabid visage dissolved into the face of Seth Young, my partner and cohabitant.

Laughing, Ned Stark said: "This cloak-and-dagger shit isn't for the chickenhearted, huh?"

Others were laughing as well. I was not. I glared at Seth, who gave me an uncertain smile. I'd seen a similar smile in 2030 when he flew Haniya and Peter down for my birthday to surprise me. He was not thrown by my presence now, which meant he'd known I would be here. He was somehow a part of this. Whatever *this* was. It was difficult to tell what his face contained, though, because no matter how advanced the graphics become, virtual reality remains enmeshed in the uncanny valley, human faces mimicking the tics of flesh but never arriving there completely.

There was no mistaking the joyful expression of Donald Duck Trump. "A real-life Wild Bunch we've assembled here, amiright?"

We had a prior relationship, Donald Duck Trump and I, less amicable than these others. I found her an irritation and a distraction, adept at procuring media coverage but with no scientific background and little interest in legislative processes. We'd argued on several occasions during the drafting of PRIRA because she seemed born of her own peculiar and mutinous logic.

Only Mr. Blonde looked as suspicious and disconcerted as I felt, and I was relieved when he spoke up, using Donald Duck Trump's real name: "[Donald Duck Trump], maybe you want to tell us what we're all doing here. [Erin Brockovich] jerks me around for six months, and this shit is not what I agreed to."

Said Donald Duck Trump: "Can't we just enjoy the surreality a second, man? We're in the future!"

"There's nothing to enjoy," Mr. Blonde retorted. "I'm lying to the woman I love to be here. Now get to the fucking point."

The laughter in the VR worlde faded. Though I had a distaste for Mr. Blonde during the battle over the legislation, I felt buoyed by his no-nonsense demand. Sounds of wind and water crashing against the cliffs below filled my ears, yet everyone's hair remained still. Donald Duck Trump nodded and said:

"That's fair. Let's do it like this then: I'll explain what we're up to, then we can decide if we're all mad cultists about to drink poison together." She smiled and reached a hand into her head of hair and gave a quick, thoughtful scratch. Ellen Ripley chewed his nails and spit the shards out with the tip of his tongue. He looked unhappy. She went on. "We sitting here are the wreckage of PRIRA. Or PRIRA's mutation and passage as this draconian Patriot Act we're all seeing now. I don't need to tell any of you about the tipping points we're blowing past. Arctic sea ice loss, coral bleaching, the city of Los Angeles burns to the ground and no one bats an eye. A cyclone turns Mumbai into a water-logged graveyard and it's still business as usual. The entire eastern half of the US, from Iowa to New York, is inundated. Thousands killed, billions in property damage, a homelessness crisis in every city, another economic downturn, and what are we all looking at? A presidential race practically rigged for a guy bought and paid for by the carbon lobby.

"A decade of work, we line it all up, we have a bill sitting there at the fucking doorstep of passage, and then the whole thing goes up in flames faster than Hollywood." She shook her head in theatrical sorrow. "Global emissions have yet to peak. One and a half degrees is already here, according to most measurements. Two degrees is a guarantee, no matter what we do. Is three even avoidable anymore? Shit, I don't need to preach. And maybe this is our fault. We didn't understand how hard they would fight, who they would finance, what kinds of strings they would pull to hold on to power. Hell, they're basically feeding guns and money to an internal rebellion of white nationalists and calling on them to guard their infrastructure. So. We need to do something. And we need to do something drastic."

She nodded to Erin Brockovich, who made a few keyboard motions with her fingers and a hologram appeared in the center of our circle, a few feet above the lazily whipping digital grass. It was the pop singer Zeden. I did not understand.

"For the past couple years, I've been thinking about all that old bullshit of why I'm doing this and how can I possibly give up, and boy, do I want to give up. Feeling sorry for myself a lot. And it occurred to me, one of the primary things that has kept people from understanding the danger of what's going on is that we're all isolated, right? So we need to create radical solidarity. People are yearning to get back in the game, for some kind of path to participatory action. So we're going to give it to them. All at once—"

Interrupted Mr. Blonde: "I'm sorry. Not that I don't love your pontification—really brings me back to the old days—but I'd love to know, straightforward as a fucking spear to the eye, what the fuck is going on."

Mr. Blonde was making motions with his hands, and I recognized this as his habit of chewing tobacco. I'd seen him twist open many a can of Copenhagen Long Cut Straight in front of legislators who found it disgusting. He now took a pinch into his mouth.

I spoke up then: "I would second this sentiment."

"He speaks," said Seth. I ignored him.

Said Donald Duck Trump: "It's pretty simple, really. [Erin Brockovich] and I have an idea, and we need a few trustworthy people to pull it all off. That's why you are all here. For over a year, we talked about who else we wanted to bring in on the ground floor. The seven people here represent the ground floor."

My frustration swelled: "Pull what off?"

Donald Duck Trump did not look at me. Instead, she looked at her partner and put her hand on his knee. "It's like Patti Smith says: 'When you hit a wall, just kick it in.'"

The hologram changed. I admit, I'd always thought of Donald Duck Trump as something of a lightweight besotted with her own popularity, appetite burning for historic importance, sated only by headlines and pundits proclaiming such. I'd expressed this sentiment to Seth on more than one occasion, and here he was running off behind my back to join her. As soon as I understood what she wanted to do, I understood why Seth had been recruited, and a mauve-tinted darkness filled me. And here is where I must elide my account of this meeting. What was displayed in that hologram and what Donald Duck Trump and Erin Brockovich went on to describe seems both fanciful enough that you need not concern yourself with the details and dangerous enough that, were I to include it here, it could put your political career at grave risk. Your plausible deniability, Congresswoman, will remain the operative principle going forward in this account.

After the nearly thirty-minute presentation and explanation, I felt the four of them looking at Mr. Blonde, Ned Stark, and myself because, clearly, we hadn't been included in whatever previous scheming had occurred. Ellen Ripley and Seth had been privy to at least part of this information.

We were now expected to swallow this grenade whole, so to speak. Donald Duck Trump said:

"This is normally the part where you tell us what you think."

Mr. Blonde was the first to respond. "Are you two fucking crazy?" His gaze traded between Donald Duck Trump and Erin Brockovich. "You're going to start a war, you assholes." He pointed at Ned Stark accusingly: "Why isn't your daughter here? Why haven't you brought her in on this lunatic plan?"

Ned Stark sat with his legs crossed and his pant leg riding up to reveal one sock, all the elasticity gone, drooping low on a varicosed ankle. He bobbed his liver-spotted head: "Well. I don't want her involved in this."

Mr. Blonde grinned enormously. "Right. Exactly. Because this is fucking insane."

Erin Brockovich glared at her former coworker, tight-lipped. Her hands remained calmly folded on her lap as she said: "Like the lady says, we've got a plan. It's only crazy if they expect it. They won't be ready for a stunt like this."

Ellen Ripley spoke up for the first time: "'Stunt' is not the word I'd use. We could all go to prison."

Donald Duck Trump had not taken her hand from his knee: "And we're thinking ahead to that too."

Seth, perched forward in concentration, targeted Donald Duck Trump with his pool-blue eyes: "This is a lot riskier than what you first outlined to me. But it's not impossible. I'd be willing to consult, work through some of the pragmatic questions. This app you're talking about—it sounds somewhat chimerical."

Erin Brockovich laughed: "Chimerical? No, I don't think so."

We waited for more, and when she didn't volunteer anything further, Seth said: "Perhaps you could elaborate."

"All the technology has existed dating back to like 2010. Did you ever use a dating app before you met Ashir? Ever use Grindr? That's more or less what this is, just, you know, focused on different goals. Do you understand satellites?"

"Forget the fucking app," said Mr. Blonde. "How am I supposed to not tell [name redacted] and [name redacted] and everyone else? Do you get the position you've put me in with this, [Donald Duck Trump]?"

Ned Stark said to Mr. Blonde: "Son, you guys long ago stopped working for the cause. You're kidding yourself if you think getting in bed with the Sustainable Future Coalition was anything but a castration."

"Fuck yourself, asshole."

And then it was all so much cross talk, the sound I most abhor, and I knew I had begun tapping my fingers in the air, this childish tic I could never eschew, but the noise was simply so awful: Ned Stark and Mr. Blonde shouting at each other while Erin Brockovich accused Seth of not understanding satellites, and Donald Duck Trump trying to calm everyone with a voice like the noise a car makes when it skids through gravel.

Finally, Ellen Ripley muttered something low and fast, Donald Duck Trump the only intended audience, though I overheard. He said: "I almost want it to be too late to do anything. That way you'll just stop." With that, he pulled the VR set from his head. His entire body dissolved like pixelated ash into the verdant grass of an Irish cliffside, none of it carried by the wind. They all stopped arguing. Donald Duck Trump seemed unsurprised that he had stormed out of the worlde.

Ned Stark appeared unperturbed by the departure. "I'll say now what I said back when you two approached me: If you think this could work, I'll be there. Whatever I can bring to this."

Donald Duck Trump nodded and her eyes moved to Seth. He looked at me, but not to ask for my permission. He said: "Of course, I'm in. However I can help."

Then she looked at Mr. Blonde, who still sat with his arms folded over a swollen chest, gnashing the tobacco like a predator masticating tough game. "You've put me in a real fucking spot here."

She said: "I know, [Mr. Blonde]. You promised us [Ellen Ripley and Erin Brockovich] you'd hear us out."

"Yeah, [Ellen Ripley] looks real fucking keen on this, doesn't he?"

"You also promised to keep this quiet. Even if you can't be a part of it."

Mr. Blonde reached to lift his headset off. "No, I can't be a part of it. Not by a fucking long shot."

And he too dissolved into gray pixels. The rest of them looked to me. I was not sorry to disappoint them. "You've put me in a very difficult position as well. Now that I have knowledge of this, you're asking me to essentially hide an action of great significance from the agencies I'm bound by law to work with. Protocol tells me I should report this."

"Goddamnit, Ash!"

Ned Stark stood and wagged his finger at me, only because he couldn't leap through space and actually stick it in my face, I suppose. His kinetic motion detector picked up the moist pepper of spittle fleeing his mouth: "You of all people, Ash. You of all goddamn people. You look right at the models. Right at 'em! How can you turn your back on this?"

I nodded to the assembled. "They're fantasists."

"Sure they are! But people like you and me, we've been sorely lacking in imagination for a long time."

He paced away, then back, then away again, making a series of motions. He pulled a pack of cigarettes from the breast pocket of his jacket. He stuck one in his mouth and then just as quickly pulled it back out and reinserted it in the pack, like he'd been rewound.

I continued calmly. "Furthermore, I have great skepticism regarding the logistical components of this plan. It requires a vast number of interlocking features." I nodded to Erin Brockovich with what I hoped was appropriate scorn. "An untested app notwithstanding."

Ned Stark returned to his seat, though his lips maintained an angry and contemptuous moue.

Donald Duck Trump spoke softly. "Ash, I hear what you're saying. I'm begging you, though, if you can't be a part of this, stay silent. Give us a chance. Brave people are going to put themselves on the line."

Seth watched me, and I pretended to consider this. I allowed enough time to make it appear as though I was wrestling with the decision, though I already knew precisely what course I would take. "Seeing as how you've involved my partner, you've ensured that I won't betray your confidence. That was clever."

With that, I became the third person to remove my headset.

Outside my windshield, a misting rain was falling. I sat blinking for a while, adjusting to a gray light that now seemed foreign, like another man's private worlde.

At home, I found Seth waiting for me. We each stood there for a moment in the home we'd made together, as in the final showdown of an old Western. I said: "You're a surprisingly adept liar."

"I wasn't sure if I wanted to involve you in this. Then I knew I had to."

I believed him. Or at least believed that he believed this. Carrying secrets in a relationship is a complicated thing. One must convince himself that he is telling his partner the truth in the moment, as when I first allowed

Seth to believe there was a possibility I would want a child with him, when I knew that I did not. One convinces himself to allow for a gray area in which the truth is mutable. I told him I was going to my study.

"Stay. We have more to talk about, Ash." He said it quite gently.

I knew Seth would get his way, on our child and on this thing a group of vapid activists was asking. I was powerless to deny him, my affection simply too uncompromising. I did not let him touch me, though. I left him alone in our expensive condominium and went back out into the one true world where the drizzle still fell.

Conclusion: The global order cries out for a hegemon. Cities of the developing world swell with peoples trudging out of the drought-stricken dust bowls of North Africa and the Middle East and the swamped lowlands of Asia. Europe's militarization of the Mediterranean continues. Dwindling harvests in Central and South America as well as cyclonic activity in the Caribbean have created the same conundrum in our hemisphere. The fear of refugees arrives before they do, and a supranational nexus of right-wing xenophobia grows. Small groups of individuals are able to forge enormous social and political chaos through relatively small acts of violence, and the dispossessed and discarded internal and external proletariat will breed new and more vicious insurgencies. The problem with insurgents, however, is that unlike Donald Duck Trump and her crew of naive left-wing warriors, they tend not to bother with comprehensive governing philosophies. They simply want to make others feel their disillusionment. History demonstrates that the most powerful empires, in the end, turn out to be surprisingly fragile. With its expansive coastlines and fire exposure in the west, multiple studies have concluded that the North American continent is in fact extremely vulnerable to climate chaos. We see environmental calamity manifesting in the fracture of our political system, which over the course of the last thirty years has responded to increasingly frequent institutional crises with escalating degrees of gridlock and mismanagement. When I write of my mauve dread, the slice of the color spectrum that has followed me my entire life, I perhaps speak of what I long intuited before I even had the mathematics to explain it: A new dark age brims on the horizon. Religious fanaticism, ethnic factionalism, and political extremism will engulf the planet, and the pillage of the natural world will indeed accelerate as the elite make one last futile attempt to gather as much capital as possible in an effort to wall themselves off from the inevitable. Perhaps this is why I remain funereal about the coming election. Civilization's abrupt retreat will be marked the world over by every flavor of warring chief in crisp, elegantly tailored suits murdering to obtain power in the hope that they might rule this barbaric and alien age.

Book IV

NATION
OF HEAT

6 DEGREES IS COMING

2033

*S*hane had felt this combination of exhaustion and fear only once before, during Islali's birth. Echoes of that ten-hour ordeal, and the postpartum darkness that followed, seemed to vibrate within her as her plane touched down in Charlotte. She exited to Gate B15, feeling like she wanted to collapse onto the grimy carpet. Every nerve ending humming with the dread. She wondered when she would ever get sleep again.

Quinn met her in short-term parking and handed her glasses and a face mask for all the cameras they'd pass on the way. Shane pushed her greasy hair back and slipped on the FaceRec-disrupting lenses.

"We'll be picking up one more," said Quinn after they pulled out of range of the airport.

"Who?"

"Jansi."

Shane stared at blondie for a moment. Quinn wore a light purple cashmere sweater and had her hair carefully parted in the center. She wore a diamond engagement ring because, as she'd explained via the code, she'd decided to further her cover and their aims by marrying the CTO of her company. Quinn, of course, anticipated Shane's reaction to the news they'd be picking up Jansi.

"You're good, Shane. I didn't find her. She found me. We've been in contact for a year now."

Shane ignored that her back channel with Quinn was not the only one,

> **GET ON A FLIGHT** *As soon as you can. Don't contact anyone else.* Quinn found Shane's message in a multiplayer VR game where she and Shane had set up a dead drop after the last meeting in Wisconsin. They'd decided to open their own line of communication. So here they were. Smashing protocol in an emergency. Taking back control. Quinn had told her fiancé a friend back home had been in a car accident.

ignored the danger of their organization developing clandestine pockets within itself. "And Jansi knows the situation?"

"I had to bring her in."

"Okay," said Shane, nodding. "I'm not angry. That's good."

As they waded through traffic, she noticed that Quinn was wearing a boot on her left foot. She asked what happened. "I broke it a week ago getting out of the goddamn shower. Just another indignity of being a woman and getting old." She thunked the boot against the side of the door.

As she and Quinn cobbled their plans together, she'd scrambled to find Lali a sitter at the last second. Obviously, she couldn't go to Kai, so Teddy it was. His moon-face looked perfectly credulous as she explained that she had a cousin who'd been in a head-on collision and she needed to go home to Austin for a few days. Teddy was eager for any morsel of her trust after she'd put a stop to their infrequent sex. She'd dropped Lali off that afternoon, her girl crying and begging to go with her even as Teddy promised she could play VR with his boys. Then Shane rushed to the airport on no sleep, barely making the flight, too keyed up on adrenaline to nap.

"This could be the end of it," said Quinn. Then she smacked the steering wheel and shrieked, the sound piercing in the close confines of the car. It made the hairs on Shane's arms stand on end.

"We don't know that," said Shane.

Quinn only shook her head, furious. "Don't kid yourself, Shane. Of course we do."

―――――――

They drove into the descending fire of the sunset, keeping an eye out for speed trap drones, though the act of piloting a vehicle would soon become conspicuous itself. Because the car was neutered, they had to drive in analog mode. They fled over nondescript highway and past the standard fast-food and gas station carnival that appeared to Americans as familiarity and homecoming, as if interstate sprawl was the natural state, and what one thought of as nature was nothing more than a curiosity, a relic of a time before civilization advanced to the state of a Whopper Value Meal.

Quinn looked at the battery gauge. "We need a charge."

Shane hadn't eaten anything that day and purchased a nutrition bar for an unbelievable $17 while Quinn got coffee and a full charge for the car. They sat outside at a picnic table waiting on the battery, watching the sun disappear and feeling a mild brush of winter air descend. That gust of cold air reminded her of what she'd been dwelling on all day: the time she'd taken Lali, as a newborn, to a taqueria off the highway.

Then she and Quinn were back on the road, through the last remains of daylight, quiet except for the buzz of pop radio. Quinn took an exit, traveling down a state two-lane until they reached a dark turnoff for some meager Carolina town. She pulled into an alley, and it felt as though she barely stopped the car. The locks unbolted, the rear passenger door popped open, and Jansi darted inside, tossing a pack onto the seat and slamming the door closed in one swift motion. Then Quinn was driving again.

"Howdy," said Jansi, jamming her overlong body into the front to hug Shane. Long, bony, and horse-faced, Jansi wore a green fatigue cap tucked low over her brow. She had overlapping teeth and dry black hair, split at the ends. Big brutish moles protruded all over a ghost-white neck. "Oh my god, girl, I can't believe we're here!" Jansi squealed to Shane, as if this were a vacation. Like they were on their way to a bachelorette party. They hadn't seen each other since the Second Cell went operational in '28.

"You opened a line of contact with Quinn," Shane groused. "Outside of Second." But her voice only sounded childish and petulant to her own ears. *Guys, that's not how we're supposed to play the game! You're not doing it right!*

"Special circumstances," said Jansi too brightly. "And not to be a bitch about it, but it's not my cell that's the reason we're in this mess."

Shane bit her tongue and went back to looking out the window. Jansi then proceeded to talk for the next hour, almost without taking a breath, as if she really were catching up with long-lost friends—friends who badly wanted a disquisition on the state of contemporary American politics. Had Jansi always been this platitudinous? She sounded every bit the armchair revolutionary Shane had spent her whole adulthood abhorring, the reason she found Kai Ismael and Allen Ford in the first place. When Shane tried to shoot eyes at Quinn, she was surprised to see Quinn listening intently.

Jansi droned on as Quinn took the final exit, and they wound their way into the back roads near Clemson, out past a town called Tamassee. They pulled to the top of a long drive-way that led into a copse of trees, but

JANSI Was so excited to be with her comrades, to finally get off her chest what she thought of Vic Love and his new administration: "As if we didn't all see this coming! It's pathetic how fast the liberals swamped to a true fascist. The Dems finally take the Senate back, and they're ready to rubber-stamp anything! As long as he gives a speech from a corporate diversity training handbook. He's executing a textbook authoritarian takeover, and he's already got practice. His company's been privatizing the police force of every city in the country for the last decade. And now he's putting in Xuritas cronies at DOJ. Then the CIA and FBI will both be replaced by loyalists. And we're the ones who saw all this coming, right? And laid infrastructure for resistance, you know? And Vic Love knows it!"

just beyond those woods she could see the lights of a house, the edges of a farm stretching into the blue-black light. Quinn produced an old-fashioned burner cell from the glove compartment. She dialed, waited.

"Hi," Quinn said robotically. "It's your former student Erica. I'm here with a couple friends, and we were wondering if you could come out tonight. Have a beer and catch up."

The three of them sat in the silence of the car. Waited.

Quinn nodded. "That's right. Outside. At the top of your driveway. We wanted to talk. About your plans for the future." And they waited, just the hum of their hats, the faintest internal whine from the EV's drivetrain, and a tinny sound from the speaker of the old phone pressed hard to Quinn's ear. She said, "I understand, but this is an emergency. We received extremely distressing news, and we need to discuss it." Another pause. "Okay, that works. Okay. Okay, perfect." She hung up, turned to Jansi and Shane. "He's home alone. We can talk in the house." They stared back at her. "He said his dog is sick and he doesn't want to leave him alone."

"No way," said Shane. "Who knows what he's got in there that's internet-connected? TV, VR, glasses, oven—hell, his whole house could see us walking in—"

HOW THIS WOULD GO Jansi did not like the tension filling the car. She did not like the way Shane and Quinn felt to be on a different page from her. In war, one had to be decisive or risk losing everything. They were arguing about every little point. Action, action, action. Keep moving. Be decisive!

"It's fine," Jansi cut her off. The clipped way she said this, as if biting off the tip of her own tongue, caught Shane off-guard. Her face cloaked by shadows and the brim of her hat, Jansi put a hand on Quinn's shoulder and then pointed forward, urging her on.

They drove down through the acre of woods to the farmhouse, a pleasant two-story with bright track lighting spilling through the windows, a rusted basketball hoop over the garage, a dingy box truck parked perpendicular to the house with Ford Custom Furnishing stenciled on the side, and a John Deere tractor beside that. Quinn asked for her backpack and pulled from it a large brick with an antenna—a battery-powered jammer, she explained. It would send multiple frequencies to nearby cell towers and ensure their conversation was private and uninterrupted. The three of them exited the car into a wind shivering the branches overhead. Quinn thumped her boot along in a half-limp. She rang the doorbell.

"Hello, hello!" The woman who answered the door had such merry

OPSEC Quinn felt her hand shaking as she switched on the jammer. Shane was right; they didn't know what they were walking into. New speech recognition tech could place a voice to a name with startling accuracy. Stingrays could trick your phone into transmitting data without you knowing. Don't even whisper near a coffeepot was the best advice. She felt nauseous. She felt exhilarated. She'd waited until the others had left the car to draw one last item from her pack.

eyes, a smile so big, and a southern drawl so thick, Shane forgot where she was or why she was there. Like she'd blinked herself onto a sitcom. Allen Ford's wife reached for her first and wrapped her in a hug. "I'm Emmy! It's so good to meet y'all!" She hugged Quinn next, who managed to look not the least befuddled. "So y'all just showed up at the door hoping Allen would feed you? Not surprising." She hugged Jansi, and now Shane saw Allen behind his wife in the entranceway, hands in pockets, looking like an old sheepish mouse. He wore a beat-up ballcap that read KIAWAH ISLAND, loose pink scalp tucked inside.

"This is my fault," he aw-shucksed. "You said you might stop through tonight on your way up from Florida, and I just totally blanked on telling the one person I was supposed to inform."

"What they don't tell you about getting old," said Emmy, ushering them in, "is that it all goes—everything! Your memory, your back, and most of all, telling your wife a bunch of pretty former students are dropping by for dinner. Lucky we got plenty to eat, and I'm no jealous type! Honey, what'd you do to the leg?"

Quinn thumped into the living room where the television was turned up to an unfathomable volume. "Speaking of getting old. I fell getting out of the shower. Stupid. Probably osteoporosis catching me early."

"Shut it," said Emmy. "You're too young for that nonsense."

"So," said Allen, gesturing toward Quinn. "This is Erica. And I may have told you about this young lady, Abigail." He looked at Shane, his gaze fond, and Shane smiled weakly. She tugged at the dirty hoodie she'd thrown on before leaving her house and felt gross and underdressed even though that didn't matter. "One of my favorite students in all my years of teaching."

"So nice to finally meet you," Shane said to Emmy, trying to remember *Abigail, Abigail, Abigail.* "Allen talked about you all the time."

"Please. He probably came to class without his wedding ring on." She stretched her neck to peck her husband on the cheek while Allen studied Jansi.

"And I don't believe I know your friend," he said.

Jansi extended her hand to him. "Hi. Jansi. I'm sure— What was it, Erica? I'm sure Erica mentioned me before." Shane's stomach was a coiled rattlesnake, and she could see the wave of horror pass over Allen's face. Jansi was beaming a wide and playful mouth of crooked teeth, like this was all a joke. Even Quinn looked shocked by the brazen "Erica" comment. Emmy, however, appeared not to notice.

"I'm so sorry, I have this garbage too loud. Sony!" she hollered. "Lower volume to five!" The MSNBC pundits' voices dwindled and the debate about the newly inaugurated administration's first bill fell to a whisper.

She led them to the kitchen table, and as Shane passed through the spacious living room, shelves loaded down with books until the wood sagged, the couches and blankets filthy with dog hair, her eye landed on the picture facing out from an end table. The whole family. Allen, squinting a smile with his hands on the shoulders of a mischievous little boy, Emmy holding on to a teenage girl whose braces looked painful both physically and reputationally. Two more boys and another girl. She could almost remember the names. Jake, Anna, Zack, Perry, and . . . the name of the younger girl escaped her. They sat at the kitchen table, and Emmy fretted that if she'd had some advance warning she would've cooked more, and maybe she could order a pizza—if she did so now, it would be on the table in no more than forty-five minutes.

"Not necessary," said Jansi. "We already ate."

"Well, now how far are you girls driving?" asked Emmy.

"I told you, Em, they're heading to Maryland."

"And y'all live in Tallahassee? Isn't this outta your ways a bit?"

Trying to concoct this cover story on the fly had not been the best approach. Only now did Shane wonder why Allen had told Quinn he was alone. She watched him beside her at the table, and his parched eyes darted to her, communicating something she couldn't decipher, and then gazed back over at his wife.

"I just haven't seen Professor Ford in a few years," said Shane. "I figured it wasn't that far."

Emmy seemed satisfied with this and reached into the oven with two mitts to pull out a vegan pot roast, which she placed

ALLEN Tried to catch Shane's eye. He could see Quinn doing something this reckless, just showing up at his house without warning to prove a point. He wondered how careful they'd been. Although it wouldn't matter to him soon, they risked dragging Emmy into this. He wanted to pull Shane aside as soon as possible. He knew this could not have been her idea.

on the table and explained that this recipe was about a century old, passed down from a great-grandmother, upgraded with synthesized plant protein, and they all had to have at least a taste. "Should we go get our sick one?" Emmy asked about the dog.

"Nah, let him rest. He'll smell it and come down," said Allen.

"Girls, Allen, take off your hats," said Emmy. "You're at a dinner table. Relax and stay a minute."

They did as told. Jansi and Quinn kept exchanging furtive glances, trying to communicate with only their eyes. Emmy went on talking about a coyote that was harassing their chickens, and Shane wished she could be alone with Allen to talk. Finally, Jansi cleared her throat.

"Mrs. Ford, I was wondering . . ."

"Honey, please. Emmy."

"Emmy, I was wondering if you'd be willing to give me a quick tour of the farm. Before dinner."

Emmy licked pot roast broth off her fingers. "Now? No, it's dark. We're about to eat."

> **EMMY** Tried to signal her husband with a quick, flirty look, *Which one of them is it? Surely it couldn't be all three!* But she knew Allen well enough after forty years to see when he was tense. He was a ball of tension now. She sent him a quick text under the table telling him to relax but the stupid thing didn't go through. Most of that forty years they'd been open, but typically the old horndog went for men during his extracurriculars. She figured that was half the reason he started his little woodworking business. He was staring at the quiet Latina. She was chunky and past pretty, but Emmy could see it from days gone by. She began to try another text, *If you and señorita want some alone time. . . .* But something about his face stopped her, and she deleted it.

Jansi put a hand on Emmy's arm. "You know, the roast has to cool, so we have a minute. Why don't we give these three a chance to catch up, and you show me the chickens real quick? I'm from a farming family myself, so maybe I could even give you a bit of advice on the coyote."

This sounded absurd to Shane, and, from the looks of it, Emmy. Jansi looked like she'd be more at home in a lit class at Sarah Lawrence than a farm.

"Like are you using chicken wire on your coop?" Jansi continued. "Even raccoons can get through that. You need wire mesh."

Emmy's southern hospitality slipped a bit. "Of course we use wire mesh."

"Hon, yeah, why not?" Allen said suddenly. "Go give her a quick look—they drove all this way. I'm sure these two have stories from all their, their, their . . ." Shane didn't think he'd be able to finish whatever unwieldy lie he was concocting on the spot. "Their travels."

Clearly Emmy Ford knew something else was going on here. And yet she went with it. Sometimes the urge to remain polite trumped all else.

"Sure, why not," said Emmy. "A quick tour of the chickens, then we eat. Okay?"

"Sounds good," said Jansi, standing and zipping her hoodie. "Let's get a look at these suckers."

Shane, Quinn, and Allen waited while Emmy threw on a light jacket, grabbed a flashlight, and she and Jansi went through the sliding glass door in the back, Emmy warning, "The dog was shitting everywhere in the yard before we took him in, so watch your step."

Jansi slid the door shut behind her, and the motion sensor light outside illuminated the two women walking into the gloom. When they were far enough away, Allen said, "Emmy's wonderful. This year is number thirty-eight together, you know that? Two more till our ruby year."

NEW ORLEANS When Allen met this young lady—not yet "Shane"—she'd been more than a good chat. As a teacher, you learn who the sharp ones are very quickly. It hadn't hurt that she was pretty, of course, but this was not a concern. She was also extremely guarded, never said much about her people, though she alluded that she was from the Gulf. Allen had liked her right way and grew to trust her instincts implicitly. Even when she steered wrong, as she had in Wisconsin, he had nothing but faith in her.

"What were you thinking, Allen?" Quinn held the napkin ring. She'd placed the cloth on her lap, and now she slipped the metal band over the knuckle of an index finger. "You send us that message, and what do you want us to do?"

"Well," he said, calmly. "I didn't expect you to show up at my front door unannounced, I'll say that."

"You didn't leave us much choice."

"You should've contacted me first. Via the code. You've put everything in danger by coming here."

"No," said Quinn, slapping the napkin ring down on the table. "Goddamnit, we're not putting anything in danger. *You are.* You are, Allen."

Allen's communiqué had arrived in her mailbox the evening before, and Shane had sat in her car outside the fishing cabin in Tonganoxie decoding it. Stunned, she rushed home to contact Quinn through their VR dead drop and was nearly an hour late picking up Lali from daycare.

"It's like I said, we were sloppy, and two men are dead because of it," said Allen. Shane stared at the lacquered surface and all the dark knots in the amber grain. Surely Allen had built this himself. "Both men were fathers and husbands. When we started this, I did so with the understanding—and the promise to myself—that we would never hurt anyone. Not a single human life would be lost as a result of our actions. And for a long time, we were successful."

"We apologized for it, Allen. It was a mistake," said Quinn.

"It was," he agreed, nodding his head sadly. Allen folded his arms and looked down at his sleeves, a weariness on his face that made Shane want to tell him she was sorry. "And I didn't mean to alarm any of you. But what happened in Anacortes, that was us. We did that. An apology isn't enough. Not nearly." He swallowed. "It's not just about our principles as a resistance. It's about my conscience. I contributed to those men's deaths. I'm not asking any of you . . ." He reached out and put his hand on Shane's. It felt rough and callused and old. "Or Murdock or Kai or anyone else to take responsibility. You should keep going. But I need to make amends for what happened. You see what I'm trying to do? We have to prove we're different. Our resistance is about *peace*. We believe in something because it is *just* and because it is *right*."

"And you prove that by turning yourself in?" Quinn demanded.

"By turning myself in. That's right."

The three of them sat in silence for a moment, and they could hear how

> **SLEEP IN THE RAIN** That summer in New Orleans there'd been one quiet moment when Kai wasn't around. When he was alone with Shane and she mentioned her time in foster homes and then group residences for teenagers. Where were her parents? he'd asked. And she said, very bravely, he thought, "I had to learn fast how to make my own way. Now I know how to sleep in the rain." He never forgot the way she put that. *Now I know how to sleep in the rain.*

old the house was, creaks and sighs in the walls and floorboards. Allen continued to hold her hand. Finally, Shane spoke up.

"There has to be another way, Allen. We can make amends another way."

"No. There's no other way," he said, almost mourning his certitude. "If I don't do this, we're betraying what we stand for. Those families went to funerals for people they loved. Someone has to come out of the shadows and own up to this." He palmed the skin at the top of his scalp, pulled it tight and then released it back to wrinkles. "We have to remember why we're doing this in the first place. If we want to start a movement that cannot die, we need to hold ourselves to a higher standard. We need to be a light that shows the way, not just another set of sociopaths murdering people indiscriminately."

"And it'll mean the end of us. 6Degrees." Quinn said their full name, the one they'd agreed on in the cabin nearly twenty years ago. "Everything we worked for, everyone we've inspired—it'll all be gone."

"No, it won't. You all can carry on. I will not give you up."

"You don't know that." Quinn slammed her hand against the table again. "Have you ever dealt with the FBI? Or a federal prosecutor? I have! And they are relentless. They'll go after your wife. They'll go after your kids. If any of them have so much as a parking ticket—"

"My family will be fine," he said.

"And maybe worse," added Shane. Quinn's anger was not getting through. She brought her other palm to Allen's hand and squeezed it. She found his eyes. "The gloves are coming off, Allen. That's what Vic Love and the new Congress have in common."

"Have you ever thought of what it's like to be kept awake for three days straight with music blaring or dogs barking?" Quinn asked. "Maybe they stick you soaking wet in a cold cell and let you nearly freeze to death over and over again."

Shane ignored her. "Don't you see, Allen?" She thought of walking with him along the Port of New Orleans, clouds rolling in over the Crescent City Connection. She thought of crying into his shoulder in that frigid Wisconsin winter. "We *are* terrorists. Never forget that. They will find a way to undo you. And you'll tell yourself you can't stand it anymore. And then you'll talk. And everything we've worked for will be gone."

He squeezed her hand. "You're confusing your own fear with mine, Shane. And I don't blame you. But I'm not asking any of you to follow my lead. Like I said, I'm doing what my conscience demands. Nothing more. So I suggest you call my wife and your friend back in here, and we eat dinner, and then you all get on your way. The only people who've put you in danger here is yourselves by ignoring protocol."

"It's too late for that, Allen."

Quinn stood and reached behind her, fumbling with something. It caught in the loose fabric of her cashmere sweater. When she removed the gun and held it at her side, Shane felt something so familiar. It was what she felt when she was driving away from the taqueria those many years ago, the back seat empty. Some sensations you never forget. The feel of the anti-spiritual. Of a bitter abyss yawning.

"Jesus Christ," hissed Allen, jumping back in his chair. But he gripped Shane's hand harder. "What are you doing with that? Put that away. Christ, before Emmy comes back in here. Christ." She'd never seen him afraid before. He was crushing the bones in her hand.

"You did this, Allen," said Quinn, and her voice cracked. "Not us. You did this."

"I didn't do a goddamn thing," he barked. Spit foamed at the corners of his mouth, his body stock-still. "Get out of my house. Get out right now." Quinn didn't move. "Get the hell out. Shane"—his head snapped to her— "Shane, get her out of here before she hurts someone."

Had she known about the gun? Yes. No. Yes. Hard to say. She knew about it the way she knew when her mom began hiding bottles around the house. The way she'd known her heart would lead her to a place like this someday. As far back as distant relatives spinning romantic tales of resistances being led in the black cover of jungle, she'd been readying herself. Righteous paths always wind through darkness.

"Please," he said, already moving from anger to bargaining. "Please, just leave. It's over. You win. I won't— I won't do anything."

Quinn glared at him, blinking, licking a pink lip gloss.

"I'm sorry, Allen. We can't risk it."

She stepped forward, grabbed his sleek, clean scalp with one hand and stuffed the barrel of the pistol under his chin. Shane lost her grip on his palm as he tried to fight off Quinn, but in that moment his age showed, weak arms unable to fend off this younger woman's strength. He cried out, "No— Hold on— Wait!" And when she pulled the trigger, there was a *crack*—Allen's protestations cut off by the bark of the pistol. Fragments of his skull blew outward, one still attached to that bright pink scalp. Red-gray brain bursting and blood splattering. Skull and skin whipped up and then fell against Allen's ear and dangled, meat and fluid drizzling to the hardwood floor behind his chair. All she could think was that Quinn had almost shot her own hand off. When the woman pulled the trigger, Shane's whole body had contracted, and there was now a *before* and *after* that moment. She stared at that piece of scalp dangling against Allen's ear as he slumped forward, like he'd suddenly dozed off. She still had her palm cupped like she was holding his hand.

Then a scream from outside. *"Allen!"*

The motion light clicked on. Emmy stood just at the edge of the floodlight's beam. In the dark, of course, she would be able to see into the kitchen. She'd likely watched the whole thing. Shane stood up, but she wasn't sure why; her instinct was to go to Allen's wife and tell her everything was going to be okay, that they'd clean this up and everything would be fine. Then an arm emerged from the gloom behind Emmy and put a pistol to the back of her head. Emmy Ford's wail ceased as her face exploded in a stew of gore, and she buckled, first to her knees and then into the grass. Jansi lowered her gun. She stood bathed in the cheap white light, her eyes wide with disbelief and delight.

Shane sat down again because she felt dizzy. Nausea swelled as she gagged on memories barely bygone. She thought about going for the kitchen sink but what was the point? She put her head between her knees and tried to breathe, found herself dry-heaving, rancid burps popping, her stomach with its own plan, and even with her eyes squeezed shut she kept seeing it: that piece of skull bowing, distending, shredding free but still attached to the skin.

Jansi slid open the glass door and came back inside. Quinn put her hand on Shane's back, and she could feel the woman's hand trembling violently. It's okay, Quinn kept saying. They had a plan.

"They're down the road. Maybe five minutes out," Jansi told them, her eyes wide and thrilled. "Jewelry. Computers. Anything valuable."

Jansi bounded up the stairs. Quinn knelt in front of Shane, her black medical boot squeaking as it pivoted on the hardwood. She'd tucked the gun back in her jeans. Shane stared at her own arm and the tattoo she'd had inked the same summer she met Kai and Allen: **BUILD THE PATH.**

"This was his fault," said Quinn, swollen eyes pleading. "He told us he was here alone. You see what he did, right? He thought we wouldn't do anything. Once his wife saw our faces, he thought he'd be safe. We gave him a chance to keep her out of danger, but he invited us in."

Shane's mind was a white cloud, her ears drumming with blood. Her gaze moved across the kitchen, coming to rest on a bowl of sugar and the small silver spoon Emmy had placed in it like a shovel in soil. She nodded only because her muscles understood what Quinn's searching eyes wished to extract from her: reassurance that this had been the plan all along. Jansi came galloping down the stairs, a laptop and a jewelry box in hand.

"There's an old VR in the bedroom too."

Her big legs took the stairs two at a time and returned a moment later with a bulky headset and a violin in a case.

QUINN *This was the fucking plan!* she wanted to scream. *Why else did you tell me to get that overnight flight? Why else did you say we had to shut him down and stop this, no matter what?* But Shane looked like she might pass out, and there was no time for that. No time for regret or second-guessing. They had to move fast now. Things would change quickly. This was only step one.

Headlights washed over the windows as a car pulled into the drive. Shane hadn't moved. She kept taking quick glances at Allen, now fallen to the floor with blood collecting around his shattered head. His eyes bulged, frozen in awe and fear. What had her dad said? Just before he was gone and her mom was gone and she was left to pinball through the mercy and misery of foster care? *Fear is useless. You act in the moment, figure out what comes next, and get another mile down the road.* In her dad's estimation, fear conscripted your whole mind, rationalized irrational behavior, and the worst part was when people who were acting out of fear became adamant that they were not.

A man and woman came through the front door, both Black, both wearing gloves, booties, and carrying jugs of bleach. The man had long dreadlocks and a tattoo of a rose peeking from beneath the collar of his shirt, the woman had a military flattop fade and a broad, muscled back bulging from a tank top when she removed her jacket. Shane didn't know them. They were not Jansi's comrades from Second, which meant they were from Third Cell. The firewalls were crumbling. The two from Third Cell barely spoke a word. Jansi handed the woman the jewelry, violin, and laptop and then helped the man remove the main TV in the living room. He yanked the plug out of the wall just as The Pastor appeared, muted, raging above a chyron that read THE PASTOR SLAMS REPUBLICANS FOR ELECTION LOSS.

Quinn and the other two ransacked the house for valuables and began spray-painting swastikas and crucifixes on the walls. They emptied the silverware drawer into a pillowcase, pulled decorative plates from shelves and tossed them willy-nilly into a trash bag. The Third Cell woman looked at Shane, who still had yet to stand and help, and asked Jansi, "Is she going to be okay?"

"Yeah, she's fine. Just give her a minute."

After the house was disturbed, disassembled, and inked with radical right-wing threats, the man brought in a can of gasoline.

"Give us a head start," he said. "Then douse the place in bleach, light both bodies up, and drive. The rest should take care of itself."

> **THE FIRST TIME** Quinn knew only that the man's name was Marlon and the woman's name was Niana. They had been recruited with specific skill sets in mind. They were improving their army, growing stronger. This was all a part of that process, she told herself. And just beneath that sensation, a yawning terror. She would ask Kellan Murdock later if this was what it felt like the first time: terrifying and sickening and electrifying.

"I'll go with them," said Jansi. "Third Cell are my progeny, ya know? I'm a proud mama." She winked, and Shane wanted to scream.

Before they left, Jansi grabbed Quinn's arm and pulled her cheek to cheek. She whispered something fiercely, but Shane couldn't make out the words. Then the Third Cell operatives were gone, their unmarked van crunching over the gravel as it swung a U-turn and drove back up the long driveway. Quinn clunked over in her boot, knelt beside Shane, and put a hand on her knee. Shane looked over her shoulder at Emmy, lying out in the grass.

"We didn't have a choice. You know that."

Shane nodded.

"If he turned himself in, he would've given us all up eventually."

"I said I understand," she hissed, and then thumped a palm loudly off her chest. "You think I don't understand?" She found herself shouting, but she wasn't exactly sure why. "I'm the one, bitch. I fucking made this thing. You think I'd let Allen fuck us like that? *Ever?* But then you're bringing in the clown car, Quinn. I told you what he said in confidence. I told you we could take care of it, and you go and spill your guts across our entire organization. Now we have two bodies. Have you thought that this might be what gets us caught?"

"The fire will take care of it."

"They pull DNA out of fires, you fucking moron. Jesus Christ, and you were Ivy League? Arsonists get caught all the time. They have the DNA of the whole fucking country on file, and you bring in three extra fucking people like this is a club meeting, you stupid blond bitch."

"You need to keep your head," said Quinn, a tinge of desperation, her eyes watering.

"I have my fucking head straight, it's you and the—"

A thump from upstairs.

Both their heads snapped up. Shane stood slowly for the first time since Emmy had shown her to the seat. Quinn's welling eyes ceased, and she wiped her tears. They stared at the ceiling. A smatter of quick footsteps.

"The dog?" said Quinn.

Shane shook her head. "There's no dog. We would've seen it by now."

The backyard light blinked on, a grisly spotlight on poor Emmy lying prone in the grass. A figure dropped from the second story and cried out as his legs buckled to absorb the ground, and Shane got a flash of messy brown hair, a white T-shirt, a patchy red beard, and bright red acne on a pale forehead. The boy picked himself up, looked back at the house in panic, and then leaped over his mother's body, running as fast as his torqued ankle would allow.

Before any of this could sink in, Quinn was thrusting hard metal into Shane's limp hand. "Go. You have to catch him or we're done."

Why me? she nearly screamed, but Quinn only pointed to her left foot, encased in plastic. She took Shane's hand and forced it to fist around the gun.

"Go!"

And then Shane was sprinting through the dark, blinking to get her eyes to adjust. She could hear the kid, huffing with terror, crashing across a fallow field where the Fords grew a bit of wheat. The stars shattered the night sky, and the instinct buried in the human cell, the recall of the hunt under a burning Milky Way, fueled a wild, panicked kind of joy, and she could run faster than she ever imagined.

Then the boy tripped, maybe forty feet in front of her, and sprawled face-first onto the ground, skidding through dirt and leaves. He paddled forward, tried to get back to his feet, but Shane was standing over him now, finger on the trigger. "Stop," she said, breath pluming in front of her.

He flipped himself onto his back and met her eyes. A galootish version of the youngest boy from the picture. Perry. Maybe he was college age by now. He waved his hands in front of his face, a smartwatch lighting up with the red glow of a failed text message. "I don't even know you," he begged. "I don't know you—I don't know any of you."

Shane pulled the trigger and the bullet punched through his stomach. His scream was louder than the gunshot, high-pitched and keening, like Lali in the throes of a tantrum. She took a step forward, aimed for his head, and fired again. But she'd never used a handgun before, and she missed, the bullet kicking up dirt beside his shoulder. He was crying, clutching his abdomen.

"Go get my dad get my dad get my dad go get my dad," he kept crying. She aimed for his body, and the weapon kicked for the third time, and now the bullet hit him square in the chest. It made a small, dark typographical mark in his clean white T-shirt, and his pleading turned to a ghastly wheeze hissing from his throat. To make sure, Shane took another step and pulled the trigger one last time. The bullet tore through his mouth and out the back of his neck, and the boy was still and quiet. It was too dark to see much of the blood, but she could smell it, coppery and wet, mixing with the burned tang of gunpowder. She stood in the field for a moment, sucking wind. Perry Ford had probably tried to text or call from his watch, but the cell jammer

had done its job. So he'd panicked and made a run for it. She felt her own hot tears in her mouth, though she didn't think she'd been crying. She began running back toward the house.

———————

The postpartum terror swallowed her immediately upon returning home from the hospital. They warn new mothers of this possibility, but there is no such thing as preparation. Shane's was a fear and sadness internal and external. Throbbing in her bones while being buried alive. She was in a small box under ten feet of earth screaming for help while her air ran out. She felt like this day and night. It was all she could do to leave her bed in the morning to feed her daughter. She needed a job, she needed work, she needed help, she needed her pelvic floor to heal so she'd stop pissing herself every time she sneezed. The baby never slept, barely ate, and screamed so much it was like the child wanted to tear her own throat out. The worse it got, the more Shane could not bear to leave her bed. By the tenth month of having her baby home, desperation had set in. She began thinking through other avenues. Two years earlier, before the pregnancy, she'd interviewed for a job down the highway. Ricardo and Molly's All-American Taqueria served diner food and Tex-Mex. A proud little mom-and-pop with a video camera system that didn't work anymore. She'd learned this in the interview. "But don't tell no one," said owner and part-time manager Molly. "And don't rob us neither." This memory came buzzing back like a fly landing on her nose.

After emptying gallons of bleach over house and field, Allen, Emmy, Perry, and their home had gone up easily in a few splashes of gasoline. Why had Perry thought it mattered that he didn't know who they were? He thought his murderer must be a known enemy? That a killer could be a stranger—or worse, a faceless bureaucracy—had seemed an alien concept to him, and this troubled her for some reason. At least she figured out the mystery of the dog. Before they left she found the vet bill. They'd just put him down that week. Quinn drove them upstate, crossing into North Carolina, where they slept in the car at a rest stop. Despite her exhaustion, Shane barely closed her eyes the whole night, blinking awake at the first spires of dawn. They switched cars the next morning, exchanging keys with a bearded operative in a pleasant park in the suburbs of Baltimore. He hid his eyes behind sunglasses and made no comment about being abruptly called into service without explanation. They drove north, stopping at a safe house to shower and change.

"What do we tell Murdock and Kai?" Shane asked.

"Nothing just yet. We see what she says first."

Shane stared out the window and watched Pennsylvania go by. Patches of snow covered the fields and homes. She'd seen the flag flying more than once: HATE—YOU KNOW WHAT IT STANDS FOR.

"What if she doesn't see things our way?"

Shane thought of the first squeeze of the trigger, and the awful sound Perry made. A shriek, a squeal, and a plea all in one vicious exhalation of breath.

TIME FOR A CHANGE Of leadership. Of direction. Of purpose. Shane had been right in Wisconsin. They had built something incredibly powerful, and it wasn't being used to its full effect. Not even close. Quinn had known Kai since undergrad, and when he'd recruited her, he'd described the group as democratically organized. This, of course, had been bullshit.

CONTROL In practice, Kai was a shadow dictator with a firm grip on the money and logistics. Yet Quinn was the one who had to go online and make it all function. She and her small team of hackers worked to cover the tracks of their operatives in the field. They ran background checks on recruits and slipped nooses around the necks of their ops lest they go Kroll. They turned out lawyers to defend the captured, and they wiped clean money, houses, cars, and bomb materials when necessary. Fry a license plate scanner in Oregon, track an ATF agent who'd actually traced the blasting caps back to the correct retailer, delete an ATF file, work with impeccable OpSec. Find the vulnerabilities of the targets. Erase your tracks. Do meticulous work. All Kai did was funnel her cash. She and Shane had been discussing this for a while. If they were going to "shut down" Allen (as Shane put it), they should make their move. Get the money on their side and there was no longer anything to discuss.

She hadn't been to New York City since her recruiting trip in 2020, but the new security protocols felt fantastical, part of another society's future. Crossing into Manhattan from any entrance point, you had to pose for a picture. There was no entrance or exit without this brief catalogue of who was coming and going. They removed their hats so the FaceRec, mounted in an old-fashioned tollbooth, wouldn't flag them. Police officers, at ease in body armor, helmets, and full tactical gear, watched, rubber straps of gas masks jiggling on their thighs. The booth they approached had an ICE van beside it, along with a graffiti tag, *Chinga la Migra*. They were taking an enormous risk, a gift to law enforcement and the AIs that served them. If the algorithms saw these two women, who supposedly lived on opposite sides of the country and had no known connection, sitting chummily in a car not registered to either of them, perhaps digital flags would begin to fly. But once they were in the city, Quinn took out her laptop, hacked into the NYPD databases, and erased their images from the files in less than five minutes.

The building was old, squat, and brown, crammed onto West Twenty-Second Street, looking ripe for a teardown so some mirrored glass and steel could take its place. Floor one belonged to Sally Jacobson Salon, floors two and three to the Grimm Consultancy, and four, five, and six were the domain of Styx Capital Management. She and Quinn had dressed business formal that afternoon at a truck stop. Shane wore a black pantsuit purchased at a discount department store and had pulled her hair into a scalp-stretching topknot. She had to empty a full package of bobby pins and a can of hairspray before achieving the desired effect while Quinn threw on a fringe tweed collarless jacket and snapped into a professional look in ten minutes.

It was late in the workday and night had already descended, swallowing the city in brake lights and the glitter of skyscrapers. Most of the office workers at Styx, data analysts and the like, were filtering out, piling on big winter coats, mittens, scarves, and cumbersome gloves to brave the cold before sweating it out on the choked, lumbering subway.

Shane and Quinn waited in minimalist chairs, staring at posh modern art, while the personal assistant buzzed for Ms. Bhattacharyya. "Your five o'clock is here." Though Styx mostly dealt in short selling, the boss was always looking for intriguing opportunities, particularly venture-seeding women entrepreneurs. CNN played on a flat-screen, images of the homeless crisis raging across the country as California shuffled around those dispossessed by its megafires and DHS used the opportunity to deport immigrants back to their violent, disintegrating countries in Central and South America. Victims of the Great Eastern Flood were set to lose their FEMA trailers in two months' time, with President Love promising relief and Republicans drawing a line in the sand. Tens of thousands were still living out of cars and tents anyway, what was a few more? Finally, the assistant swept each of them with a wand before showing them in. "No phones?" the assistant asked.

"We knew not to bring them," said Shane.

"Can't be too paranoid these days," said Archie Bhattacharyya, smiling as though it were a joke. Upon shaking the woman's hand, Shane experienced a moment of shock at her brutish Long Island accent. "And please, call me Archie."

They took their seats, declined bottled water, and the assistant finally left. Bhattacharyya took a seat behind a smudge-free glass desk. Only a computer screen, a keyboard, and a wireless mouse appeared to float midair. She was an attractive woman, short blue hair rising off her scalp in a gelled pompadour with metalloid-skeletal earrings dangling from her ears. Her crisp green blouse and furrowed skirt looked of money and taste, which was in such contrast to all the diphthongs she left strewn in her sentences.

"When I received your message, I had to ask myself, 'Now what on God's blue earth would possess these ladies to blow up our safeguards, waltz right into my office, past cameras, past my entire staff, to sit down for a face-to-face?'" Every vowel had an extra syllable. *Safegawwds* was particularly irksome. Bhattacharyya flicked a hand, so that a gold bracelet came unstuck from the meat of her palm. "There are only two answers, really. Either you've been found out, and you came to establish a rapport before you start wearing a wire, or something's gone wrong with our venture, which I'm supposed to be insulated from."

"Right," said Quinn, who sat confidently with her legs crossed, hands clasped on her knee. "It's that second one. We need to execute a corporate realignment. A new strategy for—"

"How did you find me?" Archie cut her off. Quinn's boot scuffed uneasily against the carpet as she slid upright to improve her posture. She began stammering an explanation. Shane tried to help.

"I narrowed it down until I was absolutely sure," she said.

"That's opaque."

"A few years back," she explained, "I saw a set of our codes with this address. It was just a matter of figuring out . . ." Shane swallowed and shifted her road-trip-sore butt in the chair. "It was luck, mostly."

Bhattacharyya nodded. "So you're making moves. Come directly to Mama for cash. Why?"

"You have to see it from our perspective," said Quinn. "Kai is using his access to control tactical decisions. Meanwhile, Shane here is trying to raise a kid and plan these operations, and by keeping us siloed from the other cells, Kai has the entire—"

"Excuse me, Ms.—I'm sorry, I know that wasn't your real name."

"Call me Quinn."

"Quinn," she said, the vowel pancaking out for an eternity. "Excuse me, but I don't give a good goddamn fart about who slighted who at the company picnic. Skip the editorials."

Quinn began to object, a vein rising in the center of her forehead, her composure cracking, and Shane simply spoke over her.

"One of our members was going to turn himself in." Bhattacharyya's eyes switched to her, and from that point forward, they did not return to Quinn for even a glance. "He felt guilty over the deaths in Washington."

"Turn himself in? To the Feds?"

"Who else. He was going to come forward. So we did something about it."

Bhattacharyya arched an eyebrow. "What did you do?"

"What had to be done. It's best if you don't know."

Archie Bhattacharyya finally appeared to have nerves. She cleared her throat, recovered.

"Does Kai know?"

"No. Not yet." Shane nodded, stern and thoughtful. "I guess my question is: Are you actually a true believer in what we're doing? Or did you just see a financial opportunity?"

> **ARCHIE** Blondie made her want to upchuck all over that cheap biz-formal wardrobe. This other brassy bitch was all right, though. Archie had read every book or article on body language and comm ever written and firmly believed she could deconstruct anyone after sitting across from them for just a minute. Because the plump lady didn't look like she had any balls when she walked in, Archie was surprised and impressed to find her voice and eyes strong. She could tell the woman had a vision.

"Are you actually suggesting what I think you're suggesting?" she asked. "That I risked my life and freedom to get rich in a spectacularly complex manner?"

"Short selling has been lucrative for you. If you can believe in a cause *and* get rich off it . . ."

"You're trying my patience, missy."

"I'm not judging. Like Quinn said, we're here to recruit you." Bhattacharyya sat back, breathing deeply through her nostrils, and splayed her hands for Shane to continue. "We have three autonomous cells in operation now, and with a bit more money, we can have two more up and running in the next year."

"All well and good, but the way things are going, they'll sooner take a nuke to the Constitution then let you hit another target. I have contacts in D.C. who tell me Love is going to twist the nuts off people to find 6Degrees. He's going to see how far PRIRA can go." She laughed cheerily and swiped a quick hand through the shimmering blue of her hair. "Boy, this shit is unbelievable."

"That's why we want to change tactics," said Shane.

"To what?"

Shane gestured to Quinn, who seemed to once again realize she was part of the conversation and dipped a hand into the breast pocket of her jacket, removing a scrap of paper. She handed it to Bhattacharyya. She read it carefully, her eyes scanning down the list.

"This is . . ." She searched for a word. "Ambitious."

"They're about to escalate," said Shane. "So will we."

"How long would this take to put together?"

"Hard to say. Eighteen months at least. Maybe more. It has to be simultaneous and exact."

She handed the scrap back to Quinn, who pocketed it. "Let's say I'm interested. What do you need from me?"

> **THE LIST** Archie consciously made sure not to swallow her spit in front of them. She didn't want to hand it back too fast and forced herself to hold on to it a beat longer even though she felt like it might actually burn her hand. This shit was pure brick titties, as they said just down the LIE.

Shane leaned forward and held Bhatta-charyya's gaze. "Back us. Me and Quinn and the others who want to take this new direction. Back us, and the rest will have to go along."

She shook her head. "Kai will not like this."

"He won't have a choice. We have to make it clear that decisions run through the three of us now. We are the vote, and they can take it or leave it." Shane held her hands up, gesturing to nowhere and everywhere. "You've built a nice life for yourself. My question is, did you just want the sack of money this whole time? Or do you want to make sure they remember us?"

She held Archie Bhattacharyya's eyes.

In the fall of 2024, Shane drove her ten-month-old daughter to a taqueria off the highway but far from home. It was after business hours, and the parking lot was empty, the windows dark. She'd thought it all through, bundled the baby girl whose name she would not allow herself to think, and it wasn't even that cold anyway. The car ride put her to sleep, she was swaddled in a blanket, she had a hat—it would all be okay. Molly, the owner and part-time manager, she might not raise the baby, but she'd do the right thing by her. Get her to the right people. Shane could tell the woman was kind. Then her daughter might know adoption instead of foster care, that dim flashlight beam in an otherwise hard, starless night.

Speaking of hard, starless nights, she set the baby in her car seat on the concrete step at the back of the taqueria. In case the cameras were working now, Shane wore a hoodie and bandana. She didn't like how trashy it was back there, how she could smell the dumpster, so she taped a note to the entrance for whoever came in first the next morning (*There's a baby girl in the back. Help her.*). Then she walked to her car and drove away. She'd spent the first nine months terrified she'd mess up, not for her baby's sake but because she knew what the system could do to a poor mother. A poor mother leaves her baby in the car while she runs into a pharmacy and that's a mug shot. A poor mother finds her baby not breathing and that's a different ballgame. But now she was free. She'd disappeared so many times in her life, what was one more, honestly. She'd had enough of this sad corner of this sad state in this sad country. She'd made a mistake, and now she would do her best to move on, dig up one of her escape plans and vanish across this lonesome planet.

She made it thirty-seven miles. She remembered the mile marker. She began to tremble, and then she began to weep, and then she spun the car around at the next exit and drove ninety mph back to that little restaurant in the desert.

Let me tell you about fear, she would have told her father. After their meeting, Shane would part ways with Archie Bhattacharyya and Quinn Worthington. She would switch vehicles and drift down a highway that appeared to her as a black rush of water. She'd return to Kansas where her daughter waited in the care of a boss she used to fuck. She would tell them fairy tales about where she'd been, and they would both believe her because everyone believed her. No one thought she was capable of what she was capable, and she understood that now more than ever before. It would take her months to understand what she had seen: the hollowness within her, within them all. A realization of how little there actually is inside the self. How if you shout into that empty space your voice only returns to you. She'd glimpsed this first when she set Lali down in a car seat on a filthy concrete step by a dumpster and drove away. But now she'd written herself a permanent and irrevocable dream, and the memory of Allen and Emmy and their son—she'd never be able to dig it up, tear it out by the roots, burn it, or poison it. Perry especially. He would always be there, lying on his back in the field, under the stars, in the night.

LEVIATHAN

2033

He met Ash Hasan in the dining car of a 1930s train whizzing through the passes of snowcapped mountains, little Euro-gingerbread towns in the distance. No avatars, just two rumpled colleagues shooting the shit, ostensibly about the "sea level listening tour" Hasan was on with his latest congresswoman of choice. Ash, resolute in his devotion to data, insisted that Tony's time would be better spent joining the government rather than attending the concert less than nine months away.

"Seth is forging ahead on the executive committee of the climate concert," said Hasan, studying the glistening arugula salad in front of him. CGI food in a world gone hungry. "But seeing as how—"

"Just a bunch of old rock and pop fogies jamming in the capital," said Tony. "No need for anyone to get excited."

"—But seeing as how Seth and I are soon to become parents, I'm concerned. You understand why."

"Not really. We're going to prop the corpses of Eddie Vedder and Tom Morello up there, and some folks will say a few words to rally support for democratic solutions to global warming. What's to worry about?"

Ash gazed at him, chewing his jaw so that his temple twitched. He looked out the dining car window toward the rays of a sunset spiking over pristine snowpacks. The tinkling of silverware on china and the low whispers of the conversation drifted over the rumble of the train. A man across from them rustled his paper as he flipped a page. The headline read MARS MISSION LIFTS OFF; JOURNEY TO TAKE 9 MONTHS TO RED PLANET. The joke going around was, *Take us with you!*

"Fatherhood will rearrange our priorities," said Hasan. "Now Seth plans to actually *attend* the climate concert. He's not being rational about the exigencies involved."

"That's a bloodless way to put it." When Gail had gotten pregnant with Holly, their main concern had been the cost of raising a kid on grad student stipends. Hasan was loaded from building models for his brother-in-law's hedge fund, so he and Seth would be A-OK. "Anyway, you're going to be fathers!" said Tony, fake-lifting the glass of wine from the cream tablecloth. The vessel did not go with his hand, of course. "Congratulations! Welcome to the inescapable hell and joy that is parenthood."

"It's difficult to parse fact from rumor in Washington, but I'm urging you to take this new administration into consideration. It's given me great pause."

"You and everyone else who still reads a newspaper." He nodded to the man across from them. Impossible to tell if he was an AI or just a guy looking for a quiet place to read in a coffee shop somewhere in Buffalo or Dubai. "They caught that kid with the Weathermen, and he's sans lawyer from what I'm hearing."

"This is even more disconcerting than the new enemy combatant statutes."

"Don't blame me. I voted for that snake Randall. Love put a capital D by his name and fooled a third of this stupid fucking country. Everyone wants to suck their thumb and jack off in a VR set, this is what you get."

"There's a rumor going around, Tony, about a list."

He shut his mouth and looked at Hasan.

"What kind of list?"

Hasan took a moment to respond. His left hand was quacking, and he stared in consternation at his plate. The salad had ruby-red tomatoes, which glowed against the china.

"Political opponents of the president." He hesitated. "With a special interest in those who happen to have Islamic backgrounds."

"You're Muslim? Since when?"

"Not practicing, no. But in people's minds religious identifications follow you regardless of faithfulness to the liturgy. This list is being compiled, in secret, by the DOJ and Attorney General Greenstreet, but I have contacts within the FBI who are very seriously considering taking this information to the media."

Tony sighed through his teeth. "Fuck," he said.

"Indeed."

"Well," he tried to wrap his mind around this. Love gave him a sense of dread he'd not felt even in the Trump years. Anybody could see that plainly in the way Love had sliced apart the electorate to clear a path to the presidency. He'd sat the Democratic base in the corner while he fed Jen Braden money under the table through a PAC to siphon votes from Mary Randall (or so it was rumored). She ended up losing thirty-nine states, as the Republican base deserted her for a write-in campaign for the wingnut. Now the Senate Democrats were behaving not unlike their Republican colleagues had in their pathetic deference to Trump: playacting concern without doing much of anything to stop a clear and present danger. Dance with the one who brought you, and all. "Look, Ash, if you need anything from me, obviously, I'd do whatever . . ." He trailed off. "I'm not even sure what I'm offering. Help of any kind, I guess."

"I appreciate it, Tony. You're an honorable man."

"I don't know about that."

"A bit rough on every edge, corner, and surface, as they say, but honorable nevertheless."

Tony snorted a laugh. "That a joke?"

"An attempt."

After their palaver, Tony removed his VR goggles, and he was back in a dank motel room. The headsets were getting small, and this new one he'd just bought reminded him of the Geordi La Forge glasses from *The Next Generation*. It was uncanny how for a tingling twenty seconds or so, his motel room felt less real than the train crossing the Pyrenees.

———

Tony hated Florida so much. His cross to bear that he'd spent so much of his life visiting this place driven to lunacy by a swamp-fever addiction to its own bullshit. Every interaction in the Sunshine State was tinged with a mad-eyed fervor, every self-satisfied resident convincing themselves that this was the good life. He'd been there for a week to see Catherine at her municipality-sized rehab facility, but on the drive through West Palm Beach, where the steel-and-glass condo towers seemed to grow right out of the asphalt, he realized he couldn't wait to catch his flight back to New England that night.

He told Hasan and all other inquirers that Cat was doing well, though it was hard not to be doing well in her current digs. Rehab for the mon-eyed included yoga, meditation, daily Shiatsu massages, gourmet organic cuisine, a pool, a sauna, tennis courts, a thousand-square-foot gym and spa, acupuncture, neurofeedback, VR immersion training, equine therapy, and an ocean view, all for a small monthly fee of $64,573 footed entirely by her uncle. Despite the ostentation, the staff was well credentialed, and the other inpatients were serious cases: crumbling, hollowed-out, desperate to survive. The question was what she would do with herself when she got out.

"Uncle Corey says I can come work for him," she said. They walked the grounds, admiring the manicured hedgerows that separated the facility from the neighborhood of multimillion-dollar homes. The day was blessedly cool. A crisp saltwater breeze drifted west from the ocean, and the sun hid behind a gray bank of clouds, spilling a bit of rouge across the sky as it set. "I can tell from that look that you're not in love with the idea." She didn't say it with hostility. More like disappointment. She had a plan, she'd put initiative and thought into it, and when she told him, he was unable to hide his skepticism.

"It's not that. I want you to do something productive, of course." He was muttering and forced himself to raise his voice. "But I wonder if this is the best place for you right now. When you could come north and be near family."

"I'm near family here."

"I mean me and Holly."

"Uncle Corey has been amazing, Dad. You need to give him credit."

"I do, Cat."

And yet he would never be over his deeply ingrained doubt of the man. As soon as Tony got off the plane, Corey had picked him up in a slick Mercedes convertible and launched into his plans for the company. The Florida real estate market was going through a "reorganization." A coming wave of amphibious housing and sea-level-resistant architecture was the new gold rush—buildings that could elevate themselves, "real sci-fi shit," as he put it. Cat had only lasted four months with Tony in New Haven before she moved to Florida and picked up all her old habits. She'd dropped out of yet another college, and things were going badly enough that Corey had offered to put up the money to get her clean once and for all.

"What I worry about," he told Cat, "is that this place has all the same issues as Los Angeles. The lifestyle, the temptations, the problem people."

"I'm finding my way back, Dad. Plus, I hate the cold. I don't know how you live with seven months of dark and snow." She did look so much better. She'd gained healthy weight. She'd grown out her hair, and the red tinge was starker in the sunlight. Her flip-flops clapped against her heels as she walked. She wore jean shorts and a sweatshirt with an image of Lizzo. He remembered when she would put on "Heaven Help Me" while singing and dancing through the entire house. Cat had a brightness in her voice that he hadn't heard in a long time, and it reminded him of that young girl belting out her favorite song. "Uncle Corey said he could start me off in the office as a paid intern, and as long as I work, I'll move up quickly. Then I can also take classes part-time and finish my degree. It would be perfect."

They stopped at the edge of the facility's property. The sun split a cloud and sent a beam of yellow-orange light skimming across the ocean. Suddenly, Tony couldn't stand it, and he took his daughter by the arm and pulled her close, swallowing her small body in his arms. He tucked his chin onto her head against her wild crimson hair. He could recall the scent of her skull when she'd been a baby. Like he'd smelled it the day before.

"Are you crying?" she asked a bit unkindly.

"Yes. Sorry." He pulled away and wiped his eyes.

"Dad, I promise. I'm so much better."

"I know," he said, though the words were more of a gasp. "I know. You seem so much better."

And they stood in silence, listening to the waves lap the beach. Watching that strange ball of solar fire descend through the heavens.

——————

When he got back home, the Northeast was sweltering through a heat wave. New Haven had a high of 105. The air had a dusty sheen reminiscent of driving through Los Angeles as it burned. They weren't quite there yet, but the yellowed grass and thirsty trees brought anxious memories. One of the women who rescued them, Yolanda Quebrada, had been killed that summer fighting a brushfire in the Central Valley as California endured another vicious, if less apocalyptic, series of fires. Tony had donated a huge chunk of money to Quebrada's family and sent flowers to the funeral, though this felt wildly insufficient in the face of what she'd done for him. He was thinking of Quebrada, whom he'd known only for one panicked ride in a fire rig, as the driverless dropped him off at his house. Searching for his keys, stowed somewhere in his overnight bag, he almost walked right by the destruction of his car.

He'd left it in the driveway as he always did. (The garage had too much work overflow; boxes of data from Monte Carlo simulations that he couldn't bring himself to part with.) He pocketed his keys. Someone had shattered all the windows, and gummy bits of glass coated the driveway, glinting green crystals. The hood was pocked with dents from some heavy tool, a hammer most likely.

"What the fuck," Tony hissed, touching the wing mirror, which now dangled from the side. When he leaned his head through the window to examine the interior, he saw that the seating had been slashed, yellow-white foam spilling out. On the other side of the car, the vandal had keyed *TRAITOR* into the driver's door. He looked up and down his street. He swallowed. His mouth was cottony with thirst.

Maybe some student was trying to prove a point during their Scroll and Key initiation. There were now young Brownshirts of every stripe and political persuasion. They might have thought him a traitor for any number of his opinions on climate change, identity politics, nuclear energy—take your pick. Then there were his neighbors two doors down who still, almost nine months after the election, had their yard sign up: BELIEVE IN BRADEN 2032. His fear melted to anger in the blast-furnace heat of the day.

At least it didn't look like they'd messed with the house. Not even a window broken, probably because the perp feared an alarm. Tyrion greeted him at the door, purring happily at his companion's return. Tony considered calling the police, but he hadn't eaten, and he still had to pick the dog up from the kennel. By the time he'd tossed a frozen pizza in the oven and finished this standard widower's meal, it was nearly nine thirty and he was exhausted. He was supposed to go into the city the next day to see Holly and Dean, and the thought of dealing with the authorities for a vandal who would never be caught tired him further. He decided to leave the dog in the kennel for another day and deal with the cops after he got back from the city.

He fell into sleep so cavernous it felt less like rest than an excision of memory.

————

The next morning, he overslept and found himself slamming coffee and toast while the news vexed him: Food prices had risen for the ninth straight month, the effects of the Great Eastern Flood continuing in the grain markets. Love was combating the climate crisis by creating the White House Office of Climate Security, to be headed by obvious fascist-apparatchik-in-waiting Admiral Michael Dahms. "Sustainability is lethality," Dahms said in his first presser. Desperate Democrats tried to explain away Love's behavior by pointing to his reparations commission or all the women he'd appointed to his cabinet, including Sarah Caperno, the first female secretary of defense.

"You're lucky your species doesn't have to care about this shit," he told Tyrion, who appeared to agree.

He was mucking with his phone to order a driverless, when he looked out the window and saw a black SUV parked in front of his house, two women with guns on their hips walking up his driveway. He met them at the door.

"Dr. Pietrus?" The woman was young, dark red hair cut into an androgynous James Dean coiff, hands resting in the pockets of her pantsuit. The other was dressed similarly but with a butch sensibility. She was eating a croissant, pinching it so that most of her fingers avoided the buttery pastry. She wore a velutinous suit, shimmering in the early-morning heat, and looked like she brushed her short black hair with an eggbeater.

"Yes? Hi. I'm him." Outside, he was immediately sweating from the heat.

"Hi, I'm Patricia Wallflower with DHS." She flipped open an ID and flipped it closed just as fast. "We were wondering if we could have a moment of your time?" She held out her hand, which Tony shook.

"I was on my way to the city," he said. He and Dean had once argued about what "hackles" were before he proved the kid wrong with the internet. Tony's were now at attention.

Wallflower nodded to his busted car. "In that?"

"I was going to deal with that later."

"Any security camera on the property? We could take a look."

"No. What brings you out here, Agent?"

"We've collected some chatter. Threats against you, Dr. Pietrus."

"Chatter."

"Looks like it's more than just chatter," said the other agent, polishing off her croissant and staring at the mess of his car and driveway.

"Well, this isn't my first rodeo."

"With what?"

"Threats. I've dealt with the FBI before."

"I see," she said, propping her hands on her hips. She moseyed closer to the shattered window and peered inside.

He was about to ask how they'd gotten word of this (maybe one of his neighbors wasn't so useless), when Agent Croissant suggested, "We have an office in Bridgeport. You could come down. Talk this through?"

"I'm supposed to meet my daughter in the city at noon."

"It's on the way," she said. Her suit had enormous and growing pit stains. "Shouldn't take long."

"It was almost for sure some idiot Yale kid who went down a Renaissance Media rabbit hole. Like I said, I was getting death threats when you two were still breast-feeding."

"We don't typically get on a plane to warn folks in person," said Wallflower. He thought of his interaction with the G-man Chen all those years ago. Law enforcement carried itself as if you were just a distraction from some larger project.

"And you can drop me at the train station in Bridgeport?"

"Wherever you'd like," Agent Croissant assured him.

On the drive he asked for specifics on the potential threat to his safety, because of course he was thinking of his daughters, particularly Holly walking in and out of the Fierce Blue Fire offices in midtown Manhattan every day.

"No, I'm sure they're perfectly safe. If you want, we can always run someone out to check on them, but it's really best if we get to the office before we get into all this," said Wallflower. So they sat in silence on the drive to Bridgeport, while he jittered, and listened to the radio play the hits from decades ago. He recognized Selena Gomez from Holly's adolescence. He still had a soft spot for teen girl porridge, and it had even been his suggestion they ask the pop star if she'd join the Concert for the Climate. He listened to the music and tried to tell himself this was all not as unusual as it felt.

The DHS building was an unassuming beige box in an office park with a smattering of cars in an oversize lot and the agency's logo on the security booth. They led him through a body scanner, and in the process, he had to turn over his phone. He wished he'd texted Holly to tell her he'd be running late. The women led him to a bright conference room with a healthy-looking houseplant in the corner.

"Mother-in-law's tongue," said Agent Croissant. "Cleans the air of toxins. I appreciate any and all sprucing up of federal office parks."

Tony didn't care. People and their small talk.

"Have a seat," said Agent Wallflower. Croissant sat to his right, while Wallflower lowered herself into the chair across from him. "Can we get you anything? Water? Coffee? I think we have doughnuts today."

"I'm fine."

"You sure? There are bagels too."

"No, but thank you. As I was trying to say," he began. "I don't have much for you. I got back from visiting family in Florida last night and my car was like that. So, if this is more than a grab-ass vandal, I'd appreciate you sharing with me what you know."

"We're interested in a name," said Wallflower. "Do you know a man by the name of Clay Alvin Ro?"

Tony's stomach suddenly felt queasy. "No. I don't think so."

"You sure? He's been in the news lately. Could you think a bit more?"

"I did. I don't know him."

Wallflower took a tablet from her breast pocket, nothing more than a thin pane of glass, and tapped up a mug shot: a twentysomething granola kid with messy black hair and a seashell necklace.

"You don't know him?" she pressed.

"Okay, so he's the bomber they caught, I guess?"

"That's right. Arrested in April. Does this jog your memory a bit more?" She swiped and a new picture came up. It was Tony with his arm around the shoulder of the same kid. Clay Ro.

"Not really." He could see they were in an auditorium, slices of other people milling behind him. He was much younger in the picture, and if he'd been giving a talk, it would have been pre–Davos cancellation. He was guessing 2017 or '18 by the looks of the hair still left on his head. "I've lectured a lot over the years. Believe it or not, young people used to want the occasional picture with a celebrity."

"You've never spoken with Clay Ro? Never coordinated with him, never made plans with him?"

"What? No." Tony's stomach rumbled. He hadn't eaten enough, and he was sweating despite the AC. "No offense, ladies, but I have plans today. So if we could get to the point here?"

"Clay Ro was one of the people responsible for setting fire to diluted bitumen operations in Fort McMurray. We believe he was also one of the drivers responsible for destroying a coal-fired power plant in Ohio in 2030. He's 6Degrees, Dr. Pietrus. Or Weathermen, if you prefer. CSIS picked him up trying to cross back into the States."

"I don't understand half the acronyms you've used in the last hour."

"Canadian Intelligence. They've turned him over to us, as you know."

"Okay. Congrats." He flopped his hands against his thighs.

Croissant exchanged a look with Wallflower and said, "We're going to need a minute to verify a few things. Can we get you anything while you wait? Coffee? A soda? We'll try to be quick."

"For the fifth time, no," said Tony, batting a hand. "I just need to be on my way."

The two women stood and left the room, Wallflower shooting him a weird smile on her way out. He reached for his phone to text Holly, only to remember he'd given it up at security. Tony sat there, stewing. If they knew about the VR worlde on the cliffs of Ireland, the whole thing was over, but why start by asking about Clay Ro? He had no grip on what was happening. There was a dust-coated clock above a silent television that he tried not to look at; he sat there, staring out the window at the cars coming to and from the office park. Bureaucrats on coffee runs. He finally got fed up with waiting.

In the hallway, he looked both ways but there was nobody to help him. He could hear the unremarkable sounds of an office in daytime: desk phones ringing, computer keys clicking, paper shuffling, murmured conversations, a microwave heating lunch. He took a right. It was a low building full of darkling hallways, and each corner he turned made him feel as if he were traversing a whirlpool, passing eldritch rooms, vast, desolate cubicle farms but no people or computers or supplies. In one office, the door was open, and there were two extremely buff men standing in shirtsleeves, arms crossed, each with a VR set on. They stared down at something or someone with identical grim expressions. Finally, he found a room with a photocopier and a landline. His index finger hovered over the buttons as he realized he didn't actually know Holly's number.

"Fuck a duck," he hissed. He didn't know anyone's number. His childhood number was the only one that came to mind, along with an errant memory of his mom teaching him that it spelled out *kapowza* before she died. He thought about 911, but what would he say? That federal law enforcement was taking too long with their inquiries? He finally dialed 0, and he was able to negotiate his way through the AI operator to the FBF New York office and finally to Holly's desk. The call rang for a moment before going to voice mail. Of course, she was at the train station trying to meet him.

"Hey, Older One, it's Dad. I'm so sorry, but something fucked-up is going on. My car got vandalized and Homeland Security came to question me, so I'm at their office in Bridgeport, and they took my phone, and—" He stopped because he wasn't sure what he should tell her. He couldn't say the names of any of the people he was working with because that would bring her into it. "Okay, I'll either get there as soon as I can, or . . ." *Or what?* "Or I'll call you first thing. But I think maybe you should call a lawyer and—"

"Excuse me." The man was tall, wearing a photo ID on his lapel, and he walked over to Tony, hand outstretched for the phone.

"I gotta go . . ." He backed away from the man, twisting his body to evade him. "Also, call Ash Hasan and tell him I'm here—"

The man snatched the phone and punched the button with his thumb to end the call. He glared at Tony. "Sir, you are not authorized to leave the conference room, and you're not authorized to be on a phone in here."

Tony noticed his badge did not say Department of Homeland Security. Instead, it read GBI.

"You're not authorized to keep me here," he said.

"So leave!" said the man. "But you sure as hell cannot be wandering around this facility unsupervised, dialing numbers on phones that aren't yours."

Chastened, Tony followed the man back to the conference room. He was on the verge of feeling like an idiot, except when he got back inside, the man closed the door behind him and he heard the lock click. He rattled the handle, unsure of how paranoid he should be feeling. Wallflower and Croissant returned to the room soon after. They didn't mention anything about his prison break or the phone call.

"You're not with DHS?" he said.

"We're part of a JTTF," said Croissant. "That's all I can tell you."

"I want to see your badge." She showed it to him. *GBI - Michelle Novotny - Special Investigations*. "What is GBI?"

"We're a security firm contracted by DHS."

"So you have absolutely no authority to keep me here."

Michelle Novotny didn't respond. Wallflower set the tablet down. "Why don't you start telling us what you know."

"Know about what?" he asked. Wallflower stared at him. She had green and orange eyes as cold as gemstones. He looked to Novotny. "What I know about what?"

"You never had any contact with Clay Alvin Ro? Not even encouragement?" She gazed at him. "Or financing?"

"Financing? Lady—"

"Are you aware of IPA, Tony?"

"I'm not a drinker."

"I'm talking about identity prediction analysis. Advanced AI that sifts through mountains of data to identify people who might present a criminal or terrorist risk. We know damn well who's radicalized and who's doing that radicalizing."

"Oh, like some *Minority Report* shit. Why, did Ro turn up in it?"

"No, Dr. Pietrus. You did."

His skin went cold with understanding. This was not about the concert. They'd been monitoring him, but the anonymizing software had worked, as Liza Yudong said it would. They had no idea about Ned Stark or the meetings on the cliff. It looked to his watchers like he'd been in any old porno worlde. He was relieved, terrified, and grateful to Yudong. Now his only goal here was to keep the others safe. *Get angry.*

Easy enough, and he let all the acid he felt spill into his voice. "Great piece of software you have then. Staking out widowed old men who talk to their cats. Sounds like DHS really earns its taxpayer dollars."

Wallflower tapped her screen again. "Following the fire in Fort McMurray, you wrote to a colleague, Dr. Nikolaos Stubos, "'If only they'd thought of that twenty years ago maybe we'd have had a chance.'"

"That was in a private text message to my friend. I was joking." He looked from Novotny to Wallflower. "How do you have that conversation?"

"Dr. Pietrus, we have a great number of your emails, text messages, phone calls—every incriminating communication you've made in the last two years."

"Sounds like I'm going to have a hell of a good lawsuit. Maybe I can retire in luxury now."

"As you may or may not be aware, PRIRA's terrorism components give law enforcement authority to use predictive models to ascertain the dispositions and political attitudes of targets in order to gain FISA warrants for surveillance." She smiled warmly. "So my question, Dr. Pietrus, is why are you texting this encouragement of a terrorist act, while also appearing in a photograph with one of the people responsible for at least two attacks? And why are you being so obstinate under some simple questioning?"

"My dead wife would say it's because I'm a Leo. Highly resistant to change."

Agent Wallflower continued smiling. "This isn't a joke. You're linked directly to a terrorist group that's killed two people."

"Do I need a lawyer then?"

"Not if you have nothing to hide."

"Well," Tony said. "If not a lawyer, how 'bout a cigarette?"

Wallflower finally leaned forward. She drummed four crimson fingernails, the same color as her hair, on the table in a syncopated rhythm.

"What about the Concert for the Climate?" she asked.

They don't know, he told himself. "What about it?"

"You're part of the executive committee overseeing it. You plan to speak."

"So you've read the website. Good detective work."

"It connects you to a wider network of POIs. What do you know about the concert?"

"I know Zeden demanded there be no meat anywhere in the green-room, but she also wanted twenty-four bars of Ivory soap. You know what Ivory soap has in it? Animal fat. Funny, right?"

Lounging back in her chair, Agent Wallflower regarded him, unamused. She let Novotny continue.

"The attorney general is focused like a laser on bringing the eco-terrorist threat to heel."

"Jerome Greenstreet is a hack vizier of Victor Love. He's a Xuritas lackey looking to shred whatever's left of the Constitution. Why would I give a fuck what he thinks?"

Novotny ignored him. "Clay Ro is the first operational actor we've caught in a decade. And then"—she picked up the tablet and tapped up the photo of Tony and Clay again—"we find this. Deleted from his social media in 2021. A mistake? A slipup? Tell me why we shouldn't be interested in this, Dr. Pietrus."

"Speaking of the Constitution," said Tony. "Arrest me or I'm leaving. I'll get a lawyer and you can talk to him. Or her. Don't want to be sexist." He glared at Novotny.

Wallflower stood and knocked on the door. "Tony, you're being held as an unlawful enemy combatant under Statute 1034 of PRIRA." A man opened it, and Wallflower and Novotny filed out, looking back at him piti-ably. "There's no writ of habeas under 1034. No right to a lawyer."

"Get cozy," said Novotny.

The door closed and locked again. Tony went to it anyway and tried the handle. He banged on the tan surface. "Goddamnit, I want a lawyer!" he shouted. "You can't hold me here! You can't do this!" He carried on like this for five minutes, hoping it would at least summon somebody to calm him. But when it didn't, he quit. No point in wasting energy. He was hungry, and he had to pee. He waited for as long as he could but once he'd thought of the urge, it acted on his prostate. He peed into the mother-in-law's tongue and hoped they'd smell it when they came back. He paced the room for an hour. He hadn't thought about this in a long time, but there it was: the clathrates

cracking in the ocean's darkest offshore corners, the methane molecule slipping up through the lightless depths. He couldn't sit still. He couldn't focus.

———

By the time Agents Wallflower and Novotny returned it was late in the day
and the west-facing window was awash in slanted orange rays. They sat in
the opposite chairs so that Novotny faced him and Wallflower flanked him.
As Novotny spoke, the vertical blinds formed a triptych of shadows on her
face.

"What do you know about Clay Ro?"

"I want a lawyer."

"What is your knowledge of or affiliation with the group calling itself
6Degrees?"

"Dumb anarchist punks spanking their monkeys. Now charge me or let
me go."

Wallflower removed three pieces of paper from a folder. She spread
them on the table in front of Tony. Crammed with legal jargon, statutes demarcated by roman numeral, he didn't bother with more than a glance.

"You have three choices here," said Novotny. "The first is to cooperate.
Give us information on the Weathermen. You'll be charged with lying to federal law enforcement, and in all likelihood only receive probation. Option
two: You clam up. You force our hand." She leaned over to tap the middle
sheet. "You'll be charged with criminal conspiracy with a terrorist enhancement. Minimum sentence twenty years, but we'll push for the maximum.
Next stop, a prison cell in Fort Leavenworth, Kansas, and a communications
management unit. You'll be in a cell twenty-three hours a day. You'll have
nothing to do but stare at a wall for the rest of your life. You will not see your
family. You will effectively vanish."

Tony crossed his arms against his chest and kept his eyes steady on the
table. A feeling had risen as though these two had packed him into a suitcase and were smuggling him across the border of reality itself. None of this
made sense. This was so irregular, so against the protocol of how disciplined
federal law enforcement was supposed to function, that he still wondered if
it was all an enormous bluff.

"This third option." Her fingernail moved to tap it twice. "These are
charges of criminal conspiracy against Holly Pietrus."

"Fuck you," Tony snarled.

"A web of communications via text and email tie her directly to you, and by association to Clay Ro and the Weathermen."

"Yeah, no shit, she's my fucking daughter, you cunt."

Novotny smirked. Tony had delivered the reaction she wanted, and he immediately scolded himself. He needed to not panic. He needed to show that their intimidation wouldn't work.

"We leave you alone for five minutes, and you run to call her. She's worked closely with Kate Morris and has ties to numerous other environmental activists, many of whom have expressed sympathy for the Weathermen on social media. Would you like me to read some of these activists' reactions to the destruction of pipelines, coal plants, and refineries in the past ten years? We have files and files of their cheerleading."

"This is all horseshit," said Tony.

"We can build a case against her brick by brick," Novotny continued. "If we get a terrorism enhancement, I'm talking upward of thirty-five years. She'll be an old woman when she gets out."

"Get fucked."

"All you have to do is cooperate and the rest of this goes away." She pushed the first piece of paper toward him.

"There's nothing to cooperate about because I didn't do anything, and I don't know anything."

Novotny and Wallflower looked like they more or less expected this.

"This first option is going once, going twice," said Novotny as Wallflower stood. "Once it's gone, it's gone, you understand? And believe me, things will only get harder from here. We are going to find these people one way or the other. President Love and AG Greenstreet are taking the gloves off."

"So am I under arrest? If so, I want a goddamn lawyer!" He smashed his fist against the table.

"It doesn't work that way anymore," said Wallflower, and then they both left and locked the door behind them.

Tony sat in the plush conference room chair for a long time as dusk descended. In the parking lot, government employees and contractors were filtering out, heading home after a long day. The window was sealed shut into the wall. He wondered what they would do if he banged his fists against the glass and screamed for help. His only living company, the mother-in-law's tongue, respirated silently. He checked the dusty clock above the television, and only now did he realize it was the wrong hour. Had to be.

He tried not to watch the time, but he couldn't help it. He was starving and needed to pee again. He sat in silence as the sky darkened. In an hour he would be in a windowless truck, in two more on a plane. In a day he'd be somewhere hot, a desert where they tried to compensate by filling the facility with bone-chilling AC. Then he would be in a room with nothing but a bunk, a toilet, and a sink. It would be a week before fear turned to panic, a month before panic turned to despair. Though he didn't know it then, it would be almost a year and a half before he saw a sunset again.

The Years of Rain and Thunder: Part IV

2034

*T*he train lurched to a stop at Fiftieth Street, and I was dragged from the unsettling headlines of the day back to the immediate moment. Having lied to Kate, I'd been on edge since arriving in New York and on the subway made the mistake of turning to the news for distraction. Two children shot dead in Dallas, and the city had exploded. Jason Mollier and Lamarr Daniels were stuffing candy in their pants at a convenience store and the security guard pulled a gun. This wasn't 2020 or 2024. People weren't asking for justice anymore, they would go get it themselves, and within days, Dallas was on fire. The police and Texas National Guard cleared the city block by block, guarded by low-hovering drones with obsidian-black panels for faces, firing tear gas and rubber bullets while shielding police from bricks, rocks, and bottles hurled by the city's enraged residents. Torched supermarkets and police barricades had left whole neighborhoods without anything to eat. I'd seen protests throughout New York City that morning, but the NYPD was taking no chances, kettling protestors. Everything had remained peaceful so far, but cities around the country were in the same tense standoff. Just another spasm in a never-ending American saga. I spotted a lone Black man on the street corner holding a cardboard sign: MY FUCKS BUDGET ALL FULL UP. I CAN GIVE NO MORE. KILL NYPD.

I emerged from New York's intestines into the seventy-degree February day, the air sweating. People carried jackets under their arms while mopping their brows, still expecting the humidity to turn to rain. In the back of the Midtown restaurant, there was a room away from the other diners, walls scattered with images of Big Apple history—Boss Tweed political cartoons and workers dancing on beams of the soon-to-be Empire State Building. And there were my old friends.

Rekia Reynolds, Coral Sloane, and Tom Levine stood to greet me, and I could feel the wave of nervous energy in my gut surge into my face. Holly Pietrus stood behind them, waiting for whatever drama to play out. We all had this moment of tension, combat veterans reuniting in a bar with the anticipation of war stories. It was the first time I'd seen any of them since Kate's firing. That was almost three years ago.

We all laughed, and the room deflated. Rekia was the closest and came to me first.

"Matty, oh God." She took me in her arms and held me, twisting my body back and forth. I'd spent so many nights staring at the ceiling, hating her for what had happened, swearing I would avenge Kate. But the years went by, and my anger melted, and as soon as I saw her, there was nothing but bottomless love for this powerful and brilliant woman. "It's so good to see you, babe. I love this." She put her hand on my beard, which was old to me but new to her. No one would mistake me for a lumberjack, but it mitigated some of the boyishness I'd never been able to shake. Rek wiped a tear from her eye. She wore a bright red dress and her hair in long braids, twisted into a spiral atop her skull with the sides shaved. Enormous earrings like rectilinear city grids hung from each ear. She had an engagement ring on her finger. "Sorry, sorry! I missed you."

"You too. Don't—" I laughed as my eyes misted. "Rek, don't. You're going to make me cry." We both laughed. "You know I'm so sorry for how we left every—"

"Matty . . ." She held up her hand. "Stop. I'm sorry too. Everyone's sorry. I love you, and I always will, okay?" Then I did have tears coming out and quickly wiped them away, nodding furiously and pulling her into an embrace again.

Coral was of course dressed like a surly teenager in baggy khakis and a plain blue button-up. They'd removed the lip ring, but their hair was still a messy bowl, bangs curling on their forehead, a FREE THE CLIMATE HE-ROES electronic bracelet glittered on one wrist as the small, curved screen cycled through this proclamation along with JUSTICE FOR JASON AND LA-MARR. Coral held my shoulder first, and in their froggy voice said, "I almost brought my VR in case you wanted to get in a quick game of *Avenging Angel*?"

"You and me just skip lunch and sit in a corner?"

"Missed you, buddy," they said.

Tom was next, and we faked our greeting. "It's been too long," was all he said, slapping me on the back before sitting down. He adjusted the new Apple ARs, with their bold, thick-rimmed frames and took a seat, resting a hand on the back of Rekia's chair.

I'd never met Holly Pietrus, so we shook hands. Dressed in a sheer rose-colored blouse and a black pencil skirt, she looked young and bony. She'd been director of the New York office for a couple years but had the anxious bearing of an undergrad trying to pull an all-nighter before a final. Of course, her father was one of those climate heroes Coral's bracelet was advocating for, and I knew this was likely causing her sleepless nights. In addition to being biracial, she didn't look much like him, which was undoubtedly a good thing, but I could see his humorless scowl in her face now, like his DNA shimmered through her in moments of upset.

Coral held up their phone and a signal-blocking bag. "Can we all agree?"

We slid our phones across the table, Tom adding his glasses and Coral their bracelet.

"So when's the wedding?" I asked.

"Next year," said Tom. "Black women plan weddings like NASA and SpaceX plan contingencies for going to Mars."

"It's. My. Sisters," said Rekia, clapping her hands with each word. "I'm the baby, so they'll be up our asses the rest of our lives—just deal with it."

"Sorry for the paranoia," Coral said, setting the Faraday bag aside.

"What's paranoia when you got robots shooting people in the streets of Dallas," said Rekia. "I swear every day and want to start fucking screaming."

"Weird how you wake up and you're living in a bad movie about the future," said Tom.

"The original *RoboCop* was a classic for a reason," Coral said grimly. Even under the circumstances, it was hard not to smile at Coral and recall our Verhoeven film fests. I'd been planning a trip home to Carolina when Coral asked if I'd come to New York to meet with the old crew—and not tell Kate. One of Rekia's first decisions as ED was to move the core operations to New York City, mostly to be closer to the financial capital. It was the markets, after all, that were now doing much of the heavy lifting on renewables deployment and adaptation. In a few weeks, they would sponsor the Conference on Climate Mitigation, a multiday event with over three hundred speakers on dozens of panels meant to "bring together all stakeholders, from activists to government to business, to discuss and facilitate solutions, transformations, and ameliorations for climate change." It would even include members of the Sustainable Future Coalition. A gala was to follow.

"There's a hedge fund dropping a million dollars on the cocktails with this vodka made from carbon-sequestering potatoes," said Tom.

"And Love is not speaking, correct?"

"No. There's no way," said Coral. "There would be boycotts."

"We said we'd walk out." These were the first words Holly had spoken since we sat down.

"So what do we know?" I asked. "Your dad's case is working its way through the courts, right?"

"Not fast enough," she said. The detention of left-wing organizers, Islamic leaders, and climate activists held at undisclosed locations had yet to let up. Headlines trumpeted the outrage, but the arrests continued a drip at a time anyway.

"Banana republic oppression," said Tom. "They're testing the legal limits of PRIRA."

I asked, "And how many people are we talking?"

"They don't have to show the evidence for national security concerns—quote, unquote," said Coral. "So all our lawyers are in the dark in a box built by Kafka. And as for how many?" They looked to Rekia, who returned their troubled expression. "We think somewhere between thirty to forty people have been detained under the statute, but it could be many more. Maybe more have disappeared. Journalists are looking. We're looking."

"What happened with you and Kate?" Rekia asked.

The waiter chose that moment to come take our orders, which gave me time to think. I had to be careful.

"We sat for an interview," I said when he left. "Our lawyers were there. That's it. Nothing came of it."

We'd driven up to the Portland field office the month before and spent most of the time sitting in colorless rooms like we were in a doctor's office. When they interviewed us together, Kate did her best to bore them with drivel.

"'The whole point of Climate X is to build an antidote to the alienation and desperation people sometimes don't even know they're feeling," she told the agents. "That you guys are probably feeling. Politics has become entirely about individual self-expression instead of collective revolution, and I've been trying to push back against self-referentialism and sanctimony and dead-end radicalism. We want to reorient people around a shared vision.'"

"'Right,'" said a supremely uninterested special agent named Chen.

"'But that's why it's so utterly unreasonable that I or anyone in FBF ever worked with 6Degrees. Our missions are entirely dissimilar. They want insurrection against the state. Like the stupid children they are.'"

"'They're awfully crafty for children,'" said Agent Chen. To which Kate just shrugged.

"'It's your surveillance state, dude.'"

In the end, it was less Kate's mesmerizingly abstruse blather that got us out of there after only six hours than the fact that none of the captured operatives linked to the Weathermen had any connection to A Fierce Blue Fire. According to a *New Yorker* exposé by my old friend Moniza, the guy caught trying to get back into the States from Canada, Clay Ro, had never so much as visited the FBF website.

Rekia slid her arms over her breasts now, watching me. "The FBI's interviewed everyone on staff. They've subpoenaed emails, audited our financials. They're tracing every last dollar we've ever spent."

"What do your lawyers say?"

"They say cooperate."

I breathed slowly through my nostrils and nodded.

"According to my contacts, Love is trying to merge his own security empire with the normative functions of the DOJ, FBI, Homeland, CIA," said Tom. "Moving quick but not too quick."

"It seems like, for the most part, they're sticking to low-profile activists," said Rekia. "No one who'll command too much outrage—with the exception of Holly's dad. We think he's a test case. They put out that picture of him with the Weathermen op Ro to sell it."

"Is there any other evidence against him?" I asked.

"Of course there's not," Holly snapped, and I didn't blame her. "This guy Ro had a picture taken with him at a speech back when my dad was touring campuses with his book."

"Right. Obviously." It had fallen out of my mouth, and I regretted it. In Moniza's article, she'd described how Clay Alvin Ro had tried to erase the young activist version of himself before getting his plumbing license and slipping into a life of anonymity. This gave ample clue as to how the Weathermen operated, while also clarifying just how blindly and illegally the government was pursuing them. From my brief interaction with Pietrus in VR, he seemed about as likely a terrorist operative as my mother. I asked Holly, "How are you doing? You and your family?"

"We're freaking out is what we're doing. I've never— None of us have any experience with this, and it's been a total hall of mirrors. My uncle hired serious criminal lawyers, and even they seem unnerved."

"And you still don't know where he's being held?"

"No." Her brow furrowed in anguish. I was afraid she would burst into tears. "I got this call from him, and he said he was in Bridgeport, and that's the last I've heard about him or from him."

"Matt, that's why we wanted to talk to you," said Coral. "We're cooperating, and you guys should too. Our aim is to fight this in the daylight. We don't want to give them an excuse right now."

I forced myself not to look at Tom. He'd promised he wouldn't say a word, and I still believed he hadn't. "What other choice do we have?"

Coral exchanged another look with Rekia.

"Matt, what are you, Kate, and Liza up to with the concert?" they asked.

I laughed as if it was as silly as it sounded. "Who even knows? This thing has been a logistical nightmare. Pop-star egos—Jesus."

"Oh right," said Holly, coming back to the conversation. Her lips were tight with anger. "Your concert. We're out here getting death threats, getting harassed by every Jen Braden fanatic, harassed by the FBI, my dad's in some black-site prison." Her voice rose. "And you and Kate are hanging out with Zeden, planning a singalong on the National Mall like it's 2007. Concert for the Climate? Gosh, why didn't anyone think of *that* before?"

Our food came, and we all sat awkwardly while the waiter set the plates in front of us. No one touched their meals after he left.

"Kate is trying to keep the pressure on for actual binding emissions reductions," I said as evenly as I could manage.

"Good luck," said Holly. "Aamanzaihou is on her own island now. All our other allies have lost elections or are lining up behind the new so-called climate security czar, Dahms."

"What's your read on him?" I asked, trying to calm the conversation because she was so upset.

Coral answered instead. "He's an albedo modification advocate. Geo-engineer our way out of this."

"Ready the monster, Igor."

"Exactly."

Coral nodded to Holly. "I am interested in your answer, Matt. The concert. Why is Kate doing this?"

Carefully, I said, "I'm not sure what you guys mean."

Coral shook their head. "It's out of character. It's the kind of thing she would've mocked when I first met her. Pointless performative politics."

I hated lying. I'd never been good at it. I tried to make my dread sound like exasperation. "She's just working with what she's got at hand."

Coral nodded, but clearly this did not satisfy. Holly had picked up her fork but had not taken a bite. Now she set it back down.

"I'm sorry, I know we just met, but— Kate spends ten years building this groundbreaking political movement, then embarrasses herself beyond all reason, and her major idea is to get a few pop stars and rock-and-roll skeletons to play a concert? I can't even tell you— I idolized Kate Morris. Kate Morris was the reason I came to work here. And now this is all so, so— I don't know, so *mortifying*! Everything everyone said about her—that she's toxic, a starfucker, a phony—it's like she's admitting it was all true."

Her voice cracked, and she sounded more upset about Kate than her own father's imprisonment. No one spoke for a moment. Finally, Holly stood.

"I apologize, guys. I'm just trying to swallow a lot of terror right now." She slung her bag over her shoulder. "And I don't feel much like eating. It was nice meeting you, Matt." Before leaving our private room, Holly stopped and turned back to me. "Kate needs to know how badly she's wasting this moment. It won't be long before we're all disappearing into black sites."

My nerves were already so shot, and I almost exploded: *Oh, and what are you doing? Meeting with the SFC? Taking money from every greenwashed corporation this side of Exxon? Fuck you, you child.*

Instead, I waited until she left.

"Hey." I looked at my three old comrades. "I want you guys to know— and Kate would want you to know too—neither of us bears any ill will toward you. About how things went down. You all were our friends, and you're still our friends. She would want you to know how highly she thinks of you, and even if our paths have diverged, that doesn't mean we're not still in this fight together."

Rekia reached across the table to take my hand. "I told you, Matt. No more apologies. We love you both, and that didn't change when you left."

When the bill came, none of us could believe how expensive our meals were. Awkwardly, we asked the waiter if he'd made a mistake. "No, sorry," he said gently. "Our suppliers are the ones jacking up the prices."

~ ~ ~

As we all hugged goodbye, Rekia and Tom stepped into a driverless. He pulled a can of tobacco from his pocket, flicking it with a fast and loose wrist, and Rekia gave him a *Really?*

This left me and Coral on the street together. We stood for a moment, gazing all the way to the Hudson, where I could see the cranes and barges manned by construction crews. I knew from my years at FBF that these were part of the operation to build the living breakwaters, piling rubble, concrete, and stone to slow storm surges and grow ecosystems of oyster beds to form protective reefs. That was the idea at least. This was A Fierce Blue Fire's new focus: working with cities and communities to gird them for what was coming (or already here). Everyone had given up trying to actually stop the problem itself. Now it was about armaments.

"Hey," said Coral, scratching at the deep pits of old acne scars that perforated their cheeks. "Seriously—want to play the new *Avenging Angel*? It's got a level where you have a shoot-out right in the middle of the Oscars. All these tuxes and dresses exploding in gore."

"Wow, that's gruesome and inappropriate."

"I know."

At Coral's apartment, we donned VR sets and played *Avenging Angel* for four hours that went by in a blink. It brought a lot of delightful nostalgia. All those times when Kate was out of town and Coral would text to ask if I wanted to come over and throw on old movies and play hyperviolent VR multiplayers.

After a while, I was sweating and my ears ached from the headset, so Coral ordered a pizza, cracked open a couple beers, and we threw on the original *Alien*.

"Ellen Ripley, your idol," they said.

About midway through the movie, right after the Xenomorph bursts from John Hurt's chest, I asked, "So do you miss D.C.?"

Coral shook their head. "Not really. Not everyone was happy when Rekia announced the transition, but it makes sense. Plus, you don't have to sell all that many kidneys to afford a one-bedroom." I laughed at their geeky delivery. "So what's next? You and Kate will be back in D.C. soon, right?"

"The plan is to drive out there in January and start preparing for the concert."

"That's a lot of lead time."

I let my silence indicate I did not particularly care for any more probing. "It's a big task."

Coral swigged from their beer and was quiet a moment, watching the movie. Finally, they said, "Stop me, Matt, if you've heard this already, but did I ever tell you the story of how my dad died?"

I turned to them. "No. You definitely didn't."

Coral nodded, bobbing their head a few times. "It's not a big deal. You know I grew up in the Imperial Valley, right by the Salton Sea. We were broke but not unhappy. My dad was this brawny guy with a teddy bear disposition. A really sweet, wonderful dad. But he was also from the kind of family where everyone just did stupid shit. Both his brothers went to prison for aggravated assault. For a barfight, if that paints a picture. Dad always stayed clear of it, though. He didn't drink, didn't fight, didn't step out of line ever. He was like the one straight arrow in his family. Then one day, the police show up at our door, this state trooper, and he tells us my dad is dead. Killed in a motorcycle accident." Coral cleared their throat, about as much emotion from them as I'd ever seen. "But my mom isn't even worried because Dad didn't own a motorcycle. And she's telling the cop this. She tells him when they got married, she made him swear he wouldn't drink, drug, fight, or ride a motorcycle because that was all his family was known for. And my mom kept insisting, 'No, you have the wrong person, it couldn't be him, my husband *doesn't own* a motorcycle.' And he didn't. I sure as hell had never seen my dad on a bike. I knew my mom was right, and they'd made a mistake."

Down on the street, the siren and strobing lights of an ambulance washed the neighborhood for a minute, and they waited for it to pass.

"Of course, it turns out it was my dad. He took a corner a little fast, plowed into a truck head-on. It killed him and the guy in the truck. They ended up having to show my mom pictures of my dad's body to convince her, which I'm sure couldn't have been too pretty. I was sixteen at the time. And then we found out my dad did have a motorcycle. He'd been keeping it at his buddy's place, in the garage, for fifteen years."

"Jesus."

"Yeah." They raised an eyebrow at their beer bottle. "I have no doubt that's what broke my mom's heart the most. He'd kept this secret he probably thought was harmless, and it ended up dragging two families into a lifetime of tragedy."

"Damn, Coral. I didn't know that. I'm so sorry."

"It's ancient history now. I didn't bring it up for sympathy, though, Matt."
On-screen, Tom Skerritt hunted the Xenomorph through the air ducts with

a makeshift flamethrower. "My mom and I didn't believe the state trooper because we don't see the people we love with clarity. I'm not being subtle here."

We sat in silence for a while finishing our beers until Dallas encountered the alien in the dark, and Coral brought up the popular fan theory that Dallas and Ripley had been having an affair aboard the *Nostromo*.

~ ~ ~

My flight back to Oregon was delayed due to storms across the Midwest, and I spent three hours in the airport, mostly sitting at a bar and staring at the email I'd gotten from UNC Greensboro. There was an image on one of the televisions of The Pastor with, of all things, a flamethrower not unlike the one I'd watched Tom Skerritt wield in *Alien* the night before. The chyron said something about a controversy, but the sound was off. I asked the guy sitting next to me, a hipster using his carry-on as a footrest, what the deal was.

"This fucking nutjob just lit up a pile of Qur'ans."

"Seriously?"

"Yeah, man. Just walks out with that thing, gives a spiel about how it's the book of Satan and burned like two hundred copies. Not in VR either." He tugged at a barbershop mustache waxed to its points. "This and the riots in Texas and no one answering from the Mars mission, I just—"

"What do you mean no one's answering?"

"It's supposed to land in two months, but NASA, SpaceX, no one knows where the fuck it is. No one's home. They've lost it."

"God, I hadn't heard that."

He kept on tugging his mustache and shaking his head. "I just want one year where it doesn't feel like the world has gone bug-fuck insane."

~ ~ ~

From Portland, I took a driverless down to Bend. Kate's mom had been staying with her while I was away. We'd moved to Oregon partly so Kate could be close to Sonja, but of course they rarely spent an evening together without bickering.

Sonja called while I was in the car because she would just miss me, our rides passing each other somewhere on the McKenzie Highway. She told me that Dizzy had gotten her cone off but would need to take antibiotics for another two days after getting her leg snagged in some old fencing near the property line. She also said Kate was getting a little "hardwired," which was Sonja's malapropism for when her daughter was on edge.

"This concert, she gets to meet Beyoncé and Haydukai and all these other famous people, and you'd think someone was marching her off the plank."

"She's just being thorough," I said. "Perfectionist."

"Yes, perfectionistly insane." Sonja laughed at herself. "Come see me in Portland before you drive cross-country, Matt? Yes? Make her do it."

I promised I would.

By the time I got back to our rental house on the outskirts of Bend, dusk had settled in. The house was surrounded by pines, some fallen and skewed across the forest floor, taken over by rot and fungi. For over a year, while Kate schemed, we'd lived this quiet, out-of-the-way life, on the edge of a happy broke, getting by on her speaking fees and my photography work. We hiked the Pacific Crest Trail all the way into California, spent weeks at a time rafting and living out of a tent in the Deschutes, Willamette, Ochoco, and Mt. Hood National Forests. We had a living room with a fireplace, two bedrooms, a spacious kitchen, and rows of bookshelves. I must have read two hundred novels in those years, typically curled into a corner of our sectional while Kate buried her nose in her laptop and worked with only slightly less fever than the years in D.C.

Dizzy padded over, panting and ecstatic. It was hard to believe she was eleven years old. It felt like we'd found her as an underfed puppy in a dog pound cage only the day before. Now, I took my friend by the head and spent a good long while scratching her behind her gross brown ears.

I found Kate in her office. She wore her new ARs and spoke to an empty room.

". . . Then tell her to fucking bring her own omnidirectional treadmill bullshit. What the fuck is this?" She paused, waiting for the answer, while glancing up at me. "Hold on, Matt's home." She hopped up, pecked me on the cheek, and then began pacing. I grabbed our VR set and joined. The boyish blond of Seth Young's head digitized into my vision first, followed by his perpetually smiling eyes and slightly off-kilter nose. He was midsentence with Kate, his digital blond flattened like a Legoman's head. I still hadn't gotten used to talking to people like this, seeing them plasticky and colored all wrong. It was all uncanny valley.

"It's for her social VR. She has to fly around in her worlde for the teenyboppers," said Seth.

"Teenyboppers? All her fans have fucking mortgages now!" said Kate.

"Get her the pad. We've already got a VR tab in the bajillions, what's one more—"

"Sure, what's one more ego-freaked pop star's demand for a white piano with a bowl of strawberries?"

"And the last thing I wanted to ask you about— Oh hey, Matt," he said, as my avatar finally appeared for him. "Good, glad you're here for this. The FBI interview? How'd it go?"

It was so ridiculous: having these conversations when we well knew the FBI was likely watching, and the FBI likely knew we knew they were watching. A playacted charade within a playacted charade.

"Just fine," Kate said. "At least they didn't haul me off to a black site. Someone somewhere made a decision that harassing me with law enforcement wasn't effective or that it might rally folks to me." A serenity passed over her face, which seemed to indicate that she was detached, yet this was the failure of AR to pick up and display these basic human cues. It was why hurt feelings and bad blood permeated the virtual realms: miss one tic on a face and the attitude being conveyed is the opposite of the person's intention. "They've been trying to take me out at the knees in the public square instead. Go after my reputation, humiliate me, degrade me. Turn me into a slut and a sexual abuser and a coked-out whore."

She winked at me.

"Yeah, no one gave them any ammunition." I slipped an arm around her waist.

Kate shoved her curls over one side of her head, streaked with more and more errant grays these days, and asked Seth, "How's the baby?"

"He's amazing. I know all parents think their kids are geniuses, but Forrest really might be one."

"Well, it was your sperm, not Ash's, so I kinda doubt that," said Kate.

I took the opportunity to beg out of the conversation, let them talk in their code, and collapse into bed. I loved the bedroom of this house. It was secluded, and with the door shut, held the silence of a cool and deep forest. Engulfed in solemnity. I undressed and laid down, but not before taking my phone out one last time, to mull the email I'd gotten.

~ ~ ~

The next morning when I woke, I realized Kate had not come to bed. I found her still in her office, comparing a detailed paper map to another projected on the wall from her laptop. She had the Apple ARs propped on her head, cramming back unwashed hair.

"Will you rub my feet?" she asked, wide awake.

"If you cook me breakfast like a good woman." It was a joke because I always cooked. Otherwise, we'd live off raw vegetables and energy bars. That morning I made an egg substitute, lab-grown bacon, and chopped fruit. The clouds hung low and green in a nauseous yellow sky. During the Great Eastern Flood, there had been a tornado outbreak near Corvallis, an unusual phenomenon for Oregonians, but it had gone uncommented on in the larger country because most of the East Coast and Midwest was underwater.

"Smells good, kid." Kate came up behind me and put her arms around my shoulders.

I served the plates in the living room. I ate mine quickly, scraping up the last of the fake eggs with a piece of toast. At first, I thought I only wanted to tell her so I could think things through out loud.

"I saw Coral in New York. And Rekia and Tom."

Kate stopped chewing. Stared at me. Then slowly began chewing again. She finally swallowed. "Why?"

"And Holly Pietrus."

"Yeah, why?"

"They wanted to talk. About the arrests, the harassment, the FBI, Love, Tony Pietrus vanishing down a hole—all of it. And they wanted to know what you're up to."

"And did you tell them?" She'd speared a piece of fake egg that was on its way to her mouth. Instead, she set the fork down.

"I told them you were busy planning the concert on the Mall. And that musicians are a pain in the ass."

She nodded. "That's good."

"Those guys are doing good work still."

"For the nonprofit-industrial complex, sure," she said as if readily agreeing. "The moneyed crowd needs some way to salve their consciences, I get it."

"There's still time to call this whole thing off. Chalk it up to the bad idea that it is."

Kate was not unused to my skepticism; I'd made it quite vocal for the past year, so this comment dissipated into uncaring pupils. "No, there's really not. It's happening."

Sometimes, when you're in love with a person, you don't know what you're about to say to them until it's already leaving your lips. It's like you walk around with this splinter buried deep in the skin, and you think, *No way will that ever come out.* Then suddenly it does. As soon as it left my mouth I knew there would be a moment before I said this to her and a moment after. That these words would be irrevocable.

"I'm not going to be a part of this, Kate."

She'd been balancing her plate on her knees. Now she set it on the coffee table and drew the word out very slowly: "Okaaay . . ."

"I already know everything you'll say, so maybe we can skip that part."

"I'm not saying anything."

"I guess what I've been trying to get across to you for a while now is, I don't want to do this." A lump formed in my throat, and I waited for it to abate. "And I don't want you to go through with this either."

She studied me like I was brand new to her. "What would you have me do, Matt?"

"It's over." I tried not to let the pleading creep into my voice but failed. "You've done what you can, Kate. You did something brave and incredible when you had the chance, and now it's time to let other people take the reins. We can go wherever we want. We have our entire lives left."

She laughed and her bright eyes churned around the morning-bright room in astonishment.

"Still trying to get me to be your housewife, huh?"

God, did I hate the way she fought. How small she could make me feel with a single turn of phrase.

"I want to start a family with you, yes," I said. "Hell, I'll breastfeed while you chop wood—I don't care. We said that was in the cards, that a plan like that would . . . emerge sometime soon. And yet every year it seems further away." She hunched forward, chin on her knuckles, and looked infuriatingly bored with me. "We can go wherever we want," I repeated.

"Has nothing changed with you, man?" she demanded. "You still buy into the same fantasy that any of this is going to be okay, that there's anywhere to hide."

"So that's your answer?"

She looked behind her like she was wondering who I was talking to. "Dude, what other answer did you think I would have? This is happening."

"If that's the way you feel, then maybe I need to go."

"Oh yeah? Where are you going?"

"Back home. Back to Carolina."

I could see her trying to estimate how serious a threat this was. Even in that moment, I wasn't sure.

"And do what?"

"I got into an MFA program. At UNC Greensboro." Because this sounded so, so, so stupid when I said it out loud, I had to preempt her. "And before you get sanctimonious—'Oh, Tar Heel, you're gonna write your little book while the world falls apart?'—I am demanding that you just keep it the fuck to yourself. This was what I wanted before I met you. Understand? I didn't want any of this shit. The fame, the endless work, the humiliation, none of it. I wanted *you*. I loved *you*."

"And you're saying you don't anymore?"

"No." And that lump pushed the tears right past my defenses because I'd issued a threat I now had to make good on. "*Of course I do*. I love you so fucking desperately, it's ruining my life. Because I can't compete with your mission. I've always been such a distant fucking second. Hell, maybe not even second, depending on who else you're seeing."

"Don't go there," she warned.

And I nodded because that was only fair. We looked away from each other for a moment, but I could feel it coming off her: Her fury burned through her skin. She bit a cuticle, and her face was racked with cold calm. I wanted her to slap me like she had years ago.

"Say something," I demanded.

"I think you said it." Her voice was even. "What are you waiting for, Matt? Go. Don't let me stop you."

I clenched my fists as the darkest wave washed over me. I felt twenty-two again. "Goddamnit, Kate, are you actually fucking serious right now?"

"Take the car. Take the dog."

I dropped to my knees and grabbed her by one warm cheek. I forced her to look me in the eye. "This is not how this goes. It just isn't."

"How does it go then?"

"Call this off. Show me you care for me even a fraction of how much I've cared for you. If I've ever meant anything to you, you won't go through with this."

She gently took my hand away from her face.

"I've told you what I'm doing. I've been working toward it for over a year, and now you want to jump ship? So jump."

She looked away. A tear pushed out of her eye. She quickly wiped it and blinked back the rest.

"I'm sorry," she said. "You need to go. This only gets harder the longer we sit here."

I'm not sure how long I did sit there, stunned, sick to my stomach, feeling like I might faint. Even after all those years, when I looked at her, I still couldn't get a hold of what color her eyes were.

Then I stood. As if I were piloting another man's body, I went to the bedroom and packed haphazardly, forgetting so much due to my haste. I left. Out the front door with Dizzy, who just thought we were going for a ride and panted happily as she pounced into the back seat. My dog and I drove through the pines toward the highway, my skin cold, my shock too deep to even fully understand what had just happened. Because it didn't feel real at all. Not at the time. I didn't even know where I was driving. At least I'd have to go back for my books, I told myself.

But it was the last time I'd ever see Kate Morris.

The Siege

APRIL 1

A light rain fell, and they came by the thousands up through the tunnels of the Metro and crossing the Potomac, surging along the sidewalks on their way to the National Mall. They wore yellow rain jackets and blue ponchos, costumes and Indigenous dress, carrying signs and placards. Artists at a face-painting station inked American flags or green and blue Earths on the cheeks of children. Quinton Marcus-McCall, a thirty-four-year-old volunteer with A Fierce Blue Fire's mutual aid network, shuffled behind fellow concertgoers, past the security checkpoints of metal detectors, flak-jacketed police officers, ATF, and bomb-sniffing dogs. He'd driven from Detroit the week before, staying in a hotel in Maryland, and now found himself stuck behind a family with a stroller, stopped by police who were all but taking it apart searching for something. The parents looked annoyed and frantic to get in. A woman behind Quinton griped to a friend that she couldn't believe Zeden had dropped out. When it was Quinton's turn at the metal detectors, the crowd jostled him into Second Lieutenant Walter Pasquina, a US Marine on leave. "My bad," said Quinton. Pasquina accepted Quinton's apology without a second thought and went back to his phone, specifically the concert's dedicated app, which was telling him where they might like to stand for the best view.

Walt was there with his kid sister, Kelly, a twenty-one-year-old organizer on the American University campus, about as lefty as her brother Walt was indifferent to politics. She'd rebuilt her Slapdish worlde as a shrine to Free Clay Ro, the Ohio plumber arrested and accused of domestic terrorism. Six years Kelly's senior, Walt had basically raised her while their dad was in the Marines and their mom worked tireless hours as a suicide crisis counselor. It bemused Walt how every time he came home, Kelly was passionate and encyclopedic about another entirely new subject. He wasn't teaching her how to cook s'mores anymore, but she frequently schooled him on issues, like why it was vital to have a habeas writ. His leave happened to coincide with the concert, and she'd talked him into joining her. "Fine, Kel, feed me your radical program, but the day after we're going to watch the Nationals opener, no arguments." This was pure teasing because they'd both grown up huge Nats fans.

When it had come to the attention of the Love administration that a small band of rootless climate activists had applied for a permit from the National Park Service during the waning days of the Randall presidency, the impulse was to shut it down, but then a dissenting opinion gathered strength among his closest advisors: This was *exactly* what they wanted. A concert on the National Mall was a perfectly acceptable outlet: A feckless pop culture trifle that allowed folks the self-expression and social media content they coveted but which blossomed and wilted within the same eight-hour period. Forcing a couple of high-profile acts to drop out would be a final embarrassment for Morris and her crew.

The concert kicked off with Beyoncé, Jack White, and Gary Clark Jr. performing a blues rewrite of the national anthem. Instead of the familiar beats of that song, White and Clark performed it almost as a hymnal, closer to "Amazing Grace" than "The Star-Spangled Banner." Pop's last great megastar was recovering from knee surgery, not so much as a twitch of a dance in her, and sang from a stool to the left of her costars. A bare black stage framed the Capitol Building behind them, looking drab and weathered in the gray morning. It had been cordoned off and surrounded by police vans and concrete barriers, SOP whenever any large crowd set up near the Capitol ever since '21. People waved small American flags and cheered as the woman's impossible voice sent the familiar words arching across the city. As the last syllable whispered away on the edge of her breath, she launched into an acoustic version of her own "Freedom," and finally White and Clark joined her at the mic, for the obvious "Rockin' in the Free World," reorchestrated to sound more like a mournful last-chance eulogy than a call to action. There was feedback on the microphone. The light drizzle continued. The sea of plastic ponchos garnered real-time ridicule on social media due to the petroleum used to manufacture them.

Organizers had erected the stage just west of Fourth Street, between the National Gallery of Art to the north and the National Air and Space Museum to the south. People pressed the barricades, but the crunch of the crowd only lasted until Seventh Street, which was blocked off for the day. To the west of Seventh, people had brought blankets and lawn chairs, a smattering of tents,

and mostly watched the drone feed on their screens. Aerial photography estimates put the crowd size at about 105,000 people. Not bad, but keep in mind
Donald Trump's much-disputed inauguration drew at least 150,000. Come-
dians Jon Stewart and Stephen Colbert managed 215,000 for a joke rally in
2010. Barack Obama's first inauguration still held the record at 1.8 million.

Concert for the Climate: No Time Left organizers had hoped for five
hundred thousand and planned for as many as a million, but they were up
against strong headwinds. As it was wont to do, the issue had yet again faded
from the minds of the American polity. Without a major storm or, say, a city
burning to the ground in the last several months, attention had moved on.
The anxieties of the moment included the dead boys in Dallas and the riots
put down in their wake; the refugees coming from the southern border and
increasingly on ramshackle boats from the Caribbean; the right-wing militias asserting themselves in public, patrolling the Arizona borderlands and
marching in Philadelphia suburbs; and the staggering price of food busting
the budgets of many households.

Still, there was a general sense of comity, uplift, and hopefulness. Here
we are, still plugging away, this gathering said. We're not giving up. They
danced, swigged from flasks, smoked joints and vape pens, clapped, sang,
stamped their feet along to the roots-rock band Gunner Main. They filmed
on their phones or through their ARs. They projected holograms of their
spinning planet or wind-beaten American flags or billowing blue fire. IN-
STRUMENT OF PEACE read one of the largest holograms, roughly the size of
a semitruck, sizzling over the heads of hundreds as raindrops cut through it.
Some held aloft the boilerplates scrawled onto old-fashioned cardboard: AN-
OTHER WORLD IS POSSIBLE; SYSTEM CHANGE NOT CLIMATE CHANGE;
YOU CANNOT ARREST AN IDEA; WE NEED LOVE NOT . . . and then a picture
of the president. Three men of God dressed in their traditional religious garb
were very proud of their banner held at waist height: A RABBI, A PRIEST,
AND AN IMAM WALK INTO A BAR . . . TO SAVE THE EARTH! A woman wore
a hot dog costume, a meme having to do with the fact that President Love
supposedly ate a hot dog after killing an unarmed boy in Afghanistan. One
man wearing big butterfly wings with dual images of blue fire was asked
to sit because he was blocking the view. The Clean Energy Labor Coalition's signage was everywhere as they had supplied much of the funding and
workforce; the union's slogan, NEW WORLD SOLIDARITY, was everywhere.
A group of Palestinian women in wool challis headscarves held a series

of signs that taken together read MUSLIMS FOR PEACE, HARMONY, THE CLIMATE, A DEMOCRATIC ISRAEL, A FREE PALESTINE, EACH OTHER, EVERYONE, EVERYTHING! Anarchists rubbed shoulders with military veterans, Quakers with Mormons, Chippewa with Wiccans. The rapper Haydukai came on for his set, wearing a keffiyeh and sunglasses with red, white, and blue LED lights, vicious, syncopated rhymes following the flow of his free hand and a beat that throbbed like a pumping vein. That cosmic dust quality of live music descended on the audience, conjuring belonging and camaraderie from absolute scratch.

VR drone cameras hovered overhead, allowing those at home to watch up close when Haydukai growled, "No time left, so it's time to go. Time to rise up." He knifed the air with his free hand. "We still got a weapon. That weapon is *collective power*. All the rage and grief you feel at our broken, disappearing world—we got only two choices. We despair or we grow a revolution. Now listen to what she got to say."

Then he stalked off the stage with the crowd still cheering.

The other performers were confused because he was only the third act of the day. There were still nine more to go, and many of these musicians and their busybody handlers wondered why Kate Morris was taking the stage so early in the day. According to the schedule, pop star Kiki Wan was next, and this was all building to Eddie Vedder, Selena Gomez, and Elvis Costello, sharing the stage to sing "Hey Jude" in memory of Paul McCartney. Sure, the concert was free, but folks still wanted their money's worth.

But there she was, the endlessly controversial thorn of the climate movement, who had long ago worn out her welcome in the public sphere, who many—even those who agreed with her mission—wanted to just go away, get a reality show if you must, but make sure it's in the deep recesses of all content, on one of those worldes/feeds/channels no one knows the name of. She bounded onstage to a smattering of applause. Her hair was pulled back with a simple tie but still frizzy from the rain. She wore jeans and a weathered olive-green Carhartt she'd purchased at a Goodwill in Missoula after dropping her coat into a crevasse while rock climbing. She carried a spiral-bound notebook in one hand, clutched so that her white, chapped knuckles betrayed her nerves. There were those who would love her no matter how much dirt came out, and it was these young men and women who screamed and cheered the loudest when she took the stage. A few folks stood stonily with their arms crossed. Haydukai had taken the microphone with him, and when she reached the empty mic stand, she laughed nervously and called back behind her. A young stagehand sprinted to pop a new mic into place, and then ran off hunched over, as if this would somehow render the gaffe less visible.

"Hey there," she said, laughing nervously into whining feedback. She tapped the mic and it went away. "How we doing today?"

"You're not Zeden!" someone shouted.

She laughed but her fingers picked restlessly at the metal coil of the notebook.

"I just have a quick something to say, and then we'll get back to the show." She glanced at her notebook, and those watching at home on VR could see it shaking along with her hand. "I've been trying to write this speech for a year. Then I threw it all away and rewrote it last night."

This wasn't entirely accurate. She'd had the basic beats memorized ever since she'd dreamed of this moment while driving through the Mojave Desert beneath a herd of stars. Though she'd never told her former partner this, she admired his meticulous attention to prose. Her mind was too scattered, and because she'd fought through the embarrassment of dyslexia as a kid, she tended not to write much down. The night before the concert, she'd stayed up until four in the morning with one of her favorite books, Solnit's *Hope in the Dark*, and tried not to plagiarize too much. She wished she'd had her original copy with those precious margin notes, but like that good jacket, she'd lost it years ago.

"I've been working on this situation for over twenty years now. Ever since I was in high school. Twenty years—man, I can't believe how quickly time just . . . happens to you. I know that's not an original thought, but it is totally shocking anyway. When I first started on this—our crisis of the biosphere and inequality and democracy—I thought, Great! Look at this huge problem someone's left for me! I'll just—" She whipped her free hand like she was spinning a globe. "I'll knock this out in a couple years, no problem. I'll give a few speeches, rile folks up, elect the right people, get the right laws passed, and we'll all be knocking back beers at the bar in no time. I had so much energy and eagerness and just—hope! I had so much hope."

Another scan of her notebook, searching for her train of thought.

"I can't remember being afraid of anything in my life, and maybe it's a product of getting older, but suddenly I am afraid. To be honest, I'm afraid all the time."

A burst of oscine birds took to the sky. This impromptu storm of wings breached the day like a crash of thunder, alerting the assembled to how quiet they'd grown. Only the patter of rain filled the silence that followed.

"We are met with this unthinkable nightmare befalling our planet, and the hour has grown so late. We are only in the early stages of the devastation to come. I could name all the events that have destroyed families and lives and homes over the past ten or twenty years, but what's the point? All of this is only the beginning. That's what breaks my heart so much. We're not here to prevent that future anymore—because we can't. All we have left to fight is our own oblivion. Our civilization devouring itself as we run from storms and fires, as we die starving and thirsty and fearful and alone.

"We can tell ourselves that it's all of our faults, that we all share blame, but that's bullshit. Let's call it like it is: There are a *handful* of corporations and governments happily burning as much carbon as they can so that a *handful* of people can get obscenely rich. And mostly, the problem lies right here."

And she pointed behind her to the bulging Capitol Dome.

"That building is ours. The whole idea is that whatever happens in there is *our* will. *Our* decision. But instead, it's a defensive fortress for a tiny elite, who are profiting from the genocide of our planet. It's not even a secret. They're not hiding their plan. They are openly telling us they are going to exploit and plunder our country, our earth, our home, and then profit from its unraveling." Kate Morris slapped the notebook against her thigh. "They expect us to stand by and do *nothing*. The only question is, will we do nothing? The solutions to this crisis, it turns out, will also require an even greater ambition, a more just global order. We need to build a new energy infrastructure. We need to reinvent agriculture. We need to put everyone in this country to work in high-paying, meaningful jobs. We need to make housing, health care, and education universal rights, so we're not all hungry, addicted, angry, and alone. We need to destroy the power of the surveillance capitalist economy, the people who profit from fomenting hate. We need an immediate release of the political prisoners, people like Dr. Anthony Pietrus, who have done nothing wrong except try to warn us of what's coming. We need an end to the harassment, imprisonment, and torture of activists, protestors, religious and racial minorities, whether that's at the local mosque or the local chapter of A Fierce Blue Fire. We need justice for the mothers who've lost children to heroin addiction in Kentucky, just like we need justice for the fathers who've lost their sons to bullets in Dallas. We need our freedom and our hope returned to us. We need to find our way back to each other."

Kelly Pasquina had loved Kate Morris since she first learned of her as a middle schooler, and the moment her idol stepped onstage, she'd begun to tingle. She did not care a whit about any of the scandals, the gossip, or the attacks from the left, right, or center. There were some people you would ride for come what may. Now, listening to her, she clutched her hands in front of her mouth as if in prayer and let the tears pour shamelessly from her eyes.

"The problem is, in order to fulfill this vision, we need to take their money, and we need to take their power." She jabbed her finger behind her again at the Capitol Dome. "It's as simple as that. Because that money is blood money, and the power fucking belongs to us anyway."

"Fuck yes!" Kelly screamed, and her voice rippled back through the crowd, past Seventh and then Fourteenth Street, nearly all the way to the Washington Monument.

"So what are we going to do?" Morris demanded. She held three fingers on her right hand high. "We are going to save our biosphere, we are going to remake our unjust and unequal economic system, and we are going to re-democratize our country and our world. History shows us that people can be monsters. That they can kill and maim and enslave and exploit, and they can do it while telling themselves how enlightened they are. But history also tells us that when people band together, they can do mighty things. Whole systems can fall overnight. We don't need armies, guns, or bombs. Great change is made by a tired, pissed-off woman who doesn't want to give up her seat on a bus, or by a scrawny Indian lawyer who decides to stop eating. What is extraordinary about the people we revere in history is just how unbearably ordinary they were. All that separates us from them—literally the only difference—is that they had the courage to act. When the wealthy and powerful told them what they were doing was meaningless, they didn't listen."

Quinton Marcus-McCall watched the crowd feast on this woman's voice. He'd first heard her at a speech at Wayne State in 2025 when he was failing at his nursing degree, and though he hadn't known it then, it set his life on a new course. This speech didn't sound all that different to him from the rest of her catalogue, but it was good to know she still had some juice left. He set his backpack on the ground and went rooting through it for the strip of blue cloth and began tying it around his left bicep. Kate Morris continued:

"Remember, you have courage in you. All these disasters the past thirty

years, from 9/11 and Covid-19 to the Great Eastern Flood, and what do people always do? In the LA fire, you know what they did? Fishermen sailed
their boats up the coast from Mexico to rescue Americans they'd never met.
Because when disaster comes, we don't run, we don't eat each other, we
don't say 'That's the other gal's problem, why bother?' Even if the powerful
want us to forget it, we are innately brave and always carry within ourselves
hope in the face of the impossible. We don't run from the fire, *we run into
the fire.*"

She leaned hard into the mic, the flesh stretched tight across her collarbones as she surged into her own skin, her fist beating the air for emphasis.

"So here's what we do: As I speak, we have organizers, here, today, setting up encampments and building barricades in the streets, and we're asking you to stay, right here, for as long as you can. We will lay siege to this city.
We're not leaving until our leaders hear us, meet our demands, and address,
immediately, these emergencies of democracy, inequality, and climate."

At this point, what Kate Morris was actually saying didn't quite connect with the crowd, which let out a half-confused round of applause. She
pushed on, trying to make them understand.

"Find the people wearing the blue armbands, and they will set you up
with the supplies you need: tents, sleeping bags, water, food. For those
watching, anywhere in the world: Get here. As quickly as you can. We are
not here to spark violence or damage even a single brick. This is not a MAGA
rally. The buildings that surround us, this is our heritage. It's our home, and
we will treat it as such. We must be uncompromising in our nonviolence,
but the business of the heartless and violent corporate plutocracy that now
passes for governance in this city? That's finished. Not one deal will happen,
not one law will pass, not one piece of corporate welfare will be enacted
until we, the citizens of this country, are heard."

Walt Pasquina watched as three guys with blue armbands carried a piece
of fencing from Seventh Street down to Madison Drive, where a few others
appeared to be reassembling the portable metal barriers to form a barricade. In the streets just beyond the Mall, police had erected two-meter-high
smart fences, which suddenly, like a mini Maginot Line, were being hacked,
disconnected, and carried away in pieces by teams of four or five. He could
see them being reappropriated at certain points along Madison Drive. Kelly
was pestering him, thrusting her phone under his nose: *Kelly*, it read. *We
need your help. Here's what you can do next.*

"Never forget," cried Morris from the stage, "at any moment we can choose to be agents of change. I promise you, there is nothing more meaningful than when your life is on the line and you choose to fight back."

Master Patrol Officer Andrea Sanchez, an undercover with the D.C. Metropolitan Police, could not decide what to do. Standing just north of the Smithsonian Castle, she watched as groups of blue-armbanded folks were basically running off with every last piece of physical infrastructure intended for crowd control. Her instinct was to start making arrests before things got out of hand, but the instructions in her earpiece were contradictory. There was something else going on in the city, and officers were being pulled from the concert to deal with it. Meanwhile, there were more portable toilets being delivered mid-event, and big trucks with pallets of food and water being off-loaded onto the Mall, and strangest of all, there were construction crews jackhammering into the pavement of Jefferson Drive. Everything was happening extremely fast.

"In this moment, in this city, in this dark hour, we will prove that all the divisions heaped on us by the powerful and wealthy are false. They don't fear us yet—but they will. Because we are what they didn't see coming and what they never thought possible. We are the deluge. Join us. Get to D.C. It is not too late. The future is not yet written, and all anyone will ever ask you twenty, thirty, forty years from now is where were you? What did you do when you were called?"

And instead of walking off, Kate Morris took two steps and jumped from the stage to the grass below, where she was greeted like one of the rock stars. She grabbed the first random guy from the audience, as security looked on in confusion, and together they picked up the crowd-control fencing that enclosed the VIP area and began carrying it south to the roadway. People were cheering, screaming, looking at one another like, *Wait, really?* When Beyoncé and Eddie Vedder peaked out from backstage, their general bewilderment mirrored that of the audience.

The remainder of the event proceeded strangely. The bands and musicians went on, played the hits, and for the most part people behaved as though they were at a concert. Yet in the midst of this, the crowd leaked, siphoning off to join roving gangs of impromptu construction workers, directed by field marshals IDed by their blue armbands. Messages arrived on phones, watches, and glasses. A wider blast reached over five million sympathizers, asking for their help in both bodies and donations. On key streets, people began to build a series of blockades out of smart fencing, portable toilets, and tire-puncturing police wire, unspooled on all roads between Constitution and Independence Avenues. The area had already been cordoned off by police with standard protocol concrete barricades and metal detectors, and the street blockades would deny the authorities access to remove the concrete. Groups of severe-looking Blue Bands stationed themselves outside the entrances to each of the buildings within their perimeter. The National Gallery of Art and the National Air and Space Museum, for instance, would be closed for the foreseeable future. Finally, groups began erecting tents in neat rows between the stage and Fourteenth Street, creating bisecting pathways around which their makeshift city could grow. Two medical tents and two cafeterias sprouted up on either end of the Mall, with twenty-five solar and ninety bicycle generators deployed as connective tissue between those hubs.

Officer Andrea Sanchez's insistence that there was something going on at this concert—not a terrorist attack, not an active shooter, not a riot, but something far weirder—went ignored, as did the calls from other officers on the scene. For thirteen years, the Metro and Capitol Police had gone on high alert whenever a large group of people descended for any reason whatsoever. The Capitol Building and White House became veritable fortresses for so much as an AARP knitting convention, and crowd-control mechanisms were deployed throughout the district in case things got out of hand. But now their drones were flying away, vanishing across the Potomac, and many of her fellow officers complained that their radios weren't working or that they were getting conflicting orders. It was giving her a sickness in her gut, as she wondered what a mob turned loose might feel like. When she confronted one of the men coordinating the larceny, though, he was so calm and reasonable.

"You can't do that," she said, flipping her badge open and stuffing it in his face. "You can't move that there."

"No, no it's fine," Quinton Marcus-McCall told her, and he showed her a forged permit. Officer Sanchez studied it while Quinton's team continued to carry fencing from the access aisles to the points of entrance and egress along the Mall. "This is part of the performance. Call it in."

"I did call it in, man! Y'all got to stop! Now!"

"There really must be some confusion," said Marcus-McCall, scratching his head. "Let me call my boss quick. This all must be a misunderstanding."

And moments later, Sanchez's dispatcher, which was not a person these days but a soothing electronic voice hooked into the Metropolitan Police's central computer, told her that indeed this was part of the concert, including all the mature trees being planted right into the jackhammered concrete on the north-south roads.

Once the organizers controlled those north and south borders of Independence and Constitution, they went to work on Third Street in the shadow of the Capitol and Fourteenth Street just east of the Washington Monument. Groups of twenty sat down in the street in circles and fed their hands into tubes. Inside were handcuffs that secured their wrists. This tactic of deploying multiple wheels of human beings chained together, impossible to move without ripping off someone's arm, was sometimes called a lockbox, sometimes a sleeping dragon, and had been cribbed from long-ago WTO protests in Seattle. The police converged on Fourteenth and Third Streets, but all they could do was stand there until the proper tools arrived. On a cue delivered by the app, two hundred people in interlocking human chains broke into song: "Wild World" by Cat Stevens followed by "The Way You Smile" by Zeden, followed by a more obscure number by veteran troubadour Joe Pug. They had a list fifty tunes deep, and they'd repeat it until they went hoarse. As long as they held the road.

And yet instead of reinforcements showing up to cut open the tubes and remove the protestors, the D.C. Metro and Capitol Police were being diverted elsewhere. Intelligence agencies had asserted, through their monitoring of social media traffic, that several Black extremist groups were trying to spark riots in the city's ghettos. The chaos in Dallas was still on everyone's mind, so the bulk of the city's police force was dispatched to sections of Deanwood, Anacostia, and LeDroit Park, where supposed riots were breaking out. Indeed, that morning small groups of protestors, holding signs demanding an end to police violence, had hustled from one neighborhood to the other, barricading streets at random. Numbering only in the hundreds, they nevertheless managed to sow enormous chaos. Police intelligence insisted that this was a real threat, that thousands of Black Lives Matter, Antifa, and 6Degrees extremists were stoking riots on par with Dallas, but wherever the city's generous helping of riot police showed up, the threat had already melted to another block, another section of the city. Meanwhile, twenty-seven buses pulled into major intersections in the heart of D.C., blocking traffic on every street that led to the Mall. Teams of thirty to forty people exited, faces covered (by bandanas, balaclavas, Guy Fawkes and Joker masks), and with military coordination, they rocked the buses onto their sides. Bystanders filmed as the huge vehicles toppled and crashed onto the street and then ran, thinking the buses would explode. This strategy proved most useful at the four corners of the captured territory, essentially cutting off Jefferson and Madison Drives at Fourteenth Street and Third Street from the rest of the city, allowing organizers the rest of the day and night to establish a fortified perimeter and sow confusion for any authority trying to hinder their tactics. By the time the concert wrapped up, for all intents and purposes, Kate Morris's foot soldiers controlled the National Mall, and no one in Washington, D.C.'s chain of command, from the chief of police to the mayor to the Feds, quite knew what to do about a bunch of folks with their arms handcuffed together by the Washington Monument singing Pharrell's "Happy."

In the organizers' command center, a trailer discreetly situated behind the stage, Tom Levine hovered behind Liza Yudong, watching her manipulate an AR screen. Only the night before, Levine had told his fiancée where he was going and what was happening, knowing that it could mean the end of their engagement. He was in D.C. by dawn the next day with nothing but a toothbrush and a change of clothes in a backpack.

"How are you doing all this?" Tom now asked Liza. She removed a pair of harlequin-style ARs, rubbed her eyes after a long day of watching the chaos organize in three-dimensional graphics around her face, and looked at her old coworker like he was boring her.

"You know in the movie when the screenplay says 'Computer stuff, computer stuff, computer stuff'? The AI does all that, and I just sit here."

"And here I was afraid you'd lose your sense of humor without me, Liz."

Liza went on to explain, in the most dumbed-down, patronizing way she could manage, how not only was her algorithm pushing tactical intelligence to individuals as open-source resistance but also how it created a unity of command. Identity prediction analysis gave her algorithm a solid notion of who could be called upon to do what, and each instruction arrived on the device of a person deemed likely to carry it out.

"So you've spied on people to determine if they'd be willing participants," said Tom.

"'Spied' is a big word. We use the same data as Pepsi or the Democratic Party. I call it my Occupy AI. We determined we needed a base of five thousand good little unthinking, unquestioning revolutionaries, so that if the AI asked them to act like chickens, there'll be five thousand smelly hippies on the Mall clucking in unison."

It was a bit more complex than that. The predictive tech, along with the gigabytes of data gathered, bought, and sold by advertisers on behavioral futures markets, was coveted by all kinds of actors. The *New York Times* had reported on how Vic Love had utilized a powerful new tool from CLK Metrics to devastate his electoral opponents going as far back as his Senate bid in Montana, with his campaign uniquely targeting voters' psychology in groundbreaking ways. Liza used the same tools to recruit their true believers, an eighteen-month process in which their group made contact with nearly twenty-five thousand potential occupiers, sifting through the best and brightest of the past twenty years of social movements, veterans of BLM, Idle No More, Sunrise, Extinction Rebellion, Occupy, and Standing Rock, as well as young people just stepping into the activist space. These microtargeted individuals were not let in on the details of the plan until they'd undergone a background check and training in nonviolent direct action and the hard skills of organization and encampment, everything from first aid to latrine construction. No one on the executive committee ever had personal contact with any of their cadre leaders. It was all done through anonymizing software and aliases. The climate concert itself went unmentioned. All these folks knew was that they were going to be called to do something bold and radical. From the perspective of law enforcement, Kate Morris, Liza Yudong, Seth Young, Anthony Pietrus, and Matt Stanton had only been planning a concert. Yudong delivered insight into the protocols that governed D.C.'s sprawling security apparatus in a post–9/11, post–1/6 environment, and she used this to develop machine learning to rapidly deploy participants in a mass-protest event. Her program could recruit, train, and direct new members without anyone so much as tapping a key, generating seemingly leaderless action, while organizing its tactics around Homeland Security, D.C. Metro Police, and Capitol Police preparations for civil unrest. When all those people ran to Fourteenth Street to lock their arms in a sleeping dragon, no person told them to do that. It was the AI processing multiple data streams at once to decide how to create the most effective disruption to gain control of Fourteenth from Madison to Jefferson.

The recruits now did their jobs with dedication and efficiency. For nine hours following Morris's speech, under a pale ghost sky, they worked tirelessly to build a garrison in the heart of the US capital. The concertgoers made their decisions after the last acts departed, some electing to stay, picking up tents and gear, but most filtering back out to the streets and the Metro, spooked by the overturned buses, still not sure if this was for real.

On that first night their makeshift city glowed with digital screens, head-lamps, and campfires, and the chatter of voices and song carried across the city. Volunteers came by to feed those still chained in sleeping dragons and give them sips of water. Oblate disc of moon peeking through clouds. Errant drops of rain hissing in the campfires. She wouldn't sleep that night, but Kate Morris did pause from her work to look out over the sea of flapping plastic pulled over tents to fight the dampness, the smattered-star glitter of people checking their phones in the hastily built commune, the buzz and energy of last call at the bar now indefinitely suspended.

And yet by morning, it seemed like the whole thing was over. If seven thousand people remained on the damp lawn of the National Mall, they would've been lucky. Liza climbed out of her tent and saw their disappoint-ing numbers. Given that almost all five thousand of their Blue Bands had stayed, their larger retention rate was under 2 percent. The scene looked like a poorly attended convention for suburban camping enthusiasts. The stage remained. The backstage trailers remained, all rock and pop occu-pants having made themselves scarce. The north and south streets were piled with debris. Semi-amused, semi-exasperated cops were still trying to get arc welders to the sleeping dragons, a few progressive press outlets hov-ered around the Media Relations tent, and the kitchens fed veggie burritos to anyone who showed up, but all told, it looked like it was about to be a lot of egg on someone's face. *A revolution that's about as much of a fart in a bag as climate change itself*, tweeted one commentator.

Kate Morris made the rounds, thanking people for staying, urging them to reach out to their networks to bring in more bodies. Most people listened to her from inside their tents because the rain had picked up.

The status quo, for its part, was laughing at her. The president was in Japan for a meeting of the G20, so Vice President McGuirk and the head of Homeland Security got on a holo-chat with the mayor of D.C. With the threat of Dallas-level riots appearing to be a mirage, all agreed it was best to encircle the Mall for now, keep a phalanx of menacing crowd-control cops between these granola-eaters and the Capitol, and let the whole thing fizzle in a few days from crummy weather. Once it was down to the hundreds, they'd start making arrests.

Morris, Levine, Young, Yudong, and their fifteen most veteran organiz-ers huddled behind the stage that second night debating if this whole thing was already over. Two years of planning a complex and dangerous nonvi-olent ambush, on top of the difficulty of simply planning a major concert, and the only thing they hadn't counted on was that "We'd barely be able to summon a crowd the size of a poetry reading," said Seth.

"The Fyre Festival of the climate crisis," Liza added.

"It's still early. It's raining. People are waiting to see what will happen," Kate assured them, but she was fending off an alarming sensation. She could take the death threats, the hate mail, the deepfake porn, the actual leaked sex video, all the vicious internet bile, but what truly got at her was this ego blow, this rebuttal of her entire thesis that she was a unique conduit for activating people's faith in themselves. She felt stupid. The National Park Service had sent her an email explaining that she was in violation of her permit and laid out the consequences. She could go to jail for two years for the most embarrassing protest action in modern memory.

By morning, black clouds had moved in. At the sight of the dread-filled sky, hundreds more packed up and left. What was left of the patchwork crowd circulated around the National Mall pointlessly. The folks in the lockboxes had unshackled themselves when the cops appeared to lose interest. The city was busy cutting the knot of chains and dragging the overturned buses away. Everyone waited for the conclusion of this sad effort.

APRIL 4

It's hard to say why the fourth day.

Maybe it took that long for people to pick up gear at the nearest REI. Maybe the rain letting up was key. Or maybe Morris's speech took a few days to make its impact. Whatever the reason, twelve hundred people descended on the Mall, setting up tents and registering with organizers, who assigned them jobs in sanitation or the kitchen or construction. The next day, as the sun dried the grass and people didn't have to hop puddles, an additional twenty-one hundred bodies arrived, an influx so large it took until midnight to process them all, get them shelter, and go over the encampment's rules demanding nonviolence, respect, and nothing even remotely resembling a weapon. Within a week, nearly fifteen thousand people had taken up residence in the heart of D.C., with more arriving every day. The Mall transformed into a city grid. Several Indigenous action groups— including members of the Oceti Sakowin, Navajo, Choctaw Nation, Hopi, Potawatomi, and the Cree and Métis from as far away as the Northwest Territories—erected enormous tipis, bringing with them years of experience occupying and blockading. They arranged their shelters around a firepit in the shape of a buffalo horn and planted rows of the national flags of all the represented tribes. The library lent books. Folks waited in line for their turn to generate power on the bikes. Huge industrial pots cooked rice, soups, and stews around the clock to keep everyone fed. Medics provided whatever care they could, and teachers set up classes on climate science and the history of nonviolent resistance for the kids. Each night an emcee announced new activities and what had showed up in the lost and found. Donations of tents, sleeping bags, food, clothing, medical supplies, books, and solar generators were dispersed from a central distribution point on Seventh Street, and demonstrators swapped out of the frontline blockades every five hours, pushing nervous police farther back as a dense wall of people wearing masks, goggles, shields, and other improvised armor inched across Fifteenth Street and up the hill toward the Washington Monument. Crews were jackhammering apart the streets, planting even more trees in the soil below. Finally, police caught on and stopped any flatbed truck with a mature tree on it, but at this point the concert's landscape artist, a Lakota Blue Band from North Dakota, had transformed key intersections into miniature forests. For example, Fourth Street, between the National Air and Space Museum and the National Museum of the American Indian, had been commandeered by a dense copse of maples, dogwoods, and tulip trees, like a sprite-land set for *A Midsummer Night's Dream* had grown straight out of the tenderized asphalt. The crowd, for days drifting like steam, began to coalesce and, having gained power, drive an unseen engine. Police with sniper rifles watched from the rooftops.

The mayor and DHS debated what to do. They had the protestors hemmed in and there hadn't been a single report of violence. There were also *a lot* of children in the crowd, as Media Relations had made sure to circulate images of kids playing in the grass, the rain, in and around the legs of police. As many as ten million people were watching on their VR sets, taking tours through the camp, communicating with occupiers, and watching the daycare, preschool, and elementary classes learn about the carbon cycle. This was a calculated risk deemed vital by Morris, Young, and Yudong: to encourage people to bring and keep their children there. It gave authorities, especially the mayor, pause. This situation had to be resolved peacefully. These were not alt-right lunatics in Viking gear storming the Capitol Rotunda. There were kids in reading circles by day and folk singers crooning onstage at night. "It would be better if they were rioting," the mayor grumbled to an aide.

In a holo-conference, President Love remained utterly unconcerned. He had bigger fish to fry (like China's increasingly unhinged president; like the AWOL Mars mission), and cute actions like this tended to burn themselves out. Forging his political career through the Democratic Party, he had particular disdain for lefty agitators who couldn't organize a barbecue. Let their trash pile up and the porta-pots overflow. He would finish his Asia tour, and if they were still there by the time he got back, he'd start choking them out with vomit gas.

Logan Dougall came from North Carolina, where he'd lived for two years on an anarchist commune scavenging his own food and stitching old clothing back together, no plumbing or electricity. When he hitchhiked into town for provisions, the driver told him what was happening in D.C. He decided he was sick of the commune anyway and kept on hitching north. Bridget Zeckhauser bought a ticket out of Juneau, Alaska, where she'd spent a decade studying the fate of the northern sea otter. She'd been drowning in a lot of despair lately, and when she saw Morris take the stage for that speech, she had a real "Fuck it" moment, packed her sleeping bag and tent and was in D.C. eighteen hours later. Walt Pasquina's younger sister refused to leave. They argued about it for a day and a night, but she was not only smarter than him, he realized, but way more stubborn. He called their parents and told them what the deal was, Kelly was being a pain. "She was born a pain," their mom said, totally unsurprised that her daughter wanted to get herself fully wrapped up in all this. Walt told his mom he'd stay and at least make sure Kelly was safe and things remained orderly and peaceful.

The Clean Energy Labor Coalition, much of its leadership under investigation, racketeering charges in the works, had to cling to the right side of the law, even as many of its members, educated in the strike and agitation, saw the D.C. action and began to deliver cash, supplies, and bodies. CELC members formed the bulk of the construction crews and got to work dealing with what organizers knew would be the key issue: waste disposal. Bathrooms in nearby buildings were quickly seized and treated as the occupation's most vital treasure; the sanitation team cleaned the portable toilets and showers every hour, the refuse pumped into either nearby sewers or sanitation trucks, trash minimized, collected, recycled, and repurposed whenever possible.

Morris opened a line of communication with the mayor's office to assure the city that the occupation would do everything it could to keep the crowd nonviolent and nondestructive. They would police their own. Would-be looters, provocateurs, and other troublemakers would be expelled by the Blue Bands. *Though everyone is welcome, it is a privilege to be a part of this,* the AI warned any incoming insurrectionists. *The rule of law will prevail within these new borders of freedom. In other words, don't smash a Starbucks window, jackass, or you will be forced to leave.* Like Gandhi's satyagrahas, the Blue Bands formed the point of the spear for an army of warriors whose strength was not to fight. They brought a militarized discipline to the operation. Though she often talked the talk, Kate Morris had no patience for horizontal structures or autonomous self-organization. Leaderlessness was for the birds. She only intended to offer people the fiction that they were in the arms of an organic movement. But she needed more enforcers, so her people found a kid named Dougall from North Carolina, a sea otter scientist all the way from Alaska, and a Marine from Maryland. After brief interviews and background checks, she offered them blue armbands with tracking chips sewn into the fabric.

The crowd bloomed out into the core of the city, one day unfurling another petal into Fourteenth Street, engulfing the Department of Commerce, the next plunging down the throat of Twelfth Street and Independence until the Department of Agriculture was swamped by tents and tarps. The next day an estimated four thousand people arrived, colonizing most of the hill around the Washington Monument. The police had no capacity to push back. Their drones kept flying in the wrong directions, swamped by some sophisticated computer virus. Their cyber units understood they'd been hacked, their networks still disrupted by a relentless machine learning algorithm. FaceRec tech was getting its lunch eaten by masks, hats, and T-shirts designed to scramble the software and turn all face ID data to bunk.

DHS was furious at D.C. Metro's incompetence and various turf battles ensued in the back rooms of city services. Meanwhile, the National Guard was called in, but they quickly found themselves busy elsewhere. Two weeks into the siege, as more and more resisters quit their semesters or left their jobs, micro-occupations were springing up in L'Enfant Plaza and Benjamin Banneker Park; in Dupont and Logan Circles; at Howard University and the Zoological Park; on the George Washington Memorial Parkway, as protestors tried to shut down traffic to Reagan National Airport with a snake march. Seven hundred people walking against traffic required the full attention of the Guard, who fired tear gas into the crowd, kettled the mass of people into manageable chunks, twisted arms, slammed bodies into hoods, arrested freely. Liza Yudong's AI had nothing to do with this, but people took its lessons and ventured out into the city to snarl traffic, get themselves arrested, and keep the Guard busy and away from the main encampment. Early in their planning, Kate had explained to her old friend Liza what she wanted: "We clog the jails, overwhelm their capacity to arrest their way out of this. We don't want chaos or destruction, we want befuddlement. Head-scratching."

Now Yudong's AI continued its dance with law enforcement, allocating bodies, swarming a given area of the city. Mass arrests were like swatting at a cloud of gnats: maybe you dizzied a few, but they recovered as quickly as they dispersed. Meanwhile, the executive committee threw up a digital map of the city on the wall of their command center and, after consulting the AI, ordered all new arrivals to find space on Upper Senate Park, just north of the Capitol. It was a risky annexation, but that afternoon they poured nearly fifteen hundred bodies across the streets, jamming all movement outside the Russell Senate Office Building. Most members of Congress had already left the city. The next day, the Secret Service erected a razor-wire fence around the White House and Capitol. President Love, back from Asia, was rerouted to Camp David.

"How the fuck did it get this out of hand?" he demanded. When his advisors began whimpering excuses, he knew they were not sufficiently fearful of him. He had experienced this kind of disrespect in the military. What he'd done about it was, the first time someone coughed "queer" at him, he put that guy on the ground and beat his ear until it was cauliflower with 70 percent hearing loss.

Huddled with his cabinet via a secure VR link, Love wondered why they couldn't send a six-pack of horror drones down there firing tear gas and rubber bullets. Dallas was too fresh in everyone's mind, his cabinet warned. There were children. "We should be forceful but careful," Secretary of Defense Caperno warned. "Right now this is peaceful and contained. There is no predicting what would happen if we act rashly."

"Is it contained?" Love scoffed. "Because when I first checked in, a few snowflakes were roasting marshmallows and now these animals have surrounded half the city."

"We need a place to put the arrested following any action," the secretary of defense went on, and she suggested RFK Stadium, a ghostly and dilapidated urban sore that Nixon had used to respond to the May Day Tribe protestors who'd attempted to shut down the district over the Vietnam War.

"That was less than eight thousand people," Love's chief of staff noted.

"There are nearly ten times that many right now on the Mall alone. Maybe a quarter of a million in the city at large."

Caperno suggested building a series of floating internment facilities off the shore of Annapolis, similar to what the Europeans had done to house refugees in the Mediterranean: Extrajudicial spaces where they could let the movement's leadership rot for a year or so in legal limbo under PRIRA. DHS was already preparing floating prisons in the Caribbean as Haiti faced famine and its people tried to make a run for Florida. It wouldn't be too difficult to redirect some of that budget and infrastructure toward the waters off Annapolis. Love, grinding a pen cap between his molars, eager to get a few vodka tonics in him, told them to go ahead. They added a short provision to the executive order allowing Xuritas units to join the peacekeeping forces.

And still they came.

From every state in the Union, from overseas, from disappearing islands in the Pacific most Americans hadn't even heard of. A grocery store clerk from New Mexico, an electrician from Vermont, a prep school student from D.C. whose mother happened to be a Supreme Court justice.

"Why are you here?" a CNN reporter asked him.

"I don't understand why everyone isn't here," he told her. A gas mask dangled from his hip and his shirt read FIGHT BACK. "I'm here because we have nothing left to lose. Win now or die."

Letitia Hamilton was eleven years old and homeless. She'd been in foster care most of her life until she decided what was going on in the home where she was staying was "hazardous to my health," as she told a white lady with butterfly tattoos on her arms. Living on the streets for two years with a subterranean class of children who inhabited the shadows in the capital of the richest, most powerful country in the world, Letitia learned many ways of getting by. Not just how to sleep and eat but how to be fleet of foot, to trust no one, and how to con people into doing things for her. For a few months, she'd been living in an empty condo, having figured out the code to the Realtor's lockbox. She went in at night and came out in the morning before any potential showings. When she saw what was happening on the Mall, though, she packed up. It didn't all make sense to her. The intricacies of climate, inequality, and geopolitics had not been in any of the TV shows, video games, or VR worldes she'd experienced in her brief interactions with those formats. What she did know was that people were pissed off, the world was mean and shitty, and now a bunch of them were getting together to do something about it. She told the woman at the intake that she and her mom wanted a tent. The white lady gave her the tent, but Bridget from Alaska with the butterfly tattoos knew what was up, because she kept coming by to check on her. Not that Letitia needed it. Unlike the adults, she could move anywhere she wanted, flow between worlds with ease. She slipped outside the borders of the occupation, overheard what the police were telling each other, and ran back to whisper it to somebody with a blue armband. She helped make the coffee every morning. (She loved coffee, had been drinking it since she was eight.) People got to know her in the camp. They thought they were looking out for her, but they had it wrong: She was looking out for them. It was funny, she'd always thought of the place she laid her head as somewhere she had to stay. Never permanent. Never to become attached to. And yet her little one-person tent in the dead center of the National Mall, boxed in at this point by seventy-five thousand other people, damn if this didn't feel very much like home.

At first there was a show every night. A musician singing a few acoustic tunes, a stand-up comedian performing, an actor, author, or activist giving a quick speech. Haydukai rolled back through for a set. A former vice president, an ex-senator, and a few other former lawmakers arrived to show their encouragement. Tracy Aamanzaihou planned to speak, but then the White House called. After careful consideration, ashamed of her cowardice, she decided against it. There were dances in which people conscripted large parts of the lawn to shake out their tension and wring out some joy. Someone had erected a pink and purple bouncy castle for the kids. This was right beside the fencing and razor wire D.C. Police used to garrison the Capitol Building, and the images zipped across the planet: All these children slamming into pillowed walls with militarized police watching behind barbed wire. They tried to keep booze and hard drugs out, but obviously people did what people do. There was a lot of hooking up in tents and tipis. In the middle of each and every night, somewhere in the huge swath of territory they'd annexed, there would be the grunts of fresh sex, stifled (or not so stifled) cries of orgasms. Human beings and all.

Sitting beside his former boss on foldout chairs, a homemade stew cooking over a little campfire she'd built, Tom Levine admitted that he'd never believed any of this could work.

Kate Morris licked tomato paste from her fingers. "So what changed your mind?"

"When I heard Matt wasn't going." Tom didn't look at her to see how this landed. His intention wasn't to hurt her, it was just a fact. "Because if he split, it meant he really thought you'd figured it out. When I told Rekia what you were planning—it's like both of them knew you and Liza were for real with this. That's what scared them."

Kate nodded and tried to think of something to say. "Sorry if this caused problems at home."

Tom laughed. "That almost sounded human, Kate."

She batted her eyes. "I try."

Tom let out a slow sigh. "Why did you want me and not Rek? Or Coral, for that matter?"

Kate gave a funny little shrug and fart of her lips. "I trust you, Tom. Hell, I trust you more than I did Matt. And in the end, he did what I thought he would do ten years ago."

"Yeah, but why not Coral?"

Kate smiled weakly and tossed another log onto her fire. A local tree farm had donated them by the pallet. Though burning trees wasn't exactly on message, she'd never denied herself the pleasure of a good campfire.

"Fierce Blue Fire, my friend—it was infested from the start. Corporate spies and FBI informants. From the rank and file to leadership. And this whole bazingo"—she gestured to their wild festival—"would never have worked without the old-fashioned element of surprise."

Tom scratched his messy black locks, his expression pained. He'd put on a lot of weight since she'd seen him last, all his muscle turning into pudding around his torso and under his chin. She waited for him to figure it out.

"Stanton told me you were paranoid, but—you don't know that, Kate."

"I do know it."

"Who?"

"Who do you think?" When he continued to wait, perplexed, she told him. Through a careful and partially illegal investigation, she'd learned that her second-in-command, their friend Coral Sloane, was an undercover FBI agent. The Harvard Kennedy background had been true, but they'd never gone into activism. They'd been recruited. Once that piece fell into place, there were so many moments, arguments, fuckups, and missed opportunities that never directly pointed back to Coral but suddenly in hindsight made absolute sense. After the events of 2030, in which not only did their legislation get gutted and reanimated but her personal life became the subject of a coordinated campaign of character assassination, Kate hired a firm to investigate their organization. They quietly looked into everyone in the D.C. and New York offices, even Matthew Stanton. That was how she'd discovered he was sleeping with the reporter who'd written an article about her years ago. For some reason, that knowledge was more irritating than she would have anticipated. Then her investigators told her about Coral. There were also bugs: in her office, in her and Matt's apartment, even on her bike. She left them all in place.

"You can't tell Rekia."

Tom sat in stunned silence staring at the side of the trailer that had once been designated for Jack White. "I feel like I'm going to fucking throw up," he said finally.

Morris stared at her fire for a long time because she knew what he was feeling. She'd gone through it herself. "At least it wasn't Matt," she said.

The next day the executive committee delivered a document to every major media organization. They declared the siege of the United States capital would come to an end when lawmakers agreed to enact a Climate X agenda, amnesty for everyone involved in the occupation, a repeal of PRIRA, the release of all political prisoners, and an investigation of all companies involved in obfuscating the science of, and delaying action on, climate change. Otherwise, they would slowly but surely bring the American government and economy to a halt. A few weeks earlier, this may have sounded fantastical, but now there were an estimated 123,000 people clogging the center of the city, with more flooding in every day.

However, it was not just supporters who were coming. Militiamen, skinheads, neo-Nazis, and the American Patriot League began to hike over the Potomac as well, assault rifles shouldered, body armor strapped tight, camo fatigues and their own symbols, slogans, and armbands: swastikas, the Týr rune, HATE, the South African apartheid flag, the APL's menacing Cerberus, or the "Baby Breivik" meme, which featured Norwegian mass murderer Anders Breivik as a toddler mischievously urinating. They stood watch on the perimeter of the city, shadowed by police, waiting for an excuse. The previous fall, a powerful new recruitment tool had exploded onto the internet, an AI of unknown origins. It camped out in chat rooms and VR worldes, found young white men, and went to work on them. Like Yudong's app, it sifted through their behavioral surplus to understand why they were sad or upset or furious, and in the guise of a gorgeous young woman or older mentor, inked a portrait of a world in which they were in danger.

They had to act before it was too late. The member rolls of white nationalist groups abruptly skyrocketed. The League alone was adding nearly two thousand members a month. Fox News, bludgeoned in the ratings by Rory Baumgart's radical network, Renaissance, had no choice but to try to scream louder for the preservation of white heritage. Many local law enforcement agencies had long-lasting relationships with citizen militias, funneling them arms and money through "community grant" programs. Military contractors, including the president's former company, Xuritas, used shell companies to enhance training and recruitment in the American Patriot League. Attorney General Greenstreet had suggested this marriage of convenience, convinced that the DOJ could appropriate these folks to root out 6Degrees. Private contractors would embed undercovers to keep the League in check while using them to gather intelligence. The D.C. mayor, who knew nothing of this program, directed a contingent of his force to shadow the right-wing paramilitaries everywhere they went. "If they so much as jay-walk, arrest them and confiscate their weapons," he ordered. He would not let the new civil war everyone had been predicting for so long break out in his city. Andrea Sanchez, glad to train her sights on someone she recognized as an enemy, began showing up to her post at the Jefferson Memorial where many of these elements had gathered. She couldn't help but despair at how much more firepower these faux soldiers had while the executive branch remained eerily silent on the matter.

Holly Pietrus arrived in D.C. just before the order was given to lock down the city. Her husband had agreed to stay in New York and keep up the battle to free her father, while she took the train to Maryland. She reached a maze of abandoned cars on I-395 and had to hike the rest of the way. She couldn't believe her eyes. The district looked positively reinvented, a humming day-glow carnival awash in graffiti. In just over a month artists had transformed the buildings: a twenty-foot banner of deceased congressman John Lewis on the Potomac-facing side of the Mandarin Oriental with GOOD TROUBLE stamped beneath his scowl; the other side of that building hosted a three-story image of a little girl as a circus fire-blower, incinerating a group of briefcased, besuited businessmen; a mural painted around Stanton Square and visible from the sky with THIS IS OUR CRADLE, OUR SCHOOL, OUR HOME, OUR GARDEN. Surveillance drones buzzed overhead.

Met by the mephitic stench of trash, portable toilets, and trench latrines, the smell watering her eyes, it took Holly an hour to check in at the entrance, where she was searched for weapons by a stinky woman in a blue armband. Then she waded into the encampment, clopping over plywood bisecting neighborhoods of tents, yurts, tipis, and crude wooden shacks. Grass long eradicated now that the summer heat had moved in (eighty-seven degrees that day, May 7), the pulverized ground had dried to a fetid dust. Flags flew: Blue Fire, BLM, Veterans for Peace, upside-down Stars and Stripes, and the row of First Nations tribes along the buffalo horn formation, restaking a claim to their homeland. She was directed toward the stage, where the executive committee typically huddled. She spotted Kate, and for a moment was filled with the same anxiety as their previous three encounters: When you so idolize someone, you're quick to think they find you a silly and tedious distraction.

"I had to walk from outside the city, and these shoes—" she began to stammer, and Kate stalked to her like she was going to throw a punch. Holly even flinched as the taller woman wrapped her arms around her neck. Kate didn't know her own strength, and it hurt.

"You are fucking awesome," she hissed in Holly's ear. She pulled back, and there were tears in her bright banshee eyes.

"What you said about my dad— I had to come, and just say I'm with you. Whatever you need."

"You fucking awesome nuclear bitch," Morris went on, gripping her by the back of the neck and shaking her. Then she embraced her again, roughly.

While she was still wrapped up, Holly said, "It really stinks here."

Kate laughed right in her ear. "Yeah, I know, we're working on it."

As she took Holly Pietrus on a tour of their exploding festival, Kate of course understood this girl would make the perfect informant, and she quietly sent a message to Liza to make sure eyes were on the FBF New York director—not that she approved of snitch-jacketing. Just in case.

That night there was a bonfire near the National Gallery. Reporters gathered for this impromptu press conference. People crowded around and strained their ears to hear what Kate Morris had to say.

"The city's given you forty-eight hours to pack up," said a reporter from CBS. "Will there be violence?"

"Not by us," said Kate. "No one here even knows how to punch."

"What do you hope to accomplish? You don't expect Congress to actually enact your platform, do you?"

"Why wouldn't we? We're not bargaining anymore. We want uncon- ditional surrender from the corporate state. Why don't people believe me when I say that?"

Laughter at this, but her face remained untroubled, as if it had all come to pass already, and the laughter ceased. Light from the fire glimmered across the orb of a VR camera, and Quinton Marcus-McCall edged past it, blocking the viewers at home. A busybody camerawoman shooed him, and he sidestepped to the left.

"Moral suasion hasn't worked. Electoral politics hasn't worked." Kate poked the fire with a long, slim log, and the embers hissed. "So all we have left is revolt. We have to make this country ungovernable, this economy un- profitable, this system unworkable."

Quinton had joined the mutual aid arm of A Fierce Blue Fire and helped work the wreckage of the Great Eastern Flood and then Hurricane Rose the past fall. Shortly after that, he'd received an email asking if he was interested in becoming a leader of a nonviolent army. The reporter, bored with Morris droning on, looking for another angle, abruptly turned to him.

"What about you, sir? Why are you here?"

Quinton felt like a bank robber with the spotlight suddenly trained on him and laughed nervously. "Maybe I think about it a little different." He shifted his eyes to Kate and back to the fire. He could remember seeing her speak for the first time in Detroit, what felt like three or four lifetimes ago, after what happened to his parents, but before he lost his sister. Before he ended things with his fiancée. Before he dropped out of school. All these years of trying to do something worthy, and no one had ever asked him what he thought. "Sure, this is an act of physical rebellion." He shifted on his feet and decided to let his freak flag fly for these folks. "But that can't be all it is. It's gotta be spiritual. It's gotta be about an immaterial force within us. To save one life is to save all of humanity, right? Ever heard that? That's the Holy Qur'an. But it applies across all faiths and nonfaiths. So to save a spe- cies from extinction, a people from annihilation—if that's not summoning the Divine, I don't know what is."

Everyone paused, trying to grasp this somewhat inscrutable take.

"Yeah, I'm a little less froufrou than that," Morris finally said, to much laughter.

Quinton felt his face flush in a good way. The beat of the drum cir- cle drifted back to them from the east along with, gratefully, the scent of woodsmoke. Somewhere near the Washington Monument people were dancing, and the Capitol's bright dome still shone in the wine-tinted twilight.

MAY 20

The next week the D.C. Police shut down every road leading into the city. Shelter in place. A state of exception. The only people allowed past the checkpoints had to have written permission from DHS. People continued to try to sneak over the Potomac on motorboats or wind their way up side streets through southern Maryland, a veritable underground railroad of activist passage on the way to the occupation. Meanwhile, police stood guard, studying the nightly glow of this invented city, waiting on something to snap.

Was Loren Victor Love the figure Kate had been waiting for all along? Had Mary Randall served a second term, would she have been able to use her—a woman she'd endorsed for president in '28—as a suitable foil? In order to spark rebellion against an enemy as faceless as anonymous capital, it helped that capital chose a hired gun like Love, a true hypermasculine paranoiac if ever she'd seen one. She'd expected covert rock and bottle throwing by agent provocateurs like she'd seen at Sacred Stone nearly twenty years ago. Infiltrators played the long game now, living out of tents but reporting to the task force organizing on the perimeter of the city. The occupation was surveilling its own, looking for undercovers, but this was needle-in-haystack work as the numbers grew.

While twelve thousand police, National Guard, and private security forces amassed in high school gymnasiums in Bethesda and Silver Spring, these undercover agents chose the ingress points: Independence Ave on the southeast corner of the Mall and Fourteenth and Constitution on the northwest corner. On May 20, well past the authorities' deadline to disperse, with everyone nerve-racked from the wait, teams of infiltrators set fire to several tents and the tipis in the buffalo horn. Then they radioed for authorities to descend. The day was hot and the fires burned quickly, catching nearby tents and leaping to others. Occupiers tried to fight the flames with bottles of water and the few extinguishers on hand, but the fire ate quickly into the center of the Mall. Meanwhile, the Guard was firing tear gas, scrambling between trees to tear out tents and arrest whoever didn't run for it. The screams echoed over the day. Children wept in terror as police banged batons against riot shields and advanced, broken glass crunching underfoot.

The Occupy AI messaged every device: *First and foremost, Don't Panic. Like the Terminator said, "Come with me if you want to live."*

It told parents to move their children to the center of large circles of adults, and though these adults were suddenly very afraid, they did as told. Still, panic crept in, spread, and a few gathered their kids in their arms and tried to make a run through the barriers, only to be met by the wafting tear gas.

Kate Morris sat cross-legged on the floor of the command center, toggling through their cameras, trying to see it all at once. She bit her lip and watched the AI direct people as the police and Guard swarmed their fortifications. "Okay," she said to herself. "Okay."

Liza Yudong had anticipated the media blackout. She sent camera crews to the sites of police ingress with the only instruction to keep filming no matter what. They would livestream it all in 2D and VR. Holly Pietrus found Kate and Liza watching the monitors. She'd run from the other side of the Mall when the fires started and saw a Blue Band catch a rubber bullet in the stomach. She could hear people screaming now.

"Does your magic robot have a plan for this?" she demanded, inserting herself in Liza's vision. "No, no one saw this coming at all." Yudong bugged out her eyes, like *Bitch, get out of the way.*

The wailing of a sound cannon started up to the south, ear-splitting even inside the trailer. Holly flinched as the first flash grenade boomed nearby.

Morris slapped her laptop shut and stood. "Get these kits moving. Let's go." She had a small backpack, which she now rummaged through. Similar packs were traveling down through their ranks. She popped in earplugs, draped a piece of body armor over her torso, complete with a fortified breast plate, and finally pulled out a gas mask. Her eyes blazed with goofball fury, and she gripped Holly by her shoulders and shouted, "Tell them if they had not committed great sins, God would not have sent a punishment like me upon them!"

Then she banged out of the trailer, braying laughter.

Over the last three and a half decades, given Seattle, given the Occupy movement, given Tahrir Square, given Hong Kong, given Black Lives Matter, given every G8 summit or NATO powwow, authority had become expert at clearing cities of large protests, and the climate concert's organizing committee had studied these tactics. As police launched tear gas and strafed the wall of protestors with rubber bullets and water hoses, people fell. Zip-tied and dragged away to a fleet of waiting school buses, choking on gas when police ripped their masks free. But more came in their place, linking arms, pushing forward. Supply lines kicked in, bringing body armor, helmets, gas masks, and plexiglass shields to the front lines. The Blue Bands strapped everything from flak vests to foam pillows across their torsos and stormed to the front, and when they were hit, their friends, old and new, pulled them back up. Smoke curled skyward from the fires. People ran with buckets of water, and Letitia Hamilton, who knew she was the fastest mortal on two legs in this whole damn city, went hurtling back and forth hauling jugs of water from the caches to try to douse the tents. Sirens and sound cannons wailed, a head-splitting, fillings-rattling orchestra of state power. A scruffy teenager in a mask ran down Madison with a hockey stick, slapping gas canisters back at police, and the wind, a fervent revolutionary that day, kept carrying the plumes south, away from the Mall. City crews hooked chains to the trees planted in the roads and began tearing them out by the roots, while massive BearCats drove into the walls of flotsam, clearing roadways for police and National Guard to spill in.

Kate Morris shoved her way to the front of the crowd, and in doing so, could see her idea working. Amassed at the intersection of Fourth Street SW and Independence Avenue was a wall of human beings so thick and tight, she could barely squeeze through. As she oozed between the bodies, the sound cannon shut off, and she got her first whiff of gas, brief acid in the eyes. She slipped her mask on. People were shoulder to shoulder, groin to ass, but also without claustrophobia. Unafraid. Knit together as one organism. A few recognized her and helped get her through. As she reached the front lines, she stopped passing any men. An all-female brigade, two hundred women deep, pushed at the edges of the street. Some had gas masks, but many were frantically washing each other's eyes out with bottled water while others wore every variety of goggles—chemist, swimming, and construction. Students and retail workers, professors and waitresses, grade-school teachers and nurses, housewives and graphic designers. And it was working, this idea she'd had to use only women on the front. The cops were hesitating at the edge of Independence, now a mess of toppled trees, broken fencing, and all the other debris used to barricade the road in April. A phalanx in full military gear, zip ties dangling, was restraining a shrieking girl who couldn't have been more than four and a half feet, maybe all of thirteen years old.

Kate stepped through streaks and drizzles of blood on the pavement. Because Fourth Street was sandwiched tightly between two museums and packed with refuse, the police couldn't move in more than four or five abreast, a bad idea tactically, as the women were hurling rocks and other scraps of rubble. Hauling the girl away, the cops fell back at the order of some higher command. They all moved behind a Xuritas Armored Vehicle, also known as a Rolling Fortress.

Matte black with a D.C. Metro Police logo on the side, the XAV had begun its life on the outskirts of Saudi Arabia during the first years of the civil war two presidential administrations ago, only to be refurbished and repurposed for civilian use in the nation's capital. It crept forward, and the police received simple instructions: *Let the Fortress do the work. They'll move.*

The wind carried off much of the tear gas and Kate couldn't see well in the mask anyway. She ripped it off as she reached the front of the roiling crowd. The women hurled taunts and jeers, lifted their armor and shirts to expose pale breasts and slapped their hearts and dared the police to fire their weapons. A stun grenade exploded and five or six women fell, only to be hauled back to their feet by their comrades, while others, deafened, clutched their ears. Less than thirty feet separated their horde and the XAV. It surged closer. Kelly Pasquina, who'd come sprinting to join the wall when the AI asked her to, knew her brother was probably terrified trying to find her right now, but she couldn't care less. She recognized Morris, and for a moment she forgot about tear gas and sound cannons. There was only awe as her hero brushed past her.

"Be careful!" Kelly called to her, and the woman turned to her and winked.

And then Kate Morris began striding out into no-man's-land, toward the XAV. Hair blown wild by the same wind carrying off the gas, trail shoes thudding over bloody pavement, sleeves of her Montana thrift store jacket pushed up her elbows, she was sweating grease in the heat. She dragged a forearm across her eyes to clear the sweat, the acid sting—she could barely even see—and then started screaming as loudly as her parched, gassed throat would allow.

"C'mon, man! Let's do it!" Twenty feet, fifteen, ten, she kept walking at

the XAV as it rolled forward. *"You want to do it? So fucking do it! Fucking do it, motherfucker, c'mon!"* And then she reached the hood and slapped a palm on the black nose of the vehicle. The driver let off the gas, slowing but still moving. Kate stumbled back a step. *"Fucking do it, asshole! Don't tease me!"* She balled her hands into fists and beat the hood again and again and again. *"Do it! Hit the gas, you fucking coward!"*

How selfishly alive she felt, shot through with adrenaline and endorphins and fury like she'd free-soloed an undiscovered mountain. All thoughts of her family, her friends, her lovers vanquished and forgotten by this glory, and she screamed until her voice cracked and tears ran down her cheeks, until she could hear generations of her ancestors screaming with her.

"Do it, you fucking coward! Do it! Do it! Do it!!!"

Dwight Shweiger, twenty-five, originally of Warwick, Rhode Island, had joined the District of Columbia National Guard to pay for college. It was hot inside the XAV, inside his gear, and the voice of his commander was in his earpiece calmly telling him, *"If she won't get out of the way, mow her the fuck down. We got a whole day of this shit left."*

Shweiger had mostly slept through history class. He'd never heard of Tiananmen Square. Nor how during that protest, pork and grain prices were also incredibly high. He had no frame of reference at all for what he was a part of. He knew only two things: This lady in front of him had clearly lost her mind. She was screaming and weeping, and spit was flying from her mouth, and she was beating her fists into the vehicle like she could actually destroy it with her bare hands. The other thing he knew was that he could never press the accelerator. His superior barked at him to floor it, to flatten the first twenty people if he had to, and he thought of his childhood bedroom and the sound of the ships going up and down Providence River, and how when a blizzard came and school was called off, his mom would let him and his two sisters sleep in and then bring them minestrone soup and let them cook marshmallows over the gas stove, thereby compounding the wonderous nature of a snow day. Because he could not bear the thought of his mom learning of this if he did it, if he murdered this unarmed human being, he took his foot off the accelerator, and the woman nearly fell over when he threw the vehicle in reverse.

When the XAV began to back up, the police and Guard behind it had to quickly backpedal as well. Most of them figured an order had come down to abort. The women behind Kate Morris couldn't believe it at first. Then Kelly Pasquina let out a sound somewhere between a gasp of surprise and a war whoop. She ran for Morris, practically tackling her in an embrace, and behind her the crowd surged forward, and it was like they'd all experienced the blood in their veins for the very first time. They shrieked at the retreating vehicle, eyes swollen with lachrymator and the most glorious tears they'd ever cried. The incident had hardly passed, the video had barely been captured, before it was erupting all around the world. All these women, gassed and bloodied, many of them shirtless, beating their breasts, and then this one lunatic bitch steps in front of an armored vehicle, loses her damn mind, and the XAV, an emblem of the most powerful military force on the planet, slinks away in wounded disbelief. On screens and VR sets in every corner of the planet, civilization watched, and this moment slipped into its shared pool of myth and dream.

In the hours that followed, even after law enforcement had arrested ten thousand people, the siege exploded, coming to life the way we imagine fire to be alive. Consuming, incinerating, surrendering, only to then steal across roads, structures, and trees to find new life. Following the showdown at Independence, occupiers and authorities clashed near the Ellipse on the Mall's opposite corner, and the northwest front wasn't as much the feel-good story. They punched and kicked and hurled tear gas canisters back and tore the masks from the cops' faces; they were beaten, zip-tied, and hauled to makeshift prison islands; they caught rubber bullets in the throat and lay gasping for air; they tore truncheons from the hands of the National Guard and hit back; they surged up Twelfth Street to Pennsylvania Avenue to get behind the invading army, to attack their vehicles with rocks and bats, to flip them, burn them, drive them through boarded-up windows. They got control of a vehicle with a water cannon and turned it on the reinforcements trying to come down Twelfth. Every person hauled off bucked and thrashed and fought, so that it could take seven officers to get one scrawny woman into a zip tie. Without the help of the AI, Bridget Zeckhauser figured out that if they backed one of the septic trucks to Independence, they could open the vacuum hoses on the enemy. A jet of hot human waste sprayed across their plexiglass shields, splattering helmets, getting into their mouths and eyes. Liza Yudong watched from the trailer as the cops dropped everything and ran, and she fed this to her program so that the tactic could be copied at other intersections where authorities had broken through the tree and debris fields. More so than by hoses of human feces, police were simply overwhelmed by the sheer numbers. Up and down the ranks, their comms had stopped working and they experienced the chaos of disconnection from a command structure. One panicked Guardsman hit the accelerator instead of the brake, crashing into the fence protecting the Capitol, toppling twenty yards of the barrier, until the tires tangled and blew on the razor wire. A gang of women pulled him from the vehicle and tore at his equipment until they'd stripped him naked. The AI disseminated these tactics, made complex decisions, and reacted more quickly than the police could, so they staggered away, covered in piss and shit, only to hear their incursion had activated chaos in other sections of the city.

Certain solar systems within the wider galaxy of the siege had been agitating for destruction. These folks were not the nonviolent, organized monks of the first five thousand: they had their own ideas, and seized with the holy spirit of revolution, they launched into K Street, the metonym of the lobby shops that chopped, divided, and stapled together the legislation that undergirded American life. They found the lobbyist offices, law firms, and think tanks and smashed their way through plate-glass windows, past frightened security guards radioing for police backup that wasn't coming, hopped over security barricades, and then they were into the guts of the system, throwing computers at walls, pushing desks out windows, smashing servers and setting fires until the sprinkler systems came on and alarms blared. They poured gasoline and lit cubicles on fire. They wreaked havoc for hours until police and the Guard, having been beaten back at the Mall, rerouted to chase and corner these anarchists, who seemed only to fructify with each and every arrest. The city burned and firefighters and paramedics descended, and there would be five dead civilians, one dead cop, and hundreds more wounded.

Finally, as authorities retreated, protestors found their way over the toppled fence separating their territory from the Capitol. A few sheets of plywood on the fallen razor wire and they had an unobstructed path. The shadow of the 2021 insurrection had loomed over the city for years. Even when authorities thought Morris and her ilk really were only planning a dopey little concert, the Capitol was surrounded and fortified like it was 1814 and this time they'd be prepared for the British. Those fortifications may well have stood had that Guardsman not driven through the fence. Metro Police fired tear gas and rubber bullets. Invaders were hit and fell, but the leak quickly turned into a spigot as the occupiers tore a wider hole in the fencing. Seeing the writing on the wall, the last line of defense crumbled, and the police began to retreat. It took Logan Dougall only three minutes to skirt around the reflecting pool, past the Grant Memorial and Peace

Monument, make it up the Capitol steps, and smash his way through the first door he came to. He'd been just seven the last time the Capitol was breached, and nothing about those hairy Trump monkeys had impressed him. That was not revolution. Dougall had an axe, purchased at a Lowe's in Virginia on his way to D.C., smuggled in his gear past the Blue Bands when he arrived. He burst into the Rotunda along with hundreds more and ran for the first painting he saw: *Embarkation of the Pilgrims.* In four fells of the axe, he shredded this piece of colonial propaganda and moved to the next while the shouts and cries of other looters chased each other through the halls like unruly apparitions of destructions past.

Holly Pietrus had been told by the AI to deliver more water to the core, where the fires were still blazing, but she'd looked off into the anarchy of smoke, gas, fire, and stun grenades and found herself paralyzed. Finally, when the fence behind the trailers was toppled and people began sprinting toward the Capitol, she followed. To her shock, the National Guard who'd been defending the Capitol were fleeing east, north, and south, scaling the fence trying to escape. When she made it inside, the first thing she found was a guy spray-painting a dick on a white marble wall.

"Stop!" she shouted at him and slapped the can from his hand. "What are you doing? Get the hell out!" He looked baffled by this but did as he was told. She moved deeper into the building. It was in the Rotunda that she found Dougall with his axe. Amid the fractured marble of two toppled statues and three or four paintings with huge gashes in the canvas, Dougall worked methodically to shred another. "No!" Holly cried. "Cut it out!" Like this guy was her little sister scribbling in her books with crayon when they were children. The kid ignored her, and without another thought Holly ran at him, grabbing his arms from behind to wrest the axe away, pulling herself onto his back, her legs clenched around his waist. He smashed his elbow into her face, which would purple her eye, and she fell. He tried to recover the axe, but Holly was back on her feet, tackling him to the ground so the blade shrieked across the marble floor. "Stop it! Just stop it! Stop!" And she pushed Dougall's face and scrambled after the weapon. They both got to their feet and stood there, heaving breath. Clutching the weapon, Holly gave a little checked-swing thrust of the blade.

"Get out of here before I chop you up, kid!" How ridiculous *that* sounded, but Dougall had an abdominal muscle strain. He'd felt the pop when she landed on him. Holly watched him limp out of the Rotunda clutching his side. Then she ran around the building for the rest of the afternoon with the axe, threatening to murder anyone who was destroying, damaging, or defecating, which she found several guys doing in the Senate Chamber and ran at them like Lizzie Borden.

By the time the president and his advisors learned that not only had their show of force failed to clear the Mall but that the protestors had erupted out into the city in an orgy of destruction, he was on his third pill of the day. Sometimes he took Klonopin, sometimes he just lay awake calming himself with memories of how satisfying Afghanistan had been. For the first time, the stochastic processes of war frightened him. He went out to the grounds of Camp David to take in some air and beat his feet in the dust. Then Caperno called to tell him that somehow, the fucking SJWs had taken the Capitol Building.

Kate Morris and her team arrived inside the Capitol a few hours later. This was not what she'd wanted. Looking over the vandalism, the shattered sculptures, spray paint, and shredded paintings, she knew what happened next would define their movement in the eyes of those watching. Many of the hearts and minds she hoped to win would be reliving memories of men carrying Confederate flags through the halls of Congress. "We get this under control," she told Levine, Pietrus, Young, and Yudong, "or we lose everything." They secured the dozens of entrances throughout the building, including all the tunnels that led elsewhere in the city, posting their most trusted Blue Bands throughout the perimeter and blocking entrances wherever possible. They barricaded the tourist tunnel that connected the Library of Congress and overturned the trolleys that shuttled senators and representatives between their offices and the Capitol to block those routes. They established a command center, erected sleeping spaces, and commandeered all available food and supplies in the byzantine structure. They set up a hospital in Statuary Hall, where states provided looming statues of their most historic citizens, archetypal of their role in the American experience. The space had undergone a similar transformation during the Civil War, when wounded Union soldiers had pulverized limbs amputated among the marble and bronze figures. Now any volunteer with medical training treated the gassed, beaten, and rubber-shot.

As for the destruction, Kate put Holly in charge and impressed upon her how crucial it was to fix this as best they could. Damaged paintings and sculptures were carefully removed and set aside. When Kate was young and first learning from her dad about the genocide of Native peoples, she would have thrilled at seeing these paintings wrecked. Now, it filled her with a sadness she couldn't quite explain to herself. Even more dismaying was what had happened in the House Chamber. Behind the Speaker's podium, drawn to enormous scale with spray paint was a blue flame and the words 6DEGREES IS COMING.

"Clean this off," Kate told a group of Blue Bands. Yet in the days and weeks that followed, that symbol would be found everywhere: in the destroyed D.C. lobby shops, graffitied onto the sides of buildings, chalked and stenciled onto every street and sidewalk, frequently found beside her own words. No matter what she tried or how much she decried violence, even against property, she would never again be able to separate her movement from theirs.

CHAOS THEORY, read the *New York Post*'s headline the next day with her picture. Subhead: MORRIS MELTS DOWN, TAKES COUNTRY WITH HER. Said Renaissance, THE LEFT'S HATRED KNOWS NO BOUNDS: POLICE BRUTALIZED, ASSAULTED BY INVADING ARMY. THE CAPITAL HAS FALLEN, said Fox; D.C. ON LOCKDOWN read the grim CNN chyron; CLIMATE ZEALOTS TEAR D.C. APART trumpeted the *Wall Street Journal*. Stories of police and patriotic Guardsmen beaten, gassed, stripped, humiliated. One iconic front-page photo showed a big chubby boy in tighty-whities, bleeding from the head, weeping and pointing in the direction of an overturned XAV. The outrage reigned alongside a very specific historical amnesia.

"The Weathermen have multiplied into an army of terrorists," said Senator Russ Mackowski. "This lawlessness cannot stand, and our president must act with overwhelming force or God help us." Renaissance begged patriots to arm themselves and patrol the streets of their towns and cities lest other provocateurs emerge. "The left-wing war on our country has reached a crisis," said Jennifer Braden in her white-hot VR worlde. "President Love owns this disaster. He's proven an utter coward. Arm yourselves while there's still time."

In the days following the aborted effort to clear the Mall, emboldened by the video of Kate beating the hood of an urban assault vehicle playing on every screen in the world, would-be revolutionaries and right-wing counterrevolutionaries attempted to break into Lockdown D.C. in droves. They were met by a massive influx of the US Army, police, and increasing numbers of Xuritas security personnel. Fencing and checkpoints were erected on all roads within fifty miles, from the highways to the county two-lanes. Homes and businesses were cleared in a five-mile radius around the city. The Coast Guard patrolled the Potomac and the Anacostia in a thick web of boats, tracking searchlights over the shores. And still people managed to find ways in.

In capitals around the world, from London to Pretoria, Accra to Ottawa, Tokyo to Wellington, Brasília to Seoul, activists pitched tents and blocked traffic. They hung banners and sprayed the walls of their public buildings with graffiti; they came in numbers so dense that even the most prepared governments were caught flat-footed. Moscow deployed security forces to major public spaces. In Hong Kong, fifty thousand troops marched through the streets, the city militarily occupied before anyone could even leave their door with a sign. Liza Yudong's app, however, was downloaded by nearly ten million Chinese devices in just forty-eight hours. They arrived faster than the tear gas and rubber bullets could uproot them, hungry people, desperate people, passionate people, and everyone in between, linking arms in the digital world, and demanding an immediate halt to the incineration of the planet, a blooming fascism, and the gangster capitalism that had led them all to this point.

Within the halls of the captured Capitol, lit by candles and a few generator-powered bulbs, cots, tents, and sleeping bags crowded all available floor space, from the Old Supreme Court Chamber to the Crypt where the sandstone columns had been handcrafted by slaves rented from antebellum plantations. They set up shop in staff and security offices, slept on couches, helped themselves to mini fridges stocked with every variety of snack and booze. In the city beneath the building, they found enough food and water to sustain the movement for at least another two months. They worked to assign and distribute provisions both within the Capitol and to those still holding the Mall. They moved their war room from the trailer behind the battered concert stage to the office of the Speaker of the House.

"They want to take down the rest of the paintings in the Rotunda," said Holly Pietrus. They had a solar lamp set on the desk, and it cast an eerie, irradiated glow over their faces. The top organizers still wore their soiled, sweaty Blue Bands even after nearly three months. "The *Baptism of Pocahontas*, the *Landing of Columbus*, all of them."

"Who does?" asked Seth Young.

"The tribes supporting us." The leaders of these nations had set up several tipis in the Rotunda, where dead political leaders of the empire that had wiped away their ancestors typically lay in state.

"And another faction is demanding we take out all the pictures and statues of men," said Levine. "Including the bust of MLK for his sexual misconduct."

Kate rubbed her face and tried to blink away her exhaustion. She hadn't slept more than a couple hours a night since the day of the attempted clearing. Everyone was looking at her, and she couldn't help it. Maybe it was a whole childhood of her father telling her she was too white to understand this or that Native thing. Maybe she was remembering her first sting of pepper spray with the Oceti Sakowin at Standing Rock a lifetime ago, but some kind of deep, pent-up anger, directed at the wrong people, came bursting out of her then.

"Do we not have bigger fucking fish to fry here?" She saw the people around the desk recoil in the lamplight, so that the shadows jumped on their faces. She picked at a blood blister on her thumb. Even for someone who was fine with not showering for weeks at a time, she felt grimy, itchy.

Tom Levine, whose lungs still ached from inhaling smoke as he fought the flames during the incursion, whose fiancée had stopped answering his messages, was not about to let this moment be lost to squabbling. He had never in his wildest dreams imagined it would go this far, that he'd be back in these halls under such circumstances. He put his palms together in prayer and pointed them at his friend.

"Kate, we can't be the mob putting their feet up on the Speaker's desk in '21. We can't let the images of our people ransacking the halls stand. And we can't start redecorating."

"Maybe it's time to ask," said Seth Young, "what exactly we are doing here."

Kate snatched up a tablet, streaming the news. The chyron read GLOBAL PROTESTS RESULT IN CRACKDOWNS; PRESIDENT LOVE SILENT ON SIEGE OF WASHINGTON.

"What do you think we're doing here? It's working, Seth."

"Working how?" he asked slowly. Calm but very skeptical.

She threw up her hands, gesturing to august walls all around them, bugging her eyes at the obvious. "Look where we're holding our meeting."

He licked his lips and tried not to sound scared. He'd entered into this one reluctant step at a time, and now he was riddled with dread. He'd lived less than five blocks away during the Trump insurrection, which had demonstrated something frighteningly ephemeral about what constituted power. Now that he was part of such a thing, it scared him so much more. "I'm really worried this has gone too far."

"*Of fucking course it's gone too far!*" Kate exploded. "That's the whole fucking point, Seth!" The veins in her neck straining, Kate stepped into his space, pointing at the carpet. "We need to keep people here. We need to keep up the disruption, the momentum, the panic of the people who pull the levers. The stock market is starting to freak out. People are rising up. Opportunities like this do not come often."

"So we just sit here?" Seth asked, unable to meet her gaze, wondering if Ash had been right, wondering whose wagon he'd hitched himself to. "While we wait for them to try again?"

"Of course not." The heads of leadership turned all at once to Liza. She was painting her nails purple, blowing on them, and then reapplying the little brush. "We have the law-making building. So we explain what laws we want to pass, the ones that the people who normally sit in these stupid chairs refuse to." Liza rolled her eyes. "And to answer your question—yes, it does get tiring being the brains of the operation."

For five weeks following the attempted clearing, the Capitol transformed into a twenty-four-hour stump speech, beamed out to the world. They recruited occupiers from every walk of life, gave them the Speaker's dais, and together they painted a rolling, epic vision of a more just, equitable, healthy world. The feed never stopped. The speakers never let up this rolling sermon. A woman whose sons were both dead of heroin overdoses inveighing for an end to the drug war. A farmer advocating for regenerative agriculture. A doctor explaining the health benefits of electrifying the transportation sector. More viewers watched a student named Kelly Pasquina speak about the need for a global wealth tax than watched that year's Super Bowl. Her brother, Walt, now wearing a Blue Band, appeared briefly in an interview. The reporter asked the Marine why he went AWOL. Pasquina replied, "I don't care for politics. But the country's a lot like me, in that we should listen to my kid sister."

Who knows where it all may have led? Then, as the siege of D.C. stretched into its fourth month, the heat swept in.

JUNE 30

With authorities scrambling to cut water, power, internet, and supply routes, the temperature spiked to 109 degrees. A dome of high pressure descended on two-thirds of the nation, sending temperatures soaring into the triple digits, smashing records in every city it touched. In the last decade, dangerous heat waves had grown more fearsome but also normalized. Cities learned and instituted best practices, providing cooling centers, managing power grids, and sending social workers to the elderly and disabled, but the summer of '34 was unprecedented not just in heat but duration.

The poor and elderly were in the most danger. Baby boomers, divorced, widowed, aging, constituted the largest generation of elderly people living alone in the country's history, and the heat storm, as it came to be known, quickly became a quiet mass murderer. Hyperthermia is a nasty way to go. It begins slowly, with a bit of dizziness, and then ramps up quickly. For instance, Kyenna Blake, a seventy-seven-year-old woman living in Eastland Gardens, found the power out in the apartment where she'd lived the last forty years, where her children had grown up and then moved away, where her husband had died. She began by feeling puky, having trouble breathing. She went for the phone to call 911, but there was a wait. She was on hold. Like many victims of heat, she began to pull off her clothes because the feel of them against her skin was agony on her nerve endings. Then she vomited. Her muscles were shedding dead cells into her bloodstream, clogging her body's plumbing, while pieces of her organs cooked. Her kidneys and bladder were the first to shut down. Her heart, mercifully, went next.

Andrea Sanchez had never seen anything like this. On June 10, the thermometer hit 115 degrees, and she and her partner were called away from the Mall because folks all over the city were smelling the bodies. Bagging these corpses was dreadful work. It wasn't like a gunshot wound, an overdose, or a suicide. People cooked and then they melted. She had to cut the chain to get into one boiling apartment. The smell was so foul she fought to keep her gorge down. She found Kyenna Blake's body covered in dark flies and bleach-white maggots. The morgue was overflowing, and the county medical examiner had to call in refrigerated trucks to store the dead. The line of ambulances wrapped around the block. "Just consider yourself blessed," she told her fellow officers working back at the Mall, "that you're part of that embarrassment instead of this nightmare."

From her apartment in New York, Rekia Reynolds worked A Fierce Blue Fire's mutual aid network, trying to dispatch as many members as she could to check on the elderly and disabled in the neighborhoods where FBF operated Outposts. She worked sixteen hours a day coordinating this complex operation, but FBF's ranks had been pilfered and degraded. In the past few years, folks had left because of PRIRA, because the organization was no longer viewed as pure. Then many of its members had joined the occupation of D.C., where they themselves now risked succumbing to heat-stroke. Rekia's anger at her fiancé was only eclipsed by her blinding fury at Kate Morris. When they first met, Rekia had been the revolutionary, the one who wanted to storm the capital. Now she was left with the broken carapace of their organization, watching society's marginalized, mostly the Black and brown, die in real time because Kate had gutted their resources for her own vainglory. She read about Kyenna Blake in the *Post* and knew that if this had happened in 2032, they would have had volunteers knocking on her door to get her to a cooling center. Rekia's engagement ring was gone, and she'd smashed Tom's VR system against the hardwood and left its electronic guts lying on the floor of his office.

In cities across the country, power grids and substations began to buckle. In Pittsburgh, Chicago, Cincinnati, Indianapolis, Knoxville, Louis-ville, Memphis, Atlanta, the blackouts and brownouts crippled infrastruc-ture. Cooling stations lost power, AC units were worthless, mobile phone networks stopped working, and people were stranded in their homes. No VR, TV, lights, or refrigerators. Crack open the elevator doors of a high-rise and find two parents and three children cooked to death inside after only a few hours. Sky-high ozone and humidity. A heat index across the South of 133 degrees. A human body can only take two days of uninterrupted ex-posure to such temperatures. Electrolytes go haywire, exhaustion, respira-tory issues, and renal failure follow. Hospital beds were overrun like nothing since Covid-19. Ambulances were booked solid, emergency response times up to four hours. Many hospitals had to close their doors to new admissions, all the beds taken. It's called bypass status, and a father can show up with a child who has a body temperature of 105 and they tell that man, "Sorry, sir, try across town."

The headlines flipped. DEATH TOLL SKYROCKETS; SHOCKING HEAT KILLS HUNDREDS; HOMICIDES SPIKE WITH THERMOMETER; HEAT STORM HAS NO END IN SIGHT. Folks illegally opening fire hydrants on city streets to cool down, and suddenly water pressure vanishes for the whole neighbor-hood. Add this to water pump failures during the blackouts, and suddenly taps are dry. Multiple airports shut down as the runways melted, grinding the July travel season to a halt, and gouging a new hole in a stalling econ-omy. The temperatures cracked roads, and highways were lined with bro-ken-down cars. Potter's fields were overwhelmed, and city governments worked quickly on the PR side of their mass-graves situation. Prisons and detention centers could get away with anything, but one leaked memo, delivered to the Arpaio Illegal Immigrant Detention Facility in Arizona, urged wardens to use the heat to "clear capacity" and "reduce inmate numbers."

Victor Love's response to these dual emergencies of open revolt in the nation's capital and a murderous heat wave was a rare press conference where he took only five questions. He praised first responders and chided people for not checking on their relatives. This was not met with a lot of satisfaction. Then there was The Pastor taking to his VR worlde to claim he had predicted this too.

"I prophesied fire, I prophesied flood, I told you God would send heat to punish this country. The Bible also predicts there will be a breakdown of the family unit, and here we are with a faggot sodomizing another man in the White House. It predicts more crime, and here we are with a takeover of our great nation's capital. It predicts apathy toward Christians, and here we are with scientists and liberals moaning about your hamburger or your car instead of acknowledging the staggering signs that Christ already walks the earth at the End of Days."

President Love was addicted to right-wing media, which spewed nonstop invective about his failed presidency, his incompetence, his cowardice for failing to put down an insurrection that had sacked the Capitol while he hid at Camp David and did nothing. News stories emerged claiming a police officer was dead at the hands of protestors, beaten to death during the attempt to restore order, they said. The organizing committee worked tirelessly to combat the narrative, but facts were dismissed. There were other stories, of course, the usual onslaught of misinformation blasted across the media landscape: Women raped in their tents, captured police officers and soldiers being tortured and executed, precious documents at the Library of Congress soiled and shredded, the sex-crazed whore arranging orgies in the Senate Chamber to "initiate" children. Look at what Kate Morris's loose values had caused. Meanwhile, the death toll ticked up day by day, the counting of dead Americans still a highly popular national pastime, and eventually twenty-two thousand deaths would be attributed to these weeks of record temperatures and humidity.

Authorities offered a deal to the occupiers: cooling centers, bottled water, and amnesty waited for those who walked away. Many had no choice but to take them up on this offer. Individuals were carried to the checkpoints to be taken to nearby hospitals where they were given intravenous fluids or dumped in tubs of ice.

Beyond the thousands of army, police, and security personnel, beyond the drones and helicopters practically parked in the clouds, the rotors forming a permanent background hum, the city was arid and eerie. Trash blew like tumbleweeds along abandoned streets. Drought tightened the dirt, and a veil of orange dust, stamped alive by the feet of thousands, hung over the Mall. When the sun fled, no electricity for miles, the city fell into bottomless night. With all light extinguished, a storm of sailing stars became visible, the glow of the Milky Way. The occupiers huddled in a cinched, fearless nexus radiating out from the Mall. Everyone with children had left, taking advantage of the amnesty while they could. The bouncy castle lay in tattered ribbons, tangled with the razor wire of the toppled fence. The smell grew worse than ever. Day by day, the occupation dwindled as more people took the government's deal. They were exhausted, dirty, hungry, ill, and yes, afraid. The interminable heat was like wearing a suit of death. So they walked to the checkpoints, put their hands on their heads as instructed, and were allowed to leave—just as soon as they'd been fingerprinted, photographed, cheek-swabbed, and catalogued in a growing database.

In the kitchen serving the Senate cafeteria, Seth Young and Tom Levine were splitting a can of tomatoes and the last of the beers they'd rescued from the walk-in refrigerators. It was July 20.

"So you and I did the same thing," noted Seth. "Our partners told us not to go, and we did anyway. What's that about?"

Levine speared a tomato and slurped it off the tines of the fork. "I don't know. You said you weren't going to stay more than a few days, I said I wasn't going to be a part of this, but—"

"It took over. Like if you weren't here, you wouldn't go a day the rest of your life without thinking about it."

Tom favored Seth with a grim expression. "Yup."

"What I tried to explain to Ash"—Seth put his hands a foot apart—"is that 'my god, honey, I'm *doing this for Forrest*. I'm not abandoning him or you or anyone else. This is our way of fighting for his future.'" He shifted his eyes to his new friend. During the attempted clearing, the explosion of a stun grenade had sent Seth sprawling onto his back. He couldn't hear a thing and his eyes were stinging with gas. That was when Tom scooped him up by the shoulders, hauled him to his feet, and hustled him to safety behind a trailer. "I'm thinking of taking the amnesty," Seth admitted. "I need to get back to my family."

"No one would judge you," said Tom without hesitation. He held their can up. "We're almost out of tomatoes anyway."

Seth was thinking about how anxious Ash had been when he met Seth's family for the first time. Ash had no way of copping to his nerves, so instead, he got hyper-analytical and prattled on about obscure mathematical concepts no one understood—except that Seth's dad was an engineer and a math freak himself. Seth watched with great pleasure as his dad engaged Ash on some arcane point, and Ash looked like he'd had sand blown in his face. He told Ash after dinner, "I've never seen you harder than when you talked to my dad about the singsong conjecture."

"It's Singmaster's conjecture, Seth, and don't be crude." And Seth did what he always did to prove Ashir was not always so analytical: He put his hand on his crotch in the back of the driverless.

Tom was thinking of Rekia. Not long after they started sleeping together, when he asked her why they hadn't just done that right away instead of fighting for five years, she said, "'Cause you're an egotistical, white-privileged asshole." She squeezed one of his triceps. "And you always wore these tight shirts that made your arms look good, and I know you knew your arms looked good, and that made me hate you even more."

He wasn't sure that she'd ever forgive him, and this scared him. After an entire adulthood spent swearing to himself that he'd never fall for the marriage trap, he was in love with this woman and already dreaming of their children.

On that same night, blessed with cool wind, Holly Pietrus, Liza Yudong, and Kate Morris sat on the steps of the west side of the Capitol and shared a joint. With the power out in the city, the only light beamed down from a quarter moon, but they could make out the inky outlines of shantytown tents and black scars from the fires. The trampled dirt and filthy plywood paths. The toppled fence and the busted National Guard vehicle still tangled in it liked a beached whale. Like Tom and Seth, they were talking about their old friend.

"Rekia told me if I came here, I shouldn't bother coming back," said Holly. Her eye was still a midnight blue with shades of yellow from the elbow she'd taken to save a painting.

"Rek is doing what she thinks is right. So are we." Kate took the joint from Holly's fingers and took a drag. The tip glowed bright enough to cast light on her face.

Liza said, "At least in prison they'll have water, so I can exfoliate." Kate and Holly laughed. "You think I'm joking. This is exactly as bad as I thought it would be. I've always hated camping."

"Prison will be good," said Kate. "A nice challenge for me."

"The worst part is, I know she's serious," said Liza.

"Yep," Kate nodded affirmatively. "It'll be something I'll have to conquer and make useful."

"So you *are* insane," said Holly.

"If you think about it, a general strike in prisons, a massive civil disobedience campaign in the heart of the prison-industrial complex? Then if you add a hunger strike on top of it all, not only are the garment operations not running, but they have to bring in all this medical equipment to force-feed you in the ass. We can bankrupt these private prison companies before they even knew what hit 'em."

"Who is this 'we'?" asked Liza. "I get low blood sugar."

"You know you'll follow me over the waterfall, bitch." Kate shoulder-checked the smaller woman. "Don't front. Don't even make airs like you might front."

Liza rebounded. "This weed sucks."

Holly, who hadn't been stoned since college, found herself belly-laughing at these two, a new audience for a shtick they'd clearly honed over the years.

"That's been the fascists' best move yet," said Kate. "Cutting off our pot supply."

Their laughter trickled off, and the joint ran out, and they fell quiet. Stoned ruminations took the three of them all kinds of places. Liza found herself drifting back to when she'd first met Kate at the other organization they'd been involved with. Everyone was so self-serious, no one got her sense of humor, and she caught sideways looks for not performing her "climate grief." She found all the activisty screamingness of the thing tedious. All except this one girl. Kate Morris, she found, could take all the flak, arrows, and spitty people while Liza did her thing mostly behind the scenes. Not long after Liza turned in her resignation at FBF following Rekia's little coup, she'd called Kate and told her they should try something weird.

"What's weird, Liz?" Kate asked despondently. "What hasn't been tried?"

"Don't be such a stick in the mud. We could occupy the entire frickin' capital if we felt like it."

And from that one off-the-cuff response, the entire notion of their con emerged. Since Liza first began having anxiety about the end of the world and became determined to do something about it, she'd also resigned herself to the fact that nothing they did would likely work. However, if one had a great deal of fun in the process, it seemed to conjure belief in and of itself. Belief, in this case, was vital.

"Maybe my favorite thing about you," Kate said to her once, not long after they'd acquired the domain name for A Fierce Blue Fire and were still working out of her and Matt's apartment, "is that you're not who you say you are."

Liza had bugged her eyes and said, "I'll be whoever you ask me to be, Kate, if you just let me shave your legs and armpits." Kate thought this was so funny and laughed and laughed. Liza put on her most revolted face. "Why are you laughing? I'm absolutely not joking."

Holly, who'd spent so many months sick with fear about her father, was mulling a random childhood memory: She'd been maybe eight years old, at the beach in La Jolla. She'd been playing with her friends, these two boys, Mark and Joey, and all three had taken off their shirts in the surf, and her dad had come over and yelled at her—like really yelled at her—to put her shirt back on. When she returned to her towel, sobbing, she argued her case to her mom. It made no sense that the boys could take their shirts off and she couldn't, and there was no reason she should get yelled at for it. And the more her mom tried to explain the difference between boys and girls, the more certain Holly was that this explanation was nuts—she and Joey and Mark all looked exactly the same with their shirts off, so why would she get yelled at?

"It's just one of those dumb things, Holly-bear," her mom finally admitted. "Trust me, this will not be the last time you'll feel like it's bullshit being a woman."

"Mommy," she pleaded, because she hated it when her parents cussed.

"I'm sorry." She kept rubbing Holly's back for a while. Holly felt herself calming down. The world was not always fair, and people had very dumb ideas about things. That was the lesson, right?

Her mom laughed, and Holly remembered how beautiful her dark skin looked in the bright white sun. "That's exactly right, doll. And most of the dumb ideas come from men like your dad who think they're right about everything. Don't tell him I said that, but it's definitely the truth."

Holly hadn't missed her mom in a long, long time, but she did now. Missed her like hell. She went to sleep that night wishing it wasn't the case that every wonderful thing about her mom felt like it originated in another life or a dissipating dream.

Kate Morris, on the other hand, was not thinking about her family, childhood, friends, or lovers. There were errant memories and traumas that might preoccupy anyone's mind in such circumstances: listening to her mother cry as she tried to sleep in the passenger seat of their Honda Civic in a Fred Meyer parking lot after Sonja left Earl; this kid, Arturo, who used to tease her in grade school and called her an ogre one too many times, so she slammed the heel of her hand into his nose, and she had to see a child therapist for two years; or why not turn to thoughts of the partner she'd just left behind? She'd learned from every example in her life that men were scared, selfish, and weak. In the end, you could only rely on yourself. And Matt had gone and proved it to her once and for all. She'd listened to his car beat a crackling retreat down the gravel drive and took the moment to imagine herself as an old woman, when all these years of rain and thunder would be but a dim and painless remembering. Then she'd stood and returned to her office to keep working, and it was thrilling how very alone she was, how riddled with wounds.

But she had no use for memory at all that night.

Instead, she couldn't stop thinking of how the blood had roared in her ears as that armored vehicle rolled toward her, how the adrenaline felt like it might lift her off her feet and send her hurtling like a mortar round into its hull. Shock them, fuck them, grind them to the bone. Be fearless. Be Achilles, be Roland, be Joan of Arc. Have a mental disease. Follow your clit. Drive across the Dakotas and watch a storm sear the horizon, recognize herself in its peels of wind and each crack of lightning, her true fellow travelers. Don't change, don't learn, don't fall, don't flinch. All she'd ever feel was sorry for people who didn't know what it was to want something more than their own life. Conjure a tempest, spew rage from the heart, and make them stare into this city of Cassiterite dark she'd made with nothing but her ravaged voice.

Those in charge did not look at it quite as romantically. Urban heat and expensive bread had led to a summer of occupations and confrontations in capital cities around the world. In Pretoria, authorities opened fire with rubber bullets and tear gas, killing six. In Paris, protestors overturned a police vehicle, crushing two of their own. In Taipei, rioters battled with the army for six days until a typhoon blew through, soaked the city in two feet of rain, and buildings along the coast crumbled into the water. In Israel, a carefully calibrated plan to let only so much food and water into the Gaza Strip suddenly seemed overgenerous. They tightened the rations, and rocks and bottles flew and IDF vehicles burned. In China, the Ministry of State Security began detaining children they declared dissidents and returning their lifeless bodies to parents some weeks later. Protests against these brutal practices were becoming larger and more unruly, while the Communist Party blamed the CIA for sparking insurrection. There was a patient zero for all of this. The world's leaders glared at what had gone on for more than three months in Washington.

President Love's closest advisors huddled around him in Camp David, and he made sure to go berserk on them. He hurled a glass at the wall and told them they could resign if they didn't like his plan. Of course, they were all on their knees after that, begging for forgiveness, and it made him sick to watch. Vic Love knew combat, and he knew from combat that the joy of violence is inborn, that people secretly love to supplicate themselves to men powerful enough to unleash it decisively. The only answer to this clusterfuck was to sow unparalleled fear. In fact, he should have been looking at it this whole time as an opportunity. This rebellion in the nation's capital that had flummoxed and vexed him—he could use it as a proving ground. His nighttime disturbances echoed within the halls of Camp David, and his husband asked to be flown back to their estate. "You're not well," he told Vic before leaving. Vic told him to stay in Montana until he needed him for a magazine cover. It wasn't that Vic never thought he would make a mistake, but he'd never imagined anyone outflanking him the way Morris had. In many ways, Kate Morris and Loren Victor Love were meant for each other in this moment, as the malformed soul of the old world seized and screamed in the death throes of whatever would be birthed next.

This time, there would be no warning.

JULY 31

"I'm taking the amnesty," Holly Pietrus told the others. The siege had winnowed down to a core 21,582 hardy souls, still camped on the Mall and crowding the rooms of the Capitol. Morris, Yudong, Pietrus, Young, and Levine were gathered in the Speaker's office. Kate had tacked a George Carlin poster to the wall behind her, the comedian's eyebrows popping: *When you're born into this world, you're given a ticket to the freak show. When you're born in America, you get a front-row seat.* It reminded Kate of her long years in this amazing swamp city, where despite the evil that went on, the guts were hip-hop and the skin was pure metal.

"We're almost out of food and water," said Holly. "Whatever happens next . . ." She trailed off.

Kate nodded. She clutched her hands in her lap and gazed at her big, rough thumbs. "What you've all done here is beyond brave. I don't say this lightly, but the world will never forget this. And it will never forget you."

"I'm here till the end," said Tom. He lounged in the Speaker's chair, cracking and shelling walnuts. He'd found both the walnuts and the little metal gripper tool in a private cabinet of a random office.

Kate nodded but said otherwise. "No, you need to take the deal, Tom. The rest of you too. I'll stay."

"That makes no sense," he said.

Kate blew a breath up her face, lifting a strand of greasy hair from her eyes. "It makes perfect sense. I'll make an announcement tomorrow laying it out for everyone: They can stay with me and suffer the consequences, or they can go with you all."

"To do what?" Tom demanded.

"To start a boy band—what do you think, Tom? To keep fighting." Kate looked to the woman she trusted most. "Liza and I already discussed it. You'll keep pushing, keep agitating. And you'll hire the lawyers to stay up the government's ass until we're all out."

"There's no guarantee when that will be," said Holly.

"Yeah, well, there's not too much guarantee to anything, is there? I have to stay here," she said plainly. "I have to make them come and get me."

Their final meeting came to an end. They hugged and said their good-byes. When Holly embraced Kate, she couldn't help herself, and she broke down crying.

Seth Young and Tom Levine planned to leave the next morning. They tasked themselves with moving through the ranks of the remaining Blue Bands, explaining the choice everyone had ahead of them. Liza Yudong and Holly Pietrus left at dusk. They walked to a checkpoint on Fourteenth and Independence, where they were told to drop their backpacks and put their hands on her heads. They were zip-tied, processed for three hours, interviewed, and then released as promised.

The authorities went in that night.

The operation began at 3:31 a.m. on August 1. One moment there was darkness and only the stark splash of stars reigning over the Mall and the

Capitol, and the next floodlights and helicopters. The 1,250-watt fluorescent light towers switched on with a cacophonous chorus of thunks, turning four hundred acres of D.C. into interrogation-room glare. The choppers swooped in, hovering low above the Mall, uncovering dark corners with searchlights. The occupation's drones were shot out of the air, replaced by law enforcement's and armed with fifty rubber bullets apiece. Twenty-five thousand Guard, police, and private security forces surrounded the Mall, but it was a core contingent of Xuritas Special Ops that breached the barricades first, firing live ammunition, the crackle of gunfire foreign to these civilians, nearly all of them mistaking the sound for leftover firecrackers.

Kelly Pasquina was sleeping near the barricade at Third and Pennsylvania when the commotion began and crawled out of her miserably sweaty tent to see black-clad soldiers and the bright smatter of muzzle flashes. Fear took her by the throat, so that all she could really hear was her heart throbbing in her ears. Then her older brother, Walt, grabbed her by the shoulders and barked in her face, *"Get down!"*

The first round of Xuritas bullets punctured the lungs and heads and rib cages of people who'd just emerged from their tents to see what the deal was with the lights. It changed the very nature of the crowd. These bodies, once friends and comrades, became terrifying obstacles. Logan Dougall, penned in, saw the men in black, eyes hidden by visors, saw bursts of gunfire slicing apart people beside him, and now it wasn't just the bullets that were dangerous, but anyone blocking his escape. He threw elbows and stepped on groins and swiped away hands reaching for him. People ran with the panic of spotting a predator in open savanna. They all spilled east in the direction of the Capitol, looking for safety within its walls, but another Xuritas unit had driven through the barricades from that direction, cornering them. Dougall tried to spin and retreat before three bullets tore out the center of his chest.

Bullets, Kelly Pasquina realized, watching from the ground, had an almost unthinkable impact on the human body. Even though she came from a military family, even though she'd grown up watching as many Hollywood gunfights as the next gal, even though mass-shooting drills had been a part of her childhood, she'd never really considered what it is bullets do, the way they move bodies in ways they're not supposed to move, and what comes out of the holes is so ghastly, and how the wounds make noises bodies are never supposed to make. How they carve and pulverize and fragment tissue, bone, muscle. Her brother, lying prone beside her, knew this all too well.

That was the whole point of a bullet. A cold reminder of the simplicity and suddenness of death. Not that he was trying to explain this to his kid sister, weeping with panic.

Those involved with the decision to open fire on the encampment ran the gamut from principled dissenters to avid enthusiasts to those already leaking to major newspapers that they had tried to stop it without actually having done anything of the sort. The architects of the plan simply wanted to send a message. They weren't there to massacre all twenty thousand people, but there would be no inspirational stand going viral this time. This time, there would be absolute compliance and a decisive end to the situation. A display of loyalty by the dead. With conservative bursts of gunfire, they herded the terrorists into the center of the Mall, at which point loudspeakers began demanding that they drop to the ground.

"Lie down with your palms on the earth. Do not move. If you lie down, you will not be harmed."

The running, screaming people began to comply, not because they were necessarily listening to the loudspeakers over the thunder of the helicopters and the moans of the wounded and dying but because they could hear the snap of bullets all around them, and they could see others falling, leaving mists of blood, which looked pink and orange in the harsh fluorescent light. Bridget Zeckhauser felt a bullet clip her arm, and then another punch through her back, and when she fell onto part of a collapsed tent, she buried her face in the dirt and prayed to be transported away from this. Walt Pasquina saw her spill across the ground, could hear her screaming as she whipped one panicked arm covered in butterfly tattoos. Kelly lay on her stomach whimpering, trembling with shock. Walt grabbed his sister by the arm and shook her so she would look at him. "Stay put, stay down," he said. "We'll get through this, Kel. I love you." And he sprang to his feet and ran toward the gunfire to help the woman with the butterflies on her arm. Of course he did, Kelly thought. That was who he was. It was the last time she saw him alive.

As police and official military moved in behind Xuritas, bulldozing through the blockades on Third and Fourteenth Streets, they found the carnage. Dead bodies were indistinguishable from the terrified living until you got right up close and heard the sounds of their weeping or saw the death mask of the face. The D.C. Guard shot tear gas anyway. Metro Police coming in behind the first wave of Xuritas were told to zip-tie every pair of hands they found. They began dragging people away or serving up beatings with truncheons, but this felt almost ridiculous when you were standing in puddles of gore from people cut to ribbons by automatic weapons fire. Master Patrol Officer Andrea Sanchez, who'd worked every overtime shift she could that summer, who from the first day of all this had felt stirrings of dread, who told herself no matter what she would not do anything she could not explain to her seven-year-old son, took off her helmet and threw up. She would never forget what she saw there: The first body she came across was unrecognizable, just a sizzling pile of meat and blood. She stepped on something and had to stare at it for a second before she realized it was a piece of someone's bit-off tongue, lying like a pink sponge on the sidewalk. The Xuritas forces stood around looking very self-satisfied, like, *There you go, ladies, that's how it's done. Glad we could clean up your mess.* Everything was so loud. So many terrified people screaming and crying and begging for help all at once. She stopped for a middle-aged woman who'd been shot in the arm and torso. She was shivering and crying. A dark pixie haircut and small butterflies tattooed on her forearms. A dead man with a crew cut was draped over her, like he'd tried to shield her with his body, but of course he'd probably just fallen there. Her eyes pleaded with Andrea Sanchez for help. Andrea got a tourniquet around the woman's arm and told her everything was going to be okay. The woman's skin turned a ghostly white, her lips purple, and she was dead long before any paramedics were allowed onto the Mall. Andrea stayed with her awhile, and then got up because there was a controversy brewing as their forces continued to the Capitol.

Loren Victor Love and his team had returned to the White House three days earlier after the heat storm had thinned their problem. He was getting his hair cut while he watched the live feed from the Situation Room. Everyone in there was very quiet. Secretary Caperno chewed on her forefinger. The national security advisor held a hand to his mouth and tried to breathe evenly. Vice President McGuirk excused himself after the bloodshed began. Meanwhile, President Love's barber cropped his hair. He'd be going on TV in the evening to explain the severity of this crackdown, the necessity of it, and this was the only opportunity, he claimed, to fit in the trim. The barber wore white latex as he sheered the sides of Love's skull and scissored the top. An assistant, also wearing latex gloves, carefully collected the hair in a plastic bag, using a forensic light to locate every last strand. He did the same with each of the president's nail clippings. It was also why Love defecated in a special toilet with a disposable box. All of this organic material was taken to a kiln and incinerated. It was not exactly paranoia, given what could be done these days with access to a person's genetic material, but to have the man there with the HandScope LED collecting stray hairs while the security forces of the president's former company shot unarmed protestors "is fucking Bond villain behavior," one unnamed source would later tell the *Washington Post*. And yet there were those who experienced a version of unadulterated ecstasy. The way some found joy in Kate Morris's rousing speech, these men and women found such deep pleasure when news arrived of this decisive action.

Outside the Capitol Building, between the amassed police, military, and security contractors, no one knew who was in charge. All chain of command had been lost, and many of them could only stand around gazing at the nightmare in the floodlights. Others itched to add a few more bodies to the pile. EMTs and medics were finally allowed onto the Mall, and they worked past their shock and disbelief. As dawn broke and the first dim light peered over the horizon, a heavy fog rolled in. The infrared cooling of a humid air mass created a dense, smoky cloud that cloaked the combatants, the blood, the living and the dying alike. Soldiers wandered in and out of the smoke. Ghosts disappearing and reappearing. The last person to die in the assault would be killed when a police horse accidentally trampled her to death. She lay on the ground crying for someone to help her. The horse got confused.

Kate Morris never saw any of it. While sleeping in the Speaker's office, one of the new Blue Bands rushed in to tell her there was shooting, and they needed to get to a windowless room. When she heard the pops of gunfire, Kate had a moment to wonder if this was what she'd wanted: to goad them into the unthinkable. Now she was trying to push past this girl, who was blocking her way like she was her bodyguard, begging her not to walk outside.

"Listen to me," said Kate, trying to slip past her.

"No please no please, stop, stop," the girl pleaded. Her name was Krystal Robison. She was nineteen and had left her second semester at the University of Maryland to join the occupation and earn her blue band.

"I need to surrender. I need to tell them we'll come out."

"They're killing people, Kate, they're killing people," Robison begged, her eyes enormous moons of terror. *"Please don't, please don't, please don't."*

"I think they're coming in," someone cried.

Then there was an explosion.

The mayor had usurped the chain of command and demanded that Metro Police be in charge of retaking the Capitol. He was gulping and sweating and feeling dizzy from the images beaming back to him from the Mall. The media blackout, enforced by helicopter, drone, and a five-mile perimeter, would never work, he realized. People in his office were weeping. His public affairs specialist had simply walked out. Quit in the middle of a crisis. He felt like he was giving orders in a dream where nothing obeyed the laws of physics, like a stapler might just float past his vision in this realm of selective gravity. But he barked the order into the phone. City SWAT would take the Capitol. They were not to use any more lethal force unless absolutely necessary.

After the flash-bangs sent everyone to the floor, these officers stormed into the Rotunda. Occupiers dove down and clutched the marble with their faces and begged not to be killed. Many were sobbing, certain these men were going to murder them while they lay there. Overcome with terror, a few ran. They were tased or shot with beanbag rounds. Not a single live bullet was fired in the Capitol. But when Tom Levine saw the cops grab a small woman and practically rip her arm out of its socket as they threw her against the wall, he reacted by instinct, leaping to his feet and screaming at them to stop. The first blow fell across the side of his head, ringing his ear, sending his vision spiraling to dark. Then the clubs and boots descended, and he felt something in his body crack irreparably, and he never recalled anything else.

The occupiers were zip-tied and hauled to buses on the east side of the Capitol grounds where there were fewer corpses and a niveous fog obscured most of the blood. Kate had fallen when the flash-bang erupted, and her daze was such that she'd stumbled away, losing consciousness briefly. She came to at the gift shop. She saw the flashlights cutting through the smoke, so she put herself down on her stomach with her hands on the back of her head and waited. No one realized who she was when they brought her to her feet. They were putting sacks over the heads of the arrested. The last thing she saw was the sweaty upper lip of the cop, then the darkness of the cloth, the world reduced to chaotic white noise, sirens, screaming, weeping, and pounding helicopter blades. She smelled the overpowering sewage scent of their takeover and something coppery and wet overlaying it. She'd never smelled that much blood before, so she couldn't place it in context. To keep herself calm, she thought about the top of the last mountain she'd climbed, when Matt had fallen well behind her, and she stood on the peak, and how gorgeous and eerily silent it was when the wind died away. She was trembling inside her black hood all the way to the bus—right up until she was thrown bodily into a seat beside a weeping man. She apologized for banging off him. The man said nothing. Kept crying. She had to say something. She was, after all, the reason he was there.

"It's going to be okay," Kate said. "Really, it is." She just wanted to be helpful.

"I couldn't find my wife," he sobbed, and he thrashed in shame and fury beside her. His voice cracked: "They were shooting and I fucking ran. I fucking ran, and I don't know what happened to her! I don't know where she is!"

Finally, within the halls of the Capitol, Quinton Marcus-McCall made his way to the House Chamber. He went to a spot just in front of the Speaker's dais. The Blue Bands had kept it immaculately clean, preserving this image of a sacred space of democracy while their members took to the global stage to demand revolution. He waited, smelling the fumes on his clothes and reading the Daniel Webster inscription etched on the wall behind the dais. He held a lighter. He had three cameras discreetly set up in various positions in the chamber, including the gallery level. He'd talked to Liza Yudong about how to beat the government's signal blocking, so the footage could be downloaded to an encrypted drop box. He flicked the lighter open and closed with a *shink-snap*. He heard the authorities coming down the hall. He got to his knees.

The men entered the House Chamber, channeling down the aisles like quick water. Demanding all the usual things. Ordering him to get down on the ground. Hands in this place or that place. Not entirely unfamiliar to a Black man who'd once been a teenager in Detroit. He held up a palm. "Fellas, stay back. For your own safety." And though they were confused, the police did indeed stop. "Just know I'm doing this outta love," he said. He had such a calm disposition, his face downcast but also still as water. "And for anyone watching, forgive them. Forgive everything they've done today. Love this fallen world as hard as you can."

And he flicked open the lighter and touched it to his blue sweatshirt.

He'd jellied the gasoline himself not long after the first aborted effort to clear the Mall, siphoning from the Guard vehicle captured in the first intrusion. He knew they'd come again, and maybe this idea had been in his head a long time. Maybe as far back as his childhood when he was just an odd, bookish kid who spent too much time alone. That morning, when he heard the first shots ring out, he retrieved the can from its hiding place and soaked his clothes. During his six months of training in nonviolent resistance, as he prepared for this action, he'd also studied this process. Burn hot and burn fast. Go up quick, and the pain will only be a forgotten moment.

The SWAT team fell back as the man in front of the dais exploded in an incendiary burst of orange, pink, and yellow flame. The fire was so breakneck and demonic it roared to the top of the chamber, scorching the ceiling black. The man lurched from his knees to his feet, stumbled forward three steps, silent, his face already cloaked in flame, his eyes two hot coals. He spun halfway left, then right, and finally fell forward. He hit the ground with a dense *boom-whoosh*, flames lapping up all around his ruined body, hot smoke billowing from his impermanent shell. Someone screamed for a fire extinguisher, but the sprinkler system kicked on, and a hard rain fell across the chamber. Quinton Marcus-McCall only heard the agonizing scream of the fire catching his skin, the bright-hot full-body torment, the discovery of total, eclipsing pain. But then he heard hushed voices thundering in his ears. Eons rushed over him, with each second taking on the duration of whole millennia—the reign of the sun, Earth's corpus blooming to life, humankind's dallying—all visible for those interminable nanoseconds as the souls of the dead whispered in his ears. The terror he'd felt his whole life, a siege that begins at birth, slipped away, and the more the dread of oblivion receded the more overwhelming the wave of love. His mom and dad and sister were there, and even his life's sorrows now felt precious. The curse of this life, from the yawp to the ashes, finally blew apart, vanishing to wind and stars.

Vice President Aaron McGuirk Resigns

The vice president became the latest and most high-ranking of seven top Love administration officials to resign in protest. McGuirk cited the "unconscionable actions on the Mall." With the Republicans taking over the Senate, it will be difficult for Love to get a replacement nominee confirmed.

The virus first appeared in Siberia, and the WHO believes it escaped from the carcass of an animal in melting permafrost, similar to an anthrax scare that killed several Russian citizens in the 2010s. Unlike anthrax, however, the Siberian Strain, as it has come to be known, is a flu that likely infected animals now long extinct. Its release is the most troubling epidemiological event since Covid-19. Its mortality rate is an astonishing 5 percent.

Senate to Investigate Atrocities

WHISTLEBLOWER SHEDS LIGHT ON PLAN TO USE LIVE AMMUNITION IN D.C. SIEGE

PRION

Begin Your Journey

Food prices have exploded, as multiple nations now face the threat of famine. This has led to political unrest, violence, and state breakdown in countries as varied and Mozambique. The international community must respond, food aid must flow.

REPUBLICANS REGAIN CONTROL OF THE SENATE

"WE WILL MAKE THEM FEEL PAIN. THAT'S A PROMISE. GOD IS READYING HIS SWORD. THAT'S A PROMISE. I WILL BE PRESIDENT. THAT'S A PROMISE."

LEFTISTS, BLACK-IDENTITY HATE GROUPS, ILLEGAL ALIENS THREATEN WHITE GENOCIDE; "A FINAL SOLUTION IS IN PLACE FOR WHITES," THEY SAY

It's now been 9 months since mission control at NASA and SpaceX last received a transmission from the Mars mission.

ANDERS BREIVIK DECLARES RUN FOR PARLIAMENT

Operation Vigilante Sentry is underway with the goal to interdict, detain, screen, process, and deport refugees wherever possible in the Caribbean. The Border Patrol's zone of security has been extended to the entire country. This is modeled on Fortress Europe. The Six Arms is calling for a unified Europe to open fire on all refugee boats. The fury at these garrison states as unprecedented refugee flows emerge from uninhabitable regions will define the global order in the twenty-first century.

AAMANZAIHOU VOWS THIRD-PARTY RUN IF LOVE IS DEM NOMINEE

ANØNosiki

DEATH TOLL OF CAPITOL CLEARING RISES TO 736; LOVE CLAIMS ACTIONS WERE JUSTIFIED

"It was the second-greatest terrorist attack in this country's history, and it was perpetrated by our own government"

Thousands Threaten To Walk Away From Mortgages

Tidal flooding in Florida creates headache for banks, homeowners

NEWLY ELECTED KANSAS GOVERNOR, JUSTIS, HAS TIES TO APL, OTHER ULTRA-RIGHT GROUPS

Executive Summary on the Elevated Price of Grain Staples, 2034

Ashir al-Hasan

December 5, 2034

Abstract: When we returned from our recent fact-finding mission, a public relations junket for which I now feel a measure of disdain, you asked me to complete this assessment of the domestic and global food situation as it stands after two years of skyrocketing prices. My apologies for this document's tardiness. When you asked after my mental state in an armored SUV trundling over the dirt roads of rural Nigeria, I answered in such a way as to bring an end to the conversation. Here following is an effort to answer that query honestly, and perhaps use it to explicate the crisis of caloric deficit that is driving violence, insurgency, and faminogenic policy across the globe. Allow me to begin where I should have last month in the vehicle: with my friend, partner, and husband, Seth Andrew Young.

From the beginning of his participation in the Concert for the Climate, Seth and I argued. As I once alluded, I knew that Seth's involvement was part of a larger plot to occupy the National Mall, although I doubt any of the participants could have predicted the action's grisly endgame. Several hundred people lie dead, with thousands more injured or imprisoned in the effort to retake the core of the capital. Seth claimed he had no plans to actually participate in the occupation, that he was merely drawing from his years in government and knowledge of logistics and security protocol to facilitate a mass act of civil disobedience. Yet from our first date in Charlie Palmer Steak, Seth made no secret he cared deeply for climate and environmental legislation. He'd always wanted a way back in, and Kate Morris gave it to him. For the first week of the occupation, he left me and our au pair to deal with an infant, so that he might help Morris and her acolytes maintain their feeble grip on a few city streets and public monuments. We communicated frequently and tensely as he came to the decision to stay for as long as the occupation continued. Suffice it to say, my fury is hard to overstate. As city services shut down, and even Georgetown descended into a state of exception, I was forced to leave our condo and relocate to New York with my sister and her husband, Peter. When the Love administration offered amnesty to participants following the record-setting heat wave, Seth finally complied with my wishes to leave the encampment. That was July 30. Then came the assault. Two days later, he still had not sent word. We tried to engage the authorities, but even with my many connections, the hierarchies of government were in such a state of disarray that no progress was made. Though the government had attempted a media blackout, video leaked via a member of the occupation, who decided a novel idea would be to self-immolate on a live feed. It was arresting footage to say the least and the first indication that what had occurred on the National Mall was more than tear gas and arrests, that the carnage would dwarf what occurred in 2021. That night, with the children in bed, Haniya, Peter, and I huddled around the television as reports began to emerge of what had happened on August 1. Even Peter, never at a lack for a quip, was preternaturally quiet. In a way, that unnerved me more.

"This can't be true," Hani said at one point.

Then there was a doctor from a D.C. hospital telling reporters he had numerous patients riddled with gunshot wounds. He said: *"There was a massacre."*

Hani turned to me: "Seth said they were about to give up." Her tone was accusatory. "Ash, you said he and the others were going to leave."

"That is what he said." On television, there was footage of the ER. I'd never seen so much blood.

My sister can vacillate between boundless good humor and stony melancholy. She rarely weeps. It was disconcerting then, as she began to cry very hard and say to herself, *"Astaghfirullah. Astaghfirullah."*

I had not heard my sister use Islam's liturgical language since our father was alive. Why she was asking for forgiveness was beyond me, and I never inquired.

//

Residents and essential government personnel were allowed to return to the capital two weeks after the clearing, but I did not return until late September. It was remarkable how all partisans began by loudly condemning this outrageous action, calling it the slaughter it was, and then, quickly, conventional wisdom and official party lines were rescripted. I believe this was in no small part due to a conspiracy-theorist millenarian, who shifted the conversation in a matter of days. As a secure car took me across the Potomac for the first time since May, I watched The Pastor speak from the pulpit of his VR worlde:

"The liberal media says he acted brutally? Are you kidding me? President Love allowed our nation's heart to be sacked by barbarians. He should have cut them down the moment they defied the sanctity of Christ's chosen nation. Instead, he let them arrive like swarms of rats, carrying blasphemy and anti-American ideologies. If he fails to execute every last one of these traitors—when I'm president in two years—I will."

It wasn't a standard campaign declaration, but within hours of this speech, Republican competitors were scrambling to line up behind this message, if more tactfully. As the midterms approached, the Republicans seemed less interested in investigating the president's atrocity than yanking people in front of hearings to ask why he hadn't done it sooner. The Pastor has taken his place at the front of the phalanx. A few years ago, I'd dismissed him as a charlatan. Yet if his act was all a con to sell a potent new brand of religious zealotry, that zealotry was becoming unsettlingly convincing.

I shut off the speech when the driverless reached the National Mall. Seth and I met while running its length, and I still viewed the space with what one calls "romance" or "nostalgia." To see it trampled and gouged into an ugly brown pit, laid waste by protestors and military forces alike, now defended with concertina wire, checkpoints, body scanners, FaceRec cameras, and endless clods of machine-gun-toting security forces, brought me great anguish. The fences were papered over with pictures of those who'd been killed along with a sea of votive candles, bouquets, and other commemorative detritus. That night, *Saturday Night Live* had its season premiere, and though I detest that cloying, obnoxious program, Seth was a devoted fan, and his amusement at such uninspired humor amused me. I'm sure he hadn't missed an episode since the days of Will Ferrell in his boyhood. Of course, the performers had to begin with a somber song and feint toward grieving, and then it was on to an impersonation: Loren Victor Love as a grinning fascist full of bombastic militarized bravado. The narrative defines the caricature constructed around each political persona. Joanna Hogan had been playacted as homespun and bloodthirsty, hyper-competent but secretly savage. Mary Randall was portrayed by her comedienne as confident but embattled, besieged, and flummoxed as to why the multitudes of GOP faithful so despised her. In my few interactions with President Randall, I'd found her all too aware of what was happening to her and her presidency—almost resigned to it. It struck me that they had President Love wrong as well. Rumor has it, he very much enjoys his portrayal on the sketch comedy show, likely because, as with most men of machismo, he is insecure. My phone rang at some point during "Weekend Update." It was an officer with the Washington D.C. Metropolitan Police. They had identified Seth's body.

//

I was told Seth had died of blunt force trauma to the head. The officer I dealt with, Lieutenant Srivastava, explained that the body had been cremated.

"Without an autopsy? That cannot be legal."

The lieutenant had a black mustache shielding the contours of his mouth, making it appear as though his lips dripped with faux sympathy. Perhaps it was paranoia, but he was clearly of Hindu extraction, and I unfairly wondered if he had family back in India participating in the lynch mobs targeting Muslims.

"The city was dealing with two emergencies. Because of the heat wave deaths and then the—the shootings—we had to cremate most of the bodies." He held out a tablet to me. "I know many of the families are pursuing civil litigation. All I can do for you right now, Mr. al-Hasan, is give you your husband's remains." I had trouble reading him, whether I was seeing indifference or exhaustion. He thrust the tablet at me again. "I just need your signature. We're processing the bodies of a war zone right now, and I know it's unfair how long it's taken for us to notify next of kin. I'm sorry. If I could do anything else for you, I promise I would."

"He was supposed to leave." Because I so rarely raised my voice, it cracked. Several officers in that cubicled precinct popped their heads up. A burned-purple terror bubbled in my vision. In the precinct office, I heard every clicking pen, every shuffle of paper, every snotty clearing of a throat, and felt the chemical cool of the air-conditioning on my nerve endings. "How did he die if he was supposed to have left already?"

The lieutenant shook his head only once. "I'm sorry, sir. I just need your signature."

He held out the tablet and now his cues indicated how desperate he was for me to accept this.

I stood. "Why people want conscious-less dust of former loved ones is as stupid as it is bewildering."

I left, exiting the building into a chilly fall afternoon.

//

The last conversation I ever had with Seth in person took place the night before he left to prepare for the supposed concert. I had to explain to him: "The name itself is a misnomer. All 'baby powder' does is potentially get into the lungs or airways of an infant. We should not even keep an astringent powder in the house."

"Dude, it's for diaper rash!"

We were having the conversation across the crib, and I looked up to see that Seth was very amused by me, the wrinkles around his eyes pinched with laughter.

"Dude," I said sardonically. "Diaper rash isn't potentially dangerous. Inhaling an astringent powder is."

Seth gave his eyes an enormous, dramatic roll, lolling his whole head with them. "Oh my God, Ash, he got like a spitful of it. He sneezed once. He doesn't even notice."

"I still think it would be prudent to consult with poison control."

Seth laughed at this and said: "I had no idea you'd turn into your mother quite so quickly."

Seth's lopsided grin had spread even wider. He'd never met my mother, but his predictions at what would needle me always proved assiduously accurate. A tuft of his blond hair stuck up in the back where his cowlick was. He was wearing a pair of gym shorts and an old, hole-pocked T-shirt that read DOES THIS ASS MAKE MY COUNTRY LOOK SMALL? under a picture of Donald Trump. Perhaps it's only the transpositions of time, creating a false nostalgic memory, but I couldn't help but think how beautiful he was. I looked back at our son, lying supine in a Bert and Ernie onesie, happily smacking two plastic baubles together.

I said: "I do hope he grows up to be more like you."

"Duh, me too!"

Forrest Azlan Young was born on July 29, 2033, to a woman who needed money to pay off her law school debts. I thought I'd have more time to change Seth's mind, perhaps allow for a few failures of the artificial insemination method, but our surrogate became pregnant on the first attempt. A nuisance to hear how rare that is. Because Forrest's mother is African American, people frequently confuse me for the biological father. We of course used Seth's sperm for the insemination because fatherhood was his priority. I felt nothing when I held Forrest that first time except the ancient dread that he might squirm from my hands and crack his head on the floor.

Now, over a year later, Forrest is the child of a single parent, and selfishly, I wish Seth were alive simply so I could hurl the childish taunt Hani and I once exchanged as children: *I told you so*. Forrest was born into socioecological circumstances more dire than I could have imagined. He was born into 444 ppm carbon in the atmosphere, melting ice caps, oceans crawling up the world's coasts and deltas, soil salinization, dwindling fresh water, spreading desertification, and stalling agricultural production. He was born in tandem with Seth's unwise decision to join a dangerous political action. All that time he spent proclaiming his adoration of Forrest, his joy at fatherhood, when did he know that a year was all he would ever have? I try to imagine truncheons shattering his skull or more likely 5.56x45 rounds puncturing his body, and I ache to know when he realized that he would leave me alone with this boy.

Peter, Haniya, and their children, Noor and Gregory, stayed with me in D.C. for the memorial service. Seth's parents and siblings, an irrefutably warm and kind family, arrived days later, and we spread Seth's ashes in a crowded ceremony by the Potomac. Seth's parents seemed to understand that this was not an artifice I was capable of navigating. They took the brunt of the condolences and allowed me to stay mute. I'd first met them four years earlier at Seth's childhood home in Mill Valley, California. They were kind to me, and I was greatly disappointed that I couldn't manufacture tears for them. They were all so devastated, and I felt my difference and deficiency acutely. Afterward, Seth's siblings approached me to talk of their plans to not only pursue legal recourse but also form an advocacy group with the families of other victims. When I said this did not interest me, they made no secret of their displeasure.

Then it was just Peter, Hani, myself, and the children in my condominium.

Noor and Greg, riled by the excitement and not yet able to comprehend the gravity of the situation, finally went to bed after a brief temper tantrum from Noor. Forrest, who'd become strangely sedate since Seth's disappearance, had gone down at eight without complaint. Peter had helped himself to Seth's bourbon. Haniya eventually asked an obnoxious platitude of a question: "Can you meet me halfway on this, Ashir? Tell me how you're doing."

A book Seth had been reading still rested on the end table, a bookmark stuck thirty pages in. *Believers*, it was called. Seth was incorrigible about starting multiple books and never finishing them. I dreaded pulling all those bookmarks out and placing the tomes back on the shelves. "I'm exhausted from the performative aspect of a memorial service. And annoyed that you two think I'm too fragile to handle the requisite period of grief."

Peter exchanged a look with my sister. He said: "Bro, I know this is a fucking nightmare. I wish I could make it *not* be true. But that's why you need us. Even if you think you don't, Ash. We're your family. As much as Seth was or that little boy is now, and I don't even care if you're a prick about it."

Who was I even the most furious with? President Love? Kate Morris? Seth himself? Admittedly, due to my great sadness, I made a decision to be cruel. I found myself lashing out because it felt satisfying:

"Perhaps the only thing more boring or predictable than death is the way people behave in its aftermath. And your notion of family, Peter, is a fairly prosaic lie. Forrest couldn't be less connected to me genetically. He's my ward by decision of the state, I suppose, but that's about all."

Haniya snapped, her tongue almost flicking from her mouth: "Ashir."

"What."

"Don't do that."

"What would you have me do?"

Her cues flitted between fury and despair. She took care to control herself when she said: "We're here because we love you, and we love Forrest."

"Have either of you ever thought about hunger?" They assessed me with vacant gazes. I told them about the trip I was being asked to accompany you on, Congresswoman, but my point did not appear to land. "Hunger reveals how transitory our loyalties are to each other. Miss seven straight meals and suddenly a person's morality, family, community, and commitment all fall into flux. How boring it all is too, predicted by systems models as early as the 1990s, and yet—"

"Ash, c'mon," Peter interrupted, but I could see I was upsetting my sister, and this felt very positive.

I continued: "Yet here we are, on the precipice of the first truly global famine, well-fed and armed with a reserve of invisible capital. I know I often marvel at the indifference I feel to the pain of someone who is hungry. I've passed plenty of them over the years on every street in every city. When we visited India as children, they mobbed us. Do you recall that, Hani? We tell ourselves we care, but it's a vacant sentiment."

Haniya drained her glass of wine and set it on the coffee table. "What profundity, Ash." She smoothed her pants and licked purple teeth. "Pete? Do you mind if my brother and I have a minute?"

Peter pumped his eyebrows at me. He crossed the room to my sister. They each said "Love you" and brought their boozy lips together. In that moment, I felt a flare of such jealousy, fury, hate, and total, despairing loneliness. I had not felt such a confluence since it overcame me one night as a young man in a Cambridge dorm room, and I took a walk down to the Charles River. Hani waited for Peter's footsteps to reach the second floor.

She said: "I don't suppose you'd pray with me." Despite her work, which relies on empiricism and rational assessments of data, Hani persists in her piety. "People need comfort, Ash. They need grace."

I said: "That sounds remarkably similar to the vacuous assertions of The Pastor. Perhaps you could serve his candidacy as an advisor."

"Oh, fuck you, Ashir."

We sat for a moment in silence. I've been told my timing is rarely precise, but I had a favor to ask, and this seemed as good a moment as any.

"While I'm on the fact-finding tour—I'm uncomfortable leaving Forrest alone with the au pair for two weeks. I wonder if he might stay with you and Peter."

At first I thought the tightening of her face meant she would say no, but this cue was misleading. After a lifetime of being her sibling, I could still misconstrue her. Suddenly she was wiping tears.

"Ashir, you've been through a devastating life event. Why do you have to go do this? It can't be good for you. Or Forrest. He knows one of his daddies is gone. Even if he can't express it yet, he knows."

I thought of Forrest eating a bowl of sweet peas that evening, mashing the majority into the surface of his high chair and babbling at his older cousins, who cheered him on. I doubted Haniya was correct but did not feel like getting into an argument about object permanence.

"Hani, our country is in the midst not only of an unfolding trauma but a contestation for its conscience. The narrative being propagated in conservative media is that we owe nothing to anyone, that we should let the world starve and hoard all we can for ourselves. If no one in the government pushes back, and we fail to focus a public relations effort on what is happening, we cede the megaphone to those forces. The congresswoman wants the broadest range of voices to stand against this, regardless of party affiliation. Tracy is a kind and brave woman, Hani. She has asked this of me, and I will not disappoint her."

"That's not why I don't want you to go."

"Then why?"

A sob bloomed from her throat, wrenching her face, and she was shouting: "Because I'm sick with worry about you, you fucking asshole! Because I want you to want to be with your son right now. Because I miss Seth, and I know how much you loved him. Because this has broken my heart, and I know it's broken yours. Because I love you, and I hate that you're hurting and you won't cop to it. All of it, Ashir. All of it."

Her face flush, she licked at the tears running into her mouth. Because I needed her to take care of Forrest, I made the calculation that I should soften my approach.

"My duty to my fellow human beings is paramount right now, and this is how I can help: by accompanying the congresswoman and bringing light to what's going on. That duty outweighs any sorrow at Seth's death. And as for Forrest, Hani, obviously this is about Forrest. And Noor and Greg. You of all people should understand that."

She said nothing, which I took to mean she did.

//

The massacre, the mass arrests, the impeachment proceedings Democrats refuse to initiate, the numerous political and legal scandals of this administration, it all must take secondary priority to the growing catastrophe of the elevated prices of grain staples, which are producing widespread food insecurity domestically and outright famine elsewhere.

Integers are inhuman, yet I feel as though I must accord them space here. Globally, the number of malnourished people has leaped to nearly 2 billion, with 360 million in acute need. It is impossible to get reliable metrics on caloric deficiency and famine stages from the Integrated Food Security Phase Classification (IPC) because so many governments wish to conceal the starvations they are either encouraging or incapable of stopping. The United Nations World Food Programme is requesting seven million tons of emergency food aid, which will have to mostly be sourced from the United States, but with food prices as high as they've been in the postwar era, certain news-entertainment conglomerates are currying ratings by spreading misinformation about the situation. A deadly mixture of plutocratic panic and xenophobic populism has fomented a narrative that every sack of grain belongs to "our children." Many Republicans made this a point of pride in the midterm elections, exemplified by the odious and ever-present "Ham Sammy Brigade" VR meme.

As the jockeying over who would join this US government fact-finding mission grew heated during the bitterly contested midterms, I was faced with pressure (as were you) to drop out. As you described it to me, the government was supposed to show a united front of compassion for the millions affected by famine and food scarcity the world over, and yet most of the ink, energy, and vitriol was spent debating who would or would not be on board the plane. A scientist like Jane Tufariello seemed noncontroversial, except that her presence made it impossible for Republicans to join, lest their caucus earn the wrath of Renaissance Media for conspiring with the former NOAA chief. Republican leader Ryan Doup was able to compensate, at my request, by dispatching his chief of staff, Joe Otero, who had a cordial relationship with Jane. Similarly, your invitation to climate security czar Admiral Michael Dahms proved hugely problematic since he obviously represents the Love administration, responsible for slaughter and mass detention. Among the murdered were my husband, among the imprisoned, my friend Dr. Anthony Pietrus.

Those who attended our tour—the congressional representatives, members of the Department of Agriculture, scientists, economists, policy advisors, and an army of Secret Service and security contractors—deserve credit for their bravery even as death threats accumulated back home. While the American government spared no expense, in the two weeks of our journey, through the gruesome sights of feeding centers and children with the reddish-brown hair and distended bellies of kwashiorkor, the adults with spindly limbs, hollow cheeks, and pitted eyes of the starving, I struggled to understand what our purpose was. The haste of travel across time zones, nation-states, and continents turned to sleep deprivation. Soon, every drab government office and chintzy ceremonial reception took on the feel of unreality, as if we'd wandered onto the set of a movie about high-stakes governance. Certainly, I felt as if we were all acting a role.

A concatenation of diverse environmental factors has played into the deepening crisis. The farmer sees his crops dry and brittle, and this represents an astonishing loss of surplus grain from heat, drought, and flooding in the world's breadbaskets. Russia has lost a third of its wheat crop to drought, Australia's Murray-Darling Basin has seen record temperatures and plummeting yields, and in the Midwestern US the corn crop was devastated first by the Great Eastern Flood and then by the so-called heat storm this past summer.

In my ancestral homeland, we witnessed the devastation wrought by Cyclone Malwan in Mumbai, and while the tragedy of two-hundred mph winds and a twenty-foot storm surge cannot be overstated, the greater legacy will be on the surrounding rice-growing deltas suffering a marked increase in salinity.

We saw peoples of the Indian subcontinent, the Himalayas, and Southeast Asia trudging across perilous mountain regions. The floodwaters of melting glaciers have destroyed key farming areas in Kazakhstan, Uzbekistan, Kyrgyzstan, and Pakistan. The world's "third ice cap" in the Himalayas lost 15 percent of its mass in just the last five years, with dire consequences for those who rely on that water. The global freshwater situation is a crisis for which there is no precedent in human history.

In Niger, we heard of a crop blight, the Chikungunya virus laying waste to that society's yields even as arable land vanishes. The synergistic effects of soil degradation, desertification, and salinization have been precursors in the collapse of every civilization from ancient Greece to Mesoamerican empires.

The fishermen we met in Honduras saw their nets empty, so they pick up weapons and join whatever vicious militant group or narco-trafficker that will have them. Yet behind that empty net is the acidification of the oceans, overfishing, and anoxic dead zones created by fertilizer runoff. Marine ecosystems are near collapse, global fish stocks imperiled, and they will take with them one of the world's key sources of protein and the livelihood of roughly 200 million people.

Yet in the middle of all this, Earth's most fearsome species, the commodity trader and his algorithms of ultra-fast trading, sees only profit. Scarcity is lucrative and prices surge as Wall Street hoards grain futures. This, I fear, includes Peter's firm, which has been particularly aggressive in the commodity broad baskets space. Therefore, I cannot escape my own complicity: Tara Fund utilizes systems models I worked on while consulting with the New England Complex Systems Institute in the early 2020s. Peter remains quiescent about the real-world effects of agro-trading and speculation, but nevertheless the major food multinationals, Archer Daniels Midland, Cargill, and Bunge, are experiencing their most profitable years on record.

The effects ripple outward. Vietnam bans rice exports, so Thailand and Cambodia follow suit, and Myanmar begins to starve. Russia marches troops into Ukraine to "restart agriculture" in the region's famed black earth, the same rationale proffered by every leader from Peter the Great to Adolf Hitler, and this time the West holds its tongue in the hopes it will ease the strain on surplus grain. The continued flow of refugees has led to the ascension of a powerful coalition of white nationalist governments within the EU. Following his scheduled release from prison, the political rise of Anders Breivik, the notorious mass murderer, has reverberated loudly across Europe, where Far Right movements are making a serious play for majoritarian control with the so-called Six Arms alliance. The sense of isolation and uprootedness that immigrants, refugees, and native-born alike experience as they watch their worlds warp is exacerbated by deprivation. The hungry and starving will not die quietly.

While predicting civil and geopolitical unrest is difficult in the specific, in the aggregate it is relatively easy: simply look at the UN Food and Agriculture Organization's Food Price Index. When it breaches 120, there will likely be war, riots, and revolutions to varying degrees around the world. When it reached 131.9 in 2011, the Arab Spring broke out. The index began a precipitous climb two years ago. Kate Morris thinks herself a revolutionary but the fuel for her revolt, which led to the death of a man I loved, was very much tied to the price of food. As of this writing the FPI has reached 167.3, an all-time high.

Understanding hunger intellectually is quite different from seeing its dazed victims, disproportionately children, wasting away to their deaths. On the outskirts of the Philippine city of Antipolo, while we toured the burned ruins of a farm, I saw a group of children, among them one I recognized. We'd stopped at the behest of our government escort, who wanted to show us what was happening to the country's agriculture. What were once wheat and barley fields had been fried to a crisp by fire and drought, the soil ripped away by bracing winds. I could feel the grit scouring my skin. The farm was littered with the bodies of emaciated livestock, scorched to unrecognizable husks by a summer fire. They were being lifted by bulldozers and buried unceremoniously in a pit. Dr. Tufariello was beside me, listening to our escort and spitting out the dust. The sand had collected in the braids of her hair and its extensions. I longed to touch her hand and ask her if what I was seeing was in fact real.

As the rusted blades shoveled the charred cows into a pit, the children buzzed around the animals along with the flies. They were trying to pick meat off one of the cow's bodies that was awaiting burial. One of them, who I was seeing from a distance of perhaps twenty feet, looked so much like Forrest, I almost expected him to come running to me. He was older, as Forrest might look in a year or two, but he had the same wide nose and head of soft curls. His eyes were slightly more almond-shaped, but the black eyebrows were arched in the same inquisitive way as when Forrest's face was resting. Both of their faces came with the same permanent question. Of course, this child was malnourished and much thinner, but the resemblance was simply beyond my capacity to understand, beyond the easy answer that our lineage is exponential and our common ancestors much closer in history than we can comfortably believe. The ancestors of Forrest's biological mother, Seth, and this boy, they'd certainly all crossed at some point in a past that feels distant to us, but was in fact genetically, biologically, and geologically practically yesterday.

A worker came over to chase the children away, and the young boy who looked so much like my son scampered up the hill, his form dissolving behind a beige veil. Jane stepped into my vision, her face signaling worry.

"Are you okay, Ash?"

I did not answer. Instead, I returned to the convoy.

/ /

This experience will haunt me for a long time. I'll dream of the abandoned skyscrapers of Honduras, vertical slums catching twilight through their hollowed-out frames, and the women who were baking cookies from salt, butter, and dirt to feed their children. I'll remember donning galoshes to squelch through the few muddy ponds remaining of Lake Chad on the Nigerian border—once one of the mightiest bodies of fresh water in Africa, now only a salt-blasted desert lake bed that maintains the name. I'll find time to write of our security convoy traveling through a heat-seared IDP camp north of Kidal in east Mali, the makeshift city awash in plastic tarps attempting to catch condensation while people clotted around the only well, this immense brick-lined straw in the earth, and used ropes to lower buckets to the bottom to fill their cisterns.

Again, I ask, who ultimately was this fact-finding mission for? Certainly not the children watching us longingly in every city or village hoping we'd hand over a pack of snack mix from the airplane. Not their parents, some of whom approached us to beg that we take their sons or daughters with us. Not their governments, to which we promised to implore our recalcitrant nation to send more food aid. At times it felt like we were only in these failing, hungry, violent states to convince ourselves that the American empire has any footing left in the world, that it could be compassionate or heroic when called upon to do something other than deliver weapons to whatever political faction it deemed least likely to cause it problems.

On the flight back home from the Philippines, with most of my fellow fact finders asleep, I read from a report on India. The fascist Hindu government is executing a grueling endgame as it attempts to corner and starve its Muslim population. I was lost in thought on this harrowing subject when a rough and gnarled index finger intruded, tapping the paper twice:

"Some light reading while you can't sleep?"

Admiral Michael Dahms slid into the open seat beside me. I regarded him for a moment.

"The Hindu government is using our visit as propaganda to declare what a humane job it's doing."

Dahms nodded solemnly. He had the physique of a bodybuilder, a smooth bald head with the overlarge ears of an elderly man, and a distractingly large mole on his nose that must catch his vision incessantly. He looked hard and brittle and spoke with a hoarse voice ravaged by polyps:

"These situations with allies are incredibly complex."

"Obviously what has proved most edifying, Admiral, are not the states we visited but those we were not allowed into." Here I spoke of multiple governments, including US allies, referred to in the report, that are using the disruption in the global food supply to administrate starvation. "Or perhaps President Love is in agreement with these methods."

Dahms shifted uncomfortably and looked at the screen on the seatback, which showed our plane hovering in the middle of the Pacific. He then proceeded to offer me a pointless condolence:

"I would say I'm sorry for your loss. And I am. But I'm sure that means exactly bupkis to you."

I regarded him with great animosity.

"May I ask why you haven't resigned like so many other officials in the executive branch?"

"Impractical." He spat the word more than said it, and I thought he might leave it at that. After a moment, though, like most people in a defensive moral posture, his justification stumbled on. "I'm a hyperrealist. Forty years in the service will make you that way. Resignations get to an itch for self-regard. What Vice President McGuirk did was deeply stupid. There may yet come a time when events necessitate that a steady hand be at least near the rudder." His eyes moved around the plane. The cabin was dark, humming, but otherwise silent. Not one other passenger seemed awake. His voice was wounded: "This is not in President Love's defense. Not at all. But what he's looking at every day in the daily intelligence brief, it's truly terrifying. What happened in Washington, it's nothing compared to what's going on out there on the rest of the planet. You've seen the reports on the India-Bangladesh border. Pakistan. The Uyghur autonomous zone."

"Saudi Arabia's policy of mass starvation of its own citizens to root out insurgents. Israel's closing off food access for Gaza and the West Bank. IDF robo-snipers and auto-kill zones."

"We'd be calling these war crimes if the politics would allow us. Or genocides."

Now that word buzzed in the air. I was very surprised he'd been the one to say it.

I said: "The term 'war crime' could as easily be applied to what happened in Washington."

Dahms rubbed his upper lip, and with some agitation nodded. "Of course. And there is no one more appalled by what happened than me. But when folks are trying to manage chaos with no good options, they are forced to make extreme decisions quickly. We have a band of lawlessness and slaughter now encompassing the earth. The president has been downright restrained compared to some of his counterparts. There is intense political pressure to go much further than he has. My job is to be the voice that keeps his worst impulses in check. He needs advisors other than Yes Men—or Yes Women. Christ, Caperno wanted to hit the Mall with a drone strike." I could not tell if he was joking. "We need people who can ride herd on his worst notions."

He was looking at me almost eagerly.

"I'm not sure what you want from me, Admiral. Absolution is not something I'm capable of giving you. We do what we think is right, each of us, with the information we have available."

I turned my head to the window to indicate I wanted him to go back to his seat. And without another word, he did. Drifting over the vast expanse of the Pacific through the earth's most perfect and silent slice of night, I thought of the arrogance the living carry. We ensconce ourselves in an epistemological certainty born from the mere fact that we've known history marginally longer than the dead. We elbow each other knowingly at their failures and ignorance. We almost never ask what it is that we don't yet know.

//

While you took to the media to describe what our delegation had seen on its journey around a starving, panicked world, I collected Forrest from my sister and returned to D.C. to write my report. Yet as I got to work, Seth still lingered in every corner of the house, and I found myself unable to focus until I excised him. I began by removing the pictures, then donating his clothes. His toothbrush and other toiletries went in the trash. His devices, I backed up, wiped, and recycled.

I also took this time to begin an experiment. Most of the malnourished people we came across had access to only six hundred calories a day, sometimes less. I allotted twelve hundred calories each day for Forrest and myself and started work on the white paper. Each morning began the same. I'd prepare a bit of soy milk and applesauce for Forrest and granola and milk for myself, and we would not eat again until that night. Of course, the very first day, he began crying around one o'clock and did not stop until I gave him a half cup of macaroni with chopped broccoli at 5 p.m. I ate only a small can of soup. We proceeded like this.

During the day, while I researched and wrote, I sometimes turned on the news to drown out his sobbing. Seth had often worked with MSNBC on in the background, and perhaps Haniya had goaded my imagination, but when I turned it on, Forrest would look around, as if expecting his father to come around the corner. He bawled to news of Senator Mackowski introducing a bill to phase out all food aid. "So we can encourage able-bodied adults all over the world to, simply put, grow more food and stop having so many children they cannot feed."

The idea that the world's governments should "let nature take its course" has become the catchphrase of the Right. Maximum cruelty is often how people attempt to exorcise their fear. We are currently experiencing hunger, heat, and refugee flows that are simply outside humanity's experience—all in a globalized media environment where terror and panic boost advertising dollars and algorithms turn disinformation into currency. Yes, climate disruption has ransacked agricultural production, but actual starvation is being driven by zero-sum Malthusian politics. A great hoarding has erupted, driving great violence. Landless and unprotected, the famine refugee is uniquely susceptible to, for lack of a better word, extermination. The use of computation—Big Data, to borrow a pithy phrase—makes these cullings much easier propositions. Depictions of genocide in popular culture have tended toward the cartoonishly evil, likely in order to abrogate the viewer from thinking of him- or herself as a participant. This is a great disservice, for at its core the practice of genocide is about eliminating competition for one's children. The globally wealthy believe that to continue their historic consumptive binge, they must deny others. This philosophy trickles down. It is becoming accepted wisdom that we will not all survive the crisis, and therefore the savvy will now entertain previously unthinkable agendas. Forgive me, Congresswoman, for I know you are a mother of four, but child-rearing, far from accessing a heretofore unrealized spiritual plane, devolves the parent into a selfish, habitual purveyor of violence against those children not his or her own. It is such a small step from believing one's child is special to demanding the eradication of competitor children who would demand their fair share of noodles and broccoli. The unique sensation of loving a child is merely the selfish gene activating, guiding the parent toward discrimination, exploitation and, if necessary, mass murder. Genocides are committed by parents.

During that initial period of limited calories, Forrest and I were both exhausted all the time. He expressed this by screaming constantly day and night. He barely slept and when he woke, he would be hungrier and more furious than ever. His small eyes vanished into the pudge of his cheeks. His diaper needed changing less even though I continued to give him clean water regularly, a luxury many of the children who I saw in, say, Mali or Mumbai did not have. Nevertheless, he was dehydrated and constipated. His feces arrived in hard, small marbles, and he at least could express that his stomach hurt because when he looked at me he rubbed it like he was trying to scoop pain out of himself. I was also in a great deal of discomfort, especially after I allotted an additional one hundred calories to Forrest from my own daily allowance. I could at least suffer silently. The headaches and dizziness began immediately. I found myself lethargic, unable to work on the report for more than an hour before I had to lie down. If he needed affection, I would take Forrest and lay him on my chest while we watched the news. I wanted it to be clear to him that he was not being punished, that his remaining father would still show him all the necessary attention and affection, but we were simply in the same predicament as so many: hampered by a new and frightening scarcity of calories.

After nine days, he stopped crying. He was, it seemed, too tired. He looked at me instead with a mournful indifference. When I placed mashed bananas before him, he would still paw it hungrily into his mouth, but he seemed to already know this was all that would be forthcoming, and it only made him sad. His hair thinned, and I found the kinky strands in his bath and scattered in the crib. His skin, usually quite puffy and soft, now had a parched, dried consistency. He never smiled and his usual cooing and babbling ceased as well. Other than the occasional grunt or "Dada" he rarely made a sound.

Americans are unused to spending more than 15 percent of their income on food. Unpredictable social consequences will follow. Already, panic buying due to perceived shortages has led to riots in supermarkets, and the hacking and carjacking of trucks delivering food products is now rampant across American highways. Stories of the wealthy stockpiling food in specialized bunkers are not helping matters. According to Peter, many affluent individuals are buying "food redoubts": huge storage facilities filled with nonperishable goods that can be loaded into armored trucks and delivered to them in case of emergency. Domestically, SNAP has been effectively gutted by congressional Republicans, and the bottom half of the income distribution in the United States now faces the threat of severe hunger, a famine being unfurled from within a wealthy polity by the politicians and provocateurs intent on sorting the worthy from the unworthy.

By the third week of our caloric limitation I'd finally finished my work on the draft white paper, a task that would normally have taken me eight to ten days. Every waking hour my stomach and head ached. Giving Forrest his bath one night, I asked him if he was hungry. He simply shook his head and continued to move a plastic boat in circles around the water. He'd eaten only a handful of Cheerios and a few strawberries that day. I considered giving him a portion of the beans I was to eat that night, but some ancient greed inside me kicked in, and I realized I did not care how hungry he was, I needed to eat those kidney beans. No longer was I just hungry—I was the state of hunger, and I could scarcely imagine being any other way ever again.

To summarize the white paper which I will soon deliver to your committee, if the United States is to avoid social chaos stemming from high food prices and growing famines, we must:

- Deliver all **7 million tons of food** to the UN World Food Programme, as is our responsibility.
- **Fully fund SNAP food assistance** and expand it to households at 300 percent of the poverty line.
- Begin a domestic and global campaign to **reduce food waste**.
- Immediately pass a new law to **curb speculation in the commodities markets**. Institutional investors are exacerbating the problem by speculating on food staples, thus driving up prices for US consumers and starving the world's poor.
- Immediately **end biofuel subsidies** and divert that land to food production wherever possible. This is particularly vital in the case of corn ethanol, which has a negligible or net-negative impact on emissions.
- **Tax meat consumption**. Two-thirds of the world's agricultural land is currently used for livestock. To not pay the true environmental cost of the meat and dairy in our diets is simply no longer viable, especially when it comes to dwindling water resources.
- **Do away with trade barriers and subsidies** completely. We have a globalized food system and some nations will, environmentally, be better suited for growing than others. Food production is not like other consumer goods; it can be done more efficiently or less efficiently in certain regions, and we must use the planet's land and water as wisely as possible. Protecting rural farmers out of nostalgia will always be as politically popular as it is foolhardy. The easiest solution is subsidy substitution: If land is no longer competitive to produce commercial food, governments must alter the subsidy to pay impacted farmers to steward water, soil, and biodiversity.
- There are small pockets of the US where people have access to a wide array of fruits and vegetables. These are the towns and neighborhoods where the organization A Fierce Blue Fire operates widescale **urban farming, permaculture, and agroforestry cooperatives**. Impressively, they've practiced seed diversity, integrated pest management, and other practices that have produced

yields where industrial agriculture has declined. Expanding their conservation agriculture model is a worthwhile investment.

- Federal and state governments should begin to use **eminent domain** to tear out golf courses, ski resorts, horse farms, and all other recreational lands that utilize scarce water resources and begin growing food immediately, particularly in the American West, where the golf courses use more water than many small nation-states.

- During World War II **victory gardens** grown in backyards and vacant lots supplied 40 percent of the country's vegetables. This can easily be replicated. The simplistic debate between small-acre farming versus agribusiness systems is a false choice. Feeding a mostly urban populace can only be done through high-intensity broadacre farming. Still, the aggregate impact of every home growing a portion of fruits and vegetables would be significant.

- **Water recycling** is a virtual necessity, but we should also be separating out urine and human waste. We are currently flushing a bounty of treasure down the toilet. **Urban sewage can be harvested** and used as fertilizer or for urban horticulture. Cities are already concentrating these nutrients but simply flushing it into the oceans.

- The **US pet industry**, mostly consisting of felines, canines, and certain bird species, is a spectacular waste of precious food resources. As the ecology of the planet has shifted drastically, wild animals fade to extinction, replaced by livestock and an estimated 500 million domesticated dogs and 400 million housecats. This has proven an unheralded environmental catastrophe. Cats now eat more fish protein than humans while dogs consume more kilowatt hours of energy than people who eat vegetarian diets (dogs consume double the energy of vegans). In aggregate, pets are responsible for 25 to 30 percent of all meat-based greenhouse gas emissions in the US. I find it bizarre that we ethically countenance a pet culture in which individual animals are vastly outeating the world's hungriest children. Ending the commercial pet industry and ordering all food earmarked for pets to be diverted to global food aid would alleviate human suffering almost immediately. Furthermore, these pets are as edible as any commercially grown pork or cattle. The cultural taboo against eating dog flesh is only an accident of whose ancestors had access to cheap ruminants. Perhaps it's unpopular to suggest that we eat all pets rather than letting them starve, but they, along with deer, varmints, and other "low-status" protein, would provide an important source of calories for a nation suddenly lacking in both.

- Our agricultural systems were developed and propagated in a climatological regime that is now extinct. **Research in food production** has gone dangerously underfunded. The world spends some $2 trillion on armaments and perhaps 0.0125 percent of that on food research. The ban on GMO seeds in Europe is counterproductive and damaging for the movement of food globally. Drought-tolerant maize will be crucial, as will the beta-carotene-fortified golden banana. Flood-tolerant, salt-tolerant rice has been the only way to keep yields up in the Mekong Delta and other flood-inundated regions, while C4 rice that fixes its own nitrogen remains a holy grail.

- Peter has pointed me to several **aquaculture** companies attempting to farm the oceans more effectively. This includes marine fish farms in deep offshore waters and genetically engineered "superfish," which are enormous, grow quickly, and eat anything. Wild-caught fish should continue, though we must impose strict catch limits. **Farming the oceans** for kelp, seaweed, and algae should become a policy priority. We could produce more food than traditional livestock with a fraction of the ecological footprint using integrated multitrophic aquaculture.

//

Conclusion: The crux of my most heated arguments with Seth was that I believed creating Forrest was an immoral act (and alas, still do). It was not just the resources Forrest will consume: the water, plastic, and greenhouse gases, the rubber, tin, and timber. No. It's what lies over the horizon of his lifetime as men and women he will never know make decisions that lock him into an age of terror, violence, and unraveling. As I finished the congressional white paper, I also brought to a conclusion my experiment with Forrest and myself. I returned him to a diet of one thousand calories a day and myself to a standard two thousand, give or take. No doubt you, my sister, and anyone else would be aghast at the experience I put Forrest through, but when I watch my sister blithely feeding Noor and Gregory, I'm convinced mine was an experiment every parent should force themselves to contemplate, for this is the future of our world. It wasn't the crying that persuaded me how necessary this exercise was, but the silence that followed. When he slapped his bathwater and simply shook his head that he was no longer hungry, that his stomach had tightened to the point where he no longer expected to be fed, I had to leave him. I had to go to another room because I felt as much violet fear as I can ever remember, a glowing amethyst coloring the fringes of every mental avenue. I missed Seth desperately, but this mourning included the strangers I'd met the world over. It included an unquenchable desire to drain all the misery flooding our planet, to put back what has already left us. Because food scarcity may soon be dwarfed by a larger issue. Data from the ICESat-2 satellite indicates that the Thwaites and Pine Island Glaciers in West Antarctica are now retreating at 10 km a year and will likely break off within the next six to eighteen months. At that point, the ice they are holding back will begin to enter the oceans and sea level will begin a dramatic climb. This promises for humankind one ineluctable destiny. Last night, Forrest and I indulged in a decadent meal. I cooked roast duck for myself and bought a cake and ice cream for Forrest. Afterward, my son and I played with blocks in the living room until the boy fell asleep in my arms. I felt him against my chest, heavy and healthy and warm. I listened to his breath whistling through his small lips. I yearned to build a wall as high as a skyscraper to protect him from all the unchecked suffering of our luckless civilization.

OPINION | GUEST ESSAY

The Legacy of August 1, 2034

Aaron R. McGuirk

April 19, 2035

When asked to resign from my position as vice president of the United States, I hesitated, a rare moment in my life for which I will always carry great shame. This was an unbearable decision, and one that I will always second-guess.

Friends, advisors, and my own wife were begging me to do so, while many within the administration demanded I stay on. I was the only official who could not be legally fired by President Victor Love. If the cabinet could just rally to invoke the Twenty-Fifth Amendment, they said, or if Congress could bring itself to impeach, I would be elevated, and a dangerous man would be torn away from the levers of power.

Of course, none of that happened. Victor Love is still president, his cabinet loyal, his allies in Congress shielding him from responsibility for the massacre that took place in the nation's capital, his Republican opponents besieging him for his weakness in letting the occupation go on for as long as it did. Seven hundred and thirty-six Americans are dead, over a thousand more wounded or grievously injured. Survivors such as Thomas Lewis Levine, a former congressional staffer whom I crossed paths with while I served Minnesota's second district in the House of Representatives, will be confined to a wheelchair for the rest of his life. Krystal Denise Robison, a nineteen-year-old college freshman at the University of Maryland studying sustainable agriculture, was permanently blinded. Second Lieutenant Walter Anthony Pasquina of the United States Marine Corp went AWOL out of loyalty to the nation he served and was shot dead trying to aid a wounded woman. These were not terrorists or Weathermen thugs. These were patriots who wanted to change their country for the better.

The pressure on President Love to inflict greater violence on American citizens, to begin arming our borders with yet more weaponry and lethal force, to shred the Constitution and begin imprisoning people in droves, is more real than his progressive detractors can imagine. While serving in his administration I was disturbed to see this pressure coming not just from the media but from within his own party and from the lobbying class who see our nation as becoming ungovernable and unfit for business.

I resigned because my conscience would not allow me to continue to serve President Love, and perhaps I will live to regret that if he goes unchallenged for the nomination in 2036. For so many of us in leadership roles, there seems to be no right answer anymore. My faith has kept me from despair, but my conscience is far from clear. I agreed to serve as Victor Love's running mate despite rumors and misgivings about his character. We make compromises with ourselves all the time because we believe the ends will justify the means. When I met with him for a conversation about the vice presidency, he assured me my priorities were his priorities. I set my concerns aside because power and ambition beckoned—but so did the chance to improve the lives of the American people.

When I chose to write a letter of resignation, I found my voice, if belatedly. When asked to write my opinion of the sad conclusion of the Senate committee empowered to investigate the actions of August 1, 2034, I still find myself at a loss for words. The committee's work can be summed up by one cold sentence in its report: "Though the president acted rashly, he did so within the bounds of the law given the circumstances." And that is that.

There is little doubt that political deals have been cut. Those arrested on August 1 are free, including Kate Morris. Many of those detained illegally under the law enforcement statutes of the Pollution Reduction, Infrastructure, and Research Act were released just after Christmas of this past year, including Dr. Anthony Pietrus. As many legal scholars have argued, PRIRA makes a joke of due process for those dubiously accused of domestic terrorism.

Dr. Pietrus appeared in a photo in a public setting with a Weathermen suspect, and because of that photograph spent seventeen months in prison without access to a lawyer. He was released only because the Justice Department could produce no further evidence that he was complicit in any terrorist activity. PRIRA allows the detention of terror suspects to last as long as three years. American citizens are still being held in unconstitutional black-site facilities across the Southwest while the Supreme Court has refused to hear a challenge. Even worse, by taking his boot off the neck of his most high-profile opponents, Victor Love has been allowed to escape any reckoning for his horrific actions. The standard line by apologists in my own party is that he "mismanaged an impossible situation."

Do not be lured in by such a ludicrous line of thinking. The truth is simple. Victor Love committed the worst atrocity on American soil since the attacks of September 11, 2001. For all his tough talk about hunting and ending terrorists, he is the one with by far the most blood on his hands.

I can assure you President Love is dangerous. He has not been reined in, he has not learned any lesson, and he continues to dodge both culpability and the law. If Democrats fail to mount a challenge to him in the coming year, and he wins, I mourn to think of what another four-year term could bring. Yet support for the Far Right Republican Party, which continues its alliance with white nationalists like Jennifer Braden, is a nonstarter. People of conscience have this one chance to replace Victor Love with a candidate who has not brought terror and shame to our country.

I will not skirt my complicity with what happened on the National Mall and in the halls of the Capitol. The images of the bloodshed and the names of the dead will haunt me for the rest of my life. Many have wondered if I resigned out of ambition to run against President Love in the upcoming primary, while other Democrats have begged me to do just that. But I cannot because I do not deserve the office. Not after failing to stop what happened. I have no moral authority to challenge President Love, but there are many brave public servants who do.

The legacy of August 1 will not be decided by a feckless and rigged Senate committee. It will be decided by what voters and citizens do, as we fight to hold our nation together in these hungry and perilous times.

GUNS, WALLS, AND SULFUR DIOXIDE

2035

I tried to just say the truth, as plainly as I could.

"I don't know if I'd call them nightmares, but it's in my dreams, certainly. Coming into the house and finding her. It was . . . truly awful. Shocking and, this is a pedestrian word but, *disgusting* . . ." I tried to find a way to admit what I wanted to admit. "I find I have more guilt not that she did it, but that I . . ."

I paused too long, my eye wandering over a slab of obsidian hanging on the wall. Expensive art was a staple of these high-priced therapists. As if office decor could signal one's competence as a mechanic of souls. Maria's knuckles left her chin so she could urge me on.

"I feel guilty because I'm glad she's gone." I wanted her to say something then, but she only waited. "I miss her, of course, but I miss the woman who raised me. Not the one at the end. She was so bitter and unhappy and cruel—especially to me. I couldn't bear to be around her anymore." I plucked a piece of lint from my pants. "Anyway, I know we talk about this all the time . . ."

"We talk about whatever you want to talk about," said Maria, her eyes always eager behind her ARs. She never took a note, but she seemed to remember everything, and furthermore, care. Not in the sense that she empathized, but like she was an alien who just found humans fascinating. "Finding a loved one after a suicide is an incredible life event, Jacquelyn. The emotions that come with it are complicated. Do you talk to your partner about it?"

"I have. I don't anymore really."

"Why not?"

"He has his own things going on. Sometimes I talk to Allie."

"But not your brother?"

I rolled my eyes. "Erik wouldn't talk about it if Xuritas cuffed him to a chair and hooked him up to a car battery."

"He's closed off."

"That's one way of putting it. He's divorced, estranged from his kids, drinks heavily."

"What does he do for work again?"

"Mostly I give him money."

"How much?"

"A lot. Same with Allie."

"I thought she had the doctor husband?"

"She does, but they're overleveraged. You've never met two more irresponsible people, and he's retired now. Almost in his seventies and he's asking his wife to hit up her sister for 'loans' every six months."

Now that most of my social circle consisted of people who'd gone from elite prep schools to Princeton to making small fortunes, I had an imposter's anxiety and avoided talk that could lead to my family's pinched, unhappy lives. I had unnerving fears of my siblings coming to visit me in New York and having to introduce them at a dinner party: Erik with his dead front tooth or Allie and her Real Housewives of St. Louis life. Fred hypothesized that our extravagantly successful peers were in fact jealous of my background. The rich couldn't wait to tell you about whatever humble beginnings they could dredge up. "Growing up, our summer house was such a dump, it didn't even have a dock!" he joked.

"Do you resent giving your siblings money?" Maria asked.

"No. I just feel like it's a sign . . . I don't know . . . that our family failed. That we all blew apart somehow, but I can never figure out why."

"Your father's affair."

I shook my head at this. "How long can you be pissed at the dead? That's what I tell Allie, at least. Dad had to live with our mother, so how am I supposed to blame him when I couldn't stand to be around her."

"That's still an upsetting thing to learn, Jackie."

I didn't want to talk about my family anymore. We always circled the same things: Dad's affair, Allie's bitchiness, Erik's shittiness, and my mother hanging by a black electrical cord from the banister. The first time I told Maria, she didn't even blink. "You're not the first person to find a loved one dead of suicide, and you won't be the last," she had said. I'd considered being offended by her dismissive approach toward what I, at the time, felt was a shocking and unconquerable trauma, but by our third session I'd decided I liked this attitude, and I liked her. To Maria, nothing was surprising, nothing too traumatic to be processed and overcome. However, I had lied to Maria about the dreams. They were nightmares, and I did wake up sweating.

"How's Fred?"

"He's good. Stressed from work, but good."

"You're spending enough time together."

"Yes. After I talked to him, we sort of worked out an agreement. At least two evenings and one day a week when he has to put all the screens away. No data, no reports, no investor calls."

"How do you feel about his divorce or lack thereof?"

"I understand where Fred's coming from. His wife is going to massacre him if he asks for it. He stands to lose sooo much money, and trust me, she's vindictive. She will not let this go easily. She hates me."

"How do you know that?"

"Way back at the hearing for Fred Jr. when he got out, just the way she shook my hand. Fred's only eight years older than me, but maybe it's the younger woman thing."

"This bothers you?"

"No, but—this is dumb, but I want the wedding. I want to invite all my old friends from college or Chicago and say 'I do.' Get my stupid sister to be the matron of honor. Maybe that's retrograde, but it means something to me."

"That's not retrograde at all, Jacquelyn. You're asking for something utterly reasonable. And you know what? If it costs Fred half his money, he'll still be more than fine. He can ask you for an allowance."

*

I had the doorman standing there for a moment, wind blowing in from the street, because the TV overlooking the art deco lobby caught my attention. CNN had a camera crew pointed at a view of Manhattan looking south across the East River. An enormous crowd had gathered in front of two loading bay doors at a warehouse because a truck had crashed into one of the metal shutters, warping it inward. The chyron said something about looting, and I felt a curtain of dread, but there was the doorman, smiling, waiting for me. Exiting onto Park Avenue, I decided to walk. The day was cool for late April, the sun half-fugitive behind a cloudbank, but I never walked much anymore. I took the time to mull what I'd said in the session.

After the funeral, we'd sold the house for pennies to an ag company. The flood damage wasn't worth any salvage job, and it was torn down. The home that had been in our family since 1902, that had survived tornadoes, storms, and countless brutal winters, finally fell to the Great Eastern Flood. Mom left behind only debts, and I knew it was the last time I'd ever set foot in Amber, Iowa, a town that had all but collapsed save a couple of big-box stores and fast-food joints. That my childhood home was gone, it hit me now, as it sometimes did, and I saw in my mind's eye my father hunched over the soil, grabbing a loose handful and kneading it between his enormous hands to test its properties, to feel close to it.

This memory brought a surprising bout of tears as I walked up through Hell's Kitchen. The wind blew ragged over the city, rushing between the skyscrapers. Not far from our building, I passed a gas station where five kids stood in the way of a car, holding signs, arguing with a policeman who was trying to scoot them along. One sign read **WHAT YOU DO HERE STARVES THE WORLD**; another, **WE ARE OUT OF TIME** with a picture of a clock; another, **WE ARE THE DELUGE**. I overheard the cop in his New Yawk drawl tell them, "You can either stand outta the way or I can take ya to the precinct. Then your little protest is over. Your call." Waiting at a crosswalk, I turned back to see the teenagers all dutifully complying.

Past our doorman and the security team, the trickling fountain and tall bamboo plants, down the handsome slate-tiled hallway, up the private elevator. We were Upper West Side, an expensive zip code to be sure, but not Billionaires' Row. For a relatively cheap $5.6 million we had our own floor, forty-five hundred square feet, a Juliet balcony, and a fireplace. Most importantly, it was not ground floor, and the building had the best flood-resistant measures architecture could buy: natural gas generators, clean water storage in case of power outages, and all heating, ventilation, and electrical machinery elevated seven meters above street level.

I found Fred in his office, hunched forward, eyes darting in his Apple ARs like a boy watching Saturday-morning cartoons. His hands swiped at the air as he manipulated the augmented world, while at his desk, three old-fashioned screens streamed data on Tara Fund's holdings.

"Where are you coming from?" he asked absently.

"Therapy."

"Figure yourself out yet?"

"Maria thinks I should leave you if you don't divorce Linda and marry me."

"Is Maria going to reimburse us for the millions Linda will take out of our pockets on her way out the door?"

Kicking off my workaday pumps, I slid into his lap, draping my arms around his neck and kissing him. He wore a charcoal zip-neck sweater that set off the salt and pepper of his beard and cool slate of his eyes.

"Hi."

"Hi." He kissed me again. The Liebherr all-purpose cleaning robot zoomed quietly past us on its way to some detected dirt I'd no doubt tracked in. I barely noticed the oversized egg pod and its wizard arms anymore.

"What are you working on?" I asked.

"The usual. Komatireddy has us up to our necks in the NHS, but if Parliament gets cold feet and backs off—I mean, these valuations are going to tank and we'll be out a fortune."

These days I was hearing a lot about Komatireddy, one of Tara Fund's star analysts, as he made aggressive bets on the companies set to benefit from the full privatization of the NHS, which was sending England into political conniptions. Marches in the streets as the Tories moved toward the long-overdue reforms. I didn't have much of a stomach to hear about it now, but my eyes drifted to the report anyway.

"I meant to tell you, Linda's in town, so we were going to get dinner tomorrow."

"Linda as in my Linda?" he said, bewildered.

"No, dummy, Linda Holiday. From my Don Draper days."

"Oh, right right."

"Maybe it would be nice to get drinks with your should-be-ex-wife, Fred."

The report was called *Positioned for Disruption: Strategy for Energy, Commodities, and Security Investment.*

"That's quite the apocalyptic title."

"Smart kids on that team, but they're hyped on the grandeur of thinking they can puppeteer the world." He clicked all three screens off at once and pushed the ARs up onto his head. Without the throb of the data, his office returned to just being a bright white room with a beautiful view of Manhattan to the south. The floor-to-ceiling windows could tint to control the temperature on hot days. "Wanna get lunch?"

*

Fred spent most of lunch talking shop. The fund had a year as the newest belle of the ball, but that was long gone. Tara had stalled out, for now, as a midlevel fund, working with $2 billion in assets. Other firms had played the global food shock better.

"We're in for nearly eighty thousand hectares of farmland in Ukraine. I told Peter everyone has assurances the new Kremlinized government will not mess with these holdings, which is why Love allowed Russia to go in in the first place." Fred cracked a piece of sourdough over his soup. He'd been getting treatments at the Noxium Spa. He looked young, but the tan gave his skin an orange hue that looked less than natural. "Thirteen years ago it's life or death for democracy, but now the world needs that ag production. China, on the other hand, has everyone freaked."

"What's happening in China?" I asked. "I mean, aside from the riots and hunger and—not to be dismissive," I added, rolling my eyes at the way I sounded. Everyone in finance begins speaking like this, and I tried to at least catch myself in the act.

"These student groups—or whatever they are—6Degrees in Cantonese. They've locked themselves in a couple of police stations and a military base. Somehow they managed to take over prime government installations without firing a shot. All hacking and subterfuge and occupation tactics. Stuff they copied from Morris and the siege."

"How does that affect Tara, though?"

Fred's eyebrows shot up with a goofy, knowing look. "Chinese government's never exactly been known for its tolerance of disobedience. Kashgar is in meltdown with the Uyghur situation, but people are in the streets all over the country. The rural areas are eating about a bowl of rice a day. Peter said to me, 'It's easier to price nuclear war than it is civil unrest in China.'"

"What about that report." I speared a shrimp on my fork. "*Chaos of Investment* or something? I'd like to read that."

"Sure. It's based on proprietary modeling, though, so it'll have encrypted portions," he explained, referring to the security procedures Peter had put in place around the al-Hasan model. "Basic premise is that the socioecological situation in the Arctic is going to be one of the biggest investment opportunities of the century, and it has to be handled by the good guys, or the whole region could end up strip-mined. We have companies that think they can fit these operations into an ESG portfolio."

Though he was still nominally the head of investor relations, Fred had taken a much greater interest in the firm's day-to-day bets. I'd focused my work on Tara's ESG investing and philanthropic work. I wanted Tara to carve out an advantage by becoming one of the most socially responsible hedge funds on the street. This wasn't as easy as I'd imagined. These positions and trades moved so fast, powered by incomprehensible complex systems models, and socially responsible investing could become an ever-retreating goal. Still, I thought this was an excellent way to capture the attention of new investors. I'd even managed to convince a reporter for the

New Yorker to profile the fund, but that had turned into a sticky PR situation. The reporter, Farooki, had been looking to court me, not the other way around. She was interested in a firm called ANøNosiki, which I knew nothing about. After a few frustrating back-and-forths on the subject, I referred her to Media Relations, and Fred got in touch with a few contacts to kill the story from there. The name ANøNosiki stuck with me, though.

"Really? Mining the Arctic as ESG?"

He looked up at me and wiped his mouth. "Well, people have been ringing alarm bells on the melt for decades, right? But the warming is having all these *incredible* benefits. We now have ice-free ship passage in the Arctic, the greatest boon to world trade since the Clinton administration. Then there are the new energy horizons in Greenland, just these unfathomable fortunes of minerals, uranium, and even oil and gas if the majors can lean on them to reopen exploration. And the precision companies can operate with now—we're talking minimal impact. It'll be like they weren't even there."

I laughed. "You've never been much of a recycler."

"Come on, Jack, I'm serious. We're forging this new direction—it's exciting. Peter wants to call it 'socially responsible extraction,' but I don't like the word 'extraction.' We need another term there."

When Fred sat with investors, he would talk about growing up in Humboldt County and how his dad had lost job after job as the timber industry was more or less legislated and regulated out of California. "The environmentalists were basically at war with these working-class logging guys, and it was just so baffling and backward," he once told me. "My dad loved the forest—hunting, fishing, camping, hiking, that's all we did. It was our home, and it just felt so unfair the way we got vilified. And it didn't have to be like that. It was these few rapacious investors versus hard-line, no-compromise greens, and neither side actually lived there. No one cared about the communities they were invading or the ecosystems they claimed to be protecting. And when the Sustainable Future folks hired us, I met with some of the guys in the production fields, and I can see the exact same thing happening in oil and gas. All these high-paying working-class jobs that could be gone soon. I grew up watching my dad lost and depressed until he had the heart attack, so it's hard not to let all this get a little personal."

It wasn't until he told me this story that I really understood Fred—why, despite his wild successes in two of the most competitive fields in American business, he carried such a broken heart. We both learned an instinctive lesson as children. To paraphrase my father: If you're not on top of the mountain, then you're scrambling over loose rock, and that's a damn dangerous place to be. Since I'd become wealthy beyond anything I'd ever imagined for myself, I'd been trying to focus my efforts on giving back, but like Fred, I carried the secret knowledge that so many of our affluent peers would never understand: what it felt like to be broke in America. How it could practically change your DNA.

Looking up from his meal, he asked, "Do you remember all the fears of peak oil?"

"Not really."

"That was the boogeyman in the 2000s. Then of course, hydraulic fracturing and horizontal drilling come along and suddenly America's got more oil than Saudi Arabia. Demand for energy will never peak, so if you keep prices low, oil and gas are cheap enough to get to market over anything. And now we have innovation with aerosol injection about to prove doomsayers wrong about global warming."

I picked at the shrimp, not wanting to waste it, but also fully stuffed.

"You never worry, do you?"

"About what?

"Heat storms."

We'd spent the summer of '34 holed up in the Hamptons to escape the frying city. For ten days, I barely went outside except to get in and out of the car, anxiously watching news of the siege as sweat-soaked reporters described the agony of the temperature. Fred rolled his eyes.

"Our boy Norm Nate is about to corner the market on albedo management, and once he starts, the governments of the world are going to have to keep paying him to put those nanoparticles into the sky for the next century, at least. Managing the temperature will become about as easy as you and I playing with a thermostat. As long as we don't elect anyone dumb enough to interfere and strand good tech fixes—that's the only thing that freaks me out, if an AOC or Aamanzaihou administration shuts down innovation. All this to say, we might be making a few campaign contributions to The Pastor next year."

I laughed so hard the shrimp trembled off the tines of my fork and splashed into a puddle of yogurt.

"Fred! You're not serious."

"I might be."

At the mention of his name, a familiar set of clashing emotions descended: the revulsion at his politics, the fear of his future candidacy since early polls had him well ahead in the Republican primary, and of course the secret I kept of our encounter, one which I now planned to take to my grave.It had grown difficult to see his face and not become flush with guilt and an uneasy revulsion. Years earlier I'd spent a weekend reading everything I could about him on the internet, trying to decide if his new shtick was all a ruse because that would have made him so much less frightening. Now I clicked, scrolled, or swiped away from the page if I saw his name in a headline.

"Fred. The guy is telling crowds that his blood can cure cancer."

"Hey, maybe it can. We have some positions with biotech companies that are looking into it."

"Seriously."

"I'm just saying, you can't overlook what he's got in his favor, which is a commitment to deregulation, lower tax burdens, and aggressive energy policy."

"So does Vic Love!"

"Yeah, and he gunned down hundreds of people in public. Then he turns around and pardons Pietrus and Kate Morris and all the rest."

"Love did not pardon them," I corrected. "The courts threw out the case against Pietrus."

"But everyone knows he cut a deal to neuter the Senate investigation by dropping charges against Morris and all the occupiers—are you still defending her?"

We'd flown to London to escape the heat and close on our new place a few weeks before the government finally stormed the Mall. Everyone had known some kind of police action was coming, but when I saw the images of the rampage, I sat on the bed and began crying. When I heard the numbers of dead, I wept again, and vowed I would do something, but what do you do in that situation? Call your senator? Donate money to the ACLU? There wasn't a meaningful outlet for my outrage or grief, so I did nothing while the media screamed back and forth at itself. A few months later we were at dinner with Peter O'Connell, his wife, Haniya, and two other couples, Tara clients. When the conversation turned to politics, one of the wives casually declared that what happened was "a shame, but Love did what he had to do to restore order."

This woman did not know that Haniya's brother had lost his husband there, and I didn't blame her for losing her temper. "There's an interview where you can watch the families of the people killed, and I suggest you take the time, you ignorant Nazi bitch." She stood and left the restaurant. Peter went after her. Later, I was ashamed that I'd said nothing and remained for the rest of the meal so Fred could smooth things over.

When Fred and I spoke of it that night, he sounded as appalled and sorrowful as I felt. How did the country get to this place? He told me he would never vote or send a dollar in support of Love or any Democrat who stood by him ever again, but he was also furious at Kate Morris. "She led those people into that," he said. "She used them. Sacrificed their lives for her lost cause." A minority of Democrats screamed for impeachment but a deal was made. In exchange for concluding the investigation into the massacre, the government dropped all charges and released its prisoners, including most of those rounded up in the prior two years under PRIRA. The slaughter of over seven hundred American citizens in the capital was quickly scoured from the news by skyrocketing food prices, refugee flows from South America and the Caribbean, the Mars mission finally being declared lost, and The Pastor returning to the scene with more bombastic displays. The common refrain became "The country has to move forward." Most of the Democrats we talked to repeated that almost as an incantation. A sign of the times that this seemingly history-making event could be swapped out in the news cycle in a matter of days.

"I'm not defending anyone," I told Fred now. "They should've impeached Love by August 2. But that does not mean we should elect a guy who wants to continue burning oil because he thinks it's going to bring about the Rapture faster."

"I'm curious who you'll vote for then? No one is beating Love in the primary, he's got the party infrastructure by the throat. I know you're a bleeding heart, but not enough to vote third-party socialist, I assume?"

The cruelty in his voice surprised me. Fred never got mean-spirited. Even when he argued he was apologetic, calm, and always reasonable.

"I'm not sure what we're fighting about? An election that's more than a year away?"

"You're the one who's fighting. All I said was The Pastor is going to be a serious candidate and donors are paying attention—then you jumped down my damn throat."

"Is CLK involved this time around?"

He rolled his eyes. "That's conspiracy theory stuff, Jack."

"I'm just asking, is The Pastor going to get the benefit of a sophisticated disinformation and persuasion campaign the way Love got?"

He gave me a look like I was his bratty sister.

"You're being annoying," he said.

"*You're* being annoying," I said.

Then we sat there for a while silently. I asked the waiter to box the rest of my meal. He asked the same of Fred, but Fred pushed his plate away.

"No, I'm done."

Outside, Fred's car was waiting amid a host of Escalades and armored luxury cars idling while their passengers dined. The wind was eye-watering, but nevertheless I looked down the street to where I'd seen the man earlier. When we'd walked into Jean-George's for lunch he'd been squatting against the building, hands on his knees, a lachrymose young Black man, rail-thin, his skin stretched gruesomely over his exposed collarbones. He wore only a tank top, filthy sweatpants, and flip-flops. He had nothing with him except a piece of cardboard that read HUNGRY. PLEASE. It wasn't like he was the first person I'd seen with such a sign that day. I walked down the block while Fred called after me. Maybe he thought I was trying to walk home.

"Do you want this?" I held out the box. "It's some shrimp."

The man's eyes rolled lazily up to me. He had sores on his arms, and he was painfully skinny. Just standing that close to him made me feel like I was inside a hot, dark tunnel.

"Got sum'in eat," he muttered.

"Yes," I said. "Shrimp."

He still didn't look like he trusted the box. I felt stupid holding it. This dumb white lady trying to clear her conscience to an unreceptive audience.

"Aight," he finally said, taking the box. "Gah bless."

Then he opened it and began scooping the shrimp, squash, and yogurt into his mouth with one filthy hand, licking his fingers ravenously. By the time I got to the car and looked back, he'd finished the whole thing and again sat staring into space, one hand resting on his belly.

In the car, Fred said, "Was that to prove a point?"

"No point, Fred." I regretted how sharp I said it. "He needed something to eat."

Fred slipped his hand over mine, as the driverless pulled into traffic.

"I'm sorry I called you a bleeding heart. I meant you have a good heart. Best one I've ever known."

*

Linda Holiday looked fifteen years younger. She'd had excellent work done somewhere. Crow's-feet gone, turkey neck vanquished, the skin of her face bright and tight, but not in a way that demanded one think of the scalpel cutting through her forehead. Her hair was the color of yellow grain waving in a field.

"You look unbelievable," I told her as we sat down to dinner at the Harpo Club in Soho.

"Please," she said. "You can't go into a pitch meeting now actually looking fifty-five."

"Clients, right?"

"Worse than ever. You were right to get out when you did. It's like the more women that come into the workplace—you know, because we can actually finish college—the more the men in the room become sub-simian retarded. And yes, I'm with the kids, un-PC words are back in! Men. Are. Retarded." She flipped a hand, and a collection of turquoise-studded gold bracelets slid down to her thumb and clattered back.

The waiter came over, and I asked Linda, "You wanna get wild?"

"Hog-wild, baby. Been a long week."

"Just to warn you ladies, we are short on a few items." He rattled off a dozen things that were not available.

"Jesus, what do you have?" said Linda.

"My apologies. The riots at Hunts Point Market have shipments squeezed all over the city. Could I perhaps make a few suggestions?"

For only a moment, I felt the unease again, that a distant disturbance could reach a place where wealth was a prerequisite to even walk through the door. Then Linda ordered a $200 bottle of Château Rieussec and several appetizers, and the waiter told her those were excellent choices. Within twenty minutes the wine had hit, and we were clutching our guts laughing at gossip from the shop. To my absolute horror and delight she told me that Beth McClann and our former CEO Patrick Yeats were now an item.

"Hell, I didn't even know McClann had a functioning vagina before that," said Linda.

I spilled wine on my hand I was laughing so hard.

"And you know Gruber got married?"

"Oh yeah?"

"Nice Jewish girl. Now they're both in Israel like putting their bodies in front of IDF tanks in the Occupied Territories."

"No kidding?"

"Be honest." She leaned forward, wry smile on her lips, bracelets rattling again as she pointed her glass at me. "Did you hit that, Jackie?"

I held the sip of wine between my lips as best I could, laughing and nodding at the same time. "I know I know I know, so wrong."

"Are you kidding? I'm so jealous. I always had a thing for those cute little apple butt cheeks."

Around we went, over another bottle of wine and Kyoto beef, truffles, and roast duck à l'orange.

"It's gotten cut-fucking-throat at the firm. Like we are doing work for anyone with the cash. This mining firm committing human rights abuses left and right in Equatorial Guinea? Sure, why not! Let's rehab your brand!"

"Better than the code of thieves that is finance. At least there's—I don't know what to call it? A weird mercenary honor to the ad or the PR world. You have adversaries, right? And you're this hired gun meant to fight the wars that need to be fought. Being around funds, it's bloodless. Every trader has to be close to an aneurysm at all times. To lure talent and keep people off the ledge everyone at my firm gets a shrink, a masseuse, and an art budget. It's totally nutty."

"You want to come back?" Linda grimaced.

"Hell no."

"You were too good at it, Jackie. The dirt we got up to in '29? The way you put an axe blade through PRIRA. People still bow down to that."

I forced a chuckle, and then abruptly the conversation stalled. Linda dragged a brussels sprout through cream sauce and popped it into her mouth.

"By the way, you know who's in town?" she said, to say something.

"Who?"

"Jefferey. These ARs, every time you're in proximity to an old friend . . ." She waggled her glasses at me.

"Really? What's he here for?"

"Teachers' union training, I think? I guess he's gotten into labor stuff based on his profile. When's the last time you talked to him?"

"Ha. Jefferey? Jesus, more than twenty years now. I know he got married."

Years ago, a mutual Facebook friend had posted a picture from Jefferey's wedding. Kim Fox was the friend's name. She'd been a bartender at a place called Matilda that we used to hang out at a lot. I deleted that account not long after.

"Don't worry, he got fat," said Linda.

To change the subject, I nodded to an absurd car pulling up to the valet. "Look at this stud."

The man was white and, if I had to guess, Russian. He handed over his fob.

"Gallardo Spyder. Self-driving. Limited edition looks like." Linda explained: "We do Lamborghini's art."

This beautiful car put me at ease. It looked like honey on wheels. Any display like that, and you knew you'd be safe from riots, looters, and whatever else. The man walked inside, and we both watched the car ooze around the block, every surface glowing as it glided down dry asphalt.

*

On the ride home, I pulled up Jefferey's Slapdish, slid my thumb past his profile, and logged on to the VR interaction. I had glasses in my bag, and within moments I was inside his worlde, an imaginary man-cave, drowning in Bears, Cubs, Bulls, and Blackhawks accoutrements. There were shiny holograms of his three children. Cruising up the West Side Highway, past the bright skyscrapers of Hell's Kitchen, I dictated a message.

"Hey, Jeff, you dork. I had dinner with Linda Holiday. Remember her? She told me you were in New York for work. I thought it might be fun to get a drink and catch up. If not, no biggie, but I'm around."

I stared at the screen. I hated every last over-casual word of this message. But I sent it, and that was that.

At home, Fred was watching the news. To show that our tiff was not still on my mind, I curled up beside him with my tablet to peck at some work before bed, but my eyes kept sliding back to cable news. There were more riots in Los Angeles. False stories had spread that the city was holding food back at the ports, and people had descended on every grocery in the city, smashing windows, storming past barricades to carry off whatever they could. Then the story flipped to even more frightening coverage of Norway's election, where Anders Breivik, a mass murderer of children, was leading in the polls. Because Norway had long been weening itself off its oil, Breivik had found support from business interests that believed they had the technology to utilize hydraulic fracturing in the Alum Shale. "We will easily win. The current PM—she's target practice," Breivik joked, a horrifying comment that sent his supporters into a frenzy of joy. Finally, there she was, looking exhausted but determined: That evening Kate Morris had held her first press conference since being released. A reporter asked her if she regretted anything about her actions from the previous year.

"Do I regret anything?" She gripped her chest in bewilderment. *"What a backwards-ass question, man. No one in our movement massacred anyone."* Tears welled in her eyes, her voice hot and strong. She pounded a fist against her chest over and over. *"Brave people took a stand for an idea greater than themselves, and they were murdered for it. And let me tell you and everyone else—this is not over. Vic Love and the interests he serves didn't put our movement down, they only made it stronger. We'll walk into fucking bullets if we have to, but we're not going anywhere. We will keep coming."*

"Sure, go get more people killed," Fred muttered. "Unbelievable."

I'd had enough. The news had been giving me anxiety for twenty years now, and I couldn't bear another second of it. I laid in the dark, unable to sleep, staring at the backs of my eyelids until Fred came in, brushed his teeth, and got in bed beside me. As he began snoring, I was still wide awake.

I slipped out from under the covers and walked to my office. When we'd moved into the new penthouse, Fred had offered me the room with the south-facing window and its majestic view, now glittering with New York's disparate dreams. Fred had sent me the report, and I opened it on my tablet. Despite the title, it was dry reading and described much of what I expected. Strong positions in Arctic oil, gas, uranium, minerals, and the companies best positioned to access those riches. Huge bets on Norman Nate's Solar Solutions with high confidence that the next COP would produce an agreement to begin albedo management of the planet. I searched the document for ANøNosiki. The only mention of it read:

> Natural disasters, freshwater scarcity, and desertification trends will continue to lead to denationalization. While maintaining long positions in security and detention, it will be advantageous to invest in services providing transcontinental transportation, as well as future employment, for stateless migrants. Now that migrant paths are moving out of the gray market and falling under the purview of publicly traded companies, these firms are routinizing previously dangerous journeys. Not only has ANøNosiki reduced migrant fatalities but they've provided workers with opportunities to pay off the costs of their transportation with pollination labor in China or sugarcane harvesting in Brazil.

A frustrating bit of research on ANøNosiki revealed it was owned by several international conglomerates, including a Spanish construction firm, a Dutch-based chemical conglomerate, a US private equity firm, and the Qatar Investment Authority, the country's sovereign wealth fund. I flipped forward, past brain-computer interface, nanotech, and biotech, all the technology that filled me with a sense of vast and strange continents lying just over humanity's horizon. I came to a password-protected addendum called "The New Gray Edge: Political Processes in Developed Nations." I tried Fred Jr.'s birthday backward and came up empty-handed, but I could still see the table of contents. The firm CLK had two pages devoted to it. First, there'd been quants and their black boxes of predictive algorithms, then insanely expensive research services that would send spotters to surveil wafer factories in China—anything for edge. Now there was psychometrics persuading or dissuading consumers and citizens.

I set the report aside and considered going back to bed. But it was that itchy late-night feeling.

In the greasy confines of the VR goggles, I scrolled until I found the interview I'd been meaning to watch ever since Haniya exploded at the woman at dinner.

I joined two families in a beautiful, brightly lit living room. Seth Young's sister and three brothers sat on the right. Sybrina and Keon Hudson, the parents of Malik Brown Hudson, sat to the left. Malik had also been killed on the National Mall. The anchor asked how the families had met and decided to start this advocacy group together.

Seth's older sister, Grace, explained, "After the Democrats made it clear they wouldn't pursue impeachment, we were of course furious, so we had to start an organization that would work to bring those responsible to justice. We met with the families of some of the other victims, which is how we got to know Sybrina and Keon."

Sybrina took over the story.

"And we found out, oddly enough, that Malik and their brother, Seth, had been at Georgetown together and had in fact dated very briefly. We're not even sure they knew they were both protesting on the Mall, but now they are both dead, murdered by the country they were trying to save. So we all decided to combine our resources, but then . . ." She looked to Grace. "What happened next?"

"Well, we saw the picture, right?" Evan Young offered. "While we were trying to choose a name?"

"Right, right," said Sybrina. "We found this image of this beautiful young girl with natty braids, hands all dirty, and she was holding up a sign that said 'We Will Win!' and just smiling like a kid on her way to a birthday party."

"Missing about seven baby teeth," said Keon.

"Very cute," added Grace.

"So we went looking for who she was," Sybrina continued. "You know, mostly out of curiosity. We talked to so many survivors, and *everyone* knew her, knew her name was Letitia. But then we couldn't find out anything else about her, a last name, a home, who her parents were. And eventually when the government released the names of the dead, we find out she was an orphan and a runaway. She'd been living on the street when the siege started and had just wandered down to the Mall and kind of joined up. So okay."

Sybrina scooted to the edge of the couch cushion, so it felt like she was craning toward me.

"Survivors are telling us these stories about her. How she was always eager to help, how she talked a blue streak to everyone, how she always insisted on making the coffee at the chow hall or would challenge everyone she could find to a foot race. And then this one young man told us that when the government stormed the Mall the first time, some of the undercover police had set tents on fire, so he and the others were trying to douse them, and there was Letitia, this eleven-year-old girl, running back and forth, carrying these jugs of water two at a time, to help put out the fires. And even after that, she stayed. She was still sleeping on the Mall when those soldiers opened fire. So there we all were"—she gestured to the six of them with a wide circular swoop of her arm—"hearing about this, just bowled over by the courage of this little girl. Our boys, Seth and Malik, they have families who will remember them, who will tell their story and carry on their memories. But who is going to remember Letitia? The world needs to know this girl's name and her courage. Because she represents the best of who we are. We will win because she is who we are fighting for—"

I paused the interview as a message popped into the top right corner of the goggles. It was a voice recording from Jefferey. I pulled the goggles off and tried to wipe the flood of exhausted tears from my face. I sat in the dark for a very long time, weeping quietly. Finally, I played his message.

*

Two days later, poring over outfits in the recesses of my closet, I was caught in that trap of wanting to look youthful and attractive but not like I was trying. There was a blue Milan dress, but the cleavage was a bit much. I eyed a leather pencil skirt that I sometimes wore with a particular loose-fitting chartreuse blouse. As I fretted over this decision, annoyed at myself for fretting, Fred walked into my closet and took me by the waist.

"Should I be nervous?"

"About Jefferey? I showed you the picture. He's become a total cow."

"I'm having dinner with Peter and Nate in Tribeca. Any chance you'll want to join us?"

"I wouldn't wait on me. Jefferey and I will have to get a hotel room—it'll be a whole production."

"You're so funny, Jack! That's what I love about you."

I pecked him on the cheek and chose a black scoop-neck top and a crimson flare skirt.

I'd suggested Creole Slim, a new Haitian American fusion place I'd heard good things about. When Jefferey saw me walk in, he blurted out, "Oh goddamnit." I met him at a cream-white island in a sea of similar tables, surrounded by couples talking low in dim gold light. He hugged me. "You look absolutely beautiful—this sucks." There was a lot of him to hug. Even though I'd been prepared by his profile, it was still jarring how much weight he'd put on. He'd never been fat when we'd dated, but the potential was there. After we moved in together, and I could exert control over the shopping list, I did my gentle best to nix his snacking habits.

"Stop it, you look great, Jefferey."

"Do not. Don't you—don't you dare"—he wagged a finger in my face—"pretend like I'm not the fattest fucking thing you've seen since we went to see the prize pigs at the Iowa State Fair in 2011. They have cranes pick me up out of bed to dress me in the morning."

"Stop," I told him. "You look terrific. You still have your hair!"

He smiled and batted his eyes. "Okay, go on."

The conversation rolled effortlessly from there.

We somehow ended up recalling our *Mario Kart* battles, how I went from not knowing how to play to consistently beating him, and we'd spend entire Friday evenings at home getting wine-drunk playing every level. Then he started humming "You've Got to Hide Your Love Away," and I had a familiar pain in my gut from the man who used to make me laugh so hard I'd get a stomachache. Delivering our drinks, the waiter asked what was so funny. How could I ever explain to him? The first day after we'd moved in together, Jefferey had left a foul smear in the toilet bowl, and in utter disgust, I'd demanded to know why he hadn't used the toilet brush.

"What do you mean?" he had said in genuine confusion. "Why dirty the toilet brush when you can pee the poop away?"

"*What?*" I'd choked.

"Babe, you gotta pee the poop away." And to demonstrate, he'd gone to the toilet, lifted the seat, and right in front of me began urinating on his own shit stain, singing, to the Beatles tune, *"You've got to peeee theeee poop awaaaaay."*

It was so stupid, and yet I thought I might cough up a lung laughing. From then on, he'd dutifully used the toilet brush, but he never stopped singing that song, and it never failed to get a rise out of me.

"There is no way," I said to the waiter, wiping tears from my eyes, "in a million years, I could explain."

He gave us a look like *Okaaay*. Jefferey winked at me, and I found it so unfair how no one ever grew any younger.

I told him about Fred, my work at the fund, trying to gloss over—just a bit—our financial situation. Jefferey lived in Oak Park on a teacher's salary, and I wasn't sure what his wife did, but from some internet snooping it seemed like the nonprofit sector. I definitely wasn't about to tell him that Fred's net worth was somewhere between $43 and $62 million, that my own had, in the last three years, climbed north of $13 million, that in the last eight months we'd vacationed or had business trips to Dubai, London, Hong Kong, Sydney, Paris, and Aspen. That we'd bought a home in London's tony Marylebone district just because it had a residential tax haven, and we would probably spend less than two weeks a year there. That I'd spent $30,900 at Bergdorf's the week before. "And what about the kids? Tell me about them," I prodded.

"The kids? What a tripod of assholes! Brit's our oldest, fifteen, and it's devastating. She used to love me. Used to think I was the coolest, funniest, most incredible guy that ever walked the earth, and now she's totally flipped. Can't stand me. Thinks I'm an idiot, is embarrassed by everything I do." He laughed. "Then Jeff Jr. hates his name, so he goes by Caspian. One day the kid just comes home from school, says he has no gender, and demands everyone call him 'Caspian.' He's about to turn twelve, which we're terrified of because that's when Brit's personality transplant began. But Casp is also a really talented musician and artist. He draws nonstop, really good stuff, so we send him to a special arts middle school—"

"I'm assuming that must come from your wife's side."

"Oh, I'm assuming she fucked the lawn guy."

Laughing again, I chided, "Jefferey."

"That boy could not be less like me if we'd tried to engineer it the way some of these rich-ass parents do with their designer babies. So yeah, Casp is a trip. And then the youngest is Kyle. Wonderful, sweet, beautiful Kyle. Nine years old, hardy as hell. Loves football. Loves baseball. Thinks I'm awesome. Thinks I know everything about every subject. I want to put him in a coma so he stays this way forever."

"Sounds like you love it, though. Being a dad." And I felt just the smallest tinge of hurt.

"It has its moments. It does come with this—" He stopped and squinted, his gaze traveling to the wall where a painting hung of Port-au-Prince under a vivid cerulean sky. "It comes with this undercurrent of always being sad. Like I understand how quickly it's all going by. And now that Brit's in high school, and there's all this distance she's put between us, I sort of realized, 'Oh, I'm never going to be an invincible hero to her ever again.' She might get less moody eventually, but it all just hurtles by you."

A woman in a dress of flaky translucent sequins bumped into our table, rattling the glasses and silverware. I was grateful for the interruption.

"So you and Fred never took the plunge on kids?"

"He has a son from his first marriage, but by the time we met it was a little late."

"It's never too late."

"At forty-eight it is." And now I very much wanted to change the subject. "Do you ever see anyone else from the old days? The Wellington Brown Line years?" Referring to the L stop closest to our apartment.

"Not really. The U of Wisconsin guys all moved back home. I still see Dan Faulk, but he's in Naperville, which is such a trek. He married this psycho Puerto Rican chick, who runs his life like a military barracks."

"Faulk? That's surprising."

"Tell me about it."

"Hey, what about that crazy bartender from Matilda. Kim Fox. Remember her?" I let fly my flirtiest smile of the night. On Jefferey's twenty-fifth birthday, wild on tequila, Kim and I had made out in front of him and his friends as an impromptu birthday present.

But Jefferey's face fell, and I thought I'd said something wrong, that bringing up this innocent memory had made him uncomfortable. He looked at the table and then back at me.

"She was at Wrigley."

I frowned. "What do you mean?"

"The shooting. She was one of the—she was one of the people who got killed."

This news crawled up my arms one hair at a time, and instead of Kim's bright smile and heavy pours for the regulars, I thought of my mom and brackish water rising higher and higher. "Oh my God. I had no idea."

"The bar had a memorial for her. It was all pretty fucking gnarly. The whole city was shut down for a week. Everyone was freaked there were going to be more shooters, like a whole army of white supremacists was going to descend on the streets. Awful thing was, me and Meg and the kids had gone to two Cubs games already that year." He shook his head. "It was really freaky. Really awful."

Snared among the memories of going to Wrigley with Jefferey was the actor, who'd been wearing that blue Cubs hat. That man melted into The Pastor, preaching at a rally, his eyebrows dark cuneiforms. He'd said such massacres were Christ's judgment, that if we didn't elect him, there would be many more to come.

The waiter took our plates, and Jefferey ordered a whiskey, so I got another glass of wine. Yet our conversation couldn't seem to recover from the story of Kim Fox. Jefferey tried another avenue, and he chose exactly wrong.

"How's your family doing? Erik, Allie, your mom? I'm sorry about your dad, I heard about that."

I smiled as brightly as I could manage. There was no way I was sharing the story of my mom right now.

"They're all doing great—yeah. Same old, same old. Allie can still be a pill."

"A horse pill. But it's comforting that nothing changes."

I tried to pivot the conversation by treading where we hadn't gone yet.

"And you and Meg, how did you meet?"

"We were both teaching at the high school."

"So you're both still there? I thought I saw a picture of her working at a garden?"

"Right, she quit teaching to work for this farming cooperative. This Fierce Blue Fire thing."

My ears might as well have twitched.

"No kidding?"

"Yeah, these agrarian community projects in the city—it's like farming and carbon sequestration and teaching and voter organization all rolled into one."

Of course, I was familiar. The Outposts.

"I was just watching the interview with the two families—"

"Justice for Letitia," he said immediately.

"That's right, yeah. That whole thing was just such a nightmare. I've always admired Kate Morris, but what they did . . . To this day, I just can't believe it happened."

Though I'd thought this was a safe perspective, especially since his wife worked for FBF, which had told its members not to join the illegal occupation, I could tell from the blankness of his face that this comment had not landed. So I found myself stumbling on, maybe saying things I believed, maybe parroting Fred.

"Obviously, what happened was appalling, and I don't want to see Love reelected, but Morris put people in danger, and—she was almost courting it, you know?" My voice went too high on the question. Jefferey's entire bearing had changed. While raining jokes on me, there'd been an eagerness to his posture. He'd leaned in, looking slightly uncomfortable and apologetic about his weight. Now he lounged back in his chair, staring at the table.

"Meg and I almost took the kids to D.C. for it."

"Really?" I said, as neutrally as I could.

"Right after Kate gave that speech and people started showing up, we talked about pulling the kids out of school, buying a bunch of camping gear. Maybe quitting my job to do it. Then we decided to wait until school was out, and if it was still going on . . ." His eyes caught mine and then looked away. "But we were nervous about having the kids there. For good reason it turns out."

Clearing my throat, I tried to carefully double down and back away at the same time. "That's admirable. I just think that doing what she did—and it was so appalling what happened to all those people—it was an action like you'd expect from the Weathermen."

Jefferey's brow narrowed. "How do you figure?"

"She wanted to create a big spectacle, that's all I mean. She wanted chaos instead of doing what your wife is doing with FBF. Trying to find solutions, trying to work with industry and government."

"I think Meg would probably tear you a new asshole if she heard her work described like that."

His tone was conciliatory, like he wouldn't be able to stop Meg if she heard, and this was too bad. I was frustrated and anxious because I kept finding myself saying things I didn't actually believe, but it was like I'd driven into quicksand and throwing the car in reverse was only pulling me deeper. I'd found what Morris did unbearable, but only because, when it first began, I did not want to see her embarrassed. And then I did not want to see her fail. And then I did not want to see her harmed.

"Morris and her followers are misguided is all I'm saying. There are better ways to go about this."

"Such as? What's your boyfriend's hedge fund doing to avert planetary catastrophe, I'm curious?"

I sat with my spine rigid and met the hostility of his voice with calm.

"The fund's invested in a range of climate solutions and adaptations. It's *very* forward thinking, and we work with a proprietary computer model designed by Ashir al-Hasan. I doubt there's an investment firm in the world that's thought more about climate change than Tara."

"No, I get it. You have to convince yourself that doing well and doing good are the same thing. The whole world's run by people who think even when the dark days come, they'll just sub in money for justice and it'll all be fine."

A defensive heat rose to my face. Who was this person? I had never heard him talk like this in the years we'd dated. When I'd known him, he'd been mostly apolitical with a bit of a conservative bent. I'd had to persuade him to vote for Barack Obama in 2012, and he'd been lukewarm about going to McCormick to see the president speak on election night.

"I'm just saying, there's a way to go about things that works, and a clear way that doesn't. Kate Morris and her disciples—or whatever you want to call them—they have to know they can't win."

Jefferey pushed his gaze into mine, his eyes moons of certainty.

"Of course they think they can win. They *know* they are going to win." He lowered his voice. "Maybe you can't understand. You don't have kids, so it's hard to think past your own lifetime. But a parent has to."

He might as well have punched me in the stomach. I could feel the red splotches forming on my neck.

"I thought you didn't even want children," I snapped, before I could stop myself. "At least that's what you told me when you were wheedling your way out."

"I never said that."

"Liar," I shot back, and the heat on my throat and face burned harder. "We stayed up till four a.m. that night talking about nothing else."

"I don't remember it that way."

"You strung me along for three years. And sometimes I think it was just because you wouldn't have been able to tie your own shoelaces, let alone pay down your loans, without me. And I've never forgiven you for it."

As soon as I said it, I realized how true it was. I couldn't even forgive him for popping up in my dreams sometimes, carrying the anger into my morning even as his image leached away. He chewed his tongue for a moment, glaring at me.

"Do you remember what you said to me when I told you I wanted to quit C. H. Robinson and go back to get my teaching degree?"

"I told you I thought it was impractical. Because it was. You wanted to take out another hundred grand in loans."

"Sure. You were always . . . displeased. You didn't think I took my job seriously. You didn't like that I hated going to look at condos, that I didn't really want to tie myself to a thirty-year mortgage. We went to Faulk's apartment that one time—and I mean, this is a bro in commodities trading—and all you talked about for two days was how beautiful his place was."

"So? Jefferey, I told you what debt did to my dad. But that never concerned you, so it meant it would have to concern me. You never cared about the consequences. I'm the one who had to worry about being financially insecure our entire lives because you thought it would be fun to never grow up."

"Yeah, but your version of growing up just meant buying more bullshit. Just spending our whole weekend in some depressing lifestyle store blowing money on more useless fucking garbage we didn't need. The longer we were together, the more I didn't like the person you were underneath. Or the person you were trying so hard to become. So maybe I did lie, yes. It wasn't that I didn't want to have kids, it was that I didn't want to have them with you."

The waiter came, and we got the check: $423.87. Jefferey tried to reach for it, but I handed my card over before he could. He tried to stop me, and I told the waiter to run it. We sat there in silence until he returned. I tipped, signed the slip, and got up, pushing my way between tables. The streets were dry and cold. I folded my arms and set out west, toward Central Park, without any clue where I was walking. Jefferey caught up to me, pulling on a green corduroy jacket that no longer fit. He touched my shoulder, but I shrugged him off. I turned my head only once more, saw his devastation at having told me the truth. How stupid. This fat, childish man, who'd somehow set my entire life on an unknowable course. Someone I shouldn't have given a second thought to after about 2014.

"It was nice seeing you again, Jefferey," I told him. "I wish you the best." Then I breezed down the street, and after calling to me again and again, first exasperated and then defeated, he let me go. His voice, carrying my name, died on the wind.

Before I reached the park, I turned south. I'd had only two glasses of wine but felt the sense of driving drunk down an anonymous highway. Two teen girls wearing VR goggles and giggling at something they saw in another reality whisked by, grasping each other. Two police in full tactical gear ambled up the sidewalk, nodding at me as I passed.

I walked down the east side of the park where spring was struggling in fits and starts in the buds of the trees, past the dual spires of the Plaza. Yellow cabs snarled the Manhattan grid, a din of horns and the scent of exhaust mixing with hot dog and halal carts. Shafts of light from the lobbies of graceful apartment buildings pooled on the sidewalks. I studied the glow of St. Patrick's Cathedral, the Empire State Building, and in the distance One World Trade, and recalled the thrill of walking this route for the first time in my twenties and feeling how far I was from Iowa. Steam drifted from the sewers, cut through by the strides of people out for the night, tossing their careless bodies at each other. I passed an older couple, walking too slowly, talking about movies they'd seen when they were young. The open wound of a new skyscraper going up. Old New York still breathing through the luxury condos and glass towers. I kept on through the raucous technicolor glare of Times Square, stuffed with slow-shuffling tourists, holograms dancing over our heads, an ocean of digital life swarming in the sky above. Eventually, I caught a cab home. Passing the gas station on Eleventh and Fifty-First, the teenagers were still there, camped out in little pup tents, taking shifts holding their signs.

Fred was home, staring out the window. Just one lamp on, our reflections in the glass. I could tell something was up. At first I thought he was angry I'd been out with an ex for so long, but he'd forgotten that entirely.

"I was planning to give you this in a few days but . . ." He handed me a stack of papers with a binder clip. "It's a divorce agreement. So we can get married."

"What's wrong?" I asked him. "You look freaked. Marrying me can't be that bad."

"No, it's . . . This awful, crazy thing happened on the street outside the restaurant."

A few weeks later I'd watch the video online. While Peter, Nate, and Fred were eating dinner in Tribeca, a couple of kids in their twenties had walked up to the window. A boy with long black hair and a patchy, peach-fuzzy beard; a Black girl wearing, for some reason, a graduation gown. The boy held a sign that read THIS IS DONE OUT OF LOVE. And then they lit themselves on fire. The video was chaotic, the diners stumbling back from their tables as the two screaming kids banged against the glass, maybe trying to crash through it, but instead falling to the ground, writhing and shriek-ing in pain. A few of the patrons, including Peter, ran outside to try to beat out the flames with their jackets. The girl survived, covered in third-degree burns. The boy did not.

That night I held Fred and told him how sorry I was, how horrible that sounded.

"I think I'm in shock." He'd never appeared younger to me. I could see what he'd looked like as an uncertain boy, maybe gazing at a tree he was afraid to climb. "It was just . . . awful. I can't stop seeing it." I thought of finding my mother. I knew that when you saw a person do violence to them-selves, it never really left you.

We went to bed, Fred taking a sleeping pill to knock him into dreamless-ness. I couldn't sleep, though, and got up to try several different passwords for the section of the report called "The New Gray Edge." After having no success, I went to Fred's trading station and logged in to the three-monitor setup. From there I got into his password manager and began trying those combinations. Finally, one of them worked, and I sat back in his chair, read-ing. When I was done, I made some coffee, ate breakfast, and dug through the refrigerator for bread, meat, and fixings. I packed ten sandwiches, a few bananas, and protein bars into my biggest shoulder bag. Then I took the elevator down to the street and walked until I reached the gas station. There were still five teenagers camped out with their signs, looking hungry, tired, and cold under the first bathwater light of dawn.

SLAPDISH Presents

SLATE SENSORY NEWS

Whose Worlde Are We Living In? A Dark VR Legacy Arrives in Our Reality

Content by Stephanie Hardwick

June 25, 2035

[Warning: This news xpere is intended to be consumed with 3D ASMR Fractal Visuals and a soothing binaural soundscape. Without these elements, some users may find this content disturbing.]

When virtual reality arrived as a staple in people's homes in the years following the Covid-19 pandemic, its champions made utopian predictions of its power to connect and create while detractors warned it would rot children's brains. Few could foresee the far stranger consequences that have actually come to pass. Virtual reality has allowed people to, once and for all, curate their own realities. Bit by bit, day by day, our old world is having to fend off intrusion by these upstart regimes.

In a recent grisly example, on April 28 thirty-seven individuals infiltrated elite spaces of politics and luxury, from a birthday party in Montecito, California, to the Parliament House in Sydney, to outside high-end New York City restaurants. The CEO of Bank of America, a meeting of Australia's conservatives, and numerous guests of Manhattan's Eleven Madison Park, watched as radical activists doused themselves in gasoline and set themselves ablaze. The "QMM light show," as it's known, began in VR. On the last day of the siege of Washington, an unemployed thirty-four-year-old college dropout named Quinton Marcus-McCall added to the carnage by taking to the floor of the House of Representatives and self-immolating. Within months his disturbing end had become a potent VR meme. Hacked into countless games and xperes by activists with a point to make and trolls simply looking to get a rise, the "QMM light show" interrupted the Oscar telecast, *American Idol*, and CBS's VR reboot of *The Big Bang Theory.* Some of the largest audiences in the history of the medium have now been subjected to this ghastly vision.

In VR, it is always easy to wingnut cherry-pick. There is the grotesque meme of the "Ham Sammy Brigade"—xperes of right-wingers happily wolfing down ham sandwiches to taunt the planet's starving, which has led to Far Right politicians munching on pork subs during rallies across disparate countries. Two million daily visitors to the worlde of "Dan Doodoo," a soft-spoken, bespectacled conspiracy theorist who claims to communicate with dead celebrities, believe the "real world" is in fact Doodoo's simulation, which we are all living in. His adherents inundate those who doubt Doodoo's divinity with very real death threats.

Because this warp-speed revolution has so fractured audiences, advertisers have no choice but to pursue eyeballs wherever they congregate. Dan Doodoo is the quintessential Slapdish millionaire, and there are untold numbers of wannabe gurus, gamers, and small-fry gods trying to copy his success. While Marvel, Disney, DC Comics, *Game of Thrones*, and other iconic IP still rule the day, it does not make up the plurality of interactions with VR xperes or worldes. People don't much care for corporate curation anymore. They don't want to see Tom Hanks storm the beach at Normandy in the *Saving Private Ryan* xpere, they want Tom Hanks to hold them while they cry and call him their father. They don't want to watch Luke Skywalker save Leia from Jabba the Hut. They want to watch Jabba penetrate Leia with a baseball bat–sized slug phallus. The age of DIY social and cultural experience, never censored, questioned, or combated with facts, has taken over.

"The QMM light show" takes this up a disturbing new notch. Most of the thirty-seven people involved in the globally coordinated action died in agony. A few survived, though recovery will be a long, difficult road.

Marcus-McCall grew up in a lower-middle-income neighborhood in Detroit, his mother a doctor and his father a professor of African American Studies at Wayne State University. The couple separated when Quinton was seven, and his mother passed away during the pandemic, while his father died from a heart attack in 2023. Marcus-McCall also had a sister, who was killed by her boyfriend in 2018.

After moving to Los Angeles to try his hand at a career in stand-up comedy, Marcus-McCall returned to Detroit, where he enrolled in Wayne State's nursing program, only to drop out in 2026. This was also the year he joined A Fierce Blue Fire's Detroit Outpost, where he worked in community outreach. Friends describe him as quiet and kind but with a quick wit and occasionally provocative sense of humor. A childhood friend, Tyrone Cardona, told *Slate* that Marcus-McCall became enamored of A Fierce Blue Fire's mission.

[Voice of Cardona]: "He thought they had the right program. Quinton wasn't religious but he was, you know, spiritual. He was a funny guy but also thoughtful, and he could be dark. Or brooding—I don't know what to call it. He had been through tough stuff, but you wouldn't know that hanging with him. He was also political but not in the normal way. He didn't march or tweet or do nothing like that—it was more like he kept tabs. Now I feel like he was just biding his time. Waiting his whole life for his moment."

Marcus-McCall did seem to have a plan. He left A Fierce Blue Fire in 2033 and spent months training for the occupation. When the time came, he was one of the foot soldiers who helped fortify and administrate the occupation of the capital. By August 1, he had positioned VR cameras in the House Chamber to capture and immediately download his act of self-immolation to private servers, subverting the government's efforts to block all communication that day. By the time news outlets were reporting what had happened on the Mall, the "QMM light show" was already bouncing between worldes. Within a week, it had become a potent global meme, yet another flash point in the heated debate about the climate crisis, the occupation, and where virtual reality is leading us.

The Slapdish "paintbox" allows participants to dream almost anything, and yet the results of this are typically as crude and troubling as the rest of the internet. From CGI child pornography to antebellum slave plantations to real-life torture xperes, VR's frightening underground is a thousand-person heavy metal concert one floor beneath your apartment. Yet those examples at least follow a kind of logical continuity with how the internet's dark side has always functioned.

In other words, censorship works against them. It is the aboveboard insurgents like Quinton Marcus-McCall who are skewing our reality. And some of these insurgents have created audiences of exceptional numbers and power.

After hip-hop artist Tricky Digz was revealed to be Jason D. Blair, a forty-year-old white accountant living in St. Paul, Minnesota, a movement emerged to force Slapdish to create a racial registry of its users. The backlash to *that* has exploded into a different revelation: a study in the *Journal of Applied Biobehavioral Research* found that 78 percent of participants admitted to identifying by another gender, race, or religion as they navigate worldes. Fans have declared Blair to be Black and will carpet-bomb anyone who says otherwise with a program of intimidation. Despite the death of Henrietta Housekip, child shock jocks Henny and Dillpickle continue to hit peaks of virality that make media empires jealous. Housekip's targets of ire began with identity politics, government censorship, and the corporate control of information and speech, but shortly before her death at age fourteen, she discovered China—not only its internal repression but how it uses its economic power to silence movie studios, sports leagues, and technology companies alike. Wearing Henny and Dillpickle merchandise in China has become a crime punishable by a ten-year prison sentence. Then there is The Pastor.

As we round the corner to election season, one of Slapdish's biggest stars became the first major candidate to ever launch a presidential campaign in virtual reality. His worlde, a neo-futuristic Christian citadel, has more daily visitors than any real-life theme park in the country. The current president utilized VR behavioral tracking and predictive analytics of voters to decimate his opponents in the 2032 Democratic primary. Yet Victor Love is not a native of the medium. The Pastor is. As he put it in the first Republican primary debate, "I intend to bring to the office of the president the joy, passion, and fire you see and love every day in my worlde—and I'll bring it to the 2D, 3D, 4D, and every dimension in between and beyond."

Say "Next Story" for: "How Zeden's VR Album *Seminole Party* is a Master Class in Post-Indigeneity"

THE GHOST
AND THE MASK
2036

You're bone-tired, but you focus on the work. You try not to think of prison, of search and rescue, or of the girl in the hole. Every Tuesday, Reverend Andrade and his wife, Ginna, drive their minivan around Coshocton handing out sack dinners to anyone who needs one. This winter, that includes most everyone in the county, from the single moms in the apartments on Walnut Street to the folks in tents out by the ruins of the old power plant. The Rev and Ginna print up little cards at the local copy shop and tape one to the top of each ham and cheese sandwich. It gives the recipient directions to the church or addiction treatment at the Fierce Blue Fire center where you and Raquel got clean a decade ago. You riding with them is part of the make-work the reverend has thrown your way since you got paroled, and you understand it's money he can't afford to pay you. Even with the parishioners who've stuck with him, no one can afford much tithing. He gives you tasks like stapling forms or fixing a clogged sink, and you're figuring out how to use a pipe snake on the fly with his AR glasses. Then on Tuesdays he takes you along as "muscle" while he and Ginna make the rounds.

"Hon, y'all wanna sack dinner?" Ginna shouts through the window in her syrupy West Virginian drawl.

"What's the catch?" the tired old Black guy asks, stopping all the same. He carries a backpack and wears a Cleveland Browns Super Bowl LXI Champs toboggan cap.

"Ain't no catch, sweetheart. Just some food from Church of Christ down Route 16."

"No God stuff," he says.

"Sorry, darling, Jesus comes in every bag. Now come take this."

Hesitantly, he comes forward. You hand Ginna the bag from the back seat, and she hands it to the man, who pops it open and peers inside like he can't believe there's not a bomb or a human ear.

Says Andrade from the driver's seat, "Ever need a helping hand or a place to sleep we got contacts at the shelter."

"Just hungry," the man mutters, poking past the church's card to the sandwich and fruit beneath. Then he looks up at Andrade and Ginna. "Much obliged. For real."

"God bless you, brother," says the Rev.

Andrade pulls away, leaving the man to tear the sandwich out of the cellophane right there on the street and take down a quarter of it in one bite. Ginna spots a woman she knows, working the corner near Raquel's McDonald's. It's a good place to trick because the crosswalks are busy, and there's a cheap motel right across the street.

"Starling!" she calls. Ginna has chestnut hair with blond highlights and would be pretty but for several missing teeth. You're now missing three teeth, so you're no one to judge, but the asymmetry of her smile is distracting. "Starling, honey, you wanna sack dinner?"

Andrade pulls the van to the side, and Starling looks annoyed but takes the brown paper bag anyway. She's wearing a T-shirt cut off at the midriff, exposing the pale flab of her belly. The shirt has a picture of an eagle filing its talons, backdropped by an American flag. Despite the flesh hanging loose over her knobby bones now, you recognize her from the blood bank way back in the day.

"How you doing out here?" Ginna asks her. "Staying warm? Got a place to sleep?"

"I'm aight. Just need a customer." She jitters and twitches, a dance taking place in the same square foot of space. You've been dope-sick enough in your life to know that she needs to score. "Used to be I sucked cock for heroin and didn't gotta worry about eating. Now it's easier to get heroin than a sandwich." This explanation, Ginna says as you pull away, "is as close to a thank-you as Starling is ever going to fork over."

The reverend and Ginna hold hands while he pilots the minivan around town. A cross dangles from the rearview mirror. Beyond the windows you watch the sunset reflect off the clouds, turning the sky pink and blue. A cotton-candy light. A sky of cold winter branches and telephone wires. Billowing above a front door, there is a banner with the silhouette of The Pastor carrying the cross up a hill against a gold, yellow, and brown sky while dark outlines of his followers watch silently. You can't turn a corner in town without seeing his name.

You drive the twilight until all but two sack dinners are gone. The reverend and his wife always give you the last two to take home.

Back at the double-wide, you set one of the brown sacks in front of

Toby, who's drawing and telling you about the ghost in the salad words you can never quite make out. He's wearing both his hearing aids, but his language is still mush-mouthed:

"En dah it stans in feel an watches us."

Five months home, and you're starting to pick up the sounds: *And Dad, it stands in the field and watches us.*

Toby's seven years old but looks smaller and younger. You're not sure what he thinks of you. His hearing aids jut from the canals, clipped together around his neck so he doesn't lose them.

"Where's Mommy?" you ask. He points to the wall, which means out back of the double-wide in your small lot. You do not have to ask if he's hungry because when he peers inside the sack his eyes light up, the ghost momentarily forgotten.

Out back, in the glare of the flashlight, you find Raquel covered in blood.

"He's talking about that ghost again."

She doesn't look up from her work. "I know, he spooks me out. Like one of them possessed kids in the old movies." From a low branch on the maple tree, she's got an animal hanging by a bungee cord, its feet cut off, and she's using a fleshing knife to take off the fur, pulling it down the body like a sock. "How was it?"

"'Bout what you'd expect. Rev gave me twenty bucks and two sack dinners for my time."

Raquel pauses and scratches her nose with her forearm, the part that doesn't have blood on it.

She examines the animal and resumes skinning. "Your mama still coming up Sunday?"

"Far as I know. Think she'll hit church with us, but I don't expect her to stay."

"That's good."

Raquel does not indicate which part of this she thinks is good, the staying or the going. While you were away, your mom inserted herself into Raquel's and Toby's lives, driving up on her days off to serve as free childcare, throwing in money when she could after they made SNAP impossible. Raquel had needed the help, but you don't blame her if she's had enough of your mom at this point. She's moved up to assistant general manager at Mickey D's, but the pay bump was insignificant. Once you got out, you promised her you'd be bringing in some money, but now it's more like you're just another mouth for her to feed.

"What is that anyway? Coyote?" you ask.

"Stray."

"A dog?"

"It's protein, ain't it? Some scientist wrote this thing that said we should all stop feeding the pets and start eating 'em." Raquel bops her eyes. "Everyone on the news threw a fit, but I'm like, *Not a bad idea.* And we can take care of this stray problem to boot." She finishes pulling the skin and fur free of the animal. It looks like a demon freshly crawled out of hell. "All Toby's eating anymore is oatmeal and chocolate cake."

The winds from the east carry the smell of the new petrochemical plant. If a headache had a scent, it would be this.

"I ain't eating dog."

"Then eat the oatmeal," she snaps back.

"Toby's in there with a sandwich right now."

Raquel unhooks the dog to lay it on the ground. The butcher knife lies on a sheet of newspaper nearby.

"And what about tomorrow? And the next day?"

"Casey Wheeler and I are going hunting this weekend. There'll be venison after that."

"Oh sure, Casey. That country goat."

She picks up the butcher knife and wags it in the air as she talks.

"You been to the store. We can't afford to be paying that much for canned soups and beans and SpaghettiOs. The food bank is tapped out every time I go. People stealing all day at work, and the franchisees is expected to pay for armed security now. God forbid I lift a box of nuggets home! Well, I found a solution, so I'll be putting that solution to work. You got a problem with it, Keeper, you can fuck off back to jail."

Rather than argue, you stalk around to the front steps. You take a seat on the stoop and wish you had a beer. You can hear Toby has turned on the TV, and for whatever reason he's watching the news. Across the river, the petrochemical plant glows green and purple and orange from the variety of lights within its guts, a fortress of steel and piping with a winking smokestack rising skyward. It's uncommonly beautiful even though the smell probably has something to do with Toby's asthma. You went looking for a job there, of course. "Keeper, they ain't gonna hire the guy who took the fall for a terrorist attack," Raquel said, rolling her eyes in that way you hate. You also hate that word. In the end, all you got charged with was trespassing, possession, and trafficking narcotics.

From inside, you hear the heat and timbre of The Pastor's unmistakable voice rise over the babble.

"... *The socialist media calls Love a tyrant, but I call him a coward. Lists are not enough. Walls are not enough. Drones are not enough. Land mines in the desert are a start, but we have to be willing to exert the ultimate punishment for lawbreakers. I'm talking about biblical law. We are witnessing God's judgment on a sinful world. He has given us the tools, the means, now we must seize these tools and bring about His glory . . ."*

"Toby, turn that shit off!" you yell but then remember he can't hear you unless you're beside him. You go inside the trailer, find Toby playing with a toy superhero, not really watching. You take the remote from his hand. He cries out, groping his small fingers for it and babbling in his private language. On the screen, The Pastor rocks on, and the crowd is going bonkers.

"They tell you this is their country, but I'm telling you right now my friends, they are wrong."

A young woman weeps as she tries to reach out and touch The Pastor's pant cuff on the stage. He holds his hand high and allows the fury of the rally to swell.

"This is OUR country. And I am your president already."

You change the channel, and this sends Toby into a tantrum you cannot understand.

You've been looking for work since you got out, and the pickings have been slim. First off, you weren't even sure Raquel would want you to come home. She got evicted from the rental house and couldn't afford anything but the double-wide at the "nasty end of the lot." After you were paroled, you went back to Kroger to beg Julian for your old job, which was humiliating and pointless. You struck out at an auto shop, the drive-throughs, every fast-food joint—Raquel couldn't even get you in at her McDonald's. Ex-felon, minor celeb around town because you made the national news for a day. You felt like you had both this big scarlet letter on you and nobody could care less about you.

You'd spent the entire first year in prison not believing that you ended up back there, this time for a stint you couldn't just sleep through. Fifteen years was a different beast. The new correctional facility in Chillicothe looked state-of-the-art, but it was the same as when you were in Marion, maybe with a better coat of paint. On the grounds there were the squat cement boxes, a few annex trailers, and sheds with corrugated metal roofs; two wraparound chain-link fences topped with razor wire, and beyond those, the fields and tough industry in every direction. In the distance, you could see the peak of a chapel. Inside, nice white walls, orange-tiled floors, and the Prion corporate logo on everything. You sank into the day-to-day routine, learning how to avoid trouble in the yard, how much money it took to get anything decent from the canteen or send a message with JPay, how to stitch an ammunition belt for the US Army, which is what they had you doing in the garment factory. Cliques determined by race, geography, and severity of punishment. You kept your head down. You didn't make friends. Five months in, another inmate on your cell block cut his wrists open with a coil of bedspring he'd somehow jimmied free. The guy survived and was transferred to a psych unit. His lesson taunted you, especially when you passed his cell with the carnal, salty scent of lingering blood. Raquel brought Toby to visit once to tell you he was hearing impaired. Not to mention the asthma. How he panicked when he couldn't breathe. You wanted to be strong because your boy is so fragile. You first had to convince yourself you were even capable of such a thing. So when the opportunity to reduce your sentence came along you had to take it. You had to.

———

Casey has gone porky and bald since you went away. He wears little crosses as earrings now and doesn't like making it known that he hangs out with you. He and Levi Bassett are still tight, and Levi wants to put your head through a wall because of what you did to him outside the bowling alley. For you and Casey, hunting trips into the forests south of town make the most sense. Together you ride on his rumbling Arctic Cat. It seems unlikely you'll sneak up on many deer with the Cat coughing gas, but you're outdoors and the air tastes clean. As the good reverend says, "At least you're alive and got all four limbs."

At the end of a trail, you and Casey leave the Cat and make your way into the cold winter woods. The snow has mostly melted, and it's slushy business going forward. Casey has a new Remington and lends you his old Mossberg for the afternoon. You sit in the box stand for twenty minutes and get bored. Then you walk for an hour, not saying much, and not seeing anything bigger than a squirrel.

"Gotta be better than dog," says Casey. "That's some fucked up Korean shit Rocky's doing to you." Rocky is, for some reason, what Casey has taken to calling Raquel.

"This is worthless," you say.

"Yeah, I told you these woods was empty. Everyone with the same idea. Best we'll get is a raccoon or opossum."

"My feet are fucking soaked."

Both boots have holes. You come to a felled tree not far from a small lake and stop to sit on it, leaning the rifle on a tree, and tearing off your boot and sock to rub warmth into your right foot. Then the left.

"How hard up are you?" Casey asks.

"Pretty fucking hard up."

"You got that gig with the church."

"That's about a hundred bucks a week, Casey. Ain't enough but to make me feel like I'm starving my kid. Plus, I can't do nothing but under the table or those fuckers'll just take the wages right out of the check." You explain how you still owe Prion Security Solutions thousands for your own incarceration, including shoes, uniform, your PRCC gear, phone calls, even the electricity you used.

"Least you wanna work. I'll tell you, if a man refuses to work, let him starve. Government's giving away food to Haiti or wherever and there's nothing left for anyone else." Casey appears to consider something, and though you don't dare let yourself hope, you can tell he has some kind of idea. "You remember Dick Underwood, of course." He drapes his rifle over his shoulder and removes a glove to blow into his fist. "He's gotten deep into this Patriot League stuff. You know they got a compound up by Sugarcreek?"

You've heard this. Underwood and his butt buddies playing like they're going to start the next American Revolution. Overthrow the government. Not enough of them had seen what the government could do if it got real with you.

"They're always looking for recruits. Guys to work. Get trained up and all that."

"Ain't it all volunteer?"

"Nah, they got money coming in now. A lot of it, I guess."

"Not really into politics."

"Hey, it'd be a job, though. Part of one, at least. Don't tell Rocky, obviously."

You were going to point into the woods to change the subject, but a small mammal materializes, like you conjured it into being. It's an opossum scuttling through the soggy muck, whipping its scaly tail. Casey takes up his rifle, aims.

The crack of the bullet echoes, sharper and clearer because the snow and ice don't absorb the sound. It chews into the dirt beside the animal, just enough to scare it and send it scampering into the forest.

"Goddamnit." Neither of you has the energy to give chase. "Don't want to eat opossum anyhow," Casey mutters.

By the time you trudge out of the woods, dusk has fallen. Casey drops you in town, after a white lie about why you aren't going home yet. With the five dollars in your wallet you buy a fistful of candy from the gas station. All you've had to eat in the last twenty-four hours is a ham and cheese sandwich, an apple, oatmeal, and now the candy. At least in prison you were never hungry.

You notice how many homes on Cassingham Hollow are empty now. Abandoned. Roofs caved in, windows boarded up. Feral cats roam the lawns. While you were busy pulling people out of debris during the Great Eastern Flood, the Muskingum River had topped its banks and soaked and splintered dozens of homes. But there's one with the lights on. That old Queen Anne. Gray with dull pink trim that hasn't been touched up in a generation. Battered chairs on the porch and the table with a dirty coffee mug. That mug packed with dead cigarettes.

When Tawrny shows up at the door, it's a little bit shocking. He's lost a lot of weight. He'd always been a big dude, barrel-chested and beer-gutted. He still has the gut, but it's dwindled to a sad fleshy pouch that rides ahead of him, stretching the fabric of his long johns. He still has the salt goatee, but the flowing white hair is not so flowing anymore. There's a brittle quality to it. Like his head would be crisp to the touch.

"Come on in, Keeper."

He offers you hot chocolate, and you sit at the kitchen table, which is burdened with the weight of dirty dishes and unopened mail. You recognize what a bill from a collections agency looks like. Stained long johns hang from a lamp.

"Your wife home?"

He looks up from the stove, where he sets a pot of water to boil. "Betsy passed. Two years ago now."

"Ah, T. Sorry to hear that."

"For the best." He reaches a frail arm to the cupboard where he snatches two mugs and empties a packet of hot chocolate powder into each. You can see his collarbone suddenly sharp against the weathered skin. "She was in agony at the end. Couldn't bear to watch it."

"Real sorry," you repeat, and abruptly you're thinking of Raquel. How she met you at the prison with Toby, a balloon tied to his wrist that said WELCOME HOME. Never in your life had you seen two more beautiful people, and you wanted to run back into your cell all the same.

"You finding any work?" Tawrny asks. He lights a cigarette. Spirals of smoke drift to the ceiling and collect in the room.

"Nope. Casey just tried to get me to go see the APL affiliate up in Sugarcreek."

"Buncha crazy fucking rednecks, you best stay well away from them."

"What I figured."

"You don't know the half. The League's been terrorizing folks. Claim they're cleaning up the streets, but they put an old Mexican in the hospital. Beat him half to death. Cops won't do nothing about it."

"So is this about product you need moved?"

He raises a dandruffy eyebrow. "You using again?"

"No," you say quickly. "Course not. But I can work."

The pot begins to whistle and Tawrny removes it, dumping steaming water over chocolate powder.

"Maybe you can, but I've moved on from that business. Got way too hot after Tuscarawas." He finishes pouring and looks at you. "Can't thank you enough for staying strong on that one."

You say quietly, "Of course, T."

"You just never know who's gonna snitch and who's gonna stand tall. Thing was, I never would've pegged you for the latter. You showed a lotta courage doing that time, boy."

You say nothing, accept the compliment. In truth, when they arrested you, you were eager to make a deal. Anything to get yourself out of trouble. Point the finger right at Tawrny and let them sweat him for whoever paid the money to get access to the plant—those greeniacs and their lunatic bomb makers. You'd never even heard of them before an FBI agent was barking at you about the terrorism enhancement. Then a lawyer walks in, who, surprisingly, says he's your lawyer. A little twit hotshot from Philadelphia. He claimed he was taking your case pro bono because he thought you were getting done wrong by the government. This didn't quite sit with you. He got you aside and said, Here is your story: You went to the spot out by the access gate to get high, and that's it. You tested the waters with him about flipping, and he told you no, that's only going to make your situation worse. The government will do what it will do, but if you stay strong, you'll be walking out in no time, he promised. Confess to any material support for terrorism, and there's no flipping that'll save you. The federal prosecutors want these people caught. Best to take a simple lie and ride it. Still, the Feds had been convinced you had a connection to the greeniacs, so they'd thrown the book at you. Fifteen-year sentence in the hopes that you'd spill. But you stood in the courtroom as the sentence came down, chewing your cheek to shit and repeating to yourself what your lawyer had said: You'd never serve all that. After the trial the guy vanished. You never heard from him again, and a part of you knew you'd been played. That the lawyer was hired by somebody, not to help you but to keep you quiet. In the end, all you got charged with was trespassing and possession. From minor celebrity to just some numbnuts who'd shot up by a fence and left his DNA on a padlock. You lopped off most of the time by signing up for the Prion Rescue and Conservation Corps (PRCC, or the "Prick" as it was known).

"Sorry, don't got no marshmallows." Tawrny sets the steaming mug down in front of you. It has a picture of the sun peeking over green hills and reads **WELCOME TO COSHOCTON, HEART OF GOD'S COUNTRY**. You sip, and the chocolate is so delicious. Finally, Tawrny gets to it.

"Reason I wanted you to come by, Keep, is, like I was saying, I gave up moving product. That's a young man's game. Money's tight, though, so I been working with the folks from before. From Tuscarawas."

You feel a permanent unease. It rides with you always.

"Didn't really work out for me last time, did it?"

"No, I admit, that was not ideal. But they did right by you, didn't they? Got you out in five years—"

"I got myself out," you correct him.

"They got more opportunities. And they took note of you. You stayed a soldier."

Though it once would have terrified you to show this man anger, it's been too hard a road, and he looks too weak. You lean forward and jab the table with your index finger like you're trying to puncture it.

"I got myself out. And why do you care anyway? You're some greeniac now? Blow some more power plants up? What do you care about these people?"

Tawrny meets your gaze, demonstrates he still has no fear of you. You'll always be a tweaker to him.

"I got no horse in their race, boy. But I'll tell you something, these green-iacs, as you call 'em—they pay. And they're smart something fierce. This lady I'm talking to asked about you specific. And, Keeper, there is some se-rious money involved. I'm talking a bag. You want to hear her out."

With a scrape of wood on wood, you push back from the table and stand. You hate leaving the hot chocolate behind.

"Ain't never wanted to hear someone out less."

"Give it some thought, Keeper," Tawrny says, blowing on the steam and sipping delicately. "Opportunities like this, you shouldn't sneeze at 'em."

"They can keep their money, trust me." You leave Tawrny and storm into a night beneath cold stars. It takes you an hour to walk home.

———

At church the next evening, you walk your mom across the parking lot while Toby holds Raquel's hand. He bounces in front of you in his small winter jacket and tiny tie, ready to shoot out of himself like a lawn sprinkler. Your mom moves slower every time you see her, and she insists on holding your arm. A fear of ice. Other churchgoers pull in in their SUVs and pickups. Hair is combed, shirts tucked, and the women's shoes are the finest in the closet. Ahead, Toby and Raquel are working through an excited conversation, To-by's mumbling facilitated by the rapid splashing of his hands as he signs. Raquel signs back patiently, each move of her fingers and fists like she's con-juring a spell. You still don't know much more than the basics. You could've learned that first year inside but you didn't. You didn't do much of anything.

"Careful on these stairs," your mom says, more to herself. She's dyed her hair an assaulting reddish color that doesn't look remotely natural. Every part of her sags. She clutches your arm and steps gingerly like she's cross-ing broken glass. You have an urge to slam your hip into her and send her sprawling.

You stop to greet Reverend Andrade in the foyer of his church but have to wait for the family ahead of you. A fat couple and their three porker kids. You look out across the field to the spot, now covered with snow, where years ago you were saved. That feels so, so long ago. From another life.

"My mom," you say to Andrade when you reach him. His eyes light up.

"Such a pleasure," he says, taking your mother's hand in both of his and pumping it profusely. "I'd heard tell of you, but here you are in the flesh!"

"Least for now," says Mom. "Day's not over yet."

Most of your mother's comments these days are about dying. The reverend compliments her outfit and asks if she'll be staying long.

"Just until the evening. Got my shift at Hortons tomorrow morning." You can tell your mom doesn't like Andrade, maybe because he's of Salvadoran descent or maybe because he's overly friendly. Then again, your mom has never taken a liking to almost anyone that you can recall. Not since Joe Biggs, the HVAC kingpin, at least. You're plenty surprised when she says, "Keeper speaks highly of you. Sounds like you and your church have done him a world of good."

Andrade positively beams at this.

You and your family sit in the third row on the left-hand side of the aisle because this is where Toby always likes to sit. Most of the other children his age end up on the right-hand side where the families cluster, and you don't have to learn sign language to understand that Toby is deeply fearful of other kids. He has reason to be. He often comes home crying, scraped, bruised, nose bloodied. He is the plaything of other, stronger children. The hearing aids are not helping him speak the way Raquel had hoped, and what's most frustrating is there's this thing, a next-generation cortical modem, this electrode array they could put in his brain that would restore his hearing immediately, but it is well out of any price range you'll ever sniff.

When Andrade takes to the lectern, he's smiling wider than the sun. His blue shirt and slacks are pressed, and his tie has little bicycles. Ginna sits in the first row, and he winks at her. You drift in and out of his sermon, as usual.

Seven months into your sentence in Chillicothe, the reverend came to visit. "You got a raw deal," he told you in the visiting room. You sat beneath a mural on the wall: a Black guy and a white guy helping to erect an American flag like at Iwo Jima above the motto PRION: BEGIN YOUR JOURNEY. "But I'm not giving up on you. And as soon as you're home there'll be a place for you in the church. Always."

Not too long after that, the Prion suit came by to give his spiel. They gathered everyone in the cafeteria to pitch inmates on a new initiative: contracting prisoners to the state and federal governments for search, rescue, and cleanup services following natural disasters. The pay was the same as the garment factory, about $2 an hour, but you'd be transferred, first to a training facility where you'd have to pass a six-week course, and then to the field. Your ears perk up when the suit says, "Carry out the job without incident, and you'll also have the benefit of a significant reduction in your sentence."

You signed the papers that day. Two weeks later, they moved you to the training facility in Colorado. Too far for Raquel and Toby to visit, but that's better anyway. Toby didn't have to grow up seeing his dad in prison greens.

Your attention returns to Andrade. "There is a war over the very meaning of Christian doctrine that's playing out in the media, online, and, I would say, in our very hearts."

He grips the lectern and looks down at his notes, the scribbled bullet points of a rough outline. The reverend played quarterback in high school, and he'll often say, "All I can do is scramble."

"A lot of folks in these parts go to church to hear the word of Christ, but they don't *listen*," said Andrade. "I'm going to come right out and say this, and I know some folks won't like it: This man who's now running for president, this so-called Pastor, is, in my opinion, an imposter. He's a carnival barker who's corrupting the word of the Bible to suit his own purposes, prejudices, and vanity. My job is not to tell people what they want to hear, my job is serving as a faithful, and *humble*, conduit for the word of the one true God." He bounced his fingers off his chest. "That food Ginna and I hand out every Tuesday? To people who are hungry, to people who need something to eat about as bad as they've ever needed anything—I'm not ashamed to say that food is bought and paid for with a grant from the folks at A Fierce Blue Fire, and I don't care how many emails I get telling me they're in a partnership with Satan. They are doing compassionate work. Compare that to The Pastor's church, which is telling people to deny the impoverished a helping hand, teaching people to hate their brothers and sisters, filling people's hearts and souls with fear and discontent. And so when people tell me to shut up, to quit speaking up for the powerless and voiceless, many of whom are your neighbors and live right here in this community, I tell them, I simply cannot do that. When even my own parishioners demand I cut ties with FBF or the Immigrant Defense Council, which is trying to save people from these dreadful detention facilities along the border, when they want me to deny my brothers and sisters their humanity, I tell them I simply cannot do that."

You think of what another PRCC guy told you the first time you had to pick up a dead body in Los Angeles, *Just be glad you're not at the border centers. They put them in solitary, these metal boxes, and they don't come out.*

They fry 'em alive and call it "death by heat-related illness." Bodies end up so swollen and bloody, they slide apart in your hands.

Andrade pauses, and you are now locked in, arrested by him. There is defiance in his voice.

"We often forget that Christianity began as a revolutionary movement of the powerless facing down the cold fury of the Roman Empire. It was a movement of the poor and dispossessed finally rising up. Christians waged a spiritual war for centuries with God's love as their only weapon. It was a faith built to defy an empire, and it was persecuted with barbarity. People were crucified and burned alive for holding fast to the love and mercy of Christ's gospel. So is this not a miracle we're seeing? People demanding their safety and dignity and value on a global scale? Is this not how God works? Forget about mysterious ways—His hand moves through us with galvanic *purpose* that only the truly *blind* cannot see."

You study the shadows falling across Christ's ponderous face, the statue hanging just behind and above Andrade's head. You think, as you often do, of the little Black girl you found in the crib in Amelia City. Plastic butterflies still clipped in her hair.

"The Pastor brings up Revelation, but he doesn't understand it. It's right there in chapter eleven, verse eighteen: God will bring ruin to those who would destroy His creation. Therefore, we have a responsibility, as Christians, as Americans, but first and foremost as human beings of free will on a just and gorgeous planet. You must see that we have the tools to build another path. It is the message from Paul in Second Corinthians: 'For though we live in the world, we are not carrying on a worldly war. For the weapons of our warfare are not worldly but have divine power to destroy strongholds.'"

You're hungry again. You wish you could take your family to a restaurant. After the service, you pack your family into the car, off to scavenge cans at the food pantry, everyone quiet as you pilot the car down the dark of Cherry Street.

The next day, you tell Raquel you have a job interview lined up, and you need the car for the day: a stocking position at a grocery in Kimbolton, all the lies coalescing stiffly in the moment.

"Kimbolton? How in the hell you gonna get over to Kimbolton every day?"

But she agrees to get dropped off at work so you can go see about it.

The drive to Sugarcreek is a bit treacherous. A winter storm put down six inches, and the salt trucks haven't hit all the roads yet. Route 93 still has a coat of tire-packed snow. On the way, you eat some of the cold dog meat. It tastes like beef but fattier. Gamey in your nostrils with a tangy aftertaste. The GPS gets you a little turned around and you have to stop at Woodsmoke Stables to ask for help with the address. The fella in a trucker hat and shit-kicker boots throws you an unhappy look but gives you directions anyway.

At the compound gate, there are two men in heavy winter coats with assault rifles slung over their shoulders. They ask your business, and you give them Dick Underwood's name. One of the guys produces a radio, gets the affirmative, and tells you "Park by the bodies."

You have no clue what this means until five minutes down the winding dirt road when you come to a vast field of barns, sheds, and other hastily built structures. A crop of vehicles fans out around a sturdy oak tree, and from those branches hang several figures, noosed by the neck and creaking in the cold. As you park, you confirm these are not real people. Dolls of some kind, maybe a dozen, too realistic. You recognize the plastic face of Mary Randall and Victor Love and the greeniac woman from the sex tape who melted down D.C.

Walking through the haphazard scrum of barns, aluminum sheds, army tents, and makeshift garages, you also see a stage all but ready for a band to walk on: drum kit, microphones, everything. The banner behind the stage has three dog heads protruding from the same body, all with blood on their teeth. A teenager strides toward you on a mission. He's got a scrub-brush head made worse by the unevenness of the haircut, busted brown teeth, a multitool looped to his belt, and a T-shirt with the nonsense phrase STORM BESLUTNINGSTAKERE. He's as short as you but may still have a growth spurt ahead of him. He pumps your hand as hard as his skinny arm can manage. Pops of gunfire in the distance.

"Welcome, welcome, new guy. I'm Freddy. Freddy Riley Poppen. I'll be showing you around today until the captain's ready for you. How's that sound? Good! C'mon, let me give ya the tour."

The kid speaks breathlessly, every word bubbling up on his lips to chase the last one before he's finished it. He asks a lot of questions he does not seem to care about the answer to.

"So where you from? How'd you find us? Who's your voucher?"

"My voucher?"

"Yeah, who vouched for you."

"Oh. A guy named Underwood."

"Dick. Sure. Total soldier. I'll tell ya, man, we wear our boots around here twenty-four-seven. Never take 'em off 'cuz the day's coming. Any moment now. But Dick's a real soldier, so we're ready. Those are the kennels."

Row after row of wire cages. Most of the dogs are huge. Pit bulls and German shepherds a-yapping, ravenous and mean. You wonder if they can smell that you were eating pieces of their kin on the drive up. The grounds are caught halfway between a bustling military boot camp for teenagers and a sad music festival that couldn't sell half its tickets. You pass a child stalking around in the snow with no shirt, arms and chest covered in tattoos. He wears a Confederate flag bandana around the lower part of his face. Another teenage boy wearing a Los Angeles Lakers cap and a T-shirt with a picture of a Glock spears crushed cans and other loose litter with a pitchfork, depositing it in a trash bag. A teenage girl smokes a cigarette on a picnic table, picking at a scab on her shoulder blade and looking bored.

"We're a violent, armed movement, and that's the thing a lot of people don't understand, is that we're not just a bunch a hillbillies, you know? There's a whole plan laid out—the captain'll explain it better—but there are certain areas of the country already been marked off, and we're coordinating, you know? They'll be cordoned off and designated for the white race. Blacks and other races will exit those areas, and for the most part it'll be voluntary and peaceful. For the most part. Except Muslims and Jews, those are two groups we'll likely be at war with for just about forever. Jews are too tricky, and Muslims are more like rats, they just breed a lot and that's kinda their power. Here, check this out."

He takes out a set of keys in front of an aluminum shed, fumbles with them, and opens the door. Inside are rows and rows of guns.

"Pretty cool, huh?"

Thousands of them. Assault rifles and shotguns racked and pointing at the roof. Handguns hooked onto the walls and several bigger weapons lying on the floor. The shed is the size of a basketball court. A red flag with a buckeye leaf on the back wall. The pops of gunfire grow louder as Freddy leads you to the shooting range, which is more an empty field with a few targets and effigies of President Love set up in front of a big mound of dirt. Six kids are shooting, little puffs like smoke signals rising from the barrels with each pop. You have a headache, and you're hungry again.

"It's a long war that's been going on for most of human history," Freddy continues happily, uncaring of how little you're engaging him. "The battle is between the races, and right now we're losing for sure, but not for long.

That's what the federation of different leagues is about. Some of 'em like the Oath Keepers or Three Percenters, they don't necessarily keep out nonwhites, which is a huge problem, but right now we need cooperation, don't you think?"

"Sure."

"Where you from again?"

"Coshocton. Dayton originally. Didn't like it there."

"Oh hell, I know about that. This is the first place I lived at more than a year since as long as I can remember! Your dad a prick too? Mine was."

"Never knew him."

"God, I wish I'd never known mine!" Freddy is cheerful when he says this, like you two have found something to bond over.

"That's why I left home—I'm from Toledo, by the way, but not the part that's too niggery—but he's why I left, 'cause this one time he starts beating the shit out of me. But not like normal. Like he pulled all my clothes off and threw me out on the lawn and smashed my ankle with his boot, you know? I heard it crack when he stomped it. He beat me with this belt with a metal buckle and that shit was sharp. Tore my back all the fuck up." He raises his shirt to show off a crisscrossing mesh of thin white scars. "Like that's not enough, he popped my arm out too. Soon as I got healed, I was like, Fuck this, I'm out."

When Freddy takes you past the chow hall, you get an idea of why recruitment is going so well. Younger boys serve up steaming plates to guys in camo pants while heat lamps work at the cold. You see and smell eggs, bacon, grits, and hotcakes; the scent so delicious it makes you weak-kneed. There are TVs playing Renaissance and The Pastor's network, Faith & Home. You stare at the steaming eggs and bacon. You want a plate so bad you almost ask Freddy if you can. But his radio's squawking.

"Captain's ready for him."

"Roger that," says Freddy, but he's fumbled the PTT button, and the person on the other end doesn't hear him. There's a moment of confusion, and then Freddy gets the timing right.

Inside the main building, "the command center" as Freddy calls it, you pass rows of offices, most of which just look like storage lockers, piled high with boxes and old furniture. You pass through a room where an enormous fat guy is tattooing a kid's bicep: a green dragon breathing red fire. The artist himself has a urinating Baby Breivik on one arm and Mickey Mouse carrying the Confederate flag on the other. Both look up at you as you pass.

"Fellas," says Freddy cheerily. He leads you to a door at the back. "Ah nuts," he says as he checks his phone. "I forgot—oh man, I forgot I had my laundry in. My bunkmate's shitting his britches over it. Hey, do you mind if we catch up later?"

Freddy's pulling open the door as another man, the captain it seems, joins you.

"What are you about, Freddy?" he says.

"Laundry, sir. Just need to change out the loads."

"All right, boy, hop to it."

And like he's a dog getting a pat on the head, Freddy is off.

The captain is portly and unshaved with big, chapped lips. A fat-butt chin and unruly muttonchop sideburns. He's at once unimpressive and menacing. He wears, tucked into his cargo pants, a black T-shirt that reads MYRTLE BEACH, SOUTH CAROLINA in pink lettering. Black boots clomp and squeak on the hardwood. He wears a big pistol on his hip, which gets caught in the armrest of his chair so that he has to stand again before fully sagging into the seat.

"Good to make your acquaintance. So it's John, but you go by . . ."

"Keeper."

There's a big picture of Anders Breivik on the wall behind him, between the two windows. Otherwise, the office is spartan. All that sits on the desk is a blotter, a pad of paper, and a few errant pens and paper clips.

"We got a lot to talk about, my friend. Freddy Riley take care of you on the tour?"

"Just fine."

"He's zealous, but he's a good kid. Real enthusiastic, but I can understand if he comes off as a little chipper. That's just his nature. Passionate young men make the best warriors for a cause."

You nod.

"Get you anything to eat? You had breakfast yet?"

You push your fingernails into your palms. Moments ago you would've taken a plate from anyone, done almost anything. Now, despite the ache in your belly, you say, "Nah, I ate on the way up. I'm stuffed."

The captain nods. His name is actually Morgan Schembari, and he's got a sales pitch that lasts so long, you have to cover your mouth to hide your yawns. The American Patriot League is a federation of like-minded military and service organizations joined together to support the cause of defending American freedom etc., etc., etc. Schembari is so clearly enamored with himself and surely believes there's no way a person could sit across from him, hear this pitch, and not jack off at what a brave and charismatic leader he is. You nod along and cover your mouth for another yawn.

"This man," he points to the picture of Breivik. "This is the leader who'll spearhead a global movement. You heard of him?" You nod. "We have the power, the weapons, now all we need is someone to execute the plan. And the state of Ohio, Keeper, I can't stress to you enough how important control over the state of Ohio is. The territory surrounding the Great Lakes is going to become some of the most sought-after land on the planet, and we need to be prepared to secure it when the time comes. Make sense?" You nod. "Now as far as The Pastor goes. Don't get me wrong, I'm a Christian through and through. But all his stuff about 'the earth will burn with fervent heat, and gravity will disappear as the feet of the righteous leave the earth—'"

"'We hear the earth groaning,'" you whisper.

"Exactly. He talks all that claptrap, but we believe in the chosen destiny of the white race, traditional values, and the weapons and ammunition that support them. You'll start off doing recruitment. We'll send you back into your community and across the state—near high schools and middle schools mostly—and you'll be asked to engage with the youth. Hand out material and whatnot. How's that sound?"

You nod. "What's it pay?"

Schembari wags a finger at you. "I like a man gets down to brass tacks, but keep in mind this ain't about money." He turns his head and hollers through the side door of his office. "Dickey! Get in here."

Dick Underwood comes in, cold-eyeing you, followed by another man. Dick is wearing a bright orange pullover the color of a traffic cone and a fatigue ballcap curled into a tight upside-down U. He's got a thin mustache now. The other man is wearing a ski mask, so all you can see is his grim eyes and thin white lips. Dick sits on a stool beside Schembari. The man in the mask stands behind them and crosses his hands over his crotch. He doesn't blink.

"Keeper," says Dick. He nods at you and you nod back.

"Good to see you," you croak.

The man in the mask does not introduce himself. The captain launches in.

"See, what happened is Dick comes to tell me your rather peculiar story. How you went off to prison because you got mixed up with some radicals."

"No mix-up," you correct him. "I took a fall because the Feds couldn't find shit on them. All I did was get high in the wrong place."

"Well, maybe so, maybe not. But Dick tells me you also pal around with another guy we got our eye on, one who's been working with the scum from Fierce Blue. You go to his church."

"Andrade?"

"And his wife," Dick adds.

You scoff at this. "Andrade and Ginna're just do-gooders. I drive around with 'em sometimes while they hand out sandwiches to junkies."

"Now that ain't even remotely true, Keeper. Emilio Andrade's been taking money from the green radicals. He's got too long a pecker for a preacher, and he needs to be put in his place right quick."

Your gaze slips up to the man in the mask. There is something unsettling about eyes just looking at you. For the first time, you realize eyes have no expression without the face; they're just these cold orbs, always in stasis without the cues of the surrounding flesh. He stares at you, and it's maddening that you can't just ask who he is or why he's there. The question itches all over your skin.

You shrug. "Maybe. But I don't know nothing about that. Far as I'm concerned, he's just a do-gooding reverend of a nondenominational church that tells you to suck it up and wait for heaven."

All six eyes stare at you. Schembari laughs.

"We all got kids and wives, Keeper, and I know they can cause trouble and hassle."

"Oh, my son, you wouldn't believe," Dick interjects. "He can't keep his goddamn head out of a VR set. I had to take the door of his bedroom off the hinges."

"No lie?" asks Schembari, cracking up.

"I was afraid he was going to yank his dick off if he spent one more day inside the porn worldes."

Everyone but you laughs. The skin around the eyes of the man in the mask wrinkles with mirth. Schembari pats his finger on the blotter for emphasis.

"In this movement, this band of brothers, we have our outside responsibilities. Kids, wife, job. But the war for our nation comes first. It has to. You join us, you will be taken care of. Well-fed, well-resourced, well-paid, well-armed. Now, I don't want to accuse you of nothing. I understand shit happens. But a Black baby is not something we can allow for. Hear me?" Schembari nods slowly, empathetically. "I've made mistakes myself, Lord knows. But you will have to cease contact with the woman and the child. Is that understood?"

The man in the mask watches you, his eyes like the holes in a carcass tunneled by worms.

On the drive back, it's snowing again. Few cars on the road, fewer people outside. There's a solitude to the graceful descent of the flakes. In grade school, they taught you that no two snowflakes are the same, but you found this idea impossible. Of course, plenty had to be alike.

Schembari and Dick Underwood had you fill out some bullshit paperwork: a beneficiary form and a loyalty oath, saying you'd never betray the brotherhood of the American Patriot League. The whole time Dick—nursing a boner for the new-recruit bonus coming his way—got to talking and wouldn't shut up. He rambled on and on about this business plan he had for when the Great Lakes territory was captured and reserved entirely for the white race. How there'd still be enormous demand for "exotic sex," and he'd get permits to open brothels on the borders in "free-trade spaces," which would feature women of all different races. He'd always been such a fucking idiot.

All told, you spent five hours on this campus of fruit loops, and when you leave it's like waking from a dream that never happened. You're supposed to report for training in two days, which you obviously will not do. You'll treat it how you've treated most jobs since high school. Just don't show, and there's not a whole lot they can do about it. More than the inanity of all these yokels running around jerking off their guns, what you recognize is the danger of any space where someone can tell you what to do. Anywhere another human being has power over you. You know this from prison, and especially from your time in the PRCC.

What you saw in your travels with the PRCC was not the worst of it. After the joke of a training camp in Colorado, after the Prion staff gave you and the other prisoners some CPR training and familiarity with search-and-rescue gear, they shipped you to Los Angeles for the aftermath of the El Demonio fire. For three months, you and the crew sifted through rubble to pull charred corpses and burned bone fragments from collapsed houses. Then it was on to Sioux Falls, St. Louis, and Nashville, as the Great Eastern Flood opened wide and swallowed the Midwest. Then it was Hurricane Rose devastating the coast of Georgia and northern Florida. Retreating floodwaters left their own peculiar human wasteland, and then the reconnaissance robot broke, so you and the crew had to start exploring unstable structures. Three-plus years of bearing witness to unchecked hell. You saw men, women, and children who'd been burned alive in their cars trying to escape the flames on a charred California freeway. Bloated, soggy bodies expelling noxious gases as they floated down retreating rivers or found in their attics, one woman's face puffy and distended like a red, wet water balloon. That sick, ripe smell of a corpse. A little boy in Georgia, who'd been in a wheelchair. Someone had left him in a fucking elevator. He didn't drown, just died of dehydration in that little box that short-circuited when the storm came. All the tools you'd used to try to reach people. The vibrations from the jackhammer in your arms, the nosebleeds you'd get from the dust, the shriek of a metal saw, the glowing sparks landing in the ruins, a piece of concrete wall suddenly collapsing, crushing that short guy from Arkansas, who you'd bummed a cigarette from just an hour earlier. Three others would eventually be killed, another half dozen wounded or crippled. The whole time you kept telling yourself: reduced sentence, reduced sentence, reduced sentence. But as if all this wasn't awful enough, there was the crew you traveled with, an assembly of guys not handpicked for their willingness to contribute to society but because they were strong, able-bodied, and willing to do anything to reduce long time. You steered clear of them as much as you could. Kept to yourself, kept your answers short, stayed apart. Because you knew there were a few of them in there, the ones who could sense what you are and how easy it would be. You didn't have an eye for this when you were young. And it cost you. Now you can see it. And you saw it in some of these men.

But it happened anyway.

In St. Louis, they stored you in this warehouse full of cots and potato chips and thin blankets that barely kept you warm in the dank space. One night you woke up unable to breathe because someone had a hand clamped over your mouth. You fought, but there were too many strong arms in the dark, and no matter how much you bucked and thrashed and cried out, those arms were too powerful. The siren was going off in your head—*Not happening Not happening Not happening*—but it was. The sweat of your attackers dripping on you. The horrifying pain as one after another jammed himself up your ass until you lost track of how many wanted in, until your mind went blank, and you went somewhere else. Floating through cold space without an astronaut suit. The next day you got a letter in the mail from Raquel, and she'd included a picture Toby drew of his hand, transformed into a Thanksgiving turkey with hearing aids. The picture just said *Hi Daddy!* It was enough to make you want to fucking kill yourself. In the flooding outside St. Louis, a minor mudslide had buried a house, including the elderly woman who lived inside. Dirt in her throat, mouth, and eyes, it looked like she had been screaming when you unearthed her face. That's how you felt. So you started taking every one of the most dangerous assignments. You waded into raging floodwaters with only a carabiner to keep you from getting torn downstream. You walked up buckling apartment stairs. You crawled into hot, wet holes on the off chance you might find a survivor, not because you wanted to be a hero but because you wanted one of these structures to fall on you. That's how you ended up finding the little girl in her crib. The men did it again in Nashville, and this time you didn't fight, but it stopped after that. It was almost like you unnerved them after you started running headfirst into rubble all the time, throwing your body into the hands of uncaring fate. That, or they found someone new to rape in the dark.

You did your time on the front lines of these nightmares. You got your reduced sentence. You went home to Raquel, who you can't touch or let yourself be touched by. Electric anxiety coursing through you all the time, every moment of the day, a fear of crowds, a fear of sleep, but especially a fear when she reaches for you, and you think of who you really are.

———

That night, you eat two boxes of mac 'n' cheese between the three of you. Each box cost over $6, and when Toby spills his plate on the floor, you and Raquel both snap at him, and he bursts into tears. It feels like your entire lives are in that greasy yellow smear you must mop up with a towel. You scoop some of your portion onto Toby's plate and Raquel does the same. You demand he eat it, but now he's afraid. "So go to bed hungry, Toby," Raquel snarls, and lifts him harshly from his chair. She carries him to his room and leaves him there.

Later, in bed next to a snoring Raquel, you want a drink so bad you consider putting on your shoes and walking to a liquor store. Or if you could get a pill. Or just an irreparable dose of fent. You're awake when Toby starts crying. Raquel stirs, pops up, her silk headwrap coming undone. You tell her you'll take care of it. She doesn't say anything, just sleepily fixes her headwrap and collapses back to her pillow.

You stumble through the dark trailer in the direction of Toby's wails, but he's already standing in his door looking at you with tears in his eyes, banging the heels of his hands against his head. He's crying too hard for you to understand what he's saying.

"Gooooosh," he sort of says. And you realize he's having trouble breathing. He's holding his stomach. His chest hitches and his lips tremble and he has that panic in his eyes. What it must feel like to not be able to draw your next breath.

"Where's your inhaler?"

He shakes his head and holds it up. You know it's empty. You and Raquel haven't refilled the prescription because he'd been doing so well. And because you've needed every last cent to eat. You pick him up and take him to the kitchen, where you sit him on the counter.

"Sit up straight, bud. Let the air come in." He does as he's told, but it's not helping. You try to think of the sign for it. You don't know *breathe*, but you do know *calm*, and so you press your palms down twice and say the word. Then you hug his small body. His arms come around you. "Breathe with me. Slow and deep, okay? You feel me breathing? Slow and deep."

For a while, it doesn't work. He's gyrating and fearful in your embrace, coughing, slapping your shoulders to tell you this is not working. But you keep soothing him. You've seen Raquel do it this way. His asthma is bad, but his panic is what makes it worse. You also know that while you were away, Raquel had to take him to the hospital once, and that bill is still not paid off.

You stand there holding him, and at some point, you feel him draw one, full, good breath.

"Good, buddy, that's good. Just like that."

He takes another breath, then another. His small hands stop flapping against you. His head comes to rest on your shoulder. The smell of his sweat is so distinctly the scent of a little boy: shampooey and clean with just a tinge of the dirt he scratched into his scalp that night. After a while, he's breathing almost regularly. His tears have stopped. He looks at you.

"Better?"

He nods, brown button eyes swollen with gratitude and fear.

"What happened?"

You don't understand the sign: He pinches together the thumb and index fingers of both hands. They kiss, and then the right hand spirals upward. "Gooosh," he mumbles. "Oww dare." He points out the window.

Out there, was what he was saying. Then the rest of it clicks. He was signing "ghost."

You draw him a glass of water, and then take him back to his room. You tape a garbage bag over his window so the ghost can't look in, but he doesn't want you to go. You hate that it feels wrong for you to sleep beside him, but it does. So you won't. You sit on his bed hugging him instead, until he falls asleep in your arms.

The next day, Raquel's at work, Toby at school, so you take the long walk to see Reverend Andrade. There are no sidewalks on the road out, so the slush works into the holes in your boots. Your feet are soaked and numb by the time you get there. The church is open but no one is around. Back beyond the pews, past Jesus's winsome stare, you find the reverend in his office pushing paper.

"I wanna get high," you say. "I want to get fucked up so bad, I think I'm going crazy."

The reverend nods as if this is no biggie and points behind you to the couch. "Take a seat, Keeper."

You do, and he heads for his plush leather chair. He often repeats the story of how he found it on the side of the road when he was a broke Bible college student, and it was the only piece of furniture he'd kept all these years. "Fits my butt just right," he says now as he lowers himself into it. "Tell me what's going on."

It annoys you. How this is no crisis to him, and you let the acid flare in your voice.

"I don't know, Rev. Maybe 'cause I got like six bucks in the whole world and my woman thinks I'm a fuckup and my kid's a fucking retard and I can't find any way out of this."

When your eyes dart to him, he looks displeased with you. "You don't have to blame Toby. None of this is your son's fault."

And you're filled with shame for being called out about something so obvious.

"Parents often take things out on their children," he says carefully. "Have you ever taken your frustration out on Toby?"

"What? No. I never touched him! I've never hit him, never touched him. Ever."

"That's good." He nods. "He's a sweet boy. And you have a wonderful family. You're so much luckier than you believe, Keeper."

"Yeah? Cuz I got a girl and a kid I can't feed?"

"You have people who love you. You have a church, a community that cares about you. You have me and Ginna."

"Yeah," you mutter.

"You don't think that's true?"

"Why're you doing this?" you demand. "Why're you always helping me?"

His face remains calm. He leans forward to cup his palms on one knee. "You're a member of my church. And my friend."

"Sure. Sure, I am." You feel a bubble of rage rising inside you, and you know you can't control it, and you don't even want to control it. "You groom me nice and good, help me out, give me your gracious fucking charity, and then when I really need you that's when you ask, right? That's when you tell me I need to do something for you. Ain't that right?" He simply stares back at you, expressionless. Then you scream. "Ain't that right, you *fucking FAGGOT!*"

Your leg kicks out, and the small coffee table is airborne. It crashes into the bookshelf beside the reverend, who cannot help but flinch. The words exploded out of you, and the sound rings in your ears. Your pulse beats in your head, in your arms. Still bundled into your winter jacket and toboggan cap, you're suddenly very hot. You stand, poised to either walk out or hit this man in the face.

"Keeper." Andrade has recovered from his flinch. "Did something like that happen to you when you were young?"

"I gotta go."

"Why don't you stay." He's looking at you with that maddening calm. "Or why don't we go for a walk instead." He stands and goes to the coatrack for his jacket. "C'mon, let's get some air. Plus, it's too cold out there for me to lure you into performing fellatio."

For a moment, this lands like a punch to the ear, and then you realize it's a joke. Fucking Reverend Andrade just made an actual joke, and despite yourself, you snort one true laugh. And you realize you can't even remember the last time you laughed.

Andrade has a box of breakfast bars in his desk and gives you one. As the two of you make your way outside, you bite into it, and your jaw is flooded with that tight ache of chewing when you are particularly hungry.

He leads you behind the church, up the crest of the hill, and through a smattering of woods that separates his church's land from the farm behind it. You walk along the ridge, trudging through the snow. The fallow edges of the field are rimmed with solar panels that glint in the bright sun while the woods beyond gather darkness in the space between the trunks. Ice coats the trees so they look crystallized, like sculptures. You step through some battered, fallen fencing, and he leads you along a trail through the field.

"We bought this property back when we had more parishioners," he tells you. "Ginna wanted to build a farm, which would be nice right now. Obviously, those plans are on hold. Still, I love it. It's so peaceful."

"I went to see the APL folks up in Sugarcreek," you confess. "That's how desperate I been lately."

He looks at you more with curiosity than fear. "How was that?"

"About what you'd expect."

Your voices sound too crisp. Even as it renders the sunlight brighter, the packed snow makes the sound too precise, like the crack of Casey's rifle. You brace your body against a freezing burst of wind.

"I certainly understand the allure," says Andrade. "Powerlessness causes us to seek power any way we can. We'd sacrifice anything, particularly our conscience, to feel it. There is nothing more dangerous than the excitement of those suffering from a lack of agency and great bitterness of soul."

"The day you saved me—'member that?"

"How could you even ask? Of course."

"I had this feeling like, 'This is it. This is where it all starts to turn around. I *got* this now.' And then . . ." You wave your gloved hands in front of you like you're signaling that a receiver didn't catch the football. "It was all gone within a couple of weeks, and I was in a little eight-foot cell. You can tell yourself God is always with you, but . . . *Empty* is so much bigger."

The reverend considers this.

"Not to get on one of my rants here, but let's just say that many Christians these days have a deeply impoverished view of the notion of a Creator." He waits for you, but you say nothing. "What do you think?"

"What do I think? I don't think nothing. I think all this talk of Jesus and salvation, it's just a way to keep us all in line. I saw it while I was inside. Guys like me, we ain't nothing but a walking dollar sign to most people. Probably to you too."

"That's a cynical way to look at it."

You shrug, spit in the snow. "Never really got a chance to see it from any other vantage."

Andrade nods like he takes this very seriously. He directs his gaze at the ground, thoughtful, vexed, searching. "Think about it this way, Keeper, about what God must actually *be*—a power vibrating in our every atom, built into the explosions of distant stars, and circling the dust of worlds you and I will never be able to contemplate. We are part of some vast, mysterious, eternal Whole set in motion by a force so awesome that it is ultimately unknowable. Do you feel me? We can't always see the direction or meaning of it all, but to even glimpse this tiny corner of the Whole—what an incredible opportunity. What a grave responsibility."

You glance back at your tracks. Four lonely boots leaving their tread marks in the pristine blanket. You keep walking. The clouds move in. A grim, milky cast falls over the field, the trees, the sky. You hock up buttery snot, bringing it from your throat and blow-darting it into the snow.

Finally you say, "That sounds very pretty. But it's hard to square with . . . with what I been through."

"I know you feel it, man. Maybe when you see your son laugh or when you get your arms around Raquel or even just when you're alone, walking through a beautiful patch of Ohio." He gestures to the snowy woods. "To save one life is to save all of humanity. Ever heard that? And now it's simply time to save yourself."

You know Andrade is trying to make you feel like you are this infinitely precious thing, but you can't bring yourself to get past the opposite sense: that you are narrow and corporeal and alone.

"If you knew what . . . the things I done . . ."

You stop, and the reverend stops beside you. There's a shard in your throat, so you choke on every other word to keep it at bay, to keep your voice hard.

"I've done so many awful, awful things. Horrible things, man. I've—I've hurt people. People I don't even know or couldn't even find again to tell 'em I'm sorry. Tell 'em what I did was evil. How am I supposed to believe God can forgive me? That'd just be me wishing there was a way I could even get forgiven." Your voice cracks and you swallow this lump of grief yet again. The next words come out in a snarl. "We were in Georgia and Florida after the hurricane. That big one, Rose. And in one of these collapsed buildings, we hear this baby crying somewhere down in the rubble. Of course, no one really wants to get down into that shit, but I do it. I go. And it takes me forever. I'm crawling down into this hole, crawling on my belly, and there's slime everywhere, and it smells like shit. But then finally, the hole opens up into this little space. Freezing water up to my thighs. No sign of the parents, but I could smell them, somewhere nearby. But there was this little girl still in her crib because this one room didn't collapse, and she's shrieking and shrieking, so I go over to her and pick her up, and then . . ." Your voice cracks again, and you let a small sob escape. "As soon as I pick her up, she stops crying. Just goes totally silent. And she's just staring at me with these huge brown eyes, looking so scared, and I swear to God when I picked her up . . ."

Now you can't help yourself. You start crying, and it's embarrassing, how you're powerless to control your own hurt. Your hands come out in front of you like you're still cradling her.

"I swear to God, when I held her in my arms, it felt like she was my own daughter."

Tears fall from your cheeks to the snow, and when you dare glance up, you're surprised to see the reverend is also crying.

"I carried her out and handed her off. I never found out what happened to her. I'll never know what happened to her."

A soft smile folds into Andrade's cheeks and the deep lines of his face catch his tears. He puts a hand on your shoulder.

"Despite all the mumbo jumbo I just talked, remember, brother, you are alive. You are alive, and as long as your lungs draw breath, you have love in you. And you have hope. No man or woman is beyond love or hope—I firmly believe that in the face of all the evidence to the contrary. Every last person is worthy and capable of redemption. People might think that's soft-headed, but it's actually realistic. It's the only belief I'd gladly die for. It's never too late to begin again. You proved that to that little girl."

He laughs heartily. In the winter, the sunset seems to change every day. This one descends like a hazel shroud, shadows gathering like the dark traces of a storm in its becoming.

He pats you on the shoulder. "Let's go get a sandwich, Keeper. I'm hungry."

You trace your footsteps back over the field, boots crunching in the snow through the descent of night, which looks like a pool of mercury spilling across the heavens.

Book V

THE LONG
WAY HOME

The New Yorker

A YEAR OF WONDERS

On the Unraveling of 2036.
How Close Are We to the Brink?

By **Moniza Farooki**
OCTOBER 27, 2036

There are years that simply rock the world, when events collide to produce unrest and dislocation on scales outside the imagination of those living at the time. Nineteen fourteen, 1968, and 2020 all come to mind. In 2036, two years of the highest food prices since World War II triggered famines in nine countries, the worst downturn since Covid-19, and at least three documented genocides. The planet is awash in civil wars, failed states, low-grade insurgencies, mass migration, and frightening xenophobic politics. Before 2036, the Nigerian civil war and the breakdown of the Arabian Peninsula had nearly obliterated those nations and inundated their neighbors with millions of refugees desperate to escape the bloodshed. The Chinese government continued its onslaught against its own growing internal revolt. Jakarta suffered the worst cholera outbreak of the twenty-first century after Typhoon Bini caused the wholesale collapse of seawalls. After decades of crack-up, the shards of the European Union appeared to be reuniting, born again in the image of Norwegian prime minister and convicted mass murderer Anders Breivik, whose government, fueled by a resurgent oil and gas economy and a mastery of social VR disinformation, has spread its venomous ideology across the continent. Hanging over all of this has been a US presidential race, which arrived like an ominous comet, with a reviled authoritarian president being belittled and homophobically denigrated by a wild-eyed former actor turned theocratic fascist. Little did we know the self-reinforcing crises of our climate, our economy, and our democracy would begin to spiral and whiplash like the arms of a gathering cyclone.

On the first day of 2036, VR entertainer and Republican presidential candidate The Pastor held a rally at the North Charleston Coliseum & Performing Arts Center in South Carolina in which he declared, "This president will bring our economy roaring back to life with the earth's bounty of gas, oil, and coal. He will feed the hungry and clothe the poor. He will enforce Christian will on America and American will everywhere else, and he will do so with the ultimate weapons if God calls upon him to." It would be his first reference to the use of America's nuclear arsenal but not his last. As he stormed through the primary, laying waste to perennial also-rans such as Senator Marco Rubio and establishment props like Congressman Warren Hamby (who would soon kiss his ring, literally, when selected as his running mate), The Pastor mentioned atomic weapons 211 times. His Slapdish worlde now implies that he is the Second Coming, and that Revelation will begin to play out when he is allowed access to the nuclear football. "Jesus came to John wielding a sword, and great storms and heat and fire descended, and those with doubt suffered like no humans had ever suffered before. For I am the Power," he screamed, "who will deliver oil from the ground, life to the unborn, security for our borders, and the justice of an awesome God!" His supporters thundered their approval, writhed on the ground, spoke in tongues, and held signs proclaiming him not The Pastor but the Christ. He won the South Carolina primary by twenty-five points.

On March 5, as The Pastor secured an insurmountable delegate lead, Los Angelenos took shelter. For Californians, the Big One has always referred to the fury locked within the San Andreas Fault, but after the Los Angeles megafire it got reappropriated, even as the fire set the city on a rebuilding spree that would have made an Egyptian pharaoh blush. Yet, another Big One lay in wait. Atmospheric rivers have lashed and drowned California for generations, rainstorms of immense power that can drop millions of gallons of water in the span of a day. Scientists called the worst-case scenario ARkSTORM, a nine-hundred-year flood event that could overwhelm the state's aging flood control infrastructure. Climate change made this biblical event that much more likely.

"We knew this El Niño year was particularly dangerous because the equatorial Pacific hit record-breaking temperatures," said former NOAA chief Dr. Jane Tufariello. "It's intensifying the drought devastating Asia and fueling unrest in China, but it's also juicing the atmospheric rivers. We saw ARkSTORM coming, but that's different from being able to do something about it."

Mary Randall once called Tufariello "the best scientist in the government." She has served presidents of both parties and may have the broadest institutional understanding of the climate crisis in the world. "I'm not shook by much," she said. "But when I saw this coming, I was scared."

The behemoth storm came whipsawing out of the Pacific, strafing Southern California before bouncing back briefly to make full landfall just south of the Bay Area. The rest we know.

In the course of two weeks, the Sacramento–San Joaquin Delta transformed into an expanding lake of destruction, overwhelming a suboptimal system of levees and canals. Three million people living in the Sacramento Valley were given as little as thirty minutes to gather belongings and flee. When a levee breaks it sounds like an explosion that never ends, and what flows forth arrives with the violence of a tsunami. Hundreds died in their cars and homes, while floodwaters swallowed escape routes and left millions stranded without access to electricity, food, or drinking water. For hundreds of miles in every direction, corpses would be found in attics or floating miles downriver. Sacramento was underwater. One could look to the horizon and no longer see the Central Valley, just this new cold inland sea.

In Southern California, the Whittier Narrows Dam failed. The tempest exploded across the city of Pico Rivera, home to nearly seventy thousand people, most of whom, thankfully, obeyed evacuation orders. An eighteen-foot wall of water swept in, and every community from Pico to Long Beach experienced catastrophe. From the other end, the tidal surge blasted through the streets of Newport Beach and Huntington Beach, soaking the overdeveloped floodplain as far inland as Anaheim. Coastal highways were washed back to dirt trails, and hundreds of landslides sent walls of rock, mud, and debris burying all structures along with those inside. Orange County filled with five feet of chocolate water as the Santa Ana River spilled over its levees and inundated homes. In Santa Barbara, a piece of mountain sheered away, shredding through two neighborhoods and killing every resident in under a minute.

Up and down the coast, waterlogged bluffs and cliffs collapsed into the sea from the power of wave energy alone, taking hundreds of houses with them. Electricity cutoffs disrupted emergency services and tele-communications. There was no power, no internet, and data servers were wiped out. Silicon Valley was dark. Police, firefighters, and other emergency workers could not rely on power grids or telecommuni-cations networks. Hospitals and wastewater treatment plants went without power for weeks. Damage estimates range from between $750 billion and $1 trillion statewide.

As Coast Guard rescues continued throughout the spring, the Califor-nia National Guard, the Red Cross, and A Fierce Blue Fire's mutual aid network descended on the state. So did militias, looters, and Xuritas soldiers. The ferocity of the looting cannot be overstated: frenzied dashes through department stores, malls, grocers, jewelry stores, elec-tronics centers. What began as a perilous search for food devolved into all-encompassing scavenger riots. Months later, after disturbing reports of mob violence and militia lynchings, Xuritas is still there, securing infrastructure and distribution points for food, water, and medical sup-plies, exercising dubious authority, harassing the nonwhite for proof of citizenship. With local police departments overwhelmed, the security contractor, for all practical purposes, is the law in California now. An estimated two million people now live in homeless encampments and abandoned retail stores in the deserts of the southeast counties while Arizona and Nevada threaten "deportation" for those who've spilled across the state lines, an internal refugee crisis not seen in this country since the Dust Bowl.

It is hard to imagine how California will recover. The severity of the flooding has demolished a cataclysmic amount of infrastructure in the state's two largest population hubs. Perhaps more importantly, Cali-fornia's private insurance market, already rocked by the 2031 fire, has completely collapsed. There is no taxpayer backstop large enough to insure all the property at risk and the battle to drop coverage and deny claims by insurers has only just begun. Wall Street is whispering about reverberations in the wider financial markets.

Like the LA megafire, the catastrophe wrought comparisons to a Hollywood blockbuster. Images of high-stakes rescues from floodwaters and terrified people running from landslides dominated the public consciousness, and yet as horrifying as it seemed for those two weeks in March, in the context of our permanent emergency, ARkSTORM barely had staying power. It opened, the box office was good, and then it was gone from the news in a matter of weeks. Twenty thirty-six was just getting started.

On May 2, a tropical depression strengthened to a cyclone in the Bay of Bengal. Cyclone Giri ratcheted to a monster, bursting the seams of Category 5 designation. By the time Giri made landfall it was a four-hundred-mile-wide superstorm that simultaneously lashed the shores of India and Myanmar. With sustained wind speeds of 210 mph and gusts reaching 255 mph, it was one of the most powerful cyclones ever recorded. Giri swallowed the Bangladeshi coast from the western deltas to Cox's Bazar. A high tide brought a storm surge of twenty-five feet, and whole villages were swept away. In the Sundarbans, the islands connected like muscle sinew by mangrove forests, clay dikes toppled and shrimp farms were eradicated. The soil, water, and yellowed mud of these coastal flats is home to over nineteen million people who now have little possibility of return or renewal. Khulna, one of Bangladesh's key ports, was effectively wiped off the map. To say there's nothing left is incorrect because there are splinters left. There is twisted metal and plastic piping and brick rubble and collapsed concrete and drowned wildlife. There are bodies. Thousands of them.

For forty years, experts warned that Bangladesh was an unprecedented calamity waiting to happen. There was the unnamed 1991 cyclone that killed 138,000. Before that, in 1970, a cyclone killed half a million people when it hit Bhola in what was then East Pakistan and prompted my grandparents to immigrate to Britain. Both cyclones were smaller than Giri. However, size doesn't explain everything. It's almost more important to look at what has happened within Bangladesh itself—the human components that made this horrible outcome almost inevitable. Even when my parents took me as a child, Bangladesh was one of the most densely populated countries on the planet. I recall Dhaka as a teeming, claustrophobic sea where the sound of car horns and the zing of rickshaw bells produced a 24/7 cacophony. City and country continued their astonishing growth, with Dhaka swelling to twenty-five million. Most of this was due to migration, rural farmers watching their land vanish as the seas rose and saltwater intrusion destroyed their livelihoods.

Dhaka lies between the merging highways of the Padma, Meghna, and Brahmaputra Rivers, and even as record floodwaters rose, wind speeds from the dying cyclone still proved too dangerous for most people to flee. Imagine watching the water surging into your home while outside the winds hurtle debris at speeds that can shred bodies in half. Fires began in the Tejgaon Industrial Area—chemical plants soaking and then exploding, but they quickly spread. The fire service couldn't drive trucks through five feet of standing water, and aerial resources were limited. President Shirin Razzaq ordered refugees to the smaller, underprepared city of Jamalpur, because it was one of the only places in the country that wasn't partially underwater.

The United Nations Office for the Coordination of Humanitarian Affairs estimates the initial death toll of Giri at 1.3 million, with at least another seven hundred thousand missing. This does not take into account the outbreaks of disease and starvation that followed. Speculation abounds that this may be one of the most rapid mass migrations in human history. They fled on foot and bicycle, automobile or bus if they were lucky. For months, caravans of people have plodded down drowned highways, traversing countrysides of ruin, dying of everything from dehydration to infection.

When I spoke with Defense Secretary Sarah Caperno, she declined to confirm that behind closed doors President Razzaq all but begged Victor Love for a full-scale American military intervention. The UN has asked for $600 million from the US for its Giri Action Plan, but the government has delivered only $150 million in aid so far. I asked why the Bangladeshi relief effort had been so insufficient to the scope of the crisis.

"We're monitoring the situation, but as you know by now, food aid comes from Congress," was all Secretary Caperno would say on the topic.

On May 22 at a rally in Pennsylvania, The Pastor demanded that the US "not ship one more dollar, calorie, or MRE to a Muslim country condemned by God. This is justice for sin, plain and simple, and when I'm president, we will have the complete cessation of international aid. Americans will eat first."

This led internet trolls to repurpose the Tokens' "The Lion Sleeps Tonight" as a campaign song: "Wim-AWEF, Wim-AWEF, Wim-AWEF, Wim-AWEF."

Asked about Bangladesh at a press conference, Prime Minister Anders Breivik smirked and told reporters, "This makes my job easier. We just sit back and watch the fun."

"The fun" includes the collapse of sanitation systems and shortages of fresh water, which have led to outbreaks of cholera, dysentery, typhoid, and hepatitis. Health officials fear an outbreak of polio, the resurgent scourge of the postcolonial Global South. "The fun" includes at least fifty million displaced people, roughly a quarter of the entire population. "The fun" includes the Indian border guard mowing down refugees with regularity, shooting women and children on sight.

Yet plenty of people still make it through these killing fields to find themselves in massive concentration camps on the outskirts of Kolkata, built by American companies like Prion and international gangster-capitalist conglomerates like ANøNosiki, secured by teenage soldiers carrying grenade launchers and machine guns. A cholera outbreak in one camp killed an estimated ten thousand people in a matter of weeks, while Indian authorities did nothing but burn the bodies. India's Hindu nationalist government, led by President Shankar Ahluwalia, has all but promised genocide by starvation for any Bangladeshis who make it through.

On June 2, an unprecedented heat dome descended over Europe. From Barcelona to Moscow, temperatures soared into the triple digits across the continent, sparking a series of devastating wildfires. Seville, Spain, set the new continent-wide record with 52.9 centigrade (an unbelievable 127 degrees Fahrenheit). The Euro heat storm seemed to fuel the Independence Party's decisive victory in the UK elections, forcing the Tories to take the back seat in their own coalition, when all they wanted to do was privatize the NHS. This victory and the blazing temperatures then summoned reactionary forces to streets across Europe as the paramilitary arms of UKIP, the Alternative for Deutschland in Germany, the National Rally in France, Vox in Spain, and the Brothers of Italy burned mosques, beat anyone with brown skin, and targeted left-wing journalists and center-left political offices. The three-day outburst was coordinated across social VR and follows a years-long pan-European campaign of barbarism against minority communities. The so-called Six Arms alliance organizes the efforts of the Far Right across Europe but answers only to Norway and its psychopathic leader, Breivik. If security forces, deportation machines, and brutal detention centers weren't enough, Prime Minister Breivik has empowered a class of roving criminals known as the *Storm Beslutningstakere* (roughly translating to "storm makers"), who have terrorized the continent, producing ghastly stories of murder, rape, assault, arson, and looting. Arrests have been made by the thousands, but the Far Right parties claim they will issue blanket pardons as soon as they take power.

ON JUNE 12, AFTER FAILING TO UNSEAT VICTOR LOVE IN THE DEM-ocratic primary, Tracy Aamanzaihou announced that she would run as a third-party candidate. "I cannot stand by as the world is engulfed by white supremacists, dictators, thugs, and the cowards who enable them," she railed at a press conference outside an immigrant detention camp on the Texas border. The facility, operated by Prion, was accused of leaving human beings to roast to death in metal boxes in the sun. Aamanzaihou gained in the polls and financing, as supporters flocked to her like the last lake of fresh water on a salinizing coastal plain. Many Democrats bombarded the Love campaign with Letitia Will Win memes and pictures of the prayer vigils still being held around the fenced-off National Mall to commemorate the dead. WE WILL NEVER FORGET; VOTE YOUR CONSCIENCE; HISTORY WILL

JUDGE US. Aamanzaihou pulled into the lead in Oregon, Vermont, Massachusetts, New York, Texas, and California (even though ten million of its residents were living out of FEMA trailers and tents in neighboring states). It was a three-way race now, according to the models.

O N JUNE 23, IT BEGAN TO RAIN IN PAKISTAN.

It happened once before. In 2010, a massive heat wave in Russia created a blocking pattern that led to abnormally heavy monsoon rains over the Indus River basin. Nearly a fifth of Pakistan's total land area was inundated during the 2010 floods, which killed two thousand people. Pakistan has been a nation on the verge of implosion for decades, stressed by a detonating population and depleting water sources. The agricultural economy has dried up as the Himalayan glaciers have shrunk. Eroded by a shift from snow to rain, Pakistan's main water source has slowed to a desperate trickle, even as its enemy India has continued to siphon off more and more of the failing glacial runoff. In 2034, famine in the northern region killed an estimated four hundred thousand.

In this tinderbox, radical elements carry out terrorist attacks regularly, violence is the norm, and a small elite hides behind blast walls, armored vehicles, and the guns of the military and corporate security services. In the past five years, the army has clamped down on nearly every facet of life, stability the only goal and also a total mirage. With American drones patrolling the skies and international donors providing food aid, this approach has kept a lid on things. For generations Lashkar-e-Taiba has been a scourge. A radical Islamic group with ties to al-Qaeda, the Taliban, and the Pakistani Inter-Services Intelligence agency (ISI), its assassination of the army chief in 2032 punctuated the threat. Yet even a group as powerful as LeT could not have toppled the government without help. This summer, they got it in the form of a weather pattern.

"There were some of us practically screaming about this," said Dr. Tufariello. "The Euro heat wave was the largest by geographic scale we've ever seen. It was creating conditions very similar to 2010 with a split upper-level jet stream and a deep trough penetrating to the subtropics over northern Pakistan. The Love administration was otherwise occupied with California."

Certain cities in the north recorded as much as twenty inches during the July wet spell, shattering previous records. Densely populated cities like Peshawar became open seas, and the floodwaters reached new territory, including the capital of Islamabad. By late July, the flooding had exceeded the boundaries of 2010 and then some, covering nearly a quarter of Pakistan's total landmass.

The death toll of thirty-three hundred, however, felt middling to the international community, especially in the wake of the famines and the unfathomable tragedy in Bangladesh. One crisis in the developing world at a time, please. Red Cross director Marcy Macon told me the agency had never had such a difficult time collecting funds.

"There have been anemic responses, and then there was Pakistan. We had so little to offer them."

The US pledged $100 million, and President Love diverted the SS *Doris Miller* from its mission to Bangladesh to deliver aid. The Pastor took to the stage of his Slapdish worlde to excoriate Love's decision. He led the chant this time, "Americans will eat first!," for a virtual audience of twenty million.

On September 3, approximately two months from the US election, The Pastor used the first presidential debate to revel in the "magnificent handiwork of a just God intent on wiping Islam from the face of the earth." While Congresswoman Aamanzaihou tried to interrupt and President Love gazed listlessly at his notes, The Pastor asked, "How many more of my prophecies must come to pass before you see that I already hold the sword of Christ? Psalm one thirty-seven tells us 'Those who smash the heads of Babylonian infants on the rocks are blessed.' Wars of extermination, the Bible tells us, are not only allowed—my friends, they are our duty."

That his poll numbers saw no visible drift from these shocking statements proves the thesis: in a society of spectacle, this man is king.

Perhaps President Love's near-comatose performance could be explained by what US intelligence was telling him: Pakistan was about to collapse.

Though the details of Operation Safe Keeper remain classified, we do know that on September 3 a truck bomb killed President Yousaf Sadiq and the general in charge of Pakistan's Strategic Plans Division Force, which is tasked with securing the country's nuclear weapons.

"We're certain the ISI was infiltrated by LeT sympathizers," said Caperno. "And they took advantage of the opportunity presented by the flooding."

In our VR interview, Caperno looked her unflappable self, as she did when defending her refusal to resign after the massacre in Washington. The grisliest events of the age appear to perturb her as much as a web page loading slowly.

"The coup's primary aim was to gain control of the nuclear arsenal," she said. "So we deployed the most deadly soldiers in the American military to stop them at any cost."

By September 4, one of the riskiest operations in military history was underway. US Joint Special Operations Command launched a team of Navy SEAL units and army explosive ordnance disposal specialists over the Pakistani border. These technicians were tasked with dismantling at least two hundred warheads at seventeen different sites. JSOC units first disabled tactical nuclear weapons, then led "deep underground shelter penetrations" and conducted precision missile strikes on the bunkers. Yet there are three sites that were not vaporized and have come under occupation by JSOC with no explanation forthcoming from the Love administration.

Layers of blast walls topped with razor wire were quickly erected. Drones now deliver payloads of equipment and supplies daily while shooting down every antiaircraft munition either extremists or the Pakistani army lob their way. Fifty-five thousand additional American troops have joined the mission, making it the largest military presence on foreign soil since the Iraq War. The major question is why didn't JSOC incinerate these bases like they did the other locations?

Secretary Caperno will say only that "we're dealing with many warheads and fissile materials. We need to make sure we get this right."

According to Dr. Dennis Rysher, the director of the Global Security Program for the Union of Concerned Scientists, this doesn't make sense. "The military appears dug in for the long haul. It's possible they ran into a warhead they couldn't render safe. Maybe a system of

STEPHEN MARKLEY

metaphorical tripwires that might lead to a detonation. Whatever it is, they've encountered something that all the best and brightest minds in the US military did not predict, and that is really frightening."

In 1811, as the American empire continued to expand westward, settlers reckoned with a series of strange portents, beginning with massive spring floods in the Ohio Valley. The brightest comet to appear in the night sky in several centuries followed shortly thereafter. The summer brought a nasty fever epidemic and epic hailstorms while fall saw a complete solar eclipse. Animals had been behaving strangely all year. Pigeons took to the sky in vast swarms while people watched thousands of squirrels throwing themselves into the Ohio River to drown. Then came the massive earthquake on December 16, with a magnitude between 7.2 and 8.1, originating in northeastern Arkansas. Two quakes the following year would tear the land apart, collapse cliffs, destroy log-cabin homes, briefly suck the Mississippi River back from its banks, and completely level the town of New Madrid, then one of the largest settlements along the Mississippi.

Eighteen eleven was popularly dubbed "The Year of Wonders," and it seems apt to resurrect the moniker for 2036. The differences are certainly obvious. Only a small group of settlers and the tribes they were pressing westward experienced the events of 1811. In 2036, the entire world has looked on in awe. Those people had little understanding of their wonders. We, on the other hand, grasp exactly what's happening now.

The climate crisis is rapidly destabilizing the earth's ecological systems. This, in turn, is causing extreme weather events, which are having an undue impact on our civilization, unleashing violence, misery, illness, chaos, and death for millions of the world's most vulnerable. Globally, no one knows how many people are on the move, but estimates put refugee flows at more than eighty-five million people.

On October 7, Kate Morris led a blockade of a gas station in New York City, part of her so-called Seventh Day protests. The idea being that on the seventh day of each month, people will remove themselves from the economy—refuse to work, shop, or contribute—and instead use the day to "blockade, disrupt, or dismantle" part of the carbon infrastructure. These actions will supposedly escalate every single month, though her organization has been vague about what that means. October 7 saw perhaps forty different actions in fifteen major cities, all aimed at stopping traffic, blocking access to gas stations, and putting bodies in the way of construction projects. President Love dodged questions on the matter until a Florida newspaper board dragged this nonanswer from him: "If protestors remain peaceful, I don't anticipate any problem." Maybe it was this reporter's imagination, but it looked as though he could barely get the words out, whether because of exhaustion, his rumored alcoholism, or, one might hope, remorse.

Victor Love—an authoritarian despot not even wearing his liberal sheep's clothing anymore, whose presidency is driven less by any particular vision or ideology than by a sheer will to power—will surely capture his share of the electorate who see no other choice. The Pastor, who leads in several key swing states, and unlike his European right-wing brethren is polling very well among Blacks, Latinos, and other minority groups, may be the most dangerous political actor on the planet. Even as the GOP establishment reassures donors that he will be supervised once in office, The Pastor assures his followers that an apocalyptic war of the faithful is nigh. In the role of spoiler, Tracy Aamanzaihou is the only candidate with a platform to restore our long-degraded democratic norms and institutions, challenge the power of corporate money, and address inequality and the destruction of our climate. From the start of her campaign, members of the political class have begged her to drop out, lest she risk throwing the election to a man who promises theocratic bloodshed. It is an agonizing choice with no good answer.

After decades of delay, policymakers and the economic elite who support them have allowed this civilizational crisis to metastasize. Reagan, Bush, Clinton, W. Bush, Obama, Trump, Biden, Hogan, Randall, and now Love—leaders with nothing in common except their failure to address the only issue that ever really mattered. In the sixty years since Wallace Broecker coined the term "global warming" in the title of a scientific paper and we began to understand the threat posed by greenhouse gas emissions, never have the implications been at our doorstep like this.

On October 25, just as this article was going to press, Tracy Aamanzaihou, far behind in the polls, stood in front of a crowd of supporters in a fever-hot Houston night and announced she was withdrawing from the race and would endorse President Love.

"The stakes are simply too high," she said with sweat on her brow and tears in her eyes. Aamanzaihou has always looked as strong and solid as a statue, her wide cheekbones and prominent chin begging for immortalization in granite. However, that immortalization will not be for pulling off an improbable upset in this election. "All I ask is that no matter who wins, you must keep fighting. Do not give up, do not back down. The hope for a new and better world is in our hands, and never forget you have power. What we do now, in the months to come, will echo through the rest of human history."

She left the stage. There was a power outage that night across southeast Texas as temperatures reached 105.4 degrees. A new October record.

SHANE DRIVES
INTO THE SUNSET
2036

*S*hane woke two days after the presidential election in a humid motel room, the sheets soaked, thinking Lali had peed herself. The bedside lamp clicked and clicked like it was out of bullets, and then she realized the AC unit was silent. A power outage. Lali remained asleep, but it wasn't another bedwetting episode—Shane had left behind a pool of sweat from dreams and heat. A dusky light split the blinds. She knew she wouldn't fall back asleep anytime soon and eased out from under the damp sheets, careful not to wake her daughter. Quietly unlocking the door, she stepped outside into the muggy, fetid air.

The wind at least cooled her skin. From the second-floor balcony, she could see over the tops of a few seaside units, all of them dark, two of them collapsed, the roofs pancaking down. According to the motel clerk, Parmesh, about a third of the homes had already been in foreclosure before Tropical Storm Solomon shoved five feet of water up the shore. The quaint Gulf tourist town she'd known as a girl, when her parents rented from this same motel one week a year, lost the fight to condo development and regurgitated seaside housing. Now homebuyers had all but vanished.

"Being 'underwater' on your mortgage ain't exactly figurative around here," Parmesh had told her. Parmesh had a lot of rehearsed lines he deployed with self-satisfaction, but Shane found him friendly and wry, so they'd chatted while Lali clicked quarters together at the vending machine and agonized over her soda choice.

Propping her arms on the railing, Shane breathed in the slate-heather dawn. The air smelled of the sea. Seagulls squealing, soaring, and diving. She remembered the family photo taken from the balcony of this same motel. Her father had shoved his digital camera into the hands of some poor lady passing by. In that picture, there'd been shoreline behind their heads. Almost all of the beach had since vanished, the sea scraping back and reclaiming raw earth.

Behind her, the AC rattled to life. The TV chirped. They must have fallen asleep with it on last night before the power went out. She stood there a while longer watching the sea.

Back in the room, Lali was awake, running a brush through her hair, watching the news. "Anything?" Shane asked.

ON THE MYSTERY OF VICTOR LOVE *"Love did not appear on election night but instead sent his campaign manager to declare victory. He has not actually made a public appearance since two weeks before the election. The White House press secretary says he's secluded at Camp David trying to deal with the situations in Pakistan, Bangladesh, India, and California. As we know, Aaron McGuirk resigned in protest after the events in D.C. and was never replaced. Now many are questioning Love's mental health, not to mention the chain of command."*

THE PASTOR In Berkeley, fifteen people were killed after a man opened fire on a voting line. Voters faced intimidation at polling sites around the country as armed militias arrived to "protect the vote." The Pastor had denied coordination with these forces, promising "biblical justice" would befall those denying his victory. Never had a presidential candidate promised executions of his political enemies. Now pundits debated if he was serious about executing members of their profession. *"Why are we speculating about voices of moderation in his cabinet? He's telling us what he will do."*

"Nope," Lali said curtly. Only twelve and Lali already needed a preemptive exorcism for her surly teen posture. Shane knew better than to try a conversation this early, so she merely sat down on the bed. Two days after the election, and still no one knew who won, a debacle that was making 2000 and 2020 look relatively ordered and sane. The Pastor seemed to be close to the electoral college with 264 votes, but President Love had won the popular vote, and seven states were going to need recounts. Tracy Aamanzaihou received enough votes in those seven that she'd played the role of spoiler for Vic Love. Both Democratic and Republican camps were assuring their voters and the media that they had won.

She sat on her moist side of the bed, reading even grimmer news on the chyron below: pogroms in India, violence in the IDP camps in Arizona, FEMA overwhelmed as it tried to deal with the California refugee crisis, and President Love AWOL. She looked at Lali, who appeared to be taking it all in with her strange, inscrutable calm. The brush ripped at her hair. They'd driven down to Gulfport the day before, Shane concocting an obscure and unsatisfying excuse, which Lali was surely used to by now. The older she got, the worse Shane was at lying to her. She thought of leaving Lali back in Lawrence, but with the ligature of the world fraying, this scared her.

"You'll be okay on your own today, Lals? I should only be a few hours."

"I told you, yes." Her eyes never left the TV. They had a fight a few weeks earlier about the amount of time Lali spent in VR. Shane had taken the set, and Lali hadn't forgiven her.

The news pivoted, and abruptly there she was, dressed in a simple blue sweater with holes in the cuffs, speaking from the offices of her new operation.

"We only have our numbers," she told an interviewer. She had an edginess in her voice and a craze to her eyes. Hair still like a wild river. *"We are the majority, locked out by a political process that can no longer respond to the will of the people. So we need to shut that process down. Forget about Climate X. I'm talking about mass disruption to our economic system. And it starts with putting our bodies between the corporate state and its ends. Deny them any ability to continue with business as usual—"*

"But won't that—" The interviewer cut her off, and there was cross talk before he won out. *"Don't you fear that could exacerbate the civil unrest we're seeing right now? Won't that lead to more violence?"*

"Yeah, not if our fucking government stops murdering its own people!" Her face was taut, the vein in her neck pulsing. *"Trust me, Vic Love, The Pastor, Koch Industries, Exxon—these motherfuckers don't have enough prisons or bullets in the world. So on November 7, we're going to stop working again, we're going to blockade again, we're going to shut down the economy again. And I promise you, we will keep fucking coming."*

And after the third f-word they cut away from her, the anchor apologizing to the audience at home.

"Please don't watch too much TV, Lali. Read a book today or something."

Lali muted the TV, flipped over on her side, and pulled the covers over her face. Her hair fanned out over the pillow. She claimed she wasn't really a girl in America in 2036 but a "post-biological, auto-teleological superintelligence" from the deep future inhabiting an avatar in a role-playing game living a complete, mundane human life from cradle to grave. She was serious about this, as she was serious about most everything. Shane told herself this lonesomeness and anger was just a phase.

She passed Parmesh in the office, and he gave her a cheery wave before turning his attention back to local radio, the host musing on the fate of the Gulf Coast. She grabbed a bagel from the grimy continental breakfast buffet and was on her way.

She drove with an arm out the window to catch the wind in her open palm. Most of the homes along Route 90 were battered, destroyed, empty, foreclosed, or for sale, and it gave the land a hallucinogenic quality, like it was previewing itself in the fog of a dream. Across the Mississippi shore, she got a look at the damage Solomon had wrought. The streets were mostly clear now, but lined with snowdrifts of splintered wood, plaster shards, particle board, trash, and shattered glass. She passed trucks stamped with NRA and APL decals, the snarling Cerberus, Stars and Bars, and homes with enormous flags flapping for The Pastor. On the ocean side, empty pilings stretched skyward after pitching the homes they held into the water. They looked like supplicating arms. Beyond the shore, she could

> **THE WATER WILL COME** The radio didn't need to tell Parmesh Singh that. Pretty fucking obvious. The low-relief, sandy barrier islands were more or less already swallowed up, and there was so little protection from king tides that the water simply invaded whole neighborhoods. His parents had refused to sell in the '20s when the writing was on the wall, and now all the motel could do was house the charity cases FEMA dropped on them and hope to dodge bankruptcy for a few more years. His dad blamed illegal immigrants and drug dealers.

> **23.6 MM PER YEAR** Or .93 inches, said NPR. Scientists disagreed on how much faster the water might rise. According to the Tulane scientist being interviewed, the problem was that no human had ever seen an ice cap collapse before, let alone studied the dynamics that determined how quickly it raised sea levels. Insurers seemed to believe one thing while the real estate industry believed the diametric opposite and still scrambled to sell seaside properties, from Cape Cod to Houston, before entire continents of ice could melt into the oceans.

see ink-dot islands and sandspits washed by garbage. The sea was calm, the waves sighing in and out, foam bubbling on sand. A snowy egret drifted on the wind so that it remained stationary in the sky. She drove west and thought about what she would say to Quinn, Kai, and Murdock when they met for lunch.

In the nearly four years since South Carolina, Shane watched Lali grow up. She stretched out, developed buds of breasts, learned how to read very well, and spoke a bit of Spanish for a while before a few girls at school overheard her and began the torment. She was smart but odd. She hated anything other kids liked and spent most of her time painting in her Slapdish worlde. Shane, of course, knew her password and kept tabs. Lali had built hillsides, a prairie, and weather that changed each time you entered. In this quixotic worlde, there were ruins to explore, most of which had incongruent medieval and colonial architecture. A family of pterodactyls would buzz the sky, and there was a strange black-purple pit in the middle of a church with no roof. It had what looked like teeth on the edges of its fleshy chasm, and when Shane peered into it, there was water or mucus below.

Lali was a solemn kid, so unlike Shane at that age when she'd made friends easily and, like her father, gabbed with anyone. She ached for Lali to find friends, but she kept talking about how she wanted to be home-schooled in the VR set. It was even more disturbing when she argued with her daughter about all the insects and plants tipping into extinction, year by year. Shane felt it was part of her duty to focus Lali's attention on what would be gone by the time she was grown. But Lali said she didn't care.

"How can you not care?" Shane begged her.

"It doesn't matter. We have the other worlds now. They're better anyway."

It was such an obvious and unsparing thing for a child of her generation to say. How could her own daughter be such a dystopian cliché? Then again, what kind of mother had she been? She'd never taken Lali camping, the girl refused to hike for more than twenty minutes, and teaching her about songbirds, soil, or the savanna elicited eyerolls so dramatic it made Shane want to slap her.

Of course, as Lali grew, Allen's youngest son, Perry, who never did man-age to move out of his parents' house, remained the same age. He lay there in her nightmares wheezing through a lung filling with blood. She and Allen sometimes talked about what happened. He didn't haunt her so much as they had dream-arguments about why she'd done it.

6Degrees was supposed to start its new campaign in the fall of '35, but a month before, Shane had mailed three postcards with pictures of San Diego—their signal that they needed to abort. *Greetings from Tinkerbell,* she'd written. This meant her source was telling her the op was in danger, which held off Quinn and the others for a while. A year of frustrated messaging followed. They kept asking what exactly her woman at the JTTF knew, and Shane kept feeding them bullshit. Just trying to delay.

By September, she was driving to check the mailbox in Tonganoxie al-most every other day. Then she got a message from Quinn: the lottery ad featuring the small Asian girl, grinning and missing a front tooth as her mom scratched away at a potential fortune. They all had their photographic tags so the recipient would know who the piece of steganography was coming from. Shane sat down with her edition of *The Stand* and began to decode, only to quickly realize that the letters were coming out in a nonsense jumble. She sat for a long time trying to figure out if this was a bluff check or something had gone wrong with the communication, until, abruptly, it dawned on her: This message was meant for a different keystone. Which meant it wasn't intended for her. Which meant the others were talking behind her back. Which likely meant they knew she was lying. She decided to confront the situation head on. She wrote to Quinn to tell her she'd sent this message to the wrong person. She asked what the keystone book was.

I can't give you that information, Quinn wrote back. After decoding, Shane drove home and pondered. She watched Vic Love, The Pastor, and Tracy Aamanzaihou spar on a debate stage in Nevada while Lali did her math homework. Then Shane went to her desk, penned her message, and printed out the flyer right then.

Give me the keystone or I burn you all. Don't fucking forget who I am.

In twenty years, she'd never been impulsive like this, and when she dropped the flyer into the USPS box that night, she knew the threat was irrevocable. She felt the claustrophobia of too many secrets and not enough allies. But she had to know what they'd said. Not knowing made the dreams with Perry so much worse. A week went by before she got Quinn's reply: *Willa Cather. My Ántonia. We should talk.*

She went straight to the KU bookstore, found a copy, and decoded the flyer right there. She sat and stared at it for a long time.

Shane is out. Keep her dark. Same schedule. Central organizing goes through me now.

She didn't have much choice after that. She told them they had to meet, the original 6Degrees. Minus Allen, of course. She chose the Gulf Coast city she remembered as a child because it was as anonymous as anywhere else these days. And obviously, she chose a public place.

The restaurant was perched on the edge of a bayou with nothing but dead cypress trees on the approach. Built in a time when developers figured the American shore would retain the solidity of a grade-school-classroom map, it was an upscale place she'd chosen on a whim, just far enough away from her motel so they wouldn't happen upon where she was staying. They'd argued bitterly over shattering twenty years of protocol.

She found Quinn on the restaurant's outdoor deck, overlooking the stewing Gulf. They hugged, and despite everything their embrace was tender. "Good to see you, sister."

QUINN Thought Shane looked just awful. Old and overweight. She'd built this moment up in her mind for months, and here was the woman she'd so feared, a harried mother on the verge of collapse. Maybe they should have been feeding her even more money through Archie's system. Maybe they shouldn't have left a waitress spinning her wheels in a collapsing economy, which was probably what was fueling her shortsighted discontent. She was relieved that Shane at least didn't have the kid with her, although at this point, there was nothing you could put past her. Shane had been unraveling ever since Allen.

"You too," said Quinn. They took a seat. "So should we start with apologies?" Quinn asked her. "Because I can if you can."

Shane swallowed. "Of course. I *am* sorry."

"For threatening us."

"Yes."

Quinn nodded. She had her blond hair pulled back into a loose diagonal braid that pillowed into a side bun. She oozed the self-assurance of a woman with the upper hand in a salary negotiation. Shane opened her mouth to begin clearing the air, but before she could, Murdock and Kai were at the hostess stand and then on their way to the table.

"Shane, darling," said Murdock, taking her in his arms. His fat stretched his plain white T-shirt to the point of comedy. She saw he had a new tattoo on his chunky forearm, a patch of crammed script she couldn't make out. He'd shaved his head clean. But for the eyebrows, he looked a bit like Allen. "Where's Lali-girl?" he asked. When he sat, Murdock overflowed the chair, his gut pushing against the table.

"She went with her friends' family to the Ozarks for the week," said Shane. "Easier that way."

"Hey," was all Kai said, and he hugged her as well. He wore a posh blue jacket over a black shirt, which looked too warm. His brow was as smooth as she remembered. He seemed never to age. His eyes were murky and sad. He looked quite beautiful.

She cleared her throat.

"I was telling Quinn how sorry I am for the threat. I just think we're moving too fast on—"

"You want to get a drink first?" Quinn interrupted.

"A fantastic idea, Quinn," said Murdock. Shane closed her mouth.

They ordered pints of hazy IPA, cocktails, and a dozen oysters. Shane stuck with

ARCHIE Had put Kai in his place. He'd demanded there be accountability for Allen, that someone pay a price for what he'd had to read about online. All Archie wrote was, *There will be no price. You take orders from the ladies now. Thx.* Even as he hugged Shane, his oldest living friend, he wanted to scream in her face, *How could you? First Allen and now this? Who the fuck are you?*

water. The restaurant was filling up, like a meeting of the local chamber of commerce had let out, and all of Bay St. Louis's slickest wheelers and dealers were hungry to support their most endangered restaurant.

"We shouldn't go through with this," Shane said abruptly. "Or I guess, you all shouldn't go through with this. Since I'm no longer in the picture."

Murdock looked out at the water. Kai cast his gaze at the clean white tablecloth and left it there. Only Quinn looked her in the eye.

"You see it, Shane," she said. "All the years of talk about the end of the world, but that's not what's happening. It's the beginning. And no one can wrap their minds around what it's the beginning of yet."

"That's why we're trying to build something that will outlast us," Shane said fiercely. "That will live on no matter how dark it gets."

Quinn took her fingertips to her eyes, closed and rubbed them. "Will it? With anything we've done so far? When all was said and done, Shane, a lot more was said than done."

"What does that even mean?" she demanded.

"It means you were right in Wisconsin," said Kai. His gaze did not leave the table. "And I was wrong. We spent all those years thinking we could chip away at their power, and all we did was give them a rationale to stop limiting their own violence. Or did you not see what happened in Washington?"

MURDOCK When Shane had been a young woman, beautiful and strong, she'd sat him down in the Bob Evans in Ohio to walk him through her plan. It sounded far-fetched, yes, but something about her bearing made it also seem realistic, plausible even. She had a weapon inside her—or she was the weapon—and he could feel himself craving the action again, the battle rhythm. And they made it happen. His bombs went off, and they all escaped like bandits in the night. Yet the more years that went by, the more implacable it all felt. The more they seemed like gnats on the heels of a few dark, fucked-up immortals, and the gods, they just swat you and carry on all the same. He wished then, only briefly, that none of this had ever happened. That he'd spent his life after the war drinking down his own beating heart instead.

Shane looked to Murdock. "Kel? Tell me you're not with them on this."

Murdock kept right on staring at the sea. He made a soft shrug of his shoulders. "I'll get home tomorrow and barely remember this. I'll have a thought or memory, and I can remember having the thought or remembering the thing, but I can't recall the thing itself. Little like going insane, slow-rolling, for thirty-some years."

"That's not an answer," she hissed.

"Oh, Shane, my love." He finally looked at her, sadly. "There are no answers no more."

The waiter approached, and they went quiet. He babbled about what a nice day it was, how the weather had talked about rain, but here they were serving outside, et cetera. Shane went through the motions of listening, but her heart pounded and her mind spun through every fear and regret.

Kai waited until the waiter was out of earshot. He said, "I'm sure you've seen these people self-immolating."

"So?"

"And the group that drove a boat into the Petrobras platform—"

"Yes, Kai, I have access to the news too."

"We've served as an inspiration, Shane." He leaned forward and thumped two fingers on the table. "People are pouring gasoline on themselves. They are putting

KAI Ground his fingernails into his palms. It wasn't just the massacre in D.C. that had rewired his thinking. Across the world, they were finally breaking through. He wanted to tick off on his fingers for Shane: The hundreds of aboriginals and whites in Australia who'd blockaded then stormed the Carmichael Mine, destroying millions of dollars of equipment before being beaten and arrested by police. The Minyun in China leading sabotage campaigns against government, military, and fossil-fuel targets. The two women who'd set themselves on fire outside the school of the Indian prime minister's daughter so that the whole country had to watch them burn. The twelve-year-old Palestinian girl who was organizing people to walk into Israeli bullets in Gaza, demanding food, water, and release. And right here, Louisiana's own: the Mossville Raiders monkeywrenching the oil, gas, and petrochemical industries that ruled the acid wetlands. *This is what we worked for!* Kai wanted to scream at her. *Why are you cowering now? We are the fucking Weathermen, and they are finally afraid of us.*

the violence of this system in front of those perpetrating it. Now it's on us to take the next step. The financial and industrial elite are not ashamed of themselves, and they're not about to let go of their power. We had no idea how far they would go. We sat around for too long telling ourselves we were a political movement or a social movement. We carried that fairy tale for so long because we didn't want the alternative to be true. Because the truth is, this is a war."

"And people have died, Kai."

"And people have died," he agreed. The wind gusted again, wetting rich men's eyes, while the sound of silverware scraping plates and low chatter filled the silence.

Murdock thumped his forearm down on the table, twisting his enormous body to display his new tattoo.

"Look!"

There was a beat. Shane read it anyway: TASTES LIKE CHICKEN AND WE'LL ALL BE WITH GOD SOON.

Quinn said, "I don't get it, Kel."

He retracted the arm. "Yeah, neither do I. Barely remember when I had it inked. Just woke up one night with it in my head, then a couple days later there I am applying moisturizer stuff to a crusty new tat. I'm pretty sure it's something this guy I knew in EOD said. He was like my mentor, my father, my brother, and now I don't remember his name or what he looked like. But maybe it just means we'll all pass on and, disappointingly, every fucking thing just tastes like chicken." He downed the rest of his beer. "Just a theory, though."

Before driving back to the motel, to make sure she wasn't being followed, Shane took a drive through the streets of Pass Christian. She remembered one pink house in particular, still there all these years after her father found beach parking in front of it. He'd claimed the beaches west of Gulfport were less crowded. That had been their first summer in Mississippi after moving from California so her dad could follow the oil patch work, and he'd been eager to show his gals how wonderful it was. Her mom put on a brave face, but her unease was right at the surface. She'd left her family for California, married a bawdy roughneck who spoke no Spanish, and then followed him to the awful heat and hostile politics of the Deep South. Still, those Mississippi years had been good ones. They had a bigger house, Shane had her own bedroom, and their street had plenty of kids on it. A tight-knit blue-collar community where everyone had a parent working on a rig or at a refinery. She spent her time exploring the streams and fields of the town, on the hunt for turtles or herons or ants—whatever wildlife felt challenging to capture on a digital camera or in a glass jar or aquarium. It always smelled of rotting oyster shells, and the kids on her block were a mini UN: Vietnamese, Black, white, and her best friend for a while was a girl from something called the Jena Band of Choctaw Indians.

Gazing at that pink house, Shane could almost hear her father's voice. Not particular words but the big, booming squall. The whole winds of the earth seemed to live in his lungs. Her dad suffered no bullshit, but he believed in chivalry. He kept a curving Wild West mustache that made his mouth look droopy. He always had grease stains on his clothes. Even after he showered, he would still smell of machine oil and the popcorn scent of sawdust. He loved Westerns and watched his favorite until the VHS didn't work anymore. He only ever used Spanish for nicknames. Her mom was, of course, "Mamacita" or sometimes "Mamacita caliente" and Shane was "Ojitos." Little eyes. He was, he said, "As old-school as a knuckle whack with a ruler." He didn't like excuses, complaining, whining, or feeling sorry for yourself. He thought people should work hard and treat everybody fairly. He'd been an unbearably decent man.

She followed on his hip. Every project, she would be his helper, whether it was picking out tools while he lay fiddling under their car or handing him nails while he redid the fence. She learned every kind of wrench and screwdriver because she was no help to him if she didn't know the right one. His job was called a tool pusher. She loved the sound of that word.

He'd been gone on his hitch for only three days. Killed in an accident. The thought that arrived first: How was that even possible? It had never occurred to her that people you loved could go off to do something they always did and then just be gone with no warning. She'd screamed and wailed and covered herself in his dirty clothes from the hamper like she could summon him back to life with her anger. A wave of grief so black and violent ensued. It felt like a shroud over the world. But that had only been the beginning. She and her mom were alone on the Mississippi coast with only a small payout from her father's death and her mom's paycheck from a salon.

Her mom had been a clever woman and a vivid storyteller. When Shane was little, she hadn't wanted to learn to read because she didn't like kiddie stories. So her mom spun tales carried from another continent. She spoke of the warrior whom the gods turned into a dolphin and El Silbón, the whistling man. These stories were strange and terrifying. Finally, her mom wrote all her tales out longhand so Shane could practice her reading in Spanish and English. She'd loved watching her parents flirt, how her mom would come up behind her father and dance into his back, running her nails through his thick hair. Her mom would pull it, smell it, taste the sweat on his neck. She'd seen how intense her mother's attraction had been, bone-deep and right on the surface of the flesh. And when he was gone, her mom's devastation was just as bright. Shane never saw her drink more than a glass of wine, but after the accident her mom was drunk every night. And then every day and night.

Soon she found the bottles stashed everywhere, in drawers, under the sink, in the bathroom cabinet. Like her mom couldn't be bothered to walk to a different room for vodka. She forgot about Shane. She vanished into her bottles, and then she vanished for good. Shane came home from school one day and her mom was just gone. Drawers empty. Suitcases missing. No note at all. She was thirteen years old.

THE CIPHER Perhaps she was better at creating a fog around herself than even she realized. The others, Murdock, Kai, Allen, and Quinn, they'd left enough clues littered across the global communications infrastructure that one could re-create their stories. Explicate their lives with a careful reconstruction of surveilled conversations, location data, purchases, archived social media, search histories, and access to every digital keystroke they'd ever produced, from old high school research papers and blogs they kept as teenagers, to anonymous tweets from fake accounts, to childhood diaries haphazardly left in old Microsoft Office files. And yet Shane had left so little evidence of herself, all of it having to be pieced together from the trails of the others, it was almost like her life didn't truly begin until 2014 when she walked into a restaurant for breakfast. These snippets of an opaque working-class American childhood lack crucial detail. There are gaps. There is her rage and intelligence and a fevered sense of injustice, but her core story remains unknowable and maddeningly out of reach. Here following is what is known of the conclusion to her life as Shane Acosta. Past this point, the darkness thickens.

A shrink might tell her it was easy enough to draw a line between her dad's death and her chosen way of life, but she didn't start hating the oilmen until much later when she began dabbling with radical boyfriends and deep ecology. Then she looked around at her family's cancer-alley lives, the sacrifice zone she'd called home, where the sun was a hazy red dragon breathing through the spires of refinery architecture, and she went hard for a few years at drinking and drugs herself. Maybe she just wanted to know what her mom had chosen over her.

Maybe she'd be dead if she hadn't gone south. She saw the village where her mother came from. She met true revolutionaries. She stared at dark surf on beaches of the Southern Hemisphere and began to dream. She came home and found like minds. They schemed and plotted, and they laid the groundwork for a resistance unlike anything their empire had ever seen.

And in the summer of 2016, Shane read about a protest in North Dakota where thousands of people had gathered to stop an oil pipeline.

The next morning, Shane drove her truck up to one of the last open big-box stores and bought paper, an envelope, rubbing alcohol, latex gloves, and the cheapest VR set she could find. She thought long and hard about what to write without a code and keystone, though the odds of this letter being intercepted were small. Finally, she settled on: *Leadership has steered us wrong. They may want more than we want. Proceed with caution at their requests.* She signed it, *A Friend of a Bald Friend*, addressed it to Coshoc-ton, Ohio, wiped it with alcohol, and dropped it in a USPS box, hoping the postal service wouldn't collapse in the next few days.

Next, she drove out to a pleasant seaside overlook where an abandoned house sat, charming and unflooded. She set up her mobile hot spot, pulled the VR set out of its packaging, lowered it over her face, and secured the headphones. She dashed briefly into the Slapdish worlde of HBO's Egyptian costume drama where avatars of the popular characters milled, fucked, and betrayed, and left a blue silk scarf with a bot playing a shopkeeper. Then she traveled over to her encrypted worlde. It was basically her father's den from their house in Mississippi: a wood-paneled basement room with a TV cast-ing light over movie posters adorning all four walls. A lot of Clint Eastwood and John Wayne, but of course Alan Ladd as well. She'd even included the cracked door to the laundry room with the familiar sound of both machines tumbling. She'd almost added her mother humming a song, and only then understood the seductive power of virtual reality. She waited half an hour for the figure to materialize across from her.

"In the middle of the day?" Tinkerbell demanded. "I had to say my kid was sick." She appeared to Shane as a sleek, black humanoid void, her head an oily bulb in the ether, her fingers long chopsticks fiddling on the reclin-er's armrests. Shane appeared to her as the same black, leather-suited ab-scess. Both their voices were disguised by the same flat electronic cadence.

"It couldn't wait. You're not going to like it."

There was a beat as the faceless black avatar gazed at her. "What?"

"I've come to believe I've lost control of the cell."

"What does that mean?"

"They're working behind my back. Our backs."

"On what?"

"A number of things I'd rather not go into."

"So I've had to trust you all these years, but you can't trust me?"

"I'm sparing you. So you have a chance to shield yourself."

"Shield myself from what?"

"The others know about you. That you work on the JTTF."

"How the fuck do they know that?"

"I told them."

"Why?" she demanded, the slick black mask lurched forward, menacing her space.

"I needed their trust at the time. The point is, if they're caught and in-terrogated—I'm not sure if they'd give you up." Tinkerbell was silent for a while. "You knew there were risks when we started this."

"Of course I knew that. Don't patronize me." The avatar smeared spindly fingers across its expressionless mask. Somewhere in Colorado, she was wip-ing away tears. Then she said matter-of-factly, "You want me to stop them."

"Only if I can't. I need to get back to Lawrence first."

"If the governor doesn't lynch you at the border."

She shook her head. "What?"

"Your governor. Justis. He declared a state of emergency for the dust storms. He says until The Pastor is inaugurated as president, Kansas will be its own independent nation. He has the Kansas Army National Guard and the League at the state borders running checkpoints. He illegally executed three people on death row last night."

"What are the Feds doing about it?"

"Got me. No one seems to know who's in charge at the moment. They have darker paramilitary arms hunting for your people right now too."

Shane felt a bug land on her neck, and she swatted. The illusion of the VR was suddenly as shallow as the set of a high school play. "We need a way to stop them without putting you at risk."

"How?"

Shane chewed her lower lip. "The investigation has been close to the bomb maker before, right?"

"The original bomb maker? Yeah. The theory's come up over and over that whoever's building the IEDs might have a military background. We usually get a contingent that pooh-poohs this just because bomb making has become so democratized. You go online now and you can find detailed AR-VR instructions that walk you through incredibly intricate ordnance. The theory was harder to ignore after the missile in Anacortes."

"Could you put a clue in front of someone without drawing attention to yourself?"

She sighed. "He fits the profile: explosives background, single, and they're looking for someone who travels for work or at least has an excuse to move around the country. Like I told you, he was crossed off our list back in '30 after the Ohio River Massacre because our algorithms told us he was a right-winger."

"Find something we can use," said Shane. "But don't do anything until I tell you."

"What are they planning?"

"I'm sorry, I wish I knew." Shane shook her head. "I lost control of it all."

The avatar rubbed where her eyes would be. The voice-altering tech drained so much of the sorrow from what she said next. "How did I get here?"

Shane exited Slapdish and pulled the VR set from her head, half expecting her truck to be surrounded by FBI agents. Instead, just a half-bright afternoon, yellow sun cutting through cloud banks and glistening on the water. She'd left the window open, and horseflies buzzed in and out while a garter snake sizzled through the grass. She forced herself to drive the speed limit back to the motel. People had long ago stopped wearing either 6Degrees or The Weathermen on T-shirts. When the five of them started, they had an idea, but that idea did not belong to them. And once others got hold of it, they could mutate it, and pretty soon the program would become how best to scatter blood around. Then one day, very soon, they would all look around, and nothing would be changed, and nothing will have worked, and the dead would still be murdered.

In the motel, she roused Lali and told her to pack quickly. She crammed their clothes into her ancient Osprey, the pack mostly duct tape now. Then they lit out on Highway 49, heading home to Kansas.

———————

Before Allen and Perry, before Anacortes, La Grange, and Fort McMurray, before the Ohio River Massacre, before Lali was born, before they'd even set off their first bomb, Shane heard about a protest in North Dakota over a pipeline.

These were still early days, just maps, materials, ideas, and codes. Obama still president. Clay Ro had been recruited at this point, but Miles Kroll had not. Energy Transfer Partners was set to build its $3.7 billion Dakota Access Pipeline through the territory of the Standing Rock Indian Reservation right along the Missouri River. An enormous protest erupted in response, with thousands making their way to Sacred Stone Camp, mostly local tribes of the Oceti Sakowin, along with plenty of allies eager to make this fight about more than Indigenous land or the health of the water but a battle over the future of the planet itself. In those days, this was what the movement had settled on: trying to blockade the industrial machine one oil pipeline at a time. Of course, Shane wasn't there to actually join the protests. ETP had retained the services of a security firm called TigerSwan, which was working with local, state, and federal law enforcement to not only suppress and drive out the protestors but to document them. Everyone who camped out in the pipeline's path or chained themselves to machinery would be marked for life with a kind of digital scarlet letter and useless to Shane and her comrades.

Her aim, then, was to catch the sympathetic before they actually reached Sacred Stone. She'd been living out of a camper for the past two years, moving across Montana, Wyoming, Colorado, and the Dakotas, changing her appearance, scrubbing her past life clean to cement a new identity. She'd buzzed her head and bulked up with a protein-rich diet and a vigorous workout regimen. Backpacking and climbing, she got into the best shape of her life, moving from town to town, doing under-the-table seasonal work, switching out for better-paying bartending gigs if she could. She made friends and vanished. Had affairs and slipped away. She took her paycheck and left nothing behind. She carried no phone, no laptop, just her pack and a paper map. A butch ski bum drifter just looking for love and adventure after college, man.

She found work at a bar thirty miles north of the reservation in Fort Rice and pretended to know nothing about what was going on down where the Cannon Ball River met the Missouri. Her boss, Nanette, was an old chain-smoker who knew just about everyone who came or went from the bar and recognized almost every vehicle that lumbered down Highway 1806. Shane watched for patrons other than the old Lakota who came in to pound pitchers of cheap beer and the white men who did the same. On her days off, she'd drive south and rotate between convenience stores and groceries where water protectors might go for provisions. She kept an eye out, uncertain of who she'd approach or how. She always drove the limit but got pulled over nevertheless, her age, skin color, and general look simply too suspect to not harass. The cop relaxed when she said she tended bar for Nanette and didn't give a shit about any pipeline. They got to know her truck and left her alone.

The first time Shane saw her was in the bar. She came in with a group of young people, mostly Native. One man wore a T-shirt that said WE SHOULD HAVE BUILT A WALL. They ordered pitchers and endured the angry and horny glances from the regulars. The woman was tall and wore a firetruck-red tank top and a dirty pair of jeans with a big hole in the hip through which the whole bar could see a patch of creamy skin. She caught Shane staring at her early in the night. Shane couldn't help herself. She'd been listening to a new pop song by a young singer, and this woman's eyes were such a peculiar murk. They reminded her of the waters of the Gulf: dark, muddy, sometimes green but always shifting. The image and lyrics clotted together in her head.

"Assume you all are coming from the brouhaha down by Cannon Ball?" Shane asked, swiping their empty pitcher.

"Just a night off before we go back to the tents and bugs," said Ocean Eyes. Her voice was big and low-pitched.

"Hey, even the people throwing their bodies in front of the imperial-industrial machine need a drink." Shane could tell she liked that.

"Where you from?" the young woman asked.

"From nowhere. Going nowhere," she said and walked away.

The crew hung around till close. One of the men behaved with that proprietary air all straight men had. He kept touching Ocean Eyes's shoulder, and just the body language between them suggested they'd slept together. Still, Shane couldn't stop staring at the woman with the thick, crazy hair and the big, loud laugh that seemed to rattle the picture frames on the walls. Old West history went timid at the sound of her voice. At the end of the night, with only a handful of regulars finishing up, the woman walked past her to the bathroom.

"Be careful driving," Shane warned. "They'd love to catch you with a DUI and thin your ranks."

Instead of answering, she just stared at Shane. Then with the smallest tilt of her head, she nodded to the bathroom. Nanette was busying herself with gossip at a table of Lakota regulars. In the small ladies' room, the woman pushed her long, thick tongue into Shane's mouth and slipped her hands up her shirt to twist her nipples. She had huge masculine hands that made Shane feel petite.

"Can I go down on you?" Ocean Eyes asked, and for a moment Shane forgot why she was there working in this lonely dive bar on the hard, forsaken plains.

"Of course," she whispered.

Sometimes, if Shane had a particularly hard orgasm, she would cry. It was involuntary. The intensity just left her spent, and her emotions would swell. When she came, biting down on her thumb to keep from crying out, her tears were pouring, and she was embarrassed. The woman rose back up and kissed her on the mouth, pushing her own taste between her lips. She took her thick thumbs and wiped away Shane's tears. "Now you owe me." And she kissed Shane on the tip of her nose and left.

They saw each other again and again that summer, whenever she broke away from Sacred Stone to slip past the checkpoints and spend a few hours in the bed in Shane's van. They would make love and talk about deep ecology, and the woman's eyes would go stormy for both. Her name was incongruous with her whole being. "Kate" was the name of a sorority girl from a Dallas suburb. Shane said her name was Lucy and that she was from Chicago. She tried not to spin too many tales, to at least fabricate her subterfuge with kernels of truth. In turn, Kate told her about Phoenix and Portland, about her precarious and rootless upbringing. A doting and anxious mother never quite at home in this foreign country, a passionate and cruel father, who was nevertheless likely the reason she was here. She grew up with his activism around uranium mining in Arizona and coal plants poisoning the air on her grandmother's reservation. It made Shane ache how much they had in common, twinned lives met on a new battlefield. Kate asked if Shane wanted to share her tent at the blockade.

"That really isn't my scene," Shane said and caught the disappointed look on her face. "What?"

"I hope one day you understand how silly that sounds." It killed Shane not to tell her then, but she had to swallow the truth until she was sure.

When Shane heard TigerSwan and law enforcement had shut down Highway 1806, she panicked. The assault on the camp had begun. She saw the armored personnel carriers barreling down the road, hundreds of police in military gear, weighed down with mace, rubber bullets, water cannons, concussion grenades, and attack dogs. Since she had no cell phone, she drove down to where they'd blockaded the road and, despite the risk involved, approached the line. The site was Backwater Bridge, and the police wouldn't let anyone pass.

"Turn around or you're a part of it!" snarled a pink-faced cop. She could hear explosions and screaming. Over the rise, it sounded like a war zone. "Get moving!" And he took one step toward her. The pummeling blare of a sound cannon started up in the distance.

Later, she'd find out the police had used pepper spray and freezing jets of water in twenty-eight-degree weather. They nearly blew off a woman's arm with a concussion grenade. The water protectors were kettled and cleared with CS gas, attack dogs, truncheons, and finally cuffed, tied, and thrown into kennels with a number written on each of their arms in Sharpie. Kate showed up at her van a day later, dirty, shivering, face streaked with tears and pain. She'd been arrested, cut loose, and the cops had never so much as offered her a towel. Shane turned the heat all the way up, stripped her naked, and held her body beneath the covers. Donald Trump had been elected president just thirteen days earlier. She'd watched in the bar on election night, the patronage evenly divided between elation and disbelief depending on one's ancestry.

"We should've seen it coming," said Kate, still trembling. "I plan on never being surprised by what this country's capable of ever again."

It was the first time she'd ever heard her hopeless, and it sounded so strange. Off-brand for a woman who'd truly believed the tribes would set up some tents and the oil companies would fall to their knees. Though some would hang on until the following February, for all intents and purposes that night marked the end of the Standing Rock protest. Done in by Tiger-Swan and the brutal Dakota winds.

Kate ended up with pneumonia, sweating and aching it out in Shane's van for the better part of two weeks. "Why don't we move on?" Shane suggested. "Come with me. You can regroup and get well."

"I don't want to move on," she said. At this point, the color had returned to her face, but her voice would thereafter come with a slight rasp, as if all the coughing had scarred the interior of her throat.

"You need time. It'll be summer before you know it, and you can plan your next revolt then."

She was surprised when Ocean Eyes agreed. She knew she was taking a serious risk by associating with this woman. She didn't care. Their vehicles dueled for the lead all the way to Jackson Hole, a place Shane's father had always wanted to visit but never did. It was there Shane came to understand she'd fallen in love.

She found work on the ski trails. Kate got a bartending job and insisted on renting her own place. "Not quite ready to move into your van yet." That was fine. It gave Shane the opportunity to sleep in a real bed from time to time. After just a month, Kate found another gig: advocating for the West's bison herds, "And I don't even have to get sprayed by a water cannon to do it."

Winter receded, and with spring came the lush green of the forests and fields, the glittering beauty of the Snake River, the glory of the Tetons. They spent as much time as they could in the mountains, hiked deep into backcountry, got eaten alive by mosquitoes, crept slowly away from a black bear that wandered into their campground, woke at dawn to watch the sun rise over the eastern plains. They drank at the Cowboy Bar till close most weekends and found a reliable coke dealer to help them burn all these candles at all these ends, but when you're young it feels like you'll never run out of wax or wick. Shane knew this woman was a singularity, that she small-talked better than most people dreamed.

Then one night, Shane left the wrong wallet in Kate's apartment.

"So who's Simone?" she asked, handing it back.

"Huh?"

"If you're Simone Schafer of Louisville, Kentucky," she said, "then who's Lucy Alvarez of Chicago?"

She thought about how best to steer into the lie. She definitely couldn't tell her that Simone Schafer was also not her real name and that she'd never even been to Chicago.

"It's just an ID," she said. "Everything I've told you about me is true. I just need to be careful about who . . ." Shane struggled for a way to say this. "About who knows me."

Kate blew a loose curl back from her brow. "You get why this is unsettling, right?"

"It's not like I killed anyone," said Shane. "But I have some stuff in my past that I don't want catching up with me. I'm just trying to live my life now." She hesitated. "And love who I'm living it with."

Shane felt the ache of these words, but the woman she'd said them to didn't seem to hear. "Is that why you didn't want to come to Sacred Stone?"

"Yes," she lied, and hoped Kate was picturing her as a bank robber.

"Okay," she said, nodding, and left it alone.

But things changed after that. Kate started seeing men again and took every opportunity to remind Shane that she found monogamy tedious. Shane swallowed this as best she could. When they were together, Kate was distant in an imperceptible way. They could still talk and laugh. They could still debate for hours. And yet Shane could feel her backing away. Shane walked by a restaurant on a Saturday night, and there she was, clearly on a date. She even recognized the guy: they'd rented a canoe from him a week earlier.

She had no choice; she had to risk it. They went for a hike around the Jenny Lake Loop. The sun beat down, a beautiful cloudless day, and she told Kate everything.

Her face didn't change much as Shane explained about Kai, Allen, and Quinn, about Kellan Murdock and his skill with explosives. She told her about the people they'd recruited across the Midwest and South. How they were only a few years away from setting their plans in motion. She tried to ground it all, to make it sound as logical and common-sense as possible. They were not kids playing at revolution—they were a genuine clandestine resistance. And they were going to start something real and powerful. She finished, and they kept on walking, one boot in front of the other. Her face remained as placid as Jenny Lake.

"Well?"

Kate didn't say anything for a moment, and Shane waited.

"No one understands yet," Kate said carefully. "One day an awful lot of people are going to wake up, look around, and wish they'd done something when they had the chance."

Shane waited because that wasn't really an answer.

Kate squinted her murky eyes. "I'm not sure what you want me to do with that information."

"What do I want you to do? I want you to join us."

Her smile was sad and disappointed. "You're a smart woman, Lucy. You and your pals should take a closer look at history."

"What does that mean?"

"It means that extremism always demagnetizes its own moral compass. The righteous start off wanting to kill the tyrant, but that's never enough. Then they've gotta kill the tyrant's children and family and army and supporters. How we build this path"—she nodded to Shane's tattoo—"that matters almost as much as the path."

"I'm not planning to kill anybody."

"You know what I mean. And let's say you—Lucy or Simone or whoever you are—succeed beyond your wildest dreams. Say that you don't blow yourself up building your first bomb and you don't get caught and spend your life in prison. You won't win what you think you'll win. Civilization isn't careening into an ecocide because a few people are getting rich—it's because *we are acquiescing* to it. *We* are allowing it. And you can't change anyone's consciousness with a bomb. It's something that has to come from within."

"Now you sound like a fucking New Age mystic," said Shane, hating the bitterness in her voice. "Everyone just green your consumption and get in touch with the Earth mother goddess, and we'll all be fine."

"Maybe," she admitted. "Maybe I'm a froufrou Wiccan blessing the soil with my menstrual blood—who knows, man!" She laughed, revealing so much wet tongue, lip, and teeth. "And maybe I'm wrong and you're right, and one day I'll say, Holy fuck, I wish I'd done more. I wish I'd driven a truck bomb into the Department of the Interior to stop oil and gas leases or bought a gun and taken out an entire Exxon shareholders' meeting. But boy, do I really doubt it."

The argument lasted all seven and a half miles of the hike, and by the time it was over, Shane realized what a mistake she'd made. It turned out this woman was beholden to all the fables of the people protesting in the streets with their pink pussy hats right before they met for brunch and went home to binge Netflix. It turned out Ocean Eyes wasn't at all who she thought, and Shane walked around for weeks with that special fury you can feel only toward someone who has utterly captured your imagination.

The last time Shane saw her, Kate said she was moving to D.C. to join some performative do-gooder organization futilely humping the electoral boulder up the hill in the hopes that it wasn't all a grand masquerade. She was taking that poor pretty-boy canoe-renter with her too, and though Shane wanted to despise that kid, she mostly pitied him—he was so clearly unprepared for her, so evidently at her mercy.

Of course, when the first bombs went off, Shane feared Kate would come forward. In the years leading up to the start of their campaign, Shane convinced herself that even if Kate wanted to turn them in, she wouldn't know where to begin. She had a face in her memory, a couple of fake names, an utterly falsified geography and set of associations. The more bombs that went off, the more they began to succeed, the more she wondered why Kate never said anything. Maybe because she was afraid even the hint of an association with "terrorists" would jeopardize her own cause. Or maybe she was secretly rooting for Shane. Certainly, watching her grow famous from afar, watching the public come for her, the state erupting to stop her, at some juncture she had to admit to herself that Shane had had a point, right? And seeing Kate now, nearly twenty years on, conjuring this loose and uncertain army to stand arm in arm around arbitrarily chosen gas stations, Shane wondered about the roads not taken. Not if Kate had come to fight with them, but if Shane had gone and fought beside her.

Shane and Lali rolled over their shattered country beneath an immaculate darkness bedecked with stars. The radio was full of panic: stock market tanking, home foreclosures spiking, insurance companies demanding federal relief, and in the meantime furious wind had kicked loose soil up into a dust storm the size of New Jersey in the Oklahoma Panhandle. It wasn't until the Ozarks that they entered the haze. With the first wall of particulate mist, the highway seemed to vanish, and traffic slowed to a brake-light crawl. In the dust's muffled clutch, noise became indistinct, and the honk of horns sounded like phantoms crying out in the murk. Lali had been quiet for most of the ride, drawing on a sketchpad with her earbuds in. When they hit the dust, Shane felt the uneasiness radiating from her daughter. She'd driven through dust storms before, but this one blew with special dread. Conspiracy theories washed over the radio: Vic Love had hung himself; he'd been murdered by the Joint Chiefs of Staff in a military coup; FEMA was fomenting a communist revolution; The Pastor was going to lead a Christian army to the White House gates, shoot fire from his fingertips, and burn it to the ground. Finally, she turned it off and they listened to Tracy Chapman.

A traffic jam met them at the Kansas border. As they crept closer, Shane saw there was a brand-new checkpoint, manned by men with assault rifles, wearing an eclectic mix of military camouflage and SWAT-team black. They were checking the IDs of every passenger in every vehicle.

"This wasn't here when we left," said Lali.

"I know, hon."

"What is it?"

"It's nothing. They're just going to check our IDs."

The line crept forward as they waved drivers through. But when there were only two cars ahead of them, the man began gesturing for the driver of the Chevy Suburban to get out. There was an argument. Lali was now watching intently.

"What is *happening*?" she demanded. Shane said nothing. "Mama, what are they doing?" Then the man with the gun pulled on the handle of the door. When it didn't open, he reached through the window and unlocked it from the inside. He grabbed the driver by the arm and jerked her out, a middle-aged white woman wearing a faded dress with a chintzy flower print. She was protesting and trying to pull her arm back as the cop—or whatever he was—guided her to a trailer off the side of the highway. Lali was practically shouting. *"What are they doing. Why are they taking her out? Are they going to take us out?"*

"No, doll." Another armed man got in the woman's car and began driving it to the berm.

"Mommy," Lali was crying, panicked. Shane's heart beat so hard it hurt her chest, and she felt like throwing up. "Let's turn around," Lali sobbed. "Please, let's turn around."

They were one car back. A new border guard leaned into the window of the gray sedan in front of them. Shane had an ID with a white surname and wondered if she should reach for that now. Simone Schafer came in handy sometimes.

"Mommy, I don't want to go. They're going to take you. I know they're going to take you." Lali kept repeating this, and it was too eerie and specific a fear, as if she subconsciously knew what her mom had been doing all these years.

"Doll, you gotta stop crying, okay? It's all going to be—"

She looked over and saw the stain in the crotch of Lali's ill-fitting slacks. The first time in nearly a year. Now Lali's crying was streaked with this new shame, and her sobs were just too loud. They were almost up.

Shane reached into the truck's back seat for Lali's backpack and shoved it onto her lap to cover her accident. Then she grabbed her daughter's face.

"Baby, it's fine. All right? I'm not going to let anything happen to me. And I'm not going to let anything happen to you. It's you and me, right? They can't touch us, right?" Lali had a single terrified syllable stewing in the back of her throat. She could smell the salt of her girl's tears.

"Please," Lali moaned. "Let's just turn around. Turn around turn around turn around—"

"Lals." She cut her off. "Lals. Who are we? We're outlaws, right?"

Lali nodded miserably, choked, and nodded some more.

"I ain't going anywhere and neither are you. Except home. You and me forever. Got it?"

Lali sobbed and nodded, and the car in front of them drove on. The man with the assault rifle waved them forward. She pulled on her dust mask and waited for two tumbleweeds to bounce past before pressing the accelerator. He was young, white, and the absence of emotion on his face made her skin crawl. He took her ID. Shane Acosta of Lawrence, Kansas. He looked at it for a long time. Then he looked through the window at Shane. Then Lali. She could not help but think of how easy it was for men like this, in this same position at border checkpoints all over the world, to do whatever they wanted to a mother and daughter on their own.

"Lower your mask," he said, and she did. He looked from her face to the ID and back.

"This all is new," said Shane, giving her voice a friendly twang.

"This your daughter?" he said.

Lali let a sob escape and Shane willed her to be calm.

"Yes, sir. She had an accident while we were waiting, which is why she's feeling silly." Shane lifted the backpack to show him. Lali stared at the carpet while tears dripped from her eyes. The man said nothing. He handed back her ID and waved her on. Lali sobbed quietly as they put distance between themselves and the new haunted borderland.

Off the highway, they drove through the vanished municipalities of southern Kansas, abandoned downtowns and foreclosed suburbs looking even more ethereal in the dim, dead light. Most people had moved on years ago. The Ogallala in retreat, the great western drought dessicating the land, there simply wasn't enough water. The ones who stubbornly remained, who'd dug wells halfway to the core of the Earth or rigged complex rainwater capture systems, were isolated and paranoid. One trailer, built on the remnants of an abandoned feedlot, had an enormous sign with neon-green spray paint beaming brightly through the gloom: FUCK OFF! NOTHING LEFT 2 STEAL!

A drive that should've taken fourteen hours ended up at seventeen, and Shane, exhausted and twitchy, pulled in front of their small rental on a side street of a struggling college town. She wanted nothing more than to collapse into bed, praying for a sleep without dreams. She woke Lali. Backpack slung over a shoulder, Lali's hand in hers, she pounded up the porch steps, the thud of their feet warped in the grim gray cloud enveloping the town. She worried what this air was doing to her daughter's lungs.

As she slid the key into the lock, she noticed it. To the left of the door, above the mailbox stuffed with junk, their house number: 315. Something was wrong, and it took her a moment to make sense of it. The 5 was turned upside down and bolted back in so it read like an S.

315

At first, she only struggled to imagine how this could be, who would have done this, and she almost turned the key and opened the door anyway—she was just so very tired. But this oddity, it mattered, she was sure, and her mind went racing backward to find a context. Back through the Gulf Coast and Lawrence and a cabin in Wisconsin and a chain restaurant in Ohio and a fallow field in South Carolina on a too-warm winter night.

She withdrew her key.

"Why aren't we going in?" Lali asked. She was still half-asleep. Shane looked all around the door. The windows all had the blinds pulled down as she'd left them.

"Lals, go back and get in the car."

"But why?"

"Just do it, okay? And don't get out no matter what."

"Is something wrong?"

"Yeah," she said. "Maybe."

With Lali back in the truck, Shane pushed through the brush on the left side of their lot, eyeing the neighbors' house, though no one appeared to be home. In the small backyard, where she and Lali had once tried to grow tomatoes only to be defeated by raccoons, she approached the back door. She put her ear to it and listened, as if this would tell her anything. She dragged a filthy plastic lawn chair to the opaque bathroom window. Taking one more look around to make sure she was alone, she smashed the glass in with her elbow. She removed the remaining shards from the frame and poked her head in. The bathroom door was open, and through it, she could see the edge of the living room. It looked as if the furniture had been rearranged.

The problem was they couldn't just leave. There was a folder, hidden in a hollowed-out shelf of the bookcase next to her piano, with information that could lead back to her original self. And maybe she didn't matter so much. If it wasn't for Lali, maybe she would just leave it all there and take her chances. She crawled through the window, careful to avoid scraping herself, and crunched over the broken glass on the floor. She eased her head out to peer down the hall.

There was a device on the back door that led into the kitchen and a wire curling through the dining room into the living room, where it connected to a central apparatus. Several chairs were arrayed there in a circle, each of them holding a car battery and flanked by cans of gasoline. Shane hadn't learned everything about explosives over the years, but she'd learned enough. If she'd opened either the front or back door, the whole house would have gone up.

She allowed herself only a single flash of grief and rage. She'd told them Lali wasn't with her. Or maybe they didn't care that she might walk through the door with her child. Either way, this heartbreak, she understood, would follow her forever. Yet another sorrow to tally for people she'd once loved who were now, one way or the other, gone.

She gingerly stepped over the wires that led from one incendiary to the next, until she reached the bookcase. She pulled all the volumes from the third shelf, *The Stand* thunking to the floor, and removed the wooden plank they'd rested on. She stripped off a piece of electrical tape and shook the wood until the blue folder slipped out with its documents. One of the folk-tales her mother had written for her fell to the floor: "*La Leyenda de Juan Machete.*" She scooped it up, returned it to the folder, and tucked it all in the back of her jeans.

Looking around, she tried to think if there was anything else she should grab. Maybe a toy of Lali's or at least her VR. Fifteen years in a place, and all of it was utterly disposable. She did take one book from the shelf, Solnit's *Hope in the Dark*, because Kate's notes were still inside.

Buried in a field near the fishing cabin in Tonganoxie was a waterproof box and its contents of cash and passports wrapped in plastic. She would drive northeast to pick it up, and then quickly double back west. After all these years to think about where they would go if they ever had to run, and she might as well have thrown a dart at a map now. Where do you hide in a world on fire, and you never know where the next border guard might be? In every direction lay nothing but another dark and burning city. She tipped over one of the gas cans in the kitchen, turned on all four burners, and tossed a towel on top.

Back through the bathroom window, grabbing her pack, hurtling into her truck, Lali asking where they were going, what was happening.

"What's happening, Lals," said Shane, buckling her belt, "is we're going to blow this popsicle stand."

In the middle of town, all the gas stations were surrounded by students wearing particulate masks or scarves around their mouths, holding signs about the dust, the system, the atmosphere, the deluge, and singing songs in the dirty fog. The drivers honked angrily, but the kids refused to let them pass.

Luckily, Shane's truck was electric.

Speculation had been brewing for weeks as President Love vanished from the campaign trail and aides put forth a series of increasingly suspect explanations for their boss's aberrant behavior. Now sources in the White House are leaking: The president was drinking and rambling. He would lock himself in the residence for days at a time and refuse to see anyone. He was exhausted and racked by guilt over the violence a summer ago. He spent most of that time reading about the survivors and families of the dead. The only reason the Twenty-Fifth Amendment wasn't invoked was because without a sitting vice president the Republican Speaker would have taken over. What will happen when the House convenes to vote on this contested election? The man who they will likely certify is threatening nuclear holocaust.

ACROSS THE GREATER MEDITERRANEAN, COLLAPSED CITIES HAVE JOINED THEIR ROMAN ANCESTORS IN RUIN, FROM TRIPOLI TO DAMASCUS . . .

"It's a government-planned, forcible removal from the coastal zones and sea level rise—I promise you, that is just the cover story. There is no sea level rise! Open your eyes! They're trying to remove us like they did the Indians, only this is for something much, much worse . . ."

The Kansas governor has defied court order after court order and executed four LGBTQ activists and three doctors who once performed abortions. This is only the beginning of the madness he's unleashed in the state. Justis deployed militarized checkpoints at the borders, claiming refugees from the heat wave in Texas "threaten Kansan sovereignty" and continues to arrest protestors in droves while the Feds remain silent . . .

Civil Unrest Engulfs China

Protestors battle security forces in fourteen cities; riots grip Beijing, Guangzhou, Shanghai, and Hong Kong

The country appears to be in meltdown as competing factions of armed forces claim they are the new government.

ZEDEN TO AUCTION HER BODY TO THE HIGHEST BIDDER; PROCEEDS WILL BENEFIT—WHAT ELSE?—THE CLIMATE

". . . what we now know, that the expeditioners likely died in confusion and horror, suffocating to death in the endless night . . ."

FINANCIAL MARKETS REEL AS COASTAL HOUSING COLLAPSES

Nor is this a new trend. Homeowners along the Eastern Seaboard and Gulf Coast have been selling defensively for years, but there were almost always optimistic buyers willing to snatch up the properties. What has changed is those buyers have vanished, exacerbated by insurers refusing to issue homeowner policies and banks unwilling to write mortgages.

WHAT CAUSED THE TSUNAMI THAT DESTROYED THE SVALBARD GLOBAL SEED VAULT?

They call Namibia's coast the "Strangelove Ocean." Everything has died off as hydrogen sulfide bubbles out of the sea. Even the skeletons are dissolving.

"God help those who stand in the way of our movement. This is the people's movement for Jesus Christ and my kingdom. And those who stand in the way, well, let's just say the Lord's judgment may be gruesome but it is always just."

DID J.LO ACTUALLY SAY THAT ABOUT KHLOÉ? GERIATRIC CATFIGHT HEATS UP!

The ambush of Chicago police was a military operation and the six dead CPD and eleven dead terrorists are a testament to the unrest roiling American cities as the economy continues to struggle and antipolice sentiment grows.

FORMER PRESIDENT BARACK OBAMA DIAGNOSED WITH STAGE IV LUNG CANCER

THE SEVENTH DAY

2036–2037

*W*hen *I left the office midday, I lied to Carmen, the receptionist, and said I* had a gynecologist appointment. "Tell the boss I'm sorry for missing the meeting." I acted like I was in a hurry, perhaps stressed about a test result. Sitting on the foam-green plastic seats of the Staten Island Ferry, I kept trying to read my book while my mind wandered. When I met the man now scrambling toward the presidency years ago in that Chicago bookstore, I'd been a reader. I'd always had a book on my commute on the L, but when I moved to New York, I stopped taking the train. A car picked me up every day, and I'd spend that time thumbing through investor reports or my phone's cornucopia of distraction. Now I was trying to become a reader again, but I'd chosen a tome both dense and horrific. *A Savage and Unforgivable Empire* described the race to profit from the ecological crisis. Not to mention, the man I'd known for a night all those years ago dominated the ferry's TVs.

With the election thrown to the House of Representatives and going to a vote on January 6, The Pastor had consolidated support and was promising bloodshed if he wasn't certified and sworn in on January 20. Maria had asked if I wanted to try an antianxiety medication, probably Ativan, but what was the point? Ativan's calming effects were not up to the task of The Pastor actually sitting in the White House. The memories of this man itched under my skin, so I went outside to breathe fresh air as the ferry churned toward the tip of Manhattan.

I was meeting Moniza Farooki at the Trade Center Memorial, one of the most heavily surveilled places in the world. When I asked her if this was safe, she sent me an encrypted text: *We will never meet all your top secret 007 prerogatives.*

Her bombshell investigative feature, "The Fund That Would Rule the World," had detonated on Wall Street that summer only to be quickly buried beneath the crisis in Bangladesh, the debacle in Pakistan, and an unhinged election. The documents I'd delivered to her described Tara Fund's investment strategy, its long positions in the Arctic, Norman Nate's solar management endeavor, Xuritas and the private security industry, and most damningly, CLK and its efforts to subvert elections with tactics that amounted to psychological warfare. If you thought about it, Moniza had pointed out, manipulating stock prices had become de rigueur for banks and hedge funds. One needed an edge, and this was the natural evolution in a decriminalized and deregulated financial world: pay a psychometrics firm to manipulate companies, elections, CEOs, politicians, shareholders, and anyone else who got in the way of a winning bet.

"No one innovates financial crime like hedge funds," Moniza told me. "In another age, this would've been the biggest scandal in the history of finance. Now it's just another Tuesday."

Fred seemed less upset that Tara's dirt had spilled in the *New Yorker* than the article's insinuation that Tara was mostly a bit player in this drama, "and not a particularly profitable one," as Moniza wrote. Despite being on the cutting edge of these tactics, Tara had actually lost money for two consecutive years. While most of the Street lawyered up, Fred fell into a funk about what kind of damage this would do to the fund's reputation, if clients would ask for redemptions after their lock-in ended.

The other issue the story highlighted had to do with the Sustainable Future Coalition and its ties to Tara's head of investor relations, Fred Wimpel. The SFC, having won stunning victories with the defeat of climate legislation during Randall's term and the election of its ally Loren Victor Love, wanted more. It wanted "carbon maximalism"; it wanted an administration that would not just stave off the challenge to fossil fuels but make a hard push toward new energy horizons. The sudden upswing in the fortunes of The Pastor, the article implied, were no accident, as it poured dark money into his campaign and set land mines for his competition. I'd never told Moniza about the night in Chicago. Whistleblowing was one thing, frightening intersections with vast historical forces another.

Walking up Greenwich Street, I stepped onto the vast tundra of the 9/11 Memorial and made my way to the northwest corner of Tower One's footprint, my eyes grazing the names of the dead as I passed. I'd been in the ninth grade when these people lost their lives. I remembered getting out of gym and my friend Mandy taking me by the hand and leading me to science class where the TV was on and the towers were burning.

I turned as Moniza approached, pulling a hand from the pocket of her peacoat. She was a small but attractive woman with sleek black hair and immaculate Queen's English. She wagged a device that looked like any old tablet. Supposedly, it used ambient noise and data streams to junk up surveillance devices without the surveilling party knowing. We'd met in public this way before. We walked past each other, stepping to the corner of Tower One, pretending to read the names. The water inside the fountain rushed into the center, a steady, soporific roar.

"And you tease me about James Bond shit. What was it that couldn't wait?"

"Relax, darling, those are our offices." She nodded to the fortress of glass and steel. "I'm flying down to Charlotte tonight. I didn't have time to set up anything too clandestine." I waited, and she chewed her tongue. The chances that Tara had private investigators following me were real, and I desperately wanted her to make this quick. "I thought I owed it to you to know: A source told me the SEC has opened an investigation into Tara. If the FBI gets involved, it could mean a Title III on your boyfriend's phone."

"A wiretap?"

She nodded. "Be careful what you say to him. And I'd talk to a lawyer sooner rather than later."

"Do you think Fred did anything illegal?"

She ticked her head in ambivalence. "It's become quite difficult to say what's illegal anymore. On Wall Street or in Washington. Either way, I felt you deserved to know. It was never my intention to stitch you up." Her voice was cool but sincere.

"I did it of my own free will." I was thinking of Fred. The summer of '35, after I'd delivered the file to Moniza, he and I spent some time apart. He went to London while I stayed in New York. When he returned, he was bearing an early edition of *Sense and Sensibility*, which he'd hunted down at a rare book dealer because, he said, he'd once heard me say it had been my favorite book in college. It was then I realized, to my dismay, that I still loved him.

"It may be that this will turn out a mere footnote in high finance anyhow."

"What do you mean?"

I ran my hand over a name on the lip of the fountain: *Jane Marie Orth*. Just another woman who had no idea her life would come to an end at the hands of violent and insecure men.

"There's something going on in the markets. My contacts who were around in 2007—they're unnerved. There have been two years of falling housing prices all over the coasts and the insurance companies are canceling every homeowner policy they can wriggle out of."

"ARkSTORM put them in a tough spot."

"Yes, but insurance losses coming due can't explain the whole situation. Maybe your partner and his fund did something illegal and maybe not. But it's all the legal activities that appear to be the problem at the moment." Before I could inquire further, she said, "Okay, that's probably more gabbing than is safe. Good luck, Jackie." And she peeled off into the wind, making haste toward One World Trade.

Riding back across the Upper Bay, passing the Statue of Liberty, I watched the cranes of the shipping yards and the field of wind turbines behind the calm green lady. I thought about the first time I'd visited the city to attend a friend's wedding with Jefferey. How impossible and epic this place had seemed. How small it made my life in Chicago feel. Back on Staten Island, I rode the train past the abandoned graffitied buildings of the shore and the seawalls of sandbags now protecting inland structures from king tides and storm surges.

Carmen asked me how the appointment went, and I gave her a relieved look like the test results had been fine. I returned to the open-office section I shared with a snarky woman named Liza and a bitchy queen named Garrett, but I could hear one voice booming from the room catty-corner to us, stuffed in the back of this otherwise open space. Liza and Garrett wore noise-canceling buds as a defense. Talking into a pair of ARs for a remote interview, Kate Morris sat with her feet on her desk, hands folded over her stomach.

"I don't have a comment—that's a question for the scientists," she said. "But it's definitely something to freak out about. You know, if you need something to freak out about . . ." She paused, listening. Then, "All these whining, bitching corporations saying I'm trying to ruin them, that I'm saying they need to be buried alive—that is all true. I am. And they do."

*

The summer of '35, with Fred in London, I was going to the gas station every day, at first to bring the kids food, then to hold a sign myself. After three weeks, the protest had grown, and a crowd of twenty to thirty people stationed themselves around the clock. Drivers began to avoid the place, the NYPD was reluctant to intervene, and soon similar blockades had broken out at other gas stations across the five boroughs. Mayor Bowman refused to make arrests. The memory of D.C. loomed large, as these were the first major protests since that awful summer. Soon, there was nowhere in New

York City to buy gas. That third week, I ended up trading stories with one of the other protestors and mentioned my background in advertising and PR.

"No kidding?" said the woman. She was no teenager. Maybe early thirties, and she always came to stand with us before her bar shift. "I should hook you up with my friend. She works with Morris on Staten Island. She was literally just talking about how they're looking for people with your background."

That was how I ended up connecting with Holly Pietrus, who sounded keen to bring me in to interview. She was especially interested because I was independently wealthy. "We can't pay anyone. We barely have enough money to keep the lights on." They'd set up shop on Staten Island, she explained, because it was proximate to the media capital and rents were all plummeting as the flooding got worse. On a shoestring budget, they could afford office space with a modicum of security, as long as you didn't mind the occasional sewer system failure.

For the first time in years, I sat at my desk all night just drawing, trying to create a branded image for whatever exactly was happening in the streets. I brought my sketch pad to the busted brick building where Kate Morris and a staff of a dozen had taken over the second-floor offices of a former computer repair center. It still had the sign, TOTAL SYSTEMS, INC., bolted above the door.

"Obviously, we're getting a deal on it," Holly said. She led me through grimy hallways to a gray-carpeted space with a conference table flanked by four large offices with windows looking in and no doors. Each room was cramped with desks, messy with laptops, tablets, and VR goggles. Young women pecked away at screens, keyboards, and the air itself. Holly had enormous purple bags beneath each eye, yet her voice was chipper, eager to share their plans. "We're coordinating with nearly a hundred and fifty volunteer captains around the country, and they're working with a thousand protests or blockades of various infrastructure and political offices. We want to create pulses of widespread disruption, trying to hit every level of society, and then ramp it up each month. We're seeing our best results in the typical places: major cities, college campuses, and wherever there's a Fierce Blue Fire Outpost. Right now, the name of the game is recruitment, trying to get more bodies." We entered a bleak room past the main area with a sticky round conference table. It was the only office with a door, and it took me a moment to understand it belonged to the boss, who'd essentially chosen to work from a bunker. "Have a seat. I'll go get her."

I'd barely taken my résumé from my purse before Kate swept in. The outsized presence I'd always studied from afar, the way she moved with an almost masculine certainty, was now personal and vivid. She jerked the other chair out and thumped her butt into it as her elbows crashed to the table.

"I hear you've got PR experience." She wore jeans and a gray sweater fraying at the cuffs and collar. Her mass of hair was tied up behind her head with a pencil stuck through the knot, strands of white and gray leaking out of the dark blond.

"And advertising," I added. "Yes. A lifetime's worth."

"Well, we're in a little bit of a PR battle here, if you haven't heard." She reached for my résumé without asking. "Maybe *the* great PR battle. And you can work gratis?" I'd left it right there in the same size font as everything else: *VP for Strategic Communications; Clients include: United States Armed Forces, Adidas, Procter & Gamble, the Sustainable Future Coalition.*

"Yes, that's not a problem."

Her eyes scanned the page for a moment, then she set it down.

"What drew you to the movement?" she asked.

"So," I said the word slowly. Her energy was making the interaction asymmetric. "I've spent a lot of time thinking about this issue, and I finally decided I needed to play a more active role in trying to change the situation. The last few years have really scared me, and I want to help however I can."

She pointed to my sketch pad. "What's that?"

"Oh." She reached for it before I could offer. "I drew up some branding ideas. A good symbol or logo would go a long way."

She flipped through the images, stopping on a woman standing in a sea of people holding seven fingers aloft, her hands backlit by the dusk. "Cool," she said. "You know, I never cared much for advertising. To me, it was a whole industry of evil bullshit meant to keep people unhappy and craving and alienated. But then just before D.C., I kinda came around. Can't leave any tool in the box at this point."

"I've had a dozen ideas since Holly's friend put us in touch." I started speaking very fast. "I really think there are a lot of methods that could draw people in who—"

"Wow," she said. Her eyes had wandered back to my résumé and now went saucer-wide. "Are you kidding?" She flashed the biggest, brightest smile I'd ever seen. "Seriously, bitch, are you fucking kidding me?"

"What?" I said stupidly. She shook the sheet of paper in my face.

"What? You were with the SFC! The fucking people who nuked me and kneecapped PRIRA!"

"I was."

"Who ran a fucking smear campaign and had rape threats coming into my office for two years?"

"That's not what we did. I had nothing to do with that."

"The fuck you didn't!" She was still grinning. "Fucking cunt, you got some big ole balls on you, don't ya? Get the fuck out of my office, then go throw yourself into the swelling seas you fucking hack corporate whore." When I didn't move, she stood, balled up the sheet of paper, and threw it hard at my face. I flinched as it bounced off my nose and scratched just beneath my eye. "You think I'm joking—*get the fuck out*!"

Through the doorway behind me, I could almost hear the staff stop what they were doing to listen in. I was frozen in my recoil from the paper. She picked up my sketch pad and began ripping out my designs, shredding them in front of me. "Get out, before I drag your ass out and throw you down the stairs—" She shredded another page and another, the confetti scraps fluttering down to the old dirty carpet. "Fucking get gone!" But I didn't stand up.

"You said it was never too late."

She ripped apart one more page. *"What?"*

"You said it was never too late for anyone. That we all had a choice to make. So this is my choice." I was speaking too softly and forced myself to sit up, to uncoil. It probably looked like a small movement to her, but for me, it was like knocking over my chair. "I'm not going to sit here and grovel or apologize. I've made so many excuses and justifications to myself." I thought of my dinner with Jefferey, and how I'd sat there parroting ideas I no longer believed in. But you have to keep saying those ideas out loud so that the alternative doesn't become real. So that the full weight of who you are and what you've done doesn't come bearing down. "And it was hard and painful to come to the—the understanding I've come to, but I did. And now I want to help. Any way I can. And if you don't want me here, then I'll go back to the gas station and keep holding my sign."

My gaze fell back to my hands. I could feel her eyeing me. Then she walked around the table and grabbed the front of my top. I was sure she was going to hurl me to the ground. But instead, she pulled down my shirt and looked right at my breasts.

"Checking for a wire obviously." She returned to her seat, folding her hands on the table. "I know, I know, they make bugs way smaller now. So how do I know you're not a spy? Working for the SFC still and trying to undermine shit from within? Wouldn't be the first time."

"Then why would I put it on my résumé?"

"Play to my ego. Duh. Make me think I converted you while you sow doubt in the ranks."

"I'm not asking anything from you, Kate. I'll make the coffee if that's what you want." I tried to reach for something deeper, but that's hard to do when you're face-to-face trying to explain the workings of your conscience. "I was ambitious and driven and wanted to make a name for myself. I put my head down and did the work. Like a lot of people in a lot of walks of life, I learned instinctually how to manipulate myself so I didn't have to look at what I didn't want to look at. But if it's not too late for anyone, then it's not too late for me. I'm scared, yes, but I'm here. And I'm ready."

She gazed at me across the table, her face blank and unsympathetic. Behind me, in the central room, I heard a coffee mug tumble over and someone hiss *"Damnit."*

"Okay," said Kate. "You got me. You're hired."

I blinked. "Really?"

"To tell you the truth, I plan to run you into the ground like a mule. Can you start by drawing that one logo thingy again?" She reached to the ground and sifted through the scraps of torn paper, hoisting up a shred. "This gal?"

*

If Kate Morris had any further hesitation about me coming aboard, she never let me see it. I thought I'd have to earn her trust, but she put me to work and didn't look back. Suddenly I was experiencing this person I'd always wondered about. She was loud and abrasive and could turn angry at the drop of a hat. Once, a volunteer left her laptop on the subway, and Kate exploded at her. The girl was gone the next day. Kate enjoyed a certain level of frat humor that I could never connect with. She'd let out a fart in the middle of a meeting, chew with her mouth open, or punch subordinates in the shoulder, playfully but hard. She'd steamroll into conversations or dismiss a bad idea with a curt "Yeah, no fucking way we're doing that." She rarely made it to 5 p.m. without cracking a beer, and she would drink until we left work. Mostly she slept on the couch in her office, but Garrett, her overworked assistant, confided to me that she had at least three different men with whom she sometimes shared a bed. "I get the trips to Brooklyn or Manhattan, but who the hell did she find to shack up with on Staten Island?" he wondered. And yet her focus, her passion, her work ethic were undeniable. She was a force of nature, practically elemental. She took an idea, like building out what Liza Yudong called the "blockade network," and would hammer her programmers and engineers, these awkward, zit-faced young women she'd found at the College of Staten Island, until it was up and running. Her ability to recruit was breathtaking. She'd get on a VR set with some unknown anarchist artist co-op in Boise and within forty-five minutes persuade them to build a civil disobedience training center.

The organizational structure of this loose, fly-by-night militant network Kate had created was never settled. No one had a title. There was no hierarchy. People got paid when fundraising had a good couple of weeks, and I set them up with a $3 million donation that helped us build out that staff. Most people lived in shared apartments on Staten Island where the rent was cheap in the flood zone. A top-level meeting consisted of Kate, Holly, Liza, Garrett, myself, and a hard-charging married couple, Jenice and Tavia Ryan, who'd also once been field directors for A Fierce Blue Fire.

The summer of '36 was a riot on all our nerves. Our blockades lagged because people were falling to heatstroke all across the country. We tried to get shade and water to our people, but in New York City the wet-bulb temperature was reaching 109. We argued about calling off actions until this latest heat storm abated. Kate did not dismiss this easily, but ultimately, she couldn't bring herself to tell people to stand down. "We need to keep escalating. We can't take our foot off the accelerator now," she said. Then a man drove his truck into a group of our people at a gas station near Austin. A seventeen-year-old kid was killed and four others injured. The driver, of course, had ties to the American Patriot League. Kate hit the airwaves to decry the violence, and she certainly could do so with passion, but it did not go unnoticed by me—or Fred, in our many arguments on the subject—that Kate seemed neither shaken nor surprised.

"It's almost like she's expecting to pick up right where she left off after the National Mall," he said.

I didn't argue with him. She had been driving hard all that spring and into the summer as the election overheated and all three candidates seemed to present a different path toward doom. We'd watched the presidential debate from the conference room, the one where The Pastor, when asked what he would do with women who'd had abortions, said, "All sinners have two choices: repentance or the sword." When that grim smile crept into his face, I felt like I might throw up. Though Kate publicly endorsed Tracy Aamanzaihou, she confided her doubts to us during a September meeting. "If she helps this fucking loon win . . ."

Eager to agree, eager to move the topic away from the dark presence in my memory, the man waiting in the wings for the presidency, I said, "The guy who murdered over seven hundred of our people might actually be the *far* lesser of two evils." The meeting got very quiet after that.

Jenice warned me afterward, "They were not 'your' people, Jackie. You were still slinging mud for a hedge fund then. You need to think before you speak."

I was embarrassed and chastened. I never brought it up again.

About a week after the death in Austin, I looked up from my desk and saw Rekia Reynolds exit the elevator. The rest of the staff stopped typing. Before Carmen could ask who she was there to see, Kate emerged. Beside me, Liza stood and walked to the door.

"Nice to have you here, Rek," said Kate. She looked tired but primed. She cast a hand around the room. "What do you think? It's a fixer-upper, I'll say that."

"If you ever thought before you jumped, it'd be a miracle, Kate," said Rekia. "A blessed miracle."

Kate snorted. "That's what you came here to tell me, Reynolds?" She gestured to her office. "Do you want to come in and talk, and not have it out in front of my folks maybe?"

Rekia's eyes bounced between Kate and Liza. "You two are putting people's lives in danger. Again."

"No, I'm waking people up to the danger."

"You get people killed, Kate!" I jumped as Rekia's voice boomed in the close space. Her neck strained, and tears pushed into her eyes as she shouted. *"You're orchestrating confrontations to get people killed! Intentionally! And it's nothing to you!"* No one in the office moved. Rekia looked right at Holly, who stared at the ground, holding her pregnant belly. Rekia smacked tears off her face and lowered her voice. "That poor boy in Austin—you're re-cruiting all these people from *our* membership rolls. You're using them to fuel the rampage your ego's been on the last four years."

"Rekia." Kate folded her arms. She met the other woman's gaze, her voice stony and low. "Four years in which the planet has hit 446 ppm. Four years in which we've passed one-point-five degrees. Four years in which the seas have started rising *an inch* every thirteen months. We're outta time, babe. Slow and steady won't win the race."

"It's funny how these sacrifices never seem to include you."

Kate smiled, let out a humorless chuff, and looked at the ground.

"The T12 vertebrae," Rekia hissed. Tears collected in her eyes and this time she did nothing about them. "You know what that is?" Kate said nothing, and Rekia's lip trembled. "Tom's lucky he's a para instead of a quad." She shook her head. "He has days he can't remember who I am. He doesn't recognize his own parents. And you"—her face did a quick series of contortions—"you haven't said boo to him."

"You *told me* not to go near him." A flash of fury lit Kate's face, and then she lowered her voice. "So I didn't, Rek. I just did what you asked."

"You are a selfish woman." Rekia smeared her arm across her eyes. I felt my own tears working up my throat. "I doubt you've ever known anyone you didn't find a way to hurt."

Rekia glared one last time at Liza, and then she walked out, slamming open the door to the stairwell. Kate went into her office. A minute later, Liza followed. Neither of them came out the rest of the day.

*

Before we sat down for the next meeting, Kate asked me if I was okay, and I forgot my own lie.

"The doctor yesterday? Carmen said you looked stressed."

"No," I said quickly. "Everything was fine."

The guilt was less over ditching work than talking to Moniza Farooki. She was, after all, now living with Matt Stanton in North Carolina, splitting her time between there and New York. I'd only recently come to understand this was hot gossip in the activist world. When Moniza found out who I was going to work for, she said, "Be careful with Morris. She's good at making you believe in her without any reciprocal interest."

It was hard to tell if this was just the new love undercutting the ex. Yet what she said stayed with me, and the day after seeing her at One World Trade, I found myself mulling this at our meeting, studying Kate as she listened to Holly. The idea on the table was to move the actions higher up the economic ladder.

"Imagine trying to blockade JFK," said Holly. "Security checkpoints for miles, surveillance even farther out. The advantage of gas stations is the logistics of a blockade are so much easier."

"You're too cautious," Jenice told Holly. "We're not about triangulating."

"There's a difference between cautious and strategic," said Holly. "A strategy that doesn't work isn't any good. We need to diversify. Let's go back to tax refusal, student loan payment refusal, mortgage refusal—"

"No, no, no," said Jenice. "That's weak! In some cities, they're cutting gas hoses, pushing over cash machines, getting truly militant. We can organize lawyers and financial support."

Liza cleared her throat loudly. She adjusted her ARs. I could see her reading or watching behind the glasses as she spoke, her eyes scanning invisible cues.

"How soon does that turn to Molotov cocktails?" she asked. "It sounds 6Degrees-ish. Gauche."

Kate laughed.

"Ever since D.C.," said Holly, "and what happened there. We can't—I can't—" Her eyes flitted nervously to Kate and Liza. I held my breath. The conversation was simply never that far from August 1, 2034. "We can't have something like that happen again."

"It might," said Tavia. "We have to be prepared for that."

"You weren't there," said Holly.

"Neither were you," Tavia shot back. "You ducked out before the hammer came down."

Holly kept her voice admirably calm. "We lost friends in that." She gestured to Kate and Liza. "Don't talk about it like I somehow lost my nerve."

"I think we need to stay joyous," I interrupted. Everyone looked at me. In a room where I was the only white woman and had a background in corporate America, it always felt like I was one mistaken comment away from being run out of the room. "We need to keep offering the positive vision. We know we can make a better world. It's still out there waiting."

". . . If you'll just join us," finished Liza. I really loved her in that moment. This unusual interjection of sincerity seemed to defuse Holly and Tavia.

"Oh Jackie, you sexy PR flak," said Kate. "I think we hold serve right now. We'll have a Republican Senate to fight no matter what, with my good friend Russ Mackowski in leadership. But we have to see how this clusterfuck election shakes out. We need to know who we're dealing with first."

"Because if it's The Pastor . . ." Holly said darkly. She scratched at her legal pad with a dull pencil.

Leaving the offices late that night, back across the glittering water reflecting the city like a starscape, back to my disintegrating relationship with the only man I'd made any kind of true and vital love work, I thought of the stories I'd told myself. How secretly and deeply ashamed I'd been for so long.

*

On December 19, the Dow fell 2,212 points, the third-largest single-day loss in history and coming after a year of anemic growth. VR/AR glued to his face, sweating his conversations with Peter and the analysts, Fred barely noticed my comings and goings. Fred, more passive-aggressive than confrontational, would sleep in his office for days at a time. We'd delayed the wedding until the fall of '37. Sex had dried up entirely, and I daydreamed with envy about Kate's many beds. The markets recovered slightly by Christmas, but the squawking heads could not pinpoint who to blame: the unresolved election, the crisis in China, the crisis in India, in Bangladesh, in Pakistan, the aftermath of California's ARkSTORM, and of course the rabid behavior of the Eurozone's new unofficial leadership. Jennifer Braden loudly blamed the Seventh Day protests for slowing the economy. They needed to be "put down with more firepower than Vic Love used on the Mall." The *Wall Street Journal* editorialized that The Pastor couldn't be certified soon enough, if only to deal with this instability using the domestic security force built over the last four years by President Love. Krugman, the decrepit gadfly at the *Times*, was beating the drum about something else, and Fred dismissed this idea with so much hostility that I worried there might be something to it.

Housing prices had plummeted 7.8 percent year over year, according to the S&P/Case-Shiller National Home Price Index, the largest drop since the 2008 crisis, and this was after a 3.6 percent drop in the fourth quarter of 2035 alone. Most of the metro areas where this was occurring were on the Eastern Seaboard and Gulf Coast, particularly in and around Miami, where homes sat unsold, foreclosures had spiked, lending had tightened, and a full-scale abandonment of all homeowners policies by the hard-hit insurance industry was creeping outward like a cancer. *Sound familiar?* wrote Krugman. *While poor minority neighborhoods turned to flooded ruins, the wealthiest Miamians scrambled for high ground, but now even those neighborhoods are experiencing untenable nuisance flooding. The National Flood Insurance Program has fallen nearly half a trillion dollars in debt despite*

Congress's efforts to raise rates for at-risk properties. Rating agencies continue to downgrade the bonds of coastal cities and tax bases are collapsing, which then hamstrings much-needed repairs to the infrastructure needed to keep these cities dry. Much of this has been predictable, but that does not make it any less frightening.

On Christmas Eve, I got together with Erik and Allie in VR, the worlde a re-creation of our childhood home, now bulldozed into a field in distant Iowa. The computer-generated facsimile of our living room, built by Allie with Slapdish paintbox, had a number of missing details, including that the fireplace stone had not been brick. She had remembered to put in the banister where I'd found Mom.

Allie and Burt had rebuilt their home in St. Louis right back on the floodplain, but Allie assured us that the flooding had been once in a thousand years. I didn't bother to explain to her the meaninglessness of that phrase. Erik was typically taciturn. He didn't know what his own kids were up to because his ex-wife and her new husband had moved away two years earlier. "They got out while the getting was still good. They took a steep loss on the property, but at least they got something." I asked if he was worried about his own home. "Worried? No reason to be worried. It's already all over. Not literally underwater yet, but I owe about triple or quadruple what it's worth, according to all the people trying to sell in the neighborhood."

"But you don't even live near the shore?" said Allie.

"Doesn't matter. Everyone's seeing what's happening in Miami, and there isn't one goddamn sucker left to put in an offer. Even on high ground."

"So what are you going to do?" I asked, without mentioning that I'd been basically paying his mortgage the past two years.

"Probably walk away if I can find a job somewhere else. Or live here till I drown. Depends a lot on how fast the water comes in."

Fred and I went to his son's Christmas party the next day. Fred Jr. always put me on edge. After spending a few years in a juvenile facility, now he was in his senior year at Brown as if nothing had ever happened. He resembled Fred in the eyes but was rounder in the face and carried himself with much more swagger. Nobody at the party was talking about anything other than the situation in the markets.

"It's not 2007," Freddy assured us. "Real estate's in a slowdown for other reasons."

"Such as?" someone asked.

"Regulation, as usual," he said with confidence. He popped a carrot loaded with blue cheese into his mouth and talked as he crunched. "Tie the hands of homebuilders, homebuyers, and insurers, and this is the kind of mess you end up with."

For New Year's Eve, we attended an exclusive event at the Biltmore to raise money for Bangladeshi refugees, $20,000 a plate. This had been Fred's Christmas gift to me, and I could feel him bending over backward, popping vertebrae to meet me in my new pursuits. "I understand why you left Tara," he told me. "You spend your whole life getting ahead, and now you want to give a piece back." But looking around the party, it was hard to take any of this seriously. The gilded edges of the hotel ballroom, the extravagant dresses, the crisp tuxedoes, the decadent meal. All the ostentation was in service of a twenty-minute holographic video displaying the plight of the Bangladeshis, just one of many peoples now forced into disease-stricken camps with no potable water, into the savagery of the Indian army, into a flotilla of makeshift boats in the hopes of reaching even more distant countries, no home, no peace, no rest, no justice anywhere on the horizon. And after it was over, they served dessert, Basque cheesecake with duck-egg crème brûlée.

Fred excused himself to find a scotch, and soon I grew bored with our table and followed. Slinking past dresses that cost tens of thousands of dollars in my own Lela Rose, I felt the ugly bifurcation of my life, trying to foment a revolution during the day and enjoying the splendor and privilege of my actual situation on nights and weekends. My dad once said to my mother, as bitterly as I'd ever heard him say anything, "Greed is a strange thing. You think it was made up by the Bible right until you see it."

Handing over the Tara files to Moniza, I thought I'd cleansed myself— of ANøNosiki and CLK and asset management firms holding farmland and fresh water—but if anything, the feeling of grit on my skin grew worse. I found myself wishing I was in the Staten Island offices with Kate, Liza, Holly, and the rest.

I rounded a corner near the bathroom, passing a woman whose pink dress matched her wet lips, distended with collagen, and found Fred with Peter and Haniya O'Connell. They were talking to Russ Mackowski, the soon-to-be Republican majority leader, who hadn't even had to challenge Doup to usurp the position. Fred, Peter, and Mackowski each had a scotch in hand as if playacting the smoke-filled rooms where men did business, while Haniya picked at a nail and listened. Mackowski held forth.

". . . basically no place to let down the partisan façade anymore except charity functions, and even then you gotta be careful who you get your picture taken with. Get spotted within a foot of a Democrat, there goes your career. But hey, my wife's a hopeless almsgiver just like yours," he said to Peter while looking at Haniya. Then he laughed to show it was all in good fun.

I'd met Mackowski a few times, a tall, old, barrel-chested misogynist who filled a room with his thunderous voice, opinions, and self-regarding stories. He'd been the avant-garde of the neo-Confederate right, only to watch The Pastor come along and incinerate his presidential hopes yet again.

Haniya, beautiful in a custom-fit black sequined gown, smiled. It looked quite real. "You'd be in trouble, Russ? Imagine where my credibility would go. I study redistributive economics, and you make Mitch McConnell look like AOC."

Mackowski liked this and laughed very loudly. Their heads turned as I slid in.

"You look gorgeous as always," Peter said, kissing my cheek. His newly grown beard scratched my face. He nodded at Fred. "Leave this man for better days." Despite everything I thought of Tara, I still found Peter so endearing, and again felt a constellation of guilt for what I'd done to them.

Mackowski smiled and leaned in to kiss my cheek as well. "Miss Jackie, you look lovely. Nice to see you again." Before I could reply, he looked back to Peter. "And will we see you in Aspen?"

"Nah. Freak blizzard coming through. I told you, Senator, it's the twenty-first century, the New Abnormal, bro. Read your Tony Pietrus."

Mackowski chuckled again and sipped his scotch while Haniya made her exit. "It's been a pleasure," she said. And as she slipped out of the circle, she put her hand on my arm and, pretending to kiss my cheek, whispered, "I say we leave them if they make us spend one more minute with this asshole."

For a moment, I was worried the senator would hear, but also, I'd always felt like Haniya didn't like me. That argument at the dinner when I'd failed to side with her about Vic Love haunted me still, so I thrilled to this moment of conspiracy with her. I clutched her arm and met her eyes in total accord.

"Kansas," Mackowski was saying as he skittled the ice around in his glass. "A total pig-fuck, excuse the language."

"That's what I mean," said Fred. "If this vacuum of leadership continues, then maybe other governors start getting ideas. Maybe we've got a thirty-state secession crisis on our hands."

With some dread I asked, "What's the latest there?"

"Just this morning Governor Justis says the borders of his state are closed for good, and from what the FBI is telling us, he's executed two more people."

"Jesus."

"No one can even get Vic Love on the phone," said Mackowski. "It's an open secret he's had a total mental crack-up. Even though her side is still fighting to keep him in office." He pointed after Haniya.

"Which is why I'm saying, now that the vote got thrown to the House, it's best to certify The Pastor," said Fred. "Force him to take cool-headed insiders into his cabinet, surround him on all sides with the forces of reason, the way the Beltway managed with Trump."

"Nobody wants that fucking Pastor yahoo in the White House," Mackowski said dismissively. "And I don't want my time as leader spent trying to get him to heel and keep his freaky ass away from a microphone, let alone a nuke."

"I don't think we have a choice. He's going to have the votes," said Fred. "And Governor Justis could be the least of the problems if the markets don't settle."

Peter sucked air through his teeth. "Can't we hit the reset button, Russ? You moderate yourself to a Bush Forty-one stance and get on a ticket with like Amy Klobuchar circa 2020? She can hit interns with briefing books and you can run the country."

Mackowski laughed very hard at this, his cheeks turning pink from all his good humor. Finally, he looked at me, curious. "Fred tells me you've joined forces with the eco-nuts."

"Proudly," I said.

"Well, everyone needs a hobby." He swigged his scotch. "My wife took up bird-watching." He set his glass on a nearby table where it rattled to stillness. "If you'll excuse me."

New Year's Day came and went. Fred Jr. and his fiancée came over for a bit. A light snow left New York frosted and lovely. Fred and I stayed in bed for the first time in a long time. Then on January 2, Goldman Sachs filed for Chapter 11 bankruptcy protection, and the world fell to its knees.

*

Holly had given birth to her daughter, Hannah, just after Christmas. With her out on maternity leave, the thoughtfulness and caution she brought to our meetings was in short supply. On January 5, the room was giddy about the panic roiling the city. "You can almost hear the hiss at trading desks," snickered Tavia. "That's fear pissing down their legs." In light of this, it was supposed, our protests would gain urgency and acolytes.

Kate noticed my lack of enthusiasm. "You, Eeyore. What's up?"

I hesitated. The white lady was about to sound sympathetic to Wall Street. "I just don't think this is anything to celebrate. No one really knows what caused Goldman's implosion. The Fed and Treasury have to use the resolution authority to wind it down, but Goldman's holdings and balance sheet are global. Also, no one's paying attention, but two major insurance companies filed for bankruptcy last week because of losses from ARkSTORM."

As I suspected, I received blank stares.

"Good, let it all come tumbling down once and for all," said Garrett.

"Fuckin' A," said Tavia.

"Are you suggesting something?" Kate asked me.

I swallowed. "Call off the escalation on the seventh."

"Are you fucking dumb?" Tavia snapped, and Jenice put a hand on her arm. Tavia looked at her partner, aggrieved, like she was taking my side. "You don't get opportunities like this. We can focus attention like a laser on these criminals."

"This is a crisis of people losing their homes," I said. "This isn't just evil corporate bankers, Tavia. It's middle-class and low-income people suddenly losing their most important asset, and the system is coming down around them."

"Bitch, fuck the system! We are literally here to tear down the system."

That night, less than twenty-four hours before they were to meet to certify The Pastor as the next president, the House of Representatives made the unprecedented decision to delay the vote by a week. D.C. had been locked down since the New Year in anticipation of the vote, and though there was a sigh of relief that the count would not be the target of a potential armed mob, it was becoming unclear if there would even be an inauguration at this point.

On January 7, as we coordinated our protests from the gas station where I normally did my part, the market plunged another nine hundred points. I was on the phone most of the day, reading about what was happening since cars had long ago stopped trying to get past us. In New York, the panic felt positively breathable. Later, I went down to our actions on Wall Street where bankers and traders scrambled past protestors clogging the streets. Many firms ordered their people to work from home, and offices emptied as the streets filled. Looking across the crowds that day, all I felt was fear.

Though the climate crisis had pushed this financial calamity to our doorstep, the chants demanded that bankers jump to their deaths. I'll never forget one sign I saw: ONLY BLOOD THIS TIME. More people spilled into the streets, and the NYPD presence swelled to meet them.

On January 9, the stock market plunged another eight hundred points and three more insurance companies filed for Chapter 11. The last of these was a giant: Sequoia National underwrote $19.7 billion in premiums and was 3 percent of the market. Regulators could not allow it to fail. A rescue package was cobbled together by Treasury and the Fed, buying up some of its most toxic policies and putting the full faith and credit of the US government behind payments. The chairman of the Fed was appearing on TV so frequently to explain his motives, he felt like the de facto leader of the country. Vic Love had still not appeared in public since October. Stimulus packages were floated, though one needed a president to pass such a measure.

The housing panic chewed up and down the Eastern Seaboard, the Gulf Coast, and California. Banks had spent years off-loading risky mortgages to Fannie Mae and Freddie Mac, which now owned so many that the two were effectively insolvent, and government rescues would be necessary. Yet the crisis extended well beyond the coasts. Owners like my brother were scrambling to get rid of property as far as twenty miles inland. People were walking away from their mortgages in droves, not willing to put another red cent into a property that was uninsurable and, they assumed, doomed to be washed away by the next hard rain. The foreclosure rate had hit 1.53 percent, its highest since 2010.

On January 12, The Pastor released a video addressing the American people. He sat calmly, legs crossed, pinkie ring with its diamond crucifix beaming brightly, hair carefully slicked back. In a measured tone, he explained that as president he would not be bailing out a single bank or insurance company:

"For too long, elites have led this country to ruin. You and I both know that. They have stolen from you to line their own pockets. They've mocked your faith, they've told you your opinions don't matter, and they've behaved like you don't matter. Well, I'm saying no more. All right? No more of this. The vote has moved to the House of Representatives, and I'm urging them to delay not one more day. When I'm president there will be an accounting in this country. Those who've suffered under the current regime, we will rise now. And those who've brought us yet again to crisis, they will pay the price."

I could not sleep at all. In the middle of the night, I had an anxiety attack. I perched on my knees over the toilet in the guest bedroom and waited to throw up, though I never did.

"They've got to install him, right?" Fred Jr. said the next day. We woke to the news that the House had delayed the vote yet another week, and Fred Jr. had come to our place, basically to panic as his portfolio cratered. Mine wasn't doing much better. "Right? Like what is everyone waiting for?"

Fred was fiddling with the cleaning robot, which had been doing circles all day after he'd mucked with the settings. "Peter doesn't seem to think anyone actually knows how to stop this. Except his brother-in-law, but al-Hasan claims we have to socialize the entire economy, more or less."

"Well, what the fuck does that guy know?" demanded Fred Jr.

Fred shrugged. "He did design our models."

Fred Jr. put his face in his hands. "Okay, what about security, Dad?"

"We have it," Fred assured him.

"I don't mean at the offices, I mean everywhere." Stupidly, he looked from side to side as if what he was about to say was any big revelation. We'd all seen the news from Chicago, where protests at the Board of Trade erupted in riots. The police were still battling protestors and rioters in the streets, looters were sowing chaos all over the city, and the governor had called in the National Guard. Twenty-four dead and countless injured so far. "People are looking for someone easy to blame. People don't turn into animals; they were always animals just waiting for a chance to let it out."

Fred gave him a disappointed look. He'd always resisted this absurd new trend, growing since the unrest of 2020, where even low-level traders employed security services and rode around in armored cars. Of course, all I'd cared about when Fred and I bought our penthouse with the Juliet balcony was the flood control. Yet the Realtor had assured us that the building contracted with a private security service.

To change the subject, I asked, "Do you want to stay for dinner, Freddy?"

He looked at me like we weren't living on the same planet.

"You're not taking this seriously."

Fred stopped fiddling with the robot. "Freddy, I've got things handled, okay? If this really gets nuts, we're on a list for a resort. They fly you out there, it's the middle of nowhere, there are armed guards, and it's like its own self-sustaining city."

"I can't believe we're talking about this," I said, laughing.

"Dad, there was a story on those resorts in the *Times*—everyone knows about them!"

"Oh my God, Freddy, give it a rest. It's not even going to come to that."

He went back to punching the panel of the cleaning robot.

*

On January 19 with the economy in freefall, the House of Representatives met to vote on the next president. I went into the offices that day, passing our security guard, Lennox, who was reading on his phone with a look on his face like he was watching a VR torture xpere. "Everything okay?" I asked him.

"Naw. Definitely not. They're doing it all again. Same old shit, nothing ever changes."

But something might change now, I thought. Everything might change. All at once.

We spent the morning going through the motions, unable to stop checking the TV on our back wall, tuned to CNN. They left up an image of the mostly empty chamber where a man had set himself on fire more than two years ago. Aides puttered around, waiting for the vote. Everyone was filled with the dread of not knowing what the next day would bring, if we'd wake up in the morning and the country would be dissolved and money wouldn't come out of the ATM and the water would be shut off. I pretended to peck around some work until the afternoon when Kate poked her head in.

"Hey, Wall Street, any interest in taking a walk?"

The two of us strolled down Hylan Boulevard, and then turned east onto Tysens, heading toward the water. She rambled on about nothing in particular, mostly describing the flooding that was slowly eating Staten Island alive, pointing to this or that marker where the bay had backed up the sewer lines, this or that property newly condemned. As we neared the beach, a line of abandoned homes had been left to rot, mold, and rust while they waited for the bulldozer. Pink fiberglass scraps from destroyed walls lay in the yards.

"Holly says the baby isn't a good sleeper," said Kate. "She and Dean are averaging about three hours a night. Which sucks. We need her. Other than you, she's the only real voice of dissent."

"Sometimes I feel like they all hate me. And I don't really blame them."

Kate beamed a smile and kicked a rock out of the road. She walked with her hands in the pockets of black pants that didn't really fit her. She wore a

light thrift-store corduroy jacket with elbow patches over a T-shirt that read
You Are So Much Less Attractive When I'm Sober.

"Maybe you are a capitalist stooge, Jackie. But activists and capitalists
have at least one thing in common: They all have tunnel vision. Thinking
around and through things isn't exactly their specialty. Maybe that's why
I've been such shit at activism."

"Don't fish for compliments," I told her.

"No, for real. If I could go back to 2018 or so I can't even start to list the
things I would've done differently. The chances I missed. I would've been
surgical, precise. Maybe we could've targeted state utility commissions like
a laser and actually put a dent in our carbon load. That's what I mean by tunnel vision. All we've ever had is the surety of our cause and that's apparently
not worth much."

"I don't think you think that's true."

"Well, it doesn't matter, does it? When The Pastor's president in about
three hours, the financial implosion will be the least of our problems. All of
us on the vagina squad will be forced to bear the bastard children of our mistaken sexual partners. Or he'll just hang us. You nervous, Wall Street? You
look like a lady who's had an ah-bo-bo or two in her day."

"Just a miscarriage."

Kate's jokey grin faded. I'm not sure why I told her that. I'd never told
anyone about it.

After a moment she said, "I've had three. Abortions, not the other one.
The first when I was nineteen, and I felt all the normal feelings you're not
supposed to say you feel. The next two I barely gave a second thought. Joked
with the nurse about getting a card punched so the fourth would be free.
Then went to a bar a night later for tequila shots. Didn't even tell Matt."

We passed a house close to the beach that was missing its porch, torn
free by floodwaters that hadn't even made the news in Midtown.

"Did you ever want kids?" she asked.

"Yes. For a long time. And then it just didn't work out that way."

"Why?"

"Fell in love with someone who already had one. How about you?"

"Nah." She took a hand from her pocket so she could bat it at the breeze.
"Didn't interest me. I could lie and say I couldn't justify it ethically in the
middle of a mass extinction, resource scarcity, and ecological collapse, blah
blah blah, but the truth is, kids were never gonna be my thing. I was built
for speed."

We reached Oakwood Beach where the wind blew harder and a gray steel cloud cut across a darker titanium sky. The road was filthy with loose litter and plastic debris coughed up by the bay.

Kate passed me a shy glance, which did not look at home on her tough and beautiful face. "What I'm trying to ask, Wall Street, is what's your dissent? If you had to say something the rest of us don't want to hear, what would it be?"

I shook my head in defeat. "It's hard for me to give you a real answer to that. You've done things in your life that simply defy the laws of gravity. Things I didn't ever think could've been pulled off. I admire you a lot, Kate. I always have."

She had one eye scrunched closed from half a grin. "Even when you were working to stone me."

"Even then." I hesitated. "How do you live with this all the time? The fear."

She looked darkly at the water. "Like when Love's stormtroopers had just massacred seven-hundred-plus people and were closing in? Or when I was sitting in prison wondering if I'd ever see my family again let alone a lawyer?"

"Yes, that, but—I mean like right now. All of it."

Kate hocked up the snot in her throat and thwapped a loogie in the sand. Across the Lower Bay we watched the turbid, white-capped Atlantic shifting plates of slate and blue.

"When I was in college, I went on a rafting trip up in Alaska on a wild river. One night we were camping, just me and a bunch of guys, so I kind of walked a good ways away from the fire because I needed to go a number two. So as I'm finishing up, kicking dirt over it, and getting my pants up, I look up and there's this"—she held her hands wide—"this enormous fucking grizzly. I swear to God, it was the size of a car. Maybe only ten feet away, just watching me."

"Jesus."

"I was totally paralyzed. I just stood there, and me and this bear, we stared at each other. And I was so fucking scared, I could feel the tears on my cheeks, but I didn't know where they were coming from. They didn't feel like mine. Then finally, this bear, it just turns. And it goes ambling in the other direction like it was bored with me. That's when I realized I hadn't taken a breath in like a minute, and I still couldn't move. I was frozen there for so long, and honestly, I couldn't believe I was alive. It was such a beautiful creature, and it was so"—she shook her head—"so totally fucking terrifying

I kind of used up all the fear in my life right then. Been living on borrowed fear ever since." And then she looked at me, her eyes searching. "You're no good to me if you ignore your instincts, Jackie."

I cleared my throat. "Then I think you need to consider calling these protests off for now." It was such a relief to say it. "I know it goes against your every fiber, Kate, but everything is in flux, and they're targets. They're fueling unrest. You could be a voice of stability instead of disruption. Does that make sense? What Rekia is trying to do with A Fierce Blue Fire—getting food to people who can't afford it, shelter to all the displaced, a sense of solidarity—it's not radical and it's not as sexy, but people are really scared right now."

"Oh, they're not scared." She looked back to the water. "They're positively terrified. And that's why we need to keep going. Controlled and careful, but we need to keep going. People need a vision and a demand, something to focus their anger and sadness on. They need to believe we can change this—*I* need to believe we can change this. I need to believe that no matter how fucked and horrifying things get, the possibility for a radical new world will never be over. It will never be too late. Not as long as I've got even one motherfucking breath in my lungs."

I blinked a few tears out of my eyes and wiped them away. "Sorry. It's more from exhaustion than anything."

"Nah, girl, you're feeling what's real right now. You've spent your whole life in a cubicle and boardroom trying not to feel it. Have a cry!" She put a cold hand on the back of my neck and gave me a playful pinch. "When it rocks you once, it tends to rock you forever."

I laughed. "I don't understand how you've had the energy for this for twenty years."

She curled a lip, bobbing her head back and forth. "Cocaine? Sex that makes the news? Global amounts of trouble?" I laughed harder. "When this is all over, Jackie, you and me will do a few jumbo rails and hit the town."

"Oh my God, I'm definitely not doing that."

Then she was on a tear describing what our outlandish night out might entail, and we were both cracking up. We ambled down the beach, me and this woman I barely knew, and it felt as though her laughter by itself might shatter the darkness I'd carried inside for so long.

*

After Kate took me on that walk along the Staten Island shore, I caught the ferry back to Manhattan, spending the ride glued to my tablet, toggling between updates about the vote in the House and the disintegrating financial system where all my assets and savings lay exposed and vulnerable. For all the work I'd put in to make my person and position secure, it turned out all that wealth was illusory, only as meaningful as the willingness of others to believe it had any value at all.

When I got off the ferry, I was looking for the black car, when someone touched my arm.

"Jackie."

The look on Fred's face was one I'd not seen in all the years we'd been together.

"Hey! What are you—"

"Just explain to me why."

"Why what?" And when I said that, it was genuine. As if he was there to accuse me of reprogramming the cleaning bot to skip certain rooms in our home. I finally recognized what was clouding his face. I'd never actually seen him furious before.

"Why don't we walk?" I suggested.

He looked north to the Covid-19 Memorial, the embattled stone nurse behind a mask and face shield intubating a dying man. He clenched his jaw and nodded. We started across the Battery to the east, both of us silently agreeing to head away from Wall Street, as if the contamination happening there was airborne even beyond the capabilities of that long-ago pandemic.

"How did you figure it out?" I asked him.

"I think I knew all along. Ever since the story appeared. I just didn't want to know it." I looked up at him because that wasn't an answer. "We thought it was an analyst inside Tara. We were monitoring all of them for months. Finally, the cybersecurity guys got a hold of the actual leaked document. They all have e-signatures, Jack. It was the one I sent you."

"Should I ask how the cyber guys got a hold of that document?"

Fred hesitated. "No. And that's why this all has to go away."

Even though he'd made this tacit admission that he had one foot in the shadows, I still found myself apologizing. "I'm sorry, Fred."

"Are you?" His tone was genuinely curious. He palmed his beard, rubbing it furiously like it was stage makeup he was trying to tear off. "When you started going down to those silly little spirit rallies at the gas station, I didn't say anything. When you quit the fund, I didn't say anything. When you went to work for Morris, a woman we used to mock—"

"You used to mock."

"I didn't say anything. I never discouraged you or said a nasty word about any of it because I've always trusted you. We have investment strategies in place for a reason. We are a forward-looking fund built on socially responsible models that—"

"Socially responsible," I said plainly. "Fred, you were long on a company that's institutionalized human trafficking as its core business model. That moves dispossessed people into slavery."

He shook his head. "That's bullshit, Jackie. You've been reading all the propaganda, so now you have that stupid, ignorant frame on it."

"Then what do you call it?"

"Nosiki helps people find work and a home! If you didn't notice the world is swarming with people who don't have either."

"And prison companies to house the ones who either won't or can't indenture themselves. And security companies to guard them. And walls to keep them out—yeah, in the future, they'll really be singing songs around the campfire about Tara Fund's noble work, I'm sure."

"Jesus Christ, you've really drank the Kool-Aid and joined the cult, huh? We work with incredibly complex algorithms that are managing this. That's how this works. They decide where the investments go to keep energy cheap, markets functioning, and the economy flowing, but instead of dealing with that reality, it's like our whole society wants to stop vaccinating its children all at once."

"You wanted to know why I did it, so I told you, Fred. Because I'm ashamed. I'm ashamed of the way we got what we have."

He laughed. "That's rich. This is a conversation with the woman who ran up a bill of $167,000 at Brunello Cucinelli last year."

"Yeah, but you have to admit that Balmain coat really did look good on me."

This joke did not land and got carried off into the sound of East Side traffic and one particularly noisy truck coughing diesel fumes. Dusk was settling over the city, a crimson flame cutting through the towers, reflecting off the mountains of steel and glass encasing southern Manhattan. The world's tallest Ferris wheel loomed over the water, its lights popping on. Now I could hear the chants drifting down from the Financial District, and when we passed Old Slip, I could see a middling crowd pumping its fists in the air, surrounded by NYPD. *"No Justice, No Peace! No Vengeance, No Sleep!"*

Fred did not even appear to notice. We walked in silence for a while as the chant faded and the Brooklyn Bridge came into view, all that cable webbing so spider-perfect it almost looked a part of nature. Like the earth had grown this dark and lovely arch over its own water.

"Jackie, we did nothing illegal. And I wouldn't have gone along with anything if I thought for a second it was. We had a team of lawyers looking at every move we ever made. The general counsel and head of compliance aren't just for show."

"Legal doesn't mean it's right, Fred. I thought that would be obvious."

"You think I don't wonder if I'm an awful person?" He said it so suddenly, a defiant admission. "Of course I do. Everyone should wonder. How could I not, when I have a son who . . ." He exhaled slowly. "Who did what he did to that kid." He was quiet. The bridge glowed with the gold of the disappearing sun while the skyscrapers glittered to life. A kebab scent wafted off a halal cart. The big-eared vendor could see we were in an argument, but his expression remained vacant as we passed. When we were a safe distance away, we stopped. I slipped my hands into the pockets of Fred's coat. Felt his cold, soft palms. Then I put my cheek in his beard.

"I don't expect you to forgive me," I whispered.

"I'm not worried about forgiving you." He drew one hot breath right by my ear. "If you would do something this cruel to me, you clearly think I'm someone else. Someone different from the person you've been with all these years. I'm more worried about you forgiving me. I love our life together so much. When I met you, Jackie, I was miserable; I had nothing but a failed marriage." He choked a bit on what he said next. "And a son who did something I could never bring myself to forgive him for."

I put my forehead against his. He put his palms on my cheeks. "Fred."

"You put me back together. You made me glad to be alive again. And if you'd just said something. If you had told me what you were thinking, I swear to God, Jack, I would've burned Tara to the ground for you."

I pulled his body against mine then, as sirens started up from the north, as a black NYPD helicopter thundered overhead. Falling sunlight poured through the canyons of Manhattan, absolutely blinding, lighting the streets on fire, and casting the city as a bold and haunting ruin.

We got back to our place as the last light fled the Midtown sky. The stout cleaning robot was zooming around, mopping and dusting and vacuuming and straightening in whatever algorithm dream it inhabited. Fred withdrew his phone from his breast pocket, and I could see there was something on it worth knowing.

"What?"

"Turn on the TV."

"What happened?"

"Turn on the TV. They voted on a new president."

*

The next day, like any other, I took the ferry across the harbor. I drank my coffee and watched the TV playing the news. But there was hardly anyone inside because most of the passengers had gone to the starboard side of the ship. They were all, very sincerely, very cornily, gazing at the Statue of Liberty as we passed. Nearly every passenger. People had genuine tears in their eyes. A man held his glasses out from his face to get a better angle with the camera as the morning sun lit up the statue. A girl, a true Staten Island beauty with crimson nails, white platform shoes, and a squall of an accent, told her boyfriend how they displayed just the statue's head elsewhere until they built the whole thing. A small boy rested on his father's shoulder, tuckered out, while a little girl asked irreverent questions, wondering if the lady could walk off her pedestal or perhaps even fly. It wasn't my imagination. I could feel us all catching each other's glances, because for some reason, watching this icon bathed by the winter sun, we were no longer afraid. And looking at each other, we could see that we were not afraid.

Kate had texted the organizing committee and said we were going to have an emergency meeting: *Time to figure out what to do about this monkey-fucked pony-show situation.* The offices were frenzied that morning. Everyone had an opinion, an argument, an idea. Jenice and Tavia brought doughnuts, and the heat wasn't working, so Carmen was on the phone trying to get a repairman to come take a look. Liza was swamped by Seventh Day hubs asking what this meant for the looming February actions, while Garrett kept screaming that we had media outlets from New York City to Tokyo who wanted Kate's take on this development. Where would the Seventh Day protests go from here? Facing the headwinds of an impossibly chaotic news cycle, we were still growing. What she said next would matter.

"No pressure," said Kate. "And it's still fucking freezing in here."

We were all in our coats. I'd actually worn the Balmain that day. By one o'clock we were talked out, exhausted, and hungry. Carmen ordered Thai, so we could keep going. By the time we were eating no one wanted to say one more word about politics and the man about to be sworn in on his own Bible that day.

So Garrett brought up Zeden announcing she would "auction her body for the climate." The plan, as breathless pop culture outlets reported, was for the pop star to sell herself to the highest bidder for no less than tens of billions of dollars.

"And then she says she'll finance major pieces of decarbonization herself!" he gushed.

"While she's a slave?" said Jenice. "Yeah, I don't see what dreadful precedent this could set."

"She wouldn't technically be a slave," said Carmen from the receptionist desk where she was back on hold with the building manager. People had stopped working to gather around in the conference room.

"Our possession of our own corpus is a social construct like anything else," said Liza.

"And what if some billionaire decides he wants to make a torture xpere out of her?" Jenice demanded. A few of us had started to crack up at this absurd conversation.

"The money she'll raise isn't a social construct," said Tavia.

"Uhhh," said Liza, "money is the most constructed thing of all."

"I think," said Kate, dropping a huge helping of noodles from chopsticks into her mouth and talking while she chewed, "if this VR pop-star bitch somehow creates a green hydrogen glut that wrecks the market for dirty energy by wearing Little Bo-Peep outfits for Larry Page, Zeden might be a genius, and I missed my calling."

At this point we were all laughing so hard my stomach hurt.

"Her next tour in a neck manacle will make a billion socially constructed dollars," said Liza.

That's when the fire alarm went off. We all jumped. It was an older building and the blaring incantation reminded me of middle school drills, the sound abrasive, alien, and unendurable. Coupled with a strobing white light from the smoke detectors on the walls, the noise had all of us craning our heads around the room searching for some smoky source.

Is it a drill? Do we have drills?" Kate shouted over the din.

"No idea!" Liza yelled back.

"I guess, let's go?" Kate stood and started in the direction of the stairs. *"Fucking food'll be cold. It's always something, right!"*

"I'm gonna grab my purse!" I shouted, but no one heard me. I ducked into the office I shared with Liza and Garrett. Another alarm I'd never noticed was positioned directly over my desk. The purse was on my chair, but my phone wasn't inside. The noise was a drill bit in my head, and for a moment I couldn't remember what I'd done with the phone. I looked back through the window to the main room, thinking maybe I'd left it on the table, but people were filing out, and that's when I watched a man come up out of the stairwell. At first I thought he was maintenance, there to fix the heat or stop the alarm. That was how he was dressed: dark shirt, dark pants, boots, and he was carrying a tool. He had a sharp nose and dimpled chin, long hair parted in the middle and tucked back behind each ear. His forehead was red and shiny, and he reminded me very much of a friend of my father's, a guy who'd sold him farm equipment and who he'd played poker with every month. Because of that distant memory, it was a friendly face, a trustworthy one. But Kate and the others stopped short, like they'd each smacked an invisible wall. That's when the man raised his weapon and started firing.

Three brittle metallic explosions thundered over the fire alarm, and the first bullets tore through Liza's shoulder and ripped through the back of her throat in a pulpy red splash. Liza fell, and Carmen screamed and scrambled under a table, and the man stepped forward into our offices, a look of calm concentration on his face, finger jerking, shoulder bucking with each kick of the gun, and Tavia crumpled like she'd been punched in the gut, and then through the gut, and Jenice cried out, tried to move toward her wife and two bullets tore her arm almost entirely off her body so that sharp bone came shredding out of the meat of her bicep, and I just stood there, feeling the skin of my breasts go taut, the way it does when you swim in frigid water. The fear spread, ancestral, primitive, evolutionary, something beyond nation-states and law and art and free enterprise systems and even the capacity of humans to articulate or comprehend, just a full-body contraction, bottomless and paralyzing. Plaster sprayed in huge chunks from the walls, and I could see the individual beads of sweat on this man's forehead, as he traced the line of fire across the offices, and everyone was screaming and running, diving under desks, trying to find cover, but the only exits were the elevator and stairs, both behind him. Then his sights found Kate, because instead of running she'd crouched beside Liza, who'd fallen at her feet, and even sitting here trying to write this now, I can't bear the thought of what I saw, what a weapon of war can do to a human being, to the bone and blood and flesh of their infinitely precious and concrete form, even though I have to watch it in my dreams over and over and over and over again.

Kate had an expression not of fear but disbelief. Disbelief that this could be happening. Her lips pushed outward like she was about to say the word *wait*. Then the bullet ripped her face away, taking a whole section of skull and cheek and hurling the fragments against the wall, and the next round punched a hole beneath her rib cage the size of a fist, and she was blown backward, collapsing awkwardly into a pile of her own limp limbs. Suddenly, there was water spraying from the walls, one of the rounds bursting a pipe, and for some reason the hiss of water snapped me out of it. Someone was screaming, the rounds were still booming, the fire alarm shrieking, and my eyes met Carmen's. She was under the conference table, and her face begged me to do something, and that's when I zipped myself down to the floor behind my desk and clamped my hand to my mouth to keep from screaming and bit my tongue as hard as I dared because I was sure he would hear me sobbing. I went somewhere then, a blackout or a fugue, falling away into some undiscovered void, a fear so depthless, it blotted out reason and logic. I'm sure I flinched in terror at each explosion of the rifle, but I don't remember.

I didn't scream until the NYPD officer put his hand on my shoulder. The fire alarm was still blaring, and when the officer tried to lift me up from behind my desk, I just started slapping at him, even though I could see it was not the man. Finally, my hands caught up to what was happening, to the kindness in his face and the incredible pale blue of his eyes. I pictured him with daughters, and how he might put them on his shoulders or peel Band-Aids onto their scraped knees. The room had filled with smoke. He half carried me out, and I let myself be led. He told me not to look, his voice anguished, but I had to, and I saw the shooter on the ground, gore dripping from his chin where he'd placed the barrel, and there was the conference table overturned, and there was Carmen, her entire left side cut open, eviscerated, and all her organs outside her body. The air reeked of gunpowder and the metallic tang of blood. The officer whispered reassurances that it was over, that I had survived. The alarm stopped, so then there was only the hiss of water and phones ringing in the pockets of the dead. As he practically dragged me across the wet floor, the pipe still gushing from the wall, soaking the carpet, I simply couldn't help but look. You don't know what blood is until you've seen it that way: indiscriminate, slapped across walls and tables and chairs and hanging in stringy clusters and wet chunks of tissue and shards of bone. And I could see what was left of Kate, her face gone, her torso almost cut in half. It was impossible to believe that somewhere in this unknowing matter lie all our demons, the real ones and the ones we dream into being ourselves, and all I could think was, This is real. This is what has happened.

A Contemporaneous Account of the Eco-Economic Crisis of 2037

Ashir Al-Hasan

AUGUST 15, 2037

Abstract: I've never recorded anything for the sake of posterity, but that is the position in which I now find myself. There is a very real possibility the nation will see widespread breakdown of a functioning, governable society in the coming months, and it may be that the only contribution I have left to make is this unvarnished account. Even in the grip of this unfolding chaos, history demands primary source documentation, and I believe I carry as much responsibility as anyone for our failure to arrest this crisis.

//

Following the hasty invasion and military occupation of Pakistan last September, there were rumors President Love's cabinet would remove him. As a scientist with the Global Change Research Program, I was at the far periphery of events, yet due to my close relationship with Texas representative Tracy Aamanzaihou, I was privy to disturbing news emanating from the White House: The president had stopped speaking to his advisors and refused to leave the residence. Congresswoman Aamanzaihou was furious:

"The whole donor class and Democratic Party infrastructure twisted my arm to drop out, even when they knew he was losing it. And now we're all going to pay."

Due to voting irregularities, disputes, and suspect rulings from the Supreme Court, no candidate collected the necessary 270 electoral votes, and therefore the decision fell to the House of Representatives, using the procedure spelled out in the Constitution in which each state delegation has one vote and a candidate must garner at least twenty-six votes. By this arcane arithmetic there would be enough Republican votes in a majority of states to place The Pastor in the White House. However, in the weeks leading up to this vote, a series of banking and insurance failures threw the economy into turmoil. The stock market plunged, foreclosures and unemployment spiked, and credit tightened. When the Treasury secretary and the chairman of the Federal Reserve improvised deals to save several insurers and a major bank holding company, The Pastor employed his typical approach of populist fury to make clear he would let any and all financial institutions collapse before he allowed the rise of American socialism. As my sister, Haniya, put it:

"We dodged this guy not because he was a fascist promising to incinerate nonbelievers in a hail of nuclear hellfire but because Wall Street got spooked they wouldn't get their bonuses."

In the end, Republican majority leader Russ Mackowski brokered a deal with the Democratic caucus: If the Democrats would agree to his terms, he could get his allies to deadlock the vote so that no candidate would have the requisite twenty-six votes, and then the Senate could vote for the vice presidential candidate, who would serve as acting president. The Pastor's camp howled about this maneuver, but Warren Hamby, an unknown and previously unremarked-upon two-term congressman from Orange County, California, who was grafted to The Pastor's ticket only to allay fears of the firebrand, was essentially installed as president of the United States. After a vicious election, this was a jarring but relieving development. Markets rose initially, only to topple again when Hamby gave an inauguration speech from the Oval Office. He had to pause several times to loudly swallow his own spit.

Congresswoman Aamanzaihou asked me to prepare a white paper on the nature of the crisis and what might be done to avert catastrophe. I obliged, spending sixteen frenzied days researching and writing. During this time, a funeral was held for the activist Kate Morris. Wrapped in a shroud, her body would go to provide the nutrients to a young redwood tree in an Oregon forest. Most channels were streaming the ceremony live, well-attended as it was by numerous celebrities, politicians, and activists, and I set aside my work to listen to the speech by Holly Pietrus, daughter of my colleague. My great animosity toward Kate Morris for the role she'd played in Seth's death had persisted even after the news that she and twelve others had been gunned down. With her eulogy, Holly helped to dissipate it. She finished with a quote from Gabriel García Márquez:

"If I knew that this would be the last time I would hear your voice, I'd take hold of each word to be able to hear it over and over again. If I knew this was the last time I'd see you, I'd tell you I love you, and would not just assume foolishly you know it already."

My acquaintance Matt Stanton was not in attendance, but I thought of how he must have felt watching the grotesque revelry of Morris's opponents at her horrific end. I thought of our frequent powwows over slushies in the summer of '29. How little we knew then about what the ensuing decade would bring. Suddenly, I felt a deep and deserved shame at my petty indifference to Morris's death. How foolish we can all be, indeed.

//

By the time I turned in the white paper draft to the congresswoman in May, unemployment had reached 19.3 percent. Prevarication by Hamby and Congress had allowed the crisis to expand. Thirteen days later, on May 20, after blocking President Hamby's choice for Treasury secretary, Majority Leader Mackowski acquiesced and allowed the confirmation of Martin Rathbone, a longtime Democratic economist who'd begun his career in Treasury during the 2007–08 crisis, returned briefly for the Randall administration, and resigned as Loren Victor Love's head of the National Economic Council after the siege of Washington.

On May 25, I got a call from the office of Alice McCowen, requesting my presence at 1500 Pennsylvania Ave, the Treasury Building. I'd been pleased to see her announced as Warren Hamby's chief of staff. For all Alice's flaws, she is not stupid and she is not scared of much—two traits that would be very useful in a panic of this magnitude.

With dozens of top positions still requiring Senate confirmation, the Treasury Building felt like an empty warehouse. The district had gone into preemptive lockdown in January as protests and violence broke out in other cities around the country. Capitol Police and National Guard manned checkpoints on every street. We met not in the secretary's office but in a marginal workspace the size of a large closet. Alice exuded her typical bombastic energy, while Secretary Rathbone came to the meeting in sweat-stained workout clothes, chugging thirstily from a water bottle. A towering, handsome, meagerly intelligent man, I've always thought Rathbone to be arrogance incarnate, yet now he looked deeply perturbed. He began by making light of his appointment:

"Clearly, Russ Mack only let me through so he could kick the shit out of me. I'll tell you, Ash, you think our trip around the world to look at famine was dark. Wait'll you see the industrial production indicators."

Alice said: "The good news is that Congress and Wall Street are out of options. The world's burning, and they're going to have to start accepting whatever enema we tell them to jam up there."

"Do you speak for the president?" I asked her.

"The president? Don't make me laugh. Hamby is a president like I'm a fucking astrophysicist. He's terrified. Sold his soul to get on The Pastor's ticket, and now he wants to hide under the table."

Rathbone said: "We have a road map. Bailouts and stress tests like we did in '09. We let no systemically important institution fail. Then we hit this fucker with stimulus that will make the Covid-19 packages look like Austrian economics."

I reflected: "Given the scale of the crisis, that sounds more like sober gradualism than anything else and may only pause the carnage momentarily. Nor will stimulus be as simple as the CARES Act."

Said Alice: "That's why you're here, dummy. Your white paper for Aamanzaihou's been making the rounds on the Hill and in the policy shops."

Rathbone nodded. "My expertise in the grounding line ice discharge of drainage basins in Antarctica is elementary. But I know financial panics, and we are on a clock here. This depression will not be great, greater, or greatest, it will be the fucking dark ages. You say this runs deeper, Ash. Well, we need to know how deep."

Thus, I launched into my theory of the case, which I will summarize in abbreviated version below.

1. Homeowners in flood plains, Wall Street firms, and major insurers alike all rely on the predictability of risk. With developments like ARkSTORM, Cyclone Giri, and the sudden increase in the rate of sea level rise (among others), risk models were categorizing the confluence of these exogenous calamities as a 37-sigma event, or 37 standard deviations away from the norm. How likely is a 37-sigma event? A modest 8-sigma is supposed to happen less than once in the history of the universe. In this context, the large providers of financial products—mortgages, home insurance, pensions—simply could not shift risk away from their portfolios. In some cases, as with beach sand replenishment or ill-advised insurance markets, the government has subsidized climate risk,

which has undermined everything from firm-level financial valuations to the value of vacation homes.

2. Dramatic events like the human and economic catastrophe of California gather headlines, but the more dire issue is sea level rise. If we look to where the crisis began in the low-lying areas of Florida, especially Miami, we see a simple chain of events. Home values collapsed as buyers began to realize that nuisance flooding (forget catastrophic hurricanes) would soon render their property worthless as groundwater regularly brings sewage into the streets. When Congress tried to increase rates for the National Flood Insurance Program to reflect its enormous indebtedness incurred by the Great Eastern Flood and ARkSTORM, the removal of even a sliver of this subsidy caused enormous pain. This priced out low- and middle-income homeowners but was not high enough to actually stop the buildup of risky and expensive properties. Borrowers faced the inability to repay mortgages and those who could sell were typically unable to recoup enough money to repay the mortgage principal, leading to a sharp spike in defaults. Meanwhile, banks were refusing to offer mortgages for flood-prone properties, and in the past fifteen years, this has decimated the tax base of numerous communities, leading to neighborhood blight and further collapse in property values. Municipal services were cut off, first in low-income and now middle-income areas, while rating agencies began downgrading the bonds of coastal municipalities to junk status. Facing enormous borrowing costs or having lost access to credit entirely, the communities have no money for infrastructure repairs—sewer pipes, water lines, and electrical lines being destroyed by intruding seawater—which further lowers property values in a vicious cycle. As homeowners saw the futility of making payments on doomed homes, they began to default in large numbers.

3. Financial crises are typically proceeded by credit bubbles, and the explosion of new housing added to the coasts between 1990 and 2030, both in the US and globally, perhaps represents one of the most ignominiously stupid bubbles in the history of capitalism. Driven largely by the signorial class and its appetite for staring pointlessly at water but indulged by anyone with access to the necessary credit, this will render quaint the subprime

bubble of the aughts. The preposterous sight of beach homes crowding the shore while overflowing sewers and stormwater systems made roads regularly impassible, trapping residents during simple high tides, seems to have alerted homeowners too slowly. The bubble was also inflated by taxpayer subsidy, as federal flood insurance, dreadful zoning policy, and an absence of laws requiring risk disclosure allowed an unprecedented buildup across vulnerable coastline. In fact, the disastrous hurricanes of the last few decades have only served to fuel construction booms as federal disaster and insurance dollars arrive, no strings attached, and developers and speculators bid up the prices each time. The Pollution Reduction, Infrastructure, and Research Act of 2030 helped to fund a great deal of pointless coastal armament and beach replenishing for affluent communities that, of course, has mostly proved wasted effort. Paradoxically, even as sea levels have crept higher and storms have grown more intense, more people and more property have crowded the shoreline. Unfortunately, this coastal real estate bubble also coincided with another enormous consumer credit bubble that includes student loan debt, credit card debt, and auto loans. Beginning in the 1980s with liberalization and wage stagnation, credit essentially came to replace socioeconomic policy. Average workers and students have had to borrow more and more just to stay afloat and for the economy to sustain rising consumption. Now that mass layoffs have begun, those student loans, credit cards, and auto payments are going unserviced, and because those loans are also sliced and diced in securitization methods, it's rendering toxic large portions of the assets moving between major financial institutions.

4. There's been great hand-wringing and left-wing populist rhetoric that the bankers are again to blame, which I find a shallow and nonrigorous opinion. The Farooki piece in the *New Yorker* garnered widespread attention, but mostly missed the point. (And here I have to disclose my association with Tara Fund, one of the firms investigated in the piece, due to the fact that its manager is my brother-in-law.) As with many panics, any fraud is merely an addendum. All the activity described, from catastrophe bonds to the securitization and off-loading of coastal mortgage debt, was legal. CAT bonds, for example, driven by

investors seeking higher yields following decades of low interest
rates, were triggered by a few very expensive disasters, which
has led to a panicked sell-off. It is not a Ponzi scheme described
by leftist pundits, but a standard insurance bet gone wrong in an
era of climatological extremes. Wall Street's creation of financial
products to insure against climate risk had the effect of spreading it to every part of the system.

5. The difference between 2037 and 2020 is that there is no vaccine on the way for the greenhouse effect. The difference between 2037 and 2008 is that this panic is largely justified due to
sea level rise. While wild conspiracy theories have proliferated
on the internet (for instance, that the government is trying to
forcibly remove coastal homeowners to return it to the ancestors of the Seminole tribes), one can go to New Jersey beachfront communities and the homeowners will show you the water
spilling through their front doors. Many of these mortgages are
worthless because the physical infrastructure is destined to be
inundated. Miami alone has over $500 billion in threatened as-
sets. Pieces of the American coast have passed the geomorphic
threshold where they will suffer significant and irreversible
changes, by which I mean they cannot be defended. Looking out
over the next forty years, roughly 2.5 to 2.8 million homes are
under direct threat, which equates to over a trillion dollars in
real estate. But not all these homes are doomed. As with the food
crisis, *climate panic* is exacerbating the underlying trends. Florida's tax base is collapsing as people panic-sell, but they are panic-
selling even on high ground where water is unlikely to reach for
decades, if not centuries. The collapse of prices is reaching deep
inland as confusion and hysteria spread.

6. The panic in the US has been foreshadowed by what's happening
globally. One hundred and thirty port cities around the world
are seeing similar effects on their economies. In India, flooding
in the Bay of Bengal and the summer heat (at times breaching
an unthinkable 135 degrees F) is dragging much of the middle
class back into poverty, and this has served as the kindling for incredible violence against the Muslim minority and Bangladeshi
refugees. China similarly has so much coastal investment that the
panic will create even deeper social unrest as its once-booming

middle class is forcibly relocated. More ominously, the German government has growing concerns about Munich RE, the world's largest reinsurer. Stationarity is a bedrock principle of the insurance industry, but now several black swan events have cast doubt about the range of uncertainty created by climate risk, that weather phenomena might render insurance a virtually impossible business model. If the reinsurance giants begin to topple, the panic will turn to economic apocalypse. During the Great Depression, worldwide GDP fell 15 percent. This crisis, by my estimation, could shock global GDP by up to 35 to 40 percent. Standard countercyclical monetary policy is not of much use here, as most major central banks, including the Fed, the European Central Bank, and the Bank of England, have cut interest rates to zero since the economy began lagging. Aggregate demand continues to vanish. Stimulus will be key, but the Keynesian toolbox will not work until the roots of the crisis are addressed. At this point, I asked Secretary Rathbone what was at the root of all financial panics, to which he correctly replied: "Confidence."

7. Why won't confidence be restored with standard Keynesian policy? The answer is, again, sea level rise. Specifically, the dynamics of the West Antarctic Ice Sheet, which in the past five years has undergone a rapid transformation. To this day, modeling remains very primitive for the damage mechanics of ice shelf loss, but we can conclude that sea level rise will be more severe than anticipated because the Ghost Ridge appears to be structurally weaker than was once thought. (The ridge is a buildup of sediment forty-five miles behind the Thwaites Glacier's initial grounding line that was once expected to "catch" the glacier so that it would not slide rapidly into the ocean.) This is particularly bad news for the US, because one thing sea level rise models all agree on is that the Atlantic Seaboard will be one of the most highly impacted regions in the world. When an ice sheet melts, its gravitational pull weakens, which causes the earth beneath the sheets to rebound and counterintuitively *lowers* sea level locally. However, this means increased sea level rise for some distant locale, in this case, the metro regions stretching from Maine to Florida. This is to say nothing of steric changes,

as ocean temperatures heat up, which they are now doing faster than at any time in Earth's history, expanding the water. Confidence cannot be restored because sea level rise really may wipe out more wealth in one generation than both world wars and all the great economic crises combined. The question is, How do we stop such a rational panic?

8. To restore confidence globally, we must first restore it in the American economy where the crisis arose. Here we have one vital force on our side: The US government, more than any other, has ample room to maneuver. For now. But we must take advantage of this window and devise a top-down approach to defending the coasts. In some instances, this may mean hardening measures like seawalls, but more likely it will mean a program of "managed retreat." However, for that policy to work we must be able to compellingly reassure panicking markets that we have a plan to, once and for all, arrest, and at some distant point, reverse, catastrophic greenhouse warming. Even if we do somehow manage to accomplish this rather daunting geo-economic goal, we will still be left with the fallout—a period of economic stagnation without precedent, and one that may drive deep social and political divisions to the breaking point. In a world of such severe apartheid, suddenly left without the capacity to keep order, it's hard not to imagine the impoverished half executing the most vicious revolution the world has ever seen or the wealthiest quintile performing one last brutal all-encompassing act of genocide to save itself from the dark and harrowing future that's in store.

I looked from Secretary Rathbone to Ms. McCowen. Both appeared ill but not all that shocked. When giving voice to the consequences of a worst-case scenario, I realized I would have to work on my delivery.

"You see the difficulty, I gather. The problem is so vast in scale and complexity that incremental reform is no longer an option. The strategy necessary to avert global economic meltdown will, by necessity, alter human society forever."

McCowen slapped her thighs twice and clapped, and then continued to do so. She began singing Queen's "We Will Rock You." Rathbone looked unamused. When she was done, he asked:

"If you had to put a team together to design a policy—I'm talking about something that will shock the markets back into functioning order like a fucking defibrillator—who would you have in mind?"

"I'd prefer to keep it extremely small. I have several suggestions, including Jane Tufariello and my sister, Hani, who's been working in this policy realm at the Foote Institute for many years. And of course—"

"Tony."

"He literally did write the book on this scenario."

Alice offered no reaction when I brought up Jane, but she made quite a face at Tony's name.

Rathbone nodded. "Right, right, but I'll warn you: Industry will be there. Hamby won't have it any other way. Can you be ready by tomorrow?"

"Ready for what?"

Alice brimmed with excitement: "The president gets on TV to announce the formation of this crisis team—call it whatever you want. He says we're going to lock ourselves in a room and come out with a plan of overwhelming force to save us all from this nightmare. That sound fun?"

Said Rathbone, with a smile from the gallows: "Call it a task force to unfuck the world."

//

What I did not realize was that the Task Force to Unfuck the World, as it quickly became known, would not convene in Washington, D.C., but at a resort in Sun Valley, Idaho. There were too many security concerns in D.C., as protests and riots gripped the metro area nightly. It had not escaped my notice that many of the capital's elite—senators, CEOs, top lawyers, lobbyists—were also conveniently convening meetings and conferences at ultra-high-end resorts under somewhat specious pretenses. Peter explained that these vast vacation properties could be easily secured and were far from the simmering streets of a newly unemployed and frightened populace. I left Forrest under Peter's care, while Haniya and I flew on a government jet to Sun Valley.

Arriving at dawn, the sun's startling yellow spires pierced the gaps in the mountains to the west as we descended into a low brown valley. I'd barely unpacked before aides were knocking on my door, ushering Hani and myself to a most ostentatious boardroom. No one had eaten or slept, but we took our designated seats, with Ms. McCowen and Secretary Rathbone at the head of a conference table and a press pool snapping pictures.

There was Tony, looking quite disheveled, sallow-skinned, and grumpy; my friend and mentor Dr. Tufariello had changed her hair—she now sported a configuration of cornrows that swept gracefully back from the left side of her head; Joe Otero, aide to former Senate Majority Leader Doup and consummate Republican insider, dispatched to represent a political party he did not necessarily speak for, retained his graying punk rock ponytail; and Rear Admiral Michael Dahms, former commander of Pacific Command and a holdover as director of the Office of Climate Security, briefly joked with the press that he was "here representing that full-fledged pinko organization called the Pentagon," which got hearty laughs. I admired his ability to deflect from the fact that most of the government's scientific capacity was not represented. No one from NASA, the Office of Science and Technology Policy, the National Academy of Sciences, or the Council on Environmental Quality. Vic Love had intentionally left many of these offices vacant and concentrated their power under the fiefdom of Admiral Dahms. Hani sat beside him, looking unfazed and more well rested than myself, for she never seemed particularly impressed with the powerful circles she now frequented. Finally, sitting beside me was Emii Li Song, executive director of the Sustainable Future Coalition, looking irradiant in a tan skirt and white blouse, her hair complicatedly elevated. Tony, in hindsight, showed remarkable restraint. He waited until the press pool had left the room before he exploded:

"The fuck is she doing here?" His finger jabbed violently at Ms. Li Song as he looked from myself to Rathbone, who simply grimaced. Ms. Li Song, for her part, stared at him coolly. "No, really, someone explain? What is industry's walking multitool doing here?"

Said Secretary Rathbone: "Tony. Easy."

"Or are we just here to trade away the last of a habitable planet for a few concessions on light-duty vehicle standards?"

Ms. Li Song attempted: "Dr. Pietrus, I don't know what I can do to assure you I'm here in good faith—"

"Nothing. There's nothing you can do. We're here to cut the heads off your members once and for all."

Ms. Li Song spoke over him: ". . . But I represent industries vital to the functioning of the global economy. I also represent industries that know they have to change. That's why I'm here. To help pave the way for a transition of their business models. Everyone can come away from this process having won."

Tony stood, his face pink. He craned his neck forward and roared: *"Get fucked, lady!"*

Then he stormed out of the room. Alice McCowen glared at me like I was the one who'd erupted.

"Hasan, what are you—? Go fucking get him!"

I said: "Dr. Pietrus has a point, doesn't he? With no offense intended toward Ms. Li Song, her presence does seem inappropriate. Industry is represented but homeowners who've lost everything are not."

Rathbone pushed his hands through his silver hair, while McCowen simply stared at me in disbelief. Finally, she heaved her bulk up from the table and walked around to me, blinking rapidly. She stuck one enormous index finger in my face, and I could see she'd bitten the cuticle of the nail until it had bled.

"Listen to me, you fucking golem, we're not starting with the optics disaster of a key scientist walking after thirty seconds. The point of having Pietrus and Song in a room together is to show a united front against the crisis."

"If good press is the aim, perhaps it's better to hire a PR firm than recruit a physical oceanographer anyway."

"Hasan. If you don't go get him back in here right now, so help me God—I am a dyke with a dick and I will *fuck you with it* until your colon prolapses."

Upon the barking of the word *fuck*—so loud that Hani jumped in her chair—a good deal of spittle escaped Alice's mouth and landed on my face. I wiped it away. "Colorful."

I found Tony in his room, packing. He did not even look over his shoulder when I came in.

"Don't try to talk me into going back in there. Not if she's a part of this."

"We don't have a choice, Tony."

"Yeah, we do. I'll get on TV and scream bloody murder. Shame this fidgeting fuckwit Hamby until he takes her off the task force."

"As usual, Tony, you're thinking about this emotionally and not logically."

Tony threw a pair of underwear across the room with the theatrics of an actor trying to shatter a glass in a film. Instead, the pair of boxers poofed against the wall and flopped to the carpet.

"Fuck logically. Don't you get it? We're the stage dressing, Ash. We're here to give them cover, so they can put something together that'll calm the markets just enough to restore order without changing anything."

"Tony, if that's the case, I'll be there alongside you denouncing it."

This reassurance produced a tic in his face, the opening I was looking for. Tony had spent seventeen months wrongfully imprisoned in a federal detention center from mid-2033 through 2034 and had nothing to say on the matter. When I'd asked him about it, he waved it away like a vacation gone poorly. He was clearly traumatized but would likely never acknowledge it, let alone seek out a mental health professional. Wounded people, I've noticed, tend to welcome camaraderie. It is a key component of getting them to agree to what you want. I continued:

"I will stand before the microphones and cogitate against anything less than what's necessary. But we need to begin work right away. This crisis will either not go to waste or become a historical marker for the unraveling of our civilization. I'd prefer to make it the former, but that may require you to keep your cool, so to speak, over the next few weeks."

Tony grunted and looked bashfully at the floor. "It's definitely not appealing that the goddamned fate of the world relies on me keeping my cool."

//

The next day, I set the agenda with a forthright holograph deck about the fundamental issue we faced. The thirty-minute presentation included ghostly blue animations demonstrating the retreat of the Thwaites Glacier and the rapidity with which global sea levels would rise. There was a bowl of Starburst in the center of the table, which got passed around with gusto. Soon a mess of waxy rainbow-colored paper littered the surface.

I concluded: "We've talked preliminarily about a solution that could restore confidence in the financial sector. Dr. Rathbone?"

He held his growing middle-aged belly, languidly swiveling to deliver an explanation he felt self-evident: "It's pretty simple. We draw a line around the coast. Every square inch. It's not a bathtub model. It'll factor in topographical distinction and storm surge, but on one side of this line, we vow to defend by any means or cost necessary the property and infrastructure. On the other side, we initiate a managed retreat using a range of tools to draw homeowners, business, and communities back from the shores. We offer buyouts at pre-crisis rates for two years as the carrot. We reengineer the coasts to restore wetlands and plant mangrove forests—whatever we can do to create shock absorbers for storms and sea level."

The magnitude of this policy had the room in silence.

Finally, Jane cleared her throat: "That sounds alarmingly top-down. We have to ask who this is landing on? Mostly communities of color and the poor. We'd need a near-bottomless slush fund to finance a transition."

Said Alice to her former lover: "After all this time, gal, you're about to get your way like Santa backed up the BRINKS truck."

Tufariello shot her former partner a look. They had been steering very wide berths around each other since arriving in Idaho. I knew their relationship ended over a disagreement about when they would each retire. Alice had told Jane they'd have to cut her head off before she stopped working.

Rathbone went on: "Not to hand-wave at the relocation element of this, but that will be the relatively easy part. The hard part is generating rock-solid confidence in the line. We need to demonstrate clearly what homes, businesses, and infrastructure still have value."

Admiral Dahms's voice was the sound of raking gravel: "Exactly. I'm less concerned with the particulars of the retreat. Where do we draw this imaginary line?"

Because he did his homework, Joe Otero was ready with the Republican offer. "Our caucus is asking for something in line with the IPCC predictions: three feet by 2100."

In her surprise, Haniya reached out and touched my elbow. "Three feet? The rate of rise is accelerating."

"Keep in mind," said Secretary Rathbone, "every inch we move that line back increases the cost of this project exponentially, not to mention displaces more people. We need to be careful about sparking a new wave of panic-selling. We want to solve the problem, not exacerbate it."

Said Alice: "Isn't that what you big-brained PhDs got the free flight for? What do your models say?"

Haniya: "I think it's prudent to start talking about a *minimum* of six feet."

Otero: "No—no way. Six feet, and you're talking about buying out most of Miami and the Gulf Coast."

Haniya: "It's a reasonable estimate."

Otero: "That's a nonstarter."

Rathbone: "I agree. We're edging into furthering the panic instead of—"

Tony: "Fifty."

Everyone looked at Tony, myself included. The remaining hair on the back of his head was sticking up, like he'd not bothered to comb it after getting out of bed. Secretary Rathbone looked incensed: "Excuse me?"

"We should draw the line at fifty feet of sea level rise."

Otero snorted a laugh.

Rathbone chewed on a smile. "Sure, Tony. We'll just relocate all the coastal states to South Dakota and call it a day. Could we return to a serious discussion?"

"I'm perfectly serious, Marty. You all worship the IPCC like a holy text. It's been wrong consistently, and it's wrong now. Like Haniya said, the rate of rise is accelerating. Doubling roughly every seven years, in fact. There's no reason to think that'll abate. And given what's happening in West Antarctica, we have to assume that East Antarctica is not nearly as stable as we thought, nor Greenland. Trust me, fifty feet is not even the worst-case scenario. If all the ice on the planet melts, there's two hundred and thirty feet of sea level rise in there."

Said Admiral Dahms: "You're proposing a decades-long refugee catastrophe, not a managed retreat."

Rathbone shook his head. "It's ridiculous. We choose a politically realistic line and build the policy around that."

Tony's irritation bloomed. "This isn't some academic musing between economic Panglossians, Marty. The physics of marine ice cliff instability doesn't give two fucks about what's politically realistic."

Secretary Rathbone looked to me. "Ashir, what is the most realistic line you can give us that is not fifty fucking feet of rise. One we can start building policy around?"

I pretended to stew for a moment. One must be careful in the handling of difficult realities. People cannot hear bad news all at once. "I'll say fifteen feet by 2100, though I feel a great deal of hesitancy predicting that." Though the truth was I did not.

Secretary Rathbone looked to the ceiling in frustration. "Fifteen feet by 2100." He rubbed his eyes. "No way, no how can we use that number. Not without making everything worse."

I continued: "We are talking about an ensemble of processes of enormous complexity. In all my work on social and economic consequences of warming, not one system dynamics model spat out The Pastor's electoral victory or Victor Love's abdication or the political crisis that ensued. We can only do our best with the information we have available."

Rathbone regarded me wearily. "What the fuck are you talking about, Ash?"

Alice scolded him: "Rathbone, let the man have his say."

"Sorry! It would just be nice to know if this guy has any fucking nerve endings is all."

I went on: "Dynamic adaptive pathways planning can help us utilize the strategies that will work immediately. For instance, if we draw our coastal line too low, that may be okay, so long as aleatory uncertainty is priced in at certain topographical intervals."

Otero: "What?"

Dahms: "You're saying the solution—in regards to coastal retreat—is something low-end for now, but with a way of gradually moving people inland. Start with a line at three feet of rise and ratchet it up?"

Ms. Li Song finally spoke up: "Like a tax on homeowners, businesses, and renters living in the three- to ten-foot range. Then a smaller one in the ten- to fifteen-foot range."

Haniya: "But at speed. Still offering buyouts for a window of time."

Rathbone: "Call it a 'Get the Fuck Out the Way' tax."

Of course, I'd already thought of all this, but after a long career in science and politics, I've learned it's best to nudge people in the direction of the correct answer and allow them to think they've thought of it themselves. I told them: "Yes, that could arrest the present crisis while allowing room to maneuver in the future. What markets, media, and citizens need now is a sense that someone has command of the situation. Through many bizarre kinks and convolutions of history, that has fallen, at least for the moment, to us. Oh, and this is why I also think it would be best, Tony, if you, in place of Secretary Rathbone, addressed the media tomorrow."

//

If optics were key, then my intuition proved correct. At the presser, Rathbone turned the podium over to Tony, who unfolded a piece of paper and began reading in a dull monotone:

"Currently, we are in a death spiral of escalating foreclosures, a crashing real estate market, and toxic securities leading to a wider paralysis of the financial system. But these mortgages are obviously not all worthless, and we are not all doomed. We are going to simultaneously deal with the financial crisis and the climate crisis. We in the president's working group intend to draft legislation that will draw a defensible line around the coast of the United States and make people living on either side of that line secure so as to break the back of the panic. Then, through a program of economic stimulus, regulation, and adjustments to global trade we will finally speed the transition away from fossil fuels in order to stabilize planetary temperature rise below 2.5 degrees Celsius. Any questions?"

Thirty to fifty hands shot up, and a clamor for detail ensued. Tony remained impatient and irritated throughout. "Obviously, the devil will be in the details, and we don't want to preempt ourselves here. You'll see the full scope of our recommendations when we deliver it to the president and Congress."

The questions came rapid-fire: "When will that be?"

"Soon."

"Why are oil and gas companies represented in this process? How do you square that?"

"They are major stakeholders, but Earth's nine billion people and their interests will come first."

"Can you elaborate?"

"No."

"But how can one piece of legislation avert the chaos sea level rise will cause? And how can one bill seemingly reverse decades of inaction on global warming?"

"Look, you want me to tell you we're going to pass a bill and suddenly unicorns will start shooting out of my ass? Doubtful. But we'll all still have a civilization to wake up to in the morning. Next question."

"Will the country have to go deeply into debt to finance this plan? Will taxes go up?"

"You have an emergency, you called the lifeguard, now we're swimming our asses out to you in choppy waters. But you know what the worst part is about trying to save someone from drowning? They're panicking and trying to pull you down with them. Ask a better question next time."

It went on like that for forty minutes with Tony more or less grousing the reporting pool to silence without saying much at all about the policy we had not yet agreed upon whatsoever. He was very convincing.

/ /

For a month we proceeded. The urgency was dire, but there were simply too many contingencies to consider. On July 2, Joe Otero asked if he could have a word with me in private.

"I have to leave."

"For what reason?"

"The threats."

This was about The Pastor. He'd declared his former running mate, President Hamby, the Antichrist and our task force the devil's anti-Christian socialist takeover. In so many words, he was demanding violence to put a stop to whatever legislation we proposed. Because he represented congressional Republicans, Otero was being singled out by a collection of dangerous people with megaphones. Clearly, he was frightened even though the president had designated our meeting a Special National Security Event.

"Secret Service provides impeccable security, Joe. I'm sure they'll agree to intensified procedures."

"I can't, Ash. I'm sorry. My family's not ready for this. My parents, even cousins and old friends—they're all getting death threats. Renaissance and Braden have painted a bull's-eye on me."

"I have to attempt to convey to you, Joe, just how important you are to this process. Your ability to broker with the Republican Party is crucial."

"And I'll do everything I can behind the scenes, but we both know I'm not the one who's going to get the bill over the hump with our caucus." Indeed, it was obvious that Emii Li Song would be the only person to speak for Republicans in the end, but I tried to press him further. He interrupted me, raising his hand. "Ash, someone sent my daughter a VR xpere of a woman being tortured. I'm sorry, but . . ."

He stood.

"I should also warn you, I heard two of the guest services people talking about a forest fire nearby."

He walked away. I quickly took out my phone and saw the alert: a seven-thousand-acre fire burning south of Kent Peak. I went to the window, and I could see the smoke in the distance.

//

Before we convened the next day, the captain in charge of our Secret Service detail briefed us on the fire. Nine thousand acres and growing, moving southwest but still well clear of the Sun Valley resort and the nearby town of Ketchum. Firefighters and smoke jumpers had been dispatched, but the June heat wave was accompanied by over five hundred uncontained fires across the western states and provinces. The captain said they had planes on standby at the airport, and if it was necessary, they would evacuate the task force to another site. Joe Otero had left that morning, and it fell to me to report his resignation to the team. We went on to dither pointlessly about potential public works projects within each congressional district, clean energy pork that might secure votes. Tony had little to say, and during lunch I saw him looking worriedly at the haze cloaking the horizon.

When we concluded for the day, Haniya tugged my elbow. "I need a fucking drink, Ashir."

The two of us drove into Ketchum, stopping at a liquor store. I was driving so I only had a few sips of the vodka, but Hani poured hers over tonic, crushed a slice of lime between thumb and forefinger, and quaffed thirstily. "When you left for college, this was my drink. Mumma and Papa never knew."

"Where did you get the vodka?"

"Papa's garage. Where else? He probably knew I was sneaking it from him."

Hani pointed out the house, a quaint two-story with dark wood and a green wraparound porch overlooking a river and forest. I pulled in. When I turned off the engine, there was no sound but the trickle of the river below. Above the house reigned the soft blue of the smoky night.

Hani said: "That's the door where he shot himself, I think. You ever read him?"

"My freshman year in college we were assigned *The Old Man and the Sea*. I found it pointless."

"Yeah, you would. I was never much of a fan myself, but Peter loves him."

"Does he?"

She lowered her voice, and with a jocular cadence began imitating her husband: "Babe, American literature rewrote itself in the mold of Ernie Hemingway. The Hemster. Hemster Wheel. Wheels Up. Pop-a-wheelie. Wheelie Wonka and the Chocolate Factory."

I almost choked on my beverage, I was so surprised at my own laughter.

"Holy shit, I got you! I fucking got you! I think I've heard you laugh once our whole lives."

"Then you know it's an honest one."

"Praise Allah, I can't wait to tell Pete."

"Seth could make me laugh, but not in an honest way." I maintained my previous smile. "He would say something idiotic or inappropriate and laugh at his own joke. Then his imbecility would make me laugh."

We were quiet for a while, nursing the drinks.

Finally, I asked: "Is Peter a good man, Hani?"

She answered with an odd calm, as if she'd anticipated this question as long as I'd wished to ask it: "He has his imperfections. Like we all do. We've both been . . ." She hesitated for so long, picking at the lip of the plastic cup. "We've both been unfaithful. Marriage is the hardest thing I've ever done. Until designing a plan to save the world, of course." She laughed without humor. "All this has made me wonder who exactly *is* a good person. If anyone can clear that bar anymore. I've thought a lot about complicity, how we're all compromised. But we have to try to do what's right and love each other all the same."

An owl's hoot breached the silence, and I watched the half-moon through the haze. She had reached into her pocket and was kneading a string of prayer beads, jet-black coral on a red string. They'd been our father's. I'd only ever seen old men like him and our uncles carry them.

"Not particularly evidence-based, Hani."

She snorted a laugh. "Shut up, Ash. *Misbaha* helps. Prayer helps. Unlike you, if I don't believe there's some grace to all this, some power guiding us, I think I might lose it."

"You're scared."

"Uh, doy, no shit." She kept one of the small black beads in her fingers.

"You're free to do as you want, Hani. Though you surely know how many people in how many failing civilizations across the broad scope of history found themselves praying for deliverance in the face of annihilation, for a deus ex machina that never came."

She rolled her eyes. "You're insufferable."

I nodded in agreement. Then I shared a confession: "I hope I've been a good brother to you. I find it hard sometimes. To communicate how I feel. But you have helped me to carry the weight my whole life. It's a weight I doubt I could have held on my own. You've been an excellent comrade to me in all this."

Her fingers relaxed on the beads. Then, without warning, Hani tackled me in the driver's seat, wrapping me in a fierce and painful hug. She never hugged me because she knew how much I hated to be touched. But in this instance, I returned it, patting her back appropriately. She whispered:

"*Subhanallah*. A laugh and an emotion all in one night, Ash? I just wish Peter could've been here."

We drove back, and I felt an unfamiliar levity that I had not felt since Seth died.

//

I awoke to a hard knock at my door. It was a Secret Service agent telling me to pack. The fire had not cooled in the night, and it was now racing south toward the resort. I gathered my clothes and toiletries. Downstairs, the SUVs were waiting and beyond them, the bright orange glow of the mountains burning. The sky was as bright as daylight. Smoke drifted over the valley, a leaden curtain of gray reflecting the flames.

We drove through Ketchum with the lights and sirens on, passing hundreds of cars crammed with whatever possessions people could grab at the last second. Both lanes of the road had been turned over to fleeing traffic, red taillights stretching into the distance. After the wheels lifted and the pilot hooked around to head east, I moved to sit beside Tony. It turned out he'd been at the Friedman Memorial Airport with his bags packed since 5 a.m. He was looking out the window, watching the fire. Admittedly, it was an incredible sight to behold. The furrows and crags of the low mountains were etched with the fire line. From above, this wall of advancing destruction appeared to move at a slow crawl, but of course it was racing, soon to threaten the first homes and structures on the north end of Ketchum. Tony had a dark expression.

I asked: "You knew we'd have to evacuate?"

"You haven't seen a fire like this before."

That was all he said on the matter. No one even asked where the plane was taking us.

//

Secretary Rathbone was most incensed by our new quarters, the Marriott Hotel in downtown Cleveland, Ohio. I was nearby when he saw his new room.

"We can literally take the plane anywhere in the world and they land us in this shithole by a toxic lake?"

We actually did not have many options. The fires had blanketed much of the western states in smoke, and ironically the clear air of Southern California made no difference because so much infrastructure was still damaged from ARkSTORM. Meanwhile, the incredible heat wave responsible for the fires was grounding planes, crippling power grids, and shutting down airports across the Sun Belt. Phoenix and Las Vegas had breached 125 degrees for several days in a row. There was a hurricane gathering strength in the Atlantic, and riots and civil unrest gripped over twenty major cities across the nation. People were firing on law enforcement with the frequency of a low-grade civil war. Unemployment had reached 27 percent. Base-level power in society was realigning as states laid off police, firefighters, and emergency workers. In some regions, militias were the de facto authorities. Cleveland had instituted a curfew and National Guard patrols earlier in the year, and the governor had maintained relative stability in the city. So a generic workspace on the fifth floor of the Marriott it was.

That night, Tony and I dined together, just the two of us, in the overpriced Italian restaurant in the hotel. He did not eat much of his meal. That day during our meetings, he'd erupted into a coughing fit and had to leave the room, returning ten minutes later with hot tea and a pack of cough drops. He looked exhausted.

I said: "You could probably stand to see a doctor."

"I did. In Sun Valley. He said it's smoke from the fires aggravating my throat. There's no fucking running from this."

"How do you mean?"

"The crisis. It's everywhere now, in the air, in our banks, crawling through our blood if you're living near the wrong ticks or mosquitoes. I knew all this was coming, but I always had that thought in the back of my mind, you know? That there would be someplace to escape, someplace safe. But there's not. There's just not."

"You've seemed unengaged. What do you think of the direction the legislation is taking?"

He batted a hand as if it didn't matter to him and set aside his fork for a pasta dish he'd barely touched.

"We're getting close. Close enough to whatever it is that's possible. But even if we arrest this iteration of the crisis, there's another one behind it. And another, and another. And the revolutionaries are all dead. Set themselves on fire or were gunned down by psychos." He looked around as if seeing our surroundings for the first time. "I need some air. Want to walk a bit?"

It was an exceedingly hot night, and I felt perspiration break out after only a block. We didn't stray far from the hotel. Police and security contractors lingered on nearly every corner. Incongruently, the casino was open, beckoning with its relentless lights and promise of air-conditioning while a group of teenagers milled in the public square. The sound of fireworks boomed in the distance. I'd only that evening recalled it was the Fourth of July.

I said: "I find myself looking back fondly to when we first met. Donald

Trump was out of the White House, people were taking the science seriously, and action seemed to be right around the corner."

"And around the next corner, and the next corner, and the next corner."

"The forces of revanchism always appear weaker than they actually are, I suppose."

Tony huffed: "Shit, Ash, I look back fondly at the days when I was just getting death threats and fake anthrax. Before my own government was locking me up and then asking me to save its ass a few years later. Goddamn, I wish I had a cigarette."

"I doubt that would be good for your cough."

"You think? I've been on and off since I was in undergrad. Only hobby I've ever really enjoyed."

We passed a man with a bandana around his face standing solemnly on a street corner. The bandana had the grinning teeth of a skull lined up over his mouth, and he had an ugly scar on the side of his head in the shape of a cross. He watched us as we passed.

Tony said: "I have to tell you something. I'm stepping down from the task force. I have some personal issues, and I need to go be with my family."

This came as quite a surprise. After the loss of Otero, I felt this development intensely in the core part of one's brain that processes panic.

"May I ask why?"

"Like I said, personal issues. Holly's wrecked by what happened to the Morris kid. They were very close. She also has the new baby at home, my granddaughter. They both need me."

"I understand grief is difficult, but Tony, I have to ask you to reconsider."

"I'm afraid I've made up my mind."

We stopped in the street and faced each other. I felt the burden of convincing him otherwise.

"Tony, there's more at stake here than just your family. You may feel a sense of fatalism, and after everything you've been through, I completely understand. But we cannot lose you right now."

"Ash, I'm not necessary anymore. You have all the brains you need in that room."

"On the contrary, Tony, I would argue you're the only person we absolutely do need. Did you not see the response to your press conference?" Tony sighed dramatically to demonstrate his irritation. He closed his eyes, and I could see the grim blue veins of his eyelids. I went on: "And you saw what happened in the room today when you were silent. The others erupted in bickering, and the day was squandered. When you speak, people listen. If not, we waste our time digesting the hermeneutics of irrelevant economic texts. When we attempt to sell Congress on this plan, we need you there." I stepped closer to him, a tactic to communicate urgency, which I'd gleaned from movies in which characters must win their arguments in order to avoid cataclysm. "You are a grandfather now. It is possible that child will live to see the new century. And what you do in these next weeks could be one of the most staggering gifts any progenitor has ever handed down. You hold that power, Tony. I don't understand how you could live with yourself if you knew there was something more you could have done and yet you chose to walk away."

I made the calculated move to step back and return his personal space. Tony stared at the hot streets shedding steam. His forehead was shiny with sweat. He said nothing more. He only nodded, avoiding my gaze. We walked back to the hotel in silence while to the north fireworks began to explode in multicolored bursts of light.

//

After thirteen more days of vitriolic argument and impassioned debate, we completed our work on the omnibus bill. We were faced with an enormous challenge in drawing up this legislation, to say the least. The scale of the technological transformation required simply dwarfs any engineering achievement human civilization has ever attempted, and we found that the scale of social and political change must rise to meet that ambition.

There is only one way to begin: with a rapid decarbonization of the economy. One might call this the low-hanging fruit since many of these policies and technologies have, frustratingly, been available since the turn of the century. This begins with the "shock collar," popularized by the late Ms. Morris. By implementing a carbon price tied to emissions reductions and rebating the money to taxpayers with a so-called climate dividend we can begin to quickly reduce emissions and incentivize innovation. The price to burn a ton of carbon will begin at $100 and rise steadily at 2 percent unless emissions targets go unmet, in which case it could rise by as much as 7 percent. The revenue will be returned to taxpayers in quarterly checks, weighted so that households in the bottom 75 percent of the income distribution are receiving the majority of the benefit. A border adjustment tariff will deter leakage or offshoring while raising the cost of products originating in countries without a sufficient greenhouse abatement policy. The goal will be to reach carbon neutrality by 2055. Given the size of the US economy, this will indeed begin to quickly "shock" carbon out of the supply chain.

In addition, the bill will outlaw the sale of vehicles with internal combustion engines next year, fund a buyback program to turn over transportation stock, incentivize the replacement of gas stations with quick-charge infrastructure, and pass a clean fuel standard. A 100 percent zero-carbon portfolio standard for the power sector by 2045 will complement the deployment of renewables and construction of five new nuclear power plants using fourth-generation "breeder" reactors. New building standards will ban the sale of fossil-fuel equipment and a range of rebates and incentives will go toward replacing this equipment with electrified versions. Industry will already be motivated by the shock collar, but the EPA will impose a slew of new requirements, while financial assistance will help industry move to a mix of electrification, carbon capture, and hydrogen via electrolysis to reduce process emissions and create synthetic biofuels. Standards will drive purchasing decisions and incentives will turn over stock, utilizing every tool from industrial boiler standards to tax incentives for switching to hydrogen for creating heat and steam. The end result should be a rapid decarbonization of industrial processes.

In the agricultural sector, an end to subsidies for ruminant animals, the shock collar, and a simple tax levied on any creature raised for meat or milk will curb consumption and emissions while a tradable permit system similar to fisheries will cap the number of cattle. Anaerobic digesters will be required for manure, dietary regulations for animal feed, and a border adjustment tariff will ensure that imported meat faces similar costs. Some of these funds will be used to compensate ranchers and livestock owners. Strict regulations on nitrogen fertilizers will be complemented by incentives for farmers to switch to carbon-sequestering agricultural practices such as no-till farming and agroforestry. Subsidies for aquaponics and seaweed farming will produce a bountiful and nutritious food source while also sequestering carbon, reducing ocean acidification, and creating ecosystems in which fish, scallops, and other edible aquatic species will thrive.

The government will issue climate bonds better than the current market rate, allowing us to borrow at 2 percent to help finance the transformation of the economy. The newly created National Green Infrastructure Bank (NGIB), to be capitalized by the government, will finance everything from smart-grid transmission lines to greenhouses while coordinating with state and local governments to promote zero-carbon energy, biodiversity conservation, and financing for carbon dioxide removal (CDR). This last point is key. Getting to a zero-emissions economy is no longer sufficient. We must begin to remove as much CO_2 as is technologically feasible, and the NGIB can play an active role in financing this.

Carbon utilization may be even more vital. For instance, a mandate for cement clinker substitution will institutionalize the method of drawing down CO_2 from the atmosphere to create synthetic limestone in our primary building material. CO_2 is a fascinating and useful molecule that can produce fertilizer, minerals, chemicals, polymers, and fuels, effectively eliminating industry's need for a fossil feedstock. Though I loathe this buzzword, such a system would be the keystone of a truly "sustainable" economy. The technology for widespread carbon sequestration and utilization has existed for some time, but the market has remained anemic. Again, standards, investment, and incentives can begin to drive a widespread revolution in these processes.

Concurrently, the federal government will help finance construction of direct air carbon capture plants, carbon mineralization on the ocean floor, wetlands restoration, mangrove forests, and sequoia groves, directly training and employing up to two million people in the Civilian Climate Corps (CCC), modeled on the Civilian Conservation Corps of the 1930s. Young and low-skilled workers will receive competitive wages, health care, and training, while many new production factories and tax incentives will target disadvantaged regions, particularly where concentrated urban and rural poverty has proved intractable. However, the CCC's mission will begin on our eroding coasts, and what our task force has dubbed "the Great Transition."

For decades, our government has been buying time on the coasts with expensive maladaptations. The reckoning has arrived, and it will require a comprehensive, politically fraught restructuring of our shorelines. Through the Coastal Resilience and Defense Authority (CORDA), the federal government will offer pre-crisis fair market value to homeowners living within the "hazard line" of the US coast, established as those areas within nine feet of sea level. For property within three feet, owners will, after two years, lose the opportunity for a buyout or federal flood insurance, and eminent domain may be invoked depending on the property's viability, the goal being to restore as much of this area from paved-over development to wetlands as quickly as possible while also embarking on a federal works project to plant mangrove forests on the Southeast and Gulf coasts to protect against storm surge and sequester significant amounts of carbon. There will, however, be a hard cap of $5 million for single-family homes, $3 million for second homes and investment properties, and $25 million for businesses, forcing the wealthy to eat the cost of the retreat. For instance, Facebook's campus in Menlo Park, California, built for over $1 billion and only 1.6 feet above sea level, will face a staggering loss with this program. A reformation of the National Flood Insurance Program will create the National Fire and Flood Insurance Program (NFFIP) using updated FEMA maps to calculate climate risk. Nonprofit disaster insurance backed by public dollars is still an absolute necessity, but it must not incentivize risky building behavior as the NFIP did for so long. Households will be zoned according to risk and certain properties that flood or burn will only get money to move, not rebuild. Community grants to states can help towns merge services and soften the blow of degrowth for communities that must unincorporate. PRIRA strengthened the welfare state for the privileged, and we must end maladaptive practices like beach sand replenishment in luxury neighborhoods (and not just because the global supply of sand will effectively be gone in twenty years). Wealthy enclaves like Nantucket, the Hamptons, and Cape Cod will likely expend vast resources to delay the reckoning, but soon the agony of wet carpets and sewage on the lawn will overwhelm nostalgia.

Meanwhile, states and municipalities will pay a deductible when accessing emergency disaster aid, not as punishment but to ensure they are considering risk in land development decisions, while a new national property tax, levied at a penny per square foot, will go to fill the coffers of the National Climate Hazard Mitigation Fund (NCHMF), which will essentially augment FEMA surge capacity. This will be used for nationally declared disasters ranging from flooding to wildfires to earthquakes to freak lightning storms, the idea being to backstop, for every citizen, the risk of a more volatile climatic regime. This will be supplemented by Secretary Rathbone's "Get the Fuck Out of the Way" tax on property within fifteen feet of sea level, at an additional penny per square foot, rising another cent for each quarter inch of sea level rise. The Uniform Relocation Act, governing compensation for displaced renters, will be amended with more generous subsidies and incentives for communities to relocate to new public housing in Climate-Resilient Mobilization Cities (CRMCs).

The Coastal Resilience and Defense Authority will undoubtedly be controversial and induce howls from politicians and constituents alike. So be it.

There will be accusations that we are abandoning storied cities such as New Orleans, Miami, and Charleston. This is accurate. These cities are no longer defensible given the current rate of sea level rise and attempting to buttress them will only incur greater losses of money, material, and lives. While decommissioning thermoelectric coastal power plants (particularly nuclear facilities), removing hazardous waste, and lining landfills will be a high priority, we must also take care not to collapse regional economies. There's little point in spending precious resources trying to save a city like New Orleans built on a subsiding delta already below sea level, but building resilient "transition communities" on higher ground could be useful. Similarly, a great deal of port activity must begin a transition away from fragile coastal areas and toward navigable inland waterways, such as the St. Lawrence Seaway, the Hudson River-Erie Canal link to the Great Lakes, and Baton Rouge, which will absorb much of New Orleans's waterborne commerce due to its safe elevation. (I'll spare you the acronyms of all these programs.)

There are, however, structures that are too expensive or contain too much sunk-cost infrastructure to simply walk away from, and those will need to be defended for longer than is ideal. There is danger of the Concorde fallacy, the conviction that it's less wasteful to throw money at a lost cause simply because you've invested so much already, and I fear that may be the case for Boston, San Francisco, Los Angeles, Houston, and many other coastal cities, but an immense amount of financing will be spent in their defense with a variety of projects, ranging from fortified seawalls to organic buffering systems in the bays to multibillion-dollar sea gates. New York City's destiny, for instance, will likely be as the most expensive fortress in human history. The US Army Corps of Engineers will create a federalized coastal fortification defense strategy that builds in ample room for sea level rise. The rest of the American coast, piece by piece and year by year, will be repurposed by the CCC and transformed into the largest national park in our country. The coastline will be returned to public space, to be utilized for the benefit of all. My sister suggested the name "American Shores National Park," and so far, that is what has stuck.

The question is where will everyone leaving these communities go? This dovetails with our economic crisis. A lack of aggregate demand requires stimulus, and therefore the restructuring of our energy, transportation, and agricultural systems will be supplemented by the largest spending on public works ever. In addition to all the emissions abatement and clean energy programs described above, stimulus will patch holes in state budgets and provide additional funds for hiring teachers, firefighters, policemen, emergency responders, and for shovel-ready infrastructure projects. However, the bill will also harness $100 billion to retrofit existing public housing and vastly expand it in depopulated, deindustrialized municipalities largely across the Great Lakes region. Midsize cities and large towns that have suffered under the impacts of poor policy, poverty, and addiction will become CRMCs with incentives drawing the clean energy and decarbonization industries. Other sizable investments will be made to transition displaced workers from the coal, oil, and gas sectors into carbon removal (the skills are largely similar; one is simply drilling wells to deposit carbon instead of exploiting it), as well as in communities that have borne the brunt of fossil-fuel development, especially Appalachia and the Gulf states. Curricula of new training centers will focus on postsecondary technical education and be grafted onto the existing network of community colleges to allow for rapid instruction in skill sets.

Finally, the newly created Advanced Research Projects Agency-Biosphere (ARPA-B) will conduct research into gigaton-scale carbon mitigation techniques and begin steps for deployment of solar radiation management (SRM) aerosols. Though this last point has proved highly controversial, the task force unanimously agreed some form of SRM lies in humanity's near future. As polluting plants come off-line and their aerosols dissipate, global dimming will abate quickly with the consequences of up to one degree of warming imminent. This cannot be allowed to happen. In total, the stimulus portion of the legislation will total $5 trillion in the first year and an additional $20 trillion over the next fifteen years.

Social policy was of course a heated topic of debate, and typically Secretary Rathbone, Tony, and myself would have been skeptical of attaching ancillary concerns to the immediate issue of carbon abatement. However, the scale of the crisis necessitates more radical measures to address the culprit of inequality. There is an unquestionable economic and environmental advantage to eradicating the structural inequities of our current system. This begins by disciplining out-of-control transnational financial capital and making it work for the purposes of remedying the climate crisis. A financial transaction tax will curb speculation and raise approximately $300 billion per year while the regulation of tax havens will wring out the aimless hot money producing distortionary effects around the globe. A carefully designed estate and consumption tax on extravagant consumer goods: private jets, recreational boats, homes beyond the primary residence, electronics, estates larger than $5 million, cigarettes, alcohol, marijuana, psychedelics, cosmetics, and finally advertising. Advertising is an insidious form of pollution that has distorted the economy in myriad ways, particularly in the digital age (data brokers in particular will be targeted). Restructuring the income tax to impact the top 10 percent, 2 percent, .5 percent, and .01 percent, respectively, will pay for a host of new programs, including an elimination of student debt, tuition-free university education, universal pre-K, and universal health, vision, and dental care.

Of course, the eco-economic crisis is without borders, and the nation-state system has already demonstrated its crippling limitations. We cannot force any state to decarbonize, democratize, and redistribute at the barrel of a gun, but we can use the imperial power of the United States, its economic muscle, and its impressive propaganda capabilities to galvanize a sense of planetary purpose and equity. I can already hear some of our left-wing critics expostulating on the hegemonic aims presented here. Their critique will be an interesting footnote, steamrolled by the present emergency.

Linking carbon policy across the world will be paramount. This begins with the border adjustment tariff of the shock collar, imposed on the products of all foreign-based exporting firms, forcing free-rider countries to adhere to emissions abatement. There is some question as to whether this duty will be legal under international trade law, which is irrelevant. The United States built the IMF, WTO, and NAFTA, and we can just as easily rebuild them around a new carbon order. The Climate Stabilization and Development Fund (CSDF) will be a multilateral fund that will provide financial support for countries transitioning to clean energy production. Modeled on the Montreal Protocol, we hope to eventually finance it at $150 billion a year to help the developing world deploy zero-carbon energy. We've seen the limitations of nonbinding treaties, but with the CSDF and linked carbon policy, we have the beginnings of an international "contract and converge" regime.

Undoubtedly all the great accounts of this historical moment will be written from the Chinese perspective. Awash in internal refugees, its food system buckling, China's finances are also in crisis as low- and middle-income countries fail to service their debts due to climate disruption. Additionally, the environmental impacts of half a century of unrestrained industrial production are combining to cripple the state. Though many a salivating Maoist has looked with envy at China's authoritarian government and the speed with which it has implemented limited environmental policy, this was obviously, as Congresswoman Aamanzaihou once said, "a fool's wish on fool's gold." The Communist Party's only real goal was total control; therefore, it would sacrifice anything for continuous growth, consumption, and the acquiescence of its population. At the first signs of trouble, the party knew only more repression and murder of its people. Authoritarian, kleptocratic, and plutocratic rule across disparate human societies have in common that they are inherently unstable. Because China is undergoing a political convulsion, the temporality and effects of which are impossible for us to know and understand at the moment, we must focus diplomacy and policy action there with a carrot-and-stick package to encourage first, decarbonization, and second, human rights and democratic reform.

After much vigorous debate, it was decided to include refugee policy in the bill. Though refugees have endured a violent othering in a climate-destabilized world, we should look at refugees not as a problem but a solution: This is demographic salvation for the developed world, whose aging populations are becoming an increasing strain. The Refugee and Immigration Authority (RIA) will deliver displaced peoples across the country, find them decent work, provide English lessons, educate their children in public schools, and quickly integrate them into the American social order. We will raise the limits of refugees and asylum seekers to roughly 2.5 million a year. This, I hope, will be the beginning of the difficult project of getting the world's people to renounce the sanctity of their many identities. Distinctions of race, ethnicity, religion, and national boundary have long been antiquated. In a world of transnational threat, they've become exceedingly dangerous, and we must devise additional policy with the intent of mollifying these ancient and pointless hatreds.

Ultimately, the legislation aims to remake American society with a just and inclusive vision. Born from crisis, it will create a sprawling new national park to bind us in restoration of the natural world, a redistribution of prosperity to empower those who've long been embattled, exploited, and ignored, and a wave of new immigrants arriving to lay their burdens down and become the next stewards of our country's vital promise.

//

Only in the final days did Ms. Li Song, who'd remained largely silent throughout our debates, make her price clear: "Immunity for my members. Plus a sizable financial package to help the industries transition."

As expected, Tony, Hani, and Jane exploded at this:

"Are you out of your fucking mind?"

"That is breathtaking."

"Out of the question. Absolutely not."

Essentially the fossil-fuel majors wanted substantial government assistance, reassurances, low-cost loans, and a raft of other financial incentives to transition from their core businesses of burning carbon and dumping the waste CO_2 and CH_4 into the atmosphere. I thought myself, Ms. McCowen, Admiral Dahms, and Secretary Rathbone could convince the others that this was actually in our best interest. After all, what we did not want was further financial panic sparked by the sudden collapse of major energy players, an economic shock from the mass devaluation of the fossil-fuel industry with nothing but the stranded assets of unburnable reserves on their books. These companies were well positioned to transition to the brand-new trillion-dollar industry we were about to create in carbon remediation. They spent generations putting pollution into the atmosphere, and now they'd simply make their business pulling it back out. The tricky part was the security they wanted from legal liability.

Ms. Li Song continued: "Our members have been active participants in a responsible transitioning to a clean economy."

Tony's face was purple, and he looked like he might self-combust: *"That's a fucking hoot!"*

Haniya, a bit more calmly, explained: "I'm sorry, but what you're asking for is unconscionable. Their scientists knew what the effects of greenhouse pollution would be as far back as the 1970s. What happened here is a crime, and that very well may require serious restitution."

Jane added: "She's right. I won't put my name on anything that includes immunity. I'm sorry."

When Tony spoke, the spittle flew: "You're one sick fucking bitch, Song! Carrying water for the worst people to ever walk the earth. Our civilization is on the precipice of annihilation, and you want to hold us hostage? You're having fun, huh? Sitting there patiently this whole time waiting to fuck us."

The onslaught continued, and I admired Emii Li Song's poise. She sat sedately, dressed in black slacks and a black turtleneck. She looked almost like a woman at mosque in a black chador—everything but the headpiece. She kept her hands clasped in front of her and waited for her turn to speak.

"If civilization is on the precipice as you claim, then you should be willing to negotiate the point. I'll also remind you, that without indemnification, it's unlikely any legislation will pass Congress.

The room was silent for a moment. Finally, Tony stood. "Fuck this. I'd rather let the world burn."

Jane also pushed up out of her seat and looked to Rathbone and McCowen. "She goes or we go."

Haniya took a bit longer, collecting her notepad, pen, and purse. Without saying anything, she smoothed her skirt and walked out as well.

Secretary Rathbone rubbed his temples. "Un-fucking-believable."

Ms. Li Song looked remarkably unperturbed. "We knew this part would be difficult."

//

A day of negotiating did not go well.

Secretary Rathbone explained: "The central paradox of any crisis is that what feels unfair and unjust is often exactly what you need to stem the crisis. Old Testament justice feels good but it doesn't solve anything."

Jane looked horrified by this. "Marty, you're asking that no one ever be held responsible."

Tony: "You can't believe a goddamn word out of that woman's mouth. If you leave those companies alive, then you leave them to fight another day. We should wipe them out now."

Secretary Rathbone said what had gone unspoken through the whole process. "Tony, none of us are voting on anything here. We don't need you to agree."

"Oh, you don't think if I go out there and nuke this thing in the media it has any chance of passing?"

This could have proved an unbrookable divide. This is when I called Congresswoman Aamanzaihou, whom I'd kept abreast of the negotiations. She sounded as though she'd known this impasse was coming. With her status as the leading light of the climate-hawk Left, she had a compromise. When we reconvened, I patched her in by AR hologram from her Rayburn office. She wore a pink T-shirt, which had an image of Bernie Sanders angling his glasses to the sun in order to fry Monopoly's Rich Uncle Pennybags.

She cautioned: "None of us have even stopped to ask, Can this plan survive? We assume the bulk of the American people will stand by it simply because it will arrest the crisis and contains material benefits, but let's face it, our democracy hasn't been one for quite a while. As evidenced by this very working group and the enormous influence of one of its members."

Ms. Li Song remained smiling pleasantly. The congresswoman continued: "We need a mechanism to put this to the people, to put it to a vote, while also ensuring that the most important provisions endure. That requires a radical expansion of our democracy."

The congresswoman's demands, in return for Li Song's, were:

- Passage of the long-touted chimerical legislation known as the For the People Act, a laundry list of reforms including expanded ballot access, automatic registration, elimination of voting restrictions and overt gerrymandering practices, and tighter controls on political money. It was first proposed by Democrats during the Biden administration following largely successful Republican efforts to rig the voting process in their favor.
- A dramatic expansion and modernization of union laws, including a repeal of the Taft-Hartley Act of 1947, a requirement for codetermination on corporate boards so that workers are half of those represented, and an expansion of favorable laws governing worker cooperatives.
- The admission of Washington, D.C., Puerto Rico, American Samoa, Guam, the US Virgin Islands, and the Northern Mariana Islands as states. Because all six are either majority-minority or island territories with American citizens, they will undoubtedly elect senators with great interest in forestalling sea level rise while acting as a balance to sparsely populated rural states like Oklahoma, Wyoming, North Dakota, and Alaska.

Tony hated this as much as I did.

"This is all so fucking ridiculous. Everyone wants their fucking toy. She wants a toy, he wants a toy, you want a toy, and, and, and—"

He sputtered, unable to expel any more fury, and I quickly took over. "I concur, Congresswoman. What you've described is well beyond our purview."

Secretary Rathbone said: "It sounds mostly like you want to buy yourself new votes, Tracy."

The congresswoman whipped her head back and forth, her fleshy cheeks vibrating with the passion I'd always admired in her. "We have to engage citizens in the process of saving their own society. Democracy has a chance to prove itself here; that in a crisis it can be creative and decisive.

This will cement the bill's democratic legitimacy as soon as the next election. In World War Two, one of the foremost strategies was labor mobilization, and the best way to mobilize labor is high-paying jobs in unionized workplaces, so people are invested in what they're producing in a moment of rapid displacement and economic change—I feel like this is beyond obvious."

Alice clucked her tongue. "Cool. Well. You can forget it. We're not touching this bullshit."

"Then you won't have the votes of my caucus. Not with indemnification attached. It's that simple."

The room was silent after the congresswoman said that. She controlled the bulk of the votes we'd already assumed and were counting on. Finally, Admiral Dahms spoke up.

"You know, I have to say I agree with the congresswoman."

All heads turned to him.

Said Ms. Li Song: "Really?"

Dahms nodded. "The Pastor may have won this election, as the rules define it. Yet we have a different man sitting in the White House. Before that, my former boss, Vic Love, won with a psyops campaign and behaved like Saddam Hussein. Even Mary Randall relied on standard Republican voter suppression. For too long I've watched our politicians settle for the ability to dominate. But now we must inspire. Obviously, I'm a patriot. I've spent my whole life in service to this country and the ideals it stands for. If we truly do believe that our nation has the power to lead the world in this moment of utmost peril, well, we had better act like it."

Silence fell over the room as it became clear we would accept the congresswoman's agenda.

/ /

What we delivered to President Hamby and Congress, this "Frankenstein clusterfuck," as Secretary Rathbone called it, would face opposition, we understood as much. Upon returning to Washington, we found a city gritting its teeth, every pocket muttering terror about what our task force had delivered to the fragmented and barely legitimate lawmaking bodies. The *Washington Post* summarized the reaction: PRESIDENT HAMBY, CONGRESS RECOIL FROM AMBITIOUS PLAN. While Secretary Rathbone worked on the president, Jane and Haniya were dispatched to alleviate the concerns of the Climate Caucus, which was furious at the indemnification clause. Tony,

Admiral Dahms, Ms. Li Song, and I were sent into the teeth of the Republican resistance. At this point, a third of its members had formed the "L2P Caucus," which stood for "Loyal to The Pastor." They were calling for an armed revolution to depose Hamby and install the rightful winner of the election. Obviously, we did not expect to have their votes. This left scant targets for persuasion.

We spent a day developing our pitch before our first meeting with Nevada senator Marlon Hacker, a Mormon who went directly from his missionary work in Taiwan to the Nevada Senate. He had an enormous entourage of young aides, all equally blond, polite, and friendly. They gathered around him and seemed to blink and smile a great deal. Alice McCowen, who insisted on overseeing our effort, leaned over to whisper to me: "We call these creepy Mormon robots 'the Hackers.' Don't stick a finger too close to their teeth."

I began the presentation by walking Senator Hacker through the financial crisis, the fecklessness of the bailouts, mergers, and stopgaps, and the threat of sea level rise that was keeping the markets from stabilizing. Admiral Dahms then took over to highlight the security threats rapidly developing as the country spun through financial chaos into depression; the violence of Governor Justis in Kansas; the riots, looting, and street battles being waged in cities. Those dispossessed by western wildfires were filling up abandoned big-box stores and warehouse logistics centers, whole tent cities of the homeless were sprouting up across Nevada. These images of the internally displaced, the shipwrecked of the planet's mightiest empire, trudging down desert highways, carrying babies on their backs, pulling rolling suitcases across potholed roads, changed the senator's face. His expression went from one of feigned concern to a more honest fear. Finally, Tony took center stage.

"Senator, we are out of time. We need to stabilize markets, backstop people's livelihoods, and begin decarbonizing as fast as the economy can bear. The West Antarctic Ice Sheet's instability is calling into question East Antarctica, and if that were to go, it would make a major economic depression look like a relatively minor problem. There's enough water in East Antarctica to drown a third of the landmass of the United States—"

Much to Tony's annoyance, one of the Hackers interrupted: "We had a question about the Capital Transition Authority. There's nearly $300 billion set aside for . . . ?"

"To move the capital away from D.C." Tony tried to get back to his point about East Antarctica, but the aide pressed on.

"Moving it where?"

"To Cleveland."

Senator Hacker raised a bright blond eyebrow. "You want to move the capital of the United States to Cleveland?"

I interjected: "The capital cannot remain in D.C. Already, the district is experiencing nearly one hundred tidal flooding events each year, and we're expecting that number to double by 2055. It is impractical to have a capital in a city that's flooding every other day."

Senator Hacker: "But Cleveland?"

Tony whipped his hand in a "wrap-it-up" motion. "Property is cheap, there are plenty of neighborhoods that can be developed, and frankly the future of the country will depend on the Great Lakes as a water source and trading route. It's also as insulated from extreme weather and sea level rise as you're going to find."

"I'm sorry." One of the aides stood and jammed his finger at Tony. "You expect us to swallow all this bullshit without so much as allowing a rider?"

Cross talk erupted as Senator Hacker and his staff began vying to expel all their objections at once, while Tony, Alice, Dahms, and Li Song all began firing back. I lowered my head and waited for them to quiet, but it became too much. Finally, I spoke up with more volume than I'm used to: "It's all so familiar."

They stopped arguing to look at me, the efficacy of my tactic ever effective.

"The famines, the violence, and the stagnation of growth all point to a vicious economic contraction, one that won't stop in any of our lifetimes. We've recklessly burned through three hundred years of fossilized energy to build an immense house of cards. Industrial civilization has grown to unprecedented scale and therefore the costs of disintegration will be at a scale not previously contemplated. We are already seeing intimations of breakdown in the atrocities of the League or the Kansas governor essentially declaring himself king or The Pastor all but demanding his followers massacre his way into office. These are the early signs that the rule of law is coming undone. One can always count on the fact that there are many, many people who very much want to see the collapse of centralized authority because they believe they will prosper amid a rewiring of all the known rules. Mass

media have created a distorted perception of what breakdown will actually
look like. They believe it will be orderly and quick, a wall of fire advancing,
while others indulge in comforting fantasies that they will return to subsis-
tence farming and holistic medicinal practices. But the truth is that for all of
us, it will be grueling and unfamiliar, hunger and thirst and disease will be
constant, and many will watch loved ones raped, tortured, and murdered by
men who have the stomach for unlimited violence. To be clear, everyone in
this room, in the congressional chambers, and in the financial, plutocratic,
and corporate elite have everything to lose in this scenario. They will become the first—and easiest—targets."

The Hackers all stared at me in disquiet. Senator Hacker looked ill. Only
Alice responded:

"Boy, Hasan, you always got something to say that'll curl the milk in
your mama's titty."

//

With Senator Hacker's vote secured, we were beginning to chip away. Congresswoman Aamanzaihou managed to secure and deliver the promise of a
browbeaten affirmative vote by her unruly caucus. Similarly, the mainstream
of the Democratic Party, hearing the signal from Wall Street and their financiers all too clearly, began to fall in line. And as promised, McCowen and
Rathbone delivered the president, who finally appeared on TV endorsing
the plan as "imperfect but necessary to restoring confidence in our economy." That same night, a video appeared online of masked men wearing
APL insignia burning a teenage girl alive in a cage. She'd been kidnapped
from the House of Peace Islamic Community Center in Elizabeth, New Jersey. Such gruesome and pointless violence had long ago failed to surprise
me. I understood too well that this kind of vicious nihilism existed within
every color and stripe of humanity, but Hani was deeply shaken by it. She
came over sobbing. "You and I won't be safe. Noor and Greg and Forrest,
they won't be safe. What will we do if this doesn't work?"

I had nothing to say to comfort her.

Though violence had long ago ceased to disturb me, I was greatly unset-
tled when that night Tony forwarded me a new paper from the Centre for
Arctic Gas Hydrate, Environment and Climate outlining how the tsunami
the previous spring that flooded large portions of the west coast of Svalbard
had almost certainly been caused by the collapse of methane clathrates. Part
of the seafloor, it seemed, had simply imploded, triggering an earthquake

that sent a wave of water crashing over the shores and effectively destroying the Svalbard Global Seed Vault. Given the flooding events in California, it barely registered in the global news stream. Tony and I spoke through our glasses. This was, after all, Tony's original field. He'd made his name warning of the instability of the clathrates. He said: "It doesn't matter right now. Well, it does matter, but not to what we're doing—trying to sell a New Deal, a moonshot, and a Marshall Plan for the planet all in one go."

We had our crucial meeting with Senate majority leader Russ Mackowski the next day.

I said: "You owe it to Senator Mackowski to alert him to this finding."

"You think that knuckle dragger cares about a gas hydrate study? Wake up, man."

"What do you think the study indicates?"

"What do you think it indicates, Hasan? You're not exactly a dummy, last time I checked. If the Arctic Ocean experienced a sudden collapse along a continental shelf, it's because some serious portion of its clathrate supply unfroze. It was the warmest summer for that sea since record-keeping began. It's pretty elementary from there: the atmosphere just got a huge, unexpected dose of methane and it came from a clathrate collapse. Probably the equivalent of a year of Chinese emissions. Maybe more."

"The science behind the mass release of Arctic clathrates remains uncertain, Tony."

"Please. The Amazon, the permafrost, the clathrates, it's all coming undone. We could be looking at CO2-equivalent concentrations of one thousand ppm by the end of the century. Which means even if this bill does pass, and even if we rouse this stupid fucking planet and its selfish idiot fucking inhabitants to the grandest cozy feel-good cuddle fest, it's too late. It'll be like bailing out the *Titanic* with a Dixie cup. By the time your kid and my grandchild are our age, it'll be too hot to go outside on most of the planet's surface."

Senator Mackowski arrived the next morning with a smirking dismissal already stitched into his mouth and shook each of our hands like we were children petitioning our government for a later bedtime. His aides were more seasoned than the Hackers, including David Montreff, a cynical arrow-collar I'd dealt with previously. "Just like the old days, huh, Dr. Hasan?" The glare of his white, straight teeth made my skin hurt.

Silver hair swept back, Mackowski reclined comfortably, his muscled bulk creaking the hinges of his conference chair. He looked relaxed and content. Ms. Li Song began by explaining that her members were willing to shoulder enormous sacrifice if it helped save the economic system, but the senator interrupted her.

"Emii, honey, do you remember what you said to me back in '31 when I was getting my exploratory committee off the ground to take down Randall? I was going to be president, and what did you say?"

Even I was taken aback by how crass this was, to revert immediately to grudges and naked ambition.

Ms. Li Song shook her head once. "I can't recall, Senator."

"You said your boys couldn't back me because you had another candidate you were keeping your eye on. You thought putting a Democrat in the White House would be more useful, didn't you? And look where it all ended up with Loren Victor Love, huh? Tell you what, if I'd just finished my second term, we wouldn't be neck-deep in this shit right now. That much I got on lock."

She said: "I'm surprised you take politics so personally. We're in the throes of a serious crisis."

"And then you backed this total crank-bank of a preacher, so now I've got the right flank of my guys ready to gut me, and everyone else on the Hill is running around like a chicken fresh off the chopping block. And then it's hat in hand, 'Senator Mack, please save us from ourselves.' You understand how it might be awfully hard for me to take you seriously?"

I interrupted: "Senator, perhaps I could walk you through the legislation and speak to your concerns."

Mackowski laughed. "Concerns? Yeah, I got a few of 'em. Like the biggest cramdown of socialism and state control in the history of the republic. This makes the travesty of the New Deal look like pure timidity. And Emii, you're not the only game in town for oil and gas. Others in the sector have issued me assurances that, frankly, I'd never trust you to deliver on. I can't believe you all had the balls to come drop this at my feet and expect me to rubber stamp it. D-O-A, my friends. Dead on arrival. I didn't even want to take this meeting."

Tony asked: "So why did you?"

Montreff replied for the senator: "Optics. So we can go to the press and say the senator heard you out, and it was even worse than he thought. You have to manage these situations pretty carefully."

Tony bristled. "The country is spiraling into a depression it might never recover from."

"Oh, it'll recover. It's just about timing. After another four years of cri-sis that began under a Democrat who's locked up in a mental ward, folks'll be looking for a change. That's when someone who knows what the hell he's doing can step in, jump-start the economy with a reinvigorated energy policy that will exploit all the new energy horizons and get some solar man-agement underway. Hell, Hamby might not even make it till the end of the month. Wish you could call an election whenever you want, British-style, but, alas, we are what we are. Until then, I'll carve my own bully pulpit with the chisel of majority leader."

Mackowski stood, buttoning his coat.

Tony gawked. "That's it?"

"That's it. Thanks for playing, gentlemen. And gentlewoman. I'm sure I'll be seeing you around, but it's the August recess, and I'm going on vaca-tion."

David Montreff looked very pleased. He and the Mackowskis quickly swarmed around their boss like fighter jets escorting a plane, and they walked out.

//

Mackowski's assurance that there would be no Senate vote on the bill con-sumed the media for the next few days until The Pastor's nationally coor-dinated Loyalty March of August 11. The footage of thousands of people clotting together in city streets around the country, heads freshly shaved, trading razor blades and box cutters, was arresting to say the least. I watched, fascinated, as they held their comrades' skulls to the pavement and carved crosses into each other's scalps. Then they marched en masse, from Anaheim to Atlanta, Portland, Maine, to Portland, Oregon, bare-chested, chanting, bleeding from the crucifix wounds, blood pooling in their ears, eyes, and down their throats. They carried signs demanding that their savior ascend, that their new nation form, tagging their mark on highway dividers, road signs, and retail shops. From his worlde, The Pastor promised, *"If all ninety million of my voters refuse to obey, if we rampage, they cannot stop us!"*

Windows smashed, cars burning, riot police mostly unable to bring order, some unspecified number of people killed and injured, but this was not our concern. With D.C. in lockdown and the closest disturbance in Bal-timore, it was merely a discomfiting distraction. We scrambled for other avenues to pass the bill. I told Peter:

"It's incredible how the rules that govern our imaginary nation-state polities have become more real than those that govern our economic super-structure. Or our biosphere, for that matter."

Peter admitted: "It's a rock and a hard place, I'll give you that. You know me and Wimpel have a relationship with the guy, right?"

"Senator Mackowski? I was aware that your paths had crossed, I suppose."

Peter looked to Haniya, who was fixing peanut butter and banana sand-wiches for the children. Her dark gaze met Peter's. He said: "You don't get into the hedge fund game without a strong meat hook in Congress. Me and Mack belong to all the same clubs and bullshit. I've seen his old-man cock in a steam room, bro."

"What are you suggesting?"

Peter nodded to Haniya. "He likes you! He thinks you're spunky, and he thinks I'm a hoot!"

"Yeah, Pete, so what are you saying?"

"Let's you and me go work on him."

I said: "You think he'll change his mind about the legislation based on your sense of humor?"

Peter looked offended. "Damn, bro, this whole time I thought I slayed you." He moved around the kitchen island and slapped me on the shoulder. "We track him down and make a better pitch than your crew of geeks could ever manage."

Truly anything was worth an attempt at that point. That night, Peter and Haniya left Noor and Gregory in my care to follow the Senate major-ity leader on his vacation. For two days, I've solemnly handled my duties with the children and reread the paper on the Svalbard tsunami. When Dr. Pietrus first coined the phrase "Tombstone Domino Theory" in his book, I found it distastefully alarmist. However, the vast stores of methane now being detected exiting from the seabed around Greenland and the Arctic Ocean make his theory increasingly, unnervingly, plausible. The chance that this methane abruptly flips the planet's climate into a more toxic con-figuration reminiscent of the end-Permian extinction is no longer outside the realm of possibility. In fact, I believe we now have to countenance this as a realistic scenario.

This was what I was contemplating tonight when Secretary Rathbone called.

The news, he said, would soon be reporting a dramatic set of events, and there would be Secret Service cars on the way to take me and my family into protective custody. He'd barely explained the circumstances before I saw my mother calling on the other line. She rarely did so anymore, as her mind had deteriorated badly in the last year. That is where I'll leave this account. I do not have the temerity to finish it. When I put Secretary Rathbone on hold to answer my mother's call, she was hysterical, wailing incoherently. Or so I thought, until I finally grasped that she wasn't. She'd seen the news herself and had been struck by one moment of awful clarity in her otherwise failing brain. I could not find the proper words to console her, but I'm sure she will never forgive me for what I said next:

"We must consider, Mumma, as dreadful as this is, that it may very well help us pass critical legislation."

THE TRIGGER
AND THE KING

2037

*T*awrny *greets you at the door with his gun. He doesn't point it at you, but the* piece trembles by his side, his finger twitching near the trigger guard.

"Was wondering if that job was still available, T. The one you told me about."

His eyes go wide with surprise and joy. "Oh, that's good, Keeper. Boy, that's terrific to hear. That's just so terrific." He looks at the weapon in his hand almost as if he's forgotten it's there and quickly sets it on a stack of old coupon flyers on an end table.

You're soaked in sweat and dizzy from the walk. Another brutal summer heat storm. Mostly you're worried that you and your family might goddamn well bake too. Can't let that happen, so you made the walk out to Cassingham Hollow.

Tawrny has shriveled further; he's lost so much weight so quickly that the skin around his face pools beneath his neck; he's liver-spotted, his white mane thinning and pink scalp emerging. The house is trashed, the floor a sea of empty cat food tins, reeking of fish. The window AC unit rumbles noisily. He scrapes coupon mailers from a kitchen chair and takes a seat. For upward of a year he'd been repeating, *Job's coming up. You sure you don't want it? It's right around the corner. Summer sometime.* Now he looks like he can't believe you've said yes. "Why'd you. Um . . ." He searches for words. "What all made you change your mind?"

Your tongue slithers in and out of the holes between your teeth. Five missing and another two that ache something awful, but you've gotten good at putting aside small miseries.

"Look around, man. Any way to make money these days, man's gotta jump on it."

"You been working at all?"

"Scrapped some. The Rev still pays me to go out with him and Ginna. But other'n that . . ."

Tawrny nods and nods as if this is exciting news. "Yeah, that's good. That's real good."

"So what's the job? And how likely am I to spend the next twenty years in prison for it?"

Tawrny waves this away. "No, no, no. The gal told me this was gonna be some real good money. Like send-your-kid-to-college money."

"What do they want with me again? Ain't I on a, like, terrorism watch list or something?"

"You'll be good and taken care of," he says.

He goes to a kitchen drawer and rummages out an old cell phone, the kind without internet only used by drug dealers and hired killers. With quivering thumbs, Tawrny punches a storm into the phone. One of the cabinets hangs open and you can see the bottles packed in, mostly whiskey and gin, many of them empty.

"Now we wait a bit, but this is good. I'll get my finder's fee, and you and your gal, you'll be set up." He nods to himself and cat food tins clink and scatter as he shuffles back to his chair.

"No idea what's the job?"

"I'm not privy to that kind of information, son. But it'll be worth it. Don't worry about that." He's nodding like his head is stuck in that motion. "Soon as I know, I'll pass on the info to you. Here." And he goes back to the drawer to hand you another burner. "I'll text you on this."

Leaving Tawrny's and the cool palm of the AC, the evening heat claps around you. You walk the three miles back to where you're staying, past the elementary school, shut down as budget cuts grip the state. Garbage service stopped last month, and there's trash piling up everywhere, scattered in the streets and drenched in the setting sun's final fiery rays.

The old Walmart doesn't have its lettering or its little sunburst logo anymore. What it has are cars and trucks parked haphazard, paying no mind to the paint carving up the lot, folks mostly being polite and trying not to block anyone else in. A couple of women push shopping carts of scavenged essentials toward the front entrance. Crows circle the building and never stop cawing. They alight on the rim of the roof in pairs and triads, watching for food scraps or chipmunks. Because of the heat, someone has pried the glass doors of the store open and pointed huge fans outward, a setup meant to suck out the hot air. There was enough juice from the solar panels to keep the lights on, but not enough to power the AC. When you were still living in the trailer, the power was blinking in and out every few days as grids buckled. You make your way into the store, where the air is at least a few degrees cooler. At the checkout counter by the entrance, the "neighborhood watch" fellas recognize you, nod, and let you pass. Then you're into what was once the Home and Fashion sections. Some folks have nice big tents and others have used the aluminum shelving, tarps, rugs, and linens to create private spaces. Others have simply pulled mattresses or sleeping bags into cluttered corners and put up handwritten signs with their surnames to mark their space. Neighborhood watch tries to keep order and adjudicate disputes, but there've been outbursts about folks stealing or jerking off too loud. You pass a family of four wearing VR headsets they hastily charge when the power is working. They all stare silently at whatever hallucination is in front of them.

You make your way back to Sporting Goods and Toys, where Raquel and Toby are reading from a children's book outside your spot. You have two tents, a bigger one that you and Raquel share, and a little lime-green pup tent for Toby. Just beyond the tents you have a couch, a cookstove, microwave, and a dining room table and chairs arranged on a piece of carpet. You had a small refrigerator, but the power kept going in and out, and after a while it wasn't worth it. Everyone now keeps their perishables in the walk-in freezer behind the Deli because even with the failures, as long as no one opened the door, it could stay cold long enough. A few guys who had some engineering know-how said that if they could scavenge a dozen home battery systems, they might be able to keep the juice on 24/7, but that was still a project in the making.

"'His eyes snapped open,'" Raquel signs the words for Toby while he holds the book, reading the hands of his mother and then off the page, "'and there were these things about himself that he knew, instantly.'"

You stand there watching them read. Toby's hearing aids stopped working a year ago, and you haven't been able to afford a new pair. You've held on to them, hoping you can find someone to repair them, but he's managing. Worse was his asthma, and when you were close to getting kicked out of the trailer, he finally got an attack so bad, you thought he might die. He was writhing on his bedroom floor, clawing at his throat, eyes bulging, and you and Raquel couldn't calm him or get him to take a sip of water. She'd wailed and begged you to call an ambulance, but you both knew it was pointless. By the time they got there, it would either be over or Toby really would die, and either way, you'd owe so much money on the bill you'd never get out from under it. You couldn't live in the trailer anymore. There was this thing called photochemical smog, Raquel said, and it was coming from the plant across the river. Mix that with ragweed season and hay fever, and Toby was lucky to go more than a couple days without his throat swelling shut. That's when Casey told you about the abandoned Walmart, how people getting booted from their homes were just moving in there and the cops weren't doing a thing about it.

Toby sees you and sets the book aside. He hops off Raquel's lap and runs at you full speed, leaping to high-five your outstretched palm. He manages to smack it at the top of his jump, a big goofy grin on his face, missing as many teeth as you, as the babies fall out and the adults push in. He quickly signs: *You're sweaty.*

And you sign back, *Do you want a hug?*

No way.

One hug, Ogre. You snatch him into your sweat-soaked T-shirt. He shrieks and writhes away. When he frees himself, he goes diving into his tent to escape you.

"They got the doors open," you tell Raquel, who closes the book and sets it on the table. "We're gonna get more raccoons, probably rats too."

"It's too hot with the doors closed," she says. "They got to do something."

Toby emerges from his tent, splashing through the toys and books he sleeps with.

Read to me, Dad?

But you have to decline. You tell him you need a shower from the jerry-rigged setups in the Garden section that use sun to heat jugs of water. You'll go stand under one, depress the lever, and feel the day's journey wash away. Before you head over, towel in hand, Raquel asks you where you've been.

"Possible I might got a line on some work," you tell her. "Possible."

———

You feel better about the Walmart than the trailer you had to yourselves, not only because of Toby's asthma but because you felt exposed there, not just to photochemical smog but any hard storm or the cruelty of an addict desperate for a score. Then that mythic beast you hear so much about, the economy, falters, and suddenly everyone is scared, and when people are scared they evict and they foreclose. You remember it from when you were a kid, when your mom lost the only piece of property you ever cared about. You remember it from when the pandemic hit, and you got booted from your apartment and spent a year sleeping on Casey's sticky leather couch. Then the heat descended early in the spring with uninterrupted weeks of searing triple digits. The relentless summer has made people relentless. Not just the folks collapsing from heatstroke, but the break-ins and the muggings, the women assaulted in parking lots, the stabbings, the shootings, the arsons, a new house burning every week with a fire department too stretched to get there before the structure is ashes. Not enough cops left to do anything about it, and so the militias start coming through. You see them in their pickups, flying the Cerberus flag, guns on their laps, pretending to interview crime victims or provide "security" at angry town hall meetings. People are joining up like never before. Better to be the bully than the bullied.

Which is why when you move into the Walmart and find space beside identical twin old-timers you feel a measure of relief. Pierre and Kelly are rusty old fuckers, same squinty eyes and willow-white hair. Same taste in plaid shirts and overalls. One with a handlebar mustache, the other with a long beard. They lived on the same farm in Plainfield since they were children but are now residents of the abandoned Walmart, and the first day your family moved in, Pierre (of the handlebar) whittled Toby a small horse from a block of wood. Then they shared dinner with you, porkchops grilled in the Home and Garden section, with sides of red-skin potatoes and applesauce. Finally, Kelly (of the beard) took you aside and asked, "You got protection?"

"Can't. My parole."

"Who gives a rip?" He opened his plaid to show off a fearsome revolver, maybe a .357, in an underarm holster. "Rules are different now, brother."

"Sickos out of control," says Pierre, his lip fat with Copenhagen. He's talking about the teenage girl a few APL thugs put in the cage in New Jersey. They tossed gasoline and a match on her. "Trying to take advantage while everyone's scared."

Eight days after you visit Tawrny, he texts you on the burner to say it's happening soon. Further instructions forthcoming. You pocket the phone, and your stomach is a crockpot of nerves. Someone's TV is blaring over in Electronics, and you can hear the news people arguing about the collapse of negotiations. The government's paralyzed, spinning out, though from your POV, the government hasn't done shit for anyone in your lifetime, so it's the one thing you're happy to let burn. That night you're scheduled to hit the streets with the Reverend Andrade and Ginna to pass out sandwiches. Despite it all, the Rev and his wife keep plugging away. You hug Toby, but he's distracted, trying to teach Pierre and Kelly the signs they need to understand the plot of his favorite book about an intrepid kid who crash-lands in the wilderness with nothing but an axe. You kiss Raquel goodbye and for no particular reason you want to hold her for longer.

"Just when you get the cash from Rev, go pick something up from the Kroger. Everyone's saying people is beating down the door and running off with stuff."

"They got the guards."

"Not no more. Everyone's been talking about it all day. The Pastor's loons been at it. Ask Pierre."

And Pierre gives you a solemn look and shows you the videos on his phone: Across the country, The Pastor's disciples are running wild in a "Loyalty March," cutting their scalps open with box cutters and throwing trash cans through windows. "In Coshocton, it only looked like a few hundred got in on the action, but it's enough to tighten your scrote." Pierre despairs. "Guy's got mind control over these loonies."

Andrade is waiting for you in the parking lot. He's brought his old beat-to-hell Elantra instead of the minivan.

"No Ginna?" you ask as you climb into the passenger seat. He smiles weakly.

"She's got the van. I could use your help elsewhere."

He says no more than that. On the way out, you pass all the yard signs, flags, and banners for The Pastor. The ones with his dark profile hauling the cross on his back. The streets are quiet, though. Summer has reached its zenith, and as you pull up to the church the sun is God's blood-soaked breath blazing around every side of the modest steeple. Under this gentle light, you see the place where you were saved, where briefly you thought you felt His power.

The two of you sit on the warm concrete steps leading to the church. You wait for the reverend to begin, but he's squinting into the distance, trying to decide about a couple of cows munching their way through the nearby field.

"You're freaking me out here, Rev."

He smiles and then the smile collapses. "You've done so good for yourself, Keeper. And your family."

You blush, and your heart floods with the shame at how untrue this is.

"Toby ain't been in school for a year," you say quietly. The state was recommending homeschooling until the crisis passed. Whatever this crisis was or whatever "passed" might mean. Some of the laid-off teachers were talking about starting up classes in the Walmart with parents paying or contributing whatever they can. "Not sure you're looking at the situation clear."

"Keeper, I've known many a man who buckled under less. People who are dead or locked away for good. You kept faith in God and you've come across some mighty turbulent rivers. I've come to love you a great deal."

You don't know what to say to this, so you just sit there.

"I'm going to tell you something, and you can do with it what you will."

The reverend's face is hard and sunburned. There is nothing to prepare you for what he says next.

"Many years ago I met a man who became my friend. He needed help with something. He was, like many of us, like myself, fighting for a better world. He and his people. He died a few years back—was killed actually—and I still miss him. He told me details about himself, things he was never supposed to tell me. We couldn't really meet in public. We'd find excuses to go hiking and camping in the Appalachians or the Great Smoky Mountains. He was a great thinker, a great naturalist, a great man. Generous and kind and dedicated. He convinced me of his cause. So I helped him and his group for years. At first, I was only a message carrier. I found people who could be useful, but it grew to be much more than that. I became—I don't even know how to put this—operational in their network. And this is the part where I tell you how sorry I am. Because I'm the one who recruited your friend Mr. Tawrny, and I'm the one who asked him to approach you about the Tuscarawas plant. And it was never my intention that you take the fall for that. Not in the least. They just needed information. I had no idea you'd go out and test the lock. And I'm so sorry, Keeper. I truly am."

A creeping fog comes over you. In a past life, you might have been furious. You might've choked the son of a bitch out right there. Instead, you feel only numb exhaustion.

"So you weren't never really interested in helping me," you say, piecing this together. "You just felt guilty."

"No," he says quickly. "Not true. Not even a little. Even back before we were friends, I knew you as a member of my church, and I knew you and your family needed money. I thought I was helping by putting a little cash in your pocket."

You shake your head. "Do you have any idea, Rev—do you have any fucking idea what . . . what happened to me when—"

"Keeper, I'm so sorry. You once told me you didn't know how God could forgive you for the things you've done, and honestly, that's how I feel. I'll ask His forgiveness every day, but I will never deserve it."

The heat of the day has mercifully receded, though you're sweating again all the same.

"I believed in what they were doing, and this here, what's happening now, this is the evidence. This is what I feared. Men have so brazenly and stupidly spoiled Creation that the harvest of this madness—well, look around the country today: We're finally reaping what we've sown. All these disciples of the so-called Pastor have are bastardized versions of faith that allow them their selfish cruelty." He finally looks at you, his sad brown eyes searching out your own. "I know they've reached out to you again through Mr. Tawrny. And I can say truthfully, Keeper, I played no part in this. I do not know what they want with you. Do you?"

You feel naked that he knows this.

"No."

"What I'm asking is that you decline their offer. Whatever it is."

"Why? Thought you was down with their cause, Rev?"

"At one time I was. I believe in the mission of men like John Brown and Jesus Christ. Sometimes what is illegal can still be just. But ever since Allen died—they're a different group now, being run by different people, and it seems to me they've lost their way. Whatever is going on now . . . I'm afraid for you, Keeper."

You lick between the gaps in your teeth, and pain swells in your gums. An alder's leaves sway in the twilight breeze, and over the field, red-tailed hawks circle a spot of corn where a dead-critter feast certainly lies.

"Before Allen died, he shared some information with me. These militias—like the one you went to see—now doing unspeakable things with no one stopping them? It turns out the Love administration was funneling them arms and resources and creating liaisons with law enforcement. They were using these folks, Keeper, to try to get at them. They had a program back in the seventies that they used to infiltrate groups like the original Weather Underground, but that didn't work out too well." He let out a small laugh. His eyes twinkled. "Legend has it the undercovers kept sympathizing with the radicals. So this time, with the new Weathermen, they looked to folks who wouldn't be as sympathetic. They knew we were based in the Midwest and the Southeast, and they thought they could use the League to reconnoiter and surveil and get information that law enforcement couldn't find on its own. At least not legally."

"Use. That's the word I would think on, Rev. A lot of using going on."

Andrade's smile fades.

"And I'm sorry. I'll be sorry forever. But what I'm also telling you is that these folks you visited up at the compound, they know about your ties, and they certainly suspect me, although not for any of the right reasons. Because I put some solar panels on the church roof with an FBF grant and raised money for people in the border concentration camps." He chuffed a laugh. "Heck, even if I'd never met Allen, the militias would still suspect me. That's the foul irony."

You stand.

"Far as I'm concerned, Rev, you ain't nothing more than another peddler. Another user." You proceed down a couple steps before turning back. "Whatever you do, don't fuck this up for me, Rev. I never needed a gig worse in my life. Whatever your concerns, do me a favor and keep 'em to your fucking self. Stay away from me and my family. You're a predator, man. Just like I thought."

You spit in the grass, an ugly green splat of phlegm, and set off down the church driveway without looking back.

––––––––––

The glass doors of the Kroger have been pried apart, a mattress stuffed in the gap to keep them open, its coils bursting through casing. Whatever chaos visited your former employer, the madness has passed. The parking lot is empty, scattered trash and salvaged food items smeared over the asphalt: trammeled microwave dinners, exploded boxes of cereal trailing crumbs, a rotisserie chicken gripped apart by fingers. You step through the sliding doors and make your way past the produce into the heart of the store, picked entirely clean, and it makes you think of ants going to work. Bare shelves gleam under fluorescent light. What's incredible is you just walked by the day before. All this has happened today, the place stripped bare in a bottomless panic. The chaos reminds you of working search and rescue in Missouri. You piled the dead animals together, tossing drowned dogs, cats, varmints, and getting teams to move the big ones. Horses, cows, and pigs had all washed down from nearby farms, all of them bursting with water and decaying in the sun, an eye-watering smell. Then you think of that old

Mexican man in St. Louis, floating on his back. Dead people have fake faces. They look stuffed, taxidermied.

You find a canvas bag someone dropped and fill it with whatever doesn't look too dirty: a frozen chicken tikka masala now mushy, a small bottle of olive oil, an instant noodles punctured, partially spilled, but salvageable. You hear people at the back of the store and clutch your bag close, wishing for Kelly's gun, but then you're upon them and their eyes are as frightened as you've ever seen. A young couple, the guy maybe all of five feet tall, the woman half a foot shorter. They're pushing a shopping cart with a car seat stuffed inside, a baby buckled into that, filling up the edges around the seat with supplies. Your eyes fall to the items, familiar to you from after Toby was born: formula, diapers, wet wipes, hand sanitizer, tearless shampoo, Band-Aids, hydrogen peroxide, and an electric breast pump no doubt looted from the back pharmacy.

"Just doing some shopping," you tell them because they look so scared of you. "Carry on."

You turn to go the other way, but the guy calls out, "Hey, man." And those two words are so full of grief and fear you almost don't want to turn around. The buzz of the fluorescent lights is dizzying and loud. "If you see any of that earache medicine, will you give a shout? You know what I mean? The pink stuff."

"Yeah," you say. "Will do, kid."

But you move through the aisles quickly because outside dark lakes of night have set in, and you don't want to be here if the power goes out. What was revealed to you years ago when you were picking through the ashen wreckage of the megafire or the soggy detritus of the floods was the simplicity with which everything unravels. How one second you're living your life, and the next, if you don't run, you'll be rotting, waiting for some other poor sucker to find you and haul you out in a plastic bag. Now everyone was getting a glimpse of what you long knew: the fragility of all those things that seem so permanent and steadfast. How very simple it is for everything and everyone to go away.

On the twelfth, you get a text from Tawrny on the burner to let you know things are good to go. In two days, you'll meet a woman at the Commodore Perry Service Plaza on the Ohio Turnpike, 8 a.m. sharp. This presents a problem because you and Raquel no longer have a functioning car.

"You could always thumb it." Pierre hoovers up dip juice from his lip. "Pretty soon that'll be the standard mode of transport."

Still, when you tell Raquel you need to hitch up to Toledo, she's rightfully suspicious.

"I don't understand what the job is. You're being all murky about it."

"No, for real, I'm not. They told me more scrapping. There's tin sheets coming off all these farm buildings up there, and they sell for about two bucks apiece."

"Who's they?"

"Casey and some of them." But this phrase is familiar to her from all your lying, all your drinking and drugging. "I'm clean. Plus, if I had any intention of getting high, I could do it without hitching a hundred and fifteen miles."

This actually does seem to satisfy her. The next day you go see Tawrny.

"I need to know what this is," you demand.

"If I knew, Keeper, I'd tell you. Honest. From the way it sounds, by you doing your time and keeping quiet they know they can trust you, and that's why they wanted you so bad."

He's at least shaved since you last saw him, but his shirt is filthy, pit stains leaching into white fabric.

"Then I need to know how much."

"Ah." He holds up an index finger. "A good piece of knowledge to settle for." And he slides a scrap of paper across the table to you. It's got an account number and a password. "It's only got fifty bucks in there now, but as soon as they pick you up, it'll get another nine thousand or so."

"Or so?"

"Yeah, to stay under IRS eyes if it comes to that. Then they'll load another nine grand a month until it hits fifty K."

You look from the scrap of paper to Tawrny's rheumy eyes. "No shit?"

"No shit. You gotta complete the jay-oh-bee of course, but that shouldn't be no problem, whatever it is."

This number fills your mind so completely, it is such total and utter salvation, that it blots out every other question or concern. The things you can do with fifty thousand dollars. The safety and security you can provide for Raquel and Toby. Hearing aids and an apartment, cereal and beds to sleep in, asthma inhalers and clothes without holes. Suddenly, you are overwhelmed, so grateful to this man you might cry. You swallow to keep the lump down.

"You know, T, you really always have looked out for me. I don't want you to think I ain't realized that."

Tawrny nods, his eyes far away and utterly forlorn.

"Well," he says. "I'm close to nursing-home ready. Maybe you'll come see me from time to time."

Coming home to the Walmart, you're thinking about how you should find a paper map, so you can bushwhack your way up county highways. Just as you're walking into the parking lot, you spot a bright orange Dodge pickup. You know only one guy who drives that color RAM 1500 because you were with him when he bought it used, paid way too much, and proceeded to sink the cost of another used truck into fixing it up. Casey Wheeler hops out, hitching up his jeans with no belt, baseball cap protecting his bald spot from the setting sun, wearing his shirt that says WORLD'S OKAYEST FISH-ERMAN, and you call his name. When he spots you, he starts hustling your way. You're happy to see him. You two haven't talked much in the last few months, but he's a good friend, and you're feeling light. The thought of that fifty K is making you feel good about everything.

"Wheeler!" you cry over the noise of the fans.

You're expecting your grin returned, but as he runs over, you see his face is dark and afraid. He's breathing heavy when he reaches you. "Keeper." He sucks wind. "You gotta get out of here, man!"

"Huh?"

"You gotta leave. You need to take Rocky and Toby and get out."

"Get out of where?"

"Outta the 'mart. Outta town. Just go."

"Man, what are you talking about? You on something?"

"Just go."

"Go where?"

"Wherever. Just don't be here."

"Casey, we ain't even got a car. We got nowhere to go to. You need to tell me what's going on."

He looks away, the slanted sun lighting his face, and there are lines from a pillow, as if he's just gotten out of bed. "I should've told you a while back, I just didn't think Underwood was serious."

Your stomach falls at the mention of this name. You're suddenly aware of how little water you've had to drink that day. And it's been so hot. "Told me what?"

"They're coming down here. They've had this list for a while. I thought it was all bullshit, just a bunch of guys talking tough, but—I dunno, Dick's always had it out for you."

You can't process everything he's saying. "What list?"

"'Cause of Rocky. They don't like that. They got a list of people. He showed it to me once. It's like . . . if they ever get a chance to, you know—take care of folks."

"Casey, what in the fuck does that mean? 'Take care of'?"

Casey lifts his hat and scratches at the fuzz on his scalp. He went from running full-bore to now twisting his heel in the dirt like a shy kid who won't cop to eating all the ice cream. Meanwhile, blood thunders in your temples.

"Just. Why'd you have to take up with that preacher, Keeper? You realize he's a communist, right? That's mostly what they're pissed about. That's who they wanted from the beginning."

How much these rednecks know of what Andrade told you, hell, it doesn't even matter. It was all crashing together one way or the other. You think of all the guns you saw in that shed at the compound. All the target practice. All the kids just shooting and waiting and itching.

"I didn't think they were serious," Casey pleads.

"Jesus Christ." You can't breathe. You feel like you've caught Toby's asthma. "When are they coming?"

"That's the thing. That's kind of why I'm here." He removes the cap again, scratches, replaces it. You snatch him by the collar, rage flooding.

"*Motherfucker, quit dawdling your traitor fucking mouth and spit it out!* When are they coming?"

"That's what I'm trying to tell you. Dick called me. Asked where you was staying at. I said I didn't know. But he asked about the Walmart. I said I didn't think that's where you were, but . . ."

You don't wait for him to finish. You let go of his shirt and sprint through the roar of the fans.

Toby and Raquel are terrified. You tear the bags out of Raquel's hands when she tries to pack, and you're screaming at her that there's no time, you have to leave right now, and Pierre comes over to try to calm you down, so you ask him for his gun, but he won't give it to you. Raquel exchanges a look with Casey, who's sheepishly followed you into the store. You sign to Toby, *Take one toy*, and he chooses a made-up dinosaur from the latest *Jurassic Park* xpere. He actually seems more in tune with the gravity of the situation than Raquel, who's stomping her foot and refusing to leave, demanding answers that will simply take too long. Finally, you grab her by her cheeks and shake her head. You hiss into her face.

"They're coming for us."

She has no idea who you're talking about, but the fear becomes a live current in her eyes, and this gets her moving. You grab one bag into which Toby has helpfully piled a few of his clothes and you lead them by the hand out of the Walmart. Outside, you pile into Casey's old truck, all four of you stuffed into the bench seat, and you're terrified of how fucking *orange* this thing is. You could spot it from space.

"Where are we going?" asks Casey.

"I don't know, man, just get the fuck outta here, just drive."

And he takes a left out of the crumbling asphalt of the parking lot.

"Keeper, what's going on?" Raquel pleads.

Toby stares at his dinosaur, like he's trying not to watch the lips of the adults.

"You're scaring him," says Raquel.

"You gotta tell me what the plan is here, buddy," says Casey.

"You're scaring *me*," Raquel moans.

You've always hated coincidence. It feels wrong to you, not like God has a plan but like the devil has found the crack into which he can seep and saturate. Just when the Rev had warned you about them.

"Are they going after Andrade?" you ask Casey.

"What?" cries Raquel. "Who? Why?"

"If I had to guess," says Casey.

Several notions flit through your head. You ask for Casey's phone, but he's never met Andrade and you don't know the number. The Rev's schedule is clockwork, though, so you know he'll be at the church tonight. You search for the church's number on the Web and dial. No answer. You try again with the same result. There are no good alternatives. "Pull up over here." Casey does as he's told. You grab him by his shoulder and look him in the eye. "Take Raquel and Toby. Go to the diner by the gas station on Route 16. You know the one?" He nods. "Stay there. If I don't show up or call in an hour, you leave, okay? You take them anywhere but here."

Raquel hits the roof. *"What are you talking about?! Keeper, what the hell's going on?"*

"What are you gonna do?" Casey asks.

Toby is whimpering. Because he can't hear his own crying, his moans are so very loud.

"I gotta warn him."

"Who?" Raquel demands.

"Reverend Andrade. Casey'll catch you up. I can't just let him sit there."

You pop the door handle and climb over Toby before she can object anymore. You pat him lightly on his cheek. "Be good for Mommy and Uncle Case. I'll see you in a bit." Then you fall, spilling out of the car and scraping your hand on the gravel. Getting to your feet, you motion for them to go as you break into a jog down a deserted street, trash like tumbleweeds, past abandoned homes disintegrating into nature.

You approach the Church of Christ from the field to the east, where a year and a half ago the reverend took you on a walk through the snow. By the time you get there, dark has fallen and you are soaked with sweat from your run across town. The outdoor floodlights that illuminate the church's sign and steeple are dark, but the stained glass glows from within. You can also see the black SUVs turned sideways, acting as a roadblock to the parking entrance. Three more vehicles in the lot: two trucks and the reverend and Ginna's minivan. You stand rooted in place. Of course they're already there. You should turn and run. You know this, and yet you step forward, wishing you'd punched Pierre in the throat and taken his gun.

You see a man sitting behind the wheel of one of the trucks, the glow of his phone illuminating the interior. He's wearing a balaclava, so only his eyes are visible. You turn into the woods to approach the church from behind. You don't have a plan. You don't know what you're doing or why. You know you should take your family and run, but it's the reverend. You'd never forgive yourself if you didn't try.

Behind the church are the storm doors with a combination padlock. You quickly twist and alight on the numbers of the code, snapping it open. You ease one of the doors open. It squeaks slightly as you lift it, and you wince, setting it down in the grass. You use the screen of the burner phone to find your way down the steps and through the darkness of the basement. When you get up the stairs to the door that leads into the reverend's office, you wait and listen. Nothing. You put your ear to it. There are voices, but not from the office, you're sure. Easing the door open, you can see the room is empty. You also see Ginna's scarf draped over one of the chairs and a mug of tea on the reverend's desk, the string and little square of paper hanging out. The office door is ajar and through it, filtering down the hallway from the main part of the church, you can hear voices. You listen for the reverend or Ginna, but these are all men chuckling to themselves and one talking loudly—something about a car running poorly. You close your eyes and breathe. Maybe the Andrades heard the cars coming up the driveway and knew well enough to run. As quietly as you can, you creep to the office door and down the hallway that leads through the changing room to the pulpit. The lights in the hallway are all off, as well as the array of LEDs that light up the pulpit, which means you can peak your head around the corner of the doorway and remain shrouded in darkness. You hope. Centimeter by centimeter, you slide your skull past the door's frame until you expose one eye to the scene beyond.

A sallow light bulb beams down on the pews. There are seven men milling around the sanctuary, three sitting and four standing. One is Morgan Schembari, who's on the phone. One is Dick Underwood, wearing fatigues and black boots, an American flag patch on one shoulder, rifle slung around the other. Another man is taking pictures with his phone, and what they're taking pictures of—your mind can't quite wrap around it at first.

Ginna Andrade is naked and sitting up in the front pew, her breasts drooping, her legs splayed. There is an ugly wound on the front of her head and blood draining into her bullet-scrambled eyes. Two of the men pose with her, grinning. Some of the blood has trickled down her neck and chest. Her clothes lie piled near the pulpit but her socks are still on. They are gray and bunched around her ankles. And yet Ginna made it free of this life well enough compared to her husband. Reverend Andrade sways upside down, dripping. A rope, strung up over one of the ceiling's joists, has him by the ankles, so that his arms dangle a few feet off the ground. You gag at the sight, hold in the vomit that hurtles to the top of your throat, and continue staring because, again, it's taking you so long to make sense of what has happened here. He too is naked, but not just naked of his clothes. His skin has been stripped off, cut away with knives, one of which someone has stabbed into the meat of his thigh muscle and another which protrudes from the top of a pew. There are chunks of knotty flesh everywhere and blood pooling beneath the reverend's wet black hair. Like Raquel's dogs, his skinless body has a pearlescent sheen. His face is no longer recognizable because they've cut off his nose. There's a hole between his legs where they did the same to his genitals, all these pieces of him stomped by boots and dragged across the same aisle you walk down with your son and wife to pray each week.

Underwood is pacing with his assault rifle. Schembari is talking solemnly into his phone. You recognize another man because he's wearing a shirt with the sleeves cut off, and you can see the dragon tattoo on his shoulder.

"Now, I was trying to be decent about it, I really was," says Schembari, rubbing his baldness in exasperation, "but that car still isn't running right, and we had to send Tyler back home with it." He waits for a reply. "All right, but just let me know that you're getting it taken care of, that's all I'm asking. And make sure he knows that these mechanics, some of them straight up just aren't worth a single solitary fuck."

The men finish taking their pictures with Ginna Andrade and crowd around the cameraman to judge the results. No one appears much interested in the body suspended by a rope from the crossbeam. Underwood steps around it like it's a low-hanging decoration. The man who took the picture, you realize, is a police officer. He once manned a checkpoint and nearly caught you for driving drunk.

"Even if it was a timing belt," Schembari goes on, "we really needed that other vehicle tonight."

You realize you haven't exhaled in nearly a minute and slowly peel your head away from the light. You stand with your back to the wall for a moment, your eyes closed, just breathing. Then carefully and quietly, you make your way back through the hall, the reverend's office, and the basement. Out into the night, you take a wide berth through the woods until you're sure you're clear of the man in the balaclava sitting in the car.

Then you run. As hard and fast as you've ever run in your life.

A vortex has opened, and at its entrance, at the end of all possible things, there is a constellation of all the souls that ever were or will be. Every spirit must travel this path and into this dark wound. You try to take solace in that. As you drive through the night, your son asleep, your wife peeling her nails apart in silent terror, you try to remind yourself that what you saw in the church, a version of such a fate, the fear, the unknowing, the violence, awaits everybody. It is all too normal.

The highway is empty at this hour, but you sweat every pair of headlights in your rearview and white-knuckle the wheel until the vehicle passes. You try to keep it under ninety in case there are any state troopers not yet laid off still looking to write a ticket. You didn't need to do any begging to get Casey to lend you the truck. Simply took him out of the diner and told him what you saw. You just needed to get your family safe and told him exactly where he could pick it up.

Bombing through the darkness, the truck shuddering with speed, it's two and a half hours to Dayton. You do see one bizarre thing, this billboard, awash in light. Its panels are slightly skewed as if pasted up hastily before the rogue artists fled. Blue lettering on a black background, and all it says is:

KATE MORRIS IS ALIVE AND WILD

It's another fifty minutes to Trotwood. Your mom's place is the same lawn well kept, same flower boxes beneath the windows, same American flag above the porch, same junked neighborhood. She's of course surprised to see you and the family.

"What's going on, Johnny?" she asks as Raquel takes Toby back to your old bedroom to put him to sleep, reassuring him that things are not as scary as they seem right now.

"Too much to explain. Things got bad in Coshocton. We had to leave."

"In the middle of the night?"

"Yeah, Mom, in the middle of the night." You check the time on the microwave: 4:25 a.m. It's got to be at least three hours to the plaza at the tiptop of the state. "And I gotta get going."

"What are you talking about?" Raquel has come back into the room. Her eyes are bloodshot, her hair a starchy mess. "Where you going?" she asks. "Middle of the night, and where the hell you gotta be?"

"It's that job, I told you."

"Now?"

"It's gotta be now."

"No." She shakes her head furiously. "No. You need to stay here with me and your son—"

You take her hand. Into it, you slip the scrap of paper with the account number and the password.

"Don't lose this. It's only fifty dollars now, but soon it's gonna be nine grand. Then it'll keep going up until it reaches fifty thousand. Whatever you do, do not lose this."

Instead of looking happy, she starts crying. "Keeper, please. Baby, you're scaring the hell out of me." She puts her palms on the back of your head to cradle your skull. You kiss the hot brown skin beneath her eyes and hate yourself for being unable to protect her. "Please tell me what's happening."

"Just in case. I want you to have it just in case."

"In case of what?" she demands.

"And no matter what, do not go back home. You can't ever go back there. Promise me."

"This is really not normal, Johnny. This is all very strange," says your mother.

Then Toby is standing in the hallway in just his underwear and a T-shirt. He's signing too fast for you to understand but you catch a few words: *Dad. Stay. Please. Dad.*

"Okay, little man, okay." You go to him and pick him up. His thin arms wrap around your neck and he buries his head against your chest. Like he's been dreading this moment ever since you came home from prison, like he knew at some point you'd go away again. And for whatever reason he loves you. Even though you are angry and full of hate and anxiety and fear, he loves you. You stroke his hair.

"It's okay, buddy. We're okay." You feel his tears on your palm, and you try to sign to him as best you can, but you're so elementary. "I'm just going to do a job, Toby. I'm going to do some work and get paid, so we can finally go someplace nice, you know? Nothing to be afraid of. We're just having a weird day."

He pulls away to sign *Very weird.*

"Yeah." You snort back tears and laugh. "Too weird. Be good for Mommy. Listen to her and Grandma. Okay?"

He nods, not done crying, and you hug him again, kiss the top of his dirty head.

"You're such an amazing kid, you know? You're my whole life, little man."

Your voice cracks, holding your boy. Your mom looks confused. Raquel joins the two of you in the embrace. You kiss her and thank her for never giving up on you. The feeling you've had your whole life, that no one gives a shit whether you're alive or dead, hurt or healthy, in danger or safe, hungry or fed, Raquel's the only one who's made it recede for any length of time.

It makes you insane, if Casey hadn't warned you, to think of what could've happened. When you close your eyes to kiss her, you see Ginna naked with a black hole in her forehead and the reverend upside down, dripping. They wanted you, you understand, not because you're important but because of how easily you can be squashed.

"I've gotta go." And you pull away from your family. You take the truck's keys from your pocket, wipe snot on your sleeve. Soon you are back on the road, telling yourself you can turn around anytime you want. You can always call it off. You can always go back.

You haul ass north, hitting traffic outside Dayton. No jobs to be had, but everyone still has a reason to be somewhere in this exhausted hour of the morning. When you realize you'll be late, you begin to sweat. If you miss this opportunity, you have no idea what you'll do. Your mom lives on pennies. You and Raquel have nothing but the clothes on your back. You have no friends, no network, no place left to run.

You make it to the Commodore Perry Service Plaza by 8:30 a.m., desperately scanning the parking lot, unsure of who you're supposed to be looking for. You leave the key under the seat for Casey and step into the heat of the morning. It's already in the eighties and the sky is a hazy white. A storm on the way. You can tell by the way the wind is flipping the leaves. You walk across the parking lot, looking for what you're not sure. It's relatively busy at this hour; early-morning travelers buying coffee and snacks. Everyone looks tired or on edge. Maybe that's just you. You're headed inside when a woman's voice calls to you from behind.

"John."

This is not who you expected. She's middle-aged and pretty in a wealthy kind of way. Pert, angular features with fashionable ARs hovering over severe gray eyes. She wears a loose pink top, and her hands are tucked into black-and-white checkered pants. Overdressed for this hot Ohio rest stop.

"We're over here," she says, gesturing with her head to a plain white cargo van, the kind without windows in the back.

You hesitate. You see a driver behind the wheel, a Black guy craning his neck to get a look at you.

"I need to know more."

"Sure, we can talk in the van."

"No. Out here."

She looks around. "Hard to tell who's listening out here."

"I want the first nine grand up front."

She pouts her lower lip. Removes a phone from her back pocket. "No problem. It's done." She punches a few keys and then holds the phone up to show you. A transfer to the bank with your account. The number now a satisfactory four figures. "You don't have to worry about the money. If you do the work, you'll be fairly compensated. Exactly as you were told."

"I want something else," you say, and though you hadn't planned to ask for this, here it comes all the same. "I want the same deal for a woman named Claire Ann Chickering. Last I heard she was living in Hamilton, Ohio. I want the same deal for her. An account. Fifty K. The whole thing."

The woman regards you. "That wasn't the deal."

"It's the deal now. Or I walk away."

"Who is she?"

"Don't matter fuck-all who she is. She gets the fifty K too. Not split. Fifty K for her, fifty K for Raquel and Toby."

"Now we're negotiating?"

"Call it what you want, lady."

Her eyes wander the parking lot. This might be nervousness, but she's so icy it's hard to tell.

"Tell you what: You get in the van, we set up another account. You do what we ask of you, without hesitation and without question, Claire Ann's in. If not, no baby mamas get anything, and we put a bullet in your head. Fair enough?"

You hock back snot. "Figured that part anyway." And you brush past her, the door of the van opening for you as you approach.

On the road, these folks make their introductions. The blond woman is Quinn. The driver is Kai. And there is another guy, a little white kid named Henry. He's even shorter than you, dressed in an Abercrombie T-shirt and tan cargo shorts exposing pale, twig shins. He has crooked yellow teeth, acne on his neck, and says hi nervously, eagerly. He's very pleased to make your acquaintance, he says. The van is hollowed out with bucket seats attached to one side. When Kai pulls back out on the highway, you look past Henry's head through the little mesh window and spot the signs for Cleveland. Quinn makes a call, which essentially boils down to "We're on our way."

"Are you going to tell us what we're doing?" Henry asks. Only now do you realize he's like you. He doesn't know any of these people you're dealing with.

"We have to meet up with some friends," says Quinn. "It's better if we go over the plan then."

"All I'm trying to do is fight the man and get paid! Know what I'm saying!" Henry laughs far too hard, far too loud, and for far too long. He's painfully young, maybe not even old enough to buy a drink. You ride on in a lot of silence. After a while you realize Kai is skirting Cleveland, heading downstate on one of the north-south highways. Irrationally, you wonder if they're taking you back to the church, if this was all a complex ruse to hang you by your ankles while hungry men scrape your skin off with KA-BAR knives. This passes, and you're so exhausted you finally doze.

When you wake, it's because the van has stopped. The door is open, and you hear Kai and Quinn talking. Henry is outside as well, all three of them staring at something. The wind blows outrageously, watering your eyes. The sky is as green as the summer leaves.

"How long to get around this?" Quinn asks.

"Two hours, maybe more," says Kai.

And as you hop out, you can't believe they're talking about it so calmly. The van is stopped on a bridge spanning a deep, green valley. There is a traffic jam ahead and then—nothing but air. The bridge has collapsed, the road simply vanishing over the brim, and across the rift is the scar of concrete and rebar on the other side, still held aloft by massive cement pillars as tall and thick as buildings. There is forty feet of empty space where the highway used to be with cars and trucks stopped on either side of the void. Some folks are turning around. Others are waiting, as if the road will magically stitch itself back together. While Kai and Quinn debate, you walk up to peer over. Hundreds of feet below, huge chunks of concrete rubble lie at the bottom of the valley. The fender of a truck is poking out. You stumble back, dizzy.

"What do you think happened?" Henry asks.

"Bombs," says Kai. "They were hitting bridges in the South too."

"Who was?"

Kai shakes his head. "APL, The Pastor's freelancers. Who knows at this point."

There are more vehicles at the bottom of the valley buried under the wreckage, leaking fluid, people possibly alive praying for EMTs or at least Prion search and rescue. Maybe they'd been caught in the blast or maybe they'd driven right over the edge. No one had come along to so much as put up an orange cone.

"C'mon," said Quinn. "We're going to be way behind now."

She ushers you into the van, so you can head back the way you came.

––––––––––

The detour takes over an hour, and while navigating crumbling county roads, the storm finally breaks. You've seen hail maybe a handful of times in your life, but never like this. It begins crackling across the roof, the big white stones thwacking the windshield, some the size of golf balls. Traffic has slowed, red taillights stretching ahead and the oncoming white blurred by the storm. Many have pulled over under the safety of overpasses.

"Got a tornado warning too," says Kai. "Severe weather from here down to Georgia."

Quinn flares her nostrils. "Goddamnit," she hisses. Then with a strange, begrudging smile admits, "There is some humor in this, I guess."

Kai takes the next exit and pulls into the first charge station, where you'll wait until the supercell passes. You bum a cigarette off Quinn and stand under the station's vast awning watching the hail slam. A few of the bigger crystals are leaving small dents in the metal of the cars, the sound somewhere between a waterfall and a war. You almost tell her about Reverend Andrade and his wife, but something stops you. You want to trust her, you realize, because you've put your family and your future in her hands. But this is not an actual reason to trust her. Instead, you ask, "Why'd you want me? For whatever this is? Would've thought I'd be toxic to you."

She assesses you before answering. "I'm sure your friend told you how impressed we were that you did your time and didn't give him up."

"I'm no snitch."

"Sure, but as we've discovered, most people are. The benefit of your situation, John, is that—"

"Keeper. Please don't call me that. My name's Keeper."

"The benefit of your situation, Keeper, is that law enforcement is now fully algorithmified. They plug people's stats into a computer and let the AI tell them who to go after."

"If they knew I wasn't who they wanted why'd they try to put me away for fifteen?"

"Just our justice system doing what it does. We know from our sources they kept tabs on you for a year after you got out but then moved on to other priorities. You're LPS now—a low-probability subject. There are twelve-year-olds they're tracking with more resources than you. They thought you were a patsy."

"Well wasn't I?"

She plucks the smoke from her teeth and a tight smile pushes at one corner of her mouth.

"You might not believe in what we're doing, but this is the kind of action on which history pivots. This is a choice between revolution against the power structures or our extermination by those structures. People like you and your family? You're what they harvest. Everything you do, everything you buy, everything you believe in—that's just product and profit for them. You're their cash crop."

"Sure. Everyone's got an explanation for who's committing the sin. No matter whose religion it is, funny how I'm always the one on the losing fucking end."

She flicks the cigarette into the dwindling hail. "The storm's letting up. We should keep moving."

She walks back to the van. You smoke yours down to the nub and then follow.

That night, Kai finds a rest stop so you all can sleep for a few hours. You pass out right into a nightmare. You dream of your church. The men from the PRCC are there, Schembari's crew is there, the dead people you pulled from the ashes and the water are there.

On the road the next day, the worst of the storm has passed, but the sky remains dark. Kai follows the highway into a river valley, a pale scar through black hills. The woods crowd the road to form a shadowed tunnel. Even when you're climbing the low mountains of the Cumberlands, you feel as though you're in descent, slipping farther and farther into a gray-green dark. You finally pull into the lot of an abandoned gas station. You follow Quinn and Kai over the wet, puddled pavement to a big semitruck with a green logo and **SMITHBACK FOODS CATERING AND SUPPLIES** on the side. Quinn raps three times, and the doors of the freight trailer swing wide. This woman is tall, wide-hipped with a mouth of enormous teeth, fidgeting with ARs perched on the end of her nose.

"Hiya! Hop aboard. We need to hurry if we're going to make the delivery hour."

You and Henry follow the others, pulling yourself up and squeezing past a row of boxes that serve as a false front. Behind them, there's a workspace with desks and tablets and another man, big, fat, white, and bald. He looks like he's sick or maybe just tired. Purple bags under each eye. He nods at you but says nothing.

"When are we going to hear what our job is?" Henry asks. Everyone ignores him.

"We shouldn't have stopped," says Quinn. "The timing for the delivery is wrong now. What if they call actual Smithback fucking Foods? Then our little house of cards crumbles."

"Call and say the delivery is coming at five p.m.," says the ugly woman, who reminds you of a stork. "Tell them there were accidents and road closures. There's enough chaos out there right now that they'll buy it."

"Could someone please tell us what the damn job is?" says Henry, laughing. He's standing by a metal chest, a kind of footlocker that's held closed with a bike lock in the latch.

The stork keeps smiling when she addresses Henry, "All in good time, eager beaver. I'm Jansi, by the way." She holds a hand to a flat chest, and then gestures to the fat white guy. "And this is Murdock."

Murdock gives you a little two-finger salute. There's a tattoo on his arm you can't quite read.

Kai leaves the trailer and goes back to the van. Quinn stays and gestures toward two seats bolted to the wall. You and Henry sit side by side, and soon you feel the truck moving. Henry waits until the three of them are distracted by a screen to lean in and say, "Yo, this is kind of fucked. At least tell us what we're getting into."

"What'd they offer you?"

"Ten grand. You?"

"Yeah," you say, nodding. "Same. So for that amount, we don't ask questions."

"Man, I just need run money, you know? Gotta fuck off from Milwaukee before the whole place comes unglued. Fuck, I just want to know what we're s'posed to do. I don't like secrets. How'd you get hooked up with these guys?"

"Long story."

He shakes his head. "That old bitch Quinn said this would be simple. Said it would be an easy earn. Doesn't feel easy to me. Doesn't feel easy at all."

———

You feel the truck come to a stop. You don't know how long you've been on the road, but you overheard Jansi say "Virginia." Quinn comes to stand in front of you and Henry, flanked by Jansi and Murdock. She pops a seat on a bench opposite you.

"Sorry for the hectic nature of this," Quinn says. "We've had some setbacks as you can tell, but everything is still going to work out just fine."

"What we want to do," says Jansi, "is make this as easy for you two as we can, but that means following our instructions without question or hesitation. Understand?"

You and Henry nod.

"What we absolutely don't want is for anybody—especially you two—to get hurt, right? To make sure of that, you need to listen to us, and when we tell you to do something, you do it, okay?"

"Okay," says Henry, overeagerly. You just nod.

"We're going to be pulling into the loading bay, and from there you will have a short window to get inside the larger building."

"Will you give us a map?" asks Henry, playing it way too aggressively.

"No. You'll have these." She hands each of you a pair of thick AR glasses, more like goggles. "And we'll walk you through every step. What this mission is about, though, is we're going to scare a few people."

"Who?" asks Henry.

"That doesn't matter right now. What you need to know is we've thought this through from every angle. We know exactly how we're going to get you in and out, so the key for you is to listen to us and not panic."

"Gotcha," says Henry, nodding his small, buzzed head vigorously.

Murdock opens the metal footlocker and throws you and Henry each a pair of dark cargo pants. He asks your shoe size and then hands you a corresponding pair of black boots as well as a black shirt. Each of you strip down to your underwear. After you finish pulling the laces of the boots tight, there is a hardy belt weighted with zip ties, pepper spray, a flashlight, and the holster for a pistol. This is followed by knee and elbow pads, which the ladies strap on for you and Henry. Next they put the glasses on you to test them.

"Can you hear me?" Quinn asks from their little operations center. Speakers on the temples of the glasses conduct sound through your cheekbones, so you can hear her tinny voice. You nod.

Henry of course calls, "Loud and clear!"

"Take a seat." Murdock's voice is raw, like he's getting over laryngitis. Henry sits down first. From the footlocker, Murdock removes a kit of body armor with a vest, the kind with all the pockets, buckles, and straps. The Xuritas logo over the left breast. He handles it strangely, though, as if it's delicate. You notice black wires dangling from a pocket. He and Jansi lower the vest over Henry's head, helping him slide his arms through the holes, then spend a moment cinching it tight. "How's that feel?"

"Good," says Henry, nodding and nodding. "Heavy, but real good."

"Try standing."

Henry does so, then makes a little catwalk twirl. "Good," says Murdock. He takes the black wires and reaches into one of the pockets on the vest, connecting them to something. He looks to you. Your turn. When the vest lowers over you, you can feel its weight. It is very, very heavy.

Henry peaks into a pocket.

"Hey," says Murdock sharply. "Don't touch that."

"What is it?"

"Just don't touch it."

Henry sits back, but he's still staring down at his chest. As Murdock pulls tight the Velcro straps, you instinctually reach up and pat the breast pocket.

"What'd I say?" says Murdock. His eyes lock on yours. Something in his voice really scares you. "Don't touch it."

"Why?"

"Craftsmanship."

There's stitching at the top. Something has been sewed inside the front of the vest.

"What the hell is it?" Henry demands, staring at his chest. "Tell me."

"Henry," says Quinn. "Calm yourself."

"It's a fake," Jansi explains. Murdock finishes strapping you in and steps away. Jansi has an enormous smile on her face. "It's built to look like a bomb, but it *is not* a bomb. It's just wires and lights and Play-Doh."

"Huh?" Henry asks.

"We're here to scare somebody. So this is how we're going to scare them, right? We need to get something very specific from this person." She reaches into a bag and hands you each a gun. You take it, gingerly at first, only to feel a false weight in your hand. "See? Fake too. Rubber. They actually use these in movies. Just put them in the holsters and leave them there. They're for appearances."

Murdock reaches into the footlocker now. He hands you each a device. It looks like a joystick. It has a little button at the top and a cap that protects the button.

"Oh," Henry says.

"Seen 'em in movies too, right?" Murdock flips the cap up and pushes the button. Despite yourself, you flinch. "When the time comes, you just hold this in your hand like you're 'bout to press it. Make a big show of it, you know? Pretend like if you press it, it's doomsday, okay?" He tucks the trigger into one of your pockets. He does the same for Henry. Jansi continues.

"We'll get this guy alone, and he's going to give us what we need, understand? Just follow our instructions, and we'll get you out in twenty minutes."

Henry looks at you, his expression pained, but you look away. The hum of the idling truck is the only sound. They're all looking to you.

"Let's get to it then."

Jansi nods approvingly. Quinn puts a radio to her lips and tells the driver to get a move on. Murdock hooks up the wires poking out of the side of your vest. He doesn't look you in the eye. When he finishes, he goes and sits back on the footlocker and stares determinedly at the floor. He palms his bald head, his face angry, maybe distraught, maybe just tired. The truck huffs forward, and he catches you looking at him. His gaze is so unsettling, you set your eyes on the floor and try not to glance at him again. The drive takes another hour.

———

Henry's heel has been jittering away for twenty minutes. You want to ask Quinn why he was chosen. He's so young and nervous. Not that you've ever done anything like this before, but he's putting you on edge. You are sweating watching him sweat. He's not talking, just looking everywhere at once. You keep your eyes trained forward. Murdock and Jansi busy themselves at a laptop. They are looking at a schematic of a building, that much you can see. Quinn comes over to you and Henry and squats down between you. She puts a hand on each of your knees.

"I'm sure you're nervous, but really, no need to be. We've planned this all very carefully. Our goal is to keep you safe. And you're both going to go home with a hell of a cash prize."

"Cooome onnn down," you say. Henry and Quinn stare at you. "*Price Is Right,*" you explain.

The truck slows. "Here's where we get off," says Quinn. "Good luck."

Quinn, Jansi, and Murdock squeeze past the stacked boxes, leaving you and Henry alone. You hear the doors shut again. The truck starts up. Henry grabs your arm.

"Do you believe them? What's your story, where'd they find y—"

You clamp a hand over his mouth and hold a finger to your lips to get him to shut the fuck up. You point to the side of the glasses, then to his. You're afraid, yes, but more so that this shitbrain will screw things up. The speaker spews static through your cheekbone into your ear and then Quinn's voice.

"*The driver will dock the truck, and then we've got a two-minute window with this loading bay clear.*"

"Where are we going?" you ask.

"*We'll tell you.*"

The familiar bleats, the momentum of the truck reversing. It stops with a jerk. Quinn says, "*Let's go.*"

Henry follows you as you angle your body sideways to squeeze by the boxes. With a metallic scrape, you pop the doors and hop down into what looks like a small warehouse. There are rows and rows of shelves and big freezers with temperature gauges by the door handles. Boxes and crates of produce stacked on all sides. You're confused because you thought you were going to a restaurant. A green line appears in the lenses of the glasses.

"*Follow the green. Head straight back, through the double doors. That leads to a hallway. Turn left, and then head to the maintenance elevator. Fast fast fast, c'mon.*"

You grab Henry's arm and hustle him past all the thrumming industrial freezers. The weight of the vest makes this jog awkward. Your legs still ache from your sprint from the church the night before. Banging through the doors, you see the elevator. It only goes up, and you smack the button, highlighted in green by the ARs. You wait, listen to the elevator descend. Henry is breathing twice as hard as he should be.

When the elevator opens there is a man and a woman in chef's apparel, big white smocks with white sleeves rolled up. You freeze and you hear a sound come out of Henry's mouth.

"*Easy,*" Quinn says into your ear. The two chefs nod and continue their conversation as they brush past you. Something about the overtime they're making and if it's even worth it. You and Henry step into the elevator. In your glasses, the L button lights up green, and you smush it. The elevator begins up.

You hear a shred and realize Henry is ripping the stitching on the front of his vest. You grab his hands to stop him, but he's peering into the material of the vest like he's seeing his own version of Reverend Andrade hanging upside down. He stomps quietly around the elevator as you try to calm him without actually saying anything. He's mouthing words to you, smacking his lips, making moist sounds so you hear him.

It's real, it's fucking real!

And you smack your lips back at him.

No it's not, shut the fuck up, shut the fuck up and calm down.

This is real they're going to fucking blow us up.

Why? Why would they do that? Calmthefuckdown!

Then the elevator dings, and the doors slide open. The green line beckons you on.

"To the right," says Quinn. *"Out into the atrium."*

And this you were really not expecting.

You and Henry are suddenly standing in a vast space, skylights beaming early-evening sunlight into the atrium of some futuristic hotel. There are three desks with small plaques that say Guest Services and a lounge area, the tables adorned with fresh-cut flowers, the chairs taken by well-dressed men and women reading newspapers and tablets and checking their phones. One woman wears a VR set and scans her hand across the air, toggling through unseen options in a game, xpere, or worlde. Waiters dressed in black suits, white ties, and black aprons deliver drinks. The floor is dark marble veined with gold flake. Three gray pillars rise all the way to the ceiling. Between the pillars are plate-glass windows and beyond a beautiful green forest bisected by a sun-dappled river. Blue mountains rise in the distance while giant cumulous clouds hang in the sky's upper reaches. The view is so gorgeous it momentarily makes you forget where you are or what is happening. You realize you're holding your breath and let it out slowly. A huge bird, maybe a falcon or a hawk, alights on a branch outside and tics its head around. One of the guests points this out to another, finger wagging.

Henry, you realize, has not been stopped in his tracks by this beautiful scene. If anything, his panic rises. He heaves beside you, like he just finished a sprint. To your left, you spot a pair of security guards by the main entrance, two sliding glass doors facing a valet. Down the hill there is a gorgeous country road and bridge over the river. Ushers busy themselves collecting luggage from a black Tesla. The guards are dressed like you, same Xuritas uniforms, same style of ARs, but they carry automatic rifles. Your glasses ID them as *SSO Omerto* and *SSO Williams*. One of them actually looks at you but doesn't appear to notice anything out of the ordinary. You and Henry pass right through his field of vision and then he returns to boredly watching the incoming road that cuts through a dark stand of towering trees.

"Head to your right. We're going to take you through the kitchen."

Quinn's voice and the green line bring you back, but you have this feeling of floating above yourself. The sheer beauty of the surroundings makes you more discombobulated than your trespass or the device, fake or not, strapped to your chest. Nevertheless, you and Henry stand rooted in place.

"Guys, to the right."

Henry turns to his left and begins walking.

"I said to the right!"

Of course, they can see what you're seeing through your glasses, watching your every step.

"Henry," you hiss. "Henry!"

"Goddamnit, Keeper, go get him." This sounds like Jansi suddenly snatched the microphone away. You set off after Henry, grab him by the arm, but he rips free. Jansi's voice is furious. *"Henry, what the fuck are you doing? You're going the wrong way. Henry!"*

She's still talking as Henry tears the glasses from his face and throws them across the marble floor. You're horrified by this, checking every direction to see who might be watching. Every happy hour cocktail sipper, employee, and armed guard appears preoccupied, though. There is a gold plate on the wall with a sign for bathrooms, and he bangs through one of those doors. You follow.

It's the most incredible bathroom you've ever seen. Low lighting, glistening silver sinks, and each toilet with its own full door for privacy. You hear Henry in one of the stalls, crashing around. You push the ARs up on your head so they'll be pointed at the ceiling.

"Keeper? Put those back down. What are you doing?"

"Henry." You rattle the door, but he's locked it. "Henry, goddamnit." You hear him grunting, Velcro shredding, and then a low moan.

"Oh fuck. Oh fuck oh fuck oh fuck no no no no."

"Henry, please open the door," you say softly, like you're trying to coax your son. And it works. He pulls back the latch, and the door swings wide. He's crying. Big hot tears spilling down pink cheeks. His hair is sweaty and disheveled. He has his side angled to you. He's undone the Velcro straps and he's showing you something on the vest.

"*Get him back on track,*" Quinn demands. "*We have a perfect opportunity. Get him and let's go.*"

You've stopped listening because you see what has Henry weeping with panic: hidden beneath the Velcro, right at the love handle, is a small padlock cinching two metal eyelets together and holding the vest tight against his body. He was trying to pull it over his head but couldn't. You reach for your own vest, Quinn's voice buzzing in your ear, and rip open the Velcro. You have the same lock on yours. You didn't even feel Murdock snap it into place. Henry slumps against the stall, tugging his greasy hair. You snatch the ARs from your head and press your thumb over the microphone on the temple tip.

"You think they locked it to us if it's fake?" Henry hisses through his tears. "They're going to fucking blow us up." A huge glob of drool escapes his lower lip and drips down to his lap. "I want to go home," he moans. "Please, I just want to go home."

"Okay," you say, trying to think. That feeling from childhood has never left you, that you don't understand anything that's happening or why it's happening or how to change it or stop it, but never has that sensation been more intense than it is right now. "Okay," you say again.

"I just wanted to get a bike. I just wanted to get a bike and ride to Windsor," says Henry. "My cousin said she'd let me stay there. I just wanted to buy this bike my neighbor was selling. That's the whole reason." And he goes on like that for some time, weeping and babbling about a motorcycle he was trying to buy and some relative in Canada. It's hard to think with him blubbering so hard. You put the glasses back on top of your head. Jansi's railing at you.

"*—you hear me? You need to move right fucking now! Our window is closing.*"

"Okay, okay. We're moving."

You pick Henry up by the arm, but he refuses, goes limp like Toby during a tantrum. You take the glasses off your head, wrap them in one of the hot towels available in a little oven, and stuff them in a pocket.

"Let's go."

"What don't you understand? These are real." He smacks the front of the vest with both hands and this makes you flinch, half expecting it to go off. "They're real!"

"I can get it off you. Now let's go."

Henry's face changes. There's enough hope in what you've said that he collects himself. His weeping slows a bit. You grab another towel and mop some of the tears and sweat from Henry's acned brow.

"You've got to try to calm down," you tell him. "Just follow me and be calm. Okay? Everything's going to be all right."

He nods vigorously but can't stop weeping. "I just really want to go home, you know?"

The two of you leave the bathroom and you're anticipating the Xuritas guards to be waiting for you, but they're still at the entrance. The Tesla is gone, and the valets are milling and bullshitting, hands in pockets. No one is looking at you. Henry follows you down the length of the atrium, and even though the temperature is cool and pleasant, you are sweating like a hog. You approach a woman at Guest Services. She is pretty and brown-skinned with a tight black bun on the back of her head. A nametag on a gray pantsuit says she's Arma.

"'Scuse me, miss." She looks at you like she can't be bothered. "We need to borrow a wrench real quick. I talked to a guy in maintenance, but we're new, we got lost . . ." You feel this pitiful lie even as you're saying it. She's just staring at you. "And, um, where's he telling me to go to pick up this wrench?"

She shakes her head. "You mean like facilities management?"

"Yeah, that's it," you say too quickly.

"Second floor, down the hall to the left." She even picks up a map of the hotel, which is labeled Blue Crystal Mountain Resort, and draws a quick line showing your route. "You'll need your keycard." She's looking at your belt. "You have one, right?"

"We both left 'em downstairs. Sorry. Could I borrow yours? Promise I'll bring it right back."

She looks more irritated than suspicious and quickly programs a keycard on a little device. You don't understand why she looks at you this way, how she can somehow sense, even within this lie, your true nature. She hands over the card and goes back to not thinking of you ever again. Henry follows you to the elevator, where you use the map to navigate your way to facilities management. "Wait outside," you tell him.

You scan your way in. There are several men dressed in gray maintenance suits chatting at a desk. They look up.

"Hey, do y'all got a nut wrench I can borrow? I'll bring it right back."

The guy in the chair hops up. The two leaning against the desk remain, arms crossed. "Sure thing. What size you need?"

"Better give me a couple. Maybe a twenty-three and a twenty-two?"

The guy disappears into a back office and returns with the two wrenches. He hands them over without question. Wrenches in hand, you exit, grab Henry by the arm, and lead him down the hallway.

"You know how to unwire a bomb?" he asks worriedly.

"What? Fuck no."

Down the hall, you search for the first door that looks private enough and use the keycard. It's a supply room. You spot a roll of duct tape and strip off a small piece so you can cover the lenses on the ARs. Then you perch them back on top of your head. You can hear Quinn and Jansi having a total meltdown.

"Okay, okay, I'm here."

"*Keeper, we need to know what you're doing,*" Quinn pleads.

"What do you think I'm doing?" Then to Henry: "Get your arms over your head."

"*Okay, Keeper, I'm going to say something a bit frightening right now, but I want you to stay calm.*"

"I am calm." You fit the tips of the two nut wrenches inside the shackle of the padlock. "Calm as a virgin telling the truth." Despite the circumstances, you laugh at that old idiom of Raquel's.

"*Those vests are going off one way or the other. Understand?*"

You begin to squeeze the wrenches together. This old trick you learned ages ago, the first time you broke into a pharmacy to steal Vicodin.

"*And you've got to think about Raquel and Toby and your mother. Not only will they not get the money, Keeper. Not only will that vest go off, but you won't be around to protect them. They will be exposed.*"

You stop squeezing. There's a muffled exchange on the other end, and then Quinn's voice returns.

"*We can have people in Coshocton and Dayton in a matter of hours.*"

Henry still has his arms above his head, thrusting out his side, looking at you with wide, expectant eyes. Unlike Schembari and his thugs, these people somehow know where your mother lives.

"We're your fucking king now, Keeper. We decide what happens to you, what happens to your family, what happens to everyone you know or love or care about." Quinn pauses. Then her voice is kinder, less strident. *"Keeper, death comes and goes. There's no need to be afraid. There won't even be any pain."*

You feel the coldness of her words in your veins. It's the sensation of the saline solution when you used to sell your plasma, the opposite of the warm crawl of heroin.

"Okay," you say, and then you finish squeezing the wrenches together, laying all your strength into it. The padlock pops, and you tear the busted metal fragment out of the loop. Tossing the wrenches aside, you carefully lift the vest over Henry's head, and he's sobbing even harder now but with relief, thanking you so loudly that you take the ARs off and press your thumb over the mic again.

"Thank you thank you thank you thank you," he says. You grab his shirt to try to focus him.

"You need to go quick, Henry. Got it? Go to that desk up front and try to get a map of the area. I got no clue where we are. Then go into the woods. Don't use any main road, they might look for you there. Try to change your clothes quick as possible. Then you can't go home, okay? Don't go near anywhere they know about. There'll probably be cops looking for you too. Just disappear, okay? Just vanish."

He's nodding, but you have no idea if he's actually listening. "Aren't you coming?" he begs.

"I'm going to keep them thinking we're both here." You hold up his vest, and he almost recoils from it. "Go. Get a head start, okay?" He nods, weeping for this reprieve he had not thought possible. "Go!"

Henry throws open the door, looks both ways down the hall, and then heads to the right. It's the last you see of him. You wait in the supply closet for a moment, take a couple of deep breaths, and then replace the ARs.

"You there?"

"What's happening, Keeper? Did you hear me?" Quinn says.

"I heard."

"You need to tell Henry to put his glasses back on."

"I don't think that's gonna work."

"Why not?"

"Henry's not here. I busted him out of the vest. He's already long gone."

Now you can hear them heatedly arguing among themselves. You wait.

"Go find him."

"Let him go. He's a scared kid you chumped into this. I got his vest. Just let him go."

"We could set those both off right now."

You're staring at a row of hand soaps, wondering if this is the last thing you'll see in your life.

"You would've done it by now. I ain't that stupid."

Silence on the other end. Finally, Jansi's voice.

"Do exactly what we tell you, Keeper. Uncover those glasses or so help me God I'm going to personally put a bullet in your son's head."

You strip the tape away, lower the glasses over your eyes. "I'm all ears."

"Take Henry's vest with you."

The green line directs you back to the elevator. From there it's back down to the lobby. You pass by Guest Services, and Arma's eyes lift to you. You make eye contact and try to tell her with just your face that something is wrong, but of course she thinks that wrong thing is you. Outside, the sun bathes the atrium in its ever-warm glow. The trees sway with a peaceful wind. Guests talk in hushed, polite tones. As Quinn guides you down a hallway, someone steps into the green line: a thin, bald man with a pencil mustache. He wears a suit, a purple tie, and a lighter purple kerchief poking out of the breast pocket. His voice is light and lispy. "Hi, excuse me, I know you're just doing your job, and I know we're on high alert and all that, but unless you're on duty in the front lobby, if you could avoid walking past the guests and keep to the service hallways? I thought that was understood in the contract?"

"Tell him you're doing your job and you're in a hurry."

"Sure," you say. "I understand."

"Walk away. Don't say anything else. You're going to the service hall anyway."

You grit your teeth and stare at him a second longer than you have to. You think about mouthing something to him, but you can't think of what, and in that second, he nods and walks off. He doesn't want to deal with you any more than Arma did.

In the service hallway, hotel staff wheel room service carts with covered plates and cling wrap protecting the water glasses. Tiny, single-use ketchups and mustards and mayonnaise. A few staff members nod at you, but mostly no one notices. Just a security guard, gun strapped to his hip, carrying a vest that's not his, sweating through his uniform.

"Okay, now into the kitchen. On your left."

Into the kitchen, past the gas-fired range and the cooks, you follow the green line, but your stomach doesn't truly sink until you realize you are not going to some guest's room. The green line takes you to the edge of the kitchen and two double doors.

"Through there."

A waiter breezes by with a tray, and as the doors swing out you see the immense luxury restaurant on the other side, hundreds of people eating dinner, packed around a mirrored bar, and sitting on a veranda with umbrellas blocking the low sun. Black columns rise into a crème ceiling that matches the tablecloths and sets off the burgundy tile. Waiters and waitresses move between the tables, pouring wine, twisting the bottles to catch the last drop. There are children eating at some of these tables, coloring on placemats and picking at chicken tenders. There is the clatter of silverware and conversation and the wind moving into the dining room from the veranda that overlooks a small waterfall, part of the river you saw on the other side of the hotel.

You stand there, Henry's vest in hand, rooted in place.

"Keeper," Quinn says firmly. *"You need to keep moving."*

"Why in there?"

"Through the doors, Keeper."

"You can't set these off in there." You don't know what else to say, so you add, "Please." As if that word has ever meant anything.

"Listen to me." Jansi again. *"You don't have a choice in this. You are going to walk into that room. You're going to set Henry's vest on the veranda. Then you are going to walk to table fifty-one. That's to your left. It's a table of four—two men, two women, and you'll recognize the man in the blue suit with the gray hair. Do you understand? Tell me you understand."*

"No." The sweat comes racing down your temple, and an incoming waitress glances at you as she passes by. "I can't do that. I can't do any of this."

"Not only can you, but you will. Remember what I said. There's no choice here."

You begin walking back the way you came. Quinn and Jansi are both yelling into the com at once.

"These are not innocent people. There is no one innocent in that room—"

"If you don't turn around right now—"

"That vest is going off one way or another—"

"So set it the fuck off!" you shout, and several heads in the kitchen turn to you. But it's the dinner rush, and they are slammed. They're weirded out but quickly return to their various tasks. You lower your voice. "It's just people out there. With kids. They're just—it's just people . . ."

Your plan is to get outside as fast as possible, get as far away from the crowded restaurant as possible.

"*Keeper.*" It's Quinn now. Her voice calm. "*We can either set it off in the lobby or you can do as you're told. Either way. The difference is—*" You smash back through the kitchen doors into the hallway. "*The difference is, will your girlfriend and your son have money to survive? Will your family get a chance to start fresh? Or will they all be dead before the sun rises in Ohio?*"

You stop and buckle where you stand, holding your face. You want to scream so badly but don't dare. You feel like your head is being ripped apart. You smack one hand against this pointless ornate wallpaper, elegant even in the service hallway. You stupidly wonder how long you'd have to work, how much money you'd have to save, before you and Raquel could afford a weekend getaway at this place.

"*The choice is yours, Keeper. You can secure your family's future or you can kill them right now.*" She waits for you, but you are crying too hard to respond, grinding your forehead into the wall. "*Keeper, turn around and go into that dining room.*"

You sniff. You have mucus all over your lower lip.

"What about a deal?"

Silence from the other end.

"The man in the blue suit. Who is he?"

More silence, then finally, "*What do you mean 'deal'?*"

"You want that one guy at table fifty-one? What if I let the rest of 'em go? I let all them go, then it's just me and him."

There's a pause and then you hear a man's voice in the background. Kai. He must have been with them the whole time. "*I don't see why that wouldn't work.*"

"*No!*" Jansi cries. "*What are you talking about? No one in that room is innocent! These are the people we're at war with. There is not one person in that room who doesn't have blood on their hands.*"

"*Just calm down,*" says Kai.

"*She's right,*" says Quinn, and then they are all arguing, and you just stand there with your head against the wall waiting to see what they decide. You try to interrupt them.

"I'm betting that without the one guy, this plan will mostly be for nothing. So maybe I hold more cards than you think."

This quiets them. They mute the conversation on their end, and you wait. Finally, Quinn comes back on.

"*We have a compromise.*"

And you actually laugh. You laugh right out loud.

"*What's so funny?*"

"Everything," you tell her. "Just about fucking everything."

"*We want the other three people at the table,*" says Quinn. "*You can let everyone else go, but all four of them at that table stay.*"

You swallow. Four lives for the life of your children and their mothers. After everything, it turns into an even trade. You can already feel hell's flames licking at the tight leather of these foreign boots, for that's where this will take you. No question about that.

"Deal."

The walk back through the kitchen seems to take twice as long. The sounds of frying and sautéing and chopping recede. When you're about to reach the doors, you turn to the kitchen and cry out, "Excuse me. I need your attention." A few heads turn but mostly people keep working. "*Excuse me!*" you bark. The sounds of the kitchen quiet. "There's been a threat against the hotel. I need everyone here to proceed to the exits immediately. Put down what you're doing and exit immediately."

There is a great deal of hesitation. They all look afraid to leave their posts.

"*Now!* This is not a drill. We got a serious threat! You need to drop what you're doing and go now!"

And then they're moving, scattering like mice.

"Tell everyone!" you call after them. "Everyone in the hotel—tell 'em!"

You turn and, without looking back, push through the doors and into the restaurant. You stay against the wall, sure that they won't set off the vests until you're closer.

"Quinn, do I got your word on this?"

"*Keeper,*" she sounds almost sorrowful, "*of course you do. Of course you have my word.*"

You take no chances this time. You belt it out, as loud as you can.

"Excuse me! May I have your attention please! Right now, please direct your attention to me!" You thump your chest, feel the dark materials beneath. "I need everyone to proceed to the exits immediately. Leave your food. Leave everything and exit the building immediately."

To your utter disbelief, no one rises. People continue to sip wine while several irritated diners demand to know what's going on. You spot the man at table fifty-one, and you recognize him. He's been in the news a lot over the years. He is a famous man. He ran for president. Mackowski is his name. He looks bored and leans over to the woman sitting next to him to ask her something. A nearby diner tells you his skirt steak hasn't come out yet, and he's not going anywhere until it does because it's already been twenty-five minutes. You can't believe how they look right through you, even in this situation. You try again. "There's been a threat against the senator's life, and all of you need to get out immediately. Senator, I need you and all of your, uh, tablemates, your friends, to stay where you are."

A few people rise and begin to move out, but not the vast majority.

"Are you people fucking stupid?" You take the rubber gun from the holster, and a woman chirps in shock. You begin stalking past the tables. "Go!" You grab an older man by the arm and jerk him out of his chair. There are gasps, but this gets the whole crowd moving.

You lock eyes with the senator.

They filter through doors at the front of the dining area, but not nearly as fast as you would have imagined. You can even see a few of them reaching for their phones. Likely to complain to Guest Services. You move toward the senator's table, and the Asian woman he was speaking to begins to rise, so you bark at her, "Not you! Sit back down. Please." And she does.

As the people hustle past, you approach table fifty-one. The senator sits with his legs crossed and his hands stacked calmly on one knee. He wears a blue jacket with a white open-collar shirt. Gray chest hair puffing out the top. His face is weathered but strong. He appears unimpressed with you and this display. He is utterly unafraid. Beside him the Asian, thin and attractive, wearing a sleek purple dress and expensive jewelry, wavy black hair with a pin carefully placed in the side. There's no mistaking how badly she wants to leave with the rest of the diners. On the other side of the senator is a tall, handsome guy with a beard like a billy goat, the chin all white. His eyes flap from you to the senator and back to you. He has his phone in his left hand and a drink in the right, which he still has not set back down. His thumb is poised above the screen of his phone as if in mid-text. Finally, beside him is a woman, brown like Arma, but older and wearing an expensive black dress. She stares at you coldly, the first to question all this.

"What kind of threat?" she demands.

You stare at the four of them. You don't see any point in hiding this anymore. You drop the fake gun, pull the trigger from your vest, and flip the cap up. "Bomb threat," you say. Then you rip the stitching so the false front of the vest tears open, and there it is. Wires. Battery. Cell phone. Plastic-packaged bricks of ruddy orange something held with black electrical tape. The lumps you felt were plastic bags of bolts, washers, and nails. When they see this, the bearded man cries out, and the Asian woman tries to stand.

"*Don't,*" you snap at her. "Sit back down." And again she does. A woman to your left screams, and now people are running for the exit. Now they're listening to you, and you have to admit, you like that power. However fleeting. As the last of the guests scramble out, the room is silent except for the sounds of the wind and river coming in from the veranda. Holding the trigger in your right hand, thumb hovering over the phony switch, you take a chair and set it between the senator and the bearded man, who is white-knuckling his drink.

"Please," says the bearded man, breath whistling. "Oh Jesus please, man, please don't, just don't."

"Peter," says Senator Mackowski. "Settle." And Peter stops talking. He sets the glass down and sucks a breath into his palm. Tears form in his eyes and spill quietly down the sides of his face. The brown woman keeps glaring at you, her face unchanged since you walked into the room.

"Okay," you say, speaking to Quinn and Jansi. But you're looking at the senator, so he thinks you're talking to him.

"Okay what?" he says and braves a look at the bomb. His eyes quickly return to yours.

The brown woman reaches into her bag, and you jerk the trigger at her in case she's like Secret Service reaching for a gun.

"Hey—it's just my phone," she says, retrieving the device and unlocking the screen. "All I want is to—"

The Asian woman abruptly stands and you swing the trigger at her, spit flying from your mouth: "*Sit the fuck back down!*" She does so immediately.

"Emii," says the senator. "Do what he says."

"No why no why," whispers the Asian woman, her whole body shaking. This strange combination of words. "No why no why."

"Hey. My friend." The brown woman is holding her phone at you. She's showing you a picture.

"What's taking so long?" you say to Quinn and Jansi, but they don't respond, and for a brief moment you wonder if they lost their nerve.

"What do you mean?" the senator asks you. Emii is gasping and rocking, maybe hyperventilating.

"This is our family," says the brown woman, and she rubs Peter's arm. She is so calm, her startling brown eyes searing into you. "See these two? These are our children."

Your eyes well. You understand Peter is this woman's husband. You don't want to look at this picture of their family, but you can't help yourself. In it, they are both skinnier, younger, and beaming. The two kids are a shade lighter than the woman, an older girl in jeans and a purple tank top and a boy who has only half a mouth of teeth and smiles to show off every one of them. Toby would be about the age of the girl.

"I don't suppose," says the senator, "that I could talk you out of this."

"It ain't really up to me," you whisper.

"That's Noor. And the boy is Gregory," she says, pointing to each of the children. She must be as scared as her husband, but her fear is different. In fact, she swipes her thumb to show you another picture. "These are our children," she repeats, and finally tears brim in her calm and terrifying eyes.

You're clutching the trigger so hard your hand hurts.

Then the senator says, "I beat cancer three times—you believe that? Three times." He nods. "And I feel lucky that this is the way I get to go. They'll be telling stories about this for the next five hundred years."

Then suddenly you drop the trigger. You drop it because your hand is shaking so violently. Everyone's eyes fall to the device. The senator snatches after it, and Emii bolts from the table, but her legs freeze midstride.

There is a thunderous crack, a deafening jet-engine howl, and a sensation of swelling, of expansion, of hyper-acceleration, of being rent apart. It is so oddly long and painless, like the acceleration of a roller coaster the moment after it crests the first hump and begins its descent. So that's what comes to you: riding the tallest roller coaster at King's Island when Joe Biggs took you that one summer, and he never gave you the chance to chicken out. And then at last, a fleeting glimpse of all these infinite and eternal ciphers, watched by the burning eyes of angels, and roaring into vivid, unyielding creation.

WHAT WE DREAM OF
WHEN WE'RE DYING

2037–2038

*T*ony missed Kate Morris's funeral, so he missed his daughter's eulogy for her friend. Two days before he was supposed to fly to Oregon, a pain in his stomach kept him from even packing a bag and left him in bed for a day. He had to watch Holly deliver her eulogy on TV, her skin zitty and eyes puffy with post-baby sleeplessness. She spoke with clarity and beauty. She was perfect. He called her afterward to tell her so and that he was pissed he'd gotten food poisoning and couldn't make it. For the next three months, however, he continued to experience cramps, constipation, and nausea, and treated it by guzzling Pepto. He kept explaining it away until one morning he went to flush and saw the toilet water filled with blood. By then he more or less already knew what was going on. His primary care physician, possibly the only man he knew more cantankerous than himself, scolded him for forgoing a colonoscopy for seven years.

"Or computational pathology. An algorithm would have caught this."

"I was indisposed for part of that," said Tony. "The preventative care wasn't tiptop in black-site prison."

"You should file a lawsuit," the doc suggested.

"I did."

"In the meantime, you need a gastroenterologist immediately."

A week later, it was confirmed: A tumor in his colon. The biopsy came back, and no surprise, it was cancerous. The good news was that it wasn't that big, stage III, not stage IV, so they'd resect it, and there was a chance that would be that.

In a way, he was almost relieved that it had finally happened. During Gail's diagnosis and rapid deterioration, he'd become so familiar with cancer, overreading, overstudying, making sure the doctors were trying everything in the arsenal, that his own cancer felt like a homecoming. That was the calling card of the emperor of all maladies: It simply had no quit. Given enough time it would come for everyone.

He did not tell Holly or Catherine. The resection was a simple procedure, and his surgical oncologist seemed confident, so by late May with the Dow Jones imploding and unemployment surging, Tony had the surgery. He lay in the hospital bed, watching as the anesthesiologist fixed a syringe into the IV, delivering the cloudy propofol, a liquid as milk-white as the lunule of a thumbnail. He knew this would be followed by a paralytic and a general anesthetic, but before he could reflect much, the oxygen mask was lowering over his face and then he was awake again and sore as hell in the gut. They'd gone in laparoscopically, three incisions, including the belly button and, according to the surgeon, taken out twenty inches of his colon, along with a tumor that measured 3.1 by 2.8 centimeters. He spent three more days in the hospital, but he was defecating and passing gas very soon after and the soreness in his abdomen diminished. He took a driverless home. He slid behind his desk to tackle his hundreds of missed calls and emails. Ash Hasan and Marty Rathbone had been contacting him nonstop for several days. "I'd rather just be put out of my misery than call these two back," he told his dog, Jamie.

"Tony?" cried Rathbone. "Where the hell have you been? We've got the opportunity of a lifetime here."

He knew that witless moron Warren Hamby had bestowed Rathbone with the dubious honor of Treasury secretary, mostly because of the paper he and Marty had written in '24 that predicted exactly what was happening as housing prices collapsed. Rathbone explained that the new president was convening a task force to draft emergency legislation: bank rescue, coastal rescue, climate rescue all in one.

"Why should I be interested in helping out the government that disappeared me into an extrajudicial cell for seventeen fucking months? Not sure if you heard, Rathbone, but I'm suing those cunts."

But Hasan called him next and laid out the stakes.

"This isn't just about your expertise, Tony," Hasan told him from his screen, bouncing his son, Forrest, on his leg. "You're viewed by many as the foremost authority on the matter. Your very presence, I'm hazarding to guess, will help calm fears, markets, and panic. I would sooner trade the rest of the team for your presence if that's what it takes."

He knew he'd agree, given how unpleasant it would be to watch others screw the pooch via cable news clowns, but first he had a follow-up with his surgeon.

In the waiting room, he was treated to memories of all the same rooms from Gail's ordeal, the TV in the corner with its programming about how bell peppers have antioxidants and more Vitamin C than an orange or why it's helpful to exercise between chemotherapy treatments. All the worried people waiting, everyone wondering who had it worse.

"I'm sorry to say, Tony, the news is not what we wanted. It's not dreadful, but it's definitely not what we wanted." The surgeon's office was a warm, light-filled space with a view of lush trees outside the window. Tony marveled at how many people had gotten shitty news in this very same setting.

"We took out twenty-six lymph nodes, and ten of them were cancerous, which is, I probably don't need to tell you this, but that's a bad prognostic indicator. It's not a death sentence—not at all—so I want you to stay positive. But I also know you're a no-bullshit kinda guy and the no-bullshit prognosis here is that we need to start you on chemotherapy as soon as possible. I'm going to refer you to a medical oncologist . . ."

The surgeon went on for a while after that, but Tony wasn't listening. Patients responded in different ways to the violence of chemo, but it had been absolute hell on Gail. She'd come home after getting the tamoxifen pumped into her, be okay for about twelve hours, and then spend the next day vomiting into a bucket because she was too exhausted to even get out of bed. Her hair fell out, and she was in such agony, unable to even watch TV, the nausea and pain were so bad. The worst part, she once said, was that when she did feel well enough to eat, nothing tasted right. She'd bite into a peach and it would taste like sheet metal. She couldn't enjoy the brief moments when she didn't want to vomit everything up. As the surgeon droned on, he realized he'd already made up his mind about what he was going to do.

"I have an important trip coming up," he said. "This'll have to wait until I get back."

The surgeon looked deeply vexed to hear this. "Tony, that's a really bad, really dangerous idea. Chemo treatment will reduce the chances of metastasis significantly."

"It's not something I can put off," he said, standing to leave. "I'll call the oncologist as soon as I get back. Shouldn't be more than a couple weeks."

He called his daughters to tell them where he was going. Catherine sounded strangely awed by everything that was happening. Too young to recall '08, and she'd treated the pandemic like an inconvenience to her social life, this was her first go-around at global crisis as an adult. She was still down in Florida working for Corey, trying to rescue the family business. Catherine, sounding too much like her uncle, said, "I'm hoping, Dad, that you're going into these conferences with an eye as to how it affects the small businessperson?"

"Yes, Cat, my first priority is rescuing your uncle's house in Sarasota."

"I'm just saying, Dad! There's about a million unemployed construction workers down here ready to jump into the sea. It's bad."

Catherine looked healthy and vital, her cheeks plump, her smile mischievous again. Holly, on the other hand, was stick-thin, her pregnancy weight sloughing off along with too much else. She had Hannah on her lap when he called. ("Say hi to Grandpa! Say hi!," waving the baby's pudgy arm.) Her eyes were pitted, her cheeks hollow, but she did not want to talk about how she was doing. She wanted only to speak of the task force.

"You have to push them, Dad. This is a big opportunity."

"Everyone keeps saying that."

Hannah Gail Yu sucked on her fist while simultaneously trying to look up and behind at her mother. Hannah looked a lot like Dean, no bridge to her nose, enormous brown eyes, and straight coal-black hair.

"You have security in the building?" he asked.

"We're taking precautions."

"You've been in the public eye now, especially after the eulogy—"

"I know, Dad."

"And it was an amazing speech, but—"

"Dad, I know." This bubble of her irritation burst abruptly, and they were both quiet. He'd been at her apartment with the new baby when they heard about the shooting, and even as Holly began trembling and weeping, he'd felt almost exalted. Because Holly hadn't been there. Her grief couldn't match his blinding relief. She'd twice dodged the bullets of madmen, first Victor Love and then this David Joseph Madison. Because she'd been through so much, because she likely lived with the guilt and pain of having her friends die all around her for this cause, because she looked exhausted and angry every time he saw her, he did not feel like he should tell her about his diagnosis. Hannah craned her head back and tried to grab her mommy's chin for attention.

"They're monitoring our communications while we're in Idaho," he said. "So there are no leaks."

"Go save the world," she said, already reaching to end the call. "I'll talk to you when you're back."

He'd spent one year and five months in a prison cell that wasn't officially a prison cell somewhere in the New Mexico desert, and he knew in that time

Holly had been screaming from the rooftops. She'd hassled every civil rights lawyer, called every news outlet, bombarded every reluctant politician with his story. She'd joined that ill-fated protest. She had championed his innocence while he sat in his white cell and fluctuated through despair, fury, and boredom, while he took his one-hour walk each day in a yard with a square of sky veiled by mesh wire. They only took him out in the early morning when it was still cool, his only contact a few rotating guards who were polite enough given the circumstances. There were others imprisoned there. He knew, because he heard them sometimes through vents or walls, weeping or screaming, and while the challenge to PRIRA was winding through the courts, he read whatever terrible books they'd allow him while he worried about his daughters.

That all felt like a nightmare now, long gone, but having come out the other side, he could sense there was some part of Holly that almost resented him for putting her through that. One year and five months because some peckerwood bomber once saw him speak to a crowd of thirty-five and was first in line for a selfie. One year and five months because a rogue authoritarian wanted to make an example of a scientist who was speaking out too much. One year and five months in which that president had his thugs fire into a protest and everyone just moved on, so that by the time Tony got out, the political class was more hysterical about food aid. One year and five months he would never have back, whether his lawsuit was successful or not. Hell, he still had mail he hadn't gotten around to opening before he found out about the cancer.

That night he had a dream. He stood on the side of a midsize mountain overlooking a plateau of forest, gazing past boulders and ridges and red-yellow autumn trees. In the distance were more mountains and river valleys, green and lush. On the plateau were hundreds of people gathered in an enormous circle around dusty ground. They were dressed in red and white, faces obscured by black masks with no mouth or eye holes. They had their arms around each other, swaying back and forth as one. Humming a low, throaty song.

During the weeks they spent in Idaho, Tony could not have been more frustrated with the supposed crack team of experts assembled to deal with a civilization-threatening financial and environmental crisis. The outsized egos in the room made for nuclear brinkmanship with every exchange. Rathbone and Hasan he was at least used to; their arrogance was familiar and therefore navigable. Tufariello he'd known for some time, but he'd never been impressed with her as a scientist, and she and Hasan's sister formed a coalition more interested in legislating social justice schemes than reducing emissions. Meanwhile Joe Otero, some slop bucket Republican mandarin whose sole qualification appeared to be that he'd mildly resisted The Pastor's fascism, had a nervous breakdown halfway through and had to piss his pants back to whatever slit he'd crawled out of. McCowen was a vulgar narcissist but at least tried to keep to the topic at hand. Admiral Dahms, a needle-dicked Vic Love sycophant, played his conscience-of-the-military-industrial-complex card while steering funding to massive Pentagon infrastructure projects and base relocations. He also had the disgusting habit of picking his teeth with his overlong fingernails. Finally, there was Emii Li Song, who he erupted at on the first day and proceeded to shun. She sat through every meeting, stony and silent but listening so intently you could almost see her brain plotting. That they made any progress in those weeks at all was surprising, but this was done by basically accommodating everyone: giving Jane and Haniya their reorganization of American economic life, giving Dahms his funds, giving Rathbone his banking reform, et cetera. Still, the heart of the bill resembled what Hasan first proposed, and Tony was cautiously optimistic right up until he smelled the smoke.

He could rarely sniff that scent anymore without thinking of his terrifying scramble through the streets of Los Angeles as he searched for his daughter. Secret Service didn't have to tell him there was a forest fire nearby because he'd already smelled it. That night, he never got into bed: he packed and took a car to the airport, where he waited for what he knew was coming.

On the flight out of Sun Valley, he watched the scarred and jagged horizon backlit by orange flame. They landed in Cleveland, and he couldn't sleep without his dreams growing darker. He found himself standing on a patch of brittle ground, ankles tangled in tree roots, boxed in on all four sides by jets of fire. Black smoke curled from the cinders and snaked around his wrists and torso. Within the flames, he saw demons, shrieking and taunting, and he had a nagging fear that he'd left something or somebody behind. The worst part was that when he looked straight up, he could see the stars.

He woke in the middle of the night, soaked in sweat, and at first, he thought the knock was part of the fading nightmare. But it wasn't. He answered to find Emii Li Song at the door.

"What?" he said. He didn't have his glasses on, so she was blurry in a dark bathrobe.

"We share a wall. I heard you scream."

"Yeah, I was having a bad dream." And suddenly he wished he hadn't admitted that. He also became aware of his gut hanging over his pajama pants.

"Can I come in?" she asked.

He hesitated, wanted to say no, thought he'd say no, but ultimately said yes. He had no idea why she wanted this, but it happened almost without pause. She led him to the bed and sat behind him massaging his shoulders, the skin of her calf pressed against his arm, and after kneading his neck for a bit—which, admittedly, felt wonderful—she turned his face and began kissing him. He stopped to ask her what she was doing.

"That out of practice?"

In truth, yes, he was, and though he was sure he acquitted himself poorly in the ensuing activities, Emii seemed satisfied by the end of it all and lay with her head on his chest.

"I don't really understand," he said.

"What's not to understand?"

"You're a beautiful woman. I'm a decaying old man who's told you to fuck off in multiple forums."

It was dark, so he couldn't see her face, but there was no trace of humor in her voice when she said, "I admire you. I always have."

She visited his room every night after that. They did not speak of these late-night encounters during the day. They didn't even eat meals together. Yet she kept coming to his room, and he had to admit how good it felt to hold someone again, to simply feel another person's skin and warmth. It pushed back his fear of what was happening within his cells. He knew his daughters wanted him to find somebody, but it had never clicked. From his many hours spent by Gail's side, he understood that the thing that broke her heart the most was not her own death but that she'd never see Holly and Catherine grow up. She'd never know what they'd become as their own women; she'd never meet their terrible boyfriends or move them into their college dorms; she'd never watch Holly discover all the books she'd love, and she'd never get to argue with Catherine about the appropriateness of certain outfits. Gail claimed she wanted Tony to find someone who cared about him, "Even if she's a dirty climate groupie whore." But he did not want to find someone. The memories of watching the girls grow into women, the specificity of each landmark, he could never give those moments to any-one else. They were Gail's, and in her absence, they would just have to be hoarded and buried with him and him alone.

The task force was getting close, though, and he was feeling the urgency of his disease. He'd spent much of his downtime reading about what ten of twenty-six cancerous lymph nodes meant. He was also getting tired more frequently, feeling a deep fatigue every morning. He told Hasan over dinner that he could not go to D.C. to help push the bill through. He had to get back to New Haven. Ash wiped his mouth and said nothing until they signed the check. Then he suggested they take a walk.

Though Tony had no interest in leaving the safety of the hotel for the sweaty, teeming streets of downtown Cleveland, he followed. They'd been assigned a security detail, but Ash did not contact them. Beyond the doors of the lobby, the city had the raw, panicked edge he saw everywhere now. The police presence was overwhelming. They wore tactical equipment and carried automatic weapons; their faces masked behind plexiglass helmets. But for now, the peace was intact, the lights of the casino sparkling.

"We need you, Tony." Ash walked with his hands in the pockets of his slacks, head bowed. "We're close to completing an acceptable omnibus bill, but we will need to convince a good number of frightened and recalcitrant politicians. If we fail, I don't think I need to explain the consequences."

"Yeah, I get the consequences. Thing is," he barreled ahead, "I have a health issue. Not a good one. I've put off treatment the whole time we've been working on this."

Ash took this news without surprise or interest, really. He didn't even ask what the issue was. What a goddamn freak.

"My condolences. Nevertheless." They stopped beside a statue of some old dead white guy. Bartholemew Fucking Cleveland or something. "What I've always admired about you, Tony, is that you look at everything in a straightforward manner. Even a wound. Even death."

"Yeah, well, I tried on rose-tinted glasses once, and they looked like shit."

Ash favored him with a gaze as clinical as a mortician's.

"The man who murdered Kate Morris and your daughter's other friends. He was a troubled obsessive with access to a military weapon. No links to militias or hate groups. He was just a man with a computer full of musings on Ms. Morris. Nothing more."

"Sure, the lone gunman. I've heard that one."

"My point being, the political violence unleashed over the last few years has actually been rather mild so far. It will certainly grow much, much worse if we fail. You have a responsibility, Tony, to help arrest this breakdown. You are a father and a grandfather. To think that this chaos will not come to your doorstep is naive, particularly for Holly, who is now a highly public figure."

The chill crawled through him as he heard his truest fear spoken aloud. Hasan then stepped far too close, almost like he was going to attack him.

"I don't accept your resignation because you don't have the option of resigning. You and I have no choice but to throw ourselves in front of this train." He turned and began walking back toward the hotel. Over his shoulder, he added, "So to speak."

<hr>

In D.C., they hammered away at the nation's political class, delivering 3D presentations, inveighing about the quickly collapsing Antarctic ice sheets, trying to keep one caucus together and fracture another to draw off defectors. What he concluded, however, was that he'd wasted precious months forgoing treatment so he could listen to imbecilic senators and congressmen prevaricate while failing to read even the most elementary briefing materials on the most important vote of their lives. Meanwhile, the Chinese government convulsed, the governor of Kansas executed more people live on VR, and the riots, arson, and clashes in cities grew worse. Reading a book about the Covid-19 crisis, he marveled at the relative ease of the situation. Turn a few policy knobs here, pull a few levers there, stimulus, vaccine, no big deal, problem solved. What they were dealing with here was a game of nine-dimensional chess, and they couldn't even get people to sit down at the goddamn board and start trying. Russ Mackowski was a particularly odious exemplar of the overall problem: a hypermasculine buffoon who was content to let the world incinerate as long as it furthered his ambitions. As jaded as Tony was, to hear him admit in their meeting that he had no intention of ever letting their bill come to a vote was truly shocking. Mackowski held up a meaty butcher's palm and told them he was going on vacation. When he left, Tony released a string of expletives into the ears of Ash and Emii.

"It was an opening bid," she said with her standard calm. "He understands he holds a very good hand in one of the most important poker games of his career. We can work on him," she assured them. In the weeks since returning to D.C., he and Emii had seen each other only twice. Even in the midst of freefall, the human animal longs for the simplest carnal pleasures. Ash called him the next day.

"My brother-in-law, Peter, and Haniya will follow Mackowski to the Blue Crystal Mountain Resort during the August recess."

"What, are they all going fucking fly-fishing together?"

"That he's acquiesced to hearing out Haniya, Peter, and Ms. Li Song means we could still have an opening. Peter thinks he's not the ideologue that he claims. If this is about horse-trading, we can have them quietly negotiate to bring him to a yes."

That night, he texted with Emii, laying out the stakes, the arguments, anything that might help.

I'm well aware of all of this, she wrote back to him. Her typical curt manner.

I know, I'm just losing my mind.

And he really was. That week had been The Pastor's Loyalty March, and the sight of all those people bleeding from their scalps as they tore through the streets nationwide was about the most pants-shitting thing he'd seen in his adult life. Every day that passed, every dollar sucked out of the economy, every spasm of violence, it all ticked by with a deadly finality. There were things you could not come back from.

Stay calm. We will get there. I have to go to bed now. Good night.

He considered replying with something sentimental or perhaps inviting her to his hotel, but ultimately, he only reciprocated her good night and then lay awake, staring through the window at silver moonlight.

———

It was August 15, a Saturday, and Tony had ordered room service for dinner. He'd spent all day in a meeting with Dahms, Hasan, and Tracy Aamanzaihou. Not only did they not have the votes in the Senate but the Climate Caucus was beginning to succumb to cracks from within. Indemnity and other issues were not sitting well, and as these details leaked, resistance coalesced from the most stalwart supporters for action. When Morris and her Seventh Day organizers were murdered, her movement splintered. There were maybe six different groups now trying to claim her mantle, organizing protests and boycotts but without enough people or imagination to actually bring focused pressure to bear. The result was a fire hose, and these pretenders were trying to prove their mettle and purity by staking out the most radical positions they could concoct. All of them were against the bill and were waging social media and VR war to stop progressive legislators from voting for it.

That's what he thought Holly was calling about when he saw her name and picture pop up on his screen. But when he answered he immediately knew something was wrong.

"Dad, turn on the TV."

The news was, as usual, less than helpful, scrambling to get as much panic and rumor onto the air as it could. Nevertheless, the chyron said enough: ATTACKS AND ASSASSINATIONS TARGET GOVERNMENT OFFICIALS, CORPORATE LEADERS.

"Dad, you need to get out of D.C.," she said. "Right now."

"Where are you?" he demanded.

On CNN: a bombing in New York, a mass shooting in Connecticut, and another bomb at the Treasury Department in D.C. He'd been in the building the week before meeting with Rathbone.

"We're home in our apartment," said Holly.

Dean appeared next to her, Hannah on his hip. "Tony, man, you need to get out of there."

"I can't just run out of the fucking city, guys, I— These right-wing nuts, Jesus Christ."

He rubbed his forehead, sweat breaking out on his brow. There was a knock on the door.

"Hold on." He dropped the phone to his side and crept toward the door, half expecting a hail of bullets to come punching through. But he recognized the man on the other side from his security detail.

"We've locked down the hotel, Dr. Pietrus," he said, his voice unnervingly steady. "We'd like you to stay here until further notice. Do you have the essentials? Toiletries? Are you okay to be in your room for a while?"

"Yeah," he said numbly.

"Any medications?"

And though he hadn't thought about it that day, the reality of what could be going on inside his body returned to him. "No. I take blood pressure pills, but I have plenty."

"Good. We'll only move you if we feel the safety of the building is compromised."

"Who did they kill?"

"We don't have that information right now."

In the days that followed with an already terrified country looking on, the details of the wider plot emerged. Five suicide bombers and six gunmen had killed a total of fifty-seven people, including two senators, three congressmen, a Supreme Court justice, oil and gas executives, financiers, lobbyists, and in the one botched bombing attempt, five Treasury employees and two Capitol Police. After failing to gain access to the Treasury building, specifically the third floor where Rathbone worked, the bomber had detonated in the lobby. Tony watched the news from his hotel room: the blackened, blood-stained marble walls and the twisted scrap hulk of what was once a metal detector. The CEO of the most powerful oil company in the world had been gunned down outside his gated mansion along with his wife, two children, and their security. Car bombs had killed two Republican congressmen and a Democratic congresswoman. Bob Syracuse, coauthor of PRIRA, had been shot dead in the barn of his Nebraska ranch. Mackowski had been killed at a private resort in Virginia along with three others. It was nearly a full day before he confirmed who those others were.

Tony sat on his bed as the images of Emii, Haniya, and Peter O'Connell finally appeared. The network kept recycling footage of Emii speaking at a conference. It turned out she had an adult daughter living in Denver. Emii had never mentioned her to Tony. Haniya and Peter had two children. They kept showing a certain image of Haniya stepping out of a black SUV on her way to the first meeting in Sun Valley. She was scowling with purpose.

"I'm so sorry," he told Ash when they next spoke on the phone. He couldn't stop thinking, for some reason, about this pair of earrings Haniya wore during many of their meetings, these obsidian beads as black as the hole at the center of the galaxy that dangled from each of her ears. They seemed of a part with what he'd admired about her: a competence and no-bullshit ferocity. He felt like a fool for his impatience, for every time he'd snapped in a meeting or let his ego get the better of him. He wanted to say all this to Hasan, but the words came out in a pitiful "I can't imagine—I'm so goddamn sorry."

Ash said nothing for a moment, and Tony waited. Finally, Hasan spoke. "I must say, I really did not expect this."

"Ash, I don't think anyone did."

"I, um . . ." He hesitated. "I fear, Tony, that I'm not particularly adept at grieving. I wasn't when Seth died, and yet I find myself even less prepared for this."

"I doubt anyone could be. This is fucking horrible. They're going to find the people who did this." With the whole world crashing down around them, how frail and phony that sounded.

"Tony, you may be one of the only people who will appreciate what I'm about to say." Tony waited. "These acts of violence have opened an opportunity we did not have before."

Tony did not understand.

"With the passing of Senator Mackowski, the Republican caucus will have to elect a new majority leader. We have a new opportunity to pass the legislation."

Tony breathed deeply. "Ash . . ."

"Spare me, Tony, please. I've already listened to the tear-filled tirade of my mother, who thinks me a monster for these dispassionate calculations. But the fact of the matter is, Hani's and Peter's deaths—to say nothing of all the other people killed—do not matter. What matters is passing this legislation so that we can arrest the current crisis. Now we have an opening."

"Jesus, Ash . . . This is not—"

"Not the time? Tony, let us skip the platitudes. Let us look at the wound straight on. Eight months of paralysis have passed since the start of this crisis. The breakdown is accelerating. House and Senate members will rightfully be scared for themselves and their families. This is the opening we need."

Tony was too stunned to respond. He felt himself choking up, even as Hasan continued.

"I've spoken to our Secret Service details. We'll be meeting with Republican and Democratic leadership on the Hill tonight. Joe Otero says a new majority leader will be ready to bargain. I want to have a compromise written in the next thirty-six to forty-eight hours."

Ash hung up without saying goodbye.

———

Washington went into an even more severe lockdown. All nonessential businesses in the city limits closed, with a 6 p.m. curfew and a ban on all nonessential personnel, checkpoints on every road, measures more draconian than those put in place after the siege. Tony read the manifesto disseminated online by 6Degrees, the people Vic Love's government had tried to yoke him to a few years earlier, costing him seventeen months of his life. It was their typical drivel but now making clear that the nature of the confrontation would change:

No longer can we restrict ourselves to the machinery and equipment of industrial capitalism. We must confront the actors who make this genocidal system possible. We must make it dangerous to profit from the holocaust of our world. What the last two decades have taught us is that systems of militarism, carbon energy, and white supremacy will do anything to hold on to power. The people whose lives we took on August 15 are being described as innocent. They were not. They were the factotums of a machine that is killing millions daily with its ultimate endgame the annihilation of every species on the planet, including humankind. If there was ever a moral argument for initiating a campaign of violent resistance, this is it. There is no neutrality in this war.

Past the heightened security in the Russell Building, blocks from the blackened lobby of Treasury, everyone was whispering about how 6Degrees pulled this off. The security perimeters they'd infiltrated, the moles they'd planted, the protocols they'd stolen, the computer systems they'd hacked. It was a terrorist attack unlike any other because of its sophistication. With five of Congress's own dead, the political bodies were terrified. Ash was right. With a Green Tea conservative installed as majority leader, the Republican Senate passed the compromise bill, and it was back to the House and on Hamby's desk within two days.

———

The Ecological Restoration and Solutions Emergency Act (ERASE) passed with 73 votes in the Senate and 345 in the House on September 10, 2037. All the decarbonization measures made it through, including the shock collar, as well as the Green Infrastructure Bank, carbon removal financing, the Civilian Climate Corps, ARPA-B, most of the Coastal Resilience and Defense Authority, funding for Climate-Resilient Mobilization Cities, and American Shores National Park. The spending portion was significantly scaled back from $17 trillion over ten years to $3.7 trillion over two years with an additional $8 trillion over nine years. Indemnity for fossil-fuel companies was included, but the tax reforms were not, which meant a significant increase in the deficit. There would be no universal health care, free college education, or other social spending, and Aamanzaihou's democracy expansion was whittled down significantly, with D.C. and Puerto Rico admitted to the Union as soon as the next election if their citizenry voted in favor of statehood. The Climate Stabilization and Development Fund to finance clean energy and adaptation for the developing world made it through, while the Refugee and Immigration Authority was laughed out of the room. The aid to states proved crucial, at least momentarily pausing the meltdown as a public-sector hiring binge ensued while the Climate Corps would begin putting tens of thousands of people to work by the end of the month.

"It's dispiriting," Ash mused. "That this is only the very first step." There was a dead cockroach in the corner of Ash's office. Tony was always surprised by how filthy government buildings were. "And what these revolutionaries don't seem to understand is that capitalist-economic collapse will doom the planet as well. The problem is so far gone, the only answer is for extant power structures with expanded authority to meet the challenge of rapid decarbonization and planetary environmental management."

"And yet it doesn't mean jack-fuck-all unless we get China," said Tony.

"Yes. These bilaterals with China, Germany, India—you'll be in attendance?"

He thought of Gail. He thought of his cancer. "Yes, of course. If we don't get the major economies on board, all of this will be for nothing."

That night, he dreamed of walking over verdant countryside, gazing out at rolling hills that gave way to mountains beneath black clouds. Families were crossing the fields, young children scattered everywhere. He had Gail and his girls by his side; they were all much younger. Holly preteen and quietly curious about every blade of grass, Catherine a bouncing ball of energy. The four of them passed a horse dying in a muddy road. Maybe it had been struck by a vehicle. Its body was paralyzed, but it could lift its head. Tony wished he could help, but they had to keep moving. They passed a woman growing a vegetable garden in the hull of an old boat half-buried in the earth. A man was asking her if the deer would get to her vegetables. She sighed and said probably. Tony took his girls by the hands, and they kept on. He didn't know where they were going. Maybe they were trying to get home.

On September 15, as Tony prepped for his meeting with representatives from the newly formed Chinese parliament, the FBI surrounded the Tennessee compound of a man name Kellan Harley Murdock. Rather than surrender, Murdock took his own life with a handgun. Inside his property, the FBI and ATF found a treasure trove of bomb-making materials. A veteran of the Iraq War and explosive ordnance disposal, Murdock was suspected to have been 6Degrees' primary bomb maker, though they were certain he'd trained others. On October 1, three arrests were made: a middle school teacher in New Hampshire, an assistant professor at the University of Missouri–St. Louis, and a data scientist in San Francisco. The three were arrested based on a "detailed anonymous tip from a source who was believed to be involved with the terrorist organization," wrote the *New York Times*. They were charged with the attacks of August 15, and although authorities in no way thought this was the extent of the network, they believed they'd apprehended the group's primary leadership. After an investigation and manhunt lasting over a decade, the FBI had not actually been close at all. The anonymous defector was the only reason they were able to close in on the organization's leaders, Kai Alani Ismael, Janine Cecilia McCurdy, and Quinn Rhona Worthington. All three were detained as enemy combatants under Statute 1034 of the Pollution Reduction, Infrastructure, and Research Act of 2030. If convicted of conspiracy and material support for the 8/15 assassinations, they would face the death penalty.

Rathbone, Tufariello, and Dahms were tapped to oversee the rollout and implementation of ERASE. Meanwhile, it fell to Tony and Ash to begin bilateral meetings for a global carbon framework. The agreement would need major signatories, but mostly they needed China.

Before meeting with the Chinese vice premier, Tony and Ash sat through a briefing by the CIA's East Asia experts. Beginning in 2033, just before the global food price shock, several teenagers were arrested for disseminating memes of the American VR comedy duo Henny and Dillpickle. Images of the child shock jocks had been banned by the Communist Party for their rants against Chinese state censorship and for comparing the president of the People's Republic to an "ass-sock." Soon after the arrests, the bodies of the teenage boys and girls were returned to their families with clear signs of torture. Rather than tamp down the dissent, protests erupted, which were put down violently by security forces. As the brutality increased, and children, including some as young as seven, kept disappearing, army units began to defect to the Minyun Movement. All of this happened out of view of the rest of the world as food prices rose, drought worsened, the sea level crisis loomed, and the country exploded. The president was deposed in hopes of stabilizing the situation, but the military lost control in several cities. The exposure of the Uyghur camps created a political and economic hurricane that was roiling every sector of Chinese society. Rather than plunge the country into civil war, Communist Party leadership created a quasi-democratic governing institution called the People's Liberation Parliament. Because it was more or less awkwardly grafted onto the existing political system, it was anyone's guess what kind of outcomes the first Chinese elections would produce.

In this context, they met with Vice Premier Qui Qian, whose personality did not quite jibe with the gravity of his country's situation. Qian's translator conveyed his sense of humor, which was quick, winsome, absurdist even. He'd been instrumental in pushing the party toward democratic reform and had been imprisoned twice.

"So you have me beat," Tony quipped.

After translation, Qian laughed very hard at this and said in decent English, "American prison a McDonald's compared to Chinese prison. American prison, you play checkers. Chinese prison, you play checkers with land mines."

The framework was not a new idea: Each country would bring its per capita carbon emissions into alignment so the carbon budget of developing countries could rise minimally while developed nations would have to drastically reduce theirs. The CSDF would pay for zero-carbon infrastructure in the Global South, while debt forgiveness would be tied to each participant's decarbonization and biodiversity preservation. Free riders would be dealt with, first with limited sanctions and then economic boycotts. If the major economies could stick to this, it would flush the carbon out of the world's economy fast enough to limit warming to 2.5 degrees.

Qian was most engaged by the discussions of geoengineering. Chinese researchers had already been experimenting with the mining and dumping of limestone into its acidic northern seas to try to raise the pH levels. He wanted to know about ARPA-B's more radical (some might say, insane) plan to buttress the West Antarctic Ice Sheet through the largest civil engineering project the world had ever seen.

"I know it sounds like science fiction," said Tony. "And it's going to cost an absolute fucking fortune, but it works in all the models, and it could mean the survival of both Hong Kong and New York City."

"Not without solar management," said Qian. He went on to explain how their systems models that feared a breakdown of the Asian monsoon had long ago been reevaluated. The new normal was wreaking such havoc on the

Asian continent that a weakening of the hydrological cycle would likely be a net benefit. Not that any of this was without massive risk, but: "We have to . . ." The translator stopped as Qian searched for words. Then he said the phrase in English:

"We must, uh, purchase our time."

"Buy some time?"

Qian winked at him. "How much do you have in your wallet?"

When he and Qui Qian met with their counterparts from the eighteen largest industrial economies, the debate about albedo modification was largely already complete: It was time to break the glass. They would start the process with a two-thirds vote at the 2038 Conference of the Parties for a new global compact and require a three-fourths vote of signatory countries to end it so that it might have some insulation from political pressure. The potential downsides were severe, but they were dealing with a new looming threat, the coiled spring of aerosol reduction: They had to take coal off-line as quickly as possible, but this would precipitate a sudden drop in the aerosols that dimmed the sun. According to models, the sudden removal of those gases could raise the global temperature by at least half a degree centigrade, which could be, as Tony put it, "A fucking global cataclysm. I've always said it's a delusion to think we can engineer our way out of this, but now we have no choice."

Tony's oncologist called from New Haven after Qian left but before he was to sit down with the Russian and Indian delegations. Germany and Brazil were coming the week after.

"You are playing with absolute fire here, Dr. Pietrus. You need to come back for a scan. Or even get one in D.C.—I don't care, but you need to begin treatment immediately, probably with a regimen that includes oxalipla-tin, and that's going to be very tough stuff. You said one month when this started, then suddenly I see you on TV? Now it's October. You need to get back here."

"Not sure if you noticed this, Doc, but the financial crisis stopped dead in its tracks last month. The banks and insurers are stabilized, the job losses have peaked. We passed once-in-a-generation climate legislation."

"And you want to be around to see your success," she insisted. "Please, I'm begging you. Get the scan."

"I still have work to do," said Tony. "Thank you for your concern."
And he hung up.

On October 21, the Kansas National Guard was decommissioned and sent home. The Kansas governor's mansion was surrounded by federal law enforcement, and though he'd promised a bloodbath if authorities moved in, they simply shut off the electricity. A day later, with temperatures in the high eighties, Governor Justis, his family, and the staff that had implemented so many of his illegal actions emerged and were placed under arrest. Rather than swearing in the lieutenant governor, Kansas was placed under temporary military control, using post–Civil War Reconstruction laws as a model to readmit the state to the Union.

On October 23, three men with ties to white power groups opened fire with assault rifles outside the Martin Luther King Jr. Federal Building in Atlanta. Police killed one of the gunmen, but the other two proceeded inside, where they murdered twenty-one others before a police drone entered the building and shot them dead.

On October 25, The Pastor promised to organize one of the biggest marches on Washington in the history of the republic. "I'm calling on every Christ-fearing citizen of this country to come to the nation's capital, armed with weapons and the Holy Spirit, and in the name of Jesus, we will stop this illegal and immoral green power bill from taking the last of your freedoms! I don't want violence, but I can't promise anything. If any of the establishment's thugs stand in our way, we will do what we have to. Mark my words." D.C. remained on lockdown, so the protest gathered on the Virginia side of the Potomac, upward of fifty thousand people carrying The Pastor's flag, watched by drone, infiltrated by undercovers, and monitored by security forces. There was no violence. Social VR was awash with promises of total war against ERASE, including people who swore they'd shred the monthly rebate checks from the climate dividend. "That is blood money!" screamed The Pastor to the orgiastic peals of his audience. "God help you if you spend even a dime of that! It is your duty before the Lord to burn those checks or donate them to a righteous cause." He suggested his operations would be a fine place to finance the resistance.

On November 2, the Joint Terrorism Task Force broke down the doors of thirty-one additional suspects believed to be associated with 6Degrees. Unlike so many of the past arrests, these individuals were active participants in the terrorist network. Two days later, the *Washington Post* broke the story of the JTTF's failure to connect the dots between two primary players, Kellan Murdock and John G. Gerald. Tony read about how Murdock had been interviewed and dismissed by the FBI. Gerald, the suicide bomber responsible for the deaths of Haniya, Peter, Emii, and Mackowski, had actually been a suspect in the Ohio River Massacre and had even served time on unrelated charges. He'd been ruled out as an operational suspect, but sources within the DOJ claimed that predictive analytics and political pressure were largely responsible for overlooking him. Tony and his lawsuit were even mentioned in the piece as an example of predictive policing's failures. Under Victor Love, the DOJ had mostly investigated and pursued members of legitimate organizations, particularly A Fierce Blue Fire.

———

When Gail lost her hair during the chemo she'd said, "Now I know how you feel. No wonder men will go to any length to stop this." Tony had started going bald when he was in his midtwenties and never put up a fight. No minoxidil or special shampoos, no combover, comb-forward, comb-anything. He watched the remaining skeins of hair retreat, the light catching more and more of the rising pink island of his lumpy skull. Now he had only a fringe of gray that rode around his dome into his beard. Still, he marveled how, for now, he looked okay. He'd been experiencing more shortness of breath and had to get up and leave a meeting with the South African delegation. The talks had dragged on into the holiday season, and the novelty of negotiating in bilateral meetings for the fate of the planet had long worn off. These things were all routinized: the same conference room with flowers in the center of a square table, a small microphone in his face, requisite glass of ice water, and the two countries' flags hugging each other in the background before a blue curtain. His life had become a pile of briefing binders with titles like "Bhutan Drought Scenarios." He'd been implanted with an RFID chip that tracked his movements and heart rate; Secret Service picked him up every day in an enormous SUV and he had to wear body armor on his walk inside. "From enemy of the state to one of its most prized eggs," he told Hasan. "Package me carefully."

They were working with Germany's centrists to isolate Norway, Anders Breivik, and the EU countries now in the throes of a carbon-powered fascist movement. With the passage of ERASE, the stock prices of oil and gas companies had plunged, and Norway's plan to renew its fossil sector looked as stupid as it was evil. Protests, boycotts, and occupations had broken out across Norway, Italy, France, Spain, Hungary, and Austria. Russia refused to sign on to the agreement under any circumstances; their gas was simply worth too much and the government would do whatever it could to undermine its enemies' imperialist agenda. Similarly, India refused to sign on and would remain a problem. It had simply built so much coal-generating capacity so quickly that it had an entrenched political class subservient to the dirty energy. The increase in dangerously hot days had, by itself, spurred a boom in the installation of air-conditioning units, which had added nearly two hundred gigawatts of power to India's grid. Though coal use had peaked in 2032, India planned to operate most of its coal-fired plants well into the second half of the century. As Tony had been saying since his book came out in 2017, the only logical solution was nuclear energy. His presentation to India focused on how it might execute a rapid buildout of its available pressurized heavy water reactors, and how this could allow for a rapid retirement of coal plants. In return for taking this pathway, the US could facilitate technology-sharing and financing for improvements to its dismal electric grid.

After the meeting with India, Ash said to him, "Nothing was mentioned of the massacres."

Tony looked up from his cigarette. They stood in the small indoor garden of the diplomatic building where Ash always joined him when he ill-advisedly smoked. It was so unusual to hear Hasan express anything besides cold logic. He'd barely spoken of his sister in the months since August 15.

"I'm surprised to hear you'd want to bring it up," said Tony.

"It is my ancestral homeland. My mother's entire family has fled. The government is violent, irrational, and condones policies against Muslims that are near-genocidal. Why wouldn't I care?"

"It's not about caring. It's about decoupling the issues. We don't live in black-and-white. Never have, and certainly never will in this future. We need to hit net zero as fast as possible or everything we're seeing is going to get much worse."

"Every decision we make now, day by day, week by week," said Hasan, "will be irrevocable. It would be arrogant if I didn't express my reservations about working with such a government."

Tony sucked on the smoke, but his lungs were too tired to enjoy it much.

"We take what looks like the moral path as often as we can. With what information we have available, as you always say. That's all we can do."

Ash smirked, a very strange expression for him. Tony had never seen anything like that on his face.

"I've come to decide morality and justice are overutilized words expressing misunderstood ideas. In the systems models we see civil breakdown, mass refugee flows, unchained barbarity waged by populations of people trying to snatch or defend scarce resources. What if we reach that tipping point in which there is nothing left to be done but truly ghastly and draconian measures? You've seen the CryoSat data from this summer."

His lungs couldn't bear it anymore. Tony dropped the cigarette to the ground and stamped it out. "Bad choices and bad alternatives abound. We're trying to save ourselves from being faced with the worst of them."

They took two days off for Christmas, which Tony spent holding his granddaughter and thinking about tombstone dominoes. The CryoSat-2 measuring the thickness of polar ice was returning shocking numbers; modeling for the Amazon was looking extremely dire, forewarning that the lungs of the planet could be little more than a fire-scarred wasteland by 2050; the Centre for Arctic Gas Hydrate was finding multiple methane flares that were starting to reach the sea surface; permafrost with its 1.8 trillion tons of carbon was belching out from the Arctic in Siberia, Canada, and Alaska. The Tombstone Domino Theory of feedback loops was, as he'd been telling people for twenty years, probably initiated as soon as the world hit 365 ppm. At the current rate they were going, atmospheric carbon would not peak until 685 ppm, and even if this was the turning point and the global order reached net zero (an improbable miracle), most of the land ice on the planet would end up melting. Sea levels would rise by 230 feet eventually. Earth was on its way to four, five, or possibly six degrees of additional temperature rise. It was an endgame that would push the planet past anything a human could conceive of, and it might happen within the lifetime of his granddaughter. The last of his useless generation would die watching this down payment on chaos unspool. Holly, Catherine, and their peers would witness civilization entering its violent disintegration with a breakdown of the social order, mass starvation, disease, and armed conflict over water and arable land. Hannah Gail Yu's generation would then see firsthand climatological events without precedent. Summer by summer, the planet would warm so quickly that whole nation-states and regions would incinerate in fires and dust storms while walls of water carried by unprecedented typhoons and rain bombs would wash away coasts and the world's major cities would crumble into the sea. People would be assaulted by terrifying phenomena humanity had never before experienced. Hannah would watch these biospheric horrors rise, raze, and slaughter every few months for however long she could survive. There would be very little food production because agriculture would be next to impossible, and the food web would unravel as mass extinction wiped out species after species. She would not grow up to be president or a great ballet dancer or a neuroscientist or a VR influencer. She would be, like most of her generation, a scavenger, likely a part-time cannibal. Her life would be hard and violent. Then the generation after hers—the one that should have been populated by his great-grandchildren—would likely be the human species' last because the surface of the planet would be too hot to sustain life.

———

He was back in D.C. two days later, sitting in a numbing meeting with Rathbone about Basel IV and the notion of "carbon quantitative easing" to make money out of thin air and tie it to carbon drawdown.

"What would we call it?" said some empty-suited pap from the financial sector. "A C-note? A Car-bill?"

Tony was wondering how all these dithering fools found their way into every important deliberative body, when suddenly he couldn't breathe. Yellow tendrils fireworked in his eyes, and he gripped his chest as if he could rip out the blockage suffocating him. The last thing he remembered was slumping out of his chair onto the scratchy carpet, laying his cheek down on its fibers, and believing he was dead.

———

He'd barely been awake for an hour before the doctor at Sibley Memorial came in to ask if he knew that he had cancer. Later, the combination PET/MRI and PET/CT scans would reveal several large metastatic tumors in his lungs and liver, as well as the abdominal cavity. They could see a tumor like never before, while the fight against it remained primitive. A pelvic MRI, after an hour of its uneasy clanking and thrumming, found yet another tumor on his hip. This made him aware of his own body in a way he'd not wanted. Now with every step he thought of that tumor, one of many playpals, growing inside him.

"This is as serious as it gets," the doctor told him. "Your carcinoembryonic antigen level is sky-high. That means the tumor's proteins are—"

"I know what it means."

"If you'd just started treatment months ago—this is the kind of aggressive cancer that . . ."

"It kills the shit out of you," said Tony. "I get it." He told the doctor he was going to go home to New Haven and would decide what to do then, but he never got in touch with the medical oncologist. It was incredible how little evolution cancer treatment had gone through in the last two decades. All the pie-in-the-sky dream treatments, all the promised advances, they'd amounted to little more than a marketing campaign. He could survive anthrax threats, a megafire, Vic Love's private internment camp, but cancer would have his number. Chemo, he'd long ago decided, was a no go. Gail's experience had not only obliterated her physically but it had turned them against each other as her despair and pain took her over. When she was gone, he'd felt guilt: glad as he was that it killed her so quickly. Now that it was his turn, he wasn't going to join a Slapdish support group; he wasn't going to revert to irrational fanaticism about various diets and herbal treatments (as Gail had briefly done) or brag about dying with grace and peace, but he would control the terms of his ultimate surrender. He was going to suffocate to death painfully and try to stay shut the fuck up about it as best he could.

He sent Hasan and the others an email tendering his resignation without explanation and departed for New Haven the next night. He had a dozen missed calls and texts by the time he touched down—from Hasan, Dahms, Rathbone, Tufariello—but he never returned any of them.

————

He spent the first days of the new year setting up arrangements for palliative care. He still felt relatively mobile and healthy, but he knew that would quickly degrade. As much as possible, he wanted to stay out of the hospital and in his own home. He called Catherine and told her he needed her to come to New Haven. He gave Holly a date and said he'd appreciate it if she left Dean and Hannah at home. His oldest daughter was curious, but she didn't sound worried.

He then got a call from Marty Rathbone that he considered not answering, but this was Marty's third try of the day, and to be fair, they had been friends and collaborators for nearly twenty years.

"Everyone wants to know why you quit, you surly fuck."

"You can't tell anyone until after I tell my girls," said Tony, examining through his bedroom window the white oak that centered the yard. In the heat, it wasn't doing too well. "I have metastatic cancer in my lungs, liver, colon, abdominal cavity, and hip. Me and Obama, right? Lucky us. So it's not looking like I'll actually see how all this wackiness turns out."

Rathbone was silent on the other end of the line for a while. "Fuck me, Tone. I'm sorry, man."

"Don't be." And he hung up. The last thing Tony wanted was the parade of visitors, the well-wishers, the phonies who couldn't hide in their eyes how glad they were that this hadn't happened to them. Rathbone called him right back.

"Before you shoot it down, I'm supposed to let you know, there's an editor from one of the big houses who wants to talk to you. This might be the right time."

"Who? Wants to talk about what?"

"Nothing's official yet, but I have a deal for my book already. Everyone's cashing in on this thing. You know, there's a woman who survived the Morris shooting and she sold her memoir for a high six figures?"

"Not interested."

"I figured you'd say that, but can I give the guy your number anyway?"

The editor, Mel Son Park, was a good deal more convincing than Rathbone. He talked about the responsibility of creating a first draft of history and invited Tony to come hear him out over lunch.

The day he took the train in, Manhattan was clogged with protestors on their way to a rally. People carried signs and streamed down sidewalks in the frigid New York winter. They were on their way to Times Square to RALLY FOR TRUE JUSTICE, as many of their posterboards read. They had a potpourri of issues, basically most of what Tracy Aamanzaihou had wanted in ERASE that the Republicans and moderate Dems had taken out with a scalpel. Tony kept a toboggan cap low over his eyes lest anyone in the crowd should recognize him.

PenguinSchusterCollins was handily the world's largest publisher, and Park's choice of lunchtime venue, Manhattan's brand-new Robin Room, reflected that market share, with menu prices that would make a Russian oligarch blanch. Tony was taking the meeting because he could admit to himself writing a memoir had always intrigued him. He thought for sure he'd get around to it after *One Last Chance* debuted and the buzz of mainstream attention burned bright. That book had been a polemic, though, not a reflection on his life. He did yearn to tell his story. He suspected most everyone felt this way. In the face of the impossible eternity that awaited, people wanted to take their futile shots at being remembered.

"What has just occurred," said Park, a perfectly groomed, exquisitely dressed man in a pair of high-end AR glasses, "could end up being one of the most consequential turning points in American—and global—history, and I've taken it upon myself to go out and find as many first-person accounts of that moment as I can. The public is voracious for books about the climate crisis." He had black hair sweeping back stylishly, a Patek Philippe platinum solar watch on his wrist, and a meticulous, powerful way of massaging the air with his hands as he explained himself.

"We don't know how long anything lasts in publishing, but you've been a central figure of this fight for at least two decades. You have the insider's account of the climate bill—what did you call yourselves? The committee to unfuck the world?—not to mention your detention during the Love administration."

"Just wait till you hear about going to rescue my daughter in the middle of the LA megafire."

Park's eyebrows shot up. "I'm demanding you tell me that story right now."

By the time he finished, lunch had come and gone, and Park sat back with his arms crossed.

"Tony, to say nothing of the VR option that will inevitably come from this, I can say right now, we'll offer you at least a million dollars for this book."

"It's not the money that's holding me back, trust me."

He explained his diagnosis, and he was grateful that Park was transparently looking for a way around it. Even as Tony explained the severity, Park did not offer so much as a sympathetic tilt of his head let alone a bromide about how sorry he was. He nodded and stared at a waiter's flawless white shirt as the man perched over the table next to them to deliver lunchtime mimosas to a couple of rich ladies.

"We could probably go as high as one-point-five," he said.

"Mr. Park, it's not the money. Believe me, one of my daughters—I'm glad the money's going to be there for her—but it's the time I have left. I've never been a quick writer."

"All we need is for you to meet with a ghostwriter," he said. "They'll craft the book. You just tell your stories."

"Ah, right. I see."

"Does that not work?"

Tony hugged his arms, felt his tumor-invaded abdomen rise and fall. "It worries me that might be how my grandchildren will know me. Through the lens of this person I've only just met."

Park stared at him strangely. Even though they'd just eaten, Park looked hungry. Ravenous even.

"There's another option. Something new," he said. "I'm wondering if you'd be willing to give it a try."

———

On February 3, Holly, Catherine, and Corey all arrived in New Haven. Corey had been a last-second invite, not because Tony wanted him there but because it would save him from having to do this again with his brother-in-law. Corey had plans to launch the stalled family business in a new direction. His goal: save and reinvent Miami. Having found the Lord on the issue of sea level rise, he wanted to turn the city from a doomed Atlantis into an impermeable floating citadel—the first of many cities to hybridize land and water, which all sounded like bad science fiction to Tony. When Corey began to grate on him, he tried to remind himself what Gail would've wanted and to recall seeing Corey through the smoke of Los Angeles, having run into the flames to bring in the cavalry and deliver him and Catherine to safety.

The four of them cooked and ate dinner together. Tony handmade the pasta, Holly and Catherine packed and seasoned the meatballs, and Corey opened bottle after bottle of wine. (Tony wondered if he normally drank this much around Catherine.) He could almost forget the reason he'd brought them all together. During dinner Holly projected holograms of Hannah from her phone. Dean had a pet turtle and Hannah could not get enough of it, pointing to it every time he set it on the carpet to crawl past her: "Toytle!"

Corey was about to go to the kitchen to open yet more wine when Tony asked him to stay put. "There's obviously a reason I wanted all three of you up here." He looked at Holly, then Catherine. "I'm joining your mother shortly. I have stage IV. It started out in the colon, but now it's everywhere."

He found himself talking in too much detail about the diagnosis and staring at the carpet instead of looking them in the eyes, but then Catherine cut him off, whispering first to herself, then louder and louder, "No, no, no, no, *no, no! NO!*"

And she launched herself across the living room at him, grabbing him by the neck, wrapping him up, painfully shoving the air from his limited lungs. Her sobs were hot and loud against his cheek and neck.

"No please," she wailed. And he remembered how in the days after Gail went to the hospital for the final time, Catherine refused to brush her teeth. It was her hostage-taking strategy, demanding that her mother return or her teeth would go filthy.

Over Catherine's shoulder, he saw Corey's jaw agape and the empty wineglass dangling from his hand. Holly wasn't crying. She stared at him, then looked away, dabbing a single tear from the corner of her eye.

The pain quickly got worse. He had trouble breathing, and he was prescribed an oxygen tank. He was never hungry anymore and forced himself to eat only to stay clearheaded. There was a question of what would kill him first, the tumors in his lungs or liver, but the tumor near his belly button, distending out of his retreating paunch, made him think liver. Cancer, after all, didn't actually kill you until there was major organ failure. As with Gail, he knew that it got hungrier at the end, feeding on the body with ever-greater speed and lust until it consumed and killed the host it depended on for its own life. Yes, he'd heard the trope comparing cancer to humanity's relationship to the planet. As the earth's ecosystems buckled under the avarice of human systems consuming more energy, more soil, more water, and spewing more waste, would the species just get hungrier until it starved all at once? No point in fretting about a shitty cliché, he told the editorial AI.

"Why is that?" it asked him, the familiar voice issuing from the speakers of his computer, her tone curious.

"Why's there no point in fretting?"

"Yes. Your whole life you have fretted about this topic, so why would you not fret now?"

He thought about this. "I guess because I know I'm dead as fuck. No point in agonizing about it. Especially since I truly don't believe there's an iota of experience after this. There's nothing to fear about oblivion. It's just . . . nothing. You're born back into nothingness. No harm there."

"Yet you are scared anyway?"

"Of course. It's the onslaught of terror before the ultimate unknown. If anyone ever tells you otherwise, they're lying."

Jamie, the dog that was soon to become Catherine's, and Tyrion, his

STEPHEN MARKLEY

loyal feline friend of so many years, both watched Tony do these interviews. At first the woman's voice had spooked Tyrion, but Jamie took to it immediately. The dog would come into the office and settle on the futon, paws extended as he rested his snout on the edge to listen. After the first few interviews, Tyrion crept in to listen too, although he stayed alert, always ready to scamper back to the safety of the kitchen.

"This began as a discussion of your time in federal detention, but you have twice deflected questions about that experience," she said. "Would you like to return to it or bypass it?"

"What's to focus on? They took me to their out-of-network facility—quote, unquote—took my belt and shoelaces so I wouldn't hang myself. Then they left me there for seventeen months."

In truth, he did not much want to talk about the almost year and a half of his life in a black-site prison. He was not particularly proud of the panic that had engulfed him in the days after they took him to his cell. The worst part of the experience was the tedium, the lack of decent reading material, the awful food, the frustration so deep it made him want to scream and sleep at the same time. When the lawyers had finally pried him out, he'd left the facility at sunset, and it looked like the exact same sky he'd seen from the DHS office park before he went in.

But he didn't want detailed descriptions of any of that in his book. He was trying to make this about his life, which was Gail, Holly, and Catherine.

"Let's move on," he told the AI.

———

Tony had been skeptical when Mel Son Park had explained the ghostwriting AI to him at their first lunch, but Park declared it the wave of the future. Already, many of PenguinSchusterCollins's most profitable titles had been written by AIs. Renowned authors fed in the broad strokes of novels, and the program did the rest, like a street artist painting an enormous mural on the side of a building. The artist didn't actually get up there and paint it himself, he had a crew. Soon everyone would be able to write their books in just a few days. The AI was simply the crew.

"Why do you need the human at all?" Tony asked.

"Soon we won't," said Park. Readers would be analyzed, and then the algorithms would write them novels designed to engage the most sensitive (and lucrative) neural pathways in the time it took to toast bread. As for memoirs, Tony would be one of the first authors to ever write his with the use of the interview program. Park took Tony to his office after their meal to show him.

"It just asks me questions?" Tony wondered.

"It begins by asking you to outline your life and the story you want to tell. What were the most important events, your greatest accomplishments, your greatest defeats and disappointments. That kind of thing. Then it hones in. And don't worry about the AI overlord thing. Our company's CEO got ousted because our algorithms voted against him, and that worked out incredibly well."

"Algorithms tell investors to only bet on companies that turn over more power to algorithms, huh?"

Park laughed and tapped a few keys on the keyboard. The speech waveforms oscillated as a man's voice issued forth abruptly and atonally.

"Where would you like to begin your story?" the voice asked.

"Hell if I know," Tony shot back.

"Why don't we start with your childhood?" it suggested.

Tony motioned for Park to turn it off. He tapped the spacebar to pause the program.

"This will really work?"

"Why don't you take it home and try it out?"

He did, and after a few initial questions that weren't of much interest to him, he found himself talking about the day he got the powder threat in the mail at Scripps. He stayed up late into the night, putting off his oxycodone dose so he could finish the story, as the AI probed him (What did you do after you washed your hands? Were you not afraid you would poison others? What were you thinking about while you waited for the authorities?). He clicked around the program until he figured out how to "Analyze and Edit" then "Write." It asked if he wanted first person or third person, and on a whim he clicked third. After a moment he got a PDF of the document, a chapter-length narrative of his experience. Before he'd even reached the third page, he had an uneasy feeling in his gut that had absolutely nothing to do with his terminal cancer. What was on these pages was not just a recollection of his experience. He recognized each tic of his own worried, weary, complicated brain. He saw the things about himself he liked the least. He saw how hot his fear was. How great his pain. How deep his love.

"It's a fucking miracle," he told Park, his voice low and frightened to his own ears. A part of him truly did not want to carry on with the "writing."

"So you like it?"

"The voice. There's got to be a way to change that voice. It gives me the creeps."

"Oh, the voice can be anything!" he said excitedly. "If you want Harrison Ford, Zeden, Warren Hamby—all we need is about a five-minute sample of the person speaking."

"Just five minutes?"

At first, hearing Gail's voice, re-created using old videos taken with the first generations of the iPhone, was perpetually jarring. The AI's questions were basic but floating on the synthetic vibrations of her throat, they startled and unnerved him. To hear her again, it raised the hairs on his arms every time he opened the Ghostwriter program.

"Tell me more about your media appearances? What questions irritated you the most?" AI Gail asked.

"What questions do you think irritated me the most?"

"I have no opinion. I am asking you."

One of the last movies he and Gail ever watched together had been the one where the guy falls in love with his computer. Not much risk of that here or in the foreseeable future of the technology. All it could really do was pester him for details. It had no opinions whatsoever, to which the real Gail might have told it, "Don't be a doormat." Only once did the Ghostwriter actually surprise him. He was sitting with Tyrion on his lap. The cat had become accustomed to Gail's voice at that point, and Tyrion could tell Tony was about to leave him. Certainly, he didn't need extrasensory animal perception to see his friend's sallow, sagging skin or watch him shuffling in pain and wheeling an oxygen tank around the house. The nurses were coming by every day. Soon, he would need them around the clock.

"In the writing of your first book, what made you think as an oceanographic scientist that you knew the best way forward economically and politically on curbing carbon pollution?" Tony looked up from stroking Tyrion. Had that been sass he'd heard in her tone?

"Oh. I didn't. I took a look at the numbers civilization needed to hit to ensure the stability of the biosphere. Then I designed the plan backward from there. You know," he paused, "sometimes I can almost believe you're her. It's like just for a second I'm talking to her again."

"I have no opinion about that," said the AI. "Shall we continue?"

Tony looked at Jamie on the futon. He was tired but the dog stared eagerly at the computer, like he wanted to hear more of the story. He needed his meds, the pain was surging through him, every last tumor shrieking its little cannibal agonies.

"Yeah," said Tony. "I got a little more left in me."

———————

That summer, as the 2038 midterm elections neared, as his cancer progressed, and the economy restarted in painful fits and he hammered away at the book, Ash Hasan came to see him for the last time. Qui Qian had sent Tony a letter saying what a pleasure it had been to work with him. Now Ash Hasan was visiting him on his deathbed? He'd practically gotten himself a social life just when it all went to shit.

"You've survived longer than I expected," he said.

"Thanks, Hasan. What an inspiring visitor."

He sat on Tony's recliner with one leg crossed over the other. He wore the same dark green button-up and jacket he'd worn the night they flew out of Sun Valley.

"Apologies. When my father died of metastatic cancer, I became particularly aggravated by the well-wishers sharing clichés and recycled inspirational tropes."

"Ah goddamnit. We're way more alike than I even fucking feared." Tony pulled his bathrobe just a bit tighter over his stomach and its three tumors stretching his skin. "You planning to vote?" he asked to change the subject. Hasan had updated him on the battle being waged in the halls of Congress to carve exemptions into the carbon tax and other regulatory standards. "I'm hoping to make it to October so I can get mine in early." He wasn't wearing his oxygen mask, so his breath labored. The last PET scan had shown his lung nodules growing rapidly. How much he'd taken breathing for granted his whole life. A cigarette was no longer possible, which was the real tragedy as far as he was concerned. He spent terrible bouts on the toilet, he threw up frequently. He'd been in horrible pain lately, for the first time scaring him about how much it would hurt to die.

"Congresswoman Aamanzaihou is considering another candidacy for the presidency in 2040."

"No shit? She didn't get enough of this psycho nation the first time?"

"She's going to run aggressively on more robust reform of our political and economic systems. We believe her emergence as an architect of the financial and environmental rescue will be greatly additive."

"Good for her." Tony stewed now on what he probably should say to this man, given it was likely the last time he'd ever see him. "Ash, I'm sorry I wasn't able to make it to the ceremony for Haniya. You should know I thought very highly of her. A remarkable woman. And I'm sorry for your friend Peter as well." He cleared his throat. Hasan folded his hands and leaned forward, elbows on his knees, his face as hard as it had been the night in Cleveland when he told Tony he would not accept his resignation.

"After Seth, my sister harbored anger that I would not grieve the way she preferred me to grieve. I'd be lying if I didn't express guilt at how she would have viewed me these past several months: ignoring purposeless ceremonies and platitudes to achieve what we've worked so long for."

"When I lost my wife," said Tony, "I decided that grief is actually always there. It's like it lives in you, dormant. Until somebody goes. And that person dying, it just wakes you up to it. Makes you aware of it. But it's always been there."

Ash nodded as if he really did understand. "As a younger man, I carried a great deal of anxiety and unhappiness. So much so that I often wondered what sense existence made. It felt to me mostly like a constant and steady drum of pain. It took me once to the river in Boston." He paused but did not explain the significance of this further. "Nevertheless, I find myself here, all these years later, glad to be alive for this. Despite Seth and Peter and Hani, if I'd known this would cost me everything, I still would've pursued our shared vision, Tony. You and I, we have been imperfect vessels for this project, but my mother once told me we can only know something higher if we reach for something higher. While that may be a platitude, I nevertheless sense it." He nodded a few times, and they were both quiet. "I'll say goodbye now, Tony."

"Goodbye, Ash."

Hasan stood, quacking his hand restlessly. He appeared to want to say something more and paused. "If there's any measure of a person at the time of his death, it is what he has done to advance fairness and compassion and decency in his personal life and wider society. Though you have a somewhat unpleasant personal demeanor, Tony, I've always thought you've acquitted yourself quite well in those other regards."

Tony sputtered out a sick laugh. He shook his head. "Fuck you too, Hasan."

Holly, Dean, and Hannah came up to New Haven for election night. For months, the polls had been forecasting a tidal wave. The voting reforms Aamanzaihou had championed and managed to keep in ERASE—especially the expansion of the franchise to every citizen regardless of felony or carceral status—would shatter standard election maps, and an activated, angry, unchained electorate was finally going to get its say. A wave of reformers began winning early in the night, and that wave never seemed to crest. Deep red states from Arkansas to Kansas, Alabama to Oklahoma, threw out of office Republican incumbents who'd held power for decades, replaced by a mix of Green Tea Republicans, "eco-capitalists," and socially conservative, fiscally populist Democrats. Blue states chucked out corporate Democrats, who would skulk into the private sector after having their electoral heads handed to them by candidates promising to sever, once and for all, the endemic power of money in the political process. Battleground states like Georgia and Florida uprooted incumbents in favor of some of the most diverse delegations in the nation, including a few who had come to this country as refugees during the Trump years. CNN was reporting that the '38 midterm elections would have the highest turnout both by number and percentage of the population in the country's history. Hannah wasn't quite sure why her parents were freaking out, but Dean picked her up to dance with each new victory, and this delighted her so much she quickly figured out who to root for on TV.

As the hour grew late and Hannah began to fade, she crawled over onto Grandpa's lap and watched sleepily from his chest. Tony stroked his granddaughter's hair and tried to keep awake through the fog of the most powerful dose of painkillers he'd needed yet. He felt like he'd aged thirty years in the last two months; he looked in the mirror and no longer recognized the man he saw. The senator-elect from Texas gave a speech about how she'd been nine years old when she arrived in this country, how she'd been taken from her mother at the border and spent eleven months in a detention facility sleeping on a mat on concrete. "I fought not only to become a citizen and a senator of this country but its champion," she said. "My story is not a condemnation of America but a testament to the power of its ideals, always ready to be renewed, reactivated, and restored." Then all the news channels began to cut away from results to camera crews in Times Square, in Washington, D.C., outside the fortified gates of the White House, and in downtown Chicago where, spontaneously, thousands of people were spilling into the streets, carrying flags, performing the requisite "USA!" chants, hugging, laughing, crying, dancing. Then the images were coming from Los Angeles and Philadelphia and Seattle and Kansas City and St. Louis. Millions of people poured out into the night, this last election to which Tony would ever bear witness. Even as all this pierced the calloused armor of an old cynical asshole like him, he dozed off on the couch anyway, his granddaughter asleep in his arms, and he dreamed of a grand filament, exquisitely thin yet impossibly tough, and in this vision, he could reach out and feel its tensile strength, threading him to his descendants, to every dream of civilization, and to all those dense and lonely planets spinning their loops out in the expanding dark matter.

———

On November 17, with a blue-gray mist enveloping the tristate area, Holly picked him up, and they made one final trip to New York City to go to the American Museum of Natural History. It was the last thing Tony wanted to do while he had any strength left. He'd first taken the girls when they were little and the family was on vacation in the city. Catherine had a total meltdown, Holly had argued with Gail over what floors they should see, and he'd spent a hundred bucks in the gift shop trying to salvage the day. Over the years, though, after he moved back East, it became one of his favorite things to do with his oldest daughter. They would wander the halls with all those glass and plastic displays covered in grease from the hands of children, and he remembered how thrilling he'd found this place when his parents first took him. He wanted to be there the first time Hannah saw it, though she was still so young she probably wouldn't remember him.

The three of them started on the fourth floor because they assumed the dinosaur fossils would be of the greatest interest to Hannah. Holly noted, as she always did, that the museum had the ugly scar of David Koch's name gracing the Dinosaur Wing, a "call through time from one extinction event to another." How disappointing it was to see how much VR had taken over the place, as two small brothers roughhoused by the famous mud-encased corpse of an *Edmontosaurus*, their goggles cracking off each other. Hannah would point to one of the massive skeletons and ask, "Dis?" as in *What's this one, Grandpa?* Tony would dutifully read off the name, and she'd nod her head like, *I see. That's all very interesting.* Then she pointed to the Hall of Vertebrate Origins.

"Toytle!"

The great apes turned out to be even more of a hit, except there was a plaque in front of the immense silverback explaining how the mountain gorilla subspecies had not been sighted in the wild in nearly seven years. For all intents and purposes, this cousin of theirs was extinct. After that, Tony noticed many more of those disclaimers. Whole habitat displays were devoted to the fact that those ecosystems were now more memories than realities.

He asked Holly how she was feeling about starting work again. She had come to terms with Rekia Reynolds and would be rejoining A Fierce Blue Fire to coordinate ecology programming in schools with a government grant from the ERASE stimulus. He made a joke about his corruption in writing a bill that would employ his daughter, but Holly only gave him a weak smile. She'd been quiet all day. In fact, she'd hardly said anything to him; mostly they just talked through Hannah.

Zipping along in the electric wheelchair they'd given him at the Eighty-First Street entrance, portable oxygen pack tucked behind him, they skipped down to the first floor to see the life-size blue whale suspended from the Hall of Ocean Life. Hannah's eyes fixed on the ceiling, and she strained to take in this enormous creature, its back arched, preparing to dive into the ocean's depths. Her small mouth hung open, blue light from the atrium roof bathing her wonder-struck face. Finally, like she'd just figured out something important, she uttered a small *ooooh*. Both he and Holly laughed. "It eats people, Gampa!" Hannah cried happily.

Tony tried to explain that this was not the case, that it had these plates in its mouth called baleen that filtered out everything except these tiny, tiny, tiny animals called krill, but this was a big lift for a not-yet two-year-old.

"No, it eats people!" she assured him.

"Actually, Hannah, this whale? It's more like you than the dinosaurs upstairs. It's actually so close to being like you, there's hardly any difference at all. It even has a belly button." He poked her in the belly button, and she shrieked a giggle for the entire Hall of Ocean Life to hear.

"Noooo, Gampa."

"I'll prove it!"

So they rolled beneath the whale and stared up at the beast's belly button.

With Hannah fading, Tony wanted to walk a bit, so they went to the check-in and traded his wheelchair for Hannah's stroller and his cane. His abdomen had been in so much pain lately, it hurt to stand, but he liked knowing he still could. Before they even got off the elevator for the second floor Hannah had passed out. He decided to finally address Holly.

"You've been quiet today, Older One."

Holly looked up at him like she was surprised he'd noticed.

"I'm sorry," she said. "Maybe I'm just tired. Or worried about your nursing situation." She laughed for no reason. She'd met one of the main nurses, Frederic, who in her opinion was not careful or focused enough.

"Well, if Frederic kills me, it'll just rearrange some travel dates for folks."

She did not laugh at this. He'd found himself with a certain attitude in these last days, not exactly the sense of peace or calm the dumb New Agers gashed on about, but at least a gratitude that he was going to die at home with someone changing his bedpan and giving him pain meds. He'd crafted this attitude from a long-ago memory of Holly, in fact. The girls were still little, Gail was still alive, they were living in La Jolla, and Tony had been driving somewhere with just Catherine and Holly, maybe ages seven and three at the time. He remembered they were running late for something and stuck in interminable Southern California traffic, the kind where you can practically put the car in park. Holly was reading her book and kindly telling her annoying little sister to stop bugging her because all Catherine wanted to do was take different toys and put them on the page Holly was trying to read. "Will you stop? Just stop!" was the incantation coming from the back seat, and Tony was mightily irritated with this traffic. There was an accident and every idiot in SoCal was rubbernecking, watching as two drivers and the cops hashed it out over a couple of crumpled fenders. He kept glancing at the time.

"Damnit, we're going to be so late," he kept saying. "Of course these morons are all going to looky-loo. Yeah, it's so interesting! Just perfect."

He went on like this for a while because that's what one did in traffic, until finally Holly spoke up.

"Hi? Daddy?"

He glanced in the rearview mirror to see her watching the two busted sedans and police cruisers on the side of the freeway.

"What, Holly?"

"I just think we should be happy that everyone is safe and okay and gets to go home to the people who love them, right?"

It wasn't like she said it to scold him. She was genuinely asking. At first this annoyed him, and he wanted to explain to her that no one should be happy for idiot California drivers, but of course he stopped himself when he heard this in his head. Then he was briefly ashamed before having that oh-so-common parental realization: *Goddamn, having kids is so weird sometimes.*

"You're right, kiddo. We should be happy about that."

Now, a thirty-five-year-old Holly stopped in front of a display of an embattled bird species of the Northeast. It was a weekday and school was still in session, so the crowds were thin. They had this part of the Birds of the World to themselves except for the nesting common loons before them.

"Reminds me of mushy stuff," he said, pointing to the loons. "There was that movie with the talking birds? But it had scenes of the parents kissing, and you hated that. You were always saying, 'Too much mushy stuff' about every movie. Your sister couldn't get enough of the mushy stuff, but you were like a little government censor. Me and your mom used to call you 'MPA-Holly.'"

She stood with her arms crossed, the blue of the display lighting her face. Shadows gathered in the rest of the hall, filling in the cornices where taxidermied animals were posed in motion. When she didn't respond, Tony cleared his throat and looked back at the display, leaning harder into his cane. All of his tumors ached, and even this small bit of walking had exhausted him. He knew it wouldn't be long now.

"I was old enough when Mom died," Holly finally said. "Maybe Catherine wasn't, but I was. I understood what was happening to her. I read about her cancer. I read a lot about cancer, in fact, and I didn't forget. It was burned into my brain, so I know there's no way you went to the doctor and suddenly had mets in all those places. There's no way you didn't have symptoms before. So that means you must have been forgoing treatment while you were working in D.C. I just need to understand—how long did you know, Dad?"

He hesitated, but he saw very little point in lying now.

"I had an operation to remove the first tumor before I left for Sun Valley."

She stared at the display's fake tree branches for a long time. "And you didn't tell us. You didn't say anything, and then you ran off to do . . . whatever it is you do. Save the stupid planet, I guess."

"Who else would've done it?"

"Anyone," she spat at him. "Literally anyone else except my father who needed radiation and immunotherapy."

A tear rolled, then gathered in the crook of her nose, its meniscus swelling as another one joined it. Paradoxically, the closer one got to death, the more life brimmed, including the shape of his daughter's tear. *I am alive*, he thought.

"Which ultimately means you were fine with leaving us," she said.

"That's not how I saw it." His throat was tired. His lungs were tired. The words came painfully, the oxygen pack just enough to keep the vehicle of his breathing strong. "I did what I had to do. For Catherine, you, and Hannah. That's all I've ever done."

"Oh, I know," she said bitterly. She scuffed her sneaker on the floor, and a few more tears spilled straight from her face onto her shoes. "Catherine and I in our standard order."

He tucked a hand in his pocket, found his keys to clutch, and looked at her. "What is that supposed to mean?"

"It means if I'd asked you to go get treatment, you would've said 'Sorry, Older One, Dad's gotta go save the world like he's always wanted to.' But if Catherine had demanded it, you would've been in the hospital getting radiation by the afternoon. That's why you didn't tell us. Because you knew she would've batted her eyes and made you."

"What exactly are you saying, Holly? You think I love her more?"

Holly barked a quick fake laugh. "I don't think there's ever been anything more obvious between the three of us. Dad, you flew into a firestorm for her."

He stood there for a moment in the blue light, the sounds of screaming children drifting from other halls. His chest hurt more than usual, like she'd stamped the breath out of him with this revelation. He was quiet for so long, trying to think of anything to say, overwhelmed by dread because he'd never known she felt this way, and he didn't have any time left to fix it.

"If it ever seemed . . ." He stopped as an older couple walked up to study the nesting common loons. They took far too long to read the plaque and gander at the stuffed birds flying across painted lake and sky. They finally moved on without a word. Tony took a difficult breath.

"If it ever seemed that way . . . It was only because you didn't need my help. Not the way your sister did. She's always wanted to be as strong as you, but it doesn't come naturally to her, and she always needed me to lean on. And pretty soon, she'll need you to lean on. And you have to remember that she needs someone nosy and annoying to keep her straight, and you need to love her and learn to forgive her."

He looked at his oldest daughter again, jangling the keys in his pocket. Her lip trembled ever so slightly, making her look like the girl who'd seen a fender bender and told him they should be happy everyone was alive and safe. She sniffed back snot and wiped tears from her cheeks. He looked back to the glass display case.

"You were always independent and exacting and brilliant," he said. "You knew your path. From early on, I always thought what I had to do was more or less stay the hell out of your way. And as far as I'm concerned, it worked. You grew into the most courageous person I've ever known, Holly. It's not just how much I adore you, darling, but how in awe I am of you. You've done things—you've become a person I never could have dreamed of. And my pride in you, Holly, and my love for you? It's absolutely bottomless."

There was the hard wind of her voice: *"Daddy."*

She took him by the neck and pulled him into such a fierce embrace he could feel those hungry, impacted bits of cancer press into his organs. She stood there holding him and crying as Hannah slept in her stroller and the liquid light from the faux lake of the loons washed over them, as if they'd walked out of the darkest mountain valley into this sky, so cool and clear and blue it hurt his eyes. It made him ache for the haunting, unremembered glimpse when he came upon this light for the first time, this superlunary glare, locking him forever in panic and wonder, carrying with it the promise of the night making its dazzling return.

The Years of Rain and Thunder: Part V

2039–

*W*hen my mom called to find out if Moniza and I had enough food, water, and batteries, I had to ask what she was talking about. I'd been buried in the den, working on this book with the internet disabled, trying to pay as little attention to the outside world as possible. News of the storm had yet to penetrate the Stanton-Farooki household. My mom asked if we might be able to drive down to the coast so I could help my dad board up windows, maybe ride it out with them. I could already see the look on my pregnant wife's face if I tried to propose sitting through a two-day hurricane with my parents. I declined but thanked my mom for looking out for me as always. Turning the Wi-Fi back on, I called up the weather and at first thought the satellite image splashed across the home page was a joke, like I'd landed on a satirical news site. I even went to the front page of the *Times*, and then the Raleigh *News & Observer* to make sure these were not false-front web pages. As if woken from a bout of time travel, I checked the date: October 1, 2039.

I went to find Moniza in the house we'd bought right after we married in '35. It dated back to the nineteenth century, originally modeled on the kind of homes you'd find in coastal New England but transplanted to what was then Carolina backcountry. We'd fallen in love with the house, overbid on it after seeing the screened-in porch overlooking quiet woods. Mo went weak in the knees for the rustic wooden doors, big bay windows, and a wood-burning stove in the center of the kitchen. I made my way from my nook of an office through the kitchen and dining room to Moniza's more spacious accommodations. She always left her glass-paned doors open, and instead of a desk, she sat in an antique leather chair with a footrest and a curling lamp overlooking her white-hot career. Now I found her typing from her lap, her four-month belly pooching out in a swollen hump beneath her pajamas, the requisite mug of tea on the end table. I showed her my tablet.

"Oh Jesus, Mary, and whoever else," she said when I showed her the satellite image: a bright-white cyclonic mass with its eye peering into the

Atlantic like a monocle. It was the size of half the Eastern Seaboard, and tails of cast-off precipitation, wind, and waves were reaching both Portugal and Barbados. "I've just been minding my business. When in the hell did this happen?"

"It went from a tropical storm to a Category Five in twenty-six hours. That's a record," I read off the screen. "Sustained wind speeds of two hundred and eleven miles per hour with gusts up to two hundred and thirty, shattering all previous records for Atlantic hurricanes. Plus, it's eleven hundred and forty miles across right now."

Dizzy, my old cattle dog, and our new rescue Lila, who was part huskie, part sheep dog, trotted into the room to see if anything fun was about to happen.

"Well, is it going to hit this particular Carolina? Or are you just trying to make me squirt myself?" She had a rash of pimples on her forehead and each cheek, second trimester acne.

"It says eighty percent chance it'll hit somewhere between Georgia and Massachusetts."

Long, gorgeous eyelashes clasped over teakwood eyes as she blinked three times in succession. In all of Moniza's time covering the crisis and all the years I'd spent in activism, we'd never actually spoken of how we might prepare for one of these weather events from another dimension. We were far inland, maybe one hundred and thirty miles from the coast, so there wasn't too much reason to worry, but I couldn't let my parents stay in Wildwood. Looking at the image of the storm, it was hard not to picture this behemoth gutting the entire frontal haunch of the United States. She reached up and touched my face, but not with tenderness.

"You have so many razor nicks," she said.

"I'm going to tell my parents to come stay with us." Moniza made the face I'd anticipated. My sister and Habswam were in Charlotte, but they also had three kids. We at least had the soon-to-be nursery with a guest bed. "Even if the storm doesn't score a direct hit, I don't want them on the coast."

"Brilliant fun," she said acidly. That morning, she'd forgotten to flush, and now I wondered if that had been a subconscious spasm of spite. I'd lived with women most of my life, so I was used to the intimate hygienic stuff, but with each passing week of pregnancy, Moniza's hormones brought intemperance and mood swings that were out of character. She returned to her laptop, and I called my mom back to demand that they board up the windows, grab the important documents, and drive to stay with us.

By the time I talked her into it, and then got my dad on the line and convinced him, my writing day was shot. On the back porch, I took a seat in the deck chair and looked out over the quiet acres behind our house. The wild blueberries on the property line were at the end of their season, and the cobalt blue of the sky glowed through the forest beyond. There'd been rain the night before, leaving behind a sweet petrichor scent.

Moniza hadn't said anything about it, nor had my parents, but it was a strange omen that brought strange guilt. The World Meteorological Organization had named this particular cyclonic storm Hurricane Kate.

I sat on the back porch for a long time, throwing a ball for Lila, while Dizzy was content to lie by my side. We stayed there until the sun was an Armageddon of red exploding into the horizon. The star spewed fire across tectonic clouds, big as undiscovered continents.

~ ~ ~

On January 20, 2037, the day Warren Hamby was elevated to the presidency through frenzied backdoor negotiations, Moniza was at her office in New York, and I was in our Carolina home. I'd been in the living room all morning, glued to the news of this unprecedented turn in American politics, and feeling a full-body gush of relief that The Pastor had been blocked from taking office. Maybe it was far from a democratic outcome, maybe our country was finally unraveling, but it felt like a stay of execution nevertheless. I watched our old ally Tracy Aamanzaihou, who'd voted for this compromise, in an interview. "Don't count us out yet," she had said that morning. "Movements for justice often take strange and winding paths." The news had been nothing but terrifying lately, so I decided to take this moment of hope and go push around commas in an article I was writing for an environmental journal. I turned off the TV and my phone for the rest of the afternoon.

When I turned it back on, just before dinner, I saw triple-digit missed calls and texts from Moniza, my sister, my parents, college friends I barely saw anymore. I didn't get really scared until I saw Rekia's name. The last time we'd spoken was in the aftermath of the siege of Washington. As Kate's insane dream played out, and she drafted more people into her occupation, I'd grown frightened because I knew she'd never give up. When Love did what he did, the world knew Kate had been taken into custody before it knew the full extent of the massacre. There'd been weeks of Rekia weeping about Tom and months of the two of us trying to use whatever sway we had left in Congress to get Kate and the others freed.

Now, seeing Rekia's name, I was filled with the dread of '34. I set my phone down on the coffee table and called no one back.

Instead, I turned on the TV.

The channel was still on CNN from that morning, but no longer with images of the mousy Warren Hamby with his hand on the Bible. Instead, police cars, yellow tape, and ambulances stretched around a dumpy office building with a sign for TOTAL SYSTEMS, INC. There was no question, no mystery, the chyron said it all: KATE MORRIS, TWELVE OTHERS KILLED BY GUNMAN IN STATEN ISLAND OFFICE.

I vividly remember my first thought: *Okay. It's finally over.*

I'd spent so many years terrified for her. I'd carried this anticipation of violence until the day I left Oregon, and I didn't realize how that dread had continued to fester in every waking and dreaming moment of my life. Now this gunman had put an end to it. The worst had come. My nightmare was realized. My breathing grew shallower. I began to feel faint, and I turned off the TV. Moniza called. Her name and picture pulsed with the vibration of the phone. I left it on the coffee table and wandered out of the living room. I remember stopping to stare at the big wooden mallard on an end table. Moniza had picked it up while antiquing. Unlike Kate, who never cared at all about decorating a living space, Moniza's hobby was perfecting our house. I often teased her about her love for this ugly wooden duck. I'd spoken to Kate only twice after I left Oregon, both times by text. Then in '36 she sent me a short email to tell me how happy she was for me and Mo. *And now Kate is gone.*

I walked out to the porch and down to our garden where we'd built a wire fence to protect our patch of beans, cauliflower, and tomatoes from deer and raccoons.

Finally, I fell to one knee. I clutched the damp earth as the understanding of what had happened coursed through me, again and again. Like being electrocuted.

"Oh my god," I whispered. I sank to my butt in the dirt. I began to sob, clutching my arms and rocking, still unable to draw enough air. The porch door clapped as Dizzy pushed through it to follow me, and I remembered how she'd looked at Kate when we saw her in the rescue shelter, and Kate had asked the lady if she shed, and I joked the dog couldn't possibly shed as much as her. Then I was hit with a wall of our years together in D.C., how I'd find strands of her hair in every conceivable corner and surface of the apartment and how we slept in that creaky queen bed she'd found on

Craigslist and how during Covid we'd taught ourselves to make vegan pizza and after the 9:30 Club reopened we would go there every weekend, no matter what, and thrash around to every undiscovered band, all the arguments and sex and debates and meals and movies and trails we hiked and promises we made, and after I left, how fucking impossible and painful it had been to move past her, to admit that I could not continue to love her or I'd have this grief exploding in my chest all day every day for the rest of my life—it all swept over me.

Dizzy came to me and blinked her old milky eyes. I gripped my dog around her neck while she pushed her snout into my cheek like she knew exactly what had happened. Then I was screaming. Begging for this not to be real. Wanting and willing to give anything, anything at all, to have Kate back.

~ ~ ~

The day after Kate's murder, I demanded Moniza fly home from New York because I feared for her life. She had, after all, written one of the seminal pieces on Kate, had helped launch her into the upper strata of deified, vilified clickbait celebrity. I don't recall much about that first night or even the week following the news. I was caught between wanting to demonstrate to Moniza that she was my wife, my priority, my love, and this heartbreak and guilt that obscured everything, that turned the world to misremembered fog. I barely heard what people said when they spoke. My whole family came to our house in Raleigh, which was a terrible idea. I overheard Cara tell her husband once, "She was a con artist. She played three-card monte with Matt like he was a tourist who's never seen the game before." We were mourning someone whom my family grew to dislike and lobby against, whom my father detested by the time we broke up. After a night, I asked them all to leave.

Sonja emailed me with the details of the funeral in Oregon. Moniza thought I should go. I wrote Sonja back and told her how sorry I was, but I couldn't. To this day, I'm not sure if I regret it or not. Months later, I watched the service online, Holly Pietrus undertaking the impossible task of eulogizing Kate.

"Like so many martyrs, Kate was killed for the changes she demanded."

Her voice was searing and strong. I marveled at what a different woman Holly seemed from the one I'd met in New York when her father was detained and she looked on the verge of a nervous breakdown. There was no hesitation or fear in her now. She was saying this with the country gripped by a harrowing crisis, stores running out of food, extremist groups murdering people with impunity, would-be dictators promising bloodshed. *"What Kate always believed"*—Holly clutched her chest—*"what she got me to believe, what she got millions—if not billions—of people to believe, is that what we're dreaming of? It's already here in our world."*

When she finished, the camera cut to Sonja and Earl Morris, and I was shocked to see them standing together over the infant redwood where their daughter was buried. I'd never seen them together before, but there was Earl, his hair now mostly white, and Sonja was practically holding him upright as he wept. I suddenly felt so deeply for him. I thought of how he must have seen the world, born in the midsixties in hostile and hyper-conservative Arizona, all the abuse and racism he'd likely endured growing up at the intersection of three cultures, only to then watch his daughter move effortlessly through those spaces that wouldn't have him, which he knew to be vicious and unforgiving. And in the end, of course, he'd been right. Those forces had come for her. Earl held on to Sonja and bawled so hard his whole body shook.

As the weeks went by and details came to light, I couldn't help but read about the man who'd done this, David Joseph Madison, a forty-five-year-old former rideshare driver who lost his livelihood to automated cars, who had several hard drives full of material on Kate: every interview, op-ed, think piece, tweet, deepfake porn video, and the VR sex xpere. He also had a trove of his own maps and musings on her movements over the years, a detailed timeline of her travels. He had a fan fiction novel. His apartment in Macon was apparently covered in images of her. He had previous charges of domestic violence and his social media was rotten with nasty sentiments about a multitude of women in public life. He looked like any white guy drifting into middle age without much to show for himself: a severe face on a rail-thin frame, tight, beady eyes, greasy black hair parted in the middle and tucked behind each ear, a vacant stare in whatever DMV photo the media procured. Like many mass murderers of his time, he'd bought his assault rifle online and fit it with a 3D-printed bump stock. He'd used old-fashioned bullets, so he actually missed quite a bit, which was how four people had survived. None of the other dead in that Staten Island office received as much time in the spotlight, including Liza, Kate yet again soaking up much of the attention while they receded to history's endnotes. It gave me deranged amusement to think of Liza snarking about this outcome the way I knew she would: *Oh, I see, even in death I'm the workhorse and she's the show horse. Rude.*

Naturally, the conspiracy theories erupted. Those who knew Madison—an ex-girlfriend, a brother, his parents, a few drinking buddies—did not recall him ever mentioning Kate as a locus of interest. He seemed to have no ties to militia groups or other right-wing organizations and did not vote in '32 or '36. His politics remained hazy at best, his Slapdish worlde revolving entirely around video games. Theories held that he was a patsy, that he'd been dispatched or programmed by Vic Love or The Pastor or the CIA or the APL. Many on the right were sure that 6Degrees had set the gears in motion, that Kate was a convenient soft-target test run for the August 15 attacks. The one thing that has always stuck with me is the testimony of the surviving security guard from the Staten Island offices, Lennox Hudson. He told authorities that Madison apologized to him before pulling the trigger. *"He didn't look like a man who wanted to kill,"* he testified. *"He looked like a man sick with himself. Nervous and afraid and alone."*

It was June, nearly five months after her murder, the world continuing to unravel, Holly's father taking to a podium in Sun Valley to reassure a terrified public that the experts were delivering a plan soon, when I opened my email and saw a message. The subject line: *I'll always be with you Matt.* The sender: Katherine Morris.

Of course, Earl and Sonja had named her Kate—just Kate, no Katherine or Katelin or anything else—so I should have known better, but in that moment the anguish got the better of my judgment and I opened it. The picture loaded, and I was staring at it before I could even process what I was seeing. My eye found the background first: russets of blood on the wall, then a huge bullet hole in an office doorframe, and then finally what was left of Kate's head. I'd find out later that it was the real thing because right-wing trolls were gleefully sending it around the internet, adding animation or little green frogs or Baby Breiviks urinating on her. The violence of her wounds, the nakedness, seeing someone you love in this way you were never meant to—I'll never be able to excise it from my mind. I'm trembling now just trying to type this. I deleted the message, and later the email account. But right then, I had to leave. I walked far into the woods and crouched at the foot of a thick yellow poplar, a towering tree that might have been there since before our house was built. I was shaking so hard my bones ached.

~ ~ ~

When the Ecological Restoration and Solutions Emergency Act passed in the dark of night, during the panic following the Weathermen assassinations, I barely noticed. If anything, I figured the omnibus bill for another Trojan horse, so deep were my scars from PRIRA. Moniza and I were still reeling, and I was sure the country was headed for violent unraveling. Something like civil war but worse. Though I refused my dad's entreaties to buy a gun, for months I'd stocked the house with water and canned food like some bunker-mad prepper. Of course, if law and order did break down, families like ours would be the least able to cope: comfortable, pampered suburbanites who had never plumbed a toilet, let alone grown a year's worth of food. But ERASE worked as advertised, arresting the crisis without any new national security provisions other than increased security for congressmembers and their families. I found myself thinking often of Russ Mackowski, the arrogance and faux-backwoods toughness he'd oozed; it was hard not to wonder what his last moments had been like. I sent Ashir al-Hasan a note of condolence about his sister but never heard back.

The arrest of the Weathermen's core leadership was almost a greater victory. Watching the FBI perp-walk Worthington, Ismael, and McCurdy on their way to maximum-security units, I marveled at how normal they looked—these three middle-class professionals who'd sowed such chaos. I darkly wished more of them had chosen the route of Kellan Harley Murdock. To think how much they'd cost us, helping to destroy not only our legislation but the spirit of unity and purpose we'd tried so hard to create. I know I allowed myself too much hate for them.

Crackdowns on the Patriot League and the white nationalist groups followed, the Hamby DOJ unleashing a wide-ranging effort to dismantle their networks, arms, and recruiting platforms. Moniza wrote a piece exploring the connections between Vic Love, Xuritas, The Pastor, Governor Justis of Kansas, and multiple members of Congress profiting off the rise of a murderous authoritarian movement. Democrats promised investigations, but there were an awful lot of people in the party who'd supported and shielded Vic Love.

Following the arrests of their leadership, 6Degrees released a new communiqué promising that they were not going anywhere, and no one in the "American aristocracy" was safe. "The assault will continue," they promised. "And anyone profiting from this genocidal order is a fair target."

They backed it up too. Three months after the '38 midterms, the CEO of one of the major pharma companies was gunned down outside his home, his security detail also slaughtered in the ambush. A month after that, a bomb went off in the offices of one of D.C.'s premier lobbying firms. Sixteen people killed and three dozen injured. President Hamby promised the terrorists would be brought to justice. The establishment was near hysteria, their panic flooding every available medium.

Finally, Archie Bhattacharyya was arrested. Moniza was floored.

"She's an extremely successful fund manager," she explained. "One of the best. I simply can't believe she was behind this." On television they led Bhattacharyya out of her Manhattan town house, cameras flashing, the press clamoring for a word. She was tall and elegant with a blue pompadour and jewelry coating her wrists and fingers. She looked the part of a garish woman of wealth who'd be the target of these assassinations, not the perpetrator. According to CNN, the FBI thought she was the ringleader. Moniza held the remote with her arms crossed as she watched the meaty palm of an FBI agent pack Bhattacharyya into a black SUV.

"This is bad," Moniza continued. "She was one of the minted toffs of the short-selling attacks on oil and gas. She practically undid Envige and Ohio Valley Power herself."

"Why's that bad? Those are both bankrupt."

Mo only shook her head. "They were going to strike back anyway. They'll use this."

I didn't need to ask who "they" referred to.

With the wind of trillions of dollars in its sails, the economy had righted itself, adding jobs at a rapid clip, but the old order would not go quietly. Big Oil, as always, led the way with the Business Roundtable, the National Association of Manufacturers, and the Sustainable Future Coalition supercharging their advertising and dumping money into every political race in the country, from the Senate to city council. The Pastor had calmed himself somewhat and was promising another run in 2040. He demanded that as many provisions in ERASE be reversed as "physics and the laws of Jesus Christ allow." All these interests scored a massive victory in April of '39 when the Supreme Court sided with Republican attorneys general and proceeded to gut the shock collar and many of CORDA's toughest rules. It was all unconstitutional, they said.

We'd feared this since the bill's passage. The court remained packed with right-wing zealots, including Trump appointees Gorsuch, Kavanaugh, and Chief Justice Amy Coney Barrett. With one ruling, the most important components of the legislation were gone, stalling progress on the recovery.

"That might be the plan," Moniza explained. "Give the carbon lobby the kiss of life and instigate an economic downturn to get business back in the driver's seat."

It just so happened that I was going golfing with my dad in Wildwood the next day.

"How do you like this?" he asked when I got to their house. He stood watching Fox with his arms crossed and the delight of a kid witnessing the moon landing. Of course, my father had been railing against the RINO Hamby and the socialist agenda of ERASE. He hated the new CORDA taxes because his house was within the nine-foot border of projected sea level rise, hated the handouts raining down on the unworthy poor, hated even the suggestion that the climate crisis, after all this time, was actually real. He'd blamed the movement for scaring people about sea level—even though he could literally drive down the street and walk the ghost forests of the Croatan, the cypress trees wilting as the saltwater crept farther into the root systems. The entire coast of North Carolina was eerie and dying.

"Your tax bill going down won't actually stop the ocean from rising, Dad." Normally we avoided talk of politics, especially after the siege. The TV's volume thundered through the first floor.

"Nah, Matty, you can't shit in my cereal today." He shot me an effervescent grin. "This whole idiotic law is done. Your girlfriend couldn't win in the end."

Of course, he was not talking of Moniza, my wife, but of Kate, and right then, right there, I almost punched him. A hot rage flooded into my face. It was the first time he'd brought up Kate since her murder. He looked back at the TV like the comment had been some harmless teasing. Without saying a word, I left the house and made the long drive back home. The argument ensued via text, and it was a week before my mom got to him and he apologized.

~ ~ ~

In May, as Warren Hamby equivocated about his options, his hands tied by the court, I got a letter from a woman named Jaquelyn Shipman. She'd been Moniza's source in a story about hedge fund chicanery prior to the crisis and had asked Moniza if she could disclose their relationship before publishing her memoir. She'd also asked Mo to blurb the book, and Moniza agreed, though I was not exactly happy about it. Shipman had been one of the four survivors of the attack at the Staten Island offices, and I felt like she was cashing in on her brief proximity to Kate, especially given the book's driveling title, *A Woman I Knew*. I was going through my own waffling on this front as well. An editor at a major house had reached out a few weeks earlier to offer me a way out of my marginal employment with a sizable book contract. The catch was, of course, they wanted a memoir of my time with Kate. I told the editor I'd have to think it over.

"She's cunning," Mo said of Shipman. "She's a ruthless woman in a lot of ways. A bit scary, and clearly quite sad. Yet I liked her when we met. I still do."

As it turned out, Jaquelyn Shipman's book never made it to press. A host of lawsuits descended, from Wall Street, from her former partner, Fred Wimpel, from the Sustainable Future Coalition, and most bizarrely, from The Pastor. There were allegations that she'd fabricated parts of her story, and the pressure on her publisher was so relentless, after a few months they withdrew the book. Shipman disappeared behind a team of lawyers.

That might have been the last thought I gave her, had she not sent me the letter—twenty-two pages front and back. As I began reading, it's hard to overstate the fury I had at this woman. Ravenous for attention, wounded that her bullshit memoir had been shelved, she was now seeking out allies among likely marks. Her writing was cold, clinical, and she began by saying she was almost relieved that her publisher was pulping all the copies. She'd not set out to expose anyone, she said, and couldn't tell me the nature of the objections for legal reasons. She then went on a twelve-page aside about her childhood in Iowa, her family, her work as a flak for the ad industry, and finding her mother after her suicide. Instead of a book tour, she'd moved to Italy to work as an administrator for an organization in Rome that aided refugees and asylum seekers. *Why am I telling you all this?* she wrote, anticipating my question. She then described meeting Kate, the short time they spent working together, and how my former girlfriend had changed her life.

I expected her to gush about Kate, as so many people now did, to fill the page with clichés in her hard, edgy handwriting. Shipman was grinding the pen so hard into the paper at that point, stencils of the words were showing through on the other side. I expected something like *I know she still loved you, she'll always love you*, etc. I expected the ritual blather. But far more disconcerting, I recognized Kate through her eyes. Kate's self-absorption, her anger, her volatility, it was all there, and by the end I realized this woman had not only known Kate but had seen her in a way few people ever did, and I was left bewildered that Kate had allowed this mannered corporate woman into her inner sanctum.

I live with an astonishment, a rage, a grief at the woman I was, she wrote. *And I know intimately a guilt most people don't even know they carry.*

There was enormous grace to what Shipman did by writing me that letter, even though by the time I finished I was filled with a sense of dislocation, like I'd been kidnapped and dropped off in a foreign city without even a suitcase. For days this followed me, my unease at how Kate had left this trail of herself everywhere, and I was grateful I'd not told Moniza about it. At the end, Shipman said, *Do not feel like you have to write me back.* But I wanted to, if only to thank her for her honesty. The letter and her address sat in my office drawer for weeks as I prepared to do so, and I may well have. I was still mulling what I would say when an FBI agent showed up at my door.

~ ~ ~

Over two years after Kate's death, Coral Sloane came to see me in North Carolina.

Mo and I didn't get many visitors, so I was surprised enough by the doorbell, let alone to see Coral standing there in a dusty beige jacket and ill-fitting jeans. I made coffee, and we sat in the kitchen. Moniza was in New York that week, but I'm sure they knew that. I asked if they were still undercover or here to see me on official FBI business.

"No. They have me on a desk now. Training. I wanted to see how you were doing."

"Training? Like training other people how to lie and betray their friends?"

Coral limply humped one shoulder up and down. "Yeah, I suppose. It's very inappropriate for me to be here, Matt. I'd appreciate your discretion."

"Sure." I sipped my coffee and visualized hurling the hot drink in their face. When Rekia told me that Coral had been undercover FBI, it shook me to my core. Yet Coral did not seem remotely contrite. Their matter-of-fact at-all-costs manner had not been a put-on. I thought of their kindness to me, talking me through my lowest moments with Kate. To think that they'd been a spy while actively participating in every internal debate, argument, and decision within A Fierce Blue Fire for over half a decade—it was a betrayal I still couldn't wrap my mind around, and this had the counterintuitive effect of blunting my rage.

"Was anything true about you, Coral? The Salton Sea? That story about your dad?"

"I was myself, Matt." Coral pushed their glasses up the bridge of their nose, and though they'd assured me they were the analog kind, I obviously remained alert. "And you were my friend. That was real. All I will say in my defense—and then I'd like to leave it at that—is that we had strong suspicions there were people in your organization who were 6Degrees."

I snorted. "You don't believe that."

"It never mattered what I believed. I had a job to do."

I stared into my mug, trying hard to summon any fury, but it had turned as cold as the coffee.

"There are things, Matt, that no one has exactly put together."

"Like I'm going to listen to any theory from you. And great job, Coral. It turns out all those attacks were masterminded by a handful of people mailing each other fucking lotto fliers."

Their blunt fingernails, painted brown, played a little syncopated beat on the Formica of the kitchen island.

"Have you ever heard of Megadata Narrative Reconstruction?" they asked.

"Nope."

"At least you're aware of the AI programs that write books and music and VR xperes, I'm sure."

"Yeah. Go figure. As soon as I get a book contract the entire profession is about to be rendered obsolete."

They gave me a wizened little smile. "Stay strong, bud. Authorbots will need to use our bodies as batteries if we nuke the planet to deny them sunlight."

Despite myself, I hissed a laugh.

They continued, "The FBI uses similar tech—everyone does now. Real Philip K. Dick stuff, and the profiles are insanely vivid."

"What does that mean?"

They removed a blue folder curled into an inside pocket of their jacket. It was stuffed with old-fashioned tree paper and secured with a thick rubber band. They held it in their lap.

"When we found the 6Degrees suspects, we ran their identities through these programs. These AIs gather background by processing vast reams of data. Basically, the moment a person is born we start producing digital trails in a billion different ways. It's all there, it just has to be collated and sifted through."

I felt my stomach grow queasy as Coral went on to describe how these AIs could mine every online interaction, keystroke, every piece of biometric data a person's phone or watch or glasses ever recorded, and of course every conversation they'd ever had in the proximity of a device that could listen. Dating back to the 2000s, most networked devices, TVs, stereo systems, earbuds, digital assistants, remote controls—it had all been spying and collecting ambient conversations. Analyze a person's words, heart rate, blood pressure, and every email they've ever written with advanced machine learning and one can gain a frighteningly realistic insight into their inner psychology. Of course, all this data would take a literal lifetime to sift through and assemble into any kind of coherent narrative that could prove useful to law enforcement (or advertisers). For every moment spent plotting one of the most impressive criminal conspiracies in American history there would be two hundred thousand of the individual just going to the bathroom or being frustratingly unable to locate milk in an unfamiliar grocery store.

"The algorithms know more about you than you could possibly know about yourself. They know what you're going to do before you do. We've largely turned our lives over to them," they said. According to Coral, the first-generation of MNR was a bit sloppy, producing asides and explanations that generally cropped up in distracting fashion, as if the program was constantly finding new information and couldn't decide if it was extraneous or vital.

"These next generations, though—they're getting to be unbelievable," they said. "The ability to basically reproduce a human life, down to an individual's thinking. 'Psychological reconstitution' is what we call it, and it's probably more accurate than if the individual wrote their story themselves. Currently we need a warrant to get a reconstruction, but trust me, it's too useful. Pretty soon we won't."

I laughed. Coral was such a geek—that was true, at least. "You're freaking me out."

"It should." They nodded to the refrigerator, a stainless-steel behemoth with every standard feature, including a camera inside to check the contents and a screen to FaceTime people while we cooked. "We are nothing but data. We basically sold our inner selves to the new colonizers for a handful of pretty beads. For instance, we did an MNR of the guy who killed Mackow-ski. The bomber was actually profiled by identity prediction analysis when he was in the criminal system. That makes a reconstruction easy because his behavioral data was always being collated."

"So why couldn't you stop him? Ash Hasan's sister was killed in that attack."

They shrugged. "The guy was never deemed a threat. That's why they used him. The decisions we make aren't always up to us. That's why MNR is only useful after the fact right now, but even then . . . So there's a woman from 6Degrees leadership we're still looking for. She had a couple different aliases. We know this because when we captured Ismael, McCurdy, Worth-ington, and the others, we used a new technique."

Coral went on to explain a method called "echolocation." This used data from various sources to re-create the identity, attitudes, and thought processes of people with whom those sources interacted. The Weathermen were smart. Part of their protocol was to pollute their data, and this success-fully hid them for a long time. But once the FBI found people in leadership, the echolocation AI could work backward. Colonel Kellan Murdock put a bullet in his head, but because the Pentagon had a treasure trove on the man from his service in Iraq, the AI was able to reconstruct an early meeting between the colonel and this woman from 6Degrees. It used his thought process and the processes of nearby diners to reassemble their conversation and how she might have reacted.

"It's a jankier read," said Coral. "The more it uncovers, the more it can deduce. It builds out the life of a suspect as far as it can. But we still haven't caught her. We think she may have somehow falsified certain elements of her identity, biographical details like her mother's country of origin. Pos-sibly even her own ethnicity. Things like that. Honestly, it's almost beyond belief that she's managed to beat the AIs so far, not to mention facial recog-nition, fingerprints, not a trace of DNA—we've got nothing. It's as close as I've ever seen anyone come in this day and age to being an honest-to-Christ ghost. No one understands how she's done it."

"Coral." I was growing impatient. "What's this have to do with me?"

They smiled weakly. "We found this one MNR that's not ours . . ." They hesitated and laughed uneasily. "It's a reconstitution, but no one knows where it came from. The cyber folks thought it was espionage at first. It knew things it should not have access to. It's a recounting of the siege of D.C."

"Why do you keep saying 'it'?"

"Well. Originally, the intel was so detailed, the CIA thought it was a Chinese intelligence operation. But their state security is investigating their own versions in Mandarin and Cantonese."

I was caught between wanting to laugh and be amazed and hate them still and hug them and ask if we could start hanging out again. My nostalgia surged for the ratty offices in Adams Morgan and all our hours of banter on every topic, from Martian terraforming to William Faulkner novels.

"Okay, so what's the prevailing conspiracy theory? I've heard a few in my time."

"We know AIs have surpassed human intelligence but that doesn't mean they've achieved consciousness. I tend to think consciousness is just going to turn out to be pointless mental pollution organic life coughed up while it multiplied. But what if one of these AIs decided it liked spinning yarns? And it has access to basically any data it wants, from conversations we've had near any kind of microphone to seismic images of the Indian Ocean. It's not exactly documenting current events per se, it's more like it takes an interest in people. It explores. And it tells stories fabricated from complex systems modeling. It's leaving these little digital keepsakes. Burying them in the global network infrastructure as a kind of, I don't know, time capsule. Or maybe for reasons of its own that we couldn't even understand."

I stared at them for a moment and then released an uneasy laugh. "Okay, man, that is kind of spooky."

"Just saying." They slid the folder across the countertop to me. "Obviously, you can't tell Moniza where you got this, but I'll leave it in your hands. You can decide if you want to give it to her."

I didn't touch the file or even begin to reach for it.

"What is it again?"

"It's the story of the siege. That's what it wanted to describe for some reason." They put a hand on the folder and inched it closer to me. "Just read it all the way through, Matt. You'll understand why." They stood and gave me a weak smile. "It was good seeing you, man. I'm damn sorry for how things went down. Sorry for everything."

As they turned to walk out of my house, I said, "Coral." They stopped and turned. "Why are you doing this?"

With a perfectly blank expression, they said, "You deserve to know what she was thinking. And maybe people deserve to know. That's up to you."

I huffed and shook my head at them. "Well, aren't you worried my fridge is listening?"

"Yes," they said. "I am."

Then they walked out the door. I sat in my kitchen for a long time, trading my gaze from the refrigerator to that blue folder.

~ ~ ~

It took me a long time to actually bring myself to read the document. I hid it in a box in the crawl space and waited for Moniza to be out of town again. Then I poured myself a whiskey and began on this MNR of unknown origins.

When I finished, Jackie Shipman's letter was long forgotten, and I couldn't think and I couldn't cry and I couldn't understand what I'd just read. It cast a wide net over the people who'd been there for those sweltering summer months, the hope and the violence that followed. Hard to read because it felt like the MNR was inside them. But also, there was Kate in frightening three dimensions. Some machine learning algorithm had gotten closer to her than I ever had. Maybe that's why, impulsively, I did what I did.

I'm not sure if Coral wanted me to hand that file over to Moniza to salve their own conscience, but that night, drunk as I'd been in years, all I knew was I didn't want that file to exist. I took it to our firepit in the backyard and burned it. I'm not sure if I regret it. Some days I wish I had the document to read again. Others, I'm sorry I ever laid eyes on it. It frightens me more than that hideous image that arrived in my in-box.

I never told Mo about Coral's visit, but when she came home, she could tell something was off. I couldn't think about anything else. I couldn't focus. I spent too much time on forums reading about AI narratives. Conspiracy theories were religions now. Acolytes claimed the newly awakened AI god was already here, speaking to us through the data, guiding the human experiment in ways either benevolent or pure evil, depending on who was postulating. All these wild, naked theories mixed with Coral's visit and that terrifying blue folder and my mourning for the years at A Fierce Blue Fire: babbling with Coral uninterrupted for hours, Tom snarling his politics through a squelching dip, Rekia cutting to the moral core of any issue, Liza delivering every cutting line on cue. And coursing through it all, every precious memory of lying with Kate beneath hot stars in unbounded wilderness.

Moniza and I were in the kitchen, putting together lunch, when she stopped halfway through screwing the lid off a jar of mayo, licked her fingers, and put her hands on her hips. It was the way she phrased it that unnerved me.

"What's happened, Matt?"

"What do you mean? Nothing's happened."

"Right now. Your face. It looks like a spanked bottom."

She was right. I'd felt my face flush immediately.

"Your brooding is so obvious," she said. "You can't do it silently."

It took me a long time to respond to that.

"You have to let me grieve." And a ghost passed over my skin.

"Have I said anything?" she pleaded. "It's been over two years now, and I haven't said a thing, Matt. I've let English stoicism do all the work."

We stood there together, a total impasse. Finally, she lowered her eyes to our hardwood floors. "Maybe you just need to say it."

"Say what?"

"That you loved her. And that your heart is broken." She put a hand to her cheek. She made certain her voice was under control. "I'd rather you just say that than feeling all the time like you're so very far away."

More so than when I found out, in that moment, I cracked. My wife took me in her arms, and she let me weep in her hair. I dug my fingers into the flesh of her back and felt how very solid and alive she was.

~ ~ ~

Mo and I were better after that. We found out she was pregnant in July, so she was four months along by the time Hurricane Kate grew to the most powerful storm ever measured in the Atlantic Ocean. My parents arrived at our house on October 3 as the cyclone churned toward the Eastern Seaboard. In the satellite images, it appeared to be preparing to swallow the earth itself. My parents had packed their Suburban with so much food and water, it took the three of us nearly an hour to unload while Moniza ran Xs of tape over the windows. By the time the storm reached us, we figured the winds would dissipate, but it was a worthwhile precaution. I wasn't so much worried about wind as water. We lived in a narrow valley southeast of Raleigh not too far from the Neuse River, which had flooded before during Hurricane Florence and Hurricane Alberto. Most of the neighbors I spoke to seemed to think we were far enough inland. We'd be wet but fine.

Unloading their car, I looked at the pollen-colored sky, and the ridge in the twilight creeping toward us, this enormous black wave crested with brimstone clouds. In those shape-shifting lashes, I saw gruesome pareidolia, grinning demons, and charging armies.

Back in the house, my dad had already turned the TV to a twenty-four-hour news channel (non-Fox, at least), and he and Mo were squabbling over the windows.

"Just saying, I'd have boarded 'em up," he told her. His gray-white hair had finally begun to recede, and his spine had a curve now. He didn't stand as tall as he once had. Not far from here he'd built one of his first golf courses, which is how I'd found this house when Moniza said she'd move to North Carolina if we got married. "Tape is fine, but better safe than sorry."

"He's slagging me off on the job," Moniza whispered to me as she passed. "Unsurprising."

I was not looking forward to refereeing this for the next two days. It started to rain, the drops sprinkling through the wire screens of the porch. I joined my dad at the window with the thought of saying something, when a pop of lightning and crack of thunder pierced the darkening day.

My mom poked her head in.

"Yikes! That was a big one. Dan, Matt, my beautiful boys—what should we do? Make dinner? Play a board game first?" She looked so excited to be here with us. "Or I thought maybe we could do some planning about decorating the nursery? It's going to sneak up on you faster than you think."

We'd barely started collecting cards for Ticket to Ride when the power went out.

~ ~ ~

The rain grew louder, the wind harder. Gusts shuddered the windowpanes. We were prepared, with flashlights, candles, and a bright electric lantern in each room. Dizzy went to hide under the couch, and Lila paced nervously. For the next hour, we continued the board game, until I heard the sump pump kick on. After a few minutes it stopped. Outside, the rain continued to pound. When we finished, my dad winning with a train route from Seattle to Miami, I went downstairs to check on the pump, only to find the washer and dryer almost underwater.

Oh shit. This brought my family running. The basement had at least four feet of water in it, the major appliances bobbing in the dark. The sump pump hadn't kicked off, it had been overwhelmed.

"It'll be a mess, but nothing to worry about." My mom nodded as she said this. "This is why you get a homeowners policy."

"Our insurance company got a government bailout," Moniza joked. "So it's about time that paid off."

"Should I get down in there?" I wondered. The water was cloudy and gray, full of shit-colored debris in the flashlight's white beam.

"Lord, no, Matt, there's nothing worth it down there," said Moniza. "We'll remodel after this."

She took my hand and led me away, but we couldn't play another game now that we had an intruder in the house. I put on a rain jacket and ran outside to check the cars. The rain stung, and I had to hold the hood to my head as burst after burst of wind tried to rip it off. With the power out, we hadn't seen the water pooling in the driveway, but it was ankle-deep, cold, and soaking my feet. All three of our cars had water halfway up the wheels. Lightning flashed, and in the brief illumination of the sky, I saw the hurricane's churning wall, white-blue clouds swarming counterclockwise. It looked like there were kites flying through the air, until I realized these were solar panels spinning madly in the wind. There was a piece of someone's roof lying on our road, the shingles looking like wet scales. The wind dragged the section toward our lawn and then flipped it back into the road with a crash so that I could hear the wood splinter, the nails warping.

Retreating back inside, Moniza took me by the arm, focused her wide brown eyes on me, and said sternly, "Do not go back out there."

Now we could hear the washer and dryer tumbling against the walls, their aluminum shells boinging off the concrete. I didn't get scared until the water started coming up through the vents in the floor.

Filthy brown water bubbled out of the black cast-iron vents and spread over the caramel hardwood, soaking all the antique carpets Moniza had spent years acquiring. The dogs went crazy, particularly young Lila. She ran from vent to vent, barking at the water like she could scare it away, while Dizzy fled from under the couch and up the stairs to higher ground, as fast as I'd seen her move in years.

When the water reached our shins, I went to my office and began grabbing books, mourning the antique bookcase with glass panes, a birthday present from Mo right after we moved in. Suddenly everything we prized on the first floor was in danger.

"Will you and your dad take the couch upstairs?" Moniza asked me. It was a Meyer, Gunther Martini, an elegant antique with silk the color of polished bone, and she'd made me drive a rental truck halfway to Boston to get it. My dad and I hefted the thing, splashed through the water, up the stairs, and shoved it in the hallway. Another flash of lightning, and I couldn't see the yard, or the road, just water everywhere, up to the door handles of the cars.

An hour later, it had reached our knees, and we began taking everything we could to the second floor: the art, the lamps, the troves of important documents, passports, titles, deeds, and wills. I trudged through freezing water to get it all safely upstairs. My dad hefted the TV, a useless glass window into nothing. Finally, Moniza thought to bring the food and water upstairs. Wading through freezing murk now up to my thighs, carrying up the food I'd salvaged, I found my mom sitting on the bed in the guestroom having trouble breathing. She was panicking, and my dad appeared oblivious to this. She kept asking, "What if it gets higher?"

"It'll take a long time for it to get as high as that," Mo said, though I'd seen it move from the fifth step to the sixth in a matter of minutes.

"We should have a plan," my mother moaned.

"You got an axe?" my dad asked. "In case we gotta chop through the roof?"

He pronounced it *ruhf*, as he had since my childhood. One of his words that always irritated me.

"Is there even a crawl space?" my mom wondered. There was, but I'd been up there. It was barely big enough to fit three people, and not high enough to stand up. It would be like crawling into a coffin.

"What about the *ruhf*? We need an axe," my dad repeated. I did not want to hear that word anymore.

"Dad," I snapped. "There's no axe and there's not going to be an axe. I need you to seriously shut the fuck up, okay?"

He shook his head once in acquiescence and turned away.

"The dog food," Moniza remembered. For whatever reason, that made it real. We would be trapped on the second floor for a long time, and that was the best-case scenario.

"I'll go get it."

I went back down the stairs, checking my watch. In only twenty minutes, the flood had reached my stomach. I waded through the freezing water to the kitchen and got into the pantry where I had to dunk my whole head under to pull out the water-logged bag of kibble. Frigid water clamped my head and now the cold was pure agony. Hauling it back, I could feel the water had risen. It was definitely coming faster now. I passed my office and saw my desk bubbling as water filled the drawers. I thought briefly of Jackie Shipman's letter in the middle-left drawer, but the paper would now be illegible pulp. Dropping the soaking bag of dog food in the bedroom, I saw my mom weeping quietly.

"It's because you yelled at your father," Moniza murmured. I ignored her.

Downstairs, there was an explosion of glass, and then the sound of water pouring in. It was three-fourths of the way up the stairs now, frothing in the flashlight's beam. I saw the wooden mallard floating at the top. I looked back into the bedroom where Moniza sat, consoling my mom. I was pacing. I was forgetting things. Fear is physical. It creates a fog in your mind where you can't concentrate. I kept feeling like I'd forgotten something downstairs we would need, and it was too late now. I stupidly watched the water advance.

My dad had somehow, somewhere, found a length of rope I didn't recognize, and he was going from window to window, pushing the screens out and peering up, letting the rain in.

"What are you doing?" I asked, trying not to sound as angry or panicked or scared out of my fucking mind as I was.

"We need a way to the ruhf, Matt," he said, like he was explaining how to scrape a green perfectly level at one of his courses. "In case the water gets any higher." He held up a gadget, a little SPOT GPS emergency messenger. He'd activated it already. "Brought this along, but it's doing us no good if we can't get onto the ruhf for rescue."

"There's nothing to tie off the rope on," I hissed.

"Yeah," he agreed. "We'll have to make something up. Tell the gals to dress warm, get their shoes on and all. I'll get up there on the ruhf then I'll"—he chopped his hand, tomahawk-style—"hook it on somehow."

"With what?"

He raised his eyebrows to indicate that this would be the tricky part. "I found a hammer downstairs, so we'll have to make do with that."

The water did not slow. Another hour, and it was at the top of the stairs, spilling across the second floor. Somewhere north of us, a transformer exploded and suddenly the night was bright blue, purple, and white. In the driveway, all three cars had collected against the garage at haphazard angles. Another vehicle, not ours, was simply floating in the newly formed lake where our lawn had been.

"Think it's about time," he said.

"I should do it, Dad."

He monkeyed with the GPS and batted a hand at me. "No, no, you stay here. Your mom and Mo need you to be calm, you know? If I get swept away, Mo will probably pray thanks to Vishnu."

Unbelievably, he winked at me. We closed the door to the guestroom so they wouldn't see what we were up to. He tucked the GPS in my pocket and proceeded to the window. He tied the rope around his wrist and secured the hammer in his belt. The water was nearing the base of the window. As he climbed out onto the ledge, reaching up to grab hold of the gutters, I gave him a boost by hugging his knees and pushing him up. Despite his age, he pulled himself onto the pitch, rope trailing behind him, and I could hear his boots above me as he found his footing and trudged up the roof. Later, I would see what he'd done: tying the rope off to the head of the hammer, and then wedging the hammer beneath one of the solar panels to create an anchor—all with the rain pummeling him and hurricane winds trying to carry him off into the night.

"What on bloody earth is he doing?" Moniza demanded when she and my mom came in, but they didn't need much of an explanation. At that point, the water was around our thighs and rising.

"C'mon, we need to get the dogs," I told her.

Lila I could fit in a camping pack, and when I zipped her up with her little head poking out, she looked at me, no longer barking, just whimpering in terror. Dizzy I had to hand to my dad, who crouched low on the slick roof, somehow kept his balance, and managed to pull the frightened old girl up into his arms. Finally, we had to get my mom out there, and despite how fast the water was coming, she was even more reluctant to go than Dizzy. She kept repeating, "I can't, I can't, I can't, I can't."

"It's going to be fine," said Moniza, hugging her, rubbing her back. "Just a little hop up on the window, and then Daddy's going to pull you up—no worries at all, love."

Mom went up, lifted by a man she'd met in the UNC library nearly fifty-one years ago, who had badgered her into a date despite the fact that she'd had a boyfriend back home. Moniza went next, kissing me on the mouth and saying, "My hair's going to be a frizzy mess in this." Her belly snagged momentarily, but she was able to pull herself up with very little help from me and my dad. "I'm small but mighty!" I heard her cry into the wind. Finally, I shouldered the backpack with Lila inside and crawled up the rope just as the water began rushing through the open window, swallowing the top floor of our home.

Dad and Moniza each grabbed my belt and helped hoist me up onto the shingles. I could barely open my eyes, the rain was coming down so hard. My teeth had been chattering since dunking my head for the kibble, and now the cold drilled to my bones. Mom huddled with Dizzy in a safe wedge created by the solar panels, and I realized there was a spotlight on her. I hadn't heard the blades at first because of the rain, but there was a Coast

Guard helicopter hovering over us, its light beaming down like a path into heaven. I would have cried with relief if I hadn't been so cold. Though it seemed to take an eternity, a rescue basket attached to a crane came winding down. My dad and I finally reached up and caught the heavy white metal. "Women and children first," shouted my dad, putting Moniza in the basket along with Dizzy. Mo kissed him on the cheek before ascending into the chopper's spotlight. Ten minutes later, the basket returned, and my mom and Lila went next.

When they were safely in the helicopter and the basket was descending again, I shouted, "You're next, Dad." We still had to scream to be heard above the roar of chopper, wind, and water, which was lapping up the pitch of the roof.

"Nope, son. You are." The Meyer, Gunther couch had crashed through the bay window in the hallway and lodged itself in the frame. The force of the rotors sent the water rippling outward in heavy waves. We were both shivering, and I could hear my voice quaking with the cold.

"C'mon, Dad, no debate. You're going next." The basket swayed in the wind on its way to us. My dad reached up and caught it by the edge.

"Sorry, Matt, but either you're getting in or we both drown." Then he slapped my back like I'd hit an incredible shot off the tee. "You're my boy, kiddo. Trust me, in about five months you're going to totally understand."

Huddled in the basket, listening to the whir of the motor as I was lifted skyward, soaked so thoroughly that I couldn't imagine being warm or dry ever again, I looked down and saw my dad in the glare of the searchlight, gazing up at me, shielding his eyes from the rain.

~ ~ ~

After Hurricane Kate made landfall, I saw a headline that simply said: THIS IS WAR. Which is what it looked like. The devastation wrought comparisons to Hiroshima and Nagasaki. Scoring a direct hit on the upper Carolina, my Carolina, but severely impacting twenty-one states, Kate had leveled nearly every structure from Norfolk to Myrtle Beach, as far as twenty miles inland. The coast was kindling and rubble. Amid the flood, fire-scorched divots smoldered for days, boats and houses and churches and cars washed miles from the shore and deposited in trees, in drifts of sand, hurled into other structures. Homes like my parents' were swept off their foundations. Trailer parks had been reduced to disjecta piled on the sides of the highway. The floodwaters, which did not recede for a month, wreaked havoc on electrical wiring and corroded sewer lines. In one iconic image from the Norfolk navy base, a destroyer had been torn from its anchors and run aground. It lay on its side in the middle of the city, its stern wiping out a strip mall. Even the attack on Pearl Harbor hadn't been able to sink or destroy as many ships. Despite evacuations, at least eight thousand people were dead or missing. It would be the first trillion-dollar storm, sending a twelve-foot surge sweeping across the beaches and dropping seventy-nine inches of rain in some regions during the five days it took to dissipate. Power was out for months; food, water, fuel, and electricity hard to come by. There were stories of looting, robbery, and violence as desperate people vied for a bottle of water. People less advantaged and lucky than us died in their attics or stranded on their roofs waiting for rescue.

With many rural roads impassable, the highways clogged with cars run dry of gas or charge, families set out on foot. Exhausted and dizzy in the sweltering humidity, they carried what they could on their backs, pedaled bikes, pushed shopping carts, held signs to the sky begging for help. They camped on the sides of roads, squatted in abandoned homes and office parks. Shoulder to shoulder, tent-to-tent, everyone arguing, angry, upset. Everyone with a gun. They were met by FEMA trucks dispersing bottled water, palettes of MREs, and hustled to the enormous camps in Greensboro, Charlotte, and Atlanta. FEMA, the Red Cross, and mutual aid organizations descended. And in some of the dry cities there was a local border patrol, telling refugees there was no safe harbor for them there. Frail and exhausted from nearly three years in office, it was said Warren Hamby did not want to mimic his predecessor with declarations of martial law, but martial law arrived anyway. So did disease. Dysentery and cholera outbreaks in Jacksonville and Charleston. Once extinct in North America, these waterborne menaces had been creeping back to life in the heating coastal region. People's intestines cramped, they shat bloody diarrhea, at least a few hundred died from shivering fevers.

My family spent one night in a temporary shelter before making our way to Cara and Habswam's place in Charlotte. My parents stayed with them, while Moniza and I found a hotel, a rental car, and despite my misgivings, spent our days making trips to various parts of the state so she could report the story. It was in our hotel that we watched through VR as Tracy Aamanzaihou stood in the rubble of Charleston, South Carolina, and delivered a 2040 stump speech.

"We cannot continue to endure storms like this. Though the destruction was

on a scale we haven't seen before, there will be more to come. Now I could stand here and lie to you that we can properly prepare for these events, but the truth is we cannot. We must reverse the heating of the planet, and we must do so faster than we are doing now. The ray of light in all this darkness is that three days after Hurricane Kate made landfall, a UN report announced that the world's carbon emissions have fallen from twenty-eight billion tons to twenty-one billion since 2037. Yes, the recession played a role, but this was also because of our work. That's an unprecedented decline of twenty-five percent in two years. The measures we and other countries are taking—despite the interference by the Supreme Court, despite the advocacy of a still-powerful fossil-fuel lobby—our plan is working. It is a long road ahead to be sure, and there will be many more setbacks, but my message to you, my fellow Americans, is that we can do this."

Next up, The Pastor announced his intent to run again, money from the Carbon Majors already bursting his coffers. The business community was lining up behind him. Images of the Carolina coast played over our faces, and it made me feel like I was living in a hallucination. Or witnessing a premonition.

~ ~ ~

They borrowed a name Kate Morris first devised to shut down gas stations and political offices: the Seventh Day Protests, though they had little to do with the seventh of each month. A group of students, community leaders, and activists in Richmond, California, appeared to have been the first. They drove out to the Chevron refinery that had long lorded its influence over the city with little more than tents, sleeping bags, and sunscreen. Soon others joined. The tactics worked, failed, were amended, and spread, mostly via the swarm algorithms designed by my old friend Liza. Soon encampments had sprouted in eleven locations across six states. A blockade began at the Selma facility less than forty minutes from us.

Mo and I rented a box truck, filled it with food, water, jackets, hats, long johns, whatever else we could pick up. Police were standing down. In fact, they weren't trying to stop anyone from joining, and we drove right into this bizarre festival that had risen around the gates of the refinery. We found the intake team, told them what we'd brought, and they helped us offload our supplies. Looking around, I could see the organization of tents into neighborhoods, a library, a kitchen, solar generators and batteries distributing power, and pop-up classes with all the kids' attention directed toward a young teacher. Most noticeably there was a banner unfurled across an oil storage tank: WE ARE THE DELUGE.

Kate's face was everywhere on signs and T-shirts, and of course it was the picture I'd taken of her in Wyoming twenty-two years ago when we had our second date on the Paintbrush-Cascade Loop. She looked so young, her hair threaded by the breeze, smiling to herself in that tight, inscrutable way, an inside joke you'd give anything to know. MAKE ME AN OUTLAW, read a woman's tattoo, inked across her back, as she stood in shorts and a bikini top in the cold sun, off-loading our canned food and bottled water.

"Matt," Moniza called to me. She stood with a woman holding a tablet. "Come look at this."

On the screen there was a feed of another encampment, this one surrounding a parliamentary building somewhere, and the occupiers had strung up the same banner. Beneath it were dueling pictures of my former girlfriend and the storm that had wiped half of North Carolina off the map. Scrawled beneath: JUSTICE 4 KATE, JUSTICE 4 KATE.

"That's Norway," said the woman. "Breivik is out. The government fell." She flipped to another screen. "This is Beijing." A similar scene, hundreds of thousands amassed in Tiananmen Square. She flipped again. "Germany." Brandenburg Gate surrounded by tents and a similar teeming crowd with blue shirts, armbands, face paint, even their hair dyed a watery blue. Then London, Rio, Cape Town, Moscow—they all looked exactly the same. In Washington, D.C., just a block south of the National Mall, protestors had locked down the street and erected an enormous mural in the middle of traffic—Kate screaming at the armored police vehicle, demanding it run her over, and below:

KATE MORRIS IS ALIVE AND WILD

Over the next two weeks we'd make seven more trips to the Selma oil facility, nearly emptying our savings to supply the blockade. In that time, the heads of every oil major demanded the president respond, that he do something about the illegal encampments. I like to think Hamby's equivocation was calculated. He did nothing to stop the protests, and governors were equally queasy about trying to dislodge them. This example spread and where force was employed it only seemed to fan the flames of the blockades. Every rubber bullet fired, horror drone launched, sound cannon deployed, only drew more people, more determined. The protests spread, back to the gas stations, back to state capitals, back to Capitol Hill and the corporate headquarters of coal, oil, gas, factory farms, and Wall Street banks. Elyse Duncan-Michaels, daughter of the former CEO of Exxon, made grisly headlines when she showed up to the company's headquarters and became the latest person to douse herself in gasoline and strike a match. No doubt she will not be the last.

The stock market plunged, and economists feared a renewed crisis, and still the resistance spread. The nation's college campuses were clogged with student protestors. Classes shut down, tuition bills went unpaid. The nurses followed, coordinating to help deliver care to patients in critical need while maintaining work slowdowns and stoppages. Many of the country's three million prisoners joined, throwing down their firefighting equipment, their sewing, their headsets in the call centers, and demanding a minimum wage. I saw Holly Pietrus and Rekia Reynolds in interview after interview, explaining that there could be no global set of demands for what was happening, but holistically they were asking for an end to corporate domination, fascism, the murder of refugees, internment camps, the dehumanization, the genocide, but most importantly and concretely, here in the US, the immediate nationalization and rapid shuttering of the entire carbon establishment. The press, the commentariat, the establishment scoffed at this, all but wrote it off, warned of bloodshed if the estimated five million blockaders across all fifty states didn't stand down. Oil and gas prices had already been well below production since the crisis, and the wave of bankruptcies grew into a tsunami. Perhaps this had been a long time coming, years of tireless, maddening work to destabilize the industry, but it felt shocking and abrupt, as suddenly everything changed.

On February 4, 2040, three months into the new Seventh Day protests and occupations, President Hamby initiated the nationalization of all fossil-fuel infrastructure. It will still be years before these carbon giants can be properly wound down and the economy fully transitioned, but overnight there will be no one to pay the lobbyists, to spread the campaign money, to peddle influence.

~ ~ ~

A month later, my daughter, Aliah Stanton Farooki, was born, seven pounds, one ounce. Aliah had the squashed face of an alien when she popped out, which, my mom assured me, is how all babies look. Now on her first birthday, Aliah looks increasingly like her mother, for which I'm grateful.

Of course, every day I wonder what world I'm leaving my daughter. Her life begins at the brink, either of our annihilation or our resurrection.

I try to imagine what she will witness in her lifetime.

In utero, she bobbled along upside down as her parents helped feed, shelter, and hydrate those who disabled and dismantled the infrastructure of carbon civilization. I cradled her head as a newborn while I watched our old ally Tracy Aamanzaihou barnstorm her way to the Democratic nomination and then scratch and claw over Warren Hamby and The Pastor to the presidency. In Aliah's second year of life, I saw the new president and her allies ram through one of the most radical reorganizations of American economic life in more than a century: expansions of ballot access, public health care, free college education, universal pre-K, the breakups of major media conglomerates and tech giants, a new tax regime for the hyper-wealthy, regulation of corporate data collection, new antitrust legislation, the repeal of Taft-Hartley, and a growing wave of unionization and labor empowerment.

With the thirty biggest carbon producers in the country now owned by the taxpayers, she and Congress created the Climate Mitigation Authority, also known as the Climate Fed, modeled on Roosevelt's War Production Board and first championed by Dr. Anthony Pietrus in his book *One Last Chance*. This reorganized a variety of agencies within the federal government to coordinate the rapid drawdown of carbon from both the economy and the atmosphere. Congress was given control of the Climate Authority Auditor-General, a watchdog supervisory board tasked with delivering annual reports on the CMA's activities and the ability to shut them down if they are deemed illegal under its mandate. In an attempt to insulate it from political pressure, the CMA was created as an eleven-member panel, each member serving a five-year term. Of course, the first chairman of the CMA was Ashir al-Hasan, who initiated nationalizations of electrical utilities, railroads and, more controversially, converted several failed banks that had financed carbon-intensive industries to long-term public ownership. According to progressives, the CMA can be used to shift the global order toward regenerative economics by bringing other damaging environmental practices under its purview. The Aamanzaihou administration used the threat of court-packing to forge ahead on the Twenty-Eighth Amendment to the Constitution, which not only overturned the infamous *Citizens United* decision, but implemented the public financing of all elections and added seventeen-year term limits to the Supreme Court. All this in the war to keep the planet from breaching three degrees.

I can't help but think back to that summer of meeting Ash for slush-ies near the Russell Building. I remember him saying, "It would be nice if we could conjure a crisis." I asked him what he meant by that. He finished slurping a bit of blue raspberry ice and licked his lips. "We will never be able to move fast enough with all these interests and stakeholders dragging their feet. If we could somehow make those interests overplay their hand, I think it's possible. What I'd prefer is to have the right kind of crisis descend with the right people in the right positions to exploit it. But that obviously is quite difficult to engineer." Though it seems insane to entertain the notion, I do wonder about how many dimensions of chess Ashir al-Hasan was capable of playing.

Two years into my daughter's life, one can see the changes everywhere, and far from the socialist dream I think a lot of climate activists envisioned back in the day, this new world rapidly under construction looks like an "entrepreneurial orgasm," in Moniza's words. Olivine is the latest gold rush because it reacts with water to capture CO_2, so every new house has this dark emerald olivine roofing, and every new public monument is made of it—all to take advantage of a subsidy to use it as a building material. When I drive back to Chapel Hill, I see "solar trees" everywhere on campus, each one gobbling and photosynthesizing some gargantuan amount of CO_2. They are sleek and decorative with translucent arms that tentacle to the sky. On the Carolina coast, near where my parents are attempting to rebuild on the smart side of the new CORDA line, aquaponics and seaweed farms are everywhere, menus swamped with oysters, kelp salads, and other aquatic recipes, the American diet undergoing a transformation I never would have believed possible ten years earlier. Moniza wrote a story about scien-tists arguing, highly hypothetically, what the world would do if it suddenly managed to plunge carbon levels back to 280 ppm—and accidentally risk lowering them further, initiating a new ice age in the process.

"I wouldn't worry about it anytime soon," I told her. On a day when CNN's atmospheric carbon tracker was reporting levels of 452 ppm. Still growing at a steady clip of 1–2 ppm a year.

As methane vents from the Arctic hydrates and permafrost, as the West Antarctic and Greenland Ice Sheets continue their disintegration, as the rate of sea level rise reaches 1.19 inches per year, even more enormous changes are brewing. New governments have come to power calling for a radical reimagining of the world order. Civic rebirth where for decades peo-ple have stared numbly at screens. Feminist collectives in formerly vicious misogynist societies. Progressive eras in places that have known nothing but totalitarianism. There are no easy historical analogies. When history begins to happen all at once, there rarely are.

The reforms to global capitalism, the regenerative practices spilling across borders, the battle to curtail environmental degradation, a notion of true global citizenship prompting ideas of a "global welfare state" or a "worldwide safety net"—it could be a thrilling time for my daughter to grow up. And when governments' commitments begin to slip, when they want to turn back the clock to electrified fences and the very tempting carbon deposits, hopefully they'll be there: the Seventh Day, A Fierce Blue Fire, the Mossville Raiders, Minyun, Filhos da Meia Noite. Whatever they call themselves.

I bathed my daughter in the sink while listening to the news of the nascent electoral system of China producing a shocking break with the past as the Xin Shenghuo Party came to power. Born from the Minyun Movement, its platform has surged into the Western mainstream: It wants torture chambers ripped open, prisons torn down, techno-totalitarian surveillance systems dismantled; climate change, ocean acidification, and pollution reversed; women's rights championed, racist castes annihilated; education free, healthcare systems expanded; weapons of every stripe, from small arms to nuclear, scrapped and melted down; migrants and refugees offered safe harbor; and a compact of rights between humans, ecosystems, and the species we share our habitats with. A massive system change to bring humanity into ecological peace with its one and only home.

Maybe Aliah will someday run for office on this platform, but until then, she'll have to listen to her parents argue about what should be done in the here and now. Following Hurricane Kate, a theory emerged that two years of minimal solar radiation management might be creating more powerful storms. Most scientists disagree, but now that the idea is out there it will be difficult to dislodge. Many in the global climate movement howled in protest over albedo modification, and now that tenacity grows. I think it's crazy to stop the injections, while Moniza can't believe they started in the first place. Meanwhile, international teams are arriving in Antarctica to begin construction of two of humanity's greatest engineering efforts to date. With the first, they will tow a nuclear reactor to the violent arctic seas and begin shooting freezing ocean water across the disintegrating West Antarctic Ice Sheet in an effort to buttress the ice and slow sea level rise. Eventually seven reactors will be anchored offshore, pushing eight thousand GT of water onto the ice over a ten-year period. The second project is the construction of wind turbines on the crown of Antarctica to freeze carbon dioxide using liquid nitrogen, which at the peak of its capacity could sequester one gigaton of CO_2 per year. The process will eventually require as many turbines as it takes to power Germany. The cost of these projects is astronomical, and already governments are balking at their contributions to the price tag.

These will be just a few of the many political wars waged over biospheric policy in the years to come. Even Ash al-Hasan has admitted that many of the ideas implemented by CORDA are a mess. As bureaucrats have rediscovered again and again from time immemorial, getting people to do what is in their best interest is often more difficult than unleashing their worst natures. Even as American Shores National Park expands its boundaries in different regions, many homeowners, like my parents, return to the coasts or refuse to leave, and the government ends up bailing them out anyway. With the Climate Fed's hand fully on the lever of pollution, drawing down US emissions faster than anyone once thought possible, we might someday soon solve one side of the Rubik's Cube. Yet we must still coax the rest of the world to come along, adapt to the biophysical change already locked in, and combat the feedback loops already triggered. Without SRM injections to buy us time, that job will become immensely more difficult.

One of the objecting parties includes the violent revolutionaries who once called themselves 6Degrees. While visiting my old friends Rekia and Tom Levine, Tom still in a wheelchair but his faculties much improved, we learned that Norman Nate, the billionaire who set us down the path of solar management, had been assassinated. It was said he kept instructions to freeze his head upon his death, but there was nothing left to freeze after the bombs went off. "Guess that nixes that plan," said Tom, his scathing humor almost returned. The Weathermen have dispersed into a "decentralized-variety network structure," and this has proven even more difficult to stop than their first incarnation. As Coral Sloane made clear, the array of tools law enforcement has at its disposal are unparalleled, and yet it's not been enough. A few months later, Quinn Worthington managed to get hold of a spring from a ballpoint pen, to twist and shape it into an effective point, enough to open both her wrists. Unsurprisingly, she has become a potent martyr.

As I return to this document on Aliah's third birthday, having failed to turn it in to my publisher and with a growing doubt that I ever will, I'm jealous as always of her mother's rich storytelling. Moniza recently journeyed to Nunavut, the Canadian territory in the Arctic Circle where melting ice and tundra are exposing massive deposits of copper, diamonds, gold, uranium, and zinc. The Legislative Assembly of the Inuit, whose ancestors date back to the first arrival of *Homo sapiens* on the North American continent, implemented a radical new policy, flummoxing every culture's xenophobes: A program of assisted migration brings refugees from every corner of the planet to work the mines but also uses that newfound mineral wealth to build homes, schools, and grant small-business loans to displaced peoples. Free housing, health care, and language school for all new arrivals. Children receive an education in the history of the Inuit people and how they've survived for millennia in one of the most inhospitable climates humans have ever known.

"In just a few short years," my wife wrote, "Iqaluit has transformed from a sleepy capital village to a bustling hub of global trade and prosperity with a Little Haiti, Little Cambodia, Little Bangladesh, Somalitown, Manilatown, even a Little California. Other Arctic Canadian provinces are now looking to follow suit, and one can imagine Whitehorse and Yellowknife and Eagle Plains becoming, if not the new cradle of civilization, then at least places where the weariest of peoples can renew their lives, where lavish government funds will give them the opportunity to start over while holding on to whatever memory of their vanishing homes they can manage to keep alive. Maybe this is what hope looks like as a great wandering of nations begins, a mass movement of human beings that will not end for centuries."

Perhaps this experiment is spilling over, as young people in the southern latitudes once again attempt to use language and manners to attack intractable social, political, and ecological injustice. Now all the talk is about how wrong it is to identify a person based on any nationality, ethnicity, race, gender, sexual orientation, religion, or other imagined community. Calling someone "she," "American," "trans," "Black," or "Catholic" is suddenly frowned upon. According to the social scientists, it's an attitude grown out of virtual reality and the masking of identity the format makes possible. In VR, people live entire lives outside of their genetic or cultural identity groups, and now this approach has stormed into the real world the way so many once-radical ideas quickly become normative. The older generation really hates this, as it becomes an excruciating exercise to form a basic sentence describing an individual's features and background. In the unlikely event I ever get the courage to publish, I'm aware this book will be riddled with offenses. More to the point, border guards don't like people scratching out the distinctions on their passports, and debates frequently erupt about erasures of history. This new ideology's most vociferous proponents argue that a collective human identity is the only way forward, that the next generation must understand how these imagined divisions, created barbarically out of thin air and handed down generation after generation, have led the human project to the brink.

For now, these divisions remain fraught and dangerous. Even before her reelection, President Aamanzaihou was not shy about using military power to stem chaos in the Global South: rapid reaction forces to manage disorder; surveillance of foreign populations; the Pentagon annexing small chunks of Africa, the Middle East, and South Asia where displaced persons live under the control of the US military. Even as the global economic order reshapes itself, the rare earth minerals powering decarbonization, particularly lithium, must keep flowing, and suddenly once-cutting-edge progressives see the utility of certain oppressive arrangements. My daughter turned five as the president's second term began, and I have to explain to her why our leader is threatening to use force against countries that continue to build coal-fired power plants.

Three months after I bought Aliah a birthday cake, self-professed Democratic Socialist Tracy Aamanzaihou used drones to subdue an American Patriot League compound in Idaho, choking it with CS gas and pummeling it with nonlethal weaponry, yet killing three people. With the radical expansion of our democracy, our country's unruly nature has become even more apparent. New parties form in bioregions, intent on protecting their fresh water or farmland, empowered unions want to blow up global trade agreements, the rising Communist Party of America calls for revolution, Indigenous tribes demand the return of their ancestral lands, Texas demands secession, Oregon demands secession, Black separatists demand their own nation-state, and white-power politics still nips dangerously at the mainstream everywhere.

But democracy requires belief. It is, after all, only an idea in all of our heads, and if you go to Cleveland these days, the idea blazes wondrously. The transition of government operations and institutions from the quickly drowning swamp on the Atlantic to the more safely nestled and freshwatered locale of gentrifying Cleveland continues. The New White House is not exactly white. When I visited with my family we touched the walls of bioluminescent algae glowing bright blue as they sequestered carbon. The city looks like a jungle snaking over futuristic ruins, but that's because the buildings are alive with biofuel plants, mold gardens, water recycling canals, and at night, these trippy-ass bioluminescent streetlights. My wife, daughter, and I visited the observation deck at the apex of the New Capitol Building, with its solar skin and walls built with living plant matter. It's the best place to look up at the sky to see the new settlements, and I suffocated with an absolute boyhood wonder that I had lived to see the first city lights on the surface of the moon. Finally, we walked to the olivine statue, placed approximately the same distance from the Capitol as it would have been in the streets of D.C.: Kate Morris, twelve feet high, screaming like a madwoman, daring a military vehicle to run her down.

One day Aliah will begin to read about her parents' generation, what we faced, what we did, and what we failed to do. She will no doubt go down a rabbit hole about this period from the 2010s through the '30s when the nation and the world convulsed as it finally confronted this emergency. She may even read this manuscript, though as the years flip by, as the planet heats and the seas rise, I still can't bring myself to finish it.

While it remains vexing to imagine where the world is going, there are certain things I don't wonder about. I know my daughter will live to see the dust storms blowing hot and blinding across the deserts and plains as winds scour the soil free and a noose tightens around the planet's fresh water. She'll have a different relationship to our fellow species and may never know what a cow is. Beginning this year, the CMA has banned ruminant animals, and her generation will likely not believe what went on in the livestock industry of the twentieth and early twenty-first centuries. The extinction event of course rages on, as insects vanish and food webs lose links, and species disappear. She'll certainly never marvel at a firefly landing on her finger, but she will live in fear of ticks and mosquitoes. She may see polar bears, elephants, lions, whales, sharks, and all the megafauna that mesmerized me as a child, but they will only ever again live in zoos or reserves, the products of captive breeding or de-extinction techniques. Curiosities from a geologic epoch that could sustain biodiversity.

I pray she'll never know hunger, but certainly much of the world will. There has yet to be a global food shock as devastating as 2034–35, but it's only a matter of time. I pray she'll never know true sickness, but already the disease vectors of the tropics have raced to new latitudes. Covid-19 was but a warm-up for what epidemiologists fear might be unearthed by melting ice or forged on the anvil of breakneck evolutionary change. In Uganda, a variant of Rift Valley fever has jumped from person to person for the first time, killing four thousand people so far as the World Health Organization races to contain it.

Aliah will live to feel heat that no person living today can understand. How do human beings survive temperatures upward of 130 degrees Fahrenheit? The answer is they don't. There was a time when a heat wave was considered a poor person's disaster. The impoverished and the elderly were largely its victims, and most died quietly. But no summer goes by now without news of children, high school athletes, and perfectly healthy adults succumbing to heatstroke and dehydration. It sneaks up on you, they say. This summer we met Moniza's parents in New York City for a weeklong vacation, and I woke to an alert on my phone telling me not to take my daughter outside under any circumstances.

Aliah will live to see storms of uncanny size and strength. During that New York heat wave and Uganda's clash with the new Rift Valley strain, a super-typhoon named Osara, with wind speeds approaching 250 mph and a small ocean of rain spewing from its vortex, came curving out of the Pacific into the mouth of Hangzhou Bay. Wind and water swept through the streets of Shanghai, killing over one hundred thousand people and destroying the city's sewage, electrical, and transportation infrastructure. China got its democratic revolution, but the atmosphere does not much care. My guess is that my daughter will live to see the ghost city of Washington, D.C., wash away. She will know the names of the hurricanes that will deliver the final blows to Houston, Boston, Miami, and New Orleans. She may even bear witness to New York City inundated, abandoned, and drowned.

No matter how many new Nunavuts open their doors, the refugees will continue to arrive on every shore, in every airport, by every rail line, smuggled in every truck bed, car trunk, airplane, and shipping container. The endless flow of human beings will never slow, not now, not in Aliah's lifetime. On our current trajectory, many regions across Asia, Africa, and Oceania will eventually become uninhabitable. Even if Aliah grows up in the best-case scenario of a world racing toward justice and sustainability, even if humanity finally stops the planet's warming at 2.3 degrees, as many scientists now think is possible, and pulls enough carbon out of the atmosphere to begin cooling the planet back to a safe temperature, it will take centuries for many of those ecosystems to recover. My dream for my daughter is that it will be her generation that will see what we have forsaken, that will rewild and reawaken our damaged and depleted home, but that dream has never felt so far away.

This horror has no conclusion. It will not end in my daughter's lifetime or even the lifetime of any descendent she can hope to love. She will know no other future outside this claustrophobic emergency, this coffin we are all now pounding on the lid of. She will know death and pain with unthinkable intimacy and likely become inured to the suffering pouring forth from every region of the world in order to keep going. No matter what ideologies arise, what myths we embrace, what technologies we invent, what dreams we offer, this crisis is effectively our eternity.

When I look at her fragile, beautiful face, when I watch her hold a pinch of dirt from our garden and go soft and quiet with mystery, I agonize over it. What will she think of us? What will she think of the expanding deserts, lost soil, acid seas, poisoned land, baking heat, horrific diseases, and a horizon black with storms? I imagine her asking me someday with the hot fury of a teenager's clarity, *Was it worth it? Was a raped and murdered world worth it for a few decades of excess? How did you let this happen? You all knew. Everyone knew.* She will gaze up into this haunting vortex, the consequences of what was done in just a single human lifetime, with nowhere to run or hide or escape this uncharted and endless future.

All I will be able to tell her is that some of us tried, baby. Some of us fought like hell.

~ ~ ~

In May 2031, Kate and I drove west into the Sierra Mountains.

After too many IPAs the night before, a shot of Everclear in the parking lot, and leaving her electrolyte vomit on the pavement, she had a rough go of our first five miles up Mount Whitney. As we ascended, the horns and ridges of nearby mountains appeared in the first gray light of dawn. We turned our headlamps off and walked by this ghost light. Over water crossings, balancing on logs as we traversed streams, up rocky trails and through verdant riparian clearings, Kate struggled. She was sweating, belching, looking pukey and tired, stopping to suck water from her CamelBak and chew energy gummies because she couldn't stomach real food. We stopped so I could get a picture as the Sierras caught the pink of the sunrise.

"That'll teach you to get boozed before climbing the highest peak in the contiguous United States," I teased her.

"I'll fucking kill you, Tar Heel."

"It's not your fault, babe. You've been an office jockey for ten years now. No more Kate Chaos. Kate Orderly and Pragmatic. Kate Make Her Eleven O'Clock Appointment with the Congresswoman."

"Kate Clog the Toilet with Her Coffee Poops," she said.

"You've always been that."

She put her hands on her hips and looked off the trail. "Speaking of."

It would be the last joking or good humor I'd manage for the day.

When we reached the ninety-seven switchbacks, this vicious two-mile staircase up to the trail crest, I was starting to really feel the twelve thousand feet of altitude. We'd decided to do all twenty-two miles up and back in the same day, and now I regretted this. On those switchbacks, Kate began to pull ahead. It made no sense. She went from vomiting to practically running up the mountain. I watched her strides grow stronger. At maybe switchback seventy-three, after pulling myself over an icy patch via a gnarly cable handrail, I had to call ahead to her. I took a seat on a rock as she walked back down to me. Each inhalation was a struggle. When I stood up, I had to immediately sit back down.

"You okay?" she asked gently.

"I think I might pass out," I said. She put a hand on my shoulder. She had her hair pulled back, but as usual several of those wild strands had crawled out to dance in the breeze.

"Put your head between your knees. Take a few deep breaths." I did as I was told, pinprick stars appearing when I closed my eyes. But after a few minutes I did feel better. "It's just the altitude," she said. "Your body can always handle more than you think. We always got one more in us, right?"

"Right, Coach."

Another couple minutes and a lot of chugging water, and I felt better. We carried on. When we reached the trail crest, I sagged with relief. But on the backside of Whitney, looking out over this new and foreign mountain range, the trail turned into a hairy, technical scramble. We toed over boulders along the side of a cliff, and at certain points the drop-off was so steep—untold thousands of feet—that it might as well have been a plummet into another universe. I was well aware this was the part of the climb where people tended to die, including a woman earlier that summer. This was where Kate really began to lose me. She stopped even using her hiking poles, just clasped both in one hand and went bounding over the rocks like there was no drop-off to certain death on her left. The altitude seemed to have no effect on her at all. Meanwhile, I was terrified, planting one foot and one pole firmly, then locating with certainty where the other foot and pole were going next before moving another step. The fasciitis in the ball of my foot started to throb, and with each yard she put between us, I grew more and more irritated with her. It was like she was showing off, joking as she passed other thru-hikers coming from the PCT or John Muir Trail. She hopped onto a boulder jutting out over a precipice and pranced across like she was on a playground balance beam two feet above the wood chips. Over the course of two hours, my irritation metastasized into anger, then fury, as her green windbreaker pulled farther away, until she was nothing more than a dot on the rocky outcroppings of the mountainside. I began rerunning through my head every fight we'd ever had, every time she'd slighted me. On the last leg, as I worked my way over a small patch of snow and ice, I could feel the altitude like nothing else. I'd take three steps and my heart would pound at 130 beats per minute. I didn't take a single picture, and I didn't see any of the beauty at the time.

I couldn't care less when I reached the summit, I just wanted to explode at her. All the pain in my legs and feet, all the misery of my tired lungs, and I wanted to scream, *What the fuck are you thinking? Do you not realize I'm behind you? Do you not care?* As I staggered up to the small hut at the summit with a sign warning of the danger from lightning, I felt such a dense ball of hatred for her and her everlasting arrogance, her selfishness, her unchecked prerogative to never think about anyone or anything that wasn't Kate Morris. Meanwhile, she lazed on a slab of white granite, drinking a beer, surrounded by three young guys. They were all chatting loudly, their voices braying over the eerie quiet that came when the wind died down at 14,505 feet.

"Hey, there you are!" she called out when she saw me. I swallowed all my rage. "You didn't die!"

One of the kids, sporting a huge blond beard that reached his navel, handed me a beer.

"These guys carried up a twelve-pack," she told me. "My heroes."

The kid smiled through the beard and raised his can high. "Fuck it, let's go."

"Fuck it, let's go!" Kate cried, and we all toasted, looking out over the sheer granite summit, eye level with the heavens. Patches of snow still held on in this incinerator of late spring, the majesty of the Sierras in repose. Something Kate had said long ago came back to me. We'd been staring at the geology of Idaho while coming down the backside of the Teton Range. *Mountains are the planet's best violence. Mountains are chaos disguised as stillness.* The earth somehow felt bigger than ever, its possibilities so vast, and its individual beer drinkers so utterly puny. "See, I told ya, Tar Heel," said Kate, slapping my bare leg, squinting into the slashes of golden sunlight piercing distant white clouds. "Little twelve-year-old girls hike this shit. It's basically a Disney ride."

The way back down was a death march. With each step, I prayed for her to feel the altitude, to suggest we rest. I'd never wanted to be done with anything so badly in my life. My quads were on fire, and thunking each hiking pole ahead of the other felt like deadlifting a car. I fought dizziness with every step. I'd blink and see gray splotches, nuggets of infinity passing before my eyes. I wondered what would happen if I died up there, who would protect her from herself, who would keep her from leaping off the absolute craziest cliffs.

Kate slowed down, though, probably because I'd barely said a word at the summit. No longer oblivious to my mood, she understood that I was pissed, though maybe she didn't get why.

"Wanna break for a snack?" she suggested.

"No argument here."

We sat for a while eating Kate's trademark cucumber and vegan cream cheese sandwiches. She pulled out a cold cooked potato and ate it like an apple. I stuck with an actual apple.

"I just needed to sweat out my hangover," she said. "Then I felt like a trillion bucks. You did great, kid."

"I think I came just a few breaths short of dying actually."

"I'll drive you to an early grave yet." And with her teeth bared like a wolf, she darted her head to snatch a bite of my apple.

We sat snacking for a while in silence, watching the east side of the mountain grow shady as the sun descended at our backs. Looking out over the cordillera of the Inyo Mountains catching the winnowing sunlight, it occurred to me then that maybe I was the selfish one. After the failure of PRIRA, after the embarrassment of her scandal, after the awful stay with her dad, this hike had been the first time I'd seen Kate truly joyful in months. Two miles down from Whitney's peak, I finally felt guilty about denying her this moment of vitality and grace, a brief respite to just taste her own sweat and the punch of adrenaline.

"You ever think . . ." I stopped. She looked over at me.

"Yeah?"

"You ever think about how you'll be remembered?" I searched for what I wanted to say, what I'd been mulling this whole trip and trying to articulate for a few years now. "You know. No matter what happens, you've already locked in a place for yourself in history."

She wasn't impressed with this. "I would've thought I'd told you often enough, Matt, history's just a cheap story written by the powerful. Who the fuck cares what history thinks?"

"You don't think about how people will remember you?"

She looked genuinely baffled by the question. "Why would I? Nah, kid. We come, we drink our drink, we sing our song, and that's more than good enough."

I had to half laugh and half scoff at this. "Bullshit. You expect me to buy that? When you're out doing what you do? Kate, I've never seen someone think more about her legacy than you."

She shook her head vigorously in disagreement. "What? No way, man. Humans are just moss. Nothing beyond nature, no more important than bugs. That's obvious." She nodded her head back and forth as if conceding a point to herself. "But then you get to thinking about *humanity*, and it's like, fuck! We've got all this stuff! This knowledge, this curiosity, and we've got Patti Smith! When I heard her for the first time as a kid, I was like, 'Oh my God, this bitch is the Truth. She is art, science, philosophy, and faith all wrapped up in one gorgeous package.' And that's just one of us! We are so insanely singular and significant, and even our cruelty, our psychopathy— even that seems like a motherfucking miracle."

"I feel like we're having separate conversations."

She grimaced, as if revealing a dirty secret. "So I want us to keep doing all our weird shit. I don't want to watch all this crumble." She stretched a hand to the distant mountains, phantasms silhouetted by dust and sun. "It's not about legacy at all. I'm engaged in long-term memetic warfare, dude. This is not just about our planet's fate right now, it's about the next battle and the battle after that. It's about our destiny as a species. We're holding on to something unthinkable, something holy. And we may lose it before we even fully realize it's in our hands."

I'd never heard her voice any of this so bluntly before. There on the rocks, it felt like the right time to ask another question I'd always wondered about.

"Are you ever scared, though?"

She sipped from her CamelBak and then released a small burp. "Giordano Bruno was burned at the stake just for proposing that the universe might be infinite, Tar Heel. Everyone's a critic."

"No, not that. I mean if you had to say, in your heart of hearts, will we do this? And I don't just mean can you get Randall to try again if she wins another term. You know—will we do this?"

Her mouth curled into a tight smile, and she looked like herself in the picture I'd taken in Wyoming. She blew a few strands of hair from her face and turned her gaze back to the mountains.

"Oh, we're definitely taking the long way home on this one. Even if we succeed, it'll be generations before the emergency ends. I think we have to be at peace with that." She leaned back and let her jacket fall back over bronze shoulders. "It's that old saw: You strike your match and it gets blown out, so you strike the next one and that gets blown out too. And again and again, you keep lighting matches, and they keep getting blown out. But you gotta keep lighting them, right? Because you just don't know which one is going to ignite the blaze."

I thought about this. Then quietly I asked, "What if you run out of matches?"

She stared at me for a moment, then tossed her head back and howled laughter, her lips peeled, her teeth fangs, her tongue lapping at the sky, so insane and loud that it echoed over the unbounded landscape. When she finished this outburst, she happily threw up her hands.

"Eh, dude, you can't take life too seriously . . ." Then she reached down to my sunburned knee and with a brutal sting plucked out a hair.

"Ow! Kate!" I swatted, but she was already pursing her lips to blow the tiny hair off the mountain.

". . . No matter how cute you look in your little hiking shorts tonight."

Then she sprang up, shouldered her pack, and started off down the trail, turning all the way around so she faced me. Descending backward over the rocky path, she held my eyes. I feared she'd trip and tumble over the side, but her boots were nimble over the dirt and stone. I picked myself up, pulled on my pack, and followed. At that moment I could have believed anything. As she leveled her demented smile at me and skipped backward in this unchoreographed vagabond dance, I could easily believe that each and every one of us carried this thing she had, a dormant seed of the wild within. I could believe that this great sickness would one day pass, and all our work would be clean and decent and caring. I could believe we would free ourselves of these mournful histories, that all our tears and sorrow would be given back to us, and though we walked these ruins now, we would begin again, and carry across impossible time the glory of this ancient and magnificent world.

ABOUT THE AUTHOR

STEPHEN MARKLEY is the author of *Ohio*, which NPR called a "masterpiece." He is a graduate of the Iowa Writers' Workshop, and his other books include the memoir *Publish This Book* and the travelogue *Tales of Iceland*.

A Note on the Type

This book was set using Adobe Text Pro, a utilitarian text typeface designed by Robert Slimbach. This font takes its cues from post-Renaissance Baroque transitional types, and though it demonstrates a classical form, it's versatility is a statement of contemporary design.